ARTHUR HAILEY

ARTHUR HAILEY

AIRPORT
HOTEL
WHEELS

CHANCELLOR
PRESS

Airport first published in Great Britain in 1968 by Michael Joseph Ltd
in association with Souvenir Press Ltd
Hotel first published in Great Britain in 1965 by Michael Joseph Ltd
 in association with Souvenir Press Ltd
Wheels first published in Great Britain in 1971 by Michael Joseph Ltd
in association with Souvenir Press Ltd

This collected volume first published in Great Britain in 1994 by
Chancellor Press an imprint of
Reed Consumer Books Ltd
Michelin House, 81 Fulham Road, London SW3 6RB
and Auckland, Melbourne, Singapore and Toronto

ISBN 1 85152 744 3

A CIP catalogue record for this book is available from the British
Library

Printed in Great Britain by The Bath Press

Contents

AIRPORT

Oh! I have slipped the surly bonds of earth
And danced the skies on laughter-silvered wings

from *High Flight* by John Gillespie Magee, Jr (1922–1941)
sometime Flight Lieutenant, Royal Canadian Air Force

PART ONE

6.30 pm-8.30 pm (CST)

I

At half-past six on a Friday evening in January, Lincoln International Airport, Illinois, was functioning, though with difficulty.

The airport was reeling – as was the entire Midwestern United States – from the meanest, roughest winter storm in half a dozen years. The storm had lasted three days. Now, like pustules on a battered, weakened body, trouble spots were erupting steadily.

A United Air Lines food truck, loaded with two hundred dinners, was lost and presumably snowbound somewhere on the airport perimeter. A search for the truck – in driving snow and darkness – had so far failed to locate either the missing vehicle or its driver.

United's Flight 111 – a non-stop DC-8 for Los Angeles, which the food truck was to service – was already several hours behind schedule. The food snafu would make it later still. Similar delays, for varying reasons, were affecting at least a hundred flights of twenty other airlines using Lincoln International.

Out on the airfield, runway three zero was out of use, blocked by an Aéreo-Mexican jet – a Boeing 707 – its wheels deeply mired in waterlogged ground beneath snow, near the runway's edge. Two hours of intensive effort had failed to get the big jet moved. Now, Aéreo-Mexican, having exhausted its own local resources, had appealed to TWA for help.

Air Traffic Control, hampered by the loss of runway three zero, had instituted flow control procedures, limiting the volume of incoming traffic from adjoining air route centres at Minneapolis, Cleveland, Kansas City, Indianapolis, and Denver. Despite this, twenty incoming flights were stacked up over head, and orbiting, some nearing low fuel limits. On the ground, twice that number were readying for takeoff. But until the backlog of flights in the air could be reduced, ATC had ordered further delays of outbound traffic. Meanwhile, terminal gates, taxiways, and ground holding areas were increasingly crammed with waiting aircraft, many with engines running.

Air freight warehouses – of all airlines – were stacked to their palletized limits with shipments, their usual high speed transit impeded by the storm. Freight supervisors were nervously watching perishables – hothouse flowers from Wyoming for New England; a ton of Pennsylvania cheese for Anchorage, Alaska; frozen peas for Iceland; live lobsters – trans-shipped from the east for a polar route flight – destination Europe. The lobsters were for tomorrow's menus in Edinburgh and Paris where they would be billed as 'fresh local seafood', and American tourists would order them unknowingly. Storm or not, contracts decreed that air freight perishables must arrive at destination fresh, and swiftly.

Causing special anxiety in American Airlines Freight was a shipment of several

1

thousand turkey poults, hatched in incubators only hours earlier. The precise hatching-shipping schedule – like a complex order of battle – was set up weeks ago, before the turkey eggs were laid. It called for delivery of the live birds on the West Coast within forty-eight hours of birth, the limit of the tiny creatures' existence without their first food or water. Normally, the arrangement provided a near-hundred per cent survival. Significant also – if the poults were fed en route, they would stink, and so would the aeroplane conveying them, for days afterwards. Already the poults' schedule was out of joint by several hours. But an aeroplane had been diverted from passenger to freight service, and tonight the fledgling turkeys would have priority over everything else travelling, human VIPs included.

In the main passenger terminal, chaos predominated. Terminal waiting areas were jammed with thousands of passengers from delayed or cancelled flights. Baggage, in piles, was everywhere. The vast main concourse had the combined appearance of a football scrimmage and Christmas Eve at Macy's.

High on the terminal roof, the airport's immodest slogan, LINCOLN INTERNATIONAL – AVIATION CROSSROADS OF THE WORLD, was entirely obscured by drifting snow.

The wonder was, Mel Bakersfeld reflected, that anything was continuing to operate at all.

Mel, airport general manager – lean, rangy, and a powerhouse of disciplined energy – was standing by the Snow Control Desk, high in the control tower. He peered out into the darkness. Normally, from this glass-walled room, the entire airport complex – runways, taxi strips, terminals, traffic of the ground and air – was visible like neatly aligned building blocks and models, even at night their shapes and movements well defined by lights. Only one loftier view existed – that of Air Traffic Control which occupied the floor above.

But tonight only a faint blur of a few nearer lights penetrated the almost-opaque curtain of wind-driven snow. Mel suspected this would be a winter to be discussed at meteorologists' conventions for years to come.

The present storm had been born five days ago in the lee of the Colorado mountains. At birth it was a tiny low pressure area, no bigger then a foothills homestead, and most forecasters on their air route weather charts had either failed to notice, or ignored it. As if in resentment, the low pressure system thereupon inflated like a giant malignancy and, still growing, swung first southeast, then north.

It crossed Kansas and Oklahoma, then paused at Arkansas, gathering assorted nastiness. Next day, fat and monstrous, it rumbled up the Mississippi Valley. Finally, over Illinois the storm unloaded, almost paralysing the state with blizzard winds, freezing temperatures, and a ten-inch snowfall in twenty-four hours.

At the airport, the ten-inch snow had been preceded by a continuous, if somewhat lighter, fall. Now it was being followed by more snow, whipped by vicious winds which piled new drifts – at the same time that ploughs were clearing the old. Maintenance snow crews were nearing exhaustion. Within the past few hours several men had been ordered home, over-fatigued despite their intermittent use of sleeping quarters provided at the airport for just this kind of emergency.

At the Snow Control Desk near Mel, Danny Farrow – at other times an assistant airport manager, now snow shift supervisor – was calling Maintenance Snow Centre by radio phone.

2

'We're losing the parking lots. I need six more Payloaders and a banjo team at Y-seventy-four.'

Danny was seated at the Snow Desk, which was not really a desk at all, but a wide, three-position console. Confronting Danny and his two assistants – one on either side – was a battery of telephones, teleautographs, and radios. Surrounding them were maps, charts, and bulletin boards recording the state and location of every piece of motorized snow-fighting equipment, as well as men and supervisors. There was a separate board for banjo teams – roving crews with individual snow shovels. The Snow Desk was activated only for its one seasonal purpose. At other times of year, this room remained empty and silent.

Danny's bald pate showed sweat globules as he scratched notations on a large-scale airport grid map. He repeated his message to Maintenance, making it sound like a desperate personal plea, which perhaps it was. Up here was the snow clearance command post. Whoever ran it was supposed to view the airport as a whole, juggling demands, and deploying equipment wherever need seemed greatest. The problem though – and undoubtedly a cause of Danny's sweating – was that those down below, fighting to keep their own operations going, seldom shared the same view of priorities.

'Sure, sure. Six more Payloaders.' An edgy voice from Maintenance, which was on the opposite side of the airfield, rattled the speakerphone. 'We'll get 'em from Santa Claus. He ought to be around in this lot.' A pause, then more aggressively, 'Any other damnfool stupid notions?'

Glancing at Danny, Mel shook his head. He recognized the speakerphone voice as belonging to a senior foreman who had probably worked continuously since the present snowfall started. Tempers wore thin at times like this, with good reason. Usually, after an arduous, snow-fighting winter, airport maintenance and management had an evening stag session together which they called 'kiss-and-make-up night'. They would certainly need one this year.

Danny said reasonably, 'We sent four Payloaders after that United food truck. They should be through, or almost.'

'They might be – if we could find the frigging truck.'

'You haven't located it *yet*? What are you guys doing – having a supper and ladies' night?' Danny reached out, turning down the speakerphone volume as a reply slammed back.

'Listen, do you birds in that crummy penthouse have any idea what it's like out on the field? Maybe you should look out the windows once in a while. Anybody could be at the goddam North Pole tonight and never know the difference.'

'Try blowing on your hands, Ernie,' Danny said. 'It may keep 'em warm, and it'll stop you sounding off.'

Mentally, Mel Bakersfeld filtered out most of the exchange, though he was aware that what had been said about conditions away from the terminal was true. An hour ago, Mel had driven across the airfield. He used service roads, but although he knew the airport layout intimately, tonight he had trouble finding his way and several times came close to being lost.

Mel had gone to inspect the Maintenance Snow Centre and then, as now, activity had been intensive. Where the tower Snow Control Desk was a command post, the Maintenance Snow Centre was a front line headquarters. From here, weary crews and supervisors came and went, alternately sweating and freezing, the ranks of regular workers swelled by auxiliaries – carpenters, electricians, plumbers, clerks, police. The auxiliaries were pulled from their regular airport duties and paid time-and-a-half until the snow emergency was over. But they knew what was expected, having rehearsed snow manoeuvres, like weekend soldiers, on runways and taxi strips during summer and fall. It sometimes amused outsiders to see snow removal groups, plough blades down, blowers roaring, on a hot, sunny day. But if any expressed surprise at the extent of preparation, Mel Bakersfeld would remind them that removing snow from the airport's operating area was equal to clearing seven hundred miles of highway.

Like the Snow Desk in the control tower, the Maintenance Snow Centre was activated for its winter function only. It was a big, cavernous room above an airport truck garage and, when in use, was presided over by dispatcher. Judging from the present radio voice, Mel guessed that the regular dispatcher had been relieved for the time being, perhaps for some sleep in the 'Blue Room', as Airport Standing Orders – with a trace of humour – called the snow crew's bunk-house.

The maintenance foreman's voice came on the radiophone again. 'We're worried about that truck too, Danny. The poor bastard of a driver could freeze out there. Though if he has any gumption, he isn't starving.'

The UAL food truck had left the airline flight kitchen for the main terminal nearly two hours ago. Its route lay around the perimeter track, a journey which usually took fifteen minutes. But the truck had failed to arrive, and obviously the driver had lost his way and was snowbound somewhere in the airport boondocks. United flight dispatch had first sent out its own search party, without success. Now airport management had taken over.

Mel said, 'That United flight finally took off, didn't it? Without food.'

Danny Farrow answered without looking up. 'I hear the captain put it to the passengers. Told them it'd take an hour to get another truck, that they had the movie and liquor aboard, and the sun was shining in California. Everybody voted to get the hell out. I would, too.'

Mel nodded, resisting a temptation to take over and direct the search himself for the missing truck and driver. Action would be a therapy. The cold of several days, and dampness with it, had made Mel's old war injury ache again – a reminder of Korea which never left him – and he could feel it now. He shifted, leaning, letting the good foot take his weight. The relief was momentary. Almost at once, in the new position, the ache resumed.

He was glad, a moment later, that he had not interfered. Danny was already doing the right thing – intensifying the truck search, pulling ploughs and men from the terminal area and directing them to the perimeter road. For the time being, the parking lots would have to be abandoned, and later there would be plenty of beefs about *that*. But the missing driver must be saved first.

Between calls, Danny warned Mel, 'Brace yourself for more complaints. This search'll block the perimeter road. We'll hold up all the other food trucks till we find the guy.'

Mel nodded. Complaints were a stock-in-trade of an airport manager's job. In this case, as Danny predicted, there would be a flood of protests when other airlines realized their food trucks were not getting through, whatever the reason.

There were some who would find it hard to believe that a man could be in peril of death from exposure at the centre of civilization like an airport, but it would happen just the same. The lonelier limits of the airport were no place to wander without bearings on a night like this. And if the driver decided to stay with his truck and keep the motor running for warmth, it could quickly be covered by drifts, with deadly carbon monoxide accumulating beneath.

With one hand, Danny was using a red telephone; with the other, leafing through emergency orders – Mel's orders, carefully drawn up for occasions such as this.

The red phone was to the airport's duty fire chief. Danny summarized the situation so far.

'And when we locate the truck, let's get an ambulance out there, and you may need an inhalator or heat, could be both. But better not roll until we know where exactly. We don't want to dig you guys out, too.'

The sweat, in increasing quantity, was gleaming on Danny's balding head. Mel was aware that Danny disliked running the Snow Control Desk and was happier in his own department of airport planning, sifting logistics and hypotheses of aviation's future. Such things were comfortably projected well ahead, with time to think, not disconcertingly here-and-now like the problems of tonight. Just as there were people who lived in the past, Mel thought, for the Danny Farrows, the future was a refuge. But unhappy or not, and despite the sweat, Danny was coping.

Reaching over Danny's shoulder, Mel picked up a direct line phone to Air Traffic Control. The tower watch chief answered.

'What's the story on the Aéreo-Mexican 707?'

'Still there, Mr Bakersfeld. They've been working a couple of hours trying to move it. No luck yet.'

That particular trouble had begun shortly after dark when an Aéreo-Mexican captain, taxiing for takeoff, mistakenly passed to the right instead of left of a blue taxi light. Unfortunately, the ground to the right which was normally grass covered, had a drainage problem, due to be worked on when winter ended. Meanwhile, despite the heavy snow, there was still a morass of mud beneath the surface. Within seconds of its wrong-way turn, the hundred and twenty ton aircraft was deeply mired.

When it became obvious that the aircraft could not get out, loaded, under its own power, the disgruntled passengers were disembarked and helped through the mud to hastily hired buses. Now, more than two hours later, the big jet was still stuck, its fuselage and tail blocking runway three zero.

Mel inquired, 'The runway and taxi strip are still out of use?'

'Affirmative,' the tower chief reported. 'We're holding all outbound traffic at the gates, then sending them the long route to the other runways.'

'Pretty slow?'

'Slowing us fifty per cent. Right now we're holding ten flights for taxi clearance, another dozen waiting to start engines.'

It was a demonstration, Mel reflected, of how urgently the airport needed additional runways and taxiways. For three years he had been urging construction of a new runway to parallel three zero, as well as other operational improvements. But the Board of Airport Commissioners, under political pressure from downtown, refused to approve. The pressure was because city councilmen, for reasons of their own, wanted to avoid a new bond issue which would be needed for financing.

'The other thing,' the tower watch chief said, 'is that with three zero out of use, we're having to route takeoffs over Meadowood. The complaints have started coming in already.'

Mel groaned. The community of Meadowood, which adjoined the southwest limits of the airfield, was a constant thorn to himself and an impediment to flight operations. Though the airport had been established long before the community, Meadowood's residents complained incessantly and bitterly about noise from aircraft overhead. Press publicity followed. It attracted even more complaints, with increasingly bitter denunciations of the airport and its management. Eventually, after long negotiations involving politics, more publicity and – in Mel Bakersfeld's opinion – gross misrepresentation, the airport and the Federal Aviation Administration had conceded that jet takeoffs and landings directly over Meadowood would be made only when essential in special circumstances. Since the airport was already limited in its available runways, the loss in efficiency was considerable.

Moreover, it was also agreed that aircraft taking off towards Meadowood would – almost at once after becoming airborne – follow noise abatement procedures. This, in turn, produced protests from pilots, who considered the procedures dangerous. The airlines, however – conscious of the public furore and their corporate images – had ordered the pilots to conform.

Yet even this failed to satisfy the Meadowood residents. Their militant leaders were still protesting, organizing, and – according to latest rumours – planning legal harassment of the airport.

Mel asked the tower watch chief, 'How many calls have there been?' Even before the answer, he decided glumly that still more hours of his working days were going to be consumed by delegations, arguments, and the same insoluble discussions as before.

'I'd say fifty at least, we've answered; and there've been others we haven't. The phones start ringing right after every takeoff – our unlisted lines, too. I'd give a lot to know how they get the numbers.'

'I suppose you've told the people who've called that we've a special situation – the storm, a runway out of use.'

'We explain. But nobody's interested. They just want the aeroplanes to stop coming over. Some of 'em say that problems or not, pilots are still supposed to use noise abatement procedures, but tonight they aren't doing it.'

'Good God! – if I was a pilot neither would I.' How could anyone of reasonable intelligence, Mel wondered, expect a pilot, in tonight's violent weather, to chop back his power immediately after takeoff, and then go into a steeply banked turn on instruments – which was what noise abatement procedures called for.

'I wouldn't either,' the tower chief said. 'Though I guess it depends on your point of view. If I lived in Meadowood, maybe I'd feel the way they do.'

'You wouldn't live in Meadowood. You'd have listened to the warnings we gave people, years ago, not to build houses there.'

'I guess so. By the way, one of my people told me there's another community meeting over there tonight.'

'In this weather?'

'Seems they still plan to hold it, and the way we heard, they're cooking up something new.'

'Whatever it is,' Mel predicted, 'we'll hear about it soon.'

6

Just the same, he reflected, if there *was* a public meeting at Meadowood, it was a pity to provide fresh ammunition so conveniently. Almost certainly the press and local politicians would be present, and the direct flights overhead, however necessary at this moment, would give them plenty to write and talk about. So the sooner the blocked runway – three zero – was back in use, the better it would be for all concerned.

'In a little while,' he told the tower chief, 'I'll go out on the field myself and see what's happening. I'll let you know what the situation is.'

'Right.'

Changing the subject, Mel inquired, 'Is my brother on duty tonight?'

'Affirmative. Keith's on radar watch – west arrival.'

West arrival, Mel knew, was one of the tough, tense positions in the tower. It involved supervising all incoming flights in the west quadrant. Mel hesitated, then remembered he had known the tower watch chief a long time. 'Is Keith all right? Is he showing any strain?'

There was a slight pause before the answer. 'Yes, he is. I'd say more than usual.'

Between the two men was the knowledge that Mel's younger brother had lately been a source of anxiety to them both.

'Frankly,' the tower chief said, 'I wish I could let him take things easier. But I can't. We're short-staffed and everybody is under the gun.' He added, 'Including me.'

'I know you are, and I appreciate your watching out for Keith the way you have.'

'Well, in this job most of us have combat fatigue at one time or another.' Mel could sense the other choosing his words carefully. 'Sometimes it shows up in the mind, sometimes in the gut. Either way, when it happens we try to help each other.'

'Thanks.' The conversation had not eased Mel's anxiety. 'I may drop in later.'

'Right, sir.' The tower chief hung up.

The 'sir' was strictly a courtesy. Mel had no authority over ATC, which answered only to the Federal Aviation Administration with headquarters in Washington. But relationships between controllers and airport management were good, and Mel saw to it they stayed that way.

An airport, any airport, was an odd complexity of overlapping authority. No single individual had supreme command, yet no one segment was entirely independent. As airport general manager, Mel's was closest to an over-all assignment, but there were areas where he knew better than to intrude. Air Traffic Control was one, airline internal management another. He could, and did, intervene in matters affecting the airport as a whole or the welfare of people using it. He could peremptorily order an airline to remove a door sign which was misleading or failed to conform to terminal standards. But what went on behind the door was, within reason, the airline's exclusive business.

This was why an airport manager needed to be a tactician as well as versatile administrator.

Mel replaced the Snow Desk telephone. On another line, Danny Farrow was arguing with the parking lot supervisor, a harassed individual who for several hours had been fielding irate complaints from marooned car owners. People were asking: didn't whoever ran the airport know it was snowing? And if they did, why didn't someone get on the ball and move the stuff so a man could drive his car anywhere at any time, as was his democratic right?

'Tell 'em we declared a dictatorship.' The non-covered lots, Danny insisted, would have to wait until priorities eased. He would send men and equipment when he could. He was interrupted by a call from the tower watch chief. A new weather forecast predicted a wind shift in an hour. It would mean a change of runways, and could they hurry the ploughing of runway one seven, left? He would do his best, Danny said. He'd check with the Conga Line supervisor and call the tower back.

It was the kind of pressure, unremitting, which had gone on for three days and nights since the present snowfall started. The fact that the pressure had been met made all the more irritating a note, delivered to Mel by messenger, fifteen minutes ago. The note said:

m –

thought shd warn u–airlines snow committee (on vern demerest's urging . . . why does your bro-in-law dislike you?) filing critical report becos runways & taxiways snow clearance (v.d. says) lousy, inefficient . . . .

report blames airport (meaning u) for main hunk of flight delays . . . also claims stuck 707 wouldn't have if taxiway ploughed sooner, better . . . so now all airlines being penalized, etc, etc. You get the drift . . . and where are you – in one? (drift, i mean) . . . climb out & buy me coffee soon.

luv

t

The 't' was for Tanya – Tanya Livingston, passenger relations agent for Trans America, and a special friend of Mel's. Mel read the note again, as he usually did messages from Tanya, which became clearer the second time around. Tanya, whose job straddled trouble-shooting and public relations, objected to capitals. ('Mel, doesn't it make sense? If we abolished capitals there'd be scads less trouble. Just look at the newspapers.') She had actually coerced a Trans America mechanic into chiselling all capitals from the type bars of her office typewriter. Someone higher up raised hob about that, Mel had heard, quoting the airline's rigid rule about wilful damage to company property. Tanya had got away with it, though. She usually did.

The Vern Demerest in the note was Captain Vernon Demerest, also of Trans America. As well as being one of the airline's most senior captains, Demerest was a militant campaigner for the Air Line Pilots Association, and, this season, a member of the Airline Snow Committee at Lincoln International. The committee inspected runways and taxiways during snow periods and pronounced them fit, or otherwise, for aircraft use. It always included an active flying captain.

Vernon Demerest also happened to be Mel's brother-in-law, married to Mel's older sister, Sarah. The Bakersfeld clan, through precedent and marriage, had roots and branches in aviation, just as older families were once allied with seafaring. However, there was little cordiality between Mel and his brother-in-law, whom Mel considered conceited and pompous. Others, he knew, held the same opinion. Recently, Mel and Captain Demerest had had an angry exchange at a meeting of the Board of Airport Commissioners, where Demerest appeared on behalf of the pilots' association. Mel suspected that the critical snow report – apparently initiated by his brother-in-law – was in retaliation.

Mel was not greatly worried about the report. Whatever shortcomings the airport might have in other ways, he knew they were coping with the storm as well as any organization could. Just the same, the report was a nuisance. Copies would go to all airlines, and tomorrow there would be inquiring phone calls and memos, and a need for explanations.

Mel supposed he had better stay briefed, in readiness. He decided he would make an inspection of the present snow clearance situation at the same time that he was out on the airfield checking on the blocked runway and the mired Aéreo-Mexican jet.

At the Snow Desk, Danny Farrow was talking with Airport Maintenance again. When there was a moment's break, Mel interjected, 'I'll be in the terminal, then on the field.'

He had remembered what Tanya said in her note about having coffee together. He would stop at his own office first, then, on his way through the terminal, he would drop by Trans America to see her. The thought excited him.

2

Mel used the private elevator, which operated by passkey only, to descend from the tower to the administrative mezzanine. Though his own office suite was silent, with stenographers' desks cleared and typewriters covered, the lights had been left on. He entered his own interior office. From a closet, near the wide mahogany desk he used in daytime, he took out a heavy topcoat and fur-lined boots.

Tonight Mel himself was without specific duties at the airport. This was as it should be. The reason he had stayed, through most of the three-day storm, was to be available for emergencies. Otherwise, he mused, as he pulled on the boots and laced them, by now he would have been home with Cindy and the children.

Or would he?

No matter how objective you tried to be, Mel reasoned, it was hard to be sure of your own real motives. Probably, if it had not been the storm, something else would have arisen to justify not going. Not going home, in fact, seemed lately to have become the pattern of his life. His job was a cause, of course. It provided plenty of reasons to remain extra hours at the airport, where lately there had been big problems facing him, quite apart from tonight's imbroglio. But – if he was honest with himself – the airport also offered an escape from the incessant wrangling between himself and Cindy which seemed to occur nowadays whenever they spent time together.

'Oh, hell!' Mel's exclamation cut across the silence of the office.

He plodded in the fur-lined boots towards his desk. A glance at the typed reminder from his secretary confirmed what he had just recalled. Tonight there was another of his wife's tedious charity affairs. A week ago, reluctantly, Mel had promised to attend. It was a cocktail party and dinner (so the typed note said), downtown at the swank Lake Michigan Inn. What the charity was, the note didn't specify, and, if it had ever been mentioned, he had since forgotten. It made no difference, though. The causes with which Cindy Bakersfeld involved herself were depressingly similar. The test of worthiness – as Cindy saw it – was the social eminence of her fellow committee members.

Fortunately, for the sake of peace with Cindy, the starting time was late – almost two hours from now and in view of tonight's weather, it might even be later. So he could still make it, even after inspecting the airfield. Mel could come back, shave and change in his office, and be downtown only a little late. He had better warn Cindy though. Using a direct outside line, Mel dialled his home number.

Roberta, his elder daughter, answered.

'Hi,' Mel said. 'This is your old man.'

Roberta's voice came coolly down the line. 'Yes, I know.'

'How was school today?'

'Could you be specific, Father? There were several classes. Which do you want to know about?'

Mel sighed. There were days on which it seemed to him that his home life was disintegrating all at once. Roberta, he could tell, was in what Cindy called one of her snotty moods. Did all fathers, he wondered, abruptly lose communication with their daughters at age thirteen? Less than a year ago, the two of them had seemed as close as father and daughter could be. Mel loved both his daughters deeply – Roberta, and her younger sister, Libby. There were times when he realised they were the only reasons his marriage had survived. As to Roberta, he had known that as a teenager she would develop interests which he could neither share nor wholly understand. He had been prepared for this. What he had not expected was to be shut out entirely or treated with a mixture of indifference and condescension. Though, to be objective, he supposed the increasing strife between Cindy and himself had not helped. Children were sensitive.

'Never mind,' Mel said. 'Is your mother home?'

'She went out. She said if you phoned to tell you you have to be downtown to meet her, and for once try not to be late.'

Mel curbed his irritation. Roberta was undoubtedly repeating Cindy's words exactly. He could almost hear his wife saying them.

'If your mother calls, tell her I might have to be a little late, and that I can't help it.' There was a silence, and he asked, 'Did you hear me?'

'Yes,' Roberta said. 'Is there anything else, Father? I have homework to do.'

He snapped back, 'Yes, there is something else. You'll change your tone of voice, young lady, and show a little more respect. Furthermore, we'll end this conversation when I'm good and ready.'

'If you say so, Father.'

'And stop calling me Father!'

'Very well, Father.'

Mel was tempted to laugh, then supposed he had better not. He asked, 'Is everything all right at home?'

'Yes. But Libby wants to talk to you.'

'In a minute. I was just going to tell you – because of the storm I may not be home tonight. There's a lot happening at the airport. I'll probably come back and sleep here.'

Again a pause, as if Roberta was weighing whether or not she could get away with a smart answer: *So what else is new?* Apparently she decided not. 'Will you speak to Libby now?'

'Yes, I will. Goodnight, Robbie.'

'Goodnight.'

There was an impatient shuffle as the telephone changed hands, then Libby's small breathless voice. 'Daddy, Daddy! Guess what!'

Libby was always breathless as if, to a seven-year-old, life was excitingly on the run and she must forever keep pace or be left behind.

'Let me think,' Mel said. 'I know – you had fun in the snow today.'

10

'Yes, I did. But it wasn't that.'

'Then I can't guess. You'll have to tell me.'

'Well, at school, Miss Curzon said for homework we have to write down all the good things we think will happen next month.'

He thought affectionately: he could understand Libby's enthusiasm. To her, almost everything was exciting and good, and the few things which were not were brushed aside and speedily forgotten. He wondered how much longer her happy innocence would last.

'That's nice,' Mel said. 'I like that.'

'Daddy, Daddy! Will you help me?'

'If I can.'

'I want a map of February.'

Mel smiled. Libby had a verbal shorthand of her own which sometimes seemed more expressive than conventional words. It occurred to him that he could use a map of February himself.

'There's a calendar in my desk in the den.' Mel told her where to find it and heard her small feet running from the room, the telephone forgotten. It was Roberta, Mel assumed, who silently hung up.

From the general manager's office suite, Mel walked on to the executive mezzanine which ran the length of the main terminal building. He carried the heavy topcoat with him.

Pausing, he surveyed the thronged concourse below, which seemed to have become even busier within the past half-hour. In waiting areas, every available seat was occupied. News stands and information booths were ringed by crowds, among them many military uniforms. In front of all airline passenger counters were line-ups, some extending around corners out of sight. Behind the counters, ticket agents and supervisors, their normal numbers swelled by colleagues from earlier shifts retained on overtime, had schedules and passage coupons spread out like orchestral scores.

Delays and reroutings which the storm had caused were taxing both scheduling and human patience. Immediately below Mel, at Braniff ticketing, a youngish man with long blond hair and a yellow scarf was proclaiming loudly, 'You've got the effrontery to tell me I must go to Kansas City to get to New Orleans. You people are rewriting geography! You're mad with power!'

The ticket agent facing him, an attractive brunette in her twenties, brushed a hand over her eyes before answering with professional patience, 'We can route you directly, sir, but we don't know when. Because of the weather, the longer way will be faster and the fare is the same.'

Behind the yellow-scarfed man, more passengers with other problems pressed forward urgently.

At the United counter, a small pantomime was being played. A would-be passenger – a well-dressed businessman – leaned forward, speaking quietly. By the man's expression and actions, Mel Bakersfeld could guess what was being said. 'I would very much like to get on that next flight.'

'I'm sorry, sir, the flight is fully booked. There's also a long standby . . .' Before the ticket agent could complete his sentence, he glanced up. The passenger had laid his brief case on the counter in front of him. Gently, but pointedly, he was tapping a plastic baggage tag against a corner of the case. It was a 100,000-Mile Club tag, one of those United issued to its favoured friends – an inner elite which all airlines had helped create.

The agent's expression changed. His voice became equally low. 'I think we'll manage something, sir.' The agent's pencil hovered, crossed out the name of another passenger – an earlier arrival whom he had been about to put on the flight – and inserted the newcomer's name instead. The action was unobserved by those in line behind.

The same kind of thing, Mel knew, went on at all airline counters everywhere. Only the naïve or uninformed believed waiting lists and reservations were operated with unwavering impartiality.

Mel observed that a group of new arrivals – presumably from downtown – was entering the terminal. They were beating off snow from their clothing as they came in, and judging from their appearance, it seemed that the weather outside must be worsening. The newcomers were quickly absorbed in the general crowds.

Few among the eighty thousand or so air travellers who thronged the terminal daily ever glanced up at the executive mezzanine, and fewer still were aware of Mel tonight, high above them, looking down. Most people who thought about airports did so in terms of airlines and aeroplanes. It was doubtful if many were even aware that executive offices existed or that an administrative machine – unseen, but complex and employing hundreds – was constantly at work, keeping the airport functioning.

Perhaps it was as well, Mel thought, as he rode the elevator down again. If people became better informed, in time they would also learn the airport's weaknesses and dangers, and afterwards fly in and out with less assurance than before.

On the main concourse, he headed towards the Trans America wing. Near the check-in counters, a uniformed supervisor stepped forward. 'Evening, Mr Bakersfeld. Were you looking for Mrs Livingston?'

No matter how busy the airport became, Mel thought, there would always be time for gossip. He wondered how widely his own name and Tanya's had been linked already.

'Yes,' he said. 'I was.'

The supervisor nodded towards a door marked AIRLINE PERSONNEL ONLY.

'You'll find her through there, Mr Bakersfeld. We just had a bit of a crisis here. She's taking care of it.'

3

In a small private lounge which was sometimes used for VIPs, the young girl in the uniform of a Trans America ticket agent was sobbing hysterically.

Tanya Livingston steered her to a chair. 'Make yourself comfortable,' Tanya said practically, 'and take your time. You'll feel better afterwards, and when you're ready we can talk.'

Tanya sat down herself, smoothing her trim, tight uniform skirt. There was no one else in the room, and the only sound – apart from the crying – was the faint hum of air-conditioning.

There was fifteen years or so difference in age between the two women. The girl was not much more than twenty, Tanya in her late thirties. Watching, Tanya felt the gap to be greater than it was. It came, she supposed, from having been exposed to marriage, even though briefly, and a long time ago – or so it seemed.

She thought: it was the second time she had been conscious of her age today. The first was while combing her hair this morning; she had seen telltale strands of grey among the short-cropped, flamboyant red. There was more of the grey than last time she had checked a month or so ago, and both occasions were reminders that her forties – by which time a woman ought to know where she was going and why – were closer than she liked to think about. She had another thought: in only fifteen years from now, her own daughter would be the same age as the girl who was crying.

The girl, whose name was Patsy Smith, wiped reddened eyes with a large linen handkerchief which Tanya had given her. She spoke with difficulty, choking back more tears. 'They wouldn't talk that way . . . so mean, rudely . . . at home . . . not to their wives.'

'You mean passengers wouldn't?'

The girl nodded.

'Some would,' Tanya said. 'When you're married, Patsy, you may find out, though I hope not. But if you're telling me that men behave like adolescent boors when their travel plans get crossed up, I'll agree with you.'

'I was doing my best . . . We all were . . . All day today; and yesterday . . . the day before . . . But the way people talk to you . . .'

'You mean they act as if you started the storm yourself. Especially to inconvenience them.'

'Yes . . . And then that last man . . . Until him, I was all right . . .'

'What happened exactly? They called me when it was all over.'

The girl was beginning to regain control of herself.

'Well . . . he had a ticket on Flight 72, and that was cancelled because of weather. We got him a seat on 114, and he missed it. He said he was in the dining room and didn't hear the flight called.'

'Flight announcements aren't made in the dining room,' Tanya said. 'There's a big notice saying so, and it's on all the menus.'

'I explained that, Mrs Livingston, when he came back from the departure gate. But he was still nasty. He was going on as if it were my fault he'd missed the flight, not his. He said we were all inefficient and half asleep.'

'Did you call your supervisor?'

'I tried to, but he was busy. We all were.'

'So what did you do?'

'I got the passenger a seat – on the extra section, 2122.'

'And?'

'He wanted to know what movie was showing on the flight. I found that out, and he said he'd seen it. He got nasty again. The movie he'd wanted to see was on the first flight which was cancelled. He said, could I get him another flight which was showing the same movie as the first one? All the time, there were other passengers; they were pressing up against the counter. Some were making remarks out loud about how slow I was. Well, when he said that about the movie, that was when I . . .' The girl hesitated. 'I guess something snapped.'

Tanya prompted. 'That was when you threw the timetable?'

Patsy Smith nodded miserably. She looked as if she were going to cry again. 'Yes. I don't know what got into me, Mrs Livingston . . . I threw it right over the counter. I told him he could fix his own flight.'

ARTHUR HAILEY

'All I can say,' Tanya said, 'is that I hope you hit him.'

The girl looked up. In place of tears, there was the beginning of a smile. 'Oh, yes; I did.' She thought, then giggled. 'You should have seen his face. He was so surprised.' Her expression became serious. 'Then, after that . . .'

'I know what happened after that. You broke down, which was a perfectly natural thing to do. You were sent in here to finish your cry, and now you have, you're going home in a taxi.'

The girl looked bemused. 'You mean . . . that's all?'

'Certainly it's all. Did you expect us to fire you?'

'I . . . I wasn't sure.'

'We might have to,' Tanya said, 'much as we'd dislike it, Patsy, if you did the same thing again. But you won't, will you? Not ever.'

The girl shook her head firmly. 'No, I won't. I can't explain, but having done it just once is enough.'

'That's the end of it, then. Except that you might like to hear what happened after you left.'

'Yes, please.'

'A man came forward. He was one of those in the line-up, and he said he heard, and saw, the whole thing. He also said he had a daughter the same age as you, and if the first man had talked to his daughter the same way he talked to you, he would personally have punched him on the nose. Then the second man – the one from the line-up – left his name and address, and said if the man you had been talking to ever made any kind of complaint, to let him know and he would report what really happened.' Tanya smiled. 'So, you see – there are nice people, too.'

'I know,' the girl said. 'There aren't many, but when you do get one like that, who's nice to you, and cheerful, you feel you want to hug him.'

'Unfortunately we can't do that, any more than we should throw timetables. Our job is to treat everyone alike, and be courteous, even when passengers are not.'

'Yes, Mrs Livingston.'

Patsy Smith would be all right, Tanya decided. Apparently she hadn't thought of quitting, as some girls did who suffered similar experiences. In fact, now that she was over her emotion, Patsy seemed to have the kind of resilience which would be helpful to her in future.

God knows, Tanya thought, you needed resilience – and some toughness – in dealing with the travelling public, whatever job you held.

Take Reservations.

Downtown in reservation departments, she was aware, personal pressures would be even greater than at the airport. Since the storm began, reservation clerks would have made thousands of calls advising passengers of delays and rearrangements. It was a job the clerks all hated because people whom they called were invariably bed-tempered and frequently abusive. Airline delays seemed to arouse a latent savagery in those affected by them. Men talked insultingly to women telephonists, and even people who at other times were courteous and mild-mannered, turned snarly and disagreeable. New York-bound flights were worst of all. Reservation clerks had been known to refuse the assignment of telephoning news of delay or cancellation to a flight load of passengers destined for New York, preferring to risk their jobs rather than face the torrent of invective they knew awaited them. Tanya had often speculated on what it was about New York which infected those headed there with a kind of medicine-dance fervour to arrive.

But for whatever reasons, she knew there would be resignations among airline staffs – in Reservations and elsewhere – when the present emergency was over. There always were. A few nervous breakdowns could be counted on, too, usually among the younger girls, more sensitive to passengers' rudeness and ill humour. Constant politeness, even when you were trained for it, was a strain which took a heavy toll.

She was glad, though, that Patsy Smith would not be among the casualties.

There was a knock at the outer door. It opened, and Mel Bakersfeld leaned in. He was wearing fleece-lined boots and carrying a heavy topcoat. 'I was coming by,' he told Tanya. 'I can drop back later, if you like.'

'Please stay.' She smiled a welcome. 'We've almost finished.'

She watched him as he walked to a chair across the room. He looked tired, Tanya thought.

She switched her attention back, filled in a voucher, and handed it to the girl. 'Give this to the taxi dispatcher, Patsy, and he'll send you home. Have a good night's rest, and we'll expect you back tomorrow, bright and breezy.'

When the girl had gone, Tanya swung her chair around to face Mel's. She said brightly, 'Hullo.'

He put down a newspaper he had been glancing at, and grinned, 'Hi!'

'You got my note?'

'I came to thank you for it. Though I might have made it here without.' Gesturing to the door through which the girl had gone, he asked, 'What was all that about? Battle fatigue?'

'Yes.' She told him what had happened.

Mel laughed. 'I'm tired, too. How about sending *me* off in a taxi?'

Tanya looked at him, inquiringly. Her eyes – a bright, clear blue – had a quality of directness. Her head was tilted, and an overhead light reflected red highlights from her hair. A slim figure, yet with a fullness which the trim airline uniform heightened . . . Mel was conscious, as at other times, of her desirability and warmth.

'I might consider it,' she said. 'If the taxi goes to my place, and you let me cook you dinner. Say, a Lamb Casserole.'

He hesitated, weighing conflicting claims, then reluctantly shook his head. 'I wish I could. But we've some trouble here, and afterwards I have to be downtown.' He got up. 'Let's have coffee, anyway.'

'All right.'

Mel held the door open, and they went out into the bustling, noisy main concourse.

There was a press of people around the Trans America counter, even greater than when Mel arrived. 'I mustn't take long,' Tanya said. 'I've still two hours more on duty.'

As they threaded their way through the crowds and increasing piles of luggage, she moderated her normally brisk pace to Mel's slower one. He was limping rather more than usual, she noticed. She found herself wanting to take his arm and help him but supposed she had better not. She was still in Trans America uniform. Gossip spread fast enough without helping it actively. The two of them had been seen a good deal lately in each other's company, and Tanya was sure that the airport rumour machine – which operated like a jungle telegraph with IBM speed – had already taken note. Probably it was assumed

15

that she and Mel were bedding down together, though, as it happened, that much was untrue.

They were headed for the Cloud Captain's Coffee Shop in the central lobby.

'About that Lamb Casserole,' Mel said. 'Could we make it another night? Say, the day after tomorrow?'

The sudden invitation from Tanya had surprised him. Although they had had several dates together – for drinks or dinner – until now she had not suggested visiting her apartment. Of course, going there could be for dinner only. Still . . . there was always the possibility that it might not.

Lately, Mel had sensed that if their meetings away from the airport continued, there could be a natural and obvious progression. But he had moved cautiously, instinct warning him that an affair with Tanya would be no casual romance but a deeply emotional involvement for them both. A consideration, also, was his own problems with Cindy. Those were going to take a lot of working out, if they could be worked out at all, and there was a limit to the number of complications a man could handle at one time. It was a strange commentary, he thought, that when a marriage was secure it seemed easier to manage an affair than when the same marriage was shaky. Just the same, Tanya's invitation seemed too enticing to pass up.

'The day after tomorrow is Sunday,' she pointed out. 'But I'll be off duty, and if you can manage it, I'll have more time.'

Mel grinned. 'Candles and wine?'

He had forgotten it would be Sunday. But he would have to come to the airport anyway because, even if the storm moved on, there would be after effects. As to Cindy, there had been several Sundays when she had been out, herself, without an announced reason.

Momentarily, Mel and Tanya separated as she dodged a hurrying, florid-faced man, followed by a redcap with a loaded luggage cart, topped by golf clubs and tennis rackets. Wherever that load was going, Tanya thought enviously, it was a long way south.

'Okay,' she said when they rejoined. 'Candles and wine.'

As they entered the coffee shop, a pert hostess recognized Mel and ushered him, ahead of others, to a small table at the rear, marked RESERVED, which airport officials often used. About to sit down, he stumbled slightly and grasped Tanya's arm. The observant hostess flicked her eyes over them both with a half-smile. Rumour machine, stand by for a bulletin, Tanya thought.

Aloud, she said, 'Did you ever see such crowds? This has been the wildest three days I remember.'

Mel glanced around the packed coffee shop, its bedlam of voices punctuated by the clatter of dishes. He nodded towards the outer door through which they could both see a moving, surging swarm of people. 'If you think this is a big horde tonight, wait until the Lockheed L-500s go into service.'

'I know – we can barely cope with the 747s; but a thousand passengers arriving all at once at a check-in counter . . . God help us!' Tanya shuddered. 'Can you imagine what it will be like when they collect their baggage. I don't even want to think about it.'

'Nor do a good many other people – who *ought* to be thinking about it right now.' He was amused to find that their conversation had already drifted into aviation. Aeroplanes and airliners held a fascination for Tanya, and she liked talking about them. So did Mel, which was one of the reasons he enjoyed her company.

'Which people aren't thinking?'

'Those who control policy on the ground – airport and air traffic. Most are acting as if today's jets will fly for ever. They seem to believe that if everybody keeps quiet and still, the new, big aeroplanes will go away and not bother us. That way we needn't have ground facilities to match them.'

Tanya said thoughtfully, 'But there's a lot of building at airports. Wherever you go, you see it.'

Mel offered her a cigarette and she shook her head negatively. He lit one for himself before answering.

'Mostly the building going on is patchwork – changes and additions to airports built in the 1950s or early '60s. There's little that's far-seeing. There are exceptions – Los Angeles is one; Tampa, Florida, and Dallas-Fort Worth are others; they'll be the first few airports in the world ready for the new mammoth jets and supersonics. Kansas City, Houston, and Toronto look good; San Francisco has a plan, though it may get sunk politically. In North America there's not much else that's impressive.'

'How about Europe?'

'Europe is routine,' Mel said, 'except for Paris – the new Nord airport to replace Le Bourget will be among the finest yet. London is the kind of inefficient mess which only the English can create.' He paused, considering. 'We shouldn't knock other countries, though; back home is bad enough. New York is frightening, even with changes being made at Kennedy; there simply isn't enough air space above New York – I'm thinking of travelling there by train in future. Washington, DC, is floundering – Washington National's a Black Hole of Calcutta. Dulles was a giant step sideways. And Chicago will wake up one day to find it let itself get twenty years behind.' He stopped, considering. 'You remember a few years ago, when the jets first started flying – what conditions were like at airports which had been designed for DC-4s and Constellations.'

'I remember,' Tanya said. 'I worked at one. On normal days you couldn't move for the crowds; on busy days you couldn't breathe. We used to say it was like holding the World Series in a sand lot.'

'What's coming in the 1970s,' Mel predicted, 'is going to be worse, far worse. And not just people congestion. We'll be choking on other things, too.'

'Such as what?'

'Airways and traffic control for one, but that's another whole story. The really big thing, which most airport planning hasn't caught on to yet, is that we're moving towards the day – fast – when air freight business will be bigger than passenger traffic. The same thing's been true with every form of transportation, starting with the birchbark canoe. To begin with, people are carried, plus a little freight, but before long, there's more freight than people. In airline business we're already closer to that than is generally known. When freight does get to be top dog – as will happen in the next ten years or so – a lot of our present airport ideas will be obsolete. If you want a sign of the way things are moving, watch some of the young men who are going into airline management now. Not long ago, hardly anybody wanted to work in air freight departments; it was backroom stuff; passenger business had the glamour. Not any more! Now the bright boys are heading for air freight. They know that's where the future and the big promotions lie.'

Tanya sighed. 'I'll be old-fashioned and stick with people. Somehow freight . . .'

A waitress came to their table. 'The special's off, and if we get many more people in here tonight, there won't be much else either.'

They ordered coffee, Tanya cinnamon toast, and Mel a fried egg sandwich.

When the waitress had gone, Mel grinned. 'I guess I started to make a speech. I'm sorry.'

'Maybe you need the practice.' She regarded him curiously. 'You haven't made many lately.'

'I'm not president of the Airport Operators Council any more. I don't get to Washington as much, or other places either.' But it was not the whole reason for not making speeches and being less in the public eye. He suspected Tanya knew it.

Curiously, it was a speech of Mel's which had brought them together to begin with. At one of the rare inter-line meetings which airlines held, he had talked about coming developments in aviation, and the lag in ground organization compared with progress in the air. He had used the occasion as a dry run for a speech he intended to deliver at a national forum a week or so later. Tanya had been among the Trans America contingent, and next day had sent him one of her lower case notes:

mr. b

spch great. all'v us earthside slaves cheering u 4 admitting airport policy-makers asleep at drawing boards. somebody needed 2 say it. mind suggestion? wd all be more alive if fewer fax, more abt people . . . passenger, once inside belly (airplane or whale, remember jonah?) thinks only of self, not system much. i'll bet orville/wilbur felt same way once off ground. wright?

tl

As well as amusing him, the note had caused him to think. It was true, he realized – he *had* concentrated on facts and systems to the exclusion of people as individuals. He revised his speech notes, shifting the emphasis as Tanya suggested. The result was the most successful presentation he had ever made. It gained him an ovation and was widely reported internationally. Afterwards he had telephoned Tanya to thank her. That was when they had started seeing each other.

The thought of Tanya's first message was a reminder of the note she had sent this evening. 'I appreciate that tip about the snow committee report, though I'm curious how you managed to see it before I have.'

'No mystery. It was typed in the Trans America office. I saw our Captain Demerest checking it, and chortling.'

'Vernon showed it to you?'

'No, but he had it spread out, and I'm adept at reading upside down. Which reminds me, you didn't answer my question: Why does your brother-in-law dislike you?'

Mel grimaced. 'I guess he knows I'm not overly keen on *him*.'

'If you wanted to,' Tanya said, 'you could tell him now. There's the great man himself.' She nodded towards the cashier's desk, and Mel turned his head.

Captain Vernon Demerest of Trans America was counting out change as he paid a bill. A tall, broad-shouldered, striking figure, he towered above others around him. He was dressed informally in a Harris tweed jacket and impeccably creased slacks, yet managed to convey an impression of authority – like a Regular Army General, Mel thought, temporarily in civilian clothes. Demerest's strong, aristocratic features were unsmiling as he addressed a four-striper Trans America captain – in uniform – who was with him. It

18

appeared that Demerest was giving instructions; the other nodded. Captain Demerest glanced briefly around the coffee shop and, observing Mel and Tanya, gave a curt, cool nod. Then, checking his watch, and with a final word to the other captain, he strode out.

'He appeared in a hurry,' Tanya said. 'Though wherever he's going, it won't be for long. Captain D. is taking Flight Two to Rome tonight.'

Mel smiled. *'The Golden Argosy?'*

'No less. I see, sir, you read our advertising.'

'It's hard not to.' Mel was aware, as were millions of others who admired the four-colour double-page spreads in *Life, Look,* the *Post* and other national magazines, that Trans America Flight Two – *The Golden Argosy* – was the airline's crack, prestige flight. He also knew that only the line's most senior captains ever commanded it.

'It seems to be agreed,' Mel said, 'that Vernon is one of the finest pilots extant.'

'Oh yes, indeed. Extant and arrogant.' Tanya hesitated, then confided, 'If you're in a mood for gossip, you aren't alone in not caring for your brother-in-law. I heard one of our mechanics say not long ago, he was sorry there weren't propellers any more because he'd always hoped Captain Demerest would walk into one.'

Mel said sharply, 'That's a pretty savage thought.'

'I agree. Personally, I prefer what Mr Youngquist, our president, is supposed to have said. I understand his instructions about Captain Demerest are: "Keep that bumptious bastard out of my hair, but book me on his flights".'

Mel chuckled. Knowing both men, he felt sure the sally was true. He should not have let himself be drawn into a discussion about Vernon Demerest, he realized, but news of the adverse snow report and the nuisance effect it would have, still rankled. He wondered idly where his brother-in-law was going at the moment and if it involved one of his amorous adventures, of which – reportedly – there were a good many. Looking towards the central lobby, Mel saw that Captain Demerest had already been swallowed up in the crowds outside.

Across the table, Tanya smoothed her skirt with a swift stroking gesture which Mel had noticed before and liked. It was a feminine habit and a reminder that few women looked as good in uniform, which often seemed to have a desexing effect, but with Tanya worked the opposite way.

Some airlines, Mel knew, let their senior passenger agents out of uniform, but Trans America liked the authority which its jaunty blue and gold commanded. Two gold rings edged with white, on Tanya's cuffs, proclaimed her job and seniority.

As if surmising his thoughts, she volunteered, 'I may be out of uniform soon.'

'Why?'

'Our District Transportation Manager is being transferred to New York. The Assistant DTM is moving up, and I've applied for his job.'

He regarded her with a mixture of admiration and curiosity. 'I believe you'll get it. And that won't be the end, either.'

Her eyebrows went up. 'You think I might make vice-president?'

'I believe you could. That is, if it's the kind of thing you want. To be a lady executive; all that.'

Tanya said softly, 'I'm not sure if it's what I want, or not.'

The waitress brought their order. When they were along again, Tanya said, 'Sometimes us working girls don't get a lot of choice. If you're not satisfied to stay in the job you have

19

through to pension time – and lots of us aren't – the only way out is up.'

'You're excluding marriage?'

She selected a piece of cinnamon toast. 'I'm not excluding it. But it didn't work for me once, and it may not again. Besides which, there aren't many takers – eligible ones – for used bride with baby.'

'You might find an exception.'

'I might win the Irish Sweep. Speaking from experience, Mel dear, I can tell you that men like their women unencumbered. Ask my ex-husband. If you can find him, that is; I never could.'

'He left you after your baby was born?'

'Goodness, no! That way Roy would have had six months of responsibility. I think it was on a Thursday I told him I was pregnant; I couldn't have kept it to myself much longer. On Friday, when I came home from work, Roy's clothes were gone. So was Roy.'

'You haven't seen him since?'

She shook her head. 'In the end, it made the divorce much simpler – desertion; no complications like another woman. I have to be fair, though, Roy wasn't all bad. He didn't empty our joint checking account, though he could have. I must admit I've sometimes wondered if it was kindness, or if he just forgot. Anyway, I had all that eighty dollars to myself.'

Mel said, 'You've never mentioned that before.'

'Should I have?'

'For sympathy, maybe.'

She shook her head. 'If you understood me better, you'd know the reason I'm telling you now is because I don't need sympathy. Everything has worked out fine.' Tanya smiled. 'I may even get to be an airline vice-president. You just said so.'

At an adjoining table, a woman said loudly, 'Geez! Lookit the time!'

Instinctively, Mel did. It was three quarters of an hour since he had left Danny Farrow at the Snow Control Desk. Getting up from the table, he told Tanya, 'Don't go away. I have to make a call.'

There was a telephone at the cashier's counter, and Mel dialled one of the Snow Desk unlisted numbers. Danny Farrow's voice said, 'Hold it,' then, a few moments later, returned on the line.

'I was going to call you,' Danny said, 'I just had a report on that stuck 707 of Aéreo-Mexican.'

'Go ahead.'

'You knew Mexican had asked TWA for help?'

'Yes.'

'Well, they've got trucks, cranes, God knows what out there now. The runway and taxiway are blocked off completely, but they still haven't shifted the damn aeroplane. The latest word is that TWA has sent for Joe Patroni.'

Mel acknowledged, 'I'm glad to hear it, though I wish they'd done it sooner.'

Joe Patroni was an airport maintenance chief for TWA, and a born troubleshooter. He was also a down-to-earth, dynamic character and a close crony of Mel's.

'Apparently they tried to get Patroni right away,' Danny said. 'But he was at home and the people here had trouble reaching him. Seems there's a lot of phone lines down from the storm.'

20

'But he knows now. You're sure of that?'

'TWA's sure. They say he's on his way.'

Mel calculated. He knew that Joe Patroni lived at Glen Ellyn, some twenty-five miles from the airport, and even with ideal driving conditions the journey took forty minutes. Tonight, with snowbound roads and crawling traffic, the airline maintenance chief would be lucky to make it in twice that time.

'If anyone can get that aeroplane moved tonight,' Mel conceded, 'it'll be Joe. But meanwhile I don't want anybody sitting on their hands until he gets here. Make it clear to everyone that we need runway three zero usable, and urgently.' As well as the operational need, he remembered unhappily that flights must still be taking off over Meadowood. He wondered if the community meeting, which the tower chief had told him about, was yet in session.

'I've been telling 'em,' Danny confirmed. 'I'll do it some more. Oh, a bit of good news – we found the United food truck.'

'The driver okay?'

'He was unconscious under the snow. Motor still running, and there was carbon monoxide, the way we figured. But they got an inhalator on him, and he'll be all right.'

'Good! I'm going out on the field now to do some checking for myself. I'll radio you from there.'

'Wrap up well,' Danny said. 'I hear it's a lousy night.'

Tanya was still at the table when Mel returned, though preparing to go.

'Hold on,' he said, 'I'm coming, too.'

She motioned to his untouched sandwich. 'How about dinner? if that's what it was.'

'This will do for now.' He bolted a mouthful, washed it down hastily with coffee, and picked up his topcoat. 'Anyway, I'm having dinner downtown.'

As Mel paid their check, two Trans America ticket agents entered the coffee shop. One was the supervising agent whom Mel had spoken to earlier. Observing Tanya, he came across.

'Excuse me, Mr Bakersfeld . . . Mrs Livingston, the DTM's looking for you. He has another problem.'

Mel pocketed his change from the cashier. 'Let me guess. Somebody else threw a timetable.'

'No, sir.' The agent grinned. 'I reckon if there's another thrown this evening it'll be me. This one's a stowaway – on Flight 80 from Los Angeles.'

'Is that all?' Tanya appeared surprised. Aerial stowaways – though all airlines had them – were seldom a cause of great concern.

'The way I hear it,' the agent said, 'this one's a dilly. There's been a radio message from the captain, and a security guard has gone to the gate to meet the flight. Anyway, Mrs Livingston, whatever the trouble is, they're calling for you.' With a friendly nod, he went off to rejoin his companion.

Mel walked with Tanya from the coffee shop into the central lobby. They stopped at the elevator which would take Mel to the basement garage where his car was parked.

'Drive carefully out there,' she cautioned. 'Don't get in the way of any aeroplanes.'

'If I do, I'm sure you'll hear about it.' He shrugged into the heavy topcoat. 'Your stowaway sounds interesting. It'll try to drop by before I leave, to find out what it's all about.' He hesitated, then added, 'It'll give me a reason to see you again tonight.'

They were close together. As one, each one reached out and their hands touched. Tanya said softly, 'Who needs a reason?'

In the elevator, going down, he could still feel the warm smoothness of her flesh, and hear her voice.

4

Joe Patroni – as Mel Bakersfeld had learned – was on his way to the airport from his home at Glen Ellyn. The cocky, stocky Italian-American, who was airport maintenance chief for TWA, had left his suburban, ranch-style bungalow by automobile some twenty minutes earlier. The going was exceedingly slow, as Mel had guessed it would be.

At the moment, Joe Patroni's Buick Wildcat was halted in a traffic tie-up. Behind and ahead, as far as visibility extended, were other vehicles, also stopped. While waiting, his actions illuminated by the tail-lights of the car in front, Patroni lit a fresh cigar.

Legends had grown up around Joe Patroni: some professional, others personal.

He had begun his working life as a grease monkey in a garage. Soon after, he won the garage from his employer in a dice game, so that at the end of the game they reversed roles. As a result, young Joe became heir to various bad debts, including one which made him owner of an ancient, decrepit Waco biplane. With a mixture of resourcefulness and sheer mechanical ability he repaired the aeroplane then flew it successfully – without benefit of flying lessons, which he could not afford.

The aeroplane and its mechanical functioning absorbed Joe Patroni completely – so much so, that he enticed his former employer into another dice game and allowed him to win the garage back. Joe thereupon quit the garage and took a job as an airline mechanic. He studied at night school, became a lead mechanic, then a foreman with a reputation as a top-notch troubleshooter. His crew could change an engine faster than an aeroplane manufacturer said it could be done; and with absolute reliability. After a while, whenever there was pressure, or a difficult repair job, the word went out: *get Joe Patroni.*

A contributing reason for his success was that he never wasted time on diplomacy. Instead, he went directly to the point, both with people and aeroplanes. He also had a total disregard for rank, and was equally forthright with everyone, including the airline's senior executives.

On one occasion, still talked about when airline men reminisced, Joe Patroni walked off his job and, without word to anyone, or prior consultation, rode an aeroplane to New York. He carried a package with him. On arrival, he went by bus and subway to the airline's Olympian headquarters in midtown Manhattan where, without announcement or preamble, he strode into the president's office. Opening the package, he deposited an oily, disassembled carburettor on the immaculate presidential desk.

The president, who had never heard of Joe Patroni, and whom no one ever got to see without prior appointment, was apoplectic until Joe told him, 'If you want to lose some aeroplanes in flight, throw me out of here. If you don't, sit down and listen.'

The president sat down – while Joe Patroni lighted a cigar – and listened. Afterwards he called in his engineering vice-president who, later still, ordered a mechanical modification affecting carburettor icing in flight, which Patroni had been urging –

unsuccessfully at lower level – for months.

Later, Patroni received official commendation, and the incident became one more to add to an already growing fund of Patroni stories. Soon after, Joe was promoted to senior supervisor, and a few years later was given the important post of maintenance chief at Lincoln International.

On a personal level, another report said that Joe Patroni made love to his wife, Marie, most nights, the way other men enjoyed a pre-dinner drink. This was true. In fact, he had been thus engaged when the telephone message came from the airport about the mired Aéreo-Mexican jet which TWA had been asked to help extricate.

The same rumour continued: Patroni made love the same way he did everything else – with a long, thin cigar stuck jauntily in the side of his mouth. This was untrue, at least nowadays. Marie, having coped with several pillow fires during their early years of marriage – drawing on her training as a TWA air hostess to extinguish them – had emphatically forbidden any more cigars in bed. Joe complied with the edict because he loved his wife. He had reason to. When he married her, she was probably the most popular and beautiful hostess in the entire airline system, and twelve years and three children later she could still hold her own with most successors. There were some who wondered aloud why Marie – who had been pursued ardently by captains and first officers – had ever chosen Joe Patroni at all. But Joe, even as a young maintenance foreman, which he was when they met, had a way with him, and had kept Marie satisfied – in all important ways – ever since.

Another thing about Joe Patroni was that he never panicked in emergencies. Instead, he quickly assessed each situation, deciding what priority the emergency rated, and whether or not he should complete other tasks before coping with it. In the case of the mired 707, instinct told him it was a moderate-to-acute crisis, which meant there was time to finish what he was doing, or have dinner, but not both. Accordingly, he abandoned dinner. Soon after, Marie raced to the kitchen in her robe and threw sandwiches together for Joe to eat during his twenty-five mile drive to the airport. He nibbled on a sandwich now.

Being recalled to the airport after performing a full day's work was not a new experience, but tonight the weather was worse than any other occasion he remembered. Accumulated effects of the three-day storm were everywhere, making driving exacting and hazardous. Huge snowpiles lined the streets and, in the darkness, more snow was falling. Both on and off freeways, traffic was moving at a crawl, or not at all. Even with mud-snow tyres, which Patroni's Buick Wildcat had, traction was poor. Windshield wipers and defrosters were barely coping with gusting snow outside and steam within, while headlight beams illuminated only short distances ahead. Stalled vehicles, some abandoned by their drivers, turned roads into obstacle courses. It was obvious that only those with good reason would be out on such a night.

Patroni checked his watch. Both his car and the one immediately ahead had been stationary for several minutes. Farther ahead still, he could make out others, also stopped, and to his right was another halted lane of traffic. Moreover, for some time, no vehicles had come from the opposite direction, so obviously something had happened to obstruct all four lanes. If nothing more occurred in the next five minutes, he decided, he would get out of the car to investigate, though observing the slush, drifts, and still falling snow outside, he hoped he would not have to go. There would be plenty of time to become cold and miserable – as he was undoubtedly going to be before the night was out – after arrival at the airport. Meanwhile, he turned up the volume of the car radio, which was tuned to a rock-and-roll station, and puffed at his cigar.

Five minutes went by. Ahead, Joe Patroni could see people getting out of cars and walking forward, and he prepared to join them. He had brought a fleece-lined parka and pulled it tightly around him, slipping the hood over his head. He reached for the heavy-duty electric lantern which he always carried. As he opened the car door, wind and snow rushed in. He eased out, closing the door quickly.

He plodded forward while other car doors slammed and voices called, 'What's happened?' Someone shouted, 'There's been an accident. It's a real mess.' As he progressed, flashing lights became visible ahead, and shadows moved and separated, becoming a cluster of people. A new voice said, 'I'm telling you they won't clear that lot in a hurry. We'll be stuck here for hours.' A large, darker shadow loomed, partially lighted by sputtering red flares. It proved to be a massive tractor-trailer unit on its side. The cumbersome sixteen-wheeled vehicle was spread across the road, blocking all traffic movement. Part of its cargo – apparently cases of canned goods – had spewed out, and already a few opportunists were braving the snow and collecting cases, then hurrying them to their cars.

Two state police patrol cars were at the scene. State troopers were questioning the truck driver, who appeared unhurt.

'All I did was touch the goddam brakes,' the driver protested loudly. 'Then she jackknifed and rolled over like a whore in heat.'

One of the policeman wrote in his notebook, and a woman murmured to a man beside her, 'Do you think he's putting that last bit down?'

Another woman shouted, 'Lotta good that'll do.' Her voice was shrill against the wind. 'Whyn't you cops get this thing moved?'

One of the state troopers walked across. Most of his uniform coat was already snow-covered. 'If you'll give us a hand to lift, madam, we'd be glad to oblige.'

A few people tittered, and the woman muttered, 'Smart ass cops.'

A tow truck, amber roof-beacon flashing, approached, moving slowly, on the opposite side of the obstruction. The driver was using the now unoccupied lanes on what would normally be the wrong side of the road. He stopped and got out, shaking his head doubtfully as he saw the size and position of the tractor-trailer.

Joe Patroni shoved forward. He puffed on his cigar, which glowed redly in the wind, and prodded the state trooper sharply on the shoulder. 'Listen, son, you'll never move that rig with one tow truck. It'll be like hitching a tomtit to a brick.'

The policeman turned. 'Whatever it's like, mister, there's spilled gasoline around here. You'd better get that cigar out.'

Patroni ignored the instruction, as he ignored almost all smoking regulations. He waved the cigar towards the overturned tractor-trailer. 'What's more, son, you'd be wasting everybody's time, including mine and yours, trying to get that hunk of junk right side up tonight. You'll have to drag it clear so traffic can move, and to do that you need two more tow trucks – one on this side to push, two over there to pull.' He began moving around, using his electric lantern to inspect the big articulated vehicle from various angles. As always, when considering a problem, he was totally absorbed. He waved the cigar once more. 'The two trucks together'll hitch on to three points. They'll pull the cab first, and faster. That'll overcome the jackknifing. The other truck . . .'

'Hold it,' the state trooper said. He called across to one of the other officers. 'Hank, there's a guy here sounds as if he knows what he's talking about.'

Ten minutes later, working with the police officers, Joe Patroni had virtually taken charge. Two additional tow trucks, as he suggested, were being summoned by radio. While awaiting their arrival, the driver of the first tow truck was attaching chains, under Patroni's direction, to the axles of the capsized tractor-trailer. The situation had already assumed a proficient, get-on-with-it pattern – a trademark of any proceeding in which the energetic TWA maintenance chief became involved.

Patroni himself had remembered several times, with concern, his reason for being out at all tonight, and the fact that by now he was long overdue at the airport. But helping to clear the blocked highway, he calculated, was the fastest means of getting there. Obviously, his own car and others could not move forward until the wrecked tractor-trailer had been dragged clear from the centre of the road. To go back and try an alternate route was equally impossible because traffic behind was backed up, with continuous lines of vehicles extending – so the police assured him – for miles to the rear.

He went back to his car to use the radio telephone he had installed at his employers' suggestion, and for which they picked up the monthly bills. He called the airline's maintenance department at the airport to report on his delay, and, in return, was informed of Mel Bakersfeld's message about the urgent need for runway three zero to be cleared and usable.

Joe Patroni gave some instructions over the telephone, but was aware that the most important thing was to be on the airfield himself as speedily as possible.

When he left the Buick for the second time, snow was still falling heavily. Dodging drifts which had formed around the line of waiting cars, he returned to the road block at a jog trot and was relieved to see that the first of the two extra tow trucks had arrived.

5

The elevator, which Mel Bakersfeld had taken after leaving Tanya, deposited him in the terminal basement. His official airport car – mustard yellow, and radio-equipped – was in a privileged parking stall close by.

Mel drove out, meeting the storm where the building exit joined an aircraft parking ramp outside. As he left the shelter of the terminal, wind and whirling snow slammed savagely against the car's windshield. The wiper blades slapped swiftly back and forth, though barely maintaining sufficient clear space for forward vision. Through a fractionally opened window, a blast of icy air and snow rushed in. Mel closed the window hastily. The transition from the terminal's warm snugness to the harshness of the night outside was startling.

Immediately ahead were aeroplanes parked at gate positions on the ramp. Through breaks in the snow, as the wind whipped and eddied around concourse buildings, Mel could see into the lighted interiors of several aircraft, which had passengers already seated. Obviously, several flights were ready to leave. These would be awaiting word from the tower to start engines, their continued delay a result of the blockage of runway three zero. Farther out on the airfield and runways, he could make out blurred shapes and

25

navigation lights of other aeroplanes – recent arrivals, with engines running. These were in a holding area, which pilots called the penalty box, and would move in as gate positions became vacant. Undoubtedly, the same thing was happening in the other seven aircraft concourses grouped around the terminal.

The two-way radio in Mel's car, tuned to ground control frequency, crackled alive.

'Ground to Eastern seventeen,' a controller intoned, 'you are cleared to runway two five. Change frequency now for your airways clearance.'

A burst of static. 'Eastern seventeen. Roger.'

A stronger voice rasped irritably. 'Ground control from Pan Am fifty-four on outer taxiway to two five. There's a private Cessna in front – a twin-engine tortoise. I'm standing on my brakes to keep behind.'

'Pan Am fifty-four, stand by.' The briefest pause, then the controller's voice again: 'Cessna seven three metro from ground control. Enter the next right intersection, hold and let Pan American pass you.'

Unexpectedly, a pleasant woman's voice responded. 'Ground control from Cessna seven three metro. I'm turning now. Go ahead, Pan Am, you great big bully.'

A chuckle, then, 'Thanks honey. You can fix your lipstick while you wait.'

The controller's voice rebuked, 'Tower to all aircraft. Confine your messages to official business.'

The controller was edgy, Mel could tell, despite the routine, studied calmness. But who wouldn't be tonight, with conditions and traffic the way they were? He thought uneasily again about his brother, Keith, involved with the unrelenting pressure of west arrival control.

The talk between tower and aircraft was continuous, with no gaps between transmissions. When one exchange ended, Mel snapped his own mike button down. 'Ground control from mobile one. I'm at gate sixty-five, proceeding to runway three zero, site of the stuck 707.'

He listened while the controller gave taxiing instructions to two other flights which had just landed. Then: 'Tower to mobile one. Roger, follow the Air Canada DC-9 pulling out of the gate ahead of you. Hold short of runway two one.

Mel acknowledged. He could see the Air Canada flight, at this moment easing out from a terminal gate, its high graceful tail an angular silhouette.

While still in the ramp area, he drove outwards the airfield carefully, watching for ramp lice – as airport men called the proliferation of vehicles which surrounded aeroplanes on the ground. As well as the usual ones, tonight there were several cherry pickers – trucks with high, manoeuvrable platforms at the end of steel, articulated arms. On the platforms, service crews were reaching out to clear snow from aircraft wings, and spraying glycol to retard ice formation. The men themselves were snow-covered in their exposed position.

Mel braked hastily, avoiding a speeding honey wagon, on its way from the ramp area to disgorge its malodorous four-hundred gallon load of contents pumped out from aircraft toilets. The load would eject into a shredding machine in a special building which other airport employees avoided, and then be pumped to city sewers. Most times the procedure worked efficiently, except when passengers reported losses of items – dentures, purses, wallets, even shoes – dropped accidentally in aircraft toilets. It happened once or twice a day. Then loads had to be sifted, while everyone hoped the missing item could be located quickly.

26

Even without incidents, Mel realised, this would be a busy night for sanitary crews. Airport managements knew from experience that demands on toilet facilities on the ground and in the air, increased as weather worsened. Mel wondered how many people were aware that airport sanitary supervisors received hourly weather forecasts and made their plans – for extra cleaning and increased supplies – accordingly.

The Air Canada jet he was to follow had cleared the terminal and was increasing taxi speed. Mel accelerated to keep up. It was reassuring – with windshield wipers barely coping with the snow – to have the DC-9's tail light as a reference point ahead. Through the rear mirror he could make out the shape of another, larger jet now following. On radio, the ground controller cautioned, 'Air France four-o-four, there is an airport ground vehicle between you and Air Canada.'

It took a quarter of an hour to reach the intersection where runway three zero was blocked by the Aéreo-Mexican 707. Before then, Mel had separated from the stream of taxiing aircraft which were destined for takeoff on the two other active runways.

He stopped the car and got out. In the dark and loneliness out here, the storm seemed even more wintry and violent than nearer the terminal. The wind howled across the deserted runway. If wolves appeared tonight, Mel thought, it would not be surprising.

A shadowy figure hailed him. 'Is that Mr Patroni?'

'No, it isn't.' Mel found that he, too, had to shout to make himself heard above the wind. 'But Joe Patroni's on the way.'

The other man came closer. He was huddled into a parka, his face blue with cold. 'When he gets here, we'll be glad to see him. Though I'm damned if I know what Patroni'll do. We've tried about everything to get this bastard out.' He gestured to the aeroplane looming, shadowy, behind them. 'She's stuck, but good.'

Mel identified himself, then asked, 'Who are you?'

'Ingram, sir. Aéreo-Mexican maintenance foreman. Right now, I wish I had some other job.'

As the two men talked, they moved nearer to the stalled Boeing 707, instinctively seeking shelter under the wings and fuselage, high above them. Under the big jet's belly, a red hazard light winked rhythmically. In its reflection Mel could see the mud beneath snow in which the aircraft's wheels were deeply mired. On the runway and adjoining taxiway, clustered like anxious relatives, were a profusion of trucks and service vehicles, including a fuel tanker, baggage tenders, a post office van, two crew buses, and a roaring power cart.

Mel pulled the collar of his topcoat tightly around him. 'We need this runway urgently – tonight. What have you done so far?'

In the past two hours, Ingram reported, old-fashioned boarding ramps had been trundled from the terminal, man-handled to the aircraft, and passengers guided down them. It had been a slow, tricky job because steps were icing as fast as they were cleared. An elderly woman had been carried down by two mechanics. Babies were passed from hand to hand in blankets. Now, all passengers were gone – in buses, along with the stewardesses and the second officer. The captain and first officer remained.

'Since the passengers left – have you tried to get the aeroplane moving?'

The foreman nodded affirmatively. 'Had the engine running twice. The captain's put on all the power he dare. But she won't come free. Just seems to dig herself in deeper.'

'What's happening now?'

27

'We're taking off more weight, hoping that'll help.' Most of the fuel, Ingram added, had been sucked out by tankers – a heavy load since tanks were full for takeoff. Baggage and freight compartments in the belly had been emptied. A post office truck was retrieving mailbags.

Mel nodded. The mail, he knew, would have come off anyway. The airport post office kept a minute-to-minute watch on airline schedules. They knew exactly where their mailbags were and, if delays occurred, postal employees quickly switched mail from one airline to another. Mail from the stranded jet, in fact, would fare better than passengers. In half an hour at most, it would be on its way by another flight, if necessary, on an alternate route.

Mel asked, 'Have you all the help you need?'

'Yes, sir – for all we can do now. I've got most of our crew from Aéreo-Mexican here – a dozen men. Right now, half of 'em are thawing out in one of the buses. Patroni may want more people, depending on what his ideas are.' Ingram turned, surveying the silent aircraft gloomily. 'But if you ask me, it's going to be a long job and we'll need heavy cranes, jacks, and maybe pneumatic bags to lift the wings. For most of those, we'd have to wait until daylight. The whole thing could take most of tomorrow.'

Mel said sharply, 'It can't take most of tomorrow, or even tonight. This runway has to be cleared . . .' He stopped abruptly, shivering with a suddenness which startled him. The intensity was unexpected, almost eerie.

Mel shivered again. What was it? He assured himself: the weather – the fierce, harsh wind across the airport, driving the whirling snow. Yet, strangely, since leaving the car until this moment, his body had adjusted to the cold.

From the opposite side of the airfield, above the wind, he could hear the thunder of jet engines. They rose to a crescendo, then diminished as a flight took off. Another followed, and another. Over there, all was well.

And here?

It was true, wasn't it? – for the briefest instant he had had a premonition. A hint, no more; an intuition; the smell of greater trouble brewing. He should ignore it, of course; impulse, premonitions, had no place in pragmatic management. Except that once, long ago, he had had the selfsame feeling – a conviction of events accumulating, and progressing to some disastrous, unenvisaged end. Mel remembered the end, which he had been unable to avert . . . entirely.

He glanced at the 707 again. It was snow-covered now, its outline blurring. Commonsense told him: apart from the runway blockage and the inconvenience of takeoffs over Meadowood, the situation was harmless. There had been a mishap, with no injuries, no apparent damage. Nothing more.

'Let's go to my car,' he told the Aéreo-Mexican foreman. 'We'll get on the radio and find out what's happening.'

On the way, he reminded himself that Cindy would shortly be waiting impatiently downtown.

Mel had left the car heater turned on, and inside the car it was comfortingly warm. Ingram grunted appreciatively. He loosened his coat and bent forward to hold his hands in the stream of warm air.

Mel switched the radio to the frequency of airport maintenance.

'Mobile one to Snow Desk. Danny, I'm at the blocked intersection of three zero. Call

TWA maintenance and check on Joe Patroni. Where is he? When coming? Over.'

Danny Farrow's voice crisped back through the speaker on the dash. 'Snow Desk to mobile one. Wilco. And, Mel, your wife called.'

Mel pressed the mike button. 'Did she leave a number?'

'Affirmative.'

'Mobile one to Snow Desk. Please call her, Danny. Tell her I'm sorry, I'll be a little late. But check on Patroni first.'

'Understood. Stand by.' The radio went silent.

Mel reached inside his topcoat for a packet of Marlboros. He offered them to Ingram. 'Thanks.'

They lit up, watching the windshield wipers slap back and forth.

Ingram nodded towards the lighted cockpit of the Aéreo-Mexican jet. 'Up there, that son-of-a-bitch of a captain is probably crying into his sombrero. Next time, he'll watch blue taxi lights like they was altar candles.'

Mel asked, 'Are your ground crews Mexicans or American?'

'We're all American. Only meatheads like us would work in this lousy weather. Know where that flight was going?'

Mel shook his head.

'Acapulco. Before this happened, I'd have given up six months' screwing to be on it.' The foreman chuckled. 'Can you imagine, though – getting aboard, and your ass all settled, then having to get off in this. You should have heard the passengers cursing, especially the women. I learned some new words tonight.'

The radio came alive again.

'Snow Desk to mobile one,' Danny Farrow said. 'I talked with TWA about Joe Patroni. They've heard from him, but he's held up in traffic. He'll be another hour, at least. He sent a message. You read me so far?'

'We read,' Mel said. 'Let's have the message.'

'Patroni warns not to get the aeroplane deeper in the mud than it is already. Says it can happen easily. So, unless the Aéreo-Mexican crowd are real sure of what they're doing, they should hold off any more tries until Joe gets there.'

Mel glanced sideways at Ingram. 'How does the Aéreo-Mexican crowd feel about that?'

The foreman nodded. 'Patroni can have all the tries he wants. We'll wait.'

Danny Farrow said, 'Did you get that? Is it clear?'

Mel thumbed the mike button. 'It's clear.'

'Okay. There's more. TWA is rounding up some extra ground crew to help. And, Mel, your wife phoned again. I gave her your message.' Mel sensed Danny hesitating, aware that others whose radios were on the airport maintenance frequency were listening, too.

Mel said, 'She wasn't happy?'

'I guess not.' There was a second's silence. 'You'd better get to a phone when you can.'

It was a safe bet, Mel thought, that Cindy had been more than usually snippy with Danny, but, loyally, he wasn't saying so.

As for the Aéreo-Mexican 707, obviously there was nothing more to be done until Joe Patroni arrived. Patroni's advice about not getting the aircraft more deeply mired made good sense.

Ingram was pulling on heavy mitts and refastening his coat. 'Thanks for the warm-up.' He went out, into the wind and snow, slamming the door quickly. A few moments later,

Mel could see him plodding through deep drifts towards the assembled vehicles on the taxiway.

On radio, the Snow Desk was speaking to Maintenance Snow Centre. Mel waited until the exchange finished, then held the transmit button down. 'This is mobile one, Danny. I'm going to the Conga Line.'

He eased the car forward, picking his way carefully in the blowing snow and darkness, with only widely spaced runway lights to guide him.

The Conga Line, both spearhead and prime mover of the airport snow fighting system, was – at the moment – on runway one seven, left. In a few minutes, Mel thought grimly, he would find out for himself if there was truth, or merely malice, in the critical report of Captain Demerest's Airline Snow Committee.

6

The subject of Mel's thoughts – Captain Vernon Demerest of Trans America – was, at the moment, some three miles from the airport. He was driving his Mercedes 230 SL Roadster and, compared with the journey he had made to the airport earlier from home, was having little trouble negotiating local streets, which had been recently ploughed. Snow was still falling heavily, abetted by a strong wind, but the fresh covering on the ground was not yet deep enough to make conditions difficult.

Demerest's destination was a group of three-storey apartment blocks, close to the airport, known colloquially to flying crews as Stewardess Row. It was here that many of the stewardesses based at Lincoln International – from all airlines – maintained apartments. Each apartment was usually shared by two or three girls, and the initiated also had a name for the individual ménages. They were known as stewardess nests.

The nests were often the scene of lively, off-duty parties, and sometimes headquarters for the amorous affairs which occurred, with predictable regularity, between stewardesses and male flying crews.

Taken as a whole, the stewardess nests were neither more nor less freewheeling than other apartments occupied by single girls elsewhere. The difference was that most of what transpired in the way of swinging, amoral activities, involved airline personnel.

There was good reason for this. Both the stewardesses and male crew members whom they met – captains, and first and second officers – were, without exception, high-calibre people. All had reached their jobs, which many others coveted, through a tough, exacting process of elimination in which those less talented were totally eclipsed. The comparative few who remained were the brightest and best. The result was a broth of sharp, enlightened personalities with a zest for life and the perceptiveness to appreciate one another.

Vernon Demerest, in his time, had appreciated many stewardesses, as they had appreciated him. He had, in fact, had a succession of affairs with beautiful and intelligent young women whom a monarch or a male movie idol might well have desired without attaining. The stewardesses whom Demerest and fellow pilots knew, and regularly made love to, were neither whores nor easy lays. They were, however, alive, responsive, and sexually endowed girls, who valued quality, and took it when so obviously and conveniently close to hand.

One who had taken it – so to speak – from Vernon Demerest, and seemed inclined to continue to, was a vivacious, attractive, English-born brunette, Gwen Meighen. She was a farmer's daughter who had left home to come to the United States ten years earlier at the age of eighteen. Before joining Trans America she was briefly a fashion model in Chicago. Perhaps because of her varied background, she combined an uninhibited sexuality in bed with elegance and style when out of it.

It was to Gwen Meighen's apartment that Vernon Demerest was headed now.

Later tonight, the two of them would leave for Rome on Trans America Flight Two. On the flight deck, Captain Demerest would command. In the passenger cabins, aft, Gwen Meighen would be senior stewardess. At the Rome end of the journey, there would be a three-day layover for the crew, while another crew – already in Italy for its own layover – would fly the aeroplane back to Lincoln International.

The word 'layover' had long ago been adopted officially by airlines and was used deadpan. Possibly, whoever coined the term had a sense of humour; in any case, flying crews frequently gave it a practical application as well as its official one. Demerest and Gwen Meighen were planning a personal definition now. On arrival in Rome, they would leave immediately for Naples for a forty-eight hour 'layover' together. It was a halcyon, idyllic prospect, and Vernon Demerest smiled appreciatively at the thought of it. He was nearing Stewardess Row, and as he reminded himself of how well other things had gone this evening, his smile broadened.

He had arrived at the airport early, after leaving Sarah, his wife, who – placidly as usual – had wished him a pleasant trip. In an earlier age, Sarah might have busied herself with needlepoint or knitting during her liege's absence. As it was, he knew that as soon as he had left, she would become immersed in her curling club, bridge, and amateur oil painting which were the mainstays of her life.

Sarah Demerest's placidity, and her dullness which naturally went with it, were qualities her husband had come to accept and, in a perverse way, valued. Between flying trips and affairs with more interesting women, he thought of his sojourns at home, and sometimes spoke of them to intimates, as 'going into the hangar for a stand down'. His marriage had another convenience. While it existed, the women he made love to could become as emotional and demanding as they liked, but he could never be expected to meet the ultimate demand of matrimony. In this way, he had a perpetual protection against his own hasty action in the heat of passion. As to sexual intimacy with Sarah, he still obliged her occasionally, as one would play 'throw the ball' with an old dog. Sarah responded dutifully, with conventional body heavings and quickened breath, though he suspected both were more from rote than passion, and that if they quit copulation entirely she would not be overly concerned. He was also sure that Sarah suspected his philandering, if not in fact, then at least by instinct. But, characteristically, she would prefer not to know, an arrangement in which Vernon Demerest was happy to co-operate.

Another thing which had pleased him this evening was the Airlines Snow Committee report in which he had delivered a verbal kick in the crotch, aimed at his stuffed-shirt-brother-in-law, Mel Bakersfeld.

The critical report had been solely Demerest's idea. The other two airline representatives on the committee had at first taken the view that the airport management was doing its best under exceptional conditions. Captain Demerest argued otherwise. The others had finally gone along with him and agreed that Demerest would personally write the report, which he made as scathing as he could. He had not bothered about accuracy or otherwise of the indictment; after all, with so much snow around, who could be sure of anything? He had, however, made certain that the widely circulated report would cause a maximum of embarrassment and irritation to Mel Bakersfeld. Copies were now being Xeroxed and would be sent to regional vice-presidents of all airlines, as well as airline headquarters, in New York and elsewhere. Knowing how everyone enjoyed finding a scapegoat for operational delays, Captain Demerest was confident that telephones and teletypes would be busy after its receipt.

A revenge, Vernon Demerest thought pleasurably – small but satisfying – had been exacted. Now, perhaps, his limping, quarter-cripple brother-in-law would think twice before antagonizing Captain Demerest and the Air Line Pilots Association, as Mel Bakersfeld had presumed to do – in public – two weeks ago.

Captain Demerest swung the Mercedes into an apartment building parking lot. He stopped the car smoothly and got out. He was a little early, he noticed – a quarter of an hour before the time he had said he would collect Gwen and drive her to the airport. He decided to go up, anyway.

As he entered the building, using the pass key Gwen had given him, he hummed softly to himself, then smiled, realizing the tune was *O Sole Mio*. Well, why not? It was appropriate. Naples . . . a warm night instead of snow, the view above the bay in starlight, soft music from mandolins, Chianti with dinner, and Gwen Meighen beside him . . . all were less than twenty-four hours away. Yes, indeed! – *O Sole Mio*. He continued humming it.

In the elevator going up, he remembered another good thing. The flight to Rome would be an easy one.

Tonight, though Captain Demerest was in command of Flight Two – *The Golden Argosy* – he would do little of the work which the flight entailed. The reason was that he was flying as a line check captain. Another four-striper captain – Anson Harris, almost as senior as Demerest himself – had been assigned to the flight and would occupy the command pilot's left seat. Demerest would use the right seat – normally the first officer's position – from where he would observe and report on Captain Harris's performance.

The check flight arrangement had come up because Captain Harris had elected to transfer from Trans America domestic operations to international. However, before flying as a full-fledged international captain, he was required to make two flights over an overseas route with a regular line captain who also held instructor's qualifications. Vernon Demerest did.

After Captain Harris's two flights, of which tonight's would be the second, he would be given a final check by a senior supervisory captain before being accepted for international command.

Such checks – as well as regular six-monthly check flights, which all pilots of all airlines were required to undergo – entailed an aerial scrutiny of ability and flying habits. The checks took place on ordinary scheduled flights, and the only indication a passenger might have that one was in progress would be the presence of two four-striper captains on the flight deck up front.

Despite the fact that captains checked each other, the tests, both regular and special, were usually serious, exacting sessions. The pilots wanted them that way. Too much was at stake – public safety and high professional standards – for any mutual back-scratching, or for weaknesses to be overlooked. A captain being checked was aware that he must measure up to required standards in all respects. Failure to do so would mean an automatic adverse report which, if serious enough, could lead to an even tougher session with the airline's chief pilot, with the testee's job in jeopardy.

Yet, while performance standards were not relaxed, senior captains undergoing flight checks were treated by their colleagues with meticulous courtesy. Except by Vernon Demerest.

Demerest treated any pilot he was assigned to test, junior or senior to himself, in precisely the same way – like an errant schoolboy summoned to the headmaster's presence. Moreover, in the headmaster's role, Demerest was officious, arrogant, condescending, and tough. He made no secret of his conviction that no one else's ability as a pilot was superior to his own. Colleagues who received this brand of treatment raged inwardly, but had no choice but to sit and take it. Subsequently they vowed to one another that when Demerest's own time came they would give him the meanest, toughest check ride he had ever had. They invariably did, with a single consistent result – Vernon Demerest turned in a flawless performance which could not be faulted.

This afternoon, characteristically, Demerest prefaced his check session by telephoning Captain Anson Harris at home. 'It'll be a bad night for driving,' Demerest said without preamble. 'I like my crew to be punctual, so I suggest you allow plenty of time to get to the airport.'

Anson Harris, who in twenty-two unblemished years with Trans America had never been late for a single flight, was so outraged, he almost choked. Fortunately, before Harris could get any words out, Captain Demerest hung up.

Still fuming, but to make absolutely sure that Demerest would not catch him out, Captain Harris had arrived at the airport almost three hours ahead of flight time instead of the usual one hour. Captain Demerest, fresh from his stint with the Airlines Snow Committee, had encountered Harris in the Cloud Captain's Coffee Shop. Demerest was wearing a sports jacket and slacks; he kept a spare uniform in his airport locker and planned to change into it later. Captain Harris, a greying, grizzled veteran whom many younger pilots addressed as 'sir', was in Trans America uniform.

'Hi, Anson.' Vernon Demerest dropped into an adjoining seat at the counter. 'I see you took my good advice.'

Captain Harris's grip on his coffee cup tightened slightly, but all he said was, 'Good evening, Vern.'

'We'll start the pre-flight briefing twenty minutes earlier than usual,' Demerest said. 'I want to check your flight manuals.'

Thank God, Harris thought, his wife had gone through his manuals only yesterday, inserting the very latest amendments. But he had better check his mail slot in the dispatch office. This bastard was likely to fault him for not making an amendment published only this afternoon. To give his hands – which were itching – something to do, Captain Harris filled and lit his pipe.

He was aware of Vernon Demerest looking at him critically.

'You're not wearing a regulation shirt.'

For a moment, Captain Harris could not believe his colleague was serious. Then, as he realized he was, Harris's face suffused a deep plum red.

Regulation shirts were an irritant to Trans American pilots, as they were to pilots of other airlines. Obtainable through company sources, the official shirts cost nine dollars each, and were often ill fitting, their material of dubious quality. Though contrary to regulations, a much better shirt could be purchased independently for several dollars less, with the difference in appearance scarcely noticeable. Most pilots bought the unofficial shirts and wore them. *Vernon Demerest did too.* On several occasions Anson Harris had heard Demerest speak disdainfully of the company's shirts and point to the superior quality of his own.

Captain Demerest motioned to a waitress for coffee, then reassured Harris, 'It's all right. I won't report on your wearing a non-reg shirt here. As long as you change it before you come on my flight.'

Hold on! Anson Harris told himself. *Dear God in heaven, give me strength not to blow, which is probably what the ornery son-of-a-bitch wants. But why? Why?*

All right. All right, he decided; indignity or not, he would change his unofficial shirt for a regulation one. He would not give Demerest the satisfaction of having a single miniscule check point on which to fault him. It would be difficult to get a company shirt tonight. He would probably have to borrow one – exchange shirts with some other captain or first officer. When he told them why, they would hardly believe him. He hardly believed it himself.

But when Demerest's own check flight came up . . . *the next, and all others from this moment on . . . let him beware.* Anson Harris had good friends among the supervisory pilots. Let Demerest be wearing a regulation shirt; let him hew to regulations in every other trifling way . . . *or else.* Then Harris thought glumly: The foxy bastard will remember; he'll make sure he does.

'Hey, Anson!' Demerest seemed amused. 'You've bitten off the end of your pipe.'

And so he had.

Remembering, Vernon Demerest chuckled. Yes, it *would* be an easy flight tonight – for him.

His thoughts returned to the present as the apartment block elevator stopped at the third floor. He stepped into the carpeted corridor and turned to the left familiarly, heading for the apartment which Gwen Meighen shared with a stewardess of United Air Lines. The other girl, Demerest knew because Gwen had told him, was away on an overnight flight. On the apartment door bell he tapped out their usual signal, his initials in Morse . . . dit-dit-dit-dah dah-dit-dit . . . then went in, using the same key which opened the door below.

Gwen was in the shower. He could hear the water running. When he went to her bedroom door, she called out, 'Vernon, is that you?' Even competing with the shower, her voice – with its flawless English accent, which he liked so much – sounded mellow and exciting. He thought: Small wonder Gwen had so much success with passengers. He had seen them appear to melt – the men especially – when her natural charm was turned towards them.

He called back, 'Yes, honey.'

Her filmy underthings were laid out on the bed – panties, sheer nylons; a transparent bra, flesh coloured, with a girdle of the same material; a French silk, hand-embroidered slip. Gwen's uniform might be standard, but beneath it she believed in expensive individuality. His senses quickened; he moved his eyes away reluctantly.

'I'm glad you came early,' she called again. 'I want to have a talk before we leave.'

'Sure, we've time.'

'You can make tea, if you like.'

'Okay.'

She had converted him to the English habit of tea at all times of day, though he had scarcely ever drunk tea at all until knowing Gwen. But now he often asked for it at home, a request which puzzled Sarah, particularly when he insisted on it being correctly made – the pot warmed first, as Gwen had taught him, the water still boiling at the instant it touched the tea.

He went to the tiny kitchen, where he knew his way around, and put a kettle of water on the stove. He poured milk into a jug from a carton in the refrigerator, then drank some milk himself before putting the carton back. He would have preferred a gin and tonic, but, like most pilots, abstained from liquor for twenty-four hours before a flight. Out of habit he checked his watch; it showed a few minutes before 8.00 pm. At this moment, he realized, the sleek, long-range Boeing 707 jet which he would command on its five-thousand mile flight to Rome, was being readied for him at the airport.

He heard the shower stop. In the silence he began humming once again. Happily. *O Sole Mio.*

7

The blustering, biting wind across the airfield was as strong as ever, and still driving the heavily falling snow before it.

Inside his car, Mel Bakersfeld shivered. He was heading for runway one seven, left, which was being ploughed, after leaving runway three zero and the stranded Aéreo-Mexican jet. Was the shivering due to the cold outside, Mel wondered, or to memory, which the scent of trouble a few minutes ago, plus the nagging reminder from the old injury of his foot, had triggered.

The injury had happened sixteen years ago off the coast of Korea when Mel had been a Navy pilot flying fighter missions from the carrier *Essex*. Through the previous twelve hours (he remembered clearly, even now) he had had a presentiment of trouble coming. It wasn't fear – like others, he had learned to live with that; rather, a conviction that something fateful, possibly final, was moving inexorably towards him. Next day, in a dogfight with a MIG-15, Mel's Navy F9F-5 had been shot down into the sea.

He managed a controlled ditching, but though unhurt himself, his left foot was trapped by a jammed rudder pedal. With the aeroplane sinking fast – an F9F-5 had the floating characteristics of a brick – Mel used a survival-kit hunting knife to slash desperately, wildly, at his foot and the pedal. Somehow, underwater, his foot came free. In intense pain, half-drowned, he surfaced.

He had spent the next eight hours in the sea before being picked up, unconscious. Later he learned he had severed the ligaments in front of his ankle, so that the foot extended from his leg in an almost straight line.

In time, Navy medics repaired the foot, though Mel had never flown – as a pilot – since then. But at intervals the pain still returned, reminding him that long ago, as on other later occasions, his instinct for trouble had been right. He had the same kind of instinct now.

Handling his car cautiously, being careful to retain his bearings in the darkness and restricted visibility, Mel was nearing runway one seven, left. This was the runway which, the tower chief indicated, Air Traffic Control would seek to use when the wind shifted as was forecast to happen soon.

At the moment, on the airfield, two runways were in use: one seven, right, and runway two five.

Lincoln International had five runways altogether. Through the past three days and nights they had represented the front line of the battle between the airport and the storm.

The longest and widest of the five was three zero, the runway now obstructed by Aéreo-Mexican. (With a change of wind and an aircraft approaching from the opposite direction, it could also be runway one two. The figures indicated compass headings of 300 and 120 degrees.) This runway was almost two miles long and as wide as a short city block; an airport joke claimed that one end could not be seen from the other because of the earth's curvature.

Each of the other four runways was half a mile or so shorter, and less wide.

Without ceasing, since the storm began, the miles of runways had been ploughed, vacuumed, brushed, and sanded. The motorized equipment – several million dollars' worth of roaring diesels – had stopped only minutes at a time, mainly for refuelling or relieving crews. It was work which air travellers never saw at close hand because no aircraft used a fresh-cleared runway until the surface had been inspected and declared safe. Standards were exacting. Half an inch of slush or three inches of powdery snow were maximums allowable for jets. More than that would be sucked into engines and endanger operation.

It was a pity, Mel Bakersfeld reflected, that runway snow teams were not more on public view. The sight was spectacular and stirring. Even now, in storm and darkness, approaching the massed equipment from the rear, the effect was impressive. Giant columns of snow cascaded to the right in arcs of a hundred and fifty feet. The arcs were framed in vehicle searchlights, and shimmered from the added colour of some twenty revolving beacons – one on the roof of each vehicle in the group.

Airport men called the group a Conga Line.

It had a head, a tail, a body, and an entourage, and it progressed down a runway with the precision of choreography.

A convoy leader was the head. He was a senior foreman from airport maintenance and drove an airport car – bright yellow, like all other equipment in the Line. The leader set the Conga Line pace, which was usually fast. He had two radios and remained permanently in touch with the Snow Desk and Air Traffic Control. By a system of lights, he could signal drivers following – green for 'speed up', amber for 'maintain pace', red for 'slow down', and flashing red for 'stop'. He was required to carry in his head a detailed map of the airport, and must know precisely where he was, even on the darkest night, as now.

Behind the convoy leader, its driver, like an orchestra's first violinist, was the number one plough – tonight a mammoth Oshkosh with a big main blade ahead, and a wing blade to the side. To the rear of number one plough, and on its right, was number two. The first plough heaved the snow aside; the second accepted the load from the first and, adding more, heaved both lots farther.

36

Then came a Snowblast, in echelon with the ploughs, six hundred roaring horsepower strong. A Snowblast cost sixty thousand dollars and was the Cadillac of snow clearance. With mighty blowers it engulfed the snow which both ploughs piled, and hurled it in a herculean arc beyond the runway's edge.

In a second echelon, farther to the right, were two more ploughs, a second Snowblast.

After the ploughs and Snowblasts came the graders – five in line abreast, with plough blades down to clear any mounds the front ploughs missed. The graders towed revolving brushes, each sixteen feet wide and independently diesel powered. The brushes scoured the runway surface like monstrous yard brooms.

Next were sanders. Where the eleven vehicles ahead had cleared, three hulking FWD trucks, with hoppers holding fourteen cubic feet apiece, spread sand out evenly.

The sand was special. Elsewhere around the airport, on roadways and areas which the public used, salt was added to the sand as a means of melting ice. But never for aeronautical areas. Salt corroded metal, shortening its life, and aeroplanes were treated with more respect than cars.

Last in the Conga Line itself – 'tail-end Charlie' – was an assistant foreman in a second car. His job was to ensure that the line stayed intact and to chivvy stragglers. He was in radio touch with the convoy leader, often out of sight ahead in snow and darkness.

Finally came the entourage – a standby plough, in case one faltered in the Line; a service truck with a detail of mechanics; refuelling tankers – diesel and gasoline; and – when summoned by radio at appointed times – a coffee and doughnut wagon.

Mel accelerated around the entourage and positioned his car alongside the assistant foreman's. His arrival was noticed. He heard the convoy leader notified by radio, 'Mr Bakersfeld just joined us.'

The Line was moving fast – close to forty miles an hour instead of its usual twenty-five. The leader had probably speeded up because of the expected wind shift and the need to have the runway open soon.

Switching his radio at ATC ground frequency, Mel heard the convoy leader call the tower, '. . . on one seven, left, approaching intersection with runway two five. Request clearance over intersection.'

Runway two five was an active runway, now in use.

'Convoy leader from ground control, hold short of the intersection. We have two flights on final approach. You may not, repeat not, cross runway intersection. Acknowledge.'

The voice from the tower was apologetic. Up there, they understood the difficulty of stopping a rolling Conga Line, and getting it started again. But the approaching flights had undoubtedly made a tricky instrument descent and now were close to landing, one behind the other. Only a desperate emergency would justify sending them round again on such a night.

Ahead of Mel, red lights were going on, flashing commandingly as the Conga Line slowed and stopped.

The assistant foreman, a cheerful young Negro, jumped from his car and came across to Mel's. As he opened the door, the wind swept in, but could only be felt, not heard, above the encompassing roar of idling diesels. The assistant put his mouth against Mel's ear. 'Say, Mr B, how's about joining the Line? One of the boys'll take care of your car.'

Mel grinned. The pleasure he got, whenever he could spare time, from riding and occasionally handling heavy motorized equipment was well known around the airport.

Why not? he reasoned. He had come out to inspect the snow clearance as a result of the adverse report by Vernon Demerest's Airlines Snow Committee. Clearly, the report was unjustified, and everything was going well. But maybe he should watch a few minutes longer from a ringside perch.

Nodding agreement, he shouted, 'Okay, I'll ride the second Snowblast.'

'Yessir!'

The assistant foreman, carrying a hand searchlight and leaning against the wind, preceded Mel past the now stationary lines of sand trucks and brushes. Mel observed that already fresh snow was starting to cover the runway area cleared only moments ago. To the rear, a figure ducked from a service truck and hastened to Mel's car.

'Better hurry, Mr B. It's only a short stop.' The young Negro flashed his light at the Snowblast cab, then held it steady, illuminating the way, as Mel clambered up. High above, the Snowblast driver opened the cab door and held it while Mel eased inside. On the way up, his impaired foot pained him sharply, but there was no time to wait. Ahead, the flashing red lights had already changed to green, and presumably the two approaching aircraft had now landed and were past the intersection. The Conga Line must hurry across before the next landing, perhaps only a minute or two away. Glancing to the rear, Mel could see the assistant foreman sprinting back towards his tail-end-Charlie car.

The Snowblast was already moving, picking up speed with a deep-throated roar. Its driver glanced sideways as Mel slipped into one of the two soft, padded seats.

'Hi, Mr Bakersfeld.'

'How are you, Will?' Mel recognized the man, who when there was no snow emergency, was employed by the airport as a payroll clerk.

'I'm pretty good, sir. Tired some.'

The driver was holding position carefully behind the third and fourth ploughs, their beacon lights just visible. Already the Snowblast's huge auger blades were engorging snow, cramming it to the blower. Once more, a continuous white stream was arcing outwards, clear of the runway.

Up here was like the bridge of a ship. The driver held his main control wheel lightly, like a helmsman. A multitude of dials and levers, glowing in the darkness, were arranged for fingertip control. Circular, high-speed windshield wipers – as on a ship – provided ports of clear vision through encrusted snow.

'I guess everyone's tired,' Mel said. 'All I can tell you is that this can't last for ever.'

He watched the forward speed needle climb – from twenty-five to thirty, thirty to thirty-five. Swinging in his seat, Mel surveyed outside. From this position, at the centre of the Conga Line, he could see the lights and shapes of the other vehicles. He noted approvingly that the formation was exact.

A few years ago, in a storm like this, an airport would have closed completely. Now it didn't, mainly because ground facilities – in this one area – had caught up with progress in the air. But of how many areas of aviation could the same thing be said? Mel reflected ruefully: very few.

'Oh, well,' the driver said, 'it makes a change from working an adding machine, and the longer this keeps up, the more extra pay there'll be when it's over.' He touched a lever, tilting the cab forward to inspect the auger blades. With another control he adjusted the blades, then relevelled the cab. 'I don't have to do this; you know that, Mr Bakerfeld, I volunteer. But I kinda like it out here. It's sort of . . .' He hesitated. 'I dunno.'

Mel suggested, 'Elemental?'

'I guess so.' The driver laughed. 'Maybe I'm snow happy.'

'No, Will, I don't believe you are.' Mel swung forward, facing the way the Conga Line was moving. It *was* elemental here. More to the point, amid the airfield's loneliness there was a feeling of closeness to aviation, the real aviation which in its simplest sense was man against the elements. You lost that kind of feeling if you stayed too long in terminals and airline office buildings; there, the extraneous, non-essential things confused you. Maybe all of us in aviation management, Mel thought, should stand at the distant end of a runway once in a while, and feel the wind on our faces. It could help to separate detail from fundamentals. It might even ventilate our brains as well.

Sometimes in the past Mel had gone out on to the airfield when he needed to think, to reason quietly and alone. He had not expected to tonight, but found himself doing so now . . . wondering, speculating, as he had so often in recent days, about the airport's future and his own.

8

Less than a lustrum ago, the airport was considered among the world's finest and most modern. Delegations inspected it admiringly. Civic politicians were given to pointing with pride and would huff and puff about 'air leadership' and 'a symbol of the jet age'. Nowadays, the politicians still huffed and puffed but with less reason. What most failed to realize was that Lincoln International, like a surprising number of other major airports, was close to becoming a whited sepulchre.

Mel Bakersfeld pondered the phrase *whited sepulchre* while riding in darkness down runway one seven, left. It was an apt definition, he thought. The airport's deficiencies were serious and basic, yet, since they were mostly out of public view, only insiders were aware of them.

Travellers and visitors at Lincoln International saw principally the main terminal – a brightly lighted, air-conditioned Taj Mahal. Of gleaming glass and chrome, the terminal was impressively spacious, its thronged concourses adjoining elegant waiting areas. Opulent service facilities ringed the passenger area. Six specialty restaurants ranged from a gourmet dining room, with gold-edged china and matching prices, to a grab-it-and-run hot dog counter. Bars, cosily darkened or stand-up and neon lit, were plentiful as toilets. While waiting for a flight, and without ever leaving the terminal, a visitor could shop, rent a room and bed, and take a steam bath with massage, have his hair cut, suit pressed, shoes shined, or even die and have his burial arranged by Holy Ghost Memorial Gardens which maintained a sales office on the lower concourse.

Judged by its terminal alone, the airport was still spectacular. Where its deficiencies lay were in operating areas, notably runways and taxiways.

Few of the eighty thousand passengers who flew in and out each day were aware of how inadequate – and, therefore, hazardous – the runway system had become. Even a year previously, runways and taxiways were barely sufficient; now, they were dangerously overtaxed. In normally busy periods, on two main runways, a takeoff or landing occurred every thirty seconds. The Meadowood situation and the consideration the airport showed to community residents, made it necessary, at peak periods, to use an alternative runway which bisected one of the other two. As a result, aircraft took off and landed on converging courses, and there were moments when air traffic controllers held their breath and prayed. Only last week Keith Bakersfeld, Mel's brother, had predicted grimly, 'Okay, so we stay on our toes in the tower, and we cope with the hairy ones, and we haven't brought two aeroplanes together at that intersection yet. But someday there'll be a second's inattention or misjudgement, and one of us will. I hope to God it isn't me, because when it happens it'll be the Grand Canyon all over again.'

The intersection Keith had spoken of was the one which the Conga Line had just passed over. In the cab of the Snowblast, Mel glanced to the rear. The Conga Line was well clear of the intersection now, and, through a momentary gap in the snow, aeroplane navigation lights were visible on the other runway, moving swiftly as a flight took off. Then, incredibly, there were more lights only a few yards behind as another flight landed, it seemed at the same instant.

The Snowblast driver had turned his head also. He whistled. 'Those two were pretty close.'

Mel nodded. They *had* been close, exceptionally so, and for an instant his flesh had prickled with alarm. Obviously, what had happened was that an air traffic controller, instructing the pilots of both aeroplanes by radio, had cut tolerances exceedingly fine. As usual, the controller's skilled judgement had proved right, though only just. The two flights were safe – one now in the air, the other on the ground. But it was the need for a multiplicity of such hair-breadth judgements which created an unceasing hazard.

Mel had pointed out the hazard frequently to the Board of Airport Commissioners and to members of City Council, who controlled airport financing. As well as immediate construction of more runways and taxiways, Mel had urged purchase of additional land around the airport for long-term development. There had been plenty of discussion and sometimes angry argument, as a result. A few Board and Council members saw things the way Mel did, but others took a strongly counter view. It was hard to convince people that a modern jetport, built in the late 1950s, could so quickly have become inadequate to the point of danger. It made no difference that the same was true of other centres – New York, San Francisco, Chicago, and elsewhere; there were certain things which politicians simply did not want to see.

Mel thought: maybe Keith was right. Perhaps it would take another big disaster to arouse public awareness, just as the 1956 Grand Canyon disaster had spurred President Eisenhower and the Eighty-fourth Congress to revamp the airways. Yet, ironically, there was seldom any difficulty in getting money for non-operational improvements. A proposal to triple-deck all parking lots had won city approval without dissent. But that was something which the public – including those who had votes – could see and touch. Runways and taxiways were different. A single new runway cost several million dollars and took two years to build, yet few people other than pilots, air traffic controllers, and airport management, ever knew how good or bad a runway system was.

But at Lincoln International a showdown was coming soon. It had to. In recent weeks, Mel had sensed the signs, and when it happened the choice would be clear – between advancement on the ground, matching new achievements in the air, or impotently drifting backwards. In aviation, there was never a status quo.

There was another factor.

As well as the airport's future, Mel's personal future was at stake. Whichever way airport policies veered, so would his own prestige advance or lessen in places where it counted most.

Only a short time ago, Mel Bakersfeld had been a national spokesman for ground logistics of aviation, had been touted as the rising young genius in aviation management. Then, abruptly, a single, calamitous event had wrought a change. Now, five years later, the future was no longer clear, and there were doubts and questioning about Mel Bakersfeld, in others' minds as well as in his own.

The event which caused the change was the John F. Kennedy assassination.

'Here's the end of the runway, Mr Bakersfeld. You riding back with us, or what?' The voice of the Snowblast driver broke in on Mel's reverie.

'Hm?'

The man repeated his question. Ahead of them, once more, warning lights were flashing on, the Conga Line slowing. Half the width of a runway was cleared at one time. Now, the Line would reverse itself and go back the way it had come, clearing the remaining portion. Allowing for stops and starts, it took forty-five minutes to an hour to plough and sand a single runway.

'No,' Mel said. 'I'll get off here.'

'Right, sir.' The driver directed a signal light at the assistant foreman's car which promptly swung out of line. A few moments later, as Mel clambered down, his own car was waiting. From other ploughs and trucks, crews were descending and hurrying to the coffee wagon.

Driving back towards the terminal, Mel radioed the Snow Desk, confirming to Danny Farrow that runway one seven, left would be usable shortly. Then, switching to ATC ground control, he turned the volume low, the subdued, level voices a background to his thoughts.

In the Snowblast cab he had been reminded of the event which, of all others he remembered, had struck with greatest impact.

It had been four years ago.

He thought, startled, was it really that long ago? – four years since the grey November afternoon when, dazedly, he had pulled the p.a. microphone across his desk towards him – the microphone, rarely used, which overrode all others in the terminal – and cutting in on a flight arrival bulletin, had announced to concourses which swiftly hushed, the shattering news which seconds earlier had flashed from Dallas.

His eyes, as he spoke then, had been on the photograph on the facing wall across his office, the photograph whose inscription read: *To my friend Mel Bakersfeld, concerned, as I am, with attenuating the surly bonds of earth – John F. Kennedy.*

The photograph still remained, as did many memories.

The memories began, for Mel, with a speech he had made in Washington, DC.

At the time, as well as airport general manager, he had been president of the Airport Operators Council – the youngest leader, ever, of that small but influential body linking major airports of the world. AOC headquarters was in Washington, and Mel flew there frequently.

His speech was to a national planning congress.

Aviation, Mel Bakersfeld had pointed out, was the only truly successful international undertaking. It transcended ideological boundaries as well as the merely geographic.

41

Because it was a means of intermingling diverse populations at ever-diminishing cost, it offered the most practical means to world understanding yet devised by man.

Even more significant was aerial commerce. Movement of freight by air, already mammoth in extent, was destined to be greater still. The new, giant jet aeroplanes, to be in service by the early 1970s, would be the fastest and cheapest cargo carriers in human history; within a decade, ocean going ships might be dry-dock museum pieces, pushed out of business in the same way that passenger aeroplanes had clobbered the *Queen Mary* and *Queen Elizabeth.* The effect could be a new, world-wide argosy of trade, with prosperity for now impoverished nations. Technologically, Mel reminded his audience, the airborne segment of aviation offered these things, and more, within the lifetimes of today's middle-aged people.

Yet, he had continued, while aeroplane designers wove the stuff of dreams into fabrics of reality, facilities on the ground remained, for the most part, products of short-sightedness or misguided haste. Airports, runway systems, terminals, were geared to yesterday, with scant – if any – provision for tomorrow; what was lost sight of, or ignored, was the juggernaut speed of aviation's progress. Airports were set up piecemeal, as individually as city halls, and often with as small an imagination. Usually, too much was spent on showplace terminals, too little on operating areas. Co-ordinated, high level planning, either national or international, was non-existent.

At local levels, where politicians were apathetic about problems of ground access to airports, the situation was as bad, or worse.

'We have broken the sound barrier,' Mel declared, 'but not the ground barrier.'

He listed specific areas for study and urged international planning – US led and presidentially inspired – for aviation on the ground.

The speech was accorded a standing ovation and was widely reported. It produced approving nods from such diverse sources as *The Times* of London, *Pravda*, and *The Wall Street Journal*.

The day after the speech, Mel was invited to the White House.

The meeting with the President had gone well. It had been a relaxed, good-humoured session in the private study on the White House second floor. J.F.K., Mel found, shared many of his own ideas.

Subsequently, there were other sessions, some of them 'brain trust' affairs involving Kennedy aides, usually when the Administration was considering aviation matters. After several such occasions, with informal aftermaths, Mel was at home in the White House, and less surprised than he had been at first to find himself there at all. As time went on, he drifted into one of those easygoing relationships which J.F.K. encouraged among those with expertise to offer him.

It was a year or so after their first encounter that the President sounded Mel out about heading the Federal Aviation Agency. (It was an Agency then, an Administration later.) Sometime during the Kennedy second term, which everyone assumed would be automatic, the incumbent FAA Administrator, Halaby, would move on to other things. How did Mel feel about implementing, from within, some of the measures he had advocated from without? Mel had replied that he was very interested indeed. He made it clear that if an offer was made, his answer would be yes.

Word filtered out, not from Mel, but through others who had had it from the top. Mel was 'in' – a dues-paid member of the inner circle. His prestige, high before, went higher still. The Airport Operators Council re-elected him president. His own airport commissioners voted him a handsome raise. Barely in his late thirties, he was considered the Young Harold of aviation management.

Six months later, John F. Kennedy made his fateful Texas journey.

Like others, Mel was first stunned, then later wept. Only later still, did it dawn on him that the assassin's bullets had ricocheted on to the lives of others, his own among them. He discovered he was no longer 'in' in Washington. Najeeb Halaby did, in fact, move on from FAA – to a senior vice-presidency of Pan American – but Mel did not succeed him. By then, power had shifted, influences waned. Mel's name, he later learned, was not even on President Johnson's short list for the FAA appointment.

Mel's second tenure as AOC president ran out uneventfully and another bright young man succeeded him. Mel's trips to Washington ceased. His public appearances became limited to local ones, and, in a way, he found the change to be a relief. His own responsibilities at Lincoln International had already increased as air traffic proliferated beyond most expectations. He became intensely occupied with planning, coupled with efforts to persuade the Board of Airport Commissioners to his own viewpoints. There was plenty to think about, including troubles at home. His days and weeks and months were full.

And yet, there was a sense that time and opportunity had passed him by. Others were aware of it. Unless something dramatic occurred, Mel surmised, his career might continue, and eventually end, precisely where he was.

'Tower to mobile one – what is your position?' The radio enjoinder broke through Mel's thoughts, returning him abruptly to the present.

He turned up the radio volume and reported. By now, he was nearing the main passenger terminal, its lights becoming clearer, despite the still heavily falling snow. The aircraft parking areas, he observed, were as fully occupied as when he left, and there was still a line of arriving aircraft waiting for gate positions to be vacated.

'Mobile one, hold until the Lake Central Nord crosses ahead of you, then follow it in.'

'This is mobile one. Roger.'

A few minutes later, Mel eased his car into the terminal basement parking area.

Near his parking stall was a locked box with an airport telephone. He used one of his keys to open the box and dialled the Snow Desk. Danny Farrow answered. Was there any fresh news, Mel inquired, about the mired Aéreo-Mexican jet?

'Negative,' Danny said. 'And the tower chief said to tell you that not being able to use runway three zero is still slowing traffic fifty per cent. Also, he's getting more phone complaints from Meadowood every time there's a takeoff over there.'

Mel said grimly, 'Meadowood will have to suffer.' Community meeting or not, there was nothing he could do to eliminate overhead noise for the time being. The most important thing at the moment was to reduce the lag in operations. 'Where's Joe Patroni now?'

'Same place. Still held up.'

'Can he make it for sure?'

'TWA says so. He has a phone in his car, and they've been in touch.'

'As soon as Joe gets here,' Mel instructed, 'I want to be notified. Wherever I am.'

'That'll be downtown, I guess.'

Mel hesitated. There was no reason, he supposed, why he need remain at the airport any longer tonight. Yet again, unaccountably, he had the same sense of foreboding which had disturbed him on the airfield. He remembered his conversation earlier with the tower watch chief, the line of waiting aircraft on the ramp apron outside. He made a spontaneous decision.

'No, I won't be downtown. We need that runway badly, and I'm not leaving until I know positively that Patroni is out there on the field, in charge.'

'In that case,' Danny said, 'I suggest you call your wife right now. Here's the number she's at.'

Mel wrote it down, then depressed the receiver rest and dialled the downtown number. He asked for Cindy, and after a brief wait heard her voice say sharply, 'Mel, why aren't you here?'

'I'm sorry, I was held up. There've been problems at the airport. It's a pretty big storm . . .'

'Damn you, *get down here fast!*'

From the fact that his wife's voice was low, Mel deduced there were others within hearing. Just the same, she managed to convey a surprising amount of venom.

Mel sometimes tried to associate the voice of Cindy nowadays with the Cindy he remembered before their marriage fifteen years ago. She had been a gentler person then, it seemed to him. In fact, her gentleness had been one of the things which appealed to Mel when they first met in San Francisco, he on leave from the Navy and Korea. Cindy had been an actress at the time, though in a minor way because the career she had hoped for had not worked out, and clearly wasn't going to. She had had a succession of diminishingly small parts in summer stock and television, and afterwards, in a moment of frankness, admitted that marriage had been a welcome release from the whole thing.

Years later, that story had changed a little, and it became a favourite gambit of Cindy's to declare that she had sacrificed her career and probable stardom because of Mel. More recently, though, Cindy didn't like her past as an actress being mentioned at all. That was because she had read in *Town and Country* that actresses were seldom, if ever, included in *The Social Register,* and addition of her own name to the *Register* was something Cindy wanted very much indeed.

'I'm coming downtown to join you just as soon as I can,' Mel said,

Cindy snapped, 'That isn't good enough. You should be here already. You knew perfectly well that tonight was important to me, and a week ago you made a definite promise.'

'A week ago I didn't know we were going to have the biggest storm in six years. Right now we've a runway out of use, there's a question of airport safety . . .'

'You've people working for you, haven't you? Or are the ones you've chosen so incompetent they can't be left alone?'

Mel said irritably, 'They're highly competent. But I get paid to take some responsibility, too.'

'It's a pity you can't act responsibly to me. Time and again I make important social arrangements which you enjoy demolishing.'

Listening, as the words continued, Mel sensed that Cindy was getting close to boiling point. Without any effort, he could visualize her now, five feet six of imperious energy in her highest heels, clear blue eyes flashing, and her blonde coiffed head tilted back in that dammnably attractive way she had when she was angry. That was one reason, Mel supposed, why, in their early years of marriage, his wife's temper outbursts seldom dismayed him. The more heated she became, it always seemed, the more desirable she grew. At such moments, he had invariably let his eyes rove upwards, beginning at her ankles – not hurriedly, because Cindy possessed extraordinarily attractive ankles and legs; in fact, better than those of most other women Mel knew – to the rest of her which was just as proportionate and physically appealing.

In the past, when his eyes had made their appreciative assessment, some two-way physical communion sprang into being, prompting each to reach out, to touch one another, impulsively, hungrily. The result was predictable. Invariably, the origin of Cindy's anger was forgotten in a wave of sensuality which engulfed them. Cindy had an exciting, insistent savagery, and in their lovemaking would demand, *'Hurt me, goddam you, hurt me!'* At the end, they would be spent and drained, so that picking up the skein of a quarrel was more than either had the wish or energy to do.

It was, of course, a way of shelving, rather than resolving, differences which – Mel realized, even early on – were fundamental. As the years passed, and passion lessened, accumulated differences became more sharply accented.

Eventually, they ceased entirely to use sex as a panacea and, in the past year or so, physical intimacy of any kind had become more and more occasional. Cindy, in fact, whose bodily appetites had always needed satisfying whatever the state of mind between them, appeared in recent months to have become indifferent altogether. Mel had wondered about that. Had his wife taken a lover? It was possible, and Mel supposed he ought to care. The sad thing was, it seemed easier not to be concerned.

Yet there were still moments when the sight or sound of Cindy in her wilful anger could stir him physically, arousing old desires. He had that feeling now as he listened to her excoriating voice on the telephone.

When he was able to cut in, he said, 'It isn't true that I enjoy demolishing your arrangements. Most of the time I go along with what you want, even though I don't think the things we go to are all that important. What I would enjoy are a few more evenings at home with the children.'

'That's a lot of crap,' Cindy said, 'and you know it.'

He felt himself tense, gripping the telephone more tightly. Then he conceded to himself; perhaps the last remark was true, to an extent. Earlier this evening he had been reminded of the times he had stayed at the airport when he could have gone home – merely because he wanted to avoid another fight with Cindy. Roberta and Libby had got left out of the reckoning then, as children did, he supposed, when marriages went sour. He should not have mentioned them.

But apart from that, tonight *was* different. He ought to stay on at the airport, at least until it became known for sure what was happening about the blocked runway.

'Look,' Mel said, 'let's make one thing clear. I haven't told you this before, but last year I kept some notes. You wanted me to come to fifty-seven of your charitable whingdings. Out of that I managed forty-five, which is a whole lot more than I'd attended from choice, but it isn't a bad score.'

'You bastard! I'm not a ball game where you keep a scorecard. I'm your wife.'

Mel said sharply, 'Take it easy!' He was becoming angry, himself. 'Also, in case you don't know it, you're raising your voice. Do you want all those nice people around to know what kind of a heel you have for a husband?'

'I don't give a goddam!' But she said it softly, just the same.

'I do know you're my wife, which is why I intend to get down there just as soon as I can.' What would happen, Mel wondered, if he could reach out and touch Cindy now? Would the old magic work? He decided not. 'So save me a place, and tell the waiter to keep my soup warm. Also, apologize and explain why I'm late. I pressume some of the people there have heard there *is* an airport.' A thought struck him. 'Incidentally, what's the occasion tonight?'

'I explained last week.'

'Tell me again.'

'It's a publicity party – cocktails and dinner – to promote the costume ball which is being given next month for the Archidona Children's Relief Fund. The press is here. They'll be taking photographs.'

Now Mel knew why Cindy wanted him to hurry. With him there, she stood a better chance of being in the photographs – and on tomorrow's newspaper social pages.

'Most other committee members,' Cindy insisted, 'have their husbands here already.'

'But not all?'

'I said most.'

'And you did say the Archidona Relief Fund?'

'Yes.'

'Which Archidona? There are two. One's in Ecuador, the other in Spain.' At college, maps and geography had fascinated Mel, and he had a retentive memory.

For the first time, Cindy hesitated. Then she said testily, 'What does it matter? This isn't the time for stupid questions.'

Mel wanted to laugh out loud. *Cindy didn't know.* As usual, she had chosen to work for a charity because of *who* was involved, rather than what.

He said maliciously, 'How many letters do you expect to get from this one?'

'I don't know what you mean.'

'Oh, yes, you do.'

To be considered for listing in *The Social Register,* a new aspirant needed eight sponsoring letters from people whose name already appeared there. At the last count, Mel had heard, Cindy had collected four.

'By God, Mel, if you say anything – tonight or any other time . . .'

'Will the letters be free ones, or do you expect to pay for them like those other two?' He was aware of having an advantage now. It happened very rarely.

Cindy said indignantly, 'That's a filthy allegation. It's impossible to buy your way in . . .'

'Nuts!' Mel said. 'I get the cancelled cheques from our joint account. Remember?'

There was a silence. Then Cindy asserted, low-voiced and savagely, 'Listen to me! You'd better get here tonight, and soon. If you don't come, or if you do come and embarrass me by saying anything of what you did just now, it'll be the end. Do you understand?'

'I'm not sure that I do.' Mel spoke quietly. Instinct cautioned him that this was an important moment for them both. 'Perhaps you'd better tell me exactly what you mean.'

Cindy countered, 'You figure it out.'

She hung up.

On his way from the parking area to his office, Mel's fury seethed and grew. Anger had always come to him less quickly than to Cindy. He was the slow-burn type. But he was burning now.

He was not entirely sure of the focus of his anger. A good deal was directed at Cindy, but there were other factors, too: His professional failure, as he saw it, to prepare effectually for a new era of aviation; a seeming inability to infuse others any longer with his own convictions; high hopes, unfulfilled. Somehow, between them all, Mel thought, his personal and professional lives had become twin testaments to inadequacy. His marriage was on the rocks, or apparently about to go there; if and when it did, he would have failed his children, also. At the same time, at the airport, where he was trustee for thousands who passed through daily in good faith, all his efforts and persuasion had failed to halt deterioration. There, the high standards he had worked to build were eroding steadily.

En route to the executive mezzanine, he encountered no one he knew. It was just as well. If he had been spoken to, whatever question had been put, he would have snarled a heated answer. In his office, he peeled off the heavy outdoor clothing and let it stay on the floor where it fell. He lit a cigarette. It had an acrid taste, and he stubbed it out. As he crossed to his desk, he was aware that the pain in his foot had returned, increasingly.

There was a time – it seemed long ago – when on nights like this, if his wounded foot pained him, he would have gone home, where Cindy would have insisted he relax. He would have a hot bath first, then after, while he lay face downwards on their bed, she would massage his back and neck with cool, firm fingers until pain ebbed out of him. It was unthinkable, of course, that Cindy would ever do the same thing again; but if she did, he doubted that it would work. You could lose communication in other ways besides the spoken word.

Seated at his desk, Mel put his head in his hands.

As he had done on the airfield earlier, he shivered. Then, abruptly in the silent office a telephone bell jangled. For a moment he ignored it. It rang again, and he realized it was the red alarm system telephone on a stand beside the desk. In two swift strides he reached it.

'Bakersfeld here.'

He heard clicks and more acknowledgements as others came on the line.

'This is Air Traffic Control,' the tower chief's voice announced. 'We have an airborne emergency, category three.'

9

Keith Bakersfeld, Mel's brother, was a third of the way through his eight-hour duty watch in the air traffic control radar room.

In radar control, tonight's storm was having a profound effect, though not a directly physical one. To a spectator, Keith thought, lacking an awareness of the complex story which a conglomeration of radarscopes was telling, it might have seemed that the storm, raging immediately outside, was a thousand miles away.

The radar room was in the control tower, one floor down from the glass-surrounded

47

eyrie – the tower cab – from which ATC directed aircraft movement on the ground and immediate local flying. The radar section's jurisdiction extended beyond the airport, and radar controllers reached out to bridge the gap between local control and the nearest ATC regional centre. The regional centres – usually miles from any airport – controlled main trunk airways and traffic coming on and off them.

In contrast to the top portion of the tower, the radar room had no windows. Day and night, at Lincoln International, ten radar controllers and supervisors laboured in perpetual semi-darkness under dim moonglow lights. Around them, tightly packed equipment – radarscopes, controls, radio communications panels – lined all four walls. Usually, controllers worked in shirtsleeves since the temperature, winter or summer, was maintained at an even seventy degrees to protect the delicate electronic gear.

The pervading tone in the radar room was calm. However, beneath the calmness, at all times, was a constant nervous strain. Tonight, the strain had been added to by the storm and, within the past few minutes, it had heightened further still. The effect was like stretching an already tensioned spring.

Cause of the added tension was a signal on a radarscope which, in turn, had triggered a flashing red light and alarm buzzer in the control room. The buzzer had now been silenced, but the distinctive radar signal remained. Known as a double blossom, it had flowered on the semi-darkened screen like a tremulous green carnation and denoted an aircraft in distress. In this case, the aircraft was a US Air Force KC-135, high above the airport in the storm, and seeking an immediate emergency landing. Keith Bakersfeld had been working the flatface scope on which the emergency signal appeared, and a supervisor had since joined him. Both were now transmitting urgent, swift decisions – by interphone to controllers at adjoining positions, and by radio to other aircraft.

The tower watch chief on the floor above had been promptly informed of the distress signal. He, in turn, had declared a category three emergency, alerting airport ground facilities.

The flatface scope, at the moment the centre of attention, was a horizontal glass circle, the size of a bicycle tyre, set into a table top console. Its surface was dark green, with brilliant green points of light showing all aircraft in the air within a forty-mile radius. As the aircraft moved, so did the points of light. Beside each light point was a small plastic marker, identifying it. The markers were known colloquially as 'shrimp boats' and controllers moved them by hand as aircraft progressed and their positions on the screen changed. As more aircraft appeared, they were identified by voice radio and similarly tagged. New radar systems dispensed with shrimp boats; instead, identifying letter-number codes – including altitude – appeared directly on the radar screen. But the newer method was not yet in wide use and, like all new systems, had bugs which needed elimination.

Tonight there was an extraordinary number of aircraft on the screen, and someone had remarked earlier that the green pin points were proliferating like fecund ants.

Keith was seated closest to the flatface, his lean, spindly figure hunched forward in a grey steel chair. His body was tense; his legs, hooked underneath the chair, were as rigid as the chair itself. He was concentrating, his face strained and gaunt, as it had been for months. The green reflection of the scope accentuated, eerily, deep hollows beneath his eyes. Anyone who knew Keith well, but had not seen him for a year or so, would have been shocked both by his appearance and his change in manner. Once, he had exuded an amiable, relaxed good-nature; now, all signs of it were gone. Keith was six years younger than his brother, Mel, but nowadays appeared a good deal older.

The change in Keith Bakersfeld had been noticed by his colleagues, some of whom were working tonight at other control positions in the radar room. They were also well aware of the reason for the change, a reason which had evoked genuine sympathy. However, they were practical men with an exacting job, which was why the radar supervisor, Wayne Tevis, was observing Keith covertly at this moment, watching the signs of increasing strain, as he had for some time. Tevis, a lanky, drawling Texan, sat centrally in the radar room on a high stool from where he could peer down over the shoulders of operators at the several radar-scopes serving special functions. Tevis had personally equipped the stool with castors, and periodically he rode it like a horse, propelling himself by jabs of his hand-tooled Texan boots wherever he was needed at the moment.

During the preceding hour, Wayne Tevis had at no point moved far away from Keith. The reason was that Tevis was ready, if necessary, to relieve Keith from radar watch, a decision which instinct told him might have to be made at any time.

The radar supervisor was a kindly man, despite his mild flamboyance. He dreaded what he might have to do, and was aware of how far-reaching, for Keith, its effect could be. Nevertheless, if he had to, he would do it.

His eyes on Keith's flatface scope, Trevis drawled, 'Keith, old son, that Braniff flight is closing on Eastern. If you turn Braniff right, you can keep Eastern going on the same course.' It was something which Keith should have seen himself, but hadn't.

The problem, which most of the radar room crew was working at feverishly, was to clear a patch for the Air Force KC-135, which had already started down on an instrument landing approach from two thousand feet. The difficulty was – below the big Air Force jet were five airline flights, stacked at intervals of a thousand feet, and orbiting a limited airspace. All were awaiting their turn to land. A few miles on either side were busy departure corridors, other columns of aircraft, similarly stacked and, lower still, were three more airliners, already on landing approaches. Somehow, the military flight had to be threaded down through the stacked civilian aeroplanes without a collision occurring. Under normal conditions the assignment would test the strongest nerves. As it was, the situation was complicated by radio failure in the KC-135, so that voice contact with the Air Force pilot had been lost.

Keith Bakersfeld thumbed his microphone. 'Braniff eight twenty-nine, make an immediate right turn, heading zero-niner-zero.' At moments like this, even though pressures built to fever pitch, voices should stay calm. Keith's voice was high-pitched and betrayed his nervousness. He saw Wayne Tevis glance at him sharply. But the blips on the radar screen, which had been uncomfortably close, began separating as the Braniff captain obeyed instructions. There were moments – this was one – when air traffic controllers thanked whatever gods they acknowledged for the swift, alert responses of airline pilots. The pilots might beef, and often did subsequently, at being given sudden course changes which required tight, abrupt turns and shook up passengers. But when a controller gave the *'immediate'*, they obeyed instantly and argued later.

In another minute or so the Braniff flight would have to be turned again, and so would Eastern, which was at the same level. Even before that, there must be new courses for two TWAs – one higher, the other lower – plus a Lake Central Convair, an Air Canada Vanguard, and a Swissair just coming on the screen. Until the KC-135 had come through,

49

these and others must be given zigzag courses, though for brief distances only, since none must stray into adjoining airspaces. In a way, it was like an intricate chess game, except that all the pieces were at various levels and moving at several hundred miles an hour. Also as part of the game, pieces had to be raised or lowered while they still moved forward, yet none must come closer than three miles laterally or a thousand feet vertically from another, and none must go over the edge of the board. And while all of it happened, the thousands of passengers, anxious for their journeys to end, had to sit in their airborne seats – and wait.

In occasional moments of detachment, Keith wondered how the Air Force pilot, in difficulty and letting down through storm and crowded airspace, was feeling at this moment. Lonely, probably. Just as Keith himself was lonely; just as all life was lonely, even with others physically close beside you. The pilot would have a co-pilot and crew, in the same way that Keith had fellow-workers who, at this moment, were near enough to touch. But that was not the kind of nearness which counted. Not when you were alone in that inner room of the mind, where no one else could enter, and where you lived – apart and solitary – with awareness, memory, conscience, fear. Alone, from the moment you were born until you died. Always, and for ever, alone.

Keith Bakersfeld knew how much alone a single human being could be.

In succession, Keith gave fresh courses to Swissair, one of the TWAs, Lake Central, and Eastern. Behind him he could hear Wayne Tevis trying to raise the Air Force KC-135 on radio again. Still no response, except that the distress radar blip, actuated by the KC-135 pilot, still blossomed on the scope. The position of the blip showed the pilot was doing the right thing – following exactly the instructions he had been given before the radio failure happened. In doing so, he would be aware that air traffic control could anticipate his movements. He would also know that his position could be seen by radar on the ground, and trusted that other traffic would be routed out of his way.

The Air Force flight, Keith knew, had originated in Hawaii and come non-stop after mid-air refuelling over the West Coast, its destination Andrews Air Force Base, near Washington. But west of the Continental Divide there had been an engine failure, and afterwards electrical trouble, causing the aeroplane commander to elect an unscheduled landing at Smoky Hill, Kansas. At Smoky Hill, however, snow clearance of runways had not been completed, and the KC-135 was diverted to Lincoln International. Air Route Control nursed the military flight northeast across Missouri and Illinois. Then, thirty miles out, West Arrivals Control, in the person of Keith Bakersfeld, took over. It was soon afterwards that radio failure had been added to the pilot's other troubles.

Most times, when flying conditions were normal, military aircraft stayed clear of civil airports. But in a storm like tonight's help was asked – and given – without question.

In this darkened, tightly packed radar room, other controllers, as well as Keith, were sweating. Yet no hint of pressures or tension must be betrayed by controllers' voices when speaking with pilots in the air. The pilots had plenty to concern themselves with at any time. Tonight, buffeted by the storm, and flying solely on instruments with nil visibility outside their cockpits, demands upon their skill were multiplied. Most pilots had already flown extra time because of delays caused by heavy traffic; now they would have to stay even longer in the air.

From each radar control position a swift, quiet stream of radio orders was going out to hold even more flights clear of the danger area. The flights were awaiting their own turn to land and every minute or two were being joined by new arrivals coming off airways. *A controller, his voice low but urgent, called over his shoulder. 'Chuck, I've got a hot one. Can you take Delta seven three?'* It was a controller's way of saying he was in trouble and had more than he could handle. *Another voice. 'Hell! – I'm piled up, too . . . Wait! . . . Affirmative, I got it.' A second's pause. 'Delta seven three from Lincoln approach control. Turn left; heading one two zero. Maintain altitude, four thousand!'* Controllers helped each other when they could. A few minutes from now the second man might need help himself. *'Hey, watch that Northwest; he's coming through from the other side. Christ! it's getting like the Outer Drive at rush hour.' . . . 'American four four, hold present heading, what's your altitude?' . . . 'That Lufthansa departure's way off course. Get him the hell out of the approach area!' . . .* Departing flights were being routed well around the trouble area, but arrivals were being held up, valuable landing time lost. Even later, when the emergency would be over, everyone knew it would take an hour or more to unravel the aerial traffic jam.

Keith Bakersfeld was trying hard to maintain his concentration, to retain a mental picture of his sector and every aircraft in it. It required instant memorizing – identifications, positions, types of aircraft, speeds, altitudes, sequence of landing . . . a detailed diagram, in depth, with constant changes . . . a configuration which was never still. Even at quieter times, mental strain was unceasing; tonight, the storm was taxing cerebral effort to its limit. A controller's nightmare was to 'lose the picture', a situation where an overtaxed brain rebelled and everything went blank. It happened occasionally, even to the best.

Keith had been the best. Until a year ago, he was one whom colleagues turned to when pressures built to unreason. *Keith, I'm getting swamped. Can you take a couple?* He always had.

But, lately, roles had changed. Now, colleagues shielded him as best they could, though there was a limit to how much any man could help another and do his own job, too.

More radio instructions were needed. Keith was on his own; Tevis, the supervisor, had propelled himself and his high stool across the room to check another controller. Keith's mind clicked out decisions. *Turn Braniff left, Air Canada right, Eastern through a hundred and eighty degrees.* It was done; on the radar screen, blips were changing direction. *The slower-moving Lake Central Convair could be left another minute. Not so, the Swissair jet; it was converging with Eastern. Swissair must be given a new course immediately, but what? Think fast! Forty-five degrees right, but for a minute only, then right again. Keep an eye on TWA and Northwest! A new flight was coming in from the west at high speed – identify, and find more airspace. Concentrate, concentrate!*

Keith determined grimly: *He would not lose the picture; not tonight, not now.*

There was a reason for not doing so; a secret he had shared with no one, not even Natalie, his wife. Only Keith Bakersfeld, and Keith alone, knew that this was the last time he would ever face a radarscope or stand a watch. Today was his last day with air traffic control. It would be over soon.

It was also the last day of his life.

'Take a break, Keith.' It was the tower watch chief's voice.

Keith had not seen the tower chief come in. He had done so unobtrusively, and was standing by Wayne Tevis, the radar supervisor.

A moment earlier, Tevis had told the tower chief quietly, 'Keith's all right, I reckon. For a few minutes I was worried, but he seemed to pull together.' Tevis was glad he had not

51

had to take the drastic action he had contemplated earlier, but the tower chief murmured, 'Let's take him off a while, anyway'; and, as an afterthought, 'I'll do it.'

Glancing at the two men together, Keith knew at once why he was being relieved. There was still a crisis, and they didn't trust him. The work break was a pretext; he wasn't due for one for half-an-hour. Should he protest? For a controller as senior as himself, it was an indignity which others would notice. Then he thought: Why make an issue now? It wasn't worth it. Besides, a ten-minute break would steady him. Afterwards, when the worst of the emergency was over, he could return to work for the remainder of his shift.

Wayne Tevis leaned forward. 'Lee will take over, Keith.' He motioned to another controller who had just returned from his own work break – a scheduled one.

Keith nodded, without comment, though he remained in place and continued to give radio instructions to aircraft while the new man got the picture. It usually took several minutes for one controller to hand over to another. The man coming in had to study the radar display, letting the over-all situation build in his mind. He also needed to become mentally tensed.

Getting tensed – consciously and deliberately – was a part of the job. Controllers called it 'sharpening to an edge', and in Keith's fifteen years in air traffic control, he had watched it happen regularly, to others and to himself. You did it, because you had to, when you took over a duty, as now. At other times it became a reflex action, such as when controllers drove to work together – in car pools, as some did. On leaving home, conversation would be relaxed and normal. At that point in the journey, a casual question like, 'Are you going to the ball game Saturday?' would elicit an equally casual answer – 'Sure am,' or 'No, I can't make it this week.' Yet, nearing the job, conversation tautened, so that the same question – a quarter mile from the airport – might produce a terse 'affirmative' or 'negative', and nothing more.

Coupled with tense mental sharpness was another requirement – a controlled, studied calmness at all times on duty. The two requirements – contradictory in terms of human nature – were exhausting mentally and, in the long run, took a toll. Many controllers developed stomach ulcers which they concealed through fear of losing their jobs. As part of the concealment, they paid for private medical advice instead of seeking free medical help to which their employment entitled them. At work, they hid bottles of Maalox – 'for the relief of gastric hyperacidity' – in their lockers and, at intervals, sipped the white, sweetish fluid surreptitiously.

There were other effects. Some controllers – Keith Bakersfeld knew several – were mean and irascible at home, or flew into rages, as a reaction to pent-up emotions at work. Coupled with irregular hours of working and sleeping, which made it difficult to regulate a household, the effect was predictable. Among air traffic controllers, the list of broken homes was long, divorce rates high.

'Okay,' the new man said. 'I have the picture.'

Keith slid out from his seat, disconnecting his headset as the relieving controller took his place. Even before the newcomer was seated, he had begun transmitting fresh instructions to the lower TWA.

The tower chief told Keith, 'Your brother said he might drop around later.'

Keith nodded as he left the radar room. He felt no resentment against the tower chief, who had his own responsibilities to contend with, and Keith was glad he had made no protest about being relieved prematurely. More than anything else at the moment, Keith wanted a cigarette, some coffee, and to be alone. He was also glad – now the decision had been made for him – to be away from the emergency situation. He had been involved in too many in the past to regret missing the culmination of one more.

Air traffic emergencies of one kind or another occurred several times a day at Lincoln International, as they did at any major airport. They could happen in any kind of weather – on the clearest day, as well as during a storm like tonight's. Usually, only a few people knew about such incidents, because almost all were resolved safely, and even pilots in the air were seldom told the reason for delays or abrupt instructions to turn this way or that. For one thing, there was no need for them to know; for another, there was never time for radio small talk. Ground emergency staffs – crash crews, ambulance attendants, and police – as well as airport senior management, were always alerted, and the action they took depended on the category of emergency declared. Category one was the most serious, but was rarely invoked, since it signalled an actual crash. Category two was notification of imminent danger to life, or physical damage. Category three, as now, was a general warning to airport emergency facilities to stand by; they might be needed, or they might not. For controllers, however, any type of emergency involved additional pressures and after effects.

Keith entered the controllers' locker room which adjoined the radar control room. Now that he had a few minutes to think more calmly, he hoped, for the sake of everyone, that the Air Force KC-135 pilot, and all others in the air tonight, made it safely down through the storm.

The locker room, a small cubicle with a single window, had three walls of metal lockers, and a wooden bench down the centre. A notice board beside the window held an untidy collection of official bulletins and notices from airport social groups. An unshaded light bulb in the ceiling seemed dazzling after the radar room's semi-darkness. No one else was in the locker room, and Keith reached for the light switch and turned it off. There were floodlights on the tower outside, and enough light came in for him to see.

He lit a cigarette. Then, opening his locker, he took out the lunch pail which Natalie had packed before his departure from home this afternoon. As he poured coffee from a Thermos, he wondered if Natalie had put a note in with his meal, or, if not a note, some inconsequential item she had clipped from a newspaper or a magazine. She often did one or both, hoping, he supposed, that it might cheer him. She had worked hard at doing that, right from the beginning of his trouble. At first, she had used obvious means; then, when those hadn't worked, less obvious ones, though Keith had always realized – in a detached, dispassionate kind of way – exactly what Natalie was doing, or trying to. More recently there had been fewer notes and clippings.

Perhaps Natalie, too, had finally lost heart. She had had less to say lately, and he knew, from the redness of her eyes, there were times she had been crying.

Keith had wanted to help her when he saw it. But how could he – when he couldn't help himself?

A picture of Natalie was taped to the inside of his locker door – a snapshot, in colour, which Keith had taken. He had brought it here three years ago. Now, the light from outside shone on the picture only dimly, but he knew it so well, he could see what was there, whether highlighted or not.

The picture showed Natalie in a bikini. She was seated on a rock, laughing, one slim hand held above her eyes to shield them from the sun. Her light brown hair streamed behind; her small, pert face showed the freckles which always appeared in summer. There was an impudent, pixyish quality to Natalie Bakersfeld, as well as strength of will, and the camera had caught both. In the rear of the picture was a blue-water lake, high firs, and a rock out-cropping. They had been on a motoring holiday in Canada, camping among the Haliburton lakes, and for once their children, Brian and Theo, had been left behind in Illinois, with Mel and Cindy. The holiday proved to be one of the happier times that Keith and Natalie had ever known.

Perhaps, Keith thought, it wasn't a bad thing to be remembering it tonight.

Pushed in behind the photo was a folded paper. It was one of the notes he had been thinking about, which Natalie put occasionally in his lunch pail. This was one from a few months ago which, for some reason, he had saved. Though knowing what was there, he took the paper out and walked to the window to read. It was a clipping from a news magazine, with some lines below in his wife's handwriting.

Natalie had all kinds of odd interests, some far-ranging, which she encouraged Keith and the boys to share. This clipping was about continuing experiments, by US geneticists. Human sperm, it reported, could now be fast frozen. The sperm was placed in a deep freeze for storage where it remained in good condition indefinitely. When thawed, it could be used for fertilization of women at any time – either soon or generations hence.

Natalie had written:

The Ark could have been 50 per cent smaller, if Noah
Had know the facts about frozen spermatazoa;
It appears you can have babies by the score
Merely by opening a refrigerator door.
I'm glad we had our ration
With love and passion.

She had been trying then; still trying desperately to return their lives . . . the two of them; and as a family . . . to the way they had been before. *With love and passion.*

Mel had joined forces, too, attempting with Natalie, to induce his brother to fight free from the tide-race of anguish and depression which engulfed him totally.

Even then a part of Keith had wanted to respond. Summoning, from some deep consciousness, a spark of spirit, he had sought to match their strength by drawing on his own; to respond to proffered love with love himself. But the effort failed. It failed – as he had known it would – because there was no feeling or emotion left within him. Neither warmth, nor love, nor even anger to be kindled. Only bleakness, remorse, and all-enveloping despair.

Natalie realized their failure now; he was sure of that. It was the reason, he suspected, that she had been crying, somewhere out of sight.

And Mel? Perhaps Mel, too, had given up. Though not entirely – Keith remembered what the tower chief had told him. 'Your brother said he might drop around . . .'

It would be simpler if Mel didn't. Keith felt unequal to the effort, even though they had been as close as brothers could be all their lives. Mel's presence might be complicating.

Keith was too drained, too weary, for complications any more.

He wondered again if Natalie had put in a note with his meal tonight. He took out the contents of the lunch pail carefully, hoping that she had.

There were ham and watercress sandwiches, a container of cottage cheese, a pear, and wrapping paper. Nothing more.

Now that he knew there was none, he wished desperately there had been some message; any message, even the most trifling. Then he realized – it was his own fault; there had been no time. Today, because of the preparations he needed to make, he had left home earlier than usual. Natalie, to whom he had given no advance warning, had been rushed. At one point, he had suggested not taking a lunch at all; he would get a meal, he said, at one of the airport cafeterias. But Natalie, who knew the cafeterias would be crowded and noisy, which Keith disliked, had said no, and gone ahead as quickly as she could. She had not asked why he wanted to leave early, though he knew she was curious. Keith was relieved that there had been no questioning. If there had been, he would have had to invent something, and he would not have wanted the last words between them to have been a lie.

As it was, there had been enough time. He had driven to the airport business area and registered at the O'Hagan Inn where, earlier in the day, he had made a reservation by telephone. He had planned everything carefully, using a plan worked out several weeks ago, though he had waited – giving himself time to think about it, and be sure – before putting the plan into effect. After checking into his room, he had left the Inn and arrived at the airport in time to go on duty.

The O'Hagan Inn was within a few minutes drive of Lincoln International. In a few hours from now, when Keith's duty watch was ended, he could go there quickly. The room key was in his pocket. He took it out to check.

10

The information – which the tower watch chief had relayed earlier to Mel Bakersfeld – about a meeting of Meadowood citizenry, was entirely accurate.

The meeting in the Sunday school hall of Meadowood First Baptist Church – fifteen seconds, as a jet flies, from the end of runway two five – had been in session half-an-hour. Its proceedings had started later than planned, since most of the six hundred adults who were present had had to battle their way, in cars and on foot, through deep snow. But somehow they had come.

It was a mixed assemblage, such as might be found in an averagely prosperous dormitory community. Of the men, some were medium-level executives, others artisans, with a sprinkling of local tradespeople. In numbers, men and women were approximately equal. Since it was Friday night, the beginning of a weekend, most were casually dressed, though exceptions were half a dozen visitors from outside the community and several press reporters.

The Sunday school hall was now uncomfortably crowded, stuffy and smoke-filled. All available chairs were occupied, and at least a hundred people were standing.

That so many had turned out at all on such a night, leaving warm homes to do so, spoke eloquently of their mettle and concern. They were also, at the moment, unanimously angry.

The anger – almost as tangible as the tobacco smoke – had two sources. First was the long-standing bitterness with the airport's by-product – the thunderous, ear-assaulting noise of jet propulsion which assailed the homes of Meadowood, day and night, shattering peace and privacy, both waking and sleeping. Second was the immediate frustration that, through a large part of the meeting so far, those assembled had been unable to hear one another.

Some difficulty in hearing had been anticipated. After all, it was what the meeting was about, and a portable p.a. system had been borrowed from the church. What had not been expected, however, was that tonight jet aircraft would be taking off immediately overhead, rendering both human ears and the p.a. system useless. The cause, which the meeting neither knew nor cared about, was that runway three zero was blocked by the mired Aéreo-Mexican 707, and other aircraft were being instructed to use runway two five instead. The latter runway pointed directly at Meadowood, like an arrow, whereas runway three zero, when usable, at least routed takeoffs slightly to one side.

In a momentary silence the chairman, red-faced, shouted, 'Ladies and gentlemen, for years we have tried reasoning with the airport management and the airline companies. We have pointed to the violation of our homes. We have proved, with independent testimony, that normal living – under the barrage of noise we are forced to endure – is impossible. We have pleaded that our very sanity is in danger and that our wives, our children, and ourselves live on the edge of nervous breakdowns, which some among us have suffered already.'

The chairman was a heavy-jowled, balding man named Floyd Zanetta, who was a printing firm manager and Meadowood home-owner. Zanetta, sixtyish, was prominent in community affairs, and in the lapel of his sports jacket was a Kiwanis long-service badge.

Both the chairman and an impeccably dressed younger man were on a small raised platform at the front of the hall. The younger man, seated, was Elliott Freemantle, a lawyer. A black leather briefcase stood open at his side.

Floyd Zanetta slammed a hand on the lectern in front of him. 'What do the airport and airlines do? I'll tell you what they do. They pretend; pretend to listen. And while they are pretending they make promises and more promises which they have no intention of fulfilling. The airport management, the FAA, and the airlines are cheats and liars . . .'

The world 'liars' was lost.

It was engulfed in a shattering, almost unbelievable crescendo of sound, a monstrous roar of power which seemed to seize the building and shake it. As if protectively, many in the hall covered their ears. A few glanced upwards nervously. Others, their eyes transmitting anger, spoke heatedly to those beside them, though only a lip reader could have known what was said; no words were audible. A water pitcher near the chairman's lectern trembled. If Zanetta had not grasped it quickly, it would have fallen to the floor and shattered.

As swiftly as it had begun and built, the roar lessened and faced. Already miles away and several thousand feet above, Flight 58 of Pan American was climbing through storm and darkness, reaching for higher, clearer altitudes, swinging on to course for Frankfurt, Germany. Now, Continental Airlines 23, destination Denver, Colorado, was rolling on the farther end of runway two five, cleared for takeoff – over Meadowood. Other flights, already in line on an adjoining taxiway, were waiting their turn to follow.

It had been the same way all evening, even before the Meadowood meeting started. And after it started, business had had to be conducted in brief intervals between the overwhelming din of takeoffs.

56

Zanetta continued hastily, 'I said they are cheats and liars. What is happening here and now is conclusive evidence. At the very least we are entitled to noise abatement procedures, but tonight even this . . .'

'Mr Chairman,' a woman's voice cut in from the body of the hall, 'we've heard all this before. We all know it, and going over it again won't change anything.' All eyes had turned to the woman, who was now standing. She had a strong, intelligent face and shoulder-length brown hair which had fallen forward, so that she brushed it back impatiently. 'What I want to know, and so do others, is what else can we do, and where do we go from here?'

There was an outburst of applause and cheering.

Zanetta said irritably, 'If you'll kindly let me finish . . .' He never did.

Once again, the same encompassing roar dominated the Sunday school hall.

The timing, and the last remark, provided the only laughter, so far, of the evening. Even the chairman grinned ruefully as he raised his hands in a despairing gesture.

A man's voice called peevishly, 'Get on with it!'

Zanetta nodded agreement. He continued speaking, picking his way – like a climber over rocks – between recurring peaks of sound from overhead. What the community of Meadowood must do, he declared, was to discard politeness and reasonable approaches to the airport authority and others. Instead, a purely legalistic attack must be the order from now on. The residents of Meadowood were citizens with legal rights, which were being infringed upon. Along with those legal rights went recourse to the courts; therefore, they must be prepared to fight in the courts, with toughness, even viciousness, if necessary. As to what form a legalistic offensive should take, it so happened that a noted lawyer, Mr Elliott Freemantle, whose offices were downtown in the Loop, had consented to be present at the meeting. Mr Freemantle had made a study of laws affecting excessive noise, privacy and airspace, and, very soon, those who had braved the weather to attend would have the pleasure of hearing this distinguished gentleman. He would in fact, present a proposal . . .

As the clichés rolled on, Elliott Freemantle fidgeted. He passed a hand lightly over his barber-styled, grey-streaked hair, fingering the smoothness of his chin and cheeks – he had shaved an hour before the meeting – and his keen sense of smell confirmed that the exclusive face lotion, which he always used after shaving and sunlamp sessions, still lingered. He recrossed his legs, observing that his two-hundred dollar alligator shoes still gleamed with mirror clearness, and was careful not to spoil the crease in the trousers of his tailored Blue Spruce pebble-weave suit. Elliott Freemantle had long ago discovered that people preferred their lawyers – unlike their doctors – to look prosperous. Prosperity in a lawyer conveyed an aura of success at the bar, success which those about to engage in litigation wanted for themselves.

Elliott Freemantle hoped that most of those in the hall would shortly become litigants, and that he would represent them. Meanwhile, he wished the old cluck of a chairman, Zanetta, would get the hell off his feet so that he, Freemantle, could take over. There was no surer way to lose the confidence of an audience or a jury, than by letting them think faster than yourself, so that they became aware of what you were going to say before you said it. Freemantle's finely honed intuition told him this was what was happening now. It meant that when his own turn came, he would have to work that much harder to establish his competence and superior intellect.

Some among his legal colleagues might have questioned if Elliott Freemantle's intellect

57

was, in fact, superior. They might even have objected to the chairman's description of him as a gentleman.

Fellow lawyers sometimes regarded Freemantle as an exhibitionist who commanded high fees mainly through a showman's instinct for attracting attention. It was conceded, though, that he had an enviable knack for latching early on to causes which later proved spectacular and profitable.

For Elliott Freemantle, the Meadowood situation seemed custom made.

He had read about the community's problem and promptly arranged, through contacts, to have his name suggested to several home-owners as the one lawyer who could most likely help them. As a result, a home-owners committee eventually approached him, and the fact that they did so, rather than the other way around, gave him a psychological advantage he had planned from the beginning. Meanwhile, he had made a superficial study of the law, and recent court decisions, affecting noise and privacy – a subject entirely new to him – and when the committee arrived, he addressed them with the assurance of a lifetime expert.

Later, he had made the proposition which resulted in this meeting tonight, and his own attendance.

Thank God! It looked as if Zanetta, the chairman, was finally through with his windy introduction. Banal to the last, he was intoning, '. . . and so it is my privilege and pleasure to present . . .'

Scarcely waiting for his name to be spoken, Elliott Freemantle bounded to his feet. He began speaking before Zanetta's buttocks had made contact with his chair. As usual, he dispensed with all preliminaries.

'If you are expecting sympathy from me, you can leave right now, because there won't be any. You won't get it at this session, or others we may have later. I am not a purveyor of crying towels, so if you need them, I suggest you get your own, or supply each other. My business is law, law, and nothing else!'

He had deliberately made his voice harsh, and he knew he had jolted them, as he intended to.

He had also seen the newspaper reporters look up and pay attention. There were three of them at the press table near the front of the hall – two young men from the big city dailies and an elderly woman from a local weekly. All were important to his plans, and he had taken the trouble to find out their names and speak to them briefly before the meeting started. Now, their pencils were racing. Good! Co-operation with the press always ranked high in any project of Elliott Freemantle's, and he knew from experience that the best way to achieve it was by providing a lively story with a fresh angle. Usually he succeeded. Newspaper people appreciated that – a lot more than free drinks or food – and the livelier and more colourful the story, the more friendly their reportage was inclined to be.

He returned his attention to the audience.

Only a shade less aggressively, he continued, 'If we decide between us, that I am to represent you, it will be necessary for me to ask you questions about the effect of airport noise on your homes, your families, your own physical and mental health. But do not imagine I shall be asking the questions because I care personally about these things, or you as individuals. Frankly, I don't. You may as well know that I am an extremely selfish man. If I ask these questions, it will be to discover to what extent wrong has been done you under the law. I am already convinced that some wrong has been done – perhaps

58

considerable wrong – and, in that event, you are entitled to legal redress. But you may as well know that whatever I learn, and however deeply I become involved, I am not given to losing sleep about the welfare of my clients when I'm away from my office or the courts. But . . .' Freemantle paused dramatically, and stabbed a finger forward to underscore his words. 'But, in my office and in the courts, as clients, you would have the utmost of my attention and ability, *on questions of law*. And on those occasions, if we work together, I promise you will be glad I am on your side and not against you.'

Now he had the attention of everyone in the hall. Some, both men and women, were sitting forward in their chairs, striving not to miss any words as he paused – though for the minimum time – as aircraft continued overhead. A few faces had become hostile as he spoke, but not many. It was time, though, to relax the pressure a little. He gave a swift, short smile, then went on seriously.

'I inform you of these things, so that we understand each other. Some people tell me that I am a mean, unpleasant man. Maybe they are right, though personally if ever I want a lawyer for myself, I'll make sure of choosing someone who *is* mean and unpleasant, also tough – on my behalf.' There were a few approving nods and smiles.

'Of course, if you want a nicer guy who'll hand you more sympathy, though maybe a bit less law' – Elliott Freemantle shrugged – 'that's your privilege.'

He had been watching the audience closely and saw a responsible-looking man, in heavy rimmed glasses, lean towards a man and whisper. From their expressions, Freemantle guessed the man was saying, 'This is more like it! – what we wanted to hear.' The woman, probably the whisperer's wife, nodded agreement. Around the hall, other faces conveyed the same impression.

As usual on occasions like this, Elliott Freemantle had shrewdly judged the temper of the meeting and calculated his own approach. He sensed early that these people were weary of platitudes and sympathy – well-meaning but ineffective. His own words, blunt and brutal, were like a cold, refreshing douche. Now, before minds could relax and attention wander, he must take a new tack. The moment for specifics had arrived – tonight, for this group, a discourse on the law of noise. The trick to holding audience attention, at which Elliott Freemantle excelled, was to stay half a mental pace ahead; that much and no more, so that those listening could follow what was being said, but must remain sufficiently alert to do so.

'Pay attention,' he commanded, 'because I'm going to talk about your particular problem.'

The law of noise, he declared, was increasingly under study by the nation's courts. Old concepts were changing. New court decisions were establishing that excessive noise could be an invasion of privacy as well as trespass on property rights. Moreover, courts were in a mood to grant injunctions and financial recompense where intrusion – including aircraft intrusion – could be proven.

Elliott Freemantle paused while another takeoff thundered overhead, then gestured upwards. 'I believe you will have no difficulty in proving it here.'

At the press table all three reporters made a note.

The United States Supreme Court, he went on, had already set a precedent. In *US* v. *Causby* the court ruled that a Greensboro, North Carolina, chicken farmer was entitled to compensation because of 'invasion' by military planes flying low above his house. In handing down the *Causby* decision, Mr Justice William O. Douglas had stated, '. . . if the landowner is to have full enjoyment of the land, he must have exclusive control of the immediate reaches of the enveloping atmosphere.' In another case reviewed by the Supreme Court, *Griggs* v. *County of Allegheny*, a similar principal was upheld. In state courts of Oregon and Washington, in *Thornburg* v. *Port of Portland* and *Martin* v. *Port of Seattle*, damages for excessive aircraft noise had been awarded, even though air space directly above the plaintiffs had not been violated. Other communities had begun, or were contemplating, similar legal action, and some were employing sound trucks and movie cameras as aids to proving their case. The trucks took decibel readings of noise; the cameras recorded aircraft altitudes. The noise frequently proved greater, the altitudes lower, than airlines and airport management admitted. In Los Angeles, a home-owner had filed suit against LA International Airport, asserting that the airport, by permitting landings on a newly extended runway close to his home, had taken an easement on his property without due process of law. The home-owner was claiming ten thousand dollars which he believed to be equivalent to the decrease in value of his home. Elsewhere, more and more similar cases were being argued in the courts.

The recital was succinct and impressive. Mention of a specific sum – ten thousand dollars – evoked immediate interest, as Elliott Freemantle intended that it should. The entire presentation sounded authoritative, factual, and the produce of years of study. Only Freemantle himself knew that his 'facts' were the result, not of poring over law reports, but of two hours, the previous afternoon, spent studying newsclippings in a downtown newspaper morgue.

There were also several facts which he had failed to mention. The chicken farmer ruling of the Supreme Court was made more than twenty years earlier, and total damages awarded were a trifling three hundred and seventy-five dollars – the actual value of some dead chickens. The Los Angeles suit was merely a claim which had not yet come to trial and might never do so. A more significant case, *Batten* v. *US*, on which the Supreme Court had ruled as recently as 1963, Elliott Freemantle knew about but conveniently ignored. In *Batten*, the court accepted that only an actual 'physical invasion' could create liability; noise alone did not do so. Since, at Meadowood, there had been no such invasion, the Batten precedent meant that if a legal case was launched, it might well be lost before it was begun.

But lawyer Freemantle had no wish for this to be know, at least not yet; nor was he overly concerned whether a case, if brought to court, might eventually be won or lost. What he wanted was this Meadowood home-owners group as clients – at a whopping fee.

On the subject of fee, he had already counted the house and done some mental arithmetic. The result delighted him.

Of six hundred people in the hall, he estimated that five hundred, probably more, were Meadowood property owners. Allowing for the presence of husbands and wives together, it meant that there was a minimum of two hundred and fifty prospective clients. If each of these two hundred and fifty could be persuaded to sign a one hundred dollar retainer agreement – which Elliott Freemantle hoped they would before the evening was over – a total fee in excess of twenty-five thousand dollars seemed decidedly within reach.

On other occasions he had managed precisely the same thing. It was remarkable what you could accomplish with audacity, particularly when people were white hot in pursuing their own interests. An ample supply of printed retainer forms was in his bag. *This memorandum of agreement between . . . hereinafter known as plaintiff/s and Freemantle and Sye, attorneys at law . . . who will undertake plaintiff/s legal representation in promotion of a claim for damages sustained due to aircraft use of the Lincoln International Airport facility . . . Plaintiff/s agrees to pay the said Freemantle and Sye one hundred dollars, in four instalments of twenty-five dollars, the first instalment now due and payable, the balance quarterly on demand . . . Further, if the suit is successful Freemantle and Sye will receive ten per cent of the gross amount of any damages awarded . . .*

The ten per cent was a long shot because it was highly unlikely that there would ever be any damages to collect. Just the same, strange things sometimes happened in law, and Elliott Freemantle believed in covering all bases.

'I have informed you of the legal background,' he asserted. 'Now I intend to give you some advice.' He flashed one of his rare, quick smiles. 'This advice will be a free sample, but – like toothpaste – any subsequent tubes will have to be paid for.'

There was a responsive laugh which he cut off brusquely with a gesture. 'My advice is that there is little time for anything else but action. Action now.'

The remark produced handclapping and more nods of approval.

There was a tendency, he continued, to regard legal proceedings as automatically slow and tedious. Often that was true, but on occasions, if determination and legal skill were used, the law could be harried along. In the present instance, legal action should be begun at once, before airlines and airport, by perpetuation of noise over a period of years, could claim custom and usage. As if to underline the point, still another aircraft thundered overhead. Before its sound could die, Elliott Freemantle shouted, 'So I repeat – my advice to you is wait no longer! You should act tonight. Now!'

Near the front of the audience, a youngish man in an alpaca cardigan and hopsack slacks sprang to his feet. 'By God! – tell us how we start.'

'You start – if you want to – by retaining me as your legal counsel.'

There was an instant chorus of several hundred voices. 'Yes, we want to.'

The chairman, Floyd Zanetta, was now on his feet again, waiting for the shouting to subside. He appeared pleased. Two of the reporters had craned around and were observing the obvious enthusiasm throughout the hall. The third reporter – the elderly woman from the local weekly – looked up at the platform with a friendly smile.

It had worked, as Elliott Freemantle had known it would. The rest, he realized, was merely routine. Within the next half hour a good many of the retainer blanks in his bag would be signed, while others would be taken home, talked over, and most likely mailed tomorrow. These people were not afraid of signing papers, or of legal procedures; they had become accustomed to both in purchasing their homes. Nor would a hundred dollars seem an excessive sum; a few might even be surprised that the figure was that low. Only a handful would bother doing the mental arithmetic which Elliott Freemantle had done himself, and even if they objected to the size of the total amount, he could argue that the fee was justified by responsibility for the large numbers involved.

Besides, he would give them value for their money – a good show, with fireworks, in court and elsewhere. He glanced at his watch; better get on. Now that his own involvement was assured, he wanted to cement the relationship by staging the first act of a drama. Like everything else so far, it was something he had already planned and it would gain attention – much more than this meeting – in tomorrow's newspapers. It would also confirm to these people that he meant what he said about not wasting any time.

The actors in the drama would be the residents of Meadowood, here assembled, and he hoped that everyone present was prepared to leave this hall and to stay out late.

The scene would be the airport.

The time: tonight.

▌▌

At approximately the same time that Elliott Freemantle was savouring success, an embittered, thwarted, former building contractor named D.O. Guerrero was surrendering to failure.

Guerrero was fifteen miles or so from the airport, in a locked room of a shabby walk-up apartment on the city's South Side. The apartment was over a noisome, greasy-spoon lunch counter on 51st Street, not far from the stockyards.

D.O. Guerrero was a gaunt, spindly man, slightly stoop-shouldered, with a sallow face and protruding, narrow jaw. He had deep-set eyes, pale thin lips, and a slightly sandy moustache. His neck was scrawny, with a prominent Adam's apple. His hairline was receding. He had nervous hands, and his fingers were seldom still. He smoked constantly, usually lighting a fresh cigarette from the stub of the last. At the moment he needed a shave and a clean shirt, and was perspiring, even though the room in which he had locked himself was cold. His age was fifty; he looked several years older.

Guerrero was married, and had been for eighteen years. By some standards, the marriage was good, if unspectacular. D.O. (through most of his life he had been known by his initials) and Inez Guerrero accepted each other equably, and the idea of coveting some other partner seemed not to occur to them. D.O. Guerrero, in any case, had never been greatly interested in women; business, and financial manoeuvring, occupied his thoughts far more. But in the past year, a mental gulf had opened between the Guerreros which Inez, though she tried, was unable to bridge. It was one result of a series of business disasters which reduced them from comparative affluence to near poverty, and eventually forced a succession of moves – first from their comfortable and spacious, if heavily mortgaged, surburban home to other quarters less pretentious, and later still to this seamy, draughty, cockroach-infested, two-room apartment.

Even though Inez Guerrero did not enjoy their situation, she might have made the best of it if her husband had not become increasingly moody, savagely bad tempered, and at times impossible to talk with. A few weeks ago, in a rage, he had struck Inez, bruising her face badly, and though she would have forgiven him, he would neither apologize nor discuss the incident later. She feared more violence and, soon after, sent their two teen-age children – a boy and a girl – to stay with her married sister in Cleveland. Inez herself stayed on, but took a job as a coffee-house waitress, and although the work was hard and the pay small, it at least provided money for food. Her husband seemed scarcely to notice the children's absence, or her own; his mood recently had been a deep self-contained dejection.

Inez was now at her job. D.O. Guerrero was in the apartment alone. He need not have locked the door of the small bedroom where he was occupied, but had done so as an added guarantee of privacy, even though he would not be there for long.

Like others this night, D.O. Guerrero would shortly leave for the airport. He held a confirmed reservation, plus a validated ticket – for tonight – on Trans America Flight Two to Rome. At this moment, the ticket was in a pocket of his topcoat, also in the locked room, slung over a rickety wooden chair.

Inez Guerrero had no knowledge of the ticket to Rome, nor did she have the slightest inkling of her husband's motive in obtaining it.

The Trans America ticket was for a round trip excursion which normally cost four hundred and seventy-four dollars. However, by lying, D.O. Guerrero had obtained credit. He paid fort-seven dollars down, acquired by pawning his wife's last possession of any value – her mother's ring (Inez had not yet missed it) – and promised to remit the balance, plus interest, in monthly instalments over the next two years.

It was highly unlikely that the promise would ever be fulfilled.

No self-respecting finance company or bank would have loaned D.O. Guerrero the price of a bus ticket to Peoria, leave alone an airline fare to Rome. They would have investigated his background thoroughly, and discovered he had a long history of insolvency, a parcel of long standing personal debts, and that his home-building company, Guerrero Contracting Inc., had been placed in bankruptcy a year earlier.

An even closer check into Guerrero's tangled finances might have disclosed that during the past eight months – using his wife's name – he had attempted to raise capital for a speculative land deal, but failed to do so. In course of this failure he incurred even more debts. Now, because of certain fraudulent statements, as well as being an undischarged bankrupt, exposure, which seemed imminent, would involve criminal prosecution and almost certainly a prison term. Slightly less serious, but just as immediate, was the fact that the rent of this apartment, wretched as it was, was three weeks overdue, and the landlord had threatened eviction tomorrow. If evicted, they would have nowhere else to go.

D.O. Guerrero was desperate. His financial rating was minus zero.

Airlines, though, were notably easygoing about extending credit; also, if a debt went sour they were usually less tough in collection procedures than other agencies. This was calculated policy. It was based on the fact that fare-paying air travellers, over the years, had proved themselves an unusually honest cross-section of society, and bad debt losses of most airlines were remarkably low. Deadbeats like D.O. Guerrero troubled them rarely; therefore they were not geared – because it was not worth while – to defeat the kind of subterfuge he had used.

He avoided, by two simple means, more than a cursory credit investigation. First he produced an 'employer's reference' which he had typed himself on the letterhead of a defunct company he once operated (not the bankrupt one), the company's address being his own post office box. Second, in typing the letter he deliberately misspelled his surname, changing the initial from 'G' to 'B', so that a routine consumer credit check for 'Guerrero' would produce no information, instead of the harmful data recorded under his correct name. For further identification he used his Social Security card and driver's licence, on both of which he carefully changed the same initial beforehand, and had since changed it back again. Another point he remembered was to make sure that his signature on the time payment contract was indecipherable, so it was not clear whether he had signed 'G' or 'B'.

The misspelling was perpetuated by the clerk who yesterday made out his airline ticket in the name of 'D.O. Buerrero', and D.O. Guerrero had weighed this carefully in light of his immediate plans. He decided not to worry. If any query was raised afterwards, the error of a single letter, both on the 'employer's reference' and the ticket, would appear to be a genuine mistake. There was nothing to prove he had arranged it deliberately. In any case, when checking in at the airport later tonight, he intended to have the spelling corrected – on the Trans American flight manifest as well as on his ticket. It was important, once he was aboard, to be sure there was no confusion about his correct identity. That was part of his plan, too.

Another part of D.O. Guerrero's plan was to destroy Flight Two by blowing it up. He would destroy himself along with it, a factor which did not deter him since his life, he reasoned, was no longer of value to himself or others.

But his death could be of value, and he intended to make sure it was.

Before departure of the Trans America flight, he would take out flight insurance for seventy-five thousand dollars, naming his wife and children as beneficiaries. He rationalized that he had done little for them until now, but his final act would be a single transcendent gesture on their behalf. He believed that what he was doing was a deed of love and sacrifice.

In his warped, perverted mind – driven by desperation – he had given no thought to other passengers who would be aboard Flight Two, nor to the aircraft's crew, all of whose deaths would accompany his own. With a psychopath's total lack of conscience he had considered others only to the extent that they might circumvent his scheme.

He believed he had anticipated all contingencies.

The business about his ticket would not matter once the aircraft was en route. No one could prove he had not intended to pay the instalments he contracted for; and even if the fake 'employer's reference' was exposed – as it probably would be – it demonstrated nothing except that he had obtained credit under false pretences. That, in itself, would have no bearing on a subsequent insurance claim.

Another thing was that he deliberately bought a round-trip ticket to create the appearance of not only intending to complete the outward flight, but also to return. As to choosing a Rome flight, he had a second cousin in Italy whom he had never seen, but occasionally talked of visiting – a fact which Inez knew. So at least there would seem an element of logic to his choice.

D.O. Guerrero had had his plan in mind for several months while his fortunes were worsening. During that time he studied carefully the histories of air disasters where airliners were destroyed by individuals seeking to profit from flight insurance. The number of instances was surprisingly large. In all cases on record the motive had been exposed by post-crash investigation and, where conspirators remained alive, they had been charged with murder. The flight insurance policies of those involved had been invalidated.

There was no means of knowing, of course, how many other disasters, where causes remained unknown, had been the result of sabotage. The key factor was the presence or absence of wreckage. Wherever wreckage was recovered, trained investigators pieced it together in an attempt to learn its secrets. They usually succeeded. If there was an explosion in mid-air, its traces remained, and the nature of the explosion could be determined. Therefore, D.O. Guerrero reasoned, his own plan must preclude the recovery of wreckage.

This was the reason he had selected Trans America's non-stop flight to Rome.

A large proportion of the journey of Flight Two – *The Golden Argosy* – was above ocean, where wreckage from a disintegrated aeroplane would never be found.

Using one of the airline's own passenger brochures which conveniently showed air routes, aircraft speeds, and even had a feature called *Chart Your Own Position*, Guerrero calculated that after four hour's flying – allowing for average winds – Flight Two would be over mid-Atlantic. He intended to check the calculation and amend it, if necessary, as the journey progressed. He would do so, first by noting the exact time of takeoff, then by listening carefully to the announcements which captains always made over cabin p.a. systems about the aircraft's progress. With the information it would be a simple matter to decide if the flight was behind schedule, or ahead, and by how much. Finally, at approximately a point he had already decided on – eight hundred miles east of Newfoundland – he would trigger an explosion. It would send the aircraft, or what remained of it, plummeting towards the sea.

No wreckage could ever be found.

The debris of Flight Two would remain for ever, hidden and secret, on the Atlantic Ocean floor. There would be no examination, no later exposure of the cause of the aircraft's loss. Those left might wonder, question, speculate; they might even guess the truth, but they could never *know*.

Flight insurance claims – in the absence of any evidence of sabotage – would be settled in full.

The single element on which everything else hinged was the explosion. Obviously it must be adequate to destroy the aeroplane, but – equally important – it must occur at the right time. For the second reason D.O. Guerrero had decided to carry the explosive device aboard and set it off himself. Now, within the locked bedroom, he was putting the device together, and despite his familiarity – as a building contractor – with explosives, was still sweating, as he had since he started a quarter of an hour ago.

There were five main components – three cartridges of dynamite, a tiny blasting cap with wires attached, and a single cell transistor radio battery. The dynamite cartridges were Du Pont Red Cross Extra – small but exceedingly powerful, containing forty per cent nitroglycerine; each was an inch and a quarter in diameter and eight inches long. They were taped together with electrician's black tape and, to conceal their purpose, were in a Ry-Krisp box, left open at one end.

Guerrero had also laid out several other items, carefully, on the ragged coverlet of the bed where he was working. These were a wooden clothespin, a square inch of clear plastic, and a short length of string. Total value of the equipment which would destroy a six and a half million dollar aeroplane was less than five dollars. All of it, including the dynamite – a 'leftover' from D.O. Guerrero's days as a contractor – had been bought in hardware stores.

Also on the bed was a small, flat attaché case of the type in which businessmen carried their papers and books when travelling by air. It was in this that Guerrero was now installing the explosive apparatus. Later, he would carry the case with him on the flight.

It was all incredibly simple. It was so simple, in fact, Guerrero thought to himself that most people, lacking a knowledge of explosives, would never believe that it would work. And yet it would – with shattering, devastating deadliness.

He taped the Ry-Krisp box containing the dynamite securely in place inside the attaché case. Close to it he fastened the wooden clothespin and the battery. The battery would fire the charge. The clothespin was the switch which, at the proper time, would release the current from the battery.

His hands were trembling. He could feel sweat, in rivulets, inside his shirt. With the blasting cap in place, one mistake, one slip, would blow himself, this room, and most of the building, apart here and now.

He held his breath as he connected a second wire from the blasting cap and dynamite to one side of the clothespin.

He waited, aware of his heart pounding, using a handkerchief to wipe moisture from his hands. His nerves, his senses, were on edge. Beneath him, as he sat on the bed, he could feel the thin, lumpy mattress. The decrepit iron bedstead screeched a protest as he moved.

He resumed working. With exquisite caution, he connected another wire. Now, only the square inch of clear plastic was preventing the passage of an electric current and thereby an explosion.

The plastic, less than a sixteenth of an inch thick, had a small hole near its outer edge. D. O. Guerrero took the last item left on the bed – the string – and passed one end through the hole in the plastic, then tied it securely, being cautious not to move the plastic. The other end of the string he pushed through an inconspicuous hole, already drilled, which went through to the outside of the attaché case, emerging under the carrying handle. Leaving the string fairly loose inside the case, on the outside he tied a second knot, large enough to prevent the string from slipping back. Finally – also on the outside – he made a fingersize loop, like a miniature hangman's noose, and cut off the surplus string.

And that was it.

A finger through the loop, a tug on the string! Electric current would flow, and the explosion would be instant, devastating, final, for whoever or whatever was nearby.

Now that it was done, Guerrero relaxed and lit a cigarette. He smiled sardonically as he reflected again on how much more complicated the public – including writers of detective fiction – imagined the manufacture of a bomb to be. In stories he had read there were always elaborate mechanisms, clocks, fuses which ticked or hissed or spluttered, and which could be circumvented if immersed in water. In reality, no complications were required – only the simple, homely components he had just put together. Nor could anything stop the detonation of this kind of bomb – neither water, bullets, nor bravery – once the string was pulled.

Holding the cigarette between his lips, and squinting through its smoke, D. O. Guerrero put some papers carefully into the attaché case, covering the dynamite, clothespin, wires, battery, and string. He made sure the papers would not move around, but that the string could move freely under them. Even if he opened the case for any reason, its contents would appear innocent. He closed the case and locked it.

He checked the cheap alarm clock beside the bed. It was a few minutes after 8.0 pm, a little less than two hours to flight departure time. Time to go. He would take the subway uptown to the airline terminal, then board an airport bus. He had just enough money left for that, and to buy the flight insurance policy. The thought reminded him that he must allow sufficient time at the airport to get insurance. He pulled on his topcoat quickly, checking that the ticket to Rome was still in the inside pocket.

He unlocked the bedroom door and went into the mean, shabby living room, taking the attaché case with him, holding it gingerly.

One final thing to do! A note for Inez. He found a scrap of paper and a pencil and, after thinking for several seconds, wrote:

I won't be home for a few days. I'm going away. I expect to have some good news soon which will surprise you.

He signed it D.O.

For a moment he hesitated, softening. It wasn't much of a note to mark the end of eighteen years of marriage. Then he decided it would have to do; it would be a mistake to say too much. Afterwards, even without wreckage from Flight Two, investigators would put the passenger list under a microscope. The note, as well as all other papers he had left, would be examined minutely.

He put the note on a table where Inez would be sure to see it.

As he went downstairs D. O. Guerrero could hear voices, and a jukebox playing, from the greasy-spoon lunch counter. He turned up the collar of his topcoat, with the other hand holding the attaché case tightly.Under the carrying handle of the case, the loop of string like a hangman's noose was close to his curled fingers.

Outside, as he left the south side building and headed for the subway, it was still snowing.

PART TWO

8.30 pm-ll pm (CST)

I

Once more, Joe Patroni returned to the warmth of his car and telephoned the airport. The TWA maintenance chief reported that the road between himself and the airport was still blocked by the traffic accident which had delayed him, but the chances of getting through soon looked good. Was the Aéreo-Mexican 7O7, he inquired, still stuck in mud out on the airfield? Yes, he was informed, it was; furthermore, every few minutes, everyone concerned was calling TWA to ask where he was, and how much longer he would be, because his help was needed urgently.

Without waiting to warm himself fully, Patroni left the car and hurried back down the highway, through the still falling snow and deep slush underfoot, to where the accident had occurred.

At the moment, the scene around the wrecked tractor-trailer transport looked like a staged disaster for a wide screen movie. The mammoth vehicle still lay on its side, blocking all four traffic lanes. By now it was completely snow covered and, with none of its wheels touching ground, seemed like a dead, rolled-over dinosaur. Floodlights and flares, aided by the whiteness of the snow, made the setting seem like day. The floodlights were on the three tow trucks which Patroni had urged sending for, and all had now arrived. The brilliant red flares had been planted by state police, of whom several more had appeared, and it seemed that when a state trooper lacked something to do, he lit another flare. As a result, the display of pyrotechnics was worthy of the Fourth of July.

The arrival of a TV camera crew, a few minutes earlier, he heightened the stage effect. The self-important crew had come with blaring horn and illegal flashing beacon, driving down a shoulder of the road in a maroon station wagon blazoned WSHT. Typically, the four young men who comprised the TV crew had taken over as if the entire event had been arranged for their convenience, and all further developments could now await their pleasure. Several state troopers, having ignored the illegal beacon on the station wagon, were engaged in waving the tow trucks from their present positions into new ones, as the TV men directed.

Before he left to make his telephone call, Joe Patroni had carefully coaxed the tow trucks into locations which would give them the best leverage, together, to move the disabled tractor-trailer. As he left, the truck drivers and helpers were connecting heavy chains which he knew would take several more minutes to secure. The state police had been glad of his aid, and a burly police lieutenant, by that time in charge at the scene, had told the tow truck drivers to take their instructions from Patroni. But now, incredibly, the chains were removed, except for one which a grinning tow truck operator was handling as photofloods and a portable TV camera focused on him.

Behind the camera and lights a crowd of people, even larger than before, had assembled from other blocked vehicles. Most were watching the TV filming interestedly, their earlier impatience and the cold bleak misery of the night apparently forgotten for the moment.

A sudden gust of wind slapped icy wet snow into Joe Patroni's face. Too late, his hand went to the neck of his parka. He felt some of the snow slide in, penetrate his shirt, and soak him miserably. Ignoring the discomfort, he strode towards the state police lieutenant and demanded, 'Who in hell changed the trucks? The way they're lined now, you couldn't move a peck of coondirt. All they'll do is pull each other.'

'I know, mister.' The lieutenant, tall, broad-shouldered, and towering above the short, stocky figure of Patroni, appeared fleetingly embarrassed. 'But the TV guys wanted a better shot. They're from a local station, and it's for the news tonight – all about the storm. Excuse me.'

One of the television men – himself huddled into a heavy coat – was beckoning the lieutenant into the filming. The lieutenant, head up, and ignoring the falling snow, walked with brisk authority towards the tow truck which was the centre of the film shot. Two state troopers followed. The lieutenant, being careful to keep his face towards the camera, began giving instructions, with gestures, to the tow truck operator, instructions which were largely meaningless, but on screen would look impressive.

The maintenance chief, remembering his need to get to the airport speedily, felt his anger rise. He braced himself to race out, grab the TV camera and lights, and smash them all. He could do it, too; instinctively his muscles tightened, his breathing quickened. Then, with an effort, he controlled himself.

A trait of character of Joe Patroni's was a white-hot, violent temper; fortunately the violent part was not easily set off, but once it was, all reason and logic deserted him. The exercise of control over his temper was something he had tried to learn through his years of manhood. He had not always succeeded, though nowadays a single memory helped.

On one occasion he had failed to have control. The result, for ever after, haunted him.

In the Army Air Forces of World War II, Joe Patroni had been a redoubtable amateur boxer. He fought as a middle-weight and, at one point, came within sight of the Air Forces championship, within his division, of the European Theatre.

In a bout staged in England shortly before the Normandy invasion, he had been matched against a crew chief named Terry O'Hale, a rough, tough Bostonian with a reputation for meanness in the ring, as well as out of it. Joe Patroni, then a young Pfc. aviation mechanic, knew O'Hale and disliked him. The dislike would not have mattered if O'Hale, as a calculated part of his ring technique, had not whispered constantly, '*You greasy dago wop...Whyn't you fighting for the other side, you mother lovin' Eytie?...You cheer when they shoot our ships down, dago boy?*' and other pleasantries. Patroni had seen the gambit for what it was – an attempt to get him rattled – and ignored it until O'Hale landed two low blows near the groin in swift succession, which the referee, circling behind, did not observe.

The combination of insults, foul blows, and excruciating pain, produced the anger which Patroni's opponent had counted on. What he did not count on was that Joe Patroni would deliver an onslaught so swift, savage, and utterly without mercy that O'Hale went down before it and, after being counted out, was pronounced dead.

Patroni was exonerated. Although the referee had not observed the low blows, others at ringside had. Even without them, Patroni had done no more than was expected – fought to the limit of his skill and strength. Only he was aware that for the space of seconds he had been berserk, insane. Alone and later, he faced the realization that even if he had known O'Hale was dying, he could not have stopped himself.

In the end, he avoided the cliché of abandoning fighting, or 'hanging up his gloves for good', as the usual fiction sequence went. He had gone on fighting, employing in the ring the whole of his physical resource, not holding back, yet testing his control to avoid crossing the hairline between reason and beserk savagery. He succeeded, and knew that he had, because there were tests of anger where reason struggled with the wild animal inside him – and reason won. Then, and only then, did Joe Patroni quit fighting for the remainder of his life.

But control of anger did not mean dismissing it entirely. As the police lieutenant returned from camera range, Patroni confronted him heatedly. 'You just blocked this road an extra twenty minutes. It took ten minutes to locate those trucks where they should be; it'll take another ten to get them back.'

As he spoke, there was the sound of a jet aircraft overhead – a reminder of the reason for Joe Patroni's haste.

'Now listen, mister.' The lieutenant's face suffused a deeper red than it already was from cold and wind. 'Get through your head that I'm in charge here. We're glad to have help, including yours. But I'm the one who's making decisions.'

'Then make one now!'

'I'll make what I'm . . .'

'No! – *you* listen to *me*.' Joe Patroni stood glaring, uninhibited by the policeman's bulk above him. Something of the maintenance chief's contained anger, and a hint of authority, made the lieutenant hesitate.

'There's an emergency at the airport. I already explained it; and why I'm needed there.' Patroni stabbed his glowing cigar through the air for emphasis. 'Maybe other people have reasons for hightailing it out of here too, but mine's enough for now. There's a phone in my car. I can call my top brass, who'll call your brass, and before you know it, somebody'll be on that radio of yours asking why you're polishing your TV image instead of doing the job you're here for. So make a decision, the way you said! Do I call in, or do we move?'

The lieutenant glared wrathfully back at Joe Patroni. Briefly, the policeman seemed ready to vent his own anger, then decided otherwise. He swung his big body towards the TV crews. 'Get all that crap out of here! You guys have had long enough.'

One of the television men called over his shoulder, 'We'll just be a few minutes more, chief.'

In two strides the lieutenant was beside him. 'You heard me! Right now!'

The policeman leaned down, his face still fierce from the encounter with Patroni, and the TV man visibly jumped. 'Okay, okay.' He motioned hastily to the others and the lights on the portable camera went out.

'Let's have those two trucks back the way they were!' The lieutenant began firing orders at the state troopers, who moved quickly to execute them. He returned to Joe Patroni and gestured to the overturned transport; it was clear that he had decided Patroni was more use as an ally than an antagonist. 'Mister, you still think we have to drag this rig? You sure we can't get it upright?'

'Only if you want to block this road till daylight. You'd have to unload the trailer first, and if you do . . .'

'I know, I know! Forget it! We'll pull and shove now, and worry about damage later.' The lieutenant gestured to the waiting line of traffic. 'If you want to get moving right after, you'd better hustle your car out of line and move up front. You want an escort to the airport?'

Patroni nodded appreciatively. 'Thanks.'

Ten minutes later the last spindle tow hook snapped into place. Heavy chains from one tow truck were secured around the axles of the disabled transport tractor; a stout wire cable connected the chains to the tow truck winch. A second tow truck was connected to the toppled trailer. The third tow truck was behind the trailer, ready to push.

The driver from the big transport unit, which, despite its overturning, was only partially damaged, groaned as he watched what was happening. 'My bosses ain't gonna like this! That's a near-new rig. You're gonna tear it apart.'

'If we do,' a young state trooper told him, 'we'll be finishing what you started.'

'Wadda you care? Ain't nothing to you I just lost a good job,' the driver grumbled back. 'Maybe I should try for a soft touch next time – like bein' a lousy cop.'

The trooper grinned. 'Why not? You're already a lousy driver.'

'You figure we're ready?' the lieutenant asked Patroni.

Joe Patroni nodded. He was crouching, observing the tautness of chains and cables. He cautioned, 'Take it slow and easy. Get the cab section sliding first.'

The first tow truck began pulling with its winch; its wheels skidded on snow and the driver accelerated forward, keeping the tow chain straining. The overturned transport's front portion creaked, slid a foot or two with a protesting scream of metal, then stopped.

Patroni motioned with his hand. 'Keep it moving! And get the trailer started!.

The chains and cable between the trailer axles and the second tow truck tightened. The third tow truck pushed against the trailer roof. The wheels of all three tow trucks skidded as they fought for purchase on the wet, packed snow. For another two feet the tractor and trailer, still coupled together, as they had been when they rolled over, moved sideways across the highway to an accompanying ragged cheer from the crowd of onlookers. The TV camera was functioning again, its lights adding brightness to the scene.

A wide, deep gash in the road showed where the big transport had been. The tractor cab and the body of the loaded trailer were taking punishment, the trailer roof beginning to angle as one side of the trailer dragged against the road. The price to be paid – no doubt by insurers – for reopening the highway quickly would be a steep one.

Around the road blockage, two snow ploughs – one on either side like skirmishers – were attempting to clear as much as they could of the snow which had piled since the accident occurred. Everything and everyone, by this time, was snow covered, including Patroni, the lieutenant, state troopers, and all others in the open.

The truck motors roared again. Smoke rose from tyres, spinning on wet, packed snow. Slowly, ponderously, the overturned vehicle shifted a few inches, a few feet, then slid clear across to the far side of the road. Within seconds, instead of blocking four traffic lanes, it obstructed only one. It would be a simple matter now for the three tow trucks to nudge the tractor-trailer clear of the highway on to the shoulder beyond.

State troopers were already moving flares, preparatory to untangling the monumental traffic jam which would probably occupy them for several hours to come. The sound, once again, of a jet aircraft overhead was a reminder to Joe Patroni that his principal business this night still lay elsewhere.

The state police lieutenant took off his cap and shook the snow from it. He nodded to Patroni. 'I guess it's your turn, mister.'

A patrol car, parked on a shoulder, was edging on to the highway. The lieutenant pointed to it. 'Keep closed up behind that car. I've told them you'll be following, and they've orders to get you to the airport fast.'

Joe Patroni nodded. As he climbed into his Buick Wildcat, the lieutenant called after him, 'And mister . . . Thanks!'

2

Captain Vernon Demerest stood back from the cupboard door he had opened, and emitted a long, low whistle.

He was still in the kitchen of Gwen Meighen's apartment on Stewardess Row. Gwen had not yet appeared after her shower and, while waiting, he had made tea as she suggested. It was while looking for cups and saucers that he had opened the cupboard door.

In front of him were four tightly packed shelves of bottles. All were miniature bottles of liquor – the ounce-and-a-half size which airlines served to passengers in flight. Most of the bottles had small airline labels above their brand names, and all were unopened. Making a quick calculation, Demerest estimated there were close to three hundred.

He had seen airline liquor in stewardesses' apartments before, but never quite so much at one time.

'We have some more stashed away in the bedroom,' Gwen said brightly from behind him. 'We've been saving them for a party. I think we've enough, don't you?'

She had come into the kitchen quietly, and he turned. As always since the beginning of their affair, he found the first sight of her enchanting and refreshing. Unusually for one who never lacked confidence with women, he had at such moments a heady sense of wonder that he had ever possessed Gwen at all. She was in a trim uniform skirt and blouse which made her seem even younger than she was. Her eager, high-cheekboned face was tilted upwards, her rich black hair lustrous under the kitchen lights. Gwen's deep dark eyes regarded him with smiling, frank approval. 'You can kiss me hard,' she said. 'I haven't put on make-up yet.'

He smiled, her clear melodious English voice delighting him again. As girls from British middle-class boarding schools somehow managed to do, Gwen had captured all that was best in English intonation and avoided the worst. At times, Vernon Demerest encouraged Gwen to talk, merely for the joy of hearing her speak.

Not talking now, they held each other tightly, her lips responding eagerly to his.

After a minute or so, Gwen pushed herself away. 'No!' she insisted firmly. 'No, Vernon dear. Not here.'

'Why not? We've time enough.' There was a thickness to Demerest's voice, a rough impatience.

'Because I told you – I want to talk, and we don't have time for both.' Gwen rearranged her blouse which had parted company with the skirt.

'Hell!' he grumbled. 'You bring me to the boil, then . . . Oh, all right; I'll wait till Naples.' He kissed her more gently. 'All the way to Europe you can think of me up there on the flight deck, turned to "simmer".'

'I'll bring you to the boil again. I promise.' She laughed, and leaning close against him, passed her long slim fingers through his hair and around his face.

He groaned. 'My God! – you're doing it right now.'

'Then that's enough.' Gwen took his hands, which were around her waist, and pushed them resolutely from her. Turning away, she moved to close the cupboard he had been looking into.

'Hey, wait a minute. What about all those?' Demerest pointed to the miniature liquor bottles with their airline labels.

'Those?' Gwen surveyed the four crowded shelves, her eyebrows arched, then switched to an expression of injured innocence. 'They're just a few little old leftovers that passengers didn't want. Surely, Captain, sir, you're not going to report me for possession of leftovers.'

He said sceptically, 'That many?'

'Of course.' Gwen picked up a bottle of Beefeater gin, put it down and inspected a Canadian Club whisky. 'One nice thing about airlines is, they always buy the best brands. Care for one now?'

He shook his head. 'You know better than that.'

'Yes, I do; but you shouldn't sound so disapproving.'

'I just don't want you to get caught.'

'Nobody gets caught, and almost everybody does it. Look – every first class passenger is entitled to two of these little bottles, but some passengers use only one, and there are always others who won't have any.'

'The rules say you turn back all the unused ones.'

'Oh, for heaven's sake! So we do – a couple for appearances, but the rest the girls divide between them. The same thing goes for wine that's left over.' Gwen giggled. 'We always like a passenger who asks for more wine near the end of a trip. That way, we can officially open a fresh bottle, pour off one glass . . .'

'I know. And take the rest home?'

'You want to see?' Gwen opened another cupboard door. Inside were a dozen filled wine bottles.

Demerest grinned. 'I'll be damned.'

'This isn't all mine. My roommate and one of the girls next door have been saving theirs for the party we're planning.' She took his arm. 'You'll come, won't you?'

'If I'm invited, I guess.'

Gwen closed both cupboard doors. 'You will be.'

They sat down in the kitchen, and she poured the tea he had made. He watched admiringly while she did it. Gwen had a way of making even a casual session like this seem an occasion.

He noticed with amusement that she produced cups from a pile in another cupboard, all bearing Trans America insignia. They were the kind the airline used in flight. He supposed he should not have been stuffy about the airline liquor bottles; after all, stewardess 'perks' were nothing new. It was just that the size of the hoard amazed him.

All airline stewardesses, he was aware, discovered early in their careers that a little

74

husbandry in aeroplane galleys could relieve their cost of living at home. Stewardesses learned to board their flights with personal hand baggage which was partially empty, using the space for surplus food – always of highest quality, since airlines purchased nothing but the best. A Thermos jug, brought aboard empty, was useful for carrying off spare liquids – cream or even decanted champagne. If a stewardess was really enterprising, Demerest was once assured, she could cut her weekly grocery bill in half. Only on international flights where, by law, all food – untouched or otherwise – was incinerated immediately after landing, were the girls more cautious.

All this activity was strictly forbidden by regulations of all airlines – but it still went on.

Another thing stewardesses learned was that no inventory check of removable cabin equipment was ever made at the termination of a flight. One reason was that airlines simply didn't have time; another, it was cheaper to accept some losses than make a fuss about them. Because of this, many stewardesses managed to acquire home furnishings – blankets, pillows, towels, linen napkins, glasses, silverware – in surprising quantity, and Vernon Demerest had been in stewardess nests where most items used in daily living seemed to have come from airline sources.

Gwen broke in on his thoughts. 'What I was going to tell you, Vernon, is that I'm pregnant.'

It was said so casually that at first the words failed to register. He reacted blankly. 'You're what?'

'Pregnant – p-r-e-g-n . . .'

He snapped irritably, 'I know how to spell it.' His mind was still groping. 'Are you sure?'

Gwen laughed – her attractive silvery laugh – and sipped her tea. He sensed she was making fun of him. He was also aware that she had never looked more lovely and desirable than at this moment.

'That line you just said, darling,' she assured him, 'is an old cliché. In every book I've ever read where there's a scene like this, the man asks, "Are you sure?"'

'Well, goddammit, Gwen!' His voice rose. *'Are you?'*

'Of course. Or I wouldn't be telling you now.' She motioned to the cup in front of him. 'More tea?'

'No!'

'What happened,' Gwen said calmly, 'is perfectly simple. On that layover we had in San Francisco . . . you remember! – we stayed at that gorgeous hotel on Nob Hill; the one with the view. What was it called?'

'The Fairmont. Yes, I remember. Go on.'

'Well, I'm afraid I was careless. I'd quit taking pills because they were making me overweight; then I thought I didn't need any other precautions that day, but it turned out I was wrong. Anyway, because I was careless, now I have a teensy-weensy little Vernon Demerest inside me who's going to get bigger and bigger.'

There was a silence, then he said awkwardly, 'I suppose I shouldn't ask this . . .'

She interrupted. 'Yes, you should. You're entitled to ask.' Gwen's deep dark eyes regarded him with open honesty. 'What you want to know is, has there been anyone else, and am I positive it's you? Right?'

'Look, Gwen . . .'

She reached out to touch his hand. 'You don't have to be ashamed of asking. I'd ask too, if things were the other way round.'

He gestured unhappily. 'Forget it. I'm sorry.'

'But I want to tell you.' She was speaking more hurriedly now, a shade less confidently. 'There hasn't been anybody else; there couldn't be. You see . . . I happen to love you.' For the first time her eyes were lowered. She went on, 'I think I did . . . I know I did . . . love you, I mean – even before that time we had in San Francisco. When I've thought about it, I've been glad of that, because you ought to love someone if you're to have their baby, don't you think so?'

'Listen to me, Gwen.' He covered her hands with his own. Vernon Demerest's hands were strong and sensitive, accustomed to responsibility and control, yet capable of precision and gentleness. They were gentle now. Women he cared about always had that effect on him, in contrast to the rough brusqueness with which he dealt with men. 'We have to do some serious talking, and make some plans.' Now that the first surprise was over, his thoughts were becoming orderly. It was perfectly clear what needed to be done next.

'You don't have to do anything.' Gwen's head came up; her voice was under control. 'And you can stop wondering if I'm going to be difficult, or if I'll make things awkward for you. I won't. I knew what I was getting into; that there was the chance this would happen. I didn't really expect it to, but it has. I had to tell you tonight because the baby's yours; it's part of you; you ought to know. Now you do, I'm also telling you you don't have to worry. I intend to work things out myself.'

'Don't be ridiculous; of course I'll help. You don't imagine I'd walk away and ignore the whole bit.' The essential thing, he realized, was speed; the trick with unwanted foetuses was to get the little beggars early. He wondered if Gwen had any religious scruples about abortions. She had never mentioned having a religion, but sometimes the most unlikely people were devout. He asked her, 'Are you Catholic?'

'No.'

Well, he reflected, that helped. Maybe, then, a quick flight to Sweden would be the thing; a few days there was all Gwen would need. Trans America would co-operate, as airlines always did, providing they were not officially involved – the word 'abortion' could be hinted at, but must never be mentioned. That way, Gwen could fly deadhead on a Trans America flight to Paris, then go by Air France to Stockholm on a reciprocal employee pass. Of course, even when she got to Sweden, the medical fees would still be damnably expensive; there was a jest among airline people that the Swedes took their overseas abortion customers to the clinic and the cleaners at the same time. The whole thing was cheaper in Japan, of course. Lots of airline stewardesses flew to Tokyo and got abortions there for fifty dollars. The abortions were supposed to be therapeutic, but Demerest mistrusted them; Sweden – or Switzerland – were more reliable. He had once declared: when he got a stewardess pregnant, she went first class.

From his own point of view, it was a bloody nuisance that Gwen had got a bun in the oven at this particular time, just when he was building an extension on his house which, he remembered gloomily, had already gone over budget. Oh well, he would have to sell some stock – General Dynamics, probably; he had a nice capital gain there, and it was about time to take a profit. He would call his broker right after getting back from Rome – and Naples.

He asked, 'You're still coming to Naples with me?'

'Of course; I've been looking forward to it. Besides, I bought a new negligee. You'll see it tomorrow night.'

He stood up from the table and grinned. 'You're a shameless hussy.'

'A shameless *pregnant* hussy who shamelessly loves you. Do you love me?'

She came to him, and he kissed her mouth, face, and an ear. He probed her pinna with his tongue, felt her arms tighten in response, then whispered, 'Yes, I love you.' At the moment, he reflected, it was true.

'Vernon, dear.'

'Yes.'

Her cheek was soft against his. Her voice came, muffled, from his shoulder. 'I meant what I said. You don't have to help me. But if you really want to, that's different.'

'I want to.' He decided he would sound her out about an abortion, on their way to the airport.

Gwen disengaged herself and glanced at her watch; it was 8.20. 'It's time, Captain, sir. We'd better go.'

'I guess you know you really don't have to worry,' Vernon Demerest said to Gwen as they drove. 'Airlines are used to having their unmarried stewardesses get pregnant. It happens all the time. The last report I read, the national airline average was ten per cent, per year.'

Their discussion, he noted approvingly, was becoming increasingly matter-of-fact. Good! – it was important to steer Gwen away from any emotional nonsense about this baby of hers. If she did become emotional, Demerest knew, all sorts of awkward things could happen, impeding commonsense.

He was handling the Mercedes carefully, with the delicate yet firm touch which was second nature to him when controlling any piece of machinery, including a car or aeroplane. The surburban streets, which were newly cleared when he drove from the airport to Gwen's apartment, were thickly snow-covered again. Snow was still coming down continuously, and there were deepening drifts in wind-exposed places, away from the shelter of buildings. Captain Demerest warily skirted the larger drifts. He had no intention of getting stuck nor did he even want to get out of the car until the shelter of the enclosed Trans America parking lot was reached.

Curled into the leather bucket seat beside him, Gwen said incredulously, 'Is that really true – that every year, ten out of every hundred stewardesses get pregnant?'

He assured her, 'It varies slightly each year, but it's usually pretty close. Oh, the pill has changed things a bit, but the way I hear it, not as much as you'd expect. As a union officer I have access to that kind of information.'

He waited for Gwen to comment. When she made none, he went on, 'What you have to remember is that airline stewardesses are mostly young girls, from the country, or modest city homes. They've had a quiet upbringing, an average life. Suddenly, they have a glamour job; they travel, meet interesting people, stay in the best hotels. it's their first taste of *la dolce vita.*' He grinned. 'Once in a while that first taste leaves some sediment in the glass.'

'That's a rotten thing to say!' For the first time since he had known her, Gwen's temper flared. She said indignantly, 'You sound so superior, just like a man. If I have any sediment in *my* glass, *or* in me, let me remind you that it's yours, and even if we didn't plan to leave it there, I think I'd find a better name for it than that. Also, if you're lumping me together with all those girls you talked about from the country and "modest city homes", I don't like that one damn bit either.'

There was heightened colour in Gwen's cheeks; her eyes flashed angrily.

'Hey!' he said. 'I like your spirit.'

'Well, keep on saying things like you did just now, and you'll see more of it.'

'Was I that bad?'

'You were insufferable.'

'Then I'm sorry.' Demerest slowed the car and stopped at a traffic light which shone with myriad red reflections through the falling snow. They waited in silence until, with Christmas card effect, the colour winked to green. When they were moving again, he said carefully, 'I didn't mean to lump you with anybody, because you're an exception. You're a sophisticate who got careless. You said you did, yourself. I guess we were both careless.'

'All right.' Gwen's anger was dissipating. 'But don't ever put me in bunches. I'm me; no one else.'

They were quiet for several moments, then Gwen said thoughtfully, 'I suppose we could call him that.'

'Call who what?'

'You made me remember what I said earlier – about a little Vernon Demerest inside me. If we had a boy, we could call him Vernon Demerest the second, the way Americans do.'

He had never cared much for his own name. Now he began to say, 'I wouldn't want my son . . .' then stopped. This was dangerous ground.

'What I started to say, Gwen, was that airlines are used to this kind of thing. You know about the Three-Point Pregnancy Programme?'

She said shortly. 'Yes.'

It was natural that Gwen did. Most stewardesses were aware of what airlines would do for them if they became pregnant, providing the stewardess herself agreed to certain conditions. Within Trans America the system was referred to familiarly as the '3-PPP'. Other airlines used differing names, and arrangements varied slightly, but the principle was the same.

'I've known girls who've used the 3-PPP,' Gwen said. 'I didn't think I'd ever need to.'

'Most of the others didn't, I guess.' He added: 'But you wouldn't need to worry. It isn't something that airlines advertise, and it all works quietly. How are we for time?'

Gwen held her wrist watch under the light of the dash. 'We're okay.'

He swung the Mercedes into a centre lane carefully, judging his traction on the wet, snowy surface, and passed a lumbering utilities truck. Several men, probably an emergency crew, were clinging to the sides of the truck as it moved along. They looked weary, wet, and miserable. Demerest wondered what the men's reaction would be if they knew that he and Gwen would be under warm Neapolitan sunshine only hours from now.

'I don't know,' Gwen said; 'I don't know if I could ever do it.'

Like Demerest, Gwen knew the reasoning of management which lay behind airline pregnancy programmes. No airline liked losing stewardesses for any reason. Their training was expensive; a qualified stewardess represented a big investment. Another thing: the right kind of girls, with good looks, style, and personality, were hard to find.

The way the programmes worked was practical and simple. If a stewardess became pregnant, and did not plan to be married, obviously she could return to her job when her pregnancy was over, and usually her airline would be delighted to have her back. So, the arrangement was, she received official leave of absence, with her job seniority protected. As to her personal welfare, airline personnel departments had special sections which, among other things, would help make medical or nursing home arrangements, either where a girl lived or at some distant point, whichever she preferred. The airline helped psychologically, too, by letting the girl know that someone cared about her, and was looking out for her interests. A loan of money could sometimes be arranged. Afterwards, if a stewardess who had had her child was diffident about returning to her original base, she would be quietly transferred to a new one of her own choosing.

In return for all this, the airline asked three assurances from the stewardess – hence the Three-Point Pregnancy Programme.

First, the girl must keep the airline personnel department informed of her whereabouts at all times during her pregnancy.

Second, she must agree that her baby be surrendered for adoption immediately after birth. The girl would never know the baby's adoptive parents; thus, the child would pass out of her life entirely. However, the airline guaranteed that proper adoption procedures would be followed, with the baby being placed in a good home.

Third – at the outset of the three-point programme the stewardess must inform the airline of the name of the child's father. When she had done so, a representative from Personnel – experienced in such situations – promptly sought out the father with the objective of obtaining financial support for the girl. What the personnel man tried to obtain was a promise in writing, of enough money to cover medical and nursing home expenses, and if possible, some or all of the stewardess's lost wages. Airlines preferred such arrangements to be amicable and discreet. If they had to, though, they could get tough, using their considerable corporate influence to bring pressure on non-co-operating individuals.

It was seldom necessary to be tough where the father of the stewardess's baby was a flying crew member – a captain, or first or second officer. In such cases, gentle company suasion, plus the father's wish to keep the whole thing quiet, were usually enough. As to keeping quiet, the company obliged. Temporary support payments could be made in any reasonable way, or, if preferred, the airline made regular deductions from the employee's pay checks. Just as considerately, to avoid awkward questions at home, such deductions appeared under the heading: 'personal misc.'.

All money received by these means was paid, in its entirety, to the pregnant stewardess. The airline deducted nothing for its own costs.

'The whole point about the programme,' Demerest said, 'is that you're not alone, and there's all kinds of help.'

He had been careful of one thing – to avoid any reference, so far, to abortion. That was a separate subject because no airline would, or could, become directly involved in abortion arrangements. Advice on the subject was frequently given unofficially to those who sought it – by stewardess supervisors who learned, through experience of others, how such arrangements could be made. Their objective, if a girl was determined on abortion, was to ensure its performance under safe medical conditions, avoiding at all costs the dangerous and disreputable practitioners whom desperate people sometimes resorted to.

Gwen regarded her companion curiously. 'Tell me one thing. How is it you know so much about all this?'

'I told you, I'm a union officer . . .'

'Your part of the ALPA's for pilots. You don't have anything to do with stewardesses – not in that way, anyhow.'

'Maybe not directly.'

'Vernon, this has happened to you before . . . getting a stewardess pregnant . . . Vernon, hasn't it?'

He nodded reluctantly. 'Yes.'

'It must come pretty easily to you, knocking up stewardesses – those gullible country girls you were talking about. Or were they mostly from "modest city homes"?' Gwen's voice was bitter. 'How many have there been altogether? Two dozen, a dozen? Just give me an idea in round figures.'

He sighed. 'One; only one.'

He had been incredibly lucky, of course. It could have been many more, but his answer was the truth. Well . . . almost the truth; there was that other time, and the miscarriage, but that shouldn't count.

Outside the car, traffic density was increasing as they neared the airport, now less than a quarter of a mile away. The bright lights of the great terminal, though dimmed tonight by snow, still filled the sky.

Gwen said, 'The other girl who got pregnant. I don't want to know her name . . .'

'I wouldn't tell you.'

'Did she use the thingummy – the three-point programme?'

'Yes.'

'Did you help her?'

He answered impatiently, 'I said earlier – what kind of a man do you think I am? Of course I helped her. If you must know, the company made deductions from my pay checks. That's how I knew about the way it's done.'

Gwen smiled. '"Personal misc."?'

'Yes.'

'Did your wife ever know?'

He hesitated before answering. 'No.'

'What happened to the baby?'

'It was adopted.'

'What was it?'

'Just a baby.'

'You know perfectly well what I mean. Was it a boy or a girl?'

'A girl, I think.'

'You *think*.'

Gwen's questioning made him vaguely uncomfortable. It revived memories he would as soon forget.

They were silent as Vernon Demerest swung the Mercedes into the airport's wide and imposing main entry. High above the entry, soaring and floodlighted, were the futuristic parabolic arches – acclaimed achievement of a world-wide design contest – symbolizing, so it was said, the noble dreams of aviation. Ahead of an impressive, serpentine complex of roads, interchanges, flyovers, and tunnels, designed to keep the airport's unceasing vehicular traffic flowing at high speed, though tonight the effects of the three-day storm were making progress slower than usual. Great mounds of snow were occupying normally usable road space. Snowploughs and dump trucks, trying to keep remaining areas open, were adding their own confusion.

After several brief hold-ups, Demerest turned on to the service road which would bring them to the Trans America main hangar area, where they would leave the car and take a crew bus to the terminal.

Gwen stirred beside him. 'Vernon.'

'Yes.'

'Thank you for being honest with me.' She reached out, touching his nearer hand on the steering wheel. 'I'll be all right. I expect it was just a bit much, all at once. And I *do* want to go with you to Naples.'

He nodded and smiled, then took his hand off the wheel and clasped Gwen's tightly. 'We'll have a great time, and I promise we'll both remember it.'

He would do his best, he decided, to ensure the promise came true. For himself, it would not be difficult. He had been more attracted to Gwen, had felt more loving in her company, and closer in spirit, than with anyone else he remembered. If it were not for his marriage . . . He wondered, not for the first time, about breaking with Sarah, and marrying Gwen. Then he pushed the thought away. He had known too many others in his profession who had suffered upheaval – pilots who forsook wives of many years, for younger women. More often than not, all the men had in the end were shattered hopes and heavy alimony.

Sometime during their trip, though, either in Rome or Naples, he must have another serious discussion with Gwen. Their talk, so far, had not gone exactly as he would have liked, nor had the question of an abortion yet been raised.

Meanwhile – the thought of Rome reminded him – there was the more immediate matter of his command of Trans America Flight Two.

3

The key was to room 224 of the O'Hagan Inn.

In the semi-darkened locker area adjoining the air traffic control radar room, Keith Bakersfeld realized he had been staring at the key and its identifying plastic tag for several minutes. Or had it been seconds only? It might have been. Just lately, like so much else, the passage of time seemed inconstant and disoriented. Sometimes at home recently, Natalie had found him standing quite still, looking into nothingness. And when she had asked, with concern, *Why are you there?*, only then had he become awakened to where he was and had resumed movement and conscious thinking.

What had happened, he supposed – then and a moment ago – was that his worn, weary mind had switched itself off. Somewhere inside the brain's intricacies – of blood vessels, sinew, stored thought, and emotion – was a tiny switch, a self-defence mechanism like a thermal cutout in an electric motor, which worked when the motor was running too hot and needed to be saved from burning itself out. The difference, though, between a motor and a human brain, was that a motor stayed out of action if it needed to.

A brain would not.

The floodlights outside, on the face of the control tower, still reflected enough light inward through the locker room's single window for Keith to see. Not that he needed to see. Seated on one of the wooden benches, the sandwiches Natalie had made, untouched, beside him, he was doing nothing more than holding the O'Hagan Inn key and thinking, reflecting on the paradox of the human brain.

A human brain could achieve soaring imagery, conceive poetry and radarscopes, create the Sistine Chapel and a supersonic Concorde. Yet a brain, too – holding memory and conscience – could be compelling, self-tormenting, never resting, so that only death could end its persecution.

Death . . . with oblivion, forgetfulness; with rest at last.

It was the reason that Keith Bakersfeld had decided on suicide tonight.

He must go back soon to the radar room. There were still several hours of his shift remaining, and he had made a pact with himself to finish his air traffic control duty for tonight. He was not sure why, except that it seemed the right thing to do, and he had always tried to do the right thing, conscientiously. Perhaps being conscientious was a family trait; he and his brother Mel always seemed to have that much in common.

Anyway, when the duty was done – his final obligation finished – he would be free to go to the O'Hagan Inn, where he had registered late this afternoon. Once there, without wasting time, he would take the forty Nembutal capsules – sixty grains in all – which were in a drugstore pillbox in his pocket. He had husbanded the capsules, a few at a time, over recent months. They had been prescribed to give him sleep, and from each prescription which Natalie's druggist had delivered, he had carefully extracted half and hidden it. A few days ago he had gone to a library, checking a reference book on clinical toxicology to assure himself that the quantity of Nembutal he had was well in excess of a fatal dose.

His present duty shift would end at midnight. Soon after, when he had taken the capsules, sleep would come quickly and with finality.

He looked at his watch, holding its face towards the light from outside. It was almost nine o'clock. Should he return to the radar room now? No – stay a few minutes longer. When he went, he wanted to be calm, his nerves steady for whatever these last few hours of duty might contain.

Keith Bakersfeld fingered the O'Hagan Inn key again. Room 224.

It was strange about the coincidence of figures, that his room number tonight, allocated by chance, should have in it a '24'. There were people who believed in that kind of thing – numerology; the occult significance of numbers. Keith didn't, though if he did, those second and third figures, prefaced by a '2', could be taken to mean 24 for the second time.

The first 24 had been a date, a year and a half ago. Keith's eyes misted, as they had so many times before, when he remembered. The date was seared – with self-reproach and anguish – in his memory. It was the wellspring of his darksome spirit, his utter desolation. It was the reason he would end his life tonight.

A summer's day; morning. Thursday, June the twenty-fourth.

It was a day for poets, lovers, and colour photographers; the kind of day which people stored up in their minds, to open like a scrapbook when they wanted to remember, years later, all that was best of any time and place. In Leesburg, Virginia, not far from historic Harpers Ferry, the sky was clear at dawn – CAVU, the weather report said, which is aviation shorthand for 'ceiling and visibility unlimited'; and conditions stayed that way, except for a few cotton-wool tufts of scattered cumulus by afternoon. The sun was warm, but not oppressive. A gentle breeze from the Blue Ridge Mountains carried the scent of honeysuckle.

On his way to work that morning – driving to the Washington Air Route Traffic Control Centre at Leesburg – Keith Bakersfeld had seen wild roses blooming. He thought of a line from Keats which he had learned in high school – *'For Summer has o'erbrimmed . . .'* It seemed appropriate to such a day.

He had driven, as usual, across the Virginia border – from Adamstown, Maryland, where he and Natalie, with their two boys, shared a pleasant rented home. The top of the Volkswagen convertible was down; he had travelled without haste, enjoying the benevolence of air and sun, and when the familiar low, modern buildings of the Air Route Centre came in sight, he had felt less tense than usual. Afterwards, he wondered if that, in itself, had been a cause of the events which followed.

Even inside the Operations Wing – thick-walled and windowless, where daylight never penetrated – Keith had an impression that the glory of the summer's day outside had somehow percolated inwards. Among the seventy or more shirtsleeved controllers on duty there seemed a sense of lightness, in contrast to the pressure-driven earnestness with which work proceeded on most days of the year. One reason, perhaps, was that the traffic load was less than usual, due to the exceptionally clear weather. Many non-commercial flights – private, military, even a few airliners – were operating on VFR – 'visual flight rules', or the see-and-be-seen method by which aircraft pilots kept track of their own progress through the air, without need to report by radio to ATC air route controllers.

The Washington Air Route Centre at Leesburg was a key control point. From its main operations room all air traffic on airways over six eastern seaboard states was observed and directed. Added up, the control area came to more than a hundred thousand square miles. Within that area, whenever an aircraft which had filed an instrument flight plan left an airport, it came under Leesburg observation and control. It remained under that control either until its journey was complete or it passed out of the area. Aircraft coming into the area were handed over from other control centres, of which there were twenty across the continental United States. The Leesburg centre was among the nation's busiest. It included the southern end of the 'northeast corridor' which daily accommodated the world's heaviest concentration of air traffic.

Oddly, Leesburg was distant from any airport, and forty miles from Washington, DC, from which the Air Route Centre took its name. The centre itself was in Virginia countryside – a cluster of low, modern buildings with a parking lot – and was surrounded on three sides by rolling farmland. Nearby was a small stream named Bull Run – its fame enshrined for ever by two battles of the Civil War. Keith Bakersfeld had once gone to Bull Run after duty, reflecting on the strange and diametric contrast between Leesburg's past and present.

This morning, despite awareness of the summer's day outside, everything in the spacious, cathedral-like main control room was operating as usual. The entire control area – larger than a football field – was, as always, dimly lighted to allow proper viewing of the several dozen radar screens, arranged in tiers and rows under overhanging canopies. The control room noise level was what any newcomer noticed first. From a flight data area, with great banks of computers, assorted electronic gear and automatic teletypes, arose the continuous whir and chatter of machinery. Nearby, from dozens of positions where controllers sat, directing aerial traffic, came a ceaseless hum of voice radio exchanges on a host of frequencies. The machinery and human voices merged, producing a constant noise level which was all-pervading, yet strangely muted by acoustic, sound-absorbent walls and ceilings.

Above the working level of the control room was an observation bridge, running the room's full width, where occasional visitors were brought to watch proceedings below. The control room activity looked, from this eyrie, not unlike that of a stock exchange. Controllers rarely glanced up at the bridge, being trained to ignore anything which might diminish concentration on their work, and since only a few especially privileged visitors ever made it to the control room floor, controllers and outsiders rarely met. Thus the work was not only high pressure, but also monastic – the last condition added to by the total absence of women.

In an annex to the control room Keith slipped off his jacket, and came in wearing the crisp white shirt which was like a uniform for air traffic controllers. No one knew why controllers wore white shirts on duty; there was no rule about it, but most of them did. As he passed other control positions while heading for his own, a few colleagues wished him a friendly 'good morning', and that was unusual too. Normally, the immediate sense of pressure on entering the control area made it customary to give a hurried nod or a brief 'Hi!' – sometimes not even that.

The control sector which Keith regularly worked comprised a segment of the Pittsburgh-Baltimore area. The sector was monitored by a team of three. Keith was radar controller, his job to maintain contact with aircraft and to issue radio instructions. Two assistant controllers handled flight data and airport communications; a supervisor co-ordinated activities of the other three. Today, in addition, the team had a trainee controller whom Keith had been instructing, at intervals, over the past several weeks.

Others of the team were drifting in at the same time as Keith Bakersfeld, taking position behind the men they were to relieve, and allowing a few minutes while they absorbed the 'picture' in their minds. All through the big control room, at other positions, the same thing was happening.

Standing at his own sector, behind the radar controller about to go off duty, Keith already felt his mental acuity sharpen, his speed of thinking consciously accelerate. For the next eight hours, except for two brief work breaks, his brain must continue to operate that way.

Traffic, he observed, was averagely busy for the time of day, taking into account the widespread good weather. On the scope's dark surface, some fifteen pinpoints of bright green light – or 'targets', as radarmen called them – indicated aircraft in the air. Allegheny had a Convair 440 at eight thousand feet, approaching Pittsburgh. Behind the Allegheny flight, at varying altitudes, were a National DC8, an American Airlines 727, two private aircraft – a Lear jet and a Fairchild F-27 – and another National, this time a prop-jet Electra. Several other flights, Keith noted, were due to come on the screen at any moment, both from other sectors and as a result of takeoffs from Friendship Airport, Baltimore. Going the opposite way, towards Baltimore, was a Delta DC-9, about to be taken over by Friendship approach control; behind this flight were a TWA, a Piedmont Airlines Martin, another private flight, two Uniteds, and a Mohawk. Height and distance separations of all aircraft were satisfactory, Keith observed, except that the two Uniteds heading for Baltimore were a little close. As if the controller still at the scope had read Keith's mind, he gave the second United a delaying diversionary course.

'I have the picture,' Keith said quietly. The other controller nodded and moved out.

Keith's supervisor, Perry Yount, plugged in his headset above Keith's head and leaned over, making his own assessment of the traffic situation. Perry was a tall, lean Negro, a few years younger than Keith. He had a quick, retentive memory which could store a mass of flight data, then repeat it back, as a whole or in pieces, with computer accuracy. Perry was a comforting man to have around when there was trouble.

Keith had already accepted several new flights and handed over others when the supervisor touched his shoulder. 'Keith, I'm running two positions this shift – this and the next one. We're a man short. You okay for a while?'

Keith nodded. 'Roger.' He radioed a course correction to an Eastern 727, then motioned towards the trainee controller, George Wallace, who had slipped into a seat beside him. 'I've got George to keep an eye on me.'

'Okay.' Perry Yount unplugged his headset and moved to the adjacent console. The same kind of thing had happened occasionally before, and was handled without difficulty. Perry Yount and Keith had worked together for several years; each was aware that he could trust the other.

Keith told the trainee beside him. 'George, start getting the picture.'

George Wallace nodded and edged closer to the radarscope. He was in his mid-twenties, had been a trainee for almost two years; before that, he had served an enlistment in the US Air Force. Wallace had already shown himself to have an alert, quick mind, plus the ability not to become rattled under tension. In one more week he would be a qualified controller, though for practical purposes he was fully trained now.

Deliberately, Keith allowed the spacing between an American Airlines BAC-400 and a National 727 to become less than it should be; he was ready to transmit quick instructions if the closure became critical. George Wallace spotted the condition at once, and warned Keith, who corrected it.

That kind of first-hand exercise was the only sure way the ability of a new controller could be gauged. Similarly, when a trainee was at the scope himself, and got into difficulties, he had to be given the chance to show resourcefulness and sort the situation out unaided. At such times, the instructing controller was obliged to sit back, with clenched hands and sweat. Someone had once described it as 'hanging on to a brick wall by your fingernails'. When to intervene or take over was a critical decision, not to be made too early or too late. If the instructor did take over, the trainee's confidence might be permanently undermined, and a potentially good controller lost. On the other hand, if an instructor failed to take over when he should, a ghastly mid-air collision could result.

The risks involved, and extra mental pressures, were such that many controllers refused to take them. They pointed out that the task of teaching their work to others carried neither official recognition nor extra pay. Moreover, if anything went wrong, the instructing controller was wholly responsible. Why suffer so much strain and liability for nothing?

Keith, however, had shown an aptitude as an instructor as well as patience in bringing trainees along. And although he, too, suffered and sweated at times, he did the job because he felt he should. At this moment, he took a personal pride in the way George Wallace had developed.

Wallace said quietly again, 'I'd turn United 284 right until you get altitude separation with Mohawk.'

Keith nodded agreement as he thumbed his microphone button. 'United Flight 284, from Washington centre. Turn right, heading zero six zero.'

Promptly the reply crackled back. 'Washington control, this is United 284. Roger; zero six zero.' Miles distant, and high above in clear bright sunshine while passengers dozed or read, the powerful sleek jet would be easing into a smooth controlled turn. On the radarscope, the bright green half-inch-wide blip which was United 284 began moving in a new direction.

Below the control area, in a room devoted to rack upon rack of ponderously turning tape recorders, the exchange between ground and air had been recorded – for playback later if need arose. Every such conversation, from each position in the control room, was recorded and stored. Periodically, some of the tapes were replayed and listened to critically by supervisors. If a procedure was wrong, a controller heard about it; yet no controller knew when a recording of his own might be selected for analysis. On a door of the tape-recorder room was the grimly humorous reminder, *'Big Brother Is Listening.'*

The morning progressed.

Periodically, Perry Yount appeared. He was still overseeing two positions and stayed long enough to assess the current traffic situation. What he saw seemed to satisfy him, and he spent less time behind Keith than at the other position, where several problems seemed to be occurring. Around mid-morning the air traffic volume eased slightly; it would pick up again before midday. Soon after 10:30 am Keith Bakersfeld and George Wallace exchanged positions. The trainee was now at the scope, Keith checking from alongside. There was no need, Keith found, for intervention; young Wallace was proving competent and alert. As far as was possible in the circumstances, Keith relaxed.

At ten to eleven, Keith was aware of a need to visit the toilet. In recent months, he had had several bouts with intestinal flu; he had a suspicion that this was the beginning of another. He signalled Perry Yount and told him.

The supervisor nodded. 'Is George doing okay?'

'Like a veteran.' Keith said it loud enough so George could hear.

'I'll hold things down,' Perry said. 'You're relieved, Keith.'

'Thanks.'

Keith signed the sector log sheet and noted his time of checking out. Perry scribbled an initial on the next line of the log, accepting responsibility for monitoring Wallace. In a few minutes time, when Keith returned, they would follow the same procedure.

As Keith Bakersfeld left the control room, the supervisor was studying the scope, his hand lightly on George Wallace's shoulder.

The washroom Keith had gone to was on an upper level; a frosted-glass window admitted some of the brightness of the day outside. When Keith had finished, and freshened himself with a wash, he went to the window and opened it. He wondered if the weather was still as superb as when he had arrived earlier. It was.

From the rear of the building into which the window was set, he could see – beyond a service area – green meadows, trees, and wild flowers. The heat was greater now. All around was a drowsy hum of insects.

Keith stood looking out, aware of a reluctance to leave the cheerful sunlight and return to the control room's gloom. It occurred to him that lately he had had similar feelings at other times – too many times, perhaps; and he thought – if he was honest, it was not the gloom he minded so much, but the mental pressures of his job, unrelenting as they were, had never bothered him. Nowadays they did, and on occasions he had to force himself, consciously, to meet them.

While Keith Bakersfeld was standing at the window, thinking, a Northwest Orient 727 jet, en route from Minneapolis-St Paul, was nearing Washington, DC. Within its cabin a stewardess was bending over an elderly male passenger. His face was ashen; he seemed unable to speak. The stewardess believed he had had, or was having, a heart attack. She hurried to the flight deck to inform the captain. Moments later, acting on the captain's orders, the Northwest first officer asked Washington Air Route Centre for special clearance down, with priority handling to Washington National Airport.

Keith wondered sometimes – as he was wondering now – how many more years he could force his occasionally weary mind to go on. He had been a controller for a decade and a half. He was thirty-eight.

The depressing thing was – in this business you could be mentally drained, an old man, at age forty-five or fifty, yet honourable retirement was another ten or fifteen years away. For many air traffic controllers, those final years proved an all-too-gruelling trail, whose end they failed to reach.

Keith knew – as most controllers did – that strains on the human systems of those employed in air traffic control had long been recognized. Official flight surgeons' files bulged with medical evidence. Case histories, directly attributable to controllers' work, including hypertension, heart attacks, gastric ulcers, tachycardia, psychiatric breakdowns, plus a host of lesser ailments. Eminent, independent medics in scholarly research studies, had confirmed such findings. In the words of one: 'A controller will spend nervous, sleepless hours every night wondering how in the name of heaven he kept all those planes from running into each other. He managed not to cause a disaster today, but will he have the same luck tomorrow? After a while, something inside him – physical, mental, oftentimes both – inevitably breaks down.'

Armed with this knowledge, and more, the Federal Aviation Agency had urged Congress to allow air traffic controllers to retire at age fifty, or after twenty years of service. The twenty years, doctors declared, were equal to forty in most other jobs. The FAA warned legislators: public safety was involved; controllers, after more than twenty years of service, were potentially unsafe. Congress, Keith remembered, had ignored the warning and refused to act.

Subsequently, a Presidential Commission also turned thumbs down on early retirement for controllers, and the FAA – then a presidential agency – had been told to cease and desist in its argument. Now, officially, it had. Privately, however – as Keith and others knew – Washington FAA officials were as convinced as ever; they predicted that the question would arise again, though only after an air disaster, or a series, involving worn-out controllers, followed by press and public furore.

Keith's thoughts switched back to the countryside. It *was* glorious today; the fields inviting, even when viewed from a washroom window. He wished he could go out there and sleep in the sun. Well, he couldn't and that was that. He supposed he had better get back to the control room. He would – in just a moment more.

The Northwest Orient 727 had already started down, on authority from Washington Centre.

At lower altitudes, other flights were being hurriedly diverted, or ordered to orbit, safe distances away. A slanting hole, through which Northwest would continue descending, was being cleared in the growing midday traffic. Approach control at Washington National Airport had been alerted; its function would come shortly when it accepted the Northwest jet from Washington Centre. At this moment, responsibility for the Northwest flight and other aircraft devolved on the sector team next to Keith's – the extra sector which the young Negro, Perry Yount, was supervising.

Fifteen aircraft with combined speeds totalling seven thousand five hundred miles per hour were being juggled in an airspace a few miles wide. No aeroplane must come near another. The Northwest flight must be brought down, safely, through them all.

Similar situations happened several times a day; in bad weather it could be several times an hour. Sometimes emergencies came together, so that controllers numbered them – emergency one, emergency two, emergency three.

In the present situation, as always, Perry Yount – quiet-spoken, cool, and capable – was responding with experienced skill. Working with others in the sector team, he was co-ordinating emergency procedures – calmly, level voiced, so that from his tone no bystander listening would be aware that an emergency existed. Other aircraft could not hear transmissions to the Northwest flight, which had been instructed to switch to a separate radio frequency.

Everything was going well. The Northwest flight was steady on course, descending. In a few minutes, the emergency situation would be over.

Amid the pressures, Perry Yount even found time to slip across to the adjoining position – which normally would have his undivided attention – to check George Wallace. Everything looked good, though Perry knew he would be easier in mind when Keith Bakersfeld was back. He glanced towards the control room door. No sign of Keith yet.

Keith – still at the open window, still looking out at the Virginia countryside – was remembering Natalie. He sighed. Lately, there had been disagreements between them, triggered by his work. There were points of view which his wife could or would not see. Natalie was concerned about Keith's health. She wanted him to give up air traffic control; to quit, and choose some other occupation while some of his youth and most of his health remained. It had been a mistake, he realized now, to confide his doubts to Natalie, to describe what he had seen happen to other controllers whose work had made them prematurely old and ailing. Natalie had become alarmed, perhaps with reason. But there were considerations to giving up a job, walking away from years of training and experience; considerations which it was hard for Natalie – or for any woman, he supposed – to grasp.

Over Martinsburg, West Virginia – some thirty miles northwest of Washington Route Centre – a private, four-place Beech Bonanza, at seven thousand feet, was leaving Airway V166 and entering Airway V44. The little Beech Bonanza, identifiable visually by its butterfly tail, was cruising at 175 mph, its destination Baltimore. It contained the Redfern family: Irving Redfern, a consulting engineer-economist, his wife Merry, and their two children – Jeremy, ten years old, and Valerie, nine.

Irving Redfern was a cheerful, thorough man. Today, because of favourable weather conditions, he could have flown using visual flight rules. However, he considered it more prudent to file an instrument flight plan and, since leaving his home airport of Charleston, West Virginia, had stayed on airways, remaining in touch with air traffic control. A few moments earlier, Washington Route Centre had given him a new course on Airway V44. He had already turned on it and now his magnetic compass, which had been swinging slightly, was settling down nicely.

The Redferns were going to Baltimore partly for Irving Redfern's business, and partly for pleasure, which would include a family theatre outing tonight. While their father was concentrating on his flying, the children, with Merry, were chattering about what they would have for lunch at Friendship Airport.

The Washington Centre controller who had given Irving Redfern his latest instructions was George Wallace, the almost-qualified trainee still filling in for Keith Bakersfeld. George had correctly identified the Redferns' Beechcraft on his radarscope, where it appeared as a bright green dot, though smaller and moving more slowly than most other traffic – at the moment, principally airline jets. There was nothing closing up on the Beechcraft, however, which appeared to have plenty of airspace all around it. Perry Yount, the sector supervisor, had by now returned to the adjoining position. He was helping sort out the aftermath confusion now that the critical Northwest Orient 727 had been handed over safely to Washington National Airport approach control. Periodically, Perry glanced across at George and once called out, 'Is everything okay?' George Wallace nodded, though he was beginning to sweat a little. Today's heavier noontime traffic seemed to be building up earlier than usual.

Unknown to George Wallace or Perry Yount or Irving Redfern, an Air National Guard T-33 jet trainer was flying – at the moment idly in circles – a few miles north of Airway V44. The T-33 was from Martin Airport, near Baltimore, and its National Guard pilot was an automobile salesman named Hank Neel.

Lieutenant Neel, who was fulfilling his part-time military training requirements, had been sent up solo for VFR proficiency flying. Because he had been cautioned to do only local flying in an authorized area northwest of Baltimore, no flight plan had been filed; therefore, Washington Air Route Centre had no knowledge that the T-33 was in the air. This would not have mattered, except that Neel had become bored with his assignment and was also a careless pilot. Looking out casually, as he held the jet trainer in lazy circles, he realized he had drifted south while practising manoeuvres, though in reality he had come a good deal farther than he imagined. He was so far south that several minutes ago the National Guard jet had entered George Wallace's radar control area and now appeared on Wallace's screen at Leesburg as a green dot, slightly larger than the Redfern family's Beech Bonanza. A more experienced controller would have recognized the dot instantly for what it was. George, however, still busy with other traffic, had not yet observed the extra, unidentified signal.

Lieutenant Neel, at fifteen thousand feet, decided he would finish his flying practice with some aerobatics – two loops, a couple of slow rolls – and then return to base. He swung the T-33 into a steep turn and circled again while he took the standard precaution of looking for other aeroplanes above and below. He was now even closer than before to Airway V44.

The thing his wife failed to realize, Keith Bakersfeld thought, was that a man couldn't just quit his job irresponsibly, on a whim, even if he wanted to. Especially when the man had a family to support, children to educate. Especially when the job you possessed, the skills you so patiently acquired, had fitted you for nothing else. In some branches of government service, employees could leave and utilize their proficiency elsewhere. Air traffic controllers could not. Their work had no counterpart in private industry; no one else wanted them.

Being trapped that way – which was what it amounted to, Keith recognized – was a disillusion which came with other disillusions. Money was one. When you were young, enthusiastic, wanting to be a part of aviation, the civil service pay scale of an air traffic controller seemed adequate or better. Only later did it become clear how inadequate – in relation to the job's awesome responsibility – that pay scale was. The two most skilful specialists involved in air traffic nowadays were pilots and controllers. Yet pilots earned thirty thousand dollars a year while a senior controller reached his ceiling at ten thousand. No one believed pilots should earn less. But even pilots, who were notoriously selfish in taking care of themselves, believed air traffic controllers should earn more.

Nor was promotion – as in most other occupations – something an air traffic controller could look forward to. Senior supervisory posts were few; only a fortunate handful ever attained them.

And yet . . . unless you were reckless or uncaring – which controllers, by the nature of their work, were not – there was no way out. So there would be no quitting for himself, Keith decided. He must have another talk with Natalie; it was time she accepted that for better of worse, it was too late for change. He had no intention, at this stage, of scratching inadequately for some other kind of living.

He really must go back. Glancing at his watch, he realized guiltily that it was almost fifteen minutes since he left the control room. For part of the time he had been daydreaming – something he rarely did, and it was obviously the somniferous effect of the summer's day. Keith closed the washroom window. From the corridor outside, he hurried downward to the main control room.

High over Frederick County, Maryland, Lieutenant Neel straightened up his National Guard T-33 and eased on forward trim. Neel had completed his somewhat casual inspection and had seen no other aircraft. Now, beginning his first loop and slow roll, he put the jet trainer into a steep dive.

Entering the control room, Keith Bakersfeld was aware at once of an increased tempo. The hum of voices was louder than when he left. Other controllers were too pre-occupied to glance up – as they had done earlier this morning – as he passed by them on the way to his own position. Keith scribbled a signature in the sector log and noted the time, then moved behind George Wallace, getting the picture, letting his eyes adjust to the control room semi-darkness, in sharp contrast to the bright sunlight outside. George had murmured 'Hi!' as Keith returned, then continued transmitting radio instructions to traffic. In a moment or two, when Keith had the picture, he would relieve George and slip into his seat. It had probably been good for George, Keith reasoned, to be on his own for a while; it would improve his confidence. From the adjoining sector console, Perry Yount had noted Keith's return.

Keith studied the radarscope and its moving pinpoints of light – the aircraft 'targets' which George had identified, then noted on small movable markers on the screen. A bright green dot without identification caught Keith's eye. He asked George sharply, 'What's the other traffic near the Beech Bonanza 403?'

Lieutenant Neel had finished his first loop and slow roll. He had climbed back to fifteen thousand feet, and was still over Frederick County, though a little farther south. He levelled the

T-33 jet, then put the nose down sharply and began a dive into a second loop.

'What other traffic . . .?' George Wallace's eyes followed Keith's across the radarscope. He gasped; then in a strangled voice 'My God!'

With a swift, single movement, Keith ripped the radio headset from George and shouldered him aside. Keith flung a frequency switch open, snapped a transmit button down. 'Beech Bonanza NC-403, this is Washington Centre. There is unidentified traffic to your left. Make an immediate right turn *now*!'

The National Guard T-33 was at the bottom of its dive. Lieutenant Neel pulled the control column back and, with full power on, began a fast, steep climb. Immediately above was the tiny Beech Bonanza, containing Irving Redfern and his family, cruising steadily on Airway V44.

In the control room . . . breathlessly . . . silently . . . praying hard . . . they watched the closing, bright green dots.

The radio crackled with a burst of static. 'Washington Centre, this is Beech . . .' Abruptly the transmission stopped.

Irving Redfern was a consulting engineer-economist. He was a competent amateur pilot, but not a commercial one.

An airline pilot, receiving the Washington Centre message, would have flung his aircraft instantly into a steep right turn. He would have caught the urgency in Keith's voice, would have acted, without waiting to trim, or acknowledge, or – until later – question. An airline pilot would have ignored all minor consequences except the overriding urgency of escaping the nearby peril which the route centre message unmistakably implied. Behind him, in the passenger cabin, scalding coffee might have spilled, meals scattered, even minor injuries resulted. Later there would have been complaints, apologies, denunciations, perhaps a Civil Aeronautics Board inquiry. But – with ordinary luck – there could have been survival. Quick action could have ensured it. It would have ensured it for the Redfern family, too.

Airline pilots were conditioned, by training and usage, to swift, sure reflexes. Irving Redfern was not. He was a precise, scholarly man, accustomed to think before acting, and to follow correct procedures. His first thought was to acknowledge the Washington Centre message. Thus, he used up two or three seconds – all the time he had. The National Guard T-33, swooping upwards from the bottom of its loop, struck the Redferns' Beech Bonanza on the left side, slicing off the private aircraft's port wing with a single screeching rip of metal. The T-33, mortally damaged itself, continued upwards briefly while its forward section disintegrated. Scarcely knowing what was happening – he had caught only the briefest glimpse of the other plane – Lieutenant Neel ejected and waited for his parachute to open. Far below, out of control and spinning crazily, the Beechcraft Bonanza, with the Redfern family still inside, was plummeting to earth.

Keith's hands were trembling as he tried again. 'Beech Bonanza NC-403, this is Washington Centre. Do you read?'

Beside Keith, George Wallace's lips moved silently. His face was drained of colour.

As they watched in horror, the dots on the radarscope converged, blossomed suddenly, then faded.

Perry Yount, aware of something wrong, had joined them. 'What is it?'

Keith's mouth was dry. 'I think we've had a mid-air.'

It was then it happened: the nightmarish sound which those who heard it wished they had not, yet afterwards would not be able to erase from memory.

In the pilot's seat of the doomed, spinning Beech Bonanza, Irving Redfern – perhaps involuntarily, perhaps as a last despairing act – pressed the transmit button of his microphone and held it down. The radio still worked.

At Washington Centre, the transmission was heard on a console speaker which Keith had switched on when his emergency transmissions began. At first there was a burst of static, then immediately a succession of piercing, frantic chilling screams. Elsewhere in the control room, heads turned. Faces nearby paled. George Wallace was sobbing hysterically. Senior Supervisors came hurrying from other sections.

Suddenly, above the screaming clearly, a single voice – terrified, forlorn, beseeching. At first, not every word was audible. Only later, when the tape recording of the last transmission was played and replayed many times, were the full words put together, the voice identified as that of Valerie Redfern, nine years old.

'. . . *Mummy! Daddy! . . . Do something! I don't want to die . . . Oh, Gentle Jesus, I've been good . . . Please, I don't want . . .*'

Mercifully, the transmission stopped.

The Beech Bonanza crashed and burned near the village of Lisbon, Maryland. What remained from the four bodies was unrecognizable and was buried in a common grave.

Lieutenant Neel landed safely by parachute, five miles away.

All three controllers involved in the tragedy – George Wallace, Keith Bakersfeld, Perry Yount – were at once suspended from duty, pending investigation.

Later, the trainee, George Wallace, was held technically not to blame, since he was not a qualified controller when the accident occurred. He was, however, dismissed from government service and barred for ever from further employment in air traffic control.

The young Negro supervisor, Perry Yount, was held wholly responsible. The investigating board – taking days and weeks to play back tapes, examine evidence, and review decisions which Yount himself had had to make in seconds, under pressure – decided he should have spent less time on the emergency involving the Northwest Orient 727 and more in supervising George Wallace during the absence of Keith Bakersfeld. The fact that Perry Yount was doing double duty – which, had he been less co-operative, he could have refused – was ruled not relevant. Yount was officially reprimanded, and reduced in civil service grade.

Keith Bakersfeld was totally exonerated. The investigating board was at pains to point out that Keith had requested to be temporarily relieved from duty, that his request was reasonable, and he followed regulations in signing out and in. Furthermore, immediately on return, he perceived the possibility of a mid-air collision and tried to prevent it. For his quick thinking and action – though the attempt was unsuccessful – he was commended by the board.

The question of the length of Keith's absence from the control room did not arise initially. Near the end of the investigation – perceiving the way things were going for Perry Yount – Keith attempted to raise it himself, and to accept the major share of blame. His attempt was treated kindly, but it was clear that the investigating board regarded it as a chivalrous gesture – and no more. Keith's testimony, once its direction became clear, was cut off summarily. His attempted intervention was not referred to in the board's final report.

An independent Air National Guard inquiry produced evidence that Lieutenant Henry Neel had been guilty of contributory negligence in failing to remain in the vicinity of Middletown Air Base, and for allowing his T-33 to drift near Airway V44. However, since his actual position could not be proved conclusively, no charges were preferred. The lieutenant went on selling automobiles, and flying during weekends.

On learning of the investigating board's decision, the supervisor, Perry Yount, suffered a nervous collapse. He was hospitalized and placed under psychiatric care. He appeared to be moving towards recovery when he received by mail, from an anonymous source, a printed bulletin of a California right-wing group opposing – among other things – Negro civil rights. The bulletin contained a viciously biased account of the Redfern tragedy. It portrayed Perry Yount as an incompetent, bumbling dullard, indifferent to his responsibilities, and uncaring about the Redfern family's death. The entire incident, the bulletin argued, should be a warning to 'bleeding heart liberals' who aided Negroes in attaining responsible positions for which they were not mentally equipped. A 'housecleaning' was urged of other Negroes employed in air traffic control, 'before the same thing happens again'.

At any other time, a man of Perry Yount's intelligence would have dismissed the bulletin as a maniacal diatribe, which it was. But because of his condition, he suffered a relapse after reading it, and might have remained under treatment indefinitely if a government review board had not refused to pay hospital bills for his care, maintaining that his mental illness had not been caused through government employment. Yount was discharged from the hospital but did not return to air traffic control. When Keith Bakersfeld last heard of him, he was working in a Baltimore waterfront bar, and drinking heavily.

George Wallace disappeared from sight. There were rumours that the former trainee controller had re-enlisted – in the US Army Infantry, not the Air Force – and was now in serious trouble with the Military Police. According to stories, Wallace repeatedly started fist fights and brawls in which he appeared to go out of his way to bring physical punishment on himself. The rumours were not confirmed.

For Keith Bakersfeld, it seemed for a while as if life would go on as usual. When the investigation ended, his temporary suspension was lifted; his qualifications and government service rating remained intact. He returned to work at Leesburg. Colleagues, aware that Keith's experience could easily have been their own, were friendly and sympathetic. His work, at first, went well enough.

After his abortive attempt to raise the subject before the investigating board, Keith confided in no one – not even to Natalie – the fact of his washroom loitering that fateful day. Yet the secret knowledge was seldom far from the forefront of his mind.

At home, Natalie was understanding and, as always, loving. She sensed that Keith had undergone a traumatic shock from which he would need time to recover, and she attempted to meet his moods – to talk or be animated when he felt like it, to stay silent when he did not. In quiet, private sessions, Natalie explained to the boys, Brian and Theo, why they, too, should show consideration for their father.

In an abstracted way, Keith understood and appreciated what Natalie was trying to do. Her method might eventually have succeeded, except for one thing – an air traffic controller needed sleep. Keith was getting little sleep and, some nights, none.

On the occasions he did sleep, he had a persistent dream in which the scene in the Washington Centre control room, moments before the mid-air collision, was re-created . . . the merging pinpoints of light on the radarscope . . . Keith's last desperate message . . . the screams; the voice of little Valerie Redfern . . .

Sometimes the dream had variations. When Keith tried to move towards the radarscope to seize George Wallace's radio headset and transmit a warning, Keith's limbs resisted, and would change position only with frustrating slowness, as if the air surrounding them were heavy sludge. His mind warned frantically: If he could only move freely, the tragedy could be averted . . . Although his body strained and fought, he always reached his goal too late. At other times he attained the headset, but his voice would fail. He knew that if he could articulate words, a warning would suffice, the situation could be saved. His mind would race, his lungs and larynx strain, but no sound came.

But even with variations, the dream always ended the same way – with the Beech Bonanza's last radio transmission as he heard it so many times during the inquiry, on the played-back tape. And afterwards, with Natalie asleep beside him, he would lie awake, thinking, remembering, longing for the impossible – to change the shape of things past. Later still, he would resist sleep, fighting for wakefulness, so he would not endure the torture of the dream again.

It was then that in the loneliness of night, his conscience would remind him of the stolen, wasted minutes in the route centre washroom; crucial minutes when he could have returned to duty, and should have done, but through idleness and self-concern had failed to do so. Keith knew – as others did not – that the real responsibility for the Redfern tragedy was his own, not Perry Yount's. Perry had been a circumstantial sacrifice, a technical victim. Perry had been Keith's friend, had trusted Keith that day to be conscientious, to come back to the control room as quickly as he could. Yet Keith, though knowing his friend was standing double duty, aware of the extra pressures on him, had been twice as long as he needed to be, and had let Perry down; so in the end, Perry Yount stood accused and convicted in Keith's place.

Perry for Keith – a sacrificial goat.

But Perry, though grievously wronged, was still alive. The Redfern family was dead. Dead because Keith doodled mentally, dallying in the sunshine, leaving a semi-experienced trainee too long with responsibilities which were rightly Keith's, and for which Keith was better qualified.

There could be no question that had he returned sooner, he would have spotted the intruding T-33 long before it neared the Redferns' plane. The proof was that he *had* spotted it when he did return – too late to be of use.

Around and around . . . over and over in the night . . . as if committed to a treadmill . . . Keith's mind laboured on, self-torturing, sick with grief, recrimination. Eventually he would sleep from exhaustion, usually to dream, and to awake again.

In daytime, as well as night, the memory of the Redferns persisted. Irving Redfern, his wife, their children – though Keith had never known them – haunted him. The presence of Keith's own children, Brian and Theo – alive and well – appeared a personal reproach. Keith's own living, breathing, seemed to him an accusation.

The effect of sleepless nights, the mental turmoil, showed quickly in his work. His reactions were slow, decisions hesitant. A couple of times, under pressure, Keith 'lost the picture' and had to be helped. Afterwards he realized he had been under close surveillance. His superiors knew from experience what might happen, and half-expected some such signs of strain.

Informal, friendly talks followed, in upper-level offices, which achieved nothing. Later, on a suggestion from Washington, and with Keith's consent, he was transferred from the East Coast to the Midwest – to Lincoln International for control tower duty. A change of locale, it was believed, would prove therapeutic. Officialdom, with a touch of humanity, was also aware that Keith's older brother, Mel, was general manager at Lincoln; perhaps Mel Bakersfeld's influence would be steadying too. Natalie, though loving Maryland, made the transition without complaint.

The idea hadn't worked.

Keith's sense of guilt persisted; so did the nightmares, which grew, and took on other patterns, though always the basic one remained. He slept only with the aid of barbiturates prescribed by a physician friend of Mel's.

Mel understood part of his brother's problem, but not all; Keith still kept the secret knowledge of his washroom dawdling at Leesburg solely to himself. Later, watching Keith's deterioration, Mel urged him to seek psychiatric help, but Keith refused. His reasoning was simple. Why should he seek some panacea, some ritualistic mumbo-jumbo to insulate his guilt, when the guilt was real, when nothing in heaven or earth or clinical psychiatry could ever change it?

Keith's dejection deepened until even Natalie's resilient nature rebelled against his moods. Though aware that he slept badly, Natalie had no knowledge of his dreams. One day she inquired in anger and impatience, 'Are we supposed to wear hair shirts for the rest of our lives? Are we never to have fun again, to laugh the way we used to? If you intend to go on this way, you'd better understand one thing – I don't, and I won't let Brian and Theo grow up around this kind of misery either.'

When Keith hadn't answered, Natalie went on, 'I've told you before: our lives, our marriage, our children, are more important than your work. If you can't take that kind of work anymore – and why should you if it's that demanding? – then give it up now, get something else. I know what you always tell me: the money'll be less; you'd throw away your pension. But that isn't everything; we'd manage somehow. I'll take all the hardship you can give me, Keith Bakersfeld, and maybe I'd complain a little, but not much, because anything would be better than the way we are right now.' She had been close to tears, but managed to finish. 'I'm warning you I can't take much more. If you're going on like this, it may have to be alone.'

It was the only time Natalie had hinted at the possibility of their marriage breaking up. It was also the first time Keith considered suicide.

Later, his idea hardened to resolve.

The door of the darkened locker room opened. A switch snapped on. Keith was back again in the control tower at Lincoln International, blinking in the overhead light's glare.

Another tower controller, taking his own work break, was coming in. Keith put away his untouched sandwiches, closed his locker, and walked back towards the radar room. The other man glanced at him curiously. Neither spoke.

Keith wondered if the crisis involving the Air Force KC-135, which had had radio failure, had ended yet. Chances were, it had; that the aircraft and its crew had landed safely. He hoped so. He hoped that something good, for someone, would survive this night.

As he went in, he touched the O'Hagan Inn key in his pocket to be sure, once again, that it was there. He would need it soon.

4

It was almost an hour since Tanya Livingston had left Mel Bakersfeld in the central lobby of the main terminal. Even now, though other incidents had intervened, she remembered the way their hands touched at the elevator, the tone he used when he had said, 'It'll give me a reason to see you again tonight.'

Tanya hoped very much that Mel remembered too, and – though she was aware he had to go downtown – that he would find time to stop by first.

The 'reason' Mel referred to – as if he needed one – was his curiosity about the message received by Tanya while in the coffee shop. 'There's a stowaway on Flight 80,' a Trans America agent had told her. 'They're calling for you,' and 'the way I hear it, this one's a dilly.'

The agent had already been proved right.

Tanya was once more in the small, private lounge behind the Trans America check-in counters where earlier this evening she had comforted the distraught young ticket agent, Patsy Smith. But now, instead of Patsy, Tanya faced the little old lady from San Diego.

'You've done this before,' Tanya said. 'Haven't you?'

'Oh yes, my dear. Quite a few times.'

The little old lady sat comfortably relaxed, hands folded daintily in her lap, a wisp of lace handkerchief showing between them. She was dressed primly in black, with an old-fashioned high-necked blouse, and might have been somebody's great-grandmother on her way to church. Instead she had been caught riding illegally, without a ticket, between Los Angeles and New York.

There had been stowaways, Tanya recalled reading somewhere, as long ago as 700 BC, on ships of the Phoenicians, which plied the eastern Mediterranean. At that time, the penalty for those who were caught was excruciating death – disembowelment of adult stowaways, while children were burned alive on sacrificial stones.

Since then, penalties had abated, but stowaways had not.

Tanya wondered if anyone, outside a limited circle of airline employees, realized how much of a stowaway epedemic there had been since jet aeroplanes increased the tempo and pressures of passenger aviation. Probably not. Airlines worked hard to keep the whole subject under wraps, fearing that if the facts became known, their contingent of non-paying riders would be greater still. But there *were* people who realized how simple it all could be, including the little old lady from San Diego.

Her name was Mrs Ada Quonsett. Tanya had checked this fact from a Social Security card, and Mrs Quonsett would undoubtedly have reached New York undetected if she had not made one mistake. This was confiding her status to her seat companion, who told a stewardess. The stewardess reported to the captain, who radioed ahead, and a ticket agent and security guard were waiting to remove the little old lady at Lincoln International. She had been brought to Tanya, part of whose job as passenger relations agent was to deal with such stowaways as the airline was lucky enough to catch.

Tanya smoothed her tight, trim uniform skirt in the gesture which had become a habit. 'All right,' she said, 'I think you'd better tell me about it.'

The older woman's hands unfolded and the lace handkerchief changed position slightly. 'Well, you see, I'm a widow and I have a married daughter in New York. Sometimes I get lonely and want to visit her. So what I do is go to Los Angeles and get on an aeroplane that's going to New York.'

'Just like that? without a ticket.'

Mrs Quonsett seemed shocked. 'Oh, my dear, I couldn't possibly afford a ticket. I just have Social Security and this small pension my late husband left. It's all I can do to manage the bus fare from San Diego to Los Angeles.'

'You *do* pay on the bus?'

'Oh, yes. The Greyhound people are very strict. I once tried buying a ticket to the first stop on the line, then staying on. But they made a check at every city, and the driver found my ticket wasn't good. They were quite unpleasant about it. Not like the airlines at all.'

'I'm curious,' Tanya said, 'why you don't use San Diego airport.'

'Well, I'm afraid, my dear, they know me there.'

'You mean you've been caught at San Diego?'

The little old lady inclined her head. 'Yes.'

'Have you been a stowaway on other airlines? Besides ours?'

'Oh, yes. But I like Trans America best.'

Tanya was trying hard to remain severe, though it was difficult when the conversation sounded as if they were discussing a stroll to the corner store. But she kept her face impassive as she asked, 'Why do you like Trans America, Mrs Quonsett?'

'Well, they're always so reasonable in New York. When I've stayed with my daughter a week or two, and I'm ready to go home, I go to your airline offices and tell them.'

'You tell them the truth? That you came to New York as a stowaway?'

'That's right, my dear. They ask me the date and the flight number – I always write it down so I'll remember. Then they look up some papers.'

'The flight manifest,' Tanya said. She wondered: was this conversation real or just imagination.

'Yes, dear, I think that's what it's called.'

'Please go on.'

The little old lady looked surprised. 'There isn't anything else. After that, they just send me home. Usually the same day, on one of your aeroplanes.'

'And that's everything? Nothing else is said?'

Mrs Quonsett gave a gentle smile, as she might have done at a vicarage afternoon tea. 'Well, I do sometimes get a little scolding. I'm told I've been naughty, and not to do it again. But that really isn't much, is it?'

'No,' Tanya said. 'It certainly isn't.'

The incredible thing, Tanya realised, was that it was all so obviously true. As airlines were aware, it happened frequently. A would-be stowaway merely boarded an aeroplane – there were plenty of ways it could be done – and sat quietly, waiting for departure. As long as the stowaway stayed away from the first class compartment, where passengers could be identified easily, and unless the flight was full, detection was unlikely. It was true that stewardesses would count heads, and their tally might disagree with the gate agent's manifest. At that point a stowaway would be suspected, but the agent in charge would be faced with two choices. Either he could let the aeroplane go, recording on the manifest that the head and ticket counts did not agree, or a recheck could be made of the tickets of everybody aboard.

A recheck, if decided on, would take most of half an hour; meanwhile, the cost of holding a six-million-dollar jet aeroplane on the ground would soar. Schedules, both at origin and down the line, would be disrupted. Passengers with connections to make, or appointments, would grow angrily impatient, while the captain, conscious of his punctuality record, would fume at the agent. The agent would reason that he might have made a mistake anyway; moreover, unless he could show good reason for a delay, he would get a roasting later on from his District Transportation Manager. In the end, even if a stowaway was found, the loss in dollars and goodwill would far exceed the cost of providing a free ride for a single individual.

So what happened was that the airline did the only sensible thing – it closed the doors, and sent the aeroplane on its way.

That was usually the end of it. Once in flight, stewardesses were too busy to do a ticket check, and passengers would certainly not submit to the delay and annoyance of one at journey's end. Therefore the stowaway walked off, unquestioned and unhindered.

What the little old lady had told Tanya about returning was just as accurate. Airlines took the view that stowaway incidents should not happen and, when they did, it was their own fault for failing to prevent them. On the same basis, airlines accepted responsibility for ensuring that stowaways were returned to their point of origin and – since there was no other way to convey them – offenders went back in regular seats, getting normal service, including airline meals.

'You're nice, too,' Mrs Quonsett said. 'I can always tell nice people when I meet them. But you're a lot younger than the others in the airline – those I get to meet, I mean.'

'You mean the ones who deal with cheats and stowaways.'

'That's right.' The little old lady seemed unabashed. Her eyes moved appraisingly. 'I should say you're twenty-eight.'

Tanya said shortly, 'Thirty-seven.'

'Well, you have a young mature look. Perhaps it comes from being married.'

'Come off it,' Tanya said. 'That isn't going to help you.'

'But you are married.'

'I was. I'm not now.'

'Such a pity. You could have beautiful children. With red hair like your own.'

Red hair, perhaps, but not with the beginnings of grey, Tanya thought – the grey she had noticed again this morning. As to children, she might have explained that she did have a child, who was at home in their apartment and, she hoped, asleep. Instead, she addressed Mrs Ada Quonsett sternly.

'What you've done is dishonest. You've defrauded; you've broken the law. I suppose you realize you can be prosecuted.'

For the first time a gleam of triumph crossed the older woman's innocent face. 'But I won't be, will I? They never do prosecute anybody.'

There was really no point in continuing, Tanya thought. She knew perfectly well, and so apparently did Mrs Quonsett, that airlines never prosecuted stowaways, on the theory that publicity would be more harmful than otherwise.

There was just a chance, though, that some more questions might produce information useful in the future.

'Mrs Quonsett,' Tanya said, 'since you've had so much free travel from Trans America, the least you can do is help us a little.'

'I'll be glad to if I can.'

'What I'd like to know is how you get aboard our flights.'

The little old lady smiled. 'Well, my dear, there are quite a few ways. I try to use different ones as much as I can.'

'Please tell me about them.'

'Well, most times I try to be at the airport early enough so I can get myself a boarding pass.'

'Isn't that difficult to do?'

'Getting a boarding pass? Oh, no; it's very easy. Nowadays airlines use their ticket folders as passes. So I go to one of the counters and say I've lost my ticket folder, and please may I have another. I pick a counter where the clerks are busy, with a lot of people waiting. They always give me one.'

Naturally they would, Tanya thought. It was a normal request which occurred frequently. Except that, unlike Mrs Quonsett, most people wanted a fresh ticket folder for a legitimate reason.

'But it's just a blank folder,' Tanya pointed out. 'It isn't made out as a gate pass.'

'I make it out myself – in the ladies' room. I always have some old passes with me, so I know what to write. And I keep a big black pencil in my purse.' Depositing the lace handkerchief in her lap, Mrs. Quonsett opened her black beaded purse. 'See?'

'I do see,' Tanya said. She reached out, removing the crayon pencil. 'Do you mind if I keep this?'

Mrs Quonsett looked faintly resentful. 'It's really mine. But if you want it, I suppose I can get another.'

'Go on,' Tanya said. 'So now you have a boarding pass. What happens after that?'

'I go to where the flight is leaving from.'

'The departure gate.'

'That's right. I wait until the young man checking the tickets is busy – he always is when a lot of people come together. Then I walk past him, and on to the aeroplane.'

'Suppose someone tries to stop you?'

'No one does, if I have a pass.'

'Not even the stewardesses?'

'They're just young girls, my dear. Usually they're talking to each other, or interested in the men. All they look at is the flight number, and I always get that right.'

'But you said you don't always use a boarding pass.'

Mrs Quonsett blushed. 'Then, I'm afraid, I have to tell a little white lie. Sometimes I say I'm going aboard to see my daughter off – most airlines let people do that, you know. Or, if the plane has come in from somewhere else, I say I'm going back to my seat, but I left my ticket on board. Or, I tell them my son just got on, but he dropped his wallet and I want to give it to him. I carry a wallet in my hand, and that works best of all.'

'Yes,' Tanya said, 'I imagine it would. You seem to have thought everything out very carefully.' She had plenty of material, she mused, for a bulletin to all gate agents and stewardesses. She doubted, though, if it would have much effect.

'My late husband taught me to be thorough. He was a teacher – of geometry. He always said you should try to think of every angle.'

Tanya looked hard at Mrs Quonsett. Was her leg being gently pulled?

The face of the little old lady from San Diego remained impassive. 'There's one important thing I haven't mentioned.'

On the opposite side of the room a telephone rang. Tanya got up to answer it.

'Is that old biddy still with you?' The voice was the District Transportation Manager's. The DTM was responsible for all phases of Trans America operations at Lincoln International. Usually a calm, good-natured boss, tonight he sounded irascible. Clearly, three days and nights of flight delays, rerouting unhappy passengers, and endless needlings from the airline's Eastern head office were having their effect.

'Yes.' Tanya said.

'Get anything useful out of her?'

'Quite a lot. I'll send you a report.'

'When you do, use some goddam capitals for once, so I can read it.'

'Yes, sir.'

She made the 'sir' sufficiently pointed, so there was a momentary silence at the other end. Then the DTM grunted. 'Sorry, Tanya! I guess I'm passing on to you what I've been getting from New York. Like the cabin boy kicking the ship's cat, only you're no cat. Can I do anything?'

'I'd like a one-way passage to Los Angeles, tonight, for Mrs Ada Quonsett.'

'Is that the old hen?'

'The same.'

The DTM said sourly, 'I suppose, a company charge.'

'I'm afraid so.'

'What I hate about it is putting her ahead of honest-to-goodness fare-paying passengers who've been waiting hours already. But I guess you're right; we're better off to get her out of our hair.'

'I think so.'

'I'll okay a requisition. You can pick it up at the ticket counter. But be sure to alert Los Angeles, so they can have the airport police escort the old hag off the premises.'

Tanya said softly, 'She could be Whistler's Mother.'

The DTM grunted. 'Then let Whistler buy her a ticket.'

Tanya smiled and hung up. She returned to Mrs Quonsett.

'You said there was an important thing – about getting aboard flights – that you hadn't told me.'

The little old lady hesitated. Her mouth had tightened noticeably at the mention, during Tanya's conversation, of a return flight to Los Angeles.

'You've told me most of it,' Tanya prompted. 'You might as well finish. *If* there's anything else.'

'There certainly is.' Mrs Quonsett gave a tight, prim nod. 'I was going to say it's best not to choose the big flights – the important ones, I mean, that go non-stop across the country. They often get full, and they give people seat numbers, even in Economy. That makes it harder, though I did it once when I could see there weren't many others going.'

'So you take flights that aren't direct. Don't you get found at intermediate stops?'

'I pretend to be asleep. Usually they don't disturb me.'

'But this time you were.'

Mrs Quonsett pressed her lips in a thin, reproving line. 'It was that man sitting beside me. He was very mean. I confided in him, and he betrayed me to the stewardess. That's what you get for trusting people.'

'Mrs Quonsett,' Tanya said. 'I imagine you heard; we're going to send you back to Los Angeles.'

There was the slightest gleam behind the elderly, grey eyes. 'Yes, my dear, I was afraid that would happen. But I'd like to get a cup of tea. So, if I can go now, and you'll tell me what time to come back . . .'

'Oh, no!' Tanya shook her head decisively. 'You're not going anywhere alone. You can have your cup of tea, but an agent will be with you. I'm going to send for one now, and he'll stay with you until you board the Los Angeles flight. If I let you loose in this terminal I know exactly what would happen. You'd be on an aeroplane for New York before anybody knew it.'

From the momentary hostile glare which Mrs Quonsett gave her, Tanya knew she had guessed right.

Ten minutes later, all arrangements were complete. A single seat reservation had been made on Flight 103 for Los Angeles, leaving in an hour and a half. The flight was non-stop; there was to be no chance of Mrs Quonsett getting off en route and heading back. DTM Los Angeles had been advised by teletype; a memo was going to the crew of Flight 103.

The little old lady from San Diego had been handed over to a male Trans America agent – a recently recruited junior, young enough to be her grandson.

Tanya's instructions to the agent, Peter Coakley, were precise. 'You're to stay with Mrs Quonsett until flight time. She says she wants some tea, so take her to the coffee shop and she can have it; also something to eat if she asks, though there'll be dinner on the flight. But whatever she has, stay with her. If she needs the ladies' room, wait outside; otherwise, don't let her out of your sight. At flight time, take her to the departure gate, go aboard with her and hand her over to the senior stewardess. Make it clear that once aboard, she is not to be allowed off the aeroplane for any reason. She's full of little tricks and plausible excuses, so be careful.'

Before leaving, the little old lady grasped the young agent's arm. 'I hope you don't mind, young man. Nowadays an old lady needs support, and you do so remind me of my dear son-in-law. He was good-looking, too, though of course he's a lot older than you are now. Your airline does seem to employ nice people.' Mrs Quonsett glanced reproachfully at Tanya. 'At least, most of them are.'

'Remember what I said,' Tanya cautioned Peter Coakley. 'She's got a barrelful of tricks.'

Mrs Quonsett said severely, 'That isn't very kind. I'm sure this young man will form his own opinion.'

The agent was grinning sheepishly.

At the doorway, Mrs Quonsett turned. She addressed Tanya. 'Despite the way you've behaved, my dear, I want you to know that I don't bear any grudge.'

A few minutes later, from the small lounge which she had used for tonight's two interviews, Tanya returned to the Trans America executive offices on the main mezzanine. The time, she noticed, was a quarter to nine. At her desk in the big outer office she speculated on whether the airline had heard the last, or not, of Mrs Ada Quonsett. Tanya rather doubted it. On her capital-less typewriter she began a memo to the District Transportation Manager.

> to: dtm
> from: tanya liv'stn
> sbject: whistler's mum

She stopped, wondering where Mel Bakersfeld was, and if he would come.

5

He simply couldn't, Mel Bakersfeld decided, go downtown tonight.

Mel was in his office, in the mezzanine administrative suite. His fingers drummed thoughtfully on the surface of his desk, from where he had been telephoning, obtaining latest reports on the airport's operating status.

Runway three zero was still out of use, still blocked by the mired Aéreo-Mexican jet. As a result, the general runway availability situation was now critical, and traffic delays – both in the air and on the ground – were worsening. The possibility of having to declare the airport closed, some time within the next few hours, was very real.

Meanwhile, aircraft takeoffs were continuing over Meadowood, which was a hornet's nest all its own. The airport switchboard, as well as air traffic control's, was being swamped with bitterly complaining calls from Meadowood householders – those who were at home. A good many others, Mel had been informed, were at the protest meeting he had heard about earlier this evening, and now there was a rumour – which the tower chief had passed along a few minutes ago – that some kind of public demonstration was being planned, to take place at the airport tonight.

Mel thought glumly: a bunch of demonstrators underfoot was all he needed.

One good thing was that the category three emergency had just been declared concluded, the air force KC-135 which caused it, having landed safely. But one emergency ended was no assurance another would not begin. Mel had not forgotten the vague unease, the presentiment of danger he had felt while on the airfield an hour ago. The feeling, impossible to define or justify, still bothered him. Yet even without it, the other circumstances were enough to require his remaining here.

Cindy, of course – still waiting for him at her charity whingding – would raise all hell. But she was angry, anyway, because he was going to be late; he would have to brace himself to absorb the extra wrath as a result of not appearing at all. He supposed he might as well get Cindy's first salvo over with. The slip of paper with the downtown number where he had reached his wife earlier was still in his pocket. He took it out, and dialled.

As before, it took several minutes for Cindy to come to the telephone, and when she did, surprisingly, there was none of the fire she had shown during their previous conversation, only an icy chill. She listened in silence to Mel's explanation – why it was essential he should remain at the airport. Because of the lack of argument, which he had not expected, he found himself floundering, with laboured excuses not wholly convincing to himself. He stopped abruptly.

There was a pause before Cindy inquired coldly, 'Have you finished?'

'Yes.'

She sounded as if she were talking to someone distasteful and remote. 'I'm not surprised, because I didn't expect you to come. When you said you would, I assumed as usual you were lying.'

He said heatedly, 'I wasn't lying, and it isn't as usual. I told you earlier tonight, how many times I've been . . .'

'I thought you said you'd finished.'

Mel stopped. What was the use? He conceded wearily, 'Go on.'

'As I was trying to say when you interrupted – also as usual . . .'

'Cindy, for God's sake!'

'. . . knowing you were lying, gave me the chance to do some thinking.' She paused. 'You say you're staying at the airport.'

'Considering that's what this conversation is all about . . .'

'How long?'

'Until midnight; perhaps all night.'

'Then I'll come out there. You can expect me.'

'Listen, Cindy, it's no good. This isn't the time or the place.'

'Then we'll make it the time. And for what I have to say to you, any place is good enough.'

'Cindy, please be reasonable. I agree there are things we have to discuss, but not . . .'

Mel stopped, realizing he was talking to himself. Cindy had hung up.

He replaced his own phone and sat in the silent office, meditatively. Then, not quite knowing why, he picked up the telephone again and, for the second time tonight, dialled home. Earlier, Roberta had answered. This time it was Mrs Sebastiani, their regular baby-sitter.

'I was just calling to check,' Mel said. 'Is everything all right? Are the girls in bed?'

'Roberta is, Mr Bakersfeld. Libby's just going.'

'May I speak to Libby?'

'Well . . . just for a moment, if you promise to be very quick.'

'I promise.'

Mrs Sebastiani, Mel perceived, was her usual didactic self. When on duty she exacted obedience, not just from children, but from entire families. He sometimes wondered if the Sebastianis – there was a mousy husband who appeared occasionally – ever had emotional marriage problems. He suspected not. Mrs Sebastiani would never permit it.

He heard the patter of Libby's feet approach the phone.

'Daddy,' Libby said, 'does our blood keep going round inside for ever and ever?'

Libby's questions were always intriguingly different. She opened new subjects as if they were presents under a Christmas tree.

'Not for ever, dear; nothing's for ever. Just so long as you live. Your blood has been going around for seven years, ever since your heart started pumping.'

'I can feel my heart,' Libby said. 'In my knee.'

He was on the point of explaining that hearts were not in knees, and about pulses and arteries and veins, then changed his mind. There was plenty of time for all that. As long as you could feel your heart – wherever it seemed to be – that was the important thing. Libby had an instinct for essentials; at times he had the impression that her little hands reached up and gathered stars of truth.

'Goodnight, Daddy.'

'Goodnight, my love.'

Mel was still not sure why he had called, but he felt better for having done so.

As to Cindy, when she determined to do something she usually did it, so it was entirely likely that she would arrive at the airport later tonight. And perhaps she was right. There were fundamental things they had to settle, notably whether their hollow shell of marriage was to continue for the children's sake, or not. At least they would have privacy here, out of hearing of Roberta and Libby, who had overheard too many of their fights before.

At the moment there was nothing specific for Mel to do, except be available. He went out from his office on to the executive mezzanine, looking down on the continued bustling activity of the main terminal concourse.

It would not be many years, Mel reflected, before airport concourses changed dramatically. Something would have to be done soon to revise the present inefficient way in which people boarded aeroplanes and got off them. Simply walking on and off, individually, was far too cumbersome and slow. As each year passed, individual aeroplanes cost more and more millions of dollars; at the same time, the cost of letting them stay idle on the ground grew greater. Aircraft designers, airline planners, were striving to arrange more flying hours, which produced revenue, and fewer ground hours, which produced none at all.

Already plans were afoot for 'people-pods' – based on American Airline-type 'igloos' now used for pre-loading air freight. Most other airlines had their own variations of the igloo system.

Freight igloos were self-contained compartments, shaped to fit tightly in a jet plane fuselage. Each igloo was pre-loaded with freight of assorted shapes and sizes, and could be lifted to fuselage level, and stowed inside a jet, in minutes. Unlike conventional passenger planes, the inside of a jet freighter was usually a hollow shell. Nowadays when an all-cargo plane arrived at an airport freight terminal, igloos already in the aeroplane were off-loaded, and new ones put in. With a minimum of time and labour, an entire jet could be swiftly unloaded, reloaded, and be ready again for takeoff.

'People-pods' would be an adaptation of the same idea, and Mel had seen drawings of the type now contemplated. They would comprise small, comfortable cabin sections complete with seats, which passengers would step into at an airport check-in point. The pods would then be whisked on conveyor lines – similar to present baggage conveyor systems – to ramp positions. While their occupants remained seated, the people-pods would be slid into an aircraft which might have arrived only a few minutes earlier, but had already discharged other people-pods containing incoming passengers.

When the pods were loaded and in place, windows in them would correspond with windows in the aircraft fuselage. Doors at the end of each pod would fold back so that stewardesses and passengers could pass through to other sections. Galley compartments, complete with fresh food and fresh stewardesses, would be inserted as separate pods.

A refinement of the system might eventually allow boarding of people-pods downtown, or permit interline transfers by passengers without ever leaving their seats.

A related concept was a 'sky-lounge' already under development in Los Angeles. Each lounge, holding forty passengers, would be part-bus, part-helicopter. On local routes it could travel surburban or downtown streets under its own power, then, at a local heliport become a pod beneath an outsize helicopter – the entire unit whisked to and from an airport.

And these things would happen, Mel Bakersfeld reflected. Or if not those precisely, then something similar, and soon. A fascination, for those who worked in the aviation milieu, was the speed with which fantastic dreams came true.

A shout, abruptly, from the concourse below, broke into his thoughts.

'Hey, Bakersfeld! Hey up there!'

Mel searched with his eyes, seeking the source of the voice. Locating it was made more difficult by the fact that fifty or so faces, their owners curious about who was being called, had simultaneously swung up. A moment later he identified the caller. It was Egan Jeffers, a tall, lean Negro in light tan slacks and a short-sleeved shirt. One sinewy brown arm gestured urgently.

'You get down here, Bakersfeld. You hear me! You got troubles!'

Mel smiled. Jeffers, who held the terminal shoeshine concession, was an airport character. With a challenging, broad grin across his homely features, he could make the most outrageous statements and somehow get away with it.

'I hear you, Egan Jeffers. How about you coming up instead?'

The grin widened. 'Nuts to that, Bakersfeld! I'm a lessee and don't forget it.'

'If I do, I suppose you'll read me the Civil Rights Act.'

'You said it, Bakersfeld. Now haul your ass down here.'

'And you watch your language in my airport.' Still amused, Mel turned away from the mezzanine rail and headed for the staff elevator. At the main concourse level, Egan Jeffers was waiting.

Jeffers operated four shoeshine parlours within the terminal. As concessions went, it was not a major one, and the airport's parking, restaurant and newsstand concession produced revenues which were astronomical by comparison. But Egan Jeffers, a one-time kerbside bootblack, blithely behaved as if he alone kept the airport solvent.

'We gotta contract, me and this airport. Check?'

'Check.'

'Down in all that fancy rig-y-marole it says I got the exclu-sive right to shine shoes in these here premises. *Ex-clu-sive.* Check?'

'Check.'

'Like I said, man, you got troubles. Follow me, Bakersfeld.'

They crossed the main concourse to a lower level escalator which Jeffers descended in long strides, two steps at a time. He waved genially to several people as they passed. Less athletically, favouring his weaker foot, Mel followed.

At the foot of the escalator, near the group of car-rental booths occupied by Hertz, Avis, and National, Egan Jeffers gestured. 'There it is, Bakersfeld! Look at it! Taking the shoe polish outa the mouths of me and the boys who work for me.'

Mel inspected the cause of complaint. At the Avis counter a bold display card read:

A SHINE WHILE YOU SIGN
With our compliments

. . . .

We're Trying Harder Still!

Beneath, at floor level, was a rotating electric shoe polisher, positioned so that anyone standing at the counter could do what the notice said.

Mel was half amused; the other half of his mind accepted Egan Jeffers' complaint. Half-kidding or not, Jeffers was within his rights. His contract spelled out that no one else at the airport could shine shoes, just as Jeffers himself could not rent cars or sell newspapers. Each concessionaire received the same kind of protection in return for the substantial portion of his profits which the airport appropriated for itself.

With Egan Jeffers watching, Mel crossed to the car-rental booth. He consulted his pocket panic list – a slim booklet containing private telephone numbers of senior airport personnel. The Avis manager was listed. The girl behind the counter switched on an automatic smile as he approached. Mel instructed her, 'Let me use your phone.'

She protested, 'Sir, it's not a public . . .'

'I'm the airport manager.' Mel reached across, picked up the telephone, and dialled. Not being recognized in his own airport was a frequent experience. Most of Mel's work kept him behind the scenes, away from public areas, so that those who worked there seldom saw him.

Listening to the ringing tone, he wished that other problems could be settled as swiftly and simply as this one was going to be.

It took a dozen rings, then several minutes more of waiting, before the Avis manager's voice came on the line. 'Ken Kingsley here.'

'I might have needed a car,' Mel said. 'Where were you?'

'Playing with my kid's trains. Takes my mind of automobiles – and people who call me about them.'

'Must be great to have a boy,' Mel said. 'I just have girls. Is your boy mechanically minded?'

'An eight-year-old genius. Any time you need him to run that toy airport of yours, let me know.'

'Sure will, Ken.' Mel winked at Egan Jeffers. 'There is one thing he might do now. He could set up a shoeshine machine at home. I happen to know where there's one surplus. So do you.'

There was a silence, then the Avis manager sighed. 'Why is it you guys always want to stifle a little honest sales promotion?'

'Mostly because we're mean and ornery. But we can make it stick. Remember that contract clause? – any change in display space must have prior approval of airport management. Then there's the one about not infringing on other lessees' business.'

'I get it,' Kingsley said. 'Egan Jeffers has been beefing.'

'Let's say he isn't cheering.'

'Okay, you win. I'll tell my people to yank the damn thing. Is there any fat rush?'

'Not really,' Mel said. 'Any time in the next half hour will do.'

'You bastard.'

But he could hear the Avis man chuckling as he hung up.

Egan Jeffers nodded approvingly, his wide grin still in place. Mel brooded: I'm the friendly airport fun man; I make everybody happy. He wished he could do the same thing for himself.

'You handled that A-OK, Bakersfeld,' Jeffers said. 'Just stay on the ball, so it don't happen again.' At a businesslike pace, still beaming, he headed for the 'up' escalator.

Mel followed more slowly. On the main concourse level, at the Trans America counters, a milling crowd was in front of two positions marked:

Special Check-in
Flight Two – *The Golden Argosy*
Rome Nonstop

Nearby, Tanya Livingston was talking animatedly with a group of passengers. She signalled Mel and, after a moment or two, came over to join him.

'I mustn't stop; it's like a madhouse here. I thought you were going downtown.'

'My plans changed,' Mel said. 'For that matter, I thought you were going off duty.'

'The DTM asked if I'd stay. We're trying to get *The Golden Argosy* away on time. It's supposed to be for prestige, though I suspect the real reason is, Captain Demerest doesn't like to be kept waiting.'

'You're letting prejudice carry you away.' Mel grinned. 'Though sometimes I do, too.'

Tanya gestured down the concourse to a raised platform with a circular counter surrounding it, a few yards from where they were standing. 'That's what your big fight with your brother-in-law was all about; why Captain Demerest is so mad at you. Isn't it?'

Tanya was pointing to the airport's insurance-vending booth. A dozen or more people were ranged around the circular counter, most of them completing application forms for air trip insurance. Behind the counter, two attractive girls, one a striking blonde with big breasts, were busy writing policies.

'Yes,' Mel acknowledged, 'that was most of our trouble – at least recently. Vernon and the Air Line Pilots Association think we should abolish insurance booths at airports, and insurance policy vending machines. I don't. The two of us had a battle about it in front of the Board of Airport Commissioners. What Vernon didn't like, and still doesn't, is that I won.'

'I heard.' Tanya looked at Mel searchingly. 'Some of us don't agree with you. This time we think Captain Demerest is right.'

Mel shook his head. 'Then we'll have to disagree. I've been over it so many times; Vernon's arguments just don't make sense.'

They hadn't made any more sense – in Mel's opinion – that day a month ago, at Lincoln International, when Vernon Demerest had appeared before an Airport Commissioners meeting. Vernon requested the hearing, and had represented the Air Line Pilots Association, which was waging a campaign to outlaw insurance vending at airports everywhere.

Mel remembered the details of the session clearly.

It was a regular Board of Airport Commissioners meeting, on a Wednesday morning in the airport board room. All five commissioners were present: Mrs Mildred Ackerman, an attractive brunette housewife who was rumoured to be a mistress of the mayor, hence her appointment; and her four male colleagues – a university professor, who was Board

107

chairman, two local businessmen, and a retired union official.

The board room was a mahogany panelled chamber, in the terminal, on the executive mezzanine. At one end, on a raised platform, the commissioners sat in reclining leather chairs behind a handsome elliptical-shaped table. At a lower level was a second table, less elaborate. Here Mel Bakersfeld presided, flanked by his department heads. Alongside was a press table and, at the rear, a section for the public, since Board meetings were nominally open. The public section was rarely occupied.

Today the only outsider, apart from commissioners and staff, was Captain Vernon Demerest, smartly attired in Trans America uniform, his four gold stripes of rank bright under the overhead lights. He sat waiting in the public section, with books and papers spread over two other chairs beside him. Courteously, the Board elected to hear Captain Demerest first, ahead of its regular business.

Demerest rose. He addressed the Board with his usual self-assurance, and referred only occasionally to his notes. He was appearing, he explained, on behalf of the Air Line Pilots Association, of which he was a local council chairman. However, the views he would expound were equally his own, and were shared by most pilots of all airlines.

The commissioners settled back in their reclining chairs to listen.

Airport insurance vending, Demerest began, was a ridiculous, archaic hangover from flying's early days. The very presence of insurance booths and machines, their prominence in airport concourses, were insults to commercial aviation, which had a finer safety record, in relation to miles travelled, than any other form of transportation.

In a railway station or bus depot, or on boarding an ocean liner, or driving his own car from a parking garage, did a departing traveller have special insurance policies, against death and mutilation, thrust beneath his nose with subtle sales pressure? Of course not!

Then why aviation?

Demerest answered his own question. The reason, he declared, was that insurance companies knew a rick bonanza when they saw it, 'and never mind the consequences'.

Commercial aviation was still sufficiently new so that many people thought of travelling by air as hazardous, despite the provable fact that an individual was safer in a commercial airliner than in his own home. This inherent mistrust of flying was magnified on the exceedingly rare occasions when an airline accident occurred. The impact was dramatic, and obscured the fact that far more deaths and injuries occurred in other, more accepted ways.

The truth about the safety of flying, Demerest pointed out, was attested by insurance companies themselves. Airline pilots, whose exposure to air travel was far greater than that of passengers, could buy standard life insurance at regular rates and, through their own group plans, at even lower rates than the general populace.

Yet other insurance companies, abetted by greedy airport managements, and with the docile acquiescence of airlines, continued to batten on the fears and gullibility of air travellers.

Listening, at the staff table, Mel conceded mentally that his brother-in-law was making a lucid presentation, though the reference to 'greedy airport managements' had been unwise. The remark had produced frowns from several of the five commissioners, including Mrs Ackerman.

Vernon Demerest seemed not to notice. 'Now, madam and gentlemen, we come to the most significant, the vital point.'

This, he declared, was the very real danger, to every air passenger and to all flying crews, created by irresponsible, casual sales of insurance policies at airport counters, and by vending machines . . . 'policies promising vast sums, fortunes, in return for a mere few dollars' premium'.

Demerest continued heatedly: 'The system – if you choose to dignify a public disservice by calling it a system . . . and most pilots don't – offers a gilt-edged, open invitation to maniacs and criminals to engage in sabotage and mass murder. Their objectives need be only the simplest: personal reward for themselves or their expected beneficiaries.'

'Captain!' The woman commissioner, Mrs Ackerman, was leaning forward in her chair. From her voice and expression, Mel guessed she was doing a slow burn about the 'greedy airport managements' remark. 'Captain, we're hearing a whole lot of your opinions. Do you have any facts to back up all this?'

'Indeed I do, madam. There are many facts.'

Vernon Demerest had prepared his case thoroughly. Using charts and graphs, he demonstrated that known in-flight disasters caused by bombings or other acts of violence averaged one and one half per year. Motives varied, but a consistent, prevalent cause was financial gain from flight insurance. As well, there had been additional bombing attempts which either failed or were prevented, and other disasters where sabotage was suspected but not proved.

He named classic incidents: Canadian Pacific Airlines, 1949 and 1965; Western Airlines, 1957; National Airlines, 1960 and a suspected sabotage in 1959; two Mexican airlines, 1952 and 1953; Venezuelan Airlines, 1960; Continental Airlines, 1962; Pacific Airlines, 1964; United Airlines, 1950, 1955, and a suspected sabotage in 1965. In nine of the thirteen incidents, all passengers and crew members perished.

It was true, of course, that where sabotage was exposed, any insurance policies which had been taken out by those involved were automatically invalidated. In short: sabotage didn't pay, and normal, informed people were aware of this. They also knew that even after an air disaster from which there were no survivors, providing wreckage was located, it was possible to tell if an explosion had occurred and, usually, by what means.

But it was not normal people, Demerest reminded the commissioners, who committed bombings or savage acts of violence. It was the abnormal, the psychopaths, the criminally insane, the conscienceless mass killers. Those kind of people were seldom well-informed, and even if they were, the psychopathic mind had a way of perceiving only what it wanted to, of bending facts to suit what was convenient to believe.

Mrs Ackerman made an interjection again; this time her hostility to Demerest was unmistakable. 'I'm not sure any of us, even you, Captain, have qualifications to discuss what goes on in the minds of psychopaths.'

'I wasn't discussing it,' Demerest said impatiently. 'In any case, that isn't the point.'

'Pardon me, you *were* discussing it. And I happen to think it is the point.'

Vernon Demerest flushed. He was accustomed to command, not to being questioned. His temper, never far below the surface flashed. 'Madam, are you normally stupid or just being deliberately obtuse?'

The Board chairman rapped sharply with his gavel, and Mel Bakersfeld resisted the urge to laugh.

Well, Mel thought, we might as well finish right now. Vernon should stick to flying, which he was good at, and avoid diplomacy, where he had just struck out. The chances of the Airport Board doing anything which Captain Demerest wanted were, at this moment, minus nil – at least unless Mel helped Demerest out. For a moment he wondered if he should. He suspected Demerest realized he had gone too far. However, there was still time to turn what had just happened into a joke which everyone could laugh at, including Mildred Ackerman. Mel had a knack of doing that kind of thing, for making differences amenable, at the same time saving face for those on both sides. Also, he knew he was a favourite of Millie Ackerman's; they got on well together, and she always listened attentively to anything Mel might say.

Then he decided: the hell with it. He doubted if his brother-in-law would do the same thing if their situations were reversed. Let Vernon get out of the mess himself. In any case, Mel was going to have his own say in a few minutes' time.

'Captain Demerest,' the Board chairman observed coldly, 'that last remark is uncalled for, out of order, and you will please withdraw it.'

Demerest's features were still flushed. Momentarily he hesitated, then nodded. 'Very well, I withdraw it.' He glanced at Mrs Ackerman. 'I beg the lady's pardon. Perhaps she can understand that this is a subject which I, like most commercial flying crews, feel strongly about. When there's something which seems to be so obvious . . .' He left the sentence incomplete.

Mrs Ackerman was glaring. The apology, such as it was, Mel thought, had been handled badly. Now it was too late to smooth things over, even if he wanted to.

One of the other commissioners asked, 'Captain, what exactly do you want from us?'

Demerest took a pace forward. His voice became persuasive. 'I'm appealing to you for abolition of insurance machines and over-the-counter insurance vending at this airport, and a promise that you will refuse to rent space, ever again, for the same purpose.'

'You'd abolish insurance sales entirely?'

'At airports – yes. I may say, madam and gentlemen, that the Air Line Pilots Association is urging other airports to do the same thing. We're also asking Congress to take action to make airport insurance sales illegal.'

'What would be the point of doing that in the United States, when air travel is international?'

Demerest smiled faintly. 'This campaign is international, too.'

'How international?'

'We have the active support of pilots' groups in forty-eight other countries. Most believe that if an example were set in North America, either by the US or Canada, others would follow.'

The same commissioner said sceptically, 'I'd say you're all expecting quite a lot.'

'Surely,' the chairman interjected, 'the public is entitled to buy air travel insurance if they want it.'

Demerest nodded agreement. 'Of course. No one is saying they can't.'

'Yes, you are.' It was Mrs Ackerman again.

The muscles around Demerest's mouth tightened.

'Madam, anyone can get all the travel insurance they want. All they need have is the elementary foresight to make arrangements in advance – through any insurance broker or even a travel agency.' His glance took in the other commissioners. 'Nowadays a good many people carry a blanket accident policy for travel; then they make all the trips they want, and they're insured permanently. There are plenty of ways of doing it. As an example, the major credit card companies – Diners, American Express, Carte Blanche – all offer permanent travel insurance to their card holders; it can be renewed automatically each year, and billed.'

Most businessmen who travelled, Demerest pointed out, had at least one of the credit cards he had named, so abolition of airport insurance need impose no hardship nor inconvenience on business people.

'And with all these blanket policies, the rates are low. I know, because I have that kind of policy myself.'

Vernon Demerest paused, then continued. 'The important thing about all these insurance policies is that they go through channels. The applications are handled by experienced people; a day or so elapses between an application and the issuance of the policy. Because of this, there is a far better chance of the psychotic, the maniac, the unbalanced individual being noticed, his intentions questioned.

'Another thing to remember – an insane or unbalanced person is a creature of impulse. Where flight insurance is concerned, this impulse is catered to by the quickie, no-questions-asked policies available from airport vending machines and at insurance counters.'

'I think we all get the point you're making,' the chairman said sharply. 'You're beginning to repeat yourself, Captain.'

Mrs Ackerman nodded. 'I agree. Personally, I'd like to hear what Mr Bakersfeld has to say.'

The eyes of the commissioners swung towards Mel. He acknowledged, 'Yes, I do have some observations. But I'd prefer to wait until Captain Demerest is completely finished.'

'He's finished,' Mildred Ackerman said. 'We just decided.'

One of the other commissioners laughed, and the chairman rapped with his gavel. 'Yes, I really think so . . . If you please, Mr Bakersfeld.'

As Mel rose, Vernon Demerest returned, glowering, to his seat.

'I may as well make it clear,' Mel began, 'that I take the opposite point of view to just about everything Vernon has said. I guess you could call it a family disagreement.'

The commissioners, who were aware of Mel's relationship by marriage to Vernon Demerest, smiled, and already, Mel sensed, the tension of a few minutes earlier had lessened. He was used to these meetings and knew that informality was always the best approach. Vernon could have found that out, too – if he had taken the trouble to inquire.

'There are several points we ought to think about,' Mel continued. 'First, let's face up to the fact that most people have always had an inherent fear of flying, and I'm convinced that feeling will always exist, no matter how much progress we make, and however much we improve our safety record. Incidentally, the one point on which I agree with Vernon is that our safety record is exceedingly good already.'

He went on: Because of this inherent fear, many passengers felt more comfortable, more reassured, with air trip insurance. They wanted it. They also wanted it to be obtainable at airports, a fact proven by the enormous volume of sales from vending machines and airport insurance booths. It was a matter of freedom that passengers should have the right, and the opportunity, to buy insurance or not. As for getting the insurance ahead of time, the plain fact was that most people didn't think of it. Besides, Mel added, if flight insurance was sold this way, a great deal of revenue to airports – including Lincoln International – would be lost. At the mention of airport revenue, Mel smiled. The airport commissioners smiled with him.

That was the crux of it, of course, Mel realized. Revenue from the insurance concessions was too important to lose. At Lincoln International, the airport gained half a million dollars annually from commissions on insurance sales, though few purchasers realized that the airport appropriated twenty-five cents from every premium dollar. Yet insurance represented the fourth largest concession, with only parking, restaurants, and auto rentals producing larger sums for the airport's coffers. At other big airports, insurance revenue was similar or higher. It was all very well, Mel reflected, for Vernon Demerest to talk about 'greedy airport managements', but that kind of money had a way of talking, too.

Mel decided not to put his thoughts into speech. His single brief reference to revenue was enough. The commissioners, who were familiar with the airport's financial affairs, would get the point.

He consulted his notes. They were notes which one of the insurance companies doing business at Lincoln International had supplied him with yesterday. Mel had not asked for the notes, nor had he mentioned to anyone outside his own office that today's insurance debate was coming up. But the insurance people had somehow learned, and it was extraordinary how they always did – then acted promptly to protect their interests.

Mel would not have used the notes if they had run counter to his own honestly held opinions. Fortunately they did not.

'Now,' Mel said, 'about sabotage – potential and otherwise.' He was aware of the board members listening intently.

'Vernon has talked quite a lot about that – but I must say, having listened carefully, that most of his remarks seemed to me to be over-statements. Actually, the proven incidents of air disasters because of insurance-inspired bombings have been very few.'

In the spectator section, Captain Demerest shot to his feet. 'Great God! – how many disasters do we need to have?'

The chairman rapped sharply with his gavel. 'Captain . . . if you please!'

Mel waited until Demerest subsided, then continued calmly, 'Since the question has been asked, the answer is "none". A more pertinent question is: Might not the disasters still have occurred, even if airport-purchased insurance had not been available?'

Mel paused, to let his point sink home, before continuing.

'It can be argued, of course, that if airport insurance had not been available, the disasters we are talking about might never have happened at all. In other words, these were crimes of impulse, triggered by the ease with which airport insurance can be bought. Similarly, it can be contended that even if the crimes were contemplated in advance, they might not have been carried through had flight insurance been less readily available. Those, I think, are Vernon's arguments – and the ALPA's.'

Mel glanced briefly at his brother-in-law who gave no sign beyond a scowl.

'The glaring weakness of all those arguments,' Mel maintained, 'is that they are purely suppositional. It seems to me just as likely that someone planning such a crime would not be deterred by the absence of airport insurance, but would merely obtain their insurance elsewhere, which – as Vernon himself pointed out – is a simple thing to do.'

Expressed another way, Mel pointed out, flight insurance appeared only an afterthought of would-be saboteurs, and not a prime motive for their crime. The real motives, when aerial sabotage occurred, were based on age-old human weaknesses – love triangles, greed, business failures, suicide.

As long as there had been human beings, Mel argued, it had proved impossible to eliminate these motives. Therefore, those concerned with aviation safety and sabotage prevention should seek, not to abolish airport flight insurance, but to strengthen other precautionary measures in the air and on the ground. One such measure was stricter control of the sale of dynamite – the principal tool used by most aerial saboteurs to date. Another proposal was development of 'sniffer' devices to detect explosives in baggage. One such device, Mel informed the attentive Airport Commissioners, was already in experimental use.

A third idea – urged by flight insurance companies – was that passengers' baggage be opened for examination *before* flight, in the same way that happened with Customs inspection now. However, Mel concluded, the last idea presented obvious difficulties.

There should be stricter enforcement, he claimed, of existing laws prohibiting the carrying of side arms on commercial airliners. And aeroplane design should be studied in relation to sabotage, with the objective that aircraft could better endure an internal explosion. In that connection, one idea – also advocated by the insurance vending companies – was for an inner skin of baggage compartments to be made stronger and heavier than at present, even at the price of increased weight and decreased airline revenue.

The FAA, Mel pointed out, had made a study of airport insurance and subsequently opposed any ban on airport sales. Mel glanced at Vernon Demerest, who was glowering. Both knew that the FAA 'study' was a sore point with the airline pilots since it had been made by an insurance company executive – an aviation insurance man himself – whose impartiality was highly suspect.

There were several more points remaining in the insurance company notes which Mel had not yet touched on, but he decided he had said enough. Besides, some of the remaining arguments were less convincing. He even had serious doubts, now that he had made it, about the baggage compartment suggestion of a moment or two ago. Who would the extra weight be for, he wondered – the passengers, airlines, or mostly for the flight insurance companies? But the other arguments, he thought, were sound enough.

'So,' he concluded, 'what we have to decide is whether, because of supposition and very little else, we should deprive the public of a service which they so obviously want.'

As Mel resumed his seat, Mildred Ackerman said promptly and emphatically, 'I'd say no.' She shot Vernon Demerest a glance of triumph.

With minimum formality the other commissioners agreed, then adjourned, leaving other business until afternoon.

In the corridor outside, Vernon Demerest was waiting for Mel.

'Hi, Vernon!' Mel spoke quickly, making an effort at conciliation before his brother-in-law could speak. 'No hard feelings, I hope. Even friends and relatives have to differ now and then.'

The 'friends' was, of course, an overstatement. Mel Bakersfeld and Vernon Demerest had never liked each other, despite Demerest's marriage to Mel's sister, Sarah, and both men knew it; also, of late, the dislike had sharpened to open antagonism.

'You're damn right there are hard feelings,' Demerest said. The peak of his anger had passed, but his eyes were hard.

The commissioners, now filing out from the Board room, looked curiously at them both. The commissioners were on their way to lunch. In a few minutes Mel would join them.

Demerest said contemptuously, 'It's easy for people like you – ground-bound, desk-tied, with penguins' minds. If you were in the air as often as I am, you'd have a different point of view.'

Mel said sharply, 'I wasn't always flying a desk.'

'Oh, for Christ's sake! Don't hand me that hero veteran crap. You're at zero-feet now; the way you think shows it. If you weren't, you'd see this insurance deal the way any self-respecting pilot does.'

'You're sure you mean self-respecting, not self-adoring?' If Vernon wanted a slanging match, Mel decided, he could have one. There was no one else within hearing now. 'The trouble with most of you pilots is you've become so used to thinking of yourselves as demigods and captains of the clouds, you've convinced yourselves your brains are something wonderful too. Well, except in a few specialized ways, they're not. Sometimes I think the rest of what you have has addled through sitting up in that rarefied air too long while automatic pilots do the work. So when someone comes up with an honest opinion which happens to run counter to your own, you behave like spoiled little children.'

'I'll let all that stuff go,' Demerest said, 'though if anybody's childish it's you right now. What's more to the point is that you're dishonest.'

'Now look, Vernon . . .'

'An honest opinion, you said.' Demerest snorted in disgust. 'Honest opinion, my eye! In there, you were using an insurance company poop sheet. You were reading from it! I could see from where I was sitting, and I know because I have a copy myself.' He touched the pile of books and papers he was carrying. 'You didn't even have the decency, or take the trouble, to prepare a case yourself.'

Mel flushed. His brother-in-law had caught him out. He *should* have prepared his own case, or at least adapted the insurance company's notes and had them retyped. It was true he had been busier than usual for several days before the meeting, but that was no excuse.

'Some day you may regret this,' Vernon Demerest said. 'If you do, and I'm around, I'll be the one to remind you of today. Until then, I can do without seeing you any more than I have to.'

Before Mel could reply, his brother-in-law had turned and gone.

Remembering, now, with Tanya beside him in the main terminal concourse, Mel wondered – as he had several times since – if he could not have handled the clash with Vernon a good deal better. He had an uneasy feeling that he had behaved badly. He could still have differed with his brother-in-law; even now Mel saw no reason to change his point of view. But he could have done it more good-naturedly, avoiding the tactlessness which was a part of Vernon Demerest's makeup, but not of Mel's.

There had been no confrontation, since that day, between the two of them; the near-encounter with Demerest in the airport coffee shop tonight had been Mel's first sight of his brother-in-law since the airport commissioners' meeting. Mel had never been close to his older sister, Sarah, and they seldom visited each other's homes. Yet sooner or later, Mel and Vernon Demerest would have to meet, if not to resolve their differences, at least to shelve them. And, Mel thought, judging by the strongly worded snow committee report – unquestionably inspired by Vernon's antagonism – the sooner it happened, the better.

'I wouldn't have mentioned the insurance bit,' Tanya said, 'if I'd known it would send you so far away from me.'

114

Though the recollections which had flashed through his mind occupied only seconds of time, Mel was conscious once again of Tanya's perceptiveness concerning himself. No one else that he could remember had ever had quite the same facility for divining his thoughts. It argued an instinctive closeness between them.

He was aware of Tanya watching his face, her eyes gentle, understanding, but beyond the gentleness was a woman's strength and a sensuality which instinct told him could leap to flame. Suddenly, he wanted their closeness to become closer still.

'You didn't send me far away,' Mel answered. 'You brought me nearer. At this moment I want you very much.' As their eyes met directly, he added, 'In every way.'

Tanya was characteristically frank. 'I want you too.' She smiled slightly. 'I have for a long time.'

His impulse was to suggest that they both leave now, and find some quiet place together . . . Tanya's apartment perhaps . . . and hang the consequences! Then Mel accepted what he already knew; he couldn't go. Not yet.

'We'll meet later,' he told her. 'Tonight. I'm not sure how much later, but we will. Don't go home without me.' He wanted to reach out, and seize and hold her, and press her body to his, but the traffic of the concourse was all around them.

She reached out, her fingertips resting lightly on his hand. The sense of contact was electric. 'I'll wait,' Tanya said. 'I'll wait as long as you want.'

A moment later she moved away, and was instantly swallowed up in the press of passengers around the Trans America counters.

6

Despite her forcefulness when she had talked with Mel a half-hour earlier, Cindy Bakersfeld was uncertain what to do next. She wished there was someone she could trust to advise her. Should she go to the airport tonight, or not?

Alone and lonely, with the cocktail party babel of the Friends of the Archidona Children's Relief Fund around her, Cindy brooded uneasily over the two courses of action she could take. Through most of the evening, until now, she had moved from group to group, chatting animatedly, meeting people she knew, or wanted to. But for some reason tonight – rather more than usual – Cindy was aware of being here unaccompanied. For the past few minutes she had been standing thoughtfully, preoccupied, by herself.

She reasoned again: She didn't feel like going unescorted into dinner, which would begin soon. So on the one hand she could go home; on the other, she could seek out Mel and face a fight.

On the telephone with Mel she had insisted she would go to the airport and confront him. But if she went, Cindy realized, it would mean a showdown – almost certainly irreversible and final – between them both. Commonsense told her that sooner or later the showdown must come, so better to have it now and done with; and there were other related matters which had to be resolved. Yet fifteen years of marriage were not to be shrugged off lightly like a disposable plastic raincoat. No matter how many deficiencies and disagreements there were – and Cindy could think of plenty – when two people lived together that long, there were connecting strands between them which it would be painful, emotionally and physically, to sever.

Even now, Cindy believed, their marriage could be salvaged if both of them tried hard enough. The point was: Did they want to? Cindy was convinced she did – if Mel would meet some of her conditions, though in the past he had refused to, and she doubted very much if he would ever change as much as she would like. Yet without some changes, continuing to live together as they were would be intolerable. Lately there had not even been the consolation of sex which once upon a time made up for other inadequacies. Something had gone wrong there too, though Cindy was not sure what. Mel still excited her sexually; even now, just thinking about him in that way was enough to arouse her, and at this moment she was conscious of her body stirring. But somehow, when the opportunity was there, their mental separation inhibited them both. The result – at least in Cindy – was frustration, anger, and later a sexual appetite so strong that she had to have a man. Any man.

She was still standing alone, in the plush La Salle Salon of the Lake Michigan Inn, where tonight's reception for the press was being held. The buzz of conversation around her was mostly about the storm and the difficulty everyone had had in getting there; but at least – unlike Mel, Cindy thought – they had made it. Occasionally there was a mention of Archidona, reminding Cindy that she still hadn't found out which Archidona – Ecuador or Spain . . . *damn you, Mel Bakersfeld! Okay, so I'm not as smart as you are* – her charity was directed at.

An arm brushed against hers and a voice said amiably, 'No drink, Mrs Bakersfeld? Can I get you one?'

Cindy turned. The questioner was a newspaperman named Derek Eden, whom she knew slightly. His by-line appeared in the *Sun-Times* frequently. Like many of his kind, he had an easy, confident manner and air of mild dissipation. She was aware that each of them had taken note of the other on previous occasions.

'All right,' Cindy said. 'A Bourbon and water, go lightly on the water. And please use my first name; I think you know it.'

'Sure thing, Cindy.' The newspaperman's eyes were admiring and frankly appraising. Well, Cindy thought, why not? She knew she looked good tonight; she had dressed well and made up carefully.

'I'll be back,' Derek Eden assured her, 'so don't go away now I've found you.' He headed purposefully for the bar.

Waiting, surveying the crowded La Salle Salon, Cindy caught the glance of an older woman in a flowered hat. At once Cindy smiled warmly and the woman nodded, but her eyes moved on. She was a society page columnist. A photographer was beside her and together they were planning pictures of what would probably be a full-page layout in tomorrow's paper. The woman in the flowered hat motioned several of the charity workers and their guests together, and they crowded in, smiling obligingly, trying to look casual, but pleased that they had been selected. Cindy knew why she had been passed over; alone she was not important enough, though she would have been if Mel were there. In the city's life, Mel rated. The galling thing was – socially, Mel didn't care.

Across the room the photographer's light gun flashed; the woman in the hat was writing names. Cindy could have cried. *For almost every charity* . . . she volunteered, worked hard, served on the meanest committees, did menial chores which more socially prominent women rejected; then to be left out like this . . .

Damn you again, Mel Bakersfeld! Damn the bitching snow! And screw that demanding, stinking, marriage-wrecking airport.

The newspaperman, Derek Eden, was coming back with Cindy's drink and one of his own. Threading his way across the room, he saw her watching him and smiled. He looked sure of himself. If Cindy knew men, he was probably calculating what his chances were of laying her tonight. Reporters, she supposed, knew all about neglected, lonely wives.

Cindy did some calculating of her own concerning Derek Eden. Early thirties, she thought; old enough to be experienced, young enough to be taught a thing or two and to get excited, which was what Cindy liked. A good body from the outward look of him. He would be considerate, probably tender; would give as well as take. And he was available; even before he left to get the drinks he had already made that clear. Communication didn't take long between two reasonably sensitive people with a similar idea.

A few minutes earlier she had weighed the alternatives of going home or to the airport. Now, it seemed, there might be a third choice.

'There you are.' Derek Eden handed her the drink. She glanced at it; there was a lot of bourbon, and he had probably told the barman to pour heavily. Really! – men were so obvious.

'Thank you.' She sipped, and regarded him across the glass.

Derek Eden raised his own drink and smiled. 'Noisy in here, isn't it?'

For a writer, Cindy thought, his dialogue was deplorably unoriginal. She supposed she was expected to say *yes*, then the next thing he would come up with would be, *Why don't we go some place where it's quieter?* The lines to follow were equally predictable.

Postponing her response, Cindy took another sip of Bourbon.

She considered. Of course, if Lionel were in town she would not have bothered with this man. But Lionel, who was her storm anchor at other times, and who wanted her to divorce Mel so that he, Lionel, could marry her, Cindy . . . Lionel was in Cincinnati (or was it Columbus?) doing whatever architects did when they went on business trips, and wouldn't be back for another ten days, perhaps longer.

Mel didn't know about Cindy and Lionel, at least not specifically, though Cindy had an idea that Mel suspected she had a lover somewhere, stashed away. She also had a parallel notion that Mel didn't mind much. It gave him an excuse to concentrate on the airport, to the total exclusion of herself; that goddamned airport, which had been fifty times worse than a mistress in their marriage.

It had not always been that way.

Early in their marriage, soon after Mel left the Navy, Cindy had been proud of his ambitions. Later, when Mel was rapidly ascending the lower rungs of aviation management, she was happy when promotions, new appointments, came his way. As Mel's stature grew, so did Cindy's – especially socially, and in those days they had social engagements almost every evening. On behalf of them both, Cindy accepted invitations to cocktail parties, private dinners, opening nights, charity soirees . . . and if there were two the same night, Cindy was expert at judging which was more important, and turning down the other. That kind of socializing, getting to know prominent people, was important to a young man on the rise. Even Mel saw that. He went along with everything Cindy arranged, without complaining.

The trouble was, Cindy now realized, she and Mel had two different long-term aims. Mel saw their social life as a means to fulfilling his professional ambitions; his career was the essential, the socializing a tool which eventually he would dispense with. Cindy, on the other hand, envisaged Mel's career as a passport to an even greater – and higher level – social life. Looking back, it sometimes occurred to her that if they had understood each other's point of view better in the beginning, they might have compromised. Unfortunately, they hadn't.

Their differences began around the time that Mel – in addition to being general manager of Lincoln International – was elected president of the Airport Operators Council.

When Cindy learned that her husband's activity and influence now extended to Washington, DC, she had been overjoyed. His subsequent summons to the White House, the rapport with President Kennedy, led Cindy to assume they would plunge forthwith into Washington society. In roseate daydreams she saw herself strolling – and being photographed – with Jackie or Ethel or Joan, at Hyannis Port or on the White House lawn.

It hadn't happened; not any of it. Mel and Cindy had not become involved in Washington social life at all, although they could have done so quite easily. Instead, they began – at Mel's insistence – declining some invitations. Mel reasoned that his professional reputation was now such that he no longer needed to worry about being 'in' socially, a status he had never cared for, anyway.

When she caught on to what was happening, Cindy exploded, and they had a first-class row. That was a mistake, too. Mel would sometimes respond to reason, but Cindy's anger usually made him stand firm to the point of obstinacy. Their dispute raged for a week, Cindy becoming bitchier as it progressed, thus making things worse. Being bitchy was one of Cindy's failings, and she knew it. Half the time she didn't intend to be that way, but sometimes, faced with Mel's indifference, her fiery temper got the better of her – as it had on the telephone tonight.

After the week-long argument, which never really ended, their quarrels became more frequent; they also stopped trying to conceal them from the children, which was impossible, anyway. Once – to the shame of them both – Roberta announced that in future after school she would be going to a friend's house first, 'Because when I stay home, I can't do my homework while you're fighting.'

Eventually a pattern was established. Some evenings Mel accompanied Cindy to certain social events which he had agreed on in advance. Otherwise he stayed longer hours at the airport and came home less frequently. Finding herself alone much more, Cindy concentrated on what Mel sneered at as her 'junior league charities' and 'silly social climbing'.

Well, maybe at times, Cindy thought, it did look silly to Mel. But she didn't have much else, and it so happened she enjoyed the social status competition – which was what it was, really. It was all very well for a man to criticize; men had plenty of activities to occupy their time. In Mel's case there was his career, his airport, his responsibilities. What was Cindy supposed to do? Stay home all day and dust the house?

Cindy had no illusions about herself so far as mental acuity went. She was no great intellect, and she knew that in lots of ways, mentally, she would never measure up to Mel. But then, that was nothing new. In their early years of marriage, Mel used to find her occasional mild stupidities amusing, though nowadays when he derided her – as he had taken to doing lately – he seemed to have forgotten that. Cindy was also realistic about her former career as an actress – she would never have made the grade to stardom, or have

118

come close to it. It was true that, in the past, she sometimes implied that she might have done so if marriage had not ended her theatrical activity. But that was merely a form of self-defence, a need to remind others – including Mel – that she was an individual as well as being the airport manager's wife. Within herself Cindy knew the truth – that as a professional actress she would almost certainly not have risen above bit parts.

The involvement in social life, however – in the *mise en scène* of local society – was something Cindy could handle. It gave her a sense of identity and importance. And although Mel scoffed, and denied that what Cindy had done was an achievement, she *had* managed to climb, to be accepted by socially conspicuous people whom she would not have met otherwise, and to be involved in events like tonight's . . . except that on this occasion she needed Mel as escort, and Mel – thinking first of his goddamned airport, as always – had let her down.

Mel, who had so much in the way of identity and prestige, had never understood Cindy's need to carve out some kind of individuality for herself. She doubted if he ever would.

Just the same, Cindy had gone ahead. She also had plans for the future which she knew would entail a monstrous family battle if she and Mel stayed married. It was Cindy's ambition to have her daughter Roberta, and later Libby, presented as debutantes at the Passavant Cotillion, glittering apex of the Illinois deb season. As the girls' mother, Cindy herself would garner social status.

She had once mentioned the notion casually to Mel, who reacted angrily, 'Over my dead body!' Debutantes and their silly, simpering mothers, he advised Cindy, belonged to an age that was gone. Debutante balls, he declared – and thank goodness there were few of them left – were an anachronistic perpetuation of a snobbery and class structure which the nation was fortunately shedding, though – judging by people who still thought like Cindy did – not nearly fast enough. Mel wanted his children to grow up (he told Cindy) with the knowledge that they were equal to others, but not with some conceited, misguided notion that they were socially superior. And so on.

Unusually for Mel, whose policy declarations were normally brief and concise, he had gone on for some time.

Lionel, on the other hand, thought the whole thing was a good idea.

Lionel was Lionel Urquhart. At the moment he hovered alongside Cindy's life in the shape of a question mark.

Curiously, it was Mel who brought Cindy and Lionel together to begin with. Mel introduced them at a civic luncheon which Lionel was attending because of something architectural he had done for the city, and Mel was there because of the airport. The two men had known each other casually for years.

Afterwards, Lionel telephoned Cindy, and they met a few times for luncheons and dinners, then more frequently, and eventually for the ultimate intimacy between a man and a woman.

Unlike many people who made a practice of extra-marital sex, Lionel had taken the experience extremely seriously. He lived alone, having been separated from his wife for several years, but was not divorced. Now he wanted to get a divorce, and have Cindy do the same, so they could marry. By this time, he knew that Cindy's own marriage was shaky.

Lionel and his estranged wife had never had children – a fact, he confided to Cindy, that he greatly regretted. It was not too late, he declared, for Cindy and himself to have a child if they married soon. Also, he would be more than happy to provide a home for Roberta and Libby, and would do his best to be a substitute father.

Cindy had put off a decision for several reasons. Principally, she hoped that relations between herself and Mel would improve, making their marriage closer to what it used to be. She could not say with assurance that she was still in love with Mel; love, Cindy found, was something you became more sceptical about as you grew older. But at least she was used to Mel. He was there; so were Roberta and Libby; and, like many women, Cindy dreaded a major upheaval in her life.

Initially, too, she believed that a divorce and remarriage would be damaging to her socially. On this point, however, she had now changed her mind. Plenty of people had divorces without dropping out of sight socially, even temporarily, and one saw wives with old husbands one week, new ones the next. Cindy even had the impression sometimes that not to have been divorced, at least once, was somewhat square.

It was possible that marriage to Lionel might improve Cindy's status socially. Lionel was much more amenable to partying and entertaining than Mel. Also, the Urquharts were an old, respected city family. Lionel's mother still presided, dowager-like, over a decaying mansion near the Drake Hotel, where an antique butler ushered visitors in, and an arthritic maid brought afternoon tea on a silver tray. Lionel had taken Cindy there for tea one day. Afterwards he reported that Cindy had made a good impression, and he was sure he could persuade his mother to sponsor Roberta and Libby as debutantes when the time came.

There and then – because her differences with Mel had grown even more intense – Cindy might have plunged ahead, commiting herself to Lionel, except for one thing. Sexually, Lionel was a dying duck.

He tried hard, and occasionally he managed to surprise her, but most of the times they made love he was like a clock whose mainspring is running down. He said gloomily one night, after an abortive session in the bedroom of his apartment, which had been frustrating for both of them, 'You should have known me when I was eighteen; I was a young ram.' Unfortunately, Lionel was now a long way from eighteen; he was forty-eight.

Cindy envisaged that if she married Lionel, such limited sex as they now enjoyed as lovers would drift into nothingness when they came to live together. Of course, Lionel would try to make up in other ways – he was kind, generous, considerate – but was that enough? Cindy was far from being on the wane sexually; she had always been strongly sensual, and lately her desire and sexual appetite seemed to have grown. But even if Lionel failed in that area, she wasn't batting any better with Mel right now, so what was the difference? Over-all, Lionel would give her more.

Perhaps the answer was to marry Lionel Urquhart and do some bedding down on the side. The latter might be difficult, especially when she was newly married, but if she was cautious it could be managed. Other people she knew of – men and women, some in high places – did the same thing to keep themselves satiated physically, and their marriages intact. After all, she had succeeded in deceiving Mel. He might suspect her in a general sense, but Cindy was positive that Mel had no definite knowledge about Lionel or anyone else.

Now, how about tonight? Should she go to the airport for a showdown with Mel, as she had considered earlier? Or should she let herself get involved for the evening with this newspaperman, Derek Eden, who was standing beside her waiting for an answer to his question.

It occurred to Cindy that perhaps she could manage both.

She smiled at Derek Eden. 'Tell me again. What was it you said?'

'I said it was noisy in here.'

'Yes, it is.'

'I wondered if we might skip the dinner and go somewhere quieter.'

Cindy could have laughed aloud. Instead, she nodded. 'All right.'

She glanced around at the other hosts and guests of the Archidona Children's Relief Fund press party. The photographers had stopped taking pictures, so there was really no point in staying any longer. She could slip out quietly, and not be noticed.

Derek Eden asked, 'Do you have a car here, Cindy?'

'No, do you?' Because of the weather, Cindy had come in a taxi.

'Yes.'

'All right,' she said, 'I won't leave here with you. But if you're waiting in your car, outside, I'll come through the main doors in fifteen minutes.'

'Better make it twenty minutes. I'll need to make a couple of phone calls.'

'Very well.'

'Do you have any preference? I mean where we'll go?'

'That's entirely up to you.'

He hesitated, then said, 'Would you like dinner first?'

She thought amusedly: the 'first' was a message – to make quite sure she understood what she was getting into.

'No,' Cindy said. 'I haven't time. I have to be somewhere else later.'

She saw Derek Eden's eyes glance down, then return to her face. She sensed the intake of his breath, and had the impression that he was marvelling at his own good fortune. 'You're the greatest,' he said. 'I'll only believe my good luck when you come out through those doors.'

With that, he turned away and slipped quietly from the La Salle Salon. A quarter of an hour later, unnoticed, Cindy followed him.

She collected her coat and, as she left the Lake Michigan Inn, drew it closely around her. Outside it was still snowing, and an icy, shrieking wind swept across the open spaces of the Lakeshore and the Outer Drive. The weather made Cindy remember the airport. A few minutes ago she had made a firm resolve: she would still go there, later tonight; but it was early yet – not quite half-past nine – and there was plenty of time – for everything.

A porter forsook the shelter of the Inn doorway and touched his hat. 'Taxi, ma'am?'

'I don't think so.'

At that moment the lights of a car in the parking lot came on. It moved forward, skidding once on the loose snow, then came towards the door where Cindy was waiting. The car was a Chevrolet, several models old. She could see Derek Eden at the wheel.

The porter held the car door open and Cindy got in. As the door slammed closed, Derek Eden said, 'Sorry about the car being cold. I had to call the paper, then make some arrangements for us. I got here just ahead of you.'

Cindy shivered, and pulled her coat even tighter. 'Wherever we're going, I hope it's warm.'

Derek Eden reached across and took her hand. Since the hand was resting on her knee, he held that too. Briefly she felt his fingers move, then he returned his hand to the wheel. He said softly, 'You'll be warm. I promise.'

7

Forty-five minutes before its scheduled departure time of 10.0 pm, Trans America Airlines Flight Two – *The Golden Argosy*, Captain Vernon Demerest commanding – was in the final stages of preparation for its five-thousand mile, non-stop journey to Rome.

General preparations for the flight had been under way for months and weeks and days. Others, more immediate, had continued for the past twenty-four hours.

An airline flight from any major terminal is, in effect, like a river joining the sea. Before it reaches the sea, a river is fed by tributaries, originating far back in time and distance, each tributary joined along its length by others, either greater or smaller. At length, at the river's mouth, the river itself is the sum of everything which flowed into it. Translated into aviation terms, the river at the sea is an airliner at its moment of takeoff.

The aircraft for Flight Two was a Boeing 707-320B Intercontinental Jetliner, registered Number N-731-TA. It was powered by four Pratt & Whitney turbofan jet engines, providing a cruising speed of six hundred and five miles per hour. The aircraft's range, at maximum weight, was six thousand miles, or the straight line distance from Iceland to Hong Kong. It carried a hundred and ninety-nine passengers and twenty-five thousand US gallons of fuel – enough to fill a good-sized swimming pool. The aircraft's cost to Trans America Airlines was six and a half million dollars.

The day before yesterday N-731-TA had flown from Dusseldorf, Germany, and, two hours out from Lincoln International, an engine overheated. As a precaution, the captain ordered it shut down. None of the aircraft's passengers were aware that they were operating with three engines instead of four; if necessary, the aircraft could have flown on one. Nor was the flight even late arriving.

Trans America Maintenance, however, was advised by company radio. As a result, a crew of mechanics was waiting, and whisked the aeroplane to a hangar as soon as passengers and freight were disembarked. Even while taxiing to the hangar, diagnostic specialists were at work, seeking out the aeroplane's trouble, which they located quickly.

A pneumatic duct – a stainless steel pipe around the affected engine – had cracked and broken in flight. The immediate procedure was for the engine to be removed and a replacement installed. That was relatively simple. More complicated was the fact that for several minutes before the overheating engine was shut down, extremely hot air must have escaped into the engine nacelle. This heat could conceivably have damaged one hundred and eight pairs of wires from the aircraft's electrical system.

Close examination of the wires showed that while some had been heated, none apparently had suffered damage. If a similar condition had occurred within an automobile, bus, or truck, the vehicle would have been put back into service without question. But airlines took no such chances. It was decided that all one hundred and eight pairs of wires must be replaced.

The work of replacement was highly skilled, but exacting and tedious because only two men at a time could operate in the confined space of the engine nacelle. Moreover, each pair of wires must be identified, then connected painstakingly to cannon plugs. A non-stop, day-and-night effort was planned with teams of electrical mechanics relieving each other.

The entire job would cost Trans America Airlines thousands of dollars in skilled man-hours and lost revenue while the big aircraft was unproductive on the ground. But the loss was accepted without question, as all airlines accepted such losses in pursuit of high safety standards.

The Boeing 707 – N-731-TA – which was to have flown to the West Coast and back before its flight to Rome, was taken out of service. Operations was advised, and hastily shuffled schedules to help bridge the gap. A connecting flight was cancelled and several dozen passengers transferred to competitive airlines. There was no substitute aircraft. When it came to multi-million-dollar jets, airlines did not carry spares.

Operations, however, urged Maintenance to have the 707 ready for Flight Two to Rome, which was then thirty-six hours away from scheduled departure. An operations vice-president in New York personally called the Trans America base maintenance chief, and was told: 'If we can get it ready for you, we will.' A top-notch foreman and a crack crew of mechanics and electricians were already on the job, all of them aware of the importance of finishing quickly. A second crew, to relieve the others through the night, was being rounded up. Both crews would work extra hours until the job was done.

Contrary to general belief, aircraft mechanics took a close interest in the operational flights of aeroplanes they serviced. After a complex job, or a rush one such as this, they would follow the progress of a particular aeroplane to learn how their work had stood up. It was a source of satisfaction to them when, as usually happened, the aeroplane functioned well. Months later, they might say to each other, observing an aeroplane taxiing in, 'There's old 842. Remember that time . . . and the trouble we had with her. I guess we cured it.'

Through the critical day and a half following discovery of the trouble with N-731-TA, work on the aeroplane, though slow by its nature, continued as speedily as possible.

At length, three hours from Flight Two's departure time, the last of the hundred-odd pairs of wires was reconnected. It took another hour to replace the engine cowlings and for an engine run-up on the ground. Then, before the aeroplane could be accepted for service, an air test was required. By this time, urgent calls from Operations demanded: Would N-731-TA be ready for Flight Two or not? If not, would Maintenance for Chrissake say so, so Sales could be informed of a possible long delay, and passengers notified before they left their homes.

His fingers crossed, and touching wood, the maintenance chief replied that, barring complications on the air test, the aircraft would be available on time.

It was – but only just. The chief Trans America pilot at the base, who had been standing by for just that purpose, test flew the aircraft, barrelling up through the storm to clearer altitudes above. He reported on return: 'You guys down here'd never know it, but the moon's still there,' then certified N-731-TA as completely airworthy. Executive pilots liked that kind of assignment, it helped build up their needed flying hours without going far from their desks.

There was so little time left when the chief pilot landed, that he taxied the aeroplane directly to gate forty-seven of the terminal, where – as Flight Two, *The Golden Argosy* – it was to load.

Thus Maintenance had come through – as Maintenance did so often – but no corners had been cut.

Once the aeroplane was at its gate, knots of workers bustled in and around it like scurrying elves.

Food was a major item to go aboard. Seventy-five minutes before departure time, Departure Control called the caterer's flight kitchen, ordering food for the flight, according to the number of passengers expected. Tonight the first-class section of Flight Two would have only two vacant seats; the economy section would be three-quarters full. First-class, as usual, was allocated six meals extra; economy had the same number of meals as passengers. Thus, first-class passengers could have a second dinner if they asked for it; economy passengers couldn't.

Despite the exact count, a last-minute passenger would always get a meal. Spare meals – including Kosher meals – were available in lockers near the departure gate. If an unexpected passenger went aboard as doors were closing, his food tray was passed in after him.

Liquor stocks, requiring a signed stewardess receipt, came aboard too. Liquor for first-class passengers was free; tourist passengers paid a dollar a drink (or the equivalent in foreign currency) unless they took advantage of a piece of inside information. The information was that stewardesses were issued almost no change, sometimes none, and where a stewardess could not make change, her instructions were to give the passenger his or her drinks free. Some regular travellers had drunk free for years in tourist class, merely by proffering a fifty- or twenty-dollar bill and insisting they had nothing smaller.

At the same time that the food and liquor went aboard, other commissary supplies were checked and replenished. There were several hundred items, ranging from babies' diapers, blankets, pillows, airsick bags, and a Gideon Bible to accessories like 'Tray, beverage service, 8-hole, qty.5.' All were expendable. At the conclusion of a flight, airlines never bothered with checking inventories. Whatever was missing was replaced without question, which was why passengers who walked from an aeroplane with anything portable were seldom stopped.

Included in commissary supplies were magazines and newspapers. Newspapers were usually available on flights – with an exception. The Trans America commissary had a standing order: if a newspaper front page featured an air disaster, the newspapers were not to go aboard, but were thrown away. Most other airlines had the same rule.

Tonight, on Flight Two, there were plenty of newspapers. The principal news was weather – the effect, on the entire Midwest, of the three-day winter storm.

Baggage was now coming aboard Flight Two as passengers were beginning to check in. When a passenger saw his bag disappear at the check-in counter it went, by a series of conveyor belts, to a room deep below the departure gates which baggage men privately called 'the lion's den'. It acquired that name because (so baggage men confided after several drinks) only the brave or innocent would allow a bag they cared about to enter here. Some bags – as saddened owners could testify – came into the lion's den and were never seen again.

In the den, an attendant on duty watched each bag arrive. According to its destination label, he flicked a lever on a panel and, a moment later, an automatic arm reached out and grabbed the bag, setting it beside others for the same flight. From this point, the others, a crew of several men transferred all bags to the proper aeroplanes.

It was an excellent system – when it worked. Unfortunately, if often didn't.

Baggage handling – airlines conceded privately – was the least efficient part of air travel. In an age where human ingenuity could place a capsule the size of a houseboat in outer space, it was a fact that an airline passenger's bag could not be counted on to arrive safely at Pine Bluff, Arkansas, or Minneapolis-St Paul, or even at the same time as the passenger. An astounding amount of airline baggage – at least one bag in every hundred – went to the wrong destinations, was delayed, or lost entirely. Executives pointed woefully to the many opportunities for human error which existed with baggage handling. Efficiency experts periodically examined airline baggage systems, and periodically they were improved. Yet no one had come up with a system which was infallible, or even close to it. The result was that all airlines employed staffs, at every major terminal, whose job was solely to trace missing baggage. Such staffs were seldom idle.

An experienced, cagey traveller did the best he could by making sure that the tags which agents or porters put on his bags when he checked in showed his correct destination. Often they didn't. With surprising frequency, wrong tags were slapped on in haste, and had to be changed when the error was pointed out. Even then, when the bags disappeared from sight, there was the sense of having entered a lottery, and at that point the traveller could only pray that some day, somewhere, he would be reunited with his luggage again.

Tonight at Lincoln International – though no one knew it yet – the baggage for Flight Two was already incomplete. Two bags, which should have gone to Rome, were at this moment being loaded aboard a flight for Milwaukee.

Freight was now going aboard Flight Two in a steady stream. So was mail. Tonight there were nine thousand pounds of mail in coloured nylon bags, some for Italian cities – Milan, Palermo, Vatican City, Pisa, Naples, Rome; other for onward transmission to faraway places, whose names read like pages from Marco Polo . . . Zanzibar, Khartoum, Mombasa, Jerusalem, Athens, Rhodes, Calcutta . . .

The heavier-than-usual mail load was a bonus for Trans America. A flight of British Overseas Airways Corporation, scheduled to leave shortly before Trans America Flight Two, had just announced a three-hour delay. The post office ramp supervisor, who kept constant watch on schedules and delays, promptly ordered a switch of mail from the BOAC airliner to Trans America. The British airline would be unhappy because carriage of mail was highly profitable, and competition for post office business keen. All airlines kept uniformed representatives at airport post offices, their job to keep an eye on the flow of mail and ensure that their own airline got a 'fair share' – or more – of the outgoing volume. Post office supervisors sometimes had favourites among the airline men, and saw to it that business came their way. But in cases of delay, friendships didn't count. At such moments there was an inflexible rule: the mail went by the fastest route.

Inside the terminal, at lower level, and a few hundred feet from the Boeing 707 aircraft which was now Flight Two, was Trans America Control Centre (Lincoln International). The centre was a bustling, jam-packed, noisy conglomeration of people, desks, telephones, teletypes, Tel-Autographs, private-line TV, and information boards. Its personnel were responsible for directing the preparation of Flight Two and all other Trans America flights. On occasions like tonight, with schedules chaotic because of the storm, the atmosphere was pandemonic, the scene resembling an old-time newspaper city room, as seen by Hollywood.

In a corner of the control centre was the Load Control Desk – the desk top invisible beneath a sea of paper – occupied by a young, bearded man with the improbable name of Fred Phirmphoot. In his spare time Phirmphoot was an amateur abstract painter; recently he had taken to throwing paint on canvas, then riding over it with a child's tricycle. He was reputed to dabble – at weekends – with LSD, and also suffered from body odour. The last was a constant annoyance to his fellow workers in the control centre – hot and stuffy tonight, despite the cold, bitter weather outside – and more than once Fred Phirmphoot had been told that he should take a bath more often.

Yet, paradoxically, Phirmphoot had a keen mathematician's mind, and his superiors swore that he was one of the best load control men in the business. At the moment he was masterminding the loading of Flight Two.

An aeroplane (Fred Phirmphoot would occasionally explain to his bored beat friends), 'She's a bird that's a teeter-totter, man. If you ain't hep, that aeroplane chick'll teeter or totter, maybe the twain; but me, baby, I don't let it none.'

The trick was to distribute the weight correctly through the aeroplane so that its fulcrum point and centre of gravity were at predetermined places; hence the aircraft would be balanced, and stable in the air. Fred Phirmphoot's job was to calculate how much could be stowed aboard Flight Two (and other flights) and where. No mailbag, no individual piece of freight, went into any position in the aircraft hold without his say-so. At the same time, he was concerned with cramming in as much as possible. 'Illinois to Rome, man,' Fred was apt to declare, 'That's long spaghetti. It don't pay off in marmalade.'

He worked with charts, manifests, tabulations, an adding machine, last-minute messages, a walkie-talkie, three telephones – and an uncanny instinct.

The ramp supervisor had just asked, by walkie-talkie, for permission to load another three hundred pounds of mail in the forward compartment.

'Roger-dodger,' Fred Phirmphoot acknowledged. He shuffled papers, checking the passenger manifest which had lengthened in the past two hours. Airlines allowed an average weight for passengers – a hundred and seventy pounds in winter, ten pounds less in summer. The average always worked out, with one exception: when a football team was travelling. The husky ballplayers threw all calculations out of joint, and at the time load dispatchers added their own estimates, which varied according to how well they knew the team. Baseball and hockey players were no problem; being smaller they fitted the average. Tonight the manifest showed that Flight Two had only normal passengers.

'It's okay for the mail, baby,' Fred Phirmphoot replied into the walkie-talkie, 'but I want that coffin moved back to the rear compartment; from the look of the weight slip, that dead guy was a fatso. Also, there's a packaged generator from Westinghouse. Locate that midships; the rest of the freight can fit about it.'

Phirmphoot's problems had just been added to by an order from the crew of Flight Two that an extra two thousand pounds of fuel were to be added for taxiing and ground running, in addition to the normal reserve for that purpose. Out on the airfield tonight, all aircraft were being subjected to long delays, with engines running, before takeoff. A jet engine, operating at ground level, drank fuel like a thirsty elephant, and Captains Demerest and Harris didn't want to waste precious gallonage which they might require on the way to Rome. At the same time, Fred Phirmphoot had to calculate that all that extra fuel, which was now being pumped into the wing tanks of NC-731-TA, might not be burned before takeoff; therefore, some of it could be added to the total takeoff weight. The question was, how much?

There were safety limits for gross weights at takeoff, yet with every airline flight the objective was to carry as much as possible, to earn maximum revenue. Fred Phirmphoot's dirty fingernails danced over his adding machine, making hasty computations. He pondered the result, fingering his beard, his body odour rather worse than usual.

The decision about extra fuel was one of the many decisions which Captain Vernon Demerest had been making for the past half-hour. Or rather, he had been letting Captain Anson Harris make the decisions, then – as check captain with the final responsibility – Demerest approved them. Vernon Demerest was enjoying his passive role tonight – having someone else do most of the work, yet relinquishing none of his own authority. So far Demerest had not faulted any of Anson Harris's decisions, which was not surprising since Harris's experience and seniority were almost as great as Demerest's own.

Harris had been dour and huffy when they met for the second time tonight in the crew room at the Trans America hangar. Demerest noted with amusement that Anson Harris was wearing a regulation shirt, though it was on the small side, and every now and then Harris's hand would go up to ease the collar. Captain Harris had managed to switch shirts with an obliging first officer who later related the story zestfully to his own captain.

But after a few minutes, Harris relaxed. A professional to his bushy, greying eyebrows, he was aware that no flight crew could function efficiently with hostility in the cockpit.

In the crew room both captains inspected their mail slots, and there was a pile of mail as usual, some of it company bulletins which must be read before tonight's flight. The remainder – memos from the chief pilot, medical branch, the research department, cartographer's office, and the rest, they would take home to go through later.

While Anson Harris inserted a couple of amendments in his flight manuals – which Demerest had announced his intention of checking – Vernon Demerest studied the Crew Schedule Board.

The Schedule Board was made up monthly. It showed the dates on which captains and first and second officers would fly, and on which routes. There was a similar board for stewardesses in their crew room down the hall.

Every pilot bid, each month, for the route he wanted to fly, and those who were most senior got first choice. Demerest invariably got what he bid for; so did Gwen Meighen, whose seniority among the stewardesses was correspondingly high. It was the bidding system which made it possible for pilots and stewardesses to make mutual layover plans much as Demerest and Gwen had done in advance of tonight.

Anson Harris had finished the hasty amending of his flight manuals.

Vernon Demerest grinned. 'I guess your manuals are okay, Anson. I've changed my mind; I won't inspect them.'

Captain Harris gave no sign, except a tightening around his mouth.

The second officer for the flight, a young two-striper named Cy Jordan, had joined them. Jordan was flight engineer; also a qualified pilot. He was lean and angular, with a hollow-cheeked, mournful face, and always looked as if he needed a good meal. Stewardesses heaped extra food upon him, but it never seemed to make any difference.

The first officer who usually flew as second-in-command to Demerest, tonight had been told to stay home, though under his union contract he would receive full pay for the round-trip flight. In the first officer's absence, Demerest would do some of the first officer duties, Jordan the rest. Anson Harris would do most of the flying.

'Okay,' Demerest told the other two, 'let's get moving.'

The crew bus, snow-covered, its windows steamed inside, was waiting at the hangar door. The five stewardesses for Flight Two were already in the bus, and there was a chorus of 'Good evening, Captain . . . good evening, Captain,' as Demerest and Anson Harris clambered in, followed by Jordan. A gust of wind, and snow flurries, accompanied the pilots. The bus driver hastily closed the door.

'Hi, girls!' Vernon Demerest waved cheerfully, and winked at Gwen. More conventionally, Anson Harris added a 'Good evening.'

The wind buffeted the bus as the driver felt his way warily around the ploughed perimeter track, the snowbanks high on either side. Word had filtered around the airport of the experience of the United Air Lines food truck earlier in the evening, and all vehicle drivers were being cautious as a result. As the crew bus neared its destination, the bright terminal lights were a beacon in the darkness. Farther out on the airfield a steady stream of aircraft was taking off and landing.

The bus stopped and the crew scrambled out, diving for the shelter of the nearest door. They were now in the Trans America wing of the terminal, at lower level. The passenger departure gates – including gate forty-seven, where Flight Two was being readied – were above.

The stewardesses went off to complete their own pre-flight procedures while the three pilots headed for the Trans America international dispatch office.

The dispatcher, as always, had prepared a folder with the complex information which the flight crew would need. He spread it out on the dispatch office counter and the three pilots pored over it. Behind the counter a half-dozen clerks were assembling world-wide information on airways, airport conditions, and weather which other international flights of Trans America would require tonight. A similar dispatch room for domestic flights was down the hall.

It was at that point that Anson Harris tapped a preliminary load report with his pipestem and asked for the extra two thousand pounds of fuel for taxiing. He glanced at the second officer, Jordan, who was checking fuel consumption graphs, and Demerest. Both nodded agreement, and the dispatcher scribbled an order which would be relayed to the ramp fuelling office.

The company weather forecaster joined the other four. He was a pale young man, scholarly behind rimless glasses, who looked as if he rarely ventured out into the weather personally.

Demerest inquired, 'What have the computers given us tonight, John? Something better than here, I hope.'

More and more, airline weather forecasts and flight plans were being spewed out by computers. Trans America and other airlines still maintained a personal element, with individuals liaising between computers and flight crews, but predictions were that the human weathermen would disappear soon.

The forecaster shook his head as he spread out several facsimile weather charts. 'Nothing better until you're over mid-Atlantic, I'm afraid. We have some improved weather coming in here soon, but since you're going east you'll catch up with what's already left us. The storm we're in now extends all the way from here to Newfoundland, and beyond.' He used a pencil point to trace the storm's wide swathe. 'Along your route, incidentally, Detroit Metropolitan and Toronto airports are both below limits and have closed down.'

The dispatcher scanned a teletype slip which a clerk had handed him. He interjected, 'Add Ottawa; they're closing right now.'

'Beyond mid-Atlantic,' the weatherman said, 'everything looks good. There are scattered disturbances across southern Europe, as you can see, but at your altitudes they shouldn't bother you. Rome is clear and sunny, and should stay that way for several days.'

Captain Demerest leaned over the southern Europe map. 'How about Naples?'

The weatherman looked puzzled. 'Your flight doesn't go there.'

'No, but I'm interested.'

'It's in the same high pressure system as Rome. The weather will be good.'

Demerest grinned.

The young forecaster launched into a dissertation concerning temperatures, and high and low pressure areas, and winds aloft. For the portion of the flight which would be over Canada he recommended a more northerly course than usual to avoid strong headwinds which would be encountered farther south. The pilots listened attentively. Whether by computer or human calculation, choosing the best altitudes and route was like a game of chess in which intellect could triumph over nature. All pilots were trained in such matters; so were company weather forecasters, more attuned to individual airline needs than their counterparts in the US Weather Bureau.

'As soon as your fuel load permits,' the Trans America forecaster said, 'I'd recommend an altitude of thirty-three thousand feet.'

The second officer checked his graphs; before N-731-TA could climb that high, they would have to burn off some of their initially heavy fuel load.

After a few moments the second officer reported, 'We should be able to reach thirty-three thousand around Detroit.'

Anson Harris nodded. His gold ballpoint pen was racing as he filled in a flight plan which, in a few minutes' time, he would file with air traffic control. ATC would then tell him whether or not the altitudes he sought were available and, if not, what others he might have. Vernon Demerest, who normally would have prepared his own flight plan, glanced over the form when Captain Harris finished, then signed it.

All preparations for Flight Two, it seemed, were going well. Despite the storm, it appeared as if *The Golden Argosy*, pride of Trans America, would depart on time.

It was Gwen Meighen who met the three pilots as they came aboard the aircraft. She asked, 'Did you hear?'

Anson Harris said, 'Hear what?'

'We're delayed an hour. The gate agent just had word.'

'Damn!' Vernon Demerest said. 'Goddam.'

'Apparently,' Gwen said, 'a lot of passengers are on their way, but have been held up – I guess because of the snow. Some have phoned in, and Departure Control decided to allow them extra time.'

Anson Harris asked, 'Is boarding being delayed too?'

'Yes, Captain. The flight hasn't been announced. It won't be for another half-hour, at least.'

Harris shrugged. 'Oh, well; we might as well relax.' He moved towards the flight deck.

Gwen volunteered, 'I can bring you all coffee, if you like.'

'I'll get coffee in the terminal,' Vernon Demerest said. He nodded to Gwen. 'Why don't you come with me?'

She hesitated. 'Well, I could.'

'Go ahead,' Harris said. 'One of the other girls can bring mine, and there's plenty of time.'

A minute or two later, Gwen walked beside Vernon Demerest, her heels clicking as she kept pace with his strides down the Trans America departure wing. They were heading for the main terminal concourse.

Demerest was thinking: the hour's delay might not be a bad thing after all. Until this moment, with the essential business of Flight Two to think about, he had pushed all thoughts of Gwen's pregnancy from his mind. But, over coffee and a cigarette, there would be a chance to continue the discussion they had begun earlier. Perhaps, now, the subject which he had not broached before – an abortion – could be brought into the open.

8

Nervously, D.O. Guerrero lit another cigarette from the stub of his previous one. Despite his efforts to control the motion of his hands, they trembled visibly. He was agitated, tense, anxious. As he had earlier, while putting his dynamite bomb together, he could feel rivulets of perspiration on his face and beneath his shirt.

The cause of his distress was time – the time remaining between now and the departure of Flight Two. It was running out, remorselessly, like sand from an hourglass; and much – too much – of the sand was gone.

Guerrero was in a bus en route to the airport. Half an hour ago the bus had entered the Kennedy Expressway, from which point, normally, there would have been a swift, fifteen-minute ride to Lincoln International. But the expressway, like every other highway in the state, was impeded by the storm, and jammed with traffic. At moments the traffic was halted, at other times merely inching along.

Before departure from downtown, the dozen or so bus passengers – all destined for Flight Two – had been told of their flight's delay by one hour. Even so, at the present rate of progress, it appeared as if it might take another two hours, perhaps three, to get to the airport.

Others in the bus were worried too.

Like D.O. Guerrero, they had checked in at the Trans America downtown terminal in the Loop. Then, they had been in plenty of time, but now, in view of the mounting delay, were wondering aloud whether Flight Two would wait for them indefinitely, or not.

The bus driver was not encouraging. In reply to questions he declared that usually, if a bus from downtown terminal was late, a flight was held until the bus arrived. But when conditions got really bad, like tonight, anything could happen. The airline might figure that the bus would be held up for hours more – as it could be – and that the flight should go. Also, the driver added, judging by the few people in the bus, it looked as if most passengers for Flight Two were out at the airport already. That often happened with international flights, he explained; relatives came to see passengers off, and drove them out by car.

The discussion went back and forth across the bus, though D.O. Guerrero, his spindly body hunched into his seat, took no part in it. Most of the other passengers appeared to be tourists, with the exception of a voluble Italian family – a man and woman with several children – who were talking animatedly in their own language.

'If I were you, folks, I wouldn't worry,' the bus driver had announced a few minutes earlier. 'The traffic ahead looks as if it's loosenin' up some. We might just make it.'

So far, however, the speed of the bus had not increased.

D.O. Guerrero had a double seat section, three rows back from the driver, to himself. The all-important attaché case was held securely on his lap. He eased forward, as he had done several times already, straining to peer ahead into the darkness beyond the bus; all he could see, through the twin arcs cleared by the big, slapping windshield wipers, was what appeared to be an endless string of vehicle lights, disappearing into the falling snow. Despite his sweating, his pale, thin lips were dry; he moistened them with his tongue.

For Guerrero, 'just making it' to the airport in time for Flight Two would simply not do. He needed an extra ten or fifteen minutes, at least, to buy flight insurance. He cursed himself for not having gone out to the airport sooner, and bought the flight insurance he needed in plenty of time. In his original plan, purchasing the insurance at the last minute, and thus minimizing any chance of inquiry, seemed a good idea. What he had not foreseen was the kind of night this had turned out to be – though he ought to have foreseen it, remembering the time of year. It was just that kind of thing – overlooking some significant, variable factor – which had dogged D.O. Guerrero through his business enterprises, and time after time brought grandiose schemes to naught. The trouble was, he realized, whenever he made plans, he convinced himself that everything would go exactly as he hoped; therefore he failed to allow for the unexpected. More to the point, he thought bitterly, he never seemed able to learn from past experience.

He supposed that when he got to the airport – assuming Flight Two had not already left – he could go to the Trans America flight counter and announce himself as being present. Then he would insist on being allowed time to buy flight insurance before the flight took off. But it would involve the one thing he desperately wanted to avoid: drawing attention to himself, in the same way that he had drawn attention already – and for the stupidest omission he could possible have made.

He had failed to bring any baggage, other than the small, slim attaché case in which he was carrying the dynamite bomb.

At the check-in counter downtown the ticket agent had asked, 'Is that your baggage, sir?' He pointed to a large pile of suitcases belonging to a man in line behind.

'No,' D.O. Guerrero hesitated, then held up the small attaché-briefcase. 'I . . . er . . . don't have anything except this.'

The agent's eyebrows went up. 'No baggage for a trip to Rome, sir? You really are travelling light.' He motioned to the attaché case. 'Do you wish to check that?'

'No, thank you.' All D.O. Guerrero wanted at that moment was his airline ticket, and to get away from that counter, and secure an inconspicuous seat on the airport bus. But the agent glanced curiously at him a second time, and Guerrero knew that, from this moment onwards, he would be remembered. He had stamped himself indelibly on the ticket agent's memory – all because he forgot to bring a suitcase, which he could so easily have done. Of course the reason he had not done so was instinctive. D.O. Guerrero knew – as others did not – that Flight Two would never reach its destination; therefore no baggage was necessary. But he *ought* to have had baggage, as a cover. Now, at the inquiry which would inevitably follow the flight's loss, the fact that one passenger – himself – had boarded without baggage, would be remembered and commented on. It would underscore whatever other suspicions about D.O. Guerrero investigators might, by that time, have.

But if there were no wreckage, he reminded himself, *what could they prove?*

Nothing! The flight insurance people would have to pay.

The children from the Italian family were running noisily up and down the aisle of the bus. A few seats back the mother was still jabbering in Italian to the husband; she held a baby which was crying lustily. Neither the woman nor the man seemed aware of the baby's crying.

Guerrero's nerves were stretched and raw. He wanted to seize the baby and throttle it; to shout to the others, *Shut up! Shut up!*

Couldn't they sense? . . . Didn't the fools know that this was no time for stupid chattering? . . . No time, when Guerrero's whole future – at least, his family's future . . . the success of the plan so painstakingly worked out . . . everything, *everything*, was predicated on getting to the airport with time to spare.

One of the running children – a boy of five or six, with an attractive, intelligent face – stumbled in the aisle and fell sideways into the empty seat beside D.O. Guerrero. In regaining his balance, the boy's hand went out, striking the attaché case still on Guerrero's lap. The case slipped sideways and Guerrero grabbed it. He managed to stop it before it fell, then turned to the child, his face contorted to a snarl, his hand raised to strike.

Wide-eyed, the boy regarded him. He said softly, *'Scusi.'*

With an effort, Guerrero controlled himself. Others in the bus might be watching. If he were not careful, he would draw attention to himself again. Groping for some of the words he had picked up from Italians who had worked for him on construction projects, he said awkwardly, *'E troppo rumorosa.'*

The child nodded gravely. *'Sì.'* He stood where he was.

'All right,' Guerrero said. 'That's all. Get lost! *Se ne vada!*'

'Sì,' the boy said again. His eyes were uncomfortably direct, and for a moment Guerrero was reminded that this child, and others, would be aboard Flight Two. Well, it made no difference. There was no point in becoming sentimental; nothing would change his intentions now. Besides, when it happened, when he pulled the string of the attaché case and the aeroplane ripped apart, everything would be over quickly, before anyone – especially the children – had time to know.

The boy turned away, and went back in the bus to his mother.

At last! – the bus was moving faster . . . now it was speeding up! Ahead, through the windshield, D.O. Guerrero could see that the traffic had thinned, other lights in front were moving quickly. They might . . . just might . . . arrive at the airport in time for him to buy flight insurance without any need to arouse attention. But it was going to be close. He hoped the insurance booth would not be busy.

He noticed that the children from the Italian family had returned to their seats, and he congratulated himself about not attracting attention a moment ago. If he had struck the child – as he almost had – people would have made a fuss. At least he had avoided that. It was still a pity that he had got himself noticed when checking in, though when he thought about it, he supposed that no irreparable harm had been done.

Or had it?

A new worry nagged him.

Supposing the ticket agent who had been curious about the absence of any baggage remembered the incident again, after the bus had gone. Guerrero knew he had appeared nervous at the time; supposing the agent had noticed, had later become suspicious. The agent would talk to someone else, a supervisor perhaps, who might already have telephoned the airport. Even at this moment, someone – the police? – might be waiting for the bus to arrive; to interrogate D.O. Guerrero; to open and inspect his single small attaché case, with the damning evidence inside. For the first time Guerrero wondered what would happen if he were caught. It would mean arrest, imprisonment. Then he thought: before he would allow that to happen . . . if he were accosted, if exposure seemed imminent . . . he would pull the loop of string on the outside of the case and blow himself, along with everyone nearby, to pieces. His hand went out. Beneath the attaché case handle he touched the loop of string and held it. It was reassuring . . . Now, for the moment, he would try to think of something else.

He wondered if Inez had yet found his note.

She had.

Inez Guerrero came tiredly into the miserable 51st Street apartment, and slipped off her shoes, which had been hurting, and her coat and kerchief, which were soaked from melted snow. She was aware of a cold coming, and an all-engulfing weariness. Her work as a waitress had been harder than usual today, the customers meaner, the tips smaller. Besides, she was not yet accustomed to it, which took a greater toll.

Two years ago, when the Guerreros lived comfortably in a congenial home in the suburbs, Inez, though never beautiful, had been a pleasant-appearing, well-preserved woman. Since then, ravages of time and circumstance had come swiftly to her face, so that where once she seemed younger than she was, now she looked considerably older. Tonight, if Inez had been in a house of her own, she would have sought the solace of a hot bath, which always seemed to relax her in times of trouble – of which there had been plenty in the Guerreros' married life. Although there was a bathroom of sorts down the hall, which three apartments shared, it was unheated and draughty, with old paint peeling, and a gas water heater which had to be appeased with quarters. The thought of it defeated her. She decided she would sit still for a while in the shabby living room, then go to bed. She had no idea where her husband was.

It was some time before she noticed the note on the living-room table.

I won't be home for a few days. I'm going away. I expect to have some good news soon which will surprise you.

Few things surprised Inez where her husband was concerned; he had always been unpredictable, and more recently, irrational. Good news would certainly be a surprise, but she couldn't bring herself to believe that there would be any. Inez had watched too many of her husband's ambitious schemes totter and collapse to believe in the likelihood of one more possibility succeeding.

But the first part of the note puzzled her. Where was D.O. going 'for a few days'? Equally mystifying: What did he intend to use for money? The night before last the Guerreros pooled the last of the money they had in the world. The total was twenty-two dollars and some cents. Besides the money, they had only one thing left worth pawning; it belonged to Inez – her mother's ring, and so far she had resisted parting with it. It might have to go soon.

Of the twenty-two dollars-odd, Inez had taken fourteen, to use for food and as a token payment towards the rent. She had seen the desperation in D.O.'s face as he pocketed the remaining eight dollars and small change.

Inez decided to stop puzzling, and to go to bed as she had planned. She was too weary even to worry about how her children were faring, though she had not heard from her sister in Cleveland – with whom the children were staying – for more than a week. She turned out the single light in the living room and went into the cramped, shabby bedroom.

She had trouble finding her nightgown. Some of the contents of the rickety dressing chest seemed to have been moved around. Eventually she found the nightgown in a drawer with the three of D.O.'s shirts; they were the last he had, so wherever he had gone, he had not taken a change of clothing. Under one of the shirts a folded sheet of yellow paper caught her eye. She took it out and opened it.

The yellow sheet was a printed form which had been filled in by typewriter; what Inez was holding was a carbon copy. When she saw what it was, she sat down, unbelieving, on the bed. To make sure she had not misunderstood, she read the contents of the form again.

It was a time-payment contract between Trans America Airlines and D.O. 'Buerrero' – the name, she noticed, was misspelled. The contract acknowledged that 'Buerrero' had received a round-trip ticket to Rome, economy class; that he had made a down payment of forty-seven dollars, and hereby promised to pay the balance of four hundred and twenty-seven dollars, plus interest, in instalments over twenty-four months.

It didn't make sense.

Inez stared dazedly at the yellow form. Within her mind, questions chased one another. Why did D.O. need an air ticket at all? And if a ticket, why to Rome? And what about the money? He couldn't possibly pay the instalments, though that part, at least, was understandable. There had been plenty of other obligations D.O. Guerrero incurred that he couldn't meet; debts never disturbed him, as they did Inez. But apart from the debt, where had the forty-seven dollars down payment come from? The form acknowledged receipt; the money had been paid. Yet two nights ago, D.O. declared that he had no more money than they pooled, and whatever else he might do, Inez knew he never lied to her.

Yet that forty-seven dollars came from somewhere. Where?

Suddenly, she remembered the ring; it was gold with a single diamond in a platinum setting. Until a week or two ago, Inez wore it regularly, but recently her hands had swollen and she took the ring off, leaving it in a small box in one of the bedroom drawers. For the second time tonight she searched the drawers. The box was there – empty. Obviously, to get the forty-seven dollars, D.O had pawned the ring.

Her first reaction was regret. To Inez, the ring had meant something; it was a last tenuous link between herself and the past, her scattered family, her dead mother whose memory she revered. More realistically: the ring, though not exceptionally valuable, had been a last resort. While it was there, there was the knowledge that however bad things became, the ring would always provide a few days more of living. Now it was gone, and along with it, the minor reassurance.

Yet knowing where the down payment came from for the airline ticket still provided no answer to the question – why? Why an air journey? Why to Rome?

Still seated on the bed, Inez applied herself to thinking carefully. For the moment, she ignored her tiredness.

Inez was not a highly intelligent woman. If she had been, probably she would not have endured marriage to D.O. Guerrero for almost twenty years; and even now, if better equipped mentally, she would have been more than a coffee-house waitress at a paltry wage. But occasionally, through slow, careful reasoning aided by instinct, Inez could reach right conclusions. Especially where her husband was concerned.

Now, instinct more than reason warned her that D.O. Guerrero was in trouble – more serious trouble than they had yet encountered. Two things convinced her: his irrationality of late, and the length of his intended journey; in the Guerreros' present circumstances, only some monumental, desperate undertaking could require a trip to Rome. She went to the living room and returned with the note, which she read again. Over the years there had been many notes; Inez sensed that this one did not mean what it said.

Beyond that, her reasoning failed to go. But she had the feeling, a conviction growing as each minute passed, that there must be something, *ought* to be something, she should do.

It did not occur to Inez to abdicate entirely, to abandon D.O. to the outcome of whatever new folly he might have begun. She was essentially a simple soul with an uncomplicated nature. Eighteen years ago she accepted D.O. Guerrero 'for better or worse'. That it had turned out to be mostly 'worse' did not, as Inez saw it, change her responsibility as a wife.

Her cautious, measured reasoning continued. She supposed the first thing to do was find out if D.O. had already left by air; if not, perhaps there was time to stop him. Inez had no idea how much of a start D.O. had, or how many hours ago his note to her was written. She looked again at the yellow time-payment form; it said nothing about when the flight would be, or its departure time, though she could telephone the airline – Trans America. As quickly as she could, Inez began putting on the clothes, which, a few minutes earlier, she had taken off.

Her outdoor shoes hurt her feet again, and her coat was still sodden and uncomfortable as she went down the narrow stairs from the apartment to the street. In the mean lower hallway, snow had blown under the outer door and covered the bare boards of the floor. Outside, Inez saw, the snow was even deeper than when she came in. The cold, bleak wind assaulted her as she left the building's shelter, whipping more snow into her face.

There was no telephone in the Guerreros' apartment, and although Inez could have used a pay phone in the lunch counter on the lower floor, she wanted to avoid a meeting with the proprietor, who was also the building landlord. He had threatened eviction tomorrow if the Guerreros' arrears of rent were not paid in full. That was something else which Inez had pushed from her mind tonight, and which – if D.O. failed to return by morning – she would have to face alone.

A drugstore, with a pay phone, was a block and a half away. Picking her way through deep snow on uncleared sidewalks, Inez headed there.

The time was a quarter to ten.

The drugstore telephone was in use by two teenage girls, and Inez waited almost ten minutes for it to be free. Then, when she dialled the Trans America number, a recording informed her that all lines to Reservations were busy, and would she please wait. She waited while the recording repeated itself several times before a brisk woman's voice declared that she was Miss Young, and could she help?

'Please,' Inez said, 'I want to ask about flights to Rome.'

As if a button had been pressed, Miss Young replied that Trans America had direct non-stop flights from Lincoln International to Rome on Tuesdays and Fridays; through New York there were connections daily, and did the caller wish to make a reservation now?

'No,' Inez said. 'No, I'm not going. It's about my husband. Did you say there was one on Fridays . . . a flight . . . tonight?'

'Yes, madam – our Flight Two, *The Golden Argosy*. It departs at ten o'clock local time, except that tonight the flight has been delayed one hour, due to weather conditions.'

Inez could see the drugstore clock. By now, it was nearly five past ten.

She said quickly, 'You mean the flight hasn't gone yet?'

'No, madam, not yet.'

'Please . . .' As she often did, Inez found herself groping for words. 'Please, it's important for me to find out if my husband is on that flight. His name is D.O. Guerrero, and . . .'

'I'm sorry; we're not permitted to give out that information.' Miss Young was polite but firm.

'I don't think you understand, miss. It's my husband I'm asking about. This is his wife.'

'I do understand, Mrs Guerrero, and I'm sorry; but it's a company rule.'

Miss Young, and others like her, were well drilled in the rule and understood its reason. Many businessmen took secretaries or mistresses along on air trips, listing them as wives, to take advantage of family plan fare reductions. In the past, a few suspicious, genuine wives had checked up, causing trouble for the airlines' customers – the men. Later, it was the men who complained bitterly about breaches of confidence, with the result that airlines nowadays made a policy of not disclosing passenger names.

Inez began, 'Isn't there any way . . .'

'There really isn't.'

'Oh, dear.'

'Do I understand,' Miss Young inquired, 'that you think your husband might be leaving on Flight Two, but you're not sure?'

'Yes, that's right.'

'Then the only thing you might do, Mrs Guerrero, is to go out to the airport. Probably the flight hasn't boarded yet; so if your husband is there, you could see him. Even if the flight has boarded, they might help you at the departure gate. But you'd have to hurry.'

'All right,' Inez said. 'If that's the only thing, I suppose I'd better try.' She had no idea how she would get to the airport – more than twenty miles away – in less than an hour, in the storm.

'Just a moment.' Miss Young sounded hesitant, her voice more human, as if some of Inez's distress had penetrated through the phones. 'I really shouldn't do this, Mrs Guerrero, but I'll give you a little tip.'

'Please.'

'At the airport, when you get to the departure gate, don't say you *think* your husband is aboard. Say you know he's aboard and you'd like to speak to him. If he isn't, you'll find out. If he is, it will make it easier for the gate agent to tell you what you want to know.'

'Thank you,' Inez said. 'Thank you very much.'

'You're entirely welcome, madam.' Miss Young was her machine-like self once more. 'Goodnight, and thank you for calling Trans America.'

Replacing the telephone, Inez remembered something she had noticed coming in. A taxi was parked outside; now she saw the driver. In a yellow, peaked cap, he was at the drug-store soda fountain, in conversation with another man.

A taxi would be costly, but if she was to get to the airport by 11.0 pm, it was probably the only means.

Inez crossed to the soda fountain and touched the driver on the arm. 'Excuse me.'

The cab driver turned. 'Yeah, waddya want?' He had a mean, flabby face, and needed a shave.

'I was wondering how much it would cost for a taxi to the airport.'

The driver inspected her through narrow, calculating eyes. 'From here, maybe nine, ten dollars on the meter.'

Inez turned away. It was too much – more than half the small amount of money she had remaining; and she was not even sure that D.O. would be on the flight.

'Hey, you! Hold it!' The cabbie downed a Coke he had been drinking and hurried after Inez. He caught her at the door. 'How much dough ya got?'

'It isn't that.' Inez shook her head. 'It's just . . . it's more than I can afford.'

The cabbie snorted, 'Summa you people think ya can get them kinda rides for peanuts. 'S long drag out there.'

'Yes, I know.'

'Why you wanna go? Whyn't yer get th'bus?'

'It's important; I have to be there . . . ought to be there . . . by eleven o'clock.'

'Here,' the cab driver said, 'maybe it's bargain night. I'll take yer for seven, even.'

'Well . . .' Inez still hesitated. Seven dollars was most of what she had planned to offer the apartment landlord tomorrow in an attempt to appease him about the arrears of rent. She would have no wages from the coffee house until the end of next week.

The cab driver said impatiently, ''S th' best offer you'll get. You wanna take it, or not?'

'Yes,' Inez said. 'Yes, I'll take it.'

'Okay, lessgo.'

While Inez climbed into the cab unaided, the driver smirked as he used a whisk broom to clear snow from the windshield and windows. When Inez approached him in the drugstore, he was already off duty and, since he lived near the airport, was about to deadhead home. Now, he had a fare. Also, he lied in declaring the meter fare to the airport to be nine or ten dollars; it was actually less than seven. But the lie made it possible to concoct what his passenger believed to be a deal, so now he could drive with his flag up, and pocket the seven dollars for himself. High-flagging was illegal, but no cop, the driver reasoned, would be likely to spot him on a lousy night like this.

Thus, the cab driver thought smugly, in a single move he had managed to cheat both this stupid old crone of a passenger and his son-of-a-bitch employer.

As they moved off, Inez asked anxiously, 'Are you sure you can get there by eleven o'clock?'

Over his shoulder the driver snarled, 'I said so, didn't I, so lemme do the drivin'.'

Just the same, he conceded to himself, he was not certain that they would. The roads were bad, the other traffic slow. They might just make it, but it was going to be close.

Thirty-five minutes later, the taxi containing Inez was crawling tediously along the snowbound, still-plugged Kennedy Expressway. Sitting tensely on the back seat, her fingers working nervously, Inez was wondering how much longer the journey would take.

At the same moment, the airport bus containing the contingent of Flight Two passengers swung on to the departure ramp entrance at Lincoln International. The bus, after shaking itself free from the slow-moving traffic nearer town, had continued to make good time; now, the clock above the terminal showed a quarter to eleven.

As the bus stopped, D.O. Guerrero was first to alight.

9

'Bring along that portable public address system,' Elliott Freemantle commanded. 'We might be glad of it.'

The Meadowood community meeting in the Sunday school hall of Meadowood First Baptist Church was sizzling with excitement which Lawyer Freemantle had skilfully generated. The meeting was also about to move on to Lincoln International Airport.

'Don't hand me any bilgewater about it being too late, or not wanting to go,' Elliott Freemantle had exhorted his audience of six hundred a few minutes earlier. He stood before them confidently, impeccable as ever in his elegant Blue Spruce suit and gleaming alligator shoes; not a single barber-styled hair was out of place, and he radiated confidence. The meeting was enthusiastically with him now, and the rougher tongued he was, it seemed, the more they liked him.

He continued, 'And don't let's have a lot of footling excuses for not going. I don't want to hear about baby-sitters, mother-in-law left alone, or stews on the stove simmering, because I couldn't care less; neither – at this moment – should you. If your car's stuck in the snow, leave it there and ride in someone else's. The point is: I'm going to the airport tonight, on your behalf, to make myself obnoxious.' He paused as another aircraft thundered overhead. 'By God! – it's time somebody did.' The last remark had caused applause and laughter.

'I need your support, and I want you there – all of you. Now I'll ask you a plain, straight question: Are you coming?'

The hall resounded to a roar of 'Yes!' People were on their feet, cheering.

'All right,' Freemantle said, and the hall had hushed. 'Let's get a few things clear before we go.'

He had already told them, he pointed out, that legal proceedings must be the basis of any action to gain relief for Meadowood community from its overwhelming airport noise. Such legal proceedings, however, should not be the kind which nobody noticed, or which took place in some out-of-the-way, unpeopled courtroom. Instead, they must be conducted in the spotlight of public attention and public sympathy.

'How do we get that kind of attention and sympathy?' Lawyer Freemantle paused, then answered his own question.

'We get it by making our point of view known in such a way that it becomes newsworthy. Then, and only then, can the attention-getting media – press, radio, and television – feature our viewpoint prominently, in the kind of way we want.'

The press were good friends, he declared. 'We do not ask them to share our point of view, merely to report it fairly, which – in my experience – they always do. But it helps our reporter friends if a cause can engender some drama; that way, they get a better story.'

The three reporters at the press table were grinning as Freemantle added, 'We'll see if we can stage some drama for them tonight.'

While Elliott Freemantle was speaking, he was also observing shrewdly the progress of the legal forms, retaining himself as legal counsel for individual homeowners, which were now circulating through the hall. Many of the forms – at least a hundred, he estimated – had been signed and passed forward. He had watched ballpoint pens appear, husbands and wives bend over the documents to sign jointly, thus committing each family to payment of a hundred dollars. Lawyer Freemantle did some happy calculation: a hundred completed retainers meant ten thousand dollars for himself. Not a bad fee for – so far – an evening's work, and in the end the total fee would be a great deal more.

While the forms were still circulating, he decided, he would continue talking for a few minutes longer.

As to what was going to happen at the airport tonight, he instructed his listeners, they were to leave that to him. He hoped there would be a confrontation with the airport's management; in any case, he intended to stage a demonstration – within the airport terminal – which people would remember.

'All I ask is that you stay together and that you raise your voices only when I tell you.'

Emphatically, he cautioned, there would be no disorder. No one must be able to say next day that the Meadowood anti-noise delegation violated any law.

'Of course' – Freemantle smiled suggestively – 'we may get in the way and cause some inconvenience; I understand that the airport is extremely busy tonight. But we can't help that.'

There was laughter again. He sensed that people were ready to go.

Still another aircraft reverberated overhead, and he waited until the sound had died.

'Very well! let us be on our way!' Lawyer Freemantle raised his hands like a jet-age Moses, and misquoted: 'For I have promises to keep, with much ado before I sleep.'

The laughter changed to renewed cheering, and people began moving towards the doors.

It was then that he had noticed the portable p.a. system, borrowed from the Meadowood First Baptist Church, and instructed that it be brought along. Floyd Zanetta, the meeting's chairman – virtually ignored since Elliott Freemantle eclipsed him in attention – hurried to comply.

Freemantle himself was stuffing signed retainer forms into his briefcase. A quick count showed that he had underestimated earlier – there were over a hundred and sixty forms, or more than sixteen thousand dollar's worth of collectable fees. In addition, many who had come forward to shake his hand within the past few minutes, assured him they would mail their own forms, along with cheques, in the morning. Lawyer Freemantle glowed.

He had no real plan as to what would happen at the airport, any more than he had arrived tonight with a fixed idea about how to take over this meeting. Elliott Freemantle disliked fixed ideas. He preferred to improvise, to get situations rolling, then direct them this way or that, to his own advantage. His freewheeling methods had worked once already this evening, he saw no reason why they should not do so again.

The main thing was to keep these Meadowood home-owners convinced that they had a dynamic leader who would eventually produce results. Furthermore, they must remain convinced until the four quarterly payments, which the legal retainer agreements called for, were made. After that, when Elliott Freemantle had his money in the bank, the opinions were less important.

So he had to keep this situation lively, he reasoned, for ten or eleven months – and he would do it. He would give these people all the dynamism they could want. There would be need for some more meetings and demonstrations like tonight's because those made news. Too often, court proceedings didn't. Despite what he had said a few minutes ago about legal proceedings being a base, any sessions in court were likely to be unspectacular and possibly unprofitable. Of course, he would do his best to introduce some histrionics, though quite a few judges nowadays were wise to Lawyer Freemantle's attention-creating tactics, and curtailed them sternly.

But there were no real problems, providing he remembered – as he always did in these affairs – that the most important factor was the care and feeding of Elliott Freemantle.

He could see one of the reporters, Tomlinson of the *Tribune*, using a pay phone just outside the hall; another reporter was nearby. Good! It meant that downtown city desks were being alerted, and would cover whatever happened at the airport. There would also, if earlier arrangements Freemantle had made worked out, be some TV coverage, too.

The crowd was thinning. Time to go!

10

Near the airport's floodlighted main entrance, the flashing red beacon of the state police patrol car died. The patrol car, which had preceded Joe Patroni from the site of the wrecked tractor-trailer, slowed, and the state trooper at the wheel pulled over to the kerb, waving the TWA maintenance chief past. Patroni accelerated. As his Buick Wildcat swept by, Patroni waved his cigar in salutation and ponked his horn twice.

Although the last stage of Joe Patroni's journey had been accomplished with speed, overall it had taken more than three hours to cover a distance – from his home to the airport – which normally took forty minutes. Now, he hoped, he could make good some of the lost time.

Fighting the snow and slippery road surface, he cut swiftly through the stream of terminal-bound traffic and swung on to a side road to the airport's hangar area. At a sign, 'TWA Maintenance', he wheeled the Buick sharply right. A few hundred yards farther on, the airline's maintenance hangar loomed towering and massive. The main doors were open; he drove directly in.

Inside the hangar a radio-equipped pickup truck, with driver, was waiting; it would take Patroni on to the airfield – to the mired Aéreo-Mexican jet, still obstructing runway three zero. Stepping from his car, the maintenance chief paused only long enough to relight his cigar – ignoring 'no smoking' regulations – then hoisted his stocky figure into the truck cab. He instructed the driver, 'Okay, son, push that needle round the dial.'

The truck raced away, Patroni obtaining radio clearance from the tower as they went. Once again from the lighted hangar area, the driver stayed close to taxi lights, the only guide – in the white-tinted gloom – to where paved surfaces began and ended. On instructions from the tower they halted briefly near a runway while a DC-9 of Delta Air Lines landed in a flurry of snow and rolled by with a thunder of reversed jet thrust. The ground controller cleared them across the runway, then added, 'Is that Joe Patroni?'

'Yep.'

There was an interval while the controller dealt with other traffic, then: 'Ground control to Patroni. We have a message from the airport manager's office. Do you read?'

'This's Patroni. Go ahead.'

'Message begins: Joe, I'll bet you a box of cigars against a pair of ball tickets that you can't get that stuck aeroplane clear of three zero tonight, and I'd like you to win. Signed, Mel Bakersfeld. End of message.'

Joe Patroni chuckled as he depressed the transmit button. 'Patroni to ground control. Tell him he's on.'

Replacing the radio mike, he urged the truck driver, 'Keep her moving, son. Now I got me an incentive.'

At the blocked intersection of runway three zero, the Aéreo-Mexican maintenance foreman, Ingram – whom Mel Bakersfeld had talked with earlier – approached the pickup as it stopped. The foreman was still huddled into a parka, shielding his face as best he could from the biting wind and snow.

Joe Patroni bit off the end of a fresh cigar, though this time without lighting it, and descended from the truck cab. On the way out from the hangar he had changed from the overshoes he had been wearing into heavy fleece-lined boots; high as the boots were, the deep snow came over them.

Patroni pulled his own parka around him and nodded to Ingram. The two men knew each other slightly.

'Okay,' Patroni said; he had to shout to make himself heard above the wind. 'Gimme the poop.'

As Ingram made his report, the wings and fuselage of the stalled Boeing 707 loomed above them both, like an immense ghostly albatross. Beneath the big jet's belly a red hazard light still winked rhythmically, and the collection of trucks and service vehicles, including a crew bus and roaring power cart, remained clustered on the taxiway side of the aircraft.

The Aéreo-Mexican maintenance foreman summarized what had been done already: the removal of passengers, and the first abortive attempt to get the aeroplane moving under its own power. Afterwards, he informed Joe Patroni, as much weight had been taken off as possible – freight, mail, baggage, with most of the fuel load being sucked out by tankers. Then there had been a second attempt to blast the aeroplane out, again with its own jets, which also ended in failure.

Chewing his cigar instead of smoking it – one of Patroni's rare concessions to fire precaution, since the smell of aviation kerosene was strong – the TWA maintenance chief moved closer to the aircraft. Ingram followed, and the two were joined by several ground crewmen who emerged from the shelter of the crew bus. As Patroni surveyed the scene, one of the crewmen switched on portable floodlights which were rigged in a semicircle in front of the aeroplane's nose. The lights revealed that the main landing gear was partially out of sight, embedded in a covering of black mud beneath snow. The aircraft had stuck in an area which was normally grass-covered, a few yards off runway three zero, near an intersecting taxiway – the taxiway which the Aéreo-Mexican pilot had missed in the dark and swirling snow. It was sheer bad luck, Patroni realized, that at that point the ground must have been so waterlogged that not even three days of snow and freezing temperatures had been sufficient to harden it. As a result, the two attempts to blast the aeroplane free with its own power had merely succeeded in settling it deeper. Now, nacelles of the four jet engines beneath the wings were uncomfortably close to ground level.

Ignoring the snow, which swirled about him like a scene from *South with Scott*, Patroni considered, calculating the possibilities of success.

There was still a worthwhile chance, he decided, of getting the aeroplane out by use of its own engine power. It would be the fastest way, if it could be done. If not, they would have to employ giant lifting bags – eleven altogether, made of nylon fabric – placed under wings and fuselage, and inflated by pneumatic blowers. When the bags were in place, heavy-duty jacks would be used to raise the aircraft's wheels, then a solid floor built under them. But the process would be long, difficult, and wearying. Joe Patroni hoped it could be avoided.

He announced, 'We gotta dig deep and wide in front of the gear. I want two six-foot-wide trenches down to where the wheels are now. Coming forward from the wheels, we'll level the trenches at first, then slope 'em up gradually.' He swung to Ingram. 'That's a lot of digging.'

The foreman nodded. 'Sure is.'

'When we've finished that part, we'll start the engines and pull full power with all four.' Patroni motioned to the stalled silent aircraft. 'That should get her moving forward. When she's rolling, and up the slope of the trenches, we'll swing her this way.' Stomping with the heavy boots he had put on in the truck, he traced an elliptical path through the snow between the soft ground and the taxiway paved surface. 'Another thing – let's lay big timbers, as many as we can, in front of the wheels. You got any at all?'

'Some,' Ingram said. 'In one of the trucks.'

'Unload 'em, and send your driver round the airport to round up as many as he can. Try all the airlines, and airport maintenance.'

The ground crewmen nearest Patroni and Ingram hailed others, who began scrambling from the crew bus. Two of the men rolled back a snow-covered tarpaulin on a truck containing tools and shovels. The shovels were passed around among figures, moving and shadowy outside the semicircle of bright lights. The blowing snow, at times, made it difficult for the men to see each other. They waited for orders to begin.

A boarding ramp, leading to the forward cabin door of the 707, had been left in place. Patroni pointed to it. 'Are the flyboys still aboard?'

Ingram grunted. 'They're aboard. The goddam captain and first officer.'

Patroni looked at him sharply. 'They been giving you trouble?'

'It isn't what they gave me,' Ingram said sourly, 'it's what they wouldn't. When I got here, I wanted 'em to pull full power, the way you just said. If they'd done it the first time, I reckon she'd have come out; but they didn't have the guts, which is why we got in deeper. The captain's made one big screwup tonight, and knows it. Now he's scared stiff of standing the ship on its nose.'

Joe Patroni grinned. 'If I were him, I might feel the same way.' He had chewed his cigar to shreds; he threw it into the snow and reached inside his parka for another. 'I'll talk to the captain later. Is the interphone rigged?'

'Yeah.'

'Call the flight deck, then. Tell 'em we're working, and I'll be up there soon.'

'Right.' As he moved closer to the aircraft, Ingram called to the twenty or so assembled ground crewmen, 'Okay, you guys; let's get digging!'

Joe Patroni seized a shovel himself and, within minutes, the group was shifting mud, earth, and snow.

When he had used the fuselage interphone to speak to the pilots in their cockpit high above, Ingram – with the aid of a mechanic – began groping through icy mud, with cold numbed hands, to lay the first of the timbers in front of the aircraft's wheels.

Across the airfield occasionally, as the snow gusted and limits of visibility changed, the lights of aircraft taking off and landing could be seen, and the whine-pitched roar of jet engines was carried on the wind to the ears of the men working. But close alongside, runway three zero remained silent and deserted.

Joe Patroni calculated: It would probably be an hour before the digging would be complete and the Boeing 707's engines could be started in an attempt to taxi the big airliner out. Meanwhile, the men now excavating the twin trenches, which were beginning to take shape, would have to be relieved in shifts, to warm themselves in the crew bus, still parked on the taxiway.

It was ten thirty now. With luck, he thought, he might be home in bed – with Marie – soon after midnight.

To bring the prospect nearer, also to keep warm, Patroni threw himself even harder into shovelling.

In the Cloud Captain's Coffee Shop, Captain Vernon Demerest ordered tea for Gwen, black coffee for himself. Coffee – as it was supposed to do – helped keep him alert; he would probably down a dozen more cups between here and Rome. Although Captain Harris would be doing most of the flying of Flight Two tonight, Demerest had no intention of relaxing mentally. In the air, he rarely did. He was aware, as were most veteran pilots, that aviators who died in their beds of old age were those who throughout their careers had been ready to cope instantly with the unexpected.

'We're both unusually quiet,' Gwen said in her gentle English voice. 'We scarcely said a word coming into the terminal.'

It was just a few minutes since they left the departure concourse, after announcement of the one-hour flight delay. They had managed to snare a booth near the rear of the coffee shop, and now Gwen was looking into the mirror of her compact, patting her hair into place where it flowed superbly from beneath the smart Trans America stewardess cap. Her dark, expressive eyes switched briefly from the mirror to Vernon Demerest's face.

'I wasn't talking,' Demerest said, 'because I've been thinking; that's all.'

Gwen moistened her lips, though not applying lipstick – airlines had strict rules against stewardesses applying make-up in public. In any case, Gwen used very little; her compexion was the milk and roses kind which so many English girls seemed born with.

'Thinking about what? Your traumatic experience – the announcement we're to be parents?' Gwen smiled mischievously, then recited, 'Captain Vernon Waldo Demerest

143

and Miss Gwendolyn Aline Meighen announce the approaching arrival of their first child, a . . . what? . . . We don't know, do we? We won't for another seven months. Oh well, it isn't long to wait.'

He remained silent while their coffee and tea was set before them, then protested, 'For God's sake, Gwen, let's be serious about this!'

'Why should we be? Especially if I'm not. After all, if anyone's worrying, it ought to be me.'

He was about to object again when Gwen reached for his hand under the table. Her expression changed to sympathy. 'I'm sorry. I suppose it really is a bit shattering – for both of us.'

It was the opening Demerest had been waiting for. He said carefully, 'It needn't be shattering. What's more, we don't have to be parents unless we choose to be.'

'Well,' Gwen said matter-of-factly, 'I was wondering when you'd get around to it.' She snapped her compact closed, and put it away. 'You almost did in the car, didn't you? Then thought better of it.'

'Thought better of what?'

'Oh really, Vernon! Why pretend? We both know perfectly well what it is you're talking about. You want me to have an abortion. You've been thinking about it ever since I told you I was pregnant. Well, haven't you?'

He nodded reluctantly. 'Yes.' He still found Gwen's directness disconcerting.

'What's the matter? Did you think I'd never heard about abortions before?'

Demerest glanced over his shoulder, wondering if they could be overheard, but the clatter of the coffee shop, the buzz of conversation generally, were all-pervading.

'I wasn't sure how you'd feel.'

'I'm not sure either.' It was Gwen's turn to be serious. She was looking down at her hands, the long slender fingers he admired so much now clasped in front of her. 'I've thought about it. I still don't know.'

He felt encouraged. At least there was no slammed door, no blank refusal.

He tried to make himself the voice of reason. 'It's really the only sensible thing to do. Maybe in some ways it's unpleasant to think of, but at least it's over quickly, and if it's done properly, therapeutically, there's no danger involved, no fear of complications.'

'I know,' Gwen said. 'It's all terribly simple. Now you have it; now you don't.' She looked at him directly. 'Right?'

'Right.'

He sipped his coffee. Perhaps this was going to be easier than he thought.

'Vernon,' Gwen said softly, 'have you considered that what's inside me is a human being: that it's alive, a person – even now? We made love. It's us, you and me; a part of us.' Her eyes, more troubled than he had yet seen them, searched his face for a response.

He said emphatically, his voice deliberately harsh, 'That isn't true. A foetus at this stage is not a human being; nor is it a person, not yet. It could be later, but it isn't now. It doesn't have life or breath or feeling. An abortion – particularly this soon – isn't the same as taking a human life.'

Gwen reacted with the same quick temper she had shown in the apartment earlier. 'You mean it might not be such a good thing later on? If we waited, then had an abortion, it might not be so ethical when the baby was perfectly formed, its fingers and toes all there. To kill it then might be a little worse than now. Is that it, Vernon?'

144

Demerest shook his head. 'I didn't say that.'

'But you implied it.'

'If I did, I didn't mean to. In any case, you're twisting words around.'

Gwen sighed. 'I'm being womanly.'

'No one's more entitled to be.' He smiled; his eyes moved over her. The thought of Naples and Gwen . . . a few hours from now . . . still excited him.

'I do love you, Vernon. I really do.'

Under the table he retrieved her hand. 'I know. It's why this is hard for us both.'

'The thing is,' Gwen said slowly, as if thinking aloud, 'I've never conceived a child before, and until it happens a woman always wonders if she can. When you find out, as I have, that the answer's yes, in a way it's a gift, a feeling . . . that only a woman knows . . . that's great and wonderful. Then, suddenly in our kind of situation, you're faced with ending it all, of squandering what was given.' Her eyes were misty. 'Do you understand, Vernon? Really understand?'

He answered gently, 'Yes, I think so.'

'The difference between you and me is that you've had a child.'

He shook his head. 'I've no children. Sarah and I . . .'

'Not in your marriage. But there *was* a child; you told me so. A little girl; the one from the 3-PPP programme' – Gwen gave the ghost of a smile – 'who was adopted. Now, whatever happens there's always someone, somewhere that's you again.'

He remained silent.

Gwen asked, 'Do you ever think about her? Don't you ever wonder where she is, what she's like?'

There was no reason to lie. 'Yes,' he said. 'Sometimes I do.'

'You've no means of finding out?'

He shook his head. He had once inquired, but was told that when an adoption was sealed, they threw away the files. There was no way to know – ever.

Gwen drank from her teacup. Over its rim she surveyed the crowded coffee shop. He sensed that her composure had returned; the trace of tears was gone.

She said with a smile, 'Oh dear, what a lot of trouble I'm causing you.'

He answered, and meant it: 'It isn't my worrying that matters. It's what's best for you.'

'Well, I suppose in the end I'll do what's sensible. I'll have an abortion. I just have to think it through, talk it out, first.'

'When you're ready, I'll help. But we shouldn't lose much time.'

'I suppose not.'

'Look, Gwen,' he assured her, 'the whole thing is fast, and I promise you it'll be medically safe.' He told her about Sweden; that he would pay whatever the clinic cost; that the airline would co-operate in getting her there.

She acknowledged, 'I'll make up my mind, for sure, before we get back from this trip.'

He picked up their check, and they rose to leave. It was nearing time for Gwen to be on hand to greet passengers boarding Flight Two.

As they left the coffee shop, she said, 'I guess I'm pretty lucky you're the way you are. Some men would have walked away and left me.'

'I won't leave you.'

But he *would* leave her; he knew that now. When Naples and the abortion were over, he would finish with Gwen, break off their affair – as considerately as he could, but completely and definitely just the same. It would not be too difficult. There might be an uncomfortable moment or two when Gwen learned of his intention, but she was not the kind to make a fuss; she had demonstrated that already. In any event, he could handle the situation, which would not be a new one. Vernon Demerest had disentangled himself successfully from amorous affairs before.

It was true that this time there was a difference. No one before had ever had quite the same effect on him as Gwen. No other woman had stirred him quite so deeply. No one else – at least, whom he remembered – had caused him to enjoy her company, just being with her, quite so much. Parting, for himself, would not be easy, and he knew he would be tempted, later on, to change his mind.

But he would not. Through all his life so far, once he had decided on a course of action, Vernon Demerest had seen it through. Self-discipline was a habit he enforced.

Besides, commonsense told him that if he did not break with Gwen soon, the time might come when he could not, when – self-discipline or not – he could never bring himself to give her up. If that happened, it would entail a need for permanence and, along with that, the kind of catastrophic upheaval – marital, financial, emotional – which he was determined to avoid. Ten or fifteen years ago, maybe; not now.

He touched Gwen's arm. 'You go on. I'll follow in a minute.'

Ahead of them, as the crowds in the central concourse parted briefly, he had observed Mel Bakersfeld. Vernon Demerest had no particular objection to being seen with Gwen; just the same, there was no sense in advertising their relationship around the family.

His brother-in-law, he noticed, was talking earnestly with Lieutenant Ned Ordway, the efficient, amiable Negro who commanded the airport police detachment. Perhaps Mel would be too absorbed to notice his sister's husband, which was perfectly all right with Demerest, who had no particular wish for a meeting, though at the same time he had no intention of avoiding one.

Gwen disappeared into the crowd; his last glimpse of her was of shapely, nylon-sheathed legs, and ankles equally as attractive and proportionate. *O Sole Mio* . . . hurry up!

Damn! Mel Bakersfeld had seen him.

'I was looking for you,' Lieutenant Ordway had told Mel a few minutes earlier. 'I've just heard we're having visitors – several hundreds.'

Tonight the airport police chief was in uniform; a tall, striking figure who looked like an African emperor, though for one so big, he spoke with surprising softness.

'We already have visitors.' Mel glanced around the crowded, bustling concourse. He had been passing through on the way to this office on the executive mezzanine. 'Not hundreds; thousands.'

'I don't mean passengers,' Ordway said. 'The ones I'm talking about may cause us more trouble.'

He told Mel about the Meadowood mass meeting to protest airport noise; now the meeting had adjourned and most of its members were on their way to the airport. Lieutenant Ordway had learned about the meeting, and its intended follow-up, from a TV news crew which had requested permission to set up cameras inside the terminal. After talking with the TV people, Ordway telephoned a friend on the *Tribune* city desk downtown, who read him the gist of a news story which a reporter at the original meeting had just phoned in.

'Hell!' Mel grumbled. 'Of all the nights to choose! As if we don't have enough trouble, already.'

'I guess that's the idea; they'll get noticed more that way. But I thought you'd better be warned because they'll probably want to see you, and maybe someone from the FAA.'

Mel said sourly, 'The FAA goes underground when they hear of something like this. They never come out until the all clear's sounded.'

'How about you?' The policeman grinned. 'You plan to start tunnelling?'

'No. You can tell them I'll meet a delegation of half a dozen, though even that's a waste of time tonight. There's nothing I can do.'

'You realize,' Ordway said, 'that providing they don't create a disturbance or damage property, there's nothing I can do legally to keep the rest of them out.'

'Yes, I realize it, but I'm not going to talk to a mob, though just the same, let's not look for trouble. Even if we get pushed around a little, make sure we don't do any pushing ourselves unless we have to. Remember that the press will be here, and I don't want to create any martyrs.'

'I already warned my men. They'll make with the jokes and save the jujitsu.'

'Good!'

Mel had confidence in Ned Ordway. The policing of Lincoln International was handled by a self-administering detachment of the city force, and Lieutenant Ordway represented the best type of career policeman. He had been in charge of the airport detail a year, and would probably move on to a more important assignment downtown soon. Mel would be sorry to see him go.

'Apart from this Meadowood thing,' Mel inquired, 'how's everything else been?' He was aware that Ordway's force of a hundred policemen, like most others at the airport, had done extra hours of duty since the storm began.

'Mostly routine. More drunks than usual, and a couple of fist fights. But that figures because of all the flight delays and your busy bars.'

Mel grinned. 'Don't knock the bars. The airport takes a percentage from every drink, and we need the revenue.'

'So do airlines, I guess. At least judging by the passengers they try to sober up, so they can put them aboard. I have my usual beef about that.'

'Coffee?'

'Right. The moment a passenger in his cups shows up at an airline check-in counter, somebody from passenger relations gets assigned to pour coffee into him. Airlines never seem to learn that when the coffee's in, all you have is a wide-awake drunk. Mostly, that's when they call us.'

'You can handle it.'

Ordway's men, Mel was aware, were expert at dealing with airport drunks, who were rarely charged unless they became obstreperous. Mostly they were salesmen and businessmen from out of town, sometimes exhausted after a gruelling, competitive week, whom a few drinks on the way home hit hard. If flight crews wouldn't allow them aboard – and captains, who had the last word on such matters, were usually adamant about it – the drunks were escorted to the police detention building and left to sober up. Later, they were allowed to go – usually sheepishly.

'Oh, there is one thing,' the police chief said. 'The parking lot people think we have several more dumped cars. In this weather it's hard to be sure, but we'll check it out as soon as we can.'

Mel grimaced. Worthless cars abandoned on parking lots were currently a plague at every big city airport. Nowadays, when an old jalopy became useless, it was surprisingly hard to get rid of it. Scrap and salvage dealers were jammed to the limits of their yards and wanted no more – unless car owners paid. So an owner was faced with the alternatives of paying for disposal, renting storage, or finding a place to abandon his vehicle where it could not be traced back to him. Airports had become obvious dumping grounds.

The old cars were driven into airport parking lots, then licence plates and other obvious identification quietly removed. Engine serial numbers could not be removed, of course, but the time and trouble involved in tracing them was never worth while. It was simpler for the airport to do what the ex-owner would not – pay for the car to be taken away and junked, and as quickly as possible since it was occupying revenue parking space. Recently, at Lincoln International, the monthly bill for old car disposal had become formidable.

Through the shifting throng in the concourse, Mel caught sight of Captain Vernon Demerest.

'Aside from that,' Ordway said genially, 'we're in great shape for your Meadowood visitors. I'll let you know when they get here.' With a friendly nod, the policeman moved on.

Vernon Demerest – in Trans America uniform, his bearing confident as usual – was coming Mel's way. Mel felt a surge of irritation, remembering the adverse snow committee report which he had heard about, but still hadn't seen.

Demerest seemed disinclined to stop until Mel said, 'Good evening, Vernon.'

'Hi.' The tone was indifferent.

'I hear that you're an authority, now, on snow clearance.'

'You don't have to be an authority,' Vernon Demerest said brusquely, 'to know when there's a lousy job being done.'

Mel made an effort to keep his tone moderate. 'Have you any idea how much snow there's been?'

'Probably better than you. Part of my job is studying weather reports.'

'Then you're aware we've had ten inches of snow on the airport in the past twenty-four hours; to say nothing of what was there already.'

Demerest shrugged. 'So clear it.'

'It's what we're doing.'

'Goddamned inefficiently.'

'The maximum recorded snowfall here – ever,' Mel persisted, 'was twelve inches in the same period. That was an inundation, and everything closed down. This time we've come near to it, but we haven't closed. We've fought to stay open, and we've managed it. There isn't an airport anywhere that could have coped better than we have with this storm. We've had every piece of snow-moving machinery manned around the clock.'

'Maybe you haven't got enough machinery.'

'Good God, Vernon! Nobody has enough equipment for the kind of storm we've had these past three days. Anybody could use more, but you don't buy snow-clearing machinery for occasional maximum situations – not if you've any economic sense. You buy for optimums, then when an emergency hits you, you use everything you have, deploying it to best advantage. That's what my men have been doing, and they've done damned well!'

'Okay,' Demerest said, 'you have your opinion. I have mine. I happen to think you've done an incompetent job. I've said so in my report.'

'I thought it was a committee report. Or did you elbow the others out so you could take a personal stab at me?'

'How the committee works is our business. The report is what matters. You'll get your copy tomorrow.'

'Thanks a lot.' His brother-in-law, Mel noticed, had not bothered to deny that the report was directed personally. Mel went on, 'Whatever it is you've written won't change anything, but if it gives you satisfaction, it'll have a nuisance value. Tomorrow I'll have to waste time explaining how ignorant – in some areas – you really are.'

Mel had spoken heatedly, not bothering to conceal his anger, and for the first time Demerest grinned. 'Got under your skin a little, eh? Well, that's too bad about the nuisance value and your precious time. I'll remember it tomorrow while I'm enjoying Italian sunshine.' Still grinning, he walked away.

He had not gone more than a few yards when the grin changed to a scowl.

The cause of Captain Demerest's displeasure was the central lobby insurance booth – tonight, clearly doing a brisk business. It was a reminder that Demerest's victory over Mel Bakersfeld had been picayune, a pinprick only. A week from now, the adverse snow committee report would be forgotten, but the insurance counter would still be here. So the real victory was still with his smooth, smug brother-in-law, who had defeated Demerest's arguments in front of the Board of Airport Commissioners, and made him look a fool.

Behind the insurance counters two young girls – one of them the big-breasted blonde – were rapidly writing policies for applicants, while another half dozen people waited in line. Most of those waiting were holding cash in their hands – representing more quick profits for the insurance companies, Demerest reflected sourly – and he had no doubt the automatic vending machines in various locations in the terminal were just as busy.

He wondered if any of his own Flight Two passengers-to-be were among those in line. He was tempted to inquire and, if so, do some proselytizing of his own; but he decided not. Vernon Demerest had tried the same thing once before – urging people at an insurance counter not to buy airport flight insurance, and telling them why; and afterwards there had been complaints, resulting in a sharply worded reprimand from Trans America management. Though airlines did not like airport insurance vending any more than aircrews did, the airlines were subject to differing pressures which forced them to stay neutral. For one thing, airport managements claimed they needed the insurance companies' revenue; if they didn't get it from that source, they pointed out, maybe the airlines would have to make up the difference in higher landing fees. For another, airlines were not eager to offend passengers, who might resent not being able to buy insurance in a way they had become used to. Therefore the pilots alone had taken the initiative – along with the abuse.

Preoccupied with his thoughts, Captain Demerest had paused for a few seconds, watching the insurance booth activity. Now he saw a newcomer join the queue – a nervous-looking man – spindly and stoop-shouldered, and with a small, sandy moustache. The man carried a small attaché case and seemed to be worrying about the time; he cast frequent glances at the central lobby clock, comparing it with his own watch. He was clearly unhappy about the length of the line-up ahead of him.

149

Demerest thought disgustedly: the man had left himself with too little time; he should forget about insurance and get aboard his flight.

Then Demerest reminded himself: he should be back on the flight deck of Flight Two. He began to walk quickly towards the Trans America departure concourse; at any moment now the first boarding announcement would be made. Ah! – there it was.

'Trans America Airlines announce the departure of Flight Two, The Golden Argosy, *for Rome . . .'*

Captain Demerest had stayed in the terminal longer than he intended. As he hurried, the announcement, clear and audible above the babel in the concourses, continued.

12

' . . . Flight Two, The Golden Argosy, *to Rome. The flight is now ready for boarding. All passengers holding confirmed reservations . . .'*

An airport flight departure announcement meant diverse things to those who heard it. To some, it was a routine summons, a prefix to another tedious, work-oriented journey which – had free choice been theirs – they would not have made. For others, a flight announcement spelled a beginning of adventure; for others still, the nearing of an end – the journey home. For some it entailed sadness and parting; for others, in counterpoint, the prospect of reunion and joy. Some who heard flight announcements heard them always for other people. Their friends or relatives were travellers; as to themselves, the names of destinations were wistful not-quite-glimpses of faraway places they would never see. A handful heard flight announcements with fear; few heard them with indifference. They were a signal that a process of departure had begun. An aeroplane was ready; there was time to board, but no time to be tardy; only rarely did airliners wait for individuals. In a short time the aeroplane would enter man's unnatural element, the skies; and because it was unnatural there had always been, and would for ever remain, a component of adventure and romance.

There was nothing romantic about the mechanics of a flight announcement. It originated in a machine which in many ways resembled a juke box, except that push buttons instead of coins were required to actuate it. The push buttons were on a console in Flight Information Control – a miniature control tower (each airline had its own FIC or equivalent) – located above the departure concourse. A woman clerk pushed the buttons in appropriate sequence; after that the machinery took over.

Almost all flight announcements – the exceptions were those for special situations – were pre-recorded on cartridge tapes. Although, to the ear, each announcement seemed complete in itself, it never was, for it consisted of three separate recordings. The first recording named the airline and flight; the second described the loading situation, whether preliminary, boarding, or final; the third recording specified gate number and concourse. Since the three recordings followed one another without a pause, they sounded – as they were intended to – continuous.

People who disliked quasi-human automation were sometimes cheered when flight announcement machines went wrong. Occasionally part of the machinery would jam, with such results as passengers for half a dozen flights being misdirected to the same gate.

The resultant debacle, involving a thousand or more confused, impatient passengers, was an airline agent's nightmare.

Tonight, for Flight Two, the machinery worked.

'. . . *passengers holding confirmed reservations please proceed to gate forty-seven, the Blue Concourse D.*'

By now, thousands in the terminal had heard the announcement of Flight Two. Some who heard were more concerned than others. A few, not yet concerned, would be, before the night was done.

More than a hundred and fifty Flight Two passengers heard the announcement. Those who had checked in, but had not reached gate forty-seven, hastened towards it, a few recent arrivals still knocking snow from their clothing as they went.

Senior Stewardess Gwen Meighen was pre-boarding several families with small children when the announcement echoed down the boarding walkway. She used the flight deck interphone to notify Captain Anson Harris, and prepared herself for an influx of passengers within the next few minutes. Ahead of the passengers, Captain Vernon Demerest ducked aboard and hurried forward, closing the flight deck door behind him.

Anson Harris, working with Second Officer Cy Jordan, had already begun the pre-flight check.

'Okay,' Demerest said. He slipped into the first officer's right-hand seat, and took the check list clipboard. Jordan returned to his regular seat behind the other two.

Mel Bakersfeld, still in the central concourse, heard the announcement and remembered that *The Golden Argosy* was Vernon Demerest's flight. Mel genuinely regretted that once again an opportunity to end, or even lessen, the hostility between himself and his brother-in-law had ended in failure. Now, their personal relationship was – if possible – worse than before. Mel wondered how much of the blame was his own; some, certainly, because Vernon seemed to have a knack for probing out the worst in Mel, but Mel honestly believed that most of their quarrel was of Vernon's making. Part of the trouble was that Vernon saw himself as a superior being, and resented it when others didn't. A good many pilots whom Mel knew – especially captains – felt that way about themselves.

Mel still seethed when he remembered Vernon, after the airport commissioners' meeting, asserting that people like Mel were 'ground-bound, desk-tied, with penguins' minds'. As if flying an aeroplane, Mel thought, were something so damned extra-special compared with other occupations!

Just the same, Mel wished that tonight for a few hours he was a pilot once again, and was about to leave – as Vernon was leaving – on a flight for Rome. He remembered what Vernon had said about enjoying Italian sunshine tomorrow. Mel could do with a little of that, a little less, at this moment, of aviation's logistics of the ground. Tonight the surly bonds of earth seemed surlier than usual.

Police Lieutenant Ned Ordway, who had left Mel Bakersfeld a few minutes earlier, heard the announcement of Flight Two through the opened doorway of a small security office just off the main concourse. Ordway was in the office receiving a telephoned report from his desk sergeant at airport police headquarters. According to a radio message from a patrol car, a heavy influx of private automobiles, crammed with people, was coming into the parking lots, which were having difficulty accommodating them. Inquiries had revealed that most of the cars' occupants were from Meadowood community – members of the anti-noise demonstration which Lieutenant Ordway had already heard about. As per the lieutenant's orders, the desk sergeant said, police reinforcements were on their way to the terminal.

A few hundred feet from Lieutenant Ordway, in a passenger waiting area, the little old lady from San Diego, Mrs Ada Quonsett, paused in her conversation with young Peter Coakley of Trans America, while both listened to the announcement of Flight Two.

They were seated, side by side, on one of a series of black, leather padded benches. Mrs Quonsett had been describing the virtues of her late husband in the same kind of terms which Queen Victoria must have used when speaking of Prince Albert. 'Such a dear person, so very wise, and handsome. He came to me in later life, but I imagine, when he was young, he must have been very much like you.'

Peter Coakley grinned sheepishly, as he had done many times in the past hour and a half. Since leaving Tanya Livingston, with instructions to remain with the old lady stowaway until the departure of her return flight for Los Angeles, their talk had consisted chiefly of a monologue by Mrs Quonsett in which Peter Coakley was compared frequently and favourably with the late Herbert Quonsett. It was a subject of which Peter was becoming decidedly weary. He was unaware that that was what Ada Quonsett astutely intended.

Surreptitiously, Peter Coakley yawned; this was not the kind of work he had expected when he became a Trans America passenger agent. He felt an absolute fool, sitting here in uniform, playing dry nurse to a harmless, garrulous old dame who could have been his great-grandmother. He hoped this duty would be over soon. It was bad luck that Mrs Quonsett's flight to Los Angeles, like most others tonight, was being further delayed by the storm; otherwise the old girl would have been on her way an hour ago. He hoped to goodness that the LA flight would be called soon. Meanwhile, the announcement about Flight Two, which was continuing, made a welcome, if brief, respite.

Young Peter Coakley had already forgotten Tanya's cautioning words: 'Remember . . . she's got a barrelful of tricks.'

'Fancy that!' Mrs Quonsett said when the announcement ended. 'A flight to Rome! An airport is so interesting, don't you think, especially for a young, intelligent person like you? Now there was a place – Rome – which my late, dear husband wanted us both to visit.' She clasped her hands, a wispy lace handkerchief between them, and sighed. 'We never did.'

While she talked, Ada Quonsett's mind was ticking like a fine Swiss watch. What she wanted was to give this child in a man's uniform the slip. Although he was plainly becoming bored, boredom itself was not enough; he was still here. What she had to do was develop a situation in which boredom would become carelessness. But it needed to be soon.

Mrs Quonsett had not forgotten her original objective – to stow away on a flight to New York. She had listened carefully for New York departure announcements, and five flights of various airliners had been called, but none was at the right moment, with any reasonable chance of getting away from her young custodian, unnoticed. Now, she had no means of knowing if there would be another New York departure before the Trans America flight to Los Angeles – the flight which she was supposed to go on, but didn't want to.

Anything, Mrs Quonsett brooded, would be better than going back to Los Angeles tonight. Anything – even . . . a sudden thought occurred to her . . . even getting aboard that flight to Rome.

She hesitated. Why not? A lot of things she had said tonight about Herbert were untrue, but it *was* true that they had once looked at some picture postcards of Rome together . . . If she got no farther than Rome airport, she would at least have been there; it would be something to tell Blanche when she finally got to New York. Just as satisfying, it would be spitting in the eye of that red-headed passenger agent bitch . . . But could she manage it? And what was the gate number they had just announced? Wasn't it . . . gate forty-seven in the Blue Concourse 'D'? Yes, she was sure it was.

Of course, the flight might be full, with no space for a stowaway or anyone else, but that was always a chance you took. Then for a flight to Italy, she supposed, people needed passports to get aboard; she would have to see how that worked out. And even now, if there was a flight announcement for New York . . .

The main thing was not just to sit here, but to do *something*.

Mrs Quonsett fluttered her frail, lined hands. 'Oh dear!' she exclaimed. 'Oh dear!' The fingers of her right hand moved, hovering near the top of her old-fashioned, high-necked blouse. She dabbed at her mouth with the lace handkerchief and emitted a soft, low moan.

A look of alarm sprang to the young ticket agent's face. 'What is it, Mrs Quonsett? What's wrong?'

Her eyes closed, then opened; she gave several short gasps. 'I'm so sorry. I'm afraid I don't feel at all well.'

Peter Coakley inquired anxiously. 'Do you want me to get help? A doctor?'

'I don't want to be a nuisance.'

'You won't be . . .'

'No.' Mrs Quonsett shook her head weakly. 'I think I'll just go to the ladies' room. I expect I'll be all right.'

The young ticket agent appeared doubtful. He didn't want the old girl dying on him, though she looked ready for it. He asked uneasily, 'Are you sure?'

'Yes, quite sure.' Mrs Quonsett decided she didn't want to attract attention here, not in the main part of the terminal. There were too many people nearby who would be watching. 'Please help me up . . . thank you . . . now, if you'll just give me your arm . . . I believe the ladies' room is over there.' On the way, she threw in a couple of low moans, producing anxious glances from Peter Coakley. She reassured him, 'I've had an attack like this before. I'm sure I'll feel better soon.'

At the door to the women's room she released young Coakley's arm. 'You're very kind to an old lady. So many young people nowadays . . . Oh, dear! . . .' She cautioned herself: that was enough; she must be careful not to overdo it. 'You'll wait here for me? You won't go away?'

'Oh, no. I won't go.'

'Thank you.' She opened the door and went in.

There were twenty or thirty women inside; everything at the airport was busy tonight, Mrs Quonsett thought, including washrooms. Now she needed an ally. She looked the field over carefully before selecting a secretary-type woman in a beige suit, who didn't seem to be in a hurry. Mrs Quonsett crossed to her.

'Excuse me, I'm not feeling very well. I wonder if you'd help me.' The little old lady from San Diego fluttered her hands and closed and opened her eyes, as she had for Peter Coakley.

The younger woman was concerned at once. 'Of course I'll help. Would you like me to take you . . .'

'No . . . please.' Mrs Quonsett leaned against a washbasin, apparently for support. 'All I want is to send a message. There's a young man outside the door in airline uniform – Trans America. His name is Mr Coakley. Please tell him . . . yes, I would like him to get a doctor after all.'

'I'll tell him. Will you be all right until I get back?'

Mrs Quonsett nodded. 'Yes, thank you. But you will come back . . . and tell me.'

'Of course.'

Within less than a minute the younger woman had returned. 'He's sending for a doctor right away. Now, I think you should rest. Why don't . . .'

Mrs Quonsett stopped leaning on the basin. 'You mean he's already gone?'

'He went immediately.'

Now all she had to do, Mrs Quonsett thought, was get rid of this woman. She closed and opened her eyes again. 'I know it's asking a great deal . . . you've already been so good . . . but my daughter is waiting for me by the main door, near United Air Lines.'

'You'd like me to get her for you? Bring her here?'

Mrs Quonsett touched the lace handkerchief to her lips. 'I'd be so grateful, though really it's an imposition.'

'I'm sure you'd do as much for me. How will I know your daughter?'

'She's wearing a long mauve coat and a small white hat with yellow flowers. She has a little dog – a French poodle.'

The secretary-type woman smiled. 'That should be easy. I won't be long.'

'It *is* so good of you.'

Ada Quonsett waited only a moment or two after the woman had gone. Mrs Quonsett hoped, for her temporary helper's sake, she did not spend too much time searching for an imaginary figure in a mauve coat, accompanied by a non-existent French poodle.

Smiling to herself, the little old lady from San Diego left the washroom, walking spryly. No one accosted her as she moved away and was absorbed in the surging terminal crowds.

Now, she thought, which was the way to the Blue Concourse 'D', and gate forty-seven?

To Tanya Livingston, the Flight Two announcement was like a scoreboard change at a quadruple-header ball game. Four Trans America flights were, at the moment, in various stages of departure; in her capacity as passenger relations agent, Tanya was liaising with them all. As well, she had just had an irritating session with a passenger from an incoming flight from Kansas City.

The aggressive, fast-talking passenger complained that his wife's leather travelling case, which appeared on the arrivals carousel with a rip in its side, had been damaged as a result of careless handling. Tanya did not believe him – the rip looked like an old one – but, as

Trans America and other airlines invariably did, she offered to settle the claim on the spot, for cash. The difficulty had been in arriving at an agreeable sum. Tanya offered thirty-five dollars, which she considered to be more than the bag's value; the passenger held out for forty-five. Finally they settled at forty dollars, though what the complainant didn't know was that a passenger relations agent had authority to go to sixty dollars to get rid of a nuisance claim. Even when suspecting fraud, airlines found it cheaper to pay up quickly than enter into a prolonged dispute. In theory, ticket agents were supposed to note damaged bags at check-in, but seldom did; as a result, passengers who knew the ropes sometimes replaced worn-out luggage in that way.

Though the money was not her own, Tanya always hated parting with it when, in her opinion, the airline was being cheated.

Now, she turned her attention to helping to round up stragglers for Flight Two, some of whom were still coming in. Fortunately, the bus with downtown check-ins had arrived several minutes earlier, and most of its passengers had by now been directed to Concourse 'D', gate forty-seven. In a minute or two, Tanya decided, in case there were any last-minute passenger problems during boarding, she would go to gate forty-seven herself.

D.O. Guerrero heard the announcement of Flight Two while in line at the insurance counter in the terminal central concourse.

It was Guerrero, appearing hurried and nervous, whom Captain Vernon Demerest had seen arrive there, carrying his small attaché case which contained the dynamite bomb.

Guerrero had come directly from the bus to the insurance counter where he was now fifth in line. Two people at the head of the line were being dealt with by a pair of girl clerks – a heavy-chested blonde in a low-cut blouse – was having a prolonged conversation with her present customer, a middle-aged woman. The clerk was apparently suggesting that the woman take out a larger policy than had been asked for; the woman was being indecisive. Obviously, it would take at least twenty minutes for Guerrero to reach the head of the line, but by then Flight Two would probably be gone. Yet he *had* to buy insurance; he *had* to be aboard.

The p.a. announcement had said that the flight was being boarded at gate forty-seven. Guerrero should be at the gate *now*. He felt himself trembling. His hands were clammy on the attaché case handle. He checked his watch again, for the twentieth time, comparing it with the terminal clock. Six minutes had gone by since the announcement of Flight Two. The final call . . . the aeroplane doors closing . . . could come at any moment. He would have to do *something*.

D.O. Guerrero pushed his way roughly to the head of the line. He was past caring about being noticed, or offending. A man protested, 'Hey, buddy, we're waiting too.' Guerrero ignored him. He addressed the big-breasted blonde. 'Please . . . my flight has been called – the one to Rome. I need insurance. I can't wait.'

The man who had spoken before interjected. 'Then go without. Another time, get here sooner.'

Guerrero was tempted to retort: *There won't be another time.* Instead, he addressed himself to the blonde again. 'Please!'

To his surprise, she smiled warmly; he had been expecting a rebuff. 'You did say Rome?'

'Yes, yes. The flight's been called.'

'I know.' She smiled again. 'Trans America Flight Two. It is called *The Golden Argosy*.'

Despite his anxiety, he was aware that the girl had a sexy European accent, probably Hungarian.

D.O. Guerrero made an effort to speak normally. 'That's right.'

The girl turned her smile on the others who were waiting. 'This gentleman really does not have much time. I'm sure you will not mind if I oblige him first.'

So much had gone wrong tonight that he could scarcely believe his good luck. There was some muttered grumbling in the line of people waiting, but the man who had done the talking until now was silent.

The girl produced an insurance application form. She beamed at the woman she had been dealing with. 'This will only take a moment.' Then she turned her smile again on D.O. Guerrero

For the first time he realized how effective the smile was, and why there had been no real protest from the others. When the girl looked at him directly, Guerrero – who was seldom affected by women – had the feeling he was going to melt. She also had the biggest tits he had ever seen.

'My name is Bunnie,' the girl said in her European accent. 'What is yours?' Her ballpoint was poised.

As a vendor of airport insurance, Bunnie Vorobioff was a remarkable success.

She had come to the United States, not from Hungary as D.O. Guerrero had supposed but from Glauchau in the southern portion of East Germany, via the Berlin Wall. Bunnie (who was then Gretchen Vorobioff, the homely, flat-chested daughter of a minor Communist official and a Young Communist herself) crossed the wall at night with two male companies. The young men were caught by searchlights, shot and killed; their bodies hung for twenty-four hours on barbed wire, in public view. Bunnie avoided the searchlights and small arms fire and survived, survival being a quality which seemed to come to her naturally.

Later, on arrival as a US immigrant at age twenty-one, she had embraced American free enterprise and its goodies with the enthusiasm of a religious convert. She worked hard as a hospital aide, in which she had some training, and moonlighted as a waitress. Into the remaining time she somehow crammed a Berlitz course in English, and also managed to get to bed – occasionally to sleep, more often with interns from the hospital. The interns repaid Gretchen's sexual favours by introducing her to silicone breast injections, which started casually and ended by being a joyous group experiment to see just how big her breasts would get. Fortunately, before they could become more than gargantuan, she exercised another new-found freedom by quitting her hospital job for one with more money. Somewhere along the way she was taken to Washington, DC, and toured the White House, the Capitol, and the Playboy Club. After the last, Gretchen further Americanized herself by adopting the name Bunnie.

Now, a year and a half later, Bunnie Voribioff was totally assimilated. She was in an Arthur Murray dancing class, the Blue Cross and Columbia Record Club, had a charge account at Carson Pirie Scott, subscribed to *Reader's Digest* and *TV Guide*, was buying the *World Book Encyclopedia* on time, owned a wig and a Volkswagen, collected trading stamps, and was on pills.

Bunnie also loved contests of all kinds, especially those which held a hope of tangible reward. Along these lines, a reason she enjoyed her present job more than any other she had had so far, was that periodically her insurance company employers held sales contests for its staff, with merchandise prizes. One such contest was in progress now. It would end tonight.

The contest was the reason why Bunnie had reacted so agreeably when D.O. Guerrero announced that he was on his way to Rome. At this moment Bunnie needed forty more points to win her objective in the present sales contest – an electric toothbrush. For a while tonight she had despaired of completing her total points before the deadline, since insurance policies she had sold today were mostly for domestic flights; these produced lower premiums and earned fewer contest points. However, if a maximum size policy could be sold for an overseas flight, it would earn twenty-five contest points, bring the remainder within easy reach. The question was: How big an insurance policy did this Rome passenger want and, assuming it was less than the maximum, could Bunnie Vorobioff sell him more?

Usually she could. Bunnie merely turned on her most sexy smile, which she had learned to use like an instant warming oven, leaned close to the customer so that her breasts bemused him, then announced how much more benefit could be had for an additional small sum of money. Most times the ploy worked and was the reason for Bunnie's success as an insurance saleswoman.

When D.O. Guerrero had spelled out his name, she asked, 'What kind of policy were you considering, sir?'

Guerrero swallowed. 'Straight life – seventy-five thousand dollars.'

Now that he had said it, his mouth was dry. He had a sudden fear that his words had alerted everyone in the line-up; their eyes were boring into his back. His entire body was trembling; he was sure it would be noticed. To cover up, he lit a cigarette, but his hand was shaking so much that he had trouble bringing match and cigarette together. Fortunately, the girl, with her pen hovering over the entry 'principal sum', appeared not to notice.

Bunnie pronounced, 'That would cost two dollars and fifty cents.'

'What? . . . Oh, yes.' Guerrero managed to light the cigarette, then dropped the match. He reached into his pocket for some of the small amount of money he had remaining.

'But it is quite a tiny policy.' Bunnie Vorobioff had still not marked in the principal sum. Now she leaned forward, bringing her breasts nearer to the customer. She could see him looking down at them with fascination; men always did. Some, she sensed at times, wanted to reach out and touch. Not this man, though.

'Tiny?' Guerrero's speech was awkward, halting. 'I thought . . . it was the biggest.'

Even to Bunnie, the man's nervousness was now apparent. She supposed it was because he would be flying soon. She directed a dazzling smile across the counter.

'Oh no, sir; you could buy a three hundred thousand dollar policy. Most people do, and for just ten dollars premium. Really, it isn't much to pay for all that protection, is it?' She kept her smile switched on; the response could mean a difference of nearly twenty contest points; it might gain or lose her the electric toothbrush.

'You said . . . ten dollars?'

'That's right – for three hundred thousand dollars.'

D.O. Guerrero thought: *He hadn't known.* All along, he had believed that seventy-five thousand dollars was the top limit for airport-purchased insurance for an overseas flight.

He had obtained the information from an insurance application blank which, a month or two ago, he had picked up at another airport. Now he remembered – the earlier blank came from an automatic vending machine. It had not occurred to him that over-the-counter policies could be that much greater.

Three hundred thousand dollars!

'Yes,' he said eagerly. 'Please . . . yes.'

Bunnie beamed. 'The full amount, Mr Guerrero?'

He was about to nod assent when the supreme irony occurred to him. He probably did not possess ten dollars. He told Bunnie, 'Miss . . . wait!' and began searching his pockets, pulling out whatever money he could find.

The people in line were becoming restive. The man who had objected to Guerrero to begin with, protested to Bunnie, 'You said he'd just take a minute!'

Guerrero had found four dollars and seventy cents.

Two nights ago, when D.O. Guerrero and Inez had pooled their last remaining money, D.O. had taken eight dollars, plus small change, for himself. After pawning Inez's ring and making the downpayment on the Trans America ticket, there had been a few dollars left; he wasn't sure how many, but since then he had paid for meals, subway fares, the airport bus . . . He had known that he would need two and a half dollars for flight insurance, and had kept it carefully in a separate pocket. But beyond that he hadn't bothered, aware that once aboard Flight Two, money would be of no further use.

'If you don't have cash,' Bunnie Vorobioff said, 'you can give me a cheque.'

'I left my chequebook home.' It was a lie; there were cheques in his pocket. But if he wrote a cheque, it would bounce and invalidate the insurance.

Bunnie persisted, 'How about your Italian money, Mr Guerrero? I can take lire and give you the proper rate.'

He muttered, 'I don't have Italian money,' then cursed himself for having said it. *Downtown he had checked in without baggage for a flight to Rome. Now, insanely, he had demonstrated before onlookers that he had no money, either American or Italian.* Who would board an overseas flight unequipped and penniless, except someone who knew the flight would never reach its destination?

Then D.O. Guerrero reminded himself . . . except in his own mind . . . the two incidents – downtown and here – were unconnected. They would not be connected until afterwards, and by then it wouldn't matter.

He reasoned, as he had on the way out: It was not the strength of suspicion which was important. The crucial factor would still be the absence of wreckage, the absence of proof.

Surprisingly, despite his latest gaffe, he discovered he was growing more confident.

He added some dimes and pennies to the pile of change on the insurance counter. Then, miraculously, in an inside pocket, he found a five-dollar bill.

Not concealing his excitement, Guerrero exclaimed, 'That's it! I have enough!' There was even a dollar or so in small change left over.

But even Bunnie Vorobioff was doubtful now. Instead of writing the three hundred thousand dollar policy which the man was waiting for, she hesitated.

While he had searched his pockets, she had been watching the customer's face.

It was strange, of course, that this man was going overseas without money, but, after all, that was his own business; there could be plenty of reasons for it. What really bothered her was his eyes; they held a hint of frenzy, desperation. Both were qualities which Bunnie

Vorobioff recognized from her past. She had seen them in others. At moments – though it seemed long ago – she had been close to them herself.

Bunnie's insurance company employers had a standing instruction: If a purchaser of flight insurance seemed irrational, unusually excited, or was drunk, the fact was to be reported to the airline on which he was travelling. The question for Bunnie was: Was this an occasion to invoke the rule?

She wasn't sure.

The company standing instruction was sometimes discussed among themselves, by flight insurance sales clerks. Some of the girls resented or ignored it, arguing that they were hired to sell insurance, not to act as unpaid, unqualified psychologists. Others pointed out that many people who bought flight insurance at an airport were nervous to begin with; how could anyone, without special training, decide where nervousness ended and irrationality began? Bunnie herself had never reported a keyed-up passenger, though she knew a girl who had, and the passenger turned out to be an airline vice president, excited because his wife was going to have a baby. There had been all kinds of trouble over *that*.

Still Bunnie hesitated. She had covered her hesitation by counting the man's money on the counter. Now she wondered if Marj, the other clerk working beside her, had noticed anything unusual. Apparently not. Marj was busy writing a policy, earning *her* contest points.

In the end, it was Bunnie Vorobioff's past which swayed her decision. Her formative years . . . occupied Europe, her flight to the West, the Berlin Wall . . . had taught her survival and conditioned her to something else: to curb curiosity, and not to ask unnecessary questions. Questions had a way of leading to involvement, and involvement – in other people's problems – was something to be avoided when one had problems of one's own.

Without further questioning, at the same time solving her problem of how to win an electric toothbrush, Bunnie Vorobioff wrote a flight insurance policy, for three hundred thousand dollars, on D.O. Guerrero's life.

Guerrero mailed the policy to his wife, Inez, on his way to gate forty-seven and Flight Two.

13

US Customs Inspector Harry Standish did not hear the announcement of Flight Two's impending departure, but knew it had been made. Flight announcements were not relayed to the Customs Hall, since only international arriving passengers came there, so Standish obtained his information on the telephone, from Trans America Airlines. He had been informed that Flight Two was beginning to load at gate forty-seven and would depart at its rescheduled time of 11.0 pm.

Standish was watching the clock and would go to gate forty-seven in a few minutes, not on official business, but to say goodbye to his niece, Judy – his sister's child – who was leaving for a year's schooling in Europe. Standish had promised his sister, who lived in Denver, that he would see Judy off. Earlier this evening, in the terminal, he had spent some time with his niece – a pleasant, self-possessed girl of eighteen – and had said he would drop around for a final goodbye before her flight took off.

Meanwhile, Inspector Standish was trying to clear up a tiresome problem near the end of what had been an exceptionally tiresome day.

'Madam,' he said quietly to the haughty, angular woman whose several suitcases were spread open on the Customs inspection table between them, 'are you quite sure you don't wish to change your story?'

She snapped back, 'I suppose you're suggesting I should lie, when I've already told you the truth. Really! – you people are so officious, so disbelieving, I sometimes wonder if we're not living in a police state.'

Harry Standish ignored the second remark, as Customs officers were trained to ignore the many insults they received, and answered politely, 'I'm not suggesting anything, madam. I merely asked if you wished to amend your statement about these items – the dresses, the sweaters, and the fur coat.'

The woman, whose American passport showed that she was Mrs Harriet Du Barry Mossman who lived in Evanston, and had just returned from a month in England, France, and Denmark, replied acidly, 'No, I don't. Furthermore, when my husband's lawyer hears of this interrogation . . .'

'Yes, madam,' Harry Standish said. 'In that case, I wonder if you'd mind signing this form. If you like, I'll explain it to you.'

The dresses, sweaters, and fur coat were spread out on top of the suitcases. Mrs Mossman had been wearing the coat – a sable jacket – until a few minutes ago when Inspector Standish arrived at Customs inspection station number eleven; he had asked her to take the coat off so that he could look at it more closely. Shortly before that, a red light on a wall panel near the centre of the big Customs Hall had summoned Standish. The lights – one for each station – indicated that an inspecting officer had a problem and needed supervisory help.

Now, the young Customs man who had dealt with Mrs Mossman originally was standing at Inspector Standish's side. Most of the other passengers, who had arrived aboard a Scandinavian Airlines DC-8 from Copenhagen, had cleared Customs and had left. Only this well-dressed American woman posed a problem, insisting that all she had bought in Europe was some perfume, costume jewellery, and shoes. The total declared value was ninety dollars – ten dollars less than the free exemption she was allowed. The young officer had been suspicious.

'Why should I sign anything?' Mrs Harriet Du Barry Mossman demanded.

Standish glanced at an overhead clock; it was a quarter to eleven. He still had time to finish this and reach Flight Two before it left. He answered patiently, 'To make things easier for yourself, madam. We're merely asking you to confirm in writing what you've already told us. You say the dresses were purchased . . .'

'How many times must I tell you? They were bought in Chicago and New York before I left for Europe; so were the sweaters. The coat was a gift – purchased in the United States. I received it six months ago.'

Why, Harry Standish wondered, did people do it? All the statements just made, he knew with certainty, were lies.

To begin with, the dresses – six, all of good quality – had had their labels removed. No one did that innnocently; women were usually proud of the labels in quality clothes. More to the point – the workmanship of the dresses was unmistakably French; so was the tailoring of the fur coat – though a Saks Fifth Avenue label had been sewn unskilfully in the coat lining. What people like Mrs Mossman failed to realize was that a trained Customs man didn't need to see labels to know where garments originated. Cutting, stitching – even the way a zipper was put in – were like familiar handwriting, and equally distinctive.

The same thing was true of the three expensive sweaters. They also were without labels, and were unmistakably from Scotland, in typical British 'drab' shades, not available in the United States. When a US store ordered similar sweaters, the Scottish mills made them in much brighter colours, which the North American market favoured. All this, and much else, Customs officers learned as part of their training.

Mrs Mossman asked, 'What happens if I sign the form?'

'Then you may go, madam.'

'And take my things with me? All my things?'

'Yes.'

'Supposing I refuse to sign?'

'Then we shall be obliged to detain you here while we continue the investigation.'

There was the briefest hesitation, then: 'Very well. You fill out the form; I'll sign.'

'No, madam; *you* fill it out. Now here, please describe the items, and alongside where you say they were obtained. Please give the name of the stores; also from whom you received the fur coat as a gift . . .'

Harry Standish thought: He would have to leave in a minute; it was ten to eleven now. He didn't want to reach Flight Two after the doors were closed. But first he had a hunch . . .

He waited while Mrs Mossman completed the form and signed it.

Commencing tomorrow, an investigative officer would begin checking out the statement Mrs Mossman had just made. The dresses and sweaters would be requisitioned and taken to the stores where she claimed they were purchased; the fur jacket would be shown to Saks Fifth Avenue, who would undoubtedly disown it . . . Mrs Mossman – though she didn't know it yet – was in for a great of trouble, including some heavy Customs duty to be paid, and almost certainly a stiff fine.

'Madam,' Inspector Standish said, 'is there anything else you wish to declare?'

Mrs Mossman snapped indignantly, 'There certainly isn't!'

'You're sure?' It was Customs Bureau policy to give travellers the utmost opportunity to make voluntary declarations. People were not to be entrapped unless they brought it on themselves.

Not deigning to reply, Mrs Mossman inclined her head disdainfully.

'In that case, madam,' Inspector Standish said, 'will you kindly open your handbag?'

For the first time the haughty woman betrayed uncertainty. 'But surely, purses are never inspected. I've been through Customs many times . . .'

'Normally, they are not. But we do have the right.'

Asking to see the contents of a woman's handbag was a rarity; like a man's pockets, a handbag was considered personal and almost never looked into. But when an individual chose to be difficult, Customs men could be difficult too.

Reluctantly, Mrs Harriet Du Barry Mossman unclipped her purse.

Harry Standish inspected a lipstick and a gold compact. When he probed the powder in the compact, he extracted a diamond and ruby ring; he blew the powder on the ring away. There was a tube of hand lotion, partially used. Unrolling the tube, he could see that the bottom had been opened. When he pressed the tube near the top, there was something hard inside. He wondered when would-be smugglers would come up with something original. Such old tricks! He had seen them all many times.

Mrs Mossman was noticeably pale. Her hauteur had disappeared.

'Madam,' Inspector Standish said, 'I have to leave for a short while, but I'll be back. In any case, this is going to take some time.' He instructed the young Customs officer beside him, 'Inspect everything else very carefully. Check the linings of the bag and cases, the seams and hems of all the clothes. Make a list. You know what to do.'

He was leaving when Mrs Mossman called after him. 'Officer!'

He stopped. 'Yes, madam.'

'About the coat and dresses . . . perhaps I did make a mistake . . . I was confused. I did buy them, and there are some other things . . .'

Standish shook his head. What people never seemed to learn was that there had to be a cut-off point somewhere; after that, co-operation was too late. He saw that the young officer had found something else.

'Please! . . . I beg of you . . . my husband . . .' As the Inspector turned away, the woman's face was white and drawn.

Walking briskly, Harry Standish used a short cut, below the public portion of the terminal, to reach Concourse 'D' and gate forty-seven. As he went, he reflected on the foolishness of Mrs Harriet Du Barry Mossman and the many like her. Had she been honest about the coat and dresses, and declared them, the duty payable would not have been great, especially for someone who was clearly well-to-do. The young Customs officer, though noticing the sweaters, probably would not have bothered with them; and certainly her handbag would not have been inspected. Customs men were aware that most returning travellers did a little smuggling, and were often tolerant about it. Also, if asked, they would help people lump high-duty items under their duty-free exemption, charging duty on other articles which were entitled to lower rates.

The people who got nabbed, hit hard, and were sometimes prosecuted, were invariably the greedy ones like Mrs Mossman, who tried to get away with everything. What had depressed Harry Standish today was the number of others of her kind.

He was relieved to see that the doors of Trans America Flight Two had not yet closed, and a few remaining passengers were still being checked in. His US Customs uniform was a passport anywhere within the airport, and the busy gate agent barely glanced up as Inspector Standish went past. The gate agent, Standish noticed, was being helped by a redheaded woman passenger relations agent whom he knew as Mrs Livingston.

The inspector entered the walkway to the tourist section; a stewardess was at the rear aeroplane doorway. He smiled. 'I'll only be a moment. Don't take off with me aboard.'

He found his niece, Judy, in an aisle seat of a three-seat section. She was keeping a baby amused, the baby belonging to a young couple in the two seats alongside. Like all aeroplane tourist sections, this one already seemed cramped and crowded, the seats oppressively close to one another. On the few air journeys Inspector Standish made himself, he travelled tourist, but always had a sense of claustrophobia. Tonight he didn't envy any of these people the monotonous ten-hour journey which lay ahead of them.

'Uncle Harry!' Judy said. 'I thought you weren't going to make it.' She handed the baby back to its mother.

'I just came to say God bless!' he told her. 'Have a good year, and when you come back don't try any smuggling.'

She laughed. 'I won't. Goodbye, Uncle Harry.'

His niece put her face up to be kissed, and he bussed her affectionately. He felt good about Judy. He had a feeling she would not grow up to be a Mrs Mossman.

Leaving the aircraft, with a friendly nod to the stewardesses, the Customs inspector paused a moment at the concourse gate, watching. The last moments before departure of any flight, especially one for some far distant place, always fascinated him, as they did many people. The final call . . . *Trans America Airlines announce the immediate departure of Flight Two*, The Golden Argosy . . .' . . . was just coming over the p.a. system.

The knot of people waiting to board had been reduced to two. The redheaded passenger agent, Mrs Livingston, was gathering up her papers as the regular gate agent dealt with the last arrival but one – a tall blond man, hatless, and wearing a camel-hair coat. Now, the blond man left the agent's desk and entered the tourist section walkway. Mrs Livingston left too, walking away from the departure gate, towards the main section of the terminal.

While he had been watching, Inspector Standish was aware, almost subconsciously, of someone else nearby, facing a window which looked away from the departure gate. Now the figure turned. He saw that it was an old lady; she appeared small, demure, and frail. She was dressed primly in black in an old-fashioned style, and carried a black beaded purse. She looked as if she needed somebody to take care of her, and he wondered why someone so old, and apparently alone, was here so late at night.

Moving with surprising spryness, the old lady crossed to where the Trans America ticket agent was dealing with the last Flight Two passenger. Standish heard some, though not all, of what was said; the old lady's words were punctuated by noise from outside, from the aircraft engines, which were being started. 'Excuse . . . my son just boarded . . . blond hair, no hat, camel-hair coat . . . forgot his wallet . . . all his money.' The old lady, Standish observed, was holding what looked like a man's billfold.

The gate agent glanced up impatiently. He appeared harassed; gate men usually were at the last moments of departure. The agent put out his hand to take the wallet, then observing the old lady, changed his mind and said something quickly. He pointed to the tourist boarding walkway and Standish heard, 'Ask a stewardess.' The old lady smiled and nodded, and entered the walkway. A moment later she was out of sight.

All that Customs Inspector Standish had observed had taken only moments – perhaps less than a minute. Now, he saw a newcomer arrive – a stoop-shouldered, spindly man, hurrying down Concourse 'D' towards gate forty-seven. The man had a gaunt face and a slight sandy moustache. He was carrying a small attaché case.

Standish had been about to turn away, but something about the man attracted his attention. It was the way the newcomer was holding his case – under his arm, protectively. Harry Standish had watched people, many times, doing the same thing as they came through Customs. It was a giveaway that whatever was inside the case was something they wanted to conceal. If this man had been coming in from overseas, Standish would have had him open the case, and would have examined its contents. But the man was going *out* of the United States.

Strictly speaking, it was none of Harry Standish's business.

Yet something . . . instinct, a sixth sense which Customs men developed, plus a personal connection, through Judy, with Flight Two . . . something kept the inspector watching, his eyes directed at the small attaché case which the spindly man still cradled.

The feeling of confidence which returned to D. O. Guerrero at the insurance counter had remained. As he approached gate forty-seven, observing that he was still in time for Flight Two, he had a conviction that most of his difficulties were over; from now on, he assured himself, everything would work out as he had foreseen. In keeping with this belief, there was no problem at the gate. As he had planned from the beginning, at this point he drew attention to the minor discrepancy between the name 'Buerrero' on his ticket and 'Guerrero' on his passport. Barely glancing at the passport, the gate agent corrected both the ticket and his passenger list, then apologized, 'Sorry, sir; sometimes our reservation machines get careless.' Now, Guerrero noted with satisfaction, his name was recorded properly; later, when Flight Two was reported missing, there would be no doubt about his own identification.

'Have a pleasant flight, sir.' The gate agent returned his ticket folder and motioned towards the tourist section walkway.

As D. O. Guerrero went aboard, still holding his attaché case carefully, the starboard engines were already running.

His numbered seat – by a window in a three-seat section – had been allocated when he checked in downtown. A stewardess directed him to it. Another male passenger, already in the aisle seat, stood up partially as Guerrero squeezed by. The centre seat, between them, was unoccupied.

D. O. Guerrero balanced his case cautiously on his knees as he strapped himself in. His seat was midway in the tourist section, on the left side. Elsewhere in the cabin, other passengers were still settling down, arranging hand baggage and clothing; a few people were blocking the centre aisle. One of the stewardesses, her lips moving silently, and looking as if she wished everyone would keep still, was making a count of heads.

Relaxing for the first time since leaving the south side apartment, D. O. Guerrero leaned back in his seat and closed his eyes. His hands, steadier than at any other time this evening, were firmly on the attaché case. Without opening his eyes, his fingers groped under the handle and located the all-important loop of string. The feel of it was reassuring. He would sit precisely like this, he decided, when in approximately four hours from now he would pull the string, releasing the electrical current which would fire the massive charge of dynamite within the case. When the moment came, he wondered, how much would he have time to know? In answer, he reasoned: there would be an instant . . . one fleeting particle of a second only . . . when he would savour, triumphantly, the knowledge of success. Then, mercifully, no more . . .

Now that he was aboard and ready, he wished the flight would go. But when he opened his eyes, the same stewardess was still counting.

There were two stewardesses, at the moment, in the tourist cabin. The little old lady from San Diego, Mrs Ada Quonsett, had been observing them both, intermittently, peering through the slightly opened door of a toilet where she was hiding.

The pre-takeoff head count by a stewardess, now being made, was something which Mrs Quonsett knew about; she was also aware that this was the moment when anyone who was aboard illegally was closest to exposure. But if a stowaway could survive the count, chances were that she (or he) would not be detected until much later, if at all.

Fortunately the stewardess now making the head count was not the one whom Mrs Quonsett encountered when she came aboard.

Mrs Quonsett had had a few anxious moments outside while she cautiously watched the redheaded passenger agent bitch, whom she had been distressed to find on duty at gate forty-seven. Fortunately, the woman had left just before the flight finished loading, and getting past the male gate agent proved easy.

After that, Mrs Quonsett repeated her story about the wallet to the stewardess on duty at the aircraft doorway. The stewardess, who was trying to cope with queries from several other people milling in the entranceway, declined to accept the wallet when she learned there was 'a lot of money in it' – a reaction Mrs Quonsett had counted on. Also as expected, the little old lady was told she could take the wallet to her son herself, if she was quick.

The tall blond man who, all unknowingly, had been a 'son' to Mrs Quonsett, was getting into a seat near the front of the cabin. Mrs Quonsett moved in his direction, but only briefly. She was watching covertly, waiting for the attention of the stewardess near the door to be diverted. Almost at once it was.

Mrs Quonsett had left her plans flexible. There was a seat close by, which she could have occupied; however, a sudden movement by several passengers at once left a clear path to one of the aircraft toilets. A moment or two later, through the partially opened toilet door, she saw the original stewardess go forward out of sight and another stewardess begin the head count, starting at the front.

When the second stewardess – still counting – neared the back of the aeroplane, Mrs Quonsett emerged from the toilet and walked quickly past with a muttered 'Excuse me'. She heard the stewardess cluck her tongue impatiently. Mrs Quonsett sensed that she had now been included in the count – but that was all.

A few rows forward, on the left side, there was an unoccupied seat in the middle of a section of three. In her experience as an aerial stowaway, the little old lady from San Diego had learned to seek such seats because most passengers disliked them; therefore they were the last to be chosen from seat selection boards and, where an aeroplane was less than full, were usually left empty.

Once in the seat, Mrs Quonsett kept her head down, trying to be as inconspicuous as possible. She had no illusion that she could avoid discovery indefinitely. At Rome there would be Immigration and Customs formalities, making it impossible for her to walk away unimpeded, as she was accustomed to doing after her illegal flights to New York; but, with luck, she would have the thrill of reaching Italy, plus an agreeable journey back. Meanwhile, on this flight, there would be a good meal, a movie, and, later, perhaps, a pleasant conversation with her two seat companions.

Ada Quonsett wondered about her seat companions. She had noticed that both were men, but for the time being avoided looking at the man on her right since it would mean turning her face towards the aisle and the stewardesses, both of whom were now moving back and forth, making another head count. Mrs Quonsett took covert stock, however, of the man on her left, a survey made easier by the fact that he was reclining and had his eyes closed. He was a gaunt, thin man, she observed, with a sallow face and scrawny neck, who looked as if a hearty meal might do him good. He had a small sandy moustache.

On his knees, Mrs Quonsett noticed, the man on her left had an attaché case, and, despite the fact that his eyes were closed, he was holding it firmly.

The stewardesses had finished their head count. Now a third stewardess appeared from the first class compartment forward, and the three of them were holding a hurried consultation.

The man on Mrs Quonsett's left had opened his eyes. He was still gripping the case tightly. The little old lady from San Diego – an habitually curious soul – wondered what was inside.

Walking back towards the Customs Hall – this time through the passenger section of the terminal – Inspector Harry Standish was still thinking about the man with the attaché case. Standish could not have questioned the man; outside a Customs enclosure a Customs officer had no right to interrogate anyone, unless believing they had evaded Customs inspection. The man at the departure gate quite obviously had not.

What Standish could do, of course, was telegraph the man's description to Italian Customs, advising that he might be carrying contraband. But Standish doubted if he would. There was little co-operation between Customs departments internationally, only an intense professional rivalry. Even with Canadian Customs, close at hand, the same thing was true; incidents were on record where US Customs had been tipped off that illegal diamond shipments were being smuggled into Canada, but – as a matter of policy – Canadian authorities were never told. Instead, US agents spotted the suspects on arrival in Canada and tailed them, only making an arrest if they crossed the United States border. The US reasoning was: the country which seized that kind of contraband kept it all, and Customs departments were averse to sharing loot.

No, Inspector Standish decided, there would be no telegram to Italy. He would, however, tell Trans America Airlines of his doubts and leave a decision to them.

Ahead of him he had seen Mrs Livingston, the passenger relations agent who had been at the Flight Two departure gate. She was talking with a Skycap and a group of passengers. Harry Standish waited until the Skycap and passengers had gone.

'Hullo, Mr Standish,' Tanya said. 'I hope things are quieter in Customs than around here.'

'They aren't,' he told her, remembering Mrs Harriet Du Barry Mossman, no doubt still being questioned in the Customs Hall.

As Tanya waited for him to speak again, Standish hesitated. Sometimes he wondered if he was becoming too much of the super sleuth, too aware of the keenness of his instincts. Most times, though, his instincts proved right.

'I was watching your Flight Two load,' Standish said. 'There was something bothered me.' He described the gaunt, spindly man and the suspicious way he had been clasping an attaché case.

'Do you think he's smuggling something?'

Inspector Standish smiled. 'If he were arriving from abroad, instead of leaving, I'd find out. All I can tell you, Mrs Livingston, is that there's something in that case which he'd prefer other people not to know about.'

Tanya said thoughtfully, 'I don't quite know what I can do.' Even if the man *was* smuggling she was not convinced it was the airline's business.

'Probably there's nothing to do. But you people cooperate with us, so I thought I'd pass the information on.'

'Thank you, Mr Standish, I'll report it to our DTM, and perhaps he'll want to notify the captain.'

As the Customs inspector left, Tanya glanced at the overhead terminal clock; it showed a minute to eleven. Heading for Trans America Administration on the executive mezzanine, she reasoned: it was too late now to catch Flight Two at the departure gate; if the flight had not yet left the gate, it certainly would within the next few moments. She wondered if the District Transportation Manager was in his office. If the DTM thought the information important, he might notify Captain Demerest by radio while Flight Two was still on the ground and taxiing. Tanya hurried.

The DTM was not in his office, but Peter Coakley was.

Tanya snapped, 'What are you doing here?'

The young Trans America agent, whom the little old lady from San Diego had eluded, described sheepishly what had happened.

Peter Coakley had already received one dressing down. The doctor, summoned to the women's washroom on a fool's errand, had been articulate and wrathful. Young Coakley clearly expected more of the same from Mrs Livingston. He was not disappointed.

Tanya exploded, 'Damn, damn, damn!' She remonstrated, 'Didn't I warn you she had a barrelful of tricks?'

'Yes, you did, Mrs Livingston. I guess I . . .'

'Never mind that now! Get on the phone to each of our gates. Warn them to be on the lookout for an old, innocent-looking woman in black – you know the description. She's trying for New York, but may go a roundabout way. If she's located, the gate agent is to detain her and call here. She is not to be allowed on any flight, no matter what she says. While you're doing that, I'll call the other airlines.'

'Yes, ma'am.'

There were several telephones in the office. Peter Coakley took one, Tanya another.

She knew by memory the airport numbers of TWA, American, United, and Northwest; all four airlines had direct New York flights. Talking first with her opposite number in TWA, Jenny Henline, she could hear Peter Coakley saying, 'Yes, very old . . . in black . . . when you see her, you won't believe it . . .'

A contest of minds had developed, Tanya realized, between herself and the ingenious, slippery Ada Quonsett. Who, in the end, Tanya wondered, would outwit the other?

For the moment she had forgotten both her conversation with Customs Inspector Standish and her intention to locate the DTM.

Aboard Flight Two, Captain Vernon Demerest fumed, 'What in hell's the holdup?'

Engines numbers three and four, on the starboard side of aircraft N-731-TA, were running. Throughout the aeroplane their subdued but powerful jet thrumming could be felt.

The pilots had received ramp supervisor's clearance by interphone, several minutes ago, to start three and four, but were still awaiting clearance to start engines one and two, which were on the boarding side and normally not activated until all doors were closed. A red panel light had winked off a minute or two earlier, indicating that the rear fuselage door was closed and secure; immediately after, the rear boarding walkway was withdrawn. But another bright red light, still glowing, showed that the forward cabin door had not been closed, and a glance backwards through the cockpit windows confirmed that the front boarding walkway was still in place.

Swinging around in his right-hand seat, Captain Demerest instructed Second Officer Jordan, 'Open the door.'

Cy Jordan was seated behind the other two pilots at a complex panel of instruments and engine controls. Now he half rose and, extending his long, lean figure, released the flight deck door which opened outwards. Through the doorway, in the forward passenger section, they could see a half dozen figures in Trans America uniform, Gwen Meighen among them.

'Gwen!' Demerest called. As she came into the flight deck, 'What the devil's happening?'

Gwen looked worried. 'The tourist passenger count won't tally. We've made it twice; we still can't agree with the manifest and tickets.'

'Is the ramp supervisor there?'

'Yes, he's checking our count now.'

'I want to see him.'

At this stage of any airline flight there was always a problem of divided authority. Nominally the captain was already in command, but he could neither start engines nor taxi away without authorization from the ramp supervisor. Both the captain and ramp chief had the same objective – to make an on-schedule departure. However, their differing duties sometimes produced a clash.

A moment later, the uniformed ramp supervisor, a single silver stripe denoting his rank, arrived on the flight deck.

'Look, chum,' Demerest said, 'I know you've got problems, but so have we. How much longer do we sit here?'

'I've just ordered a ticket recheck, captain. There's one more passenger in the tourist section than there ought to be.'

'All right,' Demerest said. 'Now I'll tell *you* something. Every second we sit here we're burning fuel on three and four, *which you gave the okay to start* . . . precious fuel which we need in the air tonight. So unless this aeroplane leaves right now, I'm shutting everything down and we'll send for Fuelling to top off our tanks. There's another thing you ought to know: air traffic control just told us they have a temporary gap in traffic. If we taxi out right away, we can be off the ground fast; in ten minutes from now that may have changed. Now, you make the decision. What's it to be?'

Torn between dual responsibilities, the ramp supervisor hesitated. He knew the captain was right about burning fuel; yet to stop engines now, and top off tanks, would mean a further half hour's costly delay on top of the hour which Flight Two was late already. On the other hand, this was an important international flight on which the head count and ticket collection *ought* to agree. If there was really an unauthorized person aboard, and he was found and taken off, later the ramp supervisor could justify his decision to hold. But if the difference in tallies turned out to be a clerical error – as it might – the DTM would roast him alive.

He made the obvious decision. Calling through the flight deck door, he ordered, 'Cancel the ticket recheck. This flight is leaving now.'

As the flight deck door closed, a grinning Anson Harris was on the interphone to a crewman on the ground below. 'Clear to start two?'

The reply rattled back, 'Okay to start two.'

The forward fuselage door was closed and secured; in the cockpit, its red indicator light winked out.

Number two engine fired and held at a steady roar.

'Okay to start one?'

'Okay to start one.'

The forward boarding walkway, like a severed umbilical cord, was gliding back towards the terminal.

Vernon Demerest was calling ground control on radio for permission to taxi.

Number one engine fired and held.

In the left seat, Captain Harris, who would taxi out and fly the takeoff, had his feet braced on the rudder pedal toe brakes.

It was still snowing hard.

'Trans America Flight Two from ground control. You are clear to taxi . . .'

The engine tempo quickened.

Demerest thought: *Rome . . . and Naples . . . here we come!*

It was 11.0 pm, Central Standard Time.

In Concourse 'D', half running, half stumbling, a figure reached gate forty-seven.

Even if there had been breath to ask, questions were unneeded.

The boarding ramps were closed. Portable signs denoting the departure of Flight Two, *The Golden Argosy*, were being taken down. A taxiing aircraft was leaving the gate.

Helplessly, not knowing what she should do next, Inez Guerrero watched the aeroplane's lights recede.

PART THREE

11 pm–1.30 am (CST)

I

As always at the beginning of a flight, Senior Stewardess Gwen Meighen experienced a sense of relief as the forward cabin door slammed closed and, a few moments later, the aircraft began moving.

An airliner in a terminal was like a dependent relative, subject to the whims and succour of its family. Such life as it had was never independent. Its identity was blurred; supply lines hobbled it; strangers, who would never join its airborne complement, moved in and out.

But when the doors were sealed as the aeroplane prepared for takeoff, it became once more an entity. Crew members were most keenly aware of the change; they were returned to a familiar, self-contained environment in which they could function with skill and independence for which they had been trained. No one impeded them; nothing was underfoot, except what they were used to and at home with. Their tools and equipment were the finest; their resources and limitations were inventoried and known. Self-reliance returned. The camaraderie of the air – intangible, yet real to all who shared it – was theirs once more.

Even passengers – the more sensitive ones – were attuned to a mental transformation and, once in the air, awareness of the change increased. At high altitude, looking down, concerns of the everyday world seemed less important. Some, more analytical than others, saw the new perspective as a shedding of the pettiness of earth.

Gwen Meighen, occupied with pre-takeoff rituals, had no time for such analysis. While four of the five stewardesses busied themselves with housekeeping chores around the aeroplane, Gwen used the p.a. system to welcome passengers aboard. With her soft English voice, she did the best she could with the treacly, insincere paragraph from her stewardess manual, which the company insisted must be read on every flight.

'On behalf of Captain Demerest and your crew . . . our most sincere wish that your flight will be pleasant and relaxing . . . shortly we shall have the pleasure of serving . . . if there is anything we can do to make your flight more enjoyable. . .'

Gwen wondered sometimes when airlines would realize that most passengers found such announcements, at the beginning and end of every flight, a boring intrusion.

More essential were the announcements about emergency exits, oxygen masks, and ditching. With two of the other stewardesses demonstrating, she accomplished them quickly.

They were still taxiing, Gwen observed – tonight more slowly than usual, taking longer to reach their takeoff runway. No doubt the reason was traffic and the storm. From outside she could hear an occasional splatter of wind-driven snow on windows and fuselage.

There was one more announcement to be made – that which aircrews liked least. It was required before takeoffs at Lincoln International, New York, Boston, Cleveland, San Francisco, and other airports with residential areas nearby.

'Shortly after takeoff you will notice a marked decrease in engine noise, due to a reduction in power. This is perfectly normal and is done as a courtesy to those who live near the airport and in the direct flight path.'

The second statement was a lie. The power reduction was neither normal nor desirable. The truth was: it was a concession – some said a mere public relations gesture – involving risk to aircraft safety and human life. Pilots fought noise abatement power restrictions bitterly. Many pilots, at risk of their careers, refused to observe them.

Gwen had heard Vernon Demerest parody, in private, the announcement she had just made . . . 'Ladies and gentlemen, at the most critical point of takeoff, when we need our best power and have a hundred other things to do in the cockpit, we are about to throttle back drastically, then make a steep climbing turn at high gross weight and minimum speed. This is an exceedingly foolish manoeuvre for which a student pilot would be thrown out of flying school. However, we are doing it on orders from our airline employers and the Federal Aviation Administration because a few people down below, who built their houses long after the airport was established, are insisting that we tiptoe past. They don't give a damn about air safety, or that we are risking your lives and ours. So hang on tight, folks! Good luck to us all, and please start praying.'

Gwen smiled, remembering. There were so many things she appreciated about Vernon. He was energetically alive; he possessed strong feelings; when something interested him, he became actively involved. Even his failings – the abrasive manner, his conceit – were masculine and interesting. He could be tender, too – and was, in lovemaking, though responding eagerly to passion as Gwen had cause to know. Of all the men she knew, there was no one whose child she would bear more gladly than Vernon Demerest's. In the thought there was a bitter sweetness.

Replacing the p.a. microphone in its forward cabin niche, she was aware that the aircraft's taxiing pace had slowed; they must be near the takeoff point. These were the last few minutes she would have – for several hours to come – with any opportunity for private thoughts. After takeoff there would be no time for anything but work. Gwen had four stewardesses to supervise, as well as her own duties in the first class cabin. A good many overseas flights had male stewards directing cabin service, but Trans America encouraged senior women staffers like Gwen to take charge when they proved themselves capable.

Now the aircraft had stopped. From a window Gwen could see the lights of another aircraft ahead, several others in line behind. The one ahead was turning on to a runway; Flight Two would be next. Gwen pulled down a folding seat and strapped herself in. The other girls had found seats elsewhere.

She thought again: a bitter sweetness, and always the same single question recurring. Vernon's child, and her own – an abortion or not? . . . Yes or no? To be or not to be? . . . *They were on the runway* . . . Abortion or no abortion? . . . *The engines' tempo was increasing. They were rolling already, wasting no time; in seconds, no more, they would be in the air* . . . Yes or no? To permit to live or condemn to die? How, between love and reality, conscience and commonsense, did anyone decide?

As it happened, Gwen Meighen need not have made the announcement about power reduction.

On the flight deck, taxiing out, Captain Harris told Demerest gruffly, 'I plan to ignore noise abatement procedures tonight.'

Vernon Demerest, who had just copied their complicated route clearance, received by radio – a task normally performed by the absent First Officer – nodded. 'Damn right! I would too.'

Most pilots would have let it go at that, but, characteristically, Demerest pulled the flight log towards him and made an entry in the 'Remarks' column: 'NAP not observed. Reason: weather, safety.'

Later, there might be trouble about that log entry, but it was the kind of trouble Demerest enjoyed and would meet head on.

The cockpit lights were dimmed. Pre-takeoff checks had been completed.

They had been lucky in the temporary traffic lull; it had allowed them to reach their takeoff point, at the head of runway two five, quickly, and without the long ground hiatus which had plagued most other flights tonight. Already though, for others following, the delay was building up again. Behind Trans America Flight Two was a growing line of waiting aircraft and a procession of others taxiing out from the terminal. On radio, the ATC ground controller was issuing a swift stream of instructions to flights of United Air Lines, Eastern, American, Air France, Flying Tiger, Lufthansa, Braniff, Continental, Lake Central, Delta, TWA, Ozark, Air Canada, Alitalia, and Pan Am, their assorted destinations like an index of world geography.

Flight Two's additional fuel reserves, ordered by Anson Harris to allow for extra ground running time, had not, after all, been needed. But even with the heavy fuel load, they were still within safe takeoff limits, as Second Officer Jordan had just calculated, spreading out his graphs once more, as he would many times tonight and tomorrow before the flight ended.

Both Demerest's and Harris's radios were now switched to runway control frequency.

On runway two five, immediately ahead of Trans America, a British VC-10 of BOAC received word to go. It moved forward, with lumbering slowness at first, then swiftly. Its company colours – blue, white, and gold – gleamed briefly in the reflection of other aircrafts' lights, then were gone in a flurry of whirling snow and black jet exhaust. Immediately the ground controller's voice intoned, 'Trans America Two, taxi into position, runway two five, and hold; traffic landing on runway one seven left.'

One seven left was a runway which directly bisected runway two five. There was an element of danger in using the two runways together, but tower controllers had become adept at spacing aircraft – landing and taking off – so that no time was wasted, but no two aeroplanes reached the intersection at the same moment. Pilots, uncomfortably aware of the danger of collison when they heard by radio that both runways were in use, obeyed controllers' orders implicitly.

Anson Harris swiftly and expertly jockeyed Flight Two on to runway two five.

Peering out, through snow flurries, Demerest could see the lights of an aeroplane, about to touch down on one seven. He thumbed his mike button. 'Trans America Two, Roger. In position and holding. We see the landing traffic.'

Even before the landing aircraft had bisected their own runway, the controller's voice returned. 'Trans America Two, cleared for takeoff. Go, man, go!'

The final three words were not in any air traffic control manual, but to controllers and pilots they had identical meaning: *Get the hell moving, now! There's another flight landing right after the last.* Already a fresh set of lights – ominously close to the airfield – was approaching runway one seven.

Anson Harris had not waited. His outspread fingers slid the four main throttles forward to their full extent. He ordered, 'Trim the throttles,' and briefly held his toe brakes on, allowing power to build, as Demerest set pressure ratios evenly for all four engines. The engines' sound deepened from a steady whine to a thunderous roar. Then Harris released the brakes and N-731-TA leaped forward down the runway.

Vernon Demerest reported to the tower, 'Trans America Two on the roll,' then applied forward pressure to the control yoke while Harris used nose wheel steering with his left hand, his right returning to the throttles.

Speed built. Demerest called, 'Eighty knots.' Harris nodded, released nose wheel steering, and took over the control yoke . . . Runway lights flashed by in swirling snow. Near crescendo, the big jets' power surged . . . At a hundred and thirty-two knots, as calculated earlier, Demerest called out 'V-one' – notification to Harris that they had reached 'decision speed' at which the takeoff could still be aborted and the aircraft stopped. Beyond V-one the takeoff must continue . . . Now they were past V-one . . . Still gathering speed, they hurtled through the runways' intersection, glimpsing to their right a flash of landing lights of the approaching plane; in mere seconds the other aircraft would cross where Flight Two had just passed. Another risk – skilfully calculated – had worked out; only pessimists believed that one day such a risk might not . . . As speed reached a hundred and fifty-four knots, Harris began rotation, easing the control column back. The nose wheel left the runway surface; they were in lift-off attitude, ready to quit the ground. A moment later, with speed still increasing, they were in the air.

Harris said quietly, 'Gear up.'

Demerest reached out, raising a lever on the central instrument panel. The sound of the retracting landing gear reverberated through the aircraft, then stopped with a thud as the doors to the wheel wells closed.

They were going up fast – passing through four hundred feet. In a moment, the night and clouds would swallow them.

'Flaps twenty.'

Still performing first officer duty, Demerest obediently moved the control pedestal flap selector from thirty degrees to twenty. There was a brief sensation of sinking as the wing flaps – which provided extra lift at takeoff – came partially upward.

'Flaps up.'

Now the flaps were fully retracted.

Demerest noted, for his report later, that at no point during takeoff could he have faulted Anson Harris's performance in the slightest degree. He had not expected to. Despite the earlier needling, Vernon Demerest was aware that Harris was a top-grade captain, as exacting in performance – his own and others – as Demerest was himself. It was the reason Demerest had known in advance that their flight to Rome tonight would be, for himself, an easy journey.

Only seconds had passed since leaving the ground; now, still climbing steeply, they passed over the runway's end, the lights below already dimming through cloud and falling snow. Anson Harris had ceased looking out and was flying on instruments alone.

Second Officer Cy Jordan was reaching forward from his flight engineer's seat, adjusting the throttles to equalize the power of all four engines.

Within the clouds there was a good deal of buffeting; at the outset of their journey, the passengers behind were getting a rough ride. Demerest snapped the 'No Smoking' light switch off; the 'Fasten Seat Belts' sign would remain on until Flight Two reached more stable air. Later, either Harris or Demerest would make an announcement to the passengers; but not yet. At the moment, flying was more important.

Demerest reported to departure control. 'Turning portside one eight zero; leaving fifteen hundred feet.'

He saw Anson Harris smile at his use of the words 'turning portside' instead of 'turning left'. The former was correct but unofficial. It was one of Demerest's own phrases; many veteran pilots had them – a minor rebellion against ATC officialese which nowadays all flying people were supposed to hew to. Controllers on the ground frequently learned to recognize individual pilots by such personal idioms.

A moment later Flight Two received radio clearance to climb to twenty-five thousand feet. Demerest acknowledged while Anson Harris kept the aircraft climbing. Up there in a few minutes from now they would be in clear, calm air, the storm clouds far below, and high above, in sight, the stars.

The 'turning portside' phrase *had* been noticed on the ground – by Keith Bakersfeld.

Keith had returned to radar watch more than an hour ago, after the time spent in the controllers' locker room alone, remembering the past and reaffirming his intention of tonight.

Several times since then Keith's hand had gone instinctively into his pocket, touching the key of his covertly rented room at the O'Hagan Inn. Otherwise, he had concentrated on the radarscope in front of him. He was now handling arrivals from the east and the continuing heavy traffic volume demanded intensive concentration.

He was not concerned directly with Flight Two; however, the departure controller was only a few feet away and in a brief interval between his own transmissions Keith heard the 'turning portside' phrase and recognized it, along with his brother-in-law's voice. Until then, Keith had no idea that Vernon Demerest was flying tonight; there was no reason why he should. Keith and Vernon saw little of each other. Like Mel, Keith had never achieved any close rapport with his brother-in-law, though there had been none of the friction between them which marred relations between Demerest and Mel.

Shortly after Flight Two's departure, Wayne Tevis, the radar supervisor, propelled his castor-equipped chair across to Keith.

'Take five, buddyboy,' Tevis said in his nasal Texan drawl. 'I'll spell you. Your big brother dropped in.'

As he unplugged his headset and turned, Keith made out the figure of Mel behind him in the shadows. He remembered his earlier hope that Mel would not come here tonight; at the time Keith feared that a meeting between the two of them might be more than he could handle emotionally. Now he found that he was glad Mel had come. They had always been good friends as well as brothers, and it was right and proper there should be a leave-taking, though Mel would not know that it was that – at least, until he learned tomorrow.

'Hi,' Mel said. 'I was passing by. How have things been?'

Keith shrugged. 'I guess, all right.'

'Coffee?' Mel had picked up two take-out coffees from one of the airport restaurants on his way. They were in a paper bag; he offered one of the cups to Keith and took the other himself.

'Thanks.' Keith was grateful for the coffee as well as for the break. Now that he was away from the radarscope, if only briefly, he realized that his own mental tension had been accumulating again within the past hour. He observed, as if watching someone else, that his hand holding the coffee cup was not entirely steady.

Mel glanced around the busy radar room. He was careful not to look too obviously at Keith whose appearance – the gaunt, strained face with deep hollows beneath the eyes – had shocked him. Keith's appearance had deteriorated over recent months; tonight, Mel thought, his brother looked worse than at any time before.

His mind still on Keith, he nodded towards the profusion of radar equipment. 'I wonder what the old man would have thought of all this.'

The 'old man' was – had been – their father, Wally (Wild Blue) Bakersfeld, stick-and-goggles aviator, stunt flier, crop duster, night mail carrier, and parachute jumper – the last when he needed money badly enough. Wild Blue had been a contemporary of Lindbergh, a crony of Orville Wright, and had flown to the end of his life, which terminated abruptly in a filmed Hollywood stunt sequence – an aeroplane crash, intended to be simulated, but which turned out to be real. It happened when Mel and Keith were in their teens, but not before Wild Blue had inculcated in both boys an acceptance of aviation as their way of life, which persisted into adulthood. In Keith's case, Mel sometimes thought, the father had done his younger son a disservice.

Keith shook his head without answering Mel's question, which didn't matter because it had been only rhetorical, Mel marking time while wondering how best to approach what was uppermost in his mind. He decided to do it directly.

Keeping his voice low, Mel said, 'Keith, you're not well; you're looking damned awful. I know it, you know it; so why pretend? If you'll let me, I'd like to help. Can we talk about whatever the trouble is? We've always been honest with each other.'

'Yes,' Keith acknowledged, 'we've always been that.' He sipped his coffee, not meeting Mel's eyes.

The reference to their father, though casual, had moved Keith strangely. He remembered Wild Blue well; he had been a poor provider – the Bakersfeld family was perpetually short of money – but a genial man with his children, especially if the talk was about flying, as the two boys usually wanted it to be. Yet in the end it was not Wild Blue who had been a father figure to Keith, but Mel; Mel Bakersfeld who possessed the sound sense and stability, as far back as Keith remembered, which their father lacked. It was Mel who always looked out for Keith, though never being ostentatious about it, or over protective as some older brothers were, robbing a younger boy of dignity. Mel had a facility, even then, for doing things for people and making them feel good at the same time.

Mel had shared things with Keith, had been considerate and thoughtful, even in small ways. He still was. Bringing the coffee tonight was an example, Keith thought, then checked himself: Don't wax sentimental over a carton of coffee just because this is a last meeting. This time, Keith's aloneness, his anguish and guilt were beyond Mel's fixing. Even Mel could not bring back to life little Valerie Redfern and her parents.

Mel motioned with his head and they moved to the corridor outside the radar room.

'Listen, old chum,' Mel said. 'You need a break from all this – a long one; perhaps more than a break. Maybe you need to get away for good.'

For the first time Keith smiled. 'You've been listening to Natalie.'

'Natalie's apt to talk a lot of sense.'

Whatever Keith's other problems might be, Mel reflected, he had been outstandingly fortunate in Natalie. The thought of his sister-in-law reminded Mel of his own wife, Cindy, who presumably was still on her way to the airport. Comparing your own marriage unfavourably with someone else's was disloyal, Mel supposed; at times, though, it was hard not to do it. He wondered if Keith really knew just how lucky – at least in that important area – he had been.

'There's something else,' Mel said. 'I haven't brought it up before, but maybe now's the time. I don't think you've ever told me the whole of what happened at Leesburg – that day, the accident. Maybe you didn't tell anyone, because I've read all the testimony. *Is* there something else; that you've never told?'

Keith hesitated only momentarily. 'Yes.'

'I figured there might be.' Mel chose his words carefully; he sensed that what was passing between them could be of critical importance. 'But I also figured if you wanted me to know, you'd tell me; and if you didn't, well, it was none of my business. Sometimes, though, if you care about someone enough – say, like a brother – you ought to make it your business, whether they want you to butt in or not. So I'm making this mine now.' He added softly, 'You hear me?'

'Yes,' Keith said, 'I hear you.' He thought: He could stop this conversation, of course; perhaps he should stop it now, at once – since it was pointless – by excusing himself and going back to the radarscope. Mel would assume they could resume later, not knowing that for the two of them together, there would be no later.

'That day at Leesburg,' Mel insisted. 'The part you've never told – it has something to do with the way you feel, the way you *are*, right now. Hasn't it?'

Keith shook his head. 'Leave it alone, Mel. Please!'

'Then I'm right. There *is* a relationship, isn't there?'

What was the point of denying the obvious? Keith nodded. 'Yes.'

'Won't you tell me? You have to tell someone; sooner or later you have to.' Mel's voice was pleading, urgent. 'You can't live with this thing – whatever it is – inside you for ever. Who better to tell than me? I'd understand.'

You can't live with this . . . Who better to tell than me?

It seemed to Keith that his brother's voice, even the sight of Mel, was coming to him through a tunnel, from the distant end, far away. At the farther end of the tunnel, too, were all the other people – Natalie, Brian, Theo, Perry Yount, Keith's friends – with whom he had lost communication long since. Now, of them all, Mel alone was reaching out, striving to bridge the gap between them . . . but the tunnel was long, their apartness – after all the length of time that Keith had been alone – was too great.

And yet . . .

As if someone else were speaking, Keith asked, 'You mean tell you here? Now?'

Mel urged, 'Why not?'

Why not, indeed? Something within Keith stirred; a sense of wanting to unburden, even though in the end it could change nothing . . . Or could it? Wasn't that what the Confessional was all about; a catharsis; an exorcism of sin through acknowledgement and contrition? The difference, of course, was that the Confessional gave forgiveness and expiation, and for Keith there could be no expiation – ever. At least . . . he hadn't thought so. Now he wondered what Mel might say.

Somewhere in Keith's mind a door, which had been closed, inched open.

'I suppose there's no reason,' he said slowly, 'why I shouldn't tell you. It won't take long.'

Mel remained silent. Instinct told him that if wrong words were spoken they could shatter Keith's mood, could cut off the confidence which seemed about to be given, which Mel had waited so long and anxiously to hear. He reasoned: if he could finally learn what bedevilled Keith, between them they might come to grips with it. Judging by his brother's appearance tonight, it had better be soon.

'You've read the testimony,' Keith said. His voice was a monotone. 'You just said so. You know most of what happened that day.'

Mel nodded.

'What you don't know, or anybody knows except me; what didn't come out at the inquiry, what I've thought about over and over . . .' Keith hesitated; it seemed as if he might not continue.

'For God's sake! For your own reason, for Natalie's sake, for mine – go on!'

It was Keith's turn to nod. 'I'm going to.'

He began describing the morning at Leesburg a year and a half before; the air traffic picture when he left for the washroom; supervisor Perry Yount; the trainer controller left in immediate charge. In a moment, Keith thought, he would admit how he had loitered; how he had failed the others through indifference and negligence; how he returned to duty too late; how the accident, the triple tragedy of the Redferns' deaths, had been solely his own doing; and how others were blamed. Now that at last he was doing what he had longed to, without knowing it, there was a sense of blessed relief. Words, like a cataract long dammed, began tumbling out.

Mel listened.

Abruptly, a door farther down the corridor opened. A voice – the tower watch chief's – called, 'Oh, Mr Bakersfeld!'

His footsteps echoing along the corridor, the tower chief walked towards them. 'Lieutenant Ordway has been trying to reach you, Mr Bakersfeld; so has the Snow Desk. They both want you to call.' He nodded. 'Hi, Keith!'

Mel wanted to cry out, to shout for silence or delay, plead to be alone with Keith for a few minutes more. But he knew it was no good. At the first sound of the tower chief's voice Keith had stopped in mid-sentence as if a switch were snapped to 'off'.

Keith had not, after all, reached the point of describing his own guilt to Mel. As he responded automatically to the tower chief's greeting, he wondered: Why had he begun at all? What could he have hoped to gain? There could never be any gain, never any forgetting. No confession – to whomever made – would exorcise memory. Momentarily he had grasped at what he mistook for a faint flicker of hope, even perhaps reprieve. As it had to be, it proved illusory. Perhaps it was as well that the interruption occurred when it did.

Once more, Keith realized, a mantle of loneliness, like an invisible thick curtain, surrounded him. Inside the curtain he was alone with his thoughts, and inside his thoughts was a private torture chamber where no one, not even a brother, could reach through.

From that torture chamber . . . waiting, always waiting . . . there could be only one relief. It was the way he had already chosen, and would carry through.

'I guess they could use you back inside, Keith,' the tower watch chief said. It was the gentlest kind of chiding. Keith had already had one work-break tonight; another inevitably threw a heavier load on other people. It was also a reminder to Mel, perhaps unintended, that as airport general manager his writ did not run here.

Keith mumbled something and gave a distant nod. With a sense of helplessness, Mel watched his brother return to the radar room. He had heard enough to know that it was desperately important he should hear more. He wondered when that would be, and how. A few minutes ago he had broken through Keith's reserve, his secrecy. Would it happen again? With despair, Mel doubted it.

For sure, there would be no more confidences from Keith tonight.

'I'm sorry, Mr Bakersfeld.' As if belatedly guessing Mel's thoughts, the tower chief spread his hands. 'You try to do the best for everybody. It isn't always easy.'

'I know.' Mel felt like sighing, but restrained himself. When something like this happened, you could only hope for the right occasion to occur again; meanwhile you got on with other things you had to do.

'Tell me please,' Mel said, 'what were those messages again?'

The tower chief repeated them.

Instead of telephoning the Snow Control Desk, Mel walked down one floor of the control tower and went in. Danny Farrow was still presiding over the busy snow clearance command console.

There was a query about priorities in clearing the aircraft parking areas of competing airlines, which Mel settled, then checked on the situation concerning the blocked runway, three zero. There was no change, except that Joe Patroni was now on the airfield and had taken charge of attempts to move the mired Aéreo-Mexican 707, which was still preventing the runway being used. A few minutes earlier, Patroni had reported by radio that he expected to make a new attempt to move the aircraft within an hour. Knowing Joe Patroni's reputation as a top-notch troubleshooter, Mel decided there was nothing to be gained by demanding a more detailed report.

At the Snow Desk Mel remembered the message to call Police Lieutenant Ordway. Assuming that the lieutenant was still in the terminal, Mel had him paged and, a few moments later, Ordway came on the line. Mel expected the lieutenant's call to be about the anti-noise delegation of Meadowood residents. It wasn't.

'The Meadowood people are starting to come in, but they haven't been a problem and they haven't asked for you yet,' Ned Ordway said when Mel raised the question. 'I'll let you know when they do.'

What he had called about, the policeman reported, was a woman who had been picked up by one of his men. She was crying, and apparently wandering aimlessly in the main terminal. 'We couldn't get any sense out of her, but she wasn't doing anything wrong so I didn't want to take her to the station house. She seemed upset enough without that.'

'What did you do? '

Ordway said apologeticaly, 'There aren't many quiet places around here tonight, so I put her in the anteroom outside your office. I thought I'd let you know in case you got back and wondered.'

'That's all right. Is she alone?'

'One of my men was with her, though he may have left by now. But she's harmless; I'm sure of that. We'll check on her again soon.'

179

'I'll be back at my office in a few minutes,' Mel said. 'I'll see if I can do any good myself.' He wondered if he would have more success talking with the unknown woman than he had had with Keith; he doubted if he could do worse. The thought of Keith, who seemed close to breaking point, still troubled Mel deeply.

As an afterthought, he asked, 'Did you find out the woman's name?'

'Yes, we got that much. It's a Spanish-sounding name. Just a minute. I have it written down.'

There was a pause, then Lieutenant Ordway said, 'Her name is Guerrero. Mrs Inez Guerrero.'

Tanya Livingston said incredulously, 'You mean Mrs Quonsett's aboard Flight Two?'

'I'm afraid there's no doubt of it, Mrs Livingston. There was a little old lady, exactly the way you've described her.' The gate agent who had supervised boarding of *The Golden Argosy* was in the DTM's office with Tanya and young Peter Coakley, the latter still mortified at having been bamboozled by Mrs Ada Quonsett while she was in his charge.

The gate agent had come to the office a few minutes ago in response to Coakley's telephoned warning, to all Trans America gate positions, about the elusive Mrs Quonsett.

'It just didn't occur to me there was anything wrong,' the gate agent said. 'We let other visitors aboard tonight; they came off.' He added defensively, 'Anyway, I'd been under pressure all evening. We were short staffed, and apart from the time you were there helping, I was doing the work of two people. You know that.'

'Yes,' Tanya said, 'I know.' She had no intention of passing out blame. If anyone was responsible for what had happened, it was Tanya herself.

'It was just after you left, Mrs Livingston. The old lady said something about her son, I think it was, leaving his wallet. She even showed it to me. It had money in it, she said, which was why I didn't take it.'

'She'd already figured that. It's one of her regular gags.'

'I didn't know it, so I let her go aboard. From then until a few minutes ago when I got the phone call, I never gave her another thought.'

'She fools you,' Peter Coakley said. He gave a sideways glance at Tanya. 'She sure fooled me.'

The agent shook his head. 'If I didn't have to believe it, I wouldn't, even now. But she's aboard, all right.' He described the discrepancy between the tourist section head count and the ticket tally, then afterwards, the ramp supervisor's decision to let the aircraft go, rather than incur further delay.

Tanya said quickly, 'I suppose there's no doubt Flight Two's already taken off.'

'Yes, they have. I checked on my way here. Even if they hadn't, I doubt they'd bring the aircraft back in, especially tonight.'

'No they wouldn't.' Nor was there the slightest chance, Tanya knew, of *The Golden Argosy* changing course and returning for a landing, merely because of Ada Quonsett. The time and cost to disembark one stowaway would run to thousands of dollars – far more than to take Mrs Quonsett to Rome and bring her back.

'Is there a refuelling stop?' Sometimes, Tanya knew, Europe-bound flights made non-scheduled stops for fuel at Montreal or Newfoundland. If so, there would be a chance to pull Mrs Quonsett off, robbing her of the satisfaction of getting all the way to Italy.

'I asked Operations about that,' the agent answered. 'The flight plan shows they're going right through. No stops.'

Tanya exclaimed, 'Damn that old woman!'

So Ada Quonsett was going to get her ride to Italy and back, with probably a night's lodging in between, and with meals supplied – all at airline expense. Tanya thought angrily: she had underestimated the old lady's determination not to be sent back to the West Coast; she had erred also in assuming that Mrs Quonsett would head only for New York.

Barely fifteen minutes earlier Tanya had thought of the developing contest between herself and Ada Quonsett as a battle of wits. If it was, without doubt the little old lady from San Diego had won.

With uncharacteristic savageness, Tanya wished that the airline would make an exception and prosecute Mrs Quonsett. But she knew they wouldn't.

Young Peter Coakley started to say something.

Tanya snapped, 'Oh, shut up!'

The District Transportation Manager returned to his office a few minutes after Coakley and the gate agent left. The DTM, Bert Weatherby, was a hard-working, hard-driving executive in his late forties, who had come up the hard way, beginning as a ramp baggage handler. Normally considerate, and with a sense of humour, tonight he was tired and testy from three days of continuous strain. He listened impatiently to Tanya's report in which she accepted the main responsibility herself, mentioning Peter Coakley only incidentally.

Running a hand through his sparse greying hair, the DTM observed, 'I like to check that there's still some left up there. It's things like this that are making the rest of it fall out.' He considered, then rasped, 'You got us into this mess; you'd better do the salvaging. Talk to Flight Dispatch; ask them to call the captain of Flight Two on company radio and fill him in on what happened. I don't know what he can do. Personally, I'd like to throw the old hag out at thirty thousand feet, but that'll be up to him. By the way, who is the captain?'

'Captain Demerest.'

The DTM groaned. 'It would be. He'll probably think it's all a great joke because management boobed. Anyway, advise him the old biddy's to be detained on board after landing, and is not to be allowed off without escort. If the Italian authorites want to jail her, so much the better. Then get a signal off to our station manager in Rome. When they arrive it'll be his baby, and I hope he's got more competent people around him than I have.'

'Yes, sir,' Tanya said.

She started to tell the DTM of the other matter concerning Flight Two – the suspicious-looking man with an attaché case whom Customs Inspector Standish had seen going aboard. Before she could finish, the DTM cut her off.

'Forget it! What do the Customs people want us to do – their job? As long as the airline's not involved, I don't give a damn what the guy's carrying. If Customs here want to know what's in his case, let them ask Italian Customs to check, not us. I'll be damned if I'll interrogate, and maybe offend, a fare-paying passenger for something that's none of our business.'

Tanya hesitated. Something about the man with the attaché case – even though she hadn't actually seen him – bothered her. There were instances she had heard of where . . . Of course, the idea was absurd . . .

'I was wondering,' she said. 'He might not be smuggling at all.'

The DTM snapped, 'I said forget it.'

Tanya left. Back at her desk, she began writing the message to Captain Demerest of Flight Two concerning Mrs Ada Quonsett.

2

In a taxi en route to the airport from downtown, Cindy Bakersfeld leaned back against the rear seat and closed her eyes. She was neither aware, nor cared, that outside it was still snowing, nor that the taxi was moving slowly in heavy traffic. She was in no hurry. A wave of physical pleasure and contentment (was the right word euphoria? Cindy wondered) swept over her.

The cause was Derek Eden.

Derek Eden, who had been at the Archidona Relief Fund cocktail party (Cindy still didn't know *which* Archidona); who had brought her a triple-strength Bourbon, which she hadn't drunk, then had propositioned her in the most unimaginative way. Derek Eden, until today only a slightly known *Sun-Times* reporter with a second-grade by-line; Derek Eden with the dissolute face, the casual air, the nondescript unpressed clothes; Derek Eden and his beat-up filthy-inside-and-out Chevrolet; Derek Eden, who had caught Cindy in a barriers-down moment, when she needed a man, any man, and she hadn't hoped for much; Derek Eden who had proved to be the finest and most exciting lover she had ever known.

Never, never before had Cindy experienced anyone like him. Oh, God! she thought; if ever there was sensual, physical perfection, she attained it tonight. More to the point; now that she had known Derek Eden . . . dear Derek . . . she wanted him again – often. Fortunately, it was unmistakable that he now felt the same way about her.

Still leaning back in the rear of the taxi, she relived mentally the past two hours.

They had driven, in the awful old Chevrolet, from the Lake Michigan Inn to a smallish hotel near the Merchandise Mart. A doorman accepted the car disdainfully – Derek Eden didn't seem to notice – and inside, in the lobby, the night manager was waiting. Cindy gathered that one of the phone calls which her escort had made was to here. There was no formality of checking in, and the night manager showed them directly to a room on the eleventh floor. After leaving the key, and with a quick 'goodnight', he left.

The room was so-so; old fashioned, spartan, and with cigarette burns on the furniture, but clean. It had a double bed. Beside the bed, on a table, was an unopened bottle of Scotch, some mixes and ice. A card on the liquor tray read, '*With the manager's compliments*'; Derek Eden inspected the card, then put it in his pocket.

When Cindy inquired, later on, Derek explained, 'Sometimes a hotel will oblige the press. When they do, we don't make any promises; the paper wouldn't go for it. But maybe sometimes a reporter or a deskman will put the hotel's name in a story if it's an advantage; or if the story's a bad one – like a death; hotels hate that – we might leave it out. As I say, no promises. You do the best you can.'

They had a drink, and chatted, then another and during the second drink he began to kiss her. It was soon after that she became aware of the gentleness of his hands, which he passed through her hair quite a lot to begin with, in a way which she could feel through her entire body; then the hands began exploring slowly, oh, so slowly . . . and it was also then that Cindy began to realize this might be something special.

While he was undressing her, demonstrating a finesse which he had lacked earlier, he whispered, 'Don't let's hurry, Cindy – either of us.' But soon after, when they were in bed, and wonderfully warm, as Derek Eden promised in the car they would be, she *had* wanted to hurry, and cried out, 'Yes, yes! . . . Oh, please! I can't wait!' But he insisted gently, 'Yes, you can. You must.' And she obeyed him, being utterly, deliciously in his control, while he led her as if by the hand like a child, close to the brink, then back a pace or two while they waited with a feeling like floating in air; then near once more, and back, and the same again and again, the bliss of it all near-unendurable; and finally when neither of them could wait longer, there was a shared crescendo like a hymn of heaven and a thousand sweet symphonies; and if Cindy had been able to choose a moment for dying, because nothing afterwards could ever be that moment's equal, she would have chosen then.

Later, Cindy decided that one of the things she liked about Derek Eden was his total lack of humbug. Ten minutes after their supreme moment, at a point where Cindy's normal breathing was returning and her heart regaining its regular beat, Derek Eden propped himself on an elbow and lighted cigarettes for them both.

'We were great, Cindy.' He smiled. 'Let's play a return match soon, and lots of others after that.' It was, Cindy realized, an admission of two things: that what they had experienced was solely physical, a sensual adventure, and neither should pretend that it was more; yet together they had attained that rare Nirvana, an absolute sexual compatibility. Now, what they had available, whenever needed, was a private physical paradise, to be nurtured and increasingly explored.

The arrangement suited Cindy.

She doubted if she and Derek Eden would have much in common outside a bedroom, and he was certainly no prize to be exhibited around the social circuit. Without even thinking about it, Cindy knew she would have more to lose than gain by being seen publicly in Derek's company. Besides, he had already intimated that his own marriage was solid, though Cindy guessed he wasn't getting as much sex at home as he needed, a condition with which she sympathized, being in the same situation herself.

Yes, Derek Eden was someone to be treasured – but not to become involved with emotionally. She *would* treasure him. Cindy resolved not to be demanding, nor let their lovemaking become too frequent. A single session like tonight's would last Cindy a long time, and could be relived just by thinking about it. Play a little hard-to-get, she told herself; see to it that Derek Eden went on wanting her as much as she wanted him. That way, the whole thing could last for years.

Cindy's discovery of Derek had also, in a strange way, provided her with a freedom she had not possessed before.

Now that she had better-than-average sex available as it were, on a separate shelf, she could view the choice between Mel and Lionel Urquhart more objectively.

Her marriage to Mel had, in some ways, already terminated. Mentally and sexually they were estranged; their slightest disagreement resulted in bitter quarrelling. All that Mel appeared to think about nowadays was his damned airport. Each day, it seemed, thrust Mel and Cindy farther apart.

Lionel, who was satisfactory in all respects except in bed, wanted divorces all around so that he could marry Cindy.

Mel detested Cindy's social ambitions. Not only would be do nothing to advance them; he impeded them. Lionel, on the other hand, was well established in Illinois society, saw nothing unusual in Cindy's social aims and would, and could, help her fulfil them.

Until now, Cindy's choice had been complicated by the remembrance of her fifteen years of marriage to Mel and the good times together, mental and physical, they had once enjoyed. She had hoped vaguely that the past – including the satisfactions of sex – might somehow be rekindled. It was, she admitted to herself, a delusive hope.

Lionel, as a sexual partner, had little or nothing to offer. Neither – at least for Cindy, any more – had Mel.

But if sex were eliminated – an elimination which Derek Eden, like a secretly stabled stallion, had now made possible – Lionel, as a competitor to Mel, came out far ahead.

In the taxi, Cindy opened her eyes and mused.

She wouldn't make any firm decision until she had talked with Mel. Cindy didn't like decisions, anyway, and invariably put them off until they could be delayed no longer. Also, there were still imponderables involved: the children; memories of the years with Mel, which hadn't *all* been bad; and when you once cared deeply for someone, you never shook it off entirely. But she was glad she had decided, after all, to come out here tonight.

For the first time since leaving downtown Cindy leaned forward, peering out into the darkness to see if she could determine where they were. She couldn't. Through misted windows she could see snow and many other cars, all moving slowly. She guessed they were on the Kennedy Expressway, but that was all.

She was aware of the cab driver's eyes watching her in his rear-view mirror. Cindy had no idea what kind of a man the driver was; she hadn't taken notice when she got into the cab back at the hotel, which she and Derek left separately since they decided they might as well start being discreet immediately. Anyway, tonight all faces and bodies merged into the face and body of Derek Eden.

'That's Portage Park over there, madam,' the driver said. 'We're getting close to the airport. Won't be long.'

'Thank you.'

'Lotsa traffic going out there besides us. Guess those airport people must have had their problems, what with the storm and all.'

Who the hell cares? Cindy thought. *And didn't* anyone *ever think or talk of anything besides that cruddy airport?* But she kept quiet.

At the main terminal entrance Cindy paid off the cab and hurried inside to avoid wet snow which gusted under canopies and swirled along sidewalks. She threaded the crowds in the main concourse, moving around one sizeable group which seemed to intend some kind of demonstration because several people were helping assemble a portable public address system. A Negro police lieutenant, whom Cindy had met several times with Mel, was talking to two or three men from the group who appeared to be leaders. The policeman was shaking his head vigorously. Not really curious – nothing about this place really interested her – Cindy moved on, heading for the airport administrative offices on the mezzanine.

Lights were on in all the offices, though most were unoccupied and there was none of the clatter of typewriters or hum of conversation as during daytime working hours. At least some people, Cindy thought, had sense enough to go home at night.

The only person in sight was a middle-aged woman, in drab clothes, in the anteroom to Mel's office. She was seated on a settee from where she seemed to be looking into space, and took no notice as Cindy came in. The woman's eyes were red as if she had been crying. Judging by her clothes and shoes, which were sodden, she had been outside in the storm.

Cindy gave the other woman only a midly curious glance before going into Mel's office. The office was empty, and Cindy sat down in a chair to wait. After a few moments she closed her eyes and resumed her pleasant thoughts about Derek Eden.

Mel hurried in – he was limping more than usual, Cindy noticed – about ten minutes later.

'Oh!' He appeared surprised when he saw Cindy, and went back to close the door. 'I really didn't think you'd come.'

'I suppose you'd have preferred me not to.'

Mel shook his head. 'I still don't think there's anything to be gained by it – at least, not for what you seem to have in mind.' He looked at his wife appraisingly, wondering what her real purpose was in coming here tonight. He had learned long ago that Cindy's motives were usually complicated, and frequently quite different from what they appeared to be. He had to admit, though, that she looked her best tonight; positively glamorous, with a kind of radiance about her. Unfortunately, the glamour no longer affected him personally.

'Suppose you tell me,' Cindy said, 'what you think I have in mind.'

He shrugged. 'I got the impression that what you wanted was a fight. It occurred to me that we had enough of them at home without arranging another here.'

'Perhaps we'll *have* to arrange something here, since you're hardly ever home any more.'

'I might be home, if the atmosphere was more congenial.'

They had been talking for just a few seconds, Cindy realized, and already were sniping at each other. It seemed impossible nowadays for the two of them to hold a conversation without that happening.

Just the same, she could not resist answering, 'Oh, really! That isn't usually the reason you give for not being at home. You're always claiming how all-fired important it is for you to be here at the airport – if necessary, twenty-four hours a day. So many important things – or so you say – are always happening.'

Mel said curtly, 'Tonight they are.'

'But not other times?'

'If you're asking if I've sometimes stayed here in preference to coming home, the answer's yes.'

'At least this is the first time you've been honest about it.'

'Even when I do come home, you insist on dragging me to some stupid stuffed-shirt affair like tonight's.'

His wife said angrily, 'So you never did intend to come tonight!'

'Yes, I did. I told you so. But . . .'

'But nothing!' Cindy could feel the short fuse of her temper burning. 'You counted on something turning up to prevent you, the way it always does. So that you could weasel out and have an alibi; so you could convince yourself, even if you don't convince me, because I think you're a liar and a fake.'

'Take it easy, Cindy.'

'I won't take it easy!'

They glared at each other.

What had happened to them, Mel wondered, that they had come to this? – squabbling like ill-bred children; dealing in pettiness; exchanging vicious gibes; and in all of it, he himself no better than Cindy. Something happened when they quarrelled which demeaned them both. He wondered if it was always this way when things went sour with two people who had lived together for a long time. Was it because they knew, and therefore could probe painfully, each other's weaknesses? He once heard someone say that a disintegrating marriage brought out the worst in both partners. In his own and Cindy's case it was certainly true.

He tried to speak more reasonably. 'I don't think I'm a liar, or a fake. But maybe you have a point about my counting on something turning up, enough to keep me away from the social things, which you know I hate. I just hadn't thought of it that way.'

When Cindy remained silent, he went on, 'You can believe it or not, but I did intend to meet you tonight downtown – at least I think so. Maybe I didn't really, the way you said; I don't know. But I do know that I didn't arrange the storm, and, since it started, a lot of things have happened that – for real this time – have kept me here.' He nodded towards the outer office. 'One of them is that woman sitting out there. I told Lieutenant Ordway I'd talk to her. She seems to be in some sort of trouble.'

'Your wife's in trouble,' Cindy said. 'The woman out there can wait.'

He nodded. 'All right.'

'We've had it,' Cindy said. 'You and me. Haven't we?'

He waited before answering, not wanting to be hasty, yet realizing that now this had come up, it would be foolish to avoid the truth. 'Yes,' he said finally. 'I'm afraid we have.'

Cindy shot back, 'If only you'd change! If you'd see things my way. It's always been what *you* want to do, or don't. If you'd only do what *I* want . . .'

'Like being out six nights a week in black tie, and white tie on the seventh?'

'Well, why not?' Emotionally, imperiously, Cindy faced him. He had always admired her in that kind of spunky mood, even when it was directed at himself. Even now . . .

'I guess I could say the same kind of thing,' he told her. 'About changing; all that. The trouble is, people don't change – not in what they are basically; they adapt. It's that – two people adapting to each other – that marriage is supposed to be about.'

'The adapting doesn't have to be one-sided.'

'It hasn't been with us,' Mel argued, 'no matter what you think. I've tried to adapt; I guess you have, too. I don't know who's made the most effort; obviously I think it's me, and you think it's you. The main thing is: though we've given it plenty of time to work, it hasn't.'

Cindy said slowly, 'I suppose you're right. About the last bit, anyway. I've been thinking the same way too.' She stopped, then added, 'I think I want a divorce.'

'You'd better be quite sure. It's fairly important.' Even now, Mel thought, Cindy was hedging about a decision, waiting for him to help her with it. If what they had been saying were less serious, he would have smiled.

'I'm sure,' Cindy said. She repeated, with more conviction. 'Yes, I'm sure.'

Mel said quietly, 'Then I think it's the right decision for us both.'

For a second, Cindy hesitated. 'You're sure, too?'

'Yes,' he said. 'I'm sure.'

The lack of argument, the quickness of the exchange, seemed to bother Cindy. She asked, 'Then we've made a decision?'

'Yes.'

They still faced each other, but their anger was gone.

'Oh hell!' Mel moved, as if to take a pace forward. 'I'm sorry, Cindy.'

'I'm sorry, too.' Cindy stayed where she was. Her voice was more assured. 'But it's the most sensible thing, isn't it?'

He nodded. 'Yes. I guess it is.'

It was over now. Both knew it. Only details remained to be attended to.

Cindy was already making plans. 'I shall have custody of Roberta and Libby, of course, though you'll always be able to see them. I'll never be difficult about that.'

'I didn't expect you would be.'

Yes, Mel mused, it was logical that the girls would go with their mother. He would miss them both, Libby especially. No outside meetings, however frequent, could ever be a substitute for living in the same house day by day. He remembered his talks with his younger daughter on the telephone tonight; what was it Libby had wanted the first time? *A map of February.* Well, he had one now; it showed some unexpected detours.

'And I'll lhave to get a lawyer,' Cindy said. 'I'll let you know who it is.'

He nodded, wondering if all marriages went on to terminate so matter-of-factly once the decision to end them had been made. He supposed it was the civilized way of doing things. At any rate, Cindy seemed to have regained her composure with remarkable speed. Seated in the chair she had been occupying earlier, she was inspecting her face in a compact, repairing her make-up. He even had the impression that her thoughts had moved away from here; at the corners of her mouth there was the hint of a smile. In situations like this, Mel thought, women were supposed to be more emotional than men, but Cindy didn't show any signs of it, yet he himself was close to tears.

He was aware of sounds – voices and people moving – in the office outside. There was a knock. Mel called, 'Come in.'

It was Lieutenant Ordway. He entered, closing the door behind him. When he saw Cindy, he said, 'Oh, excuse me, Mrs Bakersfeld.'

Cindy glanced up, then away, without answering. Ordway, sensitive to atmosphere, stood hesitantly. 'Perhaps I should come back.'

Mel asked, 'What is it, Ned?'

'It's the anti-noise demonstration, those Meadowood people. There are a couple of hundred in the main concourse; more coming in. They all wanted to see you, but I've talked them into sending a delegation, the way you suggested. They selected half a dozen, and there are three newspaper reporters; I said the reporters could come too.' The policeman nodded towards the anteroom. 'They're all waiting outside.'

He would have to see the delegation, Mel knew. He had never felt less like talking to anyone.

'Cindy,' he pleaded, 'this won't take long. Will you wait?' When she didn't answer, he added, 'Please!'

She continued to ignore them both.

'Look,' Ordway said, 'if this is a bad time, I'll tell these people they'll have to come back some other day.'

Mel shook his head. The commitment had been made; it was his own suggestion. 'You'd better bring them in.' As the policeman turned away, Mel added, 'Oh, I haven't talked to that woman . . . I've forgotten her name.'

'Guerrero,' Ordway said. 'And you don't have to. She looked as if she was leaving when I came in.'

A few moments later the half dozen people from Meadowood – four men and two women – began filing in. The press trio followed. One of the reporters was from the *Tribune* – an alert, youngish man named Tomlinson who usually covered the airport and general aviation beat for his paper; Mel knew him well and respected his accuracy and fairness. Tomlinson's by-line also appeared occasionally in national magazines. The other two reporters were also known slightly to Mel – one a young man from the *Sun-Times*, the other an older woman from a local weekly.

Through the open doorway, Mel could see Lieutenant Ordway talking to the woman outside, Mrs Guerrero, who was standing, fastening her coat.

Cindy remained where she was.

'Good evening.' Mel introduced himself, then motioned to settees and chairs around his office. 'Please sit down.'

'Okay, we will,' one of the men in the delegation said. He was expensively well-dressed, with precisely combed, grey-streaked hair, and seemed to be the group's leader. 'But I'll tell you we're not here to get cosy. We've some plain, blunt things to say, and we expect the same kind of answers, not a lot of double-talk.'

'I'll try not to give you that. Will you tell me who you are?'

'My name is Elliott Freemantle. I'm a lawyer. I represent these people, and all the others down below.'

'All right, Mr Freemantle,' Mel said. 'Why don't you begin?'

The door to the anteroom was still open. The woman who had been outside, Mel noticed, had gone. Now, Ned Ordway came in, closing the office door.

3

Trans America Airlines Flight Two was twenty minutes out of Lincoln International, and in a steady climb which would continue until reaching thirty-three thousand feet near Detroit, in eleven more minutes. Already the flight was on its airway and great circle course for Rome. For the past several minutes the aircraft had been in smooth air, the storm clouds and accompanying turbulence now far below. A three-quarter moon hung above and ahead like a lopsided lantern; all around, the stars were sharp and clear.

On the flight deck, initial pressures were over. Captain Harris had made a progress announcement to the passengers over the p.a. system. The three pilots were settling down to routines of their long flight.

Under the second officer's table, behind Captain Harris and Demerest, a chime sounded loudly. At the same instant, on a radio panel forward of the throttles, an amber light winked on. Both chime and light indicated a radio call on Selcal radio system through which most airliners could be called individually, as if by private telephone. Each aircraft, of Trans America and other major airlines, had its own separate call code, transmitted and received automatically. The signals which had just been actuated for aircraft N-731-TA would be seen or heard on no other flight.

Anson Harris switched from the radio to which he had been listening on air route control frequency, and acknowledged, 'This is Trans America Two.'

'Flight Two, this is Trans America dispatcher, Cleveland. I have a message for the captain from DTM, LIA. Advise when ready to copy.'

Vernon Demerest, Harris observed, had also changed radio frequencies. Now Demerest pulled a notepad towards him and nodded.

Harris instructed, 'We're ready, Cleveland. Go ahead.'

The message was that which Tanya Livingston had written concerning Flight Two's stowaway, Mrs Ada Quonsett. As it progressed, with the description of the little old lady from San Diego, both captains began smiling. The message ended by asking confirmation that Mrs Quonsett was aboard.

'We will check and advise,' Harris acknowledged. When the transmission ended, he clicked the radio controls back to air route control frequency.

Vernon Demerest and Second Officer Jordan, who had heard the message from an overhead speaker near his seat, were laughing aloud.

The second officer declared, 'I don't believe it!'

'I believe it.' Demerest chuckled. 'All those boobs on the ground, and some ancient old duck fooled them all!' He pushed the call button for the forward galley phone. 'Hey!' he said, when one of the stewardesses answered. 'Tell Gwen we want her in the office.'

He was still chuckling when the flight deck door opened. Gwen Meighen came in.

Demerest read Gwen the Selcal message with Mrs Quonsett's description. 'Have you seen her?'

Gwen shook her head. 'I've hardly been back in tourist yet.'

'Go back,' Demerest told her, 'and see if the old woman's there. She shouldn't be hard to spot.'

'If she is, what do you want me to do?'

'Nothing. Just come back and report.'

Gwen was gone only a few minutes. When she returned, she was laughing like the others.

Demerest swung around in his seat. 'Is she there?'

Gwen nodded. 'Yes, in seat fourteen-B. She's just the way the message said, only more so.'

The second officer asked, 'How old?'

'At least seventy-five, probably nearer eighty. And she looks like something out of Dickens.'

Over his shoulder, Anson Harris said, 'More likely *Arsenic and Old Lace*.'

'Is she *really* a stowaway, Captain?'

Harris shrugged. 'On the ground they say so. And I guess it explains why your head count was wrong.'

'We can easily find out for sure,' Gwen volunteered. 'All I have to do is go back again and ask to see her ticket counterfoil.'

'No,' Vernon Demerest said. 'Let's not do that.'

As best they could in the darkened cockpit, the others regarded him curiously. After a second or so, Harris returned his eyes to the flight instruments; Second Officer Jordan

189

swung back to his fuel charts.

'Hold on,' Demerest told Gwen. While she waited, he made a check point report on company radio.

'All we were told to do,' Demerest said when he had finished the report, 'was to see if the old lady's aboard. Okay, she is; and that's what I'll tell Flight Dispatch. I guess they'll have somebody waiting for her at Rome; we can't do anything about that, even if we wanted to. But if the old girl's made it this far, and since we're not turning back, why make her next eight hours miserable? So leave her alone. Maybe, just before we get to Rome, we'll let her know she's been found out; then it won't be a whole big shock. But for the time being, let her enjoy her flight. Give Grandma some dinner, and she can watch the movie in peace.'

'You know,' Gwen said; she was watching him thoughtfully. 'There are times when I quite like you.'

As Gwen left the flight deck, Demerest – still chuckling – changed radio channels and reported back himself to the Cleveland dispatcher.

Anson Harris, who had his pipe alight, looked up from adjusting the auto-pilot and said drily, 'I didn't think you were much of a one for the old ladies.' He emphasized the 'old'.

Demerest grinned. 'I prefer younger ones.'

'So I'd heard.'

The stowaway report, and his reply, had put Demerest in a thoroughly good humour. More relaxed than earlier, he added, 'Opportunities change. Pretty soon you and I will have to settle for the not-so-young ones.'

'I already have.' Harris puffed at his pipe. 'For quite some time.'

Both pilots had one earpiece of their radio headsets pushed upwards. They could converse normally, yet hear radio calls if any came in. The noise level of the flight deck – persistent but not overwhelming – was sufficient to give the two of them privacy.

'You've always played it straight down the line, haven't you?' Demerest said. 'With your wife, I mean. No mucking around; on layovers I've seen you reading books.'

This time Harris grinned. 'Sometimes I go to a movie.'

'Any special reason?'

'My wife was a stewardess – on DC-4s; that was how we met. She knew what went on: the sleeping around, pregnancies, abortions, all that stuff. Later, she got to be a supervisor and had to deal with a lot of it in her job. Anyway, when we were married I made her a promise – the obvious one. I've always kept it.'

'I guess all those kids you had helped.'

'Maybe.'

Harris made another minute adjustment to the auto-pilot. As they talked, the eyes of both pilots, out of training and habit, swept the illuminated banks of instruments in front of them, as well as those to each side and above. An incorrect instrument reading would show at once if anything in the aircraft was malfunctioning. Nothing was.

Demerest said, 'How many children is it? Six?'

'Seven.' Harris smiled. 'Four we planned, three we didn't. But it all worked out.'

'The ones you didn't plan – did you ever consider doing anything about them? Before they were born.'

Harris glanced sharply sideways. 'Abortion?'

Vernon Demerest had asked the question on impulse. Now he wondered why.

Obviously, his two conversations earlier with Gwen had begun the train of thought about children generally. But it was uncharacteristic of him to be doing so much thinking about something – like an abortion for Gwen – which was essentially simple and straightforward. Just the same, he was curious about Harris's reaction.

'Yes,' Demerest said. 'That's what I meant.'

Anson Harris said curtly, 'The answer's no.' Less sharply, he added, 'It happens to be something I have strong views about.'

'Because of religion?'

Harris shook his head negatively. 'I'm an agnostic.'

'What kind of views, then?'

'You sure you want to hear?'

'It's a long night,' Demerest said. 'Why not?'

On radio they listened to an exchange between air route control and a TWA flight, Paris-bound, which had taken off shortly after Trans America Flight Two. The TWA jet was ten miles behind and several thousand feet lower. As Flight Two continued to climb, so would TWA.

Most alert pilots, as a result of listening to other aircraft transmissions, maintained a partial picture of nearby traffic in their minds. Demerest and Harris both added this latest item to others already noted. When the ground-to-air exchange ended, Demerest urged Anson Harris, 'Go ahead.'

Harris checked their course and altitude, then began refilling his pipe.

'I've studied a lot of history. I got interested in college and followed through after. Maybe you've done the same.'

'No,' Demerest said. 'Never more than I had to.'

'Well, if you go through it all – history, that is – one thing stands out. Every bit of human progress has happened for a single, simple reason: the elevation of the status of the individual. Each time civilization has stumbled into another age that's a little better, a bit more enlightened, than the one before it, it's because people cared more about other people and respected them as individuals. When they haven't cared, those have been the times of slipping backwards. Even a short world history – if you read one – will prove it's true.'

'I'll take your word for it.'

'You don't have to. There are plenty of examples. We abolished slavery because we respected individual human life. For the same reason we stopped hanging children, and around the same time, we invented habeas corpus, and now we've created justice for all, or the closest we can come to it. More recently, most people who think and reason are against capital punishment, not so much because of those to be executed, but for what taking a human life – any human life – does to society, which is all of us.'

Harris stopped. Straining forward against his seat harness, he looked outward from the darkened cockpit to the night surrounding them. In bright moonlight he could see a swirl of darkened cloud-tops far below. With a forecast of unbroken cloud along the whole of their route until mid-Atlantic, there would be no glimpses tonight of lights on the ground. Several thousand feet above, the lights of another aircraft, travelling in an opposite direction, flashed by and were gone.

From his seat behind the other two pilots, Second Officer Cy Jordan reached forward, adjusting the throttle settings to compensate for Flight Two's increased altitude.

Demerest waited until Jordan had finished, then protested to Anson Harris, 'Capital punishment is a long way from abortion.'

'Not really,' Harris said. 'Not when you think about it. It all relates to respect for individual human life; to the way civilization's come, the way it's going. The strange thing is, you hear people argue for abolition of capital punishment, then for legalized abortion in the same breath. What they don't see is the anomaly of raising the value of human life on one hand, and lowering it on the other.'

Demerest remembered what he had said to Gwen this evening. He repeated it now. 'An unborn child doesn't have life – not an individual life. It's a foetus; it isn't a person.'

'Let me ask you something,' Harris said. 'Did you ever see an aborted child? Afterwards, I mean.'

'No.'

'I did once. A doctor I know showed it to me. It was in a glass jar, in formaldehyde; my friend kept it in a cupboard. I don't know where he got it, but he told me that if the baby had lived – not been aborted – it would have been a normal child, a boy. It was a foetus, all right, just the way you said, except it had been a human being, too. It was all there; everything perfectly formed; a good-looking face, hands, feet, toes, even a little penis. You know what I felt when I saw it? I felt ashamed; I wondered where the hell was I; where were all other decent-minded, sensitive people when this kid, who couldn't defend himself, was being murdered? Because that's what happened; even though, most times, we're afraid to use that word.'

'Hell! I'm not saying a baby should be taken out when it's that far along.'

'You know something?' Harris said. 'Eight weeks after conception, everything's present in a foetus that's in a full-term baby. In the third month the foetus *looks* like a baby. So where do you draw the line?'

Demerest grumbled, 'You should have been a lawyer, not a pilot.' Just the same, he found himself wondering how far Gwen was along, then reasoned: if she conceived in San Francisco, as she assured him, it must be eight or nine weeks ago. Therefore, assuming Harris's statements to be true, there was almost a shaped baby now.

It was time for another report to air route control. Vernon Demerest made it. They were at thirty-two thousand feet, near the top of their climb, and in a moment or two would cross the Canadian border and be over southern Ontario. Detroit and Windsor, the twin cities straddling the border, were ordinarily a bright splash of light, visible for miles ahead. Tonight there was only darkness, the cities shrouded and somewhere down below to starboard. Demerest remembered that Detroit Metropolitan Airport had closed shortly before their own takeoff. Both cities, by now, would be taking the full brunt of the storm, which was moving east.

Back in the passenger cabins, Demerest knew, Gwen Meighen and the other stewardesses would be serving a second round of drinks, and in first class, hot hors d'oeuvres on exclusive Rosenthal china.

'I warned you I had strong feelings,' Anson Harris said. 'You don't need a religion, to believe in human ethics.'

Demerest growled, 'Or to have screwball ideas. Anyway, people who think like you are on the losing side. The trend is to make abortion easier; eventually, maybe, wide open and legal.'

'If it happens,' Harris said, 'we'll be a backward step nearer the Auschwitz ovens.'

'Nuts!' Demerest glanced up from the flight log, where he was recording their position, just reported. His irritability, seldom far below the surface, was beginning to show. 'There are plenty of good arguments in favour of easy abortion – unwanted children who'll be born to poverty and never get a chance; then the special cases – rape, incest, the mother's health.'

'There are always special cases. It's like saying, "okay, we'll permit just a little murder, providing you make out a convincing argument",' Harris shook his head, dissenting. 'Then you talked about unwanted children. Well, they can be stopped by birth control. Nowadays everyone gets that opportunity, at every economic level. But if we slip up on that, and a human life starts growing, that's a new human being, and we've no moral right to condemn it to death. As to what we're born into, that's a chance we all take without knowing it; but once we have life, good or bad, we're entitled to keep it, and not many, however bad it is, would give it up. The answer to poverty isn't to kill unborn babies, but to improve society.'

Harris considered, then went on, 'As to economics, there are economic arguments for everything. It makes economic logic to kill mental deficients and mongoloids right after birth; to practise euthanasia on the terminally ill; to weed out old and useless people the way they do in Africa, by leaving them in the jungle for hyenas to eat. But we don't do it because we value human life and dignity. What I'm saying, Vernon, is that if we plan to progress we ought to value them a little more.'

The altimeters – one in front of each pilot – touched thirty-three thousand feet. They were at the top of their climb. Anson Harris eased the aircraft into level flight while Second Officer Jordan reached forward again to adjust the throttles.

Demerest said sourly to Harris, 'Your trouble is cobwebs in the brain.' He realized he had started the discussion; now, angrily, he wished he hadn't. To end the subject, he reached for the stewardess call button. 'Let's get some hors d'oeuvres before the first class passengers wolf them all.'

Harris nodded. 'Good idea.'

A minute or two later, in response to the telephoned order, Gwen Meighen brought three plates of aromatic hors d'oeuvres, and coffee. On Trans America, as on most airlines, captains got the fastest service.

'Thanks, Gwen,' Vernon Demerest said; then, as she leaned forward to serve Anson Harris, his eyes confirmed what he already knew. Gwen's waist was as slim as ever, no sign of anything yet; nor would there be, no matter what was going on inside. The heck with Harris and his old woman's arguments! Of course Gwen would have an abortion – just as soon as they got back.

Some sixty feet aft of the flight deck, in the tourist cabin, Mrs Ada Quonsett was engaged in spirited conversation with the passenger on her right, whom she had discovered was an amiable, middle-aged oboe player from the Chicago Symphony. 'What a wonderful thing to be a musician, and *so* creative. My late husband loved classical music. He fiddled a little himself, though not professionally, of course.'

Mrs Quonsett was feeling warmed by a Dry Sack sherry for which her oboist friend had paid, and he had just inquired if she would like another. Mrs Quonsett beamed, 'Well, it's exceedingly kind of you, and perhaps I shouldn't, but I really think I will.'

The passenger on her left – the man with the little sandy moustache and scrawny neck – had been less communicative; in fact, disappointing. Mrs Quonsett's several attempts at conversation had been rebuffed by monosyllabic answers, barely audible, while the man

193

sat, mostly expressionless, still clasping his attaché case on his knees.

For a while, when they had all ordered drinks, Mrs Quonsett wondered if the left-seat passenger might unbend. But he hadn't. He accepted Scotch from the stewardess, paid for it with a lot of small change that he had to count out, then tossed the drink down almost in a gulp. Her own sherry mellowed Mrs Quonsett immediately, so that she thought: Poor man, perhaps he has problems, and I shouldn't bother him.

She noticed, however, that the scrawny-necked man came suddenly alert when the captain made his announcement, soon after takeoff, about their speed, course, time of flight and all those other things which Mrs Quonsett rarely bothered listening to. The man on her left, though, scribbled notes on the back of an envelope and afterwards got out one of those *Chart Your Own Position* maps, which the airline supplied, spreading it on top of his attaché case. He was studying the map now, and making pencil marks, in between glances at his watch. It all seemed rather silly and childish to Mrs Quonsett, who was quite sure that there was a navigator up front, taking care of where the aeroplane ought to be, and when.

Mrs Quonsett then returned her attention to the oboist who was explaining that not until recently, when he had been in a public seat during a Bruckner symphony performance, had he realized that at a moment when his section of the orchestra was going 'pom-tiddey-pom-pom', the cellos were sounding 'ah-diddley-ah-dah'. He mouthed both passages in tune to illustrate his point.

'Really! How remarkably interesting; I'd never thought of that,' Mrs Quonsett exclaimed. 'My late husband would have so enjoyed meeting you, though, of course, you are very much younger.'

She was now well into the second sherry and enjoying herself thoroughly. She thought: she had chosen such a nice flight; such a fine aeroplane and crew, the stewardesses polite and helpful, and with delightful passengers, except for the man on her left, who didn't really matter. Soon, dinner would be served and later, she had learned, there was to be a movie, with Michael Caine, one of her favourite stars. What more could anyone possibly ask?

Mrs Quonsett had been wrong in assuming that there was a navigator up front on the flight deck. There wasn't. Trans America, like most major airlines, no longer carried navigators, even on overseas flights, because of the multitude of radar and radio systems available on modern jet aircraft. The pilots, aided by constant air route control surveillance, did what little navigation was needed.

However, had there been an old-time air navigator aboard Flight Two, his charted position of the aircraft would have been remarkably similar to that which D. O. Guerrero had achieved by rough-and-ready reckoning. Guerrero had estimated several minutes earlier that they were close to Detroit; the estimate was right. He knew, because the captain had said so in his announcement to passengers, that their subsequent course would take them over Montreal; Fredericton, New Brunswick; Cape Ray; and later St John's, Newfoundland. The captain had even been helpful enough to include the aircraft's groundspeed as well as airspeed, making Guerrero's further calculations just as accurate.

The east coast of Newfoundland, D. O. Guerrero calculated, would be passed over in two-and-a-half hours from the present time. However, before then, the captain would probably make another position announcement, so the estimate could be revised if necessary. After that, as already planned, Guerrero would wait a further hour to ensure that the flight was well over the Atlantic Ocean before pulling the cord on his case and exploding the dynamite inside. At this moment, in anticipation, his fingers clasping the attaché case tensed.

Now that the time of culmination was so close, he wanted it to come quickly. Perhaps, after all, he thought, he would not wait the full time. Once they had left Newfoundland, really any time would do.

The shot of whisky had relaxed him. Although most of his earlier tension had disappeared on coming aboard, it had built up again soon after takeoff, particularly when the irritating old cat in the next seat had tried to start a conversation. D. O. Guerrero wanted no conversation, either now or later; in fact, no more communication with anyone else in this life. All that he wanted was to sit and dream – of three hundred thousand dollars, a larger sum than he had ever possessed at one time before, and which would be coming to Inez and the two children, he presumed, in a matter of days.

Right now he could have used another whisky, but had no money left to pay for it. After his unexpectedly large insurance purchase, there had been barely enough small change for the single drink; so he would have to do without.

As he had earlier, he closed his eyes. This time he was thinking of the effect on Inez and the children when they heard about the money. They ought to care about him for what he was doing, even though they wouldn't know the whole of it – that he was sacrificing himself, giving his own life for them. But perhaps they might guess a little. If they did, he hoped they would be appreciative, although he wondered about that, knowing from experience that people could be surprisingly perverse in reactions to what was done on their behalf.

The strange thing was: In all his thoughts about Inez and the children, he couldn't quite visualize their faces. It seemed almost as though he were thinking about people whom he had never really known.

He compromised by conjuring up visions of dollar signs, followed by threes, and endless zeros. After a while he must have dropped off to sleep because, when he opened his eyes a quick glance at his watch showed that it was twenty minutes later, and a stewardess was leaning over from the aisle. The stewardess – an attractive brunette who spoke with an English accent – was asking, 'Are you ready for dinner, sir? If so, perhaps you'd like me to take your case.'

4

Almost from their initial moment of meeting, Mel Bakersfeld had formed an instinctive dislike of the lawyer, Elliott Freemantle, who was leading the delegation of Meadowood residents. Now, ten minutes or so after the delegation filed into Mel's office, the dislike was sharpening to downright loathing.

It seemed as if the lawyer was deliberately being as obnoxious as possible. Even before the discussion opened, there had been Freemantle's unpleasant remark about not wanting 'a lot of doubletalk', which Mel parried mildly, though resenting it. Since then, every rejoinder of Mel's had been greeted with equal rudeness and scepticism. Mel's instinct cautioned him that Freemantle was deliberately baiting him, hoping that Mel would lose his temper and make intemperate statements, with the press recording them. If it was the lawyer's strategy, Mel had no intention of abetting it. With some difficulty, he continued to keep his own manner reasonable and polite.

Freemantle had protested what he termed 'the callous indifference of this airport's management to the health and well-being of my clients, the good citizen families of Meadowood.'

Mel replied quietly that neither the airport nor the airlines using it had been callous or indifferent. 'On the contrary, we have recognized that a genuine problem about noise exists, and have done our best to deal with it.'

'Then your best, sir, is a miserable, weak effort! And you've done *what?*' Lawyer Freemantle declared, 'So far as my clients and I can see – and hear – you've done no more than make empty promises which amount to nothing. It's perfectly evident – and the reason we intend to proceed to law – is that no one around here really gives a damn.'

The accusation was untrue, Mel countered. There had been a planned programme of avoiding takeoffs on runway two five – which pointed directly at Meadowood – whenever an alternative runway could be used. Thus, two five was used mostly for landings only, creating little noise for Meadowood, even though entailing a loss in operating efficiency for the airport. In addition, pilots of all airlines had instructions to use noise abatement procedures after any takeoff in the general direction of Meadowood, on whatever runway, including turns away from Meadowood immediately after leaving the ground. Air traffic control had co-operated in all objectives.

Mel added, 'What you should realize, Mr Freemantle, is that this is by no means the first meeting we have had with local residents. We've discussed our mutual problems many times.'

Elliot Freemantle snapped, 'Perhaps at the other times there was not enough plain speaking.'

'Whether that's true or not, you seem to be making up for it now.'

'We intend to make up for a good deal – of lost time, wasted effort, and bad faith, the latter not on my clients' part.'

Mel decided not to respond. There was nothing to be gained, for either side, by this kind of harangue – except, perhaps, publicity for Elliott Freemantle. Mel observed that the reporters' pencils were racing; one thing which the lawyer clearly understood was what made lively copy for the press.

As soon as he decently could, Mel resolved, he would cut this session short. He was acutely conscious of Cindy, still seated where she had been when the delegation came in, though now appearing bored, which was characteristic of Cindy whenever anything came up involving airport affairs. This time, however, Mel sympathized with her. In view of the seriousness of what they had been discussing, he was finding this whole Meadowood business an intrusion himself.

In Mel's mind, too, was his recurring concern for Keith. He wondered how things were with his brother, over in air traffic control. Should he have insisted that Keith quit work for tonight, and pursued their discussion which – until the tower watch chief's intervention cut it off – had seemed to be getting somewhere? Even now, perhaps, it was not too late . . . But then there was Cindy, who certainly had a right to be considered ahead of Keith; and now this waspish lawyer, Freemantle, still ranting on . . .

'Since you chose to mention the so-called noise abatement procedures,' Elliott Freemantle inquired sarcastically, 'may I ask what happened to them tonight?'

Mel sighed. 'We've had a storm for three days.' His glance took in the others in the delegation. 'I'm sure you're all aware of it. It's created emergency situations.' He explained the blockage of runway three zero, the temporary need for takeoffs on runway two five, with the inevitable effect on Meadowood.

'That's all very well,' one of the other men said. He was a heavy-jowled, balding man whom Mel had met at other discussions about airport noise. 'We know about the storm, Mr Bakersfeld. But if you're living directly underneath, knowing *why* aeroplanes are coming over doesn't make anyone feel better, storm or not. By the way, my name is Floyd Zanetta. I was chairman of the meeting . . .'

Elliott Freemantle cut in smoothly. 'If you'll excuse me, there's another point before we go on.' Obviously the lawyer had no intention of relinquishing control of the delegation, even briefly. He addressed Mel, with a sideways glance at the press. 'It isn't solely noise that's filling homes and ears of Meadowood, though that's bad enough – shattering nerves, destroying health, depriving children of their needed sleep. But there is a physical invasion . . .'

This time Mel interrupted. 'Are you seriously suggesting that as an alternative to what's happened tonight, the airport should close down?'

'Not only am I suggesting that you do it; we may compel you. A moment ago I spoke of a physical invasion. It is that which I will prove, before the courts, on behalf of my clients. And we will win!'

The other members of the delegation, including Floyd Zanetta, gave approving nods.

While waiting for his last words to sink home, Elliott Freemantle deliberated. He supposed he had gone almost far enough. It was disappointing that the airport general manager hadn't blown a fuse, as Freemantle had been carefully goading him to do. The technique was one which he had used before, frequently with success, and it was a good technique because poeple who lost their tempers invariably came off worse in press reports, which was what Freemantle was mainly concerned about. But Bakersfeld, though clearly annoyed, had been too smart to fall for that ploy. Well, never mind, Elliott Freemantle thought; he had been successful just the same. He, too, had seen the reporters industriously getting his words down – words which (with the sneer and hectoring tone removed) would read well in print; even better, he believed, than his earlier speech at the Meadowood meeting.

Of course, Freemantle realized, this whole proceeding was just an exercise in semantics. Nothing would come of it. Even if the airport manager, Bakersfeld, could be persuaded to their point of view – a highly unlikely happening – there was little or nothing he could do about it. The airport was a fact of life and nothing would alter the reality of it being where and how it was. No, the value of being here at all tonight was partly in gaining public attention, but principally (from Lawyer Freemantle's viewpoint) to convince the Meadowood population that they had a stalwart champion, so that those legal retainer forms (as well as cheques) would keep on flowing into the offices of Freemantle and Sye.

It was a pity, Freemantle thought, that the remainder of the crowd from Meadowood, who were waiting downstairs, could not have heard him up here, dishing out the rough stuff – on their behalf – to Bakersfeld. But they would read about it in tomorrow's papers; also, Elliott Freemantle was not at all convinced that what was happening here and now would be the last Meadowood item on tonight's airport agenda. He had already promised the TV crews, who were waiting down below because they couldn't make it in here with their equipment, a statement when this present session was over. He had hopes that by now – because he had suggested it – the TV cameras would be set up in the main terminal concourse, and even though that Negro police lieutenant had forbidden any demonstration there, Freemantle had an idea that the TV session, astutely managed, might well develop into one.

Elliott Freemantle's statement of a moment ago had concerned legal action – the action which, he had assured Meadowood residents earlier this evening, would be his principal activity on their behalf. 'My business is law,' he had told them. 'Law and nothing else.' It was not true, of course; but then, Elliott Freemantle's policies were apt to back and fill as expediency demanded.

'What legal action you take,' Mel Bakersfeld pointed out, 'is naturally your own affair. All the same I would remind you that the courts have upheld the rights of airports to operate, despite adjoining communities, as a matter of public convenience and necessity.'

Freemantle's eyebrows shot up. 'I didn't realize that you are a lawyer too.'

'I'm not a lawyer. I'm also quite sure you're aware of it.'

'Well, for a moment I was beginning to wonder.' Elliott Freemantle smirked. 'Because I am, you see; and with some experience in these matters. Furthermore, I assure you that there are legal precedents in my clients' favour.' As he had at the meeting earlier, he rattled off the impressive-sounding list of cases – *US v. Causby, Griggs v. County of Allegheny, Thornburg v. Port of Portland, Martin v. Port of Seattle.*

Mel was amused, though he didn't show it. The cases were familiar to him. He also knew of others, which had produced drastically different judgements, and which Elliott Freemantle was either unaware of or had cagily avoided mentioning. Mel suspected the latter, but had no intention of getting into a legal debate. The place for that, if and when it happened, was in court.

However, Mel saw no reason why the lawyer – whom he now disliked even more intensely – should have everything his own way. Speaking to the delegation generally, Mel explained his reason for avoiding legal issues, but added, 'Since we are all here, there are some things I would like to say to you on the subject of airports and noise generally.'

Cindy, he observed, was yawning.

Freemantle responded instantly. 'I doubt if that will be necessary. The next step so far as we are concerned . . .'

'Oh!' For the first time Mel dispensed with mildness, and bore down heavily. 'Am I to understand that after I've listened patiently to you, you and your group are not prepared to extend the same courtesy?'

The delegate, Zanetta, who had spoken before, glanced at the other. 'I do think we ought . . .'

Mel said sharply, 'Let Mr Freemantle answer.'

'There's really no need' – the lawyer smiled suavely – 'for anyone to raise their voice, or be discourteous.'

'In that case, why have you been doing both those things ever since you came in?'

'I'm not aware . . .'

'Well, I *am* aware.'

'Aren't you losing your temper, Mr Bakersfeld?'

'No.' Mel smiled. 'I'm sorry to disappoint you, but I'm not.' He was conscious of having seized an advantage, catching the lawyer by surprise. Now he went on, 'You've had a good deal to say, Mr Freemantle, and not much of it politely. But there are a few things I'd like to get on the record, too. I'm sure the press will be interested in both sides even if no one else is.'

'Oh, we're interested all right. It's just that we've heard all the wishy-washy excuses already.' As usual, Elliott Freemantle was recovering fast. But he admitted to himself that he had been lulled by Bakersfeld's earlier mild manner, so that the sharp counter-attack caught him unawares. He realized that the airport general manager was more astute than he appeared.

'I didn't say anything about excuses,' Mel pointed out. 'I suggested a review of airport noise situations generally.'

Freemantle shrugged. The last thing he wanted was to open up some new approach which might be newsworthy and, therefore, divert attention from himself. At the moment, though, he didn't see how he could prevent it.

'Ladies and gentlemen,' Mel began, 'when you first came here tonight something was said about plain, blunt speaking on both sides. Mr Freemantle has had his turn at that; now I will be equally candid.'

Mel sensed he had the full attention of the two women and four men in the delegation; also of the press. Even Cindy was watching him covertly. He continued to speak quietly.

'All of you know, or should, the measures which we have taken at Lincoln International Airport to make life easier, more bearable, from the point of view of aircraft noise, for those who live in the airport vicinity. Some of these measures have been mentioned already, and there are others, such as using remote airport areas for the testing of engines, and even then during prescribed hours only.'

Elliott Freemantle, already fidgeting, cut in. 'But you've admitted that these so-called systems fail to work.'

Mel snapped back, 'I admitted nothing of the kind. Most of the time they *do* work – as well as any compromise can. Tonight I've admitted that they are not working because of exceptional circumstances, and frankly if I were a pilot, taking off in weather like this, I'd be reluctant to reduce power right after takeoff, and make a climbing turn too. Furthermore, these kind of conditions are bound to recur from time to time.'

'Most of the time!'

'No, sir! And please allow me to finish!' Without pausing, Mel went on, 'The fact is: airports – here and elsewhere – have come close to doing as much as they can in the way of noise reduction. You may not like hearing this, and not everyone in this business admits it, but the truth is: there isn't a lot more that anyone can do. You simply cannot tiptoe a three hundred thousand pound piece of high-powered machinery into any place. So when you do bring a big jet aeroplane in – or take it out – inevitably it shakes hell out of a few people who are nearby.' There were several quick smiles, though not from Elliott Freemantle, who was scowling. Mel added, 'So if we need airports – and obviously we do – somebody, somewhere has to put up with some noise, or move away.'

It was Mel's turn to see the reporters' pencils racing with his words.

'It's true,' Mel continued, 'that aircraft manufacturers are working on noise reduction devices, but – again to be honest with you – few people in the aviation industry take them seriously, and certainly they do not represent a major effort like, for example, development of a new aircraft. At best, they'll be palliatives. If you don't believe me, let me remind you that even though trucks have been in use for many years more than aeroplanes, no one has yet invented a really effective truck muffler.

'Another thing to bear in mind is that by the time one type of jet engine gets quietened a little – if it ever does – there'll be new, more powerful engines in use which, even with suppressors fitted, will be noisier than the first engine was to begin with. As I said,' Mel added, 'I'm being absolutely frank.'

One of the women in the delegation murmured gloomily, 'You sure are.'

'Which brings me,' Mel said, 'to the question of the future. There are new breeds of aircraft coming – another family of jets after the Boeing 747s, including behemoths like the Lockheed 500, which will come into use soon; then, shortly afterwards, the supersonic transports – the Concorde, and those to follow. The Lockheed 500 and its kind will be subsonic – that is, they'll operate at less than the speed of sound, and will give us the kind of noise we have now, only more of it. The supersonics will have a mighty engine noise too, *plus* a sonic boom as they breach the sound barrier, which is going to be more of a problem than any other noise we've had so far.

'You may have heard or read – as I have – optimistic reports that the sonic booms will occur high, far from cities and airports, and that the effect on the ground will be minor. Don't believe it! We're in for trouble, all of us – people in homes, like you; people like me, who run airports; airlines, who'll have a billion dollars invested in equipment which they must use continuously, or go bankrupt. Believe me, the time is coming when we'll wish we had the simplicity of the kind of noise we're talking about tonight.'

'So what are you telling my clients?' Elliott Freemantle inquired sarcastically. 'To go jump in the lunatic asylum now, rather than wait until you and your behemoths drive them there?'

'No,' Mel said firmly. 'I'm not telling them that. I'm merely saying candidly – the way you asked me to – that I haven't any simple answers; nor will I make you promises that the airport cannot keep. Also I'm saying that in my opinion, airport noise is going to become greater not less. However, I'd like to remind all of you that this problem isn't new. It's existed since trains started running, and since trucks, buses, and automobiles joined them; there was the same problem when freeways were built through residential areas; and when airports were established, and grew. All these things are for the public good – or so we believe – yet all of them create noise and, despite all kinds of efforts, they've continued to. The thing is: trucks, trains, freeways, aeroplanes, and the rest are here. They're part of the way we live, and unless we change our way of life, then their noise is something we have to live with too.'

'In other words, my clients should abandon any idea of serenity, uninterrupted sleep, privacy and quietness for the remainder of their natural lives?'

'No,' Mel said. 'I think, in the end, they'll have to move. I'm not speaking officially, of course, but I'm convinced that eventually this airport and others will be obliged to make multibillion-dollar purchases of residential areas surrounding them. A good many of the areas can become industrial zones where noise won't matter. And of course, there would be reasonable compensation to those who owned homes and were forced to leave them.'

Elliott Freemantle rose and motioned others in the delegation to do the same.

'That last remark,' he informed Mel, 'is the one sensible thing I've heard this evening. However, the compensation may start sooner than you think, and also be larger.'

Freemantle nodded curtly. 'You will be hearing from us. We shall see you in court.'

He went out, the others following.

Through the door to the anteroom Mel heard one of the two women delegates exclaim, 'You were magnificent, Mr Freemantle. I'm going to tell everyone so.'

'Well, thank you. Thank you very . . .' The voices faded.

Mel went to the door, intending to close it.

'I'm sorry about that,' he said to Cindy. Now that the two of them were alone again, he was not sure what else they had to say to each other, if anything.

Cindy said icily, 'It's par for the course. You should have married an airport.'

At the doorway, Mel noticed that one of the men reporters had returned to the anteroom. It was Tomlinson of the *Tribune*.

'Mr Bakersfeld, could I see you for a moment?'

Mel said wearily, 'What is it?'

'I got the impression you weren't too smitten with Mr Freemantle.'

'Is this for quotation?'

'No, sir.'

'Then your impression was right.'

'I thought you'd be interested in this,' the reporter said.

'This' was one of the legal retainer forms which Elliott Freemantle had distributed at the Meadowood community meeting.

As Mel read the form, he asked, 'Where did you get it?'

The reporter explained.

'How many people were at the meeting?'

'I counted. Roughly six hundred.'

'And how many of these forms were signed?'

'I can't be sure of that, Mr Bakersfeld. My guess would be a hundred and fifty were signed and turned in. Then there were other people who said they'd send theirs by mail.'

Mel thought grimly: now he could understand Elliott Freemantle's histrionics; also why and whom the lawyer was trying to impress.

'I guess you're doing the same arithmetic I did,' the reporter, Tomlinson, said.

Mel nodded. 'It adds up to a tidy little sum.'

'Sure does. I wouldn't mind a piece of it myself.'

'Maybe we're both in the wrong business. Did you cover the Meadowood meeting too?'

'Yes.'

'Didn't anyone over there point out that the total legal fee was likely to be at least fifteen thousand dollars?'

Tomlinson shook his head. 'Either no one thought of it, or they didn't care. Besides, Freemantle has quite a personality; hypnotic, I guess you'd call it. He had 'em spellbound, like he was Billy Graham.'

Mel handed back the printed retainer form. 'Will you put this in your story?'

'I'll put it in, but don't be surprised if the city desk kills it. They're always wary about professional legal stuff. Besides, I guess if you come right down to it, there's nothing really wrong.'

'No,' Mel said, 'it may be unethical, and I imagine the bar association wouldn't like it. But it isn't illegal. What the Meadowood folk should have done, of course, was get together and retain a lawyer as a group. But if people are gullible, and want to make

201

lawyers rich, I guess it's their own affair.'

Tomlinson grinned. 'May I quote some of that?'

'You just got through telling me your paper wouldn't print it. Besides, this is off the record. Remember?'

'Okay.'

If it would have done any good, Mel thought, he would have sounded off, and taken a chance on being quoted or not. But he knew it wouldn't do any good. He also knew that all over the country, ambulance chasing lawyers like Elliott Freemantle were busily signing up groups of people, then harassing airports, airlines – and in some cases – pilots.

It was not the harassing which Mel objected to; that, and legal recourse, were everyone's privilege. It was simply that in many instances the home-owner clients were being misled, buoyed up with false hopes, and quoted an impressive-sounding, but one-sided selection of legal precedents such as Elliott Freemantle had used tonight. As a result, a spate of legal actions – costly and time-consuming – was being launched, most of which were foredoomed to fail, and from which only the lawyers involved would emerge as beneficiaries.

Mel wished that he had known earlier what Tomlinson had just told him. In that case he would have loaded his remarks to the delegation, so as to convey a warning about Elliott Freemantle, and what the Meadowood residents were getting into. Now it was too late.

'Mr Bakersfeld,' the *Tribune* reporter said, 'there are some other things I'd like to ask you – about the airport generally. If you could spare a few minutes . . .'

'Any other time I'll be glad to.' Mel raised his hands in a helpless gesture. 'Right now there are fifteen things happening at once.'

The reporter nodded. 'I understand. Anyway, I'll be around for a while. I hear Freemantle's bunch are cooking up something down below. So if there's a chance later . . .'

'I'll do my best,' Mel said, though he had no intention of being available any more tonight. He respected Tomlinson's wish to dig below the surface of any story which he covered; just the same, Mel had seen enough of delegations *and* reporters for one evening.

As to whatever else it was that Freemantle and the Meadowood people were 'cooking up down below', he would leave any worrying about that, Mel decided, to Lieutenant Ordway and his policemen.

5

When Mel turned, after closing the door of his office as the *Tribune* reporter left, Cindy was standing, pulling on her gloves. She remarked acidly, 'Fifteen things happening, I believe you said. Whatever the other fourteen are, I'm sure they'll all take priority over me.'

'That was a figure of speech,' Mel protested, 'as you know perfectly well. I already said I'm sorry. I didn't know this was going to happen – at least, not all at once.'

'But you love it, don't you? All of it. Much more than me, home, the children, a decent social life.'

'Ah!' Mel said. 'I wondered when you'd get to that.' He stopped. 'Oh, hell! Why are we fighting again? We settled everything, didn't we? There's no need to fight any more.'

'No,' Cindy said. She was suddenly subdued. 'No, I suppose not.'

There was an uncertain silence. Mel broke it first.

'Look, getting a divorce is a pretty big thing for both of us; for Roberta and Libby, too. If you've any doubts . . .'

'Haven't we been over that already?'

'Yes; but if you want to, we'll go over it fifty times again.'

'I don't want to.' Cindy shook her head decisively. 'I haven't any doubts. Nor have you, not really. Have you?'

'No,' Mel said. 'I'm afraid I haven't.'

Cindy started to say something, then stopped. She had been going to tell Mel about Lionel Urquhart, but decided against it. There was plenty of time for Mel to find that out for himself, later. As to Derek Eden, whom Cindy had been thinking about during most of the time that the Meadowood delegation had been in the office, she had no intention of disclosing his existence to Mel *or* Lionel.

There was a knock – light but definite – on the anteroom door.

'Oh, God!' Cindy muttered. 'Isn't there *any* privacy?'

Mell called out irritably, 'Who is it?'

The door opened. 'Just me,' Tanya Livingston said. 'Mel, I need some advice . . .' As she saw Cindy, she stopped abruptly. 'Excuse me. I thought you were alone.'

'He will be,' Cindy said. 'In hardly any time at all.'

'Please, no!' Tanya flushed. 'I can come back, Mrs Bakersfeld. I didn't know I was disturbing you.'

Cindy's eyes flicked over Tanya, still in Trans America uniform.

'It's probably time we were disturbed,' Cindy said. 'After all, it's been a good three minutes since the last people left, and that's longer than we usually have together.' She swung towards Mel. 'Isn't it?'

He shook his head, without answering.

'By the way.' Cindy turned back to Tanya. 'I'm curious about one thing. How you were so sure who I am.'

Momentarily, Tanya had lost her usual poise. Recovering it, she gave a small smile. 'I suppose I guessed.'

Cindy's eyebrows went up. 'Am I supposed to do the same?' She glanced at Mel.

'No,' he said. He introduced them.

Mel was aware of Cindy appraising Tanya Livingston. He had not the slightest doubt that his wife was already forming some conclusion about Tanya and himself; Mel had long ago learned that Cindy's instincts about men-women relationships were uncannily accurate. Besides, he was sure that his own introduction of Tanya had betrayed something. Husbands and wives were too familiar with each other's nuances of speech for that not to happen. It would not even surprise him if Cindy guessed about his own and Tanya's rendezvous for later tonight, though perhaps, he reflected, that was carrying imagination too far.

Well, whatever Cindy knew or guessed, he supposed it didn't really matter. After all, she was the one who had asked for a divorce, so why should she object to someone else in Mel's life, however much or little Tanya meant, and he wasn't sure of that himself? But then, Mel reminded himself, that was a logical way of thinking. Women – including Cindy, and probably Tanya – were seldom logical.

The last thought proved right.

'How nice for you,' Cindy told him with pseudo sweetness, 'that it isn't just dull old delegations who come to you with problems.' She eyed Tanya. 'You did say you have a problem?'

Tanya returned the inspection levelly. 'I said I wanted some advice.'

'Oh, really! What kind of advice? Was it business, personal? . . . Or perhaps you've forgotten.'

'Cindy,' Mel said sharply, 'that's enough! You've no reason . . .'

'No reason for what? And why is it enough?' His wife's voice was mocking; he had the impression that in a perverse way she was enjoying herself. 'Aren't you always telling me I don't take enough interest in your problems? Now I'm all agog about your friend's problem . . . that is, if there is one.'

Tanya said crisply, 'It's about Flight Two.' She added, 'That's Trans America's flight to Rome, Mrs Bakersfeld. It took off half an hour ago.'

Mel asked, 'What about Flight Two?'

'To tell the truth' – Tanya hesitated – 'I'm not really sure.'

'Go ahead,' Cindy said. 'Think of something.'

Mel snapped, 'Oh, shut up!' He addressed Tanya, 'What is it?'

Tanya glanced at Cindy, then told him of her conversation with Customs Inspector Standish. She described the man with the suspiciously held attaché case, whom Standish suspected of smuggling.

'He went aboard Flight Two?'

'Yes.'

'Then even if your man *was* smuggling,' Mel pointed out, 'it would be into Italy. The US Customs people don't worry about that. They let other countries look out for themselves.'

'I know. That's the way our DTM saw it.' Tanya described the exchange between herself and the District Transportation Manager, ending with the latter's irritable but firm instruction, 'Forget it!'

Mel looked puzzled. 'Then I don't see why . . .'

'I told you I'm not sure, and maybe this is all silly. But I kept thinking about it, so I started checking.'

'Checking what?'

Both of them had forgotten Cindy.

'Inspector Standish,' Tanya said, 'told me that the man – the one with the attaché case – was almost the last to board the flight. He must have been because I was at the gate, and I missed seeing an old woman . . .' She corrected herself. 'That part doesn't matter. Anyway, a few minutes ago I got hold of the gate agent for Flight Two and we went over the manifest and tickets together. He couldn't remember the man with the case, but we narrowed it down to five names.'

'And then?'

'Just on a hunch I called our check-in counters to see if anyone remembered anything about any of those five people. At the airport counters, nobody did. But downtown, one of the agents did remember the man – the one with the case. So I know his name; the description fits . . . everything.'

'I still don't see what's so extraordinary. He had to check in somewhere. So he checked in downtown.'

'The reason the agent remembered him,' Tanya said, 'is that he didn't have any baggage, except the little case. Also, the agent said, he was extremely nervous.'

'Lots of people are nervous . . .' Abruptly Mel stopped. He frowned. 'No baggage! For a flight to Rome!'

'That's right. Except for the little bag the man was carrying, the one Inspector Standish noticed. The agent downtown called it a briefcase.'

'But nobody goes on that kind of journey without baggage. It doesn't make sense.'

'That's what I thought.' Again Tanya hesitated. 'It doesn't make sense unless . . .'

'Unless what?'

'Unless you happen to know already that the flight you're on will never get to where it's supposed to be going. If you knew that, you'd also know that you wouldn't need any baggage.'

'Tanya,' Mel said softly, 'what are you trying to say?'

She answered uncomfortably, 'I'm not sure; that's why I came to you. When I think about it, it seems silly and melodramatic, only . . .'

'Go on.'

'Well, supposing that man we've been talking about isn't smuggling at all; at least in the way we've all assumed. Supposing the reason for him not having any luggage, for being nervous, for holding the case in the way Inspector Standish noticed . . . suppose instead of having some sort of contraband in there . . . he has a bomb.'

Their eyes held each other's steadily. Mel's mind was speculating, assessing possibilities. To him, also, the idea which Tanya had just raised seemed ridiculous and remote. Yet . . . in the past, occasionally, such things had happened. The question was: How could you decide if this was another time? The more he thought about it, the more he realized that the entire episode of the man with the attaché case could so easily be innocent; in fact, probably was. If that proved true after a fuss had been created, whoever began to fuss would have made a fool of himself. It was human not to want to do that; yet, with the safety of an aeroplane and passengers involved, did making a fool of oneself matter? Obviously not. On the other hand, there ought to be a stronger reason for the drastic actions which a bomb scare would involve than merely a possibility, plus a hunch. Was there, Mel wondered, some way conceivably in which a stronger hint, even corroboration, might be found?

Offhand, he couldn't think of one.

But there *was* something he could check. It was a long shot, but all that was needed was a phone call. He supposed that seeing Vernon Demerest tonight, with the reminder of the clash before the Board of Airport Commissioners, had made him think of it.

For the second time this evening, Mel consulted his pocket panic-list of telephone numbers. Then, using an internal airport telephone on his desk, he dialled the insurance vending booth in the main concourse. The girl clerk who answered was a long-time employee whom Mel knew well.

'Marj,' he said, when he had identified himself, 'have you written many policies tonight on the Trans America Flight Two?'

'A few more than usual, Mr Bakersfeld. But then we have on all flights; this kind of weather always does that. On Flight Two, I've had about a dozen, and I know Bunnie – that's the other girl on with me – has written some as well.'

'What I'd like you to do,' Mel told her, 'is read me all the names and policy amounts.' As he sensed the girl hesitate, 'If I have to, I'll call your district manager and get authority. But you know he'll give it to me, and I'd like you to take my word that this is important. Doing it this way, you can save me time.'

'All right, Mr Bakersfeld; if you say it's okay. But it will take a few minutes to get the policies together.'

'I'll wait.'

Mel heard the telephone put down, the girl apologize to someone at the insurance counter for the interruption. There was a rustling of papers, then another girl's voice inquiring, 'Is something wrong?'

Covering the telephone mouthpiece, Mel asked Tanya, 'What's that name you have – the man with the case?'

She consulted a slip of paper. 'Guerrero, or it may be Buerrero; we had it spelled both ways.' She saw Mel start. 'Initials D. O.'

Mel's hand still cupped the telephone. His mind was concentrating. The woman who had been brought to his office half an hour ago was named Guerrero; he remembered Lieutenant Ordway saying so. She was the one whom the airport police had found wandering in the terminal. According to Ned Ordway, the woman was distressed and crying; the police couldn't get any sense from her. Mel was going to try talking to her himself, but hadn't gotten around to it. He had seen the woman on the point of leaving the outer office as the Meadowood delegation came in. Of course, there might be no connection . . .

Through the telephone Mel could still hear voices at the insurance booth and, in the background, the noise of the main terminal concourse.

'Tanya,' he said quietly, 'about twenty minutes ago there was a woman in the outside office – middle-aged, shabbily dressed; she looked wet and draggle-tailed. I believe she left when some other people came in, but she might be still around. If she's anywhere outside, bring her in. In any case, if you find her, don't let her get away from you.' Tanya looked puzzled. He added, 'Her name is Mrs Guerrero.'

As Tanya left the office, the girl clerk at the insurance booth came back on the line. 'I have all those policies, Mr Bakersfeld. Are you ready if I read the names?'

'Yes, Marj. Go ahead.'

He listened carefully. As a name near the end occurred, he had a sudden sense of tension. For the first time his voice was urgent. 'Tell me about that policy. Did you write it?'

'No. That was one of Bunnie's. I'll let you speak to her.'

He listened to what the other girl had to say and asked two or three questions. Their exchange was brief. He broke the connection and was dialling another number as Tanya returned.

Though her eyes asked questions which for the moment he ignored, she reported immediately, 'There's no one on the mezzanine. There are still a million people down below, but you'd never pick anyone out. Should we page?'

'We can try, though I don't have a lot of hope.' On the basis of what he had heard, Mel thought, not much was getting through to the Guerrero woman, so it was unlikely that a p.a. announcement would do so now. Also, by this time she could have left the airport and be halfway to the city. He reproached himself for not having tried to talk with her, as he had intended, but there had been the other things: the delegation from Meadowood; his anxiety about his brother, Keith – Mel remembered that he had considered going back to the control tower . . . well, that would have to wait now . . . then there had been Cindy. With a guilty start, because he hadn't noticed before, he realised that Cindy was gone.

He reached for the p.a. microphone on his desk and pushed it towards Tanya.

There was an answer from the number he had dialled, which was airport police headquarters. Mel said crisply, 'I want Lieutenant Ordway. Is he still in the terminal?'

'Yes, sir.' The police desk sergeant was familiar with Mel's voice.

'Find him as quickly as you can: I'll hold. And by the way, what was the first name of a woman called Guerrero, whom one of your people picked up tonight? I think I know, but I want to make sure.'

'Just a minute, sir. I'll look.' A moment later he said, 'It's Inez; Inez Guerrero. And we've already called the lieutenant on his beeper box.'

Mel was aware that Lieutenant Ordway, like many others at the airport, carried a pocket radio receiver which gave a 'beep' signal if he was required urgently. Somewhere, at this moment, Ordway was undoubtedly hastening to a phone.

Mel gave brief instructions to Tanya, then pressed the 'on' switch of the p.a. microphone, which overrode all others in the terminal. Through the open doors to the anteroom and mezzanine he heard an American Airlines flight departure announcement halt abruptly in mid-sentence. Only twice before, during the eight years of Mel's tenure as airport general manager, had the mike and override switch been used. The first occasion – branded in Mel's memory – had been to announce the death of President Kennedy; the second, a year later, was when a lost and crying child wandered directly into Mel's office. Usually there were regular procedures for handling lost children, but that time Mel had used the mike himself to locate the frantic parents.

Now he nodded to Tanya to begin her announcement, remembering that he was not yet sure why they wanted the woman, Inez Guerrero, or even that – for certain – there was anything wrong at all. Yet instinct told him that there was; that something serious had happened, or was happening; and when you had a puzzle of that kind, the smart and urgent thing to do was gather all the pieces that you could, hoping that somehow, with help from other people, you could fit them together to make sense.

'Attention please,' Tanya was saying in her clear, unaffected voice, now audible in every corner of the terminal. 'Will Mrs Inez Guerrero, or Buerrero, please come immediately to the airport general manager's office on the administrative mezzanine of the main terminal building. Ask any airline or airport representative to direct you. I will repeat . . .'

There was a click in Mel's telephone. Lieutenant Ordway came on the line.

'We want that woman,' Mel told him. 'The one who was here – Guerrero. We're announcing . . .'

'I know,' Ordway said. 'I can hear.'

'We need her ugently; I'll explain later. For now, take my word . . .'

'I already have. When did you last see her?'

'In my outer office. When she was with you.'

'Okay. Anything else?'

'Only that this may be big. I suggest you drop everything; use all your men. And

207

whether you find her or not, get up here soon.'

'Right.' There was another click as Ordway hung up.

Tanya had finished her announcement; she pushed the 'off' button of the microphone. Outside, Mel could hear another announcement beginning, 'Attention Mr Lester Mainwaring. Will Mr Mainwaring and all members of his party report immediately to the main terminal entrance?'

'Lester Mainwaring' was an airport code name for 'policeman'. Normally, such an announcement meant that the nearest policeman on duty was to go wherever the message designated. 'All members of his party' meant every policeman in the terminal. Most airports had similar systems to alert their police without the public being made aware.

Ordway was wasting no time. Undoubtedly he would brief his men about Inez Guerrero as they reported to the main entrance.

'Call your DTM,' Mel instructed Tanya. 'Ask him to come to this office as quickly as he can. Tell him it's important.' Partly to himself, he added, 'We'll start by getting everybody here.'

Tanya made the call, then reported, 'He's on his way.' Her voice betrayed nervousness.

Mel had gone to the office door. He closed it.

'You still haven't told me,' Tanya said, 'what it was you found out.'

Mel chose his words carefully.

'Your man Guerrero, the one with no luggage except the little attaché case, and whom you think might have a bomb aboard Flight Two, took out a flight insurance policy just before takeoff for three hundred thousand dollars. The beneficiary is Inez Guerrero. He paid for it with what looked like his last small change.'

'My God!' Tanya's face went white. She whispered, 'Oh, dear God . . . no!'

6

There were times – tonight was one – when Joe Patroni was grateful that he worked in the maintenance bailiwick of aviation, and not in sales.

The thought occurred to him as he surveyed the busy activity of digging beneath and around the mired Aéreo-Mexican jet which continued to block runway three zero.

As Patroni saw it, airline sales forces – in which category he lumped all front office staff and executives – comprised inflatable rubber people who connived against each other like fretful children. On the other hand, Patroni was convinced that those in engineering and maintenance departments behaved like mature adults. Maintenance men (Joe was apt to argue), even when employed by competing airlines, worked closely and harmoniously, sharing their information, experience, and even secrets for the common good.

As Joe Patroni sometimes confided privately to his friends, an example of this unofficial sharing was the pooling of information which came to maintenance men regularly through conferences held by individual airlines.

Patroni's employers, like most major scheduled airlines, had daily telephone conferences – known as 'briefings' – during which all regional headquarters, bases, and outfield stations were connected through a continent-wide closed-circuit hookup. Directed by a head office vice-president, the briefings were, in fact, critiques and information exchanges on the way the airline had operated during the past twenty-four hours. Senior people throughout the company's system talked freely and frankly with one another. Operations and sales departments each had their own daily briefing, so did maintenance – the latter, in Patroni's opinion, by far the most important.

During the maintenance sessions, in which Joe Patroni took part five days a week, stations reported one by one. Where delays in service – for mechanical reasons – had occurred the previous day, those in charge were required to account for them. Nobody bothered making excuses. As Patroni put it: 'If you goofed, you say so.' Accidents or failures of equipment, even minor, were reported; the objective, to pool knowledge and prevent recurrence. At next Monday's session, Patroni would report tonight's experience with the Aéreo-Mexican 707, and his success or failure, however it turned out. The daily discussions were strictly no-nonsense, largely because the maintenance men were tough cookies who knew they couldn't fool one another.

After each official conference – and usually unknown to senior managements – unofficial ones began. Patroni and others would exchange telephone calls with cronies in maintenance departments of competing airlines. They would compare notes about one another's daily conferences, passing on whatever information seemed worthwhile. Rarely was any intelligence withheld.

With more urgent matters – especially those affecting safety – word was passed from airline to airline in the same way, but without the day's delay. If Delta, for example, had a rotor blade failure on a DC-9 in flight, maintenance departments of Eastern, TWA, Continental, and others using DC-9s were told within hours; the information might help prevent similar failures on other aircraft. Later, photographs of the disassembled engine, and a technical report, would follow. If they wished, foremen and mechanics from other airlines could widen their knowledge by dropping over for a look-see at the failed part, and any engine damage.

Those who, like Patroni, worked in this give-and-take milieu were fond of pointing out that if sales and administration departments of competing airlines had occasion to consult, their people seldom went to one another's headquarters, but met on neutral ground. Maintenance men, in contrast, visited competitors' premises with the assurance of a common freemasonry. At other times, if one maintenance department was in trouble, others helped as they were able.

This second kind of help had been sent, tonight, to Joe Patroni.

In the hour and a half since work began in the latest attempt to move the stranded jet from alongside runway three zero, Patroni's complement of help had almost doubled. He had begun with the original small crew of Aéreo-Mexican, supplemented by some of his own people from TWA. Now, digging steadily with the others, were ground crew from Braniff, Pan Am, American, and Eastern.

As the various newcomers had arrived, in an assortment of airline vehicles, it became evident that news of Patroni's problem had spread quickly on the airport grapevine, and, without waiting to be asked, other maintenance departments had pitched in. It gave Joe Patroni a good, appreciative feeling.

Despite the extra help, Patroni's estimate of an hour's preparatory work had already been exceeded. Digging of twin trenches, floored by heavy timbers, in front of the airliner's main landing gear had gone ahead steadily – though slowly because of the need for all the men working to seek shelter periodically, to warm themselves. The shelter and

209

the warmth, of a sort, were in two crew buses. As the men entered, they beat their hands and pinched their faces, numb from the biting wind still sweeping icily across the snow-covered airfield. The buses and other vehicles, including trucks, snow clearance equipment, a fuel tanker, assorted service cars, and a roaring power cart – most with beacon lights flashing – were still clustered on the taxiway close by. The whole scene was bathed by floodlights, creating a white oasis of snow-reflected light in the surrounding darkness.

The twin trenches, each six feet wide, now extended forwards and upwards from the big jet's main wheels to the firmer ground on to which Patroni hoped the aeroplane could be moved under its own power. At the deepest level of the trenches was a mess of mud beneath snow, which had originally trapped the momentarily strayed airliner. The mud and slush now mingled, but became less viscous as both trenches angled upwards. A third trench, less deep, and narrower than the other two, had been dug to allow passage of the nosewheel. Once the firmer ground was reached, the aircraft would be clear of runway three zero, over which one of its wings now extended. It could also be manoeuvred with reasonable ease on to the solid surface of the adjoining taxiway.

Now that preparatory work was almost complete, the success of what came next would depend on the aircraft's pilots, still waiting on the Boeing 707's flight deck, high above the current activity. What they would have to judge was how much power they could safely use to propel the aircraft forward, without upending it on its nose.

Through most of the time since he arrived, Joe Patroni had wielded a shovel with the rest of the men digging. Inactivity came hard to him. Sometimes, too, he welcomed the chance to keep himself fit; even now, more than twenty years since quitting the amateur boxing ring, he was in better shape physically than most men years his junior. The airline ground crewmen enjoyed seeing Patroni's cocky, stocky figure working with them. He led and exhorted . . . *'Keep moving, son, or we'll figure we're gravediggers, and you the corpse.'* . . . *'The way you guys keep heading for that bus, looks like you've got a woman stashed there.'* . . . *'If you lean on that shovel any more, Jack, you'll freeze solid like Lot's wife.'* . . . *'Men, we want this aeroplane moved before it's obsolete.'*

So far, Joe Patroni had not talked with the captain and first officer, having left that to the Aéreo-Mexican foreman, Ingram, who had been in charge before Patroni's arrival. Ingram had passed up a message on the aircraft interphone, telling the pilots what was happening below.

Now, straightening his back, and thrusting his shovel at Ingram, the maintenance chief advised, 'Five minutes more should do it. When you're ready, get the men and trucks clear.' He motioned to the snow-shrouded aeroplane. 'When this one comes out, she'll be like a cork from a champagne bottle.'

Ingram, huddled into his parka, still pinched and cold as he had been earlier, nodded.

'While you're doing that,' Patroni said, 'I'll yak with the fly boys.'

The old-fashioned boarding ramp which had been trundled from the terminal several hours ago to disembark the stranded passengers, was still in place near the aircraft's nose. Joe Patroni climbed the ramp, its steps covered in deep snow, and let himself into the front passenger cabin. He went forward to the flight deck – with relief, lighting his inevitable cigar as he went.

In contrast to the cold and wind-blown snow outside, the pilots' cockpit was snug and quiet. One of the communications radios was tuned to soft music of a commercial station.

As Patroni entered, the Aéreo-Mexican first officer, in shirt-sleeves, snapped a switch and the music stopped.

'Don't worry about doing that.' The chunky maintenance chief shook himself like a bull terrier while snow cascaded from his clothing. 'Nothing wrong with taking things easy. After all, we didn't expect you to come down and shovel.'

Only the first officer and captain were in the cockpit. Patroni remembered hearing that the flight engineer had gone with the stewardesses and passengers to the terminal.

The captain, a heavy-set, swarthy man who resembled Anthony Quinn, swivelled around in his port-side seat. He said stiffly, 'We have our job to do. You have yours.' His English was precise.

'That's right,' Patroni acknowledged. 'Only trouble is, our job gets fouled up and added to. By other people.'

'If you are speaking of what has happened here,' the captain said, '*Madre de Dios!* – you do not suppose that I placed this aeroplane in the mud on purpose.'

'No, I don't.' Patronic discarded his cigar, which was maimed from chewing, put a new one in his mouth and lit it. 'But now it's there, I want to make sure we get it out – this next time we try. If we don't, the aeroplane'll be in a whole lot deeper; so will all of us, including you.' He nodded towards the captain's seat. 'How'd you like me to sit there and drive it out?'

The captain flushed. Few people in any airline talked as casually to four-stripers as Joe Patroni.

'No, thank you,' the captain said coldly. He might have replied even more unpleasantly, except that at the moment he was suffering acute embarrassment for having got into his present predicament at all. Tomorrow in Mexico City, he suspected, he would face an unhappy, searing session with his airline's chief pilot. He raged inwardly: *Jesucristo y por el amor de Dios!*

'There's a lotta half-frozen guys outside who've been busting their guts,' Patroni insisted. 'Getting out now's tricky. I've done it before. Maybe you should let me again.'

The Aéreo-Mexican captain bridled. 'I know who you are, Mr Patroni, and I am told that you are likely to help us move from this bad ground, where others have failed. So I have no doubt that you are licensed to taxi aeroplanes. But let me remind you there are two of us here who are licensed to *fly* them. It is what we are paid for. Therefore we shall remain at the controls.'

'Suit yourself.' Joe Patroni shrugged, then waved his cigar at the control pedestal. 'Only thing is, when I give the word, open those throttles all the way. And I mean all the way, and don't chicken out.'

As he left the cockpit, he ignored angry glares from both pilots.

Outside, digging had stopped; some of the men who had been working were warming themselves again in the crew buses. The buses and other vehicles – with the exception of the power cart, which was needed for starting engines – were being removed some distance from the aeroplane.

Joe Patroni closed the forward cabin door behind him and descended the ramp. The foreman, huddled deeper than ever into his parka, reported, 'Everything's set.'

Remembering his cigar was still lighted, Patroni puffed at it several times, then dropped it into the snow where it went out. He motioned to the silent jet engines. 'Okay, let's light up all four.'

Several men were returning from the crew bus. A quartet put their shoulders to the ramp beside the aircraft and shoved it clear. Two others responded to the foreman's shout against the wind, 'Ready to start engines!'

One of the second pair stationed himself at the front of the aircraft, near the power cart. He wore a telephone headset plugged into the fuselage. The second man, with flashlight signal wands, walked forward to where he could be seen by the pilots above.

Joe Patroni, with borrowed protective head pads, joined the crewman with the telephone headset. The remainder of the men were now scrambling from the sheltering buses, intent on watching what came next.

In the cockpit, the pilots completed their checklist.

On the ground below, the crewman with the telephone set began the jet starting ritual. 'Clear to start engines.'

A pause. The captain's voice. 'Ready to start, and pressurize the manifold.'

From the power cart blower, a stream of forced air hit the air turbine starter of number three engine. Compressor vanes turned, spun faster, whined. At fifteen per cent speed, the first officer fed in aviation kerosene. As the fuel ignited, a smoke cloud belched back and the engine took hold with a deep-throated bellow.

'Clear to start four.'

Number four engine followed three. Generators on both engines charging.

The captain's voice. 'Switching to generators. Disconnect ground power.'

Above the power cart, electric lines came down. 'Disconnected. Clear to start two.'

Number two took hold. Three engines now. An encompassing roar. Snow streaming behind.

Number one fired and held.

'Disconnect air.'

'Disconnected.'

The umbilical air hose slipped down. The foreman drove the power cart away.

Floodlights ahead of the aircraft had been moved to one side.

Patroni exchanged headsets with the crewman near the front of the fuselage. The maintenance chief now had the telephone set, and communication with the pilots.

'This's Patroni. When you're ready up there, let's roll her out.'

Ahead of the aircraft nose, the crewman with the lighted wands held them up, ready to be a guide along an elliptical path beyond the trenches, also cleared at Joe Patroni's direction. The crewman was ready to run if the 707 came out of the mud faster than expected.

Patroni crouched close to the nosewheel. If the aeroplane moved quickly, he, too, was vulnerable. He held a hand near the interphone plug, ready to disconnect. He watched the main landing gear intently for a sign of forward movement.

The captain's voice. 'I am opening up.'

The tempo of the jets increased. In a roar like sustained thunder, the aeroplane shook, the ground beneath it trembled. But the wheels remained still.

Patroni cupped his hands around the interphone mouthpiece. 'More power! Throttles forward all the way!'

The engine noise heightened but only slightly. The wheels rose perceptibly, but still failed to move forward.

'Goddamit! All the way!'

For several seconds, the engine tempo remained as it was, then abruptly lessened. The captain's voice rattled the interphone; it had a sarcastic note. '*Patroni, por favor,* if I open my throttles all the way, this aeroplane will stand on its nose. Instead of a stranded 707, we shall both have a wrecked one.'

The maintenance chief had been studying the landing gear wheels, which had now settled back, and the ground around them. 'It'll come out, I tell you! All it needs is the guts to pull full power.'

'Look to your own guts!' the captain snapped back. 'I am shutting the engines down.'

Patroni shouted into the interphone. 'Keep those motors running; hold 'em at idle! I'm coming up!' Moving forward under the nose, he motioned urgently for the boarding ramp to be repositioned. But even as it was being pushed into place, all four engines quieted and died.

When he reached the cockpit, both pilots were unfastening their seat harnesses.

Patroni said accusingly, 'You chickened out!'

The captain's reaction was surprisingly mild. '*Es posible.* Perhaps it is the only intelligent thing I have done tonight.' He inquired formally, 'Does your maintenance department accept this aeroplane?'

'Okay,' Patroni nodded. 'We'll take it over.'

The first officer glanced at his watch and made an entry in a log.

'When you have extricated this aeroplane, in whatever way,' the Aéreo-Mexican captain stated, 'no doubt your company will be in touch with my company. Meanwhile, *buenas noches.*'

As the two pilots left, their heavy topcoats buttoned tightly at the neck, Joe Patroni made a swift, routine check of instruments and control settings. A minute or so later he followed the pilots down the outside ramp.

The Aéreo-Mexican foreman, Ingram, was waiting below. He nodded in the direction of the departing pilots, now hurrying towards one of the crew buses. 'That was the same thing they done to me; not pulling enough power.' He motioned gloomily towards the aircraft's main landing gear. 'That's why she went in deep before; now she's dug herself in deeper still.'

It was what Joe Patroni had feared.

With Ingram holding an electric lantern, he ducked under the fuselage to inspect the landing gear wheels; they were back in mud and slush again, almost a foot deeper than before. Patroni took the light and shone it under the wings; all four engine nacelles were disquietingly closer to the ground.

'Nothing but a sky hook'll help her now,' Ingram said.

The maintenance chief considered the situation, then shook his head. 'We got one more chance. We'll dig some more, bring the trenches down to where the wheels are now, then start the engines again. Only this time I'll drive.'

The wind and snow still howled around them.

Shivering, Ingram acknowledged doubtfully. 'I guess you're the doctor. But better you than me.'

Joe Patroni grinned. 'If I don't blast her out, maybe I'll blow her apart.'

Ingram headed for the remaining crew bus to call out the men; the other bus had taken the Aéreo-Mexican pilots to the terminal.

Patroni calculated: there was another hour's work ahead before they could try moving

213

the aircraft again. Therefore runway three zero would have to continue out of use for at least that long.

He went to his radio-equipped pickup to report to air traffic control.

7

The theory that an overburdened, exhausted mind can exercise its own safety valve by retreating into passive semi-awareness was unknown to Inez Guerrero. Nevertheless, for her, the theory had proved true. At this moment she was a mental walking-wounded case.

The events of tonight affecting her personally, coupled with her accumulated distress and weariness of weeks, had proved a final crushing defeat. It prompted her mind – like an overloaded circuit – to switch off. The condition was temporary, not permanent, yet while it remained Inez Guerrero had forgotten where she was, or why.

The mean, uncouth taxi driver who had brought her to the airport had not helped. When bargaining downtown, he agreed to seven dollars as the price of the ride. Getting out, Inez proffered a ten dollar bill – almost the last money she had – expecting change. Mumbling that he had no change, but would get some, the cabbie drove off. Inez waited for ten anxious minutes, watching the terminal clock which was nearing 11.0 pm – the time of Flight Two's departure – before it dawned on her that the man had no intention of returning. She had noticed neither the taxi number nor the driver's – something the driver had gambled on. Even if she had, Inez Guerrero was not the kind who complained to authority; the driver had correctly guessed that, too.

Despite the initial slowness of her journey from downtown, she could have reached Flight Two before it left – but for the time spent waiting for the non-appearing change. As it was, she arrived at the departure gate to see the aeroplane taxiing away.

Even then, to find out if her husband, D.O., was really aboard, Inez had the presence of mind to use the subterfuge which the Trans America inquiries girl, Miss Young, suggested on the telephone. A uniformed agent was just leaving gate forty-seven, where Flight Two had been. Inez accosted him.

As Miss Young advised, Inez avoided asking a direct question, and made the statement, 'My husband is on that flight which just left.' She explained that she had missed seeing her husband, but wanted to be sure he was safely aboard. Inez unfolded the yellow time-payment contract which she had discovered at home among D.O.'s shirts, and showed it to the Trans America agent. He barely glanced at it, then checked the papers he was holding.

For a moment or two Inez wondered hopefully if she had made a mistake in presuming that D.O. was leaving on the flight; the idea of his going to Rome at all still seemed fantastic. Then the agent said, yes, there was a D. O. Guerrero aboard Flight Two, and he, the agent, was sorry that Mrs Guerrero had missed seeing her husband, but everything was in a mixup tonight because of the storm, and now if she would please excuse him . . .

It was when the agent had gone and Inez realized that despite the press of people around her in the terminal, she was utterly alone, that she began to cry.

At first the tears came slowly; then, as she remembered all that had gone wrong, they streamed in great heaving sobs which shook her body. She cried for the past and for the present; for the home she had had and lost; for her children whom she could no longer keep with her; for D.O. who, despite his faults as a husband, and the failure to support his family, was at least familiar, but now had deserted her. She wept for what she herself had been and had become; for the fact that she had no money, nowhere to go but to the mean, cockroach-infested rooms downtown, from which she would be evicted tomorrow, having nothing left – after the taxi ride and the driver's theft – from the pathetically small amount with which she had hoped to stave off the landlord . . . she was not even sure if she had enough small change to return downtown. She cried because her shoes still hurt her feet; for her clothes which were shabby and sodden; for her weariness, and because she had a cold and a fever which she could feel getting worse. She cried for herself and all others for whom every hope was gone.

It was then, to avoid stares of people who were watching, that she began walking aimlessly through the terminal, still weeping as she went. Somewhere near that time, too, the defensive machinery of her mind took over, inducing a protective numbness, so that her sorrow persisted but its reasons, for a while, were mercifully blurred.

Soon after, an airport policeman found her and, with a sensitivity for which police are not always credited, placed her in as obscure a corner as he could find while telephoning his superiors for instructions. Lieutenant Ordway happened to be nearby and dealt with the matter personally. It was he who decided that Inez Guerrero, though incoherent and upset, was harmless, and had ordered her taken to the airport general manager's office – the only place Ned Ordway could think of which was quiet, yet less intimidating than police headquarters.

Inez had gone docilely, in an elevator and along a mezzanine, only half-knowing that she was being taken anywhere at all, and not caring; and after, had sat quietly in a seat she was guided to, her body, if not her mind, grateful for the rest. She had been aware of people coming and going, and some had spoken, but she had brought neither the sight nor sound of them into focus, the effort seeming too much.

But after a while, her resilience – which is another word for strength of the human spirit, which all possess, however burdened or humble – brought her back to a realization, even though vague, that she must move on, because life moved on, and always had and would, no matter how many defeats it wrought, or dreary or empty as it might seem.

So Inez Guerrero stood up, still not sure where she was or how she had come there, but prepared to go.

It was then that the Meadowood delegation escorted by Lieutenant Ordway, entered the anteroom to Mel Bakersfeld's office, where Inez was. The delegation continued into the other room, then Ned Ordway had returned to speak with Inez Guerrero, and Mel observed the two of them together briefly before the door to his office closed.

Inez, through her miasma of uncertainty, was also conscious of the big Negro policeman, whom she had a feeling she had seen somewhere before, quite recently, and he had been kind then, as he was being kind now, leading her with quiet, not-quite-questions, so that he seemed to understand, without her ever saying so, that she had to return downtown and wasn't sure she had enough money for it. She started to fumble with her purse, intending to count what was there, but he stopped her. Then, with his back to the other room, he slipped three one-dollar bills into her hand, and came with her outside, pointing the way down to where, he said, she would find a bus, and added that what he had given her would be enough for the fare, with something over for wherever she had to go when she got to the city.

The policeman had gone then, returning in the direction from which they had come, and Inez did what she was told, going down some stairs; then almost at the big door through which she was to go for the bus, she had seen a familiar sight – a hot dog counter; and at that moment she realized how hungry and thirsty she was, on top of everything else. She had groped in her purse, and found thirty-five cents, and bought a hot dog, and coffee in a paper cup, and somehow the sight of those two very ordinary things was reassuring. Not far from the food counter, she found a seat and tucked herself into a corner. She wasn't sure how long ago that was but now, with the coffee gone and the hot dog eaten, awareness which earlier had started to come back, was receding from her once more in a comfortable way. There was something comforting, too, about the crowds around her, the noises, and loudspeaker announcements. Twice Inez thought she heard her own name on the loudspeakers, but knew it was imagination and couldn't be true because no one would call her, or even know that she was here.

She realized dimly that sometime soon she would have to move on, and knew that tonight especially it would entail an effort. But for a while, she thought, she would sit here quietly, where she was.

8

With one exception, those summoned to the airport general manager's office on the administrative mezzanine arrived there quickly. The calls made to them – some by Mel Bakersfeld, others by Tanya Livingston – had stressed urgency, and the need to leave whatever they were doing.

The District Transportation Manager of Trans America – Tanya's boss, Bert Weatherby – arrived first.

Lieutenant Ordway, having started his policemen searching for Inez Guerrero, though still not knowing why, was close behind. For the time being Ordway had abandoned to their own devices the sizeable group of Meadowood residents, still milling in the main concourse, listening to Lawyer Freemantle expound their case before TV cameras.

As the DTM, Weatherby, entered Mel's office through the anteroom door, he inquired briskly, 'Mel, what's all this about?'

'We're not sure, Bert, and we haven't a lot to go on yet, but there's a possibility there could be a bomb aboard your Flight Two.'

The DTM looked searchingly at Tanya, but wasted no time in asking why she was there. His gaze swung back to Mel. 'Let's hear what you know.'

Addressing both the DTM and Ned Ordway, Mel summarized what was known or conjectured so far: the report of Customs Inspector Standish concerning the passenger with the attaché case, clasped in a way which Standish – an experienced observer – believed to be suspicious; Tanya's identification of the man with the case as one D. O. Guerrero, or perhaps Buerrero; the downtown agent's revelation that Guerrero checked in without any baggage other than the small case already mentioned; Guerrero's purchase at the airport of three hundred thousand dollars' worth of flight insurance, which he barely had enough money to pay for, so that he appeared to be setting out on a five-thousand-mile journey, not only without so much as a change of clothing, but also without funds;

216

and finally – perhaps coincidentally, perhaps not – Mrs Inez Guerrero, sole beneficiary of her husband's flight insurance policy, had been wandering through the terminal, apparently in great distress.

While Mel was speaking, Customs Inspector Harry Standish, still in uniform, came in, followed by Bunnie Vorobioff. Bunnie entered uncertainly, glancing questioningly around her at the unfamiliar people and surroundings. As the import of what Mel was saying sank in, she paled and appeared scared.

The one non-arrival was the gate agent who had been in charge at gate forty-seven when Flight Two left. A staff supervisor whom Tanya had spoken to a few minutes ago informed her that the agent was now off duty and on his way home. She gave instructions for a message to be left, and for the agent to check in by telephone as soon as he arrived. Tanya doubted if anything would be gained by bringing him back to the airport tonight; for one thing, she already knew that the agent did not remember Guerrero boarding. But someone else might want to question him by phone.

'I called everyone here who's involved so far,' Mel informed the DTM, 'in case you or someone else have questions. What we have to decide, I think – and it's mainly your decision – is whether or not we have enough to warn your captain of Flight Two.' Mel was reminded again of what he had temporarily pushed from mind: that the flight was commanded by his brother-in-law, Vernon Demerest. Later, Mel knew, he might have to do some reconsidering about certain implications. But not yet.

'I'm thinking now.' The DTM looked grim; he swung to Tanya. 'Whatever we decide, I want Operations in on this. Find out if Royce Kettering is still on the base. If so, get him here fast.' Captain Kettering was Trans America's chief pilot at Lincoln International; it was he who earlier tonight had test-flown aircraft N-731-TA, before – as Flight Two, *The Golden Argosy* – it took off for Rome.

'Yes, sir,' Tanya said.

While she was on one telephone, another rang. Mel answered.

It was the tower watch chief. 'I have the report you wanted on Trans America Two.' One of Mel's calls for a few minutes ago had been to air traffic control, requesting information on the flight's takeoff time and progress.

'Go ahead.'

'Takeoff was 11.13 local time.' Mel's eyes swung to a wall clock. It was now almost ten minutes after midnight; the flight had been airborne nearly an hour.

The tower chief continued, 'Chicago Centre handed off the flight to Cleveland Centre at 12.27 EST, Cleveland handed it to Toronto at 01.03 EST; that's seven minutes ago. At the moment, Toronto Centre reports the aircraft's position as near London, Ontario. I have more information – course, height, speed – if you want it.'

'That's enough for now,' Mel said. 'Thanks.'

'One other thing, Mr Bakersfeld.' The tower chief summarized Joe Patroni's latest bulletin about runway three zero: the runway would be out of use for at least another hour. Mel listened impatiently; at the moment, other things seemed more important.

When he hung up, Mel repeated the information about Flight Two's position to the DTM.

Tanya came off the other phone. She reported, 'Operations found Captain Kettering. He's coming.'

'That woman – the passenger's wife,' the DTM said. 'What was her name?'

217

Ned Ordway answered. 'Inez Guerrero.'

'Where is she?'

'We don't know.' The policeman explained that his men were searching the airport, although the woman might be gone. He added that city police headquarters had been alerted, and all buses from the airport to downtown were now being checked on arrival.

'When she was here,' Mel explained, 'we had no idea . . .'

The DTM grunted. 'We were all slow.' He glanced at Tanya, then at Customs Inspector Standish, who so far had not spoken. The DTM, Tanya knew, was remembering ruefully his own instructions to 'Forget it!'

Now he informed her, 'We'll have to tell the captain of the flight something. He's entitled to know as much as we do, even though so far we're only guessing.'

Tanya asked, 'Shouldn't we send a description of Guerrero? Captain Demerest may want to have him identified without his knowing.'

'If you do,' Mel pointed out, 'we can help. There are people here who have seen the man.'

'All right,' the DTM acknowledged, 'we'll work on that. Meanwhile, Tanya, call our dispatcher. Tell him there's an important message coming in a few minutes, and to get a Selcal circuit hooked into Flight Two. I want this kept private, not broadcast for everybody. At least, not yet.'

Tanya returned to the telephone.

Mel asked Bunnie, 'Are you Miss Vorobioff?'

As she nodded nervously, the eyes of the others turned to her.

Automatically, those of the men dropped to Bunnie's capacious breasts; the DTM seemed about to whistle, but changed his mind.

Mel said, 'You realize which man we're talking about?'

'I . . . I'm not sure.'

'It's a man named D. O. Guerrero. You sold him an insurance policy tonight, didn't you?'

Bunnie nodded again. 'Yes.'

'When you wrote the policy, did you get a good look at him?'

She shook her head. 'Not really.' Her voice was low. She moistened her lips.

Mel seemed surprised. 'I thought on the phone . . .'

'There were many other people,' Bunnie said defensively.

'But you told me you remembered this one.'

'It was someone else.'

'And you don't recall the man Guerrero?'

'No.'

Mel looked baffled.

'Let me, Mr Bakersfeld.' Ned Ordway took a pace forward; he put his face near the girl's. 'You're afraid of getting involved, aren't you?' Ordway's voice was a harsh, policeman's voice, not at all the gentle tone he used earlier tonight with Inez Guerrero.

Bunnie flinched, but didn't answer.

Ordway persisted, 'Well, aren't you? Answer me.'

'I don't know.'

'Yes, you do! You're afraid to help anyone for fear of what it might do to you. I know your kind.' Ordway spat out the words contemptuously. This was a savage, tough side of the lieutenant's nature which Mel had never seen before. 'Now you hear me, baby. If it's trouble you're scared of, you're buying it right now. The way to get out of trouble – *if you can* – is to answer questions. *And answer fast!* We're running out of time.'

Bunnie trembled. She had learned to fear police interrogation in the grim school of Eastern Europe. It was a conditioning never totally erased. Ordway had recognized the signs.

'Miss Vorobioff,' Mel said. 'There are almost two hundred people aboard the aeroplane we're concerned with. They may be in great danger. Now, I'll ask you again. Did you get a good look at the man Guerrero?'

Slowly, Bunnie nodded. 'Yes.'

'Describe him, please.'

She did so, haltingly at first, then with more confidence.

While the others listened, a picture of D. O. Guerrero emerged: gaunt and spindly; a pale, sallow face with protruding jaw; long scrawny neck; thin lips; a small sandy moustache; nervous hands with restless fingers. When she got down to it, Bunnie Vorobioff proved herself a keen observer.

The DTM, now seated at Mel's desk, wrote the description, incorporating it with a message for Flight Two which he was drafting.

When Bunnie came to the part about D. O. Guerrero barely having enough money – and no Italian money; the man's nervous tension, the fumbling with dimes and pennies; his excitement on discovering a five-dollar bill in an inside pocket, the DTM looked up with a mixture of disgust and horror. '*My God!* And you *still* issued a policy. Are you people *mad*?'

'I thought . . .' Bunnie started to say.

'*You thought!* But you didn't *do* anything, did you?'

Her face drained and white, Bunnie Vorobioff shook her head.

Mel reminded the DTM, 'Bert, we're wasting time.'

'I know, I know! Just the same . . .' The DTM clenched the pencil he had been using. He muttered, 'It isn't just *her*, or even the people who employ her. It's *us* – the airlines; we're as much to blame. We agree with the pilots about airport flight insurance, but haven't the guts to say so. We let them do our dirty work . . .'

Mel said tersely to Customs Inspector Standish, 'Harry, is there anything you'd add to the description of Guerrero?'

'No,' Standish said. 'I wasn't as near to him as this young lady, and she saw some things I didn't. But I did watch the way he held the case, as you know, and I'd say this: If what you think is in there really is, don't anyone try to grab that case away from him.'

'So what do you suggest?'

The Customs man shook his head. 'I'm no expert, so I can't tell you; except, I guess you'd have to get it by some kind of trickery. But if it's a bomb, it has to be self-contained in the case, and that means somewhere there's a trigger, and the chances are it'll be the kind of trigger he can get to quickly. He's possessive about the case now. If someone tried to take it away, he'd figure he was found out and had nothing to lose.' Standish added grimly, 'A trigger finger can get mighty itchy.'

'Of course,' Mel said, 'we still don't know if the man's an ordinary eccentric, and all he's got in there are his pyjamas.'

'If you're asking my opinion,' the Customs inspector said, 'I don't think so. I wish I did, because I've got a niece on that flight.'

Standish had been conjecturing unhappily: If anything went wrong, how in God's name would he break the news to his sister in Denver? He remembered his last sight of Judy: that sweet young girl, playing with the baby from the next seat. She had kissed him. *Goodbye, Uncle Harry!* Now, he wished desperately that he had been more definite, had acted more responsibly, about the man with the attaché case.

Well, Standish thought, though it might be late, at least he would be definite now.

'I'd like to say something else.' The eyes of the others swung to him.

'I have to tell you this because we haven't time to waste on modesty: I'm a good judge of people, mostly on first sight, and usually I can smell the bad ones. It's an instinct, and don't ask me how it works because I couldn't tell you, except that in my job some of us get to be that way. I spotted that man tonight, and I said he was "suspicious"; I used that word because I was thinking of smuggling, which is the way I'm trained. Now, knowing what we do – even little as it is – I'd make it stronger. The man Guerrero is dangerous.' Standish eyed the Trans America DTM. 'Mr Weatherby – get that word "dangerous" across to your people in the air.'

'I intend to, Inspector.' The DTM looked up from his writing. Most of what Standish had been saying was already included in the message for Flight Two.

Tanya, still on the telephone, was talking with Trans America's New York dispatcher by tie line. 'Yes, it will be a long message. Will you put someone on to copy, please.'

A sharp knock sounded on the office door and a tall man with a seamed, weatherworn face and sharp blue eyes came in from the anteroom. He carried a heavy topcoat and wore a blue serge suit which might have been a uniform, but wasn't. The newcomer nodded to Mel, but before either could speak, the DTM cut in.

'Royce, thanks for coming quickly. We seem to have some trouble.' He held out the notepad on which he had been writing.

Captain Kettering, the base chief pilot for Trans America, read the draft message carefully, his only reaction a tightening at the mouth as his eyes moved down the page. Like many others, including the DTM, it was unusual for the chief pilot to be at the airport this late at night. But exigencies of the three-day storm, with the need for frequent operating decisions, had kept him here.

The second telephone rang, cutting through the temporary silence. Mel answered it, then motioned to Ned Ordway who took the receiver.

Captain Kettering finished reading. The DTM asked, 'Do you agree to sending that? We've dispatch standing by with a Selcal hook-up.'

Kettering nodded. 'Yes, but I'd like you to add: "Suggest return or alternate landing at captain's discretion," and have the dispatcher give them the latest weather.'

'Of course.' The DTM pencilled in the extra words, then passed the pad to Tanya. She began dictating the message.

Captain Kettering glanced at the others in the room. 'Is that everything we know?'

'Yes, Mel said. 'It is, so far.'

'We may know more soon,' Lieutenant Ordway said. He had returned from the telephone. 'We just found Guerrero's wife.'

The message from DTM Lincoln International was addressed, CAPTAIN, TRANS AMERICA FLIGHT TWO, and began:

UNCONFIRMED POSSIBILITY EXISTS THAT MALE TOURIST PASSENGER D.O. GUERRERO ABOARD YOUR FLIGHT MAY HAVE EXPLOSIVE DEVICE IN HIS POSSESSION. PASSENGER WITH NO LUGGAGE AND APPARENTLY WITHOUT FUNDS INSURED SELF HEAVILY BEFORE DEPARTURE. WAS OBSERVED BEHAVING SUSPICIOUSLY WITH ATTACHÉ TYPE BRIEFCASE CARRIED AS HAND BAGGAGE. DESCRIPTION FOLLOWS . . .

As the DTM had foreseen, it took several minutes for a connection to be established, through company radio, with Flight Two. Since the earlier Selcal message to the flight, concerning its stowaway Mrs Ada Quonsett, the aircraft had moved out of Trans America's Cleveland dispatch area into that of New York. Now, company messages must be passed through a New York dispatcher for relaying to the flight.

The message, as Tanya dictated it, was being typed by a girl clerk in New York. Alongside the clerk a Trans America dispatcher read the first few lines, then reached for a direct phone to an operator at ARINC – a private communications network maintained co-operatively by all major airlines.

The ARINC operator – at another location in New York – set up a second circuit between himself and Trans America dispatch, then punched into a transmitter keyboard a four-letter code, AGFG, specially assigned to aircraft N-731-TA. Once more, like a telephone call to a single number on a party line, an alerting signal would be received aboard Flight Two only.

A few moments later the voice of Captain Vernon Demerest, responding from high above Ontario, Canada, was audible in New York. 'This is Trans America Two answering Selcal.'

'Trans America Two, this is New York dispatch. We have an important message. Advise when ready to copy.'

A brief pause, then Demerest again. 'Okay, New York. Go ahead.'

'CAPTAIN, FLIGHT TWO,' the dispatcher began. 'UNCONFIRMED POSSIBILITY EXISTS . . .'

Inez had still been sitting quietly, in her corner near the food counter, when she felt her shoulder shaken.

'Inez Guerrero! Are you Mrs Guerrero?'

She looked up. It took several seconds to collect her thoughts, which had been vague and drifting, but she realized that it was a policeman who was standing over her.

He shook her again and repeated the question.

Inez managed to nod. She became aware that this was a different policeman from the earlier one. This one was white, and neither as gentle nor as softly spoken as the other.

'Let's move it, lady!' The policeman tightened his grip on her shoulder in a way which hurt, and pulled her abruptly to her feet. 'You hear me? – let's go! They're screamin' for you upstairs, and every cop in the joint's bin searchin' for you.'

Ten minutes later, in Mel's office, Inez was the pivot of attention. She occupied a chair in the room's centre to which she had been guided on arrival. Lieutenant Ordway faced her. The policeman who had escorted Inez in was gone.

The others who had been present earlier – Mel, Tanya, Customs Inspector Standish, Bunnie Vorobioff, the Trans America DTM, Weatherby, and the chief pilot, Captain Kettering – were ranged about the room. All had remained at Mel's request.

'Mrs Guerrero,' Ned Ordway said. 'Why is your husband going to Rome?'

Inez stared back bleakly and didn't answer. The policeman's voice sharpened, though not unkindly. 'Mrs Guerrero, please listen to me carefully. There are some important questions which I have to ask. They concern your husband, and I need your help. Do you understand?'

'I . . . I'm not sure.'

'You don't have to be sure about *why* I'm asking the questions. There'll be time for that later. What I want you to do is help me by answering. Will you? Please.'

The DTM cut in urgently. 'Lieutenant, we haven't got all night. That aeroplane is moving away from us at six hundred miles an hour. If we have to, let's get tough.'

'Leave this to me, Mr Weatherby,' Ordway said sharply. 'If we all start shouting, it'll take a lot more time to get a great deal less.'

The DTM continued to look impatient, but kept quiet.

'Inez,' Ordway said; '. . . is it okay if I call you Inez?'

She nodded.

'Inez, *will* you answer my questions?'

'Yes . . . if I can.'

'Why is your husband going to Rome?'

Her voice was strained, barely more than a whisper. 'I don't know.'

'Do you have friends there; relatives?'

'No . . . There is a distant cousin in Milan, but we have never seen him.'

'Do your husband and the cousin correspond?'

'No.'

'Can you think of any reason why your husband would go to visit the cousin – and suddenly?'

'There is no reason.'

Tanya interjected, 'In any case, Lieutenant, if anyone was going to Milan they wouldn't use our Rome flight. They'd fly Alitalia, which is direct and cheaper – and Alitalia has a flight tonight, too.'

Ordway nodded. 'We can probably rule out the cousin.' He asked Inez, 'Does your husband have business in Italy?'

She shook her head.

'What *is* your husband's business?'

'He is . . . was . . . a contractor.'

'What kind of contractor?'

Slowly but perceptibly, Inez's grasp of things was coming back. 'He built buildings, houses, developments.'

'You said "was". Why isn't he a contractor now?'

'Things . . . went wrong.'

'You mean financially?'

'Yes, but . . . why are you asking?'

'Please believe me, Inez,' Ordway said. 'I've a good reason. It concerns your husband's safety, as well as others. Will you take my word?'

She looked up. Her eyes met his. 'All right.'

'Is your husband in financial trouble now?'

She hesitated only briefly. 'Yes.'

'Bad trouble?'

Inez nodded slowly.

'Is he broke? In debt?'

Again a whisper. 'Yes.'

'Then where did he get money for his fare to Rome?'

'I think . . .' Inez started to say something about her ring which D.O. had pawned, then remembered the Trans America Airlines time payment contract. She took the now-creased yellow sheet from her purse and gave it to Ordway who glanced over it. The DTM joined him.

'It's made out to "Buerrero",' the DTM said. 'Though the signature could be anything.'

Tanya pointed out, 'Buerrero is the name we had at first on the flight manifest.'

Ned Ordway shook his head. 'It isn't important now, but it's an old trick if anyone has a lousy credit rating. They use a wrong first letter so the bad rating won't show up in inquiry – at least, not in a hurry. Later, if the mistake's discovered, it can be blamed on whoever filled out the form.'

Ordway swung sternly back to Inez. He had the yellow printed sheet in hand. 'Why did you agree to this when you knew your husband was defrauding?'

She protested, 'I didn't know.'

'Then how is it you have this paper now?'

Haltingly, she related how she had found it earlier this evening, and had come to the airport, hoping to intercept her husband before departure.

'So until tonight you had no idea that he was going?'

'No, sir.'

'Anywhere at all?'

Inez shook her head.

'Even now, can you think of any reason for him going?'

She looked bewildered. 'No.'

'Does your husband ever do irrational things?'

Inez hesitated.

'Well,' Ordway said, 'does he?'

'Sometimes, lately . . .'

'He *has* been irrational?'

A whisper. 'Yes.'

'Violent?'

Reluctantly, Inez nodded.

'Your husband was carrying a case tonight,' Ordway said quietly. 'A small attaché case, and he seemed specially cautious about it. Have you any idea what might be inside?'

'No, sir.'

'Inez, you said your husband was a contractor – a building contractor. In the course of his work did he ever use explosives?'

The question had been put so casually and without preamble, that those listening seemed scarcely aware it had been asked. But as its import dawned, there was a sudden tenseness in the room.

'Oh, yes,' Inez said. 'Often.'

Ordway paused perceptibly before asking, 'Does your husband know a lot about explosives?'

'I think so. He always liked using them. But . . .' Abruptly, she stopped.

'But what, Inez?'

Suddenly there was a nervousness to Inez Guerrero's speech which had not been there before. 'But . . . he handles them very carefully.' Her eyes moved around the room. 'Please . . . what is this about?'

Ordway said softly, 'You have an idea, Inez, haven't you?'

When she didn't answer, almost with indifference he asked, 'Where are you living?'

She gave the address of the South Side apartment and he wrote it down. 'Is that where your husband was this afternoon; earlier this evening?'

Thoroughly frightened now, she nodded.

Ordway turned to Tanya. Without raising his voice, he asked, 'Get a line open, please, to police headquarters downtown; this extension' – he scribbled a number on a pad. 'Ask them to hold.'

Tanya went quickly to Mel's desk.

Ordway asked Inez, 'Did your husband have any explosives in the apartment?' As she hesitated, he bore in with sudden toughness. 'You've told the truth so far; don't lie to me now! Did he?'

'Yes.'

'What kind of explosives?'

'Some dynamite . . . and caps . . . They were left over.'

'From his contracting work?'

'Yes.'

'Did he ever say anything about them? Give a reason for keeping them?'

Inez shook her head. 'Only, that . . . if you knew how to handle them . . . they were safe.'

'Where were the explosives kept?'

'Just in a drawer.'

'In a drawer where?'

'The bedroom.' An expression of sudden shock crossed Inez Guerrero's face. Ordway spotted it.

'You thought of something then! What was it?'

'Nothing!' Panic was in her eyes and voice.

'Yes, you did!' Ned Ordway leaned forward, close to Inez, his face aggressive. For the second time in this room tonight he exhibited nothing of kindness; only the rough, tough savagery of a policeman who needed an answer and would get it. He shouted, 'Don't try holding back or lying! It won't work. Tell me what it was you thought.' As Inez whimpered: 'Never mind that! Tell me!'

'Tonight . . . I didn't think of it before . . . the things . . .'

'The dynamite and caps?'

'Yes.'

'You're wasting time! What about them?'

Inez whispered, 'They were gone!'

Tanya said quietly, 'I have your call, Lieutenant. They're holding.'

No one among the others spoke.

Ordway nodded, his eyes still fixed on Inez. 'Did you know that tonight, before your husband's flight took off, he insured himself heavily – very heavily indeed – naming you as beneficiary?'

'No, sir. I swear I don't know anything . . .'

'I believe you,' Ordway said. He stopped, considering, and when he spoke again his voice grated harshly.

'Inez Guerrero, listen to me carefully. We believe your husband has those explosives, which you've told us about, with him tonight. We think he carried them on to that Rome flight, and, since there can be no other explanation for having them there, that he intends to destroy the aeroplane, killing himself and everyone else aboard. Now, I've one more question, and before you answer, think carefully, and remember those other people – innocent people, including children – who are on that flight, too. Inez, you know your husband; you know him as well as anyone alive. Could he . . . for the insurance money; for you . . . could he do what I have just said?'

Tears streamed down Inez Guerrero's face. She seemed near collapse, but nodded slowly.

'Yes.' Her voice was choked. 'Yes, I think he could.'

Ned Ordway turned away. He took the telephone from Tanya and began speaking rapidly in a low tone. He gave information, interspersed with several requests.

Once Ordway paused, swinging back to Inez Guerrero. 'Your apartment is going to be searched, and we'll get a warrant if necessary. But it will be easier if you consent. Do you?'

Inez nodded dully.

'Okay,' Ordway said into the telephone, 'she agrees.' A minute or so later he hung up.

Ordway told the DTM and Mel, 'We'll collect the evidence in the apartment, if there's any there. Apart from that, at the moment, there isn't a lot we can do.'

The DTM said grimly, 'There isn't a lot any of us can do, except maybe pray.' His face strained and grey, he began writing a new message for Flight Two.

The hot hors d'oeuvres, which Captain Vernon Demerest had called for, had been served to the pilots of Flight Two. The appetizing assortment on a tray, brought by one of the stewardesses from the first class galley, was disappearing fast. Demerest grunted appreciatively as he bit into a lobster-and-mushroom tartlet garnished with Parmesan cheese.

As usual the stewardesses were pursuing their campaign to fatten the skinny young second officer, Cy Jordan. Surreptitiously they had slipped him a few extra hors d'oeuvres on a separate plate behind the two captains and now, while Jordan fiddled with fuel crossfeed valves, his cheeks bulged with chicken livers in bacon.

Soon, all three pilots, relaxing in turn in the dimly lighted cockpit would be brought the same delectable entrée and dessert which the airline served its first class passengers. The only things the passengers would get, which the crew did not, were table wine and champagne.

Trans America, like most airlines, worked hard at providing an excellent cuisine aloft. There were some who argued that airlines – even international airlines – should concern themselves solely with transportation, gear their inflight service to commuter standards, and dispense with frills, including meals of any higher quality than a box lunch. Others, however, believed that too much of modern travel had become established at box lunch level, and welcomed the touch of style and elegance which good airborne meals provided. Airlines received remarkably few complaints about food service. Most passengers – tourist and first class – welcomed the meals as a diversion and consumed them zestfully.

Vernon Demerest, searching out with his tongue the last succulent particles of lobster, was thinking much the same thing. At that moment the Selcal call chime sounded loudly in the cockpit and the radio panel warning light flashed on.

Anson Harris's eyebrows went up. A single call on Selcal was out of the ordinary; two within less than an hour were exceptional.

'What we need,' Cy Jordan said from behind, 'is an unlisted number.'

Demerest reached out to switch radios. 'I'll get it.'

After the mutual identification between Flight Two and New York dispatch, Vernon Demerest began writing on a message pad under a hooded light. The message was from DTM Lincoln International and began: UNCONFIRMED POSSIBILITY EXISTS . . . As the wording progressed, Demerest's features, in the light's reflection, tautened. At the end he acknowledged briefly and signed off without commment.

Demerest handed the message pad to Anson Harris, who read it, leaning towards a light beside him. Harris whistled softly. He passed the pad over his shoulder to Cy Jordan.

The Selcal message ended: SUGGEST RETURN OR ALTERNATE LANDING AT CAPTAIN'S DISCRETION.

As both captains knew, there was a question of command to be decided. Although Anson Harris had been flying tonight as captain, with Demerest performing first officer duty, Vernon Demerest – as check pilot – had overriding authority if he chose to exercise it.

Now, in response to Harris's questioning glance, Demerest said brusquely, 'You're in the left seat. What are we waiting for?'

Harris considered only briefly, then announced, 'We'll turn back, but making a wide, slow turn; that way, passengers shouldn't notice. Then we'll have Gwen Meighen locate this guy they're worried about, because it's a sure thing one of us can't show up in the cabin, or we'll alert him.' He shrugged. 'After that, I guess we play it by ear.'

'Okay,' Demerest assented. 'You get us faced around; I'll handle the cabin end.' He depressed the stewardess call button, using a three-ring code to summon Gwen.

On a radio frequency he had been using earlier, Anson Harris called air route control. He announced laconically, 'This is Trans America Two. We seem to have a problem here. Request clearance back to Lincoln, and radar vector from present position to Lincoln.'

Harris's swift reasoning had already ruled out landing at an alternate airport. Ottawa, Toronto, and Detroit, they had been informed at briefing, were closed to air traffic because of the storm. Besides, to deal with the man they were concerned about back in the cabin, the crew of Flight Two needed time. Returning to Lincoln International would provide it.

He had no doubt that Demerest had reached the same conclusion.

From Toronto Air Route Centre, more than six miles below, a controller's voice responded. 'Trans America Two, Roger.' A brief pause, then: 'You may begin a left turn now to heading two seven zero. Stand by for an altitude change.'

'Roger, Toronto. We are commencing the turn. We'd like to make it wide and gradual.'

'Trans America Two. A wide turn approved.'

The exchange was low key, as such exchanges usually were. Both in the air and on the ground there was mutual awareness that most would be gained by calm, least by dramatics or excitement. By the nature of Flight Two's request, the ground controller was instantly aware that an emergency – real or potential – existed. Jetliners, in flight at cruising altitude, did not abruptly reverse course without a major reason. But the controller also knew that if and when the captain was ready, he would officially declare an emergency and report its cause. Until then, the controller would not waste the time of the crew – undoubtedly occupied with urgent business of their own – by asking needless questions.

Whatever help was sought from air route control, however, would be given without query, and as speedily as possible.

Even now, on the ground, procedural wheels were turning. At Toronto Air Route Centre, located in a handsome modern building some fourteen miles beyond the city limits, the controller receiving Flight Two's transmission had summoned a supervisor. The supervisor was liaising with other sectors, clearing a path ahead of Flight Two, as well as altitudes immediately below – the last as a precaution. Cleveland Centre, which earlier had passed the flight to Toronto Centre and now would receive it back, had been alerted also. Chicago Centre, which would take over from Cleveland, was being notified.

On the flight deck of Flight Two, a new air route control message was coming in. 'Begin descent to flight level two eight zero. Report leaving flight level three three zero.'

Anson Harris acknowledged. 'Toronto Centre, this is Trans America Two. We are beginning descent now.'

On Harris's orders, Second Officer Jordan was reporting to Trans America dispatch, by company radio, the decision to return.

The door from the forward cabin opened. Gwen Meighen came in.

'Listen,' she said, 'if it's more hors d'oeuvres, I'm sorry, but you can't have them. In case you hadn't noticed, we happen to have a few passengers aboard.'

'I'll deal with insubordination later,' Demerest said. 'Right now' – he mimicked Gwen's English accent – 'we've got a spot o' bother.'

Superficially, little had changed on the flight deck since a few moments ago when the message from DTM Lincoln had come in. Yet, subtly, the relaxed mood, prevailing earlier had vanished. Despite their studied composure, the three-man crew was all-professional and sharp, their minds at peak acuity, each sensing the adjustment in the other two. It was to achieve such moments, responsively and quickly, that years of training and experience marked the long road to airline captaincy. Flying itself – controlling an aeroplane – was not a difficult achievement; what commercial pilots were paid high salaries for was their reserve of resourcefulness, airmanship, and general aviation wisdom. Demerest, Harris, and – to a lesser extent – Cy Jordan, were summoning their reserves now. The situation aboard Flight Two was not yet critical; with luck, it might not be critical at all. But if a crisis arose, mentally the crew was ready.

'I want you to locate a passenger,' Demerest told Gwen. 'He isn't to know that you're looking for him. We have a description here. You'd better read the whole thing.' He handed her the pad with the Selcal message. She moved nearer, holding it under the hooded light beside him.

As the aircraft rolled slightly, Gwen's hand brushed Vernon Demerest's shoulder. He was conscious of her closeness and a faint familiar perfume. Glancing sideways, he could see Gwen's profile in the semi-darkness. Her expression as she read was serious, but not dismayed; it reminded him of what he had admired so much earlier this evening – her strength in no way lessening her femininity. In a swift, fleeting second he remembered that twice tonight Gwen had declared she loved him. He had wondered then: had he ever truly been in love himself? When you kept tight rein on personal emotions, you were never absolutely sure. But at this moment, instinct told him, his feeling about Gwen was the closest to loving he would ever know.

Gwen was reading the message again, more slowly.

Momentarily he felt a savage anger at this new circumstance which was contriving to delay their plans – his own and Gwen's – for Naples. Then he checked himself. This was a moment for professionalism only. Besides, what was happening now would merely mean delay, perhaps for a full twenty-four hours after their return to Lincoln; but eventually the flight would go. It did not occur to him that the bomb threat might not be disposed of quickly, or that it would fail to end as tamely as most others.

Alongside Demerest, Anson Harris was still holding the aircraft in its gentle turn, using only the slightest amount of bank. It was a perfect turn, exactly executed, as demonstrated by each pilot's needle and ball indicator – the granddaddy of aviation flight instruments, still used on modern jets, as it was used in Lindbergh's *Spirit of St Louis*, and aeroplanes long before. The needle was tilted, the ball dead centre. But only compass and gyro betrayed the extent of the turn – that Flight Two was coming around a hundred and eighty degrees in course. Harris had declared that passengers would be unaware of the course reversal, and he would be right – unless someone, peering through a cabin window, happened to be familiar with positions of stars and moon in relation to westerly and easterly courses. Then they would observe the change, but that was a chance which had to be taken; fortunately, the ground being obscured by cloud meant that no one could see and identify cities. Now Harris was beginning to lose height also, the aircraft's nose lowered slightly, with throttles pulled back the barest amount, so that the note of engines would change no more than was usual during any flight. Harris was concentrating, flying with textbook precision, ignoring Gwen and Demerest.

Gwen handed the message pad back.

'What I want you to do,' Demerest instructed her, 'is go back and locate this man. See if there's any sign of the bag, and whether there's a good chance of getting it away from him. You realize that one of us from here can't go back – at least for now – in case we scare him.'

'Yes,' Gwen said. 'I understand that. But I don't need to go either.'

'Why?'

She said quietly, 'I know where he is already. In seat fourteen-A.'

Vernon Demerest regarded her searchingly. 'I don't have to tell you that this is important. If you've any doubt, go back and make sure.'

'I haven't any doubt.'

Half an hour or so ago, Gwen explained, after serving dinners in first class, she had gone aft into the tourist section to help out there. One of the passengers – in a window seat on the left – had been dozing. When Gwen spoke to him he awakened instantly. He was nursing a small attaché case on his knees and Gwen suggested that she take it, or that he put it down, while having dinner. The passenger refused. He continued to hold the case where it was, and she noticed that he clasped it as if it was important. Later, instead of letting down the folding table from the back of the seat ahead, he used the case, still held on his lap, to support his dinner tray. Accustomed to passengers' peculiarities, Gwen thought no more of it, though she remembered the man well. The description in the message fitted him exactly.

'Another reason I remember him is that he's sitting right alongside the old lady stowaway.'

'He's in a window seat, you say?'

'Yes,'

'That makes it harder – to reach across and grab.' Demerest was remembering the portion of the DTM's message: IF SUPPOSITION TRUE, LIKELY THAT TRIGGER FOR EXPLOSIVES WILL BE ON OUTSIDE OF CASE AND EASILY REACHABLE. THEREFORE USE EXTREME CAUTION IN ATTEMPTING TO SEIZE CASE FORCIBLY. He guessed that Gwen, too, was thinking of that warning.

For the first time a feeling, not of fear but doubt, intruded on his reasoning. Fear might come later, but not yet. *Was* there a possibility that this bomb scare might prove to be more than a scare? Vernon Demerest had thought and talked of this kind of situation often enough, yet could never really believe it would happen to himself.

Anson Harris was easing out of the turn as gently as he had gone into it. They were now headed around completely.

The Selcal chime sounded again. Demerest motioned to Cy Jordan, who switched radios and answered, then began copying down a message.

Anson Harris was talking once more with Toronto Air Route Centre.

'I wonder,' Vernon Demerest said to Gwen, 'if there's any chance of getting those other two passengers alongside Guerrero out of their seats. That way he'd be left there, in the three-seat section, on his own. Then maybe one of us could come from behind, lean over and grab.'

'He'd suspect,' Gwen said emphatically. 'I'm sure he would. He's edgy now. The moment we got those other people out, whatever excuse we used, he'd know something was wrong, and he'd be watching and waiting.'

The second officer passed over the Selcal message he had been copying. It was from DTM Lincoln. Using the hooded light, Gwen and Demerest read it together.

NEW INFORMATION INDICATES EARLIER POSSIBILITY OF EXPLOSIVE DEVICE IN POSSESSION OF PASSENGER GUERRERO IS NOW STRONG PROBABILITY REPEAT STRONG PROBABILITY. PASSENGER BELIEVED MENTALLY DISTURBED, DESPERATE. REPEAT PREVIOUS WARNING TO APPROACH WITH EXTREME CAUTION. GOOD LUCK.

'I like that last bit,' Cy Jordan said. 'That's real nice, wishing us that.'

Demerest said brusquely, 'Shut up!'

For several seconds – apart from routine flight deck sounds – there was silence.

'If there were some way,' Demerest said slowly, '. . . some way we could trick him into letting go of that case. All we'd need would be a few seconds to have our hands on it, then get it clear away . . . if we were quick, two seconds would be enough.'

Gwen pointed out, 'He wouldn't even put it down . . .'

'I know! I know! I'm thinking, that's all.' He stopped. 'Let's go over it again. There are two passengers between Guerrero and the aisle. One of them . . .'

'One of them is a man; he has the aisle seat. In the middle is the old lady, Mrs Quonsett. Then Guerrero.'

'So grandma's right beside Guerrero; right alongside the case.'

'Yes, but how does it help? Even if we could let her know, she couldn't possibly . . .'

Demerest said sharply, 'You haven't said anything to her yet? She doesn't know we're on to her?'

'No. You told me not to.'

'Just wanted to be sure.'

Again they were silent. Vernon Demerest concentrated, thinking, weighing possibilities. At length he said carefully, 'I have an idea. It may not work, but at the moment it's the best we have. Now listen, while I tell you exactly what to do.'

In the tourist section of Flight Two most passengers had finished dinner, and stewardesses were briskly removing trays. The meal service had gone faster than usual tonight. One reason was that due to the delayed takeoff, some passengers had eaten in the terminal and now, because of the lateness of the hour, they had either declined dinner or merely nibbled at it.

At the three-seat unit where Mrs Ada Quonsett was still chatting with her new friend, the oboe player, one of the tourist cabin stewardesses – a pert young blonde – asked, 'Have you finished with your trays?'

'Yes, I have, miss,' the oboist said.

Mrs Quonsett smiled warmly. 'Thank you, my dear; you may take mine. It was very nice.'

The dour man on Mrs Quonsett's left surrendered his tray without comment.

It was only then that the little old lady from San Diego became aware of the other stewardess standing in the aisle.

She was one whom Mrs Quonsett had observed several times previously, and appeared to be in charge of the other girls. She had deep black hair, an attractive, high-cheek-boned face, and strong dark eyes which at the moment were focussed, directly and coolly, on Ada Quonsett.

'Pardon me, madam. May I see your ticket?'

'My ticket? Why, of course.' Mrs Quonsett affected surprise, though she guessed immediately what lay behind the request. Obviously her stowaway status was either suspected or known. But she had never given up easily, and even now her wits were working. A question was: how much did this girl know?

Mrs Quonsett opened her purse and pretended to search among its papers. 'I know I had it, my dear. It must be here somewhere.' She glanced up, her expression innocent. 'That is, unless the ticket man took it when I came aboard. Perhaps he kept it and I didn't notice.'

'No,' Gwen Meighen said, 'he wouldn't have. If it was a round-trip ticket, you'd be holding a return flight coupon. And if it was one-way, you'd still have the ticket stub and boarding folder.'

'Well, it certainly seems strange . . .' Mrs Quonsett continued fumbling in her purse.

Gwen inquired coldly, 'Shall I look?' From the beginning of their exchange, she had shown none of her customary friendliness. She added, 'If there's a ticket in your purse, I'll find it. If there isn't, it will save us both wasting time.'

'Certainly not,' Mrs Quonsett said severely. Then, relenting: 'I realize you mean no harm, my dear, but I have private papers here. You, being English, should respect privacy. You *are* English, aren't you?'

'Whether I am or not doesn't matter. At this moment we're talking about your ticket. That is, *if* you have one.' Gwen's voice, pitched louder than usual, was audible several seats away. Heads of other passengers were turning.

'Oh, I have a ticket. It's just a question of where it is.' Mrs Quonsett smiled engagingly. 'About your being English, though. I could tell you were from the very first moment you spoke. So many English people – people like you, my dear – make our language sound delightful. It's such a pity so few of us Americans can do the same. My late husband always used to say . . .'

'Never mind what he said. What about your ticket?'

It was hard for Gwen to be as rude and unpleasant as she was being. In the ordinary way she would have dealt with this old woman firmly, yet remained friendly and goodnatured; Gwen also had a reluctance to bully someone more than twice her own age. But before she left the flight deck, Vernon had been explicit in his instructions.

Mrs Quonsett looked a little shocked. 'I'm being patient with you, young lady. But when I do discover my ticket I shall certainly have something to say about your attitude . . .'

'Will you really, Mrs Quonsett?' Gwen saw the old woman start at the use of her name, and for the first time there was a weakening behind the prim façade. Gwen persisted, 'You *are* Ada Quonsett, aren't you?'

The little old lady patted her lips with a lace handkerchief, then sighed. 'Since you know I am, there's no point in denying it, is there?'

'No, because we know all about you. You've got quite a record, Mrs Quonsett.'

More passengers were watching and listening now; one or two had left their seats to move closer. Their expressions were sympathetic for the old lady, critical of Gwen. The man in the aisle seat, who had been talking with Mrs Quonsett when Gwen arrived, shifted uncomfortably. 'If there's some misunderstanding, perhaps I can help . . .'

'There's no misunderstanding,' Gwen said. 'Are you travelling with this lady?'

'No.'

'Then there's nothing you need concern yourself about, sir.'

So far, Gwen had not let herself look directly at the man seated farthest away, by the window, whom she knew to be Guerrero. Nor had he looked at her, though she could tell by the inclination of his head that he was listening intently to everything that was being said. Also without being obvious, she observed that he was still clasping the small attaché case on his knees. At the thought of what the case might contain she experienced a sudden, icy fear. She felt herself tremble, with a premonition of something terrible to come. She wanted to run, return to the flight deck and tell Vernon to handle this himself. But she didn't, and the moment of weakness passed.

'I said we know all about you, and we do,' Gwen assured Mrs Quonsett. 'You were caught earlier today as a stowaway on one of our flights from Los Angeles. You were placed in custody, but you managed to slip away. Then, by lying, you got aboard this flight.'

The little old lady from San Diego said brightly, 'If you know so much, or think you do, it won't do any good arguing about it.' Well, she decided, it was no good worrying now. After all, she had expected to get caught; at least she hadn't been until after she'd had an adventure and a good dinner. Besides, what did it matter? As the redheaded woman back at Lincoln admitted airlines never prosecuted stowaways.

231

She was curious, though, about what came next. 'Are we going to turn back?'

'You're not that important. When we land in Italy, you'll be handed over to the authorities.' Vernon Demerest had warned Gwen to let it be thought that Flight Two was proceeding on to Rome, certainly not to admit that they were already turned around and heading back. He also impressed on her that she must be rough with the old lady, which Gwen had not enjoyed. But it was necessary to make an impression on the passenger Guerrero, to carry out Demerest's next step.

Though Guerrero didn't know it – and if all went well, he would not know until too late to make any difference – this entire performance was solely for his benefit.

'You're to come with me,' Gwen instructed Mrs Quonsett. 'The captain has had a signal about you, and he has to make a report. Before he does, he wants to see you.' She asked the man in the aisle seat, 'Will you let this woman out, please?'

For the first time the old lady looked nervous. 'The captain wants me?'

'Yes, and he doesn't like to be kept waiting.'

Hesitantly, Mrs Quonsett released her seat belt. As the oboe player moved out, unhappily, to let her pass, she stepped uncertainly into the aisle. Taking her arm, Gwen propelled her forward, conscious of hostile glances all around – directed at herself – as they went.

Gwen resisted an impulse to turn, to see if the man with the case was watching too.

'I'm Captain Demerest,' Vernon Demerest said. 'Please come in – as far forward as you can. Gwen, shut the door and let's see if we can squeeze everybody in.' He smiled at Mrs Quonsett. 'I'm afraid they don't design flight decks for entertaining visitors.'

The old lady from San Diego peered towards him. After the bright lights of the passenger cabin from which she had just come, her eyes were not yet adjusted to the cockpit's semi-darkness. All she could make out were shadowy figures, seated, surrounded by dozens of redly glowing dials. But there had been no mistaking the friendliness of the voice. Its effect and tone were far different from what she had braced herself to expect.

Cy Jordan pushed an armrest upward on an empty crew seat behind Anson Harris. Gwen – gently, in contrast to her behaviour of a few minutes ago – guided the old lady into the seat.

There was still no turbulence outside, which made it easy to move around. Though losing height, they were still far above the storm, and despite the aeroplane's speed of more than five hundred miles an hour, it was riding easily as if in a calm, untroubled sea.

'Mrs Quonsett,' Vernon Demerest said, 'whatever happened outside just now, you can forget it. It's not the reason you were brought here.' He asked Gwen, 'Were you pretty rough with her?'

'I'm afraid so.'

'Miss Meighen was acting on my orders. I told her to do exactly what she did. We knew one particular person would be watching and listening. We wanted it to look good, to have a plausible reason for bringing you here.'

The big shadowy figure speaking from the right-hand seat was becoming clearer to Ada Quonsett now. From what she could see of his face, he seemed a kind man, she thought. At the moment, of course, she had no idea what he was talking about. She looked about her. It was all very interesting. She had never been on a flight deck before. It was much more crowded and a smaller space than she expected. It was also warm, and the three men

232

whom she could now see were all in shirtsleeves. This would certainly be something else to tell her daughter in New York – if she ever got there.

'Grandma,' the man who had introduced himself as the captain said, 'do you get frightened easily?'

It seemed an odd question, and she thought about it before answering. 'Not easily, I think. I get nervous sometimes, though not as much as I used to. When you get older there isn't a lot left to be frightened of.'

The captain's eyes were fixed searchingly on her face. 'I've decided to tell you something, then ask for your help. We don't have too much time, so I'll make it fast. I suppose you've noticed the man sitting next to you, back in the cabin – on the window side.'

'The skinny one, with the little moustache?'

'Yes,' Gwen said. 'That's him.'

Mrs Quonsett nodded. 'He's a strange one. He won't talk to anybody, and he has a little case with him that he won't let go of. I think he's worried about something.'

'We're worried, too,' Vernon Demerest said quietly. 'We've reason to believe that in that case he has a bomb. We want to get it away from him. That's why I need your help.'

One of the surprising things about being up here with the pilots, Ada Quonsett thought, was how quiet it was. In the silence which followed what had just been said, she could hear a message coming in on an overhead speaker near where she was seated. 'Trans America Two, this is Toronto Centre. Your position is fifteen miles east of Kleinburg beacon. Advise your flight level and intentions.'

The man in the other front seat, on the left, whose face she hadn't yet seen, was answering. 'Toronto Centre from Trans America Two. Leaving flight level two niner zero. Request continued slow descent until we advise. No change in our intentions to return for landing at Lincoln.'

'Roger, Trans America. We are clearing traffic ahead of you. You may continue slow descent.'

A third man, at a little table to her right, facing still more dials, leaned across to the one who had been speaking. 'I make it an hour and seventeen minutes in. That's using forecast winds, but if the front's moved faster than expected, it could be less.'

'We *are* going back, aren't we?' Mrs Quonsett found it hard to restrain the excitement in her voice.

Demerest nodded. 'But you're the only one who knows, besides ourselves. For the time being you must keep it secret, and above all, Guerrero – that's the man with the case – mustn't find out.'

Ada Quonsett thought breathlessly: was this really happening to her? It was all quite thrilling, like something on TV. It *was* a little frightening perhaps, but she decided not to think too much about that. The main thing was – she was here, a part of it all, hobnobbing with the captain, sharing secrets, and what would her daughter say about *that*?

'Well, will you help us?'

'Oh, of course. I expect you want me to see if I can get that case away . . .'

'No!' Vernon Demerest swung farther around, leaning over the back of his seat for emphasis. He said sternly, 'You must not so much as put your hands on that case, or even near it.'

'If you say so,' Mrs Quonsett acknowledged meekly, 'I won't.'

'I do say so. And remember, it's important that Guerrero has no idea we know about his case or what's inside. Now, as I did with Miss Meighen a little while ago, I'm going to tell you exactly what to do when you go back to the cabin. Please listen carefully.'

When he had finished, the little old lady from San Diego permitted herself a small, brief smile. 'Oh, yes; yes, I think I can do that.'

She was getting out of her seat, with Gwen about to open the flight deck door for them to go, when Demerest asked, 'That flight from Los Angeles you stowed away on – they said you were trying to reach New York. Why?'

She told him about being lonely sometimes on the West Coast, and wanting to visit her married daughter in the east.

'Grandma,' Vernon Demerest said, 'if we pull this off I'll personally guarantee that not only will any trouble you're in be taken care of, but this airline will give you a ticket to New York and back, first class.'

Mrs Quonsett was so touched, she almost cried.

'Oh, thank you! Thank you!' For once she found it hard to speak. What a remarkable man, she thought; such a kind, dear man!

Her genuine emotion as she was about to leave the flight deck helped Mrs Quonsett in her progress through the first class compartment and then into the tourist cabin. With Gwen Meighen grasping her arm tightly and shoving her along, the old lady dabbed at her eyes with her lace handkerchief, giving a tearful, credible performance of acute distress. She reminded herself, almost gleefully beneath her tears, that it was her second performance tonight. The first, when she pretended to be ill, had been staged in the terminal for the young passenger agent, Peter Coakley. She had been convincing then, so why not now?

The performance was sufficiently authentic for one passenger to ask Gwen heatedly, 'Miss, whatever she's done, do you have to be so rough?'

Gwen replied tartly, already aware that she was within hearing of the man Guerrero, 'Sir, please don't interfere.'

As they passed into the tourist cabin, Gwen closed the draw curtain in the doorway separating the two passenger sections. That was part of Vernon's plan. Looking back the way they had come, towards the front of the aircraft, Gwen could see the flight deck door slightly ajar. Behind it, she knew, Vernon was watching, waiting. As soon as the curtain between first class and tourist was closed, Vernon would move aft and stand behind it, watching through a chink which Gwen was careful to leave open. Then, when the proper moment came, he would fling the curtain aside and rush through swiftly.

At the thought of what was going to happen within the next few minutes – whatever the outcome – once more an icy fear, a sense of premonition, came to Gwen. Once more she conquered it. Reminding herself of her responsibilities to the crew, and to the other passengers – who were oblivious to the drama being played out in their midst – she escorted Mrs Quonsett the remaining distance to her seat.

The passenger Guerrero glanced up quickly, then away. The small attaché case, Gwen saw, was still in the same position on his knees, his hands holding it. The man from the aisle seat next to Mrs Quonsett's – the oboe player – stood up as they approached. His expression sympathetic, he moved out to let the old lady in. Unobtrusively, Gwen moved in front of him, blocking his return. The aisle seat must remain unoccupied until Gwen moved out of the way. Gwen's eyes caught a flicker of movement through the chink she had left in the doorway curtain. Vernon Demerest was in position and ready.

'Please!' Still standing in the aisle, Mrs Quonsett turned pleading, tearfully to Gwen. 'I beg of you – ask the captain to reconsider. I don't want to be handed over to the Italian police . . .'

Gwen said harshly, 'You should have thought of that before. Besides, I don't tell the captain what to do.'

'But you can ask him! He'll listen to you.'

D. O. Guerrero turned his head, took in the scene, then looked away.

Gwen seized the old lady's arm. 'I'm telling you – get into that seat!'

Ada Quonsett's voice became a wail. 'All I'm asking is to be taken back. Hand me over there, not in a strange country!'

From behind Gwen the oboe player protested, 'Miss, can't you see the lady's upset?'

Gwen snapped, 'Please keep out of this. This woman has no business here at all. She's a stowaway.'

The oboist said indignantly, 'I don't care what she is. She's still an old lady.'

Ignoring him, Gwen gave Mrs Quonsett a shove which sent her staggering. 'You heard me! Sit down and be quiet.'

Ada Quonsett dropped into her seat. She screamed, 'You hurt me! You hurt me!'

Several passengers were on their feet, protesting.

D. O. Guerrero continued to look straight ahead. His hands, Gwen saw, were still on the attaché case.

Mrs Quonsett wailed again.

Gwen said coldly, 'You're hysterical.' Deliberately, hating what she had to do, she leaned into the section of seats and slapped Mrs Quonsett hard across the face. The slap resounded through the cabin. Passengers gasped. Two other stewardesses appeared incredulous. The oboist seized Gwen's arm; hastily she shook herself free.

What happened next occurred so swiftly that even those closest to the scene were uncertain of the sequence of events.

Mrs Quonsett, in her seat, turned to D. O. Guerrero on her left. She appealed to him, 'Sir, please help me! Help me!'

His features rigid, he ignored her.

Apparently overcome by grief and fear, she reached towards him, flinging her arms hysterically around his neck. 'Please, please!'

Guerrero twisted his body away, trying to release himself. He failed. Instead, Ada Quonsett wound her arms around his neck more tightly. 'Oh, help me!'

Red-faced and close to choking, D. O. Guerrero put up both hands to wrench her away. As if in supplication, Ada Quonsett eased her grasp and seized his hands.

At the same instant, Gwen Meighen leaned forward towards the inside seat. She reached out and in a single even movement – almost without haste – she grasped the attaché case firmly and removed it from Guerrero's knees. A moment later the case was free and in the aisle. Between Guerrero and the case, Gwen and Ada Quonsett were a solid barrier.

The curtain across the doorway from the first class cabin swept open. Vernon Demerest, tall and impressive in uniform, hurried through.

His face showing relief, he held out his hand for the attaché case. 'Nice going, Gwen. Let me have it.'

With ordinary luck, the incident – except for dealing with Guerrero later – would have ended there. That it did not was solely due to Marcus Rathbone.

Rathbone, until that moment, was an unknown, unconsidered passenger, occupying seat fourteen-D across the aisle. Although others were unaware of him, he was a self-important, pompous man, constantly aware of himself.

In the small Iowa town where he lived he was a minor merchant known to his neighbours as a 'knocker'. Whatever others in his community did or proposed, Marcus Rathbone objected to. His objections, small and large, were legendary. They included the choice of books in the local library, a plan for a community antennae system, the needed disciplining of his son at school, and the colour of paint for a civic buildiong. Shortly before departing on his present trip he had organized the defeat of a proposed sign ordinance which would have beautified his town's main street. Despite his habitual 'knocking', he had never been known to propose a constructive idea.

Another peculiarity was that Marcus Rathbone despised women, including his own wife. None of his objections had ever been on their behalf. Consequently, the humiliation of Mrs Quonsett a moment earlier had not disturbed him, but Gwen Meighen's seizure of D. O. Guerrero's attaché case did.

To Marcus Rathbone this was officialdom in uniform – and a woman at that! – impinging on the rights of an ordinary traveller like himself. Indignantly, Rathbone rose from his seat, interposing himself between Gwen and Vernon Demerest.

At the same instant, D. O. Guerrero, flushed and mouthing incoherent words, scrambled free from his seat and the grasp of Ada Quonsett. As he reached the aisle, Marcus Rathbone seized the case from Gwen and – with a polite bow – held it out. Like a wild animal, with madness in his eyes, Guerrero grabbed it.

Vernon Demerest flung himself forward, but too late. He tried to reach Guerrero, but the narrowness of the aisle and the intervening figures – Gwen, Rathbone, the oboe player – defeated him. D. O. Guerrero had ducked around the others and was heading for the aircraft's rear. Other passengers, in seats, were scrambling to their feet. Demerest shouted desperately, 'Stop that man! He has a bomb!'

The shout produced screams, and an exodus from seats which had the effect of blocking the aisle still further. Only Gwen Meighen, scrambling, pushing, clawing her way aft, managed to stay close to Guerrero.

At the end of the cabin – like an animal still, but this time cornered – Guerrero turned. All that remained between him and the aircraft's tail were three rear toilets; light indicators showed that two were empty, one was occupied. His back to the toilets, Guerrero held the attaché case forward in front of him, one hand on its carrying handle, the other on a loop of string now visible beneath the handle. In a strained voice, somewhere between a whisper and a snarl, he warned, 'Stay where you are! Don't come closer!'

Above the heads of the others, Vernon Demerest shouted again. 'Guerrero, listen to me! Do you hear me? Listen!'

There was a second's silence in which no one moved, the only sound the steady background whine of the plane's jet engines. Guerrero blinked, continuing to face the others, his eyes roving and suspicious.

'We know who you are,' Demerest called out, 'and we know what you intended. We know about the insurance and the bomb, and they know on the ground, too, so it means your insurance is no good. Do you understand? – your insurance is invalid, cancelled, worthless. If you let off that bomb you'll kill yourself for nothing. No one – least of all your family – will gain. In fact, your family will lose because they'll be blamed and hounded. Listen to me! Think.'

A woman screamed. Still Guerrero hesitated.

Vernon Demerest urged, 'Guerrero, let these people sit down. Then, if you like, we'll talk. You can ask me questions. I promise that until you're ready, no one will come close.' Demerest was calculating: If Guerrero's attention could be held long enough, the aisle might be cleared. After that, Demerest would try to persuade Guerrero to hand over the case. If he refused, there was still a chance that Demerest could leap forward, throw himself bodily on to Guerrero and wrest the case free before the trigger could be used. It would be a tremendous risk, but there was nothing better.

People were easing nervously back into their seats.

'Now that I've told you what we know, Guerrero; now *you* know that it isn't any good going on, I'm asking you to give me that case.' Demerest tried to keep his tone reasonable, sensing it was important to keep talking. 'If you do as I say, I give you my solemn word that no one in this aeroplane will harm you.'

D. O. Guerrero's eyes mirrored fear. He moistened thin lips with his tongue. Gwen Meighen was closest to him.

Demerest said quietly, 'Gwen, take it easy. Try to get in a seat.' If he had to leap, he wanted no one in the way.

Behind Guerrero the door of the occupied toilet opened. An owlish young man with thick glasses came out. He stopped, peering shortsightedly. Obviously he had heard nothing of what was going on.

Another passenger yelled, 'Grab the guy with the case! He's got a bomb!'

At the first 'click' of the toilet door, Guerrero half turned. Now he lunged, thrusting the man with glasses aside, and entered the toilet which the newcomer had vacated.

As Guerrero had moved, Gwen Meighen moved too, remaining close behind him. Vernon Demerest, several yards away, was struggling fiercely aft, down the still crowded aisle.

The toilet door was closing as Gwen reached it. She thrust a foot inside and shoved. Her foot stopped the door from closing, but the door refused to move. Despairing, as pain shot through her foot, she could feel Guerrero's weight against the other side.

In D. O. Guerrero's mind the last few minutes had been a jumbled blur. He had not fully comprehended everything that had occurred, nor had he heard all that Demerest said. But one thing penetrated. He realized that like so many of his other grand designs, this one, too, had failed. Somewhere – as always happened with whatever he attempted – he had bungled. All his life had been a failure. With bitterness, he knew his death would be a failure, too.

His back was braced against the inside of the toilet door. He felt pressure on it, and knew that at any moment the pressure would increase so that he could no longer hold the door closed. Desperately he fumbled with the attaché case, reaching for the string beneath the handle which would release the square of plastic, actuating the clothespin switch and detonating the dynamite inside. Even as he found the string and tugged, he wondered if the bomb he had made would be a failure also.

In his last split second of life and comprehension, D. O. Guerrero learned that it was not.

10

The explosion aboard Trans America Flight Two, *The Golden Argosy*, was instantaneous, monstrous, and overwhelming. In the airplane's confined space it struck with the din of a hundred thunderclaps, a sheet of flame, and a blow like a giant sledge hammer.

D. O. Guerrero died instantly, his body, near the core of the explosion, disintegrating utterly. One moment he existed; the next, there were only a few small, bloody pieces of him left.

The aircraft fuselage blew open.

Gwen Meighen, who, next to Guerrero, was nearest the explosion, received its force in her face and chest.

An instant after the dynamite charge ripped the aircraft skin, the cabin decompressed. With a second roar and tornado force, air inside the aircraft – until this moment maintained at normal pressure – swept through the ruptured fuselage to dissipate in the high altitude near-vacuum outside. Through the passenger cabins a dark engulfing cloud of dust surged towards the rear. With it, like litter in a maelstrom, went every loose object, light and heavy – papers, food trays, liquor bottles, coffee pots, hand luggage, clothing, passengers' belongings – all whirling through the air as if impelled towards a cyclopean vacuum cleaner. Curtains tore away. Internal doors – flight deck, storage, and toilets – wrenched free from locks and hinges and were swept rearwards with the rest.

Several passengers were struck. Others, not strapped in their seats, clung to any handhold as the wind and suction drew them inexorably towards the rear.

Throughout the aircraft, emergency compartments above each seat snapped open. Yellow oxygen masks came tumbling down, each mask connected by a short plastic tube to a central oxygen supply.

Abruptly the suction lessened. The aircraft's interior was filled with mist and a savage, biting cold. Noise from engines and wind was overwhelming.

Vernon Demerest, still in the aisle of the tourist cabin where he had held himself by instinctively seizing a seatback, roared, 'Get on oxygen!' He grabbed a mask himself.

Through knowledge and training, Demerest realized what most others did not: The air inside the cabin was now as rarefied as that outside, and insufficient to support life. Only fifteen seconds of full consciousness remained to everyone, unless oxygen was used at once from the aircraft's emergency system.

Even in five seconds, without the aid of oxygen, a degree of lessened judgement would occur.

In another five seconds a state of euphoria would make many decide not to bother with oxygen at all. They would lapse into unconsciousness, not caring.

Airlines had long been urged, by those who understood the hazards of decompression, to make pre-flight announcements about oxygen equipment more definite than they were. Passengers should be told, it was argued: *The instant an oxygen mask appears in front of you, grab it, stick your face into it, and ask questions after. If there is a real decompression, you haven't a single second to spare. If it's a false alarm, you can always take the mask off later; meanwhile it will do no harm.*

Pilots who took decompression tests were given a simple demonstration of the effect of oxygen lack at high altitudes. In a decompression tank, with an oxygen mask on, they were told to begin writing their signatures, and part way through the exercise their masks were removed. The signatures tailed off into a scrawl, or nothingness. Before unconsciousness occurred, the masks were put back on.

The pilots found it hard to believe what they saw on the page before them.

Yet airline managements, theorizing that more definite oxygen advice might create alarm among passengers, persisted in the use of innocuous flight announcements only. Smiling stewardesses, seeming either bored or amused, casually demonstrated the equipment while an unseen voice – hurrying to get finished before takeoff – parroted phrases like: *In the unlikely event* . . . and . . . *Government regulations require that we inform you*. No mention was ever made of urgency, should the equipment be required for use.

As a result, passengers became as indifferent to emergency oxygen facilities as airlines and their staffs appeared to be. The overhead boxes and monotonous, always-alike demonstrations were (passengers reasoned) something dreamed up by a bunch of regulation-obsessed civil servants. (Yawn!) Obviously the whole thing was largely a charade, insisted on by the same kind of people who collected income taxes and disallowed expense accounts. *So what the hell!*

Occasionally, on regular flights, oxygen mask housings opened accidentally, and masks dropped down in front of passengers. When this happened, most passengers stared curiously at the masks but made no attempt to put them on. Precisely that reaction – though the emergency was real – had occurred aboard Flight Two.

Vernon Demerest saw the reaction and in a flash of sudden anger remembered his own, and other pilots', criticisms of soft-pedalled oxygen announcements. But there was no time to shout another warning, nor even to think of Gwen, who might be dead or dying only a few feet away.

Only one thing mattered: somehow to get back to the flight deck, and help save the aeroplane if he could.

Breathing oxygen deeply, he planned his movement forward in the aircraft.

Above every seat section in the tourist cabin, four oxygen masks had dropped – one for the occupant of each seat, plus a spare to be grabbed if necessary by anyone standing in the aisle. It was one of the spares which Demerest had seized and was using.

But to reach the flight deck he must abandon this mask and use a portable one that would permit him to move forward freely.

He knew that two portable oxygen cylinders were stowed, farther forward, in an overhead rack near the first class cabin bulkhead. If he could make it to the portable cylinders, either one would sustain him for the remaining distance from the bulkhead to the flight deck.

He moved forward to the bulkhead one seat section at a time, using one spare hanging mask after another as he went. A couple of seat sections ahead, he could see that all four masks were being used by seated passengers; the three seat occupants, including a teenage girl, had one mask each; the fourth mask was being held by the teenager over the face of an infant on its mother's lap alongside. The girl seemed to have taken charge and was motioning to others near her what to do. Demerest swung towards the opposite side of the cabin, saw a spare mask hanging, and, taking a deep breath of oxygen, he let go the one he had and reached for the other spare. He made it, and breathed deeply once again. He still had more than half the tourist cabin length to go.

He had made one more move when he felt the aircraft roll sharply to the right, then dive steeply down.

Demerest hung on. He knew that, for the moment, there was nothing he could do. What happened next was dependent on two things: how much damage the explosion had done, and the skill of Anson Harris, at the flight controls, alone.

On the flight deck, the events of the last few seconds had occurred with even less warning than at the rear. After the departure of Gwen Meighen and Mrs Quonsett, followed by Vernon Demerest, the two remaining crew members – Anson Harris and Second Officer Cy Jordan – had no knowledge of what was going on in the passenger cabins behind them until the dynamite blast rocked the aircraft, followed an instant later by explosive decompression.

As in the passenger compartments the cockpit filled with a thick, dark cloud of dust, almost immediately sucked out as the flight deck door smashed free from its lock and hinges, and flew outwards. Everything loose on the flight deck was snatched up, to be carried back, joining the debris-laden whirlwind.

Under the flight engineer's table, a warning horn began blaring intermittently. Over both front seats, bright yellow lights flashed on. Both horn and lights were signals of dangerously low pressure.

A fine mist – deathly cold – replaced the cloud of dust. Anson Harris felt his eardrums tighten painfully.

But even before that, he had reacted instantly – the effect of training and experience of many years.

On the long, uphill road to airline captaincy, pilots spent arduous hours in classrooms and simulators, studying and practising airborne situations, both normal and emergency. The objective was to instil quick, correct reactions at all times.

The simulators were located at important air bases and all major scheduled airlines had them.

From outside, a simulator looked like the nose of an aircraft, with the rest of the fuselage chopped off; inside, was everything included in a normal flight deck.

Once inside a simulator, pilots remained shut up for hours, imitating the precise conditions of a long distance flight. The effect, when the outside door was closed, was uncanny; even motion and noise were present, creating the physical effect of being airborne. All other conditions paralleled reality. A screen beyond the forward windows could conjure up airports and runways, enlarging or receding to simulate takeoff and landing. The only difference between a simulator flight deck and a genuine one was that the simulator never left the ground.

Pilots in a simulator conversed with a nearby control room, as they would on radio in the air. Within the control room, skilled operators duplicated air traffic control procedures and other flight conditions. The operators could also feed in adverse situations, without warning, to pilots. These ranged through multiple engine failure, to fire, violent weather, electrical and fuel problems, explosive decompression, instrument malfunction, and other assorted unpleasantness. Even a crash could be reproduced; sometimes simulators were used in reverse to find out what had caused one.

Occasionally an operator would feed in several emergencies at once, causing pilots to emerge later, exhausted and sweat-drenched. Most pilots coped with such tests; the few who didn't had the fact noted in their records, were re-examined, and afterwards watched carefully. The simulator sessions continued, several times a year, through every stage of a pilot's career until retirement.

The result was: When a real emergency occurred, airline pilots knew exactly what to do, and did it, without fumbling or loss of precious time. It was one of many factors which made travel by scheduled airlines the safest means of transportation in human history. It had also conditioned Anson Harris to instant action, directed towards the salvation of Flight Two.

In the drill for explosive decompression one rule was fundamental: the crew took care of themselves first. Vernon Demerest observed the rule; so did Anson Harris and Cy Jordan.

They must be on oxygen at once – even ahead of passengers. Then, with full mental faculties assured, decisions could be made.

Behind each pilot's seat a quick-don oxygen mask – resembling a baseball catcher's mask – was hanging. As he had practised countless times, Harris ripped off his radio headset, then reached over his shoulder for the mask. He tugged, so that a holding clip snapped open, and slapped the mask on. As well as a connection to the aeroplane's oxygen supply, it contained a microphone. For listening, now his headset was removed, Harris changed a selector, actuating a speaker overhead.

Behind him, Cy Jordan, with identical swift movements, did the same.

In another reflex movement, Anson Harris took care of passengers. Cabin oxygen systems worked automatically in event of pressure failure; but as a precaution – in case they didn't – over the pilots' heads was an override switch. It ensured positive release of passenger masks and set oxygen flowing into them. Harris flipped the switch.

He dropped his right hand to the throttles, pulling all four off. The aircraft slowed.

It must be slowed still more.

Left of the throttles was a speed brake handle. Harris pulled it full towards him. Along the top surface of both wings, spoilers rose up inducing drag, and causing further slowing.

Cy Jordan silenced the warning horn.

So far, all procedures had been automatic. Now, a moment for decision had arrived.

It was essential that the aircraft seek a safer altitude below. From its present height of twenty-eight thousand feet, it must descend some three and a half miles to where the air was denser so that passengers and crew could breathe and survive without supplemental oxygen.

The decision Harris had to make was – should the descent be slow, or a high-speed dive?

Until the past year or two, the instruction to pilots in event of explosive decompression was: dive immediately. Tragically, however, the instruction had resulted in at least one aircraft breaking apart when a slower descent might have saved it. Nowadays, pilots were cautioned: *Check for structural damage first. If the damage is bad, a dive may worsen it, so go down slowly.*

Yet that policy too, had hazards. To Anson Harris, they were instantly apparent.

Undoubtedly Flight Two had sustained structural damage. The sudden decompression proved it, and the explosion which had occurred just before – though still less than a minute ago – might already have done great harm. In other circumstances Harris would have sent Cy Jordan to the rear to learn how bad the damage was, but since Demerest was gone, Jordan must stay.

But however serious the structural damage, there was another factor, perhaps more cogent. The air temperature outside the aircraft was minus fifty degrees centigrade. Judging by the near paralysing cold which Harris felt, the inside temperature must also be near that. In such intense cold, no one without protective clothing could survive for more than minutes.

So which was the lesser gamble – to freeze for sure, or take a chance and go down fast?

Making a decision which only later events could prove right or wrong, Harris called on interphone to Cy Jordan, 'Warn air traffic control! We're diving!'

At the same moment, Harris banked the aircraft steeply to the right and selected landing gear 'down'. Banking before the dive would have two effects: Passengers or stewardesses who were not strapped in seats, or who were standing, would be held where they were by centrifugal force; whereas a straight dive would throw them to the ceiling. The turn would also head Flight Two away from the airway they had been using, and – hopefully – other traffic below.

Putting the landing gear down would further reduce forward speed, and make the dive steeper.

On the overhead speaker, Harris could hear Cy Jordan's voice intoning a distress call. 'Mayday, mayday. This is Trans America Two. Explosive decompression. We are diving, diving.'

Harris pushed the control yoke hard forward. Over his shoulder he shouted, 'Ask for ten!'

Cy Jordan added, 'Request ten thousand feet.'

Anson Harris clicked a radar transponder switch to seventy-seven – a radar S-O-S. Now, on all monitoring screens on the ground, a double blossom signal would be seen, confirming both their distress and identity.

They were going down fast, the altimeter unwinding like a clock with a wild mainspring . . . Passing through twenty-six thousand feet . . . twenty-four . . . twenty-three . . . Climb and descent meter showed eight thousand feet descent a minute . . . Toronto Air Route Centre on the overhead speaker: 'All altitudes below you are clear. Report your intentions when ready. We are standing by.' . . . Harris had eased out of the turn, was diving straight ahead . . . No time to think about the cold; if they could get low enough fast enough, there might be survival – if the aircraft held together . . . Already Harris was aware of trouble with rudder control and elevators; rudder movement was stiff; stabilizer trim, not responding . . . Twenty-one thousand feet . . . twenty . . . nineteen . . . From the feel of the controls, the explosion had done damage to the tail; how bad, they would discover when he tried to pull out in a minute or less from now. It would be the moment of greatest strain. If anything critical gave way, they would continue plummeting in . . . Harris would have been glad of some help from the right seat, but it was too late for Cy Jordan to move there. Besides, the second officer was needed where he was – shutting air inlets, throwing in all the heat they had, watching for fuel system damage or fire warnings . . . Eighteen thousand feet . . . seventeen . . . When they reached fourteen thousand, Harris decided, he would start pulling out of the dive, hoping to level at ten . . . Passing through fifteen thousand . . . fourteen . . . Begin easing out *now*!

Controls were heavy, but responding . . . Harris pulled back on the control yoke. The dive was flattening, control surfaces holding, the aircraft coming out . . . Twelve thousand feet; descending more slowly now . . . eleven thousand . . . ten, five . . . *ten!*

They were level! So far, everything had held together. Here, the normal air was breathable and would sustain life, extra oxygen not necessary. The outside air temperature gauge showed minus five centigrade – five degrees below freezing; still cold, but not the killing cold of altitudes above.

From beginning to end, the dive had taken two and a half minutes.

The overhead speakers came alive. 'Trans America Two, this is Toronto Centre. How are you doing?'

Cy Jordan acknowledged. Anson Harris cut in. 'Level at ten thousand, returning to heading two seven zero. We have structural damage due to explosion, extent unknown. Request weather and runway information – Toronto, Detroit Metropolitan, and Lincoln.' In his mind, Harris had an instant picture of airports large enough to accommodate the Boeing 707, and with the special landing requirements he would need.

Vernon Demerest was clambering over the smashed flight deck door and other debris outside. Hurrying in, he slid into his seat on the right side.

'We missed you,' Harris said.

'Can we maintain control?'

Harris nodded. 'If the tail doesn't fall off, we may stay lucky.' He reported the impeded rudder and stabilizer trim. 'Somebody let off a firecracker back there?'

'Something like that. It's made a bloody great hole. I didn't stop to measure.'

Their casualness, both men knew, was on the surface only. Harris was still steadying the aircraft, seeking an even altitude and course. He said considerately, 'It was a good scheme, Vernon. It could have worked.'

'It could have, but it didn't.' Demerest swung around to the second officer. 'Get back in tourist. Check on damage, report by interphone. Then do all you can for the people. We'll need to know how many are hurt, and how badly.' For the first time he permitted himself an anguished thought. 'And find out about Gwen.'

The airport reports, which Anson Harris had asked for, were coming in from Toronto centre: Toronto airport still closed; deep snow and drifts on all runways. Detroit Metropolitan – all runways closed to regular traffic, but ploughs will vacate runway three left if essential for emergency approach and landing; runway has five to six inches level snow, with ice beneath. Detroit visibility, six hundred feet in snow flurries. Lincoln International – all runways ploughed and serviceable; runway three zero temporarily closed, due to obstruction, Lincoln visibility one mile; wind northwest, thirty knots, and gusting.

Anson Harris told Demerest, 'I don't intend to dump fuel.'

Demerest, understanding Harris's reasoning, nodded agreement. Assuming they could keep the aeroplane under control, any landing they made would be tricky and heavy, due to the large fuel load which in other circumstances would have carried them to Rome. Yet, in their present situation, to dump unwanted fuel could be an even greater hazard. The explosion and damage at the rear might have set up electrical short circuits, or metal friction, which even now could be producing sparks. When dumping fuel in flight, a single spark could turn an aircraft into a flaming holocaust. Both captains rationalized: better to avoid the fire risk and accept the penalty of a difficult landing.

Yet the same decision meant that a landing at Detroit – the nearest large airport – could be attempted only in desperation. Because of their heavy weight, they would have to land fast, requiring every available foot of runway and the last ounce of braking power. Runway three left – Detroit Metropolitan's longest, which they would need – had *ice beneath snow*, in the circumstances the worst possible combination.

There was also the unknown factor – wherever Flight Two landed – of how limited their control might be, due to rudder and stabilizer trim problems, which they already knew about, though not their extent.

For a landing, Lincoln International offered the best chance of safety. But Lincoln was at least an hour's flying time away. Their present speed – two hundred and fifty knots – was far slower than they had been moving at the higher altitude, and Anson Harris was holding the speed down, in the hope of avoiding further structural damage. Unfortunately, even that involved a penalty. At their present low level of ten thousand feet there was considerable buffeting and turbulence from the storm, now all around them instead of far below.

The crucial question was: Could they remain in the air another hour?

Despite everything that had happened, less than five minutes had passed since the explosion and explosive decompression.

Air route control was asking again: 'Trans America Two, advise your intentions.'

Vernon Demerest replied, requesting a direct course for Detroit while the extent of damage was still being checked. Landing intentions, either at Detroit Metropolitan or elsewhere, would be notified within the next few minutes.

'Roger, Trans America Two. Detroit has advised they are removing snowploughs from runway three left. Until informed otherwise, they will prepare for an emergency landing.'

The intercom bell chimed and Demerest answered. It was Cy Jordan calling from the rear, shouting to make himself heard above a roar of wind. 'Captain, there's a great hole back here, about six feet wide behind the rear door. Most else around the galley and toilets is a shambles. But as far as I can see, everything's holding together. The rudder power boost is blown to hell, but control cables look okay.'

'What about control surfaces? Can you see anything?'

'It looks like the skin is bulged into the stabilizer, which is why the stabilizer's jammed. Apart from that, all I can see outside are some holes and bad dents, I guess from debris blowing back. But nothing's hanging loose – at least, that shows. Most of the blast, I'd say, went sideways.'

It was this effect which D. O. Guerrero had not allowed for. He had blundered and miscalculated from the beginning. He bungled the explosion, too.

His greatest error was in failing to recognize that any explosion would be drawn outward and would largely dissipate, the moment the hull of the pressurized aircraft was pierced. Another error was in not realizing how stoutly a modern jetliner was built. In a passenger jet, structural and mechanical systems duplicated each other, so that no single malfunction or damage should result in destruction of the whole. An airliner could be destroyed by a bomb, but only if the bomb were detonated – either by plan or chance – in some vulnerable location. Guerrero made no such plan.

Demerest queried Cy Jordan, 'Can we stay in the air an hour?'

'My guess is, the aeroplane can. I'm not sure about the passengers.'

'How many are hurt?'

'I can't say yet. I checked structural damage first, the way you said. But things don't look good.'

Demerest ordered, 'Stay there as long as you need to. Do what you can.' He hesitated, dreading what the answer to his next question might be, then asked, 'Have you seen any sign of Gwen?' He still didn't know whether or not Gwen had been sucked out with the initial blast. In the past it had happened to others, including stewardesses who were near the site of an explosive decompression, unprotected. And even if that had not happened, Gwen had still been closest to the detonated bomb.

Cy Jordan answered, 'Gwen's here, but in pretty bad shape, I think. We've got about three doctors, and they're working on her and the others. I'll report when I can.'

Vernon Demerest replaced the interphone. Despite his last question and its answer, he was still denying himself the indulgence of private thoughts or personal emotion; there would be time for those later. Professional decisions, the safety of the aeroplane and its complement, came first. He repeated to Anson Harris the gist of the second officer's report.

Harris considered, weighing all factors. Vernon Demerest had still given no indication of taking over direct command, and obviously approved of Harris's decisions so far, else he would have said so. Now, Demerest appeared to be leaving the decision about where to land to Harris also.

Captain Demerest – even in utmost crisis – was behaving exactly as a check pilot should.

'We'll try for Lincoln,' Harris said. The safety of the aircraft was paramount; however bad conditions might be in the passenger cabin, they would have to hope that most people could manage to hold on.

Demerest nodded acknowledgement and began notifying Toronto Centre of the decision; in a few minutes, Cleveland Centre would take them over. Demerest requested that Detroit Metropolitan still stand by in case of a sudden change of plan, though it wasn't likely. Lincoln International was to be alerted that Flight Two would require a straight-in emergency approach.

'Roger, Trans America Two. Detroit and Lincoln are being advised.' A change of course followed. They were nearing the western shore of Lake Huron, the US-Canadian border close.

On the ground, both pilots knew, Flight Two was now the centre of attention. Controllers and supervisors in contiguous air route centres would be working intensely, coordinating removal of all traffic from the aircraft's path, sectors ahead warned of their approach, and airways cleared. Any request they made would be acted on with first priority.

As they crossed the border, Toronto Centre signed off, adding to the final exchange, 'Goodnight and good luck.'

Cleveland Air Route Centre responded to their call a moment later.

Glancing back towards the passenger cabins, through the gap where the flight deck door had been, Demerest could see figures moving – though indistinctly, because immediately after the door had gone, Cy Jordan had dimmed the first class cabin lights to avoid reflection on the flight deck. It appeared, though, as if passengers were being ushered forward, indicating that someone in the rear had taken charge – presumably Cy Jordan, who should be reporting again at any moment. The cold was still biting, even on the flight deck; back there it must be colder still. Once more, with a second's anguish, Demerest thought of Gwen, then ruthlessly cleared his mind, concentrating on what must be decided next.

Though only minutes had elapsed since the decision to risk another hour in the air, the time to begin planning their approach and landing at Lincoln International was now. As Harris continued flying, Vernon Demerest selected approach and runway charts and spread them on his knees.

Lincoln International was home base for both pilots, and they knew the airport – as well as runways and surrounding air space – intimately. Safety and training, however, required that memory should be supplemented and checked.

The charts confirmed what both already knew.

For the high speed, heavy weight landing they must execute, the longest possible length of runway was required. Because of doubtful rudder control, the runway should be the widest too. It must also be directly into wind which – the Lincoln forecast had said – was north-west at thirty knots, and gusting. Runway three zero answered all requirements.

'We need three zero,' Demerest said.

Harris pointed out, 'That last report said a temporary closing, due to obstruction.'

'I heard,' Demerest growled. 'The damn runway's been blocked for hours, and all that's in the way is a stuck Mexican jet.' He folded a Lincoln approach chart and clipped it to his control yoke, then exclaimed angrily, 'Obstruction hell! We'll give 'em fifty more minutes to pry it loose.'

As Demerest thumbed his mike button to inform air route control, Second Officer Cy Jordan – white faced and shaken – returned to the flight deck.

||

In the main terminal of Lincoln International, Lawyer Freemantle was puzzled.

It was most peculiar, he thought, that no one in authority had yet objected to the big, increasingly noisy demonstration of Meadowood residents who, at this moment, were monopolizing a large segment of the central concourse.

Earlier this evening, when Elliott Freemantle had asked the Negro police lieutenant for permission to hold a public censure meeting, he had been firmly refused. Yet here they were, with a curious crowd of spectators – and not a policeman in sight!

Freemantle thought again: it didn't make sense.

Yet what had happened was incredibly simple.

After the interview with the airport general manager, Bakersfeld, the delegation, led by Elliott Freemantle, had returned from the administrative mezzanine to the main concourse. There, the TV crews, whom Freemantle had talked with on the way in, had set up their equipment.

The remaining Meadowood residents – already at least five hundred strong, with more coming in – were gathering around the TV activity.

One of the television men told him, 'We're ready if you are, Mr Freemantle.'

Two TV stations were represented, both planning to film separate interviews for use tomorrow. With customary shrewdness, Freemantle had already inquired which TV shows the film was destined for, so that he could conduct himself accordingly. The first interview, he learned, was for a prime-time, popular show which liked controversy, liveliness, and even shock treatment. He was ready to supply all three.

The TV interviewer, a handsome young man with a Ronald Reagan haircut, asked, 'Mr Freemantle, why are you here?'

'Because this airport is a den of thieves.'

'Will you explain that?'

'Certainly. The homeowners of Meadowood community are having thievery practised on them. Thievery of their peace, their right to privacy of their work-earned rest, and of their sleep. Thievery of enjoyment of their leisure; thievery of their mental and physical health, and of their children's health and welfare. All these things, basic rights under our Constitution – are being shamelessly stolen, without recompense or recognition, by the operators of Lincoln Airport.'

The interviewer opened his mouth to smile, showing two rows of faultless teeth. 'Counsellor, those are fighting words.'

'That's because my clients and I are in a fighting mood.'

'Is that mood because of anything which has happened here tonight?'

'Yes, sir. We have seen demonstrated the callous indifference of this airport's management to my clients' problems.'

'Just what are your plans?'

'In the courts – if necessary the highest court – we shall now seek closure of specific runways, even the entire airport during night time hours. In Europe, where they're more civilized about these things, Paris airport, for example, has a curfew. Failing that, we shall demand proper compensation for cruelly wronged homeowners.'

'I assume that what you're doing at this moment means you're also seeking public support.'

'Yes, sir.'

'Do you believe the public *will* support you?'

'If they don't, I invite them to spend twenty-four hours living in Meadowood – providing their eardrums and sanity will stand it.'

'Surely, Counsellor, airports have official programmes of noise abatement.'

'A sham, sir! A fake! A public lie! The general manager of this airport confessed to me tonight that even the paltry, so-called noise abatement measures are not being observed.'

And so on.

Afterwards, Elliott Freemantle wondered if he should have qualified the statement about noise abatement procedures – as Bakersfeld had done – by referring to exceptional conditions of tonight's storm. But semi-truth or not, the way he had said it was stronger, and Freemantle doubted if it would be challenged. Anyway, he had given good performances – in the second interview as well as the first. Also during both filmings, the cameras panned several times over the intent, expressive faces of the assembled Meadowood residents. Elliot Freemantle hoped that when they saw themselves on their home screens tomorrow, they would remember who had been responsible for all the attention they were receiving.

The number of Meadowooders who had followed him to the airport – as if he were their personal Pied Piper – astonished him. Attendance at the meeting in the Sunday school hall at Meadowood had been roughly six hundred. In view of the bad night and lateness of the hour, he had thought they would be doing well if half that number made the farther trek to the airport; but not only did most of the original crowd come; some must have telephoned friends and neighbours who had joined them. He had even had requests for more copies of the printed forms retaining himself as legal counsel, which he was happy to pass out. Some revised mental arithmetic convinced him that his first hope of a fee from Meadowood totalling twenty five thousand dollars might well be exceeded.

After the TV interviews, the *Tribune* reporter, Tomlinson – who had been taking notes during the filming – inquired, 'What comes next, Mr Freemantle? Do you intend to stage some kind of demonstration here?'

Freemantle shook his head. 'Unfortunately the management of this airport does not believe in free speech, and we have been denied the elementary privilege of a public meeting. However' – he indicated the assembled Meadowooders – 'I do intend to report to these ladies and gentlemen.'

'Isn't that the same thing as a public meeting?'

'No, it is not.'

Just the same, Elliott Freemantle conceded to himself, it would be a fine distinction, especially since he had every intention of turning what followed into a public demonstration if he could. His objective was to get started with an aggressive speech, which the airport police would dutifully order him to stop. Freemantle had no intention of resisting, or of getting arrested. Merely being halted by the police – if possible in full oratorical flow – would establish him as a Meadowood martyr and, incidentally, create one more colour story for tomorrow's papers. (The morning papers, he imagined, had already closed with the earlier reports about himself and Meadowood; editors of the afternoon editions would be grateful for a new lead.)

Even more important, Meadowood homeowners would be further convinced that they had hired a strong counsel and leader, well worth his fee – the first instalment cheques for which, Lawyer Freemantle hoped, would start flooding in right after tomorrow.

'We're all set to go,' Floyd Zanetta, chairman of the earlier Meadowood meeting, reported.

While Freemantle and the *Tribune* newsman had been speaking, several of the Meadowood men had hastily assembled the portable p.a. system, brought from the Sunday school hall. One of the men now handed Freemantle a hand microphone. Using it, he began to address the crowd.

'My friends, we came here tonight in a mood of reason and with constructive thoughts. We sought to communicate that mood and thoughts to this airport's management, believing we had a real and urgent problem, worthy of careful consideration. On your behalf I attempted – in reasoned but firm terms – to make that problem known. I hoped to report back to you – at best, some promise of relief; at least, some sympathy and understanding. I regret to tell you that your delegation received none. Instead, we were accorded only hostility, abuse, and an uncaring, cynical assurance that in future the airport's noise above and around your homes is going to get worse.'

There was a cry of outrage. Freemantle raised a hand. 'Ask the others who were with me. *They* will tell you.' He pointed to the front of the crowd. 'Did this airport's general manager, or did he not, inform us that there was worse to come?' At first a shade reluctantly, then more definitely, those who had been in the delegation nodded.

Having skilfully misrepresented the honest frankness which Mel Bakersfeld had shown the delegation, Elliott Freemantle continued. 'I see others, as well as my Meadowood friends and clients, who have stopped, with curiosity, to discover what is going on. We welcome their interest. Let me inform you . . .' He continued in his customary, haranguing style.

The crowd, sizeable before, was now larger still, and continuing to grow. Travellers on their way to departure gates were having trouble getting through. Flight announcements were being drowned out by the noise. Among the Meadowooders, several had raised hastily scrawled signs which read: AEROPLANES OR PEOPLE FIRST? . . . OUTLAW JETS FROM MEADOWOOD! . . . NIX NOXIOUS NOISE . . . MEADOWOOD PAYS TAXES TOO . . . IMPEACH LINCOLN!

Whenever Freemantle paused, the shouts and general uproar grew louder. A grey-haired man in a windbreaker yelled, 'Let's give the airport a taste of their own noise.' His words produced a roar of approval.

Without question, Elliott Freemantle's 'report' had by now developed into a full-scale demonstration. At any moment, he expected, the police would intervene.

What Lawyer Freemantle did not know was that while the TV sessions were taking place and Meadowood residents assembling, the airport management's concern about Trans America Flight Two was beginning. Shortly after, every policeman in the terminal was concentrating on a search for Inez Guerrero, and thus the Meadowood demonstration escaped attention.

Even after Inez was found, Police Lieutenant Ordway remained occupied with the emergency session in Mel Bakersfeld's office.

As a result, after another fifteen minutes, Elliott Freemantle was becoming worried. Impressive as the demonstration was, unless halted officially, it would have little point. *Where in God's name,* he thought, *were the airport police, and why weren't they doing their job?*

It was then that Lieutenant Ordway and Mel Bakersfeld came down together from the administrative mezzanine.

Several minutes earlier the meeting in Mel's office had broken up. After the interrogation of Inez Guerrero and dispatch of the second warning message to Flight Two, there was nothing to be gained by retaining everyone together. Tanya Livingston, with the Trans America DTM and chief pilot, returned anxiously to the airline's offices in the terminal, to await any fresh news there. The others – with the exception of Inez Guerrero, who was being held for questioning by downtown police detectives – returned to their own bailiwicks. Tanya had promised to notify Customs Inspector Standish, who was distressed and anxious about his niece aboard Flight Two, immediately there was any new development.

Mel, not certain where he would keep his own vigil, left his office with Ned Ordway.

Ordway saw the Meadowood demonstration first and caught sight of Elliot Freemantle. 'That damn lawyer! I told him there'd be no demonstrations here.' He hurried towards the concourse crowd. 'I'll break this up fast.'

Alongside, Mel cautioned, 'He may be counting on you doing that – just so he can be a hero.'

As they came nearer, Ordway shouldering his way ahead through the crowd, Elliott Freemantle proclaimed, 'Despite assurances from the airport management earlier this evening, heavy air traffic – deafening and shattering as always – is still continuing at this late hour. Even now . . .'

'Never mind that,' Ned Ordway cut in brusquely. 'I already told you there would be no demonstration in this terminal.'

'But, Lieutenant, I assure you this is not a demonstration.' Freemantle still held the microphone, so that his words carried clearly. 'All that's happened is that I granted a television interview after a meeting with the airport management – I might say a highly unsatisfactory meeting – then reported to these people . . .'

'Report some place else!' Ordway swung around, facing others nearest him. 'Now, let's break this up!'

There were hostile glances and angry mutterings among the crowd. As the policeman turned back to Elliott Freemantle, photographers' flash bulbs popped. TV floodlights, which had been turned off, went bright once more as television cameras focused on the two. At last, Elliott Freemantle thought, everything was going just the way he wanted.

On the fringe of the crowd, Mel Bakersfeld was talking with one of the TV men and Tomlinson of the *Tribune*. The reporter was consulting his notes and reading a passage back. As he listened, Mel's face suffused with anger.

'Lieutenant,' Elliott Freemantle was saying to Ned Ordway, 'I have the greatest respect for you and for your uniform. Just the same, I'd like to point out that we did hold a meeting some place else tonight – at Meadowood – but because of noise from this airport, we couldn't hear ourselves.'

Ordway snapped back, 'I'm not here for a debate, Mr Freemantle. If you don't do as I say, you'll be arrested. I'm ordering you to get this group out of here.'

Someone in the crowd shouted, 'Suppose we won't go?'

Another voice urged, 'Let's stay here! They can't arrest all of us.'

'No!' Elliott Freemantle held up a hand self-righteously. 'Please listen to me! There will be no disorder; no disobedience. My friends and clients – this police officer has ordered us to desist and leave. We will comply with his order. We may consider it a grave restriction of free speech' . . . and there were responsive cheers and booing . . . 'but let it not be said that at any point we failed to respect the law.' More crisply, he added, 'I shall have a statement for the press outside.'

'One moment!' Mel Bakersfeld's voice cut sharply across the heads of others. He thrust his way forward. 'Freemantle, I'm interested to know what will be in that press statement of yours. Will it be more misrepresentation? Another dose of distorted law reports to delude people who don't know any better? Or just plain, old-fashioned fabrication which you're so expert at?'

Mel spoke loudly, his words carrying to those nearby. There was a buzz of interested reaction. People who had begun drifting away, stopped.

Elliott Freemantle reacted automatically. 'That's a malicious, libellous statement!' An instant later, scenting danger, he shrugged. 'However, I shall let it pass.'

'Why? If it *is* libellous, you should know how to handle it.' Mel faced the lawyer squarely. 'Or perhaps you're afraid of it proving true.'

'I'm afraid of nothing, Mr Bakersfeld. The fact is, we've been told by this policeman that the party's over. Now, if you'll excuse me . . .'

'I said it was over for you,' Ned Ordway pointed out. 'What Mr Bakersfeld does is something again. He has authority here.' Ordway had moved beside Mel; together they blocked the lawyer's way.

'If you were a real policeman,' Freemantle objected, 'you'd treat us both equally.'

Mel said unexpectedly, 'I think he's right.' Ordway glanced at him curiously. 'You *should* treat us both equally. And instead of closing this meeting, I think you should allow me the same privilege of talking to these people which Mr Freemantle just had. That is, if you want to be a real policeman.'

'I guess I want to be.' The big Negro police lieutenant, towering above the other two, was grinning. 'I'm beginning to see it your way – and Mr Freemantle's.'

Mel observed blandly to Elliott Freemantle, 'You see, he's come around. Now, since we're all here, we may as well clear up a few things.' He held out his hand. 'Let me have that microphone.'

Mel's anger of a minute or two ago was now less apparent. When the *Tribune* reporter, Tomlinson, had read back from his notes the gist of what Elliott Freemantle stated in his TV interviews and later, Mel reacted heatedly. Both Tomlinson and the TV producer asked Mel to comment on what had been said. He assured them that he would.

'Oh, no!' Freemantle shook his head decisively. The danger which he scented a few moments earlier was suddenly close and real. Once before, tonight, he had underestimated this man Bakersfeld; he had no intention of repeating that mistake. Freemantle himself now had the assembled Meadowood residents firmly under control; it was essential to his purpose that they remain that way. All he wanted at this moment was for everyone to disperse quickly.

He declared loftily, 'More than enough has been said.' Ignoring Mel, he passed the microphone to one of the Meadowood men and indicated the p.a. equipment. 'Let's get all this apart and be on our way.'

'I'll take that.' Ned Ordway reached over and intercepted the microphone. 'And leave the rest where it is.' He nodded to several other policemen who had appeared on the fringes of the crowd. They moved in. While Freemantle watched helplessly, Ordway handed the microphone to Mel.

'Thank you.' Mel faced the crowd of Meadowooders – many of their faces hostile – and others who, passing through the terminal, had stopped to listen. Though it was twenty minutes after midnight, and now Saturday morning, the heavy traffic in the main concourse showed no sign of lessening. Because of many delayed flights, pressures would probably continue through the remainder of the night, merging with a heightened weekend activity until schedules got back to normal. If one of the Meadowood objectives was to create a nuisance effect, Mel thought, it was succeeding. The extra thousand or so people were taxing available space in the concourse, arriving and departing passengers having to fight their way around like a flood tide encountering a sudden sandbank. Obviously the situation must not continue for more than a few minutes.

'I'll be brief,' Mel said. He spoke into the microphone, telling them who and what he was.

'Earlier tonight I met a delegation representing all of you. I explained some of the airport's problems; also that we understood and sympathized with yours. I expected what I said to be passed along, if not exactly, then at least in substance. Instead, I find that I have been misrepresented and you have been deceived.'

Elliott Freemantle emitted a roar of rage. 'That's a lie!' His face was flushed. For the first time tonight his impeccably styled hair was disarrayed.

Lieutenant Ordway grasped the lawyer firmly by the arm. 'Hush up, now! You had your turn.'

In front of Mel a broadcast microphone had joined the hand mike he was using. The TV lights were on as he continued.

'Mr Freemantle accuses me of lying. He's been strong in his use of words tonight.' Mel

251

consulted a note in his hand. 'I understand they include "thievery", "indifference", that I met your delegation with "hostility and abuse"; further, that the noise abatement measures we are trying to enforce are a "sham, a fake, and a public lie". Well, we'll see what *you* think about who's lying – or misrepresenting – and who is not.'

He had made an error earlier, Mel realized, in speaking to the small delegation and not to this main group. His objectives had been to achieve understanding, yet avoid disruption in the terminal. Both objectives had failed.

But at least he would aim for understanding now.

'Let me outline this airport's policy on noise suppression.'

For the second time tonight Mel described the operating limitations on pilots and their employer airlines. He added, 'At normal times these restrictions are enforced. But in difficult weather, such as tonight's storm, pilots must be given leeway, and aircraft safety must come first.'

As to runways: 'Wherever possible we avoid takeoffs over Meadowood from runway two five.' Yet, he explained, there was occasional need to use that runway, when runway three zero was out of commission, as at present.

'We do our best for you,' Mel insisted, 'and we are not indifferent, as has been alleged. But we are in business as an airport and we cannot escape our basic responsibilities, plus our concern for aviation safety.'

The hostility among his audience was still apparent, but now there was interest as well. Elliott Freemantle – glaring at Mel and fuming – was aware of the interest too.

'From what I've heard,' Mel said, 'Mr Freemantle chose not to pass on some observations I offered to your delegation on the general subject of airport noise. My remarks were made' – he consulted his notes again – 'not in "uncaring cynicism", as has been suggested, but in an attempt at honest frankness. I intend to share that frankness with you here.'

Now, as earlier, Mel admitted there was little more in the area of noise reduction which could be done; glum expressions appeared when he described the expected greater noise from new aircraft soon to be in use. But he sensed there was appreciation for objective honesty. Beyond a few scattered remarks, there were no interruptions, his words remaining audible above the background noises of the terminal.

'There are two other things which I did not mention to your delegation, but now I intend to.' Mel's voice hardened. 'I doubt if you will like them.'

The first point, he informed them, concerned Meadowood community.

'Twelve years ago your community didn't exist. It was a parcel of empty land – of low value until the airport's growth and closeness sent surrounding values soaring. To that extent your Meadowood is like thousands of communities, which have mushroomed around airports everywhere in the world.'

A woman shouted, 'When we came to live here, we didn't know about jet noise.'

'But *we* did!' Mel pointed a finger at the woman. 'Airport managements knew that jet aeroplanes were coming, and knew what jet noise would be like, and we warned people, and local zoning commissions, and pleaded with them in countless Meadowoods *not to build homes*. I wasn't at this airport then, but there are records and pictures in our files. This airport put up signs where Meadowood is now: AEROPLANES WILL TAKE OFF AND LAND OVER THIS ROUTE. Other airports did the same. And everywhere the signs appeared, real estate developers and salesmen tore them down. Then they sold land and houses to people like you, keeping quiet about the noise to come, and airport expansion plans – which usually they knew of – and I guess in the end the real estate people outwitted us all.'

This time there was no rejoinder, only a sea of thoughtful faces, and Mel guessed that what he had said had struck home. He had a sense of keen regret. These were not antagonists whom he wanted to defeat. They were decent people with a real and pressing problem; neighbours for whom he wished he could do more.

He caught sight of Elliott Freemantle's sneering features. 'Bakersfeld, I suppose you think that's pretty clever.' The lawyer turned away, shouting over nearer heads without benefit of amplifier. 'Don't believe all that! You're being softened up! If you stick with me, we'll take these airport people, and we'll take them good.'

'In case any of you didn't hear,' Mel said into the microphone, 'that was Mr Freemantle advising you to stick with him. I have something to say about that, too.'

He told the now attentive crowd, 'Many people – people like you – have had advantage taken of them by being sold land or homes in areas which should not have been developed, or should have been developed for industrial use where airport noise doesn't matter. You haven't lost out entirely, because you have your land and homes; but chances are, their values have decreased.'

A man said gloomily, 'Damn right!'

'Now there's another scheme afoot to part you from your money. Lawyers all over North America are hot-footing it to airport dormitory communities because "thar's gold in that thar noise".'

Lawyer Freemantle, his face flushed and distorted, shrilled, 'You say one more word – I'll sue you!'

'For what?' Mel shot back. 'Or have you guessed already what I'm going to say?' Well, he thought, maybe Freemantle would launch a libel action later, though he doubted it. Either way, Mel felt some of his old recklessness – a decision for plain speaking, and never mind the consequences – take command. It was a feeling which, in the past year or two, he had experienced rarely.

'Residents in the communities I spoke of,' Mel argued, 'are being assured that airports can be sued – successfully. Homeowners near airports are being promised there's a pot of dollars at every runway's end. Well, I'm not saying airports can't be sued, nor am I saying there aren't some fine, sound lawyers engaged in anti-airport litigation. What I'm warning you is that there are a good many of the other kind, too.'

The same woman who had called out before asked – more mildly this time – 'How are we supposed to know which is which?'

'It's difficult without a programme; in other words, unless you happen to know some airport law. If you don't, you can be bamboozled by a one-sided list of legal precedents.' Mel hesitated only briefly before adding. 'I've heard a few specific law decisions mentioned tonight. If you wish, I'll tell you another side to them.'

A man at the front said, 'Let's hear your version, mister.'

Several people were looking curiously at Elliott Freemantle.

Mel had hesitated, realizing that this had already gone on longer than he intended. He supposed though, that a few minutes more would make no difference.

On the fringes of the crowd he caught sight of Tanya Livingston.

'The legal cases which you and I have both heard referred to glibly,' Mel said, 'are old hat to people who run airports. The first I think, was *US v. Causby*.'

That particular case – a pillar of Lawyer Freemantle's presentation to the Meadowood group – was, Mel explained, a decision more than twenty years old. 'It concerned a chicken farmer and military aeroplanes. The aeroplanes repeatedly flew over the farmer's house, as low as sixty-seven feet – a whole lot lower than any aeroplane ever comes near Meadowood. The chickens were frightened; some died.'

After years of litigation the case found its way to the US Supreme Court. Mel pointed out: 'The total damages awarded were less than four hundred dollars – the value of the dead chickens.'

He added, 'There was no pot of dollars for the farmer, nor is there – in that legal precedent – for you.'

Mel could see Elliott Freemantle, his face alternately crimson and white with rage. Ned Ordway was once more holding the lawyer by the arm.

'There *is* one legal case,' Mel observed, 'which Mr Freemantle has chosen not to mention. It's an important one – also involving a Supreme Court ruling – and well known. Unfortunately for Mr Freemantle, it doesn't support his arguments, but runs counter to them.'

The case, he explained was *Batten v. US* in which, in 1963, the Supreme Court ruled that only an actual 'physical invasion' created liability. Noise alone was not enough.

Mel continued, 'Another ruling, along the same lines was *Loma Portal Civic Club v. American Airlines* – a 1964 decision of the California Supreme Court.' In this, he reported, the Court ruled that property owners were not entitled to restrict the flight of aircraft over houses near an airport. Public interest in continuance of air travel, the California court laid down, was paramount and overwhelming . . .

Mel had quoted the legal case unhesitatingly, without reference to notes. Clearly his audience was impressed. Now he smiled. 'Legal precedents are like statistics. If you manipulate them, you can prove anything.' He added, 'You don't have to take my word for what I've told you. Look it up. It's all on record.'

A woman near Elliott Freemantle grumbled at him, 'You didn't tell us all that. You just gave your side.'

Some of the hostility directed at Mel earlier, was now being transferred towards the lawyer.

Freemantle shrugged. After all, he decided, he still had more than a hundred and sixty signed retainer forms, which he had been careful to transfer to a locked bag in the boot of his car. Nothing that was said here could undo the fact of those.

A moment or two later he began to wonder.

Mel Bakersfeld was being asked by several people about legal contract forms which they had signed this evening. Their voices betrayed doubt. Obviously Mel's manner, as well as what he said, had made a strong impression. The crowd was dividing into small groups, most in animated discussion.

'I've been asked about a certain contract,' Mel announced. Within the crowd, other voices silences as he added, 'I think you know the contract I mean. I have seen a copy of it.'

Elliott Freemantle pushed forward. 'So what! You aren't a lawyer; we've settled that once before. Therefore you're no authority on contracts.' This time Freemantle was close enough to the microphone for his words to carry.

Mel snapped back, 'I live with contracts! Every lessee in this airport – from the biggest airline to a headache pill concessionaire – operates under a contract approved by me, and negotiated by my staff.'

He swung back to the crowd. 'Mr Freemantle points out, correctly, that I am not a lawyer, so I'll give you a businessman's advice. In certain circumstances the contracts you signed tonight could be enforceable. A contract is a contract. You *could* be taken to a debtor's court; the money might be collected. But my opinion is that, providing you serve proper notice immediately, neither thing will happen. For one thing, you have received no goods; no service has been rendered. For another, each of you would have to be sued separately.' Mel smiled. 'That, in itself, would be an undertaking.'

'One more thing.' He looked directly at Elliott Freemantle. 'I do not believe that any court would look favourably on a total legal fee in the region of fifteen thousand dollars for legal service which, at best, was nebulous.'

The man who had spoken earlier asked, 'So what do we do?'

'If you've genuinely changed your mind, I suggest that today or tomorrow you write a letter. Address it to Mr Freemantle. In it, state that you no longer want legal representation as arranged, and why. Be sure to keep a copy. Again, in my opinion – that's the last you'll ever hear.'

Mel had been blunter than he at first intended, and he had also been excessively reckless, he supposed, in going quite this far. If Elliott Freemantle chose, he could certainly make trouble. In a matter in which the airport – and therefore Mel – had active interest, Mel had interposed between clients and lawyer, casting doubt upon the latter's probity. Judging by the hatred in the lawyer's eyes, he would be delighted to do any harm to Mel he could. Yet instinct told Mel that the last thing Freemantle wanted was a searching public scrutiny of his client recruiting methods and working habits. A trial judge, sensitive about legal ethics, might ask awkward questions; later still, so might the Bar Association, which safeguarded the legal profession's ethics. The more Mel thought about it, the less inclined he was to worry.

Though Mel didn't know it, Elliott Freemantle had reached the same conclusion.

Whatever else Freemantle might be, he was a pragmatist. He had long ago recognized that in life there were gambits which you won, others that you lost. Sometimes the loss was sudden and illogical. A chance, a quirk, a nettle in the grass, could turn an almost-grasped success into mortifying defeat. Fortunately for people like Freemantle, the reverse was sometimes true.

The airport manager, Bakersfeld, had proved to be a nettle – carelessly grasped – which should have been avoided. Even after their first brush, which Elliott Freemantle now realized could have been a warning to him, he had continued to underestimate his opponent by remaining at the airport instead of quitting while ahead. Another thing Freemantle had discovered too late was that Bakersfeld, while shrewd, was a gambler too. Only a gambler would have gone out on such a limb as Bakersfeld had a moment ago. And only Elliott Freemantle – at this point – knew that Bakersfeld had won.

Freemantle *was* aware that the Bar Association might regard this night's activity unfavourably. More to the point: He had had a brush with an association investigating committee once already, and had no intention of provoking another.

Bakersfeld had been right, Elliott Freemantle thought. There would be no attempted debt collecting, through the courts, on the basis of the signed legal retainer forms. The hazards were too great, the spoils uncertain.

He would not give up entirely, of course. Tomorrow, Freemantle decided, he would draft a letter to all Meadowood residents who had signed the forms; in it he would do his best to persuade them that retention of himself as legal counsel, at the individual fee specified, should continue. He doubted, though, if many would respond. The suspicion which Bakersfeld had effectively implanted – *damn his guts!* – was too great. There might be some small pickings left, from a few people who would be willing to continue, and later it would be necessary to decide if they were worth while. But the prospect of a big killing was gone.

Something else, though, he supposed, would turn up soon. It always had.

Ned Ordway and several other policemen were now dispersing the crowd; normal traffic through the concourse was resuming. The portable p.a. system was at last being disassembled and removed.

Mel Bakersfeld noticed that Tanya, whom he had caught sight of a moment or two ago, was making her way in his direction.

A woman – one of the Meadowood residents whom Mel had noticed several times before – confronted him. She had a strong intelligent face and shoulder-length brown hair.

'Mr Bakersfeld,' The woman said quietly. 'We've all talked a lot, and we understand a few things better than we did. But I still haven't heard anything that I can tell my children when they cry, and ask why the noise won't stop so they can sleep.'

Mel shook his head regretfully. In a few words the woman had pointed out the futility of everything which had happened tonight. He knew he had no answer for her. He doubted – while airports and dwellings remained in proximity – if there would ever be one.

He was still wondering what to say when Tanya handed him a folded sheet of paper.

Opening it, he read the message which showed signs of being hastily typed:

flight 2 had mid-air explosion.
structural damage & injuries.
now heading here 4 emergency
landing, est. arrival 0130.
capt. says must have runway
three zero. tower reports runway still
blocked.

12

In the bloody shambles which was the rear of the tourist cabin of Flight Two, Dr Milton Compagno, general practitioner, was exerting the utmost of his professional skill in an attempt to save Gwen Meighen's life. He was not sure he would succeed.

When the initial explosion from D. O. Guerrero's dynamite bomb occurred, Gwen – next to Guerrero himself – was closest to the explosion's centre.

In other circumstances she would have been killed instantly, as was D. O. Guerrero. Two things – for the moment – saved her.

Interposed between Gwen and the explosion were Guerrero's body and the aircraft toilet door. Neither was an effective shield, yet the two together were sufficient to delay the blast's initial force the fraction of a second.

Within that fractional time the aeroplane's skin ripped, and the second explosion – explosive decompression – occurred.

The dynamite blast still struck Gwen, hurling her backward, gravely injured and bleeding, but its force now had an opposing force – the outward rush of air through the hole in the fuselage at the aircraft's rear. The effect was as if two tornadoes met head on. An instant later the decompression triumphed, sweeping the original explosion out with it into the high-altitude, darkened night.

Despite the forcefulness of the explosion, injuries were not widespread.

Gwen Meighen, the most critically hurt, lay unconscious in the aisle. Next to her, the owlish young man who had emerged from the toilet and startled Guerrero, was wounded, bleeding badly, and dazed, but still on his feet and conscious. A half dozen passengers nearby sustained cuts and contusions from splinters and bomb fragments. Others were struck, and stunned or bruised by hurtling objects impelled towards the aircraft's rear by the explosive decompression, but none of the latter injuries were major.

At first, after decompression, all who were not secure in seats were impelled by suction towards the gaping hole in the aircraft's rear. From this danger, too, Gwen Meighen was in gravest peril. But she had fallen so that an arm – instinctively or accidentally – encircled a seat base. It prevented her from being dragged farther, and her body blocked others.

After the initial outrush of air, the suction lessened.

Now, the greatest immediate danger for all – injured or not – was lack of oxygen.

Although oxygen masks dropped promptly from their housings, only a handful of passengers had grasped and put them on at once.

Before it was too late, however, a few people had acted. Stewardesses, responding to their training, and wherever they happened to be, seized masks and motioned others to do likewise. Three doctors, travelling with their wives as members of an off-season vacation tour, realized the need for speed, donned masks themselves and gave hasty instructions to those around them. Judy, the alert, eighteen-year-old niece of Customs Inspector Standish, placed a mask over the face of the baby in the seat beside her, as well as over her own. She then immediately signalled the baby's parents, and others across the aisle, to use oxygen. Mrs Quonsett, the old lady stowaway, having observed oxygen demonstrations many times during her illegal flights, knew what to do. She took a mask herself and handed one to her friend, the oboe player, whom she pulled back into his seat beside her. Mrs Quonsett had no idea if she was going to live or die, and found herself not greatly worried; but whatever happened, she intended to know what was going on until the very last moment.

Someone thrust a mask at the young man near Gwen who had been wounded. Though swaying, and scarcely aware of what was happening, he managed to hold it to his face.

Even so, barely half the passengers were on oxygen at the end of fifteen seconds – the critical time. By then, those not breathing oxygen were lapsing into drowsy stupor; in another fifteen seconds, most were unconscious.

Gwen Meighen received no oxygen, nor immediate help. The unconsciousness, caused by her injuries, deepened.

Then, on the flight deck, Anson Harris, accepting the risk of further structural damage and possible total destruction of the aircraft, made his decision for a high speed dive, saving Gwen and others from asphyxiation.

The dive began at twenty-eight thousand feet altitude; it ended, two and a half minutes later, at ten thousand feet.

A human being can survive without oxygen for three to four minutes without damage to the brain.

For the first half of the dive – for a minute and a quarter, down to nineteen thousand feet – the air continued to be rarefied, and insufficient to support life. Below that point, increasing amounts of oxygen were present and breathable.

At twelve thousand feet regular breathing was possible. By ten – with little time to spare, but enough – consciousness returned to all aboard Flight Two who had lost it, excepting Gwen. Many were unaware of having been unconscious at all.

Gradually, as initial shock wore off, passengers and the remaining stewardesses took stock of their situation. The stewardess who was second in seniority after Gwen – a pert blonde from Oak Lawn, Illinois – hurried towards the injured at the rear. Though her face paled, she called urgently, 'Is there a doctor, please?'

'Yes, miss.' Dr Compagno had already moved from his seat without waiting to be called. A small, sharp-featured man who moved impatiently and talked quickly with a Brooklyn accent, he surveyed the scene hurriedly, conscious of the already biting cold, the wind streaming noisily through the gaping hole in the fuselage. Where the toilets and rear galley had been was a twisted mess of charred and bloodstained wood and metal. The back of the fuselage to the interior of the tail was open, with control wires and structural assemblies exposed.

The doctor raised his voice to make himself heard above the noise of wind and engines, constant and encompassing now that the cabin was no longer sealed.

'I suggest you move as many people as you can nearer the front. Keep everyone as warm as possible. We'll need blankets for those who are hurt.'

The stewardess said doubtfully, 'I'll try to find some.' Many of the blankets normally stored in overhead racks had been swept out, along with passengers' extra clothing and other objects, in the whirlwind of decompression.

The two other doctors from Dr Compagno's tour party joined him. One instructed another stewardess, 'Bring us all the first aid equipment you have.' Compagno – already on his knees beside Gwen – was the only one of the three with a medical bag.

Carrying a bag with emergency supplies wherever he went was characteristic of Milton Compagno. So was taking charge now, even though – as a GP – he was outranked professionally by the other two doctors who were internists.

Milton Compagno never considered himself off duty. Thirty-five years ago, as a young man who had fought an upward battle from a New York slum, he hung out a shingle in Chicago's Little Italy, near Milwaukee and Grand Avenues. Since then – as his wife told it, usually with resignation – the only time he ceased practising medicine was while he slept. He enjoyed being needed. He acted as if his profession were a prize he had won, which, if not guarded, would slip away. He had never been known to refuse to see a patient at any hour, or to fail to make a house call if sent for. He never drove past an accident scene as did many of his medical brethren, fearing malpractice suits; he always stopped, got out of his car, and did what he could. He kept conscientiously up to date. Yet the more he worked, the more he seemed to thrive. He gave the impression of running through each day as if he planned to assuage the world's ailments in a lifetime, of which too little was left.

The journey to Rome – many years postponed – was to visit the birthplace of his parents. With his wife, Dr Compagno was to be away a month, and because he was growing old, he had agreed that the time should be a total rest. Yet he fully anticipated that somewhere en route, or perhaps in Italy (never mind regulations about not being licensed) he would be needed. If so, he was ready. It did not surprise him that he was needed now.

He moved first to Gwen who was clearly most critical among those hurt. He told his colleagues, over his shoulder, 'You attend to the others.'

In the narrow aisle, Dr Compagno turned Gwen over partially, leaning forward to detect if she was breathing. She was, but her breath was light and shallow. He called to the stewardess he had been speaking to, 'I need oxygen down here.' While the girl brought a portable bottle and mask, he checked Gwen's mouth for an unobstructed airway; there were smashed teeth, which he removed, and a good deal of blood; he made sure the bleeding was not preventing respiration. He told the stewardess, 'Hold the mask in place.' The oxygen hissed. Within a minute or two a vestige of colour returned to Gwen's skin, which had been ominously white.

Meanwhile, he began to control bleeding, extensive around the face and chest. Working quickly, he used a haemostat to clamp off a facial artery – worst site of external haemorrhage – and pressure dressings elsewhere. He had already detected a probable fracture of the clavical and left arm, which would need to be splinted later. He was distressed to see what appeared to be splinters from the explosion in the patient's left eye; he was less sure about the right.

Second Officer Jordan, having moved carefully around Dr Compagno and Gwen, took charge of the remaining stewardesses and was supervising the movement of passengers forward in the aircraft. As many tourist passengers as possible were being moved into the first class section, some squeezed in, two to a seat, others directed to the small, semicircular first class lounge, where spare seats were available. Such extra clothing as remained was distributed among those who appeared to need it most, without regard to ownership. As always, in such situations, people showed a willingness to help one another, unselfishness, and even flashes of humour.

The other two doctors were bandaging passengers who had received cuts, none excessively serious. The young man with glasses, who was behind Gwen at the moment of the explosion, had a deep gash in one arm, but it could be repaired and would heal. He had other minor cuts about the face and shoulders. For the time being, pressure dressings were applied to his injured arm, and he was given morphine, while being made as comfortable and warm as possible.

Both the medical attention and movement of passengers was being made more difficult by heavy buffeting which the aircraft, at its present low altitude, was taking from the storm. There was constant turbulence, punctuated every few minutes by violent pitching or sideways movements. Several passengers were finding airsickness added to their other troubles.

After reporting to the flight deck for the second time, Cy Jordan returned to Dr Compagno.

'Doctor, Captain Demerest asked me to say he's grateful for everything you and the other doctors are doing. When you can spare a moment, he'd appreciate it if you'd come to the flight deck to tell him what to radio ahead about casualties.'

259

'Hold this dressing,' Dr Compagno ordered. 'Press down hard, right there. Now I want you to help me with a splint. We'll use one of those leather magazine covers, with a towel under it. Get the biggest cover you can find, and leave the magazine in.'

A moment later: 'I'll come when I can. You can say to your captain that I think, as soon as possible, he should make an announcement to the passengers. People are getting over their shock. They could use some reassurance.'

'Yes, sir.' Cy Jordan looked down at the still unconscious figure of Gwen, his normally mournful, hollow-cheeked face accentuated by concern. 'Is there a chance for her, Doc?'

'There's a chance, son, though I wouldn't say it was the best. A lot depends on her own strength.'

'I always figured she had a lot of that.'

'A pretty girl, wasn't she?' Amid the torn flesh, blood, and dirty, tousled hair, it was difficult to be sure.

'Very.'

Compagno remained silent. Whatever happened, the girl on the floor would not be pretty any more – not without plastic surgery.

'I'll give the captain your message, sir.' Looking a little sicker than before, Cy Jordan went forward to the flight deck.

Vernon Demerest's voice came calmly on the cabin p.a. system a few moments later.

'Ladies and gentlemen, this is Captain Demerest . . .' To overcome the roar of wind and engines, Cy Jordan had turned the volume control to 'full'. Each word rang clearly.

'You know we've had trouble – bad trouble. I won't attempt to minimize it. I won't make any jokes either, because up here on the flight deck we don't see anything that's funny, and I imagine you feel the same way. We've all come through an experience which none of us in the crew has ever had before, and I hope will never have again. But we *have* come through. Now, we have the aeroplane under control, we're turned around, and expect to land at Lincoln International in about three-quarters of an hour.'

In the two passenger cabins, where first and tourist class now mingled without distinction, movement and conversation stopped. Eyes instinctively went to the overhead speakers as everyone within hearing strained to miss nothing of what was said.

'You know, of course, that the aeroplane is damaged. But it's also true that the damage could have been a whole lot worse.'

On the flight deck, with the p.a. mike in hand, Vernon Demerest wondered how specific – and how honest – he should be. On his own regular flights he always kept captain-to-passengers announcements to the barest terse minimum. He disapproved of 'long-playing captains' who bombarded their captive audience with assorted commentaries from a flight's beginning to its end. He sensed, though, that this time he should say more, and that passengers were entitled to be told the true situation.

'I won't conceal from you,' Demerest said into the microphone, 'that we have a few problems still ahead of us. Our landing will be heavy, and we're not sure how the damage we've suffered will affect it. I'm telling you this because right after this announcement the crew will start giving instructions on how to sit, and how to brace yourselves, just before we land. Another thing you'll be told is how to get out of the aeroplane in a hurry, if we need to, right after landing. If that should happen, please act calmly but quickly, and obey instructions given you by any member of the crew.

'Let me assure you that on the ground everything necessary is being done to help us.'

Remembering their need for runway three zero, Demerest hoped it was true. He also decided there was no point in going into detail about the problem of the jammed stabilizer; most passengers wouldn't understand it anyway. With a touch of lightness in his voice, he added, 'In one way you're lucky tonight because instead of one experienced captain on the flight deck, it just so happens you have two – Captain Harris and myself. We're a couple of ancient pelicans with more years of flying than we sometimes like to think about – except right now when all that combined experience comes in mighty useful. We'll be helping each other, along with Second Officer Jordan, who'll also be spending part of his time back with you. Please help us too. If you do, I promise you we'll come through this together – safely.'

Demerest replaced the p.a. mike.

Without taking his eyes from the flight instruments, Anson Harris remarked, 'That was pretty good. You should be in politics.'

Demerest said sourly, 'Nobody'd vote for me. Most times, people don't like plain talking and the truth.' He was remembering bitterly the Board of Airport Commissioners' meeting at Lincoln International where he urged curtailment of airport insurance vending. Plain speech there had proved disastrous. He wondered how the members of the Board, including his smooth, smug brother-in-law, would feel after learning about D. O. Guerrero's purchase of insurance and his maniacal intention to destroy Flight Two. Probably, Demerest thought, they would be complacent as ever, except that now instead of saying *It will never happen*, they would say, *What occurred was exceptional; the odds are against it happening again.* Well, assuming Flight Two made it back safely, and whatever was said or wasn't, sure as hell he was going to create another big fight about airport insurance vending. The difference was: this time more people would listen. Tonight's near disaster, however it turned out, was certain to attract a lot of press attention; he would make the most of it. He would talk bluntly to reporters about flight insurance, about the Lincoln airport commissioners, and not least about his precious brother-in-law, Mel Bakersfeld. Trans America's public relations flacks would do their damnedest, of course, to keep him incommunicado 'in the interests of company policy'. Just let them try!

The radio crackled alive. 'Trans America Two, this is Cleveland Centre. Lincoln advises runway three zero still temporarily out of use. They are attempting to clear obstruction before you arrive. Failing that, will land you on two five.'

Harris's face went grim as Demerest acknowledged. Runway two five was two thousand feet shorter, as well as narrower, and at the moment with a bad crosswind. Using it would compound the hazards they already faced.

Demerest's expression clearly reflected his reaction to the message.

They were still being thrown about severely by the storm. Most of Harris's time was occupied by holding the aircraft reasonably steady.

Demerest swung around to the second officer. 'Cy, go back with the passengers again, and take charge. See that the girls demonstrate the landing drill, and that everybody understands it. Then pick some key people who look reliable. Make sure they know where emergency exits are and how to use them. If we run out of runway, which'll be for sure if we use two five, everything may come apart in a hurry. If that happens we'll all try to make it back there and help, but there may not be time.'

'Yes, sir.' Once more, Jordan eased out of his flight engineer's seat.

Demerest, still anxious for news of Gwen, would have preferred to go himself, but at this stage neither he nor Harris could leave the flight deck.

As Cy Jordan left, Dr Compagno arrived. It was now easier to move into and from the flight deck, since Jordan had moved the smashed entrance door to one side.

Milton Compagno introduced himself briskly to Vernon Demerest. 'Captain, I have the report of injuries you asked for.'

'We're grateful to you, Doctor. If you hadn't been here . . .'

Compagno waved a hand in dismissal. 'Let's do all that later.' He opened a leather-covered notebook where a slim gold pencil marked a page. It was characteristic that he had already obtained names, and recorded injuries and treatment. 'Your stewardess, Miss Meighen, is the most badly hurt. She has multiple lacerations of the face and chest, with considerable bleeding. There is a compound fracture of the left arm and, of course, shock. Also, please notify whoever is making arrangements on the ground that an ophthalmic surgeon should be available immediately.'

Vernon Demerest, his face paler than usual, had been steeling himself to copy the doctor's information on to the flight log clip-board. Now, with sudden shock he stopped.

'An ophthalmic surgeon! You mean . . . her eyes?'

'I'm afraid so,' Dr Compagno said gravely. He corrected himself. 'At least, her left eye has splinters, whether wood or metal I've no means of knowing. It will require a specialist to decide if the retina is affected. The right eye, as far as I can tell, is unharmed.'

'Oh, God!' Feeling physically sick, Demerest put a hand to his face.

Dr Compagno shook his head. 'It's too early to draw conclusions. Modern ophthalmic surgery can do extraordinary things. But time will be important.'

'We'll send all you've told us on company radio,' Anson Harris assured him. 'They'll have time to be ready.'

'Then I'd better give you the rest.'

Mechanically, Demerest wrote down the remainder of the doctor's report. Compared with Gwen's injuries, those of other passengers were slight.

'I'd better get back,' Dr Compagno said. 'To see if there's any change.'

Demerest said abruptly, 'Don't go.'

The doctor stopped, his expression curious.

'Gwen . . . that is, Miss Meighen . . .' Demerest's voice sounded strained and awkward, even to himself. 'She was . . . is . . . pregnant. Does it make any difference?'

He saw Anson Harris glance sideways in startled surprise.

The doctor answered, a shade defensively, 'I had no means of knowing. The pregnancy can't be very far advanced.'

'No.' Demerest avoided the other man's eyes. 'It isn't.' A few minutes earlier he had resolved not to ask the question. Then he decided that he had to know.

Milton Compagno considered. 'It will make no difference to her own ability to recover, of course. As to the child, the mother was not deprived of oxygen long enough to do harm . . . no one was. She has no abdominal injuries.' He stopped, then went on fussily, 'So there should be no effect. Providing Miss Meighen survives – and with prompt hospital treatment her chances are fair to good – the baby should be born normally.'

Demerest nodded without speaking. Dr Compagno, after a moment's hesitation, left.

Briefly, between the two captains, there was a silence. Anson Harris broke it. 'Vernon, I'd like to rest before I make the landing. Will you fly for a while?'

Demerest nodded, his hands and feet moving automatically to the controls. He was grateful for the absence of questioning or comment about Gwen. Whatever Harris was thinking or wondering, he had the decency to keep it to himself.

Harris reached for the clipboard containing Dr Compagno's information. 'I'll send that.' He switched radio receivers to call Trans America dispatch.

For Vernon Demerest the act of flying was a physical relief after the shock and emotion of what he had just heard. Possibly Harris had considered that, possibly not. Either way, it made sense that whoever was in command for the landing should conserve his energies.

As to the landing, hazardous as it was going to be, Anson Harris obviously assumed he would make it. Demerest – on the basis of Harris's performance so far – saw no reason why he should not.

Harris completed his radio call, then eased his seat rearward and allowed his body to rest.

Beside him, Vernon Demerest tried to concentrate solely on flying. He did not succeed. To a pilot of experience and skill, total concentration during level flight – even in difficult circumstances, as now – was neither usual nor necessary. Though he tried to banish or postpone them, thoughts of Gwen persisted.

Gwen . . . whose chance of remaining alive was 'fair to good', who tonight had been bright and beautiful and full of promise, would never go to Naples now, as they had planned . . . Gwen, who an hour or two ago told him in her clear, sweet English voice, *I happen to love you . . . Gwen*, whom he loved in return, despite himself, and why not face it? . . .

With grief and anguish he visualized her – injured, unconscious, *and carrying his child*; the child he urged her to dispose of like an unwanted litter . . . She had replied with spirit, *I was wondering when you'd get around to it* . . . Later she had been troubled. *It's a gift . . . that's great and wonderful. Then suddenly, in our kind of situation you're faced with ending it all, of squandering what was given.*

But eventually, after his persuading, she conceded. *Well, I suppose in the end I'll do what's sensible. I'll have an abortion.*

There would be no abortion now. In the kind of hospital Gwen was going to, it would not be permitted unless as a direct choice between saving the mother or the unborn child. From what Dr Compagno had said, there seemed no likelihood of that; and afterwards it would be too late.

So if Gwen came through, the baby would be born. Was he relieved or sorry? Vernon Demerest wasn't sure.

He remembered somthing else, though, that Gwen had said. *The difference between you and me is that you've had a child . . . whatever happens there's always someone, somewhere, that's you again.*

She had been speaking of the child whom he had never known, even by name; the girl child, born in the limbo of the Trans America 3-PPP arrangements, who had disappeared from sight immediately and for ever. Tonight, under questioning, he admitted that sometimes he wondered about her. What he had not admitted was that he wondered, and remembered, more often than he cared to.

His unknown daughter was eleven years old; Demerest knew her birthday, though he tried not to remember it, but always did, wishing the same thing each year: that there was something he could do – even a simple thing like sending a greeting . . . He supposed it was because he and Sarah had never had a child (though both had wanted children) whose birthday he could share . . . At other times he asked himself questions to which he knew there could be no answers: Where was his daughter? What was she like? Was she happy? Sometimes he looked at children in the streets; if their ages seemed right, he speculated on whether, by merest chance . . . then chided himself for foolishness. Occasionally the thought haunted him that his daughter might be ill-treated, or need help which he had no knowledge or means to give . . . At the instinctive reminder, now, Vernon Demerest's hands tightened on the control yoke.

For the first time he realized: he could never endure the same uncertainty again. His own nature demanded positiveness. He could, and would, have gone through with the abortion because that was final, definite; moreover, nothing Anson Harris had said earlier on that subject had changed his mind. True, he might have doubts, or even sorrow, afterwards. But he would *know*.

The overhead radio speaker cut abruptly through his thoughts. 'Trans America Two, this is Cleveland Centre. Turn left on heading two zero five. Begin descent, when ready, to six thousand. Advise when leaving ten.'

Demerest's hand pulled back all four throttles to begin losing altitude. He reset the flight path indicator and eased into the turn.

'Trans America Two coming on course two zero five,' Anson Harris was advising Cleveland. 'We are leaving ten thousand now.'

The buffeting increased as they descended, but with every minute they were nearer destination and the hope of safety. They were also nearing the air route boundary point where, at any moment, Cleveland would hand them over to Chicago Centre. After that, there would be thirty minutes flying before entering the approach control of Lincoln International.

Harris said quietly, 'Vernon, I guess you know how badly I feel about Gwen.' He hesitated. 'Whatever's between the two of you is none of my business, but if there's anything I can do as a friend . . .'

'There's nothing,' Demerest said. He had no intention of unburdening himself to Anson Harris, who was a competent pilot, but still, in Demerest's eyes, an old maid.

Demerest regretted now that he had revealed as much as he did a few minutes ago, but emotion got the better of him – something which happened rarely. Now, he let his face resume a scowl, his shield against disclosing personal feelings.

'Passing through eight thousand feet,' Anson Harris told air route control.

Demerest continued to hold the aircraft in a steady descent, on course. His eyes swept the flight instruments in consistent sequence.

He remembered something about the child – his child – who had been born eleven years ago. For weeks before the birth, he debated with himself whether he should confess his infidelity to Sarah, with the suggestion that they adopt the baby as their own. In the end, his courage had failed him. He dreaded his wife's shocked reaction; he feared that Sarah would never accept the child, whose presence she would regard as a permanent reproach. Long after, and too late, he realized he had done Sarah an injustice. True, she would have been shocked and hurt, just as she would be shocked and hurt now, if she learned about Gwen. But afterwards, in a short time, Sarah's habit of coping would have taken over. For all Sarah's placidity and what Demerest thought of as her dullness, despite her suburban bourgeois activities – the curling club and amateur oil painting – his wife had a core of sane solidity. He supposed it was why they had stayed married; why, even now, he could not contemplate divorce.

Sarah would have worked something out. She would have made him squirm and suffer for a while, perhaps for a long time. But she would have agreed to the adoption, and the one who would not have suffered at all would have been the child. Sarah would have seen to that; she was that kind of person. He thought: if only . . .

Demerest said aloud, 'Life's full of goddamned "if onlys".'

He levelled out at six thousand feet, advancing the throttles to maintain speed. The jet whine rose in pitch.

Harris had been busy changing radio frequencies and – now they had passed the handoff point – reporting to Chicago Centre. He asked, 'Did you say something?' Demerest shook his head.

The storm's turbulence was as bad as ever, the aircraft still being thrown around.

'Trans America Two, we have you in radar contact,' a new voice from Chicago Centre rasped.

Harris was still attending to communications.

Vernon Demerest reasoned: So far as Gwen was concerned, he might just as well make a decision now.

All right, he decided; he would face Sarah's tears and denunciations, and perhaps her anger, but he would tell her about Gwen.

He would admit his responsibility for Gwen's pregnancy.

At home, the resulting hysteria might last several days, and the after effects for weeks or even months, during which time he would suffer mightily. But when the worst was over they would work something out. Strangely – and he supposed it showed his confidence in Sarah – he had not the slightest doubt they would.

He had no idea what they might do, and a good deal would depend on Gwen. Despite what the doctor had just said about the seriousness of Gwen's injuries, Demerest had a conviction she would come through. Gwen had spunk and courage; even unconsciously she would fight to live, and eventually, whatever impairment she suffered, would adjust to it. She would also have her own ideas about the baby. She might not give it up easily or at all. Gwen was not one to be pushed around, or to be told what to do. She did her own thinking.

The result might be that he would have two women on his hands – plus child – instead of one. *That* would take some working out!

It would also pose the question: just how far would Sarah go?

God – what a mess.

But now that his own first decision was taken, he had the conviction that something good might result. He reflected grimly: For all it was going to cost him, in anguish and hard cash, it better had.

The altimeter showed they were maintaining six thousand feet.

There would be the child, of course. Already he was beginning to think of that part in a new and different way. Naturally, he wouldn't let himself get sickly sentimental, the way some people – Anson Harris, for example – were about children; but it would be his child, after all. The experience would certainly be new.

What was it Gwen had said in the car on their way to the airport tonight? . . . *a little Vernon Demerest inside me. If we had a boy we could call him Vernon Demerest the Second, the way Americans do.*

Maybe it wasn't such a bad idea. He chuckled.

Harris glanced sideways. 'What are you laughing at?'

Demerest exploded. 'I'm not laughing! Why the hell would *I* laugh? What is there for any of us to laugh about?'

Harris shrugged, 'I thought I heard you.'

'That's the second time you've heard things that didn't happen. After this check ride I suggest you have an ear check-up.'

'There's no need to be unpleasant.'

'Isn't there? *Isn't there?*' Demerest came angrily alert. 'Maybe what this whole situation needs is for someone to get unpleasant.'

'If that's true,' Harris said, 'there's no one beter qualified than you.'

'Then when you're through with damnfool questions, start flying again, and let me talk to those duffers on the ground.'

Anson Harris slid his seat forward. 'If you want to, why not?' He nodded. 'I have it.'

Relinquishing the controls, Demerest reached for the radio mike. He felt better, stronger, for a decision taken. Now he would contend with more immediate things. He let his voice grate harshly. 'Chicago Centre, this is Captain Demerest of Trans America Two. Are you still listening down there, or have you taken sleeping pills and quit?'

'This is Chicago Centre, Captain. We're listening, and no one's quit.' The controller's voice held a note of reproach; Demerest ignored it.

'Then why in blazes aren't we getting action? This flight is in serious trouble. We need help.'

'Stand by, please.' There was a pause, then a new voice. 'This is Chicago Centre supervisor. Captain, Trans America Two, I heard your last transmission. Please understand we're doing everything we can. Before you came into our area we had a dozen people working, clearing other traffic. They're still doing it. We're giving you priority, a clear radio frequency, and a straight-in course for Lincoln.'

Demerest barked, 'It isn't enough.' He paused, holding down the mike button, then continued. 'Chicago supervisor, listen carefully. A straight-in course to Lincoln is no good if it ends on runway two five, or any runway except three zero. Don't tell me three zero's out of use; I've heard it already, and I know why. Now, write this down, and see that Lincoln understands it too: This aeroplane is heavily loaded; we'll be landing very fast. As well as that, we've structural damage including unserviceable stabilizer trim and doubtful rudder control. If we're brought in on two five, there'll be a broken aeroplane and dead people before the next hour is over. So call Lincoln, mister, and turn the screws. Tell them I don't care how they do it – they can blow apart what's blocking three zero if they have to – but we need that runway. Do you understand?'

'Yes, Trans America Two, we understand very well.' The supervisor's voice was unruffled, but a shade more human than before. 'Your message is being passed to Lincoln now.'

'Good.' Demerest held the transmit button down again. 'I have another message. This one is to Mel Bakersfeld, airport general manager at Lincoln. Give him the previous message, then add this – personal from his brother-in-law: "You helped make this trouble, you bastard, by not listening to me about airport flight insurance. Now you owe it to me and all others on this flight to climb off your penguin's butt and get that runway clear."'

This time the supervisor's voice was doubtful. 'Trans America Two, we've copied your message. Captain, are you sure you want us to use those words?'

'Chicago Centre,' Demerest's voice slammed back, 'you're damn right you'll use those words! I'm ordering you to send that message – fast, and loud, and clear.'

13

On ground control radio in his speeding car, Mel Bakersfeld could hear airport emergency vehicles being summoned and positioned.

'Ground control to city twenty-five.'

Twenty-five was the call sign of the airport fire chief.

'This is city twenty-five rolling. Go ahead ground.'

'Further information. Category two emergency in approximately thirty-five minutes. The flight in question is disabled and landing on runway three zero, if runway open. If not open, will use runway two five.'

Whenever they could, airport controllers avoided naming, on radio, an airline involved in any accident, or a potential one. The phrase 'the flight in question' was used as a cover. Airlines were touchy about such things, taking the view that the fewer times their name was repeated in that kind of context, the better.

Just the same, Mel was aware, what had happened tonight would get plenty of publicity, most likely worldwide.

'City twenty-five to ground control. Is the pilot requesting foam on runway?'

'No foam. Repeat, no foam.'

The absence of foam meant that the aircraft had serviceable landing gear and would not require a belly landing.

All emergency vehicles, Mel knew – pumpers, salvage trucks, and ambulances – would be following the fire chief, who also had a separate radio channel to communicate with them individually. When an emergency was notified, no one waited. They observed the principle: better to be ready too soon than too late. Emergency crews would now take up position between the two runways, ready to move to either as necessary. The procedure was no improvisation. Every move for situations like this was detailed in an airport emergency master plan.

When there was a break in transmissions, Mel thumbed on his own radio mike.

'Ground control from mobile one.'

'Mobile one, go ahead.'

'Has Joe Patroni, with stalled aircraft on runway three zero, been advised of new emergency situation?'

'Affirmative. We are in radio touch.'

'What is Patroni's report on progress?'

'He expects to move the obstructing aircraft in twenty minutes.'

'Is he certain?'

'Negative.'

Mel Bakersfeld waited before transmitting again. He was heading across the airfield for the second time tonight, one hand on the wheel, the other on the microphone – driving as fast as he dared in the continued blowing snow and restricted visibility. Taxi and runway lights, guidelines in the dark, flashed by. Beside him on the car's front seat were Tanya Livingston and the *Tribune* reporter, Tomlinson.

A few minutes ago, when Tanya had handed Mel her note about the explosion aboard Flight Two, the flight's attempt to reach Lincoln International, Mel had broken free instantly from the crowd of Meadowood residents. With Tanya beside him, he headed for the elevators which would take him to the basement garage two floors below, and his official airport car. Mel's place now was on runway three zero, if necessary to take charge. Shouldering his way through the crowd in the main concourse, he had caught sight of the *Tribune* reporter and said tersely, 'Come with me.' He owed Tomlinson a favour in return for the reporter's tip-off about Elliott Freemantle – both the legal contract form and the lawyer's mendacious statements later, which Mel had been able to repudiate. When Tomlinson hesitated, Mel snapped, 'I haven't time to waste. But I'm giving you a chance you may be sorry for not taking.' Without further questioning, Tomlinson fell in step beside him.

Now, as they drove, Mel accelerating ahead of taxiing aircraft where he could, Tanya repeated the substance of the news about Flight Two.

'Let me get this straight,' Tomlinson said. 'There's only one runway long enough, and facing the right direction?'

Mel said grimly, 'That's the way it is. Even though there should be two.' He was remembering bitterly the proposals he had made, over three successive years, for an additional runway to parallel three zero. The airport needed it. Traffic volume and aircraft safety cried out for implementation of Mel's report, particularly since the runway would take two years to build. But other influences proved stronger. Money had not been found, the new runway had not been built. Nor had construction – despite Mel's further pleas – yet been approved.

With a good many projects, Mel could swing the Board of Airport Commissioners his way. In the case of the proposed new runway, he had canvassed them individually and received promises of support, but later the promises were withdrawn. Theoretically, airport commissioners were independent of political pressure; in fact, they owed their appointments to the mayor and, in most cases, were political partisans themselves. If pressure was put on the mayor to delay an airport bond issue because of other projects, similarly financed and more likely to swing votes, the pressure penetrated through. In the case of the proposed new runway it not only penetrated, but three times had proved effective. Ironically, as Mel remembered earlier tonight, triple-decking of the airport's public parking lots – less necessary, but more visible – had *not* been held up.

Briefly, and in plain words, which until now he had reserved for private sessions, Mel described the situation, including its political overtones.

'I'd like to use all that as coming from you.' Tomlinson's voice held the controlled excitement of a reporter who knew he was on to a good story. 'May I?'

There would be the devil to pay after it appeared in print, Mel realized; he could imagine the indignant telephone calls from City Hall on Monday morning. But someone should say it. The public ought to know how serious the situation was.

'Go ahead,' Mel said. 'I guess I'm in a quoting mood.'

'That's what I thought.' From the far side of the car the reporter regarded Mel quizzically. 'If you don't mind my saying so, you've been in great form tonight. Just now, and with the lawyer and those Meadowood people. More like your old self. I haven't heard you speak out like that in a long while.'

Mel kept his eyes on the taxiway ahead, waiting to pass an Eastern DC-8, which was turning left. But he was thinking: Had his demeanour of the past year or two, the absence of his old fiery spirit, been so obvious that others had noticed it also?

Beside him, close enough so that Mel was conscious of her nearness and warmth, Tanya said softly, 'All the time we're talking . . . about runways, the public, Meadowood, other things . . . I'm thinking about those people on Flight Two. I wonder how they're feeling, if they're afraid.'

'They're afraid, all right,' Mel said. 'If they've any sense, and provided they know what's happening. I'd be afraid, too.'

He was remembering his own fear when he had been trapped in the sinking Navy aeroplane, long ago. As if triggered by memory, he felt a surge of pain around the old wound in his foot. In the past hour's excitement he had adjusted to ignoring it, but as always, with tiredness and overstrain, the effect forced itself on him in the end. Mel compressed his lips tightly and hoped that soon the seizure would lessen or pass.

He had been waiting for another gap in ground-to-ground radio exchanges. As one occurred, Mel depressed his mike button once more.

'Mobile one to ground control. Do you have report on how critical is the requirement of the flight in distress for runway three zero?'

'Mobile one, we understand very critical. Is that Mr Bakersfeld?'

'Yes, it is.'

'Stand by, sir. We're getting more information now.'

Still driving, nearing runway three zero, Mel waited. What came next would determine whether or not to follow the drastic course of action he was contemplating.

'Ground control to mobile one. Following message just received, via Chicago Centre, from flight in question. Message begins. Straight-in course to Lincoln no good if ends on runway two five. Aeroplane heavily loaded, will be landing very fast . . .'

The trio in the car listened tensely to the report of Vernon Demerest's message. At the words, 'If we're brought in on two five there'll be a broken aeroplane and dead people', Mel heard Tanya's sharp intake of breath, felt her shudder beside him.

He was about to acknowledge when ground control transmitted again.

'Mobile one – Mr Bakersfeld, there is an addition to previous message, personal to you, from your brother-in-law. Can you reach a phone?'

'Negative,' Mel said. 'Read it now, please.'

'Mobile one' – he sensed the controller hesitate – 'the language is very personal.'

The controller was aware – as Mel was – that many ears around the airport would be listening.

'Does it concern the present situation?'

'Affirmative.'

'Then read it.'

'Yes, sir. Message begins. "You helped make this trouble, you bastard, by not listening to me about airport flight insurance . . ." '

Mel's mouth tightened, but he waited to the end, then acknowledged non-committally, 'Roger, out.' He was sure that Vernon had enjoyed sending the message, as much as anything could be enjoyed aboard Flight Two at present, and would be even more pleased to learn the way it was received.

The extra message was unnecessary, though. Mel had already made his decision on the basis of the first.

His car was now speeding down runway three zero. The circle of floodlights and vehicles surrounding the mired Aéreo-Mexican 707 jet were coming into sight. Mel noted approvingly that the runway was only lightly snow-covered. Despite the blockage of one portion, the remainder had been kept ploughed.

He switched his radio to the frequency of airport maintenance.

'Mobile one to Snow Desk.'

'This is Snow Desk.' Danny Farrow's voice sounded tired, which was not surprising. 'Go ahead.'

'Danny,' Mel said, 'break the Conga Line. Send the Oshkosh ploughs and heavy graders across to runway three zero. They're to head for where the stuck aeroplane is, and await instructions. Get them started now, then call me back.'

'Roger, wilco.' Danny seemed about to add a question, then apparently changed his mind. A moment later, on the same frequency, the occupants of the car heard him issue orders to the Conga Line convoy leader.

The *Tribune* reporter leaned forward around Tanya.

'I'm still fitting pieces together,' Tomlinson said. 'That bit about flight insurance . . . Your brother-in-law's an Air Line Pilots Association wheel, isn't he?'

'Yes.' Mel halted the car on the runway, a few feet short of the circle of lights around the big, stalled aircraft. There was plenty of action, he could see; beneath the aircraft fuselage, and on both sides, men were digging feverishly. The stocky form of Joe Patroni was visible directing activities. In a moment Mel would join him, after the return radio call from Danny Farrow at the Snow Desk.

The reporter said thoughtfully, 'I think I heard something a while back. Didn't your brother-in-law make a big play to cancel insurance vending here – the way ALPA wants to – and you turned him down?'

'I didn't turn him down. The airport board did, though I agreed with them.'

'If it isn't an unfair question, has what's happened tonight made you change your mind?'

Tanya protested, 'Surely this isn't the time . . .'

'I'll answer that,' Mel said. 'I haven't changed my mind, at least not yet. But I'm thinking about it.'

Mel reasoned: the time for a change of heart about flight insurance – if there was to be one – was not now, in the height of emotion and the wake of tragedy. In a day or two, what had occurred tonight would be seen in better perspective. Mel's own decision – whether to urge the airport board to revise its policy, or not, should be made then. Meanwhile, no one could deny that tonight's events added strength to Vernon Demerest's – and the Air Line Pilots Association – arguments.

Possibly, Mel supposed, a compromise might be worked out. An ALPA spokesman once confided to him that the pilots did not expect their anti-airport insurance campaign to be won, either outright or quickly; success would take years and 'would have to be cut like bologna – a slice at a time'. One slice at Lincoln International might be to prohibit use of non-supervised insurance vending machines, as some airports have already done. One state – Colorado – had already outlawed the machines by Legislative Act. Other states, Mel knew, were considering similar legislation, though there was nothing to stop airports, meanwhile, from acting on their own.

It was the insurance vending machine system which Mel liked least, even though D. O. Guerrero's huge insurance policy tonight had not been bought that way. Then, if over-the-counter sales remained – for a few more years until public opinion could be moulded – there would have to be more safeguards . . .

Even though Mel had resolved not to make a firm decision, it was obvious to himself which way his reasoning was going.

The radio, still tuned to airport maintenance frequency, had been busy with calls between vehicles. Now it announced, 'Snow Desk to mobile one.'

Mel responded, 'Go ahead, Danny.'

'Four ploughs, and three graders, with convoy leader, are on their way to runway three zero as instructed. What orders, please?'

Mel chose his words carefully, aware that somewhere in an electronic maze beneath the control tower they were being recorded on tape. Later he might have to justify them. He also wanted to be sure there was no misunderstanding.

'Mobile one to Snow Desk. All ploughs and graders, under direction of convoy leader, will stand by near Aéreo-Mexican aircraft which is blocking runway three zero. Vehicles are not, repeat not, initially to obstruct the aircraft, which in a few minutes will attempt to move under its own power. But if that attempt fails, ploughs and graders will be ordered in to push the aircraft sideways, and to clear the runway. This will be done at any cost, and with all speed. Runway three zero must be open for use in approximately thirty minutes, by which time the obstructing aircraft and all vehicles must be clear. I will co-ordinate with air-traffic control to decide at what time the ploughs will be ordered in, if necessary. Acknowledge, and confirm that these instructions are understood.'

Inside the car the reporter, Tomlinson, whistled softly. Tanya turned towards Mel, her eyes searching his face.

On radio there were several seconds' silence, then Danny Farrow's voice. 'I guess I understand. But I'd better be sure.' He repeated the gist of the message, and Mel could imagine Danny sweating again, as he had been earlier.

'Roger,' Mel acknowledged. 'But be clear about one thing. If those ploughs and graders go in, I'll give the order; no one else.'

'It's clear,' Danny radioed. 'And better you than me. Mel, I guess you've figured what that equipment of ours'll do to a 707.'

'It'll move it,' Mel said tersely. 'Right now that's the important thing.' He signed off, and replaced the mike.

Tomlinson said incredulously, 'Move it! A six-million dollar aeroplane shoved sideways by snowploughs! My God, you'll tear it to pieces! And afterwards, the owners and insurers'll do the same to you.'

'I wouldn't be surprised,' Mel said. 'Of course, a lot depends on your point of view. If the owners and insurers were on that other flight coming in, they might be cheering.'

'Well,' the reporter conceded, 'I'll grant you there are some decisions that take a lot of guts.'

Tanya's hand reached down beside her and found Mel's. She said softly, emotion in her voice, 'I'm cheering – for what you're doing now. Whatever happens after, I'll remember.'

The ploughs and graders which Mel had summoned were coming into sight, travelling fast down the runway, roof beacons flashing.

'It may never happen.' Mel squeezed Tanya's hand before releasing it, then opened the car door. 'We've twenty minutes to hope it won't.'

When Mel Bakersfeld approached him, Joe Patroni was stomping his feet in an effort to be warm; the effort was largely unsuccessful despite the fleece-lined boots and heavy parka the TWA maintenance chief was wearing. Apart from the brief time Patroni had spent on the aircraft flight deck when the Aéreo-Mexican captain and first officer departed, he had been continuously out in the storm since his arrival on the scene more than three hours ago. As well as being cold and physically tired from his various exertions of the day and night, his failure to move the stranded jet despite two attempts so far, had made his temper ready to erupt.

It almost did, at the news of Mel's intention.

With anyone else, Joe Patroni would have stormed and ranted. Because Mel was a close friend, Patroni removed the unlighted cigar he had been chewing, and eyed Mel unbelievingly. 'Shove an undamaged aeroplane with snow ploughs! Are you out of your mind?'

'No,' Mel said. 'I'm out of runways.'

Mel felt a momentary depression at the thought that no one in authority, other than himself, seemed to understand the urgency of clearing three zero, at any cost. Obviously, if he went ahead as he intended, there would be few who would support his action afterwards. On the other hand, Mel had not the least doubt there would be plenty of people tomorrow with hindsight – including Aéreo-Mexican officials – who would assert he could have done this or that, or that Flight Two should have landed on runway two five after all. Obviously his decision was to be a lonely one. It did not change Mel's conviction that it should be made.

At the sight of the assembled ploughs and graders, now deployed in line on the runway, to their right, Patroni dropped his cigar altogether. As he produced another he growled, 'I'll save you from your own insanity. Keep those Dinky Toys of yours out of my hair and away from this aeroplane. In fifteen minutes, maybe less, I'll drive it out.'

Mel shouted to make himself heard above the wind and roaring engines of vehicles around them. 'Joe, let's be clear about one thing: When the tower tells us we're running out of time, that's it; there'll be no argument. People's lives are involved on the flight that's coming in. If you've engines running, they're to be shut down. At the same time, all equipment and the men must move clear immediately. Make sure in advance that all your people understand. The ploughs will move on my order. If and when they do, they won't waste time.'

Patroni nodded gloomily. Despite his outburst, Mel thought, the maintenance chief's usual cocky self-assurance seemed abated.

Mel returned to his car. Tanya and the reporter, huddled in their coats, had been standing outside, watching the work of digging around the aircraft. They got into the car with him, grateful for the warmth inside.

Once more, Mel called ground control on radio, this time asking for the tower watch chief. After a brief pause, the tower chief's voice came on the air.

In a few words Mel explained his intention. What he sought from air traffic control now was an estimate of how long he could wait before ordering the ploughs and graders to move. Once they did, it would take only minutes to have the obstructing aircraft clear.

'The way it looks now,' the tower chief said, 'the flight in question will be here sooner than we thought. Chicago Centre expects to hand over to our approach control in twelve minutes from now. After that we'll be controlling the flight for eight to ten minutes before landing, which would make time of touchdown, at latest, 01.28.'

Mel checked his watch in the dim light from the dash. It showed 01.01 am.

'A choice of which runway to use,' the tower chief said, 'will have to be made no later than five minutes before landing. After that, they'll be committed; we can't turn them.'

So what it meant, Mel calculated, was that his own final decision must be made in another seventeen minutes, perhaps less, depending on the handover time from Chicago Centre to Lincoln approach control. There was even less time remaining than he had told Joe Patroni.

Mel found he, too, was beginning to sweat.

Should he warn Patroni again, informing him of the reduced time? Mel decided not. The maintenance chief was already directing operations at the fastest pace he could. Nothing would be gained by harassing him further.

'Mobile one to ground control,' Mel radioed. 'I'll need to be kept informed of exact status of the approaching flight. Can we hold this frequency clear?'

'Affirmative,' the tower chief said. 'We've already moved regular traffic to another frequency. We'll keep you informed.'

Mel acknowledged and signed off.

Beside him, Tanya asked, 'What happens now?'

'We wait.' Mel checked his watch again.

A minute went by. Two.

Outside they could see men working, still digging feverishly near the front and on each side of the mired aircraft. With a flash of headlights, another truck arrived; men jumped down from its tailgate and hastened to join the others. Joe Patroni's stocky figure was moving constantly, instructing and exhorting.

The ploughs and graders were still in line, waiting. In a way, Mel thought, like vultures.

The reporter, Tomlinson, broke the silence inside the car.

'I was just thinking. When I was a kid, which isn't all that long ago, most of this place was fields. In summer there were cows and corn and barley. There was a grass airfield; small; nobody thought it would amount to much. If anyone travelled by air, they used the airport in the city.'

'That's aviation,' Tanya said. She felt a momentary relief at being able to think and talk of something other than what they were waiting for. She went on, 'Somebody told me once that working in aviation makes a lifetime seem longer because everything changes so often and so fast.'

Tomlinson objected, 'Not everything's fast. With airports, the changes aren't fast enough. Isn't it true, Mr Bakersfeld, that within three to four years there'll be chaos?'

'Chaos is always relative,' Mel said; the focus of his mind was still on the scene he could see through the car windshield. 'In a good many ways we manage to live with it.'

'Aren't you dodging the question?'

'Yes,' he conceded. 'I suppose I am.'

It was scarcely surprising, Mel thought. He was less concerned with aviation philosophy at this moment than with the immediacy of what was happening outside. But he sensed Tanya's need for a lessening of tension, even if illusory; his awareness of her feelings was part of the empathy they seemed increasingly to share. He reminded himself, too, that it was a Trans America flight they were waiting for, and which might land safely or might not. Tanya was a part of Trans America, had helped with the flight's departure. In a real sense, of the three of them, she had the most direct involvement.

With an effort he concentrated on what Tomlinson had said.

'It's always been true,' Mel declared, 'that in aviation, progress in the air has been ahead of progress on the ground. We sometimes think we'll catch up; in the mid-1960s we almost did; but by and large we never do. The best we can manage, it seems, is not to lag too far behind.'

The reporter persisted, 'What *should* we do about airports? What *can* we do?'

'We can think more freely, with more imagination, for one thing. We should get rid of the railway station mind.'

'You believe we still have it?'

Mel nodded. 'Unfortunately, in a good many places. All our early airports were imitation railway stations because designers had to draw on experience from somewhere, and railroad experience was all they had. Afterwards, the habit remained. It's the reason, nowadays, we have so many "straight line" airports, where terminals stretch on and on, and passengers must walk for miles.'

Tomlinson asked, 'Isn't some of that changing?'

'Slowly, and in just a few places.' As always, despite the pressures of the moment, Mel was warming to his theme. 'A few airports are being built as circles – like doughnuts; with car parking inside, instead of somewhere out beyond; with minimum distances for people to walk; with aids like high-speed horizontal elevators; with aeroplanes brought close to passengers instead of the other way around. What it means is that airports are finally being thought of as special and distinct; also as units instead of separate components. Creative ideas, even outlandish ones, are being listened to. Los Angeles is proposing a big offshore seadrome; Chicago, a man-made airport island in Lake Michigan; nobody's scoffing. American Airlines has a plan for a giant hydraulic lift to stack aeroplanes one above the other for loading and unloading. But the changes are slow, they're not co-ordinated; we build airports like an unimaginative patchwork quilt. It's as if phone subscribers designed and made their own telephones, then plugged them into a world-wide system.'

The radio cut abruptly across Mel's words. 'Ground control to mobile one and city twenty-five. Chicago Centre now estimates handoff of the flight in question to Lincoln approach control will be 01.17.'

Mel's watch showed 1.06 am. The message meant that Flight Two was already a minute earlier than the tower chief had forecast. A minute less for Joe Patroni to work; only eleven minutes to Mel's own decision.

'Mobile one, is there any change in the status of runway three zero?'

'Negative; no change.'

Mel wondered: was he cutting things too fine? He was tempted to direct the snow ploughs and graders to move now, then restrained himself. Responsibility was a two-way street, especially when it came to ordering the near-destruction of a six-million dollar aircraft on the ground. There was still a chance that Joe Patroni might make it, though with every second the possibility was lessening. In front of the stalled 707, Mel could see, some of the floodlights and other equipment were being moved clear. But the aircraft's engines had not yet been started.

'Those creative people,' Tomlinson queried, 'the ones you were talking about. Who are they?'

With only half his mind, Mel acknowledged, 'It's hard to make a list.'

He was watching the scene outside. The remainder of the vehicles and equipment in front of the stalled Aéreo-Mexican 707 had now been moved clear, and Joe Patroni's stocky, snow-covered figure was climbing the boarding ramp, positioned near the aircraft's nose. Near the top, Patroni stopped, turned, and gestured; he appeared to be shouting to others below. Now Patroni opened the front fuselage door and went inside; almost at once another, slighter figure climbed the ramp and followed him. The aircraft door slammed. Others below trundled the ramp away.

Inside the car, the reporter asked again, 'Mr Bakersfeld, could you name a few of those people – the most imaginative ones about airports and the future?'

Yes,' Tanya said, 'couldn't you?'

Mel thought: it would be like a parlour game while the house was burning. All right, he decided; if Tanya wanted him to, he would play.

'I can think of some,' Mel said. 'Fox of Los Angeles; Joseph Foster of Houston, now with ATA of America. Alan Boyd in government; and Thomas Sullivan, Port of New York Authority. In the airlines: Halaby of Pan Am; Herb Godfrey of United. In Canada, John C. Parkin. In Europe – Pierre Cot of Air France; Count Castell in Germany. There are others.'

'Including Mel Bakersfeld,' Tanya injected. 'Aren't you forgetting him?'

Tomlinson, who had been making notes, grunted. 'I already put him down. It goes without saying.'

Mel smiled. But did it, he wondered, go without saying? Once, not long ago, the statement would have been true; but he knew that on the national scene he had slipped from view. When that happened, when you left the mainstream for whatever reason, you were apt to be forgotten quickly; and later, even if you wanted to, sometimes you never did get back. It was not that he was doing a less important job at Lincoln International, or doing it less well; as an airport general manager, Mel knew he was as good as ever, probably better. But the big contribution which he had once seemed likely to make no longer was in view. He realized that this was the second time tonight the same thought had occurred to him. Did it matter? Did he care? He decided; Yes, he did!

'Look!' Tanya cried out. 'They're starting the engines.'

The reporter's head came up; Mel felt his own excitement sharpen.

Behind number three engine of the Aéreo-Mexican 707, a puff of white-grey smoke appeared. Briefly it intensified, then whirled away as the engine fired and held. Now snow was streaming rearward in the jet blast.

A second puff of smoke appeared behind number four engine, a moment later to be whisked away, snow following.

'Ground control to mobile one and city twenty-five.' Within the car the radio voice was so unexpected that Mel felt Tanya give a startled jump beside him. 'Chicago Centre advises revised handoff time of the flight in question will be 01.16 . . . seven minutes from now.'

Flight Two, Mel realized, was still coming in faster than expected. It meant they had lost another minute. A minute less for Joe Patroni to attempt to move the Aéreo-Mexican jet under its owner power; seven minutes only to Mel's decision on whether or not to use brute force and wreck an undamaged airliner to clear the runway.

Again Mel held his watch near the light of the dash.

275

On the soft ground near the opposite side of the runway from their car, Patroni now had number two engine started. Number one followed. Mel said softly, 'They could still make it.' Then he remembered that all engines had been started twice before tonight, and both attempts to blast the stuck aeroplane free had failed.

In front of the mired 707 a solitary figure with flashlight signal wands had moved out ahead to where he could be seen from the aircraft flight deck. The man with the wands was holding them above his head, indicating 'all clear'. Mel could hear and feel the jet engines' thrum, but sensed they had not yet been advanced in power.

Six minutes left. *Why hadn't Patroni opened up?*

Tanya said tensely, 'I don't think I can bear the waiting.'

The reporter shifted in his seat. 'I'm sweating, too.'

Joe Patroni was opening up! This was it! Mel could hear and feel the greater all encompassing roar of engines. Behind the stalled Aéreo-Mexican jet, great gusts of snow were blowing wildly into the darkness beyond the runway lights.

'Mobile one,' the radio demanded sharply, 'this is ground control. Is there any change in status of runway three zero?'

Patroni, Mel calculated by his watch, had three minutes left.

'The aeroplane's still stuck.' Tanya was peering intently through the car windshield. 'They're using all the engines, but it isn't moving.'

It was straining forward, though; that much Mel could see, even through the blowing snow. But Tanya was right. The aircraft wasn't moving.

The snowploughs and heavy graders had shifted closer together, their beacons flashing brightly.

'Hold it!' Mel said on radio. 'Hold it! Don't commit that flight coming in to runway two five. One way or the other, there'll be a change in three zero status any moment now.'

He switched the car radio to Snow Desk frequency, ready to activate the ploughs.

14

Ordinarily, after midnight, pressures in air traffic control relented slightly. Tonight they hadn't. Because of the storm, airlines at Lincoln International were continuing to dispatch and receive flights which were hours late. More often than not, their lateness was added to by the general runway and taxiway congestion still prevailing.

Most members of the earlier eight-hour watch in air traffic control had ended their shift at midnight and gone wearily home. Newcomers on duty had taken their place. A few controllers, because of staff shortage and illness of others, had been assigned a spreadover shift which would end at 2 am. They included the tower watch chief; Wayne Tevis, the radar supervisor; and Keith Bakersfeld.

Since the emotion-charged session with his brother, which ended abruptly and abortively an hour and a half ago, Keith had sought relief of mind by concentrating intensely on the radar screen in front of him. If he could maintain his concentration, he thought, the remaining time – the last he would ever have to fill – would pass quickly. Keith had continued handling east arrivals, working with a young assistant – a radar handoff man – seated on his left. Wayne Tevis was still supervising, riding his castor-equipped stool around the control room, propelled by his Texan boots, though less energetically, as Tevis's own duty shift neared an end.

In one sense, Keith had succeeded in his concentration; yet in a strange way he had not. It seemed almost as if his mind had split into two levels, like a duplex, and he was able to be in both at once. On one level he was directing east arrivals traffic – at the moment, without problems. On the other, his thoughts were personal and introspective. It was not a condition which could last, but perhaps, Keith thought, his mind was like a light bulb about to fail and, for its last few minutes, burning brightest.

The personal side of his thoughts was dispassionate now, and calmer than before; perhaps the session with Mel had achieved that, if nothing more. All things seemed ordained and settled. Keith's duty shift would end; he would leave this place; soon after, all waiting and all anguish would be over. He had the conviction that his own life and others were already severed; he no longer belonged to Natalie or Mel, or Brian and Theo . . . or they to him. He belonged to the already dead – to the Redferns who had died together in the wreck of their Beech Bonanza; to little Valerie . . . her family. *That was it!* Why had he never thought of it that way before; realized that his own death was a debt he owed the Redferns? With continued dispassion, Keith wondered if he were insane; people who chose suicide were said to be, but either way it made no difference. His choice was between torment and peace; and before the light of morning, peace would come. Once more, as intermittently in the past few hours, his hand went into his pocket, fingering the key to room 224 of the O'Hagan Inn.

All the while, on the other mental level, and with traces of his old flair, he coped with east arrivals.

Awareness of the crisis with Trans America Flight Two came to Keith gradually.

Lincoln air traffic control had been advised of Flight Two's intention to return there – almost an hour ago, and seconds after Captain Anson Harris's decision was made known. Word had come by 'hot line' telephone directly from Chicago Centre supervisor to the tower watch chief, after similar notification through Cleveland and Toronto centres. Initially there had been little to do at Lincoln beyond advising the airport management, through the Snow Desk, of the flight's request for runway three zero.

Later, when Flight Two had been taken over from Cleveland, by Chicago Centre, more specific preparations were begun.

Wayne Tevis, the radar supervisor, was alerted by the tower chief, who went personally to the radar room to inform Tevis of Flight Two's condition, its estimated arrival time, and the doubt about which runway – two five or three zero – was to be used for landing.

At the same time, ground control was notifying airport emergency services to stand by, and shortly after, to move with their vehicles on to the airfield.

A ground controller talked by radio telephone with Joe Patroni to check that Patroni had been advised of the urgent need for runway three zero. He had.

Contact was then established, on a reserve radio frequency, between the control tower and the flight deck of the Aéreo-Mexican jet which blocked the runway. The set-up was to ensure that when Patroni was at the aircraft's controls, there could be instant two-way communication, if needed.

In the radar room, when he had listened to the tower chief's news, Wayne Tevis's initial reaction was to glance at Keith. Unless duties were changed around, it would be Keith, in charge of east arrivals, who would accept Flight Two from Chicago Centre, and monitor the flight in.

Tevis asked the tower chief quietly, 'Should we take Keith off; put someone else on?'

The older man hesitated. He remembered the earlier emergency tonight involving the Air Force KC-135. He had removed Keith from duty then, on a pretext, and afterwards wondered if he had been too hasty. When a man was teeter-tottering between self-assurance and the loss of it, it was easy to send the scales the wrong way without intending to. The tower chief had an uneasy feeling, too, of having blundered into something private between Keith and Mel Bakersfeld when the two of them were talking earlier in the corridor outside. He could have left them alone for a few minutes longer, but hadn't.

The tower watch chief was tired himself, not only from the trying shift tonight, but from others which preceded it. He remembered reading somewhere recently that new air traffic systems, being readied for the mid-1970s, would halve controllers' work loads, thereby reducing occupational fatigue and nervous breakdowns. The tower chief remained sceptical. He doubted if, in air traffic control, pressures would ever lighten; if they eased in one way, he thought, they would increase in another. It made him sympathize with those who, like Keith – still gaunt, pale, strained – had proved victims of the system.

Still in an undertone, Wayne Tevis repeated, 'Do I take him off, or not?'

The tower chief shook his head. Low-voiced, he answered, 'Let's not push it. Keep Keith on, but stay close.'

It was then that Keith, observing the two with heads together, guessed that something critical was coming up. He was, after all, an old hand, familiar with signals of impending trouble.

Instinct told him, too, that the supervisors' conversation was, in part, about himself. He could understand why. Keith had no doubt he would be relieved from duty in a few minutes from now, or shifted to a less vital radar position. He found himself not caring.

It was a surprise when Tevis – without shuffling duties – began warning all watch positions of the expected arrival of Trans America Two, in distress, and its priority handling.

Departure control was cautioned: Route all departures well clear of the flight's anticipated route in.

To Keith, Tevis expounded the runway problem – the uncertainty of which runway was to be used, and the need to postpone a decision until the last possible moment.

'You work out your own plan, buddy boy,' Tevis instructed in his nasal Texas drawl. 'And after the handover, stay with it. We'll take everything else off your hands.'

At first, Keith nodded agreement, no more perturbed than he had been before. Automatically, he began to calculate the flight pattern he would use. Such plans were always worked out mentally. There was never time to commit them to paper; besides, the need for improvisation usually turned up.

As soon as he received the flight from Chicago Centre, Keith reasoned, he would head it generally towards runway three zero, but with sufficient leeway to swing the aircraft left – though without drastic turns at low altitude – if runway two five was forced on them as the final choice.

He calculated: He would have the aircraft under approach control for approximately ten minutes. Tevis had already advised him that not until the last five, probably, would they know for sure about the runway. It was slicing things fine, and there would be sweating in the radar room, as well as in the air. But it could be managed – just. Once more, in his mind, Keith went over the planned flight path and compass headings.

By then, more definite reports had begun to filter, unofficially, through the tower. Controllers passed information to each other as work gaps permitted . . . The flight had had a mid-air explosion. It was limping in with structural damage and injured people . . . Control of the aeroplane was in doubt. The pilots needed the longest runway – which might or might not be available . . . Captain Demerest's warning was repeated: . . . *on two five a broken aeroplane and dead people* . . . The captain had sent a savage message to the airport manager. Now, the manager was out on three zero, trying to get the runway cleared . . . The time available was shortening.

Even among the controllers, to whom tension was as commonplace as traffic, there was now a shared nervous anxiety.

Keith's radar handoff man, seated alongside, passed on the news which came to him in snatches. As he did Keith's awareness and apprehension grew. *He didn't want this, or any part of it!* There was nothing he sought to prove, or could; nothing he might retrieve, even if he handled the situation well. And if he didn't, if he mishandled it, he might send a planeload of people to their deaths, *as he had done once before already.*

Across the radar room, on a direct line, Wayne Tevis took a telephone call from the tower watch chief. A few minutes ago the chief had gone one floor above, into the tower cab, to remain beside the ground controller.

Hanging up, Tevis propelled his chair alongside Keith. 'The old man just had word from centre. Trans America Two – three minutes from handoff.'

The supervisor moved on to departure control, checking that outward traffic was being routed clear of the approaching flight.

The man on Keith's left reported that out on the airfield they were still trying frantically to shift the stranded jet blocking runway three zero. They had the engines running, but the aeroplane wouldn't move. Keith's brother (the handoff man said) had taken charge, and if the aeroplane wouldn't move on its own, was going to smash it to pieces to clear the runway. But everybody was asking: was there time?

If Mel thought so, Keith reasoned, there probably was. Mel coped, he managed things; he always had. Keith couldn't cope – at least, not always, and never in the same way as Mel. It was the difference between them.

Almost two minutes had gone by.

Alongside Keith, the handoff man said quietly, 'They're coming on the scope.' On the edge of the radarscope Keith could see the double blossom radar distress signal – unmistakably Trans America Two.

Keith wanted out! He couldn't do it! Someone else must take over; Wayne Tevis could himself. There was still time.

Keith swung away from the scope looking for Tevis. The supervisor was at departure control, his back towards Keith.

Keith opened his mouth to call. To his horror, no words came. He tried again . . . the same.

He realized: It was as in the dream, his nightmare; his voice had failed him . . . But this was no dream; this was reality! *Wasn't it?* . . . Still struggling to articulate, panic gripped him.

On a panel above the scope, a flashing white light indicated that Chicago Centre was

calling. The handoff man picked up a direct line phone and instructed, 'Go ahead, centre.'
He turned a selector, cutting in a speaker overhead so that Keith could hear.

'Lincoln, Trans America Two is thirty miles southeast of the airport. He's on a heading
of two five zero.'

'Roger, centre. We have him in radar contact. Change him to our frequency.' The
handoff man replaced the phone.

Centre, they knew, would now be instructing the flight to change radio frequency, and
probably wishing them good luck. It usually happened that way when an aircraft was in
trouble; it seemed the least that anyone could do from the secure comfort of the ground.
In this isolated, comfortably warm room of low-key sounds, it was difficult to accept that
somewhere outside, high in the night and darkness, buffeted by wind and storm, its
survival in doubt, a crippled airliner was battling home.

The east arrivals radio frequency came alive. A harsh voice, unmistakably Vernon
Demerest's; Keith hadn't thought about that until this moment. 'Lincoln approach
control, this is Trans America Two, maintaining six thousand feet, heading two five zero.'

The handoff man was waiting expectantly. It was Keith's moment to acknowledge, to
take over. *But he wanted out!* Wayne Tevis was still turned away! Keith's speech wouldn't
come.

'Lincoln approach control,' the voice from Trans America Two grated again, 'where in
hell are you?'

Where in hell . . .

Why wouldn't Tevis turn?

Keith seethed with sudden rage. *Damn Tevis! Damn air traffic control! Damn his dead
father, Wild Blue Bakersfeld, who led his sons into a vocation Keith hadn't wanted to begin with!
Damn Mel, with his infuriating self-sufficient competence! Damn here and now! Damn
everything!* . . .

The handoff man was looking at Keith curiously. At any moment Trans America Two
would call again. Keith knew that he was trapped. Wondering if his voice would work, he
keyed his mike.

'Trans America Two,' Keith said, 'this is Lincoln approach control. Sorry about the
delay. We're still hoping for runway three zero; we shall know in three to five minutes.'

A growled acknowledgement, 'Roger, Lincoln. Keep us informed.'

Keith was concentrating now; the extra level of his mind had closed. He forgot Tevis,
his father, Mel, himself. All else was excluded but the problem of Flight Two.

He radioed clearly and quietly, 'Trans America Two, you are now twenty-five miles east
of the outer marker. Begin descent at your discretion. Start a right turn to heading two six
zero . . .'

One floor above Keith, in the glass-walled tower cab, the ground controller had advised
Mel Bakersfeld that handoff from Chicago Centre had occurred.

Mel radioed back, 'Snowploughs and graders have been ordered to move, and clear the
Aéreo-Mexican aircraft from the runway. Instruct Patroni to shut down all engines
immediately. Tell him – if he can, get clear himself; if not, hold on tight. Stand by for
advice when runway is clear.'

On a second frequency, the tower chief was already informing Joe Patroni.

15

Even before it happened, Joe Patroni knew he was running out of time.

He had deliberately not started the engines of the Aéreo-Mexican 707 until the latest possible moment, wanting the work of clearing under and around the aircraft to continue as long as it could.

When he realized that he could wait no longer, Patroni made a final inspection. What he saw gave him grave misgivings.

The landing gear was still not as clear from surrounding earth, mud, and snow as it should be. Nor were the trenches, inclining upwards from the present level of the main wheels to the hard surface of the nearby taxiway, as wide or deep as he had wanted. Another fifteen minutes would have done it.

Patroni knew he didn't have the time.

Reluctantly he ascended the boarding ramp, to make his second attempt at moving the mired aircraft, now with himself at the controls.

He shouted to Ingram, the Aéreo-Mexican foreman, 'Get everybody clear! We're starting up.'

From under the aircraft, figures began to move out.

Snow was still falling, but more lightly than for several hours.

Joe Patroni called again from the boarding ramp. 'I need somebody with me on the flight deck, but let's keep the weight down. Send me a skinny guy who's cockpit qualified.'

He let himself into the aircraft's forward door.

Inside, through the flight deck windows, Patroni could see Mel Bakersfeld's airport car, its bright yellow colouring reflected through the darkness. The car was parked on the runway, to the left. Near it was the line of snowploughs and graders – a reminder, if he needed one, that he had only a few minutes more.

The maintenance chief had reacted with shocked disbelief when Mel announced his plan to shove the Aéreo-Mexican aircraft clear of runway three zero by force, if necessary. The reaction was natural, but was not through indifference to the safety of those aboard Trans America Flight Two. Joe Patroni lived with thoughts of aircraft safety, which was the object of his daily work. It was simply that the idea of reducing an undamaged aircraft to a pile of scrap metal, or something close to it, was near-impossible for him to grasp. In Patroni's eyes, an aircraft – any aircraft – represented devotion, skill, engineering know-how, hours of labour, and sometimes love. Almost anything was better than its deliberate destruction. *Almost* anything.

Patroni intended to save the aeroplane if he could.

Behind him, the fuselage door opened, and slammed closed.

A young mechanic, small and spare, came forward to the flight deck, shedding snow. Joe Patroni had already slipped off his parka and was strapping himself into the left seat.

'What's your name, son?'

'Rolling, sir.'

Patroni chuckled. 'That's what we're trying to get this aeroplane doin'. Maybe you're an omen.'

281

As the mechanic removed his own parka and slid into the right seat, Patroni looked through the window behind his left shoulder. Outside, the boarding ramp was being trundled clear.

The interphone chimed, and Patroni answered. The foreman, Ingram, was calling from below. 'Ready to start when you are.'

Joe Patroni glanced sideways. 'All set, son?'

The mechanic nodded.

'Number three starter switch – ground start.'

The mechanic snapped a switch; Patroni ordered on interphone, 'Pressurize the manifold!'

From a power cart below, air under pressure whined. The maintenance chief moved a start lever to 'idle'; the young mechanic, monitoring instruments, reported, 'Light-up on number three.' The engine note became a steady roar.

In smooth succession, engines four, two, and one followed.

On interphone, Ingram's voice was diminished by a background of wind and jet whine. 'Power cart's clear. So's everything else down here.'

'Okay,' Patroni shouted back. 'Disconnect interphone, and get the hell clear yourself.'

He told his cockpit companion, 'Sit tight son, and hang on.' The maintenance chief shifted his cigar, which contrary to regulations he had lighted a few minutes earlier, so that it was now jauntily in a corner of his mouth. Then, with chunky fingers spread, he eased the four main throttles forward.

With power at midpoint, the clamour of all four engines grew.

Ahead of the aircraft, in the snow, they could see a ground crewman with raised, lighted signal wands. Patroni grinned. 'If we come out fast, I hope that guy's a good runner.'

All brakes were off, flaps slightly down to engender lift. The mechanic held the control yoke back. Patroni worked the rudder controls alternately, hoping by sideways strain to help the aeroplane forward.

Glancing left, he saw Mel Bakersfeld's car was still in position. From an earlier calculation, Joe Patroni knew there could be only minutes – perhaps less than a minute – left.

Now, power was past three quarters. From the high-pitched note of engines, he could tell it was more power than the Aéreo-Mexican captain had used during the earlier attempt to get free. Vibration told why. Normally, at this setting, the aeroplane would be unimpeded, bowling fast down a runway. Because it was not, it was shaking severely, with every portion of its upper area straining forward, resisting the anchoring effect of the wheels below. The aeroplane's inclination to stand on its nose was unmistakable. The mechanic glanced uneasily sideways.

Patroni saw the glance and grunted. 'She'd better come out now, or she's a dead duck.'

But the aircraft was not moving. Obstinately, as it had for hours, and through two earlier attempts, it was remaining stuck.

In the hope of rocking the wheels free, Patroni slackened engine power, then increased it.

Still the aircraft failed to move.

Joe Patroni's cigar, moist from previous chewing, had gone out. Disgustedly, he flung it down and reached for another. His breast pocket was empty; the cigar had been his last.

He swore, and returned his right hand to the throttles. Moving them still farther forward, he snarled, 'Come out! Come out, you son of a bitch!'

'Mr Patroni!' the mechanic warned. 'She won't take much more.'

Abruptly, the overhead radio speakers came alive. The tower chief's voice. 'Joe Patroni, aboard Aéreo-Mexican. This is ground control. We have a message from Mr Bakersfeld: "There is no more time. Stop all engines." Repeat – stop all engines.'

Glancing out, Patroni saw the ploughs and graders were already moving. They wouldn't close in, he knew, until the aircraft engines were stopped. But he remembered Mel's warning: *When the tower tells us we're out of time, there'll be no argument.*

He thought: *Who's arguing?*

The radio again, urgently: 'Joe Patroni, do you read? Acknowledge.'

'Mr Patroni!' the mechanic shouted. 'Do you hear? We have to shut down!'

Patroni shouted back, 'Can't hear a damn thing, son. Guess there's too much noise.'

As any seasoned maintenance man knew, you always had a minute more than the panic-prone sales types in the front office said you had.

In the worst way, though, he needed a cigar. Suddenly Joe Patroni remembered – hours ago, Mel Bakersfeld bet him a box of cigars he couldn't get this aeroplane free tonight.

He called across the cockpit, 'I gotta stake in this, too. Let's go for broke.' In a single, swift motion he shoved the throttles forward to their limit.

The din and vibration had seemed great before; now they were overwhelming. The aeroplane shuddered as if it might fall apart. Joe Patroni kicked the rudder pedals hard again.

Around the cockpit, engine warning lights flashed on. Afterwards, the mechanic described the effect as 'like pinball machines at Vegas'.

Now, alarm in his voice, he called, 'Exhaust gas temperature seven hundred.'

The radio speakers were still emitting orders, including something about Patroni getting clear himself. He supposed he would have to. His hand tensed to close the throttles.

Suddenly the aeroplane shifted forward. At first, it moved slowly. Then, with startling speed, they were hurtling towards the taxiway. The mechanic shouted a warning. As Patroni snatched back all four throttles, he commanded, 'Flaps up!' Glancing below and ahead, both men had an impression of blurred figures running.

Fifty feet from the taxiway, they were still moving fast. Unless turned promptly, the aeroplane would cross the hard surface and roll into piled snow on the other side. As he felt the tyres reach pavement, Patroni applied left brakes hard and slammed open the two starboard throttles. Brakes and engines responded, and the aircraft swung sharply left, in a ninety-degree arc. Halfway around, he slid back the two throttles and applied all brakes together. The Aéreo-Mexican 707 rolled forward briefly, then slowed and halted.

Joe Patroni grinned. They had stopped with the aircraft parked neatly, in the centre of the taxiway paralleling runway three zero.

The runway, two hundred feet away, was no longer blocked.

In Mel Bakersfeld's car, on the runway, Tanya cried, 'He's done it! He's done it!'

Beside her, Mel was already radioing the Snow Desk, ordering ploughs and graders to get clear.

Seconds earlier, Mel had been calling angrily to the tower, demanding for the third time that Joe Patroni stop engines immediately. Mel had been assured the messages were relayed, but Patroni ignored them. The heat of Mel's anger still remained; even now, he could cause Joe Patroni serious trouble for the latter's failure to obey, or even acknowledge, an airport management order in a matter of urgency and safety. But Mel knew he wouldn't. Patroni had got away with it, and no one with sense quarrelled with that kind of success. Also, Mel knew, after tonight there would be one more item to add to the Patroni legend.

The ploughs and graders were already moving.

Mel switched his radio back to tower frequency. 'Mobile one to ground control. Obstructing aircraft has been moved from runway three zero. Vehicles following. I am inspecting for debris.'

Mel shone a spotlight from his car over the runway surface. Tanya and the reporter, Tomlinson, peered with him. Sometimes incidents like tonight's resulted in work crews leaving tools or debris – a hazard to aircraft taking off or landing. The light showed nothing beyond an irregular surface of snow.

The last of the snow ploughs was turning off at the nearest intersection. Mel accelerated and followed. All three in the car were emotionally drained from tensions of the past few minutes, but aware that a greater cause for tension was still to come.

As they swung left, behind the ploughs, Mel reported, 'Runway three zero clear and open.'

16

Trans America Flight Two, *The Golden Argosy*, was ten miles out, in cloud, at fifteen hundred feet.

Anson Harris, after another brief respite, had resumed flying.

The Lincoln International approach controller – with a voice vaguely familiar to Vernon Demerest, though he hadn't stopped to think about it – had guided them thus far on a series of courses, with gentle turns as they descended.

They had been, both pilots realized, skilfully positioned so that a final commitment towards either of the two possible runways could be made without major manoeuvring. But the commitment would have to be made at any moment.

Tension of the pilots grew as that moment approached.

A few minutes earlier, Second Officer Cy Jordan had returned to the flight deck, on Demerest's orders, to prepare an estimate of gross landing weight, allowing for the fuel they had used, and that remaining. Now, having done everything else necessary at his flight engineer's position, Jordan had gone back to his emergency landing station in the forward passenger compartment.

Anson Harris, aided by Demerest, had already gone through emergency trim procedures in preparation for landing with their jammed stabilizer.

As they finished, Dr Compagno appeared briefly behind them. 'I thought you'd like to know – your stewardess, Miss Meighen, is holding her own. If we can get her to a hospital soon, I'm fairly sure she'll come through.'

Demerest, finding it hard to conceal his sudden emotion, had resorted to not speaking. It was Anson Harris who half-turned and acknowledged, 'Thank you, Doctor. We've only a few minutes to go.'

In both passenger cabins, all precautions which could be taken were completed. The injured, with the exception of Gwen Meighen, had been strapped in seats. Two of the doctors had stationed themselves on either side of Gwen, ready to support her as they landed. Other passengers had been shown how to brace themselves for what might prove an exceptionally heavy landing, with unknown consequences.

The old lady stowaway, Mrs Quonsett, a little frightened at last, was tightly clutching the hand of her oboe player friend. Weariness, too, was creeping over her from the exertions of an exceedingly full day.

A short time earlier her spirits had been buoyed by a brief message from Captain Demerest, relayed through a stewardess. The captain thanked her, the stewardess said, for what she had done to help; since Mrs Quonsett had kept her part of their bargain, after they landed Captain Demerest would keep his by arranging passage for her to New York. How wonderful of that dear man, Ada Quonsett thought, to remember that when he had so much else to think of! . . . But now she wondered: would she be around to make the trip at all?

Judy, the niece of Customs Inspector Standish, had once more been holding the baby whose parents were in the seats beside her. Now she passed the child back to its mother. The baby – least concerned of anyone aboard the aeroplane – was asleep.

On the flight deck, in the right-hand seat, Vernon Demerest checked the weight information the second officer had given him against a weight-airspeed plaque on the pilots' instrument panel. He announced tersely, 'Bug speed 150 knots.'

It was the speed at which they must pass over the airfield boundary, allowing both for weight and the jammed stabilizer.

Harris nodded. Looking glum, he reached out to set a warning pointer on his airspeed indicator. Demerest did the same.

Even on the longest runway their landing would be risky.

The speed – more than 170 miles per hour – was diabolically fast for landing. Both pilots knew that it would mean an exceptionally long run after touchdown, with slow deceleration because of their heavy weight. Thus their weight became a dual liability. Yet to approach at anything less than the speed which Demerest had just computed would be suicidal; the aircraft would stall, and plummet earthwards out of control.

Demerest reached for his radio mike.

Before he could transmit, the voice of Keith Bakersfeld announced, 'Trans America Two, turn right on heading two eight five. Runway three zero is open.'

'Jesus Christ!' Demerest said. 'And about time!'

He keyed his mike and acknowledged.

Together, both pilots ran through a pre-landing check list.

There was a 'thud' through the aeroplane as their landing gear went down.

'I'm going in low,' Harris said, 'and we'll touch down early. We're still going to need every bit of real estate they have down there.'

Demerest grunted agreement. He was peering ahead, straining to penetrate cloud and darkness, to catch a glimpse of the airport lights which must be visible soon. His thoughts, despite his own outward calm, were on the damage to the plane. They still didn't know exactly how bad it was, or how it might have worsened during the rough flight in. There was that damned great hole; then there would be the heavy, fast landing . . . *God! – the whole tail assembly might come off* . . . If it does, Demerest thought, at a hundred and fifty knots we've had it . . . *That son-of-a-bitch who had set off the bomb!* A pity he had died! Demerest would like to have his hands on him now, to personally rip out his stinking life . . .

Beside him, Anson Harris, making an Instrument Landing System approach, increased their rate of descent from seven hundred to eight hundred feet per minute.

Demerest wished desperately he were flying himself. With anyone else but Harris – with a younger or less senior captain – Demerest would have taken full command. As it was, he couldn't fault Harris for a thing . . . He hoped the landing would be the same way . . . His thoughts went back to the passenger cabin. *Gwen, we're almost in! Keep on living!* His conviction about their child, that he and Gwen and Sarah would work out something, was as strong as ever.

On radio, Keith Bakersfeld's voice reported, 'Trans America Two, your course and descent look fine. There is medium to light snow on runway. Wind northwest, thirty knots. You are number one to land.'

Seconds later they emerged from cloud to see runway lights dead ahead.

'Lincoln approach control,' Demerest radioed, 'we have the runway in sight.'

'Roger, Flight Two.' Relief in the controller's voice was unmistakable. 'The tower clears you to land; monitor their frequency when ready. Good luck, and out.'

Vernon Demerest clicked his mike button twice – an airman's shorthand 'thank you'.

Anson Harris ordered crisply, 'Landing lights on. Fifty degrees flap.'

Demerest complied.

They were coming down fast.

Harris warned, 'I may need help with rudder.'

'Right.' Demerest set his feet on the rudder pedals. When speed came off, the rudder – because of the destroyed boost mechanism – would be stiff, like a car's power steering which had failed, only more so. After landing, both pilots might need to exert force, together, to maintain directional control.

They zoomed over the airfield edge, runway lights strung ahead like strands of converging pearls. On either side were piled banks of snow; beyond them, darkness. Harris had made his approach as low as he dared; the nearness to the ground revealed their exceptional speed. To both pilots, the mile and three quarters of runway in front had never looked shorter.

Harris flared out, levelling the aircraft, and closed all four throttles. The jet thrum lessened; an urgent, shrieking wind replaced it. As they crossed the runway's edge, Vernon Demerest had a blurred impression of clustered emergency vehicles which would, he knew, follow them down the runway. He thought: *We damned well might need them! Hang on, Gwen!*

They were still floating, their speed scarcely diminished.

Then the aircraft was down. Heavily. Still travelling fast.

Swiftly, Harris raised wing spoilers and slammed thrust reverse levers upward. With a roar, the jet engines reversed themselves, their force – acting as a brake – now exerted in an opposite direction to the aeroplane's travel.

They had used three quarters of the runway and were slowing, but not enough.

Harris called, 'Right rudder!' The aircraft was veering to the left. With Demerest and Harris shoving together they maintained direction. But the runway's forward limit – with piled snow and a cavern of darkness beyond – was coming up fast.

Anson Harris was applying toe brakes hard. Metal was straining, rubber screaming. Still the darkness neared. Then they were slowing . . . gradually . . . slowing more . . .

Flight Two came to rest three feet from the runway's end.

17

By the radar room clock, Keith Bakersfeld could see that another half hour of his shift remained. He didn't care.

He pushed back his chair from the radar console, unplugged his headset and stood up. He looked around him, knowing it was for the last time.

'Hey!' Wayne Tevis said. 'What gives?'

'Here,' Keith told him. 'Take this. Somebody else may need it.' He thrust the headset at Tevis, and went out.

Keith knew he should have done it years ago.

He felt a strange lightheadedness, almost a sense of relief. In the corridor outside he wondered why.

It was not because he had guided in Flight Two; he had no illusions about that. Keith had performed competently, but anyone else on duty could have done as well, or better. Nor – as he had known in advance – did anything done tonight wipe out, or counterbalance, what had gone before.

It didn't matter, either, that he had overcome his mental block of ten minutes ago. Keith hadn't cared at the time; he simply wanted out. Nothing that had happened since had changed his mind.

Perhaps, he thought, there had been a purging in his own sudden anger of a few minutes ago, in the admission, never faced before even in private thoughts, of how much he hated aviation, and always had. Now, fifteen years late, he wished he had faced the fact long ago.

He entered the controllers' locker room, with its wooden benches and cluttered notice board. Keith opened his locker and put on his outdoor clothes. There were a few personal things on the locker shelves; he ignored them. All he wanted was the colour snapshot of Natalie; he peeled it carefully from the inside surface of the metal door . . . Natalie in a bikini; laughing; her impudent pixyish face, and freckles; her hair streaming . . . When he looked at it, he wanted to cry. Behind the photograph was her note he had treasured:

I'm glad we had our ration
With love and passion.

Keith pocketed both. Someone else could clear the other things out. There was nothing he wanted to remind him of this place – ever.

He stopped.

He stood there, realizing that without intending to, he had come to a new decision. He wasn't sure of everything the decision involved, or how it might seem tomorrow, or even if he could live with it beyond then. If he couldn't live with it, there was still an escape clause; a way out – the drugstore pillbox in his pocket.

For tonight, the main thing was: he was not going to the O'Hagan Inn. He was going home.

But there was one thing he knew: If there was to be a future, it must be removed from aviation. As others who had quit air traffic control before him had discovered, that could prove the hardest thing of all.

And even if that much could be overcome – *face it now*, Keith told himself – there would be times when he would be reminded of the past. Reminded of Lincoln International; of Leesburg; of what had happened at both places. Whatever else you escaped, if you had a whole mind, there was no escaping memory. The memory of the Redfern family who had died . . . of little Valerie Redfern . . . would never leave him.

Yet memory could adapt – couldn't it? – to time, to circumstance, to the reality of living here and now. The Redferns were dead. The Bible said: *Let the dead bury their dead.* What had happened was done.

Keith wondered if . . . from now on . . . he could remember the Redferns with sadness, but do his best to make the living – Natalie, his own children – his first concern.

He wasn't sure if it would work. He wasn't sure if he had the moral or the physical strength. It had been a long time since he was sure of anything. But he could try.

He took the tower elevator down.

Outside, on his way to the FAA parking lot, Keith stopped. On sudden impulse, knowing he might regret it later, he took the pillbox from his pocket and emptied its contents into the snow.

18

From his car, which he had parked on the nearby taxiway after quitting runway three zero, Mel Bakersfeld could see that the pilots of Trans America Flight Two were wasting no time in taxiing to the terminal. The aircraft's lights, now halfway across the airfield, were still visible, moving fast. On his radio, switched to ground control, Mel could hear other flights being halted at taxiway and runway intersections to let the damaged airliner pass. The injured were still aboard. Flight Two had been instructed to head directly for gate forty-seven where medical help, ambulances, and company staff were waiting.

Mel watched the aircraft's lights diminish, and merge with the galaxy of terminal lights beyond.

Airport emergency vehicles, which had not after all been required, were dispersing from the runway area.

Tanya and the *Tribune* reporter, Tomlinson, were both on their way back to the terminal. They were driving with Joe Patroni, who had handed over the Aéreo-Mexican 707 for someone else to taxi to the hangars.

Tanya wanted to be at gate forty-seven for the disembarking of passengers from Flight Two. It was likely she would be needed.

Before leaving, she had asked Mel quietly, 'Are you still coming home?'

'If it isn't too late,' he said, 'I'd like to.'

He watched while Tanya pushed a strand of red hair back from her face. She had looked at him with her direct, clear eyes and smiled. 'It's not too late.'

They agreed to meet at the main terminal entrance in three quarters of an hour.

Tomlinson's purpose was to interview Joe Patroni, and after that the crew of Trans America Flight Two. The crew – and Patroni, no doubt – would be heroes within a few hours. The dramatic story of the flight's peril and survival, Mel suspected, would eclipse his own pronouncements on the more mundane subject of the airport's problems and deficiencies.

Though not entirely, perhaps. Tomlinson, to whom Mel had entrusted his opinions, was a thoughtful, intelligent reporter who might decide to link present dramatics with the equally serious long-term view.

The Aéreo-Mexican 707, Mel saw, was now being moved away. The aeroplane appeared undamaged, but would undoubtedly be washed down and inspected thoroughly before resuming its interrupted flight to Acapulco.

The assortment of service vehicles which had stayed with the aircraft during its ordeal by mud were following.

There was no reason for Mel not to go himself. He would – in a moment or two; but for the second time tonight he found the airfield's loneliness, its closeness to the elemental part of aviation, a stimulus to thought.

It was here, a few hours ago, Mel remembered, that he had had an instinct, a premonition, of events moving towards some disastrous end. Well, in a way they had. The disaster had happened, though through good fortune it had been neither complete, nor had the airport's facilities – or lack of them – been directly responsible.

But the disaster *could* have involved the airport; and the airport in turn might have caused complete catastrophe – through inadequacies which Mel had foreseen and had argued, vainly, to correct.

For Lincoln International was obsolescent.

Obsolescent, Mel knew, despite its good management, and gleaming glass and chrome; despite its air traffic density, its record-breaking passenger volume, its Niagara of air freight, its expectations of even more of everything, and its boastful title, 'Aviation Crossroads of the World.'

The airport was obsolescent because – as had happened so often in the short seven decades of modern aviation history – air progress had eclipsed prediction. Once more, expert prognosticators had been wrong, the visionary dreamers right.

And what was true here was true elsewhere.

Nationwide, worldwide, the story was the same. Much was talked about aviation's growth, its needs, coming developments in the air which would provide the lowest cost transportation of people and goods in human history, the chance these gave the nations of the world to know each other better, in peace, and to trade more freely. Yet little on the ground – in relation to the problem's size – had been done.

Well, one voice alone would not change everything, but each voice which spoke with knowledge and conviction was a help. It had come to Mel within the past few hours – he was not sure why or how – that he intended to continue speaking out the way he had tonight, the way he hadn't for so long.

Tomorrow – or rather, later today – he would begin by summoning, for Monday morning, an emergency special meeting of the Board of Airport Commissioners. When the Board met, he would urge an immediate commitment to build a new runway paralleling three zero.

289

The experience of tonight had strengthened, as nothing else could, the arguments for increasing runway capacity which Mel had presented long ago. But this time, he determined, he would make a fight of it – with plain, blunt words, warning of catastrophe if public safety was given lip service only, while vital operational needs were ignored or shelved. He would see to it that press and public opinion were marshalled on his side – the kind of pressure which downtown politicians, who controlled bond issues, understood.

After new runways, other projects, so far only talked about or hoped for, must be pressed on; among them – an entirely new terminal and runway complex; more imaginative ground flow of people and freight; smaller, satellite fields for the vertical and short takeoff aircraft which were coming soon.

Either Lincoln International was in the jet age, or it wasn't; if it was, it must keep pace far better than it had.

It was not, Mel thought, as if airports were an indulgence or some civic luxury. Almost all were self-sustaining, generating wealth and high employment.

Not all the battles for ground-air progress would be won; they never were. But some of them could be, and some of what was said and done here – because of Mel's stature in airport management – could spill over into national, even international, arenas.

If it did, so much the better! The English poet John Donne, Mel remembered, had once written: *No man is an island, entire of itself; every man is a piece of the continent, a part of the main.* No airport was an island either; those which called themselves International should employ the kind of thinking to justify their name. Perhaps, working with others, Mel could help to show them how.

People who hadn't heard from Mel Bakersfeld for a while might quickly learn that he was still around.

And intensive work, a resumption of more of his old industry-wide interests, might help with personal problems by keeping his mind occupied. Mel hoped so, anyway. The thought was an abrupt reminder that sometime soon – perhaps tomorrow – he would have to call Cindy and arrange to move out his clothes and personal belongings. It would be an unhappy process which he hoped the girls, Roberta and Libby, would not be around to see. To begin with, Mel supposed, he would move into a hotel until he had time to arrange an apartment of his own.

But more than ever he knew that Cindy's and his own decision for divorce had been inevitable. Both of them had known it; tonight they merely resolved to remove a façade behind which nothing existed any more. Neither for themselves nor for the children could anything have been gained by more delay.

It would still take time, though, to adjust.

And Tanya? Mel was not sure what, if anything, was ahead for them together. He thought there might be a good deal, but the time for a commitment – if there was to be one – was not yet. He only knew that tonight, before this long and complex workday ended, he craved companionship, warmth, and tenderness; and, of all the friends he possessed, Tanya had those qualities in greatest measure.

What else, between himself and Tanya, these might lead to would be known in time.

Mel put his car in gear and swung it towards the perimeter road which would take him to the terminal. Runway three zero was on his right as he drove.

Now that the runway was open, he saw, other aircraft were beginning to use it, arriving in a steady stream despite the lateness. A Convair 880 of TWA swept by and landed. Behind it, half a mile out, were the landing lights of another flight approaching. Behind the second, a third was turning in.

The fact that Mel could see the third set of lights made him aware that the cloud base had lifted. He noticed suddenly that the snowfall had stopped; in a few places to the south, patches of sky were clearing. With relief, he realized the storm was moving on.

HOTEL

*Traveller, pray lodge in this unworthy house. The bath
is ready. A peaceful room awaits you. Come in! Come in!*

Translation of a sign at the doorway of an inn, Takamatsu, Japan

Monday Evening

I

If he had had his way, Peter McDermott thought, he would have fired the chief house detective long ago. But he had not had his way and now, once more, the obese ex-policeman was missing, when he was needed most.

McDermott leaned down from his husky six and a half feet and jiggled the desk phone impatiently. 'Fifteen things break loose at once,' he told the girl by the window of the wide, broadloomed office, 'and nobody can find him.'

Christine Francis glanced at her wrist watch. It showed a few minutes before eleven p.m. 'There's a bar on Baronne Street you might try.'

Peter McDermott nodded. 'The switchboard's checking Ogilvie's hangouts.' He opened a desk drawer, took out cigarettes and offered them to Christine.

Coming forward, she accepted a cigarette and McDermott lit it, then did the same for himself. He watched as she inhaled.

Christine Francis had left her own smaller office in the St Gregory Hotel executive suite a few minutes earlier. She had been working late and was on the point of going home when the light under the assistant general manager's door had drawn her in.

'Our Mr Ogilvie makes his own rules,' Christine said. 'It's always been that way. On W. T.'s orders.'

McDermott spoke briefly into the telephone, then waited again. 'You're right,' he acknowledged. 'I tried to reorganize our tame detective force once, and my ears were properly pinned back.'

She said quietly, 'I didn't know that.'

He looked at her quizzically. 'I thought you knew everything.'

And usually she did. As personal assistant to Warren Trent, the unpredictable and irascible owner of New Orleans' largest hotel, Christine was privy to the hotel's inner secrets as well as its day-to-day affairs. She knew, for example, that Peter, who had been promoted to assistant general manager a month or two ago, was virtually running the big, bustling St Gregory, though at an ungenerous salary and with limited authority. She knew the reasons behind that, too, which were in a file marked *Confidential* and involved Peter McDermott's personal life.

Christine asked, 'What *is* breaking loose?'

McDermott gave a cheerful grin which contorted his rugged, almost ugly features. 'We've a complaint from the eleventh floor about some sort of sex orgy; on the ninth the Duchess of Croydon claims her Duke has been insulted by a room-service waiter; there's a report of somebody moaning horribly in 1439; and I've the manager off sick, with the other two house officers otherwise engaged.'

He spoke into the telephone again and Christine returned to the office window which was on the main mezzanine floor. Head tilted back to keep the cigarette smoke from her eyes, she looked casually across the city. Directly ahead, through an avenue of space between adjoining buildings, she could see into the tight, crowded rectangle of the French Quarter. With midnight an hour away, it was early yet for the Quarter, and lights in front of late night bars, bistros, jazz halls and strip joints – as well as behind darkened shutters – would burn well into tomorrow morning.

Somewhere to the north, over Lake Pontchartrain probably, a summer storm was brewing in the darkness. The beginnings of it could be sensed in muted rumblings and an occasional flash of light. With luck, if the storm moved south towards the Gulf of Mexico, there might be rain in New Orleans by morning.

The rain would be welcome, Christine thought. For three weeks the city had sweltered in heat and humidity, producing tensions all around. There would be relief in the hotel too. This afternoon the chief engineer had complained again. 'If I canna' shut down part of the air conditioning soon, I willna' be responsible for my bearings.'

Peter McDermott put down the telephone and she asked, 'Do you have a name for the room where the moaning is?'

He shook his head and lifted the phone again. 'I'll find out. Probably someone having a nightmare, but we'd better make sure.'

As she dropped into an upholstered leather chair facing the big mahogany desk, Christine realized suddenly how very tired she was. In the ordinary way she would have been home at her Gentilly apartment hours ago. But today had been exceptionally full, with two conventions moving in and a heavy influx of other guests, creating problems, many of which had found their way to her desk.

'All right, thanks.' McDermott scribbled a name and hung up. 'Albert Wells, Montreal.'

'I know him,' Christine said. 'A nice little man who stays here every year. If you like, I'll check that one out.'

He hesitated, eyeing Christine's slight, trim figure.

The telephone shrilled and he answered it. 'I'm sorry, sir,' the operator said, 'we can't locate Mr Ogilvie.'

'Never mind. Give me the bell captain.' Even if he couldn't fire the chief house detective, McDermott thought, he would do some hell raising in the morning. Meanwhile he would send someone else to look after the disturbance on the eleventh and handle the Duke and Duchess incident himself.

'Bell captain,' the phone said, and he recognized the flat nasal voice of Herbie Chandler. Chandler, like Ogilvie, was another of the St Gregory's old-timers and reputedly controlled more sideline rackets than anyone else on the staff.

McDermott explained the problem and asked Chandler to investigate the complaint about an alleged sex orgy. As he had half expected, there was an immediate protest. 'That ain't my job, Mr Mac, and we're still busy down here.' The tone was typical Chandler – half fawning, half insolent.

McDermott instructed, 'Never mind the argument, I want that complaint attended to.' Making another decision: 'And something else: send a boy with a pass key to meet Miss Francis on the main mezzanine.' He replace the phone before there could be any more discussion.

'Let's go.' His hand touched Christine's shoulders lightly. 'Take the bellboy with you, and tell your friend to have his nightmares under the covers.'

2

Herbie Chandler, his weasel face betraying an inner uneasiness, stood thoughtfully by the bell captain's upright desk in the St Gregory lobby.

Set centrally, beside one of the fluted concrete columns which extended to the heavily ornamented ceiling high above, the bell captain's post commanded a view of the lobby's comings and goings. There was plenty of movement now. The conventioneers had been in and out all evening and, as the hours wore on, their determined gaiety had increased with their liquor intake.

As Chandler watched out of habit, a group of noisy revellers came through the Carondelet Street door; three men and two women; they held drinking glasses, the kind that Pat O'Brien's bar charged tourists a dollar for over in the French Quarter, and one of the men was stumbling badly, supported by the others. All three men wore convention name tags. GOLD CROWN COLA, the cards said, with their names beneath. Others in the lobby made way good naturedly and the quintet weaved into the main floor bar.

Occasional new arrivals were still trickling in – from late planes and trains, and several were being roomed now by Chandler's platoon of bellboys, though the 'boys' was a figure of speech since none was younger than forty, and several greying veterans had been with the hotel a quarter-century or more. Herbie Chandler, who held the power of hiring and firing his bell staff, preferred older men. Someone who had to struggle and grunt a bit with heavy luggage was likely to earn bigger tips than a youngster who swung bags as if they contained nothing more than balsa wood. One old-timer, who actually was strong and wiry as a mule, had a way of setting bags down, putting a hand over his heart, then picking them up with a shake of his head and carrying on. The performance seldom earned less than a dollar from conscience-stricken guests who were convinced the old man would have a coronary around the next corner. What they did not know was that ten per cent of their tip would find its way into Herbie Chandler's pocket, plus the flat two dollars daily which Chandler exacted from each bellboy as the price of retaining his job.

The bell captain's private toll system caused plenty of low-toned growlings, even though a fast-moving bellboy could still make a hundred and fifty dollars a week for himself when the hotel was full. On such occasions, as tonight, Herbie Chandler often stayed at his post well beyond the usual hour. Trusting no-one, he liked to keep an eye on his percentage and had an uncanny knack of sizing up guests, estimating exactly what each trip to the upstairs floors would yield. In the past a few individualists had tried holding out on Herbie by reporting tips to be less than they really were. Reprisals were unfailingly swift and ruthless, and a month's suspension on some trumped-up charge usually brought non-conformists into line.

There was another cause, too, for Chandler's presence in the hotel tonight, and it accounted for his unease which had been steadily growing since Peter McDermott's telephone call a few minutes earlier. McDermott had instructed: investigate a complaint on the eleventh floor. But Herbie Chandler had no need to investigate because he knew roughly what was happening on the eleventh. The reason was simple: he had arranged it himself.

Three hours earlier the two youths had been explicit in their request and he had listened respectfully since the fathers of both were wealthy local citizens and frequent guests at the hotel. 'Listen, Herbie,' one of them said, 'there's a fraternity dance tonight – the same old crap, and we'd like something different.'

He had asked, knowing the answer, 'How different?'

'We've taken a suite.' The boy flushed. 'We want a couple of girls.'

It was too risky, Herbie decided at once. Both were little more than boys, and he suspected they had been drinking. He began, 'Sorry, gentlemen,' when the second youth cut in.

'Don't give us any crap about not being able to, because we know you run the call girls here.'

Herbie bared his weasel teeth in what passed for a smile. 'I can't imagine where you got that idea, Mr Dixon.'

The one who had spoken first insisted, 'We can pay, Herbie. You know that.'

The bell captain hesitated, despite his doubts his mind working greedily. Just lately his sideline revenues had been slower than usual. Perhaps, after all, the risk was slight.

The one named Dixon said, 'Let's quit horsing around. How much?'

Herbie looked up at the youths, remembered their fathers, and multiplied the standard rate by two. 'A hundred dollars.'

There was a momentary pause. Then Dixon said decisively, 'You got a deal.' He added persuasively to his companion, 'Listen, we've already paid for the booze. I'll lend you the rest of the split.'

'Well . . .'

'In advance, gentlemen.' Herbie moistened his thin lips with his tongue. 'Just one thing. You'll have to make sure there's no noise. If there is, and we get complaints, there could be trouble for all of us.'

There would be no noise, they had assured him, but now it seemed, there had been, and his original fears were proving uncomfortably true.

An hour ago the girls had come in through the front entrance as usual, with only an inner few of the hotel's staff aware that they were other than registered hotel guests. If all had gone well, both should have left by now, as unobtrusively as they had come.

The eleventh floor complaint, relayed through McDermott and specifically referring to a sex orgy, meant that something had gone seriously wrong. What? Herbie was reminded uncomfortably of the reference to booze.

It was hot and humid in the lobby despite the overworked air conditioning, and Herbie took out a silk handkerchief to mop his perspiring forehead. At the same time he silently cursed his own folly, wondering whether, at this stage, he should go upstairs or stay well away.

3

Peter McDermott rode the elevator to the ninth floor, leaving Christine who was to continue to the fourteenth with her accompanying bellboy. At the opened elevator doorway he hesitated, 'Send for me if there's any trouble.'

'If it's essential I'll scream.' As the sliding doors came between them her eyes met his own. For a moment he stood thoughtfully watching the place where they had been, then, long-legged and alert, strode down the carpet corridor towards the Presidential Suite.

The St Gregory's largest and most elaborate suite – known familiarly as the brasshouse – had, in its time, housed a succession of distinguished guests, including presidents and royalty. Most had liked New Orleans because after an initial welcome the city had a way of respecting its visitors' privacy, including indiscretions, if any. Somewhat less than heads of state, though distinguished in their way, were the suite's best tenants, the Duke and Duchess of Croydon, plus their retinue of secretary, the Duchess's maid and five Bedlington terriers.

Outside the double padded leather doors, decorated with gold fleur-de-lis, Peter McDermott depressed a mother-of-pearl button and heard a muted buzz inside, followed by a less muted chorus of barkings. Waiting, he reflected on what he had heard and knew about the Croydons.

The Duke of Croydon, scion of an ancient family, had adapted himself to the times with an instinct for the common touch. Within the past decade, and aided by his Duchess – herself a known public figure and cousin of the Queen – he had become ambassador-at-large and successful troubleshooter for the British government. More recently, however, there had been rumours that the Duke's career had reached a critical point, perhaps because his touch had become a shade too common in some areas, notably those of liquor and other men's wives. There were other reports, though, which said the shadow over the Duke was minor and temporary, and that the Duchess had the situation well in hand. Supporting this second view were predictions that the Duke of Croydon might soon be named British Ambassador to Washington.

From behind Peter a voice murmured, 'Excuse me, Mr McDermott, can I have a word with you?'

Turning abruptly he recognized Sol Natchez, one of the elderly room-service waiters, who had come quietly down the corridor, a lean cadaverous figure in a short white coat, trimmed with the hotel's colours of red and gold. The man's hair was slicked down flatly and combed forward into an old-fashioned forelock. His eyes were pale and rheumy, and the veins in the back of his hands, which he rubbed nervously, stood out like cords with the flesh sunk deep between them.

'What is it, Sol?'

His voice betraying an agitation, the waiter said, 'I expect you've come about the complaint – the complaint about me.'

McDermott glanced at the double doors. They had not yet opened, nor, apart from the barking, had there been any other sound from within. He said, 'Tell me what happened.'

The other swallowed twice. Ignoring the question he said in a pleading hurried whisper,

299

'If I lose this job, Mr McDermott, it's hard at my age to find another.' He looked towards the Presidential Suite, his expression a mixture of anxiety and resentment. 'They're not the hardest people to serve . . . except for tonight. They expect a lot, but I've never minded, even though there's never a tip.'

Peter smiled involuntarily. British nobility seldom tipped, assuming perhaps that the privilege of waiting on them was a reward in itself.

He interjected, 'You still haven't told me . . .'

'I'm getting to it, Mr McDermott.' From someone old enough to be Peter's grandfather, the other man's distress was almost embarrassing. 'It was about half an hour ago. They'd ordered a late supper, the Duke and Duchess – oysters, champagne, shrimp Creole.'

'Never mind the menu. What happened?'

'It was the shrimp Creole, sir. When I was serving it . . . well, it's something, in all these years it's happened very rarely.'

'For heaven's sake!' Peter had one eye on the suite doors, ready to break off the conversation the moment they opened.

'Yes, Mr McDermott. Well, when I was serving the Creole the Duchess got up from the table and as she came back she jogged my arm. If I didn't know better I'd have said it was deliberate.'

'That's ridiculous!'

'I know, sir, I know. But what happened, you see, was there was a small spot – I swear it was no more than a quarter inch – on the Duke's trousers.'

Peter said doubtfully, 'Is that *all* this is about?'

'Mr McDermott. I swear to you that's all. But you'd think – the fuss the Duchess made – I'd committed murder. I apologized. I got a clean napkin and water to get the spot off, but it wouldn't do. She insisted on sending for Mr Trent . . .'

'Mr Trent is not in the hotel.'

He would hear the other side of the story, Peter decided, before making any judgement. Meanwhile he instructed, 'If you're all through for tonight you'd better go home. Report tomorrow and you'll be told what will happen.'

As the waiter disappeared, Peter McDermott depressed the bell push again. There was barely time for the barking to resume before the door was opened by a moon-faced, youngish man with pince-nez. Peter recognized him as the Croydons' secretary.

Before either of them could speak a woman's voice called out from the suite's interior. 'Whoever it is, tell them not to *keep* buzzing.' For all the peremptory tone, Peter thought, it was an attractive voice with a rich huskiness which excited interest.

'I beg your pardon,' he told the secretary. 'I thought perhaps you hadn't heard.' He introduced himself, then added, 'I understand there has been some trouble about our service, I came to see if I could help.'

The secretary said, 'We were expecting Mr Trent.'

'Mr Trent is away from the hotel for the evening.'

While speaking they had moved from the corridor into the hallway of the suite, a tastefully appointed rectangle with deep broadloom, two upholstered chairs and a telephone side table beneath a Morris Henry Hobbs engraving of old New Orleans. The double doorway to the corridor formed one end of the rectangle. At the other end, the door to the large living-room was partially open. On the right and left were two other doorways, one to the self-contained kitchen and another to an office-cum-bed-sitting-room, at present used by the Croydons' secretary. The two main, connecting bedrooms of the suite were accessible both through the kitchen and the living-room, an arrangement contrived so that a surreptitious bedroom visitor could be spirited in and out by the kitchen if need arose.

'Why can't he be sent for?' The question was addressed without preliminary as the living-room door opened and the Duchess of Croydon appeared, three of the Bedlington terriers enthusiastically at her heels. With a swift finger-snap, instantly obeyed, she silenced the dogs and turned her eyes questioningly on Peter. He was aware of the handsome, high-cheekboned face, familiar through a thousand photographs. Even in casual clothes, he observed, the Duchess was superbly dressed.

'To be perfectly honest, Your Grace, I was not aware that you required Mr Trent personally.'

Grey-green eyes regarded him appraisingly. 'Even in Mr Trent's absence I should have expected one of the *senior* executives.'

Despite himself, Peter flushed. There was a superb hauteur about the Duchess of Croydon which – in a perverse way – was curiously appealing. A picture flashed into his memory. He had seen it in one of the illustrated magazines – the Duchess putting a stallion at a high fence. Disdainful of risk, she had been securely and superbly in command. He had an impression, at this moment, of being on foot while the Duchess was mounted.

'I'm assistant general manager. That's why I came personally.'

There was a glimmer of amusement in the eyes which held his own. 'Aren't you somewhat young for that?'

'Not really. Nowadays a good many young men are engaged in hotel management.' The secretary, he noticed, had disappeared discreetly.

'How old *are* you?'

'Thirty-two.'

The Duchess smiled. When she chose – as at this moment – her face became animated and warm. It was not difficult, Peter thought, to become aware of the fabled charm. She was five or six years older than himself, he calculated, though younger than the Duke who was in his late forties. Now she asked, 'Do you take a course or something?'

'I have a degree from Cornell University – the School of Hotel Administration. Before coming here I was an assistant manager at the Waldorf.' It required an effort to mention the Waldorf, and he was tempted to add: *from where I was fired in ignominy, and black-listed by the chain hotels, so that I am fortunate to be working here, which is an independent house.* But he would not say it, of course, because a private hell was something you lived with alone, even when someone else's casual questions nudged old, raw wounds within yourself.

The Duchess retorted, 'The Waldorf would never have tolerated an incident like tonight's.'

'I assure you, ma'am, that if we are at fault the St Gregory will not tolerate it either.' The conversation, he thought, was like a game of tennis, with the ball lobbed from one court to the other. He waited for it to come back.

'If you were at fault! Are you aware that your waiter poured shrimp Creole over my husband?'

It was so obviously an exaggeration, he wondered why. It was also uncharacteristic since, until now, relations between the hotel and the Croydons had been excellent.

'I was aware there had been an accident which was probably due to carelessness. In that event I'm here to apologize for the hotel.'

'Our entire evening has been ruined,' the Duchess insisted. 'My husband and I decided to enjoy a quiet evening in our suite here, by ourselves. We were out for a few moments only, to take a walk around the block, and we returned to our supper – and this!'

Peter nodded, outwardly sympathetic but mystified by the Duchess's attitude. It seemed almost as if she wanted to impress the incident on his mind so he would not forget it.

He suggested. 'Perhaps if I could convey our apologies to the Duke . . .'

The Duchess said firmly, 'That will not be necessary.'

He was about to take his leave when the door to the living-room, which had remained ajar, opened fully. It framed the Duke of Croydon.

In contrast to his Duchess, the Duke was untidily dressed, in a creased white shirt and the trousers of a tuxedo. Instinctively Peter McDermott's eyes sought the tell-tale stain where Natchez, in the Duchess's words, had 'poured shrimp Creole over my husband'. He found it, though it was barely visible – a tiny spot which a valet could have removed instantly. Behind the Duke, in the spacious living-room a television set was turned on.

The Duke's face seemed flushed, and more lined than some of his recent photographs showed. He held a glass in his hand and when he spoke his voice was blurry. 'Oh, beg pardon.' Then, to the Duchess: 'I say, old girl. Must have left my cigarettes in the car.'

She responded sharply, 'I'll bring some.' There was a curt dismissal in her voice and with a nod the Duke turned back into the living-room. It was a curious, uncomfortable scene and for some reason it had heightened the Duchess's anger.

Turning to Peter she snapped, 'I insist on a full report being made to Mr Trent, and you may inform him that I expect a personal apology.'

Still perplexed, Peter went out as the suite door closed firmly behind him.

But he was allowed no more time for reflection. In the corridor outside, the bellboy who had accompanied Christine to the fourteenth floor was waiting. 'Mr McDermott,' he said urgently, 'Miss Francis wants you in 1439, and please hurry!'

4

Some fifteen minutes earlier, when Peter McDermott had left the elevator on his way to the Presidential suite, the bellboy grinned at Christine. 'Doing a bit of detecting, Miss Francis?'

'If the chief house officer was around,' Christine told him, 'I wouldn't have to.'

The bellboy, Jimmy Duckworth, a balding stubby man whose married son worked in the St Gregory accounting department, said contemptuously, 'Oh him!' A moment later the elevator stopped at the fourteenth floor.

'It's 1439, Jimmy,' Christine said, and automatically both turned right. There was a difference, she realized, in the way the two of them knew the geography of the hotel: the bellboy through years of ushering guests from the lobby to their rooms; herself, from a series of mental pictures which familiarity with the printed plans of each floor of the St Gregory had given her.

Five years ago, she thought, if someone at the University of Wisconsin had asked what twenty-year-old Chris Francis, a bright co-ed with a flair for modern languages, was likely to be doing a lustrum later, not even the wildest guess would have had her working in a New Orleans hotel. That long ago her knowledge of the Crescent City was of the slightest, and her interest less. She had learned in school about the Louisiana Purchase and had seen *A Streetcar Named Desire*. But even the last was out of date when she eventually came. The street-car had become a diesel bus, and Desire was an obscure thoroughfare on the east side of town, which tourists seldom saw.

She supposed, in a way, it was that lack of knowledge which brought her to New Orleans. After the accident in Wisconsin, dully and with only the vaguest of reasoning, she had sought a place where she could be unknown and which, as well, was unfamiliar to herself. Familiar things, their touch and sight and sound, had become an ache of heart – all encompassing – which filled the waking day and penetrated sleep. Strangely – and in a way it shamed her at the time – there were never nightmares; only the steady procession of events as they had been that memorable day at Madison airport. She had been there to see her family leave for Europe; her mother, gay and excited, wearing the *bon voyage* orchid which a friend had telegraphed; her father, relaxed and amiably complacent that for a month the real and imagined ailments of his patients would be someone else's concern. He had been puffing a pipe which he knocked out on his shoe when the flight was called. Babs, her elder sister, had embraced Christine; and even Tony, two years younger and hating public affection, consented to be kissed.

'So long, Ham!' Babs and Tony had called back, and Christine smiled at the use of the silly affectionate name they gave her because she was the middle of their trio sandwich. And they had all promised to write, even though she would join them in Paris two weeks later when term ended. At the last her mother had held Chris tightly, and told her to take care. And a few minutes later the big prop-jet had taxied out and taken off with a roar, majestically, though it barely cleared the runway before it fell back, one wing low, becoming a whirling, somersaulting Catherine wheel, and for a moment a dust cloud, and then a torch, and finally a silent pile of fragments – machinery and what was left of human flesh.

It was five years ago. A few weeks after, she left Wisconsin and had never returned.

Her own footsteps and the bellboy's were muffled in the carpeted corridor. A pace ahead, Jimmy Duckworth ruminated, 'Room 1439 – that's the old gent, Mr Wells. We moved him from a corner room a couple of days ago.'

Ahead, down the corridor, a door opened and a man, well-dressed and fortyish, came out. Closing the door behind him, and ready to pocket the key, he hesitated, eyeing Christine with frank interest. He seemed about to speak but, barely perceptibly, the bellboy shook his head. Christine, who missed nothing of the exchange, supposed she should be flattered to be mistaken for a call girl. From rumours she heard, Herbie Chandler's list embraced a glamorous membership.

When they had passed by she asked, 'Why was Mr Wells's room changed?'

'The way I heard it, miss, somebody else had 1439 and raised a fuss. So what they did was switch around.'

Christine remembered 1439 now; there had been complaints before. It was next to the service elevator and appeared to be the meeting place of all the hotel's pipes. The effect was to make the place noisy and unbearably hot. Every hotel had at least one such room

– some called it the ha-ha room – which usually was never rented until everything else was full.

'If Mr Wells had a better room why was he asked to move?'

The bellboy shrugged. 'You'd better ask the room clerks that.'

She persisted, 'But you've an idea.'

'Well, I guess it's because he never complains. The old gent's been coming here for years with never a peep out of him. There are some who seem to think it's a bit of a joke.' Christine's lips tightened angrily as Jimmy Duckworth went on, 'I did hear in the dining-room they give him that table beside the kitchen door, the one no-one else will have. He doesn't seem to mind, they say.'

Christine thought grimly: Someone would mind tomorrow morning; she would guarantee it. At the realization that a regular guest, who also happened to be a quiet and gentle man, had been so shabbily treated, she felt her temper bristle. Well, let it. Her temper was not unknown around the hotel and there were some, she knew, who said it went with her red hair. Although she curbed it mostly, once in a while it served a purpose in getting things done.

They turned a corner and stopped at the door of 1439. The bellboy knocked. They waited, listening. There was no acknowledging sound and Jimmy Duckworth repeated the knock, this time more loudly. At once there was a response: an eerie moaning that began as a whisper, reached a crescendo, then ended suddenly as it began.

'Use your pass key,' Christine instructed. 'Open the door – quickly!'

She stood back while the bellboy went in ahead; even in apparent crisis a hotel had rules of decorum which must be observed. The room was in darkness and she saw Duckworth snap on the ceiling light and go around a corner out of sight. Almost at once he called back, 'Miss Francis, you'd better come.'

The room, as Christine entered, was stifling hot, though a glance at the air-conditioning regulator showed it set hopefully to 'cool'. But that was all she had time to see before observing the struggling figure, half upright, half recumbent in the bed. It was the birdlike little man she knew as Albert Wells. His face ashen grey, eyes bulging and with trembling lips, he was attempting desperately to breathe and barely succeeding.

She went quickly to the bedside. Once, years before, in her father's office she had seen a patient *in extremis*, fighting for breath. There were things her father had done then which she could not do now, but one she remembered. She told Duckworth decisively, 'Get the window open. We need air in here.'

The bellboy's eyes were focused on the face of the man in bed. He said nervously, 'The window's sealed. They did it for the air conditioning.'

'Then force it. If you have to, break the glass.'

She had already picked up the telephone beside the bed. When the operator answered. Christine announced, 'This is Miss Francis. Is Dr Aarons in the hotel?'

'No. Miss Francis; but he left a number. If it's an emergency I can reach him.'

'It's an emergency. Tell Dr Aarons room 1439, and to hurry, please. Ask how long he'll take to get here and call me back.'

Replacing the phone, Christine turned to the still struggling figure in the bed. The frail, elderly man was breathing no better than before and she perceived that his face, which a few moments earlier had been ashen grey, was turning blue. The moaning which they had heard outside had begun again; it was the effort of exhaling, but obviously most of the sufferer's waning strength was being consumed by his desperate physical exertion.

'Mr Wells,' she said, trying to convey a confidence she was far from feeling. 'I think you might breathe more easily if you kept perfectly still.' The bellboy, she noticed, was having success with the window. He had used a coat hanger to break a seal on the catch and now was inching the bottom portion upwards.

As if in response to Christine's words, the little man's struggles subsided. He was wearing an old-fashioned flannel nightshirt and Christine put an arm around him, aware of his scrawny shoulders through the coarse material. Reaching for pillows, she propped them behind, so that he could lean back, sitting upright at the same time. His eyes were fixed on hers; they were doe-like, she thought, and trying to convey gratitude. She said reassuringly. 'I've sent for a doctor. He'll be here at any moment.' As she spoke, the bellboy grunted with an extra effort and the window, suddenly freed, slid open wide. At once a draught of cool fresh air suffused the room. So the storm *had* moved south, Christine thought gratefully, sending a freshening breeze before it, and the temperature outside must be lower than for days. In the bed Albert Wells gasped greedily at the new air. As he did the telephone rang. Signalling the bellboy to take her place beside the sick man, she answered it.

'Dr Aarons is on his way, Miss Francis,' the operator announced. 'He was in Paradis and said to tell you he'll be at the hotel in twenty minutes.'

Christine hesitated. Paradis was across the Mississippi, beyond Algiers. Even allowing for fast driving, twenty minutes was optimistic. Also, she sometimes had doubts about the competence of the portly, Sazerac-drinking Dr Aarons who, as house physician, lived free in the hotel in return for his availability. She told the operator, 'I'm not sure we can wait that long. Would you check our own guests list to see if we have any doctors registered?'

'I already did that.' There was a touch of smugness in the answer, as if the speaker had studied stories of heroic telephone operators and was determined to live up to them. 'There's a Dr Koenig in 221, and Dr Uxbridge in 1203.'

Christine noted the numbers on a pad beside the telephone. 'All right, ring 221, please.' Doctors who registered in hotels expected privacy and were entitled to it. Once in a while, though, emergency justified a break with protocol.

There were several clicks as the ringing continued. Then a sleepy voice with a Teutonic accent answered, 'Yes, who is it?'

Christine identified herself. 'I'm sorry to disturb you, Dr Koenig, but one of our other guests is extremely ill.' Her eyes went to the bed. For the moment, she noticed, the blueness around the face had gone, but there was still an ashen-grey pallor, with breathing as difficult as ever. She added, 'I wonder if you could come.'

There was a pause, then the same voice, soft and agreeable: 'My dearest young lady, it would be a matter of utmost happiness if, however humbly, I could assist. Alas, I fear that I could not.' A gentle chuckle. 'You see, I am a doctor of music, here in your beautiful city to "guest conduct" – it is the word, I think – its fine symphony orchestra.'

Despite the urgency, Christine had an impulse to laugh. She apologized, 'I'm sorry for disturbing you.'

'Please do not concern yourself. Of course, if my unfortunate fellow guest becomes – how shall I put it – beyond the help of the *other* kind of doctors, I could bring my violin to play for him.' There was a deep sigh down the telephone. 'What finer way to die than to an adagio by Vivaldi or Tartini – superbly executed.'

'Thank you. I hope that won't be necessary.' She was impatient now to make the next call.

Dr Uxbridge in 1203 answered the telephone at once in a no-nonsense tone of voice. In reply to Christine's first question he responded, 'Yes, I'm a doctor of medicine – an internist.' He listened without comment while she described the problem, then said tersely, 'I'll be there in a few minutes.'

The bellboy was still at the bedside. Christine instructed him, 'Mr McDermott is in the Presidential Suite. Go there, and as soon as he's free ask him to come here quickly.' She picked up the telephone again. 'The chief engineer, please.'

Fortunately there was seldom any doubt about the chief's availability. Doc Vickery was a bachelor who lived in the hotel and had one ruling passion: the St Gregory's mechanical equipment extending from foundations to the roof. For a quarter-century, since leaving the sea and his native Clydeside, he had overseen the installation of most of it and, in lean times when money for replacement equipment was scarce, had a way of coaxing extra performance out of tired machinery. The chief was a friend of Christine's, and she knew that she was one of his favourites. In a moment his Scottish burr was on the line. 'Aye?'

In a few words she told him about Albert Wells. 'The doctor isn't here yet, but he'll probably want oxygen. We've a portable set in the hotel, haven't we?'

'Aye, we've oxygen cylinders, Chris, but we use them just for gas welding.'

'Oxygen is oxygen,' Christine argued. Some of the things her father had told her were coming back. 'It doesn't matter how you wrap it. Could you order one of your night people to have whatever's necessary sent up?'

The chief gave a grunt of agreement. 'I will; and soon as I get my breeks on, lassie, I'll be along mysel'. If I don't some clown will likely open an acetylene tank under yon man's nose, and that'll finish him for sure.'

'Please hurry!' She replaced the phone, turning back to the bed.

The little man's eyes were closed. No longer struggling, he appeared not to be breathing at all.

There was a light tap at the opened door and a tall, spare man stepped in from the corridor. He had an angular face, and hair greying at the temples. A dark blue suit, conservatively cut, failed to conceal beige pyjamas beneath. 'Uxbridge,' he announced in a quiet, firm voice.

'Doctor,' Christine said, 'just this moment . . .'

The newcomer nodded and from a leather bag, which he put down on the bed, swiftly produced a stethoscope. Without wasting time he reached inside the patient's flannel nightshirt and listened briefly to the chest and back. Then, returning to the bag, in a series of efficient movements he took out a syringe, assembled it and snapped off the neck of a small glass vial. When he had drawn the fluid from the vial into the syringe, he leaned over the bed and pushed a sleeve of the nightshirt upwards, twisting it into a rough tourniquet. He instructed Christine, 'Keep that in place; hold it tightly.'

With an alcohol swab Dr Uxbridge cleansed the forearm above a vein and inserted the syringe. He nodded to the tourniquet. 'You can release it now.' Then, glancing at his watch, he began to inject the liquid slowly.

Christine turned, her eyes seeking the doctor's face. Without looking up, he informed her, 'Aminophylline; it should stimulate the heart.' He checked his watch again, maintaining a gradual dosage. A minute passed. Two. The syringe was half empty. So far

306

there was no response.

Christine whispered, 'What is it that's wrong?'

'Severe bronchitis, with asthma as a complication. I suspect he's had these attacks before.'

Suddenly the little man's chest heaved. Then he was breathing, more slowly than before, but with fuller, deeper breaths. His eyes opened.

The tension in the room had lessened. The doctor withdrew the syringe and began to disassemble it.

'Mr Wells,' Christine said. 'Mr Wells, can you understand me?'

She was answered by a series of nods. As they had been earlier, the doe-like eyes were fixed on her own.

'You were very ill when we found you, Mr Wells. This is Dr Uxbridge who was staying in the hotel and came to help.'

The eyes shifted to the doctor. Then, with an effort: 'Thank you.' The words were close to a gasp, but they were the first the sick man had spoken. A small amount of colour was returning to his face.

'If there's anyone to thank it should be this young lady.' The doctor gave a cool, tight smile, then told Christine, 'The gentleman is still very sick and will need further medical attention. My advice is for immediate transfer to a hospital.'

'No, no! I don't want that.' The words came – a swift and urgent response – from the elderly man in the bed. He was leaning forward from the pillows, his eyes alert, hands lifted from beneath the covers where Christine had placed them earlier. The change in his condition within the space of a few minutes was remarkable, she thought. He was still breathing wheezily, and occasionally with effort, but the acute distress had gone.

For the first time Christine had time to study his appearance. Originally she had judged him to be in his early sixties; now she revised the guess to add a half dozen years. His build was slight, and shortness, plus thin peaked features and the suggestion of a stoop, created the sparrowlike effect she remembered from previous encounters. His hair, what little was left of it, was unusually combed in sparse grey strands, though now it was disarranged, and damp from perspiration. His face habitually held an expression which was mild and inoffensive, almost apologetic, and yet underneath, she suspected, was a ridge of quiet determination.

The first occasion she had met Albert Wells had been two years earlier. He had come diffidently to the hotel's executive suite, concerned about a discrepancy in his bill which he had been unable to settle with the front office. The amount involved, she recalled, was seventy-five cents and while – as usually happened when guests disputed small sums – the chief cashier had offered to cancel the charge, Albert Wells wanted to prove that he had not incurred it at all. After patient enquiry, Christine proved that the little man was right and, since she herself sometimes had bouts of parsimony – though alternating with wild feminine extravagance – she sympathized and respected him for his stand. She also deduced – from his hotel bill, which showed modest spending, and his clothes which were obviously ready-to-wear – that he was a man of small means, perhaps a pensioner, whose yearly visits to New Orleans were high points of his life.

Now Albert Wells declared. 'I don't like hospitals. I never have liked them.'

'If you stay here,' the doctor demurred, 'you'll need medical attention, and a nurse for twenty-four hours at least. You really should have intermittent oxygen too.'

The little man insisted. 'The hotel can arrange about a nurse.' He urged Christine, 'You can, can't you, miss?'

'I suppose we could.' Obviously Albert Well's dislike of hospitals must be strong. For the moment it had overcome his customary attitude of not wishing to cause trouble. She wondered, though, if he had any idea of the high cost of private nursing.

There was an interruption from the corridor. A coveralled mechanic came in, wheeling an oxygen cylinder on a trolley. He was followed by the burly figure of the chief engineer, carrying a length of rubber tubing, some wire and a plastic bag.

'This isn't hospital style, Chris,' the chief said. 'I fancy it'll work, though.' He had dressed hurriedly – an old tweed jacket and slacks over an unbuttoned shirt, revealing an expanse of hairy chest. His feet were thrust into loose sandals and beneath his bald, domed head a pair of thick-rimmed spectacles were, as usual, perched at the tip of his nose. Now, using the wire, he was fashioning a connection between the tube and plastic bag. He instructed the mechanic who had stopped uncertainly, 'Set up the cylinder beside the bed, laddie. If you move any slower, I'll think it's you should be getting the oxygen.'

Dr Uxbridge seemed surprised. Christine explained her original idea that oxygen might be needed, and introduced the chief engineer. With his hands still busy, the chief nodded, looking briefly over the top of his glasses. A moment later, with the tube connected, he announced. 'These plastic bags have suffocated enough people. No reason why one shouldna' do the reverse. Do you think it'll answer, Doctor?'

Some of Dr Uxbridge's earlier aloofness had disappeared. 'I think it will answer very well.' He glanced at Christine. 'This hotel appears to have some highly competent help.'

She laughed. 'Wait until we mix up your reservations. You'll change your mind.'

The doctor returned to the bed. 'The oxygen will make you more comfortable, Mr Wells. I imagine you've had this bronchial trouble before.'

Albert Wells nodded. He said throatily, 'The bronchitis I picked up as a miner. Then the asthma came later.' His eyes moved on to Christine. 'I'm sorry about all this, miss.'

'I'm sorry too, but mostly because your room was changed.'

The chief engineer had connected the free end of the rubber tube to the green painted cylinder. Dr Uxbridge told him, 'We'll begin with five minutes on oxygen and five minutes off.' Together they arranged the improvised mask around the sick man's face. A steady hiss denoted that the oxygen was on.

The doctor checked his watch, then enquired, 'Have you sent for a local doctor?'

Christine explained about Dr Aarons.

Dr Uxbridge nodded approval. 'He'll take over when he arrives. I'm from Illinois and not licensed to practise in Louisiana.' He bent over Albert Wells, 'Easier?' Beneath the plastic mask the little man moved his head confirmingly.

There were firm footfalls down the corridor and Peter McDermott strode in, his big frame filling the outer doorway. 'I got your message,' he told Christine. His eyes went to the bed. 'Will he be all right?'

'I believe so, though I believe we owe Mr Wells something.' Beckoning Peter into the corridor, she described the change in rooms which the bellboy had told her about. As she saw Peter frown, she added, 'If he does stay, we ought to give him another room, and I imagine we could get a nurse without too much trouble.'

Peter nodded agreement. There was a house telephone in a maid's closet across the hallway. He went to it and asked for Reception.

'I'm on the fourteenth,' he informed the room clerk who answered. 'Is there a vacant room on this floor?'

There was a perceptible pause. The night-room clerk was an old-timer, appointed many years ago by Warren Trent. He had an autocratic way of doing his job which few people ever contested. He had also made known to Peter McDermott on a couple of occasions that he resented newcomers, particularly if they were younger, senior to himself, and from the north.

'Well,' Peter said, 'is there a room or isn't there?'

'I have 1410,' the clerk said with his best southern planter's accent, 'but I'm about to allocate it to a gentleman who has this moment checked in.' He added, 'In case you're unaware, we are very close to a full house.'

Number 1410 was a room Peter remembered. It was large and airy and faced St Charles Avenue. He asked reasonably, 'If I take 1410, can you find something else for your man?'

'No, Mr McDermott. All I have is a small suite on five, and the gentleman does not wish to pay a higher rate.'

Peter said crisply, 'Let your man have the suite at the room rate for tonight. He can be relocated in the morning. Meanwhile I'll use 1410 for a transfer from 1439, and please send a boy up with the key right away.'

'Just one minute, Mr McDermott.' Previously the clerk's tone had been aloof; now it was openly truculent. 'It has always been Mr Trent's policy . . .'

'Right now we're talking about my policy,' Peter snapped. 'And another thing: before you go off duty leave word for the day clerks tomorrow I want an explanation of why Mr Wells was shifted from his original room to 1439, and you might add that the reason had better be good.'

He grimaced at Christine as he replaced the phone.

5

'You must have been insane,' the Duchess of Croydon protested. 'Absolutely, abysmally insane.' She had returned to the living-room of the Presidential Suite after Peter McDermott's departure, carefully closing the inner door behind her.

The Duke shifted uncomfortably as he always did under one of his wife's periodic tongue lashings. 'Damn sorry, old girl. Telly was on. Couldn't hear the fellow. Thought he'd cleared out.' He took a deep draught from the whisky and soda he was holding unsteadily, then added plaintively, 'Besides, with everything else I'm bloody upset.'

'Sorry! Upset!' Unusually there was an undernote of hysteria in his wife's voice. 'You make it sound as if it's all some sort of game. As if what happened tonight couldn't be the ruination . . .'

'Don't think anything of the sort. Know it's all serious. Bloody serious.' Hunched disconsolately in a deep leather armchair he seemed a little man, akin to the bowler-hatted mousy genus which English cartoonists were so fond of drawing.

The Duchess went on accusingly, 'I was doing the best I could. The very best, after your incredible folly, to establish that both of us spent a quiet evening in the hotel. I even invented a walk that we went for in case anyone saw us come in. And then crassly, stupidly, you blunder in to announce you left your cigarettes in the car.'

'Only one heard me. That manager chap. Wouldn't notice.'

'He noticed. I was watching his face.' With an effort the Duchess retained her self-control. 'Have you any notion of the ghastly mess we're in?'

'Already said so.' The Duke drained his drink, then contemplated the empty tumbler. 'Bloody ashamed too. 'F you hadn't persuaded me . . . 'F I hadn't been fuddled . . .'

'You were drunk! You were drunk when I found you, and you still are.'

He shook his head as if to clear it. 'Sober now.' It was his own turn to be bitter. 'You *would* follow me. Butt in. Wouldn't leave things be . . .'

'Never mind that. It's the other that matters.'

He repeated, '*You* persuaded me . . .'

'There was nothing we could do. Nothing! And there was a better chance my way.'

'Not so sure. 'F the police get their teeth in . . .'

'We'd have to be suspected first. That's why I made that trouble with the waiter and followed through. It isn't an alibi but it's the next best thing. It's set in their minds we were here tonight . . . or would have been if you hadn't thrown it all away. I could weep.'

'Be interesting that,' the Duke said. 'Didn't think you were enough of a woman.' He sat upright in the chair and had somehow thrown off the submissiveness, or most of it. It was a chameleon quality which sometimes bewildered those who knew him, setting them to wondering which was the real person.

The Duchess flushed, the effect heightening her statuesque beauty. 'That isn't necessary.'

'P'raps not.' Rising, the Duke went to a side table where he splashed Scotch generously into his glass, followed by a short snort of soda. With his back turned, he added, 'All the same, must admit 's'at bottom most of our troubles.'

'I admit nothing of the kind. Your habits are, perhaps, but not mine. Going to that disgusting gambling joint was madness; and to take that woman . . .'

'Y'already covered that,' the Duke said wearily. 'Exhaustively. On our way back. Before it happened.'

'I wasn't aware that what I said had penetrated.'

'Your words, old girl, penetrate thickest mists. I keep trying make them impenetrable. So far haven't succeeded.' The Duke of Croydon sipped his fresh drink. 'Why d'you marry me?'

'I suppose it was mostly that you stood out in our circle as someone who was doing something worth while. People said that the aristocracy was effete. You seemed to be proving that it wasn't.'

He held up his glass, studying it like a crystal ball. 'Not proving it now. Eh?'

'If you appear to be; it's because I prop you up.'

'Washington?' The word was a question.

'We could manage it,' the Duchess said. 'If I could keep you sober and in your own bed.'

'Aha!' Her husband laughed hollowly. 'A damn cold bed at that.'

'I already said that isn't necessary.'

'Ever wonder why I married *you*?'

'I've formed opinions.'

'Tell you most important.' He drank again, as if for courage, then said thickly. 'Wanted

310

you in that bed. Fast. Legally. Knew was only way.'

'I'm surprised you bothered. With so many offers to choose from – before and since.'

His bloodshot eyes were on her face. 'Didn't want others. Wanted you. Still do.'

She snapped. 'That's enough! This has gone far enough.'

He shook his head. 'Something you should hear. Your pride, old girl. Magnificent. Savage. Always appealed to me. Didn't want to break it. Share it. You on your back. Thighs apart. Passionate. Trembling . . .'

'Stop it! Stop it! You . . . you lecher!' Her face was white, her voice high pitched. 'I don't care if the police catch you! I hope they do! I hope you get ten years!'

6

After his quickly concluded dispute with Reception, Peter McDermott recrossed the fourteenth floor corridor to 1439.

'If you approve,' he informed Dr Uxbridge, 'we'll transfer your patient to another room on this floor.'

The tall, sparely built doctor who had responded to Christine's emergency call nodded. He glanced around the tiny ha-ha room with its mess of heating and water pipes. 'Any change can only be an improvement.'

As the doctor returned to the little man in the bed, beginning a new five-minute period of oxygen, Christine reminded Peter, 'What we need now is a nurse.'

'We'll let Dr Aarons arrange that.' Peter mused aloud: 'The hotel will have to make the engagement, I suppose, which means we'll be liable for payment. Do you think your friend Wells is good for it?'

They had returned to the corridor, their voices low.

'I'm worried about that. I don't think he has much money.' When she was concentrating, Peter noticed, Christine's nose had a charming way of crinkling. He was aware of her closeness and a faint, fragrant perfume.

'Oh well,' he said, 'we won't be too deep in debt by morning. We'll let the credit department look into it then.'

When the key arrived, Christine went ahead to open the new room, 1410. 'It's ready,' she announced, returning.

'The best thing is to switch beds,' Peter told the others. 'Let's wheel this one into 1410 and bring back a bed from there.' But the doorway, they discovered was an inch too narrow.

Albert Wells, his breathing easier and with returning colour, volunteered, 'I've walked all my life, I can do a little bit now.' But Dr Uxbridge shook his head decisively.

The chief engineer inspected the difference in widths. 'I'll take the door off its hinges,' he told the sick man. 'Then ye'll go out like a cork from a bottle.'

'Never mind,' Peter said. 'There's a quicker way – if you're agreeable, Mr Wells.'

The other smiled and nodded.

Peter bent down, put a blanket around the elderly man's shoulders and picked him up bodily.

'You've strong arms, son,' the little man said.

Peter smiled. Then, as easily as if his burden were a child, he strode down the corridor and into the new room.

Fifteen minutes later all was functioning as if on nyloned bearings. The oxygen equipment had been successfully transferred, though its use was now less urgent since the air conditioning in the more spacious quarters of 1410 had no competition from hot pipes, hence the air was sweeter. The resident physician, Dr Aarons, had arrived, portly, jovial, and breathing bourbon in an almost-visible cloud. He accepted with alacrity the offer of Dr Uxbridge to drop in in a consultant capacity the following day, and also grasped eagerly a suggestion that cortisone might prevent a recurrence of the earlier attack. A private duty nurse, telephoned affectionately by Dr Aarons ('Such wonderful news, my dear! We're going to be a team again.') was reportedly on the way.

As the chief engineer and Dr Uxbridge took their leave, Albert Wells was sleeping gently.

Following Christine into the corridor, Peter carefully closed the door on Dr Aarons who, while waiting for his nurse, was pacing the room to his own accompaniment, *pinissimo*, of the Toreador Song from *Carmen*. ('*Pom, pom, pom, pom-pom; pom-pom-pom, pom-pom . . .*') the latch clicked, cutting the minstrelsy off.

It was a quarter to twelve.

Walking towards the elevators, Christine said, 'I'm glad we let him stay.'

Peter seemed surprised. 'Mr Wells? Why wouldn't we?'

'Some places wouldn't. You know how they are: the least thing out of the ordinary, and no-one can be bothered. All they want is people to check in, check out and pay the bill; that's all.'

'Those are sausage factories. A real hotel is for hospitality; and succour if a guest needs it. The best ones started that way. Unfortunately too many people in this business have forgotten.'

She regarded him curiously. 'You think we've forgotten here?'

'You're damn right we have! A lot of the time, anyway. If I had my way there'd be a good many changes . . .' he stopped, embarrassed at his own forcefulness. 'Never mind. Most of the time I keep such traitorous thoughts to myself.'

'You shouldn't, and if you do you should be ashamed.' Behind Christine's words was the knowledge that the St Gregory *was* inefficient in many ways and in recent years had coasted under the shadow of its former glories. Currently, too, the hotel was facing a financial crisis which might force drastic transitions whether its proprietor, Warren Trent, was in favour or not.

'There's heads and brick walls,' Peter objected. 'Beating one against the other doesn't help. W. T. isn't keen on new ideas.'

'That's no reason for giving up.'

He laughed. 'You sound like a woman.'

'I *am* a woman.'

'I know,' Peter said. 'I've just begun to notice.'

It was true, he thought. For most of the time he had known Christine – since his own arrival at the St Gregory – he had taken her for granted. Recently, though, he had found himself increasingly aware of just how attractive and personable she was. He wondered what she was doing for the rest of the evening.

He said tentatively, 'I didn't have dinner tonight; too much going on. If you feel like it, how about joining me for a late supper?'

Christine said, 'I love late suppers.'

At the elevator he told her, 'There's one more thing I want to check. I sent Herbie Chandler to look into that trouble on the eleventh but I don't trust him. After that I'll be through.' He took her arm, squeezing it lightly. 'Will you wait on the main mezzanine?'

His hands were surprisingly gentle for someone who might have been clumsy because of his size. Christine glanced sideways at the strong, energetic profile with its jutting jaw that was almost lantern-like. It was an interesting face, she thought, with a hint of determination which could become obstinacy if provoked. She was aware of her senses quickening.

'All right,' she agreed. 'I'll wait.'

7

Marsha Preyscott wished fervently that she had spent her nineteenth birthday some other way, or at least had stayed at the Alpha Kappa Epsilon fraternity ball on the hotel's convention floor, eight storeys below. The sound of the ball, muted by distance and competing noises, came up to her now, drifting through the window of the eleventh-floor suite, which one of the boys had forced open a few minutes ago when the warmth, cigarette smoke and general odour of liquor in the tightly packed room became overly oppressive, even for those whose grasp of such details was rapidly diminishing.

It had been a mistake to come here. But as always, and rebelliously, she had sought something different, which was what Lyle Dumaire had promised, Lyle whom she had known for years and dated occasionally, and whose father was president of one of the city's banks as well as a close friend of her own father. Lyle had told her while they were dancing, 'This is kid stuff, Marsha. Some of the guys have taken a suite and we've been up there most of the evening. A lot of things are going on.' He essayed a manly laugh which somehow became a giggle, then asked directly, 'Why don't you come?'

Without thinking about it she had said yes, and they had left the dancing, coming upstairs to the small, crowded suite 1126-7, to be enveloped as they went in by stale air and high-pitched clamour. There were more people than she had expected, and the fact that some of the boys were already very drunk was something she had not bargained for.

There were several girls, most of whom she knew, though none intimately, and she spoke to them briefly, though it was hard to hear or be heard. One who said nothing, Sue Phillipe, had apparently passed out and her escort, a boy from Baton Rouge, was pouring water over her from a shoe he kept replenishing in the bathroom. Sue's dress of pink organdy was already a sodden mess.

The boys greeted Marsha more effusively, though almost at once returning to the improvised bar, set up by turning a glass-fronted cabinet upon its side. Someone – she wasn't sure who – put a glass clumsily into Marsha's hand.

It was obvious too that something was happening in the adjoining room, to which the door was closed, though a knot of boys whom Lyle Dumaire had joined – leaving Marsha alone – was clustered around it. She heard snatches of talk, including the question, 'What was it like?' but the answer was lost in a shout of ribald laughter.

313

When some further remarks made her realize, or at least suspect, what was happening, disgust made her want to leave. Even the big lonely Garden District mansion was preferable to this, despite her dislike of its emptiness, with just herself and the servants when her father was away, as he had been for six weeks now, and would continue to be for at least two more.

The thought of her father reminded Marsha that if he had come home as he originally expected and promised, she would not have been here now, or at the fraternity ball either. Instead, there would have been a birthday celebration, with Mark Preyscott presiding in the easy jovial way he had, with a few of his daughter's special friends who, she knew, would have declined the Alpha Kappa Epsilon invitation if it had conflicted with her own. But he had not come home. Instead, he had telephoned, apologetically as he always did, this time from Rome.

'Marsha, honey, I really tried but I couldn't make it. My business here is going to take two or three weeks more, but I'll make it up to you, honey, I really will when I come home.' He enquired tentatively if Marsha would like to visit her mother and her mother's latest husband in Los Angeles, and when she declined without even thinking about it, her father had urged, 'Well, anyway, have a wonderful birthday, and there's something on the way I think you'll like.' Marsha had felt like crying at the sweet sound of his voice, but hadn't because she had long ago taught herself not to. Nor was there any point in wondering why the owner of a New Orleans department store, with a platoon of highly paid executives, should be more inflexibly tied to business than an office boy. Perhaps there were other things in Rome which he wouldn't tell her about, just as she would never tell him what was happening in room 1126 right now.

When she made her decision to leave she had moved to put her glass on a window ledge and now, down below, she could hear them playing *Stardust*. At this time of evening the music always moved on to the old sentimental numbers, especially if the band leader was Moxie Buchanan with his All-Star Southern Gentlemen who played for most of the St Gregory's silver-plated social functions. Even if she had not been dancing earlier she would have recognized the arrangement – the brass warm and sweet, yet dominant, which was the Buchanan trademark.

Hesitating at the window, Marsha pondered a return to the dance floor, though she knew the way it would be there now: the boys increasingly hot in their tuxedos, some fingering their collars uncomfortably, a few hobbledehoys wishing they were back in jeans and sweatshirt, and the girls shuttling to and from the powder room, behind its doors sharing giggled confidences; the whole affair, Marsha decided, as if a group of children were dressed to play charades. Youth was a dull time, Marsha often thought, especially when you had to share it with others the same age as yourself. There were moments – and this was one – when she longed for companionship that was more mature.

She would not find it though in Lyle Dumaire. She could see him still in the group by the communicating door, his face flushed, starched shirtfront billowed and black tie askew. Marsha wondered how she could ever have taken him seriously, as she had for a while.

Others as well as herself were beginning to leave the suite, heading for the outer doorway in what seemed to be a general exodus. One of the older boys whom she knew as Stanley Dixon came out of the other room. As he nodded towards the door which he carefully closed behind him, she could hear snatches of his words. ' . . . girls say they're going . . . had enough . . . scared . . . disturbance.'

Someone else said, ' . . . told you we shouldn't have had all this . . .'

'Why not somebody from here?' It was Lyle Dumaire's voice, much less under control than it had been earlier.

'Yeah, but who?' The eyes of the small group swung around the room appraisingly. Marsha studiedly ignored them.

Several friends of Sue Phillipe, the girl who had passed out, were trying to help her to her feet, but not succeeding. One of the boys, more steady than the rest, called out concernedly, 'Marsha! Sue's in a pretty bad shape. Can you help her?'

Reluctantly Marsha stopped, looking down at the girl who had opened her eyes and was leaning back, her child-like face pallid, mouth slack, with its lipstick smeared messily. With an inward sigh Marsha told the others, 'Help me get her to the bathroom.' As three of them lifted her, the drunken girl began to cry.

At the bathroom one of the boys seemed inclined to follow, but Marsha closed the door firmly and bolted it. She turned to Sue Phillipe who was staring at herself in the mirror with an expression of horror. At least, Marsha thought gratefully, the shock had been sobering.

'I wouldn't worry too much,' she remarked. 'They say it has to happen once to all of us.'

'Oh God! Mother will *kill* me.' The words were a moan, ending with a dive to the toilet bowl in order to be sick.

Seating herself on the edge of the bathtub, Marsha said practically, 'You'll feel a lot better after that. When you're through I'll bathe your face and we can try some fresh make-up.'

Her head still down, the other girl nodded dismally.

It was ten or fifteen minutes before they emerged and the suite was almost cleared, though Lyle Dumaire and his cronies were still huddled together. If Lyle planned to escort her, Marsha thought, she would turn him down. The only other occupant was the boy who had appealed for help. He came forward explaining hurriedly, 'We've arranged for a girl friend of Sue's to take her home, and Sue can probably spend the night there.' As he took the other girl's arm, she went with him compliantly. Over his shoulder the boy called back, 'We've a car waiting downstairs. Thanks a lot, Marsha.' Relieved, she watched them go.

She was retrieving her wrap, which she had put down to help Sue Phillipe, when she heard the outer door close. Stanley Dixon was standing in front of it, his hands behind him. Marsha heard the lock click softly.

'Hey, Marsha,' Lyle Dumaire said. 'What's the big rush?'

Marsha had known Lyle since childhood, but now there was a difference. This was a stranger, with the mien of a drunken bully. She answered, 'I'm going home.'

'Aw, come on.' He swaggered towards her. 'Be a good sport and have a drink.'

'No, thank you.'

As if he had not heard: 'You're going to be a good sport, kid, aren't you?'

'Just privately,' Stanley Dixon said. He had a thick nasal voice with a built-in leer. 'Some of us have had a good time already. It's made us want more of the same.' The other two, whose names she didn't know, were grinning.

She snapped, 'I'm not interested in what you want.' Though her voice was firm, she was aware of an underlying note of fear. She went towards the door, but Dixon shook his head. 'Please,' she said, 'please let me go.'

'Listen, Marsha,' Lyle blustered. 'We know you want to.' He gave a coarse giggle. 'All girls want to. They never really mean no. What they mean is "come and get it".' He appealed to the others. 'Eh, fellas?'

The third boy crooned softly, 'That's the way it is. You gotta get in there and get it.'

They began to move closer.

She wheeled. 'I'm warning you: if you touch me I shall scream.'

'Be a pity if you did that,' Stanley Dixon murmured. 'You might miss all the fun.' Suddenly, without seeming to move, he was behind her, clapping a big sweaty hand across her mouth, another pinioning her arms. His head was close to hers, the smell of rye whisky overpowering.

She struggled, and tried to bit his hand, but without success.

'Listen, Marsha,' Lyle said, his face twisted into a smirk, 'you're going to get it, so you might as well enjoy it. That's what they always say, isn't it? If Stan lets go, will you promise not to make any noise?'

She shook her head furiously.

One of the others seized her arm. 'Come on, Marsha. Lyle says you're a good sport. Why don't you prove it?'

She was struggling madly now, but unavailingly. The grip around her was unyielding. Lyle had the other arm and together they were forcing her towards the adjoining bedroom.

'The hell with it,' Dixon said. 'Somebody grab her feet.' The remaining boy took hold. She tried to kick, but all that happened was her high-heeled pumps came off. With a sense of unreality Marsha felt herself being carried through the bedroom doorway.

'This is the last time,' Lyle warned. The veneer of good humour had vanished. 'Are you going to cooperate or not?'

Her answer was to struggle more violently.

'Get her things off,' someone said. And another voice – she thought it was from whoever was holding her feet – asked hesitantly. 'Do you think we should?'

'Quit worrying.' It was Lyle Dumaire. 'Nothing'll happen. Her old man's whoring it up in Rome.'

There were twin beds in the room. Resisting wildly, Marsha was forced backwards on to the nearest. A moment later she lay across it, her head pressed back cruelly until all she could see was the ceiling above, once painted white but now closer to grey, and ornamented in the centre where a light fitting glowed. Dust had accumulated on the fitting and beside it was a yellowed water stain.

Abruptly the ceiling light went out, but there was a glow in the room from another lamp left on. Dixon had shifted his grip. Now he was half sitting on the bed, near her head, but the grasp on her body as well as across her mouth was as inflexible as ever. She felt other hands, and hysteria swept over her. Contorting herself, she attempted to kick but her legs were pinned down. She tried to roll over and there was a rending sound as her Balenciaga gown tore.

'I'm first,' Stanley Dixon said. 'Somebody take over here.' She could hear his heavy breathing.

Footsteps went softly on the rug around the bed. Her legs were still held firmly, but

Dixon's hand on her face was moving, another taking its place. It was an opportunity. As the new hand came over, Marsha bit fiercely. She felt her teeth go into flesh, meeting bone.

There was an anguished cry, and the hand was withdrawn.

Inflating her lungs, Marsha screamed. She screamed three times and ended with a desperate cry. 'Help! Please help me!'

Only the last word was cut off as Stanley Dixon's hand slammed back into place with a force that made her senses swim. She heard him snarl, 'You fool! You stupid goon!'

'She bit me!' The voice was sobbing with pain. 'The bitch bit my hand.'

Dixon said savagely, 'What did you expect her to do, kiss it? Now we'll have the whole goddamned hotel on our necks.'

Lyle Dumaire urged, 'Let's get out of here.'

'Shut up!' Dixon commanded. They stood listening.

Dixon said softly, 'There's nothing stirring. I guess nobody heard.'

It was true, Marsha thought despairingly. Tears clouded her vision. She seemed to have lost the power to struggle any more.

There was a knock on the outside door. Three taps, firm and assertive.

'Christ!' the third boy said. 'Somebody did hear.' He added with a moan, 'Oh God! – my hand!'

The fourth asked nervously, 'What do we do?'

The knocking was repeated, this time more vigorously.

After a pause a voice from outside called, 'Open the door, please. I heard someone shout for help.' The caller's speech had a soft, southern accent.

Lyle Dumaire whispered. 'There's only one; he's by himself. Maybe we can stall.'

'It's worth a try,' Dixon breathed. 'I'll go.' He murmured to one of the others. 'Hold her down and this time don't make any mistake.'

The hand on Marsha's mouth changed swiftly and another held her body.

A lock clicked, followed by a squeak as the door opened partially. Stanley Dixon, as if surprised, said, 'Oh.'

'Excuse me, sir. I'm an employee of the hotel.' It was the voice they had heard a moment earlier. 'I happened to be passing and heard someone cry out.'

'Just passing, eh?' Dixon's tone was oddly hostile. Then, as if deciding to be diplomatic, he added. 'Well, thanks anyway. But it was only my wife having a nightmare. She went to bed before me. She's all right now.'

'Well . . .' The other appeared to hesitate. 'If you're sure there's nothing.'

'Nothing at all,' Dixon said. 'It's just one of those things that happen once in a while.' He was convincing, and in command of the situation. In a moment, Marsha knew, the door would close.

Since she had relaxed she had become aware that the pressure on her face had lessened also. Now she tensed herself for one final effort. Twisting her body sideways, momentarily she freed her mouth. 'Help!' she called. 'Don't believe him! Please help!' Once more, roughly, she was stopped.

There was a sharp exchange outside. She heard the new voice say, 'I'd like to come in, please.'

'This is a private room. I told you my wife is having a nightmare.'

'I'm sorry, sir; I don't believe you.'

317

'All right,' Dixon said. 'Come in.'

As if not wishing to be witnessed, the hands upon Marsha removed themselves. As they did, she rolled over, pushing herself partially upright facing the door. A young Negro was entering. In his early twenties, he had an intelligent face and was neatly dressed, his short hair parted and carefully brushed.

He took in the situation at once and said sharply. 'Let the young lady go.'

'Take a look, fellas,' Dixon said. 'Take a look at who's giving orders.'

Dimly, Marsha was aware that the door to the corridor was still partially open.

'All right, nigger boy,' Dixon snarled. 'You asked for it.' His right fist shot out expertly, the strength of his big broad shoulders behind the blow which would have felled the young Negro if it had found its target. But in a single movement, agile as a ballet step, the other moved sideways, the extending arm going harmlessly past his head, with Dixon stumbling forward. In the same instant the Negro's own left fist snapped upward, landing with a hard, sharp crack at the side of his attacker's face.

Somewhere along the corridor another door opened and closed.

A hand on his cheek, Dixon said, 'You son-of-a-bitch!' Turning to the others, he urged, 'Let's get him!'

Only the boy with the injured hand held back. As if with a single impulse, the other three fell upon the young Negro and, before their combined assault, he went down. Marsha heard the thud of blows and also – from outside – the growing hum of voices in the corridor.

The others heard the voices too. 'The roof is falling in,' Lyle Dumaire warned urgently. 'I told you we should get out of here.'

There was a scramble to the door, led by the boy who had not joined in the fighting, the others hastily behind him. Marsha heard Stanley Dixon stop to say. 'There's been some trouble. We're going for help.'

The young Negro was rising from the floor, his face bloody.

Outside, a new, authoritative voice rose above the others. 'Where is the disturbance, please?'

'There was screaming and a fight,' a woman said excitedly. 'In there.'

Another grumbled, 'I complained earlier, but no-one took any notice.'

The door opened wide. Marsha caught a glimpse of peering faces, a tall, commanding figure entering. Then the door was closed from the inside and the overhead light snapped on.

Peter McDermott surveyed the disordered room. He enquired, 'What happened?'

Marsha's body was racked with sobs. She attempted to stand, but fell back weakly against the headboard of the bed, gathering the torn dishevelled remnants of her dress in front of her. Between sobs her lips formed words: 'Tried . . . rape . . .'

McDermott's face hardened. His eyes swung to the young Negro, now leaning for support against the wall, using a handkerchief to stem the bleeding from his face.

'Royce!' Cold fury flickered in McDermott's eyes.

'No! No!' Barely coherent, Marsha called pleadingly across the room. 'It wasn't him! He came to help!' She closed her eyes, the thought of further violence sickening her.

The young Negro straightened. Putting the handkerchief away, he mocked. 'Why don't you go ahead, Mr McDermott and hit me. You could always say afterwards it was a mistake.'

Peter spoke curtly. 'I already made a mistake, Royce, and I apologize.' He had a profound dislike of Aloysius Royce who combined the role of personal valet to the hotel owner, Warren Trent, with the study of law at Loyola University. Years before, Royce's father, the son of a slave, had become Warren Trent's body servant, close companion and confidant. A quarter-century later, when the old man died, his son Aloysius, who had been born and raised in the St Gregory, stayed on and now lived in the hotel owner's private suite under a loose arrangement by which he came and went as his studies required. But in Peter McDermott's opinion Royce was needlessly arrogant and supercilious, seeming to combine a distrust of any proffered friendliness with a perpetual chip on his shoulder.

'Tell me what you know,' Peter said.

'There were four of them. Four nice white young gentlemen.'

'Did you recognize anyone?'

Royce nodded. 'Two.'

'That's good enough.' Peter crossed to the telephone beside the nearer bed.

'Who are you calling?'

'The city police. We've no choice but to bring them in.'

There was a half smile on the young Negro's face. 'If you want some advice, I wouldn't do it.'

'Why not?'

'Fo' one thing,' Aloysius Royce drawled, accenting his speech deliberately, 'I'd have to be a witness. An' let me tell you, Mr McDermott, no court in this sovereign State of Louisiana is gonna take a nigger boy's word in a white rape case, attempted or otherwise. No, sir, not when four upstanding young white gentlemen say the nigger boy is lying. Not even if Miss Preyscott supports the nigger boy, which I doubt her pappy'd let her, considering what all the newspapers and such might make of it.'

Peter had picked up the receiver; now he put it down. 'Sometimes,' he said, 'you seem to want to make things harder than they are.' But he knew that what Royce had said was true. His eyes swinging to Marsha, he asked, 'Did you say "Miss Preyscott"?'

The young Negro nodded. 'Her father is Mr Mark Preyscott. *The* Preyscott. That's right, miss, isn't it?'

Unhappily, Marsha nodded.

'Miss Preyscott,' Peter said, 'did you know the people who were responsible for what happened?'

The answer was barely audible. 'Yes.'

Royce volunteered, 'They were all from Alpha Kappa Epsilon, I think.'

'Is that true, Miss Preyscott?'

A slight movement of her head, assenting.

'And did you come here with them – to this suite?'

Again a whisper. 'Yes.'

Peter looked questioningly at Marsha. At length, he said, 'It's up to you, Miss Preyscott, whether you make an official complaint or not. Whatever you decide, the hotel will go along with. But I'm afraid there's a good deal of truth in what Royce said just now about publicity. There would certainly be some – a good deal, I imagine – and not pleasant.' He added: 'Of course, it's really something for your father to decide. Don't you think I should call, and have him come here?'

Marsha raised her head, looking directly at Peter for the first time. 'My father's in

Rome. Don't tell him, please – ever.'

'I'm sure something can be done privately. I don't believe anyone should get away with this entirely.' Peter went around the bed. He was startled to see how much of a child she was, and how very beautiful. 'Is there anything I can do now?'

'I don't know. I don't know.' She began to cry again, more softly.

Uncertainly, Peter took out a white linen handkerchief which Marsha accepted, wiped the tears, then blew her nose.

'Better?'

She nodded. 'Thank you.' Her mind was a turmoil of emotions: hurt, shame, anger, an urge to fight back blindly whatever the consequences, and a desire – which experience told her would not be fulfilled – to be enfolded in loving and protective arms. But beyond the emotions, and exceeding them, was an overwhelming physical exhaustion.

'I think you should rest a while,' Peter McDermott turned down the coverlet of the unused bed and Marsha slipped under it, lying on the blanket beneath. The touch of the pillow to her face was cool.

She said, 'I don't want to stay here. I couldn't.'

He nodded understandingly, 'In a little while we'll get you home.'

'No! Not that either! Please, isn't there somewhere else . . . in the hotel?'

He shook his head. 'I'm afraid the hotel is full.'

Aloysius Royce had gone into the bathroom to wash the blood from his face. Now he returned and stood in the doorway of the adjoining living-room. He whistled softly, surveying the mess of disarranged furniture, overflowing ash trays, spilled bottles and broken glass.

As McDermott joined him, Royce observed, 'I guess it was quite a party.'

'It seems to have been,' Peter closed the communicating door between the living-room and bedroom.

Marsha pleaded, 'There must be some place in the hotel. I couldn't face going home tonight.'

Peter hesitated. 'There's 555, I suppose.' He glanced at Royce.

Room 555 was a small one which went with the assistant general manager's job. Peter rarely used it, except to change. It was empty now.

'It'll be alright,' Marsha said. 'As long as someone phones my home. Ask for Anna the housekeeper.'

'If you like,' Royce offered, 'I'll go get the key.'

Peter nodded. 'Stop in there on the way back – you'll find a dressing gown. I suppose we ought to call a maid.'

'You let a maid in here right now, you might as well put it all on the radio.'

Peter considered. At this stage nothing would stop gossip. Inevitably when this kind of incident happened any hotel throbbed back-stairs like a jungle telegraph. But he supposed there was no point in adding postscripts.

'Very well. We'll take Miss Preyscott down ourselves in the service elevator.'

As the young Negro opened the outer door, voices filtered in, with a barrage of eager questions. Momentarily, Peter had forgotten the assemblage of awakened guests outside. He heard Royce's answers, quietly reassuring, then the voices fade.

Her eyes closed, Marsha murmured, 'You haven't told me who you are.'

'I'm sorry. I should have explained.' He told her his name and his connection with the

320

hotel. Marsha listened without responding, aware of what was being said, but for the most part letting the quiet reassuring voice flow easily over her. After a while, eyes still closed, her thoughts wandered drowsily. She was aware dimly of Aloysius Royce returning, of being helped from the bed into a dressing gown, and being escorted quickly and quietly down a silent corridor. From an elevator there was more corridor, then another bed on which she lay down quietly. The reassuring voice said, 'She's just about all in.'

The sound of water running. A voice telling her that a bath was drawn. She roused herself sufficiently to pad to the bathroom where she locked herself in.

There were pyjamas in the bathroom, neatly laid out, and afterwards Marsha put them on. They were men's, in dark blue, and too large. The sleeves covered her hands and even with the trouser bottoms turned up it was hard not to trip over them.

She went outside where hands helped her into bed. Snuggling down in the crisp, fresh linen, she was aware of Peter McDermott's calm, restoring voice once more. It was a voice she liked, Marsha thought – and its owner also. 'Royce and I are leaving now, Miss Preyscott. The door to this room is self-locking and the key is beside your bed. You won't be disturbed.'

'Thank you.' Sleepily she asked, 'Whose pyjamas?'

'They're mine. I'm sorry they're so big.'

She tried to shake her head but was too tired. 'No matter . . . nice . . .' She was glad they were his pyjamas. She had a comforting sense of being enfolded after all.

'Nice,' she repeated softly. It was her final waking thought.

8

Peter waited alone for the elevator on the fifth floor. Aloysius Royce had already taken the service elevator to the fifteenth floor, where his quarters adjoined the hotel owner's private suite.

It had been a full evening, Peter thought – with its share of unpleasantness – though not exceptional for a big hotel, which often presented an exposed slice of life that hotel employees became used to seeing.

When the elevator arrived he told the operator, 'Lobby, please,' reminding himself that Christine was waiting on the main mezzanine, but his business on the main floor would take only a few minutes.

He noted with impatience that although the elevator doors were closed, they had not yet started down. The operator – one of the regular night men – was jockeying the control handle back and forth. Peter asked, 'Are you sure the gates are fully closed?'

'Yes, sir, they are. It isn't that; it's the connections I think either here or up top.' The man angled his head in the direction of the roof where the elevator machinery was housed, then added, 'Had quite a bit of trouble lately. The chief was probing around the other day.' He worked the handle vigorously. With a jerk the mechanism took hold and the elevator started down.

'Which elevator is this?'

'Number four.'

Peter made a mental note to ask the chief engineer exactly what was wrong.

It was almost half past twelve by the lobby clock as he stepped from the elevator. As was usual by this time, some of the activity in and around the lobby had quieted down, but there was still a fair number of people in evidence, and the strains of music from the nearby Indigo Room showed that supper dancing was in progress. Peter turned right towards Reception but had gone only a few paces when he was aware of an obese, waddling figure approaching him. It was Ogilvie, the chief house officer, who had been missing earlier. The heavily jowled face of the ex-policeman – years before he had served without distinction on the New Orleans force – was carefully expressionless, though his little pig's eyes darted sideways, sizing up the scene around him. As always, he was accompanied by an odour of stale cigarette smoke, and a line of fat cigars, like unfired torpedoes, filled the top pocket of his suit.

'I hear you were looking for me,' Ogilvie said. It was a flat statement, unconcerned.

Peter felt some of his earlier anger return. 'I certainly was. Where the devil were you?'

'Doing my job, Mr McDermott.' For an outsize man Ogilvie had a surprisingly falsetto voice. 'If you want to know, I was over at police headquarters reporting some trouble we had here. There was a suitcase stolen from the baggage room today.'

'Police headquarters! Which room was the poker game in?'

The piggy eyes glowered resentfully. 'If that's the way you feel, maybe you should do some checking. Or speak to Mr Trent.'

Peter nodded resignedly. It would be a waste of time, he knew. The alibi was undoubtedly well established, and Ogilvie's friends in headquarters would back him up. Besides, Warren Trent would never take action against Ogilvie, who had been at the St Gregory as long as the hotel proprietor himself. There were some who said that the fat detective knew where a body or two was buried, and thus had a hold over Warren Trent. But whatever the reason, Ogilvie's position was unassailable.

'Well, you just happened to have missed a couple of emergencies,' Peter said. 'But both are taken care of now.' Perhaps after all, he reflected, it was as well that Ogilvie had not been available. Undoubtedly the house officer would not have responded to the Albert Wells crisis as efficiently as Christine, nor handled Marsha Preyscott with tact and sympathy. Resolving to put Ogilvie out of his mind, with a curt nod he moved on to Reception.

The night clerk whom he had telephoned earlier was at the desk. Peter decided to try a conciliatory approach. He said pleasantly, 'Thank you for helping me out with that problem on the fourteenth. We have Mr Wells settled comfortably in 1410. Dr Aarons is arranging nursing care, and the chief has fixed up oxygen.'

The room clerk's face had frozen as Peter approached him. Now it relaxed. 'I hadn't realized there was anything that serious.'

'It was touch and go for a while, I think. That's why I was so concerned about why he was moved into that other room.'

The room clerk nodded sagely. 'In that case I'll certainly pursue enquiries. Yes, you can be sure of that.'

'We've had some trouble on the eleventh, too. Do you mind telling me whose name 1126-7 is in?'

'The room clerk flipped through his records and produced a card. 'Mr Stanley Dixon.'

'Dixon.' It was one of the two names Aloysius Royce had given him when they talked briefly after leaving Marsha.

'He's the car dealer's son. Mr Dixon senior is often in the hotel.'

'Thank you.' Peter nodded. 'You'd better list it as a checkout, and have the cashier mail the bill.' A thought occurred to him. 'No, have the bill sent to me tomorrow, and I'll write a letter. There'll be a claim for damages after we've figured out what they are.'

'Very well, Mr McDermott.' The change in the night clerk's attitude was most marked. 'I'll tell the cashier to do as you ask. I take it the suite is available now.'

'Yes.' There was no point, Peter decided, in advertising Marsha's presence in 555, and perhaps she could leave unnoticed early. The thought reminded him of his promise to telephone the Preyscott home. With a friendly 'good night' to the room clerk he crossed the lobby to an unoccupied desk, used in daytime by one of the assistant managers. He found a listing for Mark Preyscott at a Garden District address and asked for the number. The ringing tone continued for some time before a woman's voice answered sleepily. Identifying himself, he announced, 'I have a message for Anna from Miss Preyscott.'

The voice, with a Deep South accent, said, 'This is Anna. Is Miss Marsha all right?'

'She's all right, but she asked me to tell you that she will stay the night at the hotel.'

The housekeeper's voice said, 'Who did you say that was again?'

Peter explained patiently. 'Look,' he said, 'if you want to check, why don't you call back? It's the St Gregory and ask for the assistant manager's desk in the lobby.'

The woman, obviously relieved, said, 'Yes, sir, I'll do that.' In less than a minute they were reconnected. 'It's all right,' she said, 'now I know who it is for sure. We worry about Miss Marsha a bit, what with her daddy being away and all.'

Replacing the telephone, he found himself thinking again about Marsha Preyscott. He decided he would have a talk with her tomorrow to find out just what happened before the attempted rape occurred. The disorder in the suite, for example, posed several unanswered questions.

He was aware that Herbie Chandler had been glancing at him covertly from the bell captain's desk. Now, walking over to him, Peter said curtly, 'I thought I gave instructions about checking a disturbance on the eleventh.'

Chandler's weasel face framed innocent eyes. 'But I went, Mr Mac. I walked right around and everything was quiet.'

And so it had been, Herbie thought. In the end he had gone nervously to the eleventh and, to his relief, whatever disturbance there might have been earlier had ended by the time he arrived. Even better, on returning to the lobby, he learned that the two call girls had left the hotel without detection.

'You couldn't have looked or listened very hard.'

Herbie Chandler shook his head obstinately. 'All I can say is, I did what you asked, Mr Mac. You said to go up, and I did, even though that isn't our job.'

'Very well.' Though instinct told him that the bell captain knew more than he was saying, Peter decided not to press the point. 'I'll be making some enquiries. Maybe I'll talk to you again.'

As he recrossed the lobby and entered an elevator, he was conscious of being watched both by Herbie Chandler and the house officer, Ogilvie. This time he rode up one floor only, to the main mezzanine.

Christine was waiting in his office. She had kicked off her shoes and curled her feet under her in the upholstered leather chair she had occupied an hour and a half before. Her eyes were closed, her thoughts far away in time and distance. She summoned them back, looking up as Peter came in.

'Don't marry a hotel man,' he told her. 'There's never an end to it.'

'It's a timely warning,' Christine said. 'I hadn't told you, but I've a crush on the new sous-chef. The one who looks like Rock Hudson.' She uncurled her legs, reaching for her shoes. 'Do we have more troubles?'

He grinned, finding the sight and sound of Christine immensely cheering. 'Other people's, mostly. I'll tell you as we go.'

'Where to?'

'Anywhere away from the hotel. We've both had enough for one day.'

Christine considered. 'We could go to the Quarter. There are plenty of places open. Or if you want to come to my place, I'm a whiz at omelets.'

Peter helped her up and steered her to the door where he switched off the office lights. 'An omelet,' he declared, 'is what I really wanted and didn't know it.'

They walked together, skirting pools of water which the rain had left, to a tiered parking lot a block and a half from the hotel. Above, the sky was clearing after its interlude of storm, with a three-quarter moon beginning to break through, and around them the city centre was settling down to silence, broken by an occasional late taxi and the sharp tattoo of their footsteps echoing hollowly through the canyon of darkened buildings.

A sleepy parking attendant brought down Christine's Volkswagen and they climbed in, Peter jack-knifing his length into the right-hand seat. 'This is the life! You don't mind if I spread out?' He draped his arm along the back of the driver's seat, not quite touching Christine's shoulders.

As they waited for the traffic lights at Canal street, one of the new air-conditioned buses glided down the centre mall in front of them.

She reminded him, 'You were going to tell me what happened.'

He frowned, bringing his thoughts back to the hotel, then in crisp short sentences related what he knew about the attempted rape of Marsha Preyscott. Christine listened in silence, heading the little car northeast as Peter talked, ending with his conversation with Herbie Chandler and the suspicion that the bell captain knew more than he had told.

'Herbie always knows more. That's why he's been around a long time.'

Peter said shortly, 'Being around isn't the answer to everything.'

The comment, as both he and Christine knew, betrayed Peter's impatience with inefficiencies within the hotel which he lacked authority to change. In a normally run establishment, with clearly defined lines of command, there would be no such problem. But in the St Gregory, a good deal of organization was unwritten, with final judgements depending upon Warren Trent, and made by the hotel owner in his own capricious way.

In ordinary circumstances, Peter – an honours graduate of Cornell University's School of Hotel Administration – would have made a decision months ago to seek more satisfying work elsewhere. But circumstances were not ordinary. He had arrived at the St Gregory under a cloud which was likely to remain – hampering his chance of other employment – for a long time to come.

Sometimes he reflected glumly on the botchery he had made of his career, for which no-one – he admitted candidly – was to blame except himself.

At the Waldorf, where he had gone to work after graduation from Cornell, Peter McDermott had been the bright young man who appeared to hold the future in his hand. As a junior assistant manager, he had been selected for promotion when bad luck, plus indiscretion, intervened. At a time when he was supposedly on duty and required elsewhere in the hotel, he was discovered *in flagrante* in a bedroom with a woman guest.

Even then, he might have escaped retribution. Good-looking young men who worked in hotels grew used to receiving overtures from lonely women, and most, at some point in their careers, succumbed. Managements, aware of this, were apt to punish a single transgression with a stern warning that a similar thing must never happen again. Two factors, however, conspired against Peter. The woman's husband, aided by private detectives, was involved in the discovery, and a messy divorce case resulted, with attendant publicity, which all hotels abhorred.

As if this was not enough, there was a personal retribution. Three years before the Waldorf débacle, Peter McDermott had married impulsively and the marriage, soon after, ended in separation. To an extent, his loneliness and disillusion had been a cause of the incident in the hotel. Regardless of the cause, and utilizing the ready-made evidence, Peter's estranged wife sued successfully for divorce.

The end result was ignominious dismissal and black-listing by the major chain hotels.

The existence of a black list, of course, was not admitted. But at a long series of hotels, most with chain affiliations, Peter McDermott's applications for employment were peremptorily rejected. Only at the St Gregory, an independent house, had he been able to obtain work, at a salary which Warren Trent shrewdly adjusted to Peter's own desperation.

Therefore when he had said a moment ago, *Being around isn't the answer to everything*, he had pretended an independence which did not exist. He suspected that Christine realized it too.

Peter watched as she manoeuvred the little car expertly through the narrow width of Burgundy Street, skirting the French Quarter and paralleling the Mississippi a half mile to the south. Christine slowed momentarily, avoiding a group of unsteady wassailers who had wandered from the more populous and brightly lighted Bourbon Street, two blocks away. Then she said, 'There's something I think you should know. Curtis O'Keefe is arriving in the morning.'

It was the kind of news that he had feared, yet half expected.

Curtis O'Keefe was a name to conjure with. Head of the world-wide O'Keefe hotel chain, he bought hotels as other men chose ties and handkerchiefs. Obviously, even to the sparsely informed, the appearance of Curtis O'Keefe in the St Gregory could have only one implication: an interest in acquiring the hotel for the constantly expanding O'Keefe chain.

Peter asked, 'Is it a buying trip?'

'It could be.' Christine kept her eyes on the dimly lighted street ahead. 'W. T. doesn't want it that way. But it may turn out there isn't any choice.' She was about to add that the last piece of information was confidential, but checked herself. Peter would realize that. And as for the presence of Curtis O'Keefe, that electrifying news would telegraph itself around the St Gregory tomorrow morning within minutes of the great man's arrival.

'I suppose it had to come.' Peter was aware, as were other executives in the hotel, that in recent months the St Gregory had suffered severe financial losses. 'All the same, I think it's a pity.'

Christine reminded him, 'It hasn't happened yet. I said W. T. doesn't want to sell.'

Peter nodded without speaking.

They were leaving the French Quarter now, turning left on the boulevard and tree-lined Esplanade Avenue, deserted except for the receding tail-lights of another car disappearing swiftly towards Bayou St John.

Christine said, 'There are problems about refinancing. W. T. has been trying to locate new capital. He still hopes he may.'

'And if he doesn't?'

'Then I expect we shall be seeing a lot more of Mr Curtis O'Keefe.'

And a whole lot less of Peter McDermott, Peter thought. He wondered if he had reached the point where a hotel chain, such as O'Keefe, might consider him rehabilitated and worth employing. He doubted it. Eventually it could happen if his record remained good. But not yet.

It seemed likely that he might soon have to search for other employment. He decided to worry when it happened.

'The O'Keefe-St Gregory,' Peter ruminated. 'When shall we know for sure?'

'One way or the other by the end of this week.'

'That soon!'

There were compelling reasons, Christine knew, why it had to be that soon. For the moment she kept them to herself.

Peter said emphatically, 'The old man won't find new financing.'

'What makes you so sure?'

'Because people with that kind of money want a sound investment. That means good management, and the St Gregory hasn't got it. It could have, but it hasn't.'

They were headed north on Elysian Fields, its wide dual lanes empty of other traffic, when abruptly a flashing white light, waving from side to side, loomed directly ahead. Christine braked and, as the car stopped, a uniformed traffic officer walked forward. Directing his flashlight on to the Volkswagen, he circled the car, inspecting it. While he did, they could see that the section of road immediately ahead was blocked off by a rope barrier. Beyond the barrier other uniformed men, and some in plain clothes, were examining the road surface with the aid of powerful lights.

Christine lowered her window as the officer came to her side of the car. Apparently satisfied by his inspection, he told them, 'You'll have to detour, folks. Drive slowly through the other lane, and the officer at the far end will wave you back into this one.'

'What is it?' Peter said. 'What happened?'

'Hit and run. Happened earlier tonight.'

Christine asked, 'Was anyone killed?'

The policeman nodded. 'Little girl of seven.' Responding to their shocked expressions, he told them, 'Walking with her mother. The mother's in hospital. Kid was killed outright. Whoever was in the car must have known. They drove right on.' Beneath his breath he added, 'Bastards!'

'Will you find out who it is?'

'We'll find out.' The officer nodded grimly, indicating the activity behind the barrier.

'The boys usually do, and this one's upset them. There's glass on the road, and the car that did it must be marked.'

More headlights were approaching from behind and he motioned them on.

They were silent as Christine drove slowly through the detour and, at the end of it, was waved back into the regular lane. Somewhere in Peter's mind was a nagging impression, an errant half-thought he could not define. He supposed the incident itself was bothering him, as sudden tragedy always did, but a vague uneasiness kept him preoccupied until, with surprise, he heard Christine say, 'We're almost home.'

They had left Elysian Fields for Prentiss Avenue. A moment later the little car swung right, then left, and stopped in the parking area of a modern, two-storey apartment building.

'If all else fails,' Peter called out cheerfully, 'I can go back to bartending.' He was mixing drinks in Christine's living-room, with its soft tones of moss-green and blue, to the accompanying sound of breaking eggshells from the kitchen adjoining.

'Were you ever one?'

'For a while.' He measured three ounces of rye whisky, dividing it two ways, then reached for Angostura and Peychaud's bitters. 'Some time I'll tell you about it.' As an afterthought he increased the proportion of rye, using a handkerchief to mop some extra drops which had fallen on the Wedgwood-blue rug.

Straightening up, he cast a glance around the living room, with its comfortable mixture of furnishings and colour – a French provincial sofa with a leaf design tapestry print in white, blue and green; a pair of Hepplewhite chairs near a marble-topped chest, and the inlaid mahogany sideboard on which he was mixing drinks. The walls held some Louisiana French prints and a modern impressionist oil. The effect was of warmth and cheerfulness, much like Christine herself, he thought. Only a cumbrous mantel clock on the sideboard beside him provided an incongruous note. The clock, ticking softly, was unmistakably Victorian, with brass curlicues and a moisture-stained, timeworn face. Peter looked at it curiously.

When he took the drinks to the kitchen, Christine was emptying beaten eggs from a mixing dish into a softly sizzling pan.

'Three minutes more,' she said, 'that's all.'

He gave her the drink and they clinked glasses.

'Keep your mind on my omelet,' Christine said. 'It's ready now.'

It proved to be everything she had promised – light, fluffy and seasoned with herbs. 'The way omelets should be,' he assured her, 'but seldom are.'

'I can boil eggs too.'

He waved a hand airily. 'Some other breakfast.'

Afterwards they returned to the living-room and Peter mixed a second drink. It was almost two a.m.

Sitting beside her on the sofa he pointed to the odd-appearing clock. 'I get the feeling that thing is peering at me – announcing the time in a disapproving tone.'

'Perhaps it is,' Christine answered. 'It was my father's. It used to be in his office where patients could see it. It's the only thing I saved.'

There was a silence between them. Once before Christine had told him, matter-of-factly, about the aeroplane accident in Wisconsin. Now he said gently, 'After it happened, you must have felt desperately alone.'

She said simply, 'I wanted to die. Though you get over that, of course – after a while.'

'How long?'

She gave a short, swift smile. 'The human spirit mends quickly. That apart – wanting to die, I mean – took just a week or two.'

'And after?'

'When I came to New Orleans,' Christine said, 'I tried to concentrate on not thinking. It got harder, and I had less success as the days went by. I knew I had to do something but I wasn't sure what – or where.'

She stopped and Peter said, 'Go on.'

'For a while I considered going back to university, then decided not. Getting an arts degree just for the sake of it didn't seem important and besides, suddenly it seemed as if I'd grown away from it all,'

'I can understand that.'

Christine sipped her drink, her expression pensive. Observing the firm lines of her features, he was conscious of a quality of quietude and self-possession about her.

'Anyway,' Christine went on, 'one day I was walking on Carondelet and saw a sign which said "Secretarial School". I thought – that's it! I'll learn what I need to, then get a job involving endless hours of work. In the end that's exactly what happened.'

'How did the St Gregory fit in?'

'I was staying there. I had since I came from Wisconsin. Then one morning the *Times-Picayune* arrived with breakfast, and I saw in the classified ads that the managing director of the hotel wanted a personal secretary. It was early, so I thought I'd be first, and wait. In those days W. T. arrived at work before everyone else. When he came, I was waiting in the executive suite.'

'He hired you on the spot?'

'Not really. Actually, I don't believe I was ever hired. It was just that when W. T. found out why I was there he called me and began dictating letters, then firing off instructions to be relayed to other people in the hotel. By the time more applicants arrived I'd been working for hours, and I took it on myself to tell them the job was filled.'

Peter chuckled. 'It sounds like the old man.'

'Even then he might never have known who I was, except about three days later I left a note on his desk. I think it read "My name is Christine Francis", and I suggested a salary. I got the note back without comment – just initialled, and that's all there's ever been.'

'It makes a good bedtime story.' Peter rose from the sofa, stretching his big body. 'That clock of yours is staring again. I guess I'd better go.'

'It isn't fair,' Christine objected. 'All we've talked about is me.' She was conscious of Peter's masculinity. And yet, she thought, there was a gentleness about him too. She had seen something of it tonight in the way that he had picked up Albert Wells and carried him to the other room. She found herself wondering what it would be like to be carried in his arms.

'I enjoyed it – a lovely antidote to a lousy day. Anyway there'll be other times.' He stopped, regarding her directly. 'Won't there?'

As she nodded in answer, he leaned forward, kissing her lightly.

In the taxi for which he had telephoned from Christine's apartment, Peter McDermott relaxed in comforting weariness, reviewing the events of the past day, which had now spilled over into the next. The daytime hours had produced their usual quota of problems, culminating in the evening with several more: the brush with the Duke and Duchess of Croydon, the near demise of Albert Wells and the attempted rape of Marsha Preyscott. There were also unanswered questions concerning Ogilvie, Herbie Chandler and now Curtis O'Keefe, whose advent could be the cause of Peter's own departure. Finally there was Christine, who had been there all the time, but whom he had not noticed before in quite the way he had tonight.

But he warned himself: women had been his undoing twice already. Whatever, if anything, developed between Christine and himself should happen slowly, with caution on his own part.

On Elysian Fields, heading back towards the city, the taxi moved swiftly. Passing the spot where he and Christine had been halted on the outward journey, he observed that the barrier across the road had disappeared and the police were gone. But the reminder produced once again the vague uneasiness he had experienced earlier, and it continued to trouble him all the way to his own apartment a block or two from the St Gregory Hotel.

Tuesday

I

As with all hotels, the St Gregory stirred early, coming awake like a veteran combat soldier after a short, light sleep. Long before the earliest waking guest stumbled drowsily from bed to bathroom, the machinery of a new innkeeping day slid quietly into motion.

Near five a.m., night cleaning parties which for the past eight hours had toiled through public rooms, lower stairways, kitchen areas and the main lobby, tiredly began disassembling their equipment, preparatory to storing it for another day. In their wake floors gleamed and wood and metalwork shone, the whole smelling pleasantly of fresh wax.

One cleaner, old Meg Yetmein, who had worked nearly thirty years in the hotel, walked awkwardly, though anyone noticing might have taken her clumsy gait for tiredness. The real reason, however, was a three-pound sirloin steak taped securely to the inside of her thigh. Half an hour ago, choosing an unsupervised few minutes, Meg had snatched the steak from a kitchen refrigerator. From long experience she knew exactly where to look, and afterwards how to conceal her prize in an old polishing rag en route to the women's toilet. There, safe behind a bolted door, she brought out an adhesive bandage and fixed the steak in place. The hour or so's cold, clammy discomfort was well worth the knowledge that she could walk serenely past the house detective who guarded the staff entrance and suspiciously checked outgoing packages or bulging pockets. The procedure – of her own devising – was foolproof, as she had proved many times before.

Two floors above Meg and behind an unmarked, securely locked door on the convention mezzanine, a switchboard operator put down her knitting and made the first morning wake-up call. The operator was Mrs Eunice Ball, widow, grandmother and tonight senior of the three operators who maintained the graveyard shift. Sporadically between now and seven a.m., the switchboard trio would awaken other guests whose instructions of the night before were recorded in a card-index drawer in front of them, divided in quarter hours. After seven o'clock the tempo would increase.

With experienced fingers, Mrs Ball flipped through the cards. As usual, she observed, the peak would be 7.45, with close to a hundred and eighty calls requested. Even working at high speed, the three operators would have trouble completing that many in less than twenty minutes, which meant they would have to start early, at 7.35 – assuming they were through with the 7.30 calls by then – and continue until 7.55, which would take them smack into the eight o'clock batch.

Mrs Ball sighed. Inevitably today there would be complains from guests to management alleging that some stupid, asleep-at-the-switchboard operator had called them either too early or too late.

One thing was to the good, though. Few guests at this time of morning were in a mood for conversation, or were likely to be amorous, the way they sometimes were at night – the reason for the locked, unmarked outer door. Also, at eight a.m., the day operators would be coming in – a total of fifteen by the day's peak period – and by nine the night shift, including Mrs Ball, would be home and abed.

Time for another wake-up. Once more abandoning her knitting, Mrs Ball pressed a key, letting a bell far above her ring out stridently.

Two floors below street level, in the engineering control room, Wallace Santopadre, third-class stationary engineer, put down a paperback copy of Toynbee's *Greek Civilization* and finished a peanut butter sandwich he had begun earlier. Things had been quiet for the past hour and he had read intermittently. Now it was time for the final stroll of his watch around the engineers' domain. The hum of machinery greeted him as he opened the control-room door.

He checked the hot-water system, noting a stepped-up temperature which indicated, in turn, that the time-controlled thermostat was doing its job. There would be plenty of hot water during the heavy demand period soon to come, when upwards of eight hundred people might decide to take morning baths or showers at the same time.

The massive air conditioners – twenty-five hundred tons of specialized machinery – were running more easily as the result of a comfortable drop in outside air temperature during the night. The comparative coolness had made it possible to shut down one compressor, and now the others could be relieved alternately, permitting maintenance work which had had to be delayed during the heat wave of the past few weeks. The chief engineer, Wallace Santopadre thought, would be pleased about that.

The old man would be less happy, though, about news of an interruption in the city power supply which had occurred during the night – around two a.m. and lasting eleven minutes, presumably due to the storm up north.

There had been no real problem in the St Gregory, and only the briefest of blackouts which most guests, soundly asleep, were unaware of. Santopadre had switched over to emergency power, supplied by the hotel's own generators which had performed efficiently. It had, however, taken three minutes to start the generators and bring them to full power, with the result that every one of the St Gregory's electric clocks – some two hundred all told – was now three minutes slow. The tedious business of resetting each clock manually would take a maintenance man most of the following day.

Not far from the engineering station, in a torrid, odorous enclosure, Booker T. Graham totted up the substance of a long night's labour amid the hotel garbage. Around him the reflection of flames flickered fitfully on smoke-grimed walls.

Few people in the hotel, including staff, had ever seen Booker T.'s domain, and those who did declared it was like an evangelist's idea of hell. But Booker T., who looked not unlike an amiable devil himself – with luminous eyes and flashing teeth in a sweat-shining black face – enjoyed his work, including the incinerator's heat.

One of the very few hotel staff whom Booker T. Graham ever saw was Peter McDermott. Soon after his arrival at the St Gregory, Peter set out to learn the geography and workings of the hotel, even to its remotest parts. In the course of one expedition he discovered the incinerator.

Occasionally since then – as he made a point of doing with all departments – Peter had dropped in to enquire at firsthand how things were going. Because of this, and perhaps through an instinctive mutual liking, in the eyes of Booker T. Graham, young Mr McDermott loomed somewhere close to God.

Peter always studied the grimed and greasy exercise books in which Booker T. proudly maintained a record of his work results. The results came from retrieving items which other people threw away. The most important single commodity was hotel silverware.

Booker T., an uncomplicated man, had never questioned how the silverware got into the garbage. It was Peter McDermott who explained to him that it was a perennial problem which management fretted about in every large hotel. Mostly the cause was hurrying waiters, busboys and others who either didn't know, or didn't care, that, along with the waste food they shovelled into bins, a steady stream of cutlery was disappearing too.

Until several years earlier the St Gregory compressed and froze its garbage, then sent it to a city dump. But in time the silverware losses became so appalling that an internal incinerator was built and Booker T. Graham employed to hand feed it.

What he did was simple. Garbage from all sources was deposited in bins on trolleys. Booker T. wheeled each trolley in and, a little at a time, spread the contents on a large flat tray, raking the mess back and forth like a gardener preparing top-soil. Whenever a trophy presented itself – a returnable bottle, intact glassware, cutlery and sometimes a guest's valuables – Booker T. reached in, retrieving it. At the end, what was left was pushed into the fire and a new portion spread out.

Today's totting up showed that the present month, almost ended, would prove average for recoveries. So far, silverware had totalled nearly two thousand pieces, each of which was worth a dollar to the hotel. There were some four thousand bottles worth two cents each, eight hundred intact glasses, value a quarter apiece, and a large assortment of other items including – incredibly – a silver soup tureen. Net yearly saving to the hotel: some forty thousand dollars.

Booker T. Graham, whose take-home pay was thirty-eight dollars weekly, put on his greasy jacket and went home.

By now, traffic at the drab brick staff entrance – located in an alley off Common Street – was increasing steadily. In ones and twos, night workers were trickling out while the first day shift, converging from all parts of the city, was arriving in a swiftly flowing stream.

In the kitchen area, lights were snapping on as early duty helpers made ready for cooks, already changing street clothes for fresh whites in adjoining locker rooms. In a few minutes the cooks would begin preparing the hotel's sixteen hundred breakfasts and later – long before the last egg and bacon would be served at mid-morning – start the two thousand lunches which today's catering schedule called for.

Amid the mass of simmering cauldrons, mammoth ovens and other appurtenances of bulk food production, a single packet of Quaker Oats provided a homey touch. It was for the few stalwarts who, as every hotel knew, demanded hot porridge for breakfast whether the outside temperature was a frigid zero or a hundred in the shade.

At the kitchen fry station, Jeremy Boehm, a sixteen-year-old helper, checked the big, multiple deep-fryer he had switched on ten minutes earlier. He had set it to two hundred degrees, as his instructions called for. Later the temperature could be brought quickly to the required three hundred and sixty degrees for cooking. This would be a busy day at the fryer, since fried chicken, southern style, was featured as a luncheon special on the main restaurant menu.

The fat in the fryer had heated all right, Jeremy observed, though he thought it seemed quite a bit smokier than usual, despite the overhanging hood and vent fan, which was on. He wondered if he should report the smokiness to someone, then remembered that only yesterday an assistant chef had reprimanded him sharply for showing an interest in sauce preparation which, he had been informed, was none of his business. Jeremy shrugged. This was none of his business either. Let someone else worry.

Someone *was* worrying – though not about smoke – in the hotel laundry half a block away.

The laundry, a bustling steamy province occupying an elderly two-storey building of its own, was connected to the main St Gregory structure by a wide basement tunnel. Its peppery, rough-tongued manageress, Mrs Isles Schulder, had traversed the tunnel a few minutes earlier, arriving as usual ahead of most of her staff. At the moment the cause of her concern was a pile of soiled tablecloths.

In the course of a working day the laundry would handle some twenty-five thousand pieces of linen, ranging from towels and bed sheets through waiters' and kitchen whites to greasy coveralls from engineering. Mostly those required routine handling, but lately a vexing problem had grown infuriatingly worse. Its origin: businessmen who did figuring on tablecloths, using ball-point pens.

'Would the bastards do it at home?' Mrs Schulder snapped at the male night worker who had separated the offending tablecloths from a larger pile of ordinarily dirty ones. 'By God! – if they did, their wives'd kick their arses from here to craptown. Plenty of times I've told those jerk head waiters to watch out and put a stop to it, but what do they care?' Her voice dropped in contemptuous mimicry. 'Yessir, yessir, I'll kiss you on both cheeks, sir. By all means write on the cloth, sir, and here's another ball-point pen, sir. As long as I get a great fat tip, who cares about the goddam laundry?'

Mrs Schulder stopped. To the night man, who had been staring open mouthed, she said irritably, 'Go on home! All you've given me is a headache to start the day.'

Well, she reasoned when he was gone, at least they'd caught this batch before they got into water. Once ball-point ink got wet, you could write a cloth off because, after that, nothing short of blasting would ever get the ink out. As it was, Nellie – the laundry's best spotter – would have to work hard today with the carbon tetrachloride. With luck they might salvage most of this pile, even though – Mrs Schulder thought grimly – she would still relish a few words with the slobs who made it necessary.

And so it went, through the entity of the hotel. Upon stage, and behind – in service departments, offices, carpenters' shop, bakery, printing plant, housekeeping, plumbing, purchasing, design and decorating, store-keeping, garage, TV repair and others – a new day came awake.

2

In his private six-room suite on the hotel's fifteenth floor, Warren Trent stepped down from the barber's chair in which Aloysius Royce had shaved him. A twinge of sciatica jabbed savagely in his left thigh like hot lancets – a warning that this would be another day during which his mercurial temper might need curbing. The private barber parlour was in an annex adjoining a capacious bathroom, the latter complete with steam cabinet, sunken Japanese-style tub and built-in aquarium from which tropical fish watched, broody-eyed, through laminated glass. Warren Trent walked stiffly into the bathroom now, pausing before a wall-width mirror to inspect the shave. He could find no fault with it as he studied the reflection facing him.

It showed a deep-seamed, craggy face, a loose mouth which could be humorous on occasion, beaked nose and deep set eyes with a hint of secretiveness. His hair, jet-black in youth, was now a distinguished white, thick and curly still. A wing collar and neatly tied cravat complemented the picture of an eminent southern gentleman.

At other times the carefully cultivated appearance would have given him pleasure. But today it failed to, the mood of depression which had grown upon him over the past few weeks eclipsing all else. So now it was Tuesday of the final week, he reminded himself. He calculated, as he had on so many other mornings. Including today, there were only four more days remaining: four days in which to prevent his lifetime's work from dissolving into nothingness.

Scowling at his own dismal thoughts, the hotel proprietor limped into the dining-room where Aloysius Royce had laid a breakfast table. The oak refectory table, its starched napery and silverware gleaming, had a heated trolley beside it which had come from the hotel kitchen at top speed a few moments earlier. Warren Trent eased awkwardly into the chair which Royce held out, then gestured to the opposite side of the table. At once the young Negro laid a second place, slipping into the vacant seat himself. There was a second breakfast on the trolley, available for such occasions when the old man's whim changed his usual custom of breakfasting alone.

Serving the two portions – shirred eggs with Canadian bacon and hominy grits – Royce remained silent, knowing his employer would speak when ready. There had been no comment so far on Royce's bruised face or the two adhesive patches he had put on, covering the worst of the damage from last night's fracas. At length, pushing away his plate, Warren Trent observed, 'You'd better make the most of this. Neither of us may be enjoying it much longer.'

Royce said, 'The trust people haven't changed their mind about renewing?'

'They haven't and they won't. Not now.' Without warning the old man slammed his fist upon the table top. 'By God! – there was a time when I'd have called the tune, not danced to a jig of theirs. Once they were lined up – banks, trust companies, all the rest – trying to lend their money, urging me to take it.'

'Times change for all of us.' Aloysius Royce poured coffee. 'Some things get better, others worse.'

Warren Trent said sourly, 'It's easy for you. You're young. You haven't lived to see everything you've worked for fall apart.'

And it had come to that, he reflected despondently. In four days from now – on Friday before the close of business – a twenty-year-old mortgage on the hotel property was due for redemption and the investment syndicate holding the mortgage had declined to renew. At first, on learning of the decision, his reaction had been surprise, though not concern. Plenty of other lenders, he assumed, would willingly take over – at a higher interest rate, no doubt – but, on whatever terms, producing the two million dollars needed. It was only when he had been decisively turned down by everyone approached – banks, trusts, insurance companies and private lenders – that his original confidence waned. One banker whom he knew well advised him frankly, 'Hotels like yours are out of favour, Warren. A lot of people think the day of the big independents is over, and nowadays the chain hotels are the only ones which can show reasonable profit. Besides, look at your balance sheet. You've been losing money steadily. How can you expect lending houses to go along with that kind of situation?'

His protestations that present losses were temporary and would reverse themselves when business improved, achieved nothing. He was simply not believed.

It was at this impasse that Curtis O'Keefe had telephoned suggesting their meeting in New Orleans this week. 'Absolutely all I have in mind is a friendly chat, Warren,' the hotel magnate had declared, his easy Texan drawl coming smoothly down the long-distance phone. 'After all, we're a couple of ageing innkeepers, you and me. We should see each other sometimes.' But Warren Trent was not deceived by the smoothness; there had been overtures from the O'Keefe chain before. The vultures are hovering, he thought. Curtis O'Keefe would arrive today and there was not the slightest doubt that he was fully briefed on the St Gregory's financial woes.

With an inward sigh, Warren Trent switched his thoughts to more immediate affairs. 'You're on the night report,' he told Aloysius Royce.

'I know,' Royce said. 'I read it.' He had skimmed the report when it came in early as usual, observing the notation, *Complaint of excessive noise in room 1126*, and then, in Peter McDermott's handwriting, *Dealt with by A. Royce and P. McD. Separate memo later.*

'Next thing,' Warren Trent growled, 'I suppose you'll be reading my private mail.'

Royce grinned. 'I haven't yet. Would you like me to?'

The exchange was part of a private game they played without admitting it. Royce was well aware that if he had failed to read the report the old man would have accused him of lack of interest in the hotel's affairs.

Now Warren Trent enquired sarcastically, 'Since everyone else is aware of what went on, would it be taken amiss if I asked for a few details?'

'I shouldn't think so.' Royce helped his employer to more coffee. 'Miss Marsha Preyscott – daughter of *the* Mr Preyscott – was almost raped. Do you want me to tell you about it?'

For a moment, as Trent's expression hardened, he wondered if he had gone too far. Their undefined, casual relationship was based for the most part upon precedents set by Aloysius Royce's father many years earlier. The elder Royce, who served Warren Trent first as body servant and later as companion and privileged friend, had always spoken out with a sprightly disregard of consequences which, in their early years together, drove Trent to white hot fury and later, as they traded insult for insult, had made the two inseparable. Aloysius was little more than a boy when his father had died over a decade ago, but he had never forgotten Warren Trent's face, grieving and tear stained, at the old Negro's funeral. They had walked away from Mount Olivet cemetery together, behind the Negro Jazz band which was playing festively *Oh, Didn't He Ramble*, Aloysius with his hand in Warren Trent's, who told him gruffly, 'You'll stay on with me at the hotel. Later we'll work something out.' The boy agreed trustingly – his father's death had left him entirely alone, his mother having died at his birth – and the 'something' had turned out to be college followed by law school, from which he would graduate in a few weeks' time. In the meanwhile, as the boy became a man, he had taken over the running of the hotel owner's suite and, though most of the physical work was done by other hotel employees, Aloysius performed personal services which Warren Trent accepted, either without comment or quarrelsomely as the mood took him. At other times they argued heatedly, mostly when Aloysius rose – as he knew he was expected to – to conversational hooks which Warren Trent baited.

And yet, despite their intimacy and the knowledge that he could take liberties which Warren Trent would never tolerate in others, Aloysius Royce was conscious of a hairline border never to be crossed. Now he said, 'The young lady called for help. I happened to hear.' He described his own action without dramatizing, and Peter McDermott's intervention, which he neither commended nor criticized.

Warren Trent listened, and at the end said, 'McDermott handled everything properly. Why don't you like him?'

Not for the first time Royce was surprised by the old man's perception. He answered, 'Maybe there's some chemistry between us doesn't mix. Or perhaps I don't like big white football players proving how kind they are by being nice to coloured boys.'

Warren Trent eyed Royce quizzically. 'You're a complicated one. Have you thought you might be doing McDermott an injustice?'

'Just as I said, maybe it's chemical.'

'Your father had an instinct for people. But he was a lot more tolerant than you.'

'A dog likes people who pat him on the head. That's because his thinking isn't complicated by knowledge and education.'

'Even if it were, I doubt he'd choose those particular words.' Trent's eyes, appraising, met the younger man's and Royce was silent. The remembrance of his father always disturbed him. The elder Royce, born while his parents were still in slavery, had been, Aloysius supposed, what Negroes nowadays contemptuously called an 'Uncle Tom nigger'. The old man had always accepted cheerfully whatever life brought, without question or complaint. Knowledge of affairs beyond his own limited horizon rarely disturbed him. And yet he had possessed an independence of spirit, as witness his relationship with Warren Trent, and an insight into fellow human beings too deep to be dismissed as cotton-patch wisdom. Aloysius had loved his father with a deep love which at moments like this transformed itself to yearning. He answered now, 'Maybe I used wrong words, but it doesn't change the sense.'

Warren Trent nodded without comment and took out his old-fashioned fob watch. 'You'd better tell young McDermott to come and see me. Ask him to come here. I'm a little tired this morning.'

The hotel proprietor mused, 'Mark Preyscott's in Rome, eh? I suppose I ought to telephone him.'

'His daughter was insistent that we shouldn't,' Peter McDermott said.

The two were in the lavishly furnished living-room of Warren Trent's suite, the older man relaxed in a deep, soft chair, his feet raised upon a footstool. Peter sat facing him.

Warren Trent said huffily, 'I'll be the one to decide that. If she gets herself raped in my hotel she must accept the consequences.'

'Actually we prevented the rape. Though I do want to find out just what happened earlier.'

'Have you seen the girl this morning?'

'Miss Preyscott was sleeping when I checked. I left a message asking to see her before she leaves.'

Warren Trent sighed and waved a hand in dismissal. 'You deal with it all.' His tone made clear that he was already tired of the subject. There would be no telephone call to Rome, Peter reasoned with relief.

'Something else I'd like to deal with concerns the room clerks.' Peter described the Albert Wells incident and saw Warren Trent's face harden at the mention of the arbitrary room change.

The older man growled, 'We should have closed off that room years ago. Maybe we'd better do it now.'

'I don't think it need be closed, proving it's understood we use it as a last resort and tell the guest what he's getting into.'

Warren Trent nodded. 'Attend to it.'

Peter hesitated. 'What I'd like to do is give some specific instructions on room changes generally. There have been other incidents and I think it needs pointing out that our guests aren't to be moved around like checkers on a board.'

'Deal with the one thing. If I want general instructions I'll issue them.'

The curt rejoinder, Peter thought resignedly, typified much that was wrong with the hotel's management. Mistakes were dealt with piecemeal after they happened, with little or no attempt to correct their root cause. Now he said, 'I thought you should know about the Duke and Duchess of Croydon. The Duchess asked for you personally.' He described the incident of the spilled shrimp Creole and the differing version of the waiter Sol Natchez.

Warren Trent grumbled, 'I know that damn woman. She won't be satisfied unless the waiter's fired.'

'I don't believe he should be fired.'

'Then tell him to go fishing for a few days – with pay – but to keep the hell out of the hotel. And warn him from me that next time he spills something, to be sure it's boiling and over the Duchess's head. I suppose she still has those damn dogs.'

'Yes.' Peter smiled.

A strictly enforced Louisiana law forbade animals in hotel rooms. In the Croydons' case, Warren Trent had conceded that the presence of the Bedlington terriers would not be noticed officially, provided they were smuggled in and out by a rear door. The Duchess, however, paraded the dogs defiantly each day through the main lobby. Already, two irate dog lovers were demanding to know why, when their own pets had been refused admittance.

'I had some trouble with Ogilvie last night,' Peter reported the chief house officer's absence and their subsequent exchange.

Reaction was swift. 'I've told you before to leave Ogilvie alone. He's responsible directly to me.'

'It makes things difficult if there's something to be done . . .'

'You heard what I said. Forget Ogilvie!' Warren Trent's race was red, but less from anger, Peter suspected, than embarrassment. The hands-off-Ogilvie rule didn't make sense and the hotel proprietor knew it. What *was* the hold, Peter wondered, that the ex-policeman had over his employer?

Abruptly changing the subject, Warren Trent announced, 'Curtis O'Keefe is checking in today. He wants two adjoining suites and I've sent down instructions. You'd better make sure that everything's in order, and I want to be informed as soon as he arrives.'

'Will Mr O'Keefe be staying long?'

'I don't know. It depends on a lot of things.'

For a moment Peter felt a surge of sympathy for the older man. Whatever criticisms might be levelled nowadays at the way the St Gregory was run, to Warren Trent it was more than a hotel; it had been his lifetime's work. He had seen it grow from insignificance to prominence, from a modest initial building to a towering edifice occupying most of a city block. The hotel's reputation, too, had for many years been high, its name ranking nationally with traditional hostelries like the Biltmore, or Chicago's Palmer House or the St Francis in San Francisco. It must be hard to accept that the St Gregory, for all the prestige and glamour it once enjoyed, had slipped behind the times. It was not that the slippage had been final or disastrous, Peter thought. New financing and a firm, controlling hand on management could work wonders, even, perhaps, restoring the hotel to its old competitive position. But as things were, both the capital and control would have to come from outside – he supposed through Curtis O'Keefe. Once more Peter was reminded that his own days here might well be numbered.

The hotel proprietor asked, 'What's our convention situation?'

'About half the chemical engineers have checked out; the rest will be clear by today. Coming in – Golden Crown Cola is in and organized. They've taken three hundred and twenty rooms, which is better than we expected, and we've increased the lunch and banquet figures accordingly.' As the older man nodded approval, Peter continued, 'The Congress of American Dentistry begins tomorrow, though some of their people checked in yesterday and there'll be more today. They should take close to two hundred and eighty rooms.'

Warren Trent gave a satisfied grunt. At least, he reflected, the news was not all bad. Conventions were the lifeblood of hotel business and two together were a help, though unfortunately not enough to offset other recent losses. All the same, the dentistry convention was an achievement. Young McDermott had acted promptly on a hot tip that earlier arrangements by the Dental Congress had fallen through, and had flown to New York, successfully selling New Orleans and the St Gregory to the convention organizers.

'We had a full house last night,' Warren Trent said. He added, 'In this business it's either feast or famine. Can we handle today's arrivals?'

'I checked on the figures first thing this morning. There should be enough checkouts, though it'll be close. Our over-bookings are a little high.'

Like all hotels, the St Gregory regularly accepted more reservations than it had rooms available. But also like all hotels, it gambled on the certain foreknowledge that some people who made reservations would fail to show up, so the problem resolved itself into guessing the true percentage of non-arrivals. Most times, experience and luck allowed the hotel to come out evenly, with all rooms occupied – the ideal situation. But once in a while an estimate went wrong, in which event the hotel was seriously in trouble.

The most miserable moment in any hotel manager's life was explaining to indignant would-be-guests, who held confirmed reservations, that no accommodation was available. He was miserable both as a fellow human being and also because he was despondently aware that never again – if they could help it – would the people he was turning away ever come back to his hotel.

In Peter's own experience the worst occasion was when a bakers' convention, meeting in New Orleans, decided to remain an extra day so that some of its members could take a moonlight cruise around Manhattan. Two hundred and fifty bakers and their wives stayed on, unfortunately without telling the hotel, which expected them to check out so an engineers' convention could move in. Recollection of the ensuing shambles, with hundreds of angry engineers and their women folk encamped in the lobby, some waving reservations made two years earlier, still caused Peter to shudder when he thought of it. In the end, the city's other hotels being already filled, the new arrivals were dispersed to motels in outlying New Orleans until next day when the bakers went innocently away. But the monumental taxi bills of the engineers, plus a substantial cash settlement to avoid a lawsuit, were paid by the hotel – more than wiping out the profit on both conventions.

Warren Trent lit a cigar, motioning to McDermott to take a cigarette from a box beside him. When he had done so, Peter said, 'I talked with the Roosevelt. If we're in a jam tonight they can help us out with maybe thirty rooms.' The knowledge, he thought, was reassuring – an ace-in-the-hole, though not to be used unless essential. Even fiercely competitive hotels aided each other in that kind of crisis, never knowing when the roles would be reversed.

'All right,' Warren Trent said, a cloud of cigar smoke above him, 'now what's the outlook for the fall?'

'It's disappointing. I've sent you a memo about the two big union conventions falling through.'

'Why have they fallen through?'

'It's the same reason I warned you about earlier. We've continued to discriminate. We haven't complied with the Civil Rights Act, and the unions resent it.' Involuntarily, Peter glanced towards Aloysius Royce who had come into the room and was arranging a pile of magazines.

Without looking up the young Negro said, 'Don't yo' worry about sparing my feelings, Mistuh McDermott' – Royce was using the same exaggerated accent he had employed the night before – 'because us coloured folks are right used to that.'

Warren Trent, his face creased in thought, said dourly, 'Cut out the comic lines.'

'Yessir!' Royce left his magazine sorting and stood facing the other two. Now his face was normal. 'But I'll tell you this: the unions have acted the way they have because they've a social conscience. They're not the only ones, though. More conventions, and just plain folks, are going to stay away until this hotel and others like it admit that times have changed.'

Warren Trent waved a hand towards Royce. 'Answer him,' he told Peter McDermott. 'Around here we don't mince words.'

'It so happens,' Peter said quietly, 'that I agree with what he said.'

'Why so, Mr McDermott?' Royce taunted. 'You think it'd be better for business? Make your job easier?'

'Those are good reasons,' Peter said. 'If you choose to think they're the only ones, go ahead.'

Warren Trent slammed down his hand hard upon the chair arm. 'Never mind the reasons! What matters is, you're being damn fools, both of you.'

It was a recurring question. In Louisiana, though hotels with chain affiliations had nominally integrated months before, several independents – spearheaded by Warren Trent and the St Gregory – had resisted change. Most, for a brief period, complied with the Civil Rights Act, then, after the initial flurry of attention, quietly reverted to their long-established segregation policies. Even with legal test cases pending, there was every sign that the hold-outs, aided by strong local support, could fight a delaying action, perhaps lasting years.

'No!' Viciously, Warren Trent stubbed out his cigar. 'Whatever's happening anywhere else, I say we're not ready for it here. So we've lost the union conventions. All right, it's time we got off our backsides and tried for something else.'

From the living-room, Warren Trent heard the outer door close behind Peter McDermott, and Aloysius Royce's footsteps returning to the small book-lined sitting-room which was the young Negro's private domain. In a few minutes Royce would leave, as he usually did around this time of day, for a law-school class.

It was quiet in the big living-room, with only a whisper from the air conditioning, and occasional stray sounds from the city below, which penetrated the thick walls and insulated windows. Fingers of morning sunshine inched their way across the broad-loomed floor and, watching them, Warren Trent could feel his heart pounding heavily – an effect of the anger which for several minutes had consumed him. It was a warning, he supposed, which he should heed more often. Yet nowadays, it seemed, so many things frustrated him, making emotions hard to control and to remain silent, harder still. Perhaps such outbursts were mere testiness – a side effect of age. But more likely it was because he sensed so much was slipping away, disappearing for ever beyond his control. Besides, anger had always come easily – except for those few brief years when Hester had taught him otherwise: to use patience and a sense of humour, and for a while he had. Sitting quietly here, the memory stirred him. How long ago it seemed! – more than thirty years since he had carried her, as a new, young bride, across the threshold of this very room. And how short a time they had had: those few brief years, joyous beyond measure, until the paralytic polio struck without warning. It had killed Hester in twenty-four hours, leaving Warren Trent, mourning and alone, with the rest of his life to live – and the St Gregory Hotel.

There were few in the hotel who remembered Hester now, and even if a handful of old-timers did, it would be dimly, and not as Warren Trent himself remembered her: like a sweet spring flower, who had made his days gentle and his life richer, as no-one had before or since.

In the silence, a swift soft movement and a rustle of silk seemed to come from the doorway behind him. He turned his head, but it was a quirk of memory. The room was empty and, unusually, moisture dimmed his eyes.

He rose awkwardly from the deep chair, the sciatica knifing as he did. He moved to the window, looking across the gabled rooftops of the French Quarter – the Vieux Carré as people called it nowadays, reverting to the older name – towards Jackson Square and the cathedral spires, glinting as sunlight touched them. Beyond was the swirling, muddy Mississippi and, in midstream, a line of moored ships awaiting their turn at busy wharves. It was a sign of the times, he thought. Since the eighteenth century New Orleans had swung like a pendulum between riches and poverty. Steamships, railways, cotton, slavery, emancipation, canals, wars, tourists . . . all at intervals had delivered quotas of wealth and disaster. Now the pendulum had brought prosperity – though not it seemed to the St Gregory Hotel.

But did it really matter – at least to himself? Was the hotel worth fighting for? Why not give up, sell out – as he could, this week – and let time and change engulf them both? Curtis O'Keefe would make a fair deal. The O'Keefe chain had that kind of reputation, and Trent himself could emerge from it well. After paying the outstanding mortgage, and taking care of minor stockholders, there would be ample money left on which he could live, at whatever standard he chose, for the remainder of his life.

Surrender: perhaps that was the answer. Surrender to changing times. After all, what was a hotel except so much brick and mortar? He had tried to make it more, but in the end he had failed. Let it go!

And yet . . . if he did, what else was left?

Nothing. For himself there would be nothing left, not even the ghosts that walked this floor. He waited, wondering, his eyes encompassing the city spread before him. It too had seen change, had been French, Spanish and American, yet had somehow survived as itself – uniquely individual in an era of conformity.

No! He would not sell out. Not yet. While there was still hope, he would hold on. There were still four days in which to raise the mortgage money somehow, and beyond that the present losses were a temporary thing. Soon the tide would turn, leaving the St Gregory solvent and independent.

Matching movement to his resolution, he walked stiffly across the room to an opposite window. His eyes caught the gleam of an aeroplane high to the north. It was a jet, losing height and preparing to land at Moisant Airport. He wondered if Curtis O'Keefe was aboard.

3

When Christine Francis located him shortly after 9.30 a.m., Sam Jakubiec, the stocky, balding credit manager, was standing at the rear of Reception, making his daily check of the ledger account of every guest in the hotel. As usual, Jakubiec was working with the quick, nervous haste which some times deceived people into believing he was less than thorough. Actually there was almost nothing that the credit chief's shrewd, encyclopaedic mind missed, a fact which in the past had saved the hotel thousands of dollars in bad debts.

His fingers were dancing now over the machine accounting cards – one for each guest and room – as he peered at names through his thick-lensed spectacles, glancing at the itemized accounts and, once in a while, making a notation on a pad beside him. Without stopping, he glanced up briefly, then down again. 'I'll be just a few minutes, Miss Francis.'

'I can wait. Anything interesting this morning?'

Without pausing, Jakubiec nodded, ' A few things.'

'For instance?'

He made a new note on the pad. 'Room 512, H. Baker. Check-in 8.10 a.m. At 8.20 a bottle of liquor ordered and charged.'

'Maybe he likes to brush his teeth with it.'

His head down, Jakubiec nodded. 'Maybe.'

But it was more likely, Christine knew, that H. Baker in 512 was a deadbeat. Automatically the guest who ordered a bottle of liquor a few minutes after arrival aroused the credit manager's suspicion. Most new arrivals who wanted a drink quickly – after a journey or a tiring day – ordered a mixed drink from the bar. The immediate bottle-orderer was often starting on a drunk, and might not intend to pay, or couldn't.

She knew, too, what would follow next. Jakubiec would ask one of the floor maids to enter 512 on a pretext and make a check of the guest and his luggage. Maids knew what to look for: reasonable luggage and good clothes, and if the guest had these the credit manager would probably do nothing more, aside from keeping an eye on the account. Sometimes solid, respectable citizens rented a hotel room for the purpose of getting drunk and, providing they could pay and bothered no-one else, that was their own business.

But if there was no luggage or other signs of substance, Jakubiec himself would drop in for a chat. His approach would be discreet and friendly. If the guest showed ability to pay, or agreed to put a cash deposit on his bill, their parting would be cordial. However, if his earlier suspicions were confirmed, the credit manager could be tough and ruthless, with the guest evicted before a big bill could be run up.

'Here's another,' Sam Jakubiec told Christine. 'Sanderson, room 1207. Disproportionate tipping.'

She inspected the card he was holding. It showed two room-service charges – one for $1.50, the other for two dollars. In each case a two-dollar tip had been added and signed for.

'People who don't intend to pay often write the biggest tips,' Jakubiec said. 'Anyway, it's one to check out.'

As with the other query, Christine knew the credit manager would feel his way warily. Part of his job – equally important with preventing fraud – was *not* offending honest guests. After years of experience a seasoned credit man could usually separate the sharks and sheep by instinct, but once in a while he might be wrong – to the hotel's detriment. Christine knew that was why credit managers occasionally risked extending credit or approved checks in slightly doubtful cases, walking a mental tightrope as they did. Most hotels – even the exalted ones – cared nothing about the morals of those who stayed within their walls, knowing that if they did a great deal of business would pass them by. Their concern – which a credit manager reflected – involved itself with a single basic question: Could a guest pay?

With a single, swift movement Sam Jakubiec flipped the ledger cards back in place and closed the file drawer containing them. 'Now,' he said, 'what can I do?'

'We've hired a private duty nurse for 1410.' Briefly Christine reported the previous night's crisis concerning Albert Wells. 'I'm a little worried whether Mr Wells can afford it, and I'm not sure he realizes how much it will cost.' She might have added, but didn't, that she was more concerned for the little man himself than for the hotel.

Jakubiec nodded. 'That private nursing deal can run into big money.' Walking together, they moved away from Reception, crossing the now-bustling lobby to the credit manager's office, a small square room behind the concierge counter. Inside, a dumpy brunette secretary was working against a wall which consisted solely of trays of file cards.

'Madge,' Sam Jakubiec said, 'see what we have on Wells, Albert.'

Without answering, she closed a drawer, opened another and flipped over cards. Pausing, she said in a single breath, 'Albuquerque, Coon Rapids, Montreal, take your pick.'

'It's Montreal,' Christine said, and Jakubiec took the card the secretary offered him.

Scanning it, he observed, 'He looks all right. Stayed with us six times. Paid cash. One small query which seems to have been settled.'

'I know about that,' Christine said. 'It was our fault.'

The credit man nodded. 'I'd say there's nothing to worry about. Honest people leave a pattern, same as the dishonest ones.' He handed the card back and the secretary replaced it, along with the others which provided a record of every guest who had stayed in the hotel in recent years. 'I'll look into it, though; find out what the charge is going to be, then have a talk with Mr Wells. If he has a cash problem we could maybe help out, give him a little time to pay.'

'Thanks, Sam.' Christine felt relieved, knowing that Jakubiec could be just as helpful and sympathetic with a genuine case, as he was tough with the bad ones.

As she reached the office doorway the credit manager called after her, 'Miss Francis, how are things going upstairs?'

Christine smiled. 'They're raffling off the hotel, Sam. I didn't want to tell you, but you forced it out of me.'

'If they pull my ticket,' Jakubiec said, 'have 'em draw again. I've troubles enough already.'

Beneath the flippancy, Christine suspected, the credit manager was as worried about his job as a good many others. The hotel's financial affairs were supposed to be confidential, but seldom were, and it had been impossible to keep the news of recent difficulties from spreading like a contagion.

She recrossed the main lobby, acknowledging 'good mornings' from bellboys, the hotel florist and one of the assistant managers, seated self-importantly at his centrally located desk. Then, bypassing the elevators, she ran lightly up the curved central stairway to the main mezzanine.

The sight of the assistant manager was a reminder of his immediate superior, Peter McDermott. Since last night Christine had found herself thinking about Peter a good deal. She wondered if the time they had spent together had produced the same effect in him. At several moments she caught herself wishing that this was true, then checked herself with an inward warning against an involvement emotionally which might be premature. Over the years in which she had learned to live alone there had been men in Christine's life, but none she had taken seriously. At times, she sometimes thought, it seemed as if instinct were shielding her from renewing the kind of close relationship which five years ago had been snatched away so savagely. All the same, at this moment she wondered where Peter was and what he was doing. Well, she decided practically, sooner or later in the course of the day their ways would cross.

Back in her own office in the executive suite, Christine looked briefly into Warren Trent's, but the hotel proprietor had not yet come down from his fifteenth-floor apartment. The morning mail was stacked on her own desk, and several telephone messages required attention soon. She decided first to complete the matter which had taken her downstairs. Lifting the telephone, she asked for room 1410.

A woman's voice answered – presumably the private duty nurse. Christine identified herself and enquired politely after the patient's health.

'Mr Wells passed a comfortable night,' the voice informed her, 'and his condition is improved.'

Wondering why some nurses felt they had to sound like official bulletins, Christine replied, 'In that case, perhaps I can drop in.'

'Not for some time, I'm afraid.' There was the impression of a guardian hand raised firmly. 'Dr Aaron will be seeing the patient this morning, and I wish to be ready for him.'

It sounded, Christine thought, like a state visit. The idea of the pompous Dr Aarons being attended by an equally pompous nurse amused her. Aloud she said, 'In that case, please tell Mr Wells I called and that I'll see him this afternoon.'

4

The inconclusive conference in the hotel owner's suite left Peter McDermott in a mood of frustration. Striding away down the fifteenth-floor corridor, as Aloysius Royce closed the suite door behind him, he reflected that his encounters with Warren Trent invariably went the same way. As he had on other occasions, he wished fervently that he could have six months and a free hand to manage the hotel himself.

Near the elevators he stopped to use a house phone, enquiring from Reception what accommodation had been reserved for Mr Curtis O'Keefe's party. There were two adjoining suites on the twelfth floor, a room clerk informed him, and Peter used the service stairway to descend the two flights. Like all sizeable hotels, the St Gregory pretended not to have a thirteenth floor, naming it the fourteenth instead.

All four doors to the two reserved suites were open and, from within, the whine of a vacuum cleaner was audible as he approached. Inside, two maids were working industriously under the critical eye of Mrs Blanche du Quesnay, the St Gregory's sharp-tongued but highly competent housekeeper. She turned as Peter came in, her bright eyes flashing.

'I might have known that one of you men would be checking up to see if I'm capable of doing my own job, as if I couldn't figure out for myself that things had better be just so, considering who's coming.'

Peter grinned. 'Relax, Mrs Q. Mr Trent asked me to drop in.' He liked the middle-aged red-haired woman, one of the most reliable department heads. The two maids were smiling. He winked at them, adding for Mrs du Quesnay, 'If Mr Trent had known you were giving this your personal attention he'd have wiped the whole thing from his mind.'

'And if we run out of soft soap in the laundry we'll send for you,' the housekeeper said with a trace of a smile as she expertly plumped the cushions of two long settees.

He laughed, then enquired, 'Have flowers and a basket of fruit been ordered?' The hotel magnate, Peter thought, probably grew weary of the inevitable fruit basket – standard salutation of hotels to visiting VIPs. But its absence might be noticed.

'They're on their way up.' Mrs du Quesnay looked up from her cushion arranging and said pointedly, 'From what I hear, though, Mr O'Keefe brings his own flowers, and not in vases either.'

It was a reference – which Peter understood – to the fact that Curtis O'Keefe was seldom without a feminine escort on his travels, the composition of the escort changing frequently. He discreetly ignored it.

Mrs du Quesnay flashed him one of her quick pert looks. 'Have a look around. There's no charge.'

Both suites, Peter saw as he walked through them, had been gone over thoroughly. The furnishings – white and gold with a French motif – were dustless and orderly. In bedrooms and bathrooms the linen was spotless and correctly folded, hand-basins and baths were dry and shining, toilet seats impeccably scoured and the tops down. Mirrors and windows gleamed. Electric lights all worked, as did the combination TV-radios. The air-conditioning responded to changes of thermostats, though the temperature now was a comfortable 68. There was nothing else to be done, Peter thought, as he stood in the centre of the second suite surveying it.

Then a thought struck him. Curtis O'Keefe, he remembered, was notably devout – at times, some said, to the point of ostentation. The hotelier prayed frequently, sometimes in public. One report claimed that when a new hotel interested him he prayed for it as a child did for a Christmas toy; another, that before negotiations a private church service was held which O'Keefe executives attended dutifully. The head of a competitive hotel chain, Peter recalled, once remarked unkindly, 'Curtis never misses an opportunity to pray. That's why he urinates on his knees.'

The thought prompted Peter to check the Gideon Bibles – one in each room. He was glad he did.

As usually happened when they had been in use for any length of time, the Bible's front pages were dotted with call girls' phone numbers, since a Gideon Bible – as experienced travellers knew – was the first place to seek that kind of information. Peter showed the books silently to Mrs du Quesnay. She clucked her tongue. 'Mr O'Keefe won't be needing these, now will he? I'll have new ones sent up.'

Taking the Bibles under her arm, she regarded Peter questioningly. 'I suppose what Mr O'Keefe likes or doesn't is going to make a difference to people keeping their jobs around here.'

He shook his head. 'I honestly don't know, Mrs Q. Your guess is as good as mine.'

He was aware of the housekeeper's eyes following him interrogatively as he left the suite. Mrs du Quesnay, he knew, supported an invalid husband and any threat to her job would be cause for anxiety. He felt a genuine sympathy for her as he rode the elevator to the main mezzanine.

In the event of a management change, Peter supposed, most of the younger and brighter staff members would have an opportunity to stay on. He imagined that most would take it since the O'Keefe chain had a reputation for treating its employees well. Older employees, though, some of whom had grown soft in their jobs, had a good deal more to worry about.

As Peter McDermott approached the executive suite, the chief engineer, Doc Vickery, was leaving it. Stopping, Peter said, 'Number four elevator was giving some trouble last night, chief. I wondered if you knew.'

The chief nodded his bald, domed head morosely. 'It's a puir business when machinery that needs money spending on it doesna' get it.'

'Is it really that bad?' The engineering budget, Peter knew had been pared recently, but this was the first he had heard of serious trouble with the elevators.

The chief shook his head. 'If you mean shall we have a big accident, the answer's no. I watch the safety guards like I would a bairn. But we've had small breakdowns and some time there'll be a bigger one. All it needs is a couple of cars stalled for a few hours to throw this building out of joint.'

Peter nodded. If that was the worse that could happen, there was no point in worrying unduly. He enquired. 'What is it you need?'

The chief peered over his thick-rimmed spectacles. 'A hundred thousand dollars to start. With that I'd rip out most of the elevator guts and replace them, then some other things as well.'

Peter whistled softly.

'I'll tell you one thing,' the chief observed. 'Good machinery's a lovely thing, and sometimes well nigh human. Most times it'll do more work than you think it could, and after that you can patch it and coax it, and it'll work for you some more. But somewhere along there's a death point you'll never get by, no matter how much you – and the machinery – want to.'

Peter was still thinking about the chief's words when he entered his own office. What was the death point, he wondered, for an entire hotel? Certainly not yet for the St Gregory, though for the hotel's present régime he suspected the point was already passed.

There was a pile of mail, memos and telephone messages on his desk. He picked up the top one and read: *Miss Marsha Preyscott returned your call and will wait in room 555 until she hears from you.* It was a reminder of his intention to find out more about last night's events in 1126-7.

Another thing: he must drop in soon to see Christine. There were several small matters requiring decisions from Warren Trent, though not important enough to have brought up at this morning's meeting. Then, grinning, he chided himself: Stop rationalizing! You want to see her, and why not?

As he debated which to do first, the telephone bell shrilled. It was Reception, one of the room clerks. 'I thought you'd want to know,' he said. 'Mr Curtis O'Keefe has just checked in.'

5

Curtis O'Keefe marched into the busy, cavernous lobby swiftly, like an arrow piercing an apple's core. And a slightly decayed apple, he thought critically. Glancing around his experienced hotel man's eye assimilated the signs. Small signs, but significant: a newspaper left in a chair and uncollected; a half dozen cigarette butts in a sand urn by the elevators; a button missing from a bellboy's uniform; two burned-out light bulbs in the chandelier above. At the St Charles Avenue entrance a uniformed doorman gossiped with a news vendor, a tide of guests and others breaking around them. Closer at hand an elderly assistant manager sat brooding at his desk, eyes down.

In the hotel of the O'Keefe chain, in the unlikely event of all such inefficiencies occurring at once, there would have been whip-cracking action, slashing reprimands and perhaps dismissals. But the St Gregory isn't my hotel, Curtis O'Keefe reminded himself. Not yet.

He headed for Reception, a slender, dapper six-foot figure in precisely pressed charcoal grey, moving with dance-like, almost mincing, steps. The last was an O'Keefe characteristic whether on a handball court, as he often was, a ballroom floor or on the rolling deck of his ocean-going cruiser *Innkeeper IV*. His lithe athlete's body had been his pride through most of the fifty-six years in which he had manipulated himself upward from a lower-middle-class nonentity to become one of the nation's richest – and most restless – men.

At the marble-topped counter, barely looking up, a room clerk pushed a registration pad forward. The hotelier ignored it.

He announced evenly, 'My name is O'Keefe and I have reserved two suites, one for myself, the other in the name of Miss Dorothy Lash.' From the periphery of his vision he could see Dodo entering the lobby now: all legs and breasts, radiating sex like a pyrotechnic. Heads were turning, with breath indrawn, as always happened. He had left her at the car to supervise the baggage. She enjoyed doing things like that occasionally. Anything requiring more cerebral strain passed her by.

His words had the effect of a neatly thrown grenade.

The room clerk stiffened, straightening his shoulders. As he faced the cool grey eyes which, effortlessly, seemed to bore into him, the clerk's attitude changed from indifference to solicitous respect. With nervous instinct, a hand went to his tie.

'Excuse me, sir. Mr Curtis O'Keefe?'

The hotelier nodded, with a hovering half smile, his face composed, the same face which beamed benignly from a half million book jackets of *I Am Your Host*, a copy placed prominently in every hotel room of the O'Keefe chain. (*This book is for your entertainment and pleasure. If you would like to take it with you, please notify the room clerk and $1.25 will be added to your bill.*)

'Yes, sir. I'm sure your suites are ready, sir. If you'll wait one moment, please.'

As the clerk shuffled reservation and room slips, O'Keefe stepped back a pace from the counter, allowing other arrivals to move in. The reception desk, which a moment ago had been fairly quiet, was beginning one of the periodic surges which were part of every hotel day. Outside, in bright, warm sunshine, airport limousines and taxis were discharging passengers who had travelled south – as he himself had done – on the breakfast jet flight from New York. He noticed a convention was assembling. A banner suspended from the vaulted lobby roof proclaimed:

WELCOME DELEGATES
CONGRESS OF AMERICAN DENTISTRY

Dodo joined him, two laden bellboys following like acolytes behind a goddess. Under the big floppy picture hat, which failed to conceal the flowing ash-blonde hair, her baby blue eyes were wide as ever in the flawless childlike face.

'Curtis, they say there's a lotta dentists staying here.'

He said drily, 'I'm glad you told me. Otherwise I might never have known.'

'Geez, well maybe I should get that filling done. I always mean to, then somehow never . . .'

'They're here to open their own mouths, not other people's.'

Dodo looked puzzled, as she did so often, as if events around her were something she ought to understand but somehow didn't. An O'Keefe Hotels manager, who hadn't known his chief executive was listening, had declared of Dodo not long ago: 'Her brains are in her tits; only trouble is, they're not connected.'

Some of O'Keefe's acquaintances, he knew, wondered about his choice of Dodo as a travelling companion when, with his wealth and influence, he could – within reason – have anyone he chose. But then, of course, they could only guess – and almost certainly underestimate – the savage sensuality which Dodo could turn on or obligingly leave quietly simmering, according to his own mood. Her mild stupidities, as well as the frequent gaucheries which seemed to bother others, he thought of as merely amusing – perhaps because he grew tired at times of being surrounded by clever, vigilant minds, forever striving to match the astuteness of his own.

He supposed, though, he would dispense with Dodo soon. She had been a fixture now for almost a year – longer than most of the others. There were always plenty more starlets to be plucked from the Hollywood galaxy. He would, of course, take care of her, using his ample influence to arrange a supporting role or two and, who knew, perhaps she might even make the grade. She had the body and the face. Others had risen high on those commodities alone.

The room clerk returned to the front counter. 'Everything is ready, sir.'

Curtis O'Keefe nodded. Then, led by the bell captain, Herbie Chandler, who had swiftly materialized, their small procession moved to a waiting elevator.

6

Shortly after Curtis O'Keefe and Dodo had been escorted to their adjoining suites, Julius 'Keycase' Milne obtained a single room.

Keycase telephoned at 10.45 a.m., using the hotel's direct line from Moisant Airport (*Talk to us Free at New Orleans' Finest*) to confirm a reservation made several days earlier from out of town. In reply he was assured that his booking was in order and, if he would kindly hasten citywards, he could be accommodated without delay.

Since his decision to stay at the St Gregory had been made only a few minutes earlier, Keycase was pleased at the news, though not surprised, for his advance planning had taken the form of making reservations at all of New Orleans' major hotels, employing a different name for each. At the St Gregory he had reserved as 'Byron Meader', a name he had selected from a newspaper because its rightful owner had been a major sweepstake winner. This seemed like a good omen, and omens were something which impressed Keycase very much indeed.

They had seemed to work out, in fact, on several occasions. For example, the last time he had come up for trial, immediately after his plea of guilty, a shaft of sunlight slanted across the judge's bench and the sentence which followed – the sunlight still remaining – had been a lenient three years when Keycase was expecting five. Even the string of jobs which preceded the plea and sentencing seemed to have gone well for the same sort of reason. His nocturnal entry into various Detroit hotel rooms had proceeded smoothly and rewardingly, largely – he decided afterwards – because all room numbers except the last contained the numeral two, his lucky number. It was this final room, devoid of the reassuring digit, whose occupant awakened and screamed stridently just as he was packing her mink coat into a suitcase, having already stowed her cash and jewellery in one of his specially capacious topcoat pockets.

It was sheer bad luck, perhaps compounded by the number situation, that a house dick had been within hearing of the screams and responded promptly. Keycase, a philosopher, had accepted the inevitable with grace, not bothering even to use the ingenious explanations – which worked so well at other times – as to why he was in a room other than his own. That was a risk, though, which anyone who lived by being light-fingered had to take, even a skilled specialist like Keycase. But now, having served his time (with maximum remission for good behaviour) and, more recently having enjoyed a successful ten-day foray in Kansas City, he was anticipating keenly a profitable fortnight or so in New Orleans.

It had started well.

He had arrived at Moisant Airport shortly before 7.30 a.m., driving from the cheap motel on Chef Menteur Highway where he had stayed the night before. It was a fine, modern terminal building, Keycase thought, with lots of glass and chrome as well as many trash cans, the latter important to his present purpose.

He read on a plaque that the airport was named after John Moisant, an Orleanian who had been a world aviation pioneer, and he noted that the initials were the same as his own, which could be a favourable omen too. It was the kind of airport he would be proud to thunder into on one of the big jets, and perhaps he would soon if things continued the way they had before the last spell inside had put him out of practice for a while. Although he was certainly coming back fast, even if nowadays he occasionally hesitated where once he would have operated coolly, almost with indifference.

But that was natural. It came from knowing that if he was caught and sent down again, this time it would be from ten to fifteen years. That would be hard to face. At fifty-two there were few periods of that length left.

Strolling inconspicuously through the airport terminal, a trim, well-dressed figure, carrying a folded newspaper beneath his arm, Keycase stayed carefully alert. He gave the appearance of a well-to-do businessman, relaxed and confident. Only his eyes moved ceaselessly, following the movements of the early rising travellers, pouring into the terminal from limousines and taxis which had delivered them from downtown hotels. It was the first north-bound exodus of the day, and a heavy one since United, National, Eastern, and Delta each had morning jet flights scheduled variously for New York, Washington, Chicago, Miami and Los Angeles.

Twice he saw the beginning of the kind of thing he was looking for. But it turned out to be just the beginning, and no more. Two men, reaching into pockets for tickets or change, encountered a hotel room key which they had carried away in error. The first took the trouble to locate a postal box and mail the key, as suggested on its plastic tag. The other handed his to an airline clerk who put it in a cash drawer, presumably for return to the hotel.

Both incidents were disappointing, but an old experience. Keycase continued to observe. He was a patient man. Soon, he knew, what he was waiting for would happen.

Ten minutes later his vigil was rewarded.

A florid-faced, balding man, carrying a topcoat, bulging flight bag and camera, stopped to choose a magazine on his way to the departure ramp. At the newsstand cash desk he discovered a hotel key and gave an exclamation of annoyance. His wife, a thin mild woman, made a quiet suggestion to which he snapped, 'There isn't time.' Keycase, overhearing, followed them closely. Good! As they passed a trash can, the man threw the key in.

For Keycase the rest was routine. Strolling past the trash can, he tossed in his own folded newspaper, then, as if abruptly changing his mind, turned back and recovered it. At the same time he looked down, observed the discarded key and palmed it unobtrusively. A few minutes later in the privacy of the men's toilet he read that it was for room 641 of the St Gregory Hotel.

Half an hour later, in a way that often happened when the breaks began, a similar incident terminated with the same kind of success. The second key was also for the St Gregory – a convenience which prompted Keycase to telephone at once, confirming his own reservation there. He decided not to press his luck by loitering at the terminal any longer. He was off to a good start and tonight he would check the railroad station, then, in a couple of days maybe, the airport again. There were also other ways to obtain hotel keys, one of which he had set in motion last night.

It was not without reason that a New York prosecuting attorney years before had observed in court, 'Everything this man becomes involved in, your honour, is a key case. Frankly, I've come to think of him as "Keycase" Milne.'

The observation had found its way into police records and the name stuck, so that even Keycase himself now used it with a certain pride. It was a pride seasoned by such expert knowledge that given time, patience and luck, the chances of securing a key to almost anything were extremely good.

His present speciality-within-a-speciality was based on people's indifference to hotel keys, an indifference – Keycase long ago learned – which was the constant despair of hoteliers everywhere. Theoretically, when a departing guest paid his bill, he was supposed to leave his key. But countless people left a hotel with their room keys forgotten in pocket or purse. The conscientious ones eventually dropped the key in a mailbox, and a big hotel like the St Gregory regularly paid out fifty dollars or more a week in postage due on keys returned. But there were other people who either kept the keys or discarded them indifferently.

The last group kept professional hotel thieves like Keycase steadily in business.

From the terminal building Keycase returned to the parking lot and the five-year-old Ford sedan which he had bought in Detroit and driven first to Kansas City, then New Orleans. It was an ideally inconspicuous car for Keycase, a dull grey, and neither old nor new enough to be unduly noticed or remembered. The only feature which bothered him a little were the Michigan licence plates – an attractive green on white. Out-of-state plates were not unusual in New Orleans, but the small distinctive feature was something he would have preferred to be without. He had considered using counterfeit Louisiana plates, but this seemed to be a greater risk, besides which, Keycase was shrewd enough not to step too far outside his own speciality.

Reassuringly, the car's motor started at a touch, purring smoothly as the result of an overhaul he had performed himself – a skill learned at federal expense during one of his various incarcerations.

He drove the fourteen miles to town, carefully observing speed limits, and headed for the St Gregory which he had located and reconnoitred the day before. He parked near Canal Street, a few blocks from the hotel, and removed two suitcases. The rest of his baggage had been left in the motel room on which he had paid several days' rent in advance. It was expensive to maintain an extra room. It was also prudent. The motel would serve as a cache for whatever he might acquire and, if disaster struck, could be abandoned entirely. He had been careful to leave nothing there which was personally identifiable. The motel key was painstakingly hidden in the carburettor air filter of the Ford.

He entered the St Gregory with a confident air, surrendering his bags to a doorman, and registered as B. W. Meader of Ann Arbor, Michigan. The room clerk, conscious of well-cut clothes and firm chiselled features which bespoke authority, treated the newcomer with respect and allocated room 830. Now, Keycase thought agreeably, there would be three St Gregory keys in his possession – one the hotel knew about and two it didn't.

Room 830, into which the bellboy ushered him a few moments later, turned out to be ideal. It was spacious and comfortable and the service stairway, Keycase observed as they came in, was only a few yards away.

When he was alone he unpacked carefully. Later, he decided he would have a sleep in preparation for the serious night's work ahead.

7

By the time Peter McDermott reached the lobby, Curtis O'Keefe had been efficiently roomed. Peter decided not to follow; there were times when too much attention could be as bothersome to a guest as too little. Besides, the St Gregory's official welcome would be extended by Warren Trent and, after making sure the hotel proprietor had been informed of O'Keefe's arrival, Peter went on to see Marsha Preyscott in 555.

As she opened the door, 'I'm glad you came,' she said. 'I was beginning to think you wouldn't.'

She was wearing a sleeveless apricot dress, he saw, which obviously she had sent for this morning. It touched her body lightly. Her long black hair hung loosely about her shoulders in contrast to the more sophisticated – though disordered – hair-do of the previous night. There was something singularly provoking – almost breathtaking – in the half-woman half-child appearance.

'I'm sorry it took so long.' He regarded her approvingly. 'But I see you've used the time.'

She smiled. 'I thought you might need the pyjamas.'

'They're just for emergency – like this room. I use it very rarely.'

'That's what the maid told me,' Marsha said. 'So if you don't mind, I thought I'd stay on for tonight, at least.'

'Oh! May I ask why?'

'I'm not sure.' She hesitated as they stood facing each other. 'Maybe it's because I want to recover from what happened yesterday, and the best place to do it is here.' But the real reason, she admitted to herself, was a wish to put off her return to the big, empty Garden District mansion.

He nodded doubtfully. 'How do you feel?'

'Better.'

'I'm glad of that.'

'It isn't the kind of experience you get over in a few hours,' Marsha admitted, 'but I'm afraid I was pretty stupid to come here at all – just as you reminded me.'

'I didn't say that.'

'No, but you thought it.'

'If I did, I should have remembered we all get into tough situations sometimes.' There was a silence, then Peter said, 'Let's sit down.'

When they were comfortable he began, 'I was hoping you'd tell me how it started.'

'I know you were.' With the directness he was becoming used to, she added, 'I've been wondering if I should.'

Last night, Marsha reasoned, her overwhelming feeling had been shock, hurt pride and physical exhaustion. But now the shock was gone and her pride, she suspected, might suffer less from silence than by protest. It was likely, too, that in the sober light of morning Lyle Dumaire and his cronies would not be eager to boast of what they had attempted.

'I can't persuade you if you decide to keep quiet,' Peter said. 'Though I'd remind you that what people get away with once they'll try again – not with you, perhaps, but someone else.' Her eyes were troubled as he continued, 'I don't know if the men who were in that room last night were friends of yours or not. But even if they were, I can't think of a single reason for shielding them.'

'One was a friend. At least, I thought so.'

'Friend or not,' Peter insisted, 'the point is what they tried to do – and would have, if Royce hadn't come along. What's more, when they were close to being caught, all four scuttled off like rats, leaving you alone.'

'Last night,' Marsha said tentatively, 'I heard you say you knew the names of two.'

'The room was registered in the name of Stanley Dixon. Another name I have is Dumaire. Were they two?'

She nodded.

'Who was the leader?'

'I think . . . Dixon.'

'Now then, tell me what happened beforehand.'

In a way, Marsha realized, the decision had been taken from her. She had a sense of being dominated. It was a novel experience, and even more surprisingly, she found herself liking it. Obediently she described the sequence of events beginning with her departure from the dance floor and ending with the welcome arrival of Aloysius Royce.

Only twice was she interrupted. Had she, Peter McDermott asked, seen anything of the women in the adjoining room whom Dixon and the others had referred to? Had she observed anyone from the hotel staff? To both questions she shook her head negatively.

At the end she had an urge to tell him more. The whole thing, Marsha said, probably would not have happened if it had not been her birthday.

He seemed surprised. 'Yesterday was your birthday?'

'I was nineteen.'

'And you were alone?'

Now that she had revealed so much, there was no point in holding back. Marsha described the telephone call from Rome and her disappointment at her father's failure to return.

'I'm sorry,' he said when she had finished. 'It makes it easier to understand a part of what happened.'

'It will never happen again. Never.'

'I'm sure of that.' He became more businesslike. 'What I want to do now is make use of what you've told me.'

She said doubtfully, 'In what way?'

'I'll call the four people – Dixon, Dumaire and the other two – into the hotel for a talk.'

'They may not come.'

'They'll come,' Peter had already decided how to make sure they would.

Still uncertain, Marsha said, 'That way wouldn't a lot of people find out?'

'I promise that when we're finished there'll be even less likelihood of anyone talking.'

'All right,' Marsha agreed. 'And thank you for all you've done.' She had a sense of relief which left her curiously light-headed.

It had been easier than he expected, Peter thought. And now he had the information, he was impatient to use it. Perhaps, though, he should stay a few minutes more, if only to put the girl at ease. He told her, 'There's something I should explain, Miss Preyscott.'

'Marsha.'

'All right, I'm Peter.' He supposed the informality was all right, though hotel executives were trained to avoid it, except with guests they knew very well.

'A lot of things go on in hotels, Marsha, that we close our eyes to. But when something like this happens we can be extremely tough. That includes anyone on our staff, if we find out they were implicated.'

It was one area, Peter knew – involving the hotel's reputation – where Warren Trent would feel as strongly as himself. And any action Peter took – providing he could prove his facts – would be backed solidly by the hotel proprietor.

The conversation, Peter felt, had gone as far as it need. He rose from his chair and walked to the window. From this side of the hotel he could see the busy mid-morning. activity of Canal Street. Its six traffic lanes were packed with vehicles, fast and slow moving, the wide sidewalks thronged by shoppers. Knots of transit riders waited on the palm-fronded centre boulevard where air-conditioned buses glided, their aluminium panels shining in the sunlight. The NAACP was picketing some businesses again, he noticed. THIS STORE DISCRIMINATES. DO NOT PATRONIZE, one placard advised, and there were others, their bearers pacing stolidly as the tide of pedestrians broke around them.

'You're new to New Orleans, aren't you?' Marsha said. She had joined him at the window. He was conscious of a sweet and gentle fragrance.

'Fairly new. In time I hope to know it better.'

She said with sudden enthusiasm, 'I know lots about local history. Would you let me teach you?'

'Well . . . I bought some books. It's just I haven't had time.'

'You can read the books after. It's much better to see things first, or be told about them. Besides, I'd like to do something to show how grateful . . .'

'There isn't any need for that.'

'Well then, I'd like to anyway. Please!' She put a hand on his arm.

Wondering if he was being wise, he said, 'It's an interesting offer.'

'Good! That's settled. I'm having a dinner party at home tomorrow night. It'll be an old-fashioned New Orleans evening. Afterwards we can talk about history.'

He protested, 'Whoa! . . .'

'You mean you've something already arranged?'

'Well, not exactly.'

Marsha said firmly, 'Then that's settled too.'

The past, the importance of avoiding involvement with a young girl who was also a hotel guest, made Peter hesitate. Then he decided: it would be churlish to refuse. And there was nothing indiscreet about accepting an invitation to dinner. There would be others present, after all. 'If I come,' he said, 'I want you to do one thing for me now.'

'What?'

'Go home, Marsha. Leave the hotel and go home.'

Their eyes met directly. Once more he was aware of her youthfulness and fragrance.

'All right,' she said. 'If you want me to, I will.'

Peter McDermott was engrossed in his own thoughts as he re-entered his office on the main mezzanine a few minutes later. It troubled him that someone as young as Marsha Preyscott, and presumably born with a gold-plated list of advantages, should be so apparently neglected. Even with her father out of the country and her mother decamped – he had heard of the former Mrs Preyscott's multiple marriages – he found it incredible that safeguards for a young girl's welfare would not be set up. If I were her father, he thought . . . or brother . . .

He was interrupted by Flora Yates, his homely freckle-faced secretary. Flora's stubby fingers, which could dance over a typewriter keyboard faster than any other he had ever seen, were clutching a sheaf of telephone messages. Pointing to them, he asked, 'Anything urgent?'

'A few things. They'll keep until this afternoon.'

'We'll let them, then. I asked the cashier's office to send me a bill for room 1126-7. It's in the name of Stanley Dixon.'

'It's here.' Flora plucked a folder from several others on his desk. 'There's also an estimate from the carpenters' shop for damages in the suite. I put the two together.'

He glanced over them both. The bill, which included several room service charges, was for seventy-five dollars, the carpenters' estimate for a hundred and ten. Indicating the bill, Peter said, 'Get me the phone number for this address. I expect it'll be in his father's name.'

There was a folded newspaper on his desk which he had not looked at until now. It was the morning *Times-Picayune*. He opened it as Flora went out and black headlines flared up at him. The hit-and-run fatality of the night before had become a double tragedy, the mother of the slain child having died in the hospital during the early hours of the morning. Peter read quickly through the report which amplified what the policeman had told them when he and Christine had been stopped at the roadblock. 'So far,' it revealed, 'there are no firm leads as to the death vehicle or its driver. However, police attach credence to the report of an unnamed bystander that a "low black car moving very fast" was observed leaving the scene seconds after the accident.' City and state police, the *Times-Picayune* added, were collaborating in a state-wide search for a presumably damaged automobile fitting this description.

Peter wondered if Christine had seen the newspaper report. Its impact seemed greater because of their own brief contact at the scene.

The return of Flora with the telephone number he had asked for brought his mind back to more immediate things.

He put the newspaper aside and used a direct outside line to dial the number himself.

A deep male voice answered, 'The Dixon residence.'

'I'd like to speak to Mr Stanley Dixon. Is he at home?'

'May I say who is calling, sir?'

Peter gave his name and added, 'The Gregory Hotel.'

There was a pause, and the sound of unhurried footsteps retreating, then returning at the same pace.

'I'm sorry, sir. Mr Dixon, junior, is not available.'

Peter let his voice take on an edge. 'Give him this message: Tell him if he doesn't choose to come to the telephone I intend to call his father directly.'

'Perhaps if you did that . . .'

'Get on with it! Tell him what I said.'

There was an almost audible hesitation. Then: 'Very well, sir.' The footsteps retreated again.

There was a click on the line and a sullen voice announced,

'This's Stan Dixon. What's all the fuss?'

Peter answered sharply. 'The fuss concerns what happened last night. Does it surprise you?'

'Who are you?'

He repeated his name. 'I've talked with Miss Preyscott. Now I'd like to talk to you.'

'You're talking now,' Dixon said. 'You got what you wanted.'

'Not this way. In my office at the hotel.' There was an exclamation which Peter ignored. 'Four o'clock tomorrow, with the other three. You'll bring them along.'

The response was fast and forceful. 'Like hell I will! Whoever you are, buster, you're just a hotel slob and I don't take orders from you. What's more you'd better watch out because my old man knows Warren Trent.'

'For your information I've already discussed the matter with Mr Trent. He left it for me to handle, including whether or not we shall start criminal proceedings. But I'll tell him you prefer to have your father brought in. We'll carry on from there.'

'Hold it!' There was the sound of heavy breathing, then, with noticeably less belligerence, 'I got a class tomorrow at four.'

'Cut it,' Peter told him, 'and have the others do the same. My office is on the main mezzanine. Remember – four o'clock sharp.'

Replacing the telephone, he found himself looking forward to tomorrow's meeting.

8

The disarranged pages of the morning newspaper lay scattered around the Duchess of Croydon's bed. There was little in the news that the Duchess had not read thoroughly and now she lay back propped against pillows, her mind working busily. There had never been a time, she realized, when her wits and resourcefulness were needed more.

On a bedside table a room-service tray had been used and pushed aside. Even in moments of crisis the Duchess was accustomed to breakfasting well. It was a habit carried over from childhood at her family's country seat of Fallingbrook Abbey where breakfast had always consisted of a hearty meal of several courses, often after a brisk cross-country gallop.

The Duke, who had eaten alone in the living-room, had returned to the bedroom a few moments earlier. He too had read the newspaper avidly as soon as it arrived. Now, wearing a belted scarlet robe over pyjamas, he was pacing restlessly. Occasionally he passed a hand through his still disordered hair.

'For goodness sake, keep still!' The tenseness they shared was in his wife's voice. 'I can't possibly think when you're parading like a stallion at Ascot.'

He turned, his face lined and despairing in the bright morning light. 'What bloody good will thinking do? Nothing's going to change.'

'Thinking always helps – if one does enough and it's the right kind. That's why some people make a success of things and others don't.'

His hand went through his hair once more. 'Nothing looks any better than it did last night.'

'At least it isn't any worse,' the Duchess said practically, 'and that's something to be thankful for. We're still here – intact.'

He shook his head wearily. He had had little sleep during the night. 'How does it help?'

'As I see it, it's a question of time. Time is on our side. The longer we wait and nothing happens . . .' She stopped, then went on slowly, thinking aloud, 'What we desperately need is to have some attention focused on you. The kind of attention that would make the other seem so fantastic it wouldn't even be considered.'

As if by consent, neither referred to their acrimony of the night before.

The Duke resumed his pacing. 'Only thing likely to do that is an announcement confirming my appointment to Washington.'

'Exactly.'

'You can't hurry it. If Hal feels he's being pushed, he'll blow the roof off Downing Street. The whole thing's damn touchy, anyway . . .'

'It'll be touchier still if . . .'

'Don't you think I bloody well know! Do you think I haven't thought we might as well give up!' There was a trace of hysteria in the Duke of Croydon's voice. He lit a cigarette, his hand shaking.

'We shall not give up!' In contrast to her husband, the Duchess's tone was crisp and businesslike. 'Even prime ministers respond to pressure if it's from the right quarter. Hal's no exception. I'm going to call London.'

'Why?'

'I shall speak to Geoffrey. I intend to ask him to do everything he can to speed up your appointment.'

The Duke shook his head doubtfully, though not dismissing the idea out of hand. In the past he had seen plenty of evidence of the remarkable influence exerted by his wife's family. All the same he warned, 'We could be spiking our own guns, old girl.'

'Not necessarily. Geoffrey's good at pressure when he wants to be. Besides, if we sit here and wait it may be worse still.' Matching action to her words, the Duchess picked up the telephone beside the bed and instructed the operator, 'I wish to call London and speak to Lord Selwyn.' She gave a Mayfair number.

The call came through in twenty minutes. When the Duchess of Croydon had explained its purpose, her brother, Lord Selwyn, was notably unenthusiastic. From across the bedroom the Duke could hear his brother-in-law's deep protesting voice as it rattled the telephone diaphragm. 'By golly, sis, you could be stirring a nest of vipers, and why do it? I don't mind telling you, Simon's appointment to Washington is a dashed long shot right now. Some of those in the Cabinet feel he's the wrong man for the time. I'm not saying I agree, but there's no good wearing blinkers, is there?'

'If things are left as they are, how long will a decision take?'

'Hard to say for sure, old thing. The way I hear, though, it could be weeks.'

'We simply cannot wait weeks,' the Duchess insisted. 'You'll have to take my word, Geoffrey, it would be a ghastly mistake not to make an effort now.'

'Can't see it myself.' The voice from London was distinctly huffy.

Her tone sharpened. 'What I'm asking is for the family's sake as well as our own. Surely you can accept my assurance on that.'

There was a pause, then the cautious question, 'Is Simon with you?'

'Yes.'

'What's behind all this? What's he been up to?'

'Even if there were an answer,' the Duchess of Croydon responded, 'I'd scarcely be so foolish as to give it on the public telephone.'

There was a silence once more, then the reluctant admission, 'Well, you usually know what you're doing. I'll say that.'

The Duchess caught her husband's eye. She gave a barely perceptible nod before enquiring of her brother, 'Am I to understand, then, that you'll act as I ask?'

'I don't like it, sis. I still don't like it.' But he added, 'Very well, I'll do what I can.'

In a few more words they said goodbye.

The bedside telephone had been replaced only a moment when it rang again. Both Croydons started, the Duke moistening his lips nervously. He listened as his wife answered.

'Yes?'

A flat nasal voice enquired, 'Duchess of Croydon?'

'This is she.'

'Ogilvie. Chief house officer.' There was the sound of heavy breathing down the line, and a pause as if the caller were allowing time for the information to sink in.

The Duchess waited. When nothing further was said she asked pointedly. 'What is it you want?'

'A private talk. With your husband and you.' It was a blunt emotional statement, delivered in the same flat drawl.

'If this is hotel business I suggest you have made an error. We are accustomed to dealing with Mr Trent.'

'Do that this time, and you'll wish you hadn't.' The cold, insolent voice held an unmistakable confidence. It caused the Duchess to hesitate. As she did, she was aware her hands were shaking.

She managed to answer, 'It is not convenient to see you now.'

'When?' Again a pause and heavy breathing.

Whatever this man knew or wanted, she realized, he was adept at maintaining a psychological advantage.

She answered, 'Possibly later.'

'I'll be there in an hour.' It was a declaration, not a question.

'It may not be . . .'

Cutting off her protest, there was a click as the caller hung up.

'Who is it? What did they want?' The Duke approached tensely. His gaunt face seemed paler than before.

Momentarily, the Duchess closed her eyes. She had a desperate yearning to be relieved of leadership and responsibility for them both; to have someone else assume the burden of decision. She knew it was a vain hope, just as it had always been for as long as she could remember. When you are born with a character stronger than those around you, there was no escaping. In her own family, though strength was a norm, others looked to her instinctively, following her lead and heeding her advice. Even Geoffrey, with his real ability and headstrong ways, always listened to her in the end, as he had just now. As reality returned, the moment passed. Her eyes opened.

'It was the hotel detective. He insists on coming here in an hour.'

'Then he knows! My God – he knows!'

'Obviously he is aware of something. He didn't say what.'

Unexpectedly the Duke of Croydon straightened, his head moving upright and shoulders squaring. His hands became steadier, his mouth a firmer line. It was the same chameleon change he had exhibited the night before. He said quietly, 'It might go better, even now, if I went . . . if I admitted . . .'

'No! Absolutely and positively no!' His wife's eyes flashed. 'Understand one thing. Nothing you can possibly do could improve the situation in the slightest.' There was a silence between them, then the Duchess said broodingly, 'We shall do nothing. We will wait for this man to come, then discover what he knows and intends.'

Momentarily it seemed as if the Duke would argue. Then, changing his mind, he nodded dully. Tightening the scarlet robe around him, he padded out to the adjoining room. A few minutes later he returned carrying two glasses of neat Scotch. As he offered one to his wife she protested. 'You know it's much too early . . .'

'Never mind that. You need it.' With a solicitousness she was unused to, he pressed the glass into her hand.

Surprised, yet yielding, she held the glass and drained it. The undiluted liquor burned, snatching away her breath, but a moment later flooded her with welcome warmth.

9

'Whatever it is can't be all that bad.'

At her desk in the outer office of the managing director's suite, Christine Francis had been frowning as she read a letter in her hand. Now she looked up to see Peter McDermott's cheerful rugged face peering around the doorway.

Brightening, she answered, 'It's another sling and arrow. But with so many already, what's one more?'

'I like that thought.' Peter eased his big frame around the door.

Christine regarded him appraisingly. 'You appear remarkably awake, considering how little sleep you must have had.'

He grinned. 'I had an early morning session with your boss. It was like a cold shower. Is he down yet?'

She shook her head, then glanced at the letter she had been reading. 'When he comes he won't like this.'

'Is it secret?'

'Not really. You were involved, I think.'

Peter seated himself in a leather chair facing the desk.

'You remember a month ago,' Christine said, ' – the man who was walking on Carondelet Street when a bottle dropped from above. His head was cut quite badly.'

Peter nodded. 'Damn shame! The bottle came from one of our rooms, no question of that. But we couldn't find the guest who did it.'

'What sort of a man was he – the one who got hit.'

'Nice little guy, as I recall. I talked to him after, and we paid his hospital bill. Our lawyers wrote a letter making clear it was a goodwill gesture, though, and not admitting liability.'

'The goodwill didn't work. He's suing the hotel for ten thousand dollars. He charges shock, bodily harm, loss of earnings and says we were negligent.'

Peter said flatly, 'He won't collect. I guess in a way it's unfair. But he hasn't a chance.'

'How can you be so sure?'

'Because there's a raft of cases where the same kind of thing has happened. It gives defending lawyers all kinds of precedents they can quote in court.'

'Is that enough to affect a decision?'

'Usually,' he assured her. 'Over the years the law's been pretty consistent. For example, there was a classic case in Pittsburgh – at the William Penn. A man was hit by a bottle which was thrown from a guest bedroom and went through the roof of his car. He sued the hotel.'

'And he didn't win?'

'No. He lost his case in a lower court, then appealed to the Supreme Court of Pennsylvania. They turned him down.'

'Why?'

'The court said that a hotel – any hotel – is not responsible for the acts of its guests. The only exception might be if someone in authority – say, the hotel manager – knew in advance what was going to happen but made no attempt to prevent it.' Peter went on, frowning at the effort of memory. 'There was another case – in Kansas City, I think. Some conventioneers dropped laundry bags filled with water from their rooms. When the bags burst, people on the sidewalk scrambled to get out of the way and one was pushed under a moving car. He was badly injured. Afterwards he sued the hotel, but couldn't collect either. There are quite a few other judgements – all the same way.'

Christine asked curiously, 'How do you know all this?'

'Among other things, I studied hotel law at Cornell.'

'Well, I think it sounds horribly unjust.'

'It's hard on anyone who gets hit, but fair to the hotel. What ought to happen, of course, is that the people who do these things should be held responsible. Trouble is, with so many rooms facing the street it's next to impossible to discover who they are. So mostly they get away with it.'

Christine had been listening intently, an elbow planted on her desk, chin cupped lightly in the palm of one hand. Sunlight, slanting through half opened venetian blinds, touched her red hair, highlighting it. At the moment a line of puzzlement creased her forehead and Peter found himself wanting to reach out and erase it gently.

'Let me get this straight,' she said. 'Are you saying that a hotel isn't responsible legally for anything its guests may do – even to other guests?'

'In the way we've been talking about, it certainly isn't. The law's quite clear on that and has been for a long time. A lot of our law, in fact, goes back to the English inns, beginning with the fourteenth century.'

'Tell me.'

'I'll give you the shortened version. It starts when the English inns had one great hall, warmed and lighted by a fire, and everyone slept there. While they slept it was the landlord's business to protect his guests from thieves and murderers.'

'That sounds reasonable.'

'It was. And the same thing was expected of the landlord when smaller chambers began to be used, because even these were always shared – or could be – by strangers.'

'When you think about it,' Christine mused, 'it wasn't much of an age for privacy.'

'That came later when there *were* individual rooms, and guests had keys. After that the law looked at things differently. The innkeeper was obliged to protect his guests from being broken in upon. But beyond that he had no responsibility, either for what happened to them in their rooms or what they did.'

'So the key made the difference.'

'It still does,' Peter said. 'On that, the law hasn't changed. When we give a guest a key it's a legal symbol, just as it was in an English inn. It means that the hotel can no longer use the room, or quarter anyone else there. On the other hand, the hotel isn't responsible for the guest once he's closed the door behind him.' He pointed to the letter which Christine had put down. 'That's why our friend from outside would have to find whoever dropped the bottle on him. Otherwise he's out of luck.'

'I didn't know you were so encyclopaedic.'

'I didn't mean to sound that way,' Peter said. 'I imagine W. T. knows the law well enough, though if he wants a list of cases I have one somewhere.'

'He'll probably be grateful. I'll clip a note on the letter.' Her eyes met Peter's directly. 'You like all this, don't you? Running a hotel; the other things that go with it.'

He answered frankly, 'Yes, I do. Though I'd like it more if we could arrange a few things here. Maybe if we'd done it earlier we wouldn't be needing Curtis O'Keefe now. By the way, I suppose you know he's arrived.'

'You're the seventeenth to tell me. I think the phone started ringing the moment he stepped on the sidewalk.'

'It's not surprising. By now a good many are wondering why he's here. Or rather, when we shall be told officially why he's here.'

Christine said, 'I've arranged a private dinner for tonight in W. T.'s suite – for Mr O'Keefe and friend. Have you seen her? I hear she's something special.'

He shook his head. 'I'm more interested in my own dinner plan – involving you, which is why I'm here.'

'If that's an invitation for tonight, I'm free and hungry.'

'Good!' He jumped up, towering over her. 'I'll collect you at seven. Your apartment.'

Peter was leaving when, on a table near the doorway, he observed a folded copy of the *Times-Picayune*. Stopping, he saw it was the same edition – with black headlines proclaiming the hit-and-run fatalities – which he had read earlier. He said sombrely, 'I suppose you saw this.'

'Yes, I did. It's horrible isn't it? When I read it I had an awful sensation of watching the whole thing happen because of going by there last night.'

He looked at her strangely. 'It's funny you should say that. I had a feeling too. It bothered me last night and again this morning.'

'What kind of feeling?'

'I'm not sure. The nearest thing is – it seems as if I know something, and yet I don't.' Peter shrugged, dismissing the idea. 'I expect it's as you say – because we went by.' He replaced the newspaper where he had found it.

As he strode out he turned and waved back to her, smiling.

As she often did for lunch, Christine had room service send a sandwich and coffee to her desk. During the course of it Warren Trent appeared, but stayed only to read the mail before setting out on one of his prowls of the hotel which, as Christine knew, might last for hours. Observing the strain in the proprietor's face, she found herself concerned for him, and noticed that he walked stiffly, a sure sign that sciatica was causing him pain.

At half past two, leaving word with one of the secretaries in the outer office, Christine left to visit Albert Wells.

She took an elevator to the fourteenth floor, then, turning down the long corridor, saw a stocky figure approaching. It was Sam Jakubiec, the credit manager. As he came nearer, she observed that he was holding a slip of paper and his expression was dour.

Seeing Christine, he stopped. 'I've been to see your invalid friend, Mr Wells.'

'If you looked like that, you couldn't have cheered him up much.'

'Tell you the truth,' Jakubiec said, 'he didn't cheer me up either. I got this out of him, but lord knows how good it is.'

Christine accepted the paper the credit manager had been holding. It was a soiled sheet of hotel stationery with a grease stain in one corner. On the sheet, in rough sprawling handwriting, Albert Wells had written and signed an order on a Montreal bank for two hundred dollars.

'In his quiet sort of way,' Jakubiec said, 'he's an obstinate old cuss. Wasn't going to give me anything at first. Said he'd pay his bill when it was due, and didn't seem interested when I told him we'd allow some extra time if he needed it.'

'People are sensitive about money,' Christine said. 'Especially being short of it.'

The credit manager clucked his tongue impatiently. 'Hell! – most of us are short of money. I always am. But people go around thinking it's something to be ashamed of when if they'd only level, a lot of the time they could be helped out.'

Christine regarded the improvised bank draft doubtfully. 'Is this legal?'

'It's legal if there's money in the bank to meet it. You can write a cheque on sheet music or a banana skin if you feel like it. But most people who have cash in their accounts at least carry printed cheques. Your friend Wells said he couldn't find one.'

As Christine handed the paper back, 'You know what I think,' Jakubiec said, 'I think he's honest and he has the money – but only just and he's going to put himself in a hole finding it. Trouble is, he already owes more than half of this two hundred, and that nursing bill is soon going to swallow the rest.'

'What are you going to do?'

The credit manager rubbed a hand across his baldness. 'First of all, I'm going to invest in a phone call to Montreal to find out if this is a good cheque or a dud.'

'And if it isn't good, Sam?'

'He'll have to leave – at least as far as I'm concerned. Of course, if you want to tell Mr Trent and he says differently' – Jakubiec shrugged – 'that's something else again.'

Christine shook her head. 'I don't want to bother W. T. But I'd appreciate it if you'd tell me before you do anything.'

'Be glad to, Miss Francis.' The credit manager nodded, then with short vigorous steps, continued down the corridor.

A moment later Christine knocked at the door of room 1410.

It was opened by a uniformed, middle-aged nurse, serious faced and wearing heavy horn-rimmed glasses. Christine identified herself and the nurse instructed, 'Wait here, please. I'll enquire if Mr Wells will see you.'

There were footsteps inside and Christine smiled as she heard a voice say insistently, 'Of course I'll see her. Don't keep her waiting.'

When the nurse returned, Christine suggested, 'If you'd like to have a few minutes off, I can stay until you come back.'

'Well . . .' The older woman hesitated, thawing a little.

The voice from inside said, 'You do that. Miss Francis knows what she's up to. If she didn't I'd have been a goner last night.'

'All right,' the nurse said. 'I'll just be ten minutes and if you need me, please call the coffee shop.'

Albert Wells beamed as Christine came in. The little man was reclining diminutively, against a mound of pillows. His appearance – the scrawny figure draped by a fresh old-fashioned nightshirt – still conveyed the impression of a sparrow, but today a perky one, in contrast to his desperate frailness of the night before. He was still pale, but the ashen pallor of the previous day had gone. His breathing, though occasionally wheezy, was regular and apparently without great effort.

He said, 'This is good of you to come 'n see me, miss.'

'It isn't a question of being good,' Christine assured him. 'I wanted to know how you were.'

'Thanks to you, much better.' He gestured to the door as it closed behind the nurse. 'But she's a dragon, that one.'

'She's probably good for you.' Christine surveyed the room approvingly. Everything in it, including the man's personal belongings, had been neatly arranged. A tray of medication was set out efficiently on a bedside table. The oxygen cylinder they had used the previous night was still in place, but the improvised mask had been replaced by a more professional one.

'Oh, she knows what she's up to all right,' Albert Wells admitted, 'though another time I'd like a prettier one.'

Christine smiled. 'You are feeling better.' She wondered if she should say anything about the talk with Sam Jakubiec, then decided not to. Instead she asked, 'You said last night, didn't you, that you started getting these attacks when you were a miner?'

'The bronchitis, I did; that's right.'

'Were you a miner for very long, Mr Wells?'

'More years'n I like to think about, miss. Though there's always things to remind you of it – the bronchitis for one, then these.' He spread his hands, palms uppermost, on the counterpane and she saw that they were gnarled and toughened from the manual work of many years.

Impulsively she reached out to touch them. 'It's something to be proud of, I should think. I'd like to hear about what you did.'

He shook his head. 'Sometime maybe when you've a lot of hours and patience. Mostly, though, it's old men's tales, 'n old men get boring if you give 'em half a chance.'

Christine sat on a chair beside the bed. 'I do have patience, and I don't believe about it being boring.'

He chuckled. 'There are some in Montreal who'd argue that.'

'I've often wondered about Montreal. I've never been there.'

'It's a mixed-up place – in some ways a lot like New Orleans.'

She asked curiously, 'Is that why you come here every year? Because it seems the same?'

The little man considered, his bony shoulders deep in the pile of pillows. 'I never thought about that, miss – one way or the other. I guess I come here because I like things old-fashioned and there aren't too many places left where they are. It's the same with this hotel. It's a bit rubbed off in places – you know that. But mostly it's homely, 'n I mean it the best way. I hate chain hotels. They're all the same – slick and polished, and when you're in 'em it's like living in a factory.'

Christine hesitated, then, realizing the day's events had dispelled the earlier secrecy, told him. 'I've some news you won't like. I'm afraid the St Gregory may be part of a chain before long.'

'If it happens I'll be sorry,' Albert Wells said. 'Though I figured you people were in money trouble here.'

'How did you know that?'

The old man ruminated. 'Last time or two I've been here I could tell things were getting tough. What's the trouble now – bank tightening up, mortgage foreclosing, something like that?'

There were surprising tides to this retired miner, Christine thought, including an instinct for the truth. She answered, smiling, 'I've probably talked too much already. What you'll certainly hear, though, is that Mr Curtis O'Keefe arrived this morning.'

'Oh no! – not him.' Albert Wells' face mirrored genuine concern. 'If that one gets his hands on this place he'll make it a copy of all his others. It'll be a factory, like I said. This hotel needs changes, but not his kind.'

Christine asked curiously, 'What kind of changes, Mr Wells?'

'A good hotel man could tell you better'n me, though I've a few ideas. I do know one thing, miss – just like always, the public's going through a fad. Right now they want the slickness 'n the chrome and sameness. But in time they'll get tired and want to come back to older things – like real hospitality and a bit of character and atmosphere; something that's not exactly like they found in fifty other cities 'n can find in fifty more. Only trouble is, by the time they get around to knowing it, most of the good places – including this one maybe – will have gone.' He stopped, then asked, 'When are they deciding?'

'I really don't know,' Christine said. The little man's depth of feeling had startled her. 'Except I don't suppose Mr O'Keefe will be here long.'

Albert Wells nodded. 'He doesn't stay long anywhere from all I've heard. Works fast when he sets his mind on something. Well, I still say it'll be a pity, and if it happens here's one who won't be back.'

'We'd miss you, Mr Wells. At least I would – assuming I survived the changes.'

'You'll survive, and you'll be where you want to be, miss. Though if some young fellow's got some sense it won't be working in any hotel.'

She laughed without replying and they talked of other things until, preceded by a short staccato knock, the guardian nurse returned. She said primly, 'Thank you, Miss Francis.' Then, looking pointedly at her watch: 'It's time for my patient to have his medication and rest.'

'I have to go anyway,' Christine said. 'I'll come to see you again tomorrow if I may, Mr Wells.'

'I'd like it if you would.'

As she left, he winked at her.

A note on her office desk requested Christine to call Sam Jakubiec. She did, and the credit manager answered.

'I thought you'd like to know,' he said. 'I phoned that bank in Montreal. It looks like your friend's OK.'

'That's good news, Sam. What did they say?'

'Well, in a way it was a funny thing. They wouldn't tell me anything about a credit rating – the way banks usually do. Just said to present the cheque for payment. I told them the amount, though, and they didn't seem worried, so I guess he's got it.'

'I'm glad,' Christine said.

'I'm glad too, though I'll watch the room account to see it doesn't get too big.'

'You're a great watchdog, Sam.' She laughed. 'And thanks for calling.'

10

Curtis O'Keefe and Dodo had settled comfortably into their communicating suites, with Dodo unpacking for both of them as she always enjoyed doing. Now, in the larger of the two living-rooms, the hotelier was studying a financial statement, one of several in a blue folder labelled *Confidential – St Gregory, Preliminary survey*.

Dodo, after a careful inspection of the magnificent basket of fruit which Peter McDermott had ordered to be delivered to the suite, selected an apple and was slicing it as the telephone at O'Keefe's elbow rang twice within a few minutes.

The first call was from Warren Trent – a polite welcome and an enquiry seeking reassurance that everything was in order. After a genial acknowledgement that it was – 'Couldn't be better, my dear Warren, even in an O'Keefe hotel' – Curtis O'Keefe accepted an invitation for himself and Dodo to dine privately with the St Gregory's proprietor that evening.

'We'll be truly delighted,' the hotelier affirmed graciously, 'and, by the way, I admire your house.'

'That,' Warren Trent said drily down the telephone, 'is what I've been afraid of.'

O'Keefe guffawed. 'We'll talk tonight, Warren. A little business if we must, but mostly I'm looking forward to a conversation with a great hotel man.'

As he replaced the telephone Dodo's brow was furrowed. 'If he's such a great hotel man, Curtie, why's he selling out to you?'

He replied seriously as he always did, though knowing in advance the answer would elude her. 'Mostly because we're moving into another age and he doesn't know it. Nowadays it isn't sufficient to be a good innkeeper; you must become a cost accountant too.'

'Gee,' Dodo said, 'these sure are big apples.'

The second call, which followed immediately, was from a pay telephone in the hotel lobby. 'Hullo, Ogden,' Curtis O'Keefe said when the caller identified himself, 'I'm reading your report now.'

In the lobby, eleven floors below, a balding sallow man who looked like an accountant which – among other things – he was, nodded confirmation to a younger male companion waiting outside the glass-panelled phone booth. The caller, whose name was Ogden Bailey and his home Long Island, had been registered in the hotel for the past two weeks as Richard Fountain of Miami. With characteristic caution he had avoided using a house phone or calling from his own room on the fourth floor. Now, in precise clipped tones he stated, 'There are some points we'd like to amplify, Mr O'Keefe, and some later information I think you'll want.'

'Very well. Give me fifteen minutes, then come to see me.'

Hanging up, Curtis O'Keefe said amusedly to Dodo, 'I'm glad you enjoy the fruit. If it weren't for you, I'd put a stop to all these harvest festivals.'

'Well, it isn't that I like it so much.' The baby blue eyes were turned widely upon him. 'But you never eat any, and it just seems awful to waste it.'

'Very few things in a hotel are wasted,' he assured her. 'Whatever you leave, someone else will take – probably through the back door.'

'My mom's mad about fruit.' Dodo broke off a cluster of grapes. 'She'd go crazy with a basket like this.'

He had picked up the balance sheet again. Now he put it down. 'Why not send her one?'

'You mean now?'

'Of course.' Lifting the telephone once more, he asked for the hotel florist. 'This is Mr O'Keefe. I believe you delivered some fruit to my suite.'

A woman's voice answered anxiously, 'Yes, sir. Is anything wrong?'

'Nothing at all. But I would like an identical fruit basket telegraphed to Akron, Ohio, and charged to my bill. One moment.' He handed the telephone to Dodo. 'Give them the address and a message for your mother.'

When she had finished, impulsively she flung her arms around him. 'Gee, Curtie, you're the sweetest!'

He basked in her genuine pleasure. It was strange, he reflected, that while Dodo had proved as receptive to expensive gifts as any of her predecessors, it was the small things – such as at this moment – which seemed to please her most.

He finished the papers in the folder and, in fifteen minutes precisely, there was a knock at the door which Dodo answered. She showed in two men, both carrying briefcases – Ogden Bailey who had telephoned, and the second man, Sean Hall, who had been with him in the lobby. Hall was a younger edition of his superior and in ten years or so, O'Keefe thought, would probably have the same sallow, concentrated look which came, no doubt, from poring over endless balance sheets and drafting financial estimates.

The hotelier greeted both men cordially. Ogden Bailey – alias Richard Fountain in the present instance – was an experienced key figure in the O'Keefe organization. As well as having the usual qualifications of an accountant, he possessed an extraordinary ability to enter any hotel and, after a week or two of discreet observation – usually unknown to the hotel's management – produce a financial analysis which later would prove uncannily close to the hotel's own figures. Hall, whom Bailey himself had discovered and trained, showed every promise of developing the same kind of talent.

Both men politely declined the offer of a drink, as O'Keefe had known they would. They seated themselves on a settee, facing him, refraining from unzipping their briefcases, as if knowing that other formalities must be completed first. Dodo, across the room, had returned her attention to the basket of fruit and was peeling a banana.

'I'm glad you could come, gentlemen,' Curtis O'Keefe informed them, as if this meeting had not been planned weeks ahead. 'Perhaps, though, before we begin our business it would benefit all of us if we asked the help of Almighty God.'

As he spoke, with the ease of long practice the hotelier slipped agilely to his knees, clasping his hands devoutly in front of him. With an expression bordering on resignation, as if he had been through this experience many times before, Ogden Bailey followed suit and, after a moment's hesitation, the younger man Hall assumed the same position. O'Keefe glanced towards Dodo, who was eating her banana. 'My dear,' he said quietly, 'we are about to ask a blessing on our intention.'

Dodo put down the banana, 'OK,' she said co-operatively, slipping from her chair, 'I'm on your channel.'

There was a time, months earlier, when the frequent prayer sessions of her benefactor – often at unlikely moments – had disturbed Dodo for reasons she never fully understood. But eventually, as was her way, she adjusted to the point where they no longer bothered her. 'After all,' she confided to a friend, 'Curtie's a doll, and I guess if I go on my back for him I might as well get on my knees, too.'

'Almighty God,' Curtis O'Keefe intoned, his eyes closed and pink-cheeked, leonine face serene, 'grant us, if it be thy will, success in what we are about to do. We ask thy blessing and thine active help in acquiring this hotel, named for thine own St Gregory. We plead devoutly that we may add it to those already enlisted – by our own organization – in thy cause and held for thee in trust by thy devoted servant who speaketh.' Even when dealing with God, Curtis O'Keefe believed in coming directly to the point.

He continued, his face uplifted, the words rolling onward like a solemn flowing river: 'Moreover if this be thy will – and we pray it may – we ask that it be done expeditiously and with economy, such treasure as we thy servants possess, not being depleted unduly, but husbanded to thy further use. We invoke thy blessing also, O God, on those who will negotiate against us, on behalf of this hotel, asking that they shall be governed solely according to thy spirit and that thou shalt cause them to exercise reasonableness and discretion in all they do. Finally, Lord, be with us always, prospering our cause and advancing our works so that we, in turn, may dedicate them to thy greater glory, Amen. Now, gentlemen, how much am I going to have to pay for this hotel?'

O'Keefe had already bounced back into his chair. It was a second or two, however, before the others realized that the last sentence was not a part of the prayer, but the opening of their business session. Bailey was first to recover and, springing back adroitly from his knees to the settee, brought out the contents of his briefcase. Hall, with a startled look, scrambled to join him.

Ogden Bailey began respectfully, 'I won't speak as to price, Mr O'Keefe. As always, of course, you'll make that decision. But there's no question that the two-million-dollar mortgage due on Friday should make bargaining a good deal easier, at least on our side.'

'There's been no change in that, then? No word of renewal, or anyone else taking it over?'

Bailey shook his head. 'I've tapped some fairly good sources here, and they assure me not. No-one in the financial community will touch it, mostly because of the hotel's operating losses – I gave you an estimate of those – coupled with the poor management situation, which is quite well known.'

O'Keefe nodded thoughtfully, then opened the folder he had been studying earlier. He selected a single typewritten page. 'You're unusually optimistic in your ideas about potential earnings.' His bright, shrewd eyes met Bailey's directly.

The accountant produced a thin, tight smile. 'I'm not prone to extravagant fancies, as you know. There's absolutely no doubt that a good profit position could be established quickly, both with new revenue sources and overhauling existing ones. The key factor is the management situation here. It's incredibly bad.' He nodded to the younger man, Hall. 'Sean has been doing some work in that direction.'

A shade self-consciously, and glancing at notes, Hall began, 'There's no effective chain of command, with the result that department heads in some cases have gained quite extraordinary powers. A case in point is in food purchasing where . . .'

'Just a moment.'

At the interruption from his employer, Hall stopped abruptly.

Curtis O'Keefe said firmly. 'It isn't necessary to give me all the details. I rely on you gentlemen to take care of those eventually. What I want at these sessions is the broad picture.' Despite the comparative gentleness of the rebuke, Hall flushed and, from across the room, Dodo shot him a sympathetic glance.

'I take it,' O'Keefe said, 'that along with the weakness in management there is a good deal of staff larceny which is siphoning off revenue.'

The younger accountant nodded emphatically. 'A great deal, sir, particularly in food and beverages.' He was about to describe his undercover studies in the various bars and lounges of the hotel, but checked himself. That could be taken care of later, after completion of the purchase and when the 'wrecking crew' moved in.

In his own brief experience Sean Hall knew that the procedure for acquiring a new link in the O'Keefe hotel chain invariably followed the same general pattern. First, weeks ahead of any negotiations, a 'spy team' – usually headed by Ogden Bailey – would move into the hotel, its members registering as normal guests. By astute and systematic observations, supplemented by occasional bribery, the team would compile a financial and operating study, probing weaknesses and estimating potential, untapped strengths. Where appropriate – as in the present case – discreet enquiries would be made outside the hotel, among the city's business community. The magic of the O'Keefe name, plus the possibility of future dealings with the nation's largest hotel chain, was usually sufficient to elicit any information sought. In financial circles, Sean Hall had long ago learned, loyalty ran a poor second to practical self-interest.

Next, armed with this accumulated knowledge, Curtis O'Keefe would direct negotiations which, more often than not, were successful. Then the wrecking crew moved in.

The wrecking crew, headed by an O'Keefe Hotels vice-president, was a tough-minded and swift-working group of management experts. It could, and did, convert any hotel to the standard O'Keefe pattern within a remarkably short time. The early changes which the wrecking crew made usually affected personnel and administration; more wholesale measures, involving reconstruction and physical plant, came later. Above all, the crew worked smilingly, with reassurance to all concerned that there were to be no drastic innovations, even as it made them. As one team member expressed it: 'When we go in, the first thing we announce is that no staff changes are contemplated. Then we get on with the firings.'

Sean Hall supposed the same thing would happen soon in the St Gregory Hotel.

Sometimes Hall, who was a thoughtful young man with a Quaker upbringing, wondered about his own part in all these affairs. Despite his newness as an O'Keefe executive, he had already watched several hotels, with pleasantly individual characters, engulfed by chain-management conformity. In a remote way the process saddened him. He had uneasy moments, too, about the ethics by which some ends were accomplished.

But always, weighed against such feelings were personal ambition and the fact that Curtis O'Keefe paid generously for services rendered. Sean Hall's monthly salary cheque and a growing bank account were cause for satisfaction, even in moments of disquiet.

There were also other possibilities which, even in extravagant day-dreaming, he allowed himself to consider only vaguely. Ever since entering this suite this morning he had been acutely aware of Dodo, though at the moment he avoided looking at her directly. Her blonde and blatant sexuality, seeming to pervade the room like an aura, did things to Sean Hall that, at home, his pretty brunette wife – a delight on the tennis courts, and recording secretary of the PTA – had never achieved. In considering the presumed good fortune of Curtis O'Keefe, it was a speculative, fanciful thought that in the great man's own early days, he too had been a young, ambitious accountant.

The musings were interrupted by a question from O'Keefe. 'Does your impression of poor management apply right down the line?'

'Not entirely, sir.' Sean Hall consulted his notes, concentrating on the subject which, in the past two weeks, had become familiar ground. 'There is one man – the assistant general manager, McDermott – who seems extremely competent. He's thirty-two, a Cornell-Statler graduate. Unfortunately there's a flaw in his record. The home office ran a check. I have their report here.'

O'Keefe perused the single sheet which the young accountant handed him. It contained the essential facts of Peter McDermott's dismissal from the Waldorf and his subsequent attempts – unsuccessful until the St Gregory – to find new employment.

The hotel magnate returned the sheet without comment. A decision about McDermott would be the business of the wrecking crew. Its members, however, would be familiar with Curtis O'Keefe's insistence that all O'Keefe's employees be of unblemished moral character. No matter how competent McDermott might be, it was unlikely that he would continue under a new régime.

'There are also a few other good people,' Sean Hall continued, 'in lesser posts.'

For fifteen minutes more the talk continued. At the end Curtis O'Keefe announced, 'Thank you, gentlemen. Call me if there's anything new that's important. Otherwise I'll be in touch with you.'

Dodo showed them out.

When she returned, Curtis O'Keefe was stretched full length on the settee which the two accountants had vacated. His eyes were closed. Since his early days in business he had cultivated the ability to catnap at odd moments during a day, renewing the energy which subordinates sometimes thought of as inexhaustible.

Dodo kissed him gently on the lips. He felt their moistness, and the fullness of her body touching his own lightly. Her long fingers sought the base of his skull, massaging gently at the hairline. A strand of soft silken hair fell caressingly beside his face. He looked up, smiling. 'I'm charging my batteries.' Then, contentedly, 'What you're doing helps.'

Her fingers moved on. At the end of ten minutes he was rested and refreshed. He stretched, opening his eyes once more, and swung upright. Then, standing, he held out his arms to Dodo.

She came to him with abandon, pressing closely, shaping her body eagerly to his own. Already, he sensed, her ever smouldering sensuality had become a fierce, demanding flame. With rising excitement, he led her to the adjoining bedroom.

The chief house officer, Ogilvie, who had declared he would appear at the Croydons' suite an hour after his cryptic telephone call, actually took twice that time. As a result the nerves of both the Duke and Duchess were excessively frayed when the muted buzzer of the outer door eventually sounded.

The Duchess went to the door herself. Earlier she had dispatched her maid on an invented errand and, cruelly, instructed the moonfaced male secretary – who was terrified of dogs – to exercise the Bedlington terriers. Her own tension was not lessened by the knowledge that both might return at any moment.

A wave of cigar smoke accompanied Ogilvie in. When he had followed her to the living room, the Duchess looked pointedly at the half-burned cigar in the fat man's mouth. 'My husband and I find strong smoke offensive. Would you kindly put that out.'

The house detective's piggy eyes surveyed her sardonically from his gross jowled face. His gaze moved on to sweep the spacious, well-appointed room, encompassing the Duke who faced them uncertainly, his back to a window.

'Pretty neat set-up you folks got.' Taking his time, Ogilvie removed the offending cigar, knocked off the ash and flipped the butt towards an ornamental fireplace on his right. He missed, and the butt fell upon the carpet where he ignored it.

The Duchess's lips tightened. She said sharply, 'I imagine you did not come here to discuss décor.'

The obese body shook in an appreciative chuckle. 'No, ma'am; can't say I did. I like nice things, though.' He lowered the level of his incongruous falsetto voice. 'Like that car of yours. The one you keep here in the hotel. Jaguar, ain't it?'

'Aah!' It was a spoken word, but an emission of breath from the Duke of Croydon. His wife shot him a swift, warning glance.

'In what conceivable way does our car concern you?'

As if the question from the Duchess had been a signal, the house detective's manner changed. His enquired abruptly, 'Who else is in this place?'

It was the Duke who answered, 'No-one. We sent them out.'

'There's things it pays to check.' Moving with surprising speed, the fat man walked around the suite, opening doors and inspecting the space behind them. Obviously he knew the room arrangement well. After reopening and closing the outer door, he returned apparently satisfied, to the living-room.

The Duchess had seated herself in a straight-backed chair. Ogilvie remained standing. 'Now then,' he said. 'You two was in that hit-'n-run.'

She met his eyes directly. 'What are you talking about?'

'Don't play games, lady. This is for real.' He took out a fresh cigar and bit off the end. 'You saw the papers. There's been plenty on radio, too.'

Two high points of colour appeared in the paleness of the Duchess of Croydon's cheeks. 'What you are suggesting is the most disgusting, ridiculous . . .'

'I told you – cut it out!' The words spat forth with sudden savagery, all pretence of blandness gone. Ignoring the Duke, Ogilvie waved the unlighted cigar under his adversary's nose. 'You listen to me, your high-an'-mightiness. This city's burnin' mad – cops, mayor, everybody else. They find who done that last night, who killed that kid an' its mother, then hightailed it, they'll throw the book, and never mind who it hits, or whether they got fancy titles neither. Now I know what I know, and if I do what by rights I should, there'll be a squad of cops in here so fast you'll hardly see 'em. But I come to you first, in fairness, so's you could tell your side of it to me.' The piggy eyes blinked, then hardened. ''F you want it the other way, just say so.'

The Duchess of Croydon – three centuries and a half of inbred arrogance behind her – did not yield easily. Springing to her feet, her face wrathful, grey-green eyes blazing, she faced the grossness of the house detective squarely. Her tone would have withered anyone who knew her well. 'You unspeakable blackguard! How dare you!'

Even the self-assurance of Ogilvie flickered for an instant. But it was the Duke of Croydon who interjected, 'It's no go, old girl, I'm afraid. It was a good try.' Facing Ogilvie, he said, 'What you accuse us of is true. I am to blame. I was driving the car and killed the little girl.'

'That's more like it,' Ogilvie said. He lit the fresh cigar. 'Now we're getting somewhere.'

Wearily, in a gesture of surrender, the Duchess of Croydon sank back into her chair. Clasping her hands to conceal their trembling, she asked, 'What is it you know?'

'Well now, I'll spell it out.' The house detective took his time, leisurely puffing a cloud of blue-cigar smoke, his eyes sardonically on the Duchess as if challenging her objection. But beyond wrinkling her nose in distaste, she made no comment.

Ogilvie pointed to the Duke. 'Last night, early on, you went to Lindy's Place in Irish Bayou. You drove there in your fancy Jaguar, and you took a lady friend. Leastways, I guess you'd call her that if you're not too fussy.'

As Ogilvie glanced, grinning at the Duchess, the Duke said sharply, 'Get on with it!'

'Well' – the smug fat face swung back – 'the way I hear it, you won a hundred at the tables, then lost it at the bar. You were into a second hundred – with a real swinging party – when your wife here got there in a taxi.'

'How do you know all this?'

'I'll tell you, Duke – I've been in this town and this hotel a long time. I got friends all over. I oblige them; they do the same for me, like letting me know what gives, an' where. There ain't much, out of the way, which people who stay in this hotel do, I don't get to hear about. Most of 'em never know I know, or know me. They think they got their little

371

secrets tucked away, and so they have – except like now.'

The Duke said coldly, 'I see.'

'One thing I'd like to know. I got a curious nature, ma'am. How'd you figure where he was?'

The Duchess said, 'You know so much . . . I suppose it doesn't matter. My husband has a habit of making notes while he is telephoning. Afterwards he often forgets to destroy them.'

The house detective clucked his tongue reprovingly. 'A little careless habit like that, Duke – look at the mess it gets you in. Well, here's what I figure about the rest. You an' your wife took off home, you drivin', though the way things turned out it might have been better if she'd have drove.'

'My wife doesn't drive.'

Ogilvie nodded understandingly. 'Explains that one. Anyway, I reckon you were lickered up, but good . . .'

The Duchess interrupted. 'Then you don't *know*! You don't know anything for sure! You can't possibly prove . . .'

'Lady, I can prove all I need to.'

The Duke cautioned, 'Better let him finish, old girl.'

'That's right,' Ogilvie said. 'Just set an' listen. Last night I seen you come in – through the basement, so's not to use the lobby. Looked right shaken, too, the pair of you. Just come in myself, an' I got to wondering why. Like I said, I got a curious nature.'

The Duchess breathed. 'Go on.'

'Late last night the word was out about the hit-'n-run. On a hunch I went over the garage and took a quiet look-see at your car. You maybe don't know – it's away in a corner, behind a pillar where the jockeys don't see it when they're comin' by!'

The Duke licked his lips. 'I suppose that doesn't matter now.'

'You might have something there,' Ogilvie conceded. 'Anyway, what I found made me do some scouting – across at police headquarters where they know me too.' He paused to puff again at the cigar as his listeners waited silently. When the cigar tip was glowing he inspected it, then continued. 'Over there they got three things to go on. They got a headlight trim ring which musta come off when the kid an' the woman was hit. They got some headlight glass, and lookin' at the kid's clothin', they reckon there'll be a brush trace.'

'A what?'

'You rub clothes against something hard, Duchess, specially if it's shiny like a car fender, say, an' it leaves a mark the same way as fingerprints. The police lab kin pick it up like they do prints – dust it, an' it shows.'

'That's interesting,' the Duke said, as if speaking of something unconnected with himself. 'I didn't know that.'

'Not many do. In this case, though, I reckon it don't make a lot o' difference. On your car you got a busted headlight, and the trim ring's gone. Ain't any doubt they'd match up, even without the brush trace *an'* the blood. Oh yeah, I shoulda told you. There's plenty of blood, though it don't show too much on the black paint.'

'Oh, my God!' A hand to her face, the Duchess turned away.

Her husband asked, 'What do you propose to do?'

The fat man rubbed his hands together, looking down at his thick, fleshy fingers. 'Like

I said, I come to hear your side of it.'

The Duke said despairingly, 'What can I possibly say? You know what happened.' He made an attempt to square his shoulders which did not succeed. 'You'd better call the police and get it over.'

'Well now, there's no call for being hasty.' The incongruous falsetto voice took on a musing note. 'What's done's been done. Rushin' any place ain't gonna bring back the kid nor its mother neither. Besides, what they'd do to you across at headquarters, Duke, you wouldn't like. No sir, you wouldn't like it at all.'

The other two slowly raised their eyes.

'I was hoping,' Ogilvie said, 'that you folks could suggest something.'

The Duke said uncertainly, 'I don't understand.'

'I understand,' the Duchess of Croydon said. 'You want money, don't you? You came here to blackmail us.'

If she expected her words to shock, they did not succeed. The house detective shrugged. 'Whatever names you call things, ma'am, don't matter to me. All I come for was to help you people outa trouble. But I got to live too.'

'You'd accept money to keep silent about what you know?'

'I reckon I might.'

'But from what you say,' the Duchess pointed out, her poise for the moment recovered, 'it would no good. The car would be discovered in any case.'

'I guess you'd have to take that chance. But there's some reasons it might not be. Something I ain't told you yet.'

'Tell us now, please.'

Ogilvie said, 'I ain't figured this out myself completely. But when you hit that kid you was going away from town, not to it.'

'We'd made a mistake in the route,' the Duchess said. 'Somehow we'd become turned around. It's easily done in New Orleans, with the streets winding as they do. Afterwards, using side streets, we went back.'

'I thought it might be that.' Ogilvie nodded understandingly. 'But the police ain't figured it that way. They're looking for somebody who was headed out. That's why, right now, they're working' on the suburbs and the outside towns. They may get around to searchin' downtown, but it won't be yet.'

'How long before they do?'

'Maybe three, four days. They got a lot of other places to look first.'

'How could that help us – the delay?'

'It might,' Ogilvie said. 'Providin' nobody twigs the car – an' seeing where it is, you might be lucky there. *An'* if you can get it away.'

'You mean out of the state?'

'I mean out o' the South.'

'That wouldn't be easy?'

'No, ma'am. Every state around – Texas, Arkansas, Mississippi, Alabama, all the rest'll be watching for a car damaged the way yours is.'

The Duchess considered. 'Is there any possibility of having repairs made first? If the work were done discreetly we could pay well.'

The house detective shook his head emphatically. 'You try that, you might as well walk over to headquarters right now an' give up. Every repair shop in Louisiana's been told to

373

holler "cops" the minute a car needing fixin' like yours comes in. They'd do it, too. You people are hot.'

The Duchess of Croydon kept a firm, tight rein on her racing mind. It was essential, she knew, that her thinking remain calm and reasoned. In the last few minutes the conversation had become as seemingly casual as if the discussion were of some minor domestic matter and not survival itself. She intended to keep it that way. Once more, she was aware, the role of leadership had fallen to her, her husband now a tense but passive spectator of the exchange between the evil fat man and herself. No matter. What was inevitable must be accepted. The important thing was to consider all eventualities. A thought occurred to her.

'The piece from our car which you say the police have. What is it called?'

'A trim ring.'

'Is it traceable?'

Ogilvie nodded affirmatively. 'They can figure what kind o'car it's from – make, model an' maybe the year, or close to it. Same thing with the glass. But with your car being foreign, it'll likely take a few days.'

'But after that,' she persisted, 'The police will know they're looking for a Jaguar?'

'I reckon that's so.'

Today was Tuesday. From all that this man said, they had until Friday or Saturday at best. With calculated coolness the Duchess reasoned: the situation came down to one essential. Assuming the hotel man was bought off, their only chance – a slim one – lay in removing the car quickly. If it could be got north, to one of the big cities where the New Orleans tragedy and search would be unknown, repairs could be made quietly, the incriminating evidence removed. Then even if suspicions settled on the Croydons later, nothing could be proved. But how to get the car away?

Undoubtedly what this oafish detective said was true: As well as Louisiana, the other states through which the car would have to pass would be alert and watchful. Every highway patrol would be on the look-out for a damaged headlight with a missing trim ring. There would probably be roadblocks. It would be hard not to fall victim to some sharp-eyed policeman.

But it *might* be done. If the car could be driven at night and concealed by day. There were plenty of places to pull off the highway and be unobserved. It would be hazardous, but no more than waiting here for certain detection. There would be back roads. They could choose an unlikely route to avoid detection.

But there would be other complications . . . and now was the time to consider them. Travelling by secondary roads would be difficult unless knowing the terrain. The Croydons did not. Nor was either of them adept at using maps. And when they stopped for petrol, as they would have to, their speech and manner would betray them, making them conspicuous. And yet – these were risks which had to be taken.

Or had they?

The Duchess faced Ogilvie? 'How much do you want?'

The abruptness took him by surprise. 'Well . . . I figure you people are pretty well fixed.'

She said coldly, 'I asked how much.'

The piggy eyes blinked. 'Ten thousand dollars.'

Though it was twice what she had expected, her expression did not change. 'Assuming we paid this grotesque amount, what would we receive in return?'

The fat man seemed puzzled. 'Like I said, I keep quiet about what I know.'

'And the alternative?'

He shrugged. 'I go down the lobby. I pick up a phone.'

'No.' The statement was unequivocal. 'We will not pay you.'

As the Duke of Croydon shifted uneasily, the house detective's bulbous, countenance reddened. 'Now listen, lady . . .'

Peremptorily she cut him off. 'I will *not* listen. Instead, you will listen to me.' Her eyes were riveted on his face, her handsome, high cheek-boned features set in their most imperious mould. 'We would achieve nothing by paying you, except possibly a few days' respite. You have made that abundantly clear.'

'That's a chance you gotta . . .'

'Silence!' Her voice was a whiplash. Eyes bored into him. Swallowing, sullenly he complied.

What came next, the Duchess of Croydon knew, could be the most significant thing she had ever done. There must be no mistake, no vacillation of dallying because of her own smallness of mind. When you were playing for the highest stakes, you made the highest bid. She intended to gamble on the fat man's greed. She must do so in such a way as to place the outcome beyond any doubt.

She declared decisively, 'We will not pay you ten thousand dollars. But we will pay you twenty-five thousand dollars.'

The house detective's eyes bulged.

'In return for that,' she continued evenly, '*you* will drive our car north.'

Ogilvie continued to stare.

'Twenty-five thousand dollars,' she repeated. 'Ten thousand now. Fifteen thousand more when you meet us in Chicago.'

Still without speaking, the fat man licked his lips. His beady eyes, as if unbelieving, were focused upon her own. The silence hung.

Then, as she watched intently, he gave the slightest of nods.

The silence remained. At length Ogilvie spoke. 'This cigar botherin' you, Duchess?'

As she nodded, he put it out.

12

'It's a funny thing.' Christine put down the immense multicoloured menu. 'I've had a feeling this week that something momentous is going to happen.'

Peter McDermott smiled across their candle-lit table, its silver and starched white napery gleaming. 'Maybe it has already.'

'No,' Christine said. 'At least, not in the way you mean. It's an uneasy kind of thing. I wish I could throw it off.'

'Food and drink do wonders.'

She laughed, responding to his mood, and closed the menu. 'You order for both of us.'

They were in Brennan's Restaurant in the French Quarter. An hour earlier, driving a car he rented from the Hertz desk in the St Gregory lobby, Peter had collected Christine from her apartment. They parked the car at Iberville, just inside the Quarter, and strolled the length of Royal Street, browsing at windows of the antique shops, with their strange mixture of objets d'art, imported bric-à-brac and Confederate weaponry – *Any sword in this box, ten dollars.* It was a warm, sultry night, with the sounds of New Orleans surrounding them – a deep growl from buses in narrow streets, the clop and jingle of a horse-drawn fiacre, and from the Mississippi the melancholy wail of an outbound freighter.

Brennan's – as befitting the city's finest restaurant – had been crowded with diners. While waiting for their table, Peter and Christine sipped a leisurely Old Fashioned, herbsaint flavoured, in the quiet, softly lighted patio.

Peter had a sense of wellbeing and a delight in Christine's company. It continued as they were ushered to a table in the cool, main floor dining-room. Now, accepting Christine's suggestion, he beckoned their waiter.

He ordered for them both: 2-2-2 huîtres – the house's speciality combining Oysters Rockefeller, Bienville and Roffignac – flounder Nouvelle Orleans, stuffed with seasoned crabmeat, chou-fleur Polonaise, pommes au four, and – from the hovering wine steward – a bottle of Montrachet.

'It's nice,' Christine said appreciatively, 'not to have to make decisions.' She would be firm, she decided, in throwing off the sense of unease she had mentioned a moment ago. It was, after all, no more than intuition, perhaps simply explained by the fact that she had had less sleep than usual the previous night.

'With a well-run kitchen, as they have here,' Peter said, 'decisions about food ought not to matter much. It's a question of choice between equal qualities.'

She chided him: 'Your hotelship's showing.'

'Sorry. I guess it does too often.'

'Not really. And if you must know, I like it. I've sometimes wondered, though, what got you started to begin with.'

'In the hotel business? I was a bellhop who became ambitious.'

'It wasn't really that simple?'

'Probably not. I had some luck along with other things. I lived in Brooklyn and in summers, between school, got a job as a bellboy in Manhattan. One night, the second summer, I put a drunk to bed – helped him upstairs, got him in pyjamas and tucked him in.'

'Did everyone get that kind of service?'

'No. It happened to be a quiet night and, besides, I'd had a lot of practice. I'd been doing the same thing at home – for my old man – for years.' For an instant a flicker of sadness touched Peter's eyes, then he continued, 'Anyway, it turned out that the one I'd put to bed was a writer for *The New Yorker*. A week or two after, he wrote about what happened. I think he called us "the hotel that's gentler than mother's milk". We took a lot of kidding, but it made the hotel look good.'

'And you were promoted?'

'In a way. But mostly I got noticed.'

'Here come the oysters,' Christine said. Two aromatic, heated plates, with the baked shells in their underlayer of rock salt, were placed dextrously in front of them.

As Peter tasted and approved the Montrachet, Christine said, 'Why is it that in Louisiana you can eat oysters all year round – "r" in the month or not?'

He answered emphatically, 'You can eat oysters anywhere, at any time. The "r"-in-the-month idea is an old canard started four hundred years ago by an English country vicar. Name of Butler, I think. Scientists have ridiculed it, the US Government says the rule is silly, but people still believe.'

Christine nibbled an Oyster Bienville. 'I always thought it was because they spawned in summer.'

'So oysters do – some seasons – in New England and New York. But not in Chesapeake Bay, which is the largest oyster source in the world. There and in the South spawning can happen at any time of year. So there isn't a single reason why northeners can't eat oysters around the calendar, just as in Louisiana.'

There was a silence, then Christine said. 'When you learn something, do you always remember it?'

'Mostly, I guess. I've a queer sort of mind that things stick to – a bit like an old-fashioned flypaper. In a way it's been lucky for me.' He speared an Oyster Rockefeller, savouring its subtle absinthe flavouring.

'How lucky?'

'Well, that same summer – the one we were talking about – they let me try other jobs in the hotel, including helping out at the bar. I was getting interested by then and had borrowed some books. One was about mixing drinks.' Peter paused, his mind leafing over events he had half-forgotten. 'I happened to be at the bar alone when a customer came in. I didn't know who he was, but he said, "I hear you're the bright boy *The Yorker* wrote about. Can you mix me a Rusty Nail?" '

'He was kidding?'

'No. But I'd have thought so if I hadn't read the ingredients – Drambuie and Scotch – a couple of hours earlier. That's what I mean by luck. Anyway, I mixed it and afterwards he said. "That's good, but you won't learn the hotel business this way. Things have changed since *Work of Art*." I told him I didn't fancy myself as Myron Weagle, but wouldn't mind being Evelyn Orcham. He laughed at that; I guess he'd read Arnold Bennett too. Then he gave me his card and told me to see him next day.'

'He owned fifty hotels, I suppose.'

'As it turned out, he didn't own anything. His name was Herb Fischer and he was a salesman – bulk canned goods, that kind of stuff. He was also pushy and a braggart, and all the time had a way of talking you down. But he knew the hotel business, and most people in it, because it was there he did his selling.'

The oyster plates were removed. Now their waiter, back-stopped by a red-coated captain, placed the steaming flounder before them.

'I'm afraid to eat,' Christine said. 'Nothing can possibly taste as heavenly as that.' She sampled the succulent, superbly seasoned fish. 'Um! Incredibly, it's even better.'

It was several minutes before she said, 'Tell me about Mr Fischer.'

'Well, at first I thought he was just a big talker – you get a million of 'em in bars. What changed my mind was a letter from Cornell. It told me to report at Statler Hall – the School of Hotel Admin – for a selection interview. The way things turned out, they offered me a scholarship and I went there from high school. Afterwards I discovered it happened because Herb badgered some hotel people into recommending me. I guess he was a good salesman.'

'You only guess!'

Peter said thoughtfully. 'I've never been quite sure. I owe a lot to Herb Fischer, but sometimes I wonder if people didn't do things, including giving him business, just to get rid of him. After it was fixed about Cornell I only saw him once again. I tried to thank him – the same way I tried to like him. But he wouldn't let me do either; just kept boasting, talking about deals he'd made, or would. Then he said I needed some clothes for college – he was right – and insisted on lending me two hundred dollars. It must have meant a lot, because I found out afterwards his commissions weren't big. I paid him back by sending cheques for small amounts. Most were never cashed.'

'I think it's a wonderful story.' Christine had listened raptly. 'Why don't you see him any more?'

'He died,' Peter said. 'I'd tried to reach him several times, but we never seemed to make it. Then about a year ago I got a phone call from a lawyer – Herb didn't have any family, apparently. I went to the funeral. And I found there were eight of us there – whom he'd all helped in the same kind of way. The funny thing was, with all his boasting he'd never told any of us about the others.'

'I could cry,' Christine said.

He nodded. 'I know. I felt I wanted to then. I suppose it should have taught me something, though I've never been quite sure what. Maybe it's that some people raise a great big barrier, all the while wishing you'd tear it down, and if you don't you never really know them.'

Christine was quiet through coffee – by agreement they had both ruled out dessert. At length she asked, 'Do any of us really know what we want for ourselves?'

Peter considered. 'Not entirely, I suppose. Though I know one thing I want to achieve – or at least something like it.' He beckoned a waiter for their bill.

'Tell me.'

'I'll do better than that,' he said. 'I'll show you.'

Outside Brennan's they paused, adjusting from interior coolness to the warm night air. The city seemed quieter than an hour earlier. A few lights around were darkening, the Quarter's night life moving on to other cantons. Taking Christine's arm, Peter piloted her diagonally across Royal Street. They stopped at the south-west corner of St Louis, looking directly ahead. 'That's what I'd like to create,' he said. 'Something at least as good, or maybe better.'

Beneath graceful grilled balconies and fluted iron columns, flickering gas lanterns cast light and shadow on the white-grey classical façade of the Royal Orleans Hotel. Through arched and mullioned windows amber light streamed outwards. On the promenade sidewalk a doorman paced, in rich gold uniform and visored pillbox cap. High above, in a sudden breeze, flags and halliards snapped upon their staffs. A taxi drew up. The doorman moved swiftly to open its door. Women's heels clicked and men's laughter echoed as they moved inside. A door slammed. The taxi pulled away.

'There are some people,' Peter said, 'who believe the Royal Orleans is the finest hotel in North America. Whether you agree or not doesn't much matter. The point is: it shows how good a hotel can be.'

They crossed St Louis, towards the site which had once been traditional hotel, a centre of Creole society; then slave mart, Civil War hospital, state capitol, and now hotel again. Peter's voice took on enthusiasm. 'They've everything going for them – history, style, a modern plant and imagination. For the new building there were two firms of New Orleans architects – one tradition steeped, the other modern. They proved you can build freshly yet retain old character.'

The doorman, who had ceased pacing, held the main door open as they strolled inside. Directly ahead two giant blackamoor statues guarded white marble stairs to the lobby promenade. 'The funny thing is,' Peter said, 'that with all that's individual, the Royal Orleans is a chain hotel.' He added tersely, 'But not Curtis O'Keefe's kind.'

'More like Peter McDermott's?'

'There's a long way to go for that. And I took a step backwards. I guess you know.'

'Yes,' Christine said. 'I know. But you'll still do it. I'd bet a thousand dollars that some day you will.'

He squeezed her arm. 'If you've that kind of money, better buy some O'Keefe Hotels stock.'

They strolled the length of the Royal Orleans lobby – white marbled with antique white, citron and persimmon tapestries – leaving by the Royal Street doors.

For an hour and a half they sauntered through the Quarter, stopping at Preservation Hall to endure its stifling heat and crowded benches for the joy of Dixieland jazz at its purest; enjoying the comparative coolness of Jackson Square, with coffee at the French market on the river side, inspecting critically some of the bad art with which New Orleans abounded; and later, at the Court of The Two Sisters, sipping cool mint juleps under stars, subdued lights and lacy trees.

'It's been wonderful,' Christine said. 'Now I'm ready to go home.'

Strolling towards Iberville and the parked car, a small Negro boy, with cardboard box and brushes, accosted them.

'Shoe shine, mister?'

Peter shook his head, 'Too late, son.'

The boy, bright eyed, stood squarely in their path, surveying Peter's feet. 'Ah bet yo' twenty-five cents ah kin tell you where yo' got those shoes. Ah kin tell you th' city and th' state; and if ah kin – you give me twenty-five cents. But if ah cain't, ah'll give yo' twenty five cents.'

A year ago Peter had bought the shoes in Tenafly, New Jersey. He hesitated, with a feeling of taking advantage, then nodded. 'OK.'

The boy's bright eyes flicked upwards. 'Mister, yo' got those shoes on yo' feet on the concrete side walk of New Orleans, in th' State o' Louisiana. Now remember – ah said ah'd tell yo' where yo' got those shoes, not where yo' bought them.'

They laughed, and Christine slipped her arm through Peter's as he paid the quarter. They were still laughing during the drive northwards to Christine's apartment.

13

In the dining-room of Warren Trent's private suite, Curtis O'Keefe puffed appraisingly at a cigar. He had selected it from a cherry-wood humidor proffered him by Aloysius Royce, and its richness mingled agreeably on his palate with the Louis XIII cognac which had accompanied coffee. To O'Keefe's left, at the head of the oak refectory table at which Royce had deftly served their superb five-course dinner, Warren Trent presided with patriarchal benevolence. Directly across, Dodo, in a clinging black gown, inhaled agreeably on a Turkish cigarette which Royce had also produced and lighted.

'Gee,' Dodo said, 'I feel like I ate a whole pig.'

O'Keefe smiled indulgently. 'A fine meal, Warren. Please compliment your chef.'

The St Gregory's proprietor inclined his head graciously. 'He'll be gratified at the source of the compliment. By the way, you may like to know that precisely the same meal was available tonight in my main dining-room.'

O'Keefe nodded, though unimpressed. In his opinion a large elaborate menu was as out of place in a hotel dining-rom as *paté de foie gras* in a lunch pail. Even more to the point – earlier in the evening he had glanced into the St Gregory's main restaurant at what should have been its peak service hour, to find the cavernous expanse barely a third occupied.

In the O'Keefe empire, dining was standard and simplified, with the choice of fare limited to a few popular, pedestrian items. Behind this policy was Curtis O'Keefe's conviction – buttressed by experience – that public taste and preferences about eating were equal, and largely unimaginative. In any O'Keefe establishment, though food was precisely prepared and served with antiseptic cleanliness there was seldom provision for gourmets, who were regarded as an unprofitable minority.

The hotel magnate observed, 'There aren't many hotels nowadays offering that kind of cuisine. Most that did have had to change their ways.'

'Most but not all. Why should everyone be as docile?'

'Because our entire business has changed, Warren, since you and I were young in it – whether we like the fact or not. The days of "mine host" and personal service are over. Maybe people cared once about such things. They don't any more.'

There was a directness in both men's voices, implying that with the meal's ending the time for mere politeness had gone. As each spoke, Dodo's baby blue eyes shifted curiously between them as if following some stage action, though barely understood, upon a stage. Aloysius Royce, his back turned, was busy at a sideboard.

Warren Trent said sharply, 'There are some who'd disagree.'

O'Keefe regarded his glowing cigar tip. 'For any who do, the answer's in my balance sheets compared with others. For example, yours.'

The other flushed, his lips tightening. 'What's happening here is temporary; a phase. I've seen them before. This one will pass, the same as others.'

'No. If you think that, you're fashioning a hangman's noose. And you deserve better, Warren – after all these years.'

There was an obstinate pause before the growling reply. 'I haven't spent my life building an institution to see it become a cheap-run joint.'

'If you're referring to my houses, none of them are that.' It was O'Keefe's turn to redden angrily. 'Nor am I so sure about this one being an institution.'

In the cold, ensuing silence, Dodo asked, 'Will it be a real fight or just a words one?'

Both men laughed, though Warren Trent less heartily. It was Curtis O'Keefe who raised his hands placatingly.

'She's right, Warren. It's pointless for us to quarrel. If we're to continue our separate ways, at least we should remain friends.'

More tractably, Warren Trent nodded. In part, his acerbity of a moment earlier had been prompted by a twinge of sciatica which for the time being had passed. Though even allowing for this, he thought bitterly, it was hard not to be resentful of this smooth successful man whose financial conquests so greatly contrasted with his own.

'You can sum up in three words,' Curtis O'Keefe declared, 'what the public expects nowadays from a hotel: an "efficient, economic package". But we can only provide it if we have effective cost accounting of every move – our guests' and our own; an efficient plant; and above all a minimum wage bill, which means automation, eliminating people and old-style hospitality wherever possible.'

'And that's all? You'd discount everything else that used to make a fine hotel? You'd deny that a good innkeeper can stamp his personal imprint on any house?' The St Gregory's proprietor snorted. 'A visitor to your kind of hotel doesn't have a sense of belonging, of being someone significant to whom a little more is given – in feeling and hospitality – than is charged for on his bill.'

'It's a delusion he doesn't need,' O'Keefe said incisively. 'If a hotel's hospitable it's because it's paid to be, so in the end it doesn't count. People see through falseness in a way they didn't used to. But they respect fairness – a fair profit for the hotel; a fair price to the guest, which is what my houses give. Oh, I grant you there'll always be a few Tuscanys for those who want special treatment and are willing to pay. But they're small places and for the few. The big houses like yours – if they want to survive my kind of competition – have to think as I do.'

Warren Trent growled, 'You'll not object if I continue to think for myself for a while.'

O'Keefe shook his head impatiently. 'There was nothing personal. I was speaking of trends, not particulars.'

'The devil with trends! I've an instinct tells me plenty of people still like to travel first class. They're the ones who expect something more than boxes with beds.'

'You're misquoting me, but I won't complain.' Curtis O'Keefe smiled coolly. 'I'll challenge your simile, though. Except for the very few, first class is finished, dead.'

'Why?'

'Because jet aeroplanes killed first-class travel, and an entire state of mind along with it. Before then, first class had an aura of distinction. But jet travel showed everyone how silly and wasteful the old ways were. Air journeys became swift and short, to the point where first class simply wasn't worth it. So people squeezed into their tourist seats and stopped worrying about status – the price was too high. Pretty soon there was a reverse kind of status in travelling tourist. The best people did it. First class, they told each other over their box lunches, was for fools and profligates. And what people realize they get from jets – the efficient, economic package – they require from the hotel business too.'

Unsuccessfully Dodo attempted to conceal a yawn behind her hand, then butted her Turkish cigarette. Instantly Aloysius Royce was beside her, proffering a fresh one and deftly lighting it. She smiled warmly, and the young Negro returned the smile, managing to convey a discreet but friendly sympathy. Unobtrusively he replaced used ash trays on the table with fresh, and refilled Dodo's coffee cup, then the others. As Royce slipped out quietly, O'Keefe observed, 'A good man you have there, Warren.'

Warren Trent responded absently, 'He's been with me a long time.' Watching Royce himself, he had been wondering how Aloysius's father might have reacted to the news that control of the hotel might soon pass on to other hands. Probably with a shrug. Possessions and money had meant little to the old man. Warren Trent could almost hear him now, asserting in his cracked, sprightly voice, 'Yo' had yo' own way so long, could be a passel o' bad times'll be fo' yo' own goodness. God bends our backs an' humbles us, remindin' us we ain't nothin' but His wayward children, 'spite our fancy notions other ways.' But then, with calculated contrariness the old man might have added, 'All th' same, 'f yo' b'lieve in somethin', yo' fight fo' it shore. After yo' dead yo' won't shoot nobody, cos yo' cain't hardly take aim.'

Taking aim – he suspected, waveringly – Warren Trent insisted, 'Your way, you make everything to do with a hotel sound so damnably antiseptic. Your kind of hotel lacks warmth or humanity. It's for automatons, with punch-card minds, and lubricant instead of blood.'

O'Keefe shrugged. 'It's the kind that pays dividends.'

'Financial maybe, not human.'

Ignoring the last remark, O'Keefe said, 'I've talked about our business the way it is now. Let's carry things a shade further. In my organization I've had a blueprint developed for the future. Some might call it a vision, I suppose, though it's more an informed projection of what hotels – certainly O'Keefe hotels – are going to be like a few years ahead.

'The first thing we'll have simplified is Reception, where checking in will take a few seconds at the most. The majority of our people will arrive directly from air terminals by helicopter, so a main reception point will be a private roof heliport. Secondly there'll be lower-floor receiving points where cars and limousines can drive directly in, eliminating transfer to a lobby, the way we do it now. At all these places there'll be a kind of instant sorting office, mater-minded by an IBM brain that, incidentally, is ready now.

'Guests with reservations will have been sent a key-coded card. They'll insert it in a frame and immediately be on their way by individual escalator section to a room which may have been cleared for use only seconds earlier. If a room isn't ready – and it'll happen,' Curtis O'Keefe conceded, 'just as it does now – we'll have small portable way stations. These will be cubicles with a couple of chairs, wash basin and space for baggage, just enough to freshen up after a journey and give some privacy right away. People can come and go, as they do with a regular room, and my engineers are working on a scheme for making the way stations mobile so that later they can latch on directly to the allocated space. That way, the guest will merely open an IBM cleared door, and walk on through.

'For those driving their own cars there'll be parallel arrangements, with coded, moving lights to guide them into personal parking stalls, from where other individual escalators will take them directly to their rooms. In all cases we'll curtail baggage handling, using high-speed sorters and conveyors, and baggage will be routed into rooms, actually arriving ahead of the guests.

'Similarly, all other services will have automated room delivery systems – valet, beverages, food, florist, drugstore, newsstand; even the final bill can be received and paid by room conveyor. And incidentally, apart from other benefits, I'll have broken the tipping system, a tyranny we've suffered – along with our guests – for years too long.'

There was a silence in the panelled dining-room as the hotel magnate, still commanding the stage, sipped coffee before resuming.

'My building design and automation will keep to a minimum the need for any guest room to be entered by a hotel employee. Beds, recessing into walls, are to be serviced by machine from outside. Air filtration is already improved to the point where dust and dirt have ceased to be problems. Rugs, for example, can be laid on floors of fine steel mesh, with air space beneath, suctioned once a day when a timed relay cuts in.

'All this, and more, can be accomplished now. Our remaining problems, which naturally will be solved' – Curtis O'Keefe waved a hand in his familiar dismissing gesture

– 'our remaining problems are principally of co-ordination, construction and investment.'

'I hope,' Warren Trent said firmly, 'that I never live to see it happen in my house.'

'You won't,' O'Keefe informed him. 'Before it can happen we'll have to tear down your house and build again.'

'You'd do that!' It was a shocked rejoinder.

O'Keefe shrugged. 'I can't reveal long-range plans, naturally. But I'd say that would be our policy before too long. If you're concerned about your name surviving, I could promise you that a tablet, commemorating the original hotel and possibly your own connection with it, would be incorporated in the new structure.'

'A tablet!' The St Gregory's proprietor snorted. 'Where would you put it – in the men's washroom?'

Abruptly Dodo giggled. As the two men turned their heads involuntarily, she remarked, 'Maybe they won't have one. I mean, all those conveyor things, who needs it?'

Curtis O'Keefe glanced at her sharply. There were moments occasionally when he wondered if Dodo were perhaps a little brighter than generally she allowed herself to seem.

At Dodo's reaction Warren Trent had flushed with embarrassment. Now he assured her in his most courteous manner, 'I apologize, my dear lady, for an unfortunate choice of words.'

'Gee, don't mind me.' Dodo seemed surprised. 'Anyway, I think this is a swell hotel.' She turned her wide and seemingly innocent eyes towards O'Keefe. 'Curtie, why'll you have to pull it down?'

He answered testily, 'I was merely reviewing a possibility. In any event, Warren, it's time you were out of the hotel business.'

Surprisingly, the response was mild compared with the asperity of a few minutes earlier. 'Even if I was willing to be, there are others to consider beside myself. A good many of my old employees rely on me in the same way I've relied on them. You tell me your plan is to replace people with automation. I couldn't walk out realizing that. I owe my staff that much, at least, in return for the loyalty they've given me.'

'Do you? Is any hotel staff loyal? Wouldn't all or most of them sell you out this instant if it meant an advantage to themselves?'

'I assure you no. I've run this house for more than thirty years and in that time loyalty builds. Or possibly you've had less experience in that direction.'

'I've formed some opinions about loyalty.' O'Keefe spoke absently. Mentally he was leafing through the report of Ogden Bailey and the younger assistant Sean Hall which he had read earlier. It was Hall whom he had cautioned against reporting too many details, but one detail which might now prove useful had been included in the written summary. The hotelier concentrated. At length he said, 'You've an old employee, haven't you, who runs your Pontalba Bar?'

'Yes – Tom Earlshore. He's been working here almost as long as I have myself.' In a way, Warren Trent thought, Tom Earlshore epitomized the older St Gregory employees whom he could not abandon. He himself had hired Earlshore when they were both young men, and nowadays, though the elderly head barman was stooped, and slowing in his work, he was one of those in the hotel whom Warren Trent counted as a personal friend. As one would a friend, he had helped Tom Earlshore too. There had been the time when the Earlshores' baby daughter, born with a deformed hip, had been sent north to Mayo Clinic for successful corrective surgery through arrangements made by Warren Trent.

And afterwards he had quietly paid the bills, for which Tom Earlshore had long ago declared undying gratitude and devotion. The Earlshore girl was now a married woman with children of her own, but the bond between her father and the hotel operator still remained. 'If there's a man I'd trust with anything,' he told Curtis O'Keefe now, 'it's Tom.'

'You'd be a fool if you did,' O'Keefe said crisply. 'I've information that he's bleeding you white.'

In the shocked silence O'Keefe recited the facts. There were a multiplicity of ways in which a dishonest bartender could steal from his employer – by pouring short measure to obtain an extra drink or two from each bottle used; by failing to ring every sale into the cash register; by introducing his own privately purchased liquor into the bar, so that an inventory check would show no shortage, but the proceeds – with substantial profit – would be taken by the bartender himself. Tom Earlshore appeared to be using all three methods. As well, according to Sean Hall's informed observations over several weeks, Earlshore's two assistants were in collusion with him. 'A high percentage of your bar profit is being skimmed off,' O'Keefe declared, 'and from the look of things generally, I'd say it's been going on a long time.'

Throughout the recital Warren Trent had sat immobile, his face expressionless, though behind it his thoughts were deep and bitter. Despite his long standing trust of Tom Earlshore, and the friendship he had believed existed, he had not the least doubt that the information provided was true. He had learned too much of chain hotel espionage methods to believe otherwise, nor would Curtis O'Keefe have made the charge without assurance of his facts. Warren Trent had long assumed that O'Keefe undercover men had infiltrated the St Gregory in advance of their chief's arrival. But what he had not expected was this searing and personal humiliation. Now he said, 'You spoke of "other things generally". What did it mean?'

'Your supposedly loyal staff is riddled with corruption. There's scarcely a department in which you aren't being robbed and cheated. Naturally, I haven't all the details, but those I have you're welcome to. If you wish I'll have a report prepared.'

'Thank you.' The words were whispered and barely audible.

'You've too many fat people working for you. It was the first thing I noticed when I arrived. I've always found it a warning sign. Their bellies are full of hotel food, and here they've battened on you every other way.'

There was a stillness in the small, intimate dining-room, broken only by the subdued ticking of a Dutch canopy clock upon the wall. At last, slowly and with a trace of weariness, Warren Trent announced, 'What you have told me may make a difference to my own position.'

'I thought it might.' Curtis O'Keefe seemed about to rub his hands together, then restrained himself. 'In any case, now we've reached that point I'd like to have you consider a proposal.'

Warren Trent said drily, 'I imagined you'd get to it.'

'It's a fair proposition, particularly in the circumstances. Incidentally, I should tell you that I'm familiar with your current financial picture.'

'I'd have been surprised if you were not.'

'Let me summarize: Your personal holdings in this hotel amount to fifty-one percent of all shares, giving you control.'

'Correct.'

'You refinanced the hotel in '39 – a four-million dollar mortgage. Two million dollars of the loan is still outstanding and due in its entirety this coming Friday. If you fail to make repayment the mortgagees take over.'

'Correct again.'

'Four months ago you attempted to renew the mortgage. You were turned down. You offered the mortgagees better terms which were still rejected. Ever since you've been looking for other financing. You haven't found it. In the short time remaining there is no chance whatever that you will.'

Warren Trent growled, 'I can't accept that. Plenty of refinancings are arranged at short notice.'

'Not this kind. And not with operating deficits as large as yours.'

Apart from tightening of the lips, there was no rejoinder.

'My proposal,' Curtis O'Keefe said, 'is a purchase price for this hotel of four million dollars. Of this, two millions will be obtained by renewing your present mortgage, which I assure you I shall have no difficulty in arranging.'

Warren Trent nodded, sourly aware of the other's complacency.

'The balance will be a million dollars cash, enabling you to pay off your minority stockholders; and one million dollars in O'Keefe Hotels stock – a new issue to be arranged. Additionally, as a personal consideration you will have the privilege of retaining your apartment here for as long as you live, with my assurance that should rebuilding be undertaken we will make other and mutually satisfactory arrangements.'

Warren Trent sat motionless, his face neither revealing his thoughts nor his surprise. The terms were better than he had expected. If accepted, they would leave him personally with a million dollars, more or less – no small achievement with which to walk away from a lifetime's work. And yet it *would* mean walking away; walking away from all he had built and cared about, or at least – he reflected grimly – that he thought he cared about until a moment or two ago.

'I should imagine,' O'Keefe said, with an attempt at joviality, 'that living here, with no worries, and your man to take care of you, would be moderately endurable.'

There seemed no point in explaining that Aloysius Royce would shortly graduate from law school and presumably have other ideas affecting his own future. It was a reminder, though, that life in this eyrie, atop a hotel he no longer controlled, would be a lonely one.

Warren Trent said abruptly, 'Suppose I refuse to sell. What are your plans?'

'I shall look for other property and build. Actually, I think you'll have lost your hotel long before that happens. But even if you don't, the competition we'll provide will force you out of business.'

The tone was studiedly indifferent, but the mind behind it astute and calculating. The truth was: the O'Keefe Hotel Corporation wanted the St Gregory very much, and urgently. The lack of an O'Keefe affiliate in New Orleans was like a missing tooth in the company's otherwise solid bite on the travelling public. It had already entailed a costly loss of referral business to and from other cities – the sustaining oxygen of a successful hotel chain. Disquieting too, competitive chains were exploiting the gap. The Sheraton-Charles were long established. Hilton, as well as having its airport inn, was building in the Vieux Carré. Hotel Corporation of America had the Royal Orleans.

Nor were the terms which O'Keefe had offered Warren Trent other than realistic. The

St Gregory mortgagees had already been sounded out by an O'Keefe emissary and were unco-operative. Their intention, it quickly became evident, was first to obtain control of the hotel and later hold out for a big killing. If the St Gregory was to be bought reasonably, the crucial moment was now.

'How much time,' Warren Trent asked, 'are you willing to allow me?'

'I'd prefer your answer at once.'

'I'm not prepared to give it.'

'Very well.' O'Keefe considered. 'I've an appointment in Naples, Saturday. I'd like to leave here no later than Thursday night. Suppose we set a deadline of noon Thursday.'

'That's less than forty-eight hours!'

'I see no reason to wait longer.'

Obstinacy inclined Warren Trent to hold out for more time. Reason reminded him: he would merely advance by a day the Friday deadline he already faced. He conceded, 'I suppose if you insist . . .'

'Splendid!' Smiling expansively, O'Keefe pushed back his chair and rose, nodding to Dodo who had been watching Warren Trent with an expression close to sympathy. 'It's time for us to go, my dear. Warren, we've enjoyed your hospitality.' Waiting another day and a half, he decided, was merely a minor nuisance. After all, there could be no doubt of the eventual result.

At the outer doorway Dodo turned her wide blue eyes upon her host. 'Thanks a lot, Mr Trent.'

He took her hand and bowed over it. 'I don't recall when these old rooms have been more graced.'

O'Keefe glanced sharply sideways, suspecting the compliment's sincerity, then realizing it was genuinely meant. That was another strange thing about Dodo: a rapport she achieved at times, as if instinctively, with the most unlikely people.

In the corridor, her fingers resting lightly on his arm, he felt his own senses quicken.

But before anything else, he reminded himself, he must pray to God, giving appropriate thanks for the way the evening had gone.

14

'There's something downright exciting,' Peter McDermott observed, 'about a girl fumbling in her handbag for the key to her apartment.'

'It's a dual symbol,' Christine said, still searching. 'The apartment shows woman's independence, but losing the key proves she's still feminine. Here! – I've found it.'

'Hang on!' Peter took Christine's shoulders, then kissed her. It was a long kiss and in the course of it his arms moved, holding her tightly.

At length, a shade breathlessly, she said, 'My rent's paid up. If we *are* going to do this, it might as well be in private.'

Taking the key, Peter opened the apartment door.

Christine put the bag on a side table and subsided into a deep settee. With relief she eased her feet from the constriction of her patent-leather pumps.

He sat beside her. 'Cigarette?'

'Yes, please.'

Peter held a match flame for them both.

He had a sense of elation and lightheartedness; an awareness of the here and now. It included a conviction that what was logical between them could happen if he chose to make it.

'This is nice,' Christine said. 'Just sitting, talking.'

He took her hand. 'We're not talking.'

'Then let's.'

'Talking wasn't exactly . . .'

'I know. But there's a question of where we're going, and if, and why.'

'Couldn't we just spin the wheel . . .'

'If we did, there'd be no gamble. Just a certainty.' She stopped, considering. 'What happened just now was for the second time, and there was some chemistry involved.'

'Chemically, I thought we were doing fine.'

'So in the course of things there'd be a natural progression.'

'I'm not only with you; I'm ahead.'

'In bed, I imagine.'

He said dreamily, 'I've taken the left side – as you face the headboard.'

'I've a disappointment for you.'

'Don't tell me! I'll guess. You forgot to brush your teeth. Never mind, I'll wait.'

She laughed. 'You're hard to talk . . .'

'Talking wasn't exactly . . .'

'That's where we started.'

Peter leaned back and blew a smoke ring. He followed it with a second and a third.

'I've always wanted to do that,' Christine said. 'I never could.'

He asked, 'What kind of disappointment?'

'A notion. That if what could happen . . . happens, it ought to mean something for both of us.'

'And would it for you?'

'It could, I think. I'm not sure.' She was even less sure of her own reaction to what might come next.

He stubbed out his cigarette, then took Christine's and did the same. As he clasped her hands she felt her assurance crumble.

'We need to get to know each other.' His eyes searched her face. 'Words aren't always the best way.'

His arms reached out and she came to him, at first pliantly, then with mounting fierce excitement. Her lips formed eager, incoherent sounds and discretion fled, the reservations of a moment earlier dissolved. Trembling, and to the pounding of her heart, she told herself: whatever was to happen must take its course; neither doubt nor reasoning would divert it now. She could hear Peter's quickening breath. She closed her eyes.

A pause. Then, unexpectedly, they were no longer close together.

'Sometimes,' Peter said, 'there are things you remember. They crop up at the damnedest times.' His arms went around her, but now more tenderly. He whispered, 'You were right. Let's give it time.'

She felt herself kissed gently, then heard footsteps recede. She heard the unlatching of the outer door and, a moment later, its closing.

She opened her eyes. 'Peter dearest,' she breathed. 'There's no need to go. Please don't go!'

But there was only silence and, from outside, the faint whirr of a descending elevator.

15

A few minutes only remained of Tuesday.

In a Bourbon Street strip joint the big-hipped blonde leaned closer to her male companion, one hand resting on his thigh, the fingers of the other fondling the base of his neck. 'Sure,' she said. 'Sure I want to go to bed with you, honey.'

Stan somebody, he had said he was, from a hick town in Iowa she had never heard of. And if he breathes at me any more, she thought, I'll puke. That's not bad breath in his mouth; it's a direct line from a sewer.

'Wadda we waitin' for, then?' the man asked thickly. He took her hand, moving it higher on the inside of his thigh. 'I got something special for you there, baby.'

She thought contemptuously: they were all the same, the loud-mouth chawbacons who came here – convinced that what they had between their legs was something exceptional which women panted for, and as irrationally proud as if they had grown it themselves like a prize cucumber. Probably, if put to a real white-hot test, this one would wind up incapable and whimpering, like others. But she had no intention of finding out. *God! – that stinking breath.*

A few feet from their table the discordant jazz combo, too inexpert to get work at one of the better Bourbon Street places like the *Famous Door* or *Paddock*, was raggedly finishing a number. It had been danced – if you choose to call untutored shuffling a dance – by one Jane Mansfield. (A Bourbon Street gimmick was to take the name of a celebrated performer, misspell it slightly, and allocate it to an unknown with the hope that the public passing by might mistake it for the real thing.)

'Listen,' the man from Iowa said impatiently. 'Whyn't we blow?'

'I already told you, sugar. I work here. I can't leave yet. I got my act to do.'

'Piss on your act!'

'Now, honey, that's not nice.' As if with sudden inspiration, the hippy blonde said, 'What hotel you staying at?'

'St Gregory.'

'That's not far from here.'

'Can have your pants off in five minutes.'

She chided: 'Won't I get a drink first?'

'You bet you will! Let's go!'

'Wait, Stanley darling! I've an idea.'

The lines were going exactly right, she thought, like a smoothly running playlet. And why not? It was the thousandth performance, give or take a few hundred either way. For the past four and a half Stan whoever-he-was from somewhere had docilely followed the tired old routine: the first drink – a try-on at four times the price he would have paid in an honest bar. Then the waiter had brought her over to join him. They had been served a succession of drinks, though, like the other girls who worked on bar commission, she had

had cold tea instead of cheap whisky which the customers got. And later she had tipped off the waiter to hustle the full treatment – a split bottle of domestic champagne for which the bill, though Stanley Sucker didn't know it yet, would be forty dollars – and just let him try to get out without paying!

So all that remained was to ditch him, though maybe in doing so – if the lines kept going right – she could earn another small commission. After all, she was entitled to some sort of bonus for enduring that stinking breath.

He was asking, 'Wha' idea, baby?'

'Leave me your hotel key. You can get another at the desk; they always have spares. Soon as I'm through here I'll come and join you.' She squeezed where he had placed her hand. 'You just make sure you're ready for me.'

'I'll be ready.'

'All right, then. Give me the key.'

It was in his hand. But held tightly.

He said doubtfully, 'Hey, you sure you'll . . .'

'Honey, I promise I'll fly.' Her fingers moved again. *The sickening slob would probably wet his pants in a minut*e. 'After all, Stan, what girl wouldn't?'

He pressed the key upon her.

Before he could change his mind she had left the table. The waiter would handle the rest, helped by a muscle man if Bad Breath made trouble about the bill. He probably wouldn't, though; just as he wouldn't come back. The suckers never did.

She wondered how long he would lie hopefully awake in his hotel room, and how long it would take him to realize she wasn't coming, and never would, even if he stayed there the rest of his useless life.

Some two hours later, at the end of a day as dreary as most - though at least, she consoled herself, a little more productive - the big-hipped blonde sold the key for ten dollars.

The buyer was Keycase Milne.

Wednesday

I

As the first grey streaks of a new dawn filtered tenuously above New Orleans, Keycase – sitting on the bed of his room at the St Gregory – was refreshed, alert, and ready for work.

Through the previous afternoon and early evening he had slept soundly. Then he had made an excursion from the hotel, returning at two a.m. For an hour and a half he had slept again, waking promptly at the time he intended. Getting up, he shaved, showered and at the end turned the shower control to cold. The icy rivulets set his body, first tingling, then glowing as he towelled himself vigorously.

One of his rituals before a professional foray was to put on fresh underwear and a clean, starched shirt. Now he could feel the pleasant crispness of the linen, supplementing the fine edge of tension to which he had honed himself. If momentarily a brief, uneasy doubt obtruded – a shadow of fear concerning the awful possibility of being sent down for fifteen years if he was caught once more – he dismissed it summarily.

Much more satisfying was the smoothness with which his preparations had gone.

Since arriving yesterday he had enlarged his collection of hotel keys from three to five.

One of the extra two keys had been obtained last evening in the simplest way possible – by asking for it at the hotel front desk. His own room number was 830. He had asked for the key of 803.

Before doing so he had taken some elementary precautions. He had made sure that an 803 key was in the rack, and that the slot beneath it contained no mail or messages. If there had been, he would have waited. When handing over mail or messages, desk clerks had a habit of asking key claimants for their names. As it was, he had loitered until the desk was busy, then joined a line of several other guests. He was handed the key without question. If there had been any awkwardness, he would have given the believable explanation that he had confused the number with his own.

The ease of it all, he told himself, was a good omen. Later today – making sure that different clerks were on duty – he would get the keys of 380 and 930 the same way.

A second bet had paid off too. Two nights earlier, through a reliable contact, he had made certain arrangements with a Bourbon Street B-girl. It was she who had provided the fifth key, with a promise of more to come.

Only the rail terminal – after tedious vigil covering the several train departures – had failed to yield result. The same thing had happened on other occasions elsewhere, and Keycase decided to profit from experience. Train travellers were obviously more conservative than air passengers and perhaps for that reason took greater care with hotel keys. So in future he would eliminate railway terminals from his plans.

He checked his watch. There was no longer any cause to delay, even though he was aware of a curious reluctance to stir from the bed where he was sitting. But, overcoming it, he made his last two preparations.

In the bathroom he had already poured a third of a tumbler of Scotch. Going in, he gargled with the whisky thoroughly, though drinking none, and eventually spitting it out into the washbasin.

Next he took a folded newspaper – an early edition of today's *Times-Picayune*, bought last night – and placed it under his arm.

Finally, checking his pockets where his collection of keys was disposed systematically, he let himself out of the room.

His crêpe-soled shoes were silent on the service stairs. He went two floors down to the sixth, moving easily, not hurrying. Entering the sixth-floor corridor he managed to take a swift, comprehensive look in both directions, though – in case he should be observed – without appearing to.

The corridor was deserted and silent.

Keycase had already studied the hotel layout and the system of numbering rooms. Taking the key of 641 from an inside pocket, he held it casually in his hand and walked unhurriedly to where he knew the room to be.

The key was the first he had obtained at Moisant Airport. Keycase, above all else, had an orderly mind.

The door of 641 was in front of him. He stopped. No light from beneath. No sound from within. He produced gloves and slipped them on.

He felt his senses sharpen. Making no sound, he inserted the key. The key turned. The door opened noiselessly. Removing the key, he went in, gently closing the door behind him.

Faint shadows of dawn relieved the inside darkness. Keycase stood still, orienting himself as his eyes became accustomed to the partial light. The greyness was one reason why skilled hotel thieves chose this time of day to operate. The light was sufficient to see and avoid obstacles but, with luck, not to be observed. There were other reasons. It was a low-point in the life of any hotel – the night staff still on duty were less alert as the end of their shift approached. Day workers had not yet come on. Guests – even party-ers and stay-out-lates – were back in their rooms and most likely to be sleeping. Dawn, too, gave people a sense of security, as if the perils of the night were over.

Keycase could see the shape of a dressing table directly ahead. To the right was the shadow of a bed. From the sound of even breathing, its occupant was well asleep.

The dressing table was the place to look for money first.

He moved cautiously, his feet exploring in an arc ahead for anything which might cause him to trip. He reached out, touching the dressing table as he came to it. Finger tips explored the top.

His gloved fingers encountered a small pile of coins. Forget it! – pocketing loose change meant noise. But where there were coins there was likely to be a wallet. Ah! – he had found it. It was interestingly bulky.

A bright light in the room snapped on.

It happened so suddenly, without any warning sound, that Keycase's quick thinking – on which he prided himself – failed him entirely.

Reaction was instinctive. He dropped the wallet and spun round guiltily, facing the light.

The man who had switched on the bedside lamp was in pyjamas, sitting up in bed. He was youngish, muscular and angry.

He said explosively, 'What the devil do you think you're doing?'

Keycase stood, foolishly gaping, unable to speak.

Probably, Keycase reasoned afterwards, the awakened sleeper needed a second or two himself to collect his wits, which was why he failed to perceived the initial guilty response of his visitor. But for the moment, conscious of having lost a precious advantage, Keycase swung belatedly into action.

Swaying as if drunkenly, he declaimed, 'Wadya mean, wha'm I doin'? Wha' you doin' in my bed?' Unobtrusively, he slipped off the gloves.

'Damn you! – this is my bed. And my room!'

Moving closer, Keycase loosed a blast of breath, whisky laden from his gargling. He saw the other recoil. Keycase's mind was working quickly now, icily, as it always had. He had bluffed his way out of dangerous situations like this before.

It was important at this point, he knew, to become defensive, not continuing an aggressive tone, otherwise the legitimate room owner might become frightened and summon help. Though this one looked as if could handle any contingency himself.

Keycase said stupidly, 'Your room? You sure?'

The man in bed was angrier than ever. 'You lousy drunk! Of course I'm sure it's my room!'

'This's 614?'

'You stupid jerk! It's 641.'

'Sorry ol' man. Guess 's my mistake.' From under his arm Keycase took the newspaper, carried to convey the impression of having come in from the street. 'Here's a mornin' paper. Special 'livery.'

'I don't want your goddam newspaper. Take it and get out!'

It had worked! Once more the well-planned escape route had paid off.

Already he was on the way to the door. 'Said I'm sorry ol' man. No need to get upset. I'm goin'.'

He was almost out, the man in bed still glaring. He used a folded glove to turn the doorknob. Then he had made it. Keycase closed the door behind him.

Listening intently, he heard the man inside get out of bed, footsteps pad to the door, the door rattle, the protective chain go on. Keycase continued to wait.

For fully five minutes he stood in the corridor, not stirring, waiting to hear if the man in the room telephoned downstairs. It was essential to know. If he did, Keycase must return to his own room at once, before a hue and cry. But there was no sound, no telephone call. The immediate danger was removed.

Later, though, it might be a different story.

When Mr 641 awoke again in the full light of morning he would remember what had occurred. Thinking about it, he might ask himself some questions. For example: Why was it that even if someone arrived at the wrong room, their key fitted and they were able to get in? And once in, why stand in darkness instead of switching on a light? There was also Keycase's initial guilty reaction. An intelligent man, wide awake, might reconstruct that part of the scene and perhaps reassess it. In any case there would be reason enough for an indignant telephone call to the hotel management.

Management – probably represented by a house detective – would recognize the signs instantly. A routine check would follow. Whoever was in room 614 would be contacted and, if possible, the occupants of both rooms brought face to face. Each would affirm that neither had seen the other previously. The house dick would not be surprised, but it would confirm his suspicion that a professional hotel thief was at large in the building. Word would spread quickly. At the outset of Keycase's campaign, the entire hotel staff would be alert and watchful.

It was likely, too, that the hotel would contact the local police. They, in turn, would ask the FBI for information about known hotel thieves who might be moving around the country. Whenever such a list came, it was a certainty that the name of Julius Keycase Milne would be on it. There would be photographs – police mug shots for showing around the hotel to desk clerks and others.

What he ought to do was pack up and run. If he hurried, he could be clear of the city in less than an hour.

Except that it wasn't quite that simple. He had invested money – the car, the motel, his hotel room, the B-girl. Now, funds were running low. He must show a profit – a good one – out of New Orleans. Think again, Keycase told himself. Think hard.

So far he had considered the worst that could happen. Look at it the other way.

Even if the sequence of events he had thought of occurred, it might take several days. The New Orleans police were busy. According to the morning paper, all available detectives were working overtime on an unsolved hit-and-run case – a double killing the whole city was excited about. It was unlikely the police would take time out from that when, in the hotel, no crime had actually been committed. They'd get around to it eventually, though. They always did.

So how long did he have? Being conservative, another clear day; probably two. He considered carefully. It would be enough.

By Friday morning he could have cleaned up and be clear of the city, covering his tracks behind him.

The decision was made. Now, what next – at this moment? Return to his own room on the eighth floor, leaving further action until tomorrow, or carry on? The temptation not to continue was strong. The incident of a moment ago had shaken him far more – if he was honest with himself – than the same kind of thing ever used to. His own room seemed a safe and comfortable haven.

Then he decided grimly: he must go on. He had once read that when a military aeroplane pilot crashed through no fault of his own, he was at once sent up again before he could lose his nerve. He must follow the same principle.

The first key he had obtained had failed him. Perhaps it was an omen, indicating that he should reverse the order and try the last. The Bourbon Street B-girl had given him 1062. Another omen! – his lucky two. Counting the flights as he went, Keycase ascended the service stairs.

The man named Stanley, from Iowa, who had fallen for the oldest sucker routine on Bourbon Street, was at last asleep. He had waited for the big-hipped blonde, hopefully, at first, then, as the hours passed, with diminishing confidence plus a discomforting awareness that he had been taken, but good. Finally, when his eyes would stay open no longer, he rolled over into a deep, alcoholic sleep.

He neither heard Keycase enter, nor move carefully and methodically around the room. He continued to sleep soundly as Keycase extracted the money from his wallet, then pocketed his watch, signet ring, gold cigarette case, matching lighter and diamond cuff links. He did not stir as Keycase, just as quietly, left.

It was mid-morning before Stanley from Iowa awoke, and another hour before he was aware – through the miasma of a whopping hangover – of having been robbed. When at length the extent of this new disaster penetrated, adding itself to his present wretchedness plus the costly and unproductive experience of the night before, he sat in a chair and blubbered like a child.

Long before then, Keycase cached his gains.

Leaving 1062, Keycase had decided it was becoming too light to risk another entry elsewhere, and returned to his own room, 830. He counted the money. It amounted to a satisfactory ninety-four dollars, mostly fives and tens, and all used bills which meant they could not be identified. Happily he added the cash to his own wallet.

The watch and other items were more complex. He had hesitated at first about the wisdom of taking them, but had given in to greed and opportunity. It meant, of course, that an alarm would be raised some time today. People might lose money and not be certain how or where, but the absence of jewellery pointed conclusively to theft. The possibility of prompt police attention was now much more likely, and the time he had allowed himself might be lessened, though perhaps not. He found his confidence increasing, along with more willingness now to take risks if needed.

Among his effects was a small businessman's valise – the kind you could carry in and out of a hotel without attracting attention. Keycase packed the stolen items in it, observing that they would undoubtedly bring him a hundred dollars from a reliable fence, though in real value they were worth much more

He waited, allowing time for the hotel to awaken and the lobby to become reasonably occupied. Then he took the elevator down and walked out with the bag to the Canal Street parking lot where he had left his car the night before. From there he drove carefully to his rented room in the motel on Chef Menteur Highway. He made one stop en route, raising the hood of the Ford and pretending engine trouble while he retrieved the motel key hidden in the carburettor air filter. At the motel he stayed only long enough to transfer the valuables to another locked bag. On the way back to town he repeated the pantomime with the car, replacing the key. When he had parked the car – on a different parking lot this time – there was nothing, either on his person or in his hotel room, to connect him with the stolen loot.

He now felt so good about everything, he stopped for breakfast in the St Gregory coffee shop.

It was afterwards, coming out, that he saw the Duchess of Croydon.

She had emerged, a moment earlier, from an elevator into the hotel lobby. The Bedlington terriers – three on one side, two on the other – frisked ahead like spirited outriders. The Duchess held their leashes firmly and with authority, though her thoughts were clearly elsewhere, her eyes focused forward, as if seeing through the hotel walls and far beyond. The superb hauteur, her hallmark, was as evident as always. Only the observant might have noticed lines of strain and weariness in her face which cosmetics and an effort of willpower had not obscured entirely.

Keycase stopped, at first startled and unbelieving. His eyes reassured him: it *was* the Duchess of Croydon. Keycase, an avid reader of magazines and newspapers, had seen too many photographs not to be sure. And the Duchess was staying, presumably, in this hotel.

His mind raced. The Duchess of Croydon's gem collection was among the world's most fabulous. Whatever the occasion, she never appeared anywhere without being resplendently jewelled. Even now his eyes narrowed at the sight of her rings and a sapphire clip, worn casually, which must be priceless. The Duchess's habit meant that, despite precautions, there would always be a part of her collection close at hand.

A half-formed idea – reckless, audacious, impossible . . . or was it? . . . was taking shape in Keycase's mind.

He continued watching as, the terriers preceding, the Duchess of Croydon swept through the St Gregory lobby and into the sunlit street.

2

Herbie Chandler arrived early at the hotel, but for his own advantage, not the St Gregory's.

Among the bell captain's sideline rackets was one referred to – in the many hotels where it existed – as 'the liquor butt hustle'.

Hotel guests who entertained in their rooms, or even drank alone, often had an inch or two of liquor left in bottles at the time of their departure. When packing their bags, most of these guests refrained from including the liquor ends, either through fear of leakage or to avoid airline excess baggage charges. But human psychology made them baulk at pouring good liquor away and usually it was left, intact, on dressing-tables of the vacated rooms.

If a bellboy observed such a residue when summoned to carry a guest's bags at checkout time, he was usually back within a few minutes to collect it. Where guests carried their own bags, as many preferred to do nowadays, the floor maid would usually notify a bellboy, who would cut her in on his eventual share of profit.

The dribs and drabs of liquor found their way to the corner of a basement storeroom, the private domain of Herbie Chandler. It was preserved as such through the agency of a storekeeper who, in turn, received help from Chandler with certain larcenies of his own.

The bottles were brought here, usually in laundry bags which bellboys could carry within the hotel without arousing comment. In the course of a day or two the amount collected was surprisingly large.

Every two or three days – more frequently if the hotel was busy with conventions – the bell captain consolidated his hoard, as he was doing now.

Herbie sorted the bottles containing gin into a single group. Selecting two of the more expensive labels, and employing a small well-worn funnel, he emptied the other miscellaneous brands into them. He ended with the first bottle full and the second three-quarters full. He capped them both, putting the second bottle aside for topping up at the next consolidation. He repeated the process with bourbon, Scotch and rye. In all, there were seven full bottles and several partial ones. A lonely few ounces of vodka he emptied, after a moment's hesitation, into the gin.

Later in the day the seven full bottles would be delivered to a bar a few blocks from the St Gregory. The bar owner, only mildly concerned with scruples about quality, served the liquor to customers, paying Herbie half the going price of regularly bottled supplies. Periodically, for those involved within the hotel, Herbie would declare a dividend – usually as small as he dared make it.

Recently the liquor butt hustle had been doing well, and today's accumulation would have pleased Herbie if he had not been preoccupied with other thoughts. Late last night there had been a telephone call from Stanley Dixon. The young man had relayed his own version of the conversation between himself and Peter McDermott. He had also reported the appointment – for himself and his cronies – in McDermott's office at four p.m. the following afternoon, which was not today. What Dixon wanted to find out was: Just how much did McDermott know?

Herbie Chandler had been unable to supply an answer, except to warn Dixon to be discreet and admit nothing. But, ever since, he had been wondering what exactly happened in rooms 1126-7 two nights earlier, and just how well informed – concerning the bell captain's own part in it – the assistant general manager was.

It was another nine hours until four o'clock. They would, Herbie expected, pass slowly.

3

As he did most mornings, Curtis O'Keefe showered first and prayed afterwards. The procedure was typically efficient since he came clean to God and also dried off thoroughly in a towel robe during the twenty minutes or so he was on his knees.

Bright sunshine, entering the comfortable air-conditioned suite, gave the hotelier a sense of well-being. The feeling transferred itself to his loquacious prayers which took on the air of an intimate man-to-man chat. Curtis O'Keefe did not forget, however, to remind God of his own continuing interest in the St Gregory Hotel.

Breakfast was in Dodo's suite. She ordered for them both, after frowning at length over a menu, followed by protracted conversation with room service during which she changed the entire order several times. Today the choice of juice seemed to be causing her the most uncertainty and she vacillated – through an exchange with the unseen order taker lasting several minutes – over the comparative merits of pineapple, grapefruit and orange. Curtis O'Keefe amusedly pictured the havoc which the prolonged call was causing at the busy room-service order desk eleven floors below.

Waiting for the meal to arrive, he leafed through the morning newspapers – the New Orleans *Times-Picayune* and an airmailed New York *Times*. Locally, he observed, there had been no fresh developments in the hit-and-run case that had eclipsed most other Crescent City news. In New York, he saw, on the Big Board, O'Keefe Hotels stock had slipped three quarters of a point. The decline was not significant – merely a normal fluctuation, and there was sure to be an off-setting rise when word of the chain's new acquisition in New Orleans leaked out, as it probably would before too long.

The thought reminded him of the annoying two days he would have to wait for confirmation. He regretted that he had not insisted on a decision last night; but now, having given his word, there was nothing to do but bide his time patiently. He had not the least doubt of a favourable decision from Warren Trent. There could, in fact, be no possible alternative.

Near the end of breakfast there was a telephone call – which Dodo answered first – from Hank Lemnitzer, Curtis O'Keefe's personal representative on the West Coast. Half-suspecting the nature of the call, he took it in his own suite, closing the communicating door behind him.

The subject he had expected to be raised came up after a routine report on various financial interests – outside the hotel business – on which Lemnitzer astutely rode hard.

'There's one thing, Mr O'Keefe' – the nasal Californian drawl came down the telephone. 'It's about Jenny LaMarsh, the doll . . . er, the young lady you kindly expressed interest in that time at the Beverly Hills Hotel. You remember her?'

O'Keefe remembered well: a striking, rangy brunette with a superb figure, coolly amused smile and a quick mischievous wit. He had been impressed both with her obvious potential as a woman and the range of her conversation. Someone had said, he seemed to recall, that she was a Vassar graduate. She had a contract of sorts with one of the smaller movie studios.

'Yes, I do.'

'I've talked with her, Mr O'Keefe – quite a few times. Anyway, she'd be pleased to go along with you on a trip. Or two.'

There was no need to ask if Miss LaMarsh knew the kind of relationship her trip would entail. Hank Lemnitzer would have taken care of that. The possibilities, Curtis O'Keefe admitted to himself, were interesting. Conversation, as well as other things with Jenny LaMarsh, would be highly stimulating. Certainly she would have no trouble holding her own with people they met together. Nor would she be torn by indecisions about things as simple as choosing fruit juice.

But, surprising himself, he hesitated.

'There's one thing I'd like to ensure, and that's Miss Lash's future.'

Hank Lemnitzer's voice came confidently across the continent. 'Don't give it a thought. I'll take care of Dodo, same's I did all the others.'

Curtis O'Keefe said sharply, 'That isn't the point.' Despite Lemnitzer's usefulness, at times there were certain subtleties he lacked.

'Just what is the point, Mr O'Keefe?'

'I'd like you to line up something for Miss Lash specifically. Something good. And I want to know about it before she leaves.'

The voice sounded doubtful. 'I guess I could. Of course, Dodo isn't the brightest . . .'

O'Keefe insisted, 'Not just anything, you understand. And take your time if necessary.'

'What about Jenny LaMarsh?'

'She doesn't have anything else . . . ?'

'I guess not.' There was the grudging sense of concession to a whim, then, breezily once more: 'OK, Mr O'Keefe, whatever you say. You'll be hearing from me.'

When he returned to the sitting-room of the other suite, Dodo was stacking their used breakfast dishes on the room-service trolley. He snapped irritably, 'Don't do that! There are hotel staff paid for that kind of work.'

'But I like doing it, Curtie.' She turned her eloquent eyes upon him and momentarily, he saw, there was a bewildered hurt. But she stopped all the same.

Unsure of the reason for his own ill humour, he informed her, 'I'm going to take a walk through the hotel.' Later today, he decided, he would make amends to Dodo by taking her on an inspection of the city. There was a harbour tour, he recalled, on an ungainly old stern-wheeler called the SS *President*. It was usually packed with sightseers and was the kind of thing she would enjoy.

At the outer doorway, on impulse, he told her about it. She responded by flinging her arms around his neck. 'Curtie, it'll be endsville! I'll fix my hair so it doesn't blow in the wind. Like this!'

She removed one lissome arm and with it pulled the flowing ash-blonde hair back from her face, twisting it into a tight, profiling skein. The effect – her face tilted upward, her unaffected joy – was of such breathtaking, simple beauty that he had an impulse to change his immediate plans and stay. Instead, he grunted something about returning soon and abruptly closed the suite door behind him.

He rode an elevator down to the main mezzanine and from there took the stairway to the lobby where he resolutely put Dodo out of his mind. Strolling with apparent casualness, he was aware of covert glances from passing hotel employees who, at the sight of him, seemed affected with sudden energy. Ignoring them, he continued to observe the physical condition of the hotel, comparing his own reactions with those in Ogden Bailey's undercover report. His opinion of yesterday that the St Gregory required a firm directing hand was confirmed by what he saw. He also shared Bailey's view about potential new sources of revenue.

Experience told him, for example, that the massive pillars in the lobby were probably not holding anything up. Providing they weren't, it would be a simple matter to hollow out a section of each and rent the derived space as showcases for local merchants.

In the arcade beneath the lobby he observed a choice area occupied by a florist shop. The rent which the hotel received was probably around three hundred dollars monthly. But the same space, developed imaginatively as a modern cocktail lounge (a riverboat theme! – why not?) might easily gross fifteen thousand dollars in the same period. The florist could be relocated handily.

Returning to the lobby, he could see more space that should be put to work. By eliminating part of the existing public area, another half-dozen sales counters – air lines, car rental, tours, jewellery, a drugstore perhaps – could be profitably squeezed in. It would entail a change in character, naturally; the present air of leisurely comfort would have to go, along with the shrubbery and thick pile rugs. But nowadays, brightly lighted lobbies with advertising everywhere you looked were what helped to make hotel balance sheets more cheerful.

Another thing; most of the chairs should be taken away. If people wanted to sit down, it was more profitable that they be obliged to do so in one of the hotel's bars or restaurants.

He had learned a lesson about free seating years ago. It was in his very first hotel – a jerry-built, false-fronted fire trap in a small South-western city. The hotel had one distinction: a dozen pay toilets which at various times were used – or seemed to be – by every farmer and ranch hand for a hundred miles around. To the surprise of young Curtis O'Keefe, the revenue from this source was substantial, but one thing prevented it becoming greater: a state law which required one of the twelve toilets to be operated free of charge, and the habit, which thrifty minded farm hands had acquired, of lining up to use the free one. He solved the problem by hiring the town drunk. For twenty cents an hour and a bottle of cheap wine the man sat on the free toilet stoically through every busy day. Receipts from the others had soared immediately.

Curtis O'Keefe smiled, remembering.

The lobby, he noticed, was becoming busier. A group of new arrivals had just come in and were registering, preceding others still checking baggage that was being unloaded from an airport limousine. A small line had formed at the reception counter. O'Keefe stood watching.

It was then he observed what apparently no-one else, so far, had seen.

A middle-aged, well-dressed Negro, valise in hand, had entered the hotel. He came towards Reception, walking unconcernedly as if for an afternoon stroll. At the counter he put down his bag and stood waiting, third in line.

The exchange, when it came, was clearly audible.

'Good morning,' the Negro said. His voice – a Midwestern accent – was amiable and cultured. 'I'm Dr Nicholas; you have a reservation for me.' While waiting he had removed a black Homburg hat revealing carefully brushed iron-grey hair.

'Yes, sir; if you'll register, please.' The words were spoken before the clerk looked up. As he did, his features stiffened. A hand went out, withdrawing the registration pad he had pushed forward a moment earlier.

'I'm sorry,' he said firmly, 'the hotel is full.'

Unperturbed, the Negro responded smilingly. 'I have a reservation. The hotel sent a letter confirming it.' His hand went to an inside pocket, producing a wallet with papers protruding, from which he selected one.

'There must have been a mistake. I'm sorry.' The clerk barely glanced at the letter placed in front of him. 'We have a convention here.'

'I know.' The other nodded, his smile a shade thinner than before. 'It's a convention of dentists. I happen to be one.'

The room clerk shook his head. 'There's nothing I can do for you.'

The Negro put away his papers. 'In that case I'd like to talk with someone else.'

While they had been speaking still more new arrivals had joined the line in front of the counter. A man in a belted raincoat enquired impatiently, 'What's the hold-up here?' O'Keefe remained still. He had a sense that in the now crowded lobby a time bomb was ticking, ready to explode.

'You can talk to the assistant manager.' Leaning forward across the counter, the room clerk called sharply, 'Mr Bailey!'

Across the lobby an elderly man at an alcove desk looked up.

'Mr Bailey, would you come here, please?'

The assistant manager nodded and, with a suggestion of tiredness, eased himself upright. As he walked deliberately across, his lined, pouched face assumed a professional greeter's smile.

An old-timer, Curtis O'Keefe thought; after years of room clerking he had been given a chair and desk in the lobby with authority to handle minor problems posed by guests. The title of assistant manager, as in most hotels, was mainly a sop to the public's vanity, allowing them to believe they were dealing with a higher personage than in reality. The real authority of the hotel was in the executive offices, out of sight.

'Mr Bailey,' the room clerk said, 'I've explained to this gentleman that the hotel is full.'

'And I've explained,' the Negro countered, 'that I have a confirmed reservation.'

The assistant manager beamed benevolently, his manifest goodwill encompassing the line of waiting guests. 'Well,' he acknowledged, 'we'll just have to see what we can do.' He placed a pudgy, nicotine-stained hand on the sleeve of Dr Nicholas's expensively tailored suit. 'Won't you come and sit down over here?' As the other allowed himself to be steered towards the alcove: 'Occasionally these things happen, I'm afraid. When they do, we try to make amends.'

Mentally Curtis O'Keefe acknowledge that the elderly man knew his job. Smoothly and without fuss, a potentially embarrassing scene had been eased from centre stage into the wings. Meanwhile the other arrivals were being quickly checked in with the aid of a second room clerk who had joined the first. Only a youthful, broad-shouldered man, owlish behind heavy glasses, had left the line-up and was watching the new development. Well, O'Keefe thought, perhaps there might be no explosion after all. He waited to see.

The assistant manager gestured his companion to a chair beside the desk and eased into his own. He listened carefully, his expression noncommittal, as the other repeated the information he had given the room clerk.

At the end the older man nodded. 'Well, doctor' – the tone was briskly businesslike – 'I apologize for the misunderstanding, but I'm sure we can find you other accommodation in the city.' With one hand he pulled a telephone towards him and lifted the receiver. The other hand slid out a leaf from the desk, revealing a list of phone numbers.

'Just a moment.' For the first time the visitor's soft voice had taken on an edge. 'You tell me the hotel is full, but your clerks are checking people in. Do *they* have some special kind of reservation?'

'I guess you could say that.' The professional smile had disappeared.

'Jim Nicholas!' The boisterously cheerful greeting resounded across the lobby. Behind the voice a small elderly man with a sprightly rubicund face surmounted by a coxcomb of unruly white hair took short hurried strides towards the alcove.

The Negro stood. 'Dr Ingram! How good to see you!' He extended his hand which the older man grasped.

'How are you, Jim, my boy? No, don't answer! I can see for myself you're fine. Prosperous too, from the look of you. I assume your practice is going well.'

'It is, thank you.' Dr Nicholas smiled. 'Of course my university work still takes a good deal of time.'

'Don't I know it! Don't I know it! I spend all my life teaching fellows like you, and then you all go out and get the big-paying practices.' As the other grinned broadly: 'Anyway you seem to have gotten the best of both – with a fine reputation. That paper of yours on malignant mouth tumours has caused a lot of discussion and we're all looking forward to a first-hand report. By the way, I shall have the pleasure of introducing you to the convention. You know they made me president this year?'

'Yes, I'd heard. I can't think of a finer choice.'

As the two talked, the assistant manager rose slowly from his chair. His eyes moved uncertainly between their faces.

The small, white-haired man, Dr Ingram, was laughing. He patted his colleague jovially on the shoulder. 'Give me your room number, Jim. A few of us will be getting together for drinks later on. I'd like to have you join us.'

'Unfortunately,' Dr Nicholas said, 'I've just been told I won't be getting a room. It seems to have something to do with my colour.'

There was a shocked silence in which the dentists' president flushed deep red. Then, his face muscles hardening, he asserted, 'Jim, I'll deal with this. I promise you there'll be an apology *and* a room. If there isn't, I guarantee every other dentist will walk out of this hotel.'

A moment earlier the assistant manager had beckoned a bellboy. Now he instructed urgently, 'Get Mr McDermott – fast!'

4

For Peter McDermott the day began with a minor piece of organization. Among his morning mail was a memo from Reservations, informing him that Mr and Mrs Justin Kubek of Tuscaloosa were due to check into the St Gregory the following day. What made the Kubeks special was an accompanying note from Mrs Kubek, advising that her husband's height was seven foot one.

Seated behind his office desk, Peter wished all hotel problems were that simple.

'Tell the carpenter's shop,' he instructed his secretary, Flora Yates. 'They probably still have that bed and mattress we used for General de Gaulle; if not, they'll have to put something else together. Tomorrow have a room allocated early and the bed made up before the Kubeks get here. Tell Housekeeping too; they'll need special sheets and blankets.'

Seated composedly on the opposite side of the desk, Flora made her notes, as usual without fuss or question. The instructions would be relayed correctly, Peter knew, and tomorrow – without his needing to remind her – Flora would check to make sure they had been carried out.

He inherited Flora on first coming to the St Gregory and had long since decided she was everything a secretary should be – competent, reliable, nudging forty, contentedly married and plain as a cement block wall. One of the handy things about Flora, Peter thought, was that he could like her immensely – as he did – without it proving a distraction. Now, if Christine had been working for him, he reflected, instead of for Warren Trent, the effect would have been far different.

Since his impetuous departure from Christine's apartment last night, she had been out of his mind only briefly. Even sleeping, he had dreamed about her. The dream was an odyssey in which they floated serenely down a green-banked river (he was not sure aboard what) to an accompaniment of heady music in which harps, he seemed to recall, were featured strongly. He had told Christine this on telephoning her early this morning and she had asked, 'Were we going upstream or down? – that ought to be significant.' But he could not remember – only that he had enjoyed the whole thing tremendously and hoped (he informed Christine) to pick up later where he had left off last night.

Before that, however – some time this evening – they were to meet again. Just when and where would be arranged later, they agreed. 'It'll give me an excuse to call you,' Peter said.

'Who needs a reason?' she had responded. 'Besides, this morning I intend to find some terribly unimportant piece of paper that suddenly has to be delivered to you personally.' She sounded happy, almost breathless, as if the excitement they had found in each other last night had spilled over into the new day.

Hoping Christine would come soon, he returned his attention to Flora and the morning mail.

It was a normal mixed batch, including several queries about conventions, which he dealt with first. As usual, Peter assumed his favourite position for dictating – feet elevated on a high leather waste-basket, and his padded swivel chair tilted precariously back, so that his body was almost horizontal. He found he could think incisively in that position, which he had refined through experimentation, so that now the chair was poised at the outer limits of balance, with only a hair's breadth between equilibrium and disaster. As she often did, Flora watched expectantly during pauses in note taking. She just sat watching making no comment.

There was another letter today – which he answered next – from a New Orleans resident whose wife had attended a private wedding reception in the hotel some five weeks earlier. During the reception she placed her wild mink jacket on a piano, along with clothes and belongings of other guests. Subsequently she had discovered a bad cigarette burn, necessitating a one-hundred-dollar repair to the coat. The husband was attempting to collect from the hotel, and his latest letter contained a strongly worded threat to sue.

Peter's reply was polite but firm. He pointed out – as he had previously – that the hotel provided checking facilities which the letter writer's wife had chosen not to use. Had she used the check room, the hotel would have considered a claim. As it was, the St Gregory was not responsible.

The husband's letter, Peter suspected, was probably just a try-on, though it could develop into a lawsuit; there had been plenty of equally silly ones in the past. Usually the courts dismissed such claims with costs for the hotel, but they were annoying because of the time and effort they consumed. It sometimes seemed, Peter thought, as if the public considered a hotel a convenient milch cow with a cornucopian udder.

He had selected another letter when there was a light tap on the door from the outer office. He looked up, expecting to see Christine.

'It's just me,' Marsha Preyscott said. 'There wasn't anyone outside, so I . . .' She caught sight of Peter. 'Oh, my goodness! – won't you fall over backwards?'

'I haven't yet,' he said – and promptly did.

The resounding crash was followed by a second's startled silence.

From the floor behind his desk, looking upwards, he assessed the damage. His left ankle stung painfully where it had struck a leg of the overturning chair on the way down. The back of his head ached as he fingered it, though fortunately the rug had cushioned most of the impact. And there was his vanished dignity – attested to by Marsha's rippling laughter and Flora's more discreet smile.

They came around the desk to help him up. Despite his discomfiture, he was aware once more of Marsha's fresh, breathtaking radiance. Today she had on a simple blue linen dress which somehow emphasized the half-woman, half-child quality he had been conscious of yesterday. Her long black hair, as it had the day before, hung lustrously about her shoulders.

'You should use a safety net,' Marsha said. 'Like they do in a circus.'

Peter grinned ruefully. 'Maybe I could get a clown outfit, too.'

Flora restored the heavy swivel chair to its upright position. As he clambered up, Marsha and Flora taking an elbow each, Christine came in. She stopped at the doorway, a sheaf of papers in her hand. Her eyebrows went up. 'Am I intruding?'

'No,' Peter said. 'I . . . well, I fell out of my chair.'

Christine's eyes moved to the solidly standing chair.

He said, 'It went backwards.'

'They do that, don't they? All the time.' Christine glanced towards Marsha. Flora had quietly left.

Peter introduced them.

'How do you do, Miss Preyscott,' Christine said. 'I've heard of you.'

403

Marsha had glanced appraisingly from Peter to Christine. She answered coolly, 'I expect, working in a hotel, you hear all kinds of gossip, Miss Francis. You do work here, don't you?'

'Gossip wasn't what I meant,' Christine acknowledged. 'But you're right, I work here. So I can come back any old time, when things aren't so hectic or private.'

Peter sensed an instant antagonism between Marsha and Christine. He wondered what had caused it.

As if interpreting his thoughts, Marsha smiled sweetly. 'Please don't go on my account, Miss Francis. I just came in for a minute to remind Peter abut dinner tonight.' She turned towards him. 'You hadn't forgotten, had you?'

Peter had a hollow feeling in his stomach. 'No,' he lied, 'I hadn't forgotten.'

Christine broke the ensuing silence. 'Tonight?'

'Oh dear,' Marsha said. 'Does he have to work or something?'

Christine shook her dead decisively. 'He won't have a thing to do. I'll see to it myself.'

'That's terribly sweet of you.' Marsha flashed the smile again. 'Well, I'd better be off. Oh, yes – seven o'clock,' she told Peter, 'and it's on Prytania Street – the house with four big pillars. Goodbye, Miss Francis.' With a wave of her hand she went out, closing the door.

Her expression guileless, Christine enquired, 'Would you like me to write that down? – the house with four big pillars. So you won't forget.'

He raised his hands in a gesture of helplessness. 'I know – you and I had a date. When I made it, I'd forgotten about the other arrangement because last night . . . with you . . . drove everything else out of my mind. When we talked this morning, I guess I was confused.'

Christine said brightly, 'Well, I can understand that. Who wouldn't be confused with so many women under foot?'

She was determined – even though with an effort – to be light-hearted and, if necessary, understanding. She reminded herself: despite last night, she had no lien on Peter's time, and what he said about confusion was probably true. She added, 'I hope you have a delightful evening.'

He shifted uncomfortably. 'Marsha's just a child.'

There were limits, Christine decided, even to patient understanding. Her eyes searched his face, 'I suppose you really believe that. But speaking as a woman, let me advise you that little Miss Preyscott bears as much resemblance to a child as a kitten to a tiger. But it would be fun I should think – for a man – to be eaten up.'

He shook his head impatiently. 'You couldn't be more wrong. It's simply that she went through a trying experience two nights ago . . .'

'And needed a friend.'

'That's right.'

'And there you were!'

'We got talking. And I said I'd go to a dinner party at her house tonight. There'll be other people.'

'Are you sure?'

Before he could reply, the telephone shrilled. With a gesture of annoyance, he answered it. 'Mr McDermott,' a voice said urgently, 'there's trouble in the lobby and the assistant manager says will you please come quickly.'

When he replaced the telephone, Christine had gone.

404

5

There were moments of decision, Peter McDermott thought grimly, which you hoped you would never have to face. When and if you did, it was like a dreaded nightmare come to reality. Even worse, your conscience, convictions, integrity and loyalties were torn asunder.

It had taken him less than a minute to size up the situation in the lobby, even though explanations were still continuing. The dignified, middle-aged Negro, now seated quietly by the alcove desk, the indignant Dr Ingram – respect president of the dentists' congress, and the assistant manager's bland indifference now that responsibility had been shifted from his shoulders – these alone told Peter all he needed to know.

It was distressingly plain that a crisis had abruptly appeared which, if badly handled, might set off a major explosion.

He was aware of two spectators – Curtis O'Keefe, the familiar, much-photographed face watching intently from a discreet distance. The second spectator was a youthful, broad-shouldered man with heavy rimmed glasses, wearing grey flannel trousers with a tweed jacket. He was standing, a well-travelled suitcase beside him, seemingly surveying the lobby casually, yet missing nothing of the dramatic scene beside the assistant manager's desk.

The dentists' president drew himself to his full five feet six height, his round rubicund face flushed and tight lipped beneath the unruly white hair. 'McDermott, if you and your hotel persist in this incredible insult, I'm giving you fair warning you've bought yourself a pile of trouble.' The diminutive doctor's eyes flashed angrily, his voice rising. 'Dr Nicholas is a highly distinguished member of our profession. When you refuse to accommodate him, let me inform you it's a personal affront to me and to every member of our congress.'

If I were on the sidelines, Peter thought, and not involved, I'd probably be cheering for that. Reality cautioned him: I *am* involved. My job is to get this scene out of the lobby, somehow. He suggested, 'Perhaps you and Dr Nicholas' – his eyes took in the Negro courteously – 'would come to my office where we can discuss this quietly.'

'No, sir! – we'll damn well discuss it right here. There'll be no hiding this in some dark corner.' The fiery little doctor had his feet set firmly. 'Now then! – will you register my friend and colleague Dr Nicholas, or not?'

Heads were turning now. Several people had paused in their progress through the lobby. The man in the tweed jacket, still feigning disinterest, had moved closer.

What quirk of fate was it, Peter McDermott wondered dismally, that placed him in opposition to a man like Dr Ingram, whom instinctively he admired. It was ironic, too, that only yesterday Peter had argued against the policies of Warren Trent which had created this very incident. The impatiently waiting doctor had demanded: *Will you register my friend?* For a moment Peter was tempted to say yes, and hang the consequences. But it was useless, he knew.

There were certain orders he could give the room clerks, but to admit a Negro as a guest was not among them. On that point there was a firm, standing instruction which could be countermanded only by the hotel proprietor. To dispute this with the room clerks would

405

merely prolong the scene and, in the end, gain nothing.

'I'm as sorry as you, Dr Ingram,' he said, 'about having to do this. Unfortunately there *is* a house rule and it prevents me offering Dr Nicholas accommodation. I wish I could change it, but I don't have authority.'

'Then a confirmed reservation means nothing at all?'

'It means a great deal. But there are certain things we should have made clear when your convention was booked. It's our fault we didn't.'

'If you had,' the little doctor snapped, 'you wouldn't have got the convention. What's more, you may lost it yet.'

The assistant manager interjected, 'I did offer to find other accommodation, Mr McDermott.'

'We're not interested!' Dr Ingram swung back to Peter. 'McDermott, you're a young man, and intelligent I should imagine. How do you feel about what you're doing at this moment?'

Peter thought: Why evade? He replied, 'Frankly, Doctor, I've seldom been more ashamed.' He added to himself, silently: If I had the courage of conviction, I'd walk out of this hotel and quit. But reason argued: If he did, would anything be achieved? It would not get Dr Nicholas a room and would effectively silence Peter's own right of protest to Warren Trent, a right he had exercised yesterday and intended to do again. For that reason alone wasn't it better to stay, to do – in the long run – what you could? He wished, though, he could be more sure.

'Goddam, Jim.' There was anguish in the older doctor's voice. 'I'm not going to settle for this.'

The Negro shook his head. 'I won't pretend it doesn't hurt, and I suppose my militant friends would tell me I should make more of a fight.' He shrugged. 'On the whole, I prefer research. There's an afternoon flight north. I'll try to be on it.'

Dr Ingram faced Peter. 'Don't you *understand?* This man is a respected teacher and researcher. He's to present one of our most important papers.'

Peter thought miserably: there must be some way.

'I wonder,' he said, 'if you'd consider a suggestion. If Dr Nicholas will accept accommodation at another hotel, I'll arrange for his attendance at the meetings here.' He was being reckless, Peter realized. It would be hard to ensure and would involve a showdown with Warren Trent. But that much he would accomplish – or go himself.

'And the social events – the dinner and luncheons?'

The Negro's eyes were directly on his own.

Slowly Peter shook his head. It was useless to make a promise he could not fulfil.

Dr Nicholas shrugged: his face hardened. 'There would be no point. Dr Ingram, I'll mail my paper so it can be circulated, I think there are some things in it that will interest you.'

'Jim.' The diminutive, white-haired man was deeply troubled. 'Jim, I don't know what to tell you, except you haven't heard the last of this.'

Dr Nicholas looked around for his bag. Peter said, 'I'll get a bellboy.'

'No!' Dr Ingram brushed him aside. 'Carrying that bag is a privilege I'll reserve for myself.'

'Excuse me, gentlemen.' It was the voice of the man in the tweed jacket and glasses. As they turned, a camera shutter clicked. 'That's good,' he said. 'Let's try it once more.' He squinted through a Rollieflex viewfinder and the shutter clicked again. Lowering the camera he remarked, 'These fast films are great. Not long ago I'd have needed flash for that.'

Peter McDermott enquired sharply, 'Who are you?'

'Do you mean who or what?'

'Whichever it is, this is private property. The hotel . . .'

'Oh, come on! Let's not go through that old routine.' The picture taker was adjusting his camera settings. He looked up as Peter took a step towards him. 'And I wouldn't try anything, buster. Your hotel's going to stink when I'm through with it, and if you want to add rough-housing a photog, go ahead.' He grinned, as Peter hesitated. 'You think fast, I'll say that for you.'

Dr Ingram asked, 'Are you a newspaperman?'

'Good question, Doctor.' The man with the glasses grinned. 'Sometimes my editor says no, though I guess he won't today. Not when I send him this little gem from my vacation.'

'What paper?' Peter asked. He hoped it was an obscure one.

'New York *Herald Trib*.'

'Good!' The dentists' president nodded approvingly. 'They'll make the most of this. I hope you saw what happened.'

'You might say I got the picture,' the newspaperman said. 'I'll need a few details from you, so I can spell the names right. First, though, I'd like another shot outside – you and the other doctor together.'

Dr Ingram seized his Negro colleague's arm. 'It's the way to fight this thing, Jim. We'll drag the name of this hotel through every newspaper in the country.'

'You're right there,' the newspaperman agreed. 'The wire services'll go for this; my pictures too, I shouldn't wonder.'

Dr Nicholas nodded slowly.

There was nothing to do, Peter thought glumly. Nothing at all.

Curtis O'Keefe, he noticed, had disappeared.

As the others moved away, 'I'd like to do this fairly quickly,' Dr Ingram was saying. 'As soon as you have your pictures I intend to start pulling our convention out of this hotel. The only way to hit these people is where they feel it most – financially.' His forthright voice receded from the lobby.

#

'Has there been any change,' the Duchess of Croydon demanded, 'in what the police know?'

It was nearing eleven a.m. Once more, in the privacy of the Presidential Suite, the Duchess and her husband anxiously faced the chief house officer. Ogilvie's great obese body overflowed the cane-seated chair he had chosen to sit on. It creaked protestingly as he moved.

They were in the spacious, sunlit living-room of the suite, with the doors closed. As on the previous day, the Duchess had dispatched the secretary and maid on invented errands.

Ogilvie considered before answering. 'They know a lotta places the car they're lookin'' for ain't. 'S far's I can find out, they been workin' the out o' town an' suburbs, usin' all the men they got. There's still more ground to cover, though I reckon by tomorrow they'll start thinkin' about closer in.'

There had been a subtle change since yesterday in the relationship between the Croydons and Ogilvie. Before, they had been antagonists. Now they were conspirators, though still uncertainly, and as if feeling their way towards an alliance, as yet not quite defined.

'If there's so little time,' the Duchess said, 'why are we wasting it?'

The house detective's mean eyes hardened. 'You figure I should pull the car out now? Right in daylight. Maybe park it on Canal Street?'

Unexpectedly, the Duke of Croydon spoke for the first time. 'My wife has been under considerable strain. It isn't necessary to be rude to her.'

Ogilvie's facial expression – a brooding scepticism – remained unchanged. He took a cigar from the pocket of his coat, regarded it, then abruptly put it back. 'Reckon we're all a bit strained. Will be, too, till it's all over.'

The Duchess said impatiently, 'It doesn't matter. I'm more interested in what's happening. Do the police have any idea yet they're looking for a Jaguar?'

The immense head with its layered jowls moved slowly from side to side. 'They do, we'll hear fast enough. Like I said, yours bein' a foreign car, it may take a few days to pin it down for sure.'

'There isn't any sign of . . . well, their not being so concerned? Sometimes when a lot of attention is given to something, after a day or two with nothing happening, people lose interest.'

'You crazy?' There was astonishment on the fat man's face. 'You seen the mornin' paper?'

'Yes,' the Duchess said. 'I saw it. I suppose my question was a kind of wishful thinking.'

'Ain't nothin' changed,' Ogilvie declared. ''Cept maybe the police are keener. There's a lot of reputations ridin' on solvin' that hit-'n-run, an' the cops know if they don't come through there'll be a shake-down, startin' at the top. Mayor's as good as said so, so now there's politics in it too.'

'So that getting the car clear of the city will be harder than ever?'

'Put it this way, Duchess. Every last cop on the beat knows if he spots the car they're lookin' for – your car – he'll be sewin' stripes on his sleeve within the hour. They got their eyeballs polished. That's how tough it is.'

There was a silence in which Ogilvie's heavy breathing was the only sound. It was obvious what the next question would have to be, but there seemed a reluctance to ask it, as if the answer might mean deliverance or the diminution of hope.

At length the Duchess of Croydon said, 'When do you propose to leave? When will you drive the car north?'

'Tonight,' Ogilvie answered. 'That's why I come to see you folks.'

There was an audible emission of breath from the Duke.

'How will you get away?' the Duchess asked. 'Without being seen.'

'Ain't no guarantee I can. But I done some figuring.'

'Go on.'

'I reckon the best time to pull out's around one.'

'One in the morning?'

Ogilvie nodded. 'Not much doin' then. Traffic's quiet. Not too quiet.'

'But you might still be seen?'

'Could be seen any time. We got to take a chance on bein' lucky.'

'If you get away – clear of New Orleans – how far will you go?'

'Be light by six. Figure I'll be in Miss'sippa. Most likely 'round Macon.'

'That isn't far,' the Duchess protested. 'Only halfway up Mississippi. Not a quarter of the way to Chicago.'

The fat man shifted in his chair, which creaked in protest. 'You reckon I should go speedin'? Break a few records? Maybe get some ticket-happy cop tailin' me?'

'No, I don't think so. I'm merely concerned to have the car as far from New Orleans as possible. What will you do during the day?'

'Pull off. Lie low. Plenty places in Miss'sippa.'

'And then?'

'Soon's it's dark, I hi' tail it. Up through Alabama, Tennessee, Kentucky, Indiana.'

'When will it be safe? Really safe.'

'Indiana, I reckon.'

'And you'll stop in Indiana Friday?'

'I guess.'

'So that you'll reach Chicago Saturday?'

'Sat'day mornin'.'

'Very well,' the Duchess said. 'My husband and I will fly to Chicago Friday night. We shall register at the Drake Hotel and wait there until we hear from you.'

The Duke was looking at his hands, avoiding Ogilvie's eyes.

The house detective said flatly, 'You'll hear.'

'Is there anything you need?'

'I best have a note to the garage. Case I need it. Sayin' I kin take your car.'

'I'll write it now.' The Duchess crossed the room to a *secrétaire*. She wrote quickly and a moment later returned with a sheet of hotel stationery, folded 'This should do.'

Without looking at the paper, Ogilvie placed it in an inside pocket. His eyes remained fixed on the Duchess's face.

There was an awkward silence. She said uncertainly, 'It isn't what you wanted?'

The Duke of Croydon rose and walked stiffly away. Turning his back, he said testily. 'It's the money. He wants money.'

Ogilvie's fleshy features shaped themselves into a smirk. 'That's it, Duchess. Ten thousan' now, like we said. Fifteen more in Chicago, Sat'day.'

The Duchess's jewelled fingers went swiftly to her temples in a distracted gesture. 'I don't know how . . . I'd forgotten. There's been so much else.'

'Don' matter none. I woulda remembered.'

'It will have to be this afternoon. Our bank must arrange . . .'

'In cash,' the fat man said. 'Nothing bigger'n twenties, an' not new bills.'

She looked at him sharply. 'Why?

'Ain't traceable that way.'

'You don't trust us?'

He shook his head. 'In somethin' like this, it ain't smart to trust anybody.'

'Then why should we trust you?'

'I got another fifteen grand ridin'.' The odd falsetto voice held an undertone of impatience. 'An' remember – that's to be cash too, an' banks don't open Sat'day.'

'Suppose,' the Duchess said, 'that in Chicago we didn't pay you.'

There was no longer a smile, or even an imitation of one.

'I'm sure glad you brought that up,' Ogilvie said. 'Just so's we understand each other.'

'I think I understand, but tell me.'

'What'll happen in Chicago, Duchess is this. I'll stash the car some place, though you won't know where. I come to the hotel, collect the fifteen g's. When I done that, you get the keys n' I tell you where the car is.'

'You haven't answered my question.'

'I'm gettin' to it.' The little pig's eyes gleamed. 'Anythin' goes wrong – like f'rinstance you say there's no cash 'cos you forgot the banks wasn't open, I holler cops – right there in Chicago.'

'You'd have a good deal of explaining to do yourself. For example, how you came to drive the car north.'

'No mystery abut that. All I'd say is, you paid me a couple hundred – I'd have it on me – to bring the car up. You said it was too far. You and the Duke here wanted to fly. Weren't until I got to Chicago an' took a good look at the car, I figured things out. So . . .' The enormous shoulders shrugged.

'We have no intention,' the Duchess of Croydon assured him, 'of failing to keep our part of the bargain. But like you, I wanted to be sure we understood each other.'

Ogilvie nodded. 'I reckon we do.'

'Come back at five,' the Duchess said. 'The money will be ready.'

When Ogilvie had gone, the Duke of Croydon returned from his self-imposed isolation across the room. There was a tray of glasses on a sideboard, replenished since last night. Pouring a stiff Scotch, he splashed in soda and tossed the drink down.

The Duchess said acidly, 'You're beginning early again, I see.'

'It's a cleansing agent.' He poured himself a second drink, though this time sipping it more slowly. 'Being in the same room with that man makes me feel dirty.'

'Obviously he's less particular,' his wife said. 'Otherwise he might object to the company of a drunken child killer.'

The Duke's face was white. His hands trembled as he put the drink down. 'That's below the belt, old girl.'

She added, 'Who also ran away.'

'By god! – you shan't get away with that.' It was an angry shout. His hands clenched and for an instant it seemed as if he might strike out. 'You were the one! – the one who pleaded to drive on, and afterwards not go back. But for you, I would have! It would do no good, you said; what was done was done. Even yesterday I'd have gone to the police. You were against it! So now we have *him* . . . that leper who'll rob us of every last vestige . . .' The voice trailed off.

'Am I to assume,' the Duchess enquired, 'that you've completed your hysterical outburst?' There was no answer, and she continued, 'May I remind you that you've needed remarkably little persuasion to act precisely as you have. Had you wished or intended to do otherwise, no opinion of mine need have mattered in the least. As for leprosy, I doubt you'll contract it since you've carefully stood aside, leaving all that had to be done with that man, to be done by me.'

Her husband sighed. 'I should have known better than to argue. I'm sorry.'

'If argument's necessary to straighten your thinking,' she said indifferently, 'I've no objection.'

The Duke had retrieved his drink and turned the glass idly in his hand. 'It's a funny thing,' he said. 'I had the feeling for a while that all this, bad as it was, had brought us together.'

The words were so obviously an appeal that the Duchess hesitated. For her, too, the session with Ogilvie had been humiliating and exhausting. She had a longing, deep within, for a moment's tranquillity.

Yet, perversely, the effort of conciliation was beyond her. She answered, 'If it has, I'm not aware of it.' Then, more astringently: 'In any case, we've scarcely time for sentimentality.'

'Right!' As if his wife's words were a signal, the Duke downed his drink and poured another.

She observed scathingly, 'I'd be obliged if you'd at least retain consciousness. I assume I shall have to deal with the bank, but there may be papers they'll require you to sign.'

7

Two self-imposed tasks faced Warren Trent, and neither was palatable.

The first was to confront Tom Earlshore with Curtis O'Keefe's accusation of the night before. 'He's bleeding you white.' O'Keefe had declared of the elderly head barman. And: 'From the look of things it's been going on a long time.'

As promised, O'Keefe had documented his charge. Shortly after ten a.m., a report – with specific details of observations, dates and times – was delivered to Warren Trent by a young man who introduced himself as Sean Hall of the O'Keefe Hotels Corporation. The young man, who had come directly to Warren Trent's fifteenth-floor suite, seemed embarrassed. The hotel proprietor thanked him and settled down to read the seven-page report.

He began grimly, a mood which deepened as he read on. Not only Tom Earlshore's but other names of trusted employees appeared in the investigators' finding. It was distressingly apparent to Warren Trent that he was being cheated by the very men and women whom he had relied on most, including some who, like Tom Earlshore, he had considered personal friends. It was obvious, too, that throughout the hotel the depredation must be even more extensive than was documented here.

Folding the typewritten sheets carefully, he placed them in an inside pocket of his suit.

He knew that if he allowed himself, he could become enraged, and would expose and castigate, one by one, those who had betrayed his trust. There might even be a melancholy satisfaction in doing so.

But excessive anger was an emotion which nowadays left him drained. He would personally confront Tom Earlshore, he decided, but no-one else.

The report, however, Warren Trent reflected, had had one useful effect. It released him from an obligation.

Until last night a good deal of his thinking about the St Gregory had been conditioned by a loyalty which he assumed he owed to the hotel's employees. Now, by the revealed disloyalty to himself, he was freed from this restraint.

The effect was to open up a possibility which earlier he had shunned, for maintaining his own control of the hotel. Even now the prospect was still distasteful, which was why he decided to take the lesser of the two unpleasant steps and seek out Tom Earlshore first.

The Pontalba Lounge was on the hotel's main floor, accessible from the lobby through double swing doors ornamented in leather and bronze. Inside, three carpeted steps led down to an L-shaped area containing tables and booths with comfortable, upholstered seating.

Unlike most cocktail lounges, the Pontalba was brightly lighted. This meant that patrons could observe each other as well as the bar itself, which extended across the junction of the L. In front of the bar were a half-dozen padded stools for unaccompanied drinkers who could, if they chose, pivot their seats around to survey the field.

It was twenty-five minutes before noon when Warren Trent entered from the lobby. The lounge was quiet, with only a youth and a girl in one of the booths and two men with lapel convention badges talking in low voices at a table near by. The usual press of lunchtime drinkers would begin arriving in another fifteen minutes, after which the opportunity to speak quietly to anyone would be gone. But ten minutes, the hotel proprietor reasoned, should be sufficient for what he had come to do.

Observing him, a waiter hurried forward but was waved away. Tom Earlshore, Warren Trent observed, was behind the bar with his back to the room and intent upon a tabloid newspaper he had spread out on the cash register. Warren Trent walked stiffly across and occupied one of the bar stools. He could see now that what the elderly bartender was studying was *Racing Form*.

He said. 'Is that the way you've been using my money?'

Earlshore wheeled, his expression startled. It changed to mild surprise, then apparent pleasure as he realized the identity of his visitor.

'Why, Mr Trent, you sure give a fellow the jumps.'

Tom Earlshore deftly folded the *Racing Form*, stuffing it into a rear pants pocket. Beneath his domed bald head, with its Santa Claus fringe of white hair, the seamed leathery face creased into a smile. Warren Trent wondered why he had never before suspected it was an ingratiating smile.

'It's been a long time since we've seen you in here, Mr Trent. Too long.'

'You're not complaining, are you?'

Earlshore hesitated. 'Well, no.'

'I should have thought that being left alone has given you a lot of opportunities.'

A fleeting shadow of doubt crossed the head barman's face. He laughed as if to reassure himself. 'You always liked your little joke, Mr Trent. Oh, while you're in there's something I've got to show you. Been meaning to come in to your office, but never got around to it.' Earlshore opened a drawer beneath the bar and took out an envelope from which he extracted a coloured snapshot. 'This is one of Derek – that's my third grandchild. Healthy young tyke – like his mother, thanks to what you did for her a long time ago. Ethel – that's my daughter, you remember – often asks after you; always sends her best wishes, same as the rest of us at home.' He put the photograph on the bar.

Warren Trent picked it up and deliberately, without looking down, handed it back.

Tom Earlshore said uncomfortably, 'Is anything wrong, Mr Trent?' When there was no answer: 'Can I mix you something?'

About to refuse, he changed his mind. 'A Ramos gin fizz.'

'Yessir! Coming right up!' Tom Earlshore reached swiftly for the ingredients. It had always been a pleasure to watch him at work. Sometimes in the past, when Warren Trent entertained guests in his suite, he would have Tom come up to handle drinks, mostly because his bartending was a performance which matched the quality of his potions. He had an organized economy of movement and the swift dexterity of a juggler. He exercised his skill now, placing the drink before the hotel proprietor with a final flourish.

Warren Trent sipped and nodded.

Earlshore asked, 'It's all right?'

'Yes,' Warren Trent said. 'It's as good as any you've ever made.' His eyes met Earlshore's. 'I'm glad of that because it's the last drink you'll ever mix in my hotel.'

The uneasiness had changed to apprehension. Earlshore's tongue touched his lips nervously. 'You don't mean that, Mr Trent. You couldn't mean it.'

Ignoring the remark, the hotel proprietor pushed his glass away. 'Why did you do it, Tom? Of all people why did it have to be you?'

'I swear to God I don't know . . .'

'Don't con me, Tom. You've done that long enough.'

'I tell you, Mr Trent . . .'

'Stop lying!' The snapped command cut sharply through the quietness.

Within the lounge the peaceful hum of conversation stopped. Watching the alarm in the barman's shifting eyes, Warren Trent guessed that behind him heads were turning. He was conscious of a rising anger he had intended to control.

Earlshore swallowed. 'Please, Mr Trent. I've worked here thirty years. You've never talked to me like this.' His voice was barely audible.

From the inside jacket pocket where he had placed it earlier, Warren Trent produced the O'Keefe investigator's report. He turned two pages and folded back a third, covering a portion with his hand. He instructed, 'Read!'

Earlshore fumbled with glasses and put them on. His hands were trembling. He read a few lines then stopped. He looked up. There was no denial now. Only the instinctive fear of a cornered animal.

'You can't prove anything.'

Warren Trent slammed his hand upon the surface of the bar. Uncaring of his own raised voice, he let his rage erupt. 'If I choose to, I can. Make no mistake of that. You've cheated and you've stolen, and like all cheats and thieves you've left a trail behind you.'

In an agony of apprehension Tom Earlshore sweated. It was as if suddenly, with explosive violence, his world which he had believed secure had split apart. For more years than he could remember he had defrauded his employer – to a point where he had long ago become convinced of his own invulnerability. In his worst forebodings he had never believed this day could come. Now he wondered fearfully if the hotel owner had any idea how large the accumulated loot had been.

Warren Trent's forefinger stabbed the document between them on the bar. 'These people smelled out the corruption because they didn't make the mistake – my mistake – of trusting you, believing you a friend.' Momentarily emotion stopped him. He continued, 'But if I dug, I'd find evidence. There's plenty more besides what's here. Isn't there?'

Abjectly Tom Earlshore nodded.

'Well, you needn't worry; I don't intend to prosecute. If I did, I'd feel I was destroying something of myself.'

A flicker of relief crossed the elderly barman's face; he tried as quickly, to conceal it. He pleaded, 'I swear if you'll give me another chance it'll never happen again.'

'You mean that now you've been caught – after years of thievery and deceit – you'll kindly stop stealing.'

'It'll be hard for me, Mr Trent – to get another job at my time. I've a family . . .'

Warren Trent said quietly, 'Yes, Tom. I remember that.'

Earlshore had the grace to blush. He said awkwardly, 'The money I earned here – this job by itself was never enough. There were always bills; things for the children . . .'

'And the bookmakers, Tom. Let's not forget them. The bookmakers were always after you, weren't they? – wanting to be paid.' It was a random shot but Earlshore's silence showed it had found a target.

Warren Trent said brusquely, 'There's been enough said. Now get out of the hotel and don't ever come here again.'

More people were entering the Pontalba Lounge now, coming in through the doorway from the lobby. The hum of conversation had resumed, its volume rising. A young assistant bartender had arrived behind the bar and was dispensing drinks which waiters were collecting. He studiedly avoided looking at his employer and former superior.

Tom Earlshore blinked. Unbelievingly he protested, 'The lunchtime trade . . .'

'It's no concern of yours. You don't work here any more.'

Slowly, as the inevitability penetrated, the ex-head barman's expression changed. His earlier mask of deference slipped away. A twisted grin took its place as he declared, 'All right, I'll go. But you won't be far behind, Mr High-and-Mighty Trent, because you're getting thrown out too, and everybody around here knows it.'

'Just what do they know?'

Earlshore's eyes gleamed. 'They know you're a useless, washed-up old half-wit who couldn't manage the inside of a paper bag, never mind a hotel. It's the reason you'll lose this place for dead damned sure, and when you do I'm one of a good many who'll laugh their guts out.' He hesitated, breathing heavily, his mind weighing the consequences of caution and recklessness. The urge to retaliate won out. 'For more years'n I remember, you acted like you owned everybody in this place. Well, maybe you did pay a few more cents in wages than some others, and hand out bits of charity the way you did to me, making like Jesus Christ and Moses rolled in one. But, you didn't fool any of us. You paid the wages to keep out the unions, and the charity made *you* feel great, so people knew it was more for you than for them. That's when they laughed at you, and took care of themselves the way I did. Believe me, there's been plenty going on – stuff you'll never learn about.' Earlshore stopped – his face revealing a suspicion he had gone too far.

Behind them the lounge was filling rapidly. Alongside, two of the adjoining bar stools were already occupied. To a growing tempo of sound Warren Trent drummed his fingers thoughtfully upon the leather-topped bar. Strangely, the anger of a few moments ago had left him. In its place was a steely resolution – to hesitate no longer about the second step he had considered earlier.

He raised his eyes to the man who, for thirty years, he believed he had known, but never had. 'Tom, you'll not know the why or how, but the last thing you've done for me has been

414

a favour. Now go – before I change my mind about sending you to jail.'

Tom Earlshore turned and, looking neither to right nor left, walked out.

Passing through the lobby on his way to the Carondelet Street door, Warren Trent coldly avoided glances from employees who observed him. He was in no mood for pleasantries, having learned this morning that betrayal wore a smile and cordiality could be a sheathing for contempt. The remark that he had been laughed at for his attempts to treat employees well had cut deeply – the more, because it had a ring of truth. Well, he thought; wait a day or two. We'll see who's laughing then.

As he reached the busy, sunlit street outside, a uniformed doorman saw him and stepped forward deferentially. Warren Trent instructed, 'Get me a taxi.' He had intended to walk a block or two, but a twinge of sciatica, knifing sharply as he came down the hotel steps, made him change his mind.

The doorman blew a whistle and from the press of traffic a cab nosed to the kerb. Warren Trent climbed in stiffly, the man holding the door open, then touching his cap respectfully as he slammed it closed. The respect was another empty gesture, Warren Trent supposed. From now on, he knew, he would look suspiciously on a good many things he once accepted at face value.

The cab pulled away, and aware of the driver's scrutiny through the rear-view mirror, he instructed, 'Just drive me a few blocks. I want a telephone.'

The man said, 'Lotsa those in the hotel, boss.'

'Never mind that. Take me to a pay phone.' He felt disinclined to explain that the call he was about to make was far too secret to risk the use of any hotel line.

The driver shrugged. After two blocks he turned south on Canal Street, once more inspecting his fare through the mirror. "S a nice day. There's phones down by the harbour.'

Warren Trent nodded, glad of a moment or two's respite.

The traffic thinned as they crossed Tchoupitoulas Street. A minute later the cab stopped at the parking area in front of the Port Commissioner's building. A telephone booth was a few paces away.

He gave the driver a dollar, dismissing the change. Then, about to head for the booth, he changed his mind and crossed Eads Plaza to stand beside the river. The midday heat bore down upon him from above and seeped up comfortingly through his feet from the concrete walkway. The sun, the friend of old men's bones, he thought.

Across the half-mile width of Mississippi, Algiers on the far bank shimmered in the heat. The river was smelly today, though that was not unusual. Odour, sluggishness and mud were part of the Father of Waters' moods. Like life, he thought; the silk and sludge unchangingly about you.

A freighter slipped by, heading seaward, its siren wailing at an inbound barge train. The barge train changed course; the freighter moved on without slackening speed. Soon the ship would exchange the river's loneliness for the greater loneliness of the ocean. He wondered if those aboard were aware, or cared. Perhaps not. Or perhaps, like himself, they had come to learn there is no place in the world where a man is not alone.

He retraced his steps to the telephone and closed the booth door carefully. 'A credit card call,' he informed the operator. 'To Washington, DC.'

It took several minutes, which included questioning about the nature of his business, before he was connected with the individual he sought. At length the bluff, blunt voice of the nation's most powerful labour leader – and, some said, among the most corrupt – came on the line.

'Go ahead. Talk.'

'Good morning,' Warren Trent said. 'I was hoping you wouldn't be at lunch.'

'You get three minutes,' the voice said shortly. 'You've already wasted fifteen seconds.'

Warren Trent said hurriedly, 'Some time ago, when we met, you made a tentative proposal. Possibly you don't remember . . .'

'I always remember. Some people wish I didn't.'

'On that occasion I regret that I was somewhat curt.'

'I've a stop watch going here. That was half a minute.'

'I'm willing to make a deal.'

'I make deals. Others accept them.'

'If time's so all-fired important,' Warren Trent shot back, 'let's not waste it hair-splitting. For years you've been trying to get a foot in the hotel business. You also want to strengthen your union's position in New Orleans. I'm offering you a chance for both.'

'How high's the price?'

'Two million dollars – in a secured first mortgage. In return you get a union shop and write your own contract. I presume it would be reasonable since your own money would be involved.'

'Well,' the voice mused. 'Well, well, well.'

'Now,' Warren Trent demanded 'will you turn off that damned stop watch?'

A chuckle down the line. 'Never was one. Be surprised, though, how the idea gets people moving. When do you need the money?'

'The money by Friday. A decision before tomorrow midday.'

'Came to me last, eh? When everybody'd turned you down?'

There was no point in lying. He answered shortly, 'Yes.'

'You been losing money?'

'Not so much that the trend can't be changed. The O'Keefe people believe it can. They've made an offer to buy.'

'Might be smart to take it.'

'If I do, you'll never get this chance from them.'

There was a silence which Warren Trent did not disturb. He could sense the other man thinking, calculating. He had not the least doubt that his proposal was being considered seriously. For a decade the International Brotherhood of Journeymen had attempted to infiltrate the hotel industry. So far, however, unlike most of the Journeymen's intensive membership campaigns, they had failed dismally. The reason had been a unity – on this one issue – between hotel operators, who feared the Journeymen, and more honest unions who despised them. For the Journeymen, a contract with the St Gregory – until now a non-union hotel – could be a crack in this massive dam of organized resistance.

As to the money, a two-million-dollar investment – if the Journeymen chose to make it – would be a small bite from the union's massive treasury. Over the years they had spent a good deal more on the abortive hotel membership campaign.

Within the hotel industry, Warren Trent realized, he would be reviled and branded a traitor if the arrangement he was suggesting went through. And among his own employees he would be heatedly condemned, at least by those informed enough to know they had been betrayed.

It was the employees who stood to lose most. If a union contract was signed there would have to be a small wage increase, he supposed, as was usual in such circumstances, as a token gesture. But the increase was due anyway – in fact, overdue – and he had intended to award it himself if the hotel refinancing had been arranged some other way. The existing employees' pension plan would be abandoned in favour of the union's, but the only advantage would be to the Journeymen's treasury. Most significant, union dues – probably six to ten dollars monthly – would become compulsory. Thus, not only would any immediate wage increase be wiped out, but employees' take-home pay would be decreased.

Well, Warren Trent reflected, the opprobrium of his colleagues in the hotel industry would have to be endured. As to the rest, he stifled his conscience by reminding himself of Tom Earlshore and the others like him.

The blunt voice on the telephone broke in on his thoughts.

'I'll send two of my financial people. They'll fly down this afternoon. Overnight they'll take your books apart. I really mean apart, so don't figure on holding back anything we should know.' The unmistakable threat was a reminder that only the brave or foolhardy ever attempted to trifle with the Journeymen's Union.

The hotel proprietor said huffily, 'I've nothing to conceal. You'll have access to all the information there is.'

'If tomorrow morning my people report OK to me, you'll sign a three-year union shop contract.' It was a statement, not a question.

'Naturally, I'll be glad to sign. Of course, there'll have to be an employees' vote, though I'm certain I can guarantee the outcome.' Warren Trent had a moment's uneasiness, wondering if he really could. There would be opposition to an alliance with the Journeymen; that much was certain. A good many employees, though, would go along with his personal recommendation if he made it strong enough. The question was: Would they provide the needed majority?

The Journeymen's president said, 'There won't be a vote.'

'But surely the law . . .'

The telephone rasped angrily. 'Don't try teaching me labour law! I know more of it, and better'n you ever will.' There was a pause, then the growled explanation, 'This will be a Voluntary Recognition Agreement. Nothing in law says it has to be voted on. There will be no vote.'

It could, Warren Trent conceded, be done in just that way.

The procedure would be unethical, immoral, but unquestionably legal. His own signature on a union contract would, in the circumstances, be binding on every hotel employee, whether they liked it or not. Well, he thought grimly, so be it. It would make everything a great deal simpler, with the end result the same.

He asked, 'How will you handle the mortgage?' It was a ticklish area, he knew. In the past, Senate investigating committees had scathingly censured the Journeymen for investing heavily in companies with whom the union had labour contracts.

'You will give a note, payable to the Journeymen's Pension Fund, for two million dollars at eight per cent. The note to be secured by a first mortgage on the hotel. The mortgage will be held by the Southern Conference of Journeymen, in trust for the pension fund.'

The arrangement, Warren Trent realized, was diabolically clever. It contravened the spirit of every law affecting use of union funds, while remaining technically inside them.

'The note will be due in three years, forfeited if you fail to meet two successive interest payments.'

Warren Trent demurred, 'I'll agree to the rest, but I want five years.'

'You're getting three.'

It was a hard bargain, but three years would at least give him time to restore the hotel's competitive position.

He said reluctantly, 'Very well.'

There was a click as, at the other end, the line went dead.

Emerging from the telephone booth, despite a renewed onset of sciatic pain, Warren Trent was smiling.

8

After the angry scene in the lobby, culminating in the departure of Dr Nicholas, Peter McDermott wondered disconsolately what came next. On reflection he decided there was nothing to be gained by hasty intervention with officials of the Congress of American Dentistry. If the dentists' president, Dr Ingram, persisted in his threat to pull the entire convention out of the hotel, it was not likely to be accomplished before tomorrow morning at the earliest. That meant it would be both safe and prudent to wait an hour or two, until this afternoon, for tempers to cool. Then he would approach Dr Ingram, and others in the congress if necessary.

As for the presence of the newspaperman during the unhappy scene, obviously it was too late to change whatever damage had been done. For the hotel's sake, Peter hoped that whoever made decisions about the importance of news stories would see the incident as a minor item only.

Returning to his office on the main mezzanine, he occupied himself with routine business for the remainder of the morning. He resisted a temptation to seek out Christine, instinct telling him that here, too, a cooling-off period might help. Some time soon, though, he realized, he would have to make amends for his monumental gaffe of earlier today.

He decided to drop in on Christine shortly before noon but the intention was eclipsed by a telephone call from the duty assistant manager who informed Peter that a guest room, occupied by Mr Stanley Kilbrick of Marshalltown, Iowa, had been robbed. Though reported only a short time earlier, the robbery apparently occurred during the night. A long list of valuables and cash was alleged to be missing, and the guest, according to the assistant manager, seemed extremely upset. A house detective was already on the scene.

Peter placed a call for the chief house officer. He had no idea whether Ogilvie was in the hotel or not, the fat man's hours of duty being a mystery known only to himself. Shortly afterwards, however, a message advised that Ogilvie had taken over the enquiry and would report as soon as possible. Some twenty minutes later he arrived in Peter McDermott's office.

The chief house officer lowered his bulk carefully into the deep leather chair facing the desk.

Trying to subdue his instinctive dislike, Peter asked, 'How does it all look?'

'The guy who was robbed's a sucker. He got hooked. Here's what's missin'.' Ogilvie laid a handwritten list on Peter's desk. 'I kept one o' these myself.'

'Thanks. I'll get it to our insurers. How about the room – is there any sign of forced entry?'

The detective shook his head. 'Key job for sure. It all figures. Kilbrick admits he was on the loose in the Quarter last night. I guess he shoulda had his mother with him. Claims he lost his key. Won't change his story. More'n likely, though, he fell for a B-girl routine.'

'Doesn't he realize that if he levels with us we stand a better chance of recovering what was stolen?'

'I told him that. Didn't do no good. For one thing, right now he feels plenty stupid. For another, he's already figured the hotel's insurance is good for what he lost. Maybe a bit more; he says there was four hundred dollars cash in his wallet.'

'Do you believe him?'

'No.'

Well, Peter thought, the guest was due for an awakening. Hotel insurance covered the loss of goods up to a hundred dollars' value, but not cash in any amount. 'What's your feeling about the rest? Do you think it was a once-only job?'

'No, I don't,' Ogilvie said. 'I reckon we got ourselves a professional hotel thief, an' he's workin' inside the house.'

'What makes you think so?'

'Somethin' that happened this mornin' – complaint from room 641. Guess it ain't come up to you yet.'

'If it has,' Peter said, 'I don't recall it.'

'Early on – near dawn's far's I can make out – some character let himself in 641 with a key. The man in the room woke up. The other guy made like he was drunk and said he'd mistook it for 614. The man in the room went back to sleep, but when he woke up started wondering how the key of 614 would fit 641. That's when I heard about it.'

'The desk could have given out a wrong key.'

'Could have, but didn't. I checked. Night-room clerk swears neither of them keys went out. And 614's a married couple; they went to bed early last night an' stayed put.'

'Do we have a description of the man who entered 641?'

'Not enough so's it's any good. Just to be sure, I got the two men – 641 and 614 – together. It wasn't 614 who went in 641's room. Tried the keys too; neither one'll fit the other room.'

Peter said thoughtfully, 'It looks as if you're right about a professional thief. In which case we should start planning a campaign.'

'I done some things,' Ogilvie said. 'I already told the desk clerks for the next few days to ask names when they hand out keys. If they smell anything funny, they're to let the key go, but get a good look at whoever takes it, then tell one of my people fast. The word's bein' passed around to maids and bellhops to watch for prowlers, an' anything else that don't sit right. My men'll be doin' extra time, with patrols round every floor all night.'

Peter nodded approvingly. 'That sounds good. Have you considered moving into the hotel yourself for a day or two? I'll arrange a room if you wish.'

Fleetingly, Peter thought, a worried expression crossed the fat man's face. Then he shook his head. 'Won't need it.'

'But you'll be around – available?'

'Sure I'll be around.' The words were emphatic but, peculiarly, lacked conviction. As if aware of the deficiency, Ogilvie added, 'Even if I ain't right here all the time, my men know what to do.'

Still doubtfully, Peter asked, 'What's our arrangement with the police?'

'There'll be a couple of plain-clothes men over. I'll tell 'em about the other thing, an' I guess they'll do some checkin' to see who might be in town. If it's some joe with a record, we could get lucky'n pick him up.'

'In the meantime, of course, our friend – whoever he is – won't sit still.'

'That's for sure. *An'* if he's smart as I think, he'll figure by now we're on to him. So likely he'll try to work fast, then get clear.'

'Which is one more reason,' Peter pointed out, 'why we need you close at hand.'

Ogilvie protested, 'I reckon I thought of everythin'.'

'I believe you did, too. In fact I can't think of anything you've left out. What I'm concerned about is that when you're not here someone else may not be as thorough or as quick.'

Whatever else might be said of the chief house officer, Peter reasoned, he knew his business when he chose to do it But it was infuriating that their relationship made it necessary to plead about something as obvious as this.

'You don't hafta worry,' Ogilvie said. But Peter's instinct told him that for some reason the fat man was worried himself as he heaved his great body upwards and lumbered out.

After a moment or two Peter followed, stopping only to give instructions about notifying the hotel's insurers of the robbery, along with the inventory of stolen items which Ogilvie had supplied.

Peter walked the short distance to Christine's office. He was disappointed to discover that she was not there. He would come back, he decided, immediately after lunch.

He descended to the lobby and strolled to the main dining-room. As he entered he observed that today's luncheon business was brisk, reflecting the hotel's present high occupancy.

Peter nodded agreeably to Max, the head waiter, who hurried forward.

'Good day, Mr McDermott. A table by yourself?'

'No, I'll join the penal colony.' Peter seldom exercised his privilege, as assistant general manager, of occupying a table of his own in the dining-room. Most days he preferred to join other executive staff members at the large circular table reserved for their use near the kitchen door.

The St Gregory's comptroller, Royall Edwards, and Sam Jakubiec, the stocky, balding credit manager, were already at lunch as Peter joined them. Doc Vickery, the chief engineer, who had arrived a few minutes earlier, was studying a menu. Slipping into the chair which Max held out, Peter enquired, 'What looks good?'

'Try the watercress soup,' Jakubiec advised between sips of his own. 'It's not like any mother made; it's a damn sight better.'

Royall Edwards added in his precise accountant's voice, 'The special today is fried chicken. We have that coming.'

As the head waiter left, a young table waiter appeared swiftly beside them. Despite standing instructions to the contrary, the executives' self-styled penal colony invariably received the best service in the dining-room. It was hard – as Peter and others had discovered in the past – to persuade employees that the hotel's paying customers were more important than the executives who ran the hotel.

The chief engineer closed his menu, peering over his thick-rimmed spectacles which had slipped, as usual, to the tip of his nose. 'The same'll do for me, sonny.'

'I'll make it unanimous.' Peter handed back the menu which he had not opened.

The waiter hesitated. 'I'm not sure about the fried chicken, sir. You might prefer something else.'

'Well,' Jakubiec said, 'now's a fine time to tell us *that*.'

'I can change your order easily, Mr Jakubiec. Yours too, Mr Edwards.'

Peter asked, 'What's wrong with the fried chicken?'

'Maybe I shouldn't have said.' The waiter shifted uncomfortably. 'Fact is, we've been getting complaints. People don't seem to like it.' Momentarily he turned his head, eyes ranging the busy dining-room.

'In that case,' Peter told him, 'I'm curious to know why. So leave my order the way it is.' A shade reluctantly, the others nodded agreement.

When the waiter had gone, Jakubiec asked, 'What's this rumour I hear – that our dentists' convention may walk out?'

'Your hearing's good, Sam. This afternoon I'll know whether it remains a rumour.' Peter began his soup, which had appeared like magic, then described the lobby fracas of an hour earlier. The faces of the others grew serious as they listened.

Royall Edwards remarked, 'It has been my observation on disasters that they seldom occur singly. Judging by our financial results lately – which you gentlemen are aware of – this could merely be one more.'

'If it turns out that way,' the chief engineer observed, 'nae doubt the first thing ye'll do is lop some mair from engineering's budget.'

'Either that,' the comptroller rejoined, 'or eliminate it entirely.'

The chief grunted, unamused.

'Maybe we'll all be eliminated,' Sam Jakubiec said. 'If the O'Keefe crowd take over.' He looked enquiringly at Peter, but Royall Edwards gave a cautioning nod as their waiter returned. The group remained silent as the young man deftly served the comptroller and credit manager while, around them, the hum of the dining-room, a subdued clatter of plates and the passage of waiters through the kitchen door, continued.

When the waiter had gone, Jakubiec asked pointedly, 'Well, what *is* the news?'

Peter shook his head. 'Don't know a thing, Sam. Except that was darn good soup.'

'If you remember,' Royall Edwards said, 'we recommended it, and I will now offer you some well-founded advice – quit while you're ahead.' He had been sampling the fried chicken served to himself and Jakubiec a moment earlier. Now he put down his knife and fork. 'Another time I suggest we listen more respectfully to our waiter.'

Peter asked, 'Is it really that bad?'

'I suppose not,' the comptroller said. 'If you happen to be partial to rancid food.'

Dubiously, Jakubiec sampled his own serving as the others watched. At length he informed them: 'Put it this way. If I were paying for this meal – I wouldn't.'

Half-rising in his chair, Peter caught sight of the head waiter across the dining-room and beckoned him over. 'Max, is Chef Hèbrand on duty?'

'No, Mr McDermott, I understand he's ill. Sous-chef Lemieux is in charge.' The head waiter said anxiously, 'If it's about the fried chicken, I assure you everything is taken care of. We've stopped serving the dish and where there have been complaints the entire meal has been replaced.' His glance went to the table. 'We'll do the same thing here at once.'

'At the moment,' Peter said, 'I'm more concerned about finding out what happened. Would you ask Chef Lemieux if he'd care to join us?'

With the kitchen door so close, Peter thought, it was a temptation to stride through and enquire directly what had gone so amiss with the luncheon special. But to do so would be unwise.

In dealing with their senior chefs, hotel executives followed a protocol as prescribed and traditional as that of any royal household. Within the kitchen the chef de cuisine – or, in the chef's absence, the sous-chef – was undisputed king. For a hotel manager to enter the kitchen without invitation was unthinkable.

Chefs might be fired, and sometimes were. But unless and until that happened, their kingdoms were inviolate.

To invite a chef outside the kitchen – in this case to a table in the dining-room – was in order. In fact, it was close to a command since, in Warren Trent's absence, Peter McDermott was the hotel's senior officer. It would also have been permissible for Peter to stand in the kitchen doorway and wait to be asked in. But in the circumstances – with an obvious crisis in the kitchen – Peter knew that the first course was the more correct.

'If you ask me,' Sam Jakubiec observed as they waited, 'It's long past bedtime for old Chef Hèbrand.'

Royall Edwards asked, 'If he did retire, would anyone notice the difference?' It was a reference, as they all knew, to the chef de cuisine's frequent absences from duty, another of which had apparently occurred today.

'The end comes soon enough for all of us,' the chief engineer growled. 'It's natural nae one wants to hurry it himsel'.' It was no great secret that the comptroller's cool stringency grated at times on the normally good-natured chief.

'I haven't met our new sous-chef,' Jakubiec said. 'I guess he's been keeping his nose in the kitchen.'

Royall Edwards' eyes went down to his barely touched plate. 'If he has, it must be a remarkably insensitive organ.'

As the comptroller spoke, the kitchen door swung open once more. A busboy, about to pass through, stood back deferentially as Max the head waiter emerged. He preceded, by several measured paces, a tall slim figure in starched whites, with high chef's hat and, beneath it, a facial expression of abject misery.

'Gentlemen,' Peter announced to the executives' table, 'in case you haven't met, this is Chef André Lemieux.'

'Messieurs!' The young Frenchman halted, spreading his hands in a gesture of helplessness. 'To 'ave this happen . . . I am desolate.' His voice was choked.

Peter McDermott had encountered the new sous-chef several times since the latter's arrival at the St Gregory six weeks earlier. At each meeting Peter found himself liking the newcomer more.

André Lemieux's appointment had followed the abrupt departure of his predecessor. The former sous-chef, after months of frustrations and inward seething, had erupted in an angry outburst against his superior, the ageing M. Hèbrand. In the ordinary way nothing might have happened after the scene, since emotional outbursts among chefs and cooks occurred – as in any large kitchen – with predictable frequency. What marked the occasion as different was the late sous-chef's action in hurling a tureen of soup at the chef de cuisine. Fortunately the soup was Vichyssoise, or consequences might have been even more serious. In a memorable scene the chef de cuisine, shrouded in liquid white and dripping messily, escorted his late assistant to the street staff door and there – with surprising energy for an old man – had thrown him through it. A week later André Lemieux was hired.

His qualifications were excellent. He had trained in Paris, worked in London – at Prunier's and the Savoy – then briefly at New York's Le Pavillon before attaining the more senior post in New Orleans. But already in his short time at the St Gregory, Peter suspected, the young sous-chef had encountered the same frustration which demented his predecessor. This was the adamant refusal of M. Hèbrand to allow procedural changes in the kitchen, despite the chef de cuisine's own frequent absences from duty, leaving his sous-chef in charge. In many ways, Peter thought sympathetically, the situation paralleled his own relationship with Warren Trent.

Peter indicated a vacant seat at the executives' table. 'Won't you join us?'

'Thank you, monsieur.' The young Frenchman seated himself gravely as the head waiter held out a chair.

His arrival was followed by the table waiter who, without bothering with instructions, had amended all four luncheon orders to Veal Scallopini. He removed the two offending portions of chicken which a hovering busboy banished hastily to the kitchen. All four executives received the substitute meal, the sous-chef ordering merely a black coffee.

'That's more like it,' Sam Jakubiec said approvingly.

'Have you discovered,' Peter asked, 'what caused the trouble?'

The sous-chef glanced unhappily towards the kitchen. 'The troubles they have many causes. In this, the fault was frying fat badly tasting. But it is I who must blame myself – that the fat was not changed, as I believed. And I, André Lemieux, I allowed such food to leave the kitchen.' He shook his head unbelievingly.

'It's hard for one person to be everywhere,' the chief engineer said. 'All of us who ha' departments know that.'

Royall Edwards voiced the thought which had occurred first to Peter. 'Unfortunately we'll never know how many didn't complain about what they had, but won't come back again.'

André Lemieux nodded glumly. He put down his coffee cup. 'Messieurs, you will excuse me. Monsieur McDermott, when you 'ave finished, perhaps we could talk together, yes?'

Fifteen minutes later Peter entered the kitchen through the dining-room door. André Lemieux hurried forward to meet him.

'It is good of you to come, monsieur.'

Peter shook his head. 'I enjoy kitchens.' Looking around, he observed that the activity of the lunchtime was tapering off. A few meals were going out, past the two middle-aged women checkers seated primly, like suspicious schoolmistresses, at elevated billing registers. But more dishes were coming in from the dining-room as busboys and waiters cleared tables while the assemblages of guests thinned out. At the big dish-washing station at the rear of the kitchen, where chrome countertops and waste containers resembled a cafeteria in reverse, six rubber-aproned kitchen helpers worked concertedly, barely keeping pace with the flow of dishes arriving from the hotel's several restaurants and the convention floor above. As usual, Peter noticed, an extra helper was intercepting unused butter, scraping it into a large chrome container. Later, as happened in most commercial kitchens – though few admitted to it – the retrieved butter would be used for cooking.

'I wished to speak with you alone, Monsieur. With others present, you understand, there are things that are hard to say.'

Peter said thoughtfully, 'There's one point I'm not clear about. Did I understand that you gave instructions for the deep fryer fat to be changed, but that it was not?'

'That is true.'

'Just what happened?'

The young chef's face was troubled. 'This morning I give the order. My nose it informed me the fat is not good. But M. Hèbrand – without telling – he countermanded. Then M. Hèbrand he has gone 'ome and I am left, without knowing, 'olding the bad fat.'

Involuntarily Peter smiled. 'What was the reason for changing the order?'

'Fat is high cost – very 'igh; that I agree with M. Hèbrand. Lately we have changed it many times. Too many.'

'Have you tried to find the reason for that?'

André Lemieux raised his hands in a despairing gesture. 'I have proposed, each day, a chemical test – for free fatty acid. It could be done in a laboratory, even here. Then, intelligently, we would look for the cause the fat has failed. M. Hèbrand does not agree – with that or other things.'

'You believe there's a good deal wrong here?'

'Many things.' It was a short, almost sullen answer, and for a moment it appeared as if the discussion would end. Then abruptly, as if a dam had burst, words tumbled out. 'Monsieur McDermott, I tell you there is much wrong. This is not a kitchen to work with pride. It is a how-you-say . . . 'odge-podge – poor food, some old ways that are bad, some new ways that are bad, and all around much waste. I am a good chef; others would tell you. But it must be that a good chef is happy at what he does or he is no longer good. Yes, monsieur, I would make changes, many changes, better for the hotel, for M. Hèbrand, for others. But I am told – as if an infant – to change nothing.'

'It's possible,' Peter said, 'there may be large changes around here generally. Quite soon.'

André Lemieux drew himself up haughtily. 'If you refer to Monsieur O'Keefe, whatever changes he may make, I shall not be 'ere to see. I have no intent to be an instant cook for a chain 'otel.'

Peter asked curiously, 'If the St Gregory stayed independent, what kind of changes would you have in mind?'

They had strolled almost the length of the kitchen – an elongated rectangle extending the entire width of the hotel. At each side of the rectangle, like outlets from a control centre, doorways gave access to the several hotel restaurants, service elevators and food preparation rooms on the same floor and below. Skirting a double line of soup cauldrons, bubbling like monstrous crucibles, they approached the glass panelled office where, in theory, the two principal chefs – the chef de cuisine and the sous-chef – divided their responsibilities. Near by, Peter observed, was the big quadruple-unit deep fryer, cause of today's dissatisfaction. A kitchen helper was draining the entire assembly of fat; considering the quantity, it was easy to see why too frequent replacement would be costly. They stopped as André Lemieux considered Peter's question.

'What changes, you say, monsieur? Most important is the food. For some who prepare food, the façade, how a dish looks, it is more important than how it tastes. In this hotel we waste much money on the décor. The parsley, it is all around. But not enough in the sauce. The watercress it is on the plate, when more is needed in the soup. And those arrangements of colour in gelatine!' Young Lemieux threw both arms upwards in despair. Peter smiled sympathetically.

'As for the wines, monsieur! *Dieu merci*, the wines they are not my province.'

'Yes,' Peter said. He had been critical himself of the St Gregory's inadequately stocked wine bins.

'In a word, monsieur, all the horrors of a low-grade table d'hôte. Such colossal disrespect for food, such abandon of money for the appearance, it is to make one weep. Weep, monsieur!' He paused, shrugged and continued. 'With less throw-away we could have a cuisine that invites the taste and honours the palate. Now it is dull, extravagantly ordinary.'

Peter wondered if André Lemieux was being sufficiently realistic where the St Gregory was concerned. As if sensing this doubt, the sous-chef insisted, 'It is true that a hotel it has special problems. Here it is not a gourmet house. It cannot be. We must cook fast many meals, serve many people who are too much in an American hurry. But in these limitations there can be excellence of a kind. Of a kind one can live with. Yet, Monsieur Hèbrand, he tells me that my ideas they are too 'igh cost. It is not so, as I 'ave proved.'

'How have you proved?'

'Come, please.'

The young Frenchman led the way into the glass-panelled office. It was a small, crowded cubicle with two desks, file cabinets, and cupboards tightly packed around three walls. André Lemieux went to the smaller desk. Opening a drawer he took out a large Manila envelope and, from this, a folder. He handed it to Peter. 'You ask what changes. It is all here.'

Peter McDermott opened the folder curiously. There were many pages, each filled with a fine, precise handwriting. Several larger, folded sheets proved to be charts, hand-drawn and lettered in the same careful style. It was, he realized, a master catering plan for the entire hotel. On successive pages were estimated costs, menus, a plan of quality control and an outlined staff reorganization. Merely leafing through quickly, the entire concept and its author's grasp of detail were impressive.

Peter looked up, catching his companion's eyes upon him. 'If I may, I'd like to study this.'

'Take it. There is no haste.' The young sous-chef smiled dourly. 'I am told it is unlikely any of my 'orses will come 'ome.'

'The thing that surprises me is how you could develop something like this so quickly.'

André Lemieux shrugged. 'To perceive what is wrong, it does not take long.'

'Maybe we could apply the same idea in finding what went wrong with the deep fryer.'

There was a responsive gleam of humour, then chagrin. 'Touché! It is true – I had eyes for this, but not the 'ot fat under my nose.'

'No,' Peter objected. 'From what you've told me, you did detect the bad fat but it wasn't changed as you instructed.'

'I should have found the cause the fat went bad. There is always a cause. Greater troubles there may be if we do not find it soon.'

'What kind of trouble?'

'Today – through much good fortune – we have used the frying fat a little only. Tomorrow, monsieur, there are six hundred fryings for convention luncheons.'

Peter whistled softly.

'Just so.' They had walked together from the office to stand beside the deep fryer from which the last vestiges of the recently offending fat were being cleaned.

'The fat will be fresh tomorrow, of course. When was it changed previously?'

'Yesterday.'

'That recently!'

André Lemieux nodded. 'M. Hèbrand he was making no joke when he complained of the 'igh cost. But what is wrong it is a mystery.'

Peter said slowly, 'I'm trying to remember some bits of food chemistry. The smokepoint of new, good fat is . . .'

'Four 'undred and twenty-five degrees. It should never be heated more, or it will break down.'

'And as fat deteriorates its smoke point drops slowly.'

'Very slowly – if all is well.'

'Here you fry at . . .'

'Three 'undred and sixty degrees; the best temperature – for kitchens and the 'ousewives too.'

'So while the smoke-point remains about three hundred and sixty, the fat will do its job. Below that, it ceases to.'

'That is true, monsieur. And the fat it will give food a bad flavour, tasting rancid, as today.'

Facts, once memorized but rusty with disuse, stirred in Peter's brain. At Cornell there had been a course in food chemistry for Hotel Administration students. He remembered a lecture dimly . . . in Statler Hall on a darkening afternoon, the whiteness of frost on window panes. He had come in from the biting, wintry air outside. Inside was warmth and the drone of information . . . *fats and catalyzing agents*.

'There are certain substances,' Peter said reminiscently, 'which, in contact with fat, will act as catalysts and break it down quite quickly.'

'Yes, monsieur.' André Lemieux checked them off on his fingers. 'They are the moisture, the salt, the brass or the copper couplings in a fryer, too much 'eat, the oil of the olive. All these things I have checked. This is not the cause.'

A word had clicked in Peter's brain. It connected with what he had observed, subconsciously, in watching the deep fryer being cleaned a moment earlier.

'What metal are your fry baskets?'

'They are chrome.' The tone was puzzled. Chromium, as both men knew, was harmless to fat.

'I wonder,' Peter said, 'how good the plating job is. If it isn't good, what's under the chrome and is it – in any places – worn?'

Lemieux hesitated, his eyes widening slightly. Silently he lifted one of the baskets down and wiped it carefully with a cloth. Moving under a light, they inspected the metal surface.

The chrome was scratched from long and constant use. In small spots it had worn away entirely. Beneath scratches and worn spots was a gleam of yellow.

'It is brass!' The young Frenchman clapped a hand to his forehead. 'Without doubt it

426

'as caused the bad fat. I have been a great fool.'

'I don't see how you can blame yourself,' Peter pointed out. 'Obviously, long before you came, someone economized and bought cheap fry baskets. Unfortunately it's cost more in the end.'

'But I should have discovered this – as you have done, monsieur.' André Lemieux seemed close to tears. 'Instead, you, monsieur, you come to the kitchen – from your *paperasserie* – to tell *me* what is 'ay-wire here. It will be a laughing joke.'

'If it is,' Peter said, 'it will be because you talked about it yourself. No-one will hear from me.'

André Lemieux said slowly, 'Others they have said to me you are a good man, and intelligent. Now, myself, I know this is true.'

Peter touched the folder in his hand. 'I'll read your report and tell you what I think.'

'Thank you, monsieur. And I shall demand new fry baskets. Of stainless steel. Tonight they will be here if I have to 'ammer someone's 'ead.'

Peter smiled.

'Monsieur, there is something else that I am thinking.'

'Yes?'

The young sous-chef hesitated. 'You will think it, how you say, presumptuous. But you and I, Monsieur McDermott – with the hands free – we could make this a 'ot-shot hotel.'

Though he laughed impulsively, it was a statement which Peter McDermott thought about all the way to his office on the main mezzanine.

A second after knocking at the door of room 1410, Christine Francis wondered why she had come. Yesterday, of course, it had been perfectly natural for her to visit Albert Wells, after his brush with death the night before and her own involvement. But now Mr Wells was being adequately cared for and, with recovery, had reverted to his role as an ordinary guest among more than a thousand and a half others in the hotel. Therefore, Christine told herself, there was no real reason to make another personal call.

Yet there was something about the little elderly man which drew her to him. Was it, she wondered, because of his fatherliness and her perception, perhaps, of some of the traits of her own father to whose loss she had never quite adjusted, even after five long years. But no! The relationship with her father had been one of her reliance on him. With Albert Wells she found herself protective, just as yesterday she had wanted to shield him from the consequences of his own action in choosing the private nursing arrangement.

Or maybe, Christine reflected, she was, at this moment, just plain lonely, wanting to offset her disappointment in learning she would not meet Peter this evening, as they had both planned. And as to that – *had* it been disappointment, or some stronger emotion on discovering that he would be dining, instead, with Marsha Preyscott?

If she was honest with herself, Christine admitted, she had been angry this morning, though she hoped she had concealed it, covering up with mild annoyance and the slight acidity of comment she had been unable to resist. It would have been a big mistake, either to have shown a possessiveness about Peter or to have given little Miss Marshmallow the satisfaction of believing she had won a feminine victory even though, in fact, she had.

There was still no response to her knock. Remembering that the nurse should be on duty, Christine knocked again, more sharply. This time there was the sound of a chair moving and footsteps approaching from inside.

The door opened to reveal Albert Wells. He was fully dressed. He looked well and there was colour in his face, which brightened as he saw Christine. 'I was hoping you'd come, miss. If you hadn't I was going to look for you.'

She said, surprised, 'I thought . . .'

The little bird-like man chuckled. 'You thought they'd keep me pinned down; well, they didn't. I felt good, so I made your hotel doctor send for that specialist – the one from Illinois, Dr Uxbridge. He's got a lot of sense; said if people feel well, they mostly are. So we bundled the nurse home, and here I am.' He beamed. 'Well, miss, come on in.'

Christine's reaction was of relief that the considerable expense of the private nursing had ended. She suspected that a realization of its cost had had a good deal to do with Albert Wells' decision.

As she followed him into the room, he asked, 'Did you knock before?'

She admitted that she had.

'Had an idea I'd heard something. I guess my mind was on this.' He pointed to a table near the window. On it was a large and intricate jigsaw puzzle, of which about two thirds was completed. 'Or maybe,' he added, 'I thought it was Bailey.'

Christine asked curiously, 'Who's Bailey?'

The old man's eyes twinkled. 'If you stay a minute, you'll meet him. Leastways, either him or Barnum.'

She shook her head, not understanding. Walking towards the window, she leaned over the jigsaw puzzle, inspecting it. There were sufficient pieces in place to recognize the scene depicted as New Orleans – the city at dusk, viewed from high above, with the shining river winding through. She said, 'I used to do these once, a long time ago. My father helped me.'

Beside her, Albert Wells observed, 'There are some who'd say it isn't much of a pastime for a grown man. Mostly, though, I set out one of these when I want to think. Sometimes I discover the key piece, and the answer to what I'm thinking about, around the same time.'

'A key piece? I've never heard of that.'

'It's just an idea of mine, miss. I reckon there's always one – to this and most other problems you can name. Sometimes you think you've found it, and you haven't. When you do, though, all of a sudden you can see a whole lot clearer, including how other things fit in around.'

Abruptly there was a sharp, authoritative knock at the outer door. Albert Wells' lips formed the word, 'Bailey!'

She was surprised, when the door opened, to see a uniformed hotel valet. He had a collection of suits on hangers over one shoulder; in front he held a pressed blue serge suit which, from its old-fashioned cut, undoubtedly belonged to Albert Wells. With practised speed the valet hung the suit in a closet and returned to the door where the little man was waiting. The valet's left hand held the suits on his shoulder; his right came up automatically, palm outstretched.

'I already took care of you,' Albert Wells said. His eyes betrayed amusement. 'When the suit was picked up this morning.'

'Not me, you didn't, sir.' The valet shook his head decisively.

'No, but your friend. It's the same thing.'

The man said stoically, 'I wouldn't know anything about that.'

'You mean he holds out on you?'

The outstretched hand went down. 'I don't know what you're talking about.'

'Come on now!' Albert Wells was grinning broadly. 'You're Bailey. I tipped Barnum.'

The valet's eyes flickered to Christine. As he recognized her, a trace of doubt crossed his face. Then he grinned sheepishly. 'Yes, sir.' He went out, closing the door behind him.

'Now what in the world was all that about?'

The little man chuckled. 'You work in a hotel, and don't know the Barnum and Bailey dodge?'

Christine shook her head.

'It's a simple thing, miss. Hotel valets work in pairs, but the one who picks up a suit is never the one who delivers it back. They figure in that way, so mostly they get tipped twice. Afterwards they pool the tips and divvy up.'

'I can see how it works,' Christine said. 'But I've never thought about it.'

'Nor do most others. Which is why it costs them a double tip for the same service.' Albert Wells rubbed his sparrow-beak nose ruminatively. 'With me it's a kind of game – to see how many hotels there are where the same thing happens.'

She laughed. 'How did you find out?'

'A valet told me once – after I let him know I'd rumbled. He told me another thing. You know in hotels with dial telephones, from some phones you can dial rooms directly. So Barnum and Bailey – whichever one's which for that day – will dial the rooms he has deliveries for. If there's no answer, he waits and calls again later. If there is an answer – which means someone's in – he'll hang up without saying anything. Then a few minutes later he'll deliver your suit and pick up the second tip.'

'You don't like tipping, Mr Wells?'

'It isn't so much that, miss. Tipping's like dying; it's here to stay, so what good's worrying? Anyway I tipped Barnum well this morning – sort of paying in advance for the bit of fun I had with Bailey just now. What I don' like, though, is to be taken for a fool.'

'I shouldn't imagine that happens often.' Christine was beginning to suspect that Albert Wells needed a good deal less protection than she had at first supposed. She found him, though, as likeable as ever.

He acknowledged: 'That's as may be. There's one thing, though, I'll tell you. There's more of that kind of malarkey goes on in this hotel than most.'

'Why do you think so?'

'Because mostly I keep my eyes open, miss, and I talk to people. They tell me things they maybe wouldn't you.'

'What kind of things?'

'Well, for one, a good many figure they can get away with anything. It's because you don't have good management, I reckon. It could be good, but it isn't, and maybe that's why your Mr Trent is in trouble right now.'

'It's almost uncanny,' Christine said. 'Peter McDermott told me exactly the same thing – almost in those words.' Her eyes searched the little man's face. For all his lack of worldliness, he seemed to have a homespun instinct for getting at the truth.

Albert Wells nodded approvingly. 'Now there's a smart young man. We had a talk yesterday.'

ARTHUR HAILEY

The disclosure surprised her. 'Peter came here?'

'That's right.'

'I didn't know.' But it was the kind of thing, she reasoned, that Peter McDermott would do – an efficient follow-up of whatever it was he was concerned with personally. She had observed before his capacity for thinking largely, yet seldom omitting detail.

'Are you going to marry him, miss?'

The abrupt question startled her. She protested, 'Whatever gave you that idea?' But to her embarrassment she felt her face was flushing.

Albert Wells chuckled. There were moments, Christine thought, when he had the mien of a mischievous elf.

'I sort of guessed – by the way you said his name just now. Besides, I'd figured the two of you must see a lot of each other, both working where you do; and if that young man has the kind of sense I think, he'll find out he doesn't have to look much further.'

'Mr Wells, you're outrageous! You . . . you read people's minds, then you make them feel terrible.' But the warmth of her smile belied the reproof. 'And please stop calling me "miss". My name is Christine.'

He said quietly, 'That's a special name for me. It was my wife's, too.'

'Was?'

He nodded. 'She died, Christine. So long ago, sometimes I get to thinking the times we had together never really happened. Not the good ones or the hard, and there were plenty of both. But then, once in a while, it seems as if all that happened was only yesterday. It's then I get weary, mostly of being so much alone. We didn't have children.' He stopped, his eyes reflective, 'You never know how much you share with someone until the sharing ends. So you and your young man – grab on to every minute there is. Don't waste a lot of time; you never get it back.'

She laughed. 'I keep telling you he isn't my young man. At least, not yet.'

'If you handle things right, he can be.'

'Perhaps.' Her eyes went to the partially completed jigsaw puzzle. She said slowly, 'I wonder if there *is* a key piece to everything – the way you say. And when you've found it, if you really know, or only guess, and hope.' Then, almost before she knew it, she found herself confiding in the little man, relating the happenings of the past – the tragedy in Wisconsin, her aloneness, the move to New Orleans, the adjusting years, and now for the first time the possibility of a full and fruitful life. She revealed, too, the breakdown of this evening's arrangements and her disappointment at the cause.

At the end Albert Wells nodded sagely. 'Things work themselves out a lot of times. Other times, though, you need to push a bit so's to start people moving.'

She asked lightly, 'Any ideas?'

He shook his head. 'Being a woman, you'll know plenty more'n me. There's one thing, though. Because of what happened, I shouldn't wonder if that young man'll ask you out tomorrow.'

Christine smiled. 'He might.'

'Then get yourself another date before he does. He'll appreciate you more, having to wait an extra day.'

'I'd have to invent something.'

'No need for that, unless you want. I was going to ask anyway, miss . . . excuse me, Christine. I'd like us to have dinner, you and me – a kind of thank you for what you did

430

the other night. If you can bear an old man's company, I'd be glad to be a stand-in.'

She answered, 'I'd love to have dinner, but I promise you won't be any stand-in.'

'Good!' The little man beamed. 'We'd best make it here in the hotel, I reckon. I told that doctor I'd not go outdoors for a couple of days.'

Briefly, Christine hesitated. She wondered if Albert Wells knew just how high were the evening prices in the St Gregory's main dining-room. Though the nursing expense had ended, she had no wish to deplete still further whatever funds he had remaining. Suddenly she thought of a way to prevent that happening.

Putting the idea aside to be dealt with later, she assured him, 'The hotel will be fine. It's a special occasion, though. You'll have to give me time to go home and change into something really glamorous. Let's make it eight o'clock – tomorrow night.'

On the fourteenth floor, after leaving Albert Wells, Christine noticed that number four elevator was out of service. Maintenance work, she observed, was being done both on the landing door and the elevator cage.

She took another elevator to the main mezzanine.

10

The dentists' president, Dr Ingram, glared at the visitor to his suite on the seventh floor. 'McDermott, if you've come here with some idea of smoothing things over, I'll tell you right now you're wasting time. *Is* that why you came?'

'Yes,' Peter admitted. 'I'm afraid it is.'

The older man said grudgingly, 'At least you don't lie.'

'There's no reason I should. I'm an employee of the hotel, Dr Ingram. While I work here I've an obligation to do the best I can for it.'

'And what happened to Dr Nicholas was the best you could do?'

'No, sir. I happen to believe it's the worst thing we could have done. The fact that I had no authority to change a hotel standing order doesn't make it any better.'

The dentists' president snorted. 'If you really felt that way, you'd have the guts to quit and get a job some other place. Maybe where the pay is poorer but the ethics higher.'

Peter flushed, refraining from a quick retort. He reminded himself that this morning in the lobby he had admired the elderly dentist for his forthright stand. Nothing had changed since then.

'Well?' The alert, unyielding eyes were focused on his own.

'Suppose I did quit,' Peter said. 'Whoever took my job might be perfectly satisfied with the way things are. At least I'm not. I intend to do what I can to change the ground rules here.'

'Rules! Rationalization! Damned excuses!' The doctor's rubicund face grew redder. 'In my time I've heard them all! They make me sick! Disgusted, ashamed, and sick of the human race!'

Between them there was a silence.

'All right.' Dr Ingram's voice dropped, his immediate anger spent. 'I'll concede you're not as bigoted as some, McDermott. You've a problem yourself, and I guess my bawling you out doesn't solve anything. But don't you see, son? – half the time it's the damned reasonableness of people like you and me which adds up to the sort of treatment Jim Nicholas got today.'

'I do see, Doctor. Though I think the whole business isn't quite so simple as you'd make it.'

'Plenty of things aren't simple,' the older man growled. 'You heard what I told Nicholas. I said if he didn't get an apology and a room, I'd pull the entire convention out of this hotel.'

Peter said guardedly, 'In the ordinary way aren't there events at your convention – medical discussions, demonstrations, that kind of thing – that benefit a lot of people?'

'Naturally.'

'Then would it help? I mean, if you wiped out everything, what could anyone gain? Not Dr Nicholas . . .' He stopped, aware of renewed hostility as his words progressed.

Dr Ingram snapped, 'Don't give me a snow job, McDermott. And credit me with intelligence to have thought of that already.'

'I'm sorry.'

'There are always reasons for *not* doing something; plenty of times they're good reasons. That's why so few people ever take a stand for what they believe in, or say they do. In a couple of hours, when some of my well-meaning colleagues hear what I'm planning, I predict they'll offer the same kind of argument.' Breathing heavily, the older man paused. He faced Peter squarely, 'Let me ask *you* something. This morning you admitted you were ashamed of turning Jim Nicholas away. If you were me, here and now, what would you do?'

'Doctor, that's a hypothetical . . .'

'Never mind the horse-shit! I'm asking you a simple, direct question.'

Peter considered. As far as the hotel was concerned, he supposed whatever he said now would make little difference to the outcome. Why not answer honestly?

He said, 'I think I'd do exactly as you intended – cancel out.'

'Well!' Stepping back a pace, the dentists' president regarded him appraisingly. 'Beneath all that hotel crap lies an honest man.'

'Who may shortly be unemployed.'

'Hang on to your black suit, son! You can get a job helping out at funerals.' For the first time Dr Ingram chuckled. 'Despite everything, McDermott, I like you. Got any teeth need fixing?'

Peter shook his head. 'If you don't mind, I'd sooner know what your plans are. As soon as possible.' There would be immediate things to do, once the cancellation was confirmed. The loss to the hotel was going to be disastrous, as Royall Edwards had pointed out at lunch. But at least some of the preparations for tomorrow and the next day could be halted at once.

Dr Ingram said crisply, 'You've levelled with me; I'll do the same for you. I've called an emergency executive session for five this afternoon.' He glanced at his watch. 'That's in two and a half hours. Most of our senior officers will have arrived by then.'

'No doubt we'll be in touch.'

Dr Ingram nodded. His grimness had returned. 'Because we've relaxed a minute, McDermott, don't let it fool you. Nothing has changed since this morning, and I intend to kick you people where it hurts.'

432

Surprisingly, Warren Trent reacted almost with indifference to the news that the Congress of American Dentistry might abandon its convention and stage a protest withdrawal from the hotel.

Peter McDermott had gone immediately to the main mezzanine executive suite after leaving Dr Ingram. Christine – a trifle coolly, he thought – had told him the hotel proprietor was in.

Warren Trent, Peter sensed, was noticeably less tense than on other occasions recently. At ease behind the black marble-topped desk in the sumptuous managing director's office, he betrayed none of the irascibility so apparent the previous day. There were moments, while listening to Peter's report, that a slight smile played around his lips, though it seemed to have little to do with events on hand. It was rather, Peter thought, as if his employer were savouring some private pleasure known only to himself.

At the end, the hotel proprietor shook his head decisively, 'They won't go. They'll talk, but that will be the end of it.'

'Dr Ingram seems quite serious.'

'He may be, but others won't. You say there's a meeting this afternoon; I can tell you what will happen. They'll debate around for a while, then there'll be a committee formed to draft a resolution. Later – tomorrow probably – the committee will report back to the executive. They may accept the report, they may amend it; either way they'll talk some more. Later still – perhaps the next day – the resolution will be debated on the convention floor. I've seen it all before – the great democratic process. They'll still be talking when the convention's over.'

'I suppose you could be right,' Peter said. 'Though I'd say it's a pretty sick point of view.'

He had spoken recklessly and braced himself for an explosive response. It failed to occur. Instead Warren Trent growled, 'I'm practical, that's all. People will cluck about so-called principles till their tongues dry out. But they won't inconvenience themselves if they can avoid it.'

Peter said doggedly, 'It might still be simpler if we changed our policy. I can't believe that Dr Nicholas, if we'd admitted him, would have undermined the hotel.'

'*He* might not. But the riff-raff who'd follow would. Then we'd be in trouble.'

'It's been my understanding we're that way already.' Perversely, Peter was conscious of indulging in verbal brinkmanship. He speculated on just how far he could go. And why – today – he wondered, was his employer in such comparative good humour?

Warren Trent's patrician features creased sardonically. 'We may have been in trouble for a while. In a day or two, however, that will not be true.' Abruptly he asked: 'Is Curtis O'Keefe still in the hotel?'

'So far as I know. I'd have heard if he'd checked out.'

'Good!' the hovering smile remained. 'I've some information that may interest you. Tomorrow I shall tell O'Keefe and his entire hotel chain to go jump in Lake Pontchartrain.'

▌▌

From his vantage point at the bell captain's upright desk, Herbie Chandler watched covertly as the four young men entered the St Gregory from the street outside. It was a few minutes before four p.m.

Two of the group Herbie recognized as Lyle Dumaire and Stanley Dixon, the latter scowling as he led the way towards the elevators. A few seconds later they were out of sight.

On the telephone yesterday, Dixon had assured Herbie that the bell captain's part in the previous night's embroilment would not be divulged. But Dixon, Herbie realized uneasily, was merely one of four. How the others – and perhaps Dixon too – would react under questioning, possibly threats, was something else again.

As he had for the past twenty-four hours, the bell captain continued to brood with growing apprehension.

On the main mezzanine, Stanley Dixon again led the way as the four youths left the elevator. They stopped outside a panelled doorway with a softly illuminated sign, EXECUTIVE OFFICES, while Dixon morosely repeated an earlier warning. 'Remember! – leave the talking to me.'

Flora Yates showed them into Peter McDermott's office. Looking up coldly, he motioned them to chairs and enquired, 'Which of you is Dixon?'

'I am.'

'Dumaire?'

Less confidently, Lyle Dumaire nodded.

'I don't have the other two names.'

'That's too bad,' Dixon said. 'If we'd known, we could have all brought calling cards.'

The third youth interjected, 'I'm Gladwin. This is Joe Waloski.' Dixon shot him an irritated glance.

'All of you,' Peter stated, 'are undoubtedly aware that I've listened to Miss Marsha Preyscott's report of what occurred Monday night. If you wish, I'm willing to hear your version.'

Dixon spoke quickly, before anyone else could intervene. 'Listen! – coming here was your idea, not ours. There's nothing we want to say to you. So if you've got any talking, get on with it.'

Peter's face muscles tightened. With an effort he controlled his temper.

'Very well. I suggest we deal with the least important matter first.' He shuffled papers, then addressed Dixon. 'Suite 1126-7 was registered in your name. When you ran away' – he emphasized the last two words – 'I assumed you had overlooked checking out, so I did it for you. There is an unpaid bill of seventy-five dollars and some cents. There is a further bill, for damage to the suite, of one hunded and ten dollars.'

The one who had introduced himself as Gladwin whistled softly.

'We'll pay the seventy-five,' Dixon said. 'That's all.'

'If you dispute the other account, that's your privilege,' Peter informed him. 'But I'll tell you we don't intend to drop the matter. If necessary, we'll sue.'

434

'Listen, Stan . . .' It was the fourth youth, Joe Waloski. Dixon waved him to silence.

Beside him, Lyle Dumaire shifted uneasily. He said softly, 'Stan, whatever happens they can make a lot of fuss. If we have to, we can split it four ways.' He addressed Peter: 'If we do pay – the hundred and ten – we might have trouble getting it all at once. Could we pay a little at a time?'

'Certainly.' There was no reason, Peter decided, not to extend the normal amenities of the hotel. 'One or all of you can see our credit manager and he'll make the arrangements.' He glanced around the group. 'Are we to regard that part as settled?'

One by one the quartet nodded.

'That leaves the matter of the attempted rape – four so-called men against one girl.' Peter made no effort to keep the contempt from his voice.

Waloski and Gladwin flushed. Lyle Dumaire uncomfortably avoided Peter's eyes.

Only Dixon maintained his self-assurance. 'That's her story. Could be we'd tell a different one.'

'I already said I'm willing to listen to your version.'

'Nuts!'

'Then I've no alternative but to accept Miss Preyscott's.'

Dixon sniggered. 'Don't you wish you'd been there, buster? Or maybe you had your piece after.'

Waloski muttered, 'Take it easy, Stan.'

Peter gripped the arms of his chair tightly. He fought back an impulse to rush out from behind the desk and strike the smugly leering face in front of him. But he knew that if he did he would give Dixon an advantage which the youth was probably, and astutely, trying to gain. He would not, he told himself, be goaded into losing control.

'I assume,' he said icily, 'you are all aware that criminal charges can be laid.'

'If they were going to be,' Dixon countered, 'somebody'd have done it by now. So don't feed us that old line.'

'Would you be willing to repeat that statement to Mr Mark Preyscott? If he's brought back from Rome after being told what happened to his daughter.'

Lyle Dumaire looked up sharply, his expression alarmed. For the first time there was a flicker of disquiet in Dixon's eyes.

Gladwin enquired anxiously 'Is he being told?'

'Shut up!' Dixon enjoined. 'It's a trick. Don't fall for it!' But there was a shade less confidence than a moment earlier.

'You can judge for yourself whether it's a trick or not.' Peter opened a drawer of his desk and took out a folder which he opened. 'I have here a signed statement, made by me, of exactly what I was informed by Miss Preyscott, and what I observed myself on arrival at suite 1126-7, Monday night. It has not been attested to by Miss Preyscott, but it can be, along with any other details she may see fit to add. There is a further statement made and signed by Aloysius Royce, the hotel employee you assaulted, confirming my report and describing what happened immediately after his arrival.'

The idea of obtaining a statement from Royce had occurred to Peter late yesterday. In response to a telephone request the young Negro had delivered it early this morning. The neatly typed document was clear and carefully phrased, reflecting Royce's legal training. At the same time Aloysius Royce had cautioned Peter, 'I still say no Louisiana court will take a nigger boy's word in a white rape case.' Though irritated by Royce's continued abrasiveness, Peter assured him, 'I'm sure it will never come to court, but I need the ammunition.'

Stan Jakubiec had been helpful also. At Peter's request the credit manager had made discreet enquiries about the two youths, Stanley Dixon and Lyle Dumaire. He reported: 'Dumaire's father, as you know, is the bank president; Dixon's father is a car dealer – good business, big home. Both kids seemingly get a lot of freedom – parental indulgence, I guess – and a fair amount of money, though not unlimited. From all I hear, both fathers wouldn't exactly disapprove of their kids laying a girl or two; more likely to say "I did the same when I was young." But attempted rape is something else again, particularly involving the Preyscott girl. Mark Preyscott has as much influence as anyone in this town. He and the other two men move in the same circle, though Preyscott probably rates higher socially. Certainly if Mark Preyscott got after the older Dixon and Dumaire, accusing their sons of raping his daughter, or trying to, the roof would fall in and the Dixon and Dumaire kids know it.' Peter had thanked Jakubiec, storing the information for use if necessary.

'All that statement stuff,' Dixon said, 'ain't worth as much as you make out. You weren't there until after, so yours is hearsay.'

'That may be true,' Peter said. 'I'm not a lawyer, so I wouldn't know. But I wouldn't discount it entirely. Also, whether you won or lost you would not come out of court smelling sweetly, and I imagine your families might give some of you a hard time.' From a glance between Dixon and Dumaire he knew the last thrust had gone home.

'Christ!' Gladwin urged the others, 'we don't want to go in any court.'

Lyle Dumaire asked sullenly, 'What are you going to do?'

'Providing you co-operate, I intend to do nothing more, at least so far as you are concerned. On the other hand, if you continue making things difficult I intend later today, to cable Mr Preyscott in Rome and deliver these papers to his lawyers here.'

It was Dixon who asked disagreeably, 'What's "co-operate" supposed to mean?'

'It means that here and now you will each write a full account of what took place Monday night, including whatever occurred in the early part of the evening and who, if anyone, was involved from the hotel.'

'Like hell!' Dixon said. 'You can stuff that . . .'

Gladwin cut in impatiently. 'Can it, Stan!' He enquired of Peter, 'Suppose we do make statements. What will you do with them?'

'Much as I'd like to see them used otherwise, you have my word they will be seen by no-one, other than internally within the hotel.'

'How do we know we can trust you?'

'You don't. You'll have to take that chance.'

There was a silence in the room, the only sounds the creaking of a chair and the muffled clatter of a typewriter outside.

Abruptly Waloski said, 'I'll take a chance. Give me something to write on.'

'I guess I will too,' It was Gladwin.

Lyle Dumaire, unhappily, nodded his assent.

Dixon scowled, then shrugged. 'So everybody's on a writing kick. What's the difference?' He told Peter, 'I like a pen with a broad nib. It suits my style.'

A half hour later Peter McDermott reread, more carefully, the several pages he had skimmed over quickly before the youths filed out.

The four versions of Monday's evening events, though differing in a few details, corroborated each other in essential facts. All of them filled in earlier gaps in information, and Peter's instructions that hotel staff be identified had been specifically followed.

The bell captain, Herbie Chandler, was firmly and unerringly impaled.

12

The original, half-formed idea in the mind of Keycase Milne had taken shape.

Unquestionably, his instinct told him, the appearance of the Duchess of Croydon at the same time he himself was passing through the lobby, had been more than coincidence. It was an omen among omens, pointing a path for him to tread, at the end of which lay the Duchess's glistening jewels.

Admittedly, the fabled Croydon gem collection was not likely to be – in its entirety – in New Orleans. On her travels, as was known, the Duchess carried only portions of her Aladdin's treasure trove. Even so, the potential loot was likely to be large and, though some jewels might be safeguarded in the hotel's vault, it was a certainty there would be others immediately at hand.

The key to the situation, as always, lay in a key to the Croydons' suite. Systematically, Keycase Milne set out to obtain it.

He rode elevators several times, choosing different cars so as not to make himself conspicuous. Eventually, finding himself alone with an elevator operator, he asked the seemingly casual question, 'Is it true the Duke and Duchess of Croydon are staying in the hotel?'

'That's right, sir.'

'I suppose the hotel keeps special rooms for visitors like that.' Keycase smiled genially. 'Not like us ordinary people.'

'Well, sir, the Duke and Duchess have the Presidential Suite.'

'Oh, really! What floor's that?'

'Ninth.'

Mentally, Keycase ticked off 'point one' and left the elevator at his own floor, the eighth.

Point two was to establish the precise room number. It proved simple. Up one flight by the service stairs, then a short walk! Double padded-leather doors with gold fleur-de-lis proclaimed the Presidential Suite. Keycase noted the number: 973-7.

Down to the lobby once more, this time for a stroll – apparently casual – past the reception desk. A quick, keen-eyed inspection showed that 973-7, like more plebian rooms, had a conventional mail slot. A room key was in the slot.

It would be a mistake to ask for the key at once. Keycase sat down to watch and wait. The precaution proved wise.

After a few minutes' observation it became obvious that the hotel had been alerted. Compared with the normal easy-going method of handing out room keys, today the desk clerks were being cautious. As guests requested keys, the clerks asked names, then checked the answers against a registration list. Undoubtedly, Keycase reasoned, his coup of early this morning had been reported, with security tightened as a result.

A cold stab of fear was a reminder of an equally predictable effect: the New Orleans police would by now be alerted and, within hours, might be seeking Keycase Milne by name. True, if the morning paper was to be believed, the hit-and-run fatalities of two nights earlier still commanded the bulk of police attention. But it was a certainty that someone at police headquarters would still find time to teletype the FBI. Once again, remembering the awful price of one more conviction, Keycase was tempted to play safe, check out and run. Irresolution held him. Then, forcing doubts aside, he comforted himself with the memory of this morning's omen in his favour.

After a time the waiting proved worth while. One desk clerk, a young man with light wavy hair, appeared unsure of himself and at moments nervous. Keycase judged him to be new to his job.

The presence of the young man provided a possible opportunity, though to utilize it would be a gamble, Keycase reasoned, and a long shot at that. But perhaps the opportunity – like other events today – was an omen in itself. He resolved to take it, employing a technique he had used before.

Preparations would occupy at least an hour. Since it was now mid-afternoon, they must be completed before the young man went off duty. Hurriedly, Keycase left the hotel. His destination was the Maison Blanche department store on Canal Street.

Using his money frugally, Keycase shopped for inexpensive but bulky items – mainly children's toys – waiting while each was enclosed in a distinctive Maison Blanche box or wrapping paper. At the end, carrying an armful of packages he could scarcely hold, he left the store. He made one additional stop – at a florist's, topping off his purchases with a large azalea plant in bloom, after which he returned to the hotel.

At the Carondelet Street entrance a uniformed doorman hurried to hold the doorway wide. The man smiled at Keycase, largely hidden behind his burden of parcels and the flowering Azalea.

Inside the hotel, Keycase loitered, ostensibly inspecting a series of showcases, but actually waiting for two things to happen. One was a convergence of several people on the reception and mail desk; the second, the reappearance of the young man he had observed earlier. Both events occurred almost at once.

Tensely, his heart pounding, Keycase approached the Reception area.

He was third in line in front of the young man with light wavy hair. A moment later there was only a middle-aged woman immediately ahead, who secured a room key after identifying herself. Then, about to leave, the woman remembered a query concerning re-addressed mail. Her questioning seemed interminable, the young desk clerk's answers hesitant. Impatiently, Keycase was aware that around him the knot of people at the desk was thinning. Already one of the other room clerks was free, and he glanced across. Keycase avoided his eye, praying for the colloquy ahead to finish.

At length the woman moved away. The young clerk turned to Keycase, then – as the doorman had done – smiled involuntarily at the awkward profusion of packages topped by the blooms.

Speaking acidly, Keycase used a line already rehearsed. 'I'm sure it's very funny. But if it isn't too much trouble I'd like the key of 973.'

The young man reddened, his smile dissolving instantly. 'Certainly, sir.' Flustered, as Keycase intended, he wheeled and selected the key from its place in the rack.

At the mention of the room number, Keycase had seen one of the other clerks glance sideways. It was a crucial moment. Obviously the number of the Presidential Suite would be well known, and intervention by a more experienced clerk would mean exposure. Keycase sweated.

'Your name, sir?'

Keycase snapped, 'What is this – an interrogation?' Simultaneously he allowed two parcels to drop. One stayed on the counter, the other rebounded to the floor behind the desk. Increasingly flustered, the young clerk retrieved both. His more senior colleague, with an indulgent smile, looked away.

'I beg your pardon, sir.'

'Never mind.' Accepting the parcels and rearranging the others, Keycase held out his hand for the key.

For a hair's breadth of time the young man hesitated. Then the image Keycase had hoped to create won out: a tired, frustrated shopper; absurdly burdened; the epitome of respectability as attested by the familiar Maison Blanche wrappings; an irritated guest, not to be trifled with further . . .

Deferentially the desk clerk handed over the key of 973.

As Keycase walked unhurriedly towards the elevators, activity at the reception desk resumed. A fleeting backward glance showed him the desk clerks were once more busy. Good! It lessened the likelihood of discussion and possible second thoughts about what had just occurred. All the same, he must return the key as quickly as possible. Its absence might be noticed, leading to questions and suspicion – especially dangerous since the hotel was already partially alert.

He instructed the elevator operator, 'Nine' – a precaution in case anyone had heard him demand a ninth-floor key. Stepping out as the elevator stopped, he loitered, adjusting parcels until the doors closed behind him, then hurried to the service stairs. It was a single flight down to his own floor. On a landing, halfway, was a garbage can. Opening it, he stuffed in the plant which had served its purpose. A few seconds later he was in his own room, 830.

He shoved the parcels hurriedly into a closet. Tomorrow he would return them to the store and claim refunds. The cost was not important compared with the price he hoped to win, but they would be awkward to take along, and to abandon them would leave a conspicuous trail.

Still moving swiftly, he unzipped a suitcase, taking out a small leather-covered box. It contained a number of white cards, some finely sharpened pencils, calipers and a micrometer. Selecting one of the cards, Keycase laid the Presidential Suite key upon it. Then, holding the key still, he painstakingly drew an outline around the edge. Next, with micrometer and calipers, he measured the thickness of the key and the exact dimensions of each horizontal groove and vertical cut, jotting the results beside the outline on the card. A manufacturer's letter-number code was stamped on the metal. He copied it; the code might help in selecting a suitable blank. Finally, holding the key to the light, he drew a careful freehand sketch of its end view.

He now had an expertly detailed specification which a skilled locksmith could follow unerringly. The procedure, Keycase often reflected amusedly, was a long way from the wax impression gambit beloved by detective fiction writers, but a good deal more effective.

He put the leather-covered box away, the card in his pocket. Moments later he was back in the main lobby.

Precisely as before he waited until the desk clerks were busy. Then, walking casually across, he laid the 973 key unnoticed upon the counter.

Again he watched. At the next lull a room clerk observed the key. Disinterestedly, he lifted it, glanced at the number and returned it to its slot.

Keycase felt a warming glow of professional achievement. Through a combination of inventiveness and skill, and overcoming the hotel's precautions, his first objective had been won.

13

Selecting a dark blue Schiaparelli tie from several in his clothes closet, Peter McDermott knotted it pensively. He was in his small downtown apartment, not far from the hotel, which he had left an hour earlier. In another twenty minutes he was due at Marsha Preyscott's dinner party. He wondered who the other guests would be. Presumably, as well as Marsha's friends – who, he hoped, would be of a different calibre from the Dixon-Dumaire quartet – there would be one or two older people, accounting for his own inclusion.

Now that the time had come, he found himself resenting the commitment, wishing instead that he had remained free to meet Christine. He was tempted to telephone Christine before leaving, then decided it would be more discreet to wait until tomorrow.

He had an unsettled sense tonight, of being suspended in time between the past and future. So much he was concerned with seemed indefinite, with decisions delayed until outcomes should be known. There was the question of the St Gregory itself. Would Curtis O'Keefe take over? If so, the other affairs seemed minor by comparison – even the dentists' convention, whose officers were still debating whether or not to march protestingly from the St Gregory. An hour ago the executive session called by the fiery dentists' president, Dr Ingram, was still in progress and looked like continuing, according to the head waiter of room service, whose staff had made several trips into the meeting to replenish ice and mixes. Although Peter had confined his behind-scenes enquiry as to whether the meeting showed signs of breaking up, the head waiter informed him there appeared to be a good deal of heated discussion. Before leaving the hotel Peter left word with the duty assistant manager that if any decision from the dentists became known, he was to be telephoned immediately. So far there had been no word. He wondered now whether Dr Ingram's forthright viewpoint would prevail or if Warren Trent's more cynical prediction about nothing happening would prove true.

The same uncertainty had caused Peter to defer – at least until tomorrow – any action concerning Herbie Chandler. What ought to be done, he knew, was immediate dismissal of the sleazy bell captain, which would be like purging the hotel of an unclean spirit. Specifically, of course, Chandler would not be dismissed for running a call girl system – which someone else would organize if Chandler didn't – but for allowing greed to overcome good sense.

With Chandler gone, a good many other abuses could be curbed, though whether Warren Trent would agree to such summary action was an open question. However, remembering the accumulated evidence and Warren Trent's concern with the hotel's good name, Peter had an idea he might.

Either way, Peter reminded himself, he must ensure that the Dixon-Dumaire group statements were safeguarded and used within the hotel only. He would keep his promise on that point. Also he had been bluffing this afternoon in threatening to inform Mark Preyscott about the attempted rape of his daughter. Then, as now, Peter remembered Marsha's entreaty: *My father's in Rome. Don't tell him, please – ever!*

The thought of Marsha was a reminder to hurry. A few minutes later he left the apartment and hailed a cruising cab.

Peter asked, 'This is the house?'

'Sure is.' The cab driver looked speculatively at his passenger. 'Leastways if you got the address right.'

'It was right.' Peter's eyes followed the driver's to the immense white-fronted mansion. The façade alone was breathtaking. Behind a yew hedge and towering magnolia trees, graceful fluted columns rose from a terrace to a high railed gallery. Above the gallery the columns soared on to a crowning, classically proportioned pediment. At either end of the main building two wings repeated the details in miniature. The entire façade was in superb repair, its wood surfaces preserved and paintwork fresh. Around the house the scent of sweet olive blossoms hung in the early evening air.

Paying off the cab, Peter approached an iron grilled gate which opened smoothly. A curving pathway of old red brick led between trees and lawns. Though barely dusk, two elevated flare pots had been lighted at either side of the pathway as it neared the house. He had reached the terrace steps when a latch clicked solidly and the double doors to the house swung open. The wide doorway framed Marsha. She waited until he reached the head of the steps, then walked towards him.

She was in white – a slim, sheath gown, her raven black hair startling by contrast. He was aware, more than ever, of the provoking woman-child quality.

Marsha said gaily, 'Welcome!'

'Thank you.' He gestured about him. 'At the moment I'm a little overwhelmed.'

'So's everybody.' She entwined her arm in his. 'I'll give you the Preyscott official tour before it's dark.'

Returning down the terrace steps, they crossed the lawn, soft underfoot. Marsha remained close. Through his coat sleeve he could feel the warm firmness of her flesh. Her finger-tips touched his wrist lightly. There was an added gentle fragrance to the scent of olive blossoms.

'There!' Abruptly Marsha wheeled. 'This is where you see it all best. It's from here they always take the pictures.'

From this side of the lawn the view was even more impressive.

'A fun-lovin' French nobleman built the house,' Marsha said. 'In the 1840s. He liked Greek revival architecture, happy laughing slaves, and also having his mistress handy, which was the reason for an extra wing. My father added the other wing. He prefers things balanced – like accounts and houses.'

'This is the new guide style – philosophy with fact?'

'Oh, I'm brimming with both. You want facts? – look at the roof.' Their eyes went up together. 'You'll see it overhangs the upper gallery. The Louisiana-Greek style – most old big houses here were built that way – makes sense because in this climate it gave shade and air. Lots of times the gallery was the most lived-in place. It became a family centre, a place of talk and sharing.'

He quoted, 'Households and families, a sharing of the good life, in a form at once complete and self-sufficient.'

'Who said that?'

'Aristotle.'

Marsha nodded. 'He'd dig galleries.' She stopped, considering. 'My father did a lot of restoration. The house is better now, but not our use of it.'

'You must love all this very much.'

'I hate it,' Marsha said. 'I've hated this place as long as I remember.'

He looked at her enquiringly.

'Oh, I wouldn't if I came to see it – as a visitor, lined up with others who'd paid fifty cents to be shown around, the way we open the house for Spring Fiesta. I'd admire it because I love old things. But not to live with always, especially alone and after dark.'

He reminded her, 'It's getting dark now.'

'I know,' she said. 'But you're here. That makes it different.'

They had begun to return across the lawn. For the first time he was conscious of the quiet.

'Won't your other guests be missing you?'

She glanced sideways, mischievously. 'What other guests?'

'You told me . . .'

'I said I was giving a dinner party; so I am. For you. If it's chaperonage you're worried about, Anna's here.' They had passed into the house. It was shadowy and cool, with ceilings high above. In the background a small elderly woman in black silk nodded, smiling. 'I told Anna about you,' Marsha said, 'and she approves. My father trusts her absolutely, so everything's all right. Then there's Ben.'

A Negro manservant followed them, soft-footed, to a small book-lined study. From a sideboard he brought a tray with decanter and sherry glasses. Marsha shook her head. Peter accepted a sherry and sipped it thoughtfully. From a settee Marsha motioned him to sit beside her.

He asked, 'You spend a lot of time alone here?'

'My father comes home between trips. It's just that the trips get longer and the time between shorter. What I'd prefer to live in is an ugly modern bungalow. Just so long as it was alive.'

'I wonder if you really would.'

'I know I would,' Marsha said firmly. 'If I shared it with someone I really cared about. Or maybe a hotel would be as good. Don't hotel managers get an apartment to live in – at the top of their hotel?'

Startled, he looked up to find her smiling.

A moment later the manservant announced quietly that dinner was served.

In an adjoining room a small circular table was set for two. Candlelight gleamed on the dinner setting and panelled walls. Above a black marble mantel the portrait of a stern-faced patriarch gazed down, giving Peter an impression of being studied critically.

'Don't let great-grandfather bother you,' Marsha said when they were seated. 'It's me he's frowning at. You see, he once wrote in his diary that he wanted to found a dynasty and I'm his last forlorn hope.'

They chatted through dinner – with lessening restraint – as the manservant served them unobtrusively. The fare was exquisite – the main course a superbly seasoned Jambalaya, followed by a deliciously flavoured Crème Brûlée. In a situation he had approached with misgiving, Peter discovered he was enjoying himself genuinely. Marsha seemed more vivacious and charming as the minutes passed, and he himself more relaxed in her company. Which was less than surprising, he reminded himself, since the gap in their ages was by no means great. And in the glow of candlelight, the old room shadowed around them, he was reminded how exceedingly beautiful she was.

He wondered if long ago the French nobleman who built the great house, and his mistress, had dined as intimately here. Or was the thought the product of a spell which the surroundings and the occasion had cast on him?

At the end of dinner Marsha said, 'We'll have coffee on the gallery.'

He held out her chair and she got up quickly, impulsively taking his arm as she had earlier. Amused, he allowed himself to be guided to a hallway and up a broad curving staircase. At the top, a wide corridor, its frescoed walls dimly lighted, led to the open gallery they had viewed from the now darkened garden below.

Demitasse cups and a silver coffee service were on a wicker table. A flickering gas lantern burned above. They took their coffee to a cushioned porch glider which swung lazily as they sat down. The night-time air was comfortably cool, with the faintest stirring of a breeze. From the garden, the hum of insects sounded sonorously; the muted sounds of traffic came over from St Charles Avenue, two blocks distant. He was conscious of Marsha, quite still beside him.

Peter chided, 'You've suddenly become quiet.'

'I know. I was wondering how to say something.'

'You might try directly. It often works.'

'All right.' There was a breathlessness to her voice. 'I've decided I want to marry you.'

For what seemed like long minutes but were, he suspected, seconds only, Peter remained unmoving, with even the gentle motion of the glider stopping. At last, with careful precision, he put down his coffee cup.

Marsha coughed, then changed the cough to a nervous laugh. 'If you want to run, the stairs are that way.'

'No,' he said. 'If I did that I'd never know why you said what you did just now.'

'I'm not sure myself.' She was looking directly ahead, out into the night, her face turned half way. He sensed that she was trembling. 'Except I suddenly wanted to say it. And quite sure I should.'

It was important, he knew, that whatever he next said to this impulsive girl should be with gentleness and consideration. He was also uncomfortably aware of a nervous constriction in his throat. Irrationally, he remembered something Christine had said this morning: *Little Miss Preyscott bears as much resemblance to a child as a kitten to a tiger. But it would be fun I should think – for a man – to be eaten up.* The comment was unfair of course, even harsh. But it was true that Marsha was not a child, nor should she be treated like one,

'Marsha, you scarcely know me, or I you.'

'Do you believe in instinct?'

'To a point, yes.'

'I had an instinct about you. From the very first moment.' Initially her voice had faltered; now she steadied it. 'Most times my instincts have been right.'

He reminded her gently, 'About Stanley Dixon, Lyle Dumaire?'

'I had the right instincts. I didn't follow them, that's all. This time I have.'

'But instinct may still be wrong.'

'You can always be wrong, even when you wait a long time.' Marsha turned, facing him directly. As her eyes searched his own, he was aware of a strength of character he had not observed before. 'My father and mother knew each other fifteen years before they married. My mother once told me that everyone they knew said it would be the perfect match. As it turned out, it was the worst. I know; I was in the middle.'

He was silent, not knowing what to say.

'It taught me some things. So did something else. You saw Anna tonight?'

'Yes.'

'When she was seventeen she was forced to marry a man she'd met just once before. It was a kind of family contract; in those days they did that kind of thing.'

Watching Marsha's face, he said, 'Go on.'

'The day before the wedding, Anna wept all night. But she was married just the same, and stayed married for forty-six years. Her husband died last year; they lived with us here. He was the kindest, sweetest man I've ever known. If ever there was a perfect marriage it belonged to them.'

He hesitated, not wishing to score a debater's point, but objected, 'Anna didn't follow her instinct. If she had, she'd not have married.'

'I know. I'm simply saying there isn't any guaranteed way, and instinct can be as good a guide as any.' There was a pause, then Marsha said, 'I know I could make you love me, in time.'

Absurdly, unexpectedly, he felt a sense of excitement. The idea was preposterous, of course; a romantic product of a girlish imagination. He, who had suffered from his own romantic notions in the past, was qualified to know. Yet was he? Was every situation an aftermath of what had gone before? Was Marsha's proposal so fantastic really? He had a sudden, irrational conviction that what she said might well be true.

He wondered what the reaction of the absent Mark Preyscott would be.

'If you're thinking about my father . . .'

Startled, he said, 'How did you know?'

'Because I'm beginning to know *you*.'

He breathed deeply, with a sense of inhaling rarefied air. 'What about your father?'

'I expect he'd be worried to begin with, and he'd probably fly home in a hurry. I wouldn't mind that.' Marsha smiled. 'But he always listens to reason and I know I could convince him. Besides, he'd like you. I know the kind of people he admires most, and you're one.'

'Well,' he said, not knowing whether to be amused or serious, 'at least that's a relief.'

'There's something else. It isn't important to me, but it would be to him. You see, I know – and my father would too – that some day you'll be a big success with hotels, and maybe own your own. Not that *I* care about that. It's you I want.' She finished breathlessly.

'Marsha,' Peter said gently, 'I don't . . . I simply don't know what to say.'

There was a pause in which he could sense Marsha's confidence leave her. It was as if, earlier, she had bolstered her self-assurance with a reserve of will, but now the reserve was gone and boldness with it. In a small, uncertain voice she said, 'You think I've been silly. You'd better say so and get it over.'

He assured her, 'I don't believe you've been silly. If more people, including me, were honest like you . . .'

'You mean you don't mind?'

'Far from minding, I'm moved and overwhelmed.'

'Then don't say any more!' Marsha leaped to her feet, her hands held out towards him. He took them and stood facing her, their fingers interlaced. She had a way, he realized, of bouncing back after uncertainty, even if her doubts were only partially resolved. She urged him, 'Just go away and think! Think, think, think! Especially about me.'

He said – and meant it – 'It will be difficult not to.'

She put up her face to be kissed and he leaned towards her. He intended to brush her cheek, but she put up her lips to his and, as they touched, her arms wound tightly around him. Dimly in his mind an alarm bell jangled. Her body pressed against him; the sense of contact was electric. Her slim fragrance was immediate and breath-taking. Her perfume filled his nostrils. It was impossible, at this moment, to think of Marsha as anything but a woman. He felt his body awaken excitedly, his senses swim. The alarm bell was silenced. He could remember only: *Little Miss Preyscott . . . would be fun . . . for a man – to be eaten up.*

Resolutely, he forced himself away. Taking Marsha's hand gently, he told her, 'I must go.'

She came with him to the terrace. His hand caressed her hair. She whispered, 'Peter, darling.'

He went down the terrace steps, scarcely knowing they were there.

14

At 10.30 p.m., Ogilvie, the chief house officer, used a staff sub-basement tunnel to walk lumberingly from the main portion of the St Gregory to the adjoining hotel garage.

He chose the tunnel instead of the more convenient main floor walkway for the same reason he had carefully picked the time – to be as inconspicuous as possible. At 10.30, guests taking their cars out for the evening had already done so, but it was too early yet for many to be returning. Nor, at that hour, were there likely to be new arrivals at the hotel, at least by road.

Ogilvie's original plan to drive the Duke and Duchess of Croydon's Jaguar north at one a.m. – now less than three hours away – had not changed. Before departure, however, the fat man had work to do and it was important that he be unobserved.

The materials for the work were in a paper bag he carried in his hand. They represented an omission in the Duchess of Croydon's elaborate scheming. Ogilvie had been aware of the omission from the beginning, but preferred to keep his own counsel.

In the double fatality of Monday night, one of the Jaguar's headlights had been shattered. Additionally, because of the loss of the trim ring, now in possession of the police, the headlight mounting had been loosened. To drive the car in darkness as planned, the headlight would have to be replaced and its mounting repaired temporarily. Yet obviously it was too dangerous to take the car to a service garage in the city and equally out of the question to have the work done by the hotel's own mechanic.

Yesterday, also choosing a time when the garage was quiet, Ogilvie had inspected the car in its out-of-the-way stall behind a pillar. He had decided that if he could obtain the right type of headlight, he could effect a temporary repair himself.

He weighed the risk of buying a replacement headlight from New Orleans' solitary Jaguar dealer, and rejected the idea. Even though the police were not yet aware – so far as Ogilvie knew – of the make of car they wee seeking, they would know in a day or two when the shattered glass fragments were identified. If he bought a Jaguar headlight now, it might easily be remembered when enquiries were made, and the purchase traced. He had compromised by buying a standard, double-filament North American sealed-beam lamp at a self-serve auto parts store. His visual inspection had shown this might be usable. Now he was ready to try it.

Getting the lamp had been one more item in a tightly-crammed day, which had left the chief house officer feeling both satisfaction and an edgy unease. He was also physically tired, a poor beginning to the long drive north which faced him. He consoled himself with remembering the twenty-five thousand dollars, ten thousand of which, as arranged, he had received this afternoon from the Duchess of Croydon. It had been a tense, cold scene, the Duchess tight-lipped and formal. Ogilvie, not caring, greedily stuffed the piled bills into a briefcase. Beside them the Duke swayed drunkenly, bleary-eyed and scarcely aware of what was happening.

The thought of the money gave the fat man a pleasant glow. It was safely hidden now, with only two hundred dollars on his person – a precaution in case anything went wrong during the journey to come.

His contrasting unease had two causes. One was awareness of the consequences to himself if he failed to get the Jaguar clear of New Orleans and later Louisiana, Mississippi, Tennessee and Kentucky. The second was Peter McDermott's emphasis on the need for Ogilvie to remain close to the hotel.

The robbery last night, and the likelihood that a professional thief was at work in the St Gregory, could not have occurred at a worse time. Ogilvie had done as much as he could. He had advised the city police, and detectives had interviewed the robbed guest. Hotel staff, including the other house officers, had been alerted and Ogilvie's second-in-command had received instructions about what to do in various contingencies. None the less, Ogilvie was well aware that he should be on hand to direct operations personally. When his absence came to McDermott's attention, as it would tomorrow, there was bound to be a first-class row. In the long run the row would not matter because McDermott and others like him would come and go while Ogilvie, for reasons known only to himself and Warren Trent, would still retain his job. But it would have the effect – which the chief house officer wanted to avoid above all else – of drawing attention to his movements in the next few days.

Only in one way had the robbery and its aftermath been useful. It provided a valid reason for a further visit to police headquarters where he enquired casually about progress of the hit-and-run investigation. Police attention, he learned, was still concentrated on the case, with the entire force alert for any break. In this afternoon's *States-Item* the police had issued a new appeal for the public to report any car with fender or headlight damage. It had been as well to have the information, but it also made the chances less of getting the Jaguar out of town without detection. Ogilvie sweated a little when he thought of it.

He had reached the end of the tunnel and was in the garage sub-basement.

The austerely lighted garage was quiet. Ogilvie hesitated, torn between going directly to the Croydons' car several floors above or to the garage office where the night checker was on duty. He decided it would be prudent to visit the office first.

Laboriously, breathing heavily, he climbed two flights of metal stairs. The checker, an elderly officious man named Kulgmer, was alone in his brightly lighted cubicle near the street entry-exit ramp. He put down an evening paper as the chief house officer came in.

'Wanted to let you know,' Ogilvie said. 'I'll be taking the Duke of Croydon's car out soon. It's stall 371. I'm doin' a favour for him.'

Kulgmer frowned. 'Don't know as I can let you do that, Mr O. Not without proper authority.'

Ogilvie produced the Duchess of Croydon's note, written this morning at his request. 'I guess this is all the authority you'll need.'

The night checker read the wording carefully, then turned the paper over. 'It seems all right.'

The chief house officer put out a pudgy hand to take the note back.

Kulgmer shook his head. 'I'll have to keep this. To cover me.'

The fat man shrugged. He would have preferred to have the note, but to insist would raise an issue, emphasizing the incident, which otherwise might be forgotten. He motioned to the paper bag. 'Just goin' up to leave this. I'll be takin' the car out, couple of hours from now.'

'Suit yourself, Mr O.' the checker nodded, returning to his paper.

A few minutes later, approaching stall 371, Ogilvie glanced with apparent casualness around him. The low-ceilinged, concrete parking area, about fifty per cent occupied by cars, was otherwise silent and deserted. The night-duty car jockeys were undoubtedly in their locker room on the main floor, taking advantage of the lull to nap or play cards. But it was necessary to work fast.

In the far corner, sheltered by the Jaguar and its partially screening pillar, Ogilvie emptied the paper bag of the headlight, a screwdriver, pliers, insulated wire and black electrician's tape.

His fingers, for all their seeming awkwardness, moved with surprising dexterity. Using gloves to protect his hands, he removed the remnants of the shattered headlight. It took only a moment to discover that the replacement headlight would fit the Jaguar, but the electrical connections would not. He had anticipated this. Working swiftly, using the pliers, wire and tape, he fashioned a rough but effective connection. With additional wire he secured the light in place, stuffing cardboard from his pockets into the gap left by the missing trim ring. He covered this with black tape, passing the tape through and securing it behind. It was a patch job which would be easily detectable in light, but adequate in darkness. It had taken almost fifteen minutes. Opening the car door on the driver's side, he turned the headlight switch to 'on'. Both headlights worked.

He gave a grunt of relief. At the same instant, from below, came the sharp staccato of a horn and the roar of an accelerating car. Ogilvie froze. The motor roared nearer, its sound magnified by concrete walls and low ceilings. Then, abruptly, headlights flashed by, sweeping up the ramp to the floor above. There was a squeal of tyres, the motor stopped, a car door slammed. Ogilvie relaxed. The car jockey, he knew, would use the manlift to return below.

When he heard footsteps receding, he put the tools and supplies back into the paper bag, along with a few larger fragments of the original headlight. He put the bag aside to take with him later.

On the way up he had observed a cleaners' closet on the floor below. Using the downward ramp, he walked to it now.

As he had hoped, there was cleaning equipment inside and he selected a broom, dustpan and a bucket. He partly filled the bucket with warm water and added a washcloth. Listening cautiously for sounds from below, he waited until two cars had passed, then hurried back to the Jaguar on the floor above.

With the broom and dustpan, Ogilvie swept carefully around the car. There must be no identifiable glass fragments left for police to compare with those from the accident scene.

There was little time left. The cars coming in to be parked were increasing in number. Twice during the sweeping he had stopped for fear of being seen, holding his breath as one car swung into a stall on the same floor, a few yards only from the Jaguar. Luckily, the car jockey had not bothered to look around, but it was a warning to hurry. If a jock observed him and came across, it would mean curiosity and questions, which would be repeated downstairs. The explanation for his presence which Ogilvie had given the night checker would seem unconvincing. Not only that, the chances of an undetected run north depended on leaving as scant a trail as possible behind.

One more thing remained. Taking the warm water and cloth, he carefully wiped the damaged portion of the Jaguar's fender and the area around it. As he wrung out the cloth, the water, which had been clear, became brown. He inspected his handiwork carefully, then grunted approval. Now, whatever else might happen, there was no dried blood on the car.

Ten minutes later, sweating from his exertions, he was back in the main building of the hotel. He went directly to his office where he intended to snatch an hour's sleep before setting out on the long drive to Chicago. He checked the time. It was 11.15 p.m.

15

'I might be able to help more,' Royall Edwards observed pointedly, 'if someone told me what this is all about.'

The St Gregory's comptroller addressed himself to the two men facing him across the long, accounting office table. Between them, ledgers and files were spread open and the entire office, normally shrouded in darkness at this time of night, was brightly lit. Edwards himself had switched on the lights an hour ago on bringing the two visitors here, directly from Warren Trent's fifteenth-floor suite.

The hotel proprietor's instructions had been explicit. 'These gentlemen will examine our books. They will probably work through until tomorrow morning. I'd like you to stay with them. Give them everything they ask for. Hold no information back.'

In issuing the instructions, Royall Edwards reflected, his employer had seemed more cheerful than for a long time. The cheerfulness, however, did not appease the comptroller, already piqued at being summoned from his home where he had been working on his stamp collection, and further irritated by not being taken into confidence concerning whatever was afoot. He also resented – as one of the hotel's most consistent nine-to-fivers – the idea of working all night.

The comptroller knew, of course, about the mortgage deadline of Friday and the presence of Curtis O'Keefe in the hotel, with its obvious implications. Presumably this latest visitation was related to both, though in what way was hard to guess. A possible clue was luggage tags on both visitors' bags, indicating they had flown to New Orleans from Washington, DC. Yet instinct told him that the two accountants – which obviously they were – had no connection with government. Well, he would probably know all the answers eventually. Meanwhile it was annoying to be treated like some minor clerk.

There had been no response to his remark that he might be able to help more if better informed, and he repeated it.

The older of the two visitors, a heavy-set middle-aged man with an immobile face, lifted the coffee cup beside him and drained it. 'One thing I always say, Mr Edwards, there's nothing quite like a good cup of coffee. Now you take most hotels, they just don't brew coffee the right way. This one does. So I reckon there can't be much wrong with a hotel that serves coffee like that. What do you say, Frank?'

'I'd say if we're to get through this job by morning, we'd better have less chit-chat.' The second man answered dourly, without looking up from the trial balance sheet he was studying intently.

The first made a placating gesture with his hands. 'You see how it is, Mr Edwards? I guess Frank's right; he often is. So, much as I'd like to explain the whole thing, maybe we'd better keep right on.'

Aware of being rebuffed, Royall Edwards said stiffly, 'Very well.'

'Thank you, Mr Edwards. Now I'd like to go over your inventory system – purchasing, card control, present stocks, your last supply check, all the rest. Say, that *was* good coffee. Could we have some more?'

The comptroller said, 'I'll telephone down.' He observed dispiritedly that it was already close to midnight. Obviously they were going to be here for hours more.

Thursday

I

If he expected to be alert for a new day's work, Peter McDermott supposed he had better head home and get some sleep.

It was a half hour past midnight. He had walked, he thought, for a couple of hours, perhaps longer. He felt refreshed and agreeably tired.

Walking at length was an old habit, especially when he had something on his mind or a problem which defied solution.

Earlier tonight, after leaving Marsha, he had returned to his downtown apartment. But he had been restless in the cramped quarters and disinclined for sleep, so he had gone out walking, towards the river. He had strolled the length of the Poydras and Julia Street Wharves, past moored ships, some dimly lighted and silent, others active and preparing for departure. Then he had taken the Canal Street ferry across the Mississippi and on the far side walked the lonely levees, watching the city lights against the darkness of the river. Returning, he made his way to the Vieux Carré and now sat, sipping *café au lait*, in the old French market.

A few minutes earlier, remembering hotel affairs for the first time in several hours, he had telephoned the St Gregory. He enquired if there was any more news concerning the threatened walk-out of the Congress of American Dentistry convention. Yes, the night assistant manager informed him, a message had been left shortly before midnight by the convention floor head waiter. So far as the head waiter could learn, the dentists' executive board, after a six-hour session, had reached no firm conclusion. However, an emergency general meeting of all convention delegates was to be held at 9.30 a.m. in the Dauphine Salon. About three hundred were expected to attend. The meeting would be *in camera*, with elaborate security precautions, and the hotel had been asked to assist in assuring privacy.

Peter left instructions that whatever was asked should be done, and put the matter from his mind until the morning.

Apart from this brief diversion, most of his thoughts had been of Marsha and the night's events. Questions buzzed in his head like pertinacious bees. How to handle the situation with fairness, yet not clumsily or hurting Marsha in doing so? One thing, of course, was clear: her proposal was impossible. And yet it would be the worst kind of churlishness to dismiss off-handedly an honest declaration. He had told her: '*If more people were honest like you . . .* '

There was something else – and why be afraid of it if honesty was to be served both ways? He had been drawn to Marsha tonight, not as a young girl but as a woman. If he

451

closed his eyes he could see her as she had been. The effect was still like heady wine.

But he had tasted heady wine before, and the taste had turned to bitterness he had vowed would never come his way again. Did that kind of experience temper judgement, make a man wiser in his choice of women? He doubted it.

And yet he *was* a man, breathing, feeling. No self-imposed seclusion could, or should, last for ever. The question: When and how to end it?

In any case, what next? Would he see Marsha again? He supposed – unless he severed their connection decisively, at once – it was inevitable he should. Then on what terms? And what, too, of their differences in age?

Marsha was nineteen. He was thirty-two. The gap between seemed wide, yet was it? Certainly if they were both ten years older, an affair – or marriage – would not be thought of as extraordinary. Also, he doubted very much if Marsha would find close rapport with a boy her own age.

The questions were endless. But a decision as to whether, and in what circumstances, he would see Marsha again had yet to be made.

In all his reasoning, too, there remained the thought of Christine. Within the space of a few days he and Christine seemed to have drawn closer together than at anytime before. He remembered that his last thought before leaving for the Preyscott house last evening had been of Christine. Even now, he found himself anticipating keenly the sight and sound of her again.

Strange, he reflected, that he, who a week ago had been resolutely unattached, should feel torn at this moment between two women!

Peter grinned ruefully as he paid for the coffee and rose to go home.

The St Gregory was more or less on the way and instinctively his footsteps took him past it. When he reached the hotel it was a few minutes after one a.m.

There was still activity, he could see, within the lobby. Outside, St Charles Avenue was quiet, with only a cruising cab and a pedestrian or two in sight. He crossed the street to take a short cut around the rear of the hotel. Here it was quieter still. He was about to pass the entry to the hotel garage when he halted, warned by the sound of a motor and the reflection of headlight beams approaching down the inside ramp. A moment later a low-slung black car swung into sight. It was moving fast and braked sharply, tyres squealing, at the street. As the car stopped it was directly in a pool of light. It was a Jaguar, Peter noticed, and it looked as if a fender had been dented; on the same side there was something odd about the headlight too. He hoped that the damage had not occurred through negligence in the hotel garage. If it had, he would hear about it soon enough.

Automatically he glanced towards the driver. He was startled to see it was Ogilvie. The chief house officer, meeting Peter's eyes, seemed equally surprised. Then abruptly the car pulled out of the garage and continued on.

Peter wondered why and where Ogilvie was driving; and why a Jaguar instead of the house officer's usual battered Chevrolet? Then, deciding that what employees did away from the hotel was their own business, Peter continued on to his apartment.

Later, he slept soundly.

2

Unlike Peter McDermott, Keycase Milne did not sleep well. The speed and efficiency with which he obtained precise details of the Presidential Suite key had not been followed by equal success in having a duplicate made for his own use. The connections which Keycase established on arriving in New Orleans had proved less helpful than he expected. Eventually a locksmith on a slum street near the Irish Channel – whom Keycase was assured could be trusted – agreed to do the job, though grumbling at having to follow specifications instead of copying an existing key. But the new key would not be ready until midday Thursday, and the price demanded was exorbitant.

Keycase had agreed to the price, as he had agreed to wait, realizing there was no alternative. But the waiting was especially trying since he was aware that the passage of every hour increased his chances of being traced and apprehended.

Tonight before going to bed he had debated whether to make a new foray through the hotel in the early morning. There were still two room keys in his collection which he had not utilized – 449, the second key obtained at the airport Tuesday morning, and 803 which he had asked for and received at the desk instead of his own key 830. But he decided against the idea, arguing with himself that it was wiser to wait and concentrate on the larger project involving the Duchess of Croydon. Yet Keycase knew, even while reaching the decision, that its major motivation was fear.

In the night, as sleep eluded him, the fear grew stronger, so that he no longer attempted to conceal it from himself with even the thinnest veil of self-deception. But tomorrow, he determined, he would somehow beat fear down and become his own lion-hearted self once more.

He fell at length into an uneasy slumber in which he dreamed that a great iron door, shutting out air and daylight, was inching close upon him. He tried to run while a gap remained, but was powerless to move. When the door had closed, he wept, knowing it would never open again.

He awoke shivering, in darkness. His face was wet with tears.

3

Some seventy miles north of New Orleans, Ogilvie was still speculating on his encounter with Peter McDermott. The initial shock had had an almost physical impact. For more than an hour afterwards, Ogilvie had driven tensely, yet at times scarcely conscious of the Jaguar's progress, first through the city, then across the Pontchartrain Causeway, and eventually northwards on Interstate 59.

His eyes moved constantly to the rear-view mirror. He watched each set of headlights which appeared behind, expecting them to overtake swiftly, with the sound of a pursuing siren. Ahead, around each turn of the road, he prepared to brake at imagined police road-blocks.

His immediate assumption had been that the only possible reason for Peter McDermott's presence was to witness his own incriminating departure. How McDermott might have learned of the plan, Ogilvie had no idea. But apparently he had, and the house detective, like the greenest amateur, had ambled into a trap.

It was only later, as the countryside sped by in the lonely darkness of early morning, that he began to wonder: Could it have been coincidence after all?

Surely, if McDermott had been there with some intent, the Jaguar would have been pursued or halted at a road-block long before now. The absence of any such attempt made coincidence more likely, in fact almost certain. At the thought, Ogilvie's spirits rose. He began to think gloatingly of the twenty-five thousand dollars which would be his at the journey's end.

He debated: Since everything had turned out so well thus far, would it be wiser to keep going? In just over an hour it would be daylight. His original plan had been to pull off the road and wait for darkness again before continuing. But there could be danger in a day of inaction. He was only halfway across Mississippi, still relatively close to New Orleans. Going on, of course, would involve the risk of being spotted, but he wondered just how great the risk was. Against the idea was his own physical strain from the previous day. Already he was tiring, the urge to sleep strong.

It was then it happened. Behind him, appearing as if magically, was a flashing red light. A siren shrieked imperiously.

It was the very thing for the past several hours he had expected to happen. When it failed to, he had relaxed. Now, the reality was a double shock.

Instinctively, his accelerator foot slammed to the floor. Like a superbly powered arrow, the Jaguar surged forward. The speedometer needle swung sharply . . . to 70, 80, 85. At ninety, Ogilvie slowed for a bend. As he did, the flashing red light drew close behind. The siren, which had stopped briefly, wailed again. Then the red light moved sideways as the driver behind pulled out to pass.

It was useless, Ogilvie knew. Even if he out-distanced pursuit now, he could not avoid others forewarned ahead. Resignedly, he let his speed fall off.

He had a momentary impression of the other vehicle flashing by: a long limousine body, light-coloured, a dim interior light and a figure bending over another. Then the ambulance was gone, its flashing red beacon diminishing down the road ahead.

The incident left him shaken and convinced of his own tiredness. He decided that no matter how the alternative risks compared, he must pull off and remain there for the day. He was now past Macon, a small Mississippi community which had been his objective for the first night's driving. A glimmer of dawn was beginning to light the sky. He stopped to consult a map and shortly afterwards turned off the highway on to a complex of minor roads.

Soon the road surface had deteriorated to a rutted, grassy track. It was rapidly becoming light. Getting out of the car, Ogilvie surveyed the surrounding countryside.

It was sparsely wooded and desolate, with no habitation in sight. The nearest main road was more than a mile away. Not far ahead was a cluster of trees. Reconnoitring on foot, he discovered that the track went into the trees and ended.

The fat man gave one of his approving grunts. Returning to the Jaguar, he drove it forward carefully until foliage concealed it. He then made several checks, satisfying himself that the car could not be seen except at close quarters. When he had finished, he climbed into the back seat and slept.

4

For several minutes after coming awake, shortly before eight a.m., Warren Trent was puzzled to know why his spirits were instinctively buoyant. Then he remembered: this morning he would consummate the deal made yesterday with the Journeymen's Union. Defying pressures, glum predictions and sundry assorted obstacles, he had saved the St Gregory – with only hours to spare – from engorgement by the O'Keefe hotel chain. It was a personal triumph. He pushed to the back of his mind a thought that the bizarre alliance between himself and the union might lead to even greater problems later on. If that happened, he would worry at the proper time; most important was removal of the immediate threat.

Getting out of bed, he looked down on the city from a window of his fifteenth-floor suite atop the hotel. Outside, it was another beautiful day, the sun – already high – shining from a near cloudless sky.

He hummed softly to himself as he showered and afterwards was shaved by Aloysius Royce. His employer's obvious cheerfulness was sufficiently unusual for Royce to raise his eyebrows in surprise, though Warren Trent – not yet far enough into the day for conversation – offered no enlightenment.

When he was dressed, on entering the living-room he immediately telephoned Royall Edwards. The comptroller, whom a switchboard operator located at his home, managed to convey both that he had worked all night and that his employer's telephone call had brought him from a well-earned breakfast. Ignoring the undertone of grievance, Warren Trent sought to discover what reaction had come from the two visiting accountants during the night. According to the comptroller's report, the visitors, though briefed on the hotel's current financial crisis, had uncovered nothing else extraordinary and seemed satisfied by Edwards' responses to their queries.

Reassured, Warren Trent left the comptroller to his breakfast. Perhaps even at this moment, he reflected, a report confirming his own representation of the St Gregory's position was being telephoned north to Washington. He supposed he would receive direct word soon.

Almost at once the telephone rang.

Royce was about to serve breakfast from the room-service trolley which had arrived a few minutes earlier. Warren Trent motioned him to wait.

An operator's voice announced that the call was long-distance. When he had identified himself, a second operator asked him to wait. At length the Journeymen's Union president came brusquely on the line.

'Trent?'

'Yes. Good morning!'

'I goddam well warned you yesterday not to hold back on information. You were stupid enough to try. Now I'm telling you: people who work trickery on me finish up wishing they hadn't been born. You're lucky this time that the whistle blew before a deal was closed. But this is a warning: don't ever try that again!'

The unexpectedness, the harsh chilling voice, momentarily robbed Warren Trent of speech. Recovering, he protested, 'In God's name, I've not the least idea what this is about.'

'No idea, when there'd been a race riot in your goddamned hotel! When the story's spewed over every New York and Washington newspaper!'

It took several seconds to connect the angry harangue with Peter McDermott's report of the previous day.

'There was an incident yesterday morning, a small one. It was certainly not a race riot or anything near. At the time we talked I was unaware that it had happened. Even if I had known, it would not have occurred to me as important enough to mention. As to the New York newspapers, I haven't seen them.'

'My members'll see them. If not those papers, then others across the country that'll carry the story by tonight. What's more, if I put money into a hotel that turns away nigs, they'd scream bloody murder along with every two-bit congressman who wants the coloured vote.'

'It's not the principle you care about, then. You don't mind what we do as long as it isn't noticed.'

'What I care about is my business. So is where I invest union funds.'

'Our transaction could be kept confidential.'

'If you believe that, you're an even bigger fool than I thought.'

It was true, Warren Trent conceded glumly: sooner or later news of an alliance would leak out. He tried another approach. 'What occurred yesterday is not unique. It's happened to Southern hotels before; it will happen again. A day or two afterwards, attention moves on to something else.'

'Maybe it does. But if your hotel got Journeymen's financing – after today – attention would damn soon switch back. And it's the kind I can do without.'

'I'd like to be clear about this. Am I to understand that despite your accountants' inspection of our affairs last night, our arrangement of yesterday no longer stands?'

The voice from Washington said, 'The trouble isn't with your books. The report my people made was affirmative. It's for the other reason all bets are off.'

So after all, Warren Trent thought bitterly, through an incident which yesterday he had dismissed as trifling, the nectar of victory had been snatched away. Aware that whatever was said would make no difference now, he commented acidly, 'You haven't always been so particular about using union funds.'

There was a silence. Then the Journeymen's president said softly, 'Some day you may be sorry for that.'

Slowly, Warren Trent replaced the telephone. On a table near by Aloysius Royce had spread open the air-mailed New York newspapers. He indicated the *Herald Tribune*. 'It's mostly in here. I don't see anything in the *Times*.'

'They've later editions in Washington,' Warren Trent skimmed the *Herald Tribune* headline and glanced briefly at the accompanying picture. It showed yesterday's scene in the St Gregory lobby with Dr Nicholas and Dr Ingram as central figures. He supposed that later he would have to read the report in full. At the moment he had no stomach for it.

'Would you like me to serve breakfast now?'

Warren Trent shook his head. 'I'm not hungry.' His eyes flickered upwards, meeting the young Negro's steady gaze. 'I suppose you think I got what I deserved.'

Royce considered. 'Something like that, I guess. Mostly, I'd say you don't accept the times we live in.'

'If it's true, that needn't trouble you any more. From tomorrow I doubt if my opinion will count for much around here.'

'I'm sorry for that part.'

'What this means is that O'Keefe will take over.' The older man walked to a window and stood looking out. He was silent, then said abruptly, 'I imagine you heard the terms I was offered – among them that I'd continue to live here.'

'Yes.'

'Since it's to be that way, I suppose that when you graduate from law school next month, I'll still have to put up with you around the place. Instead of booting you out the way I should.'

Aloysius Royce hesitated. Ordinarily, he would have tossed back a quick, barbed rejoinder. But he knew that what he was hearing was the plea of a defeated, lonely man for him to stay.

The decision troubled Royce; all the same, it would have to be made soon. For almost twelve years Warren Trent had treated him in many ways like a son. If he remained, he knew, his duties could become negligible outside of being a companion and confidant in the hours free from his own legal work. The life would be far from unpleasant. And yet there were other, conflicting pressures affecting the choice to go or stay.

'I haven't thought about it much,' he lied. 'Maybe I'd better.'

Warren Trent reflected: all things, large and small, were changing, most of them abruptly. In his mind he had not the least doubt that Royce would leave him soon, just as control of the St Gregory had finally eluded him. His sense of aloneness, and now of exclusion from the mainstream of events, was probably typical of people who had lived too long.

He informed Royce, 'You can go, Aloysius. I'd like to be alone for a while.'

In a few minutes, he decided, he would call Curtis O'Keefe and officially surrender.

5

Time magazine, whose editors recognized a newsy story when they read it in their morning papers, had hopped nimbly on to the St Gregory civil rights incident. Their local stringer – a staffer on the New Orleans *States-Item* – was alerted and told to file everything he could get on local background. *Time*'s Houston bureau chief had been telephoned the previous night, soon after an early edition of the *Herald Tribune* broke the story in New York, and had flown in on an early flight.

Now both men were closeted with Herbie Chandler, the bell captain, in a cramped, main floor cubbyhole. Loosely known as a press room, it was sparsely furnished with a desk, telephone and hat stand. The Houston man, as became his status, had the solitary chair.

Chandler, respectfully aware of *Time*'s liberality to those who smoothed its way, was reporting on a reconnaissance from which he had just returned.

'I checked about the dentists' meeting. They're closing it up tighter'n a drum. They've told the head floor waiter no-one's to get in except members, not even wives, and they'll have their own people at the door checking names. Before the meeting starts all the hotel help has to leave and doors'll be locked.'

The bureau chief nodded. An eager, crew-cut young man named Quaratone, he had already interviewed the dentists' president, Dr Ingram. The bell captain's report confirmed what he had been told.

'Sure we're having an emergency general meeting,' Dr Ingram had said. 'It was decided by our executive board last night, but it's to be a closed-door deal. If it was my say-so, son, you and nobody else could come in, and welcome. But some of my colleagues see it the other way. They think people'll speak more freely if they know the press isn't there. So I guess you'll have to sit that one out.'

Quaratone, with no intention of sitting anything out, had thanked Dr Ingram politely. With Herbie Chandler already purchased as an ally, Quaratone's immediate idea had been to employ an old ruse and attend the meeting in a borrowed bellboy's uniform. Chandler's latest report showed the need for a change of scheme.

'The room where the meeting is being held,' Quaratone queried; 'is it a good-size convention hall?'

Chandler nodded. 'The Dauphine Salon, sir. Seats three hundred. That's about how many they're expecting.'

The *Time* man considered. Any meeting involving three hundred people would obviously cease to be secret the instant it finished. Afterwards he could easily mingle with the emerging delegates and, by posing as one of them, learn what happened. That way, though, he would miss most of the minutiae of human interest which *Time* and its readers thrived on.

'Does the wotsit saloon have a balcony?'

'There's a small one, but they've already thought of it. I checked. There'll be a couple of convention people up there. Also, the p.a. microphones are being disconnected.'

'Hell!' the local newspaperman objected. 'What's this outfit afraid of – saboteurs?'

Quaratone said, thinking aloud, 'Some of them want to speak their piece but avoid getting it on the record. Professional people – on racial issues anyway – don't usually take strong stands. Here they've already got themselves in a box by admitting to a choice between the drastic action of walking out or making a token gesture, just for appearance sake. To that extent I'd say the situation's unique.' It was also, he thought, why there might be a better story here than he had supposed at first. More than ever he was determined to find a way of getting into the meeting.

Abruptly, he told Herbie Chandler. 'I want a plan of the convention floor and the floor above. 'Not just a room layout, you understand, but a technical plan showing walls, ducts, ceiling spaces, all the rest. I want it fast because if we're to do any good we've less than an hour.'

'I really don't know if there is such a thing, sir. In any case . . .' The bell captain stopped, watching Quaratone who was peeling off a succession of twenty-dollar bills.

The *Time* man handed five of the bills to Chandler. 'Get to somebody in maintenance, engineering or whatever. Use that for now. I'll take care of you later. Meet me back here in half an hour, earlier if possible.'

'Yessir!' Chandler's weasel face screwed into an obsequious smile.

Quaratone instructed the New Orleans reporter, 'Carry on with the local angles, will you? Statements from city hall, leading citizens; better talk to the NAACP. You know the kind of thing.'

'I could write it in my sleep.'

'Don't. And watch for human interest. Might be an idea if you could catch the mayor in the washroom. Washing his hands while he gave you a statement. Symbolic. Make a good lead.'

'I'll try hiding in a toilet.' The reporter went off cheerfully, aware that he too would be generously paid for his spare-time work.

Quaratone himself waited in the St Gregory coffee shop. He ordered iced tea and sipped it absently, his mind on the developing story. It would not be a major one, but providing he could find some refreshing angles, it might rate a column and a half in next week's issue. Which would please him because in recent weeks a dozen or more of his carefully nurtured stories had either been rejected by New York or squeezed out during make-up of the magazine. This was not unusual and writing in a vacuum was a frustration which *Time-Life* staffers learned to live with. But Quaratone liked to get into print and be noticed where it counted.

He returned to the undersized press room. Within a few minutes Herbie Chandler arrived, shepherding a youngish, sharp-featured man in coveralls. The bell captain introduced him as Ches Ellis, a hotel maintenance worker. The newcomer shook hands diffidently with Quaratone, then, touching a roll of whiteprints under his arm, said uneasily, 'I have to get these back.'

'What I want won't take long,' Quaratone helped Ellis roll out the plans, weighting the edges down. 'Now, where's the Dauphine Salon?'

'Right here.'

Chandler interjected, 'I told him about the meeting, sir. How you want to hear what's happening without being in.'

The *Time* man asked Ellis, 'What's in the walls and ceilings?'

'Walls are solid. There's a gap between the ceiling and the next floor above, but if you're thinking of getting in there, it wouldn't work. You'd fall through the plaster.'

'Check,' said Quaratone, who had been considering just that. His finger stubbed the plan. 'What are these lines?'

'Hot-air outlet from the kitchen. Anywhere near that you'd roast.'

'And this?'

Ellis stooped, studying the whiteprint. He consulted a second sheet. 'Cold-air duct. Runs through the Dauphine Salon ceiling.'

'How big is the duct?'

The maintenance man considered. 'I reckon about three feet square.'

Quaratone said decisively, 'I'd like you to get me in that duct. I want to get in it, and crawl out so I can hear and see what's going on below.'

It took surprisingly little time. Ellis, at first reluctant, was prodded by Chandler into obtaining a second set of coveralls and a tool kit. The *Time* man changed quickly into coveralls and hoisted the tools. Then nervously, but without incident, Ellis shepherded him to an annex off the convention floor kitchen. The bell captain hovered discreetly out of sight. Quaratone had no idea how much of the hundred dollars Chandler had passed over to Ellis – he suspected not all – but it was evidently enough.

The progress through the kitchen – ostensibly of two hotel maintenance workers – went unnoticed. In the annex a metal grille, high on the wall, had been removed by Ellis in advance. A tall step-ladder stood in front of an opening which the grille had covered.

ARTHUR HAILEY

Without conversation, Quaratone ascended the step-ladder and eased himself upwards and in. There was, he discovered, room to crawl forward, using his elbows – but only just. Darkness, except for stray glimmers from the kitchen, was complete. He felt a breath of cool air on his face; the air pressure increased as his body filled more of the metal duct.

Ellis whispered after him, 'Count four outlets! The fourth, fifth and sixth are the Dauphine Salon. Keep the noise down, sir, or you'll be heard. I'll come back in half an hour; if you're not ready, half an hour after that.'

Quaratone tried to turn his head and failed. It was a reminder that getting out would be harder than getting in. Calling back a low-voiced 'Roger!' he began to move.

The metallic surface was hard on knees and elbows. It also had agonizingly sharp projections. Quaratone winced as the business end of a screw ripped the coveralls and cut painfully into his leg. Reaching back, he disengaged himself and moved forward cagily.

The air duct outlets were easy to spot because of light filtering upwards. He eased over three, hoping grilles and duct were securely anchored. Nearing the fourth he could hear voices. The meeting, it seemed, had begun. To Quaratone's delight the voices came up clearly and, by craning, he could see a portion of the room below. The view, he thought, might be even better from the next outlet. It was. Now he could see more than half the crowded assemblage below, including a raised platform where the dentists' president, Dr Ingram, was speaking. Reaching around, the *Time* man brought out a notebook and a ballpoint pen, the latter with a tiny light in its tip.

' . . . urge you,' Dr Ingram was asserting, 'to take the strongest possible stand.'

He paused, then continued, 'Professional people like us who are by nature middle-of-the-roaders, have dilly-dallied too long on issues of human rights. Among ourselves we do not discriminate – at least most of the time – and in the past we have considered that to be enough. Generally, we've ignored events and pressures outside our own ranks. Our reasoning has been that we are professional, medical men with time for little else. Well, maybe that's true, even if convenient. But here and now – like it or not – we *are* involved up to our wisdom teeth.'

The little doctor paused, his eyes searching the faces of his audience. 'You have already heard of the unpardonable insult by this hotel to our distinguished colleague, Dr Nicholas – an insult in direct defiance of civil rights law. In retaliation, as your president, I have recommended drastic action. It is that we should cancel our convention and walk from this hotel en masse.'

There was a gasp of surprise from several sections of the room. Dr Ingram continued, 'Most of you have already learned of this proposal. To others, who arrived this morning, it is new. Let me say to both groups that the step I have proposed involves inconvenience, disappointment – to me, no less than to you – and professional as well as a public loss. But there are occasions, involving matters of great conscience, when nothing less than the most forceful action will suffice. I believe this to be one. It is also the only way in which the strength of our feelings will be demonstrated and by which we shall prove, unmistakably, that in matters of human rights this profession is not to be trifled with again.'

From the floor came several cries of 'hear, hear!' but, as well, a rumble of dissent.

Near the centre of the room a burly figure lumbered to his feet. Quaratone, leaning forward from his vantage point, had an impression of jowls, a thick-lipped smile and heavy-rimmed glasses. The burly man announced, 'I'm from Kansas City.' There was a good-natured cheer which was acknowledged with the wave of a pudgy hand. 'I've just one question for the doctor. Will he be the one who'll explain to my little woman – who's been counting on this trip like a lot of other wives, I reckon – why it is having just got here we're to turn tail and go home?'

An outraged voice protested, 'That isn't the point!' It was drowned out by ironic cheers and laughter from others in the hall.

'Yessir,' the burly man said, 'I'd like him to be the one to tell my wife.' Looking pleased with himself, he sat down.

Dr Ingram was on his feet, red-faced, indignant. 'Gentlemen, this is an urgent, serious matter. We have already delayed action for twenty-four hours which in my opinion is at least half a day too long.'

There was applause, but brief and scattered. A number of other voices spoke at once. Beside Dr Ingram, the meeting's chairman pounded with a gavel.

Several speakers followed, deploring the expulsion of Dr Nicholas, but leaving unanswered the question of reprisal. Then, as if by assent, attention focused on a slim dapper figure standing with a suggestion of authority near the front of the hall. Quaratone missed the name which the chairman announced, but caught ' . . . second vice-president and member of our executive board'.

The new speaker began in a dry crisp voice, 'It was at my urging, supported by several fellow executive members, that this meeting is being held *in camera*. As a result, we may speak freely, knowing that whatever we say will not be recorded, and perhaps misrepresented, outside this room. This arrangement, I may add, was strongly opposed by our esteemed president, Dr Ingram.'

From the platform, Dr Ingram growled, 'What are you afraid of – involvement?'

Ignoring the question, the dapper man continued, 'I yield to no-one in my personal distaste for discrimination. Some of my best . . .' – he hesitated – ' . . . my best-liked associates are those of other creeds and races. Furthermore, I deplore with Dr Ingram the incident of yesterday. It is merely on the question of procedure at this moment that we disagree. Dr Ingram – if I may emulate his choice of metaphor – favours extraction. My own view is to treat more mildly for an unpleasant but localized infection.' There was a ripple of laughter at which the speaker smiled.

'I cannot believe that our unfortunately absent colleague, Dr Nicholas, would gain in the least from cancellation of our convention. Certainly, as a profession, we would lose. Furthermore – and since we are in private session I say this frankly – I do not believe that as an organization the broad issue of race relations is any of our concern.'

A single voice near the rear protested, 'Of course it's our concern! Isn't it everybody's?' But through most of the room there was merely attentive silence.

The speaker shook his head. 'Whatever stands we take or fail to, should be as individuals. Naturally we must support our own people where necessary, and in a moment I shall suggest certain steps in the case of Dr Nicholas. But otherwise I agree with Dr Ingram that we are professional medical men with time for little else.'

Dr Ingram sprang to his feet. 'I did not say that! I pointed out that it's a view which has been held in the past. I happen to disagree strongly.'

The dapper man shrugged. 'Nevertheless the statement was made.'

'But not with that kind of implication. I will not have my words twisted!' The little doctor's eyes flashed angrily. 'Mr Chairman, we're talking here glibly, using words like "unfortunate", "regrettable". Can't all of you see that this is more than just that; that we are considering a question of human rights and decency? If you had been here yesterday and witnessed, as I witnessed, the indignity to a colleague, a friend, a good man . . .'

There were cries of 'Order! order!' As the chairman pounded with his gavel, reluctantly, his face flushed, Dr Ingram subsided.

The dapper man enquired politely, 'May I continue?' The chairman nodded.

'Thank you. Gentlemen, I will make my suggestions briefly. First, I propose that our future conventions shall be held in locales where Dr Nicholas and others of his race will be accepted without question or embarrassment. There are plenty of places which the remainder of us, I am sure, will find acceptable. Secondly, I propose that we pass a resolution disapproving the action of this hotel in rejecting Dr Nicholas, after which we should continue with our convention as planned.'

On the platform, Dr Ingram shook his head in disbelief.

The speaker consulted a single sheet of paper in his hand. 'In conjunction with several other members of your executive board, I have drafted a resolution . . .'

In his eyrie Quaratone had ceased to listen. The resolution itself was unimportant. Its substance was predictable; if necessary he could obtain a text later. He was watching, instead, the faces of the listeners below. They were average faces, he decided, of reasonably educated men. They mirrored relief. Relief, Quaratone thought, from the need for the kind of action – uncomfortable, unaccustomed – which Dr Ingram had proposed. The salve of words, paraded primly in democratic style, offered a way out. Conscience would be relieved, convenience intact. There had been some mild protest – a single speaker supporting Dr Ingram – but it was short-lived. Already the meeting had settled down to what looked like becoming a prolix discussion. 'I have drafted a resolution . . .'

The *Time* man shivered – a reminder that as well as other discomforts, he had been close to an hour in a cold air duct. But the effort had been worth while. He had a live story which the stylists in New York could re-write searingly. He also had a notion that this week his work would not be squeezed out.

6

Peter McDermott heard of the Dentistry Congress decision to continue with its convention almost as soon as the *in camera* meeting ended. Because of the obvious importance of the meeting to the hotel, he had stationed a convention department clerk outside the Dauphine Salon with instructions to report promptly whatever could be learnt. A moment or two ago the clerk telephoned to say that from the conversation of emerging delegates it was obvious that the proposal to cancel the convention had been overruled.

Peter supposed that for the hotel's sake he should be pleased. Instead, he had a feeling of depression. He wondered about the effect on Dr Ingram, whose strong motivation and forthrightness had clearly been repudiated.

Peter reflected wryly that Warren Trent's cynical assessment of the situation yesterday had proved accurate after all. He supposed he should let the hotel proprietor know.

As Peter entered the managing director's section of the executive suite, Christine looked up from her desk. She smiled warmly, reminding him how much he had wanted to talk with her last evening.

She enquired, 'Was it a nice party?' When he hesitated, Christine seemed amused. 'You haven't forgotten already?'

He shook his head. 'Everything was fine. I missed you, though – and still feel badly about getting the arrangements mixed.'

'We're twenty-four hours older. You can stop now.'

'If you're free, perhaps I could make up for it tonight.'

'It's snowing invitations!' Christine said. 'Tonight I'm having dinner with Mr Wells.'

Peter's eyebrows went up. 'He *has* recovered.'

'Not enough to leave the hotel, which is why we're dining here. If you work late, why not join us afterwards?'

'If I can, I will.' He indicated the closed double doors of the hotel proprietor's office. 'Is W. T. available?'

'You can go in. I hope it isn't problems, though. He seems depressed this morning.'

'I've some news may cheer him. The dentists just voted against cancelling out.' He said more soberly, 'I suppose you saw the New York papers.'

'Yes, I did. I'd say we got what we deserved.'

He nodded agreement.

'I also saw the local papers,' Christine said. 'There's nothing new on that awful hit-and-run. I keep thinking about it.'

Peter said sympathetically, 'I have too.' Once more the scene of three nights earlier – the roped-off, flood-lighted road, with police searching grimly for clues – came sharply back into focus. He wondered if the police investigation would uncover the offending car and driver. Perhaps by now both were safely clear and past detection, though he hoped not. The thought of one crime was a reminder of another. He must remember to ask Ogilvie if there had been any developments overnight in the hotel robbery investigation. He was surprised, come to think of it, that he had not heard from the chief house officer before now.

With a final smile for Christine, he knocked at the door of Warren Trent's office and went in.

The news which Peter brought seemed to make little impression. The hotel proprietor nodded absently, as if reluctant to switch his thoughts from whatever private reverie he had been immersed in. He seemed about to speak – on another subject, Peter sensed – then, as abruptly, changed his mind. After only the briefest of conversation, Peter left.

Albert Wells had been right, Christine thought, in predicting Peter McDermott's invitation for tonight. She had a momentary regret at having arranged – deliberately – to be unavailable.

The exchange reminded her of the stratagem she had thought of yesterday to make the evening inexpensive for Albert Wells. She telephoned Max, the head waiter of the main dining-room.

'Max,' Christine said, 'your evening dinner prices are outrageous.'

'I don't set them, Miss Francis. Sometimes I wish I did.'

'You haven't been crowded lately?'

'Some nights,' the head waiter replied, 'I feel like I'm Livingstone waiting for Stanley.

463

I'll tell you, Miss Francis, people are getting smarter. They know that hotels like this have one central kitchen, and whichever of our restaurants they eat in, they'll get the same kind of food, cooked the same way by the same chefs. So why not sit where prices are lower, even if the service isn't as fancy?'

'I've a friend,' Christine said, 'who likes dining-room service – an elderly gentleman named Mr Wells. We'll be in for dinner tonight. I want you to make sure that his bill is light, though not so small that he'll notice. The difference you can put on my account.'

The head waiter chuckled. 'Say! You're the kind of girl I'd like to know myself.'

She retorted, 'With you I wouldn't do it, Max. Everybody knows you're one of the two wealthiest people in the hotel.'

'Who's supposed to be the other?'

'Isn't it Herbie Chandler?'

'You do me no favour in linking my name with that one.'

'But you'll take care of Mr Wells?'

'Miss Francis, when we present his bill he'll think he ate in the automat.'

She hung up, laughing, aware that Max would handle the situation with tact and good sense.

With incredulous, seething anger, Peter McDermott read Ogilvie's memo, slowly, for the second time.

The memo had been waiting on his desk when he returned from the brief meeting with Warren Trent.

Dated and stamped last night, it had presumably been left in Ogilvie's office for collection with this morning's inter-office mail. Equally clear was that both the timing and method of delivery were planned so that when he received the memo it would be impossible to take any action – at least for the time being – concerning its contents.

It read:

Mr P. McDermott
Subject: Vacation
    The undersigned begs to report I am taking four days leave commencing immediately. From the seven that is due, for personal urgent reasons.
    W. Finegan, dep. chief house officer, is advised re robbery, steps taken, etc. etc. Also can act with all other matters.
    Undersigned will return on duty Monday next.

                                        Yours truly,
                                        T. I. Ogilvie
                                        Chief House Officer.

Peter remembered indignantly that it was less than twenty-four hours since Ogilvie conceded that a professional hotel thief was most likely operating within the St Gregory. At the time, Peter had urged the house officer to move into the hotel for a few days, a suggestion the fat man had rejected. Even then, Ogilvie must have known of his intention to leave within a few hours, but had kept silent. Why? Obviously, because he realized Peter would object strongly, and he had no stomach for argument and perhaps delay.

The memo said '*personal urgent reasons*'. Well, Peter theorized, that much was probably true. Even Ogilvie, despite the vaunted intimacy with Warren Trent, would realize that his absence at this time, without warning, would precipitate a major showdown on return.

But what kind of personal reason was involved? Clearly nothing straightforward, to be brought out in the open and discussed. Or it would not have been handled this way. Hotel business notwithstanding, a genuine personal crisis of an employee would be dealt with sympathetically. It always was.

So it had to be something else which Ogilvie could not disclose.

Even that, Peter thought, was no concern of his except to the extent that it obstructed efficient running of the hotel. Since it did, however, he was entitled to be curious. He decided he would make an effort to learn where the chief house officer had gone and why.

He buzzed for Flora, holding up the memo as she came in.

She made a doleful face. 'I read it. I thought you'd be annoyed.'

'If you can,' Peter said, 'I want you to find out where he is. Try his home telephone, then any other places we happen to know about. Find out if anyone's seen him today or if he's expected. Leave messages. If you locate Ogilvie, I'll talk to him myself.'

Flora wrote on her note pad.

'Another thing – call the garage. I happened to be walking by the hotel last night. Our friend drove out around one o'clock – in a Jaguar. It's possible he told someone where he was going.'

When Flora left, he sent for the deputy chief house officer, Finegan, a gaunt, slow-speaking New Englander who deliberated before answering Peter's impatient questions.

No, he had no idea where Mr Ogilvie had gone. It was only late yesterday that Finegan was informed by his superior that he would be in charge for the next few days. Yes, last night there had been continuous patrols through the hotel, but no suspicious activity was observed. Nor was there any report this morning of illicit entry into rooms. No, there had been no further word from the New Orleans police department. Yes, Finegan would personally follow up with the police as Mr McDermott suggested. Certainly, if Finegan heard from Mr Ogilvie, Mr McDermott would be informed at once.

Peter dismissed Finegan. At the moment there was nothing more to be done, though Peter's anger with Ogilvie was still intense.

It had not moderated a few minutes later when Flora announced on the office intercom, 'Miss Marsha Preyscott on line two.'

'Tell her I'm busy, I'll call later.' Peter checked himself. 'Never mind, I'll talk.'

He picked up the phone, Marsha's voice said brightly, 'I heard that.'

Irritably he resolved to remind Flora that the telephone 'hold' button should be down when the intercom was open. 'I'm sorry,' he said. 'It's a low-grade morning in contrast to a great night before.'

'I'll bet the first thing hotel managers learn is to make fast recoveries like that.'

'Some may. But this is me.'

He sensed her hesitate. Then she said, 'Was it all great – the evening?'

'All of it.'

'Good! Then I'm ready to keep my promise.'

'My impression was you had.'

'No,' Marsha said, 'I promised some New Orleans history. We could start this afternoon.'

He was about to say no; that it was impossible to leave the hotel, then realized he

ARTHUR HAILEY

wanted to go. Why not? He seldom took the two full days off duty he was entitled to each week and lately had worked plenty of extra hours as well. A brief absence could easily be managed.

'All right,' he said. 'Let's see how many centuries we can cover between two o'clock and four.'

7

Twice during the twenty-minute prayer session before breakfast in his suite, Curtis O'Keefe found his thoughts wandering. It was a familiar sign of restlessness for which he apologized briefly to God, though not belabouring the point since an instinct to be ever moving on was a part of the hotel magnate's nature, and presumably divinely shaped.

It was a relief, however, to remember that this was his final day in New Orleans. He would leave for New York tonight and Italy tomorrow. The destination there, for himself and Dodo, was the Naples-O'Keefe Hotel. Besides the change of scene, it would be satisfying to be one of his own houses once more. Curtis O'Keefe had never understood the point, which his critics made, that it was possible to travel around the world, staying at O'Keefe Hotels without ever leaving the USA. Despite his attachment to foreign travel, he liked familiar things about him – American décor, with only minor concessions to local colour; American plumbing; American food and – most of the time – American people. O'Keefe establishments provided them all.

Nor was it important that a week from now he would be as impatient to leave Italy as he was, at this moment, to depart from New Orleans. There were plenty of places within his own empire – the Taj Mahal O'Keefe, O'Keefe Lisbon, Adelaide O'Keefe, O'Keefe Copenhagen and others – where a visit from the panjandrum, although nowadays not essential to the chain's efficient running, would stimulate business as a cathedral's might quicken from the sojourn of a pope.

Later, of course, he would return to New Orleans, probably in a month or two when the St Gregory – by then the O'Keefe-St Gregory – was overhauled and moulded to the conformity of an O'Keefe hotel. His arrival for the inaugural ceremonies would be triumphal, with fanfare, a civic welcome and coverage by press, radio and television. As usual on such occasions, he would bring a retinue of celebrities, including Hollywood stars, not difficult to recruit for a lavish free-loading junket.

Thinking about it, Curtis O'Keefe was impatient for these things to happen soon. He was also mildly frustrated at not having received, so far, Warren Trent's official acceptance of the proffered terms of two nights earlier. It was now mid-morning of Thursday. The noon deadline agreed to was less than ninety minutes away. Obviously, for reasons of his own, the St Gregory's proprietor intended to wait until the last possible moment before acceptance.

O'Keefe prowled restlessly around the suite. Half an hour earlier Dodo had left on a shopping expedition for which he had given her several hundred dollars in large bills. Her purchases, he suggested, should include some lightweight clothes since Naples was likely to be even hotter than New Orleans, and there would be no time for shopping in New York. Dodo thanked him appreciatively, as she always did, though strangely without the

466

glowing enthusiasm she had shown yesterday during their boat trip around the harbour which cost a mere six dollars. Women, he thought, were perplexing creatures.

He stopped at a window, looking out, when across the living-room the telephone rang. He reached it in half a dozen strides.

'Yes?'

He expected to hear the voice of Warren Trent. Instead, an operator announced that the call was long distance. A moment later the nasal Californian drawl of Hank Lemnitzer came on the line.

'That you, Mr O'Keefe?'

'Yes, it is.' Irrationally, Curtis O'Keefe wished that his West Coast representative had not found it necessary to telephone twice within twenty-four hours.

'Got some great news for you.'

'What kind of news?'

'I inked a deal for Dodo.'

'I thought I made it clear yesterday that I insist on something special for Miss Lash.'

'How special can you geet, Mr O'Keefe? This is the greatest; a real break. Dodo's a lucky kid.'

'Tell me.'

'Walt Curzon's shooting a remake of *You Can't Take It With You*. Remember – we put money in his pot.'

'I remember.'

'Yesterday I found out Walt needed a girl to play the old Ann Miller role. It's a good supporting part. Fits Dodo like a tight brassiere.'

Curtis O'Keefe wished peevishly once again that Lemnitzer would be subtler in his choice of words.

'I assume there'll be a screen test.'

'Sure will.'

'Then how do we know Curzon will agree to the casting?'

'Are you kidding? Don't underrate your influence, Mr O'Keefe. Dodo's in. Besides, I've lined up Sandra Straughan to work with her. You know Sandra?'

'Yes.' O'Keefe was well aware of Sandra Straughan. She had a reputation as one of filmdom's most accomplished dramatic coaches. Among other achievements, she possessed a remarkable record of accepting unknown girls with influential sponsors and shaping them into box office princesses.

'I'm real glad for Dodo,' Lemnitzer said. 'She's a kid I've always liked. Only thing is, we have to move fast.'

'How fast?'

'They need her yesterday, Mr O'Keefe. It all fits, though, with the rest I've arranged.'

'The rest of what?'

'Jenny LaMarsh.' Hank Lemnitzer sounded puzzled. 'You hadn't forgotten?'

'No.' O'Keefe had certainly not forgotten the witty and beautiful Vassar brunette who had so impressed him a month or two ago. But after yesterday's talk with Lemnitzer he had shelved thoughts of Jenny LaMarsh for the time being.

'Everything's fixed, Mr O'Keefe. Jenny flies to New York tonight; she'll join you there tomorrow. We'll switch Dodo's Naples reservations to Jenny, then Dodo can fly here direct from New Orleans. Simple, eh?'

467

It was indeed simple. So simple, in fact, that O'Keefe could find no flaw in the plan. He wondered why he wanted to.

'You assure me positively that Miss Lash will get the part?'

'Mr O'Keefe, I swear it on my mother's grave.'

'Your mother isn't dead.'

'Then my grandmother's.' There was a pause, then, as if with sudden perception, Lemnitzer said, 'If you're worried about telling Dodo, why don't I do it? You just go out for a couple of hours. I'll call her, fix everything. That way – no fuss, no farewells.'

'Thank you. I'm quite capable of handling the matter personally.'

'Suit yourself, Mr O'Keefe. Just trying to help.'

'Miss Lash will telegraph you the time of her arrival in Los Angeles. You'll meet the flight?'

'Sure thing. It'll be great to see Dodo. Well, Mr O'Keefe have a swell time in Naples. I envy you having Jenny.'

Without acknowledgement, O'Keefe hung up.

Dodo returned breathlessly, loaded with packages and followed by a grinning bellboy, similarly burdened.

'I have to go back, Curtie. There's more.'

O'Keefe said gruffly, 'You could have had all this delivered.'

'Oh, this is more exciting! Like Christmas.' She told the bellboy. 'We're going to Naples. That's in Italy.'

O'Keefe gave the bellboy a dollar and waited until he had gone.

Disentangling herself from her packages, Dodo flung her arms impulsively around O'Keefe's neck. She kissed him on both cheeks. 'Did you miss me? Gee, Curtie, I'm happy!'

O'Keefe disengaged her arms gently. 'Let's sit down. I want to tell you about some changes in plan. I also have some good news.'

'We're going sooner!'

He shook his head. 'It concerns you more than me. The fact is, my dear, you're being given a movie role. It's something I've been working on. I heard this morning – it's all arranged.'

He was aware of Dodo's innocent blue eyes regarding him.

'I'm assured it's a very good part; in fact, I insisted that it should be. If things go well, as I expect them to, it could be the beginning of something very big for you.' Curtis O'Keefe stopped, conscious of a hollowness to his own words.

Dodo said slowly, 'I guess it means . . . I have to go away.'

'Unfortunately, my dear, it does.'

'Soon?'

'I'm afraid – tomorrow morning. You'll fly directly to Los Angeles. Hank Lemnitzer will meet you.'

Dodo moved her head slowly in assent. The slim fingers of one hand went absently to her face, brushing back a strand of ash-blonde hair. It was a simple movement yet, like so many of Dodo's, profoundly sensuous. Unreasonably, O'Keefe experienced a jealous twinge at the thought of Hank Lemnitzer with Dodo. Lemnitzer, who had arranged the ground work for most of his employer's liaisons in the past, would never dare to trifle with a chosen favourite in advance. But afterwards . . . Afterwards was something else again. He thrust the thought away.

'I want you to know, my dear, that losing you is a great blow to me. But we have to think of your future.'

'Curtie, it's all right.' Dodo's eyes were still upon him. Despite their innocence, he had an absurd notion they had penetrated to the truth. 'It's all right. You don't have to worry.'

'I'd hoped – about the movie role – you might be more pleased.'

'I am Curtie! Gee, I really am! I think it's swell the way you always do the sweetest things.'

The reaction bolstered his own confidence. 'It's really a tremendous opportunity. I'm sure you'll do well, and of course I shall follow your career closely.' He resolved to concentrate his thoughts on Jenny La Marsh.

'I guess . . .' There was the slightest catch in Dodo's voice. 'I guess you'll go tonight. Before me.'

Making an instantaneous decision, he answered, 'No, I'll cancel my flight and leave tomorrow morning. Tonight will be a special evening for us both.'

As Dodo looked up gratefully, the telephone rang. With a sense of relief for something else to do, he answered it.

'Mr O'Keefe?' a pleasant woman's voice enquired.

'Yes.'

'This is Christine Francis – Mr Warren Trent's assistant. Mr Trent wondered if it would be convenient for him to come to see you now.'

O'Keefe glanced at his watch. It showed a few minutes before noon.

'Yes,' he acknowledged. 'I'll see Mr Trent. Tell him to come.'

Replacing the telephone, he smiled at Dodo. 'It seems, my dear, we each have something to celebrate – you a glittering future, and me, a new hotel.'

8

An hour or so earlier Warren Trent sat brooding behind the closed double doors of his office in the executive suite. Several times already this morning he had reached out for the telephone with the intention of calling Curtis O'Keefe, accepting the latter's terms for take-over of the hotel. There no longer seemed any cause for delay. The Journeymen's Union had been the final hope of alternative financing. The brusque rejection from that source had crumbled Warren Trent's last resistance against absorption by the O'Keefe behemoth.

Yet on each occasion, after the initial motion of his hand, Warren Trent held back. He was like a prisoner, he mused, condemned to death at a specific hour but with the choice of suicide beforehand. He accepted the inevitable. He realized that he would end his own tenure because there was no alternative. Yet human nature urged him to cling to each remaining moment until all were gone and the need for decision ended.

He had been closest to capitulation when the arrival of Peter McDermott forestalled him. McDermott reported the decision of the Congress of American Dentistry to continue its convention, a fact which did not surprise Warren Trent since he had predicted it the day before. But now the entire affair seemed remote and unimportant. He was glad when McDermott left.

Afterwards, for a while, he fell into a reverie, remembering past triumphs and the satisfactions they had brought. That had been the time – not so long ago, really – when his house was sought by the great and near-great – presidents, crowned heads, nobility, resplendent women and distinguished men, the nabobs of power and wealth, famous and infamous – all with one distinction: they commanded attention and received it. And where these élite led, others followed, until the St Gregory was both a mecca and a machine for making gold.

When memories were all one had – or seemed likely to have – it was wise to savour them. Warren Trent hoped that for the hour or so which remained of his proprietorship he would be undisturbed.

The hope proved vain.

Christine Francis came in quietly, as usual sensing his mood. 'Mr Emile Dumaire would like to speak with you. I wouldn't have disturbed you, but he insisted it's urgent.'

Warren Trent grunted. The vultures were gathering, he thought. Though on second thoughts, perhaps the simile was hardly fair. A good deal of money from the Industrial Merchants Bank, of which Emile Dumaire was president, was tied up in the St Gregory Hotel. It was also Industrial Merchants which, months earlier, had refused an extension of credit as well as a larger loan for refinancing. Well, Dumaire and his fellow directors had nothing to worry about now. With the impending deal their money would be forthcoming. Warren Trent supposed he should give that reassurance.

He reached for the telephone.

'No,' Christine said. 'Mr Dumaire is here, waiting outside.'

Warren Trent stopped, surprised. It was highly unusual for Emile Dumaire to leave the fastness of his bank to make a personal call on anyone.

A moment later Christine ushered the visitor in, closing the door as she left.

Emile Dumaire, short, portly and with a fringe of curly white hair, had an unbroken line of Creole ancestry. Yet he looked – perversely – as if he had stepped from the pages of *Pickwick Papers*. His manner had a pompous fussiness to match.

'I apologize, Warren, for the abrupt intrusion without an appointment. However, the nature of my business left little time for niceties.'

They shook hands perfunctorily. The hotel proprietor waved his visitor to a chair.

'What business?'

'If you don't object, I'd prefer to take things in order. First, permit me to say how sorry I was that it was not feasible to accede to your loan request. Unfortunately, the sum and terms were far beyond your resources or established policy.'

Warren Trent nodded noncommittally. He had little liking for the banker, though he had never made the mistake of underrating him. Beneath the bumbling affectations – which lulled and deceived many – was a capable, shrewd mind.

'However, I am here today with a purpose which I hope may affect some of the unfortunate aspects of that earlier occasion.'

'That,' Warren Trent asserted, 'is extremely unlikely.'

'We'll see.' From a slim briefcase the banker extracted several sheets of ruled paper covered with pencilled notes. 'It is my understanding that you have received an offer for this hotel from the O'Keefe Corporation.'

'You don't need the FBI to tell you that.'

The banker smiled. 'You wouldn't care to inform me of the terms?'

'Why should I?'

'Because,' Emile Dumaire said carefully, 'I am here to make a counter-offer.'

'If that's the case, I'd have even less reason to speak out. What I will tell you is that I've agreed to give the O'Keefe people an answer by noon today.'

'Quite so. My information was to that effect, which is the reason for my abrupt appearance here. Incidentally, I apologize for not being earlier, but my information and instructions have taken some time to assemble.'

The news of an eleventh-hour offer – at least, from the present source – did not excite Warren Trent. He supposed that a local group of investors, for whom Dumaire was spokesman, had combined in an attempt to buy in cheaply now and sell out later with a capital gain. Whatever the suggested terms, they could hardly match the offer of O'Keefe. Nor was Warren Trent's own position likely to be improved.

The banker consulted his pencilled notes. 'It is my understanding that the terms offered by the O'Keefe Corporation are a purchase price of four millions. Of this, two millions would be applied to renewal of the present mortgage, the balance to be a million cash and a million dollars in a new issue of O'Keefe stock. There's an additional rumour that you personally would be given some kind of life tenancy of your quarters in the hotel.'

Warren Trent's face reddened with anger. He slammed a clenched fist hard upon the surface of his desk. 'Goddam, Emile! Don't play cat and mouse with me!'

'If I appeared to, I'm sorry.'

'For God's sake! If you know the details already, why ask?'

'Frankly,' Dumaire said, 'I was hoping for the confirmation that you just gave me. Also, the offer I am authorized to make is somewhat better.'

He had fallen, Warren Trent realized, for an ancient, elementary gambit. But he was indignant that Dumaire should have seen fit to play it on him.

It was also obvious that Curtis O'Keefe had a defector in his own organization, possibly someone at O'Keefe headquarters who was privy to high-level policy. In a way, there was ironic justice in the fact that Curtis O'Keefe, who used espionage as a business tool, should be spied upon himself.

'Just how are the terms better? And by whom are they offered?'

'To reply to the second first – at present I am not at liberty to say.'

Warren Trent snorted, 'I do business with people I can see, not ghosts.'

'I am no ghost,' Dumaire reminded him. 'Moreover you have the bank's assurance that the offer I am empowered to make is bona fide, and that the parties whom the bank represents have unimpeachable credentials.'

Still irked by the stratagem of a few months earlier, the hotel proprietor said, 'Let's get to the point.'

'I was about to do so.' The banker shuffled his notes. 'Basically, the valuation which my principals place upon this hotel is identical with that of the O'Keefe Corporation.'

'That's hardly surprising, since you had O'Keefe's figures.'

'In other respects, however, there are several significant differences.'

For the first time since the beginning of the interview, Warren Trent was conscious of a mounting interest in what the banker had to say.

'First, my principals have no wish that you should sever your personal connection with the St Gregory Hotel or divorce yourself from its financial structure. Second, it would be their intention – in so far as it is commercially feasible – to maintain the hotel's independence and existing character.'

Warren Trent gripped the arms of his chair tightly. He glanced at a wall clock to his right. It showed a quarter to twelve.

'They would, however, insist on acquiring a majority of the outstanding common shares – a reasonable requirement in the circumstances – to provide effective management control. You yourself would thus revert to the status of largest minority stockholder. A further requirement would be your immediate resignation as president and managing director. Could I trouble you for a glass of water?'

Warren Trent filled a single glass from the Thermos jug on his desk. 'What do you have in mind – that I become a busboy? Or perhaps assistant doorman?'

'Scarcely that.' Emile Dumaire sipped from the glass, then regarded it. 'It has always struck me as quite remarkable how our muddy Mississippi can become such pleasant tasting water.'

'Get on with it!'

The banker smiled. 'My principals propose that immediately following your resignation you be appointed chairman of the board, initially for a two-year term.'

'A mere figurehead, I suppose!'

'Perhaps. But it would seem to me that there are worse things. Or perhaps you'd prefer the figurehead to be Mr Curtis O'Keefe.'

The hotel proprietor was silent.

'I am further instructed to inform you that my principals will match any offer of a personal nature concerning accommodation here which you may have received from the O'Keefe Corporation. Now, as to the question of stock transference and refinancing. I'd like to go into that in some detail.'

As the banker talked on, closely consulting his notes, Warren Trent had a sense of weariness and unreality. Out of memory an incident came to him from long ago. Once, as a small boy, he had attended a country fair, clutching a few hoarded pennies to spend on the mechanical rides. There had been one that he had ventured on – a cake walk. It was a form of amusement, he supposed, which had long since passed into limbo. He remembered it as a platform with a multiple-hinged floor which moved continually – now up, now down, now tilting forwards, backwards, forwards . . . so that perspective was never level, and for the cost of a penny one had an imminent chance of falling before attaining the far end. Beforehand it had seemed exciting, but he remembered that nearing the finish of the cake walk he had wanted, more than anything else, merely to get off.

The past few weeks had been like a cake walk too. At the beginning he had been confident, then abruptly the floor had canted away beneath him. It had risen, as hope revived, then slanted away again. Near the end the Journeymen's Union held a promise of stability, then abruptly that too had collapsed on lunatic hinges.

Now, unexpectedly, the cake walk had stabilized once more and all he wanted to do was get off.

Later on, Warren Trent knew, his feelings would change, his personal interest in the hotel reviving, as it always had. But for the moment he was conscious only of relief that, one way or another, the burden of responsibility was shifting on. Along with relief was curiosity.

Who, among the city's business leaders, was behind Emile Dumaire? Who might care enough to run the financial risk of maintaining the St Gregory as a traditionally independent house? Mark Preyscott, perhaps? Could the department-store chieftain be seeking to augment his already widespread interests? Warren Trent recalled having heard from someone, during the past few days, that Mark Preyscott was in Rome. That might account for the indirect approach. Well, whoever it was, he supposed he would learn soon enough.

The stock transition which the banker was spelling out was fair. Compared with the offer from O'Keefe, Warren Trent's personal cash settlement would be smaller, but offset by a retained equity in the hotel. In contrast, the O'Keefe terms would cast him adrift from the St Gregory affairs entirely.

As to an appointment as chairman of the board, while it might be a token post only, devoid of power, he would at least be an inside, privileged spectator to whatever might ensue. Nor was the prestige to be dismissed lightly.

'That,' Emile Dumaire concluded, 'is the sum and substance. As to the offer's integrity, I have already stated that it is guaranteed by the bank. Furthermore, I am prepared to give you a notarized letter of intention, this afternoon, to that effect.'

'And completion, if I agree?'

The banker pursed his lips, considering. 'There is no reason why papers could not be drawn quickly, besides which the matter of the impending mortgage expiry lends some urgency. I would say completion tomorrow at this time.'

'And also at that time, no doubt, I would be told the purchaser's identity.'

'That,' Emile Dumaire conceded, 'would be essential to the transaction.'

'If tomorrow, why not now?'

The banker shook his head. 'I am bound by my instructions.'

Briefly, in Warren Trent's mind, his old ill-temper flared. He was tempted to insist on revelation as a condition of assent. Then reason argued: Did it matter, providing the stipulations pledged were met? Disputation, too, would involve effort to which he felt unequal. Once more, the weariness of a few minutes earlier engulfed him.

He sighed, then said simply, 'I accept.'

Incredulously, wrathfully, Curtis O'Keefe faced Warren Trent.

'You have the effrontery to stand there telling me you've sold elsewhere!'

They were in the living-room of O'Keefe's suite. Immediately following the departure of Emile Dumaire, Christine Francis had telephoned to make the appointment which Warren Trent was keeping now. Dodo, her expression uncertain, hovered behind O'Keefe.

'You may call it effrontery,' Warren Trent replied. 'As far as I am concerned it's information. You may also be interested to know that I have not sold entirely, but have retained a substantial interest in the hotel.'

'Then you'll lose it!' O'Keefe's face flushed with rage. It had been many years since anything he wished to buy had been denied him. Even now, obsessed with bitterness and disappointment, he could not believe the rejection to be true. 'By God! I swear I'll break you.'

Dodo reached out. Her hand touched O'Keefe's sleeve. 'Curtie!'

He wrenched the arm free. 'Shut up!' A vein pulsed visibly across his temples. His hands were clenched.

'You're excited, Curtie. You shouldn't . . .'

'Damn you! Keep out of this!'

Dodo's eyes went appealingly to Warren Trent. They had the effect of curbing Trent's own temper which had been about to erupt.

He told O'Keefe, 'You may do what you please. But I'd remind you you have no divine right of purchase. Also, you came here of your own accord with no invitation from me.'

'You'll rue this day! You and the others, whoever they are. I'll build! I'll drive this hotel down, and out of business. Every vestige of my planning will be directed at smashing this place and you with it.'

'If either of us lives that long.' Having contained himself already, Warren Trent felt his own self-control increase as O'Keefe's diminished. 'We may not see it happen, of course, because what you intend will take time. Also, the new people here may give you a run for your money.' It was an uninformed prediction, but he hoped it would prove true.

O'Keefe raged, 'Get out!'

Warren Trent, 'This is my house still. While you are my guest you have certain privileges in your own rooms. I'd suggest, though, you don't abuse them.' With a slight, courteous bow to Dodo, he went out.

'Curtie,' Dodo said.

O'Keefe did not appear to hear. He was breathing heavily.

'Curtie, are you all right?'

'Must you ask stupid questions? Of course I'm all right!' He stormed the length of the room and back.

'It's only a hotel, Curtie. You got so many others.'

'I want this one!'

'That old man – it's the only one he's got . . .'

'Oh yes! Of course you'd see it that way. Disloyally! Stupidly!' His voice was high, hysterical. Dodo, frightened, had never known him in a mood so uncontrolled before.

'Please, Curtie!'

'I'm surrounded by fools! Fools, fools, fools! You're a fool! It's why I'm getting rid of you. Replacing you with someone else.'

He regretted the words the instant they were out. Their impact, even upon himself, was of shock, snuffing out his anger like a suddenly doused flame. There was a second of silence before he mumbled, 'I'm sorry. I shouldn't have said that.'

Dodo's eyes were misty. She touched her hair abstractedly in the gesture he had noticed earlier.

'I guess I knew, Curtie. You didn't have to tell me.'

She went into the adjoining suite, closing the door behind her.

10

An unexpected bonus had revived the spirits of Keycase Milne.

During the morning, Keycase had returned his strategic purchases of yesterday to the Maison Blanche department store. There was no difficulty and he received prompt, courteous refunds. This, at the same time, relieved him of an encumbrance and filled an otherwise empty hour. There were still several more hours to wait, however, until the specially made key, ordered yesterday from the Irish Channel locksmith, would be ready for collection.

He was on the point of leaving the Maison Blanche store when his good fortune occurred.

At a main floor counter, a well-dressed woman shopper, fumbling for a credit card, dropped a ring of keys. Neither she nor anyone else but Keycase, it seemed, observed the loss. Keycase loitered, inspecting neckties at a neighbouring counter, until the woman moved on.

He walked the length of the other counter, then, as if seeing the keys for the first time, stopped to pick them up. He observed at once that as well as car keys there were several others which looked as if they fitted house locks. Even more significant was something else which his experienced eyes had spotted initially – a miniature auto licence tag. It was the kind mailed to car owners by disabled veterans, providing a return service for lost keys. The tag showed a Louisiana licence number.

Holding the keys plainly in sight, Keycase hurried after the woman, who was leaving the store. If his action of a moment earlier had been observed, it was now obvious that he was hastening to restore the keys to their owner.

But on joining the press of pedestrians on Canal Street, he palmed the keys and transferred them to a pocket.

The woman was still in sight. Keycase followed her at a cautious distance. After two blocks she crossed Canal Street and entered a beauty parlour. From outside, Keycase saw her approach a receptionist who consulted an appointment book, after which the woman sat down to wait. With a sense of elation, Keycase hurried to a telephone.

A local telephone call established that the information he sought was obtainable from the state capital at Baton Rouge. Keycase made the long-distance call, asking for the Motor Vehicle Division. The operator answering knew at once the extension he required.

Holding the keys in front of him, Keycase read out the licence number from the miniature tag. A bored clerk informed him that the car was registered to one F. R. Drummond, with an address in the Lakeview district of New Orleans.

In Louisiana, as in other states and provinces of North America, motor vehicle ownership was a matter of public record, obtainable in most instances by no greater effort than a telephone call. It was a nugget of knowledge which Keycase had used advantageously before.

He made one more telephone call, dialling the listed number for F. R. Drummond. As he had hoped, after prolonged ringing there was no answer.

It was necessary to move speedily. Keycase calculated that he had an hour, perhaps a little more. He hailed a taxi which took him quickly to where his car was parked. From there, with the aid of a street map, he drove to Lakeview, locating without difficulty the address he had jotted down.

He surveyed the house from half a block away. It was a well-cared-for-two-storey residence with a double garage and spacious garden. The driveway was sheltered by a large cypress tree, fortuitously blocking the view from neighbouring houses on either side.

Keycase drove his car boldly under the trees and walked to the front door. It opened easily to the first key he tried.

Inside the house was silent. He called out loudly, 'Anybody home?' If there had been an answer, he was ready with a prepared excuse about the door being ajar and having come to the wrong address. There was none.

He scouted the main floor rooms quickly, then went upstairs. There were four bedrooms, all unoccupied. In a closet of the largest were two fur coats. He pulled them out, piling them on the bed. Another closet revealed suitcases. Keycase selected a large one and bundled the furs in. A dressing-table drawer yielded a jewellery box which he emptied into the suitcase, adding a movie camera, binoculars and a portable radio. He closed the case and carried it downstairs, then reopened it to add a silver bowl and salver. A tape recorder, which he noticed at the last moment, he carried out to the car in one hand, the larger case in the other.

In all, Keycase had been inside the house barely ten minutes. He stowed the case and recorder in the trunk of his car and drove away. Just over an hour later he had cached the haul in his motel room on Chef Menteur Highway, parked his car once more in its downtown location, and was walking jauntily back to the St Gregory Hotel.

On the way, with a gleam of humour, he put the keys into a mail box, as the miniature licence tag requested. No doubt the tag organization would fulfil its promise and return them to the owner.

The unexpected booty, Keycase calculated, would net him close to a thousand dollars.

He had a coffee and sandwich in the St Gregory coffee shop, then walked to the Irish Channel locksmith's. The duplicate key to the Presidential Suite was ready, and despite the extortionate price demanded, he paid cheerfully.

Returning, he was conscious of the sun shining benevolently from a cloudless sky. That, and the morning's unexpected bounty, were plainly omens, portents of success for the major mission soon to come. His old assurance, Keycase found, plus a conviction of invincibility, had seeped quietly back.

11

Across the city, in leisurely disorder, the chimes of New Orleans were ringing the noon hour. Their melodies in counter-point came dimly through the ninth-floor window – closed and sealed for effective air conditioning – of the Presidential Suite. The Duke of Croydon, unsteadily pouring a Scotch and soda, his fourth since mid-morning, heard the bells and glanced at his watch for confirmation of their message. He shook his head unbelievingly and muttered, 'That's all? . . . Longest day . . . ever remember living.'

'Eventually it will end.' From a sofa where she had been attempting unsuccessfully to concentrate on W. H. Auden's *Poems*, his wife's rejoinder was less severe than most of her responses of the past several days. The waiting period since the previous night, with the awareness that Ogilvie and the incriminating car were somewhere to the north – but where? – had been a strain on the Duchess too. It was now nineteen hours since the Croydons' last contact with the chief house officer and there had been no word of a development of any kind.

'For God's sake! – couldn't the fellow telephone?' The Duke paced the living-room agitatedly as he had, off and on, since early morning.

'We agreed there should be no communication,' the Duchess reminded him, still mildly. 'It's a good deal safer that way. Besides, if the car is hidden for the daytime, as we hoped, he's probably remaining out of sight.'

The Duke of Croydon pored over an opened Esso road map, examining it as he had countless times already. His finger traced a circle around the area surrounding Macon, Mississippi. He said, half to himself, 'It's close, still so infernally close. And all of today . . . just waiting . . . waiting!' Moving away from the map, he muttered, 'Fellow could be discovered.'

'Obviously he hasn't been, or we would have heard one way or another.' Beside the Duchess was a copy of the afternoon *States-Item*; she had sent their secretary down to the lobby for an early edition. As well, they had listened to hourly radio news broadcasts throughout the morning. A radio was turned on softly now, but the announcer was describing damage from a summer storm in Massachusetts and the preceding item had been a White House statement on Vietnam. Both the newspaper and earlier broadcasts had referred to the hit-and-run investigation, but merely to note that it was continuing and nothing new had come to light.

'There were only a few hours for driving last night,' the Duchess continued, as if to reassure herself. 'Tonight it will be different. He can start immediately it's dark and by tomorrow morning everything should be safe.'

'Safe!' Her husband returned morosely to his drink. 'I suppose it's the sensible thing to care about. Not what happened. That woman . . . the child. There were pictures . . . suppose you saw.'

'We've been over that. It won't do any good again.'

He appeared not to have heard. 'Funeral today . . . this afternoon . . . at least we could go.'

'You can't, and you know you won't.'

There was a heavy silence in the elegant, spacious room.

It was broken abruptly by the jangle of the telephone. They faced each other, neither attempting to answer. The muscles of the Duke's face jerked spasmodically.

The bell sounded again, then stopped. Through intervening doors they heard the voice of the secretary indistinctly, answering on an extension.

A moment later the secretary knocked and came in diffidently. He glanced towards the Duke. 'Your Grace, it's one of the local newspapers. They say that they have had' – he hesitated at an unfamiliar term – 'a flash bulletin which appears to concern you.'

With an effort the Duchess recovered poise. 'I will take the call. Hang up the extension.' She picked up the telephone near her. Only a close observer would have noticed that her hands were trembling.

She waited for the click as the extension was replaced, then announced, 'The Duchess

477

of Croydon speaking.'

A man's crisp voice responded, 'Ma'am, this is the *States-Item* city desk. We've a flash from Associated Press and there's just been a follow-up . . .' The voice stopped. 'Pardon me.' She heard the speaker say irritably, 'Where in hell is that . . . Hey, toss over that flimsy, Andy.'

There was a rustle of paper, then the voice resuming. 'Sorry, ma'am. I'll read this to you.

LONDON (AP) – Parliamentary sources here today named the Duke of Croydon, noted British government trouble shooter, as Britain's next ambassador to Washington. Initial reaction is favourable. An official announcement is expected soon.

There's more ma'am. I won't bother you with it. Why we called was to see if your husband has a statement, then with your permission we'd like to send a photographer to the hotel.'

Momentarily the Duchess closed her eyes, letting the waves of relief, like soothing anodynes, wash over her.

The voice on the telephone cut in, 'Ma'am, are you still there?'

'Yes.' She forced her mind to function.

'About a statement, what we'd like . . .'

'At the moment,' the Duchess interjected, 'my husband has no statement, nor will he have unless and until the appointment is officially confirmed.'

'In that case . . .'

'The same applies to photography.'

The voice sounded disappointed. 'We'll run what we have, of course, in the next edition.'

'That is your privilege.'

'Meanwhile, if there's an official announcement we'd like to be in touch.'

'Should that occur, I'm sure my husband will be glad to meet the press.'

'Then we may telephone again?'

'Please do.'

After replacing the telephone, the Duchess of Croydon sat upright and unmoving. At length, a slight smile hovering around her lips, she said, 'It's happened. Geoffrey has succeeded.'

Her husband stared incredulously. He moistened his lips. 'Washington?'

She repeated the gist of the AP bulletin. 'The leak was probably deliberate, to test reaction. It's favourable.'

'I wouldn't have believed that even your brother . . .'

'His influence helped. Undoubtedly there were other reasons. Timing. Someone with your kind of background was needed. Politics fitted. Don't forget either that we knew the possibility existed. Fortunately, everything chanced to fall together.'

'Now that it's happened . . .' He stopped, unwilling to complete the thought.

'Now that it's happened – what?'

'I wonder . . . can I carry it through?'

'You can and you will. *We* will,'

He moved his head doubtfully. 'There was a time . . .'

'There is still a time.' The Duchess's voice sharpened with authority. 'Later today you will be obliged to meet the press. There will be other things. It will be necessary for you to be coherent and remain so.'

He nodded slowly. ' . . . Do best I can.' He lifted his glass to sip.

'No!' The Duchess rose. She removed the tumbler from her husband's fingers and walked to the bathroom. He heard the contents of the glass being poured into the sink. Returning she announced. 'There will be no more. You understand? No more whatever.'

He seemed about to protest, then acknowledged, 'Suppose . . . only way.'

'If you'd like me to take away the bottles, pour out this one . . .'

He shook his head. 'I'll manage.' Perceptibly, with an effort of will, he brought his thoughts to focus. With the same chameleon quality he had exhibited the day before, there seemed more strength in his features than a moment earlier. His voice was steady as he observed, 'It's very good news.'

'Yes,' the Duchess said. 'It can mean a new beginning.'

He took a half step towards her, then changed his mind. Whatever the new beginning, he was well aware it would not include that.

His wife was already responding aloud. 'It will be necessary to revise our plans about Chicago. From now on your movements will be the subject of close attention. If we go there together it will be reported prominently in the Chicago press. It could arouse curiosity when the car is taken for repair.'

'One of us must go.'

The Duchess said decisively, 'I shall go alone. I can change my appearance a little, wear glasses. If I'm careful I can escape attention.' Her eyes went to a small attaché case beside the *secrétaire*. 'I will take the remainder of the money and do whatever else is needed.'

'You're assuming . . . that man will get to Chicago safely. He hasn't yet.'

Her eyes widened as if remembering a forgotten nightmare. She whispered, 'Oh God! Now . . . above all else . . . he must! He must!'

12

Shortly after lunch, Peter McDermott managed to slip away to his apartment where he changed, from the formal business suit he wore most of the time in the hotel, to linen slacks and a lightweight jacket. He returned briefly to his office to sign letters which, on the way out, he deposited on Flora's desk.

'I'll be back late this afternoon,' he told her. Then as an afterthought: 'Did you discover anything about Ogilvie?'

His secretary shook her head. 'Not really. You asked me to find out if Mr Ogilvie told anyone where he was going. Well, he didn't.'

Peter grunted. 'I didn't really expect he would.'

'There's just one thing.' Flora hesitated. 'It's probably not important, but it seemed a little strange.'

'What?'

'The car Mr Ogilvie used – you said it was a Jaguar?'

'Yes.'

'It belongs to the Duke and Duchess of Croydon.'

'Are you sure someone hasn't made a mistake?'

'I wondered about that,' Flora said, 'so I asked the garage to double check. They told me to talk to a man named Kulgmer who's the garage night checker.'

'Yes, I know him.'

'He was on duty last night and I phoned him at home. He said Mr Ogilvie had written authority from the Duchess of Croydon to take the car.'

Peter shrugged. 'Then I guess there's nothing wrong.' It was strange, though, to think of Ogilvie using the Croydons' car; even stranger that there should be any kind of rapport between the Duke and Duchess and the uncouth house officer. Obviously, Flora had been considering the same thing.

He enquired, 'Has the car come back?'

Flora shook her head negatively. 'I wondered if I should check with the Duchess of Croydon. Then I thought I'd ask you first.'

'I'm glad you did.' He supposed it would be simple enough to ask the Croydons if they knew Ogilvie's destination. Since Ogilvie had the car, it seemed probable they would. All the same, he hesitated. After his own skirmish with the Duchess on Monday night, Peter was reluctant to risk another misunderstanding, especially since any kind of enquiry might be resented as a personal intrusion. There was also the embarrassing admission to be made that the hotel had no knowledge of the whereabouts of its chief house officer.

He told Flora, 'Let's leave it for the time being.'

There was another piece of unfinished business, Peter remembered – Herbie Chandler. This morning he had intended to inform Warren Trent of the statements made yesterday by Dixon, Dumaire and the others, implicating the bell captain in events leading up to Monday night's attempted rape. However, the hotel owner's obvious preoccupation made him decide against it. Now Peter supposed he had better see Chandler himself.

'Find out if Herbie Chandler's on duty this evening,' he instructed Flora. 'If he is, tell him I'd like to see him here at six o'clock. If not, tomorrow morning.'

Leaving the executive suite, Peter descended to the lobby. A few minutes later, from the comparative gloom of the hotel, he stepped out into the brilliant, early afternoon sunlight of St Charles Street.

'Peter! I'm here.'

Turning his head, he saw Marsha, waving from the driver's seat of a white convertible, the car wedged into a line of waiting cabs. An alert hotel doorman briskly preceded Peter and opened the car door. As Peter slid into the seat beside Marsha, he saw a trio of cab drivers grin, and one gave a long wolf whistle.

'Hi!' Marsha said. 'If you hadn't come I was going to have to pick up a fare.' In a light summer dress, she appeared as delectable as ever, but for all the light-hearted greeting he sensed a shyness, perhaps because of what had passed between them the night before. Impulsively, he took her hand and squeezed it.

'I like that,' she assured him, 'even though I promised my father I'd use both hands to drive.' With help from the taxi drivers, who moved forward and back to create a space, she eased the convertible out into traffic.

It seemed, Peter reflected as they waited for a green light at Canal Street, that he was constantly being driven about New Orleans by attractive women. Was it only three days ago that he had ridden with Christine in the Volkswagen to her apartment? That was the same night he had met Marsha for the first time. It seemed longer than three days, perhaps because a proposal of marriage by Marsha had occurred in the meantime. In the reality of daylight he wondered if she had had more rational second thoughts, though either way, he decided, he would say nothing unless she revived the subject herself.

There was an excitement, just the same, in being close together, especially remembering their parting moments of the night before – the kiss, tender, then with mounting passion as restraint dissolved; the breathless moment when he had thought of Marsha not as a girl, but as a woman; had held her, tightly, sensing the urgent promise of her body. He watched her covertly now; her eager youthfulness, the lissome movements of her limbs; the slightness of her figure beneath the thin dress. If he reached out . . .

He checked the impulse, though reluctantly. In the same self-chastening vein, he reminded himself that all his adult life so far, the immediacy of a woman had clouded his own judgement, precipitating indiscretions.

Marsha glanced sideways, diverting her attention from the traffic ahead. 'What were you thinking about just then?'

'History,' he lied. 'Where do we start?'

'The old St Louis Cemetery. You haven't been there?'

Peter shook his head. 'I've never put cemeteries high on my list of things to do.'

'In New Orleans you should.'

It was a short drive to Basin Street. Marsha parked neatly on the south side and they crossed the boulevard to the walled cemetery – St Louis number one – with its ancient pillared entrance.

'A lot of history begins here,' Marsha said, taking Peter's arm. 'In the early 1700s, when New Orleans was founded by the French, the land was mostly swamp. It would still be swamp, even now, if it weren't for the levees which kept the river out.'

'I know it's a wet city underneath,' he agreed. 'In the hotel basement, twenty-four hours a day, we pump our waste water up, not down, to meet the city sewers.'

'It used to be a whole lot wetter. Even in dry places water was just three feet down, so when a grave was dug it flooded before anyone could put a coffin in. There are stories that grave-diggers used to stand on coffins to force them down. Sometimes they punched holes in the wood to make the coffin sink. People used to say, if you weren't really dead, you'd drown.'

'Sounds like a horror movie.'

'Some books say the smell of dead bodies used to seep into the drinking water.' She made a grimace of distaste. 'Anyway, later on there was a law that all burials had to be above the ground.'

They began to walk between rows of uniquely constructed tombs. The cemetery was unlike any other Peter had ever seen. Marsha gestured around them. 'This is what happened after the law was passed. In New Orleans we call these places cities of the dead.'

'I can understand why.'

It was like a city, he thought. The streets irregular, with tombs in the style of miniature houses, brick and stuccoed, some with ironwork balconies and narrow sidewalks. The houses had several floors or levels. An absence of windows was the only consistent feature, but in their place were countless tiny doorways. He pointed. 'They're like apartment entrances.'

'They are apartments, really. And most on short leases.'

He looked at her curiously.

'The tombs are divided into sections,' Marsha explained. 'The ordinary family tombs have two to six sections, the bigger ones more. Each section has its own little door. When there's to be a funeral, ahead of time one of the doorways is opened up. The coffin already inside is emptied, and the remains from it pushed to the back where they fall through a slot into the ground. The old coffin is burned and the new one put in. It's left for a year, then the same thing happens.'

'Just a year?'

A voice behind said, "S all it needs. 'Times, though, it's longer – if the next to go ain't in a hurry. Cockroaches help some.'

They turned. An elderly, barrel-shaped man in stained denim coveralls regarded them cheerfully. Removing an ancient straw hat, he mopped his bald head with a red silk handkerchief. 'Hot, ain't it? Lot cooler in there.' He slapped his hand familiarly against a tomb.

'If it's all one to you,' Peter said. 'I'll settle for the heat.'

The other chuckled. 'Git y'anyhow in th' end. Howdy, Miss Preyscott.'

'Hullo, Mr Collodi,' Marsha said. 'This is Mr McDermott.'

The sexton nodded agreeably. 'Takin' a look at the family snuggery?'

'We were going to,' Marsha said.

'This way, then.' Over his shoulder he called out. 'We cleaned 'er up, week or two back. Lookin' mighty good now.'

As they threaded their way through the narrow, make-believe streets, Peter had an impression of ancient dates and names. Their guide pointed to a smouldering pile of rubble in an open space. 'Havin' a bit of a burn-up.' Peter could see portions of coffin amid the smoke.

They stopped before a six-sectioned tomb, built like a traditional Creole house. It was painted white and in better repair than most around it. On weathered marble tablets were many names, mostly of Preyscotts. 'We're an old family,' Marsha said. 'It must be getting crowded down among the dust.'

Sunshine slanted brightly on the tomb.

'Purty, ain't it?' The sexton stood back admiringly, then pointed to a doorway near the top. 'That's the next one for opening, Miss Preyscott. Your daddy'll go in there.' He touched another in a second tier. 'That'n 'll be fer you. Doubt, though, I'll be the one to put you in.' He stopped, then added contemplatively. 'Comes sooner than we want for all of us. Don't do neither, to waste no time; no sir!' Mopping his head once more, he ambled off.

Despite the heat of the day, Peter shivered. The thought of earmarking a place of death for someone so young as Marsha troubled him.

'It's not as morbid as it seems.' Marsha's eyes were on his face and he was aware once more of her ability to understand his thoughts. 'It's simply that here we're brought up to see all this as part of us.'

He nodded. Just the same, he had had enough of this place of death.

They were on the way out, near the Basin Street gate, when Marsha put a hand on his arm restrainingly.

A line of cars had stopped immediately outside. As their doors opened, people emerged and were gathering on the sidewalk. From their appearance it was obvious that a funeral procession was about to come in.

Marsha whispered, 'Peter, we'll have to wait.' They moved away, still within sight of the gates, but less conspicuously.

Now the group on the sidewalk parted, making way for a small cortege. A sallow man with the unctuous bearing of an undertaker came first. He was followed by a priest.

Behind the priest was a group of six pall-bearers, moving slowly, a heavy coffin on their shoulders. Behind them, four others carried a tiny white coffin. On it was a single spray of oleanders.

'Oh no!' Marsha said.

Peter gripped her hand tightly.

The priest intoned. 'May the angels take you into paradise: may the martyrs come to welcome you on your way, and lead you into the holy city, Jerusalem.'

A group of mourners followed the second coffin. In front, walking alone, was a youngish man. He wore an ill-fitting black suit and carried a hat awkwardly. His eyes seemed riveted on the tiny coffin. Tears coursed his cheeks. In the group behind, an older woman sobbed, supported by another.

' . . . May the choir of angels welcome you, and with Lazurus who was once poor, may you have everlasting rest . . .'

Marsha whispered, 'It's the people who were killed in that hit-and-run. There was a mother, a little girl. It was in the newspapers.' He saw that she was crying.

'I know.' Peter had a sense of being part of this scene, of sharing its grief. The earlier chance encounter of Monday night had been grim and stark. Now the sense of tragedy seemed closer, more intimately real. He felt his own eyes moisten as the cortege moved on.

Behind the family mourners were others. To his surprise, Peter recognized a face. At first he was unable to identify its owner, then realized it was Sol Natchez, the elderly room-service waiter suspended from duty after the dispute with the Duke and Duchess of Croydon on Monday night. Peter had sent for Natchez on Tuesday morning and conveyed Warren Trent's edict to spend the rest of the week away from the hotel, with pay. Natchez looked across to where Peter and Marsha were standing but gave no sign of recognition. The funeral procession moved farther into the cemetery and out of sight. They waited until all the mourners and spectators had followed it.

'We can go now,' Marsha said.

Unexpectedly a hand touched Peter's arm. Turning, he saw it was Sol Natchez. So he had observed them, after all.

'I saw you watching, Mr McDermott. Did you know the family?'

'No,' Peter said, 'We were here by chance.' He introduced Marsha.

She asked, 'You didn't wait for the end of the service?'

The old man shook his head. 'Sometimes there's just so much you can bear to watch.'

'You knew the family, then?'

'Very well. It's a sad, sad thing.'

Peter nodded. There seemed nothing else to say.

Natchez said. 'I didn't get to say it Tuesday, Mr McDermott, but I appreciate what you did. In speaking up for me, I mean.'

'It's all right, Sol. I didn't think you were to blame.'

'It's a funny thing when you think about it.' The old man looked at Marsha, then Peter. He seemed reluctant to leave.

'What's funny?' Peter said.

'All this. The accident.' Natchez gestured in the direction the cortege had gone. 'It must have happened just before I had that bit of trouble Monday night. Just think, while you and me were talking . . .'

'Yes,' Peter said. He felt disinclined to explain his own experience later at the accident scene.

'I meant to ask, Mr McDermott – was anything more said about that business with the Duke and Duchess?'

'Nothing at all.'

Peter supposed that Natchez found it a relief, as he himself did, to consider something other than the funeral.

The waiter ruminated, 'I thought about it a lot after. Seemed almost as if they went out of their way to make a fuss. Couldn't figure it out. Still can't.'

Natchez, Peter remembered, had said much the same thing on Monday night. The waiter's exact words came back to him. Natchez had been speaking of the Duchess of Croydon. *She jogged my arm. If I didn't know better, I'd say it was deliberate.* And later Peter had had the same general impression: that the Duchess wanted the incident remembered. What was it she had said? Something about spending a quiet evening in the suite, then taking a walk around the block. They had just come back, she said. Peter recalled wondering at the time why she had made such a point of it.

Then the Duke of Croydon had mumbled something about leaving the cigarettes in the car, and the Duchess had snapped back at him.

The Duke had left his cigarettes in the car.

But if the Croydons had stayed in the suite, then merely walked around the block . . .

Of course, the cigarettes might have been left earlier in the day.

Somehow Peter didn't think so.

Oblivious of the other two, he concentrated.

Why did the Croydons wish to conceal the use of their car on Monday night? Why create an appearance – apparently false – of having spent the evening in the hotel? Was the complaint about spilled shrimp Creole a staged device – deliberately involving Natchez, then Peter – intended to uphold this fiction? Except for the Duke's chance remark, *which angered the Duchess*, Peter would have accepted it as true.

Why conceal the use of their car?

Natchez had said a moment ago: *It's a funny thing . . . the accident . . . must have happened just before I had that bit of trouble.*

The Croydons' car was a Jaguar.

Ogilvie.

He had a sudden memory of the Jaguar emerging from the garage last night. As it stopped, momentarily, under a light, there had been something strange. He recalled noticing. But what? With an awful coldness he remembered *it was the fender and headlight; both were damaged.* For the first time the significance of police bulletins of the past few days struck home.

'Peter,' Marsha said, 'you've suddenly gone white.'

He scarcely heard.

It was essential to get away, to be somewhere alone where he could thing. He must reason carefully, logically, unhurriedly. Above all, there must be no hasty ready-made conclusions.

There were pieces of a puzzle. Superficially, they appeared to relate. But they must be considered, reconsidered, arranged, and rearranged. Perhaps discarded.

The idea was impossible. It was simply too fantastic to be true. And yet . . .

As if from a distance, he heard Marsha's voice. 'Peter! Something's wrong. What is it?' Sol Natchez, too, was looking at him strangely.

'Marsha,' Peter said, 'I can't tell you now. But I have to go.'

'Go where?'

'Back to the hotel. I'm sorry. I'll try to explain later.'

Her voice showed disappointment. 'I'd planned we'd have tea.'

'Please believe me! It's important.'

'If you must go, I'll drive you.'

'No.' Driving with Marsha would involve talking, explanations. 'Please. I'll call you later.'

He left them standing, bewildered, looking after him.

Outside, on Basin Street, he hailed a cruising cab. He had told Marsha that he was going to the hotel but, changing his mind, he gave the driver the address of his apartment. It would be quieter there.

To think. To decide what he should do.

It was approaching late afternoon when Peter McDermott summarized his reasoning.

He told himself: When you added something twenty, thirty, forty times, when every time the conclusion you arrived at was the same; when the issue was the kind of issue you were facing now; with all of this, your own responsibility was inescapable.

Since leaving Marsha an hour and a half ago, he had remained in his apartment. He had forced himself – subduing agitation and an impulse for haste – to think rationally, carefully, unexcitedly. He had reviewed, point by point, the accumulated incidents since Monday night. He had searched for alternatives of explanation, both for single happenings and the accumulation of them all. He found none that offered either consistency or sense, save the awful conclusion he had reached so suddenly this afternoon.

Now the reasoning had ended. A decision must be made.

He contemplated placing all he knew and conjectured before Warren Trent. Then he dismissed the idea as being cowardly, a shirking of his own responsibility. Whatever was to be done, he must do alone.

There was a sense of the fitness of things to be served. He changed quickly from his light suit to a darker one. Leaving, he took a taxi the few blocks to the hotel.

From the lobby he walked, acknowledging salutations, to his office on the main mezzanine. Flora had left for the day. There was a pile of messages on his desk which he ignored.

He sat quietly for a moment in the silent office, contemplating what he must do. Then he lifted the telephone, waited for a line, and dialled the number of the city police.

13

The persistent buzzing of a mosquito, which had somehow found its way into the Jaguar's interior, woke Ogilvie during the afternoon. He came awake slowly and at first had difficulty remembering where he was. Then the sequence of events came back: the departure from the hotel, the drive in early morning darkness, the alarm – unfounded, his decision to wait out the day before resuming the journey north; and finally the rutted, grassy track with a cluster of trees at its end where he had concealed the car.

The hideaway had apparently been well chosen. A glance at his watch showed that he had slept, uninterrupted, for almost eight hours.

With consciousness also came intense discomfort. The car was stifling, his body stiff and aching from confinement in the cramped rear seat. His mouth was dry and tasted foul. He was thirsty and ravenously hungry.

With grunts of anguish Ogilvie eased his bulk to a sitting position and opened the car door. Immediately, he was surrounded by a dozen more mosquitoes. He brushed them away, then glanced around, taking time to reorient himself, comparing what he saw now with his impressions of the place this morning. Then it had been barely light, and cool; now the sun was high and, even under the shade of the trees, the heat intense.

Moving to the edge of the trees he could see the distant main road with heat waves shimmering above it. Early this morning there had been no traffic. Now there were several cars and trucks, moving swiftly in both directions, the sound of their motors faintly audible.

Closer at hand, apart from a steady hum of insects, there was no sign of activity. Between himself and the main road were only drowsy meadows, the quiet path and the secluded clump of trees. Beneath the latter the Jaguar remained hidden.

Ogilvie relieved himself, then opened a package he had stowed in the trunk of the car before leaving the hotel. It included a Thermos of coffee, several cans of beer, sandwiches, a salami sausage, a jar of pickles and an apple pie. He ate voraciously, washing down the meal with copious draughts of beer, and, later, coffee. The coffee had cooled since the night before but was strong and satisfying.

While eating, he listened to the car radio, waiting for a newscast from New Orleans. When it came there was only a brief reference to the hit-and-run investigation, to the effect that no new developments had been reported.

Afterwards, he decided to explore. A few hundred yards away, on the crest of a knoll, was a second clump of trees, somewhat larger than the first. He crossed an open field towards it and, on the other side of the trees, found a mossy bank and a sluggish, muddy stream. Kneeling beside the stream, he made a rough toilet and afterwards felt refreshed. The grass was greener and more inviting than where the car was sheltered and he lay down gratefully, using his suit for a pillow.

When he was comfortably settled, Ogilvie reviewed the events of the night and the prospect ahead. Reflection confirmed his earlier conclusion that the encounter with Peter McDermott outside the hotel had been accidental and could now be dismissed. It was predictable that McDermott's reaction, on learning of the chief house officer's absence, would be explosive. But that in itself would not reveal either Ogilvie's destination or his reason for departure.

Of course, it was possible that through some other cause an alarm had been raised since last night, and that even now Ogilvie and the Jaguar were being actively sought. But in the light of the radio report it seemed unlikely.

On the whole, the outlook appeared bright, especially when he thought of the money already in safe keeping, and the remainder he would collect tomorrow in Chicago. Now he had only to wait for darkness.

14

The exhilarated mood of Keycase Milne persisted through the afternoon. It bolstered his confidence as, shortly after five p.m., he cautiously approached the Presidential Suite.

Once more he had used the service stairs from the eighth floor to the ninth. The duplicate key, manufactured by the Irish Channel locksmith, was in his pocket.

The corridor outside the Presidential Suite was empty. He stopped at the double leather-padded doors, listening intently, but could hear no sound.

He glanced both ways down the corridor then, with a single movement, produced a key and tried it in the lock. Beforehand he had brushed the key with powdered graphite, as a lubricant. It went in, caught momentarily, then turned. Keycase opened one of the double doors an inch. There was still no sound from inside. He closed the door carefully and removed the key.

It was not his purpose now to enter the suite. That would come later. Tonight.

His intention had been to reconnoitre and ensure that the key was a good fit, ready for instant use whenever he chose. Later he would begin a vigil, watching for an opportunity his planning had foreseen.

For now, he returned to his room on the eighth floor and there, after setting an alarm clock, slept.

15

Outside it was growing dusk and, excusing himself, Peter McDermott got up from his desk to switch on the office lights. He returned to face, once more, the quietly spoken man in grey flannel, seated opposite. Captain Yolles of the Detective Bureau, New Orleans Police, looked less like a policeman than anyone Peter had ever seen. He continued to listen politely, as a bank manager might consider an application for a loan, to Peter's recital of fact and surmise. Only once during the lengthy discourse had the detective interrupted, to enquire if he could make a telephone call. Informed that he could, he used an extension on the far side of the office and spoke in a voice so low that Peter heard nothing of what was said.

The absence of any measurable response had the effect of reviving Peter's doubts. At the end, he observed, 'I'm not sure all this, or even any of it, makes sense. In fact I'm already beginning to feel a little foolish.'

'If more people took a chance on that, Mr McDermott, it would make police work a lot easier.' For the first time Captain Yolles produced pencil and notebook. 'If anything should come of this, naturally we'll need a full statement. Meanwhile, there are a couple of details I'd like to have. One is the licence number of the car.'

The information was in a memo from Flora, confirming her earlier report. Peter read it aloud and the detective copied the number down.

'Thank you. The other thing is a physical description of your man Ogilvie. I know him, but I'd like to have it from you.'

For the first time Peter smiled. 'That's easy.'

As he concluded the description, the telephone rang. Peter answered, then pushed the phone across. 'For you.'

This time he could hear the detective's end of the conversation which consisted largely of repeating 'yes, sir' and 'I understand'.

At one point the detective looked up, his eyes appraisingly on Peter. He said into the telephone, 'I'd say he's very dependable.' A slight smile creased his face. 'Worried too.'

He repeated the information concerning the car number and Ogilvie's description, then hung up.

Peter said, 'You're right about being worried. Do you intend to contact the Duke and Duchess of Croydon?'

'Not yet. We'd like a little more to go on.' The detective regarded Peter thoughtfully. 'Have you seen tonight's paper?'

'No.'

'There's been a rumour – the *States-Item* published it – that the Duke of Croydon is to be British ambassador to Washington.'

Peter whistled softly.

'It's just been on the radio, according to my chief, that the appointment is officially confirmed.'

'Doesn't that mean there would be some kind of diplomatic immunity?'

The detective shook his head. 'Not for something that's already happened. *If* it happened.'

'But a false accusation . . .'

'Would be serious in any case, especially so in this one. It's why we're moving warily, Mr McDermott.'

Peter reflected that it would go hard both for the hotel and himself if word of the investigation leaked out, with the Croydons innocent.

'If it'll ease your mind a bit,' Captain Yolles said, 'I'll let you in on a couple of things. Our people have done some figuring since I phoned them first. They reckon your man Ogilvie may be trying to get the car out of the state, maybe to some place north. How he ties in with the Croydons, of course, we don't know.'

Peter said, 'I couldn't guess that either.'

'Chances are, he drove last night – after you saw him – and holed up somewhere for the day. With the car the way it is, he'd know better than to try and make a run in daylight. Tonight, if he shows, we're ready. A twelve-state alarm is going out right now.'

'Then you do take this seriously?'

'I said there were two things.' The detective pointed to the telephone. 'One reason for that last call was to tell me we've had a State lab report on broken glass and a trim ring our people found at the accident scene last Monday. There was some difficulty about a manufacturer's specification change, which was why it took time. But we know now that the glass and trim ring are from a Jaguar.'

'You can really be that certain?'

'We can do even better, Mr McDermott. If we get to the car that killed the woman and child, we'll prove it beyond the shadow of a doubt.'

Captain Yolles rose to go, and Peter walked with him to the outer office. Peter was surprised to find Herbie Chandler waiting, then remembered his own instructions for the bell captain to report here this evening or tomorrow. After the developments of the afternoon, he was tempted to postpone what would most likely be an unpleasant session, then concluded there was nothing to be gained by putting it off.

He saw the detective and Chandler exchange glances.

'Good night, Captain,' Peter said, and took a malicious satisfaction in observing a flicker of anxiety cross Chandler's weasel face. When the policeman had gone, Peter beckoned the bell captain into the inner office.

He unlocked a drawer of his desk and took out a folder containing the statements made yesterday by Dixon, Dumaire, and the other two youths. He handed them to Chandler.

'I believe these will interest you. In case you get any ideas, these are copies and I have the originals.'

Chandler looked pained, then began reading. As he turned the pages, his lips tightened. Peter heard him suck in breath through his teeth. A moment later he muttered, 'Bastards!'

Peter snapped. 'You mean because they've identified you as a pimp?'

The bell captain flushed, then put down the papers. 'What you gonna do?'

'What I'd like to do is fire you on the spot. Because you've been here so long, I intend to place the whole thing before Mr Trent.'

There was a whine to Chandler's voice as he asked, 'Mr Mac, could we talk around this for a bit?'

When there was no answer, he began, 'Mr Mac, there's a lot of things go on in a place like this . . .'

'If you're telling me the facts of life – about call girls and all the other rackets – I doubt if there's much I don't know already. But there's something else I know, and so do you: at certain things management draw the line. Supplying women to minors is one.'

'Mr Mac, couldn't you, maybe this time, not go to Mr Trent? Couldn't you keep this between you and me?'

'No.'

The bell captain's gaze moved shiftily around the room, then returned to Peter. His eyes were calculating. 'Mr Mac, if some people was to live and let live . . .' He stopped.

'Yes?'

'Well, sometimes it can be worth while.'

Curiosity kept Peter silent.

Chandler hesitated, then deliberately unfastened the button of a tunic pocket. Reaching inside he removed a folded envelope which he placed on the desk.

Peter said, 'Let me see that.'

Chandler pushed the envelope nearer. It was unsealed and contained five one-hundred-dollar bills. Peter inspected them curiously.

'Are they real?'

Chandler smirked. 'They're real all right.'

'I was curious to know how high you thought my price came.' Peter tossed the money back. 'Take it and get out.'

'Mr Mac, if it's a question of a little more . . .'

'Get out!' Peter's voice was low. He half-rose in his chair. 'Get out before I break your dirty little neck.'

As he retrieved the money and left, Herbie Chandler's face was a mask of hatred.

When he was alone, Peter McDermott sat slumped silently behind his desk. The interviews with the policeman and Chandler had exhausted and depressed him. Of the two, he thought, the second had lowered his spirits most, probably because handling the proffered bribe had left him with a feeling of being unclean.

Or had it? He thought: be honest with yourself. There had been an instant, with the money in his hands, when he was tempted to take it. Five hundred dollars was a useful sum. Peter had no illusion about his own earnings compared with those of the bell captain, who undoubtedly raked in a good deal more. If it had been anyone other than Chandler, he might possibly have succumbed. Or would he? He wished he could be sure. Either way, he would not be the first hotel manager to accept a pay-off from his staff.

The irony, of course, was that despite Peter's insistence that the evidence against Herbie Chandler would be placed before Warren Trent, there was no guarantee that it would happen. If the hotel changed ownership abruptly, as seemed likely, Warren Trent would no longer be concerned. Nor might Peter himself be around. With the advent of new management, the records of senior staff would undoubtedly be examined and, in his own case, the old, unsavoury Waldorf scandal disinterred. Had he yet, Peter wondered, lived that down? Well, there was every likelihood he would find out soon.

He returned his attention to the present.

On his desk was a printed form, which Flora had left, with a late-afternoon house count. For the first time since coming in, he studied the figures. They showed that the hotel was filling and tonight, it seemed, there was a certainty of another full house. If the St Gregory was going down to defeat, at least it was doing so to the sound of trumpets.

As well as the house count and telephone messages, there was a fresh pile of mail and memos. Peter skimmed through them all, deciding that there was nothing which could not be left until tomorrow. Beneath the memos was a Manila folder which he opened. It was the proposed master catering plan which the sous-chef, André Lemieux, had given him yesterday. Peter had begun studying the plan this morning.

Glancing at his watch, he decided to continue his reading before making an evening tour of the hotel. He settled down, the precisely hand-written pages and carefully drawn charts spread out before him.

As he read on, his admiration for the young sous-chef grew. The presentation appeared masterly, revealing a broad grasp both of the hotel's problems and the potentialities of its restaurant business. It angered Peter that the chef de cuisine, M. Hèbrand, had – according to Lemieux – dismissed the proposals entirely.

True, some conclusions were arguable, and Peter disagreed himself with a few of Lemieux's ideas. At first glance, too, a number of estimated costs seemed optimistic. But these were minor. The important thing was that a fresh and clearly competent brain had brooded over present deficiencies in food management and come up with suggested remedies. Equally obvious was that unless the St Gregory made better use of André Lemieux's considerable talents, he would soon take them elsewhere.

Peter returned the plan and charts to their folder with a sense of pleasure that someone in the hotel should possess the kind of enthusiasm for his work which Lemieux had shown. He decided that he would like to tell André Lemieux his impressions even though – with the hotel in its present uncertain state – there seemed nothing more that Peter could do.

A telephone call elicited the information that, this evening, the chef de cuisine was absent through continued sickness, and that the sous-chef, M. Lemieux, was in charge. Preserving protocol, Peter left a message that he was coming down to the kitchen now.

André Lemieux was waiting at the doorway from the main dining-room.

'Come in, monsieur! You are welcome.' Leading the way into the noisy, steaming kitchen, the young sous-chef shouted close to Peter's ear. 'You find us, as the musicians say, near the crescendo.'

In contrast to the comparative quietness of yesterday afternoon, the atmosphere now, in early evening, was pandemonic. With a full shift on duty, chefs in starched whites, their assistant cooks and juniors, seemed to have sprouted like daisies in a field. Around them, through gusts of steam and waves of heat, sweating kitchen helpers noisily hefted trays, pans, and cauldrons, while others thrust trolleys recklessly, all dodging each other as well as hurrying waiters and waitresses, the latter's serving trays held high. On steam tables the day's dinner menu dishes were being portioned and served for delivery to dining-rooms. Special orders – from à la carte menus and for room service – were being prepared by fast-moving cooks whose arms and hands seemed everywhere at once. Waiters hovered, questioning progress of their orders as cooks barked back. Other waiters, with loaded trays, moved quickly past the two austere women checkers at elevated billing registers. From the soup section, vapour rose swirling as giant cauldrons bubbled. Not far away two specialist cooks arranged, with dextrous fingers, canapés and hot hors-d'oeuvres. Beyond them, an anxious pastry chef supervised desserts. Occasionally, as oven doors clanged open, a reflection of flames flashed over concentrating faces, with the oven's interiors like a glimpse of hell. Over all, assailing ears and nostrils, was the clatter of plates, the inviting odour of food and the sweet, fresh fragrance of brewing coffee.

'When we are busiest, monsieur, we are the proudest. Or should be, if one did not look beneath the cabbage leaf.'

'I've read your report.' Peter returned the folder to the sous-chef, then followed him into the glass-panelled office where the noise was muted. 'I like your ideas. I'd argue a few points, but not many.'

'It would be good to argue if, at the end, the action was to follow.'

'It won't yet. At least, not the kind you have in mind.' Ahead of any reorganization, Peter pointed out, the larger issue of the hotel's ownership would have to be settled.

'Per'aps my plan and I must go elsewhere. No matter.' André Lemieux gave a Gallic shrug, then added, 'Monsieur, I am about to visit the convention floor. Would you care to accompany me?'

Peter had intended to include the convention dinners, scheduled for tonight, in his evening rounds of the hotel. It would be just as effective to begin his inspection from the convention floor kitchen. 'Thank you. I'll come.'

They rode in a service elevator two floors up, stepping out into what, in most respects, was a duplicate of the main kitchen below. From here some two thousand meals could be served at a single sitting to the St Gregory's three convention halls and dozen private dining-rooms. The tempo at the moment seemed as frenetic as downstairs.

'As you know, monsieur, it is two big banquets that we 'ave tonight. In the Grand Ballroom and the Bienville 'all.'

Peter nodded. 'Yes, the Dentists' Congress and Gold Crown Cola.' From the flow of meals towards opposite ends of the long kitchen, he observed that the dentists' main course was roast turkey, the cola salesmen's, flounder sauté. Teams of cooks and helpers were serving both, apportioning vegetables with machine-like rhythm, then, in a single motion, slapping metal covers on the filled plates and loading the whole on to waiters' trays.

Nine plates to a tray – the number of conventioneers at a single table. Two tables per waiter. Four courses to the meal, plus extra rolls, butter, coffee and *petits fours*. Peter calculated: there would be twelve heavily loaded trips, at least, for every waiter; most likely more if diners were demanding or, as sometimes happened under pressure, extra tables were assigned. No wonder some waiters looked weary at an evening's end.

Less weary, perhaps, would be the maître d'hôtel, poised and immaculate in white tie and tails. At the moment, like a police chief on point duty, he was stationed centrally in the kitchen directing the flow of waiters in both directions. Seeing André Lemieux and Peter, he moved towards them.

'Good evening, Chef; Mr McDermott.' Though in hotel precedence Peter out-ranked the other two, in the kitchen the maître d'hôtel deferred, correctly, to the senior chef on duty.

André Lemieux asked, 'What are our numbers for dinner, Mr Dominic?'

The maître d'hôtel consulted a slip of paper. 'The Gold Crown people estimated two hundred and forty and we've seated that many. It looks as if they're mostly in.'

'They're salesmen on salary,' Peter said. 'They have to be there. The dentists please themselves. They'll probably straggle and a lot won't show.'

The maître d'hôtel nodded agreement. 'I heard there was a good deal of drinking in rooms. Ice consumption is heavy, and room service had a run on mixes. We thought it might cut the meal figure down.'

The conundrum was how many convention meals to prepare at any time. It represented a familiar headache to all three men. Convention organizers gave the hotel a minimum guarantee, but in practice the figure was liable to vary a hundred or two either way. A reason was uncertainty about how many delegates would break up into smaller parties and pass up official banquets or, alternatively, might arrive en masse in a last-minute surge.

The final minutes before a big convention banquet were inevitably tense in any hotel kitchen. It was a moment of truth, since all involved were aware that reaction to a crisis would show just how good or bad their organization was.

Peter asked the maître d'hôtel, 'What was the original estimate?'

'For the dentists, five hundred. We're close to that and we've begun serving. But they still seem to be coming in.'

'Are we getting a fast count of new arrivals?'

'I've a man out now. Here he is.' Dodging fellow waiters, a red-coated captain was hastening through the service doors from the Grand Ballroom.

Peter asked André Lemieux, 'If we have to, can we produce extra food?'

'When I have the word of requirements, monsieur, then we will do our best.'

The maître d'hôtel conferred with the captain, then returned to the other two. 'It looks like an additional hundred and seventy people. They're flooding in! We're already setting up more tables.'

As always, when crisis struck, it was with little warning. In this case it had arrived with major impact. One hundred and seventy extra meals, required at once, would tax the resources of any kitchen. Peter returned to André Lemieux, only to discover that the young Frenchman was no longer there.

The sous-chef had sprung into action as if catapulted. He was already among his staff, issuing orders with the crackle of rapid fire. *A junior cook to the main kitchen, there to seize seven turkeys roasting for tomorrow's cold collation . . . A shouted order to the preparation room: Use the reserves! Speed up! Carve everything in sight! . . . More vegetables! Steal some from the second banquet which looked like using less than allowed! A second junior sent running to the main kitchen to round up all the vegetables he could find elsewhere . . . And deliver a message: rush up more help! Two carvers, two more cooks . . . Alert the pastry chef! One hundred and seventy more desserts required in minutes . . . Rob Peter for Paul! Juggle! Feed the dentists!* Young André Lemieux, quick thinking, confident, good natured, running the show.

Already, waiters were being reassigned: some smoothly withdrawn from the smaller banquet of Gold Crown Cola, where those remaining must do extra work. Diners would never notice; only, perhaps, that their next course would be served by someone with a vaguely different face. Other waiters, already assigned to the Grand Ballroom and the dentists, would handle three tables – twenty-seven place settings – instead of two. A few seasoned hands, known to be fast with feet and fingers, might manage four. There would be some grumbling, though not much. Convention waiters were mostly freelancers, called in by any hotel as requirements rose. Extra work earned extra money. Four dollars' pay for three hours' work was based on two tables; each extra table brought half as much again. Tips, added to a convention's bill by prior arrangement, would double the entire amount. The fast-feet men would go home with sixteen dollars; if lucky, they might have earned the same at lunch or breakfast.

A trolley with three fresh-cooked turkeys, Peter saw, was already highballing from a service elevator. The preparation-room cooks fell upon it. The assistant cook who had brought the three returned for more.

Fifteen portions from a turkey. Rapid dissection with surgeon's skill. To each diner the same proportion: white meat, dark meat, dressing. Twenty portions to a serving tray. Rush the tray to a service counter. Fresh trolleys of vegetables, steaming in like ships converging.

The sous-chef's despatch of messengers had depleted the serving team. André Lemieux stepped in, replacing the absent two. The team picked up speed, moved faster than it had before.

Plate . . . meat . . . first vegetable . . . second . . . gravy . . . slide the plate . . . cover on! A man for each move; arms, hands, ladles moving together. A meal each second . . . faster still! In front of the serving counter, a line of waiters, becoming long.

Across the kitchen, the pastry chef opening refrigerators; inspecting, selecting, slamming the doors closed. Main kitchen pastry cooks running to help. Draw on reserve desserts. More on the way from basement freezers.

Amid the urgency, a moment of incongruity.

A waiter reported to the captain, the captain to the head waiter, the head waiter to André Lemieux.

'Chef, there's a gentleman says he doesn't like turkey. May he have rare roast beef?'

A shout of laughter went up from the sweating cooks.

But the request had observed protocol correctly, as Peter knew. Only the senior chef could authorize any deviation from a standard menu.

A grinning André Lemieux said. 'He may have it, but serve him last at his table.'

That, too, was an old kitchen custom. As a matter of public relations, most hotels would change standard fare if asked, even if the substitute meal was costlier. But invariably – as now – the individualist must wait until those seated near him had begun eating, a precaution against others being inspired with the same idea.

Now the line of waiters at the serving counter was shortening. To most guests in the Grand Ballroom – late-comers included – the main course had been served. Already busboys were appearing with discarded dishes. There was a sense of crisis passed. André Lemieux surrendered his place among the servers, then glanced questioningly at the pastry chef.

The latter, a matchstick of a man who looked as if he seldom sampled his own confections, made a circle with thumb and forefinger. 'All set to go, Chef.'

André Lemieux, smiling, rejoined Peter. 'Monsieur, it seems we 'ave, as you say it, fielded the ball.'

'I'd say you've done a good deal better. I'm impressed.'

The young Frenchman shrugged. 'What you have seen was good. But it is only part of the work. Elsewhere we do not look so well. Excuse me, monsieur.' He moved away.

The dessert was *bombe aux marrons, cherries flambées*. It would be served with ceremony, the ballroom lights dimmed, the flaming trays held high.

Now, waiters were lining up before the service doors. The pastry chef and helpers were checking arrangements of the trays. When touched off, a central dish on each would spring to flame. Two cooks stood by with lighted tapers.

André Lemieux inspected the line.

At the entry to the Grand Ballroom, the head waiter, an arm raised, watched the sous-chef's face.

As André Lemieux nodded, the head waiter's arm swept down.

The cooks with tapers ran down the line of trays, igniting them. The double service doors were flung back and fastened. Outside, on cue, an electrician dimmed the lights. The music of an orchestra diminished, then abruptly stopped. Among guests in the great hall, a hum of conversation died.

Suddenly, beyond the diners, a spotlight sprang on, framing the doorway from the kitchen. There was a second's silence, then a fanfare of trumpets. As it ended, orchestra and organ swung together, *fortissimo*, into the opening bars of *The Saints*. In time to the music, the procession of waiters, with flaming trays, marched out.

Peter McDermott moved into the Grand Ballroom for a better view. He could see the overflow, the unexpected crowd of diners, the great room tightly packed.

Oh, when the Saints; Oh, when the Saints; Oh; when the Saints go marching in . . . From the kitchen, waiter after waiter, in trim blue uniform, marched out in step. For this moment, every last man had been impressed. Some, in moments only, would return to complete their work in the other banquet hall. Now, in semi-darkness, their flames reared up like beacons . . . *Oh, when the Saints; Oh, when the Saints; Oh, when the Saints go marching in* . . . From the diners, a spontaneous burst of applause, changing to hand-clapping in time with the music as waiters encircled the room. For the hotel; a commitment had been met as planned. No-one outside the kitchen could know that minutes earlier a crisis had been encountered and overcome . . . *Lord, I want to be in that number, When the Saints go marching in* . . . As waiters reached their tables, the lights went up to renewed applause and cheers.

André Lemieux had come to stand beside Peter. 'That is the all for tonight, monsieur. Unless, perhaps you 'ave a wish for the cognac. In the kitchen I have the small supply.'

'No, thank you,' Peter smiled. 'It was a good show. Congratulations!'

As he turned away, the sous-chef called after him, 'Good night, monsieur. And do not forget.'

Puzzled, Peter stopped. 'Forget what?'

'What I have already said. The 'ot-shot 'otel, monsieur, that you and I could make.'

Half amused, half thoughtful, Peter threaded his way through the banquet tables towards the ballroom outer doorway.

He had gone most of the distance when he was aware of something out of place. He stopped, glancing around, uncertain what it was. Then abruptly he realized. Dr Ingram, the fiery little president of the Dentistry Congress, should have been presiding at this, one of the main events of the convention. But the doctor was neither at the president's position nor anywhere else at the long head table.

Several delegates were table hopping, greeting friends in other sections of the room. A man with a hearing aid stopped beside Peter. 'Swell turn-out, eh?'

'It certainly is. I hope you enjoyed your dinner.'

'Not bad.'

'By the way,' Peter said. 'I was looking for Dr Ingram. I don't see him anywhere.'

'You won't.' The tone was curt. Eyes regarded him suspiciously. 'You from a newspaper?'

'No, the hotel. I met Dr Ingram a couple of times . . .'

'He resigned. This afternoon. If you want my opinion, he behaved like a damn fool.'

Peter controlled his surprise. 'Do you happen to know if the doctor is still in the hotel?'

'No idea.' The man with the hearing aid moved on.

There was a house phone on the convention mezzanine.

Dr Ingram, the switchboard reported, was still shown as registered, but there was no answer from his room. Peter called the chief cashier. 'Has Dr Ingram of Philadelphia checked out?'

'Yes, Mr McDermott, just a minute ago. I can see him in the lobby now.'

'Send someone to ask if he'll please wait. I'm on my way down.'

Dr Ingram was standing, suitcases beside him, a raincoat over his arm, when Peter arrived.

'What's your trouble now, Mr McDermott? If you want a testimonial to this hotel, you're out of luck. Besides which I've a plane to catch.'

'I heard about your resignation. I came to say I'm sorry.'

'I guess they'll make out.' From the Grand Ballroom two floors above, the sound of applause and cheering drifted down to where they stood. 'It sounds as if they have already.'

'Do you mind very much?'

'No.' The little doctor shifted his feet, looking down, then growled, 'I'm a liar, I mind like hell. I shouldn't, but I do.'

Peter said, 'I imagine anyone would.'

Dr Ingram's head snapped up. 'Understand this, McDermott: I'm no beaten rug. I don't need to feel like one. I've been a teacher all my life, with plenty to show for it: Good people I've brought on – Jim Nicholas for one, and others, procedures carrying my name, books I've written that are standard texts. All that's solid stuff. The other' – he nodded in the direction of the Grand Ballroom – 'that's frosting.'

'I didn't realize . . .'

'All the same, a little frosting does no harm. A fellow even gets to like it. I wanted to be president. I was glad when they elected me. It's an accolade from people whose opinion you value. If I'm honest, McDermott – and God knows why I'm telling you this – it's eating my heart out, not being up there tonight.' He paused, looking up, as the sounds from the ballroom were audible once more.

'Once in a while, though, you have to weigh what you want against what you believe in.' The little doctor grunted. 'Some of my friends think I've behaved like an idiot.'

'It isn't idiotic to stand up for a principle.'

Dr Ingram eyed Peter squarely. 'You didn't do it, McDermott, when you had the chance. You were too worried about this hotel, your job.'

'I'm afraid that's true.'

'Well, you've the grace to admit it, so I'll tell you something, son. You're not alone. There've been times I haven't measured up to everything I believe. It goes for all of us. Sometimes, though, you get a second chance. If it happens to you – take it.'

Peter beckoned a bellboy. 'I'll come with you to the door.'

Dr Ingram shook his head. 'No need for that. Let's not crap around, McDermott. I don't love this hotel or you either.'

The bellboy looked at him enquiringly. Dr Ingram said, 'Let's go.'

16

In the late afternoon, near the cluster of trees in which the Jaguar was hidden, Ogilvie slept again. He awoke as dust was settling, the sun an orange ball nudging a ridge of hills towards the west. The heat of the day had changed into a pleasant evening coolness. Ogilvie hurried, realizing it would soon be time to go.

He listened to the car radio first. There appeared to be no fresh news, merely a repetition of what he had heard earlier. Satisfied, he snapped the radio off.

He returned to the stream beyond the small clump of trees and freshened himself, splashing water on his face and head to banish the last vestiges of drowsiness. He made a hasty meal from what was left of his supply of food, then refilled the Thermos flasks with water, leaving them on the rear seat of the car along with some cheese and bread. The makeshift fare would have to sustain him through the night. Until daylight tomorrow he intended to make no unnecessary stops.

His route, which he had planned and memorized before leaving New Orleans, lay northwest through the remainder of Mississippi. Then he would traverse the western shoulder of Alabama, afterwards heading due north through Tennessee and Kentucky. From Louisville he would turn diagonally west across Indiana, by way of Indianapolis. He would cross into Illinois near Hammond, thence to Chicago.

The remaining journey spanned seven hundred miles. Its entire distance was too great for a single stint of driving, but Ogilvie estimated he could be close to Indianapolis by daybreak where he believed he would be safe. Once there, only two hundred miles would separate him from Chicago.

Darkness was complete as he backed the Jaguar out of the sheltering trees and steered it gently towards the main highway. He gave a satisfied grunt as he turned northward on US 45.

At Columbus, Mississippi, where the dead from the Battle of Shiloh were brought for burial, Ogilvie stopped for gas. He was careful to choose a small general store on the outskirts of town, with a pair of old-fashioned gas pumps illumined by a single light. He pulled the car forwards as far as possible from the light, so that its front was in shadow.

He discouraged conversation by ignoring the store-keeper's 'Nice night,' and 'Going far?' He paid cash for the gas and a half-dozen chocolate bars, then drove on.

Nine miles to the north he crossed the Alabama state line.

A succession of small towns came and went. Vernon, Sulligent, Hamilton, Russellville, Florence, the last – so a sign recorded – noted for the manufacture of toilet seats. A few miles farther on, he crossed the border into Tennessee.

Traffic was averagely light and the Jaguar performed superbly. Driving conditions were ideal, helped by a full moon which rose soon after darkness. There was no sign of police activity of any kind.

Ogilvie was contentedly relaxed.

Fifty miles south of Nashville, at Columbia, Tennessee, he turned on to US 31.

Traffic was heavier now. Massive tractor-trailers, their headlights stabbing the night like an endless dazzling chain, thundered south towards Birmingham and northward to the industrial Mid-west. Passenger cars, a few taking risks the truck drivers would not, threaded the stream. Occasionally, Ogilvie himself pulled out to pass a slow-moving vehicle, but he was careful not to exceed posted speed limits. He had no wish, by speeding or any other means, to invite attention. After a while, he observed a following car, which remained behind him, driving at approximately his own speed. Ogilvie adjusted the rear-view mirror to reduce the glare, then slowed to let the other car pass. When it failed to, unconcerned, he resumed his original speed.

A few miles farther on, he was aware of the northbound lanes of traffic slowing. Warning tail lights of other vehicles were flashing on. Leaning to the left, he could see what appeared to be a group of headlights, with both northbound lanes funnelling into one. The scene bore the familiar pattern of a highway accident.

Then, abruptly, rounding a curve, he saw the real reason for the delay. Two lines of Tennessee Highway Patrol cruisers, their red roof lights flashing, were positioned on both sides of the road. A flare-draped barrier was across the centre lane. At the same instant, the car which had been following switched on a police beacon of its own.

As the Jaguar slowed and stopped, State Troopers with drawn guns ran towards it.

Quaking, Ogilvie raised his hands above his head.

A husky sergeant opened the car door. 'Keep your hands where they are,' he ordered, 'and come out slowly. You're under arrest.'

17

Christine Francis mused aloud, 'There – you're doing it again. Both times, when the coffee was poured, you've held your hands around the cup. As if it gave you a kind of comfort.'

Across the dinner table, Albert Wells gave his perky sparrow's smile. 'You notice more things'n most people.'

He seemed frail again tonight, she thought. Some of the paleness of three days earlier had returned and occasionally, through the evening, a bronchial cough had been troublesome, though not diminishing his cheerfulness. What he needs, Christine reflected, is someone to take care of him.

They were in the St Gregory's main dining-room. Since their arrival more than an hour ago, most of the other diners had left, though a few still lingered over coffee and liqueurs. Although the hotel was full, attendance in the dining-room had been thin all evening.

Max, the head waiter, came discreetly to their table.

'Will there be anything else, sir?'

Albert Wells glanced at Christine who shook her head.

'I reckon not. When you'd like to, you can bring the bill.'

'Certainly,sir.' Max nodded to Christine, his eyes assuring her that he had not forgotten their arrangement of this morning.

When the head waiter had gone, the little man said, 'About the coffee. Prospecting, in the north, you never waste anything if you want to stay alive, not even the heat from a cup you're holding. It's a habit you get into. I could lose the way of it, I guess, though there's things it's wise to remind yourself of once in a while.'

'Because they were good times, or because life is better now?'

He considered. 'Some of both, I reckon.'

'You told me you were a miner,' Christine said. 'I didn't know about your being a prospector too.'

'A lot of the time, one's the other. Especially on the Canadian Shield – that's in the Northwest Territories, Christine, near as far as Canada goes. When you're there alone, just you and the tundra – the arctic desert, they call it – you do everything from driving claim stakes to burning through the permafrost. If you don't most times there's no-one else.'

'When you were prospecting, what was it for?'

'Uranium, cobalt. Mostly gold.'

'Did you find any? Gold, I mean.'

He nodded affirmatively. 'Plenty did. Around Yellowknife, Great Slave Lake. There were discoveries there from the 1890s to a stampede in 1945. Mostly, though, the country was too tough to mine and take it out.'

Christine said, 'It must have been a hard life.'

The little man coughed, then took a sip of water, smiling apologetically. 'I was tougher then. Though give the Shield half a chance, it'll kill you.' He looked around the pleasantly appointed dining-room, lighted by crystal chandeliers. 'It seems a long way from here.'

'You said that mostly it was too difficult to mine the gold. It wasn't always?'

'Not always. Some were luckier 'n others, though even for them things'd go wrong. Maybe it's partly because the Shield and the Barren Lands do strange things to people. Some you'd think'd be strong – and not just in body either – they turn out to be the weak ones. And some you'd trust with your life, you discover you can't. Then there's the other way around. One time I remember . . .' He stopped as the head waiter placed a salver on

498

the table with their bill.

She urged, 'Go on.'

'It's a kind of long story, Christine.' He turned over the bill, inspecting it.

'I'd like to hear,' Christine said and meant it. As time went on, she thought, she liked this modest little man more and more.

He looked up and there seemed to be amusement in his eyes. He glanced across the room at the head waiter, then back towards Christine. Abruptly, he took out a pencil and signed the bill.

'It was in '36,' the little man began, 'around the time that one of the last Yellowknife stampedes was gettin' started. I was prospecting near the shore of Great Slave Lake. Had a partner then. Name of Hymie Eckstein. Hymie'd come from Ohio. He'd been in the garment trade, a used-car salesman, lot of other things, I guess. He was pushy and a fast talker. But he had a way of making people like him. I guess you'd call it charm. When he got to Yellowknife he had a little money. I was broke. Hymie grubstaked the two of us.'

Albert Wells took a sip of water, pensively.

'Hymie'd never seen a snowshoe, never heard of permafrost, couldn't tell schist from quartz. From the beginning, though, we got along well. And we made out.

'We'd been out a month, maybe two. On the Shield you lose track of time. Then one day, near the mouth of the Yellowknife River, the two of us sat down to roll our cigarettes. Sitting there, the way prospectors do, I chipped away at some gossan – that's oxidized rock, Christine – and slipped a piece or two in my pocket. Later, by the lake-shore, I panned the rock. You could have shoved me over when it showed good coarse gold.'

'When it really happens,' Christine said, 'it must seem the most exciting thing in the world.'

'Maybe there are other things excite you more. If there are, they never came my way. Well, we rushed back to the place I'd chipped the rock and we covered it with moss. Two days later, we found the ground had already been staked. I guess it was the darnedest blow either of us ever had. Turned out, a Toronto prospector 'd done the staking. He'd been out the year before, then gone back east, not knowing what he had. Under Territories law, if he didn't work the claim, his rights 'd run out a year from recording.'

'How long away was that?'

'We made our find in June. If things stayed the way they were, the land 'd come clear the last day in September.'

'Couldn't you keep quiet, and just wait?'

'We aimed at that. Except it wasn't so easy. For one thing, the find we'd made was right in line with a producing mine an' there were other prospectors, like ourselves, working the same country. For another, Hymie and me'd run clean out of money and food.'

Albert Wells beckoned a passing waiter. 'I reckon I'll have more coffee after all.' He asked Christine, 'How about you?'

She shook her head. 'No, thank you. Don't stop. I want to hear the rest.' How strange, she thought, that the kind of epic adventure which people dreamed about should have happened to someone as apparently ordinary as the little man from Montreal.

'Well, Christine, I reckon the next three months were the longest any two men lived. Maybe the hardest. We existed. On fish, some bits of plants. Near the end I was thinner'n a twig and my legs were black with scurvy. Had this bronchitis and phlebitis too. Hymie wasn't a whole lot better, but he never complained and I got to like him more.'

The coffee arrived and Christine waited.

'Finally it got to the last day of September. We'd heard through Yellowknife that when the first claim ran out, there'd be others try to move in, so we didn't take chances. We had our stakes ready. Right after midnight we rammed 'em home. I remember – it was a pitch-black night, snowing hard and blowing a gale.'

His hands went around the coffee cup as they had before.

'That's about all I do remember because, after that, nature took over 'n the next clear thing I know was being in hospital in Edmonton, near a thousand miles from where we staked. I found out after, Hymie got me out from the Shield, though I never figured how he did it. And a bush pilot flew me south. Plenty of times, including in the hospital, they gave me up for dead. I didn't die. Though when I got things sorted out, I wished I had.' He stopped to drink from the coffee cup.

Christine asked, 'Wasn't the claim legal?'

'The claim was fine. The trouble was Hymie.' Albert Wells stroked his sparrow-beak nose reflectively. 'Maybe I should take the story back a bit. While we were waiting our time out on the Shield, we'd signed two bills of sale. Each of us – on paper – turned over his half of the claim to the other.'

'Why would you do that?'

'It was Hymie's idea, in case one of us didn't come through. If that happened, the survivor'd keep the paper showing that all the claim was his, and he'd tear up the other. Hymie said it'd save a lot of legal mess. At the time, it seemed to make sense. If we both made it through, the arrangement was, we'd scrap both papers.'

Christine prompted, 'So while you were in the hospital . . .'

'Hymie 'd taken both papers and registered his. By the time I was in shape to take an interest, Hymie had full title and was already mining with proper machinery and help. I found out there'd been an offer of a quarter-million dollars from one of the big smelting companies for him to sell out, and there were other bidders lining up.'

'Was there nothing at all you could do?'

The little man shook his head. 'I figured I was licked before I started. All the same, soon's I could get out of that hospital, I borrowed enough money to get back up north.'

Albert Wells stopped and waved a greeting across the dining-room. Christine looked up to see Peter McDermott approaching their table. She had wondered if Peter would remember her suggestion about joining them after dinner. The sight of him brought a delightful quickening of her senses. Then, immediately, she sensed that he was despondent.

The little man welcomed Peter warmly and a waiter hurried forward with an extra chair.

Peter sank into it gratefully. 'I'm afraid I left it a little late. There've been a few things happening.' It was, he reflected to himself, a monument of understatement.

Hoping there would be an opportunity to talk privately with Peter afterwards, Christine said, 'Mr Wells has been telling me a wonderful story. I must hear the end.'

Peter sipped his coffee which the waiter had brought. 'Go ahead, Mr Wells. It'll be like coming into a movie part way through. I'll catch the beginning later.'

The little man smiled, looking down at his gnarled and toughened hands. 'There isn't a whole lot more, though most of what there is has kind of a twist. I went north and found Hymie in Yellowknife, in what passes for a hotel. I called him every foul name I could lay my tongue to. All the while he had a great wide grin, which made me madder, till I was ready to kill him there'n then. I wouldn't have, though. He knew me well enough for that.'

Christine said, 'He must have been a hateful man.'

'I figured so. Except, when I'd quietened down some, Hymie told me to come with him. We went to a lawyer and there were papers, ready drawn, handing me back my half share, fair 'n square – in fact fairer, 'cos Hymie'd taken nothing for himself for all the work he'd done those months I'd been away.'

Bewildered, Christine shook her head. 'I don't understand. Why did he . . .'

'Hymie explained. Said he knew from the beginning there'd be a lot of legal things, papers to sign, especially if we didn't sell, and hung on to work the claim instead, which he knew I wanted to do. There were bank loans – for the machinery, wages, all the rest. With me in hospital, and most of the time not knowing up from down, he couldn't have done any of it – not with my name on the property. So Hymie used my bill of sale and went ahead. He always intended to hand my share back. Only thing was, he wasn't much of a one for writing and never let me know. Right from the beginning, though, he'd fixed things up legally. If he'd died, I'd have got his share as well as mine.'

Peter McDermott and Christine were staring across the table.

'Later on,' Albert Wells said, 'I did the same with my half – made a will so it'd go to Hymie. We had the same arrangement – about that one mine – till the day Hymie died, which was five years ago. I reckon he taught me something: When you believe in somebody, don't be in a rush to change your mind.'

Peter McDermott said, 'And the mine?'

'Well, we kept right on refusing offers to buy us out, and it turned out we were right in the end. Hymie ran it a good many years. It still goes on – one of the best producers in the north. Now 'n then I go back to take a look, for old times' sake.'

Speechless, her mouth agape, Christine stared at the little man, 'You . . . *you* . . . own a gold mine.'

Albert Wells nodded cheerfully. 'That's right. There'd be a few other things now, besides.'

'If you'll pardon my curiosity,' Peter McDermott said, 'other things such as what?'

'I'm not sure of all of it.' The little man shifted diffidently in his chair. 'There's a couple of newspapers, some ships, an insurance company, buildings, other bits 'n pieces. I bought a food chain last year. I like new things. It keeps me interested.'

'Yes,' Peter said. 'I should imagine it would.'

Albert Wells smiled mischievously. 'Matter of fact, there's something I was going to tell you tomorrow, but I may as well do it now. I just bought this hotel.'

18

'Those are the gentlemen, Mr McDermott.'

Max, the dining-room head waiter, pointed across the lobby where two men – one of them the police detective, Captain Yolles – were waiting quietly beside the hotel news-stand.

A moment or two earlier, Max had summoned Peter from the dining-table where, with Christine, he was sitting in dazed silence after Albert Wells's announcement. Both

Christine and himself, Peter knew, had been too astounded either to grasp the news entirely or assess its implications. It had been a relief to Peter to be informed that he was required urgently outside. Hastily excusing himself, he promised to return later if he could.

Captain Yolles walked towards him. He introduced his companion as Detective-Sergeant Bennett. 'Mr McDermott, is there some place handy we can talk?'

'This way.' Peter led the two men past the concierge's counter into the credit manager's office, unused at night. As they went in Captain Yolles handed Peter a folded newspaper. It was an early edition of tomorrow's *Times-Picayune*. A three-column read:

CROYDON CONFIRMED UK AMBASSADOR
NEWS REACHES HIM IN CRESCENT CITY

Captain Yolles closed the office door. 'Mr McDermott, Ogilvie has been arrested. He was stopped an hour ago, with the car, near Nashville. The Tennessee State Police are holding him and we've sent to bring him back. The car is being returned by truck, under wraps. But from an investigation on the spot, there doesn't seem much doubt it's the one we want.'

Peter nodded. He was aware of the two policemen watching him curiously.

'If I seem a little slow catching on to all that's happening,' Peter said, 'I should tell you that I've just had something of a shock.'

'Concerning this?'

'No. The hotel.'

There was a pause, then Yolles said, 'You may be interested to hear that Ogilvie has made a statement. He claims he knew nothing about the car being involved in an accident. All that happened, he says, is that the Duke and Duchess of Croydon paid him two hundred dollars to drive it north. He had that amount of money on him.'

'Do you believe that?'

'It might be true. Then again, it might not. We'll know better after we've done some questioning tomorrow.'

By tomorrow, Peter thought, a good deal might be clearer. Tonight held a quality of unreality. He enquired, 'What happens next?'

'We intend to pay a call on the Duke and Duchess of Croydon. If you don't mind, we'd like you along.'

'I suppose . . . if you think it necessary.'

'Thank you.'

'There is one other thing, Mr McDermott,' the second detective said. 'We understand that the Duchess of Croydon gave some sort of written permission for their car to be taken from the hotel garage.'

'I was told that, yes.'

'It could be important, sir. Do you suppose anyone kept that note?'

Peter considered. 'It's possible. If you like I'll telephone the garage.'

'Let's go there,' Captain Yolles said.

Kulgmer, the garage night checker, was apologetic and chagrined. 'Do you know sir, I said to myself I might need that piece of paper, just to cover me in case anything got asked.

And if you'll believe me, sir, I looked for it tonight before I remembered I must have thrown it out yesterday with the paper from my sandwiches. It isn't really my fault, though, when you look at it fair.' He gestured to the glass cubicle from which he had emerged. 'There's not much space in there. No wonder things get mixed. I was saying just last week, if that place was only bigger. Now, you take the way I have to do the nightly tally . . .'

Peter McDermott interrupted, 'What did the note from the Duchess of Croydon say?'

'Just that Mr O had permission to take away the car. I kind of wondered at the time . . .'

'Was the note written on hotel stationery?'

'Yes, sir.'

'Do you remember if the paper was embossed and had "Presidential suite" at the top?'

'Yes, Mr McDermott, I do remember that. It was just like you said, and sort of a small size sheet.'

Peter told the detectives, 'We have special stationery for that particular suite.'

The second detective queried Kulgmer, 'You say you threw the note out with your sandwich wrappings?'

'Don't see how it could have happened any other way. You see, I'm always very careful. Now, take what happened last year . . .'

'What time would that be?'

'Last year?'

The detective said patiently, 'Last night. When you threw out the sandwich wrapping. What time?'

'I'd say around two in the morning. I usually start my lunch around one. Things have quietened down by then and . . .'

'Where did you throw them?'

'Same place as always. Over here.' Kulgmer led the way to a cleaners' closet containing a garbage can. He removed the lid.

'Is there any chance of last night's stuff still being in there?'

'No, sir. You see, this is emptied every day. The hotel's fussy about that. That's right, Mr McDermott, isn't it?'

Peter nodded.

'Besides,' Kulgmer said, 'I remember the can was almost full last night. You can see there's hardly anything in there now.'

'Let's make sure,' Captain Yolles glanced at Peter for approval, then turned the garbage can upside down, emptying its contents. Though they searched carefully, there was no sign either of Kulgmer's sandwich wrappings or the missing note from the Duchess of Croydon.

Kulgmer left them to attend to several cars entering and leaving the garage.

Yolles wiped his hands on a paper towel. 'What happens to the garbage when it leaves here?'

'It goes out to our central incinerator,' Peter informed him. 'By the time it gets there, it's in big trolleys, with everything from the whole hotel mixed up together. It would be impossible to identify any one source. In any case, what was collected from here is probably burned by now.'

'Maybe it doesn't matter,' Yolles said. 'All the same, I'd like to have had that note.'

The elevator stopped at the ninth floor. As the detectives followed him out, Peter observed, 'I'm not looking forward to this.'

Yolles reassured him, 'We'll ask a few questions, that's all. I'd like you to listen carefully. And to the answers. It's possible we might need you as a witness later.'

To Peter's surprise, the doors of the Presidential Suite were open. As they approached, a buzz of voices could be heard.

The second detective said, 'Sounds like a party.'

They stopped at the doorway and Peter depressed the bell push. Through a second, partially opened door inside, he could see into the spacious living-rom. There was a group of men and women, the Duke and Duchess of Croydon among them. Most of the visitors were holding drinks in one hand, notebooks or paper in another.

The Croydons' male secretary appeared in the interior hallway. 'Good evening,' Peter said. 'These two gentlemen would like to see the Duke and Duchess.'

'Are they from the press?'

Captain Yolles shook his head.

'Then I'm sorry, it's impossible. The Duke is holding a press conference. His appointment as British Ambassador was confirmed this evening.'

'So I understand,' Yolles said. 'All the same, our business is important.'

While speaking, they had moved from the corridor into the suite hallway. Now, the Duchess of Croydon detached herself from the group in the living-room and came towards them. She smiled agreeably. 'Won't you come in?'

The secretary interjected, 'These gentlemen are not from the press.'

'Oh!' Her eyes went to Peter with a glance of recognition, then to the other two.

Captain Yolles said, 'We're police officers, madam. I have a badge but perhaps you'd prefer me not to produce it here.' He looked towards the living-room from where several people were watching curiously.

The Duchess gestured to the secretary who closed the living-room door.

Was it imagination, Peter wondered, or had a flicker of fear crossed the Duchess's face at the word 'police'? Imagined or not, she was in command of herself now.

'May I ask why you are here?'

'There are some questions, madam, that we'd like to ask you and your husband.'

'This is scarcely a convenient time.'

'We'll do our best to be as brief as possible.' Yolles' voice was quiet, but its authority unmistakable.

'I'll enquire if my husband will see you. Please wait in there.'

The secretary led the way to a room off the hallway, furnished as an office. A moment or two later, as the secretary left, the Duchess re-entered, followed by the Duke. He glanced uncertainly from his wife to the others.

'I have informed our guests,' the Duchess announced, 'that we shall be away no more than a few minutes.'

Captain Yolles made no comment. He produced a notebook. 'I wonder if you'd mind telling me when you last used your car. It's a Jaguar, I believe.' He repeated the registration number.

'Our car?' The Duchess seemed surprised. 'No, I'm not sure what was the last time we used it. No, just a moment, I do remember. It was Monday morning. It's been in the hotel garage since then. It's there now.'

'Please think carefully. Did you or your husband, either separately or together use the car on Monday evening?'

It was revealing, Peter thought, how, automatically, Yolles addressed his questions to the Duchess and not to the Duke.

Two spots of colour appeared on the Duchess of Croydon's cheeks. 'I am not accustomed to having my word doubted. I have already said that the last occasion the car was used was on Monday morning. I also think you owe us an explanation as to what this is all about.'

Yolles wrote in his notebook.

'Are either of you acquainted with Theodore Ogilvie?'

'The name has a certain familiarity . . .'

'He is the chief house officer of this hotel.'

'I remember now. He came here. I'm not sure when. There was some query about a piece of jewellery which had been found. Someone suggested it might be mine. It was not.'

'And you, sir?' Yolles addressed the Duke directly. 'Do you know, or have you had any dealings with, Theodore Ogilvie?'

Perceptibly, the Duke of Croydon hesitated. His wife's eyes were riveted on his face. 'Well . . .' He stopped. 'Only as my wife has described.'

Yolles closed his notebook. In a quiet, level voice he asked, 'Would it, then, surprise you to know that your car is at present in the State of Tennessee, where it was driven by Theodore Ogilvie, who is now under arrest? Furthermore, that Ogilvie has made a statement to the effect that he was paid by you to drive the car from New Orleans to Chicago. And, still further, that preliminary investigation indicates your car to have been involved in a hit-and-run fatality, in this city, last Monday night.'

'Since you ask,' the Duchess of Croydon said, 'I would be extremely surprised. In fact it's the most ridiculous series of fabrications I ever heard.'

'There is no fabrication, madam, in the fact that your car is in Tennessee and Ogilvie drove it there.'

'If he did so, it was without the authority or knowledge either of my husband or myself. Furthermore if, as you say, the car was involved in an accident on Monday night, it seems perfectly obvious that the same man took the car and used it for his own purposes on that occasion.'

'Then you accuse Theodore Ogilvie . . .'

The Duchess snapped, 'Accusations are your business. You appear to specialize in them. I will, however, make one to the effect that this hotel has proved disgracefully incompetent in protecting the property of its guests.' The Duchess swung towards Peter McDermott. 'I assure you that you will hear a great deal more of this.'

Peter protested, 'But you wrote an authorization. It specified that Ogilvie could take the car.'

The effect was as if he had slapped the Duchess across the face. Her lips moved uncertainly. Visibly, she paled. He had reminded her, he realized, of the single incriminating factor she had overlooked.

The silence seemed endless. Then her head came up.

'Show it to me!'

Peter said, 'Unfortunately, it's been . . .'

He caught a gleam of mocking triumph in her eyes.

505

19

At last, after more questions and banalities, the Croydons' press conference had ended.

As the outside door of the Presidential Suite closed behind the last to leave, pent-up words burst from the Duke of Croydon's lips. 'My God, you can't do it! You couldn't possibly get away with . . .'

'Be *quiet*!' The Duchess of Croydon glanced around the now silent living-room. 'Not here. I've come to mistrust this hotel and everything about it.'

'Then where? For God's sake, where?'

'We'll go outside. Where no-one can overhear. But when we do, please behave less excitably than now.'

She opened the connecting door to their bedrooms where the Bedlington terriers had been confined. They tumbled out excitedly, barking as the Duchess fastened their leads, aware of what the sign portended. In the hallway, the secretary dutifully opened the suite door as the terriers led the way out.

In the elevator, the Duke seemed about to speak but his wife shook her head. Only when they were outside, away from the hotel and beyond the hearing of other pedestrians, did she murmur. 'Now!'

His voice was strained, intense, 'I tell you it's madness! The whole mess is already bad enough. We've compounded and compounded what happened at first. Can you conceive what it will be like now, when the truth finally comes out?'

'Yes, I've some idea. *If* it does.'

He persisted, 'Apart from everything else – the moral issue, all the rest – you'd never get away with it.'

'Why not?'

'Because it's impossible. Inconceivable. We are already worse off than at the beginning. Now, with this . . .' His voice choked.

'We are *not* worse off. For the moment we are better off. May I remind you of the appointment to Washington.'

'You don't seriously suppose we have the slightest chance of ever getting there?'

'There is every chance.'

Preceded eagerly by the terriers, they had walked along St Charles Avenue to the busier and brightly lighted expanse of Canal Street. Now, turning southeast towards the river, they affected interest in the colourful store windows as groups of pedestrians passed in both directions.

The Duchess's voice was low. 'However distasteful, there are certain facts that I must know about Monday night. The woman you were with at Irish Bayou. Did you drive her there?'

The Duke flushed. 'No. She went in a taxi. We met inside. I intended afterwards . . .'

'Spare me your intentions. Then, for all she knew, you could have come in a taxi yourself.'

'I hadn't thought about it. I suppose so.'

'After I arrived – also by taxi, which can be confirmed if necessary – I noticed that when we went to our car, you had parked it well away from that awful club. There was no attendant.'

'I put it out of the way deliberately. I suppose I thought there was less chance of your getting to hear.'

'So at no point was there any witness to the fact that you were driving the car on Monday night.'

'There's the hotel garage. When we came in, someone could have seen us.'

'No! I remember you stopped just inside the garage entrance, and you left the car, as we often do. We saw no-one. No-one saw us.'

'What about taking it out?'

'You couldn't have taken it out. Not from the hotel garage. On Monday *morning* we left it on an outside parking lot.'

'That's right,' the Duke said. 'I got it from there at night.'

The Duchess continued, thinking aloud, 'We shall say, of course, that we did take the car to the hotel garage after we used it Monday morning. There will be no record of it coming in, but that proves nothing. As far as we are concerned, we have not seen the car since midday Monday.'

The Duke was silent as they continued to walk. With a gesture he reached out, relieving his wife of the terriers. Sensing a new hand on their leash, they strained forward more vigorously than before.

At length he said, 'It's really quite remarkable how everything fits together.'

'It's more than remarkable. It's meant to be that way. From the beginning, everything has worked out. Now . . .'

'Now you propose to send another man to prison instead of me.'

'No!'

He shook his head. 'I couldn't do it, even to him.'

'As far as he is concerned, I promise you that nothing will happen.'

'How could you be sure?'

'Because the police would have to prove he was driving the car at the time of the accident. They can't possibly do it, any more than they can prove it was you. Don't you understand? They may *know* that it was one or the other. They may believe they know which. But believing is not enough. Not without proof.'

'You know,' he said, with admiration, 'there are times when you are absolutely incredible.'

'I'm practical. And speaking of being practical, there's something else you might remember. That man Ogilvie has had ten thousand dollars of our money. At least we should get something for it.'

'By the way,' the Duke said, 'where is the other fifteen thousand?'

'Still in the small suitcase which is locked and in my bedroom. We'll take it with us when we go. I already decided it might attract attention to return it to the bank here.'

'You really do think of everything.'

'I didn't with that note. When I thought they had it . . . I must have been mad to write what I did.'

'You couldn't have foreseen.'

They had reached the end of the brightly lighted portion of Canal Street. Now they turned, retracing their steps towards the city centre.

'It's diabolical,' the Duke of Croydon said. His last drink had been at noon. As a result, his voice was a good deal clearer than in recent days. 'It's ingenious, devilish and diabolical. But it might, it just might work.'

20

'That woman is lying,' Captain Yolles said. 'But it'll be hard to prove, if we ever do.' He continued to pace, slowly, the length of Peter McDermott's office. They had come here – the two detectives, with Peter – after an ignominious departure from the Presidential Suite. So far Yolles had done little more than pace and ponder while the other two waited.

'Her husband might break,' the second detective suggested. 'If we could get him by himself.'

Yolles shook his head. 'There isn't a chance. For one thing, she's too smart to let it happen. For another, with them being who and what they are, we'd be walking on eggshells.' He looked at Peter. 'Don't ever kid yourself there isn't one police procedure for the poor and another for the rich and influential.'

Across the office, Peter nodded, though with a sense of detachment. Having done what duty and conscience required, what followed now, he felt, was the business of the police. Curiosity, however, prompted a question. 'The note that the Duchess wrote to the garage . . .'

'If we had that,' the second detective said, 'it'd be a clincher.'

'Isn't it enough for the night checker – and Ogilvie, I suppose – to swear that the note existed?'

Yolles said, 'She'd claim it was a forgery, that Ogilvie wrote it himself.' He mused, then added, 'You said it was on special stationery. Let me see some.'

Peter went outside and in a stationery cupboard found several sheets. They were a heavy bond paper, light blue, with the hotel name and crest embossed. Below, also embossed, were the words *Presidential Suite*.

Peter returned and the policemen examined the sheets.

'Pretty fancy,' the second detective said.

Yolles asked, 'How many people have access to this?'

'In the ordinary way, just a few. But I suppose a good many others could get hold of a sheet if they really wanted to.'

Yolles grunted. 'Rules that out.'

'There is one possibility,' Peter said. For the moment, with a sudden thought, his detachment vanished.

'What?'

'I know you asked me this, and I said that once garbage had been cleared – as it was from the garage – there was no chance of retrieving anything. I really thought . . . it seemed so impossible, the idea of locating one piece of paper. Besides, the note wasn't so important then.'

He was aware of the eyes of both detectives intently on his face.

'We do have a man,' Peter said. 'He's in charge of the incinerator. A lot of garbage he sorts by hand. It would be a long shot and it's probably too late . . .'

'For Christ's sake!' Yolles snapped. 'Let's get to him.'

They walked quickly to the main floor, then used a staff doorway to reach a freight elevator which would take them the rest of the way down. The elevator was busy on a lower level where Peter could hear packages being unloaded. He shouted down for the crew to hurry.

While they were waiting, the second detective, Bennett, said, 'I hear you've had some trouble this week.'

'There was a robbery early yesterday. With all this, I'd almost forgotten.'

'I was talking with one of our people. He was with your senior house dick . . . what's his name?'

'Finegan. He's acting chief.' Despite the seriousness, Peter smiled. 'Our regular chief is otherwise engaged.'

'About the robbery, there wasn't much to go on. Our people checked your guest list, didn't turn up anything. Today, though, a funny thing happened. There was a break-in in Lakeview – private home. A key job. The woman lost her keys downtown this morning. Whoever found them must have gone straight there. It had all the signs of your robbery here, including the kind of stuff taken, and no prints.'

'Has there been an arrest?'

The detective shook his head. 'Wasn't discovered till hours after it happened. There is a lead, though. A neighbour saw a car. Couldn't remember anything except it had licence plates that were green and white. Five states use plates with those colours – Michigan, Idaho, Nebraska, Vermont, Washington – and Saskatchewan in Canada.'

'How does that help?'

'For the next day or two, all our boys will be watching for cars from those places. They'll stop them and check. It could turn something up. We've been lucky before, with a whole lot less to go on.'

Peter nodded, though with lukewarm interest. The robbery had happened two days ago, with no recurrence. At present a good deal seemed more important.

A moment later the elevator arrived.

The sweat-shining face of Booker T. Graham beamed with pleasure at the sight of Peter McDermott, the only member of the hotel's executive staff who ever bothered visiting the incinerator room, deep within the hotel basement. The visits, though infrequent, were treasured by Booker T. Graham as royal occasions.

Captain Yolles wrinkled his nose at the overpowering odour of garbage, magnified by intense heat. The reflection of flames danced on smoke-grimed walls. Shouting to make himself heard above the roar of the furnace set into one side of the enclosure, Peter cautioned, 'Better leave this to me, I'll explain what we want.'

Yolles nodded. Like others who had preceded him here, it occurred to him that the first sight of hell might be remarkably like this moment. He wondered how a human being could exist in these surroundings for any length of time.

Yolles watched as Peter McDermott talked with the big Negro who sorted the garbage before incinerating it. McDermott had brought a sheet of the special Presidential Suite stationery and held it up for inspection. The Negro nodded and took the sheet, retaining it, but his expression was doubtful. He gestured to the dozens of overflowing bins crowded around them. There were also others, Yolles observed as they came in, lined up outside on hand trucks. He realized why, earlier on, McDermott had dismissed the possibility of locating a single piece of paper. Now, in response to a question, the Negro shook his head. McDermott returned to the two detectives.

'Most of this,' he explained, 'is yesterday's garbage, collected today. About a third of what came in has already been burned and whether what we want was in there or not, we've no means of knowing. As for the rest, Graham has to go through it, looking for things we salvage, like silverware and bottles. While he's doing that, he'll keep an eye open for a paper of the kind I've given him, but as you can see, it's a pretty formidable job. Before the garbage gets here, it's compressed and a lot of it is wet, which soaks everything else. I've asked Graham if he wants extra help, but he says there's even less chance if someone else comes in who isn't used to working the way he does.'

'Either way,' the second detective said, 'I wouldn't lay any bets.'

Yolles conceded, 'I suppose it's the best we can do. What arrangement did you make if your man finds anything?'

'He'll call upstairs right away. I'll leave instructions that I'm to be notified whatever time it is. Then I'll call you.'

Yolles nodded. As the three men left, Booker T. Graham had his hands in a mess of garbage on a large flat tray.

21

For Keycase Milne, frustration had piled upon frustration.

Since early evening he had maintained a watch upon the Presidential Suite. Near dinnertime – when he confidently expected the Duke and Duchess of Croydon to leave the hotel, as almost all visitors did – he had taken post on the ninth floor near the service stairs. From there he had a clear view of the entrance to the suite, with the advantage that he could avoid being observed himself by ducking quickly out of sight through the stairway door. He did this several times as elevators stopped and occupants of other rooms came and went, though on each occasion Keycase managed to catch a glimpse of them before his own departure. He also calculated, correctly, that at this time of day there would be little staff activity on the upper floors. In case of anything unforeseen, it was a simple matter to retreat to the eighth floor and, if necessary, his own room.

That part of the plan had worked. What had gone wrong was that through the entire evening the Duke and Duchess of Croydon had failed to leave their suite.

However, no room-service dinner had been delivered, a fact which made Keycase linger hopefully.

Once, wondering if he had somehow missed the Croydons' departure, Keycase walked gingerly down the corridor and listened at the suite door. He could hear voices inside, including a woman's.

Later, his disappointment was increased by the arrival of visitors. They appeared to come in ones and twos and, after the first few, the doors of the Presidential Suite were left open. Soon after, room-service waiters appeared with trays of hors d'oeuvres and a growing hum of conversation, mixed with the clink of ice and glass, was audible in the corridor.

He was puzzled, later still, by the arrival of a broad-shouldered youngish man whom Keycase judged to be an official of the hotel. The hotel-man's face was set grimly, as were those of two other men with him. Keycase paused long enough for a careful look at all three and, at first glance, guessed the second and third to be policemen. Subsequently he reassured himself that the thought was the product of his own too active imagination.

The three more recent arrivals left first, followed a half hour or so later by the remainder of the party. Despite the heavy traffic in the later stages of the evening, Keycase was certain he had been unobserved, except possibly as just another hotel guest.

With the departure of the last visitor, silence was complete in the ninth floor corridor. It was now close to eleven p.m. and obvious that nothing more would happen tonight. Keycase decided to wait another ten minutes, then leave.

His mood of optimism earlier in the day had changed to depression.

He was uncertain whether he could risk remaining in the hotel for another twenty-four hours. He had already considered the idea of entering the suite during the night or early tomorrow morning, then dismissed it. The hazard was too great. If someone awakened, no conceivable excuse could justify Keycase's presence in the Presidential Suite. He had also been aware since yesterday that he would have to consider the movements of the Croydons' secretary and the Duchess's maid. The maid, he learned, had a room elsewhere in the hotel and had not been in evidence tonight. But the secretary lived in the suite and was one more person who might be awakened by a night intrusion. Also, the dogs which Keycase had seen the Duchess exercising were likely to raise an alarm.

He was faced, then, with the alternative of waiting another day or abandoning the attempt to reach the Duchess's jewels.

Then, as he was on the point of leaving, the Duke and Duchess of Croydon emerged, preceded by the Bedlington terriers.

Swiftly, Keycase melted into the service stairway. His heart began to pulse faster. At last, when he had abandoned hope, the opportunity he coveted had come.

It was not an uncomplicated opportunity. Obviously the Duke and Duchess would not be away for long. And somewhere in the suite was the male secretary. Where? In a separate room with the door closed? In bed already? He looked a Milquetoast type who might retire early.

Whatever the risk of an encounter, it had to be taken. Keycase knew that if he failed to act now, his nerves would not survive another day of waiting.

He heard elevator doors open, then close. Cautiously, he returned to the corridor. It was silent and empty. Walking quietly, he approached the Presidential Suite.

His specially-made key turned easily, as it had this afternoon. He opened one of the double doors slightly, then gently released the spring pressure and removed the key. The lock made no noise. Nor did the door as he opened it slowly.

A hallway was immediately ahead, beyond it a larger room. To the right and left were two more doors, both closed. Through the one on the right he could hear what sounded like a radio. There was no-one in sight. The lights in the suite were turned on.

Keycase went in. He slipped on gloves, then closed and latched the outside door behind him.

He moved warily, yet wasting no time. Broadloom in the hallway and living-room muffled his footsteps. He crossed the living-room to a farther door which was ajar. As Keycase expected, it led to two spacious bedrooms, each with a bathroom, and a dressing-room between. In the bedrooms, as elsewhere, lights were on. There was no mistaking which room was the Duchess's.

Its furnishings included a tallboy, two dressing tables and a walk-in closet. Keycase began, systematically, to search all four. A jewel-box, such as he sought, was in neither the tallboy nor the first dressing table. There were a number of items – gold evening purses, cigarette cases and expensive-looking compacts – which, with more time and in other circumstances, he would have garnered gladly. But now he was racing, seeking a major prize and discarding all else.

At the second dressing table he opened the first drawer. It contained nothing worth while. The second drawer yielded no better result. In the third, on top, was an array of négligés. Beneath them was a deep, oblong box of hand-tooled leather. It was locked.

Leaving the box in the drawer, Keycase worked with a knife and screwdriver to break the lock. The box was stoutly made and resisted opening. Several minutes passed. Conscious of fleeting time, he began to perspire.

At length the lock gave, the lid flew back. Beneath, in scintillating, breath-taking array were two tiers of jewels – rings, brooches, necklets, clips, tiaras; all of precious metal, and most were gem-encrusted. At the sight, Keycase drew in breath. So, after all, a portion of the Duchess's fabled collection had not been consigned to the hotel vault. Once more a hunch, an omen, had proved right. With both hands he reached out to seize the spoils. At the same instant a key turned in the lock of the outer door.

His reflex was instantaneous. Keycase slammed down the jewel-box lid and slid the drawer closed. On the way in, he had left the bedroom door slightly ajar; now he flew to it. Through an inch-wide gap he could see into the living-room. A hotel maid was entering. She had towels on her arm and was headed for the Duchess's bedroom. The maid was elderly, and waddled. Her slowness offered a single slim chance.

Swinging around, Keycase lunged for a bedside lamp. He found its cork and yanked. The light went out. Now he needed something in his hand to indicate activity. Something! Anything!

Against the wall was a small attaché case. He seized it and stalked towards the door.

As Keycase flung the door wide, the maid recoiled. 'Oh!' A hand went over her heart.

Keycase frowned. 'Where have you been? You should have come here earlier.'

The shock, followed by the accusation, made her flustered. He had intended that it should.

'I'm sorry, sir. I saw there were people in, and . . .'

He cut her short. 'It doesn't matter now. Do what you have to, and there's a lamp needs fixing.' He gestured into the bedroom. 'The Duchess wants it working tonight.' He kept his voice low, remembering the secretary.

'Oh. I'll see that it is, sir.'

'Very well.' Keycase nodded coolly, and went out.

In the corridor he tried not to think. He succeeded until he was in his own room, 830. Then, in bafflement and despair, he flung himself across the bed and buried his face in a pillow.

It was more than an hour before he bothered forcing the lock of the attaché case he had brought away.

Inside was pile upon pile of United States currency. All used bills, of small denominations.

With trembling hands he counted fifteen thousand dollars.

22

Peter McDermott accompanied the two detectives from the incinerator in the hotel basement to the St Charles Street door.

'For the time being,' Captain Yolles cautioned, 'I'd like to keep what's happened tonight as quiet as possible. There'll be questions enough when we charge your man Ogilvie, whatever it's with. No sense in bringing the press around our necks until we have to.'

Peter assured him, 'If the hotel had any choice, we'd prefer no publicity at all.'

Yolles grunted. 'Don't count on it.'

Peter returned to the main dining-room to discover, not surprisingly, that Christine and Albert Wells had gone.

In the lobby he was intercepted by the night manager. 'Mr McDermott, here's a note Miss Francis left for you.'

It was in a sealed envelope and read simply:

I've gone home. Come if you can. – Christine.

He would go, he decided. He suspected that Christine was eager to talk over the events of the day, including this evening's astounding disclosure by Albert Wells.

Nothing else to do tonight at the hotel. Or was there? Abruptly, Peter remembered the promise he had made to Marsha Preyscott on leaving her at the cemetery so unceremoniously this afternoon. He had said he would telephone later, but he had forgotten until now. The crisis of the afternoon was only hours away. It seemed like days, and Marsha somehow remote. Bu he supposed he should call her, late as it was.

Once more he used the credit manager's office on the main floor and dialled the Preyscott number. Marsha answered on the first ring.

'Oh, Peter,' she said. 'I've been sitting by the telephone. I waited and waited, then called twice and left my name.'

He remembered guiltily the pile of unacknowledged messages on his office desk.

'I'm genuinely sorry, and I can't explain, at least not yet. Except that all kinds of things have been happening.'

'Tell me tomorrow.'

'Marsha, I'm afraid tomorrow will be a very full day . . .'

'At breakfast,' Marsha said. 'If it's going to be that kind of day, you need a New Orleans breakfast. They're famous. Have you ever had one?'

'I don't usually eat breakfast.'

'Tomorrow you will. And Anna's are special. A lot better, I'll bet, than at your old hotel.'

It was impossible not to be charmed by Marsha's enthusiasms. And he had, after all, deserted her this afternoon.

'It will have to be early.'

'As early as you like.'

They agreed on 7.30 a.m.

A few minutes later he was in a taxi on his way to Christine's apartment in Gentilly.

He rang from downstairs. Christine was waiting with the apartment door open.

'Not a word,' she said, 'until after the second drink. I just can't take it all in.'

'You'd better,' he told her. 'You haven't heard the half of it.'

She had mixed daiquiris, which were chilling in the refrigerator. There was a heaped plate of chicken and ham sandwiches. The fragrance of freshly brewed coffee wafted through the apartment.

Peter remembered suddenly that despite his sojourn in the hotel kitchens, and the talk of breakfast tomorrow, he had eaten nothing since lunch.

'That's what I imagined,' Christine said when he told her. 'Fall to!'

Obeying, he watched as she moved efficiently around the tiny kitchen. He had a feeling, sitting here, of being at ease and shielded from whatever might be happening outside. He thought: Christine had cared about him enough to do what she had done. More important, there was an empathy between them in which even their silences, as now, seemed shared and understood.

He pushed away the daiquiri glass and reached for a coffee cup which Christine had filled. 'All right,' he said, 'where do we start?'

They talked continuously for almost two hours, all the time their closeness growing. At the end, all they could decide on definitely was that tomorrow would be an interesting day.

'I won't sleep,' Christine said. 'I couldn't possibly. I know I won't.'

'I couldn't, either,' Peter said. 'But not for the reason you mean.'

He had no doubts; only a conviction that he wanted this moment to go on and on. He took her in his arms and kissed her.

Later, it seemed the most natural thing in the world that they should make love.

Friday

I

It was understandable, Peter McDermott thought, that the Duke and Duchess of Croydon should be rolling the chief house officer, Ogilvie – trussed securely into a ball – towards the edge of the St Gregory roof while, far below, a sea of faces stared fixedly upwards. But it was strange, and somehow shocking, that a few yards farther on, Curtis O'Keefe and Warren Trent were exchanging savage cuts with blood-stained duelling swords. Why, Peter wondered, had Captain Yolles, standing by a stairway door, failed to intervene? Then Peter realized that the policeman was watching a giant bird's nest in which a single egg was cracking open. A moment later, from the egg's interior, emerged an outsize sparrow with the cheery face of Albert Wells. But now Peter's attention was diverted to the roof-edge where a desperately struggling Christine had become entangled with Ogilvie, and Marsha Preyscott was helping the Croydons push the double burden nearer and nearer to the awful gulf below. The crowds continued to gape as Captain Yolles leaned against a doorpost, yawning.

If he hoped to save Christine, Peter realized, he must act himself. But when he attempted to move, his feet dragged heavily as if encased in glue, and while his body urged forwards, his legs refused to follow. He tried to cry out, but his throat was blocked. His eyes met Christine's in dumb despair.

Suddenly, the Croydons, Marsha, O'Keefe, Warren Trent stopped and were listening. The sparrow that was Albert Wells cocked an ear. Now Ogilvie, Yolles and Christine were doing the same. Listening to what?

Then Peter heard; a cacophony as if all the telephones on earth were ringing together. The sound came closer, swelling, until it seemed that it would engulf them all. Peter put his hands over his ears. The dissonance grew. He closed his eyes, then opened them.

He was in his apartment. His beside alarm showed 6.30 a.m.

He lay for a few minutes, shaking his head free from the wild, hodge-podge dream. Then he padded to the bathroom for a shower, steeling himself to remain under the spray with the cold tap 'on' for a final minute. He emerged from the shower fully awake. Slipping on a towel robe, he started coffee brewing in the kitchenette, then went to the telephone and dialled the hotel number.

He was connected with the night manager who assured Peter that there had been no message during the night concerning anything found in the incinerator. No, the night manager said with a trace of tiredness, he had not checked personally. Yes, if Mr McDermott wished, he would go down immediately and telephone the result, though Peter sensed a mild resentment at the unlikely errand so near the end of a long, tiring shift.

515

The incinerator was somewhere in the lower basement, wasn't it?

Peter was shaving when the return call came. The night manager reported that he had spoken with the incinerator employee, Graham, who was sorry, but the paper Mr McDermott wanted had not turned up. Now, it didn't look as if it would. The manager added the information that Graham's night shift – as well as his own – was almost ended.

Later, Peter decided he would pass the news, or rather the lack of it, to Captain Yolles. He remembered his opinion of last night, which still held good, that the hotel had done all it could in the matter of public duty. Anything else must be the business of the police.

Between sips of coffee, and while dressing, Peter considered the two subjects uppermost in his mind. One was Christine; the other, his own future, if any, at the St Gregory Hotel.

After last night, he realized that whatever might be ahead, more than anything else he wished Christine to be a part of it. The conviction had been growing on him; now it was clear and definite. He supposed it might be said that he was in love, but he was guarded in attempting to define his deeper feelings, even to himself. Once before, what he had believed was love had turned to ashes. Perhaps it was better to begin with hope, and grope uncertainly towards an unknown end.

It might be unromantic, Peter reflected, to say that he was comfortable with Christine. But it was true and, in a sense, reassuring. He had a conviction that the bonds between them would grow stronger, not weaker, as time went by. He believed that Christine's feelings were similar to his own.

Instinct told him that what lay immediately ahead was to be savoured, not devoured.

As to the hotel, it was hard to grasp, even now, that Albert Wells, whom they had assumed to be a pleasant, inconsequential little man, stood revealed as a financial mogul who had assumed control of the St Gregory, or would today.

Superficially, it seemed possible that Peter's own position might be strengthened by the unexpected development. He had become friendly with the little man and had the impression that he himself was liked in return. But liking, and a business decision, were separate things. The nicest people could be hard-headed, and ruthless when they chose. Also, it was unlikely that Albert Wells would run the hotel personally, and whoever fronted for him might have definite views on the background records of personnel.

As he had before, Peter decided not to worry about events until they happened.

Across New Orleans, clocks were chiming seven-thirty as Peter McDermott arrived, by taxi, at the Preyscott mansion on Prytania Street.

Behind graceful soaring columns, the great white house stood nobly in early morning sunlight. The air around was fresh and cool, with traces still of a predawn mist. The scent of magnolia hung fragrantly, and there was dew upon the grass.

The street and house were quiet, but from St Charles Avenue and beyond could be heard distant sounds of the awakening city.

Peter crossed the lawn by the curving pathway of old red brick. He ascended the terrace steps and knocked at the double carved doorway.

Ben, the manservant who had functioned at dinner on Wednesday night, opened the door and greeted Peter cordially. 'Good morning, sir. Please come in.' Inside, he announced, 'Miss Marsha asked me to show you to the gallery. She'll join you in a few minutes.

With Ben leading the way, they went up the broad curving staircase and along the wide corridor with frescoed walls where, on Wednesday night in semi-darkness, Peter had accompanied Marsha. He asked himself: was it really so short a time ago?

In daylight the gallery appeared as well ordered and inviting as it had before. There were deep-cushioned chairs, and planters bright with flowers. Near the front, looking down on the garden below, a table had been set for breakfast. There were two places.

Peter asked, 'Is the house stirring early on my account?'

'No, sir,' Ben assured him. 'We're early people here. Mr Preyscott, when he's home, doesn't like late starting. He always says there isn't enough of each day that you should waste the front end of it.'

'You see! I told you my father was a lot like you.'

At Marsha's voice, Peter turned. She had come in quietly behind them. He had an impression of dew and roses, and that she had risen freshly with the sun.

'Good morning!' Marsha smiled. 'Ben, please give Mr McDermott an absinthe Suissesse.' She took Peter's arm.

'Pour lightly, Ben,' Peter said, 'I know absinthe Suissesse goes with a New Orleans breakfast, but I've a new boss. I'd like to meet him sober.'

The manservant grinned. 'Yessir!'

As they sat at the table, Marsha said, 'Was that why you . . .'

'Why I disappeared like a conjurer's rabbit? No. That was something else.'

Her eyes widened as he related as much as he could of the hit-and-run investigation without mentioning the Croydons' name. He declined to be drawn by Marsha's questioning, but told her, 'Whatever happens, there will be some news today.'

To himself, he reasoned: By now, Ogilvie was probably back in New Orleans and being interrogated. If retained in custody, he would have to be charged, with an appearance in court which would alert the press. Inevitably there would be a reference to the Jaguar which, in turn, would point a finger at the Croydons.

Peter sampled the fluffy absinthe Suissesse which had appeared before him. From his own bartending days he remembered the ingredients – herbsaint, white of an egg, cream, orgeat syrup and a dash of anisette. He had seldom tasted them better mixed. Across the table Marsha was sipping orange juice.

Peter wondered: Could the Duke and Duchess of Croydon, in face of Ogilvie's accusation, continue to maintain their innocence? It was one more question which today might determine.

But certainly the Duchess's note – if it ever existed – was gone. There had been no further word from the hotel – at least, on that point – and Booker T. Graham would have long since gone off duty.

In front of both Peter and Marsha, Ben placed a Creole cream cheese Evangeline, garlanded with fruit.

Peter began to eat with enjoyment.

'Earlier on,' Marsha said, 'you started to say something. It was about the hotel.'

'Oh, yes.' Between mouthfuls of cheese and fruit, he explained about Albert Wells. 'The new ownership is being announced today. I had a telephone call just as I was leaving to come here.'

The call had been from Warren Trent. It informed Peter that Mr Dempster of Montreal, financial representative of the St Gregory's new owner, was en route to New

Orleans. Mr Dempster was already in New York where he would board an Eastern Airlines flight, arriving at mid-morning. A suite was to be reserved, and a meeting between the old and new management groups was scheduled tentatively for eleven-thirty. Peter was instructed to remain available in case he was required.

Surprisingly, Warren Trent had sounded not in the least depressed and, in fact, brighter than in recent days. Was W. T. aware, Peter wondered, that the new owner of the St Gregory was already in the hotel? Remembering that until an official change-over, his own loyalty lay with the old management, Peter related the conversation of last evening between himself, Christine and Albert Wells. 'Yes,' Warren Trent had said, 'I know. Emile Dumaire of Industrial Merchant Bank – he did the negotiating for Wells – phoned me late last night. It seems there was some secrecy. There isn't any more.'

Peter also knew that Curtis O'Keefe, and his companion, Miss Lash, were due to leave the St Gregory later this morning. Apparently they were going separate ways since the hotel – which handled such matters for VIPs – had arranged a flight to Los Angeles for Miss Lash, while Curtis O'Keefe was headed for Naples, via New York and Rome.

'You're thinking about a lot of things,' Marsha said. 'I wish you'd tell me some. My father used to want to talk at breakfast, but my mother was never interested. I am.'

Peter smiled. He told her the kind of day that he expected it to be.

As they talked, the remains of the cheeses Evangeline were removed, to be replaced by steaming, aromatic eggs Sardou. Twin poached eggs nestled on artichoke bottoms, appetizingly topped with creamed spinach and hollandaise sauce. A rosé wine appeared at Peter's place.

Marsha said, 'I understand what you meant about today being very busy.'

'And I understand what *you* meant by a traditional breakfast.' Peter caught sight of the housekeeper, Anna, hovering in the background. He called out, 'Magnificent!' and saw her smile.

Later, he gasped at the arrival of sirloin steak with mushrooms, hot French bread and marmalade.

Peter said doubtfully, 'I'm not sure . . .'

'There's *crêpes Suzette* to come,' Marsha informed him, 'and *café au lait*. When there were great plantations here, people used to scoff at the *petit déjeuner* of the continentals. They made breakfast an occasion.'

'You've made it an occasion,' Peter said. 'This, and a good deal more. Meeting you; my history lessons; being with you here. I won't forget it – ever.'

'You make it sound as if you're saying goodbye.'

'I am, Marsha.' He met her eyes steadily, then smiled. 'Right after the *crêpes Suzette*.'

There was a silence before she said, 'I thought . . .'

He reached out across the table, his hand covering Marsha's. 'Perhaps we were both day-dreaming. I think we were. But it's quite the nicest day-dream I ever had.'

'Why does it have to be just that?'

He answered gently, 'Some things you can't explain. No matter how much you like someone, there's a question of deciding what's best to do; of judgement . . .'

'And my judgement doesn't count?'

'Marsha, I have to trust mine. For both of us.' But he wondered: Could it be trusted? His own instincts had proved less than reliable before. Perhaps, at this moment, he was making a mistake which years from now he would remember with regret. How to be sure of anything, when you often learned the truth too late?

He sensed that Marsha was close to tears.

'Excuse me,' she said in a low voice. She stood up and walked swiftly from the gallery.

Sitting there, Peter wished he could have spoken less forthrightly, tempering his words with the gentleness that he felt for this lonely girl. He wondered if she would return. After a few minutes, when Marsha failed to, Anna appeared. 'Looks like you'll be finishing breakfast alone, sir. I don't believe Miss Marsha'll be back.'

He asked, 'How is she?'

'She's cryin' in her room.' Anna shrugged. 'Isn't the first time. Don't suppose it'll be the last. It's a way she has when she doesn't get all she wants.' She removed the steak plates. 'Ben'll serve you the rest.'

He shook his head. 'No, thank you. I must go.'

'Then I'll just bring coffee.' In the background. Ben had busied himself, but it was Anna who took the *café au lait* and put it beside Peter.

'Don't go away worrying over-much, sir. When she's past the most of it, I'll do the best I can. Miss Marsha has maybe too much time to think about herself. If her daddy was here more, maybe thing's be different. But he ain't. Not hardly at all.'

'You've very understanding.'

Peter remembered what Marsha had told him about Anna: how, as a young girl, Anna had been forced by her family to marry a man she scarcely knew; but the marriage had lasted happily for more than forty years until Anna's husband died a year ago.

Peter said, 'I heard about your husband. He must have been a fine man.'

'My husband!' The housekeeper cackled. 'I ain't had no husband. Never been married in my whole life. I'm a maiden lady – more or less.'

Marsha had said: *They lived with us here, Anna and her husband. He was the kindest, sweetest man I've ever known. If there was ever a perfect marriage, it belonged to them.* Marsha had used the portrayal to bolster her own argument when she asked Peter to marry her.

Anna was still chuckling. 'My goodness! Miss Marsha's been taking you in with all her stories. She makes up a good many. A lot of time she's play acting, which is why you don't need to worry none now.'

'I see.' Peter was not sure that he did, though he felt relieved.

Ben showed him out. It was after nine o'clock and the day was already becoming hot. Peter walked briskly towards St Charles Avenue where he headed for the hotel. He hoped that the walk would overcome any somnolence he might feel from the trencherman's meal. He felt a genuine regret that he would not see Marsha again, and a sorrow concerning her for a reason he could not fully comprehend. He wondered if he would ever be wise about women. He rather doubted it.

2

Number four elevator was acting up again. Cy Lewin, its elderly day-time operator, was getting thoroughly sick of number four and its capriciousness, which had started a week or more ago, and seemed to be getting worse.

Last Sunday the elevator had several times refused to respond to its controls, even though both cage and landing doors were fully closed. The relief man had told Cy that the same thing happened Monday night when Mr McDermott, the assistant general manager, was in the car.

Then, on Wednesday, there had been trouble which put number four out of service for several hours. Malfunctioning of the clutch arrangement, Engineering said, whatever that meant; but the repair job had not prevented another hiatus the following day when on three separate occasions number four refused to start away from the fifteenth floor.

Now, today, number four was starting and stopping jerkily at every floor.

It was not Cy Lewin's business to know what was wrong. Nor did he especially care, even though he had heard the chief engineer, Doc Vickery, grumbling about 'patching and patching' and complaining that he needed 'a hundred thousand dollars to rip the elevator's guts out and begin again'. Well, who wouldn't like that kind of money? Cy Lewin himself sure would, which was why every year he scraped together the price of a sweepstake ticket, though a fat lot of good it had ever done him.

But a St Gregory veteran like himself was entitled to a consideration, and tomorrow he would ask to be moved over to one of the other cars. Why not? He had worked twenty-seven years in the hotel and was running elevators before some of the young whippersnappers now around the place were born. After today, let someone else put up with number four and its contrariness.

It was a little before ten a.m., and the hotel was becoming busy. Cy Lewin took a load up from the lobby – mostly conventioneers with names on their lapels – stopping at intermediate floors until the fifteenth, which was the top of the hotel. Going down, the car was filled to capacity by the time he reached the ninth, and he highballed the rest of the way to the main lobby. On this latest trip he noticed that the jerkiness had stopped. Well, whatever *that* trouble was, he guessed it had fixed itself.

He could not have been more wrong.

High above Cy Lewin, perched like an eyrie on the hotel roof, was the elevator control room. There, in the mechanical heart of number four elevator, a small electrical relay had reached the limit of its useful life. The cause, unknown and unsuspected, was a tiny push rod the size of a household nail.

The push rod was screwed into a miniature piston head which, in turn, actuated a trio of switches. One switch applied and released the elevator break, a second supplied power to an operating motor; the third controlled a generator circuit. With all three functioning, the elevator car moved slowly up and down in response to its controls. But with only two switches working – and if the non-working switch should be that which controlled the elevator motor – the car would be free to fall under its own weight. Only one thing could cause such a failure – the overall lengthening of the push rod and piston.

For several weeks the push rod had been working loose. With movements so infinitesimal that a hundred might equal the thickness of a human hair, the piston head had turned, slowly but inexorably unscrewing itself from the push rod thread. The effect was two-fold. The push rod and piston had increased their total length. And the motor switch was barely functioning.

Just as a final grain of sand will tip a scale, so, at this moment, the slightest further twisting of the piston would isolate the motor switch entirely.

The defect had been the cause of number four's erratic functioning which Cy Lewin and others had observed. A maintenance crew had tried to trace the trouble, but had not succeeded. They could hardly be blamed. There were more than sixty relays to a single elevator, and twenty elevators in the entire hotel.

Nor had anyone observed that two safety devices on the elevator car were partially defective.

At ten past ten on Friday morning, number four elevator was – in fact, and figuratively – hanging by a thread.

3

Mr Dempster of Montreal checked in at half past ten. Peter McDermott, notified on his arrival, went down to the lobby to extend official greetings. So far this morning, neither Warren Trent nor Albert Wells had appeared on the lower floors of the hotel, nor had the latter been heard from.

The financial representative of Albert Wells was a brisk, impressive person who looked like the seasoned manager of a large branch bank. He responded to a comment of Peter's about the speed of events being breath-taking with the remark, 'Mr Wells frequently has that effect.' A bellboy escorted the newcomer to a suite on the eleventh floor.

Twenty minutes later Mr Dempster reappeared in Peter's office.

He had visited Mr Wells, he said, and spoken on the telephone with Mr Trent. The meeting arranged tentatively for eleven-thirty was definitely to proceed. Meanwhile, there were a few people who Mr Dempster wished to confer with – the hotel's comptroller for one – and Mr Trent had invited him to make use of the executive suite.

Mr Dempster appeared to be a man accustomed to exercise authority.

Peter escorted him to Warren Trent's office and introduced Christine. For Peter and Christine it was their second meeting of the morning. On arrival at the hotel he had sought her out and, though the best they could do in the beleaguered surroundings of the executive suite was to touch hands briefly, in the stolen moment there was an excitement and an eager awareness of each other.

For the first time since his arrival, the man from Montreal smiled. 'Oh yes, Miss Francis. Mr Wells mentioned you. In fact, he spoke of you quite warmly.'

'I think Mr Wells is a wonderful man. I thought so before . . .' She stopped.

'Yes?'

'I'm a little embarrassed,' Christine said, 'about something which happened last night.'

Mr Dempster produced heavy-rimmed glasses which he polished and put on. 'If you're referring to the incident of the restaurant bill, Miss Francis, it's unnecessary that you should be. Mr Wells told me – and I quote his own words – that it was one of the sweetest, kindest things that was ever done for him. He knew what was happening, of course. There's very little he misses.'

'Yes,' Christine said, 'I'm beginning to realize that.'

There was a knock at the outer office door, which opened to reveal the credit manager, Sam Jakubiec. 'Excuse me,' he said when he saw the group inside, and turned to go. Peter called him back.

'I came to check a rumour,' Jakubiec said. 'It's going round the hotel like a prairie fire that the old gentleman, Mr Wells . . .'

'It isn't rumour,' Peter said. 'It's fact.' He introduced the credit man to Mr Dempster.

Jakubiec clapped a hand to his head. 'My God! – I checked his credit. I doubted his cheque. I even phoned Montreal!'

'I heard about your call.' For the second time Mr Dempster smiled. 'At the bank they were vastly amused. But they've strict instructions that no information about Mr Wells is ever to be given out. It's the way he likes things done.'

Jakubiec gave what sounded like a moan.

'I think you'd have more to worry about,' the man from Montreal assured him, 'if you hadn't checked Mr Wells' credit. He'd respect you for doing it. He does have a habit of writing cheques on odd bits of paper, which people find disconcerting. The cheques are all good, of course. You probably know by now that Mr Wells is one of the richest men in North America.'

A dazed Jakubiec could only shake his head.

'It might be simpler for you all,' Mr Dempster remarked, 'if I explained a few things about my employer.' He glanced at his watch. 'Mr Dumaire, the banker, and some lawyers will be here soon, but I believe we've time.'

He was interrupted by the arrival of Royall Edwards. The comptroller was armed with papers and a bulging briefcase. Once more the ritual of introductions was performed.

Shaking hands, Mr Dempster informed the comptroller, 'We'll have a brief talk in a moment, and I'd like you to remain for our eleven-thirty meeting. By the way – you, too, Miss Francis. Mr Trent asked that you be there, and I know Mr Wells will be delighted.'

For the first time, Peter McDermott had a disconcerting sense of exclusion from the centre of affairs.

'I was about to explain some matters concerning Mr Wells.' Mr Dempster removed his glasses, breathed on the lenses and polished them once more.

'Despite Mr Wells' considerable wealth, he has remained a man of very simple tastes. This is in no sense due to meanness. He is, in fact, extremely generous. It is simply that for himself he prefers modest things, even in such matters as clothing, travel, accommodation.'

'About accommodation,' Peter said. 'I was considering moving Mr Wells to a suite. Mr Curtis O'Keefe is vacating one of our better ones this afternoon.'

'I suggest you don't. I happen to know that Mr Wells likes the room he has, though not the one before it.'

Mentally, Peter shuddered at the reference to the ha-ha room which Albert Wells had occupied before his transfer to 1410 on Monday night.

'He has no objection to others having a suite – me, for example,' Mr Dempster explained. 'It is simply that he feels no need for such things himself. Am I boring you?'

His listeners, as one, protested that he was not.

Royall Edwards seemed amused. 'It's like something from the Brothers Grimm!'

'Perhaps. But don't believe that Mr Wells lives in a fairy-tale world. He doesn't, any more than I do.'

Peter McDermott thought: Whether the others realized it or not, there was a hint of steel beneath the urbane words.

Mr Dempster continued, 'I've known Mr Wells a good many years. In that time I've come to respect his instincts both about business and people. He has a kind of native shrewdness that isn't taught at the Harvard School of Business.'

Royall Edwards, who was a Harvard Business School graduate, flushed. Peter wondered if the riposte was accidental or if the representative of Albert Wells had done some swift investigating of the hotel's senior staff. It was entirely possible that he had, in which case Peter McDermott's record, including his Waldorf dismissal and subsequent black-listing would be known. Was this the reason, Peter wondered, behind his own apparent omission from the inner councils?

'I suppose,' Royall Edwards said, 'we can expect a good many changes around here.'

'I'd consider it likely.' Again Mr Dempster polished his glasses; it seemed a compulsive habit. 'The first change will be that I shall become president of the hotel company, an office I hold in most of Mr Wells' corporations. He has never cared to assume titles himself.'

Christine said, 'So we'll be seeing a good deal of you.'

'Actually very little, Miss Francis. I will be a figurehead, no more. The executive vice-president will have complete authority. That is Mr Wells' policy, and also mine.'

So after all, Peter thought, the situation had resolved itself as he expected. Albert Wells would not be closely involved with the hotel's management; therefore the fact of knowing him would carry no advantage. The little man was, in fact, twice removed from active management, and Peter's future would depend on the executive vice-president, whoever that might be. Peter wondered if it was anyone he knew. If so, it could make a great deal of difference.

Until this moment, Peter reasoned, he had told himself that he would accept events as they came, including – if necessary – his own departure. Now, he discovered, he wanted to remain at the St Gregory very much indeed. Christine, of course, was one reason. Another was that the St Gregory, with continued independence under new management, promised to be exciting.

'Mr Dempster,' Peter said, 'if it isn't a great secret, who will the executive vice-president be?'

The man from Montreal appeared puzzled. He looked at Peter strangely, then his expression cleared. 'Excuse me,' he said. 'I thought you knew. That's you.'

4

Throughout last night, in the slow-paced hours when hotel guests were serenely sleeping, Booker T. Graham had laboured alone in the incinerator's glare. That, in itself, was not unusual. Booker T. was a simple soul whose days and nights were like carbon copies of each other, and it never perturbed him that this should be so. His ambitions were simple too, being limited to food, shelter and a measure of human dignity, though the last was instinctive and not a need he could have explained himself.

What had been unusual about the night was the slowness with which his work had gone. Usually, well before time to clock out and go home, Booker T. had disposed of the previous day's accumulated garbage, had sorted his retrievals, and left himself with half an hour when he could sit quietly, smoking a hand-rolled cigarette, until closing the incinerator down. But this morning, though his time on duty had been complete, the work was not. At the hour when he should have been leaving the hotel, a dozen or more tightly packed cans of garbage remained unsorted and undisposed.

The reason was Booker T.'s attempt to find the paper which Mr McDermott wanted. He had been careful and thorough. He had taken his time. And so far he had failed.

Booker T. had reported the fact regretfully to the night manager who had come in, the latter looking unfamiliarly at the grim surroundings and wrinkling his nose at the all-pervading smell. The night manager had left as speedily as possible, but the fact that he had come and the message he had brought showed that – to Mr McDermott – the missing paper was still important.

Regretful or not, it was time for Booker T. to quit and go home. The hotel objected to paying overtime. More to the point: Booker T. was hired to concern himself with garbage, not management problems, however remote.

He knew that during the day, if the remaining garbage was noticed, someone would be sent in to run the incinerator for an extra few hours and burn it off. Failing that, Booker T. himself would catch up with the residue when he returned to duty late tonight. The trouble was, with the first way, any hope of retrieving the paper would be gone for ever, and with the second, even if found, it might be too late for whatever was required.

And yet, more than anything else, Booker T. wanted to do this thing for Mr McDermott. If he had been pressed, he could not have said why, since he was not an articulate man, either in thought or speech. But somehow, when the young assistant general manager was around, Booker T. felt more of a man – an individual – than at any other time.

He decided he would go on searching.

To avoid trouble, he left the incinerator and went to the time clock where he punched out. Then he returned. It was unlikely that he would be noticed. The incinerator was not a place which attracted visitors.

He worked for another three and a half hours. He worked slowly, painstakingly, with the knowledge that what he sought might not be in the garbage at all, or could have been burned before he was warned to look.

By mid-morning he was very tired and down to the last container but one.

He saw it almost at once when he emptied the bin – a ball of waxed paper which looked like sandwich wrappings. When he opened them, inside was a crumpled sheet of stationery, matching the sample Mr McDermott had left. He compared the two under a light to be sure. There was no mistake.

The recovered paper was greased stained and partially wet. In one place the writing on it had smeared. But only a little. The rest was clear.

Booker T. put on his grimed and greasy coat. Without waiting to dispose of the remaining garbage, he headed for the upper precincts of the hotel.

5

In Warren Trent's commodious office, Mr Dempster had concluded his private talk with the comptroller. Spread around them were balance sheets and statements, which Royall Edwards was gathering up as others, arriving for the eleven-thirty meeting, came in to join them. The Pickwickian banker, Emile Dumaire, was first, a trifle flushed with self-importance. He was followed by a sallow, spindly lawyer who handled most of the St

Gregory's legal business, and a younger New Orleans lawyer, representing Albert Wells.

Peter McDermott came next, accompanying Warren Trent who had arrived from the fifteenth floor a moment earlier. Paradoxically, despite having lost his long struggle to maintain control of the hotel, the St Gregory's proprietor appeared more amiable and relaxed than at any time in recent weeks. He wore a carnation in his buttonhole and greeted the visitors cordially, including Mr Dempster whom Peter introduced.

For Peter, the proceedings had a chimeric quality. His actions were mechanical, his speech a conditioned reflex, like responding to a litany. It was as if a robot inside him had taken charge until such time as he could recover from the shock administered by the man from Montreal.

Executive vice-president. It was less the title which concerned him than its implications.

To run the St Gregory with absolute control was like fulfilment of a vision. Peter knew, with passionate conviction, that the St Gregory could become a fine hotel. It could be esteemed, efficient, profitable. Obviously Curtis O'Keefe – whose opinion counted – thought so too.

There were means to achieve this end. They included an infusion of capital, reorganization with clearly defined areas of authority, and staff changes – retirements, promotions and transplantings from outside.

When he had learned of the purchase of the hotel by Albert Wells, and its continued independence, Peter hoped that someone else would have the insight and impetus to make progressive changes. Now, he was to be given the opportunity himself. The prospect was exhilarating. And a little frightening.

There was a personal significance. The appointment and what followed, would mean a restoration of Peter McDermott's status within the hotel industry. If he made a success of the St Gregory, what had gone before would be forgotten, his account wiped clean. Hoteliers, as a group, were neither vicious nor shortsighted. In the end, achievement was what mattered most.

Peter's thoughts raced on. Still stunned, but beginning to recover, he joined the others now taking their places at a long board table near the centre of the room.

Albert Wells was last to arrive. He came in shyly, escorted by Christine. As he did, those already in the room rose to their feet.

Clearly embarrassed, the little man waved them down. 'No, no! Please!'

Warren Trent stepped forward, smiling, 'Mr Wells, I welcome you to my house.' They shook hands. 'When it becomes your house, it will be my heartfelt wish that these old walls will bring you as great a happiness and satisfaction as, at times, they have to me.'

It was said with courtliness and grace. From anyone else, Peter McDermott thought, the words might have seemed hollow or exaggerated. Spoken by Warren Trent, they held a conviction which was strangely moving.

Albert Wells blinked. With the same courtesy, Warren Trent took his arm and personally performed the introductions.

Christine closed the outer door and joined the others at the table.

'I believe you know my assistant, Miss Francis; and Mr McDermott.'

Albert Wells gave his sly, bird-like smile. 'We've had a bit to do with each other.' He winked at Peter. 'Will do some more, I reckon.'

It was Emile Dumaire who 'harrumphed' and opened the proceedings.

The terms of sale, the banker pointed out, had already been substantially agreed. The purpose of the meeting, over which both Mr Trent and Mr Dempster had asked him to preside, was to decide upon procedures, including a date for take-over. There appeared to be no difficulties. The mortgage on the hotel, due to be foreclosed today, had been assumed *pro tem* by the Industrial Merchants Bank, under guarantees by Mr Dempster, acting on behalf of Mr Wells.

Peter caught an ironic glance from Warren Trent who, for months, had tried unsuccessfully himself to obtain renewal of the mortgage.

The banker produced a proposed agenda which he distributed. There was a brief discussion of its contents, the lawyers and Mr Dempster participating. They then moved on to deal with the agenda point by point. Through most of what followed, both Warren Trent and Albert Wells remained spectators only, the former meditative, the little man sunk into his chair as if wishing to melt into the background. At no point did Mr Dempster refer to Albert Wells, or even glance his way. Obviously, the man from Montreal understood his employer's preference for avoiding attention and was used to making decisions on his own.

Peter McDermott and Royall Edwards answered questions, as they arose, affecting administration and finance. On two occasions Christine left the meeting and returned, bringing documents from the hotel files.

For all his pompousness, the banker ran a meeting well. Within less than half an hour, the principal business had been disposed of. The official transfer date was set for Tuesday. Other minor details were left for the lawyers to arrange between them.

Emile Dumaire glanced quickly around the table. 'Unless there is anything else . . .'

'Perhaps one thing.' Warren Trent sat forward, his movement commanding the attention of the others. 'Between gentlemen the signing of documents is merely a delayed formality confirming honourable commitments already entered into.' He glanced at Albert Wells. 'I assume you agree.'

Mr Dempster said, 'Certainly.'

'Then please feel free to commence at once any actions you may contemplate within the hotel.'

'Thank you.' Mr Dempster nodded appreciatively. 'There are some matters we would like to set in motion. Immediately after completion on Tuesday, Mr Wells wishes a directors' meeting to be held, at which the first business will be to propose your own election, Mr Trent, as chairman of the board.'

Warren Trent inclined his head graciously. 'I shall be honoured to accept. I will do my best to be suitably ornamental.'

Mr Dempster permitted himself the ghost of a smile. 'It is Mr Wells' further wish that I should assume the presidency.'

'A wish that I can understand.'

'With Mr Peter McDermott as executive vice-president.'

A chorus of congratulations was directed at Peter from the table. Christine was smiling. With the others, Warren Trent shook Peter's hand.

Mr Dempster waited until the conversation died. 'There remains one further point. This week I was in New York when the unfortunate publicity occurred concerning this hotel. I would like an assurance that we are not to have a repetition, at least before the change in management.'

There was a sudden silence.

The older lawyer looked puzzled. In an audible whisper, the younger one explained, 'It was because a coloured man was turned away.'

'Ah!' The old lawyer nodded understandingly.

'Let me make one thing clear.' Mr Dempster removed his glasses and began polishing them carefully. 'I am not suggesting that there be any basic change in hotel policy. My opinion, as a businessman, is that local viewpoints and customs must be respected. What I am concerned with is that if such a situation arises, it should not produce a similar result.'

Again there was a silence.

Abruptly, Peter McDermott was aware that the focus of attention had shifted to himself. He had a sudden, chilling instinct that here, without warning, a crisis had occurred – the first and perhaps the most significant of his new régime. How he handled it could affect the hotel's future and his own. He waited until he was absolutely sure of what he intended to say.

'What was said a moment ago' – Peter spoke quietly, nodding towards the younger lawyer – 'is unfortunately true. A delegate to a convention in this hotel, with a confirmed reservation, was refused accommodation. He was a dentist – I understand, a distinguished one – and incidentally a Negro. I regret to say that I was the one who turned him away. I have since made a personal decision that the same thing will never happen again.'

Emile Dumaire said, 'As executive vice-president, I doubt if you'll be put in the position . . .'

'Or to permit a similar action by anyone else in a hotel where I am in charge.'

The banker pursed his lips. 'That's a mighty sweeping statement.'

Warren Trent turned edgily to Peter. 'We've been over all this.'

'Gentlemen.' Mr Dempster replaced his glasses. 'I made it clear, I thought, that I was not suggesting any fundamental change.'

'But I am, Mr Dempster.' If there was to be a showdown, Peter thought, better to have it now, and done with. Either he would run the hotel or not. This seemed as good a time as any to find out.

The man from Montreal leaned forward. 'Let me be sure I understand your position.'

An inner cautioning voice warned Peter he was being reckless. He ignored it. 'My position is quite simple. I would insist on complete desegregation of the hotel as a condition of my employment.'

'Aren't you being somewhat hasty in dictating terms?'

Peter said quietly, 'I assume your question to mean that you are aware of certain personal matters . . .'

Mr Dempster nodded. 'Yes, we are.'

Christine, Peter observed, had her eyes intently on his face. He wondered what she was thinking.

'Hasty or not,' he said, 'I think it's fair to let you know where I stand.'

Mr Dempster was once more polishing his glasses. He addressed the room at large. 'I imagine we all respect a firmly held conviction. Even so, it seems to me that this is the kind of issue where we might temporize. If Mr McDermott will agree, we can postpone a firm decision now. Then, in a month or two, the subject can be reconsidered.'

If Mr McDermott will agree. Peter thought: With diplomatic skill, the man from Montreal had offered him a way out.

It followed an established pattern. Insistence first, conscience appeased, a belief declared. Then mild concession. A reasonable compromise reached by reasonable men. *The subject can be reconsidered.* What could be more civilized, more eminently sane? Wasn't it the moderate, non-violent kind of attitude which most people favoured? The dentists, for example. Their official letter, with the resolution deploring the hotel's action in the case of Dr Nicholas, had arrived today.

It was also true: there *were* difficulties facing the hotel. It was an unpropitious time. A change of management would produce a crop of problems, never mind inventing new ones. To wait, perhaps, would be the wisest choice.

But then, the time for drastic change was never right. There were always reasons for not doing things. Someone, Peter remembered, had said that recently. Who?

Dr Ingram. The fiery dentists' president who resigned because he believed that principle was more important than expediency, who had quit the St Gregory Hotel last night in righteous anger.

Once in a while, Dr Ingram had said, *you have to weigh what you want against what you believe in . . . You didn't do it, McDermott, when you had the chance. You were too worried about this hotel, your job . . . Sometimes, though, you get a second chance. If it happens to you – take it.*

'Mr Dempster,' Peter said. 'The law on civil rights is perfectly clear. Whether we delay or circumvent it for a while, in the end the result will be the same.'

'The way I hear it,' the man from Montreal remarked, 'there's a good deal of argument about States' rights.'

Peter shook his head impatiently. His gaze swung round the table. 'I believe that a good hotel must adapt itself to changing times. There are matters of human rights that our times have awakened to. Far better that we should be ahead in realizing and accepting these things than that they be forced upon us, as will happen if we fail to act ourselves. A moment ago I made the statement that I will never be a party to turning away a Dr Nicholas. I am not prepared to change my mind.'

Warren Trent snorted. 'They won't all be Dr Nicholas.'

'We preserve certain standards now, Mr Trent. We shall continue to preserve them, except that they will be more embracive.'

'I warn you! You will run this hotel into the ground.'

'There seem to be more ways than one of doing that.'

At the rejoinder, Warren Trent flushed.

Mr Dempster was regarding his hands. 'Regrettably, we seem to have reached an impasse. Mr McDermott, in view of your attitude, we may have to reconsider . . .' For the first time, the man from Montreal betrayed uncertainty. He glanced at Albert Wells.

The little man was hunched down in his chair. He seemed to shrink as attention turned towards him. But his eyes met Mr Dempster's.

'Charlie,' Albert Wells said. 'I reckon we should let the young fellow do it his way.' He nodded towards Peter.

Without the slightest change of expression, Mr Dempster announced, 'Mr McDermott, your conditions are met.'

The meeting was breaking up. In contrast to the earlier accord, there was a sense of constraint and awkwardness. Warren Trent ignored Peter, his expression sour. The older lawyer looked disapproving, the younger non-committal. Emile Dumaire was talking earnestly with Mr Dempster. Only Albert Wells seemed slightly amused at what had taken place.

Christine went to the door first. A moment later she returned, beckoning Peter. Through the doorway he saw that his secretary was waiting in the outer office. Knowing Flora, it would be something out of the ordinary that had brought her here. He excused himself and went outside.

At the doorway, Christine slipped a folded piece of paper into Peter's hand. She whispered, 'Read it later.' He nodded and thrust the paper into his pocket.

'Mr McDermott,' Flora said. 'I wouldn't have disturbed you . . .'

'I know. What happened?'

'There's a man in your office. He says he works in the incinerator and has something important that you want. He won't give it to me or go away.'

Peter looked startled. 'I'll come as quickly as I can.'

'Please hurry!' Flora seemed embarrassed. 'I hate to say this, Mr McDermott, but the fact is . . . well, he *smells*.'

A few minutes before midday, a lanky, slow-moving maintenance worker named Billyboi Noble lowered himself into a shallow pit beneath the shaft of number four elevator. His business there was routine cleaning and inspection, which he had already performed this morning on elevators numbers one, two and three. It was a procedure for which it was not considered necessary to stop the elevators and, as Billyboi worked, he could see the car of number four – alternately climbing and descending – high above.

7

Momentous issues, Peter McDermott reflected, could hinge upon the smallest quirk of fate.

He was alone in his office. Booker T. Graham, suitably thanked and glowing from his small success, had left a few minutes earlier.

The smallest quirk of fate.

If Booker T. had been a different kind of man, if he had gone home – as others would have done – at the appointed time, if he had been less diligent in searching, then the single sheet of paper, now staring up at Peter from his desk blotter, would have been destroyed.

The 'ifs' were endless. Peter himself had been involved.

His visits to the incinerator, he gathered from their conversation, had had the effect of inspiring Booker T. Early this morning, it appeared, the man had even clocked out and continued to work without any expectation of overtime. When Peter summoned Flora and issued instructions that the overtime be paid, the look of devotion on Booker T.'s face had been embarrassing.

Whatever the cause, the result was there.

The note, face upwards on the blotter, was dated two days earlier. Written by the

Duchess of Croydon on Presidential Suite stationery, it authorized the hotel garage to release the Croydons' car to Ogilvie *'at any time he may think suitable'*.

Peter had already checked the handwriting.

He had asked Flora for the Croydons' file. It was open on his desk. There was correspondence about reservations, with several notes in the Duchess's own hand. A handwriting expert would no doubt be precise. But even without such knowledge, the similarity was unmistakable.

The Duchess had sworn to police detectives that Ogilvie removed the car without authority. She denied Ogilvie's accusation that the Croydons paid him to drive the Jaguar away from New Orleans. She had suggested that Ogilvie, not the Croydons, had been driving last Monday night at the time of the hit-and-run. Questioned about the note, she challenged, 'Show it to me!'

It could now be shown.

Peter McDermott's specific knowledge of the law was confined to matters affecting a hotel. Even so, it was obvious that the Duchess's note was incriminating in the extreme. Equally obvious was Peter's own duty – to inform Captain Yolles at once that the missing piece of evidence had been recovered.

With his hand on the telephone, Peter hesitated.

He felt no sympathy for the Croydons. From the accumulated evidence, it seemed clear that they had committed a dastardly crime, and afterwards compounded it with cowardice and lies. In his mind, Peter could see the old St Louis cemetery, the procession of mourners, the larger coffin, the tiny white one behind . . .

The Croydons had even cheated their accomplice, Ogilvie. Despicable as the fat house detective was, his crime was less than theirs. Yet the Duke and Duchess were prepared to inflict on Ogilvie the larger blame and punishment.

None of this made Peter hesitate. The reason was simply a tradition – centuries old, the credo of an innkeeper – of politeness to a guest.

Whatever else the Duke and Duchess of Croydon might be, they were guests of the hotel.

He would call the police. But he would call the Croydons first.

Lifting the telephone, Peter asked for the Presidential Suite.

8

Curtis O'Keefe had personally ordered a late room service breakfast for himself and Dodo, and it had been delivered to his suite an hour ago. Most of the meal, however, still remained untouched. Both he and Dodo had made a perfunctory attempt to sit down together to eat, but neither, it seemed, could muster an appetite. After a while, Dodo asked to be excused, and returned to the adjoining suite to complete her packaging. She was due to leave for the airport in twenty minutes, Curtis O'Keefe an hour later.

The strain between them had persisted since yesterday afternoon.

After his angry outburst then, O'Keefe had been immediately and genuinely sorry. He continued to resent bitterly what he considered to be the perfidy of Warren Trent. But his tirade against Dodo had been inexcusable, and he knew it.

Worse, it was impossible to repair. Despite his apologies, the truth remained. He *was* getting rid of Dodo, and her Delta Air Lines flight to Los Angeles was due to leave this afternoon. He *was* replacing her with someone else – Jenny LaMarsh who, at this moment, was waiting for him in New York.

Last night, contritely, he had laid on an elaborate evening for Dodo, taking her first to dine superbly at the Commander's Palace, and afterwards to dance and be entertained at the Blue Room of the Roosevelt Hotel. But the evening had not gone well, not through any fault of Dodo's, but perversely, through his own low spirits.

She had done her best to be gay good company.

After her obvious unhappiness of the afternoon, she had, it seemed, resolved to put hurt feelings behind her and be engaging, as she always was. 'Gee, Curtie,' Dodo exclaimed at dinner, 'a lotta girls would give their Playtex girdles to have a movie part like I got.' And later, placing her hand over his, 'You're still the sweetest, Curtie. You always will be.'

The effect had been to deepen his own depression which, in the end, proved contagious to them both.

Curtis O'Keefe attributed his feelings to the loss of the hotel, though usually he was more resilient about such matters. In his long career he had experienced his share of business disappointments and had schooled himself to bounce back, getting on with the next thing, rather than waste time in lamenting failures.

But on this occasion, even after a night's sleep, the mood persisted.

It made him irritable with God. There was a distinct sharpness plus an undertone of criticism, in his morning prayers . . . *Thou hast seen fit to place thy St Gregory Hotel in alien hands . . . No doubt thou hast thine own inscrutable purpose, even if experienced mortals like thy servant can perceive no reason . . .*

He prayed alone, taking less time than usual, and afterwards found Dodo packing his bags as well as her own. When he protested, she assured him, 'Curtie. I like doing it. And if I didn't this time, who would?'

He felt disinclined to explain that none of Dodo's predecessors had ever packed or unpacked for him, or that he usually summoned someone from a hotel housekeeping department to do the job, as from now on, he supposed, he would have to do once more.

It was at that point he telephoned room service to order breakfast, but the idea hadn't worked despite the fact that when they sat down, Dodo tried again. 'Gee Curtie, we don't have to be miserable. It isn't like we'll never see each other. We can meet in LA lots of times.'

But O'Keefe, who had travelled this road before, knew that they would not. Besides, he reminded himself, it was not parting with Dodo, but the loss of the hotel which really concerned him.

The moments slipped by. It was time for Dodo to leave. The bulk of her luggage, collected by two bell-boys, had gone down to the lobby several minutes earlier. Now, the bell captain arrived for the remaining hand baggage and to escort Dodo to her specially chartered airport limousine.

Herbie Chandler, aware of Curtis O'Keefe's importance, and sensitive as always to potential tips, had supervised this call himself. He stood waiting at the corridor entrance to the suite.

O'Keefe checked his watch and walked to the connecting doorway. 'You've very little time, my dear.'

Dodo's voice floated out. 'I have to finish my nails, Curtie.'

Wondering why all women left attending to their fingernails until the very last minute,

Curtis O'Keefe handed Herbie Chandler a five-dollar bill. 'Share this with the other two.'

Charlie's weasel face brightened. 'Thank you very much, sir.' He would share it all right, he reflected, except that the other bellboys would get fifty cents each, with Herbie retaining the four dollars.

Dodo walked out from the adjoining room.

There should be music, Curtis O'Keefe thought. A blazoning of trumpets and the stirring sweep of strings.

She had on a simple yellow dress and the big floppy picture she had worn when they arrived on Tuesday. The ash-blonde hair was loose about her shoulders. Her wide blue eyes regarded him.

'Goodbye, dearest Curtie.' She put her arms around his neck and kissed him. Without intending to, he held her tightly.

He had an absurd impulse to instruct the bell captain to bring back Dodo's bags from downstairs, to tell her to stay and never to leave. He dismissed it as sentimental foolishness. In any case, there was Jenny LaMarsh. By this time tomorrow . . .'

'Goodbye, my dear. I shall think of you often, and I shall follow your career closely.'

At the doorway she turned and waved back. He could not be sure, but he had an impression she was crying. Herbie Chandler closed the door from outside.

On the twelfth floor landing, the bell captain rang for an elevator. While they waited, Dodo repaired her make-up with a handkerchief.

The elevators seemed slow this morning, Herbie Chandler thought. Impatiently he depressed the call button a second time, holding it down for several seconds. He was still tense, he realized. He had been on tenterhooks ever since the session yesterday with McDermott, wondering just how and when the call would come – a direct summons from Warren Trent perhaps? – which would mark the end of Herbie's career at the St Gregory Hotel. So far there had been no call and now, this morning, the rumour was around that the hotel had been sold to some old guy whom Herbie had never heard of.

How would that kind of change affect him personally? Regretfully, Herbie decided there would be no advantage for himself – at least, if McDermott stayed on, which seemed probable. The bell captain's dismissal might be delayed a few days, but that was all. McDermott! The hated name was like a sting inside him. If I had guts enough, Herbie thought, I'd put a knife between the bastard's shoulder blades.

An idea struck him. There were other ways, less drastic but still unpleasant, in which someone like McDermott could be given a rough time. Especially in New Orleans. Of course, that kind of thing cost money, but there was the five hundred dollars which McDermott had turned down so smugly yesterday. He might be sorry that he had. The money would be worth spending, Herbie reflected, just for the pleasure of knowing that McDermott would writhe in some gutter, a mess of blood and bruises. Herbie had once seen someone after they had received that kind of beating. The sight was not pretty. The bell captain licked his lips. The more he thought about it, the more the idea excited him. As soon as he was back on the main floor, he decided, he would make a telephone call. It could be arranged quickly. Perhaps tonight.

An elevator had arrived at last. Its doors opened.

There were several people already inside who eased politely to the rear as Dodo entered. Herbie Chandler followed. The doors closed.

It was number four elevator. The time was eleven minutes past noon.

9

It seemed to the Duchess of Croydon as if she was waiting for a slow-burning fuse to reach an unseen bomb. Whether the bomb would explode, and where, would only be known when the burning reached it. Nor was it certain how long, in time, the fuse would take.

Already it had been fourteen hours.

Since last night, when the police detectives left, there had been no further word. Troublesome questions remained unanswered. What were the police doing? Where was Ogilvie? The Jaguar? Was there some scrap of evidence which, for all her ingenuity, the Duchess had overlooked? Even now, she did not believe there was.

One thing seemed important. Whatever their inner tensions, outwardly the Croydons should maintain an appearance of normalcy. For this reason, they had breakfasted at their usual time. Urged on by the Duchess, the Duke of Croydon exchanged telephone calls with London and Washington. Plans were begun for their departure tomorrow from New Orleans.

At mid-morning, as she had most other days, the Duchess left the hotel to exercise the Bedlington terriers. She had returned to the Presidential Suite half an hour ago.

It was almost noon. There was still no news concerning the single thing that mattered most.

Last night, considered logically, the Croydons' position seemed unassailable. And yet, today, logic seemed more tenuous, less secure.

'You'd almost think,' the Duke of Croydon ventured, 'that they're trying to wear us down by silence.' He was standing, looking from the window of the suite living-room, as he had so many times in recent days. In contrast to other occasions, today his voice was clear. Since yesterday, though liquor remained available in the suite, he had not wavered in his abstinence.

'If that's the case,' the Duchess responded, 'we'll see to it that . . .'

She was interrupted by the jangling of the telephone. It honed their nervousness to an edge, as had every other call this morning.

The Duchess was nearest to the phone. She reached out her hand, then abruptly stopped. She had a sudden premonition that this call would be different from the rest.

The Duke said sympathetically, 'Would you rather let me do it?'

She shook her head, dismissing the momentary weakness. Lifting the telephone, she answered, 'Yes?'

A pause. The Duchess acknowledged, 'This is she.' Covering the mouthpiece, she informed her husband, 'The man from the hotel – McDermott – who was here last night.'

She said into the telephone, 'Yes, I remember. You were present when those ridiculous charges . . .'

The Duchess stopped. As she listened, her face paled. She closed her eyes, then opened them.

'Yes,' she said slowly. 'Yes, I understand.'

She replaced the receiver. Her hands were trembling.

The Duke of Croydon said, 'Something has gone wrong.' It was a statement not a question.

The Duchess nodded slowly. 'The note.' Her voice was scarcely audible. 'The note I wrote has been found. The hotel manager has it.'

Her husband had moved from the window to the centre of the room. He stood, immobile, his hands loosely by his sides, taking time to let the information sink in. At length he asked, 'And now?'

'He's calling the police. He said he decided to notify us first.' She put a hand to her forehead in a gesture of despair. 'The note was the worst mistake. If I hadn't written it . . .'

'No,' the Duke said. 'If it wasn't that, it would have been something else. None of the mistakes were yours. The one that mattered – to begin with – was mine.'

He crossed to the sideboard which served as a bar, and poured a stiff Scotch and soda. 'I'll just have this, no more. Be a while before the next, I imagine.'

'What are you going to do?'

He tossed the drink down. 'It's a little late to talk of decency. But if any shreds are left, I'll try to salvage them.' He went into the adjoining bedroom, returning almost at once with a light raincoat and a Homburg hat.

'If I can,' the Duke of Croydon said, 'I intend to get to the police before they come to me. It's what's known, I believe, as giving yourself up. I imagine there isn't much time, so I'll say what I have to say quickly.'

The Duchess's eyes were on him. At this moment, to speak required more effort than she could make.

In a controlled, quiet voice the Duke affirmed, 'I want you to know that I'm grateful for all you did. It was a mistake both of us made, but I'm still grateful. I'll do all I can to see that you're not involved. If, in spite of that, you are, then I'll say that the whole idea – after the accident – was mine and that I persuaded you.'

The Duchess nodded dully.

'There's just one other thing. I suppose I shall need some kind of lawyer chap. I'd like you to arrange that, if you will.'

The Duke put on the hat and with a finger tapped it into place. For one whose entire life and future had collapsed around him a few minutes earlier, his composure seemed remarkable.

'You'll need money for the lawyer,' he reminded her. 'Quite a lot, I imagine. You could start him off with some of that fifteen thousand dollars you were taking to Chicago. The rest should go back into the bank. Drawing attention to it doesn't matter now.'

The Duchess gave no indication of having heard.

A look of pity crossed her husband's face. He said uncertainly, 'It may be a long time . . .' His arms went out towards her.

Coldly, deliberately, she averted her head.

The Duke seemed about to speak again, then changed his mind. With a slight shrug he turned, then went out quietly, closing the outer door behind him.

For a moment or two the Duchess sat passively, considering the future and weighing the exposure and disgrace immediately ahead. Then, habit reasserting itself, she rose. She would arrange for the lawyer, which seemed necessary at once. Later, she decided calmly, she would examine the means of suicide.

Meanwhile the money which had been mentioned should be put in a safer place. She went into the bedroom.

It took only a few minutes, first of unbelief, then of frantic searching, to discover that the attaché case was gone. The cause could only be theft. When she considered the possibility of informing the police, the Duchess of Croydon convulsed in demented, hysterical laughter.

If you wanted an elevator in a hurry, the Duke of Croydon reflected, you could count on it being slow in coming.

He seemed to have been waiting on the ninth floor landing for several minutes. Now, at last, he could hear a car approaching from above. A moment later its doors opened at the ninth.

For an instant the Duke hesitated. A second earlier he thought he had heard his wife cry out. He was tempted to go back, then decided not.

He stepped into number four elevator.

There were several people already inside, including an attractive blonde girl and the hotel bell captain who recognized the Duke.

'Good day, Your Grace.'

The Duke of Croydon nodded absently as the doors slid closed.

10

It had taken Keycase Milne most of last night and this morning to decide that what had occurred was reality not an hallucination. At first, on discovering the money he had carried away so innocently from the Presidential Suite, he assumed himself to be asleep and dreaming. He had walked around his room attempting to awaken. It made no difference. In his apparent dream, it seemed, he was awake, already. The confusion kept Keycase genuinely awake until just before dawn. Then he dropped into a deep, untroubled sleep from which he did not stir until mid-morning.

It was typical of Keycase, however, that the night had not been wasted.

Even while doubting that his incredible stroke of fortune was true, he shaped plans and precautions in case it was.

Fifteen thousand dollars in negotiable cash had never before come Keycase's way during all his years as a professional thief. Even more remarkable, there appeared only two problems in making a clean departure with the money intact. One was when and how to leave the St Gregory Hotel. The other was transportation of the cash.

Last night he reached decisions affecting both.

In quitting the hotel, he must attract a minimum of attention. That meant checking out normally and paying his bill. To do otherwise would be sheerest folly, proclaiming dishonesty and inviting pursuit.

It was a temptation to check out at once. Keycase resisted it. A late night check-out, perhaps involving discussion as to whether or not an extra room day should be charged, would be like lighting a beacon. The night cashier would remember and could describe him. So might others if the hotel was quiet, as most likely it would be.

No! – the best time to check out was mid-morning or later, when plenty of other people would be leaving too. That way, he could be virtually unnoticed.

Of course, there was danger in delay. Loss of the cash might be discovered by the Duke and Duchess of Croydon, and the police alerted. That would mean a police stake-out in the lobby and scrutiny of each departing guest. But, on the credit side, there was nothing to connect Keycase with the robbery, or even involve him as a suspect. Furthermore, it seemed unlikely that the baggage of every guest would be opened and searched.

Also, there was an intangible. Instinct told Keycase that the presence of so large a sum in cash – precisely where and how he had found it – was peculiar, even suspicious. *Would* an alarm be raised? There was at least a possibility that it might not.

On reflection, to wait seemed the lesser risk.

The second problem was removal of the money from the hotel.

Keycase considered mailing it, using the hotel mail chute and addressing it to himself at a hotel in some other city where he would appear in a day or two. It was a method he had used successfully before. Then, ruefully, he decided the sum was too large. It would require too many separate packages which, in themselves might create attention.

The money would have to be carried from the hotel. How?

Obviously, not in the attaché case which he had brought here from the Duke and Duchess of Croydon's suite. Before anything else was done, that must be destroyed. Keycase set out carefully to do so.

The case was of expensive leather and well constructed. Painstakingly, he took it apart, then, with razor blades, cut it into tiny portions. The work was slow and tedious. Periodically, he stopped to flush portions down the toilet, spacing out his use of the toilet, so as not to attract attention from adjoining rooms.

It took more than two hours. At the end, all that remained of the attaché case were its metal locks and hinges. Keycase put them in his pocket. Leaving his room, he took a long walk along the eighth-floor corridor.

Near the elevators were several sand urns. Burrowing into one with his fingers, he pushed the locks and hinges well down. They might be discovered eventually, but not for some time.

By then, it was an hour or two before dawn, the hotel silent. Keycase returned to his room where he packed his belongings, except for the few things he would need immediately before departure. He used the two suitcases he had brought with him on Tuesday morning. Into the larger, he stuffed the fifteen thousand dollars, rolled in several soiled shirts.

Then, still dazed and unbelieving, Keycase slept.

He had set his alarm clock for ten a.m., but either he slept through its warning or it failed to go off. When he awoke, it was almost 11.30, with the sun streaming brightly into the room.

The sleep accomplished one thing. Keycase was convinced at last that the happenings of last night were real, not illusory. A moment of abject defeat had, with Cinderella magic, turned into shining triumph. The thought sent his spirits soaring.

He shaved and dressed quickly, then completed his packing and locked both suitcases.

He would leave the suitcases in this room, he decided, while he went down to pay his bill and reconnoitre the lobby.

Before doing so, he disposed of his surplus keys – for rooms 449, 641, 803, 1062 and the Presidential Suite. While shaving, he had observed a plumber's inspection plate on the bathroom wall. Unscrewing the cover, he dropped the keys in. One by one he heard them strike bottom far below.

He retained his own key, 830, for handing in when he left his room for the last time. The departure of 'Byron Meader' from the St Gregory Hotel must be normal in every way.

The lobby was averagely busy, with no sign of unusual activity. Keycase paid his bill and received a friendly smile from the girl cashier. 'Is the room vacant now, sir?'

He returned the smile. 'It will be in a few minutes. I have to collect my bags, that's all.' Satisfied, he went back upstairs.

In 830 he took a last careful look round the room. He had left nothing; no scrap of paper, no unconsidered trifle such as a match cover, no clue whatever to his true identity. With a damp towel, Keycase wiped the obvious surfaces which might have retained fingerprints. Then, picking up both suitcases, he left.

His watched showed ten past twelve.

He held the larger suitcase tightly. At the prospect of walking through the lobby and out of the hotel, Keycase's pulse quickened, his hands grew clammy.

On the eighth-floor landing he rang for an elevator. Waiting, he heard one coming down. It stopped at the floor above, started downwards once more, then stopped again. In front of Keycase, the door of number four elevator slid open.

At the front of the car was the Duke of Croydon.

For a horror-filled instant, Keycase had an impulse to turn and run. He mastered it. In the same split second, sanity told him that the encounter was accidental. Swift glances confirmed it. The Duke was alone. He had not even noticed Keycase. From the Duke's expression, his thoughts were far away.

The elevator operator, an elderly man, said, 'Going down!'

Alongside the operator was the hotel bell captain, whom Keycase recognized from having seen him in the lobby. Nodding to the two bags, the bell captain enquired, 'Shall I take those, sir?' Keycase shook his head.

As he stepped into the elevator, the Duke of Croydon and a beautiful blonde girl eased nearer the rear to make room.

The gates closed. The operator, Cy Lewin, pushed the selector handle to 'descent'. As he did, with a scream of tortured metal, the elevator car plunged downwards, out of control.

▌▌

He owed it to Warren Trent, Peter McDermott decided, to explain personally what had occurred concerning the Duke and Duchess of Croydon.

Peter found the hotel proprietor in his main mezzanine office. The others who had been at the meeting had left. Aloysius Royce was with his employer, helping assemble personal possessions, which he was packing into cardboard containers.

'I thought I might as well get on with this,' Warren Trent told Peter. 'I won't need this office any more. I suppose it will be yours.' There was no rancour in the older man's voice, despite their altercation less than half an hour ago.

Aloysius Royce continued to work quietly as the other two talked.

Warren Trent listened attentively to the description of events since Peter's hasty departure from St Louis cemetery yesterday afternoon, concluding with the telephone calls, a few minutes ago, to the Duchess of Croydon and the New Orleans police.

'If the Croydons did what you say,' Warren Trent pronounced, 'I've no sympathy for them. You've handled it well.' He growled as an afterthought. 'At least we'll be rid of those damn dogs.'

'I'm afraid Ogilvie is involved pretty deeply.'

The older man nodded. 'This time he's gone too far. He'll take the consequences, whatever they are, and he's finished here.' Warren Trent paused. He seemed to be weighing something in his mind. At length he said, 'I suppose you wonder why I've always been lenient with Ogilvie.'

'Yes,' Peter said, 'I have.'

'He was my wife's nephew. I'm not proud of the fact, and I assure you that my wife and Ogilvie had nothing in common. But many years ago she asked me to give him a job here, and I did. Afterwards, when she was worried about him once, I promised to keep him employed. I've never, really, wanted to undo that.'

How did you explain, Warren Trent wondered, that while the link with Hester had been defective and tenuous, it was the only one he had.

'I'm sorry,' Peter said. 'I didn't know . . .'

'That I was ever married?' The older man smiled. 'Not many do. My wife came with me to this hotel. We were both young. She died soon after. It all seems a long time ago.'

It was a reminder, Warren Trent thought, of the loneliness he had endured across the years, and of the greater loneliness soon to come.

Peter said, 'Is there anything I can . . .'

Without warning, the door from the outer office flew open. Christine stumbled in. She had been running and had lost a shoe. She was breathless, her hair awry. She barely got the words out.

'There's been . . . terrible accident! One of the elevators. I was in the lobby . . . It's horrible! People are trapped . . . They're screaming.'

At the doorway, already on the run, Peter McDermott brushed her aside. Aloysius Royce was close behind.

12

Three things should have saved number four elevator from disaster.

One was an overspeed governor on the elevator car. It was set to trip when the car's speed exceeded a prescribed safety limit. On number four – though the defect had not been noticed – the governor was operating late.

A second device comprised four safety clamps. Immediately the governor tripped, these should have seized the elevator guide rails, halting the car. In fact, on one side of the car two clamps held. But on the other side – due to delayed response of the governor, and because the machinery was old and weakened – the clamps failed.

Even then, prompt operation of an emergency control inside the elevator car might have averted tragedy. This was a single red button. Its purpose, when depressed, was to cut off all electrical power, freezing the car. In modern elevators the emergency button was located high, and plainly in view. In the St Gregory cars, and many others, it was positioned low. Cy Lewin reached down, fumbling awkwardly to reach it. He was a second too late.

As one set of clamps held and the other failed, the car twisted and buckled. With a thunder of wrenching, tearing metal, impelled by its own weight and speed, plus the heavy load inside, the car split open. Rivets sheared, panelling splintered, metal sheeting separated. On one side – lower than the other because the floor was now tilted at a steep angle – a gap several feet high appeared between the floor and the wall. Screaming, clutching wildly at each other, the passengers slid towards it.

Cy Lewin, the elderly proprietor, who was nearest, was first to fall through. His single scream as he fell nine floors was cut off when his body hit the sub-basement concrete. An elderly couple from Salt Lake City fell next, clasping each other. Like Cy Lewin they died as their bodies smashed against the ground. The Duke of Croydon fell awkwardly, striking an iron bar on the side of the shaft, which impaled him. The bar broke off, and he continued to fall. He was dead before his body reached the ground.

Somehow, others held on. While they did, the remaining two safety clamps gave way, sending the wrecked car plummeting the remaining distance down the shaft. Part way, a youngish conventioneer dentist slipped through the gap, his arms flailing.

He was to survive the accident, but died three days later of internal injuries.

Herbie Chandler was more fortunate. He fell when the car was near the end of its descent. Tumbling into the adjoining shaft, he sustained head injuries from which he would recover, and sheared and fractured vertebrae which would make him a paraplegic, never walking again for the remainder of his life.

A middle-aged New Orleans woman lay, with a fractured tibia and a shattered jaw, on the elevator floor.

As the car hit bottom, Dodo was last to fall. An arm was broken and her skull cracked hard against a guide rail. She lay unconscious, close to death, as blood gushed from a massive head wound.

Three others – a Gold Crown Cola conventioneer, his wife, and Keycase Milne – were miraculously unhurt.

Beneath the wrecked elevator car, Billyboi Noble, the maintenance worker who, some ten minutes earlier had lowered himself into the elevator pit, lay with legs and pelvis crushed, conscious, bleeding and screaming.

13

Running with a speed he had never used in the hotel before, Peter McDermott raced down the mezzanine stairs.

The lobby, when he reached it, was a scene of pandemonium. Screams resounded through the elevator doors and from several women near by. There was confused shouting. In front of a milling crowd, a white-faced assistant manager and a bellboy were attempting to pry open the metal doors to number four elevator shaft. Cashiers, room clerks and office workers were pouring out from behind counters and desks. Restaurants and bars were emptying into the lobby, waiters and bartenders following their customers. In the main dining-room, lunchtime music had stopped, the musicians joining the exodus.

A line of kitchen workers was streaming out through a service doorway. An excited babel of questions greeted Peter.

As loudly as he could, he shouted above the uproar. 'Quiet!'

There was a momentary silence in which he called out again, 'Please stand back and we will do everything we can.' He caught a room clerk's eye. 'Has someone called the Fire Department?'

'I'm not sure, sir. I thought . . .'

Peter snapped, 'Do it now!' He instructed another, 'Get on to the police. Tell them we need ambulances, doctors, someone to control the crowd.'

Both men disappeared, running.

A tall, lean man in a tweed jacket and drill trousers stepped forward. 'I'm a Marine Officer. Tell me what you want.'

Peter said gratefully, 'The centre of the lobby must be kept clear. Use the hotel staff to form a cordon. Keep a passageway open to the main entrance. Fold back the revolving doors.'

'Right!'

The tall man turned away and began cracking commands. As if appreciative of leadership, others obeyed. Soon, a line of waiters, cooks, clerks, bellboys, musicians, some conscripted guests extended across the lobby and to the St Charles Avenue door.

Aloysius Royce had joined the assistant manager and bellboy attempting to force the elevator doors. He turned, calling to Peter. 'We'll never do this without tools. We have to break in somewhere else.'

A coveralled maintenance worker ran into the lobby. He appealed to Peter. 'We need help at the bottom of the shaft. There's a guy trapped under the car. We can't get him out or get at the others.'

Peter snapped, 'Let's get down there!' He sprinted for the lower service stairs, Aloysius Royce a pace behind.

A grey brick tunnel, dimly lighted, led to the elevator shaft. Here, the cries they had heard above were audible again, but now with greater closeness and more eerily. The shattered elevator car was directly in front, but the way to it barred by twisted, distorted metal from the car itself and installations it had hit on impact. Near the front, maintenance workers were struggling with pry bars. Others stood helplessly behind. Screams, confused shouts, the rumble of nearby machinery, combined with a steady moaning from the car's interior.

Peter shouted to the men not occupied, 'Get more lights in here!' Several hurried away down the tunnel.

He instructed the man in coveralls who had come to the lobby, 'Get back upstairs. Guide the firemen down.'

Aloysius Royce, on his knees beside the debris, shouted, 'And send a doctor – now!'

'Yes,' Peter said, 'take someone to show him the way. Have an announcement made. There are several doctors staying in the hotel.'

The man nodded and ran back the way they had come.

More people were arriving in the corridor, beginning to block it. The chief engineer, Doc Vickery, shouldered his way through.

'My God!' The chief stood staring at the scene before him. 'My God! – I told them. I warned if we didn't spend money, something like this . . .' He seized Peter's arm. 'You heard me, laddie. You've heard me enough times . . .'

'Later, chief.' Peter released his arm. 'What can you do to get these people out?'

The chief shook his head hopelessly. 'We'd need heavy equipment – jacks, cutting tools . . .'

It was evident that the chief was in no condition to take charge. Peter instructed him, 'Check on the other elevators. Stop all service if you have to. Don't take chances of a repetition.' The older man nodded dumbly. Bowed and broken, he moved away.

Peter grasped the shoulder of a grey-haired stationary engineer whom he recognized. 'Your job is to keep this area clear. Everyone is to move out of here who is not directly concerned.'

The engineer nodded. As he began to order others back the tunnel cleared.

Peter returned to the elevator shaft. Aloysius Royce, by kneeling and crawling, had eased himself under part of the debris and was holding the shoulders of the injured, screaming maintenance man. In the dim light it was clear that a mass of wreckage rested on his legs and lower abdomen.

'Billyboi,' Royce was urging, 'you'll be all right. I promise you. We'll get you out.'

The answer was another tortured scream.

Peter took one of the injured man's hands. 'He's right. We're here now. Help is coming.'

Distantly, high above, he could hear a growing wail of sirens.

14

The room clerk's telephone summons reached the Fire Alarm Office in City Hall. His message had not concluded when two high-pitched beeps – a major alarm alert – sounded in every city fire hall. On radio, a dispatcher's calm voice followed.

'Striking box zero zero zero eight for alarm at St Gregory Hotel, Carondelet and Common.'

Automatically, four fire halls responded – Central on Decatur, Tulane, South Rampart and Dumaine. In three of the four, non-duty watch men were at lunch. At Central, lunch was almost ready. The fare was meatballs and spaghetti. A fireman, taking his turn as cook, sighed as he turned off the gas and ran with the rest. Of all the godforsaken times for a midtown, high property alarm!

Clothing and long boots were on the trucks. Men kicked off shoes, climbing aboard while rigs were rolling. Within less than a minute of the double beeps, five engine companies, two hook and ladders, a hose tender, emergency, rescue and salvage units, a deputy chief and two district chiefs were on the way to the St Gregory, their drivers fighting busy midday traffic.

A hotel alert rated everything in the book.

At other fire halls, sixteen more engine companies and two hook and ladders stood by for a second alarm.

The Police Complaint Department in the Criminal Justice Courts received its warning two ways – from the Fire Alarm Office and directly from the hotel.

Under a notice, '*Be Patient With Your Caller*', two women communications clerks wrote the information on message blanks, a moment later handed them to a radio dispatcher.

The message went out: All ambulances – Police and Charity Hospital – to the St Gregory Hotel

15

Three floors below the St Gregory lobby, in the tunnel to the elevator shaft, the noise, hasty commands, moans and cries continued. Now, penetrating them, were crisp, swift footsteps. A man in a seersucker suit hurried in. A young man. With a medical bag.

'Doctor!' Peter called urgently. 'Over here!'

Crouching, crawling, the newcomer joined Peter and Aloysius Royce. Behind them, extra lights, hastily strung, were coming on. Billyboi Noble screamed again. His face turned to the doctor, eyes pleading, features agony-contorted. 'Oh, God! Oh, God! Please give me something . . .'

The doctor nodded, scrabbling in his bag. He produced a syringe. Peter pushed back Billyboi's coverall sleeve, holding an arm exposed. The doctor swabbed hastily, jabbed the needle home. Within seconds the morphine had taken hold. Billyboi's head fell back. His eyes closed.

The doctor had a stethoscope to Billyboi's chest. 'I haven't much with me. I came off the street. How quickly can you get him out?'

'As soon as we've help. It's coming.'

More running footsteps. This time, a heavy pounding of many feet. Helmeted firemen streaming in. With them, bright lanterns, heavy equipment – axes, power jacks, cutting tools, lever bars. Little talk. Short, staccato words. Grunts, sharp orders. 'Over here! A jack under there. Get this heavy stuff moving!'

From above, a tattoo of axe blows crashing home. The sound of yielding metal. A stream of light as shaft doors opened at the lobby level. A cry. 'Ladders! We need ladders here!' Long ladders coming down.

The young doctor's command: 'I *must* have this man out!'

Two firemen struggled to position a jack. Extended, it would take the weight from Billyboi. The firemen groping, swearing, manoeuvring to find a clearance. The jack too large by several inches. 'We need a smaller jack! Get a smaller jack to start, to get the big one placed.' The demand repeated on a walkie-talkie. 'Bring the small jack from the rescue truck!'

The doctor's voice again, insistently. '*I must have this man out!*'

Peter's voice. 'That bar there! The one higher. If we move it, it will lift the lower, leave clearance for the jack!'

A fireman cautioning. 'Twenty tons up there. Shift something, it can all come down. When we start, we'll take it slow.'

'Let's try!' Aloysius Royce.

Royce and Peter, shoulders together, backs under the higher bar, arms interlocked. Strain upwards! Nothing. Strain harder again! Still harder! Lungs bursting, blood surging, senses swimming. The bar moving, but barely. Even harder! Do the impossible! Consciousness slipping. Sight diminishing. A red mist only. Straining. Moving. A shout, 'The jack is in!' The straining ended. Down. Pulled free. The jack turning, lifting. Debris rising. 'We can get him out!'

The doctor's voice, quietly. 'Take your time. He just died.'

The dead and injured were brought upwards by the ladder one by one. The lobby became a clearing station with hasty aid for those still living, a place of pronouncement for the dead. Furniture was pushed clear. Stretchers filled the central area. Behind the cordon, the crowd – silent now – pressed tightly. Women were crying. Some men had turned away.

Outside, a line of ambulances waited. St Charles Avenue and Carondelet, between Canal and Gravier Streets, were closed to traffic. Crowds were gathering behind police blockades at both ends. Singly, the ambulances raced away. First, with Herbie Chandler; next, the injured dentist who would die; a moment later, the New Orleans woman with injuries to leg and jaw. Other ambulances drove more slowly to the city morgue. Inside the hotel, a police captain questioned witnesses, seeking names of victims.

Of the injured, Dodo was brought up last. A doctor, climbing down, had applied a compression dressing to the gaping head wound. Her arm was in a plastic splint. Keycase Milne, ignoring offers of help himself, had stayed with Dodo, holding her, guiding rescuers to where she lay. Keycase was last out. The Gold Crown Cola conventioneer and his wife preceded him. A fireman passed up the bags – Dodo's and Keycase's – from the elevator's wreckage to the lobby. A uniformed city policeman received and guarded them.

Peter McDermott had returned to the lobby when Dodo was brought out. She was white and still, her body blood-soaked, the compression dressing already red. As she was laid on a stretcher, two doctors worked over her briefly. One was a young intern, the other an older man. The younger doctor shook his head.

Behind the cordon, a commotion. A man in shirtsleeves, agitated, shouting, 'Let me pass!'

Peter turned his head, then motioned to the Marine officer. The cordon parted. Curtis O'Keefe came rushing through.

His face distraught, he walked beside the stretcher. When Peter last saw him, he was on the street outside, pleading to be allowed in the ambulance. The intern nodded. Doors slammed. Its siren screaming, the ambulance raced away.

16

With shock, barely believing his own deliverance, Keycase climbed the ladder in the elevator shaft. A fireman was behind. Hands reached down to help him. Arms gave support as he stepped into the lobby.

Keycase found that he could stand and move unaided. His senses were returning. Once more, his brain was alert. Uniforms were all around. They frightened him.

His two suitcases! If the larger one had burst open! . . . But no. They were with several others near by. He moved towards them.

A voice behind said, 'Sir, there's an ambulance waiting.' Keycase turned, to see a young policeman.

'I don't need . . .'

'Everyone must go, sir. It's for a check. For your own protection.'

Keycase protested, 'I must have my bags.'

'You can collect them later, sir. They'll be looked after.'

'No, now.'

Another voice cut in. 'Christ! If he wants his bags, let him take them. Anyone who's been through that's entitled . . .'

The young policeman carried the bags and escorted Keycase to the St Charles Avenue door. 'If you'll wait here, sir, I'll see which ambulance.' He set the bags down.

While the policeman was gone, Keycase picked them up and melted into the crowd. No-one observed him as he walked away.

He continued to walk, without haste, to the outdoor parking lot where he had left his car yesterday after his successful pillaging of the house in Lakeview. He had a sense of peace and confidence. Nothing could possibly happen to him now.

The parking lot was crowded, but Keycase spotted his Ford sedan by its distinctive green-on-white Michigan plates. He was reminded that on Monday he had been concerned that the licence plates might attract attention. Obviously, he had worried needlessly.

The car was as he had left it. As usual, the motor started at a touch.

From downtown, Keycase drove carefully to the motel on Chef Menteur Highway where he had cached his earlier loot. Its value was small, compared with the glorious fifteen thousand dollars cash, but still worth while.

At the motel, Keycase backed the Ford close to his rented room and carried in the two suitcases he had brought from the St Gregory. He drew the motel room drapes before opening the larger case to assure himself that the money was still there. It was.

He had stored a good many of his personal effects at the motel, and now he repacked his several suitcases to get these in. At the end, he found that he was left with the two fur coats and the silver bowl and salver he had stolen from the house in Lakeview. There was no room to include them, except by repacking once more.

Keycase knew that he should. But in the past few minutes, he had become aware of an overwhelming fatigue – a reaction, he supposed, from the events and tensions of today. Also, time had run on, and it was important that he get clear of New Orleans as soon as possible. The coats and silver, he decided, would be perfectly safe, unpacked, in the trunk of the Ford.

Making sure he was unobserved, he loaded the suitcases into the car, placing the coats and silver beside them.

He checked out of the motel and paid a balance owing on his bill. Some of his tiredness seemed to lift as he drove away.

His destination was Detroit. He planned to make the drive in easy stages, stopping when he felt like it. On the way he would do some serious thinking about the future. For a number of years Keycase had promised himself that if ever he acquired a reasonably substantial sum of money, he would use it to buy a small garage. There, abandoning his itinerant life of crime, he would settle down to work honestly through the sunset of his days. He possessed the ability. The Ford beneath his hands was proof. And fifteen thousand dollars was ample for a start. The question was: Was this the time?

Keycase was already debating the proposition as he drove across north New Orleans, heading for the Pontchartrain Expressway and the road to freedom.

There were logical arguments in favour of settling down. He was no longer young. Risks and tension tired him. He had been touched, this time in New Orleans, by the disabling hand of fear.

And yet . . . events of the past thirty-six hours had given him fresh confidence, a new *élan*. The successful house robbery, the Aladdin's haul of cash, his survival of the elevator disaster barely an hour ago – all these seemed symptoms of his invincibility. Surely, combined, they were an omen telling him the way to go?

Perhaps after all, Keycase reflected, he should continue the old ways for a while. The garage could come later. There was really plenty of time.

He had driven from Chef Menteur Highway on to Gentilly Boulevard, around City Park, past lagoons and ancient, spreading oaks. Now, on City Park Avenue, he was approaching Metarie Road. It was here that the newer cemeteries of New Orleans – Greenwood, Metarie, St Patrick, Fireman's, Charity Hospital, Cypress Grove – spread a sea of tombstones as far as vision went. High above them all was the elevated Pontchartrain Expressway. Keycase could see the Expressway now, a citadel in the sky, a haven beckoning. In minutes he would be on it.

Approaching the junction of Canal Street and City Park Avenue, last staging point before the Expressway ramp, Keycase observed that the intersection's traffic lights had failed. A policeman was directing traffic from the centre of the road on the Canal Street side.

A few yards from the intersection, Keycase felt a tyre go flat.

Motor Patrolman Nicholas Clancy, of the New Orleans Police, had once been accused by his embittered sergeant of being 'the dumbest cop on the force, bar none'.

The charge held truth. Despite long service which had made him a veteran, Clancy had never once advanced in rank or even been considered for promotion. His record was inglorious. He had made almost no arrests, and none that was major. If Clancy chased a fleeing car, its driver was sure to get away. Once, in a mêlée, Clancy had been told to handcuff a suspect whom another officer had captured. Clancy was still struggling to free his handcuffs from his belt when the suspect was blocks away. On another occasion, a much-sought bank bandit who had got religion, surrendered to Clancy on a city street. The bandit handed over his gun which Clancy dropped. The gun went off, startling the bandit into changing his mind and fleeing. It was another year and six more holdups before he was recaptured.

Only one thing, over the years, saved Clancy from dismissal – an extreme good nature which no-one could resist, plus a sad clown's humble awareness of his own shortcomings.

Sometimes, in his private moments, Clancy wished that he could achieve one thing, attain some single worthwhile moment, if not to balance the record, at least to make it less one-sided. So far he had signally failed.

One solitary thing in line of duty gave Clancy not the slightest trouble – directing traffic. He enjoyed it. If, somehow, Clancy could have reached back into history to prevent the invention of the automatic traffic light, he would have done so gladly.

Ten minutes ago, when he realized that the lights at Canal and City Park Avenue had failed, he radioed the information in, parked his motor-cycle, and took over the intersection. He hoped that the street lighting repair crew would take its time in coming.

From the opposite side of the avenue, Clancy saw the grey Ford sedan slow and stop.

Taking his time, he strolled across. Keycase was seated, motionless, as when the car stopped.

Clancy surveyed the offside rear wheel which was resting on its rim.

'Flat tyre?'

Keycase nodded. If Clancy had been more observant, he would have noticed that the knuckle joints of the hands on the steering wheel were white. Keycase, through a veil of bitter self-recrimination, was remembering the single, simple factor his painstaking plans had overlooked. The spare tyre and jack were in the trunk. To reach them, he must open the trunk, revealing the fur coats, the silver bowl, the salver and the suitcases.

He waited, sweating. The policeman showed no sign of moving.

'Guess you'll have to change the wheel, eh?'

Again Keycase nodded. He calculated. He could do it fast. Three minutes at the most. Jack! Wheel wrench! Spin the nuts! Wheel off! The spare on! Fasten! Throw wheel, jack and wrench on the back seat! Slam the trunk closed! He could be away. On the Expressway. *If only the cop would go.*

Behind the Ford, other cars were slowing, some having to stop before easing into the centre lane. One pulled out too soon. Behind him, rubber squealed. A horn blasted in protest.

The cop leaned forward, resting his arms on the door beside Keycase.

'Gets busy around here.'

Keycase swallowed. 'Yes.'

The cop straightened up, opening the door. 'Ought to start things moving.'

Keycase drew the keys from the ignition. Slowly, he stepped down to the road. He forced a smile. 'It's all right, officer. I can handle it.'

Keycase waited, holding his breath as the cop surveyed the intersection.

Clancy said good naturedly, 'I'll give you a hand.'

An impulse seized Keycase to abandon the car and run. He dismissed it as hopeless. With resignation, he inserted the key and opened the trunk.

Scarcely a minute later, he had the hack in place, wheel nuts were loosened, and he was raising the rear bumper. The suitcases, fur coats and silver were heaped to one side in the trunk. As he worked, Keycase could see the cop contemplating the collection. Incredibly, so far, he had said nothing.

What Keycase could not know was that Clancy's reasoning process took time to function.

Clancy leaned down and fingered one of the coats.

'Bit hot for these.' The city's shade temperature for the past ten days had hovered around ninety-five.

'My wife . . . sometimes feels the cold.'

Wheel nuts were off, the old wheel free. With a single movement, Keycase opened the rear car door and flung the wheel inside.

The cop craned around the trunk lid, inspecting the car's interior.

'Little lady not with you, eh?'

'I . . . I'm picking her up.'

Keycase's hands strove frantically to release the spare wheel. The locknut was stiff. He broke a fingernail and skinned his fingers freeing it. Ignoring the hurt, he hefted the wheel from the trunk.

'Looks kind of funny, all this stuff.'

Keycase froze. He dare not move. He had come to Golgotha. Intuition told him why.

Fate had presented him with a chance, and he had thrown it away. It mattered not that the decision had been solely in his mind. Fate had been kind, but Keycase had spurned the kindness. Now, in anger, fate had turned its back.

Terror struck as he remembered what, a few minutes earlier, he had so readily forgotten – the awful price of one more conviction; the long imprisonment lasting, perhaps, for the remainder of his life. Freedom had never seemed more precious. The Expressway, so close, seemed half a world away.

At last Keycase knew what the omens of the past day and a half had really meant. They had offered him release, a chance for a new and decent life, an escape to tomorrow. If he had only known.

Instead, he had misread the portents. With arrogance and vanity, he had interpreted fate's kindness as his own invincibility. He had made his decision. This was the result. Now it was too late.

Was it? Was it ever too late – at least for hope? Keycase closed his eyes.

He vowed – with a deep resolve which, given the opportunity, he knew he would keep – that if, through merest chance, he should escape this moment, he would never again, in all his life, do one more dishonest thing.

Keycase opened his eyes. The cop was walking to another car whose driver had stopped to ask directions.

With moments swifter than he believed possible, Keycase thrust the wheel on, replaced the nuts and released the jack which he threw into the trunk. Even now, instinctively as a good mechanic should, Keycase gave the wheel nuts an extra tightening when the wheel was on the ground. He had the trunk repacked when the cop returned.

Clancy nodded approvingly, his earlier thought forgotten. 'All finished, eh?'

Keycase slammed the trunk lid down. For the first time, Motor Patrolman Clancy saw the Michigan licence plates.

Michigan. Green on white. In the depths of Clancy's brain, memory stirred.

Had it been today, yesterday, the day before? . . . His platoon commander, on parade, reading the latest bulletins aloud . . . Something about green and white . . .

Clancy wished he could remember. There were so many bulletins – wanted men, missing persons, cars, robberies. Every day the bright, eager youngsters on the force scribbled swiftly in their notebooks, memorizing, getting the information down. Clancy tried. He always had. But inevitably, the lieutenant's brisk voice, the slowness of his own handwriting, left him far behind. *Green and white.* He wished he could remember.

Clancy pointed to the plate. 'Michigan, eh?'

Keycase nodded. He waited numbly. There was just so much that the human spirit could absorb.

'Water Wonderland.' Clancy read aloud the legend on the plate. 'I hear you got some swell fishing.'

'Yes . . . there is.'

'Like to get there one day. Fisherman myself.'

From behind, an impatient horn. Clancy held the car door open. He seemed to remember he was a patrolman. 'Let's get this lane clear.' *Green and white.* The errant thought still bothered him.

The motor started. Keycase drove forward. Clancy watched him go. With precision, neither too fast nor too slow, his resolve steadfast, Keycase nosed the car on the Expressway ramp.

Green and white. Clancy shook his head and returned to directing traffic. Not for nothing had he been called the dumbest cop on the force, bar none.

17

From Tulane Avenue, the sky-blue and white police ambulance, its distinctive blue light flashing, swung into the emergency driveway of Charity Hospital. The ambulance stopped. Swiftly its doors were opened. The stretcher bearing Dodo was lifted out, then, with practised speed, wheeled by attendants through a doorway marked ADMISSION OUT-PATIENTS WHITE.

Curtis O'Keefe followed close behind, almost running to keep up.

An attendant in the lead called, 'Emergency! Make way!' A busy press of people in the admitting and discharge lobby fell back to let the small procession pass. Curious eyes followed its progress. Most were on the white, waxen mask of Dodo's face.

Swinging doors marked ACCIDENT ROOM opened to admit the stretcher. Inside were nurses, doctors, activity, other stretchers. A male attendant barred Curtis O'Keefe's way. 'Wait here, please.'

O'Keefe protested, 'I want to know . . .'

A nurse, going in, stopped briefly. 'Everything possible will be done. A doctor will talk to you as soon as he can.' She continued inside. The swinging doors closed.

Curtis O'Keefe remained facing the doors. His eyes were misted, his heart despairing.

Less than half an hour ago, after Dodo's leavetaking, he had paced the suite living-room, his thoughts confused and troubled. Instinct told him that something had gone from his life that he might never find again. Logic mocked him. Others before Dodo had come and gone. He had survived their departure. The notion that this time might be different was absurd.

Even so, he had been tempted to follow Dodo, perhaps to delay their separation for a few hours, and in that time to weigh his feelings once again. Rationality won out. He remained where he was.

A few minutes later he had heard the sirens. At first he had been unconcerned. Then, conscious of their growing number and apparent convergence on the hotel, he had gone to the window of his suite. The activity below made him decide to go down. He went as he was – in shirtsleeves, without putting on a coat.

On the twelfth-floor landing, as he waited for an elevator, disquieting sounds had drifted up. After almost five minutes, when an elevator failed to come and other guests were milling on the landing, O'Keefe decided to use the emergency stairs. As he went down, he discovered others had had the same idea. Near the lower floors, the sounds becoming clearer, he employed his athlete's training to increase his speed.

In the lobby he learned from excited spectators the essential facts of what had occurred. It was then he prayed with intensity that Dodo had left the hotel before the accident. A moment later he saw her carried, unconscious, from the elevator shaft.

The yellow dress he had admired, her hair, her limbs, were a mess of blood. The look of death was on her face.

In that instant, with searing, blinding insight, Curtis O'Keefe discovered the truth he had shielded from himself so long. He loved her. Dearly, ardently, with a devotion beyond human reckoning. Too late, he knew that in letting Dodo go, he had made the greatest single error of his life.

He reflected on it now, bitterly, surveying the accident-room doors. They opened briefly as a nurse came out. When he approached her, she shook her head and hurried on.

He had a sense of helplessness. There was so little he could do. But what he could, he would.

Turning away, he strode through the hospital. In busy lobbies and corridors, he breasted crowds, followed signboards and arrows to his objective. He opened doors marked PRIVATE, ignored protesting secretaries. He stopped before the Director's desk.

The Director rose angrily from his chair. When Curtis O'Keefe identified himself, the anger lessened.

Fifteen minutes later the Director emerged from the accident room accompanied by a slight, quietly spoken man whom he introduced as Dr Beauclaire. The doctor and O'Keefe shook hands.

'I understand that you are a friend of the young lady – I believe, Miss Lash.'

'How is she, Doctor?'

'Her condition is critical. We are doing everything we can. But I must tell you there is a strong possibility she may not live.'

O'Keefe stood silent, grieving.

The doctor continued, 'She has a serious head wound which appears superficially to be a depressed skull fracture. There is a likelihood that fragments of bone may have entered the brain. We shall know better after X-rays.'

The Director explained, 'The patient is being resuscitated first.'

The doctor nodded. 'We have transfusions going. She lost a good deal of blood. And treatment has begun for shock.'

'How long . . .'

'Resuscitation will be at least another hour. Then, if X-rays confirm the diagnosis, it will be necessary to operate immediately. Is the next-of-kin in New Orleans?'

O'Keefe shook his head.

'It makes no difference, really. In this kind of emergency, the law permits us to proceed without permission.'

'May I see her?'

'Later, perhaps. Not yet.'

'Doctor, if there's anything you need – a question of money, professional help . . .'

The Director interrupted quietly. 'This is a free hospital, Mr O'Keefe. It's for indigents and emergencies. All the same, there are services here that money couldn't buy. Two university medical schools are next door. Their staff are on call. I should tell you that Dr Beauclaire is one of the leading neurosurgeons in the country.'

O'Keefe said humbly, 'I'm sorry.'

'Perhaps there is one thing,' the doctor said.

O'Keefe's head came up.

'The patient is unconscious now, and under sedation. Earlier, there were some

549

moments of lucidity. In one of them she asked for her mother. If it's possible to get her mother here . . .'

'It's possible.' It was a relief that at least there was something he could do.

From a corridor pay phone, Curtis O'Keefe placed a collect call to Akron, Ohio. It was to the O'Keefe-Cuyahoga Hotel. The manager, Harrison, was in his office.

O'Keefe instructed, 'Whatever you are doing, leave it. Do nothing else until you have completed, with the utmost speed, what I am about to tell you.'

'Yes, sir.' Harrison's alert voice came down the line.

'You are to contact a Mrs Irene Lash of Exchange Street, Akron. I do not have the number of the house.' O'Keefe remembered the street from the day that he and Dodo had telegraphed the basket of fruit. Was it only last Tuesday?

He heard Harrison call to someone in his office, 'A city directory – fast!'

O'Keefe continued, 'See Mrs Lash yourself. Break the news to her that her daughter, Dorothy, has been injured in an accident and may die. I want Mrs Lash flown to New Orleans by the fastest possible means. Charter if necessary. Disregard expense.'

'Hold it, Mr O'Keefe.' He could hear Harrison's crisp commands. 'Get Eastern Airlines – the sales department in Cleveland – on another line. After that, I want a limousine with a fast driver at the Market Street door.' The voice returned, more strongly. 'Go ahead, Mr O'Keefe.'

As soon as the arrangements were known, O'Keefe directed, he was to be contacted at Charity Hospital.

He hung up, confident that the instructions would be carried through. A good man, Harrison. Perhaps worthy of a more important hotel.

Ninety minutes later, X-rays confirmed Dr Beauclaire's diagnosis. A twelfth-floor operating room was being readied. The neurosurgery, if continued to a conclusion, would take several hours. .

Before Dodo was wheeled into the operating room, Curtis O'Keefe was permitted to see her briefly. She was pale and unconscious. It seemed to his imagination as if all her sweetness and vitality had flown.

Now the OR doors were closed.

Dodo's mother was on her way. Harrison had notified him. McDermott of the St Gregory, whom O'Keefe had telephoned a few minutes ago, was arranging for Mrs Lash to be met and driven directly to the hospital.

For the moment there was nothing to do but wait.

Earlier, O'Keefe had declined an invitation to rest in the Director's office. He would wait on the twelfth floor, he decided, no matter for how long.

Suddenly, he had a desire to pray.

A door close by was labelled LADIES COLOURED. Next to it was another marked RECOVERY ROOM STORAGE. A glass panel showed that it was dark inside.

He opened the door and went in, groping his way past an oxygen tent and an iron lung. In the semi-darkness he found a clear space where he knelt. The floor was a good deal harder on his knees than the broadloom he was used to. It seemed not to matter. He clasped his hands in supplication and lowered his head.

Strangely, for the first time in many years, he could find no words for what was in his heart.

18

Dusk, like an anodyne to the departing day, was settling over the city. Soon, Peter McDermott thought, the night would come, with sleep and, for a while, forgetfulness. Tomorrow, the immediacy of today's events would begin receding. Already, the dusk marked a beginning to the process of time which, in the end, healed all things.

But it would be many dusks and nights and days before those who were closest to today's events would be free from a sense of tragedy and terror. The waters of Lethe were still far distant.

Activity – while not a release – helped the mind a little.

Since early this afternoon, a good deal had occurred.

Alone, in his office on the main mezzanine, Peter took stock of what had been done and what remained.

The grim sad process of identifying the dead and notifying families had been completed. Where the hotel was to aid with funerals, arrangements had begun.

The little that could be done for the injured, beyond hospital care, had been put in hand.

Emergency crews – fire, police – had long since left. In their place were elevator inspectors, examining every piece of elevator equipment the hotel possessed. They would work into tonight and through tomorrow. Meanwhile, elevator service had been partially restored.

Insurance investigators – gloomy men, already foreseeing massive claims – were intensively questioning, taking statements.

On Monday, a team of consultants would fly from New York to begin planning for replacement of all passenger elevator machinery with new. It would be the first major expenditure of the Albert Wells-Dempster-McDermott régime.

The resignation of the chief engineer was on Peter's desk. He intended to accept it.

The chief, Doc Vickery, must be honourably retired, with the pension befitting his long years of service to the hotel. Peter would see to it that he was treated well.

M. Hèbrand, the chef de cuisine, would receive the same consideration. But the old chef's retirement must be accomplished quickly, with André Lemieux promoted to his place.

On young André Lemieux – with his ideas for creation of speciality restaurants, intimate bars, an overhaul of the hotel's entire catering system – much of the St Gregory's future would depend. A hotel did not live by renting rooms alone. It could fill its rooms each day, yet still go bankrupt. Special services – conventions, restaurants, bars – were where the mother lode of profit lay.

There must be other appointments, a reorganization of departments, a fresh defining of responsibilities. As executive vice-president, Peter would be involved much of the time with policy. He would need an assistant general manager to supervise the day-to-day running of the hotel. Whoever was appointed must be young, efficient, a disciplinarian when necessary, but able to get along with others older than himself. A graduate of the School of Hotel Administration might do well. On Monday, Peter decided, he would telephone Dean Robert Beck at Cornell. The dean kept in touch with many of his bright ex-students. He might know such a man, who was available now.

Despite today's tragedy, it was necessary to think ahead.

There was his own future with Christine. The thought of it was inspiring and exciting. Nothing between them had been settled yet. But he knew it would be. Earlier, Christine had left for her Gentilly apartment. He would go to her soon.

Other – less palatable – unfinished business still remained. An hour ago, Captain Yolles of the New Orleans Police had dropped into Peter's office. He had come from an interview with the Duchess of Croydon.

'When you're with her,' Yolles said, 'you sit there wondering what's under all that solid ice. Is it a woman? Does she *feel* about the way her husband died? I saw his body. My God! – no-one deserved that. For that matter, she saw him too. Not many women could have faced it. Yet, in her, there isn't a crack. No warmth, no tears. Just her head tilted up, that way she has, and the haughty look she gives you. If I tell you the truth – as a man – I'm attracted to her. You get to feeling you'd like to know what she's really like.' The detective stopped, considering.

Later, answering Peter's question, Yolles said, 'Yes, we'll charge her as an accessory, and she'll be arrested after the funeral. What happens beyond that – whether a jury will convict if the defence claims that her husband did the conniving, and he's dead . . . Well, we'll see.'

Ogilvie had already been charged, the policeman revealed. 'He's booked as an accessory. We may throw more at him later. The DA will decide. Either way, if you're keeping his job open, don't count on seeing him back in less than five years.'

'We're not.' Reorganization of the hotel's detective force was high on Peter's list of things to do.

When Captain Yolles had gone, the office was quiet. By now, it was early evening. After a while, Peter heard the outer door open and close. A light tap sounded on his own. He called, 'Come in!'

It was Aloysius Royce. The young Negro carried a tray with a martini pitcher and a single glass. He set the tray down.

'I thought maybe you could do with this.'

'Thanks,' Peter said. 'But I never drink alone.'

'Had an idea you'd say that.' From his pocket, Royce produced a second glass.

They drank in silence. What they had lived through today was still too close for levity or toasts.

Peter asked, 'Did you deliver Mrs Lash?'

Royce nodded. 'Drove her right to the hospital. We had to go in through separate doorways, but we met inside and I took her to Mr O'Keefe.'

'Thank you.' After Curtis O'Keefe's call, Peter had wanted someone at the airport on whom he could rely. It was the reason he had asked Royce to go.

'They'd finished operating when we got to the hospital. Barring complications, the young lady – Miss Lash – will be all right.'

'I'm glad.'

'Mr O'Keefe told me they're going to be married. As soon as she's well enough. Her mother seemed to like the idea.'

Peter smiled fleetingly. 'I suppose most mothers would.'

There was a silence, then Royce said, 'I heard about the meeting this morning. The stand you took. The way things turned out.'

Peter nodded. 'The hotel is desegregated. Entirely. As of now.'

'I suppose you expect me to thank you. For giving us what's ours by right.'

'No,' Peter said. 'And you're being prickly again. I wonder, though, if you might decide now to stay with W. T. I know he'd like it, and you'd be entirely free. There's legal work for the hotel, I could see that some of it came your way.'

'I'll thank you for that,' Royce said. 'But the answer's no. I told Mr Trent this afternoon – I'm leaving, right after graduation.' He refilled the martini glasses and contemplated his own. 'We're in a way, you and me – on opposite sides. It won't be finished in our time, either. What I can do, with what I've learned about the law, I intend to do for my people. There's a lot of in-fighting ahead – legal, some of the other kind too. It won't always be fair, on our side as well as yours. But when we're unjust, intolerant, unreasonable, remember – we learned it from you. There'll be trouble for all of us. You'll have your share here. You've desegregated, but that isn't the end. There'll be problems – with people who won't like what you've done, with Negroes who won't behave nicely, who'll embarrass you because some are the way they are. What'll you do with the Negro loudmouth, the Negro smart-aleck, the Negro half-drunk Romeo? We've got 'em, too. When it's white people who behave like that, you swallow hard, you try to smile, and most times you excuse it. When they're Negroes – what'll you do then?'

'It may not be easy,' Peter said. 'I'll try to be objective.'

'You will. Others won't. All the same, it's the way the war will go. There's just one thing.'

'Yes?'

'Once in a while there'll be truces.' Royce picked up the tray with the pitcher and empty glasses. 'I guess this was one.'

Now it was night.

With the hotel, the cycle of another innkeeping day had run its course. This had differed from most, but beneath unprecedented events, routines had continued. Reservations, reception, administration, housekeeping, engineering, garage, treasury, kitchens . . . all had combined in a single, simple function. To welcome the traveller, sustain him, provide him with rest, and speed him on.

Soon, the cycle would begin again.

Wearily, Peter McDermott prepared to leave. He switched off the office lights and, from the executive suite, walked the length of the main mezzanine. Near the stairway to the lobby he saw himself in a mirror. For the first time, he realized that the suit he was wearing was rumpled and soiled. It became that way, he reflected, under the elevator debris where Billyboi died.

As best he could, he smoothed the jacket with his hand. A slight rustling made him reach into a pocket where his fingers encountered a folded paper. Taking it out, he remembered. It was the note which Christine had given him as he left the meeting this morning where he had staked his career on a principle, and won.

He had forgotten the note until now. He opened it curiously. It read: *It will be a fine hotel because it will be like the man who is to run it.*

At the bottom, in smaller lettering, Christine had written: *PS. I love you.*

Smiling, the length of his stride increasing, he went downstairs to the lobby of his hotel.

WHEELS

Henceforward, no wheeled vehicles whatsoever will be allowed within the precincts of the City, from sunrise until the hour before dusk . . . Those which shall have entered during the night, and are still within the City at dawn, must halt and stand empty until the appointed hour . . .

> – Senatus consultum of Julius Caesar, 44 BC

It is absolutely impossible to sleep anywhere in the City. The perpetual traffic of wagons in the narrow winding streets . . . is sufficient to wake the dead . . .

> – The Satires of Juvenal, AD 117

I

The president of General Motors was in a foul humour. He had slept badly during the night because his electric blanket had worked only intermittently, causing him to awaken several times, feeling cold. Now, after padding around his home in pyjamas and robe, he had tools spread on his half of the king-size bed where his wife still slept, and was taking the control mechanism apart. Almost at once he observed a badly joined connexion, cause of the night's on-again off-again performance. Muttering sourly about poor quality control of blanket manufacturers, the GM president took the unit to his basement workshop to repair.

His wife, Coralie, stirred. In a few minutes more her alarm clock would sound and she would get up sleepily to make breakfast for them both.

Outside, in suburban Bloomfield Hills, a dozen miles north of Detroit, it was still dark.

The GM president – a spare, fast-moving, normally even-tempered man – had another cause for ill humour besides the electric blanket. It was Emerson Vale. A few minutes ago, through the radio turned on softly beside his bed, the GM chief heard a news broadcast which included the hated, astringent, familiar voice of the auto industry's arch critic.

Yesterday, at a Washington Press conference, Emerson Vale had blasted anew his favourite targets – General Motors, Ford, and Chrysler. The Press wire services, probably due to a lack of hard news from other sources, had obviously given Vale's attack the full treatment.

The Big Three of the auto industry, Emerson Vale charged, were guilty of 'greed, criminal conspiracy, and self-serving abuse of public trust'. The conspiracy was their continuing failure to develop alternatives to gasoline-powered automobiles – namely, electric and steam vehicles – which, Vale asserted, 'are available now'.

The accusation was not new. However, Vale – a skilled hand at public relations and with the Press – had injected enough recent material to make his statement newsworthy.

The president of the world's largest corporation, who had a PhD in engineering, fixed the blanket control, in the same way that he enjoyed doing other jobs around the house when time permitted. Then he showered, shaved, dressed for the office, and joined Coralie at breakfast.

A copy of the *Detroit Free Press* was on the dining-room table. As he saw Emerson Vale's name and face prominently on the front page, he swept the newspaper angrily to the floor.

'Well,' Coralie said. 'I hope that made you feel better.' She put a cholesterol-watcher's breakfast in front on him – the white of an egg on dry toast, with sliced tomatoes and cottage cheese. The GM president's wife always made breakfast herself and had it with him, no matter how early his departure. Seating herself opposite, she retrieved the *Free Press* and opened it.

Presently she announced, 'Emerson Vale says if we have the technical competence to land men on the moon and Mars, the auto industry should be able to produce a totally safe, defect-free car that doesn't pollute its environment.'

Her husband laid down his knife and fork. 'Must you spoil my breakfast, little as it is?'

Coralie smiled. 'I had the impression something else had done that already.' She continued, unperturbed. 'Mr Vale quotes the Bible about air pollution.'

'For Christ's sake! Where does the Bible say anything about *that*?'

'Not Christ's sake, dear. It's in the Old Testament.'

His curiosity aroused, he growled, 'Go ahead, read it. You intended to, anyway.'

'From Jeremiah,' Coralie said. ' "*And I brought you into a plentiful country, to eat the fruit thereof and the goodness thereof; but when ye entered, ye defiled my land, and made mine heritage an abomination.*" ' She poured more coffee for them both. 'I do think that's rather clever of him.'

'No-one's ever suggested the bastard isn't clever.'

Coralie went back to reading aloud. ' "The auto and oil industries, Vale said, have together delayed technical progress which could have led, long before now, to an effective electric or steam car. Their reasoning is simple. Such a car would nullify their enormous capital investment in the pollutant-spreading internal combustion engine." ' She put the paper down. 'Is any of that true?'

'Obviously Vale thinks it's all true.'

'But you don't?'

'Naturally.'

'None of it whatever?'

He said irritably, 'There's sometimes a germ of truth in any outrageous statement. That's how people like Emerson Vale manage to sound plausible.'

'Then you'll deny what he says?'

'Probably not.'

'Why not?'

'Because if General Motors takes on Vale, we'll be accused of being a great monolith trampling down an individual. If we don't reply we'll be damned too, but at least that way we won't be misquoted.'

'Shouldn't someone answer?'

'If some bright reporter gets to Henry Ford, he's apt to.' The GM president smiled. 'Except Henry will be damned forceful and the paper won't print all his language.'

'If I had your job,' Coralie said, 'I think I'd say something. That is, if I really was convinced of being right.'

'Thank you for your advice.

The GM president finished his breakfast, declining to rise any further to his wife's bait. But the exchange, along with the needling which Coralie seemed to feel was good for him occasionally, had helped get the bad temper out of his system.

Through the door to the kitchen the GM president could hear the day maid arriving, which meant that his car and chauffeur – which picked up the girl on their way – were now waiting outside. He got up from the table and kissed his wife goodbye.

A few minutes later, shortly after 6 a.m., his Cadillac Brougham swung on to Telegraph Road and headed for the Lodge Freeway and the midtown New Center area. It was a brisk October morning, with a hint of winter in a gusty north-west wind.

Detroit, Michigan – the Motor City, auto capital of the world – was coming awake.

Also in Bloomfield Hills, ten minutes from the GM president's house, as a Lincoln Continental glides, an executive vice-president of Ford was preparing to leave for Detroit Metropolitan Airport. He had already breakfasted, alone. A housekeeper had brought a tray to his desk in the softly lighted study where, since 5 a.m., he had been alternately reading memoranda (mostly on special blue stationery which Ford vice-presidents used in implementing policy) and dictating crisp instructions into a recording machine. He had scarcely looked up, either as the meal arrived, or while eating, as he accomplished in an hour what would have taken most other executives a day, or more.

The majority of decisions just made concerned new plant construction or expansion and involved expenditures of several billion dollars. One of the executive vice-president's responsibilities was to approve or veto projects, and allocate priorities. He had once been asked if such rulings, on the disposition of immense wealth, worried him. He replied, 'No, because mentally I always knock off the last three figures. That way it's no more sweat than buying a house.'

The pragmatic, quick response was typical of the man who had risen, rocket-like, from a lowly car salesman to be among the industry's dozen top decision-makers. The same process, incidentally, had made him a multi-millionaire, though some might ponder whether the penalties for success and wealth were out of reason for a human being to pay.

The executive vice-president worked twelve and sometimes fourteen hours a day, invariably at a frenetic pace, and as often as not his job claimed him seven days a week. Today, at a time when large segments of the population were still abed, he would be en route to New York in a company Jetstar, using the journey time for a marketing review with subordinates. On landing, he would preside at a meeting on the same subject with Ford district managers. Immediately after, he would face a tough-talking session with twenty New Jersey dealers who had beefs about warranty and service problems. Later, in Manhattan, he would attend a bankers' convention luncheon and make a speech. Following the speech he would be quizzed by reporters at a freewheeling Press conference.

By early afternoon the same company plane would wing him back to Detroit where he would be in his office for appointments and regular business until dinnertime. At some point in the afternoon, while he continued to work, a barber would come in to cut his hair. Dinner – in the penthouse, one floor above the executive suite – would include a critical discussion about new models with division managers.

Later still, he would stop in at the William R. Hamilton Funeral Chapel to pay respects to a company colleague who had dropped dead yesterday from a coronary occlusion brought on by overwork. (The Hamilton funeral firm was *de rigueur* for top echelon auto men who, rank conscious to the end, passed through, en route to exclusive Woodlawn Cemetery, sometimes known as 'Executive Valhalla'.)

Eventually the executive vice-president would go home – with a filled briefcase to be dealt with by tomorrow morning.

Now, pushing his breakfast tray away and shuffling papers, he stood up. Around him, in this personal study, were book-lined walls. Occasionally – though not this morning – he glanced at them with a trace of longing; there was a time, years ago, when he had read a good deal, and widely, and could have been a scholar if chance had directed his life differently. But nowadays he had no time for books. Even the daily newspaper would have to wait until he could snatch a moment to skim through it. He picked up the paper, still folded as the housekeeper had brought it, and stuffed it into his bag. Only later would he learn of Emerson Vale's latest attack and privately curse him, as many others in the auto industry would do before the day was out.

At the airport, those of the vice-president's staff who would accompany him were already in the waiting lounge of the Ford Air Transportation hangar. Without wasting time, he said, 'Let's go.'

The Jetstar engines started as the party of eight climbed aboard and they were taxiing before the last people in had fastened seatbelts. Only those who travelled by private airfleets knew how much time they saved compared with scheduled airlines.

Yet, despite the speed, briefcases were out and opened on laps before the aircraft reached the takeoff runway.

The executive vice-president began the discussion. 'North-east Region results this month are unsatisfactory. You know the figures as well as I do. I want to know why. Then I want to be told what's being done.'

As he finished speaking, they were airborne.

The sun was halfway over the horizon; a dull red, brightening, amid scudding grey clouds.

Beneath the climbing Jetstar, in the early light, the vast sprawling city and environs were becoming visible: downtown Detroit, a square mile oasis like a miniature Manhattan; immediately beyond, leagues of drab streets, buildings, factories, housing, freeways mostly dirt encrusted: an Augean work town without petty cash for cleanliness. To the west, cleaner, greener Dearborn, abutting the giant factory complex of the Rouge; in contrast, in the eastern extremity, the Grosse Pointes, tree-studded, manicured, havens of the rich; industrial, smoky Wyandotte to the south; Belle Isle, hulking in the Detroit River like a laden grey-green barge. On the Canadian side, across the river, grimy Windsor, matching in ugliness the worst of its US senior partner.

Around and through them all, revealed by daylight, traffic swirled. In tens of thousands, like armies of ants (or lemmings, depending on a watcher's point of view) shift workers, clerks, executives, and others headed for a new day's production in countless factories, large and small.

The nation's output of automobiles for the day – controlled and masterminded in Detroit – had already begun, the tempo of production revealed in a monster Goodyear signboard at the car-jammed confluence of Edsel Ford and Walter Chrysler Freeways. In figures five feet high, and reading like a giant odometer, the current year's car production was recorded minute by minute, with remarkable accuracy, through a nationwide reporting system. The total grew as completed cars came off assembly lines across the country.

Twenty-nine plants in the Eastern time zone were operating now, their data feeding in. Soon, the figures would whirl faster as thirteen assembly plants in the Midwest swung into operation, followed by six more in California. Local motorists checked the Goodyear sign the way a physician read blood pressure or a stockbroker the Dow Jones. Riders in car pools made bets each day on the morning or the evening tallies.

The car production sources closest to the sign were those of Chrysler – the Dodge and Plymouth plants in Hamtramck, a mile or so away, where more than a hundred cars an hour began flowing off assembly lines at 6 a.m.

There was a time when the incumbent chairman of the board of Chrysler might have dropped in to watch a production start-up and personally check out a finished product. Nowadays, though, he did that rarely, and this morning was still at home, browsing through *The Wall Street Journal* and sipping coffee which his wife had brought before leaving, herself, for an early Art Guild meeting downtown.

In those earlier days the Chrysler chief executive (he was president then, newly appointed) had been an eager-beaver around the plants, partly because the declining, dispirited corporation needed one, and partly because he was determined to shed the 'book-keeper' tag which clung to any man who rose by the financial route instead of through sales or engineering. Chrysler, under his direction, had gone both up and down. One long six-year cycle had generated investor confidence; the next rang financial alarm bells; then, once more, with sweat, drastic economies and effort, the alarm had lessened, so there were those who said that the company functioned best under leanness or adversity. Either way, no-one seriously believed any more that Chrysler's slim-pointed Pentastar would fail to stay in orbit – a reasonable achievement on its own, prompting the chairman of the board to hurry less nowadays, think more, and read what he wanted to.

At this moment he was reading Emerson Vale's latest outpouring, which *The Wall Street Journal* carried, though less flamboyantly than the *Detroit Free Press*. But Vale bored him. The Chrysler chairman found the auto critic's remarks repetitive and unoriginal, and after a moment turned to the real-estate news which was decidedly more cogent. Not everyone knew it yet, but within the past few years Chrysler had been building a real-estate empire which, as well as diversifying the company, might a few decades hence (or so the dream went), make the present 'number three' as big or bigger than General Motors.

Meanwhile, as the chairman was comfortably aware, automobiles continued to flow from the Chrysler plants at Hamtramck and elsewhere.

Thus, the Big Three – as on any other morning – were striving to remain that way, while smaller American Motors, through its factory to the north in Wisconsin, was adding a lesser tributary of Ambassadors, Hornets, Javelins, Gremlins, and their kin.

2

At a car assembly plant north of the Fisher Freeway, Matt Zaleski, assistant plant manager and a greying veteran of the auto industry, was glad that today was Wednesday.

Not that the day would be free from urgent problems and exercises in survival – no day ever was. Tonight, like any night, he would go homeward wearily, feeling older than his fifty-three years and convinced he had spent another day of his life inside a pressure cooker. Matt Zaleski sometimes wished he could summon back the energy he had had as a young man, either when he was new to auto production or as an Air Force bombardier in the Second World War. He also thought sometimes, looking back, that the years of war – even though he was in Europe in the thick of things, with an impressive combat record – were less crisis-filled than his civil occupation now.

Already, in the few minutes he had been in his glass-panelled office on a mezzanine above the assembly plant floor, even while removing his coat, he had skimmed through a red-tabbed memo on the desk – a union grievance which he realized immediately could cause a plant-wide walkout if it wasn't dealt with properly and promptly. There was undoubtedly still more to worry about in an adjoining pile of paper – other headaches, including critical material shortages (there were always some, each day), or quality control demands, or machinery failures, or some new conundrum which no-one had thought of before, any or all of which could halt the assembly line and stop production.

Zaleski threw his stocky figure into the chair at his grey metal desk, moving in short jerky movements, as he always had. He heard the chair protest – a reminder of his growing overweight and the big belly he carried around nowadays. He thought ashamedly: he could never squeeze it now into the cramped nose dome of a B-17. He wished that worry would take off pounds; instead, it seemed to put them on, especially since Freda died and loneliness at night drove him to the refrigerator, nibbling, for lack of something else to do.

But at least today was Wednesday.

First things first. He hit the intercom switch for the general office; his secretary wasn't in yet. A timekeeper answered.

'I want Parkland and the union committeeman,' the assistant plant manager commanded. 'Get them in here fast.'

Parkland was a foreman. And outside they would be well aware which union committeeman he meant because they would know about the red-tabbed memo on his desk. In a plant, bad news travelled like burning gasoline.

The pile of papers – still untouched, though he would have to get to them soon – reminded Zaleski he had been thinking gloomily of the many causes which could halt an assembly line.

Halting the line, stopping production for whatever reason, was like a sword in the side to Matt Zaleski. The function of his job, his personal *raison d'être*, was to keep the line moving, with finished cars being driven off the end at the rate of one car a minute, no matter how the trick was done or if, at times, he felt like a juggler with fifteen balls in the air at once. Senior management wasn't interested in the juggling act, or excuses either. Results were what counted: quotas, daily production, manufacturing costs. But if the line stopped he heard about it soon enough. Each single minute of lost time meant that an entire car didn't get produced, and the loss would never be made up. Thus, even a two- or three-minute stoppage cost thousands of dollars because, while an assembly line stood still wages and other costs went rollicking on.

But at least today was Wednesday.

The intercom clicked. 'They're on their way, Mr Zaleski.'

He acknowledged curtly.

The reason Matt Zaleski liked Wednesday was simple. Wednesday was two days removed from Monday, and Friday was two more days away.

Mondays and Fridays in auto plants were management's most harrowing days because of absenteeism. Each Monday, more hourly paid employees failed to report for work than on any other normal weekday; Friday ran a close second. It happened because after paychecks were handed out, usually on Thursday, many workers began a long boozy or drugged weekend, and afterwards, Monday was a day for catching up on sleep or nursing hangovers.

Thus, on Mondays and Fridays, other problems were eclipsed by one enormous problem of keeping production going despite a critical shortage of people. Men were moved around like marbles in a game of Chinese checkers. Some were removed from tasks they were accustomed to and given jobs they had never done before. A worker who normally tightened wheel nuts might find himself fitting front fenders, often with the briefest of instruction or sometimes none at all. Others, pulled in hastily from labour pools or less skilled duties – such as loading trucks or sweeping – would be put to work wherever gaps remained. Sometimes they caught on quickly in their temporary roles; at other times they might spend an entire shift installing heater hose clamps, or something similar – upside down.

The result was inevitable. Many of Monday's and Friday's cars were shoddily put together, with built-in legacies of trouble for their owners, and those in the know avoided them like contaminated meat. A few big city dealers, aware of the problem and with influence at factories because of volume sales, insisted that cars for more valued customers be built on Tuesday, Wednesday, or Thursday, and customers who knew the ropes sometimes went to big dealers with this objective. Cars for company executives and their friends were invariably scheduled for one of the midweek days.

The door of the assistant plant manager's office flung open abruptly. The foreman he had sent for, Parkland, strode in, not bothering to knock.

Parkland was a broad-shouldered, big-boned man in his late thirties, about fifteen years younger than Matt Zaleski. He might have been a football fullback if he had gone to college, and, unlike many foremen nowadays, looked as if he could handle authority. He also looked, at the moment, as if he expected trouble and was prepared to meet it. The foreman's face was glowering. There was a darkening bruise, Zaleski noted, beneath his right cheekbone.

Ignoring the mode of entry, Zaleski motioned him to a chair. 'Take the weight off your feet, then simmer down.'

They faced each other across the desk.

'I'm willing to hear your version of what happened,' the assistant plant chief said, 'but don't waste time because the way this reads' – he fingered the red-tabbed grievance report – 'you've cooked us all a hot potato.'

'The hell I cooked it!' Parkland glared at his superior; above the bruise his face flushed red. 'I fired a guy because he slugged me. What's more, I'm gonna make it stick, and if you've got any guts or justice you'd better back me up.'

Matt Zaleski raised his voice to the bull roar he had learned on a factory floor. 'Knock off that goddam nonsense, right now!' He had no intention of letting this get out of hand. More reasonably, he growled, 'I said simmer down, and meant it. When the time comes I'll decide who to back and why. And there'll be no more crap from you about guts and justice. Understand?'

Their eyes locked together. Parkland's dropped first.

'All right, Frank,' Matt said. 'Let's start over, and this time give it to me straight, from the beginning.'

He had known Frank Parkland a long time. The foreman's record was good and he was usually fair with men who worked under him. It had taken something exceptional to get him as riled as this.

'There was a job out of position,' Parkland said. 'It was steering column bolts, and there was this kid doing it; he's new, I guess. He was crowding the next guy. I wanted the job put back.'

Zaleski nodded. It happened often enough. A worker with a specific assignment took a few seconds longer than he should on each operation. As successive cars moved by on the assembly line, his position gradually changed, so that soon he was intruding on the area of the next operation. When a foreman saw it happen he made it his business to help the worker back to his correct, original place.

Zaleski said impatiently, 'Get on with it.'

Before they could continue, the office door opened again and the union committeeeman came in. He was a smalll, pink-faced man, with thick-lensed glasses and a fussy manner. His name was Illas and, until a union election a few months ago, had been an assembly line worker himself.

'Good morning,' the union man said to Zaleski. He nodded curtly to Parkland, without speaking.

Matt Zaleski waved the newcomer to a chair. 'We're just getting to the meat.'

'You could save a lot of time,' Illas said, 'If you read the grievance report.'

'I've read it. But sometimes I like to hear the other side.' Zaleski motioned Parkland to go on.

'All I did,' the foreman said, 'was call another guy over and say, "Help me get this man's job back in position."'

'And I say you're a liar!' The union man hunched forward accusingly; now he swung towards Zaleski. 'What he really said was "get this *boy*'s job back." And it so happened that the person he was speaking of, and calling "boy", was one of our black brothers to whom that word is a very offensive term.'

'Oh, for God's sake!' Parkland's voice combined anger with disgust. 'D'you think I don't know that? D'you think I haven't been around here long enough to know better than to use that word that way?'

'But you *did* use it, didn't you?'

'Maybe, just maybe, I did. I'm not saying yes, because I don't remember, and that's the truth. But if it happened, there was nothing meant. It was a slip, that's all.'

The union man shrugged. 'That's your story now.'

'It's no story, you son-of-a-bitch!'

Illas stood up. 'Mr Zaleski, I'm here officially, representing the United Auto Workers. If that's the kind of language . . .'

'There'll be no more of it,' the assistant plant manager said. 'Sit down, please, and while we're on the subject I suggest you be less free yourself with the word "liar".'

Parkland slammed a beefy fist in frustration on the desk top. 'I said it was no story, and it isn't. What's more, the guy I was talking about didn't even give a thought to what I said, at least before all the fuss was made.'

'That's not the way *he* tells it,' Illas said.

'Maybe not now.' Parkland appealed to Zaleski. 'Listen, Matt, the guy who was out of position is just a kid. A black kid, maybe seventeen. I've got nothing against him; he's slow, but he was doing his job. I've got a kid brother his age. I go home, I say, "Where's the boy?" Nobody thinks twice about it. That's the way it was with this thing until this other guy, Newkirk, cut in.'

Illas persisted, 'But you're admitting you used the word "boy".'

Matt Zaleski said wearily, 'OK, OK, he used it. Let's all concede that.'

Zaleski was holding himself in, as he always had to do when racial issues erupted in the plant. His own prejudices were deep-rooted and largely anti-black, and he had learned them in the heavily Polish suburb of Wyandotte where he was born. There, the families of Polish origin looked on Negroes with contempt, as shiftless and troublemakers. In return, the black people hated Poles, and even nowadays, throughout Detroit, the ancient enmities persisted. Zaleski, through necessity, had learned to curb his instincts; you couldn't run a plant with as much black labour as this one and let your prejudices show, at least not often. Just now, after the last remark of Illas, Matt Zaleski had been tempted to inject: *So what if he did call him 'boy'? What the hell difference does it make? When a foreman tells him to, let the bastard get back to work.* But Zaleski knew it would be repeated and maybe cause more trouble than before. Instead, he growled, 'What matters is what came after.'

'Well,' Parkland said, 'I thought we'd never get to that. We almost had the job back in place, then this heavyweight, Newkirk, showed up.'

'He's another black brother,' Illas said.

'Newkirk'd been working down the line. He didn't even hear what happened; somebody else told him. He came up, called me a racist pig, and slugged me.' The foreman fingered his bruised face which had swollen even more since he came in.

Zaleski asked sharply. 'Did you hit him back?'

'No.'

'I'm glad you showed a little sense.'

'I had sense, all right,' Parkland said. 'I fired Newkirk. On the spot. Nobody slugs a foreman around here and gets away with it.'

'We'll see about that,' Illas said. 'A lot depends on circumstances and provocation.'

Matt Zaleski thrust a hand through his hair; there were days when he marvelled that there was any left. This whole stinking situation was something which McKernon, the plant manager, should handle, but McKernon wasn't here. He was ten miles away at staff headquarters, attending a conference about Orion, a super-secret car the plant would be producing soon. Sometimes it seemed to Matt Zaleski as if McKernon had already begun his retirement, officially six months away.

Matt Zaleski was holding the baby now, as he had before, and it was a lousy deal. Zaleski wasn't even going to succeed McKernon, and he knew it. He'd already been called in and shown the official assessment of himself, the assessment which appeared in a loose-leaf leather-bound book which sat permanently on the desk of the Vice-president, Manufacturing. The book was there so that the vice-president could turn its pages whenever new appointments or promotions were considered. The entry for Matt Zaleski, along with his photo and other details, read: 'This individual is well placed at his present level of management.'

Everybody in the company who mattered knew that the formal, unctuous statement was a 'kiss off'. What it really meant was: *This man has gone as high as he's going. He will probably serve his time out in his present job, but will receive no more promotions.*

The rules said that whoever received that deadly summation on his docket had to be told; he was entitled to that much, and it was the reason Matt Zaleski had known for the past several months that he would never rise beyond his present role of assistant manager. Initially the news had been a bitter disappointment, but now that he had grown used to the idea, he also knew why: He was old shoe, the hind end of a disappearing breed which management and boards of directors didn't want any more in the top critical posts. Zaleski had risen by a route which few senior plant people followed nowadays – factory worker, inspector, foreman, superintendent, assistant plant manager. He hadn't had an engineering degree to start, having been a high school dropout before the Second World War. But after the war he had armed himself with a degree, using night school and GI credits, and after that he had started climbing, being ambitious, as most of his generation were who had survived *Festung Europa* and other perils. But, as Zaleski recognized later, he had lost too much time; his real start came too late. The strong comers, the top echelon material of the auto companies – then as now – were the bright youngsters who arrived fresh and eager through the direct college-to-front office route.

But that was no reason why McKernon, who was still plant boss, should sidestep this entire situation, even if unintentionally. The assistant manager hesitated. He would be within his rights to send for McKernon and could do it here and now by picking up a phone.

Two things stopped him. One, he admitted to himself, was pride; Zaleski knew he could handle this as well as McKernon, if not better. The other: his instinct told him there simply wasn't time.

Abruptly, Zaleski asked Illas, 'What's the union asking?'

'Well, I've talked with the president of our local . . .'

'Let's save all that,' Zaleski said. 'We both know we have to start somewhere, so what is it you want?'

'Very well,' the committeeman said. 'We insist on three things. First, immediate reinstatement of Brother Newkirk, with compensation for time lost. Second, an apology to both men involved. Third, Parkland to be removed from his post as foreman.'

Parkland, who had slumped back in his chair, shot upright. 'By Christ! You don't want much.' He inquired sarcastically, 'As a matter of interest, am I supposed to apologize before I'm fired, or after?'

'The apology would be an official one from the company,' Illas answered. 'Whether you had the decency to add your own would be up to you.'

'I'll say it'd be up to me. Just don't anyone hold their breath waiting.'

Matt Zaleski snapped, 'If you'd held your own breath a little longer, we wouldn't be in this mess.'

'Are you trying to tell me you'll go along with all that?' The foreman motioned angrily to Illas.

'I'm not telling anybody anything yet. I'm trying to think, and I need more information than has come from you two.' Zaleski reached behind him for a telephone. Interposing his body between the phone and the other two, he dialled a number and waited.

When the man he wanted answered, Zaleski asked simply, 'How are things down there?'

The voice at the other end spoke softly. 'Matt?'

'Yeah.'

In the background behind the other's guarded response, Zaleski could hear a cacophony of noise from the factory floor. He always marvelled how men could live with that noise every day of their working lives. Even in the years he had worked on an assembly line himself, before removal to an office shielded him from most of the din, he had never grown used to it.

His informant said, 'The situation's real bad, Matt.'

'How bad?'

'The hopheads are in the saddle. Don't quote me.'

'I never do,' the assistant plant manager said. 'You know that.'

He had swung partially around and was aware of the other two in the office watching his face. They might guess, but couldn't know, that he was speaking to a black foreman,

Stan Lathruppe, one of the half-dozen men in the plant whom Matt Zaleski respected most. It was a strange, even paradoxical, relationship because, away from the plant, Lathruppe was an active militant who had once been a follower of Malcolm X. But here he took his responsibility seriously, believing that in the auto world he could achieve more for his race through reason than by anarchy. It was this second attitude which Zaleski – originally hostile to Lathruppe – had eventually come to respect.

Unfortunately for the company, in the present state of race relations, it had comparatively few black foremen or managers. There ought to be more, many more, and everybody knew it, but right now many of the black workers didn't want responsibility, or were afraid of it because of young militants in their ranks, or simply weren't ready. Sometimes Matt Zaleski, in his less prejudiced moments, thought that if the industry's top brass had looked ahead a few years, the way senior executives were supposed to do, and had launched a meaningful training programme for black workers in the 1940s and '50s, there would be more Stan Lathruppes now. It was everybody's loss that there were not.

Zaleski asked, 'What's being planned?'

'I think, a walkout.'

'When?'

'Probably at break time. It could be before, but I don't believe so.'

The black foreman's voice was so low Zaleski had to strain to hear. He knew the other man's problems, added to by the fact that the telephone he was using was alongside the assembly line where others were working. Lathruppe was already labelled a 'white nigger' by some fellow blacks who resented even their own race when in authority, and it made no difference that the charge was untrue. Except for a couple more questions, Zaleski had no intention of making Stan Lathruppe's life more difficult.

He asked, 'Is there any reason for the delay?'

'Yes. The hopheads want to take the whole plant out.'

'Is word going around?'

'So fast you'd think we still used jungle drums.'

'Has anyone pointed out the whole thing's illegal?'

'You got any more jokes like that?' Lathruppe said.

'No.' Zaleski sighed. 'But thanks.' He hung up.

So his first instinct had been right. There wasn't any time to spare, and hadn't been from the beginning, because a racial labour dispute always burned with a short fuse. Now, if a walkout happened, it could take days to settle and get everybody back at work; and even if only black workers became involved, and maybe not all of them, the effect would still be enough to halt production. Matt Zaleski's job was to keep production going.

As if Parkland had read his thoughts, the foreman urged, 'Matt, don't let them push you! So a few may walk off the job, and we'll have trouble. But a principle's worth standing up for, sometimes, isn't it?'

'Sometimes,' Zaleski said. 'The trick is to know which principle, and when.'

'Being fair is a good way to start,' Parkland said, 'and fairness works two ways – up and down.' He leaned forward over the desk, speaking earnestly to Matt Zaleski, glancing now and then to the union committeeman, Illas. 'OK, I've been tough with guys on the line because I've had to be. A foreman's in the middle, catching crap from all directions. From up here, Matt, you and your people are on our necks every day for production, more production; and if it isn't you it's Quality Control who say, build 'em better, even though you're building faster. Then there are those who are working, doing the jobs – including some like Newkirk, and others – and a foreman has to cope with them, along with the union as well if he puts a foot wrong, and sometimes when he doesn't. So it's a tough business, and I've been tough; it's the way to survive. But I've been fair, too. I've never treated a guy who worked for me differently because he was black, and I'm no plantation overseer with a whip. As for what we're talking about now, all I did – so I'm told – is call a black man "boy". I didn't ask him to pick cotton, or ride Jim Crow, or shine shoes, or any other thing that's supposed to go with that word. What I did was help him with his job. And I'll say another thing: if I did call him "boy" – so help me, by a slip! – I'll say I'm sorry for that, because I am. But not to Newkirk. Brother Newkirk stays fired. Because if he doesn't, if he gets away with slugging a foreman without reason, you can stuff a surrender flag up your ass and wave goodbye to any discipline around this place from this day on. That's what I mean when I say be fair.'

'You've got a point or two there,' Zaleski said. Ironically, he thought, Frank Parkland *had* been fair with black workers, maybe fairer than a good many others around the plant. He asked Illas, 'How do you feel about all that?'

The union man looked blankly through his thick-lensed glasses. 'I've already stated the union's position, Mr Zaleski.'

'So if I turn you down, if I decide to back up Frank the way he just said I should, what then?'

Illas said stiffly, 'We'd be obliged to go through further grievance procedure.'

'OK.' The assistant plant manager nodded. 'That's your privilege. Except, if we go through a full grievance drill it can mean thirty days or more. In the meantime does everybody keep working?'

'Naturally. The collective bargaining agreement specifies . . .'

Zaleski flared, 'I don't need you to tell me what the agreement says! It says everybody stays on the job while we negotiate. But right now a good many of your men are getting ready to walk off their jobs in violation of the contract.'

For the first time, Illas looked uneasy. 'The UAW does not condone illegal strikes.'

'Goddam it, then! Stop this one!'

'If what you say is true, I'll talk to some of our people.'

'Talking won't do any good. You know it, and I know it.' Zaleski eyed the union committeeman whose pink face had paled slightly; obviously Illas didn't relish the thought of arguing with some of the black militants in their present mood.

The union – as Matt Zaleski was shrewdly aware – was in a tight dilemma in situations of this kind. If the union failed to support its black militants at all, the militants would charge union leaders with racial prejudice and being 'management lackeys'. Yet if the union went too far with its support, it could find itself in an untenable position legally, as party to a wildcat strike. Illegal strikes were anathema to UAW leaders like Woodcock, Fraser, Greathouse, Bannon, and others, who had built reputations for tough negotiating, but also for honouring agreements once made, and settling grievances through due process. Wildcatting debased the union's word and undermined its bargaining strength.

'They're not going to thank you at Solidarity House if we let this thing get away from us,' Matt Zaleski persisted. 'There's only one thing can stop a walkout, and that's for us to make a decision here, then go down on the floor and announce it.'

Illas said, 'That depends on the decision.' But it was plain that the union man was weighing Zaleski's words.

Matt Zaleski had already decided what the ruling had to be, and he knew that nobody would like it entirely, including himself. He thought sourly: these were lousy times, when a man had to shove his convictions in his pocket along with pride – at least, if he figured to keep an automobile plant running.

He announced brusquely, 'Nobody gets fired. Newkirk goes back to his job, but from now on he uses his fists for working, nothing else.' The assistant plant manager fixed his eyes on Illas. 'I want it clearly understood by you and by Newkirk – one more time, he's out. And before he goes back, I'll talk to him myself.'

'He'll be paid for lost time?' The union man had a slight smile of triumph.

'Is he still at the plant?'

'Yes.'

Zaleski hesitated, then nodded reluctantly. 'OK, providing he finishes the shift. But there'll be no more talk about anybody replacing Frank.' He swung to face Parkland. 'And you'll do what you said you would – talk to the young guy. Tell him what was said was a mistake.'

'An apology is what it's known as,' Illas said.

Frank Parkland glared at them both. 'Of all the crummy, sleazy backdowns!'

'Take it easy!' Zaleski warned.

'Like hell I'll take it easy!' The burly foreman was on his feet, towering over the assistant plant manager. He spat words across the desk between them. 'You're the one taking it easy – the easy out because you're too much a goddam coward to stand up for what you know is right.'

His face flushing deep red, Zaleski roared, 'I don't have to take that from you! That'll be enough! You hear?'

'I hear.' Contempt filled Parkland's voice and eyes. 'But I don't like what I hear, or what I smell.'

'In that case, maybe you'd like to be fired!'

'Maybe,' the foreman said. 'Maybe the air'd be cleaner some place else.'

There was a silence between them, then Zaleski growled, 'It's no cleaner. Some days it stinks everywhere.'

Now that his own outburst was over, Matt Zaleski had himself in hand. He had no intention of firing Parkland, knowing that if he did, it would be a greater injustice piled on another; besides, good foremen were hard to come by. Nor would Parkland quit of his own accord, whatever he might threaten; that was something Zaleski had calculated from the beginning. He happened to know that Frank Parkland had obligations at home which made a continuing paycheck necessary, as well as too much seniority in the company to throw away.

But for a moment back there, Parkland's crack about cowardice had stung. There had been an instant when the assistant plant manager wanted to shout that Frank Parkland had been ten years old, a snot-nosed kid, when he, Matt Zaleski, was sweating bomber missions over Europe, never knowing when a hunk of jagged flak would slice through the fuselage, then horribly through his guts or face or pecker, or wondering if their B-17F would go spinning earthwards from 25,000 feet, burning, as many of the Eighth Air Force bombers did while comrades watched . . . *So think again about who you're taunting with cowardice, sonny; and remember I'm the one, not you, who has to keep this plant going, no matter how much bile I swallow doing it!* . . . But Zaleski hadn't said any of that, knowing that some of the things he had thought of happened a long time ago, and were not relevant any more, that ideas and values had changed in screwy, mixed-up ways; also that there were different kinds of cowardice, and maybe Frank Parkland was right, or partly right. Disgusted with himself, the assistant plant manager told the other two, 'Let's go down on the floor and settle this.'

They went out of the office – Zaleski first, followed by the union committeeman, with Frank Parkland, dour and glowering, in the rear. As they clattered down the metal stairway from the office mezzanine to the factory floor, the noise of the plant hit them solidly, like a barrage of bedlam.

The stairway at factory floor level was close to a section of assembly line where early subassemblies were welded on to frames, becoming the foundations on which finished cars would rest. The din at this point was so intense that men working within a few feet of one another had to shout, heads close together, to communicate. Around them showers of sparks flew upwards and sideways in a pyrotechnic curtain of intense white-blue. Volleys from welding machines and rivet guns were punctuated by the constant hiss of the power tools' lifeblood – compressed air. And central to everything, focus of activity like an ambling godhead exacting tribute, the moving assembly line inched inexorably on.

The union committeeman fell in beside Zaleski as the trio moved forward down the line. They were walking considerably faster than the assembly line itself, so that cars they passed were progressively nearer completion. There was a power plant in each chassis now, and immediately ahead, a body shell was about to merge with a chassis sliding under it in what auto assembly men called the 'marriage act'. Matt Zaleski's eyes swung over the scene, checking key points of operation, as he always did, instinctively.

Heads went up, or turned, as the assistant plant manager, with Illas and Parkland, continued down the line. There were a few greetings, though not many, and Zaleski was aware of sour looks from most workers whom they passed, white as well as black. He sensed a mood of resentment and unrest. It happened occasionally in plants, sometimes without reason, at other times through a minor cause, as if an eruption would have happened anyway and was merely seeking the nearest outlet. Sociologists, he knew, called it a reaction to unnatural monotony.

The union committeeman had his face set in a stern expression, perhaps to indicate that he hobnobbed with management only through duty, but did not enjoy it.

'How's it feel,' Matt Zaleski asked him, 'now you don't work on the line any more?'

Illas said curtly, 'Good.'

Zaleski believed him. Outsiders who toured auto plants often assumed that workers there became reconciled, in time, to the noise, smell, heat, unrelenting pressure, and endless repetition of their jobs. Matt Zaleski had heard touring visitors tell their children, as if speaking of inmates of a zoo: *They all get used to it. Most of them are happy at that kind of work. They wouldn't want to do anything else.'*

When he heard it, he always wanted to cry out: *'Kids, don't believe it! It's a lie!'*

Zaleski knew, as did most others who were close to auto plants, that few people who worked on factory production lines for long periods had ever intended to make that work a lifetime's occupation. Usually, when hired, they looked on the job as temporary until something better came along. But to many – especially those with little education – the better job was always out of reach, for ever a delusive dream. Eventually a trap was sprung.

570

It was a two-pronged trap, with a worker's own commitments on one side – marriage, children, rent, instalment payments – and on the other, the fact that pay in the auto industry was high compared with jobs elsewhere.

But neither pay nor good fringe benefits could change the grim, dispiriting nature of the work. Much of it was physically hard, but the greatest toll was mental – hour after hour, day after day of deadening monotony. And the nature of their jobs robbed individuals of pride. A man on a production line lacked a sense of achievement; he never made a car; he merely made, or put together, pieces – adding a washer to a bolt, fastening a metal strip, inserting screws. And always it was the identical washer or strip or screws, over and over and over and over and over and over and over again, while working conditions – including an overlay of noise – made communication difficult, friendly association between individuals impossible. As years went by, many, while hating, endured. Some had mental breakdowns. Almost no-one liked his work.

Thus, a production line worker's ambition, like that of a prisoner, was centred on escape. Absenteeism was a way of partial escape; so was a strike. Both brought excitement, a break in monotony – for the time being the dominating drive.

Even now, the assistant plant manager realized, that drive might be impossible to turn back.

He told Illas, 'Remember, we made an agreement. Now, I want this thing cleaned up fast.' The union man didn't answer, and Zaleski added. 'Today should do you some good. You got what you wanted.'

'Not all of it.'

'All that mattered.'

Behind their words was a fact of life which both men knew: an escape route from the production line which some workers chose was through election to a full-time union post, with a chance of moving upwards in UAW ranks. Illas, recently, had gone that way himself. But once elected, a union man became a political creature; to survive he must be re-elected, and between elections he manoeuvred like a politician courting favour with constituents. The workers around a union committeeman were his voters, and he strove to please them. Illas had that problem now.

Zaleski asked him, 'Where's this character Newkirk?'

They had come to the point on the assembly line where this morning's blow-up had occurred.

Illas nodded towards an open area with several plastic-topped tables and chairs, where line workers took their meal breaks. There was a bank of vending machines for coffee, soft drinks, candy. A painted line on the floor served in lieu of a surrounding wall. At the moment the only occupant of the area was a husky, big-featured black man; smoke drifted from a cigarette in his hand as he watched the trio which had just arrived.

The assistant plant manager said, 'All right, tell him he goes back to work, and make sure you fill in all the rest. When you're through talking, send him over to me.'

'OK,' Illas said. He stepped over the painted line and was smiling as he sat down at the table with the big man.

Frank Parkland had already gone directly to a younger black man, still working on the line. Parkland was talking earnestly. At first the other looked uncomfortable, but soon after grinned sheepishly and nodded. The foreman touched the younger man's shoulder and motioned in the direction of Illas and Newkirk, still at the lunch area table, their heads close together. The young assembly worker grinned again. The foreman put out his hand; after hesitating briefly, the young man took it. Matt Zaleski found himself wondering if he could have handled Parkland's part as gracefully or as well.

'Hi, boss man!' The voice came from the far side of the assembly line. Zaleski turned towards it.

It was an interior trim inspector, an old-timer on the line, a runtish man with a face extraordinarily like that of Hitler. Inevitably, fellow workers called him Adolf and, as if enjoying the joke, the employee – whose real name Zaleski could never remember – even combed his short hair forward over one eye.

'Hi, Adolf.' The assistant plant manager crossed to the other side of the line, stepping carefully between a yellow convertible and a mist-green sedan. 'How's body quality today?'

'I've seen worse days, boss man. Remember the World Series?'

'Don't remind me.'

World Series time and the opening days of the Michigan hunting season were periods which auto production men dreaded. Absenteeism was at a peak; even foremen and supervisors were guilty of it. Quality plummeted, and at World Series time the situation was worsened by employees paying more attention to portable radios than to their jobs. Matt Zaleski remembered that at the height of the 1968 series, which the Detroit Tigers won, he confided grimly to his wife, Freda – it was the year before she died – 'I wouldn't wish a car built today on my worst enemy.'

'This special's OK, anyway.' Adolf (or whatever his name was) had hopped nimbly in and out of the mist-green sedan. Now, he turned his attention to the car behind – a bright orange sports compact with white bucket seats. 'Bet this one's for a blonde,' Adolf shouted from inside the car. 'An' I'd like to be the one to screw her in it.'

Matt Zaleski shouted back, 'You've got a soft job already.'

'I'd be softer after her.' The inspector emerged, rubbing his crotch and leering; factory humour was seldom sophisticated.

The assistant plant manager returned the grin, knowing it was one of the few human exchanges the worker would have during his eight-hour shift.

Adolf ducked into another car, checking its interior. It was true what Zaleski had said a moment earlier: an inspector did have a softer job than most others on the line, and usually got it through seniority. But the job, which carried no extra pay and gave a man no real authority, had disadvantages. If an inspector was conscientious and drew attention to all bad work, he aroused the ire of fellow workers who could make life miserable for him in other ways. Foremen, too, took a dim view of what they conceived to be an overzealous inspector, resenting anything which held up their particular area of production. All foremen were under pressure from superiors – including Matt Zaleski – to meet production quotas, and foremen could, and often did, overrule inspectors. Around an auto plant a classic phrase was a foreman's grunted, 'Let it go,' as a substandard piece of equipment or work moved onwards down the line sometimes to be caught by Quality Control, more often not.

In the meal break area, the union committeeman and Newkirk were getting up from their table.

Matt Zaleski looked forward down the line; something about the mist-green sedan, now several cars ahead, caused his interest to sharpen. He decided to inspect that car more closely before it left the plant.

Also down the line he could see Frank Parkland near his regular foreman's station; presumably Parkland had gone back to his job, assuming his own part in the now-settled dispute to be over. Well, Zaleski supposed it was, though he suspected the foreman would find it harder, from now on, to maintain discipline when he had to. But, hell! – everybody had their problems. Parkland would have to cope with his.

As Matt Zaleski recrossed the assembly line, Newkirk and the union committeeman walked to meet him. The black man moved casually; standing up, he seemed even bigger than he had at the table. His facial features were large and prominent, matching his build, and he was grinning.

Illas announced, 'I've told Brother Newkirk about the decision I won for him. He's agreed to go back to work and understands he'll be paid for time lost.'

The assistant plant manager nodded; he had no wish to rob the union man of kudos, and if Illas wanted to make a small skirmish sound like the Battle of the Overpass, Zaleski would not object. But he told Newkirk sharply, 'You can take the grin off. There's nothing funny.' He queried Illas, 'You told him it'll be even less funny if it happens again?'

'He told me what he was supposed to,' Newkirk said. 'It won't happen no more, not if there ain't no cause.'

'You're pretty cocky,' Zaleski said. 'Considering you've just been fired and unfired.'

'Not cocky, mister, *angry*!' The black man made a gesture which included Illas. 'That's a thing you people, all of you, won't ever understand.'

Zaleski snapped, 'I can get pretty damned angry about brawls upsetting this plant.'

'Not deep soul angry. No so it burns, a *rage*.'

'Don't push me. I might show you otherwise.'

The other shook his head. For one so huge, his voice and movements were surprisingly gentle; only his eyes burned – an intense grey-green. 'Man, you ain't black, you don't know what it means; not rage, not anger. It's a million goddam pins bein' stuck in from time you was born, then one day some white motha' calls a man "boy", an' it's a million 'n one too many.'

'Now then,' the union man said, 'we settled all that. We don't have to get into it again.'

Newkirk dismissed him. 'You hush up!' His eyes remained fixed, challengly, on the assistant plant manager.

Not for the first time, Matt Zaleski wondered: had the whole free-wheeling world gone crazy? To people like Newkirk and millions of others, including Zaleski's own daughter, Barbara, it seemed a basic credo that everything which used to matter – authority, order, respect, moral decency – no longer counted in any recognizable way. Insolence was a norm – the kind Newkirk used with his voice and now his eyes. The familiar phrases were a part of it: Newkirk's *rage* and *deep soul angry* were interchangeable, it seemed, with a hundred others like *generation gap, strung out, hanging loose, taking your own trip, turned on,* most of which Matt Zaleski didn't comprehend and – the more he heard them – didn't want to. The changes which, nowadays, he could neither keep pace with nor truly understand, left him subdued and wearied.

In a strange way, at this moment, he found himself equating the big black man, Newkirk, with Barbara who was pretty, twenty-nine, college educated, and white. If Barbara Zaleski were here now, automatically, predictably, she would see things Newkirk's way, and not her father's. Christ! – he wished he were half as sure of things himself.

Tiredly, though it was still early morning, and not at all convinced that he had handled this situation the way he should, Matt Zaleski told Newkirk brusquely, 'Get back to your job.'

When Newkirk had gone, Illas said, 'There'll be no walkout. Word's going around.'

'Am I supposed to say thanks?' Zaleski asked sourly. 'For not being raped?'

The union man shrugged and moved away.

The mist-green sedan which Zaleski had been curious about had moved still farther forward on the line. Walking quickly, the assistant plant manager caught up with it.

He checked the papers, including a scheduling order and specifications, in a cardboard folder hanging over the front grille. As he had half-expected, as well as being a 'special' – a car which received more careful attention than routine – it was also a 'foreman's friend'.

A 'foreman's friend', was a *very* special car. It was also illegal in any plant and, in this case, involved more than a hundred dollar's worth of dishonesty. Matt Zaleski, who had a knack of storing away tidbits of information and later piecing them together, had more than a shrewd idea who was involved with the mist-green sedan, and why.

The car was for a company public relations man. Its official specifications were Spartan and included few, if any, extras, yet the sedan was (as auto men expressed it) 'loaded up' with special items. Even without a close inspection Matt Zaleski could see a de-luxe steering wheel, extra-ply whitewall tyres, styled steel wheels and tinted glass, none of which were in the specifications he was holding. It looked, too, as if the car had received a double paint job, which helped durability. It was this last item which had caught Zaleski's eyes earlier.

The almost-certain explanation matched several facts which the assistant plant manager already knew. Two weeks earlier the daughter of a senior foreman in the plant had been married. As a favour, the public relations man, whose car this was, had arranged publicity, getting wedding pictures featured prominently in Detroit and suburban papers. The bride's father was delighted. There had been a good deal of talk about it around the plant.

The rest was easy to guess.

The PR man could readily find out in advance which day his car was scheduled for production. He would then have telephoned his foreman friend, who had clearly arranged special attention for the mist-green sedan all the way through assembly.

Matt Zaleski knew what he ought to do. He ought to check out his suspicions by sending for the foreman concerned, and afterwards make a written report to the plant manager, McKernon, who would have no choice except to act on it. After that there would be seventeen kinds of hell let loose, extending – because of the PR man's involvement – all the way up to staff headquarters.

Matt Zaleski also knew he wasn't going to.

There were problems enough already. The Parkland-Newkirk-Illas embroilment had been one; and predictably, by now, back in the glass-panelled office were others requiring decisions, in addition to those already on his desk this morning. These, he reminded himself, he still hadn't looked at.

On his car radio, driving to work an hour or so ago from Royal Oak, he had heard Emerson Vale, the auto critic whom Zaleski thought of as an idiot, firing buckshot at the industry again. Matt Zaleski had wished then, as now, that he could install Vale on a production hot seat for a few days and let the son-of-a-bitch find out what it really took, in terms of effort, grief, compromise, and human exhaustion to get cars built at all.

Matt Zaleski walked away from the mist-green sedan. In running a plant, you had to learn that there were moments when some things had to be ignored, and this was one.

But at least today was Wednesday.

3

At 7.30 a.m., while tens of thousands in greater Detroit had been up for hours and were already working, others – either through choice or the nature of their work – were still abed.

One who remained there by choice was Erica Trenton.

In a wide, French Provincial bed, between satin sheets which were smooth against the firm surface of her young body, she was awake, but drifting back to sleep, and had no intention of getting up for at least two hours more.

Drowsily, only half-conscious of her own thoughts, she dreamed of a man . . . no particular man, simply a vague figure . . . arousing her sensually, thrusting her deeply – *again! again!* . . . as her own husband had not, for at least three weeks and probably a month.

While she drifted, as on a gently flooding tide between wakefulness and a return to sleep, Erica mused that she had not always been a late riser. In the Bahamas, where she was born, and lived until her marriage to Adam five years ago, she had often risen before dawn and helped launch a dinghy from the beach, afterwards running the outboard while her father trolled and the sun rose. Her father enjoyed fresh fish at breakfast and, in her later years at home, it was Erica who cooked it when they returned.

During her initiation to marriage, in Detroit, she had followed the same pattern, rising early with Adam and preparing breakfast which they ate together – he zestfully, and loudly appreciative of Erica's natural talent for cooking which she used with imagination, even for simplest meals. By her own wish they had no live-in help, and Erica kept busy, especially since Adam's twin sons, Greg and Kirk, who were at prep school nearby, came home during most weekends and holidays.

That was the time when she had been worried about her acceptance by the boys – Adam had divorced their mother earlier the same year, only a few months before meeting Erica and the beginning of their brief, jet-speed courtship. But Erica had been accepted at once by Greg and Kirk – even gratefully, it seemed, since they had seen little of either of their parents over several preceding years, Adam being immersed in his work, and the boys' mother, Francine, travelling frequently abroad, as she still did. Besides, Erica was closer to the boys' own age. She had been barely twenty-one then, Adam eighteen years her senior, though the differences in ages hadn't seemed to matter. Of course, the gap of years between Adam and Erica was still the same, except that nowadays – five years later – it *seemed* wider.

A reason, obviously, was that at the beginning they had devoured each other sexually. They first made love – tempestuously – on a moonlit Bahamas beach. Erica remembered still: the warm, jasmine-scented night, white sand, softly lapping water, a breeze stirring palm trees, music drifting from a lighted cruise ship in Nassau harbour. They had known each other for a few days only. Adam had been holidaying – an aftermath of his divorce – with friends at Lyford Cay who introduced him to Erica at a Nassau night spot, Charley Charley's. They spent all next day together, and others afterwards.

The night on the beach was not their first time there. But on the earlier occasions she had resisted Adam; now, she learned, she could resist no longer, and only whisper helplessly, 'I can get pregnant.'

He had whispered back, 'You're going to marry me. So it doesn't matter.'

She had not become pregnant, though many times since she wished she had.

From then on, and into marriage a month later, they made love frequently and passionately – almost unfailingly each night, then expending themselves further (but, oh, how gloriously) on awakening in the morning. Even back in Detroit the night and morning love-making persisted, despite Adam's early work start which, Erica quickly discovered, was part of an auto executive's life.

But as months went by and, after that, the first few years, Adam's passion lessened. For either of them it could never have sustained itself at the original frenetic pace; Erica realized that. But what she had not expected was that the decline would come as early as it had, or be so near-complete. Undoubtedly she became more conscious of the change because other activities were less. Greg and Kirk now came home seldom, having left Michigan for college – Greg to Columbia, en route to medical school; Kirk to the University of Oklahoma to major in journalism.

She was still drifting . . . Still not quite asleep. The house, near Quarton Lake in the northern suburb of Birmingham, was quiet. Adam had gone. Like most in the auto industry's top echelon, he was at his desk by half past seven, had done an hour's work before the secretaries came. Also, as usual, Adam had risen in time to do exercises, take a ten-minute run outside, then, after showering, get his own breakfast, as he always did these days. Erica had slipped out of the habit of preparing it after Adam told her candidly that the meal was taking too long; unlike their early years together, he chafed impatiently, wanting to be on his way, no longer enjoying their relaxed quarter-hour together at the table. One morning he had simply said, 'Honey, you stay in bed. I'll get breakfast for myself.' And he had, doing the same thing next day, and on other mornings after that, so they had drifted into the present pattern, though it depressed Erica to know she was no longer useful to Adam at the beginning of the day, that her imaginative breakfast menus, the cheerfully set table and her own presence there, were more irritating to him than pleasing.

Erica found Adam's diminishing concern about what went on at home, along with total dedication to his job, more and more an aggravating combination nowadays. He was also tediously considerate. When his alarm clock sounded, Adam snapped it off promptly before it could penetrate Erica's sleep too deeply, and got out of bed at once, though it seemed not long ago that they had reached for each other instinctively on waking, and sometimes coupled quickly, finding that each could bring the other, feverishly, to a swifter climax than at night. Then, while Erica still lay, lingering for a moment breathlessly, her heart beating hard, Adam would whisper as he slipped from her and from the bed, 'What better way to start a day?'

But not any more. Never in the morning, and only rarely, now, at night. And in the mornings, for all the contact they had, they might as well be strangers. Adam awakened quickly, performed his swift routines, and then was gone.

This morning, when Erica heard Adam moving around in the bathroom and downstairs, she considered changing the routine and joining him. Then she reminded herself that all he wanted was to move fast – like the go-go cars his Product Planning team conceived; the latest, the soon-to-be-unveiled Orion – and be on his way. Also, with his damned efficiency, Adam could make breakfast just as speedily as Erica – for a half-dozen people if necessary, as he sometimes had. Despite this, she debated getting up, and was still debating when she hear Adam's car start, and leave. Then it was too late.

Where have all the flowers gone? Where the love, the life, the vanished idyll of Adam and Erica Trenton, young lovers not so long ago? *O where, O where!*

Erica slept.

When she awakened it was mid-morning, and a watery autumn sun was slanting in through slats of the venetian blinds.

Downstairs, a vacuum cleaner whined and thumped, and Erica was relieved that Mrs Gooch, who cleaned twice a week, had let herself in and was already at work. It meant that today Erica need not bother with the house, though lately, in any case, she had paid much less attention to it than she used to do.

A morning paper was beside the bed. Adam must have left it there, as he sometimes did. Propping herself up with pillows, her long ash-blonde hair tumbling over them, Erica unfolded it.

A sizeable portion of page one was given over to an attack on the auto industry by Emerson Vale. Erica skipped most of the news story, which didn't interest her, even though there were times when she felt like attacking the auto world herself. She had never cared for it, not since first coming to Detroit, though she had tried, for Adam's sake. But the all-consuming interest in their occupations which so many auto people had, leaving time for little else, repelled her. Erica's own father, an airline captain, had been good at his job, but always put it behind him mentally when he left an Island Airways cockpit to come home. His greater interests were being with his family, fishing, pottering at carpentry, reading, strumming a guitar, and sometimes just sitting in the sun. Erica knew that even now her own mother and father spent far more time together than she and Adam did.

It was her father who had said, when she announced her sudden plans to marry Adam: '*You're your own girl and always have been. So I won't oppose this because, even if I did, it would make no difference and I'd sooner you go with my blessing than without. And maybe, in time, I'll get used to having a son-in-law almost my own age. He seems a decent man; I like him. But one thing I'll warn you of: He's ambitious, and you don't know yet what ambition means, especially up there in Detroit. If the two of you have trouble, that'll be the cause of it.*' She sometimes thought how observant – and how right – her father had been.

Erica's thoughts returned to the newspaper and Emerson Vale, whose face glared out from a two-column cut. She wondered if the youthful auto critic was any good in bed, then thought: probably not. She had heard there were no women in his life, nor men either, despite abortive efforts to smear him with a homosexual tag. Humanity, it seemed, had a depressing proportion of capons and worn-out males. Listlessly, she turned the page.

There was little that held interest, from international affairs – the world was in as much as mess as on any other day – through to the social section, which contained the usual auto names: the Fords had entertained an Italian princess, the Roches were in New York, the

Townsends at the Symphony, and the Chapins duck hunting in North Dakota. On another page Erica stopped at Ann Landers' column, then mentally began composing a letter of her own: *My problem, Ann, is a married woman's cliché. There are jokes about it, but the jokes are made by people it isn't happening to. The plain truth is – if I can speak frankly as one woman to another – I'm simply not getting enough . . . Just lately I've not been getting any . . .*

With an impatient, angry gesture Erica crumpled the newspaper and pulled the bedclothes aside. She slid from the bed and went to the window where she tugged vigorously at the blind cord so that full daylight streamed in. Her eyes searched the room for a brown alligator handbag she had used yesterday; it was on a dressing-table. Opening the bag, she riffled through until she found a small, leather-covered notebook which she took – turning pages as she went – to a telephone by Adam's side of the bed.

She dialled quickly – before she could change her mind – the number she had found in the book. As she finished, Erica found her hand trembling and put it on the bed to steady herself. A woman's voice answered, 'Detroit Bearing and Gear'.

Erica asked for the name she had written in the notebook, in handwriting so indecipherable that only she could read it.

'What department is he in?'

'I think – sales.'

'One moment, please.'

Erica could still hear the vacuum cleaner somewhere outside. At least, while that continued, she could be sure Mrs Gooch was not listening.

There was a click and another voice answered, though not the one she sought. Erica repeated the name she had asked for.

'Sure he's here.' She heard the voice call 'Ollie!' An answering voice said, 'I got it,' then, more clearly, 'Hullo.'

'This is Erica.' She added uncertainly. 'You know; we met . . .'

'Sure, sure; I know. Where are you?'

'At home.'

'What number?'

She gave it to him.

'Hang up. Call you right back.'

Erica waited nervously, wondering if she would answer at all, but when the ring back came, she did so immediately.

'Hi, baby!'

'Hullo,' Erica said.

'Some phones are better'n other phones for special kindsa calls.'

'I understand.'

'Long time no see.'

'Yes. It is.'

A pause.

'Why'd you call, baby?'

'Well, I thought . . . we might meet.'

'Why?'

'Perhaps for a drink.'

'We had drinks last time. Remember? Sat all afternoon in that goddam Queensway Inn bar.'

'I know, but . . .'

'An' the same thing the time before that.'

'That was the very first time; the time we met there.'

'OK, so you don't put out the first time. A dame cuts it the way she sees; fair enough. But the second time a guy expects to hit the coconut, not spend an afternoon of his time in a big gabfest. So I still say – what's on your mind?'

'I thought . . . if we could talk, just a little, I could explain . . .'

'No dice.'

She let her hand holding the phone drop down. *In God's name, what was she doing, even talking with this . . . There must be other men. But where?*

The phone diaphragm rasped, 'You still there, baby?'

She lifted her hands again. 'Yes.'

'Listen, I'll ask you something. You wanna get laid?'

Erica was choking back tears; tears of humiliation, self-disgust.

'Yes,' she said. 'Yes, that's what I want.'

'You're sure, this time. No more big gabfest?'

Dear God! Did he want an affidavit? She wondered: were there really women so desperate, they would respond to an approach so crude? *Obviously, yes.*

'I'm sure,' Erica said.

'That's great, kiddo! How's if we hit the sack next Wednesday?'

'I thought . . . perhaps sooner.' Next Wednesday was a week away.

'Sorry, baby; no dice. Gotta sales trip. Leave for Cleveland in an hour. Be there five days.' A chuckle. 'Gotta keep them Ohio dolls happy.'

Erica forced a laugh. 'You certainly get around.'

'You'd be surprised.'

She thought: *No, I wouldn't. Not at anything, any more.*

'Call you soon's I get back. While I'm gone, you keep it warm for me.' A second's pause, then: 'You be all right Wednesday? You know what I mean?'

Erica's control snapped. 'Of course I know. Do you think I'm so stupid not to have thought of *that*?'

'You'd be surprised how many don't.'

In a detached part of her mind, as if she were a spectator, not a participant, she marvelled: *Has he ever tried making a woman feel good, instead of awful?*

'Gotta go, baby. Back to the salt mines! Another day, another dollar!'

'Goodbye,' Erica said.

'S'long.'

She hung up. Covering her face with her hands, she sobbed silently until her long, slim fingers were wet with tears.

Later, in the bathroom, washing her face and using make-up to conceal the signs of crying as best she could, Erica reasoned: there *was* a way out.

It didn't have to happen a week from now. Adam could prevent it, though he would never know.

If only, within the next seven nights he would take her, as a husband could and should, she would weather this time, and afterwards, somehow, tame her body's urgency to reasonableness. All she sought – all she had ever sought – was to be loved and needed, and in return to give love. She still loved Adam. Erica closed her eyes, remembering the way it was when he first loved and needed her.

And she would help Adam, she decided. Tonight, and other nights if necessary, she would make herself irresistibly attractive, she'd wash her hair so it was sweet-smelling, use a musky perfume that would tantalize, put on her sheerest negligée . . . Wait! She would buy a new negligée – today, this morning, *now* . . . in Birmingham.

Hurriedly, she began to dress.

4

The handsome, grey stone staff building, which could have done duty as a state capitol, was quiet in the early morning as Adam Trenton wheeled his cream sport coupé down the ramp from outside. Adam made a fast 'S' turn, tyres squealing, into his stall in the underground, executive parking area, then eased his lank figure out of the driver's seat, leaving the keys inside. A rain shower last night had slightly spotted the car's bright finish; routinely it would be washed today, topped off with gas, and serviced if necessary.

A personal car of an executive's own choice, replaced every six months, and each time with all the extras he wanted, plus fuel and constant attention, was a fringe benefit which went with the auto industry's higher posts. Depending on which company they worked for, most senior people made their selections from the luxury ranges – Chrysler Imperials, Lincolns, Cadillacs. A few, like Adam, preferred something lighter and sportier, with a high performance engine.

Adam's footsteps echoed as he walked across the black, waxed garage floor, gleaming and immaculate.

A spectator would have seen a grey-suited, lithe, athletic man, a year or two past forty, tall, with broad shoulders and a squarish head thrust forward, as if urging the rest of the body on. Nowadays, Adam Trenton dressed more conservatively than he used to, but still looked fashionable, with a touch of flashiness. His facial features were clean-cut and alert, with intense blue eyes and a straight, firm mouth, the last tempered by a hint of humour and a strong impression, over-all, of open honesty. He backed up this impression, when he talked, with a blunt directness which sometimes threw others off balance – a tactic he had learnt to use deliberately. His manner of walking was confident, a no-nonsense stride suggesting a man who knew where he was going.

Adam Trenton carried the auto executive's symbol of office – a filled attaché case. It contained papers he had taken home the night before and had worked on, after dinner, until bedtime.

Among the few executive cars already parked, Adam noticed two limousines in vice-presidents' row – a series of parking slots near an exclusive elevator which rose nonstop to the fifteenth floor, preserve of the company's senior officers. A parking spot closest to the elevator was reserved for the chairman of the board, the next for the president; after that came vice-presidents in descending order of seniority. Where a man parked was a significant prestige factor in the auto industry. The higher his rank, the less distance he was expected to walk from his car to his desk.

Of the two limousines already in, one belonged to Adam's own chief, the Product

Development vice-president. The other was the car of the Vice-President Public Relations.

Adam bounded up a short flight of stairs, two at a time, entered a doorway to the building's main lobby, then continued briskly to a regular staff elevator where he jabbed a button for the tenth floor. Alone in the elevator, he waited impatiently while the computer-controlled mechanism took its time about starting, then on the way up experienced the eagerness he always felt to become immersed in a new day's work. As always, through most of the past two years, the Orion was at the forefront of his thoughts. Physically, Adam felt good. Only a sense of tension troubled him – a mental tautness he had become aware of lately, a nuisance, illogical yet increasingly difficult to shake off. He took a small, green-and-black capsule from an inside pocket, slipped it into his mouth and gulped it down.

From the elevator, along a silent, deserted corridor which would see little activity for another hour, Adam strode to his own office suite – a corner location, also a token of rank, rating only a little lower than a vice-president's parking slot.

As he went in, he saw a pile of newly delivered mail on his secretary's desk. There was a time, earlier in his career, when Adam would have stopped to riffle through it, to see what was interesting and new, but he had long since shed the habit, nowadays valuing his time too much for that kind of indulgence. One of the duties of a top-notch secretary was – as Adam once heard the company president declare – to 'filter out the crap' from the mountain of paper which came her boss's way. She should be allowed to go through everything first, using her judgement about what to refer elsewhere, so that an executive mind could concern itself with policy and ideas, unencumbered by detail which others, in lowlier posts, could be trusted to handle.

That was why few of the thousands of letters yearly which individual car owners addressed to heads of auto companies ever reached the person whom the sender named. All such letters were screened by secretaries, then sent to special departments which dealt with them according to set routines. Eventually the sum of all complaints and comments in a year was tabulated and studied, but no senior executive could cope with them individually and do his job as well. An occasional exception was where a correspondent was shrewd enough to write to an executive's home address – not hard to find, since more were listed in *Who's Who*, available in public libraries. Then an executive, or his wife, might well read the letter, become interested in a particular case, and follow through personally.

The first thing Adam Trenton noticed in his office was a glowing orange light on an intercom box behind his desk. It showed that the Product Development vice-president had called, almost certainly this morning. Adam touched a switch above the light and waited.

A voice, metallic through the intercom, demanded, 'What's the excuse today? Accident on the freeway, or did you oversleep?'

Adam laughed, his eyes flicking to a wall clock which showed 7.23. He depressed the key connecting him with the vice-president's office five floors above. 'You know my problem, Elroy. Just can't seem to get out of bed.'

It was rarely that the head of Product Development beat Adam in; when he did, he liked to make the most of it.

'Adam, how are you fixed for the next hour?'

'I've a few things. Nothing I can't change around.'

From the windows of his office, as they talked, Adam could see the early morning freeway traffic. At this time the volume was moderately heavy, though not so great as an hour ago when production workers were heading into factories to begin day shifts. But the traffic pattern would change again soon as thousands of office employees, now breakfasting at home, added their cars to the hurrying stream. The pressures and easings of traffic density, like variations in the wind, always fascinated Adam – not surprisingly, since automobiles, the traffic's chief constituent, were the *idée fixe* of his own existence. He had devised a scale of ohis own – like the Beaufort wind-scale, ranging from one to ten degrees of volume – which he applied to traffic as he viewed it. Right now, he decided, the flow as at Volume Five.

'I'd like you up here for a while,' Elroy Braithwaite, the vice-president, said. 'I guess you know our buddy, Emerson Vale, is off in orbit again.'

'Yes.' Adam had read the *Free Press* report of Vale's latest charges before leaving the newspaper beside the bed where Erica was sleeping.

'Some of the Press have asked for comments. This time Jake thinks we should make a few.'

Jake Earlham was the Vice-President Public Relations, whose car had also been parked below as Adam came in.

'I agree with him,' Adam said.

'Well, I seem to have been elected, but I'd like you in on the session. It'll be informal. Somebody from AP, the *Newsweek* gal, *The Wall Street Journal*, and Bob Irvin from the *Detroit News*. We're going to see them all together.'

'Any ground rules, briefing?' Usually, in advance of auto company Press conferences, elaborate preparations were made with public relations departments preparing lists of anticipated questions, which executives then studied. Sometimes rehearsals were staged at which PR men played reporters. A major Press conference took weeks in planning, so that auto company spokesmen were as well prepared as a US President facing the Press, sometimes better.

'No briefing,' Elroy Braithwaite said, 'Jake and I have decided to hang loose on this one. We'll call things the way we see them. That goes for you too.'

'OK,' Adam said. 'Are you ready now?'

'About ten minutes. I'll call you.'

Waiting, Adam emptied his attaché case of last night's work, then used a dictating machine to leave a series of instructions for his secretary, Ursula Cox, who would deal with them with predictable efficiency when she came in. Most of Adam's homework, as well as the instructions, concerned the Orion. In his role as Advanced Vehicles Planning Manager he was deeply involved with the new, still-secret car, and today a critical series of tests involving a noise-vibration problem with the Orion would be reviewed at the company's proving ground thirty miles outside Detroit. Adam, who would have to make a decision afterwards, had agreed to drive to the test review with a colleague from Design-Styling. Now, because of the Press conference just called, one of Ursula's instructions was to reschedule the proving ground arrangements for later in the day.

He had better, Adam decided, reread the Emerson Vale news story before the Press session started. Along with the pile of mail outside were some morning newspapers. He collected a *Free Press* and a *New York Times*, then returned to his office and spread them out, this time memorizing, point by point, what Vale had said in Washington the day before. ·

Adam had met Emerson Vale once when the auto critic was in Detroit to make a speech. Like several others from the industry, Adam Trenton had attended out of curiosity and, on being introduced to Vale ahead of the meeting, was surprised to find him an engagingly pleasant young man, not in the least the brash, abrasive figure Adam had expected. Later, when Vale faced his audience from the platform, he was equally personable, speaking fluently and easily while marshalling arguments with skill. The entire presentation, Adam was forced to admit, was impressive and, from the applause afterwards, a large part of the audience – which had paid for admission – felt the same way.

There was one shortcoming. To anyone with specialized knowledge, many of Emerson Vale's arguments were as porous as a leaky boat.

While attacking a highly technical industry, Vale betrayed his own lack of technical know-how and was frequently in error in describing mechanical functions. His engineering pronouncements were capable of several interpretations; Vale gave one, which suited his own viewpoint. At other moments he dealt in generalities. Even though trained in law, Emerson Vale ignored elementary rules of evidence. He offered assertion, hearsay, unsupported evidence as fact; occasionally the young auto critic – it seemed to Adam – distorted facts deliberately. He resurrected the past, listing faults in cars which manufacturers had long since admitted and rectified. He presented charges based on no more than his own mail from disgruntled car users. While excoriating the auto industry for bad design, poor workmanship, and lack of safety features, Vale acknowledged none of the industry's problems nor recent genuine attempts to improve its ways. He failed to see anything good in auto manufacturers and their people, only indifference, neglect, and villainy.

Emerson Vale had published a book, its title: *The American Car: Unsure in Any Need.* The book was skilfully written, with the attention-commanding quality which the author himself possessed, and it proved a bestseller which kept Vale in the spotlight of public attention for many months.

But subsequently, because there seemed little more for him to say, Emerson Vale began dropping out of sight. His name appeared in newspapers less frequently, then, for a while, not at all. This lack of attention goaded Vale to new activity. Craving publicity like a drug, he seemed willing to make any statement on any subject, in return for keeping his name before the public. Describing himself as 'a consumers' spokesman', he launched a fresh series of attacks on the auto industry, alleging design defects in specific cars, which the Press reported, though some were later proved untrue. He coaxed a US senator into quoting pilfered information on auto company costs which soon after was shown to be absurdly incomplete. The senator looked foolish. A habit of Vale's was to telephone reporters on big city dailies – collect, and sometimes in the night – with suggestions for news stories which just incidentally would include Emerson Vale's name, but which failed to stand up when checked out. As a result, the Press, which had relied on Vale for colourful copy, became more wary and eventually some reporters ceased trusting him at all.

Even when proved wrong, Emerson Vale – like his predecessor in the auto critic field, Ralph Nader – was never known to admit an error or to apologize, as General Motors had once apologized to Nader after the corporation's unwarranted intrusion into Nader's private life. Instead, Vale persisted with accusations and charges against all automobile manufacturers and, at times, could still draw nationwide attention, as he had succeeded in doing yesterday in Washington.

Adam folded the newspapers. A glance outside showed him that the freeway traffic had increased to Volume Six.

A moment later the intercom buzzed. 'The fourth estate just got here,' the Product Development vice-president said. 'You want to make a fifth?'

On the way upstairs, Adam reminded himself that he must telephone his wife sometime today. He knew that Erica had been unhappy lately, at moments more difficult to live with than during the first year or two of their marriage which began so promisingly. Adam sensed that part of the trouble was his own tiredness at the end of each day, which took its toll physically of them both. But he wished Erica would get out more and learn to be enterprising on her own. He had tried to encourage her in that, just as he had made sure she had all the money she needed. Fortunately there were no money problems for either of them, thanks to his own steady series of promotions, and there was a good chance of even bigger things to come, which any wife ought to be pleased about.

Adam was aware that Erica still resented the amount of time and energy which his job demanded, but she had been an automotive wife for five years now, and ought to have come to terms with that, just as other wives learned to.

Occasionally, he wondered if it had been a mistake to marry someone so much younger than himself, though intellectually they had never had the slightest problem. Erica had brains and intelligence far beyond her years, and – as Adam had seen – was seldom *en rapport* with younger men.

The more he thought about it, the more he realized they would have to find some resolution to their problems soon.

But at the fifteenth floor, as he entered high command territory, Adam thrust personal thoughts away.

In the office suite of the Product Development vice-president, Jake Earlham, Vice-President Public Relations, was performing introductions. Earlham, bald and stubby, had been a newspaperman many years ago and now looked like a donnish Mr Pickwick. He was always either smoking a pipe or gesturing with it. He waved the pipe now to acknowledge Adam Trenton's entry.

'I believe you know Monica from *Newsweek*.'

'We've met.' Adam acknowledged a petite brunette, already seated on a sofa. With shapely ankles crossed, smoke rising lazily from a cigarette, she smiled back coolly, making it plain that a representative of New York would not be taken in by Detroit charm, no matter how artfully applied.

Beside *Newsweek* on the sofa, was *The Wall Street Journal*, a florid, middle-aged reporter named Harris. Adam shook his hand, then that of AP, a taut young man whith a sheaf of copy paper, who acknowledged Adam curtly, plainly wanting the session to get on. Bob Irvin, bald and easygoing, of the *Detroit News*, was last.

'Hi, Bob,' Adam said. Irvin, whom Adam knew best, wrote a daily column about automotive affairs. He was well informed and respected in the industry, though no sycophant, being quick to jab a needle when he felt occasion warranted. In the past Irvin had given a good deal of sympathetic coverage to both Ralph Nader and Emerson Vale.

Elroy Braithwaite, the Product Development vice-president, dropped into a vacant armchair in the comfortable lounge area where they had assembled. He asked amiably, 'Who'll begin?'

Braithwaite, known among inmates as 'The Silver Fox' because of his mane of meticulously groomed grey hair, wore a tightly cut Edwardian mode suit and sported another personal trademark – enormous cuff-links. He exuded a style matching his surroundings. Like all the offices for vice-presidents and above, this one had been exclusively designed and furnished; it had African avodire wood panelling, brocaded drapes, and deep broadloom underfoot. Any man who attained this eminence in an auto company worked long and fiercely to get here. But once arrived, the working conditions held pleasant perquisities including an office like this, with adjoining dressing-room and sleeping quarters, plus – on the floor above – a personal dining room, as well as a steam bath and masseur, available at any time.

'Perhaps the lady should lead off.' It was Jake Earlham, perched on a window seat behind them.

'All right,' the *Newsweek* brunette said. 'What's the latest weak alibi for not launching a meaningful programme to develop a non-pollutant steam engine for cars?'

'We're fresh out of alibis,' the Silver Fox said. Braithwaite's expression had not changed; only his voice was a shade sharper. 'Besides, the job's already been done – by a guy named George Stephenson – and we don't think there's been a lot of significant progress since.'

The AP man had put on thin-rimmed glasses; he looked through them impatiently. 'OK, so we've got the comedy over. Can we have some straight questions and answers now?'

'I think we should,' Jake Earlham said. The PR head added apologetically, 'I should have remembered. The wire services have an early deadline for the East Coast afternoon papers.'

'Thank you,' AP said. He addressed Elroy Braithwaite. 'Mr Vale made a statement last night that the auto companies are guilty of conspiracy and some other things because they haven't made serious efforts to develop an alternative to the internal combustion engine. He also says that steam and electric engines are available now. Would you care to comment on that?'

The Silver Fox nodded. 'What Mr Vale said about the engines being available now is true. There are various kinds; most of them work, and we have several ourselves in our test centre. What Vale didn't say – either because it would spoil his argument or he doesn't know – is that there still isn't a hope in hell of making a steam or electric engine for cars, at low cost, low weight, and good convenience, in the foreseeable future.'

'How long's that?'

'Through the 1970s. By the 1980s there'll be other new developments, though the internal combustion engine – an almost totally non-polluting one – still *may* dominate.'

The Wall Street Journal interjected, 'But there've been a lot of news stories about all kinds of engines here and now . . .'

'You're damn right,' Elroy Braithwaite said, 'and most of 'em should be in the comic section. If you'll excuse my saying so, newspaper writers are about the most gullible people afloat. Maybe they want to be; I guess, that way, the stories they write are more interesting.

But let some inventor – never mind if he's a genius or a kook – come up with a one-only job, and turn the Press loose on him. What happens? Next day all the news stories say this "may" be the big break-through, this "may" be the way the future's going. Repeat that a few times so the public reads it often, and everybody thinks it must be true, just the way newspaper people, I suppose, believe their own copy if they write enough of it. It's that kind of hoopla that's made a good many in this country convinced they'll have a steam or electric car, or maybe a hybrid, soon in their own garages.'

The Silver Fox smiled at his public relations colleague, who had shifted uneasily and was fidgeting with his pipe. 'Relax Jake. I'm not taking off at the Press. Just trying to fix a perspective.'

Jake Earlham said dryly, 'I'm glad you told me. For a minute I was wondering.'

'Aren't you losing sight of some facts, Mr Braithwaite?' AP persisted. 'There are reputable people who still believe in steam power. Some big outfits other than auto companies are working on it. The California government is putting money on the line to get a fleet of steam cars on the road. And there are legislative proposals out there to ban internal combustion engines in five years from now.'

The Product Development vice-president shook his head decisively, his silver mane bobbing. 'In my book, the only reputable guy who believed in a steam car was Bill Lear. Then he gave up publicly, calling the idea "utterly ridiculous".'

'But he's since changed his mind,' AP said.

'Sure, sure. And carries around a hatbox, saying his new steam engine is inside. Well, *we* know what's inside; it's the engine's innermost core, which is like taking a spark plug and saying "there's an engine from our present cars". What's seldom mentioned, by Mr Lear and others, is that to be added are combusters, boiler, condenser, recuperation fans . . . a long list of heavy, expensive, bulky hardware, with dubious efficiency.'

Jake Earlham prompted, 'The California government's steam cars . . .'

The Silver Fox nodded. 'OK, California. Sure the state's spending lots of money; what government doesn't? If you and half a million others were willing to pay a thousand dollars more for *your* cars, maybe – just maybe – we could build a steam engine, with all its problems and disadvantages. But most of our customers – and our competitors' customers, which we have to think about too – don't have that kind of moss to sling around.'

'You're still ducking electric cars,' *The Wall Street Journal* pointed out.

Braithwaite nodded to Adam. 'You take that one.'

'There are electric cars right now,' Adam told the reporters. 'You've seen golf carts, and it's conceivable that a two-passenger vehicle can be developed soon for shopping or similar use within a small local area. At the moment, though, it would be expensive and not much more than a curiosity. We've also built, ourselves, experimental trucks and cars which are electric powered. The trouble is, as soon as we give them any useful range we have to fill most of the inside space with heavy batteries, which doesn't make a lot of sense.'

'The small, lightweight battery – zinc-air or fuel cells,' AP questioned. 'When is it coming?'

'You forgot sodium sulphur,' Adam said. 'That's another that's been talked up. Unfortunately, there's little more than talk so far.'

Elroy Braithwaite put in, 'Eventually we believe there *will* be a break-through in batteries, with a lot of energy stored in small packages. What's more, there's a big potential use for electric vehicles in downtown traffic. But based on everything we know, we can't see it happening until the 1980s.'

'And if you're thinking about air pollution in conjunction with electric cars,' Adam added, 'there's one factor which a lot of people overlook. Whatever kind of batteries you had, they'd need recharging. So with hundreds of thousands of cars plugged into power sources, there'd be a requirement for many more generating stations, each spewing out its own air pollution. Since electric power plants are usually built in the suburbs, what could happen is that you'd end up taking the smog from the cities and transferring it out there.'

'Isn't all that still a pretty weak alibi?' The cool *Newsweek* brunette uncrossed her legs, then twitched her skirt downwards, to no effect, as she undoubtedly knew; it continued to ride high on shapely thighs. One by one, the men dropped their eyes to where the thighs and skirt joined.

She elaborated, 'I mean an alibi for not having a crash programme to make a good, cheap engine – steam or electric, or both. That's how we got to the moon, isn't it?' She added pertly. 'If you'll remember, that was my first question.'

'I remember,' Elroy Braithwaite said. Unlike the other men, he did not remove his gaze from the junction of skirt and thighs, but held it there deliberately. There were several seconds of silence in which most women would have fidgeted or been intimidated. The brunette, self-assured, entirely in control, made it clear that she was not. Still not looking up, the Silver Fox said slowly, 'What was the question again, Monica?'

'I think you know.' Only then did Braithwaite, outmanoeuvred, lift his head.

He sighed. 'Oh, yes – the moon. You know, there are days I wish we'd never got there. It's produced a new cliché. Nowadays, the moment there's any kind of engineering hangup, anywhere, you can count on somebody saying: we got to the moon, didn't we? Why can't we solve this?'

'If she hadn't asked,' *The Wall Street Journal* said, 'I would. So why can't we?'

'I'll tell you,' the vice-president snapped. 'Quite apart from the space gang having unlimited public money – which we haven't – they had an objective. Get to the moon. You people are asking us, on the vague basis of things you've read or heard, to give development of a steam or electric engine for cars that kind of all-or-nothing, billions-in-the-kitty priority. Well, it so happens that some of the best engineering brains in this business think it isn't a practical objective, or even a worthwhile one. We have better ideas and other objectives.'

Braithwaite passed a hand over his silver mane, then nodded to Adam. He gave the impression of having had enough.

'What we believe,' Adam said, 'is that clean air – at least air not polluted by motor vehicles – can be achieved best, fastest, and most cheaply through refinements of the present gasoline internal combustion engine, along with more improvements in emission control and fuels. That includes the Wankel engine which is also an internal combustion type.' He had deliberately kept his voice low key. Now he added, 'Maybe that's not as spectacular as the idea of steam or electric power but there's a lot of sound science behind it.'

Bob Irvin of the *Detroit News* spoke for the first time. 'Quite apart from electric and steam engines, you'd admit, wouldn't you, that before Nader, Emerson Vale, and their kind, the industry wasn't nearly as concerned as it is now about controlling air pollution?'

The question was asked with apparent casualness, Irvin looking blandly through his glasses, but Adam knew it was loaded with explosive. He hesitated only momentarily, then answered, 'Yes, I would.'

The three other reporters looked at him, surprised.

'As I understand it,' Irvin said, still with the same casual manner, 'we're here because of Emerson Vale, or in other words, because of an auto critic. Right?'

Jake Earlham intervened from his window seat. 'We're here because your editors – and in your case, Bob, you personally – asked if we would respond to some questions today, and we agreed to. It was our understanding that some of the questions would relate to statements which Mr Vale had made, but *we* did not schedule a Press conference specifically because of Vale.'

Bob Irvin grinned. 'A bit hair-splitty, aren't you, Jake?'

The Vice-President Public Relations shrugged. 'I guess.'

From Jake Earlham's doubtful expression now and earlier, Adam suspected he was wondering if the informal Press meeting had been such a good idea.

'In that case,' Irvin said, 'I guess this question wouldn't be out of order, Adam.' The columnist seemed to ruminate, shambling verbally as he spoke, but those who knew him were aware how deceptive this appearance was. 'In your opinion have the auto critics – let's take Nader and safety – fulfilled a useful function?'

The question was simple, but framed so it could not be ducked. Adam felt like protesting to Irvin: *Why pick me?* Then he remembered Elroy Braithwaite's instructions earlier: '*We'll call things the way we see them.*'

Adam said quietly, 'Yes, they have fulfilled a function. In terms of safety, Nader booted this industry, screaming, into the second half of the twentieth century.'

All four reporters wrote that down.

While they did, Adam's thoughts ranged swiftly over what he had said and what came next. Within the auto industry, he was well aware, plenty of others would agree with him. A strong contingent of younger executives and a surprising sprinkling of topmost echelons conceded that basically – despite excesses and inaccuracies – the arguments of Vale and Nader over the past few years made sense. The industry *had* relegated safety to a minor role in car design, it *had* focused attention on sales to the exclusion of most else, it *had* resisted change until forced to change through government regulation or the threat of it. It seemed, looking back, as if auto makers had become drunken on their own immensity and power, and had behaved like Goliaths, until in the end they were humbled by a David – Ralph Nader and, later, Emerson Vale.

The David-Goliath equation, Adam thought, was apt. Nader particularly – alone, unaided, and with remarkable moral courage – took on the entire US auto industry with its unlimited resources and strong Washington lobby, and, where others had failed, succeeded in having safety standards raised and new consumer-oriented legislation passed into law. The fact that Nader was a polemicist who, like all polemicists, took rigid poses, was often excessive, ruthless, and sometimes inaccurate, did not lessen his achievement. Only a bigot would deny that he had performed a valuable public service. Equally to the point: to achieve such a service, against such odds, a Nader-type was necessary.

The Wall Street Journal observed, 'So far as I know, Mr Trenton, no auto executive has made that admission publicly before.'

'If no-one has,' Adam said, 'maybe it's time someone did.'

Was it imagination, or had Jake Earlham – apparently busy with his pipe – gone pale?

Adam detected a frown on the face of the Silver Fox, but what the hell; if necessary he would argue with Elroy later. Adam had never been a 'yes man'. Few who rose high in the auto industry were, and those who held back their honest opinions, fearing disapproval from seniors, or because of insecurity about their jobs, seldom made it higher than middle management, at best. Adam had not held back, believing that directness and honesty were useful contributions he could make to his employers. The important thing, he had learned, was to stay an individual. A misguided notion which outsiders had of auto executives was that they conformed to a standard pattern, as if stamped out by cookie cutters. No concept could be more wrong. True, such men had certain traits in common – ambition, drive, a sense of organization, a capacity for work. But, apart from that, they were highly individual, with a better-than-average sprinkling of eccentrics, geniuses, and mavericks.

Anyway, it had been said; nothing would undo it now. But there were postscripts.

'If you're going to quote that' – Adam surveyed the quartet of reporters – 'some other things should be said as well.'

'Which are?' It was the *Newsweek* girl's query. She seemed less hostile than before, had stubbed out her cigarette and was making notes. Adam stole a glance: her skirt was as high as ever, her thighs and legs increasingly attractive in filmy grey nylon. He felt his interest sharpen, then tore his thoughts away.

'First,' Adam said, 'the critics have done their job. The industry is working harder on safety than it ever did; what's more, the pressure's staying on. Also, we're consumer oriented. For a while, we weren't. Looking back, it seems as if we got careless and indifferent to consumers without realizing it. Right now, though, we're neither, which is why the Emerson Vales have become shrill and sometimes silly. If you accept their view, nothing an automobile maker does is ever right. Maybe that's why Vale and his kind haven't recognized yet – which is my second point – that the auto industry is in a whole new era.'

AP queried, 'If that's true, wouldn't you say the auto critics forced you there?'

Adam controlled his irritation. Sometimes auto criticism became a fetish, an unreasoning cult, and not just with professionals like Vale. 'They helped,' he admitted, 'by establishing directions and goals, particularly about safety and pollution. But they had nothing to do with the technological revolution, which was coming anyway. It's that that's going to make the next ten years more exciting for everybody in this business than the entire half century just gone.'

'Just how?' AP said, glancing at his watch.

'Someone mentioned break-throughs,' Adam answered. 'The most important ones, which we can see coming, are in materials which will let us design a whole new breed of vehicles by the mid- or late '70s. Take metals. Instead of solid steel which we're using now, honeycomb steel is coming; it'll be strong, rigid, yet incredibly lighter – meaning fuel economy; also it'll absorb an impact better than conventional steel – a safety plus. Then there are new metal alloys for engines and components. We anticipate one which will allow temperature changes from a hundred degrees to more than two thousand degrees Fahrenheit, in seconds, with minor expansion only. Using that, we can incinerate the remainder of unburned fuel causing air pollution. Another metal being worked on is one with a retention technique to "remember" its original shape. If you crumple a fender or a door, you'll apply heat or pressure and the metal will spring back the way it was before.

Another alloy we expect will allow cheap production of reliable, high quality wheels for gas turbine engines.'

Elroy Braithwaite added, 'That last is one to watch. If the internal combustion engine goes eventually, the gas turbine's most likely to move in. There are plenty of problems with a turbine for cars – it's efficient only at high power output, and you need a costly heat exchanger if you aim not to burn pedestrians. But they're *solvable* problems, and being worked on.'

'OK,' *The Wall Street Journal* said. 'So that's metals. What else is new?'

'Something significant, and coming soon for every car, is an on-board computer.' Adam glanced at AP. 'It will be small, about the size of a glove compartment.'

'A computer to do what?'

'Just about anything; you name it. It will monitor engine components – plugs, fuel injection, all the others. It will control emissions and warn if the engine is polluting. And in other ways it will be revolutionary.'

'Name some,' *Newsweek* said.

'Part of the time the computer will think for drivers and correct mistakes, often before they realize they're made. One thing it will mastermind is sensory braking – brakes applied individually on every wheel so a driver can never lose control by skidding. A radar auxiliary will warn if a car ahead is slowing or you're following too close. In an emergency the computer could decelerate and apply brakes automatically, and because a computer's reactions are faster than human there should be a lot less rear-end collisions. There'll be the means to lock on to automatic radar control lanes on freeways, which are on the way, with space satellite control of traffic flow not far behind.'

Adam caught an approving glance from Jake Earlham and knew why. He had succeeded in turning the talk from defensive to positive, a tactic which the public relations department was constantly urging on company spokesmen.

'One effect of all the changes,' Adam went on, 'is that interiors of cars, especially from a driver's viewpoint, will look startlingly different within the next few years. The in-car computer will modify most of our present instruments. For example, the fuel gauge as we know it is on the way out; in its place will be an indicator showing how many miles of driving your fuel is good for at present speed. On a TV-type screen in front of the driver, route information and highway warning signs will appear, triggered by magnetic sensors in the road. Having to look out for highway signs is already old-fashioned and dangerous; often a driver misses them; when they're inside the car, he won't. Then if you travel a route which is new, you'll slip in a cassette, the way you do a tape cartridge for entertainment now. According to where you are, and keyed in a similar way to the road signs, you'll receive spoken directions and visual signals on the screen. And almost at once the ordinary car radio will have a transmitter, as well as a receiver, operating on citizens' band. It's to be a nationwide system, so that a driver can call for aid – of any kind – whenever he needs it.'

AP was on his feet, turning to the PR vice-president. 'If I can use a phone . . .'

Jack Earlham slipped from his window seat and went around to the door. He motioned with his pipe for AP to follow him. 'I'll find you somewhere private.'

The others were getting up.

Bob Irvin of the *News* waited until the wire service reporter had left, then asked, 'About that on-board computer. Are you putting it in the Orion?'

God damn that Irvin! Adam knew that he was boxed. The answer was 'yes', but it was secret. On the other hand, if he replied 'no', eventually the journalists would discover he had lied.

Adam protested, 'You know I can't talk about the Orion, Bob.'

The columnist grinned. The absence of an outright denial had told him all he needed.

'Well,' the *Newsweek* brunette said; now that she was standing, she appeared taller and more lissom than when seated. 'You trickily steered the whole thing away from what we came here to talk about.'

'Not me.' Adam met her eyes directly; they were ice blue, he noted, and derisively appraising. He found himself wishing they had met in a different way and less as adversaries. He smiled, 'I'm just a simple auto worker who tries to see both sides.'

'Really!' The eyes remained fixed, still mirroring derision. 'Then how about an honest answer to this: is the outlook inside the auto industry really changing?' *Newsweek* glanced at her notebook. 'Are the big auto makers truly responding to the times – accepting new ideas about community responsibility, developing a social conscience, being realistic about changing values, including values about cars? Do you genuinely believe that consumerism is here to stay? Is there really a new era, the way you claim? Or is it all a front-office dress-up, staged by public relations flacks, while what you really hope is that the attention you're getting now will go away, and everything will slip back the way it was before, when you did pretty much what you liked? Are you people really tuned in to what's happening about environment, safety, and all those other things, or are you kidding yourselves and us? *Quo vadis?* – do you remember your Latin, Mr Trenton?'

'Yes,' Adam said, 'I remember.' *Quo vadis? Whither goest thou?* . . . The age-old question of mankind, echoing down through history, asked of civilizations, nations, individuals, groups and, now, an industry.

Elroy Braithwaite inquired, 'Say, Monica, is that a question or a speech?'

'It's a *mélange* question.' The *Newsweek* girl gave the Silver Fox an unwarmed smile. 'If it's too complicated for you, I could break it into simple segments, using shorter words.'

The public relations chief had just returned after escorting AP. 'Jake,' the Product Development Vice-President told his colleague, 'somehow these Press meetings aren't what they used to be.'

'If you mean we're more aggressive, not deferential any more,' *The Wall Street Journal* said, 'it's because reporters are being trained that way, and our editors tell us to bore in hard. Like everything else, I guess there's a new look in journalism.' He added thoughtfully, 'Sometimes it makes me uncomfortable, too.'

'Well, it doesn't me,' *Newsweek* said, 'and I still have a question hanging.' She turned to Adam. 'I asked it of you.'

Adam hesitated. *Quo vadis?* In other forms, he sometimes put the same interrogation to himself. But in answering now, how far should open honesty extend?

Elroy Braithwaite relieved him of decision.

'If Adam doesn't mind,' the Silver Fox interposed, 'I believe I'll answer that. Without accepting all your premises, Monica, this company as it represents our industry has always accepted community responsibility; what's more, it does have a social conscience and has demonstrated this for many years. As to consumerism, we've always believed in it; long before the word itself was coined by those who . . .'

The rounded phrases rolled eloquently on. Listening, Adam was relieved he hadn't answered. Despite his own dedication to his work, he would have been compelled, in honesty, to admit some doubts.

He was relieved, though, that the session was almost done. He itched to get back to his own bailiwick where the Orion – like a loving but demanding mistress – summoned him.

5

In the corporate Design-Styling Center – a mile or so from the staff building where the Press session was now concluding – the odour of modelling clay was, as usual, all-pervading. Regulars who worked in Design-Styling claimed that after a while they ceased to notice the smell – a mild but insistent mix of sulphur and glycerine, its source the dozens of security-guarded studios ringing the Design-Styling Center's circular inner core. Within the studios, sculptured models of potential new automobiles were taking shape.

Visitors, though, wrinkled their noses in distaste when the smell first hit them. Not that many visitors got close to the source. The majority penetrated only as far as the outer reception lobby, or to one of a half-dozen offices behind it, and even here they were checked in and out by security guards, never left alone, and issued colour-coded badges, defining – and usually limiting severely – the areas where they could be escorted.

On occasions, national security and nuclear secrets had been guarded less carefully than design details of future model cars.

Even staff designers were not allowed unhampered movement. Those least senior were restricted to one or two studios, their freedom increasing only after years of service. The precaution made sense. Designers were sometimes wooed by other auto companies and, since each studio held secrets of its own, the fewer an individual entered, the less knowledge he could take with him if he left. Generally, what a designer was told about activity on new model cars was based on the military principle of 'need to know'. However, as designers grew older in the company's service, and also more 'locked in' financially through stock options and pension plans, security was relaxed and a distinctive badge – worn like a combat medal – allowed an individual past a majority of doors and guards. Even then, the system didn't always work because occasionally a top-flight, senior designer would move to a competitive company with a financial arrangement so magnanimous as to outweigh everything else. Then, when he went, years of advance knowledge went with him. Some designers in the auto industry had worked, in their time, for all major auto companies, though Ford and General Motors had an unwritten agreement that neither approached each other's designers – at least, directly – with job offers. Chrysler was less inhibited.

Only a few individuals – design directors and heads of studios – were allowed everywhere within the Design-Styling Center. One of these was Brett DeLosanto. This morning he was strolling unhurriedly through a pleasant, glass-enclosed courtyard which led to Studio X. This was a Studio which, at the moment, bore somewhat the same relationship to others in the building as the Sistine Chapel to St Peter's nave.

A security guard put down his newspaper as Brett approached.

'Good morning, Mr DeLosanto.' The man looked the young designer up and down, then whistled softly. 'I shoulda brought dark glasses.'

Brett DeLosanto laughed. A flamboyant figure at any time with his long – though carefully styled – hair, deep descending sideburns and precisely trimmed Vandyke beard, he had added to the effect today by wearing a pink shirt and mauve tie, with slacks and shoes matching the tie, the ensemble topped by a white cashmere jacket.

'You like the outfit, eh?'

The guard considered. He was a grizzled ex-Army noncom, more than twice Brett's age. 'Well, sir, you could say it was different.'

'The only difference between you and me, Al, is that I design my uniforms.' Brett nodded towards the studio door. 'Much going on today?'

'There's the usual people in, Mr DeLosanto. As to what goes on, they told me when I came here: keep my back to the door, eyes to the front.'

'But you know the Orion's in there. You must have seen it.'

'Yes, sir, I've seen it. When the brass came in for the big approval day, they moved it to the showroom.'

'What do you think?'

The guard smiled. 'I'll tell you what I think, Mr DeLosanto, I think you and the Orion are a lot alike.'

As Brett entered the studio, and the outer door clicked solidly behind him, he reflected: if true, it would scarcely be surprising.

A sizeable segment of his life and creative talent had gone into the Orion. There were times, in moments of self-appraisal, when he wondered if it had been too much. On more hundreds of occasions than he cared to think about, he had passed through this same studio door, during frenetic days and long, exhausting nights – times of agony and ecstasy – while the Orion progressed from embryo idea to finished car.

He had been involved from the beginning.

Even before studio work began, he and others from Design had been apprised of studies – market research, population growth, economics, social changes, age groups, needs, fashion trends. A cost target was set. Then came the early concept of a completely new car. During months that followed, design criteria were hammered out at meeting after meeting of product planners, designers, engineers. After that, and working together, engineers devised a power package while designers – of whom Brett was one – doodled, then became specific, so that lines and contours of the car took shape. And while it happened, hopes advanced, receded; plans went right, went wrong, then right again; doubts arose, were quelled, arose once more. Within the company, hundreds were involved, led by a top half-dozen.

Endless design changes occurred, some prompted by logic, others through intuition only. Later still, testing began. Eventually – too soon, it always seemed to Brett – management approval for production came and, after that, Manufacturing moved in. Now, with production planning well advanced, in less than a year, the Orion would undergo the most critical test of all: public acceptance or rejection. And through all the time so far, while no individual could ever be responsible for an entire car, Brett DeLosanto, more than anyone else on the design team, had implanted in the Orion his own ideas, artistic flair, and effort.

Brett, with Adam Trenton.

It was because of Adam Trenton that Brett was here this morning – far earlier than his usual time of starting work. The two had planned to go together to the company proving ground, but a message from Adam, which had just come in, announced that he would be delayed. Brett, less disciplined than Adam in his working habits, and preferring to sleep late, was annoyed at having got up needlessly, then decided on a short solitude with the Orion, anyway. Now, opening an inner door, he entered the main studio.

In several brightly lighted work areas, design development was in progress on clay models of Orion derivatives – a sports version to appear three years from now, a station wagon, and on other variations of the original Orion design which might, or might not, be used in future years.

The original Orion – the car which would have its public introduction only a year from now – was at the far end of the studio on soft grey carpeting under spotlights. The model was finished in *bleu céleste*. Brett walked towards it, a sense of excitement gripping him, which was why he had come here, knowing that it would.

The car was small, compact, lean, slim-lined. It had what sales planners were already calling a 'tucked under, tubular look', clearly influenced by missile design, giving a functional appearance, yet with élan and style. Several body features were revolutionary. For the first time in any car, above the belt line there was all-around vision. Auto makers had talked bubble tops for decades, and experimented with them timidly, but now the Orion had achieved the same effect, yet without loss of structural strength. Within the clear glass top, vertical members of thin, high tensile steel – A and C pillars to designers – had been moulded almost invisibly, crossing to join unobtrusively overhead. The result was a 'greenhouse' (another design idiom for the upper body of an automobile) far stronger than conventional cars, a reality which a tough series of crashes and rollovers had already confirmed. The tumblehome – angle at which the body top sloped inwards from the vertical – was gentle, allowing spacious headroom inside. The same spaciousness, surprising in so small a car, extended below the belt line where design was rakish and advanced, yet not bizarre, so that the Orion, from every angle, merged into any eye-pleasing whole.

Beneath the exterior, Brett knew, engineering innovations would match the outward look. A notable one was electronic fuel injection, replacing a conventional carburettor – the latter an anachronistic hangover from primitive engines and overdue for its demise. Controlling the fuel injection system was one of the many functions of the Orion's on-board, shoe-box-size computer.

The model in Studio X, however, contained nothing mechanical. It was a fibreglass shell only, made from the cast of an original clay sculpture, though even with close scrutiny it was hard to realize that the car under the spotlights was not real. The model had been left here for comparison with other models to come later, as well as for senior company officers to visit, review, worry over and renew their faith. Such faith was important. A gigantic amount of stockholders' money, plus the careers and reputations of all involved, from the chairman of the board downwards, was riding on the Orion's wheels. Already the board of directors had sanctioned expenditures of a hundred million dollars for development and production, with more millions likely to be budgeted before introduction time.

Brett was reminded that he had once heard Detroit described as 'more of a gambling centre than Las Vegas, with higher stakes'. The earthy thought drew his mind to practicalities, of which one was the fact that he had not yet had breakfast.

In the design directors' dining-room, several others were already breakfasting when Brett DeLosanto came in. Characteristically, instead of ordering from a waitress, Brett dropped into the kitchen where he joshed with the cooks, who knew him well, then coerced them into preparing Eggs Benedict, which was never on the standard menu. Emerging, he joined his colleagues at the dining-room's large, round table.

Two visitors were at the table – students from Los Angeles Art Center College of Design, from where, not quite five years ago, Brett DeLosanto himself had graduated. One of the students was a pensive youth, now tracing curves on the tablecloth with a fingernail, the other a bright-eyed, nineteen-year-old girl.

Glancing around to make sure he would be listened to, Brett resumed a conversation with the students which had begun yesterday.

'If you come to work here,' he advised them, 'you should install brain filters to keep out the antediluvian ideas the old-timers will throw at you.'

'Brett's idea of an old-timer,' a designer in his early thirties said from across the table, 'is any one old enough to vote when Nixon was elected.'

'The elderly party who just spoke,' Brett informed the students, 'is our Mr Robertson. He designs fine family sedans which would be even better with shafts and a horse in front. By the way, he endorses his paycheck with a quill, and is hanging on for pension.'

'A thing we love about young DeLosanto,' a greying designer put in, 'is his respect for experience and age.' The designer Dave Heberstein, who was studio head for Colour and Interiors, surveyed Brett's carefully groomed but dazzling appearance. 'By the way, where *is* the masquerade ball tonight?'

'If you studied my exteriors more carefully,' Brett retorted, 'then used them for your interiors, you'd start customer stampedes.'

Someone else asked, 'To our competitors?'

'Only if I went to work for them.'

Brett grinned. He had maintained a brash repartee with the majority of others in the design studios since coming to work there as a novice, and most seemed to enjoy it still. Nor had it affected Brett's rise as an automobile designer, which had been phenomenal. Now, at age twenty-six, he ranked equal with all but a few senior studio heads.

A few years ago it would have been inconceivable that anyone looking like Brett DeLosanto could have got past the main gate security guards, let alone be permitted to work in the stratified atmosphere of a corporate design studio. But concepts had changed. Nowadays, management realized that avant-garde cars were more likely to be created by 'with it' designers who were imaginative and experimental about fashion, including their own appearance. Similarly, while stylist-designers were expected to work hard and produce, seniors like Brett were allowed, within reason, to decide their own working hours. Often Brett DeLosanto came in late, idled or sometimes disappeared entirely during the day, then worked through lonely hours of the night. Because his record was exceptionally good, and he attended staff meetings when told to specifically, nothing was ever said.

He addressed the students again. 'One of the things the ancient ones will tell you, including some around this table eating sunny side ups . . . Ah, many thanks!' Brett paused while a waitress placed his Eggs Benedict in front of him, then resumed. 'A thing they'll argue is that major changes in car design don't happen any more. From now on, they say, we'll have only transitions and ordered development. Well, that's what the gas works thought just before Edison invented the electric light. I tell you there are Disneyesque design changes coming. One reason: we'll be getting fantastic new materials to work with soon, and that's an area where a lot of people aren't looking because there aren't any flashing lights.'

'But you're looking, Brett, aren't you?' someone said. 'You're looking for the rest of us.'

'That's right.' Brett DeLosanto cut himself a substantial portion of Eggs Benedict and speared it with his fork. 'You fellows can relax. I'll help you keep your jobs.' He ate with zest.

The bright-eyed girl student said, 'Isn't it true that most new designs from here on will be largely functional?'

Speaking through a full mouth, Brett answered, 'They can be functional *and* fantastic.'

'You'll be functional like a balloon tyre if you eat a lot of that.' Heberstein, the Colour and Interiors chief, eyed Brett's rich dish with distaste, then told the students, 'Almost all good design is functional. It always has been. The exceptions are pure art forms which have no purpose other than to be beautiful. It's when design isn't functional that it becomes either bad design or bordering on it. The Victorians made their designs ponderously unfunctional, which is why so many were appalling. Mind you, we still do the same thing sometimes in this business when we put on enormous tail fins or excess chrome or protruding grillwork. Fortunately we're learning to do it less.'

The pensive male student stopped making patterns on the tablecloth. 'The Volkswagen is functional – wholly so. But you wouldn't call it beautiful.'

Brett DeLosanto waved his fork and swallowed hastily, before anyone else could speak. 'That, my friend, is where you and the rest of the world's public are gullibly misled. The Volkswagen is a fraud, a gigantic hoax.'

'It's a good car,' the girl student said. 'I have one.'

'Of course it's a good car.' Brett ate some more of his breakfast while the two young, would-be designers watched him curiously. 'When the landmark autos of this century are added up, the Volkswagen will be there along with the Pierce-Arrow, the Model T Ford, 1929 Chevrolet 6, Packard before the 1940s, Rolls-Royce until the '60s, Lincoln, Chrysler Airflow, Cadillacs of the '30s, the Mustang, Pontiac GTO, two-passenger Thunderbirds, and some others. But the Volkswagen is still a fraud because a sales campaign has convinced people it's an ugly car, which it isn't, or it wouldn't have lasted half as long as it has. What the Volkswagen really has is form, balance, symmetrical sense and a touch of genius; if it were a sculpture in bronze instead of a car it could be on a pedestal alongside a Henry Moore. But because the public's been beaten on the head with statements that it's ugly, they've swallowed the hook and so have you. But then, all car owners like to deceive themselves.'

Somebody said, 'Here's where I came in.'

Chairs were eased back. Most of the others began drifting out to their separate studios. The Colour and Interiors chief stopped beside the chairs of the two students. 'If you filter Junior's output – the way he advised to begin with – you might just find a pearl or two.'

'By the time I'm through' – Brett checked a spray of eggs and coffee with a napkin – 'they'll have enough to make pearl jam.'

'Too bad I can't stay!' Heberstein nodded amiably from the doorway. 'Drop in later, Brett, will you? We've a fabric report I think you'll want to know about.'

'Is it always like that?' The youth who had resumed drawing finger parabolas on the tablecloth, looked curiously at Brett.

'In here it is, usually. But don't let the kidding fool you. Under it, a lot of good ideas get going.'

It was true. Auto company managements encouraged designers, as well as others in creative jobs, to take meals together in private dining-rooms; the higher an individual's rank, the more pleasant and exclusive such privileges became. But, at whatever level, the talk at table inevitably turned to work. Then, keen minds sparked one another and brilliant ideas occasionally had genesis over entrée or dessert. Senior staff dining-rooms operated at a loss, but managements made up deficits cheerfully, regarding them as investments with a good yield.

'Why did you say car owners deceived themselves?' the girl asked.

'We know they do. It's a slice of human nature you learn to live with.' Brett eased from the table and tilted back his chair. 'Most Joe Citizens out there in communityland love snappy-looking cars. But they also like to think of themselves as rational, so what happens? They kid themselves. A lot of those same Joe C.s won't admit, even in their minds, their real motivations when they buy their next torpedo.'

'How can you be sure?'

'Simple. If Joe wants just reliable transportation – as a good many of his kind say they do – all he needs is the cheapest, simplest, stripped economy job in the Chev, Ford, or Plymouth line. Most, though, want more than that – a better car because, like a sexy-looking babe on the arm, or a fancy home, it gives a good warm feeling in the gut. Nothing wrong with that! But Joe and his friends seem to think there is, which is *why they fool themselves* . . .'

'So consumer research . . .'

'Is for the birds! OK, we send out some dame with a clipboard who asks a guy coming down the street what he wants in his next car. Right away he thinks he'll impress her, so he lists all the square stuff like reliability, gas mileage, safety, trade-in value. If it's a written quiz, unsigned, he does it so he impresses himself. Down at the bottom, both times, he may put appearance, if he mentions it at all. Yet when it comes to buy-time and the same guy's in a showroom, whether he admits it or not, appearance will be right there on top.'

Brett stood, and stretched. 'You'll find some who'll tell you that the public's love affair with cars is over. Nuts! We'll all be around for a while, kids, because old Joe C., with his hangups, is still a designer's friend.'

He glanced at his watch; there was another half-hour until he would meet Adam Trenton en route to the proving ground, which left time to stop at Colour and Interiors.

On their way out of the dining-room, Brett asked the students, 'What do you make of it all?'

The curiosity was genuine. What the two students were doing now, Brett had done himself not many years ago. Auto companies regularly invited design school students in, treating them like VIPs, while the students saw for themselves the kind of aura they might work in later. The auto makers, too, courted students at their schools. Teams from the Big Three visited design colleges several times a year, openly competing for the most promising soon-to-be graduates, and the same was true of other industry areas – engineering, science, finance, merchandising, law – so that auto companies with their lavish pay scales and benefits, including planned promotion, skimmed off a high proportion of the finer talents. Some – including thoughtful people in the industry itself – argued that the process was unjust, that auto makers corralled too much of the world's best brain-power, to the detriment of civilization generally, which needed more thinkers to solve urgent, complex human problems. Just the same, no other agency or industry succeeded in recruiting a comparable, constant flow of top-flight achievers. Brett DeLosanto had been one.

'It's exciting,' the bright-eyed girl said, answering Brett's question. 'Like being in on creation, the real thing. A bit scary, of course. All those other people to compete with, and you know how good they must be. But if you make it here, you've really made it big.'

She had the attitude it took, Brett thought. All she needed was the talent, plus some extra push to overcome the industry's prejudice against women who wanted to be more than secretaries.

He asked the youth, 'How about you?'

The pensive young man shook his head uncertainly. He was frowning. 'I'm not sure. OK, everything's big time, there's plenty of bread thrown around, a lot of effort, and I guess it's exciting all right' – he nodded towards the girl – 'just the way she said. I keep wondering, though: is it all worth it? Maybe I'm crazy, and I know it's late; I mean, having done the design course and all, or most of it. But you can't help asking: for an artist, does it matter? Is it what you want to give blood to, a lifetime?'

'You have to love cars to work here,' Brett said. 'You have to care about them so much that they're the most important thing there is. You breathe, eat, sleep cars, sometimes remember them when you're making love. You wake up in the night, it's cars you think about – those you're designing, others you'd like to. It's like a religion.' He added curtly, 'If you don't feel that way, you don't belong here.'

'I do love cars,' the youth said. 'I always have, as long as I remember, in just the way you said. It's only lately . . .' He left the sentence hanging, as if unwilling to voice heresy a second time.

Brett made no other comment. Opinions, appraisals of that kind were individual, and decisions because of them, personal. No-one else could help because in the end it all depended on your own ideas, values, and sometimes conscience. Besides, there was another factor which Brett had no intention of discussing with these two: lately he had experienced some of the same questioning and doubts himself.

The chief of Colour and Interiors had a skeleton immediately inside his office, used for anatomy studies in relation to auto seating. The skeleton hung slightly off the ground, suspended by a chain attached to a plate in the skull. Brett DeLosanto shook hands with it as he came in. 'Good morning, Ralph.'

Dave Heberstein came from behind his desk and nodded towards the main studio. 'Let's go through.' He patted the skeleton affectionately in passing. 'A loyal and useful staff member who never criticizes, never asks for a raise.'

The Colour Center, which they entered, was a vast, domed chamber, circular and constructed principally of glass, allowing daylight to flood in. The overhead dome gave a cathedral effect, so that several enclosed booths – for light-controlled viewing of colour samples and fabrics – appeared like chapels. Deep carpeting underfoot deadened sound. Throughout the room were display boards, soft and hard trim samples, and a colour library comprising every colour in the spectrum as well as thousands of sub-colours.

Heberstein stopped at a display table. He told Brett DeLosanto, 'Here's what I wanted you to see.'

Under glass, a half-dozen upholstery samples had been arranged, each identified by mill and purchase number. Other similar samples were loose on the table top. Though variously coloured, they bore the generic name 'Metallic Willow'. Dave Heberstein picked one up. 'Remember these?'

'Sure.' Brett nodded. 'I liked them; still do.'

'I did, too. In fact, I recommended them for use.' Heberstein fingered the sample which was pleasantly soft to the touch. It had – as had all the others – an attractive patterned silver fleck. 'It's crimped yarn with a metallic thread.'

Both men were aware that the fabric had been introduced as an extra cost option with the company's top line models this year. It had proved popular and soon, in differing colours, would be available for the Orion. Brett asked, 'So what's the fuss?'

'Letters,' Heberstein said. 'Customers' letters which started coming in a couple of weeks ago.' He took a key ring from his pocket and opened a drawer in the display table. Inside was a file containing about two dozen photocopied letters. 'Read a few of those.'

The correspondence, which was mainly from women or their husbands, though a few lawyers had written on behalf of clients, had a common theme. The women had sat in their cars wearing mink coats. In each case when they left the car, part of the mink had adhered to the seat, depleting and damaging the coat. Brett whistled softly.

'Sales ran a check through the computer,' Heberstein confided. 'In every case the car concerned had Metallic Willow seats. I understand there are still more letters coming in.'

'Obviously you've made tests.' Brett handed back the folder of letters. 'So what do they show?'

'They show the whole thing's very simple; trouble is, nobody thought of it before it happened. You sit on the seat, the cloth depresses and opens up. That's normal, of course, but what also open up in this case are the metallic threads, which is still OK, providing you don't happen to be wearing mink. But if you are, some of the fine hairs go down between the metallic threads. Get up, and the threads close, holding the mink hairs so they pull out from the coat. You can ruin a three-thousand-dollar coat in one trip around the block.'

Brett grinned. 'If word gets around, every woman in the country with an old mink will rush out for a ride, then put in a claim for a new coat.'

'Nobody's laughing. Over at staff they've pushed the panic button.'

'The fabric's out of production?'

Heberstein nodded. 'As of this morning. And from now on we have another test around here with new fabrics. Rather obviously it's known as the mink test.'

'What's happening about all the seats already out?'

'God knows! And I'm glad that part's not my headache. The last I heard, it had gone as high as the chairman of the board. I do know the legal department is settling all claims quietly, as soon as they come in. They've figured there'll be a few phony ones, but better to pay if there's a chance of keeping the whole thing under wraps.'

'Mink wraps?'

The studio head said dourly, 'Spare me the lousy jokes. You'll get all this through channels, but I thought you and a few others should know right away because of the Orion.'

'Thanks.' Brett nodded thoughtfully. It was true – changes would have to be made in Orion plans, though the particular area was not his responsibility. He was grateful, however, for another reason.

Within the next few days, he now decided, he must change either his car or the seats in his present one. Brett's car had Metallic Willow fabric and, coincidentally, he planned a birthday gift of mink next month which he had no wish to see spoiled. The mink, which undoubtedly would be worn in his car, was for Barbara.

Barbara Zaleski.

6

'Dad,' Barbara said, 'I'll be staying over in New York for a day or two. I thought I'd let you know.'

In the background, through the telephone, she could hear an overlay of factory noise. Barbara had had to wait several minutes while the operator located Matt Zaleski in the plant; now, presumably, he had taken the call somewhere close to the assembly line.

Her father asked, 'Why?'

'Why what?'

'Why do you have to stay?'

She said lightly, 'Oh, the usual kind of thing. Client problems at the agency. Some meetings about next year's advertising; they need me here for them.' Barbara was being patient. She really shouldn't have to explain, as if she were still a child requiring permission to be out late. If she decided to stay a week, a month, or for ever in New York, that was it.

'Couldn't you come home nights, then go back in the morning?'

'No, Dad, I couldn't.'

Barbara hoped this wasn't going to develop into another argument in which it would be necessary to point out that she was twenty-nine, a legal adult who had voted in two presidential elections, and had a responsible job which she was good at. The job, incidentally, made her financially free so that she could set up a separate establishment any time she wanted, except that she lived with her father, knowing he was lonely after her mother's death, and not wanting to make things worse for him.

'When will you be home then?'

'By the weekend for sure. You can live without me till then. And take care of your ulcer. By the way, how is it?'

'I'd forgotten it. Too many other things to think about. We had some trouble in the plant this morning.'

He sounded strained, she thought. The auto industry had that effect on everybody close to it, including herself. Whether you worked in a plant, in an advertising agency, or on design like Brett, the anxieties and pressures got to you in the end. The same kind of compulsion told Barbara Zaleski at this moment that she had to get off the telephone and back into the client meeting. She had slipped out a few minutes ago, the men assuming, no doubt, that she had left to do whatever women did in washrooms, and instinctively Barbara put a hand to her hair – chestnut brown and luxuriant, like her Polish mother's;

it also grew annoyingly fast so she had to spend more time than she liked in beauty salons. She patted her hair into place; it would have to do. Her fingers encountered the dark glasses which she had pushed upwards above her forehead hours ago, reminding her that she had heard someone recently deride dark glasses in hair as the hallmark of the girl executive. Well, why not? She left the glasses where they were.

'Dad,' Barbara said, 'I haven't much time. Would you do something for me?'

'What's that?'

'Call Brett. Tell him I'm sorry I can't make our date tonight, and if he wants to call me later, I'll be at the Drake Hotel.'

'I'm not sure I can . . .'

'Of course you can! Brett's at the Design Center, as you know perfectly well, so all you have to do is pick up an inside phone and dial. I'm not asking you to like him; I know you don't, and you've made that clear plenty of times to both of us. All I'm asking is that you pass a message. You may not even have to speak to him.'

She had been unable to keep the impatience out of her voice, so now they were having an argument after all, one more added to many others.

'All right,' Matt grumbled. 'I'll do it. But keep your shirt on.'

'You keep yours on, too. Goodbye, Dad. Take care, and I'll see you at the weekend.'

Barbara thanked the secretary whose phone she had been using and slid her full, long-limbed body from the desk where she had perched. Barbara's figure, which she was aware that men admired, was another legacy from her mother who had managed to convey a strong sexuality – characteristically Slavic, so some said – until the last few months before she died.

Barbara was on the twenty-first floor of the Third Advenue building which was New York headquarters of the Osborne J. Lewis Company – or more familiarly, OJL – one of the world's half-dozen largest advertising agencies, with a staff of two thousand, more or less, on three skyscraper floors. If she had wanted to, instead of phoning Detroit from where she had, Barbara could have used an office in the jam-packed, creative rabbit warren one floor down, where a few windowless, cupboard-size offices were kept available for out-of-town staffers like herself while working temporarily in New York. But it had seemed simpler to stay up here, where this morning's meeting was being held. This floor was client country. It was also where account executives and senior agency officers had their lavishly decorated and broadloomed office suites, with original Cézannes, Wyeths, or Picassos on the walls, as well as built-in bars – the latter remaining hidden or activated according to a client's known and carefully remembered preferences. Even secretaries here enjoyed better working conditions than some of the best creative talent down below. In a way, Barbara sometimes thought, the agency resembled a Roman galley ship, though at least those below had their martini lunches, went home at nights, and – if senior enough – were sometimes allowed topside.

She walked quickly down a corridor. In the austere Detroit offices of OJL, where Barbara worked mostly, her heels would have 'tip-tapped', but here, deep carpeting deadened their sound. Passing a door partially open, she could hear a piano and a girl singer's voice:

'One more happy user
Has joined the millions who

Say Brisk! – please bring it briskly;
It satisfies me too.'

Almost certainly a client was in there listening, and would make a decision about the jingle – aye or nay, involving vast expenditures – based on hunch, prejudice, or even whether he felt good or breakfast had given him dyspepsia. Of course, the lyric was awful, probably because the client preferred it to be banal, being afraid – as most were – of anything more imaginative. But the music had an ear-catching lilt; recorded with full orchestra and chorus, a large part of the nation might be humming the little tune a month or two from now. Barbara wondered what Brisk was. A drink? A new detergent? It could be either, or something more outlandish. The OJL agency had hundreds of clients in diverse businesses, though the auto company account which Barbara worked on was among its most important and lucrative. As auto company men were fond of reminding agency people, the car advertising budget alone exceeded a hundred million dollars annually.

Outside Conference Room 1 a red MEETING IN PROGRESS sign was still flashing. Clients loved the flashing signs for the aura of importance they created.

Barbara went in quietly and slipped into her chair halfway down the long table. There were seven others in the dignified, rosewood-panelled room with Georgian furnishings. At the table's head was Keith Yates-Brown, greying and urbanely genial, the agency management supervisor whose mission was to keep relations between the auto company and the Osborne J. Lewis agency friction free. To the right of Yates-Brown was the auto company advertising manager from Detroit, J. P. Underwood ('Call me J.P., please'), youngish, recently promoted and not entirely at ease yet with the top-rank agency crowd. Facing Underwood was bald and brilliant Teddy Osch, OJL creative director and a man who spewed ideas the way a fountain disgorges water. Osch, unflappable, schoolmasterish, had outlasted many of his colleagues and was a veteran of past, successful car campaigns.

The others comprised J. P. Underwood's assistant, also from Detroit, two other agency men – one creative, one executive – and Barbara, who was the only woman present, except for a secretary who at the moment was refilling coffee cups.

Their subject of discussion was the Orion. Since yesterday afternoon they had been reviewing advertising ideas which the agency had developed so far. the OJL group at the meeting had taken turns in presentations to the client – represented by Underwood and his assistant.

'We've saved one sequence until last, J.P.' Yates-Brown was speaking directly though informally to the auto company advertising manager. 'We thought you'd find them original, even interesting perhaps.' As always, Yates-Brown managed an appropriate mix of authority and deference, even though everyone present knew that an advertising manager had little real decision power and was off the mainstream of auto company high command.

J. P. Underwood said, more brusquely than necessary, 'Let's see it.'

One of the other agency men placed a series of cards on an easel. On each card a tissue sheet was fixed, the tissue having a sketched layout, in preliminary stage. Each layout, as Barbara knew, represented hours, and sometimes long nights of thought and labour.

Today's and yesterday's procedure was normal in the early stages of any new car campaign and the tissue sheets were called a 'rustle pile'.

'Barbara,' Yates-Brown said, 'will you skipper this trip?'

She nodded.

'What we have in mind, J.P.,' Barbara told Underwood with a glance to his assistant, 'is to show the Orion as it will be in everyday use. The first layout, as you see, is an Orion leaving a car wash.'

All eyes were on the sketch. It was imaginative and well executed. It showed the forward portion of the car emerging from a wash tunnel like a butterfly from a chrysalis. A young woman was waiting to drive the car away. Photographed in colour, whether still or on film, the scene would be arresting.

J. P. Underwood gave no reaction, not an eyelid flicker. Barbara nodded for the next tissue.

'Some of us have felt for a long time that women's use of cars has been under-emphasized in advertising. Most advertising, as we know, has been directed at men.'

She could have added, but didn't, that her own assignment for the past two years had been to push hard for the women's point of view. There were days, however, after reading the masculine-oriented advertising (the trade called it 'muscle copy') which continued to appear, when Barbara was convinced that she had failed totally.

Now she commented, 'We believe that women are going to use the Orion a great deal.'

The sketch on the easel was a supermarket parking lot. The artist's composition was excellent – the storefront in background, an Orion prominently forward with other cars around it. A woman shopper was loading groceries into the Orion's back seat.

'Those other cars,' the auto company ad manager said. 'Would they be ours or competitors'?'

Yates-Brown asnwered quickly, 'I'd say ours, J.P.'

'There should be *some* competitive cars, J.P.,' Barbara said. 'Otherwise the whole thing would be unreal.'

'Can't say I like the groceries.' The remark was from Underwood's assistant. 'Clutters everything up. Takes the eye away from the car. And if we did use that background it should be Vaselined.'

Barbara felt like sighing dispiritedly. Vaseline smeared around a camera lens when photographing cars was a photographer's trick which had become a cliché; it made background misty, leaving the car itself sharply defined. Though auto companies persisted in using it, many advertising people thought the device as dated as the Twist. Barbara said mildly, 'We're attempting to show actual use.'

'All the same,' Keith Yates-Brown injected, 'that was a good point. Let's make a note of it.'

'The next layout,' Barbara said, 'is an Orion in the rain – a real downpour would be good, we think. Again, a woman driver, looking as if she's going home from the office. We'd photograph after dark to get best reflections from a wet street.'

'Be hard not to get the car dirty,' J. P. Underwood observed.

'The whole idea *is* to get it a little dirty,' Barbara told him. 'Again – reality. Colour film could make it great.'

The assistant manager from Detroit said softly, 'I can't see the brass going for it.'

J. P. Underwood was silent.

There were a dozen more. Barbara went through each, briefly but conscientiously, knowing how much effort and devotion the younger agency staff members had put into every one. That was the way it always went. The creative oldsters like Teddy Osch held back and – as they put it – 'let the kids exhaust themselves', knowing from experience that the early work, however good it was, would always be rejected.

It was rejected now. Underwood's manager made that clear, and everyone in the room shared the knowledge, as they had shared it yesterday, before this session started. In her early days at the agency Barbara had been naïve enough to inquire why it always happened that way. Why was so much effort and quality – frequently excellent quality – utterly wasted?

Afterwards, some facts of life about auto advertising had been quietly explained. It was put to her: if the ad programme burgeoned quickly, instead of painfully slowly – far slower than advertising for most other products – then how would all the auto people in Detroit involved with it justify their jobs, the endless meetings over months, fat expense accounts, the out-of-town junkets? Furthermore, if an auto company chose to burden itself with that kind of inflated cost, it was not the agency's business to suggest otherwise, far less to go crusading. The agency did handsomely out of the arrangement; besides, there was always approval in the end. The advertising process for each model year started in October or November. By May-June, decisions had to be firm so that the agency could do its job; therefore, auto company people began making up their minds because they could read a calendar too. This was also the time that the Detroit high brass came into the picture, and they made final decisions about advertising, whether talented in that particular direction or not.

What bothered Barbara most – and others too, she discovered later – was the appalling waste of time, talent, people, money, the exercise in nothingness. And, from talking with people in other agencies, she knew that the same process was true of all Big Three companies. It was as if the auto industry, normally so time-and-motion conscious and critical of bureaucracy outside, had created its own fat-waxing bureaucracy within.

She had once asked: did any of the original ideas, the really good ones, ever get reinstated? The answer was: no, because you can't accept in June what you rejected last November. It would be embarrassing to auto company people. That kind of thing could easily cost a man – perhaps a good friend to the agency – his job.

'Thank you, Barbara.' Keith Yates-Brown had smoothly taken charge. 'Well, J.P., we realize we still have a long way to go.' The management supervisor's smile was warm and genial, his tone just the right degree apologetic.

'You sure do,' J. P. Underwood said. He pushed his chair back from the table.

Barbara asked him, 'Was there nothing you liked? Absolutely nothing at all?'

Yates-Brown swung his head towards her sharply and she knew she was out of line. Clients were not supposed to be harassed that way, but Underwood's brusque superiority had needled her. She thought, even now, of some of the talented youngsters in the agency whose imaginative work, as well as her own, had just gone down the drain. Maybe what had been produced so far wasn't the ultimate answer to Orion needs, but neither did it rate a graceless dismissal.

'Now, Barbara,' Yates-Brown said, 'no-one mentioned not liking anything.' The agency supervisor was still suave and charming, but she sensed steel beneath his words. If he wanted to, Yates-Brown, essentially a salesman who hardly ever had an original idea himself, could squash creative people in the agency beneath his elegant alligator shoes. He went on, 'However, we'd be less than professional if we failed to agree that we have not yet caught the true Orion spirit. It's a wonderful spirit, J.P. You've given us one of the great cars of history to work with.'

He made it sound as if the ad manager had designed the Orion single-handed.

Barbara felt slightly sick. She caught Teddy Osch's eye. Barely perceptibly the creative director shook his head.

'I'll say this,' J. P. Underwood volunteered. His tone was friendlier. For several years previously he had been merely a junior at this table; perhaps the newness of his job, his own insecurity, had made him curt a moment earlier. 'I think we've just seen one of the finest rustle piles we ever had.'

There was a pained silence through the room. Even Keith Yates-Brown betrayed a flicker of shocked surprise. Clumsily, illogically, the company ad man had stomped on their agreed pretence, revealing the elaborate charade for what it was. On the one hand – automatic dismissal of everything submitted; an instant later, fulsome praise. But nothing would be changed. Barbara was an old enough hand to know that.

So was Keith Yates-Brown. He recovered quickly.

'That's generous of you, J.P. Damn generous! I speak for us all on the agency side when I tell you we're grateful for your encouragement and assure you that next time around we'll be even more effective.' The management supervisor was standing now; the others followed his example. He turned to Osch. 'Isn't that so, Teddy?'

The creative chief nodded with a smile. 'We do our best.'

As the meeting broke up, Yates-Brown and Underwood preceded the others to the door.

Underwood asked, 'Did somebody get on the ball about theatre tickets?'

Barbara, close behind, had heard the ad manager ask earlier for a block of six seats to a Neil Simon comedy for which tickets, even through scalpers, were almost impossible to get.

The agency supervisor guffawed genially. 'Did you ever doubt me?' He draped an arm companionably around the other's shoulders. 'Sure we have them, J.P. You picked the toughest ticket in town, but for you we pulled every string. They're being sent to our lunch table at the Waldorf. Is that OK?'

'That's OK.'

Yates-Brown lowered his voice. 'And let me know where your party would like dinner. We'll take care of the reservation.'

And the bill, *and* all tips, Barbara thought. As for the theatre tickets, she imagined Yates-Brown must have paid fifty dollars a seat, but the agency would recoup that, along with other expenses, a thousand-fold through Orion advertising.

On some occasions when clients were taken to lunch by agency executives, people from the creative side were invited along. Today, for reasons of his own, Yates-Brown had decided against this. Barbara was relieved.

While the agency executive-J. P. Underwood group was no doubt heading for the Waldorf, she walked, with Teddy Osch and Nigel Knox, the other creative staffer who had been at the client meeting a few blocks uptown on Third Avenue. Their destination was Joe & Rose, an obscure but first-rate bistro, populated at lunchtime by advertising people from big agencies in the neighbourhood. Nigel Knox, who was an effeminate young man, normally grated on Barbara, but since his work and ideas had been rejected too, she regarded him more sympathetically than usual.

Teddy Osch led the way, under a faded red awning, into the restaurant's unpretentious interior. En route, no-one had said more than a word or two. Now, on being shown to a table in a small rear room reserved for habitués, Osch silently raised three fingers. Moments later three martinis in chilled glasses were placed before them.

'I'm not going to do anything stupid like cry,' Barbara said, 'and I won't get drunk because you always feel so awful after. But if you both don't mind, I intend to get moderately loaded.' She downed the martini. 'I'd like another, please.'

Osch beckoned a waiter. 'Make it three.'

'Teddy,' Barbara said, 'how the hell do you stand it?'

Osch passed a hand pensively across his baldness. 'The first twenty years are hardest. After that, when you've seen a dozen J. P. Underwoods come and go . . .'

Nigel Knox exploded as if he had been bottling up a protest. 'He's a beastly person. I tried to like him, but I couldn't possibly.'

'Oh shut up, Nigel,' Barbara said.

Osch continued, 'The trick is to remind yourself that the pay is good, and most times – except today – I like the work. There isn't a business more exciting. I'll tell you something else: no matter how well they've built the Orion, if it's a success, and sells, it'll be because of us and advertising. They know it; we know it. So what else matters?'

'Keith Yates-Brown matters,' Barbara said. 'And he makes me sick.'

Nigel Knox mimicked in a high-pitched voice, *'That's generous of you, J.P. Damn generous! Now I'm going to lie down, J.P., and I hope you'll pee all over me.'*

Knox giggled. For the first time since this morning's meeting, Barbara laughed.

Teddy Osch glared at them both. 'Keith Yates-Brown is my meal ticket and yours, and let's none of us forget it. Sure, I couldn't do what he does – keep snugged up to Underwood's and other people's anuses and look like I enjoyed it, but it's a part of this business which somebody has to take care of, so why fault him for a thorough job? Right now, and plenty of other times while we're doing the creative bit, which we like, Yates-Brown is in bed with the client, stroking whatever's necessary to keep him warm and happy, and telling him about *us*, how great we are. And if you'd ever been in an agency which lost an automotive account, you'd know why I'm glad he is.'

A waiter bustled up. 'Veal Parmigiana's good today.' At Joe & Rose no-one bothered with frills like menus.

Barbara and Nigel Knox nodded. 'OK, with noodles,' Osch told the waiter. 'And martinis all around.'

Already, Barbara realized, the liquor had relaxed them. Now, the session was following a familiar pattern – at first gloomy, then self-consoling; soon, after one more martini probably, it would become philosophic. In her own few years at the OJL agency she had attended several post-mortems of this kind, in New York at advertising 'in' places like Joe & Rose, in Detroit at the Caucus Club or Jim's Garage, downtown. It was at the Caucus she had once seen an elderly advertising man break down and sob because months of his work had been brusquely thrown out an hour earlier.

'I worked at an agency once,' Osch said, 'where we lost a car account. It happened just before the weekend; nobody expected it, except the other agency which took the account away from us. We called it "Black Friday".'

He fingered the stem of his glass, looking back across the years. 'A hundred agency people were fired that Friday afternoon. Others didn't wait to be fired; they knew there was nothing left for them, so they scurried up and down Madison and Third, trying for jobs at other places before they closed. Guys were scared. A good many had fancy homes, big mortgages, kids in college. Trouble is, other agencies don't like the smell of losers; besides, some of the older guys were just plain burned out. I remember, two hit the bottle and stayed on it; one committed suicide.'

'You survived,' Barbara said.

'I was young. If it happened now, I'd go the way the others did.' He raised his glass. 'To Keith Yates-Brown.'

Nigel Knox placed his partially drunk martini on the table. 'Oh no, really. I couldn't possibly.'

Barbara shook her head. 'Sorry, Teddy.'

'Then I'll drink the toast alone,' Osch said. And did.

'The trouble with our kind of advertising,' Barbara said, 'is that we offer a nonexistent car to an unreal person.' The three of them had almost finished their latest martinis; she was aware of her own speech slurring. 'We all know you couldn't possibly buy the car that's in the ads, even if you wanted to, because the photographs are lies. When we take pictures of the real cars we use a wide-angle lens to balloon the front, a stretch lens to make the side view longer. We even make the colour look better than it is with spray and powder puffs and camera filters.'

Osch waved a hand airily. 'Tricks of the trade.'

A waiter saw the hand wave. 'Another round, Mr Osch? Your food will be here soon.' The creative chief nodded.

Barbara insisted, 'It's still a nonexistent car.'

'That's jolly good!' Nigel Knox clapped vigorously, knocking over his empty glass and causing occupants of other tables to glance their way amusedly. 'Now tell us who's the unreal person we advertise it to.'

Barbara spoke slowly, her thoughts fitting together less readily than usual. 'Detroit executives who have the final word on advertising don't understand people. They work too hard; there isn't time. Therefore most car advertising consists of a Detroit executive advertising to another Detroit executive.'

'I have it!' Nigel Knox bobbed up and down exuberantly. 'Everybody knows a Detroit panjandrum is an unreal person. Clever! Clever!'

'So are you,' Barbara said. 'I don't think, at this point, I could even think panjan . . . wotsit, let alone say it.' She put a hand to her face, wishing she had drunk more slowly.

'Don't touch the plates,' the waiter warned, 'they're hot.' The Veal Parmigiana, with savoury steaming noddles was put before them, plus another three martinis. 'Complimentsa the next table,' the waiter said.

Osch acknowledged the drinks, then sprinkled red peppers liberally on his noodles.

'My goodness,' Nigel Knox warned, 'those are terribly hot.'

The creative chief told him, 'I need a new fire in me.'

There was a silence while they began eating, then Teddy Oschu looked across at Barbara. 'Considering the way you feel, I guess it's all to the good you're coming off the Orion programme.'

'What?' Startled, she put down her knife and fork.

'I was supposed to tell you. I hadn't got around to it.'

'You mean I'm fired?'

He shook his head. 'New assignment. You'll hear tomorrow.'

'Teddy,' she pleaded, 'you have to tell me now.'

He said firmly, 'No. You'll get it from Keith Yates-Brown. He's the one who recommended you. Remember? – the guy you wouldn't drink a toast to.'

Barbara had an empty feeling.

'All I can tell you,' Osch said, 'is I wish it were me instead of you.' He sipped his fresh martini; of the three of them, he was the only one still drinking. 'If I was younger I think it might have been me. But I guess I'll go on doing what I always have: advertising that nonexistent car to the unreal person.'

'Teddy,' Barbara said, 'I'm sorry.'

'No need to be. The sad thing is, I think you're right.' The creative chief blinked. 'Christ! Those peppers are hotter than I thought.' He produced a handkerchief and wiped his eyes.

7

Some thirty miles outside Detroit, occupying a half-thousand acres of superb Michigan countryside, the auto company's proving ground lay like a Balkan state bristling with defended borders. Only one entrance to the proving ground existed – through a security-policed double barrier, remarkably similar to East Berlin's Checkpoint Charlie. Here, visitors were halted to have credentials examined; no-one, without prearranged authority, got in.

Apart from this entry point, the entire area was enclosed by a high, chain-link fence, patrolled by guards. Inside the fence, trees and other protective planting formed a visual shield against watchers from outside.

What the company was guarding were some of its more critical secrets. Among them: experiments with new cars, trucks, and their components, as well as drive-to-destruction performance tests on current models.

The testing was carried out on some hundred and fifty miles of roads – routes to nowhere – ranging from specimens of the very best to the absolute worst or more precipitous in the world. Among the latter was a duplicate of San Francisco's horrendously steep Filbert Street, appropriately named (so San Franciscans say) since only nuts drive down it. A Belgian block road jolted every screw, weld, and rivet in the car, and set drivers' teeth chattering. Even rougher, and used for truck trials, was a replica of an African game trail, with tree roots, rocks, and mud holes.

One road section, built on level ground, was known as Serpentine Alley. This was a series of sharp S-bends, closely spaced and absolutely flat, so that absence of any banking in the turns strained a car to its limits when cornering at high speed.

At the moment, Adam Trenton was hurling an Orion around Serpentine Alley at 60 mph.

Tyres screamed savagely, and smoked, as the car flung hard left, then right, then left again. Each time, centrifugal force strained urgently, protestingly, against the direction of the turn. To the three occupants it seemed as if the car might roll over at any moment, even though knowledge told them that it shouldn't.

Adam glanced behind him. Brett DeLosanto, sitting centrally in the rear seat, was belted in, as well as bracing himself by his arms on either side.

The designer called over the seatback, 'My liver and spleen just switched sides. I'm counting on the next bend to get them back.'

Beside Adam, Ian Jameson, a slight, sandy-haired Scot from Engineering, sat imperturbably. Jameson was undoubtedly thinking what Adam realized – that there was no necessity for them to be going around the turns at all; professional drivers had already put the Orion through gruelling tests there which it survived handily. The trio's real purpose at the proving ground today was to review an NVH problem (the initials were engineerese for Noise, Vibration, and Harshness) which prototype Orions had developed at very high speed. But on their way to the fast track they passed the entry to Serpentine Alley, and Adam swung on to it first, hoping that throwing the car around would release some of his own tension, which he had continued to be aware of since his departure from the Press session an hour or two earlier.

The tension, which started early this morning, had occurred more frequently of late. So a few weeks ago Adam made an appointment with a physician who probed, pressed, performed assorted tests, and finally told him there was nothing wrong organically except, possibly, too much acid in his system. The doctor then talked vaguely of 'ulcer personality', the need to stop worrying, and added a kindergarten bromide, 'A hill is only as steep as it looks to the man climbing it.'

While Adam listened impatiently, wishing that medics would assume more knowledge and intelligence on the part of patients, the doctor pointed out that the human body had its own built-in warning devices and suggested easing up for a while, which Adam already knew was impossible this year. The doctor finally got down to what Adam had come for and prescribed Librium capsules with a recommended dosage. Adam promptly exceeded the dosage, and continued to. He also failed to tell the doctor that he was taking Valium, obtained elsewhere. Today, Adam had swallowed several pills, including one just before leaving downtown, but without discernible effect. Now, since the S-turns had done nothing to release his tension either, he surreptitiously transferred another pill from a pocket to his mouth.

The action reminded him that he still hadn't told Erica, either about the visit to the doctor, or the pills, which he kept in his briefcase, out of sight.

Near the end of Serpentine Alley, Adam swung the car sharply, letting the speed drop only slightly before heading for the track which was used for high-speed runs. Outside, the trees, meadows, and connecting roads sped by. The speedometer returned to 60, then edged to 65.

With one hand, Adam rechecked the tightness of his own lap straps and shoulder harness. Without turning his head, he told the others, 'OK, let's shake this baby out.'

They hurtled on the fast track, sweeping past another car, their speed still climbing. It was 70 mph, and Adam caught a glimpse of a face as the driver of the other car glanced sideways.

Ian Jameson craned left to watch the speedometer needle, now touching 75. The sandy-haired engineer had been a key figure in studying the Orion's present NVH problem.

'We'll hear it any moment,' Jameson said.

Speed was 78. The wind, largely of their own creating, roared as they flew around the track. Adam had the accelerator floored. Now he touched the automatic speed control, letting the computer take over, and removed his foot. Speed crept up. It passed 80.

'Here she comes,' Jameson said. As he spoke, the car shuddered violently – an intense pulsation, shaking everything, including occupants. Adam found his vision blurring slightly from the rapid movements. Simultaneously a metallic hum rose and fell.

The engineer said, 'Right on schedule.' He sounded complacent, Adam thought, as if he would have been disappointed had the trouble not appeared.

'At fairgrounds . . .' Brett DeLosanto raised his voice to a shout to make himself heard; his words came through unevenly because of the shaking. 'At fairgrounds, people pay money for a ride like this.'

'And if we left it in,' Adam said, 'most drivers would never know about it. Not many take their cars up to eighty.'

Ian Jameson said, 'But some do.'

Adam conceded gloomily: it was true. A handful of madcap drivers would hit 80, and among them one or two might be startled by the sudden vibration, then lose control, killing or maiming themselves and others. Even without accident, the NVH effect could become known, and people like Emerson Vale would make the most of it. It was a few freak accidents at high speed, Adam recalled, with drivers who over- or under-steered in emergencies, which had killed the Corvair only a few years ago. And although by the time Ralph Nader published his now-famous indictment of the Corvair, early faults had been corrected, the car had still gone to a precipitate end under the weight of publicity which Nader generated.

Adam, and others in the company who knew about the highspeed shake, had no intention of allowing a similar episode to mar the Orion's record. It was a reason why the company high command was being close-mouthed so that rumours of the trouble did not leak outside. A vital question at this moment was: how could the shake be eliminated and what would it cost? Adam was here to find out and, because of the urgency, had authority to make decisions.

He took back control from the car's computer and allowed the speed to fall to 20 mph. Then, twice more, at different rates of acceleration he took it up to 80. Each time, both the vibration and the point at which it occurred were identical.

'There's a difference in sheet metal on this car.' Adam remembered that the Orion he was driving was an early prototype, handmade – as were all prototypes so far – because assembly line manufacture had not yet started.

'Makes no difference to the effect,' Ian Jameson declared flatly. 'We've had an exact Orion out here, another on the dynamometer. They all do it. Same speed, same NVH.'

'It feels like a woman having an orgasm,' Brett said. 'Sounds like it, too.' He asked the engineer, 'Does it do any harm?'

'As far as we can tell, no.'

'Then it seems a shame to take it out.'

Adam snapped, 'For Christ's sake, cut the stupidity! Of course we have to take it out! If it were an appearance problem, you wouldn't be so goddam smug.'

'Well, well,' Brett said. 'Something else appears to be vibrating.'

They had left the fast track. Abruptly, Adlam braked the car, skidding so that all three were thrown forward against their straps. He turned on to a grass shoulder. As the car stopped, he unbuckled, then got out and lit a cigarette. The others followed.

Outside the car, Adam shivered slightly. The air was briskly cool, fall leaves were blowing in a gusty wind, and the sun, which had been out earlier, had disappeared behind an overcast of grey nimbostratus. Through trees, he could see a lake, its surface ruffled bleakly.

Adam pondered the decision he had to make. He was aware it was a tough one for which he would be blamed – justly or unjustly – if it went wrong.

Ian Jameson broke the uncomfortable silence. 'We're satisfied that the effect is induced by tyre and road surfaces when one or the other becomes in phase with body harmonics, so the vibration is natural body frequency.'

In other words, Adam realized, there was no structural defect in the car. He asked, 'Can the vibration be overcome?'

'Yes,' Jameson said. 'We're sure of that, also that you can go one of two ways. Either redesign the cowl side structure and underbody torque boxes' – he filled in engineering details – 'or add braces and reinforcement.'

'Hey!' Brett was instantly alert. 'The first one means exterior body changes. Right?'

'Right,' the engineer acknowledged. 'They'd be needed at the lower body side near the front door cut and rocker panel areas.'

Brett looked gloomy, as well he might, Adam thought. It would require a crash redesign and testing programme at a time when everyone believed the Orion design was fixed and final. He queries, 'And the add-ons?'

'We've experimented, and there'd be two pieces – a front floor reinforcement and a brace under the instrument panel.' The engineer described the brace which would be out of sight, extending from the cowl side structure on one side, to the steering column, thence to the cowl on the opposite side.

Adam asked the critical question. 'Cost?'

'You won't like it.' The engineer hesitated, knowing the reaction his next words would produce. 'About five dollars.'

Adam groaned. 'God Almighty!'

He was faced with a frustrating choice. Whichever route they went would be negative and costly. The engineer's first alternative – redesign – would be less expensive, costing probably half a million to a million dollars in retooling. But it would create delays, and the Orion's introduction would be put off three to six months which, in itself, could be disastrous for many reasons.

On the other hand, on a million cars, cost of the two add-ons – the floor reinforcement and brace – would be five million dollars, and it was expected that many more Orions than a million would be built and sold. Millions of dollars to be added to production expense, to say nothing of lost profit, and all for an item wholly negative! In auto construction, five dollars was a major sum, and auto manufacturers thought normally in pennies, saving two cents here, a nickel there, necessary because of the immense total numbers involved. Adam said in deep disgust, 'Goddam!'

He glanced at Brett. The designer said, 'I guess it isn't funny.'

Adam's outburst in the car was not the first clash they had had since the Orion project started. Sometimes it had been Brett who flared up. But through everything so far they had managed to remain friends. It was as well, because there was a new project ahead of them, at the moment codenamed Farstar.

Ian Jameson announced, 'If you want to drive over to the lab, we've a car with the add-ons for you to see.'

Adam nodded sourly. 'Let's get on with it.'

Brett DeLosanto looked upward incredulously. 'You mean that hunk of scrap, and the other, 'll cost five bucks!'

He was staring at a steel strip running across the underside of an Orion, and secured by bolts.

Adam Trenton, Brett, and Ian Jameson were inspecting the proposed floor reinforcement from an inspection area beneath a dynamometer, so that the whole of the car's underside was open to their view. The dynamometer, an affair of metal plates, rollers, and instrumentation, with a vague resemblance to a monstrous service station hoist, allowed a car to be operated as if on the road, while viewed from any angle.

They had already inspected, while above, the other cowl-to-steering column-to-cowl brace.

Jameson conceded, 'Possibly you could save a few cents from cost, but no more, after allowing for material, machining, then bolt fittings and installation labour.'

The engineer's manner, a kind of pedantic detachment as if cost and economics were really none of his concern, continued to irritate Adam, who asked, 'How much is Engineering protecting itself? Do we really need all that?'

It was a perennial question from a product planner to an engineer. The product men regularly accused engineers of building in, everywhere, greater strength margins than necessary, thus adding to an automobile's cost and weight while diminishing performance. Product Planning was apt to argue: *if you let the Iron Rings have their way, every car would have the strength of Brooklyn Bridge, ride like an armoured truck, and last as long as Stonehenge.* Taking an adversary view, engineers declaimed: *sure, we allow margins because if something fails we're the ones who take the rap. If product planners did their own engineering, they'd achieve light weight – most likely with a balsawood chassis and tinfoil for the engine block.*

'There's no engineering protection there.' It was Jameson's turn to be huffy. 'We've reduced the NVH to what we believe is an acceptable level. If we went a more complicated route – which would cost more – we could probably take it out entirely. So far we haven't.'

Adam said noncommittally, 'We'll see what this does.'

Jameson led the way as the trio climbed a metal stairway from the inspection level to the main floor of the Noise and Vibration Laboratory above.

The lab – a building at the proving ground which was shaped like an aeroplane hangar and divided into specialist work areas, large and small – was busy as usual with NVH conundrums tossed there by various divisions of the company. One problem now being worked on urgently was a high-pitched, girlish-sounding scream emitted by a new-type brake on diesel locomotives. Industrial Marketing had enjoined sternly: the stopping power must be retained, but locomotives should sound as if being braked, not raped. Another poser – this from Household Products Division – was an audible click in a kitchen oven control clock; a competitor's clock, though less efficient, was silent. Knowing that the public distrusted new or different sounds and that sales might suffer if the click remained, Household Products had appeared to the NVH lab to nix the click but not the clock.

Automobiles, however, produced the bulk of the laboratory's problems. A recent one stemmed from revised styling of an established model car. The new body style produced a drum sound while in motion; tests showed that the sound resulted from a windshield which had been reshaped. After weeks of hit-and-miss experimentation, NVH engineers eliminated the drum noise by introducing a crinkle in the car's metal floor. No-one, including the engineers, knew exactly why the crinkle stopped the windshield drumming; the important thing was – it did.

The present stage of Orion testing in the lab had been set up on the dynamometer. Hence the car could be operated at any speed, either manually or by remote control, for hours, days, or weeks continuously, yet never move from its original position on the machine's rollers.

The Orion which they had looked at from beneath was ready to go. Stepping over the steel floor plates of the dynamometer, Adam Trenton and Ian Jameson climbed inside, Adam at the wheel.

Brett DeLosanto was no longer with them. Having satisfied himself that the proposed add-ons would not affect the car's outward appearance, Brett had returned outside to review a minor change made recently in the Orion grille. Designers liked to see the results of their work out of doors – 'on the grass', as they put it. Sometimes, in open surroundings and natural light, a design had unexpected visual effects, compared with its appearance in a studio. When the Orion, for example, was first viewed in direct sunlight the front grille had unexpectedly appeared black instead of bright silver, as it should. A change of angle in the grille had been necessary to correct it.

A girl technician in a white coat came out from a glass-lined control booth alongside the car. She inquired, 'Is there any special kind of road you'd like, Mr Trenton?'

'Give him a bumpy ride,' the engineer said. 'Let's take one from California.'

'Yes, sir.' The girl returned to the booth, then leaned out through the doorway, holding a magnetic tape reel in her hand. 'This is State Route 17, between Oakland and San Jose.' Going back into the booth, she pressed the reel on to a console and passed the tape end through a take-up spool.

Adam turned the ignition key. The Orion's engine sprang to life.

The tape now turning inside the glass booth would, Adam knew, transfer the real road surface, electronically, to the dynamometer rollers beneath the car. The tape was one of many in the lab's library, and all had been made by sensitive recording vehicles driven over routes in North America and Europe. Thus, actual road conditions, good and bad, could be reproduced instantly for test and study.

He put the Orion in drive and accelerated.

Speed rose quickly to 50 mph. The Orion's wheels and the dynamometer rollers were racing, the car itself standing still. At the same time, Adam felt an instant pounding from below.

'Too many people think California freeways are great,' Ian Jameson observed. 'It surprises them when we demonstrate how bad they can be.'

The speedometer showed 65.

Adam nodded. Auto engineers, he knew, were critical of California road building because the state's roads – due to the absence of frost – were not made deep. The lack of depth allowed concrete slabs to become depressed at the centre and curled and broken at the edges – a result of pounding by heavy trucks. Thus, when a car came to the end of a slab, in effect it fell off and bounced on to the next. The process caused continuous bumps and vibrations which cars had to be engineered to absorb.

The Orion's speed nudged 80. Jameson said, 'Here's where it happens.'

As he spoke, a hum and vibration – additional to the roughness of the California freeway – extended through the car. But the effect was slight, the hum low-pitched, vibration minor. The NVH would no longer be startling to a car's occupants, as it had been on the test track earlier.

Adam queried, 'And that's all of it?'

'That's all that's left,' Ian Jameson assured him. 'The braces take the rest out. As I said, we consider what remains to be at an acceptable level.' Adam allowed speed to drop off, and the engineer added, 'Let's try it on a smooth road.'

With another tape on the control console – a portion of Interstate 80 in Illinois – the road unevenness disappeared while the hum and vibration seemed correspondingly lower.

'We'll try one more road,' James said, 'a really tough one.' He signalled to the lab assistant in the booth, who smiled.

As Adam accelerated, even at 60 mph the Orion jolted alarmingly. Jameson announced, 'This is Mississippi – US 90, near Biloxi. The road wasn't good to start with, then Hurricane Camille loused it up completely. The portion we're on now still hasn't been fixed. Naturally, no-one would do this speed there unless they had suicide in mind.'

At 80 mph the road, transmitted through the dynamometer, was so bad that the car's own vibration was undetectable. Ian Jameson looked pleased.

As speed came off, he commented, 'People don't realize how good our engineering has to be to cope with all kinds of roads, including plenty of others like that.'

Jameson was off again, Adam thought, in his abstract engineer's world. Of more practical importance was the fact that the Orion's NVH problem could be solved. Adam had already decided that the add-on route, despite its appalling cost, was the one they would have to travel, rather than delay the Orion's debut. Of course, the company's executive vice-president, Hub Hewitson, who regarded the Orion as his own special baby, would go through the ceiling when he heard about the five dollars added cost. But he would learn to live with it, as Adam had – almost – already.

He got out of the car, Ian Jameson following. On the engineer's instructions, Adam left the motor running. Now, the girl in the booth took over, operating the Orion by remote control. At 80 on the dynamometer, the vibration was no more serious outside than it had been within.

Adam asked Jameson, 'You're sure the bracing will stand up to long use?'

'No question about it. We've put it through every test. We're satisfied.'

So was Jameson, Adam thought; too damn satisfied. The engineer's detachment – it seemed like complacency – still irritated him. 'Doesn't it ever bother you,' Adam asked, 'that everything you people do here is negative? You don't produce anything. You only take things out, eliminate.'

'Oh, we produce something,' Jameson pointed to the dynamometer rollers, still turning swiftly, impelled by the Orion's wheels. 'See those? They're connected to a generator; so are the other dynamometers in the lab. Every time we operate a car, the rollers generate electricity. We're coupled in to Detroit Edison, and we sell the power to them.' He looked challengingly at Adam. 'Sometimes I think it's as useful as a few things which have come out of Product Planning.'

Adam smiled, conceding. 'But not the Orion.'

'No,' Jameson said. 'I guess we all have hopes for that.'

8

The nightgown which Erica Trenton finally bought was in Laidlaw-Beldon's on Somerset Mall in troy. Earlier, she had browsed through stores in Birmingham without seeing anything that appealed to her as sufficiently special for the purpose she had in mind, so she continued to cruise the district in her sports convertible, not really minding because it was pleasant, for a change, to have something special to do.

Somerset Mall was a large, modern plaza, east on Big Beaver Road, with quality stores, drawing much of their patronage from well-to-do auto industry families living in Birmingham and Bloomfield Hills. Erica had shopped there often and knew her way around most of the stores, including Laidlaw-Beldon's.

She realized, the instant she saw it, that the nightgown was exactly right. It was a sheer nylon with matching peignoir, in pale beige, almost the colour of her hair. The total effect, she knew, would be to project an image of honey blondeness. A frosted orange lipstick, she decided, would round out the sensual impression she intended to create, tonight, for Adam.

Erica had no charge account at the store, and paid by cheque. Afterwards she went to Cosmetics to buy a lipstick, since she was uncertain if she had one at home quite the right shade.

Cosmetics were busy. While waiting, glancing over a display of lipstick colours, Erica became aware of another shopper at the perfume counter close by. It was a woman in her sixties who was informing a salesclerk, 'I want it for my daughter-in-law. I'm really not sure . . . Let me try the Norell.'

Using a sample vial, the clerk – a bored burnette – obliged.

'Yes,' the woman said. 'Yes, that's nice. I'll take that. An ounce size.'

From a mirror-faced store shelf behind her, out of reach of customers, the clerk selected a white, black-lettered box and placed it on the counter. 'That's fifty dollars, plus sales tax. Will it be cash or charge?'

The older woman hesitated. 'Oh, I hadn't realized it would be that much.'

'We have smaller sizes, madam.'

'No . . . Well, you see, it's a gift. I suppose I ought . . . But I'll wait and think it over.'

As the woman left the counter, so did the perfume salesclerk. She moved through an archway, momentarily out of sight. On the counter, the boxed perfume remained where the clerk had left it.

Irrationally, incredibly, in Erica's mind a message formed: *Norell's my perfume. Why not take it?*

She hesitated, shocked at her own impulse. While she did, a second message urged: *Go on! You're wasting time! Act now!*

Afterwards, she remembered that she waited long enough to wonder: was it really her own mind at work? Then deliberately, unhurriedly, but as if a magnetic force were in control, Erica moved from Cosmetics to Perfume. Without haste or wasted motion, she lifted the package, opened her handbag and dropped it in. The handbag had a spring fastener which snapped as it closed. The sound seemed to Erica like the firing of a gun. *It would draw attention!*

What had she done?

She stood trembling, waiting, afraid to move, expecting an accusing voice, a hand on her shoulder, a shouted '*Thief!*'

Nothing happened. But it would; she knew it would, at any moment.

How could she explain? *She couldn't. Not with the evidence in her handbag.* She reasoned urgently: should she take the package out, return it to where it was before the foolish, *unbelievable impulse* swept over her and made her act as she had? She had never done this before, *never*, nor anything remotely like it.

Still trembling, conscious of her own heartbeat, Erica asked herself: *Why?* What reason was there, if any, for what she had just done? The most absurd thing was, she didn't need to steal – the perfume or anything else. There was money in her purse, a chequebook.

Even now she could call the salesclerk to the counter, could spill out money to pay for the package, and that would be that. *Providing that she acted quickly. Now!*

No.

Obviously, because still nothing had happened, no-one had seen her. If they had, Erica thought, by now she would have been accosted, questioned, perhaps taken away. She turned. Casually, feigning indifference, she surveyed the store in all directions. Business was going on as usual. No-one seemed in the least interested in her, or was even looking her way. The perfume salesclerk had not reappeared. Unhurriedly, as before, Erica moved back to Cosmetics.

She reminded herself: she had wanted some perfume anyway. The way she had got it had been foolish and dangerous and she would never, ever, do the same thing again. But she had it now, and what was done was done. Trying to undo it would create difficulties, require explanations, perhaps followed by accusation, all of which were best avoided.

A salesclerk at Cosmetics was free. With her most engaging smile and manner Erica asked to try some orange lipstick shades.

One danger, she knew, still remained: the clerk at the perfume counter. Would the girl miss the package she had put down? If so, would she remember that Erica had been close by? Erica's instinct was to leave, to hurry from the store, but reason warned her: she would be less conspicuous where she was. She deliberately dawdled over her lipstick choice.

Another customer had stopped at Perfumes. The salesclerk returned, acknowledged the newcomer, then, as if remembering, looked at the counter where the Norell package had been left. The salesgirl seemed surprised. She turned quickly, inspecting the stock shelf from where she had taken the package to begin with. Several others were on the shelf; some, the ounce-size Norell. Erica sensed the girl's uncertainty: had she put the package back or not?

Erica, being careful not to watch directly, heard the customer who had just arrived ask a question. The perfume clerk responded, but seemed worried and was looking around her. Erica felt herself inspected. As she did, she smiled at the cosmetics clerk and told her, 'I'll take this one.' Erica sensed the inspection by the other salesclerk finish.

Nothing had happened. The salesgirl was probably more worried about her own carelessness, and what might happen to her as a result of it, than anything else. As Erica paid for the lipstick, opening her handbag only a little to extract a billfold, she relaxed.

Before leaving, with a sense of mischief, she even stopped at the perfume counter to try a sample of Norell.

Only when Erica was nearing the store's outer door did her nervousness return. It became terror as she realized: she might have been seen after all, then watched and allowed to get this far so that the store would have a stronger case against her. She seemed to remember reading somewhere that that kind of thing happened. The parking mall, visible outside, seemed a waiting, friendly haven – near, yet still far away.

'Good afternoon, madam.' From nowhere, it seemed to Erica, a man had appeared beside her. He was middle-aged, greying, and had a fixed smile revealing prominent front teeth.

Erica froze. Her heart seemed to stop. So after all . . .

'Was everything satisfactory, madam?'

Her mouth was dry. 'Yes . . . yes, thank you.'

Deferentially, the man held a door open. 'Good day.'

Then, relief flooding through her, she was in the open air. Outside.

Driving away, at first, she had a let-down feeling. Now that she knew how unnecessary all the worrying had been, that there was nothing whatever she need have become concerned about, her fears while in the store seemed foolishly excessive. She still wondered, though: what had made her do it?

Suddenly, her mood became buoyant; she felt better than she had in weeks.

Erica's buoyancy persisted through the afternoon and carried over while she prepared dinner for Adam and herself. No carelessness in the kitchen tonight!

She had chosen Fondue Bourguignonne as the main course, partly because it was one of Adam's favourites, but mostly because the idea of them eating together out of the same fondue pot suggested an intimacy which she hoped would continue through the evening. In the dining-room, Erica planned her table setting carefully. She chose yellow taper candles in spiral silver holders, the candles flanking an arrangement of chrysanthemums. She had bought the flowers on the way home, and now put those left over in the living-room so that Adam would see them when he came in. The house gleamed, as it always did after a day's sprucing by Mrs Gooch. About an hour before Adam was due, Erica lit a log fire.

Unfortunately, Adam was late, which was not unusual; what *was* unusual was his failure to telephone to let Erica know. When 7.30 came and went, then 7.45 and eight o'clock, she became increasingly restless, going frequently to a front window which overlooked the driveway, then rechecking the dining-room, after that the kitchen where she opened the refrigerator to satisfy herself that the salad greens, prepared over an hour ago, had retained their crispness. The beef tenderloin for the fondue which Erica had cut into bite-size pieces earlier, as well as condiments and sauces already in serving dishes were in there too. When Adam did arrive, it would take only minutes to have dinner ready.

She had already replenished the living-room fire a couple of times, so that now the living- and dining-rooms, which opened into each other, were excessively hot. Erica opened a window, allowing cold air to blow in, which in turn made the fire smoke, so she closed the window, then wondered about the wine – a '61 Château Latour, one of a few special bottles they had squirrelled away – which she had opened at six o'clock, expecting to serve it at half past seven. Now Erica took the wine back to the kitchen and recorked it.

Returning, with everything completed, she switched on a stereo tape player. A cassette was already inserted; the last bars of a recording finished, another began.

It was *Bahama Islands*, a song she loved, which her father used to strum on his guitar while Erica sang. But tonight the soft calypso melody made her sad and homesick.

Gentle breezes swirl the shifting strand,
Clear blue waters lap this fragrant land;
Fair Bahamas!
Sweet Bahamas!
Sun and sand.

Arc of islands, set in shining seas,
White sand beaches rim these sun-kissed cays;
Island living,
Island loving,
Sand and trees.

Bright hibiscus line the path to shore,
Coral grottoes grace the ocean floor—
Nature's treasure,
Life's sweet pleasure,
Evermore.

She snapped the machine off, leaving the song unfinished, and dabbed quickly at sudden tears before they spoiled what little make-up she was wearing.

At five past eight the telephone rang and Erica hurried to it expectantly. It was not Adam, as she hoped, but long distance for 'Mr Trenton', and during the exchange with the operator, Erica realized that the caller was Adam's sister, Teresa, in Pasedena, California. When the West Coast operator asked, 'Will you speak with anyone else?' Teresa, who must have been aware that her sister-in-law was on the line, hesitated, then said, 'No, I need Mr Trenton. Please leave a message for him to call.'

Erica was irritated by Teresa's parsimony in not letting the call go through; tonight she would have welcomed a conversation. Erica was aware that since Teresa became a widow a year ago, with four children to take care of, she needed to watch finances, but certainly not to the point of worrying about the cost of a long-distance phone call.

She made a note for Adam, with the Pasadena operator's number, so he could return the call later.

Then at twenty past eight, Adam called on Citizens Band radio from his car to say he was on the Southfield Freeway, en route home. It meant he was fifteen minutes away. By mutual arrangement Erica always had a Citizens receiver in the kitchen switched to standby during early evening, and if Adam called it was usually to include a code phrase. 'Activate olive'. He used it now, which meant he would be ready for a martini as soon as he came in. Relieved, and glad she had not chosen the kind of dinner which the long delay would have spoiled, Erica put two martini glasses into the kitchen freezer and began mixing the drinks.

There was still time to hurry to the bedroom, check her hair, freshen lipstick, and renew her perfume – *the* perfume. A full-length mirror told her that the Paisley lounging pyjamas which she had chosen as carefully as everything else, looked as good as earlier. When she heard Adam's key in the lock, Erica ran downstairs, irrationally nervous as a young bride.

He came in apologetically. 'Sorry about the time.'

As usual, Adam appeared fresh, unrumpled, and clear-eyed, as if ready to begin a day's work instead of having just completed one. Lately, though, Erica had detected a tension at times beneath the outward view; she wasn't sure about it now.

'It doesn't matter.' She dismissed the lateness as she kissed him, knowing that the worst thing she could do was to be *Hausfrau*-ish about the delayed dinner. Adam returned the kiss absently, then insisted on explaining what had delayed him while she poured their martinis in the living-room.

'Elroy and I were with Hub. Hub was firing broadsides. It wasn't the best time to break off and phone.'

'Broadsides at you?' Like every other company wife, Erica knew that Hub was Hubbard J. Hewitson, executive vice-president in charge of North American automotive operations, and an industry crown prince with tremendous power. The power included an ability to raise up or break any company executive other than the chairman of the board and president, the only two who outranked him. Hub's exacting standards were well known. He could be, and was, merciless to those who failed them.

'Partly at me,' Adam said. 'But mostly Hub was sounding off. He'll be over it tomorrow.' He told Erica about the Orion add-ons, and the cost, which Adam had known would trigger the blast it had. On returning from the proving ground to staff headquarters, Adam had reported to Elroy Braithwaite. The Product Development vice-president decided they should go to Hub immediately and get the fireworks over with, which was the way it happened.

But however rough Hub Hewitson might be, he was a fair man who had probably accepted by now the inevitability of the extra items and their cost. Adam knew he had made the right decision at the proving ground, though he was still aware of tension within himself, which the martini had eased a little, but not much.

He held out his glass for refilling, then dropped into a chair. 'It's damn hot in here tonight. Why did you light a fire?'

He had seated himself alongside the table which held some of the flowers which Erica had bought this afternoon. Adam pushed the flower vase aside to make a space for his glass.

'I thought a fire might be cheerful.'

He looked at her directly. 'Meaning it isn't usually?'

'I didn't say that.'

'May be you should have.' Adam stood up, then moved around the room, touching things in it, familiar things. It was an old habit, something he did when he was restless. Erica wanted to tell him: *Try touching me! You'll get more response!*

Instead she said, 'Oh, there's a letter from Kirk. He wrote it to us both. He's been made features editor of the university paper.'

'Um.' Adam's grunt was unenthusiastic.

'It's important to him.' She could not resist adding, 'As important as when a promotion happens to you.'

Adam swung around, his back to the fire. He said harshly, 'I've told you before, I'm used to the idea of Greg being a doctor. In fact, I like it. It's tough to qualify, and when he does he'll be contributing – doing something useful. But don't expect me, now or later, to be pleased about Kirk becoming a newspaperman, or anything that happens to him on the way.'

It was a perennial topic, and now Erica wished she hadn't raised it because they were off to a bad start. Adam's boys had had definite ideas about their own careers, long before she came into their lives. Just the same, in discussions afterwards Erica had supported their choices, making clear that she was glad they were not following Adam into the auto industry.

Later, she knew she had been unwise. The boys would have gone their own ways in any case, so all she succeeded in doing was to make Adam bitter because his own career, by implication, had been denigrated to his sons.

She said as mildly as she could, 'Surely being a newspaper writer is doing something useful.'

He shook his head irritably. The memory of this morning's Press conference, which he liked less and less the more he thought about it, was still with Adam. 'If you saw as much of the Press people as I do, you might not think so. Most of what they do is superficial, out of balance, prejudiced when they claim impartiality, and riddled with inaccuracies. They blame the inaccuracies on an obsession with speed, which is used the way a cripple uses a crutch. It never seems to occur to newspaper managements and writers that being slower, checking facts before they storm into print, might be a better public service. What's more, they're critics and self-appointed judges of everybody's failings except their own.'

'Some of that's true,' Erica said. 'But not of all newspapers or everybody working for them.'

Adam looked ready for an argument which she sensed could turn into a quarrel. Determined to snuff it out, Erica crossed the room and took his arm. She smiled. 'Let's hope Kirk will do better than those others and surprise you.'

The physical contact, of which they had had so little lately, gave her a sense of pleasure which, if she had her way, would be even greater before the evening was over. She insisted, 'Leave all that for another time. I have your favourite dinner waiting.'

'Let's make it as quick as we can,' Adam said. 'I've some papers I want to go over afterwards, and I'd like to get to them.'

Erica let go his arm and went to the kitchen, wondering if he realized how many times he had used almost the same words in identical circumstances until they seemed a litany.

Adam followed her in. 'Anything I can do?'

'You can put the dressing on the salad and toss it.'

He did it quickly, competently as always, then saw the note about Teresa's call from Pasadena. Adam told Erica, 'You go ahead and start. I'll see what Teresa wants.'

Once Adam's sister was on the phone she seldom talked briefly, long distance or not. 'I've waited this long,' Erica objected, 'I don't want to have dinner alone now. Can't you call later? It's only six o'clock out there.'

'Well, if we're really ready.'

Erica had rushed. The oil-butter mix, which she had heated in the fondue pot over the kitchen range, was ready. She carried it to the dining-room, set the pot on its stand and lit the canned heat beneath. Everything else was on the dining-table, which looked elegant.

As she brought a taper near the candles, Adam asked, 'Is it worth lighting them?'
'Yes.' She lit them all.

The candlelight revealed the wine which Erica had brought in again. Adam frowned. 'I thought we were keeping that for a special occasion.'

'Special like what?'

He reminded her, 'The Hewitsons and Braithwaites are coming next month.'

'Hub Hewitson doesn't know the difference between a Château Latour and Cold Duck, and couldn't care. Why can't *we* be special, just the two of us?'

Adam speared a piece of beef tenderloin and left it in the fondue pot while he began his salad. At length he said, 'Why is it you never lose a chance to take a dig at the people I work with, or the work I do?'

'Do I?'

'You know you do. You have, ever since our marriage.'

'Perhaps it's because I feel as if I fight for every private moment that we have.'

But she conceded to herself: sometimes she did throw needless slings and arrows, just as she had a moment ago about Hub Hewitson.

She filled Adam's wineglass and said gently, 'I'm sorry. What I said about Hub was snobbish and unnecessary. If you'd like him to have Château Latour, I'll go shopping for some more.' The thought occurred to her: *Maybe I can get an extra bottle or two the way I got the perfume.*

'Forget it,' Adam said. 'It doesn't matter.'

During coffee, he excused himself and went to his upstairs study to telephone Teresa.

'Hi there, bigshot! Where were you? Counting your stock options?' Teresa's voice came clearly across the two thousand miles between them, the big-sister contralto Adam remembered from their childhood long ago. Teresa had been seven when Adam was born. Yet, for all their gap in ages, they had always been close and, strangely, from the time Adam was in his early teens, Teresa had sought her younger brother's advice and often heeded it.

'You know how it is, sis. I'm indispensable, which makes it hard to get home. Sometimes I wonder how they ever started this industry without me.'

'We're all proud of you,' Teresa said. 'The kids often talk about Uncle Adam. They say he'll be company president someday.' Another thing about Teresa was her unconcealed pleasure at her brother's success. She had always reacted to his progress and promotions that way, with far more enthusiasm – he admitted reluctantly – than Erica had ever shown.

He asked, 'How have you been, sis?'

'Lonely.' A pause. 'You were expecting some other answer?'

'Not really. I wondered if, by now . . .'

'Somebody else had shown up?'

'Something like that.'

'A few have. I'm still not a bad-looking broad for a widow lady.'

'I know that.' It was true. Though she would be fifty in a year or so, Teresa was statuesque, classically beautiful, and sexy.

'The trouble is, when you've had a man – a real one – for twenty-two years, you start comparing others with him. They don't come out of it well.'

Teresa's husband, Clyde, had been an accountant with wide-ranging interests. He had died tragically in an aeroplane accident a year ago, leaving his widow with four young children, adopted late in their marriage. Since then, Teresa had had to make major adjustments both psychologically and in financial management, the latter an area she had never bothered with before.

Adam asked, 'Is the money end all right?'

'I think so. But it's that I called you about. Sometimes I wish you were closer.'

Though Adam's late brother-in-law had left adequate provision for his family, his financial affairs had been untidy at the time of his death. As best he could from a distance, Adam had helped Teresa unravel them.

'If you really need me,' Adam said, 'I can fly out for a day or two.'

'No. You're already where I need you – in Detroit. I get concerned about that investment Clyde made in Stephensen Motors. It earns money, but it represents a lot of capital – most of what we have – and I keep asking myself: should I leave it where it is, or sell out and put the money into something safer?'

Adam already knew the background. Teresa's husband had been an auto-racing buff who haunted tracks in Southern California, so that he came to know many racing drivers well. One had been Smokey Stephensen, a consistent winner over the years who, unusually for his kind, had shrewdly held on to his prize money and eventually quit with most of his winnings intact. Later, using his name and prestige, Smokey Stephensen obtained an auto dealership franchise in Detroit, marketing the products of Adam's company. Teresa's husband had gone into silent partnership with the ex-race driver and contributed almost one-half of needed capital. The shares in the business were now owned by Teresa who received them under Clyde's will.

'Sis, you say you're getting money from Detroit – from Stephensen?'

'Yes. I haven't the figures, though I can send them to you, and the accountants who took over Clyde's office say it's a fair return. What worries me is all I read about car dealerships being risky investments, and some of them failing. If it happened to Stephensen's, the kids and I could be in trouble.'

'It can happen,' Adam acknowledged. 'But if you're lucky enough to have shares in a good dealership, you might make a big mistake by pulling out.'

'I realize that. It's why I need someone to advise me, someone I can trust. Adam, I hate to ask this because I know you're working hard already. But do you think you could spend some time with Smokey Stephensen, find out what's going on, form your own opinion about how things look then tell me what I ought to do? If you remember, we talked about this once before.'

'I remember. And I think I explained then, it could be a problem. Auto companies don't allow their staff to be involved with auto dealerships. Before I could do anything, it would have to go before the Conflict of Interest Committee.'

'Is that a big thing? Would it embarrass you?'

Adam hesitated. The answer was: it *would* embarrass him. To do what Teresa asked would involve a close study of the Stephensen dealership, which meant looking into its books and reviewing operating methods. Teresa, of course, would provide Adam with authority from her point of view, but the point of view of Adam's company – his employers – was something else again. Before Adam could cosey up with a car dealer, for whatever purpose, he would have to declare what he was doing, and why. Elroy Braithwaite would need to know; so would Hub Hewitson, probably, and it was a safe bet that neither would like the idea. Their reasoning would be simple. A senior executive of Adam's status was in a position to do financial favours for a dealer, hence the strict rules which all auto companies had about outside business interests in this and other areas. A standing Conflict of Interest Committee reviewed such matters, including personal investments of company employees and their families, reported yearly on a form resembling an income tax return. A few people who resented this, put investments in their wives' or children's names, and kept them secret. But mostly the rules made sense, and executives observed them.

Well, he would have to go to the committee, Adam supposed, and state his arguments. After all, he had nothing to gain personally; he would merely be protecting the interests of a widow and young children, which gave the request a compassionate overtone. In fact, the more he thought about it, the less trouble he anticipated.

'I'll see what I can work out, sis,' Adam said into the telephone. 'Tomorrow I'll start things moving in the company, then it may be a week or two before I get approval to go ahead. You do understand I can't do anything without that?'

'Yes, I do. And the delay doesn't matter. As long as I know you're going to be looking out for us, that's the important thing.' Teresa sounded relieved. He could picture her now, the small concentrated frown she had when dealing with something difficult had probably gone, replaced by a warm smile, the kind which made a man feel good. Adam's sister was a woman who liked to rely on a male and have him handle decisions, though during the past year she had been forced to make an unaccustomed number of her own.

Adam asked, 'How much of the Stephensen Motors stock did Clyde have?'

'It was forty-nine per cent, and I still have all of it. Clyde put up about two hundred and forty thousand dollars. That's why I've been so concerned.'

'Was Clyde's name on the franchise?'

'No. Just Smokey Stephensen's.'

He instructed, 'You'd better send me all the papers, including a record of payments you've had as dividends. Write to Stephensen, too. Tell him he'll probably be hearing from me, and that I have your authority to go in and look things over. OK?'

'I'll do that. And thank you, Adam dear; thank you very much. Please give my love to Erica. How is she?'

'Oh, she's fine.'

Erica had cleared away their meal and was on the sofa in the living-room, feet curled beneath her, when Adam returned.

She motioned to an end table. 'I made more coffee.'

'Thanks.' He poured a cup for himself, then went to the hallway for his briefcase. Returning, he sank into an armchair by the fire, which had now burned low, opened his briefcase and began to take out papers.

Erica asked, 'What did Teresa want?'

In a few words Adam explained his sister's request and what he had agreed to do.

He found Erica looking at him incredulously. 'When will you do it?'

'Oh, I don't know. I'll find time.'

'But when? I want to know when.'

With a trace of irritation, Adam said, 'If you decide to do something, you can always make the time.'

'You don't make time.' Erica's voice had an intensity which had been lacking earlier. 'You take the time from something or somebody else. Won't it mean a lot of visits to that dealer? Questioning people. Finding out about the business. I know how you do everything – always the same way, thoroughly. So it will involve a lot of time. Well, won't it?'

He conceded, 'I suppose so.'

'Will it be in office time? In the daytime, during the week?'

'Probably not.'

'So that leaves evenings and weekends. Car dealers are open then, aren't they?'

Adam said curtly, 'They don't open Sundays.'

'Well, hooray for that!' Erica hadn't intended to be this way tonight. She had wanted to be patient, understanding, loving, but suddenly bitterness swept over her. She flared on, knowing she would do better to stop, but unable to, 'Perhaps this dealer *would* open on Sunday if you asked him nicely, if you explained that you still have a little time left to spend at home with your wife, and you'd like to do something about it, like filling it with work.'

'Listen,' Adam said, 'this won't be work, and I wouldn't do it if I had the choice. It's simply for Teresa.'

'How about something simply for Erica? Or would that be too much? Wait! – why not use your vacation time as well, then you could . . . '

'You're being silly,' Adam said. He had taken the papers from his briefcase and spread them around him in a semicircle. Like a witch's circle on the grass, Erica thought, to be penetrated only by the anointed, the bewitched. Even voices entering the magic circle became distorted, misunderstood, with words and meanings twisted . . .

Adam was right. She *was* being silly. And now whimsical.

She went behind him, still conscious of the semicircle, skirting its perimeter the way children playing games avoided lines in paving stones.

Erica put her hands lightly on Adam's shoulders, her face against his. He reached up, touching one of her hands.

'I couldn't turn sis down.' Adam's voice was conciliatory. 'How could I? If things had been the other way around, Clyde would have done as much, or more, for you.'

Abruptly, unexpectedly, she realized, their moods had switched. She thought: there *is* a way into a witch's circle. Perhaps the trick was not to expect to find it, then suddenly you did.

'I know,' Erica said. 'And I'm grateful it *isn't* the other way around.' She had a sense of reprieve from her own stupidity only seconds earlier, an awareness of having stumbled without warning in to a moment of intimacy and tenderness. She went on softly, 'It's just that sometimes I want things between you and me to be the way they were in the beginning. I really do see so little of you.' She scratched lightly with her fingernails, around his ears, something she used to do but hadn't for a long time. 'I still love you.' And was tempted to add, but didn't: *Please, oh please, make love to me tonight!*

'I haven't changed either,' Adam said. 'No reason to. And I know what you mean about the time we have. Maybe after the Orion's launched there'll be more of it.' But the last remark lacked conviction. As both of them already knew, after Orion would be Farstar, which would probably prove more demanding still. Involuntarily, Adam's eyes strayed back to the papers spread out before him.

Erica told herself: *Don't rush! Don't push too hard!* She said, 'While you're doing that, I think I'll go for a walk. I feel like it.'

'Do you want me to come with you?'

She shook her head. 'You'd better finish. 'If he left the work now, she knew he would either return to it late tonight or get up ridiculously early in the morning.

Adam looked relieved.

Outside the house, Erica pulled tightly around her the suede jacket she had slipped on, and stepped out briskly. She had a scarf wound around her hair. The air was chilly, though the wind which had buffeted the Motor City through the day had dropped. Erica liked to walk at night. She used to in the Bahamas, and still did here, though friends and neighbours sometimes cautioned that she shouldn't because crime in Detroit had risen alarmingly in recent years, and now even suburban Birmingham and Bloomfield Hills – once considered almost crime-free – had muggings and armed robberies.

But Erica preferred to take her chances and her walks.

Though the night was dark, with stars and moon obscured by clouds, enough light came from the houses of Quarton Lake for Erica to see her way clearly. As she passed the houses, sometimes observing figures inside, she wondered about those other families in their own environments, their hangups, misunderstandings, conflicts, problems. Obviously, all had some, and the difference between most was only in degree. More to the point, she wondered: How fared the marriages inside those other walls, compared with Adam's and her own?

A majority of the neighbours were automotive people among whom the shedding of spouses nowadays seemed routine. American tax laws eased the way, and many a highly paid executive had discovered he could have his freedom by paying large alimony which cost him almost nothing. The alimony came off the top of his salary, so that he merely paid it to his ex-wife instead of to the government as income tax. A few people in the industry had even done it twice.

But it was always the foundered marriages which made the news. Plenty of the other kind existed – lasting love stories which had weathered well. Erica thought of names she had learned since coming to Detroit: Riccardos, Gerstenbergs, Knudsens, Iacoccas, Roches, Brambletts, others. There had been outstanding second marriages, too: the Henry Fords, Ed Coles, Roy Chapins, Bill Mitchells, Pete and Connie Estes, the John DeLoreans. As always, it depended on the individuals.

Erica walked for half an hour. On her way back, a soft rain began to fall. She held her face towards the rain until it was wet and streaming, yet somehow comforting.

She went in without disturbing Adam who was still in the living-room, immersed in papers. Upstairs, Erica dried her face, combed out her hair, then undressed and put on the nightgown she had bought earlier today. Surveying herself critically, she was aware that the sheer beige nylon did even more for her than she had expected in the store. She used the orange lipstick, then applied Norell generously.

From the living-room doorway she asked Adam, 'Will you be long?'

He glanced up, then down again at a blue-bound folder in his hand. 'Maybe half an hour.'

Adam had not appeared to notice the see-through nightgown which could not compete, apparently, with the folder, lettered, *Statistical Projection of Automobile and Truck*

Registration by States. Hoping that the perfume might prove more effective Erica came behind his chair as she had earlier, but all that happened was a perfunctory kiss with a muttered, 'Good night; don't wait for me.' She might as well, she thought, have been drenched in camphorated oil.

She went to bed, and lay with top sheet and blanket turned back, her sexual desire growing as she waited. If she closed her eyes, she could imagine Adam poised above her . . .

Erica opened her eyes. A bedside clock showed that not half an hour, but almost two hours, had passed. It was 1 a.m.

Soon after, she heard Adam climb the stairs. He came in, yawning, with a, 'God, I'm tired,' then undressed sleepily, climbed into bed, and was almost instantly asleep.

Erica lay silently beside him, sleep for herself far away. After a while she imagined that she was once more walking, out of doors, the softness of the rain upon her face.

9

The day after Adam and Erica Trenton failed to bridge the growing gap between them, after Brett De Losanto renewed his faith in the Orion yet pondered his artistic destiny, after Barbara Zaleski viewed frustrations through the benthos of martinis, and after Matt Zaleski, her plant-boss father, survived another pressure-cooker work day, a minor event occurred in the inner city of Detroit, unconnected with any of those five, yet whose effect, over months ahead, would involve and motivate them all.

Time: 8.30 p.m. *Place*: Downtown, Third Avenue, near Brainard. An empty police cruiser parked beside the kerb.

'Get your black ass against the wall,' the white cop commanded. Holding a flashlight in one hand, a gun in the other, he ran the flashlight's beam down and up Rollie Knight, who blinked as the light reached his eyes and stayed there.

'Now turn around. Hands over your head. Move! – you goddam jailbird.'

As Rollie Knight turned, the white cop told his Negro partner, 'Frisk the bastard.'

The young, shabbily dressed black man whom the policemen had stopped, had been ambling aimlessly on Third when the cruiser pulled alongside and its occupants jumped out, guns drawn. Now he protested, 'Wad'd I do?' then giggled as the second policeman's hands moved up his legs, then around his body. 'Hey man, oh man, that tickles!'

'Shaddup!' the white cop said. He was an old-timer on the force, with hard eyes and a big belly, the last from years of riding in patrol cars. He had survived this beat a long time and never relaxed while on it.

The black policeman, who was several years younger and newer, dropped his hands. 'He's OK.' Moving back, he inquired softly, 'What difference does the colour of his ass make?'

The white cop looked startled. In their haste since moving from the cruiser he had forgotten that tonight his usual partner, also white, was off sick, with a black officer substituting.

'Hell!' he said hastily. 'Don't get ideas. Even if you are his colour, you don't rate down with that crumb.'

The black cop said dryly, 'Thanks.' He considered saying more, but didn't. Instead, he told the man against the wall, 'You can put your hands down. Turn around.'

As the instruction was obeyed, the white cop rasped, 'Where you been the last half-hour, Knight?' He knew Rollie Knight by name, not only from seeing him around here frequently, but from a police record which included two jail convictions, for one of which the officer had made the arrest himself.

'Where I bin?' The young black man had recovered from his initial shock. Though his cheeks were hollowed, and he appeared underfed and frail, there was nothing weak about his eyes, which mirrored hatred. 'I bin layin' a white piece o' ass. Doan know her name, except she says her old man's a fat white pig who can't get it up. Comes here when she needs it from a man.'

The white cop took a step forward, the blood vessels in his face swelling red. His intention was to smash the muzzle of his gun across the contemptuous, taunting face. Afterwards, he could claim that Knight struck him first and his own action was in self-defence. His partner would back up his story, in the same way that they always corroborated each other, except – he remembered abruptly – tonight his partner was one of *them*, who might just be ornery enough to make trouble later. So the policeman checked himself, knowing there would be another time and place, as this smart-aleck nigger would find out.

The black cop growled at Rollie Knight, 'Don't push your luck. Tell us where you were.'

The young Negro spat on the sidewalk. A cop was an enemy, whatever his colour, and a black one was worse because he was a lackey of the Man. But he answered, 'In there,' motioning to a basement bar across the street.'

'How long?'

'An hour. Maybe two. Maybe three.' Rollie Knight shrugged. 'Who keeps score?'

The black cop asked his partner, 'Should I check it out?'

'No, be a wasta time. They'd say he'd been there. They're all damn liars.'

The black officer pointed out, 'To get here in this time from West Grand and Second he'd have needed wings, anyway.'

The call had come in minutes earlier on the prowl car radio. An armed robbery near the Fishery Building, eighteen blocks away. It had just happened. Two suspects had fled in a late model sedan.

Seconds later, the patrolling duo had seen Rollie Knight walking alone on Third Avenue. Though the likelihood of a single pedestrian, here, being involved with the uptown robbery was remote, when the white cop had recognized Knight, he shouted to halt the car, then jumped out, leaving his partner no choice but to follow. The black officer knew why they had acted. The robbery call provided an excuse to 'stop and frisk', and the other officer enjoyed stopping people and bullying them when he knew he could get away with it, though it was coincidental, of course, that those he picked on were invariably black.

There was a relationship, the black officer believed, between his companion's viciousness and brutality – which were well known around the force – and fear, which rode him while on duty in the ghetto. Fear had its own stink, and the black policeman had smelled it strongly from the white officer beside him the moment the robbery call came in, and when they had jumped from the car, and even now. Fear could, and did, make a mean man meaner still. When he possessed authority as well, he could become a savage.

Not that fear was out of place in these surroundings. In fact, for a Detroit policeman not to know fear would betray a lack of knowledge, an absence of imagination. In the inner city, with a crime rate probably the nation's highest, police were targets – always of hate, often of bricks and knives and bullets. Where survival depended on alertness, a degree of fear was rational; so were suspicion, caution, swiftness when danger showed, or seemed to. It was like being in a war where police were on the firing line. And as in any war, the niceties of human behaviour – politeness, psychology, tolerance, kindness – got brushed aside as nonessential, so that the war intensified while antagonisms – often with cause on both sides – perpetuated themselves and multiplied.

Yet a few policemen, as the black cop knew, learned to live with fear while remaining decent human beings, too. These were ones who understood the nature of the times, the mood of black people, their frustrations, the long history of injustice behind them. This kind of policemen – whether white or black – helped relieve the war a little, though it was hard to know how much because they were not in a majority.

To make moderates a majority, and to raise standards of the Detroit force generally, were declared aims of a recently appointed police-chief. But between the chief and his objectives was the physical presence of a contingent of officers, numerically strong, who through fear or rooted prejudice were frankly racist like the white cop here and now.

'Where you working, crumb?' he demanded of Rollie Knight.

'I'm like you. I ain't workin', just passin' time.'

The policeman's face bulged again with anger. If he had not been there, the black cop knew, his partner would have smashed his fist into the frail young black face leering at him.

The black cop told Rollie Knight, 'Beat it! You flap your mouth too much.'

Back in the prowl car the other policeman fumed, 'So help me, I'll nail that bastard.'

The black officer thought: *And so you will, probably tomorrow or the next day when you've got your regular sidekick back, and he'll look the other way if there's a beating or an arrest on some trumped-up charge.* There had been plenty of other vendettas of the same kind.

On impulse, the black cop, who was behind the wheel, said, 'Hold it! I'll be back.'

As he got out of the car, Rollie Knight was fifty yards away.

'Hey, you!' When the young black man turned, the officer beckoned, then walked to meet him.

The black cop leaned towards Rollie Knight, his stance threatening. But he said quietly. 'My partner's out to get you, and he will. You're a stupid jerk for letting your mouth run off, and I don't owe you favours. All the same, I'm warning you: stay out of sight, or better – get out of town 'till the man cools.'

'A Judas nigger cop! Why'd I take the word from you?'

'No reason.' The policeman shrugged. 'So let what's coming come. No skin off me.'

'How'd I leave? Where'd I get wheels, the bread?' Though spoken with a sneer, the query was a shade less hostile.

'Then don't leave. Keep out of sight, the way I said.'

'Ain't easy here, man.'

No, it was not easy, as the black cop knew. Not easy to remain unnoticed through each long day and night when someone wanted you and others knew where you were. Information came cheap if you knew the pipelines of the inner city; all it took was the price of a fix, the promise of a favour, even the right kind of threat. Loyalty was not a plant which flourished here. But being somewhere else, absence for part of the time, at least, would help. The policeman asked, 'Why aren't you working?'

Rollie Knight grinned. 'You hear me tell your pig friend . . .'

'Save the smart talk. You want work?'

'Maybe.' But behind the admission was the knowledge that few jobs were open to those with criminal records like Rollie Knight's.

'The car plants are hiring,' the black cop said.

'That's honky land.'

'Plenty of the blood work there.'

Rollie Knight said grudgingly. 'I tried one time. Some whitey fink said no.'

'Try again. Here.' From a tunic pocket the black cop pulled a card. It had been given him, the day before, by a company employment office man he knew. It had the address of a hiring hall, a name, some hours of opening.

Rollie Knight crumpled the card and thrust it in a pocket. 'When I feel like it, baby, I'll piss on it.'

'Suit yourself,' the black cop said. He walked back to the car.

His white partner looked at him suspiciously. 'What was all that?'

He answered shortly, 'I cooled him down,' but did not elaborate.

The black policeman had no intention of being bullied, but neither did he want an argument – at least, not now. Though Detroit's populace was forty per cent black, only in most recent years had its police force ceased to be nearly a hundred per cent white, and within the police department old influences still predominated. Since the 1967 Detroit riots, under public pressure the number of black policemen had increased, but blacks were not yet strong enough in numbers, rank, or influence to offset the powerful, white-oriented Detroit Police Officers Association, or even to be sure of a fair deal, departmentally, in any black-white confrontation.

Thus, the patrol continued in an atmosphere of hostile uncertainty, a mood reflecting the racial tension of Detroit itself.

Bravado in individuals, black or white, is often only skin shallow, and Rollie Knight, inside his soul, was frightened.

He was frightened of the white cop whom he had unwisely baited, and he realized now that his reckless, burning hatred had briefly got the better of ordinary caution. Even more, he feared a return to prison where one more conviction was likely to send him down for a long time. Rollie had three convictions behind him, and two prison terms; whatever happened now, all hope of leniency was gone.

Only a black man in America knows the true depths of animal despair and degradation to which the prison system can reduce a human being. It is true that white prisoners are often treated badly, and suffer also, but never as consistently or universally as black. It is also true that some prisons are better or worse than other prisons, but this is like saying that certain parts of hell are ten degrees hotter or cooler than others. The black man, whichever prison he is in, knows that humiliation and abuse are standard, and that physical brutality – sometimes involving major injury – is as normal as defecating. And when the prisoner is frail – as Rollie Knight was frail, partly from a poor physique which he was born with, and partly from accumulated malnutrition over years – the penalties and anguish can be greater still.

Coupled, at this moment, with these fears was the young Negro's knowledge that a police search of his room would reveal a small supply of marijuana. He smoked a little grass himself, but peddled most, and while rewards were slight, at least it was a means to eat because, since coming out of prison several months ago, he had found no other way. But the marijuana was all the police would need for a conviction, with jail to follow.

For this reason, later the same night while nervously wondering if he was already watched, Rollie Knight dumped the marijuana in a vacant lot. Now, instead of a tenuous hold on the means to live from day to day, he was aware that he had none.

It was this awareness which, next day, caused him to uncrumple the card which the black cop had given him and go to the auto company hiring center in the inner city. He went without hope because . . . (and this is the great, invisible gap which separates the 'have-nots-and-never-hads' of this world, like Rollie Knight, from the 'haves', including some who try to understand their less-blessed brothers yet, oh so sadly, fail) . . . he had lived so long without any reason to believe in anything, that hope itself was beyond his mental grasp.

He also went because he had nothing else to do.

The building near 12th Street, like a majority of others in the inner city's grim 'black bottom', was decrepit and unkempt, with shattered windows, of which only a few had been boarded over for inside protection from the weather. Until recently the building had been disused and was disintegrating rapidly. Even now, despite patching and rough painting, its decay continued, and those who went to work there daily sometimes wondered if the walls would be standing when they left at night.

But the ancient building, and two others like it, had an urgent function. It was an outpost for the auto companies' 'hard-core' hiring programmes.

So-called hard-core hiring had begun after the Detroit riots and was an attempt to provide work for an indigent nucleus of inner city people – mostly black – who, tragically and callously, had for years been abandoned as unemployable. The lead was taken by the auto companies. Others followed. Naturally, the auto companies claimed altruism as their motive and, from the moment the hiring programmes started, public relations staffs proclaimed their employers' public spirit. More cynical observers claimed that the auto world was running scared, fearing the effect of a permanently strife-ridden community on their businesses. Others predicted that when smoke from the riot-torn, burning city touched the General Motors Building in '67 (as it did), and flames came close, some form of public service was assured. The prediction came true, except that Ford moved first.

But whatever the motivations, three things generally were agreed: the hard-core hiring programme was good. It ought to have happened twenty years before it did. Without the '67 riots, it might never have happened at all.

On the whole, allowing for errors and defeats, the programme worked. Auto companies lowered their hiring standards, letting former deadbeats in. Predictably, some fell by the way, but a surprising number proved that all a deadbeat needed was a chance. By the time Rollie Knight arrived, much had been learned by employers and employed.

He sat in a waiting-room with about forty others, men and women, ranged on rows of chairs. The chairs, like the applicants for jobs, were of assorted shapes and sizes, except that the applicants had a uniformity: all were black. There was little conversation. For Rollie Knight, the waiting took an hour. During part of it he dozed off, a habit he had acquired and which helped him, normally, to get through empty days.

When, eventually, he was ushered into an interview cubicle – one of a half-dozen lining the waiting area – he was still sleepy and yawned at the interviewer, facing him across a desk.

The interviewer, a middle-aged, chubby black man, wearing horn-rimmed glasses, a sports jacket and dark shirt, but no tie, said amiably, 'Gets tiring waiting. My daddy used to say, "A man grows wearier sitting on his backside than chopping wood." He had me chop a lot of wood that way.'

Rollie Knight looked at the other's hands. 'You ain't chopped much lately.'

'Well, now,' the interviewer said, 'you're right. And we've established something else. You're a man who looks at things and thinks. But are *you* interested in chopping wood, or doing work that's just as hard?'

'I dunno.' Rollie was wondering why he had come here at all. Soon they would get to his prison record, and that would be the end of it.

'But you're here because you want a job?' The interviewer glanced at a yellow card which a secretary outside had filled in. 'That's correct, isn't it, Mr Knight?'

Rollie nodded. The 'Mr' surprised him. He could not remember when he had last been addressed that way.

'Let's begin by finding out about you.' The interviewer drew a printed pad towards him. Part of the new hiring technique was that applicants no longer had to complete a pre-employment questionnaire themselves. In the past, many who could barely read or write were turned away because of inability to do what modern society thought of as a standard function: fill in a form.

They went quickly through the basic questions.

Name: Knight, Rolland Joseph Louis. *Age*: 29. *Address*: he gave it, *not mentioning that the mean, walk-up room belonged to someone else who had let him share it for a day or two, and that the address might not be good next week if the occupant decided to kick Rollie out. But then a large part of his life had alternated between that kind of accommodation, or a flophouse, or the streets when he had nowhere else.*

Parents: He recited the names. The surnames differed since his parents had not married or ever lived together. The interviewer made no comment; it was normal enough. Nor did Rollie add: *He knew his father because his mother had told him who he was, and Rollie had a vague impression of a meeting once: a burly man, heavy-jowled and scowling, with a facial scar, who had been neither friendly not interested in his son. Years ago, Rollie had heard his father was in jail as a lifer. Whether he was still there, or dead, he had no idea. As for his mother, with whom he lived, more or less, until he left home for the streets at the age of fifteen, he believed she was now in Cleveland or Chicago. He had not seen or heard from her for several years.*

Schooling: Until grade eight. *He had had a quick, bright mind at school, and still had when something new came up, but realized how much a black man needed to learn if he was to beat the stinking honky system, and now he never would.*

Previous employment: He strained to remember names and places. *There had been unskilled jobs after leaving shcool – a bus boy, shovelling snow, washing cars. Then in 1957, when Detroit was hit by a national recession, there were no jobs of any kind and he drifted into idleness, punctuated by shooting craps, hustling, and his first conviction: auto theft.*

The interviewer asked, 'Do you have a police record, Mr Knight?'

'Yeah.'

'I'm afraid I'll need the details. And I think I should tell you that we check up afterwards, so it looks better if we get it correctly from you first.'

Rollie shrugged. Sure the sons-of-bitches checked. He knew that, without being given all this grease.

He gave the employment guy the dope on the auto theft rap first. He was nineteen then. He'd been put on a year's probation.

Never mind now about the way it happened. Who cared that the others in the car had picked him up, that he'd gone along, as a back-seat passenger, for laughs, and later the cops had stopped them, charging all six occupants with theft? Before going into court next day, Rollie was offered a deal: plead guilty and he'd get probation. Bewildered, frightened, he agreed. The deal was kept. He was in and out of court in seconds. Only later had he learned that with a lawyer to advise him – the way a white kid would have had – a not guilty plea would probably have got him off, with no more than a warning from the judge. Nor had he been told that pleading guilty would ensure a criminal record, to sit like an evil genie on his shoulder the remainder of his life.

It also made the sentence for the next conviction tougher.

The interviewer asked, 'What happened after that?'

'I was in the pen.' It was a year later. Auto theft again. *This time for real, and there had been two other times he wasn't caught.* The sentence: two years.

'Anything else?'

This was the clincher. Always, after this, they closed the books – no dice, no work. Well, they could stick their stinking job; Rollie still wondered why he had come. 'Armed robbery. I drew five to fifteen, did four years in Jackson Pen.'

A jewellery store. Two of them had broken in at night. All they got was a handful of cheap watches and were caught as they came out. Rollie had been stupid enough to carry a .22. Though he hadn't pulled it from his pocket, the fact that it was found on him ensured the graver charge.

'You were released for good behaviour?'

'No. The warden got jealous. He wanted my cell.'

The middle-aged Negro interviewer looked up. 'I dig jokes. They make a dull day brighter. But it *was* good behaviour?'

'If you say so.'

'All right, I'll say so.' The interviewer wrote it down.

'Is your behaviour good now, Mr Knight? What I mean is, are you in any more trouble with the police?'

Rollie shook his head negatively. He wasn't going to tell this Uncle Tom about last night, that he *was* in trouble if he couldn't keep clear of the white pig he had spooked, and who would bust him some way, given half a chance, using scum bag honky law. The thought was a reminder of his earlier fears, which now returned: the dread of prison, the real reason for coming here. The interviewer was asking more questions, busier than a dog with fleas writing down the answers. Rollie was surprised they hadn't stopped, baffled that he wasn't already outside on the street, the way it usually went after he mouthed the words 'armed robbery'.

What he didn't know – because no-one had thought to tell him, and he was not a reader of newspapers or magazines – was that hard core hiring had a new, less rigid attitude to prison records, too.

He was sent to another room where he stripped and had a physical.

The doctor, young, white, impersonal, working fast, took time out to look critically at Rollie's bony body, his emaciated cheeks. 'Whatever job you get, use some of what they pay you to eat better, and put some weight on, otherwise you won't last at it. You wouldn't last, anyway, in the foundry where most people go from here. Maybe they can put you in Assembly. I'll recommend it.'

Rollie listened contemptuously, already hating the system, the people in it. Who in hell did this smug whitey kid think he was? Some kind of God? If Rollie didn't need bread badly, some work for a while, he'd walk out now, and screw 'em. One thing was sure: whatever job these people gave him, he wouldn't stay on it one day longer than he had to.

Back through the waiting-room, in the cubicle again. The original interviewer announced, 'The doctor says you're breathing, and when you opened your mouth he couldn't see daylight, so we're offering you a job. It's in final assembly. The work is hard, but pay is good – the union sees to that. Do you want it?'

'I'm here, ain't I?' What did the son-of-a-bitch expect? A bootlick job?

'Yes, you're here, so I'll take that to mean yes. There will be some weeks of training; you get paid for that, too. Outside, they'll give you details – when to start, where to go. Just one other thing.'

Here came the preaching. Sure as glory, Rollie Knight could smell it. Maybe this white nigger was a Holy Roller on the side.

The interviewer took off his horn-rimmed glasses, leaned over the desk and put his fingertips together. 'You're smart. You know the score. You know you're getting a break, and it's because of the times, the way things are. People, companies like this one, have a conscience they didn't always have. Never mind that it's late; it's here, and a lot of other things are changing. You may not believe it, but they are.' The chubby, sports-jacketed interviewer picked up a pencil, rolled it through his fingers, put it down. 'Maybe you never had a break before, and this is the first. I think it is. But I wouldn't be doing my job if I didn't tell you that with your record it's the only one you'll get, leastways here. A lot of guys pass through this place. Some make it after they leave; others don't. Those who do are the ones who want to.' The interviewer looked hard at Rollie. 'Stop being a damn fool, Knight, and grab this chance. That's the best advice you'll get today.' He put out a hand. 'Good luck.'

Reluctantly, feeling as if he had been suckered but not knowing exactly how, Rollie took the proffered hand.

Outside, just the way the man said, they told him how to go to work.

The training course, sponsored jointly by the company and through federal grants, was eight weeks long. Rollie Knight lasted a week and a half.

He received the first week's pay cheque, which was more money than he had possessed in a long time. Over the following weekend he tied one on. However, on Monday he managed to awaken early and catch a bus which took him to the factory training centre on the other side of town.

But on Tuesday, tiredness won. He failed to wake until, through the curtainless dirty windows of his room, the sun shone directly on his face. Rollie got up sleepily, blinking, and went to the window to look down. A clock in the street below showed that it was almost noon.

He knew he had blown it, that the job was gone. His reaction was indifference. He did not experience disappointment because, from the beginning, he had not expected any other outcome. How and when the ending came were merely details.

Experience had never taught Rollie Knight – or tens of thousands like him – to take a long-term view of anything. When you were born with nothing, had gained nothing since, had learned to live with nothing, there *was* no long-term view – only today, this moment, here and now. Many in the white world – nescient, shallow thinkers – called the attitude 'shiftless', and condemned it. Sociologists, with more understanding and some sympathy, named the syndrome 'present time orientation' or 'distrust of the future'. Rollie had heard neither phrase, but his instincts embraced both. Instinct also told him, at this moment, he was still tired. He went back to sleep.

He made no attempt, later, to return to the training centre or the hiring hall. He went back to his haunts and street corner living, making a dollar when he could, and when he couldn't, managing without. The cop he had antagonized – miraculously – left him alone.

There was only one postscript – or so it seemed at the time – to Rollie's employment.

During an afternoon some four weeks later, he was visited at the rooming house, where he was still sharing space on sufferance, by an instructor from the factory training course. Rollie Knight remembered the man – a beefy, florid-faced ex-plant foreman with thinning hair and paunch, now puffing from the three flights of stairs he had been forced to climb.

He asked tersely, 'Why'd you quit?'

'I won the Irish Sweep, man. Doan need no job.'

'You people!' The visitor surveyed the dismal quarters with disgust. 'To think we have to support your kind with taxes. If I had my way . . . ' He left the sentence unfinished and produced a paper. 'You have to sign here. It says you're not coming any more.'

Indifferently, not wanting trouble, Rollie signed.

'Oh, yes, and the company made out some cheques. Now they have to be paid back in.' He riffled through some papers, of which there seemed to be a good many. 'They want you to sign those, too.'

Rollie endorsed the cheques. There were four.

'Another time,' the instructor said unpleasantly, 'try not to cause other people so much trouble.'

'Go screw yourself, fatso,' Rollie Knight said, and yawned.

Neither Rollie nor his visitor was aware that while their exchange was taking place, an expensive, late-model car was parked across the street from the rooming house. The car's sole occupant was a tall, distinguished-appearing, grey-haired Negro who had watched with interest while the training course instructor went inside. Now, as the beefy, florid-faced man left the building and drove his own car away, the other car followed, unobserved, at a discreet distance, as it had through most of the afternoon.

10

'C'mon baby, leave the goddam drink, I gotta bottle in the room.'

Ollie, the machinery salesman, peered impatiently at Erica Trenton in the semi-darkness, across the small black table separating them.

It was early afternoon. They were in the bar of the Queensway Inn, not far from Bloomfield Hills, Erica dawdling over her second drink which she had asked for as a delaying device, even though recognizing that delay was pointless because either they were or weren't going through with what they had come here for, and if they were they might as well get on with it.

Erica touched her glass. 'Let me finish this. I need it.'

She thought: he wasn't a bad-looking man, in a raffish kind of way. He was trimly built and his body was obviously better than his speech and manners, probably because he worked on it – she remembered him telling her with pride that he went to a gym somewhere for regular workouts. She supposed she could do worse, though wished she had done better.

The occasion when he had told her about workouts in the gym had been at their first meeting, here in the same bar. Erica had come for a drink one afternoon, the way other lonely wives did sometimes, in the hope that something interesting might happen, and Ollie had struck up a conversation – Ollie, cynical, experienced, who knew this bar and why some women came to it. After that, their next meeting had been by arrangement, when he had taken a room in the residential section of the inn, and assumed she would go to it with him. But Erica, torn between a simple physical need and nagging conscience, had insisted on staying at the bar all afternoon, and in the end left for home, to Ollie's anger and disgust. He had written her off, it seemed, until she telephoned him several weeks ago.

Even since then, they had had to delay their arrangement because Ollie had not come back from Cleveland as expected, and instead went on to two other cities – Erica had forgotten where. But they *were* here now, and Ollie was becoming impatient.

He asked, 'How about it, baby?'

Suddenly she remembered, with a mixture of wryness and sadness, a maxim on Adam's office wall: DO IT TODAY!

'All right,' Erica said. She pushed back her chair and stood up.

Walking beside Ollie, down the inn's attractive, picture-hung corridors – where many others had walked before her on the same kind of assignation – she felt her heart beat faster, and tried not to hurry.

Several hours later, thinking about it calmly, Erica decided the experience was neither as good as she had hoped for, nor as bad as she had feared. In a basic, here-and-now way, she had found sensual satisfaction; in another way, which was harder to define, she hadn't. She was sure, though, of two things. First, such satisfaction as she had known was not lasting, as it had been in the old days when Adam was an aggressive lover and the effect of their love-making stayed with her, sometimes for days. Second, she would not repeat the experience – at least, not with Ollie.

In such a mood, from the Queensway Inn in late afternoon, Erica went shopping in Birmingham. She bought a few things she needed, and some others she didn't, but most of her pleasure came from what proved to be an exciting, challenging game – removing items from stores without payment. She did so three times, with increasing confidence, acquiring an ornamental clothes hanger, a tube of shampoo, and – especial triumph! – an expensive fountain pen.

Erica's earlier experience, when she had purloined the ounce of Norell, had showed that successful shoplifting was not difficult. The requirements, she decided now, were intelligence, quickness, and cool nerve. She felt proud of herself for demonstrating that she possessed all three.

■ ■

On a dismal, grimy, wet November day, six weeks after the meeting with Adam Trenton at the proving ground, Brett DeLosanto was in downtown Detroit – in a grey, bleak mood which matched the weather.

His mood was uncharacteristic. Normally, whatever pressures, worries and – more recently – doubts assailed the young car designer, he remained cheerful and good-natured. But on a day like today, he thought, to a native Californian like himself, Detroit in winter was just too much, too awful.

He had reached his car, moments earlier, on a parking lot near Congress and Shelby, having battled his way to it on foot, through wind and rain and traffic, the last seeming to flow interminably the instant he sought to cross any intersection, so that he was left standing impatiently on kerbs, already miserably sodden, and getting wetter still.

As for the inner city around him . . . ugh! Always dirty, preponderantly ugly and depressing at any time, today's leaden skies and rain – as Brett's imagination saw it – were like spreading soot on a charnel house. Only one worse time of the year existed: in March and April, when winter's heavy snows, frozen and turned black, began to melt. Even then, he supposed, there were people who became used to the city's hideousness eventually. So far, he hadn't.

Inside his car, Brett started the motor and got the heater and windshield wipers going. He was glad to be sheltered at last; outside, the rain was still beating down heavily. The parking lot was crowded, and he was boxed in, and would have to wait while two cars ahead of him were moved to let him out. But he had signalled an attendant as he came into the lot, and could see the man now, several rows of cars away.

Waiting, Brett remembered it was on such a day as this that he had first come to Detroit himself, to live and work.

The ranks of auto company designers were heavy with expatriate Californians whose route to Detroit, like his own, had been through the Art Center College of Design, Los Angeles, which operated on a trimester system. For those who graduated in winter and came to Detroit to work, the shock of seeing the city at its seasonal worst was so depressing that a few promptly returned West and sought some other design field as a livelihood. But most, though jolted badly, stayed on as Brett had done, and later the city revealed compensations. Detroit was an outstanding cultural centre, notably in art, music, and drama, while beyond the city, the State of Michigan was a superb sports-vacation area, winter and summer, boasting some of the lovelier unspoiled lakes and country in the world.

Where in hell, Brett wondered, *was the parking-lot guy to move those other cars?*

It was this kind of frustration – nothing major – which had induced his present bad temper. He had had a luncheon date at the Pontchartrain Hotel with a man named Hank Kreisel, an auto parts manufacturer and friend, and Brett had driven to the hotel, only to find the parking garage full. As a result he had to park blocks away, and got wet walking back. At the Pontchartrain there had been a message from Kreisel, apologizing, but to say he couldn't make it, so Brett lunched alone, having driven fifteen miles to do so. He had several other errands downtown, and these occupied the rest of the afternoon; but in walking from one place to the next, a series of rude, horn-happy drivers refused to give him the slightest break on pedestrian crossings, despite the heavy rain.

The near-savage drivers distressed him most. In no other city that he knew – including New York, which was bad enough – were motorists as boorish, inconsiderate, and unyielding as on Detroit streets and freeways. Perhaps it was because the city lived by automobiles, which became symbols of power, but for whatever reason a Detroiter behind the wheel seemed changed into a Frankenstein. Most newcomers, at first shaken by the 'no quarter asked or given' driving, soon learned to behave similarly, in self-defence. Brett never had. Used to inherent courtesy in California, Detroit driving remained a nightmare to him, and a source of anger.

The parking-lot attendant had obviously forgotten about moving the cars ahead. Brett knew he would have to get out and locate the man, rain or not. Seething, he did: when he saw the attendant, however, he made no complaint. The man looked bedraggled, weary, and was soaked. Brett tipped him instead and pointed to the blocking cars.

At least, Brett thought, returning to his car, he had a warm and comfortable apartment to go home to, which probably the attendant hadn't. Brett's apartment was in Birmingham, a part of swanky Country Club Manor, and he remembered that Barbara was coming in tonight to cook dinner for the two of them. The style of Brett's living, plus an absence of money worries which his fifty thousand dollars a year salary and bonus made possible, were compensations which Detroit had given him, and he made no secret of enjoying them.

At last the cars obstructing him were being moved. As the one immediately ahead swung clear, Brett eased his own car forward.

The exit from the parking lot was fifty yards ahead. One other car was in front, also on the way out. Brett DeLosanto accelerated slightly to close the gap and reached for money to pay the exit cashier.

Suddenly, appearing as if from nowhere, a third car – a dark green sedan – shot directly across the front of Brett's, swung sharply right and slammed into second place in the exit line. Brett trod on his brakes hard, skidded, regained control, stopped and swore. 'You goddam maniac!'

All the frustrations of the day, added to his fixation about Detroit drivers, were synthesized in Brett's actions through the next five seconds. He leaped from his car, stormed to the dark green sedan and wrathfully wrenched open the driver's door.

'You son-of-a . . . ' It was as far as he got before he stopped.

'Yes?' the other driver said. He was a tall, greying, well-dressed black man in his fifties. 'You were saying something?'

'Never mind,' Brett growled. He moved to close the door.

'Please wait! I do mind! I may even complain to the Human Rights Commission. I shall tell them: a young white man opened my car door with every intention of punching me in the nose. When he discovered I was of a different race, he stopped. That's discrimination, you know. The human rights people won't like it.'

'It sure would be a new angle.' Brett laughed. 'Would you prefer me to finish?'

'I suppose, if you must,' the greying Negro said. 'But I'd much rather buy you a drink, then I can apologize for cutting in front like that, and explain it was a foolish, irrational impulse at the end of a frustrating day.'

'You had one of those days, too?'

'Obviously we both did.'

Brett nodded. 'OK, I'll take the drink.'

'Shall we say Jim's Garage, right now? It's three blocks from here and the doorman will park your car. By the way, my name is Leonard Wingate.'

The green sedan led the way.

The first thing they discovered, after ordering Scotches on the rocks, was that they worked for the same company. Leonard Wingate was an executive in Personnel and, Brett gathered from their conversation, about two rungs down from vice-president level. Later, he would learn that his drinking companion was the highest-ranking Negro in the company.

'I've heard your name,' Wingate told Brett. 'You've been Michelangelo-ing the Orion, haven't you?'

'Well, we hope it turns out that way. Have you seen the prototype?'

The other shook his head.

'I could arrange it, if you'd like to.'

'I would like. Another drink?'

'My turn.' Brett beckoned a bartender.

The bar of Jim's Garage, colourfully festooned with historic artifacts of the auto industry, was currently an 'in' place in downtown Detroit. Now, in early evening, it was beginning to fill, the level of business and voices rising simultaneously.

'A whole lot riding on that Orion baby,' Wingate said.

'Damn right.'

'Especially jobs for my people.'

'Your people?'

'Hourly paid ones, black *and* white. The way the Orion goes, so a lot of families in this city'll go: the hours they work, what their take-home is – and that means the way they live, eat, whether they can meet mortgage payments, have new clothes, a vacation, what happens to their kids.'

Brett mused. 'You never think of that when you're sketching a new car or throwing clay to shape a fender.'

'Don't see how you could. None of us ever knows the half of what goes on with other people; all kinds of walls get built between us – brick, the other kind. Even when you do get through a wall once in a while, and find out what's behind it, then maybe try to help somebody, you find you haven't helped because of other stinking, rotten, conniving parasites . . . ' Leonard Wingate clenched his fist and hammered it twice, silently but intensely, on the bar counter. He looked sideways at Brett, then grinned crookedly. 'Sorry!'

'Here comes your other drink, friend. I think you need it.' The designer sipped his own before asking, 'Does this have something to do with those lousy aerobatics in the parking lot?'

Wingate nodded. 'I'm sorry about that, too. I was blowing steam.' He smiled, this time less tensely. 'Now, I guess, I've let the rest of it out.'

'Steam is only a white cloud,' Brett said. 'Is the source of it classified?'

'Not really. You've heard of hard core hiring?'

'I've heard. I don't know all the details.' But he did know that Barbara Zaleski had become interested in the subject lately because of a new project she had been assigned by the OJL advertising agency.

The grey-haired Personnel man summarized the hard core hiring programme its objective in regard to the inner city and former unemployables; the Big Three hiring halls downtown; how, in relation to individuals, the programme sometimes worked and sometimes didn't.

'It's been worth doing, though, despite some disappointments. Our retention rate – that is, people who've held on to jobs we've given them – has been better than fifty per cent, which is more than we expected. The unions have cooperated; news media give publicity which helps; there's been other aid in other ways. That's why it hurts to get knifed in the back by your own people, in your own company.'

Brett asked, 'Who knifed you? How?'

'Let me go back a bit.' Wingate put the tip of a long, lean finger in his drink and stirred the ice. 'A lot of people we've hired under the programme have never, in their lives before, kept regular hours. Mostly they've had no reason to. Working regularly, the way most of us do, breeds habits: like getting up in the morning, being on time to catch a bus, becoming used to working five days of the week. But if you've never done any of that, if you don't have the habits, it's like learning another language; what's more, it takes time. You could call it changing attitudes, or changing gears. Well, we've learned a lot about all that since we started hard core hiring. We also learned that some people – not all, but some – who don't acquire those habits on their own, can get them if they're given help.'

'You'd better help *me*,' Brett said. 'I have trouble getting up.'

His companion smiled. 'If we did try to help, I'd send someone from employee relations staff to see you. If you've dropped out, quit coming to work, he'd ask you why. There's another thing: some of these new people will miss one day, or even be an hour or two late, then simply give up. Maybe they didn't intend to miss; it just happened. But they have the notion we're so inflexible, it means automatically they've lost their jobs.'

'And they haven't?'

'Christ, no! We give a guy every possible break because *we* want the thing to work. Something else we do is give people who have trouble getting to work a cheap alarm clock; you'd be surprised how many have never owned one. The company let me buy a gross. In my office I've got alarm clocks the way other men have paper clips.'

Brett said, 'I'll be damned!' It seemed incongruous to think of a gargantuan auto company, with annual wage bills running into billions, worrying about a few sleepy-head employees waking up.

'The point I'm getting at,' Leonard Wingate said, 'is that if a hard core worker doesn't show up, either to finish his training course or at the plant, whoever's in charge is supposed to notify one of my special people. Then, unless it's a hopeless case, they follow through.'

'But that hasn't been happening? It's why you're frustrated?'

'That's part of it. There's a whole lot more.' The Personnel man downed the last of his Scotch. 'Those courses we have where the hard core people get oriented – they last eight weeks; there are maybe two hundred on a course.'

Brett motioned for a refill to their drinks. When the bartender had gone, he prompted, 'OK, so a course with two hundred people.'

'Right. An instructor and a woman secretary are in charge. Between them, these two keep all course records, including attendance. They pass out paychecks, which arrive weekly in a bunch from Headquarters Accounting. Naturally, the cheques are made out on the basis of the course records.' Wingate said bitterly, 'It's the instructor and the secretary – one particular pair. They're the ones.'

'The ones what?'

'Who've been lying, cheating, stealing from the people they're employed to help.'

'I guess I can figure some of it,' Brett said. 'But tell me, anyway.'

'Well, as the course goes along, there are dropouts – for the reasons I told you, and for others. It always happens; we expect it. As I said, if our department's told, we try to persuade some of the people to come back. But what this instructor and secretary have been doing is *not* reporting the dropouts, and recording them present. So the cheques for the dropouts have kept coming in, and then that precious pair has kept those cheques themselves.'

'But the cheques are made out by name. They can't cash them.'

Wingate shook his head. 'They can and they have. What happens is eventually this pair does report that certain people have stopped coming, so the company cheques stop, too. Then the instructor goes around with the cheques he's saved and finds the people they're made out to. It isn't difficult; all addresses are on file. The instructor tells a cock-and-bull story about the company wanting the money back, and gets the cheques endorsed. After that, he can cash them anywhere. I know it happens that way. I followed the instructor for an afternoon.'

'But how about later, when your employee relations people go visiting? You say they hear about the dropouts eventually. Don't they find out about the cheques?'

'Not necessarily. Remember, the people we're dealing with aren't communicative. They're dropouts in more ways than one, usually, and never volunteer information. It's hard enough getting answers to questions. Besides that, I happen to think there've been some bribes passed around. I can't prove it, but there's a certain smell.'

'The whole thing stinks.'

Brett thought: compared with what Leonard Wingate had told him, his own irritations of today seemed minor. He asked, 'Were you the one who uncovered all this?'

'Mostly, though one of my assistants got the idea first. He was suspicious of the course attendance figures; they looked too good. So the two of us started checking, comparing the new figures with our own previous ones, then we got comparable figures from other companies. They showed what was going on, all right. After that, it was a question of watching, catching the people. Well, we did.'

'So what happens now?'

Wingate shrugged, his figure hunched over the bar counter. 'Security's taken over; it's out of my hands. This afternoon they brought the instructor and the secretary downtown – separately. I was there. The two of them broke down, admitted everything. The guy cried, if you'll believe it.'

'I believe it,' Brett said. 'I feel like crying in a different way. Will the company prosecute?'

'The guy and his girlfriend think so, but I know they won't.' The tall Negro straightened up; he was almost a head higher than Brett DeLosanto. He said mockingly, 'Bad public relations, y'know. Wouldn't want it in the papers, with our company's name. Besides, the way my bosses see it, the main thing is to get the money back; seems there's quite a few thousand.'

'What about the other people? The ones who dropped out, who might have come back, gone on working . . . '

'Oh come, my friend, you're being ridiculously sentimental.'

Brett said sharply. 'Knock it off! I didn't steal the goddam cheques.'

'No, you didn't. Well, about those people, let me tell you. If I had a staff six times the size I have, and *if* we could go back through all the records and be sure which names to follow up on, and *if* we could locate them after all these weeks . . . '

The bartender appeared. Wingate's glass was empty, but he shook his head. For Brett's benefit he added, 'We'll do what we can. It may not be much.'

'I'm sorry,' Brett said. 'Damn sorry.' He paused, then asked, 'You married?'

'Yes, but not working at it.'

'Listen, my girlfriend's cooking dinner at my place. Why not join us?'

Wingate demurred politely. Brett insisted.

Five minutes later they left for Country Club Manor.

Barbara Zaleski had a key to Brett's apartment and was there when they arrived, already busy in the kitchen. An aroma of roasting lamb was drifting out.

'Hey, scullion!' Brett called from the hallway. 'Come, meet a guest.'

'If it's another woman,' Barbara's voice sailed back, 'you can cook your own dinner. Oh, it isn't. Hi!'

She appeared with a tiny apron over the smart, knit suit she had arrived in, having come directly from the OJL agency's Detroit office. The suit, Brett thought appreciatively, did justice to Barbara's figure; he sensed Leonard Wingate observing the same thing. As usual, Barbara had dark glasses pushed up into her thick, chestnut-brown hair, which she had undoubtedly forgotten. Brett reached out, removed the glasses and kissed her lightly.

He introduced them, informing Wingate, 'This is my mistress.'

'He'd like me to be,' Barbara said, 'but I'm not. Telling people I am is his way of getting even.'

As Brett had expected, Barbara and Leonard Wingate achieved a rapport quickly. While they talked, Brett opened a bottle of Dom Perignon which the three of them shared. Occasionally Barbara excused herself to check on progress in the kitchen.

During one of her absences, Wingate looked around the spacious apartment living-room. 'Pretty nice pad.'

'Thanks.' When Brett leased the apartment a year and a half ago he had been his own interior decorator, and the furnishings reflected his personal taste for modern design and flamboyant colouring. Bright yellows, mauves, vermilions, cobalt greens predominated, yet were used imaginatively, so that they merged as an attractive whole. Lighting complemented the colours, highlighting some areas, diminishing others. The effect was to create – ingeniously – a series of moods within a single room.

At one end of the living-room was an open door to another room.

Wingate asked, 'Do you do much of your work here?'

'Some,' Brett nodded towards the open door. 'There's my Thinkolarium. For when I need to get creative and be uninterrupted away from that wired-for-sound Taj Mahal we work in.' He motioned vaguely in the direction of the company's Design-Styling Center.

'He does other things there, too,' Barbara said. She had returned as Brett spoke. 'Come in, Leonard. I'll show you.' Wingate followed her, Brett trailing.

The other room, while colourful and pleasant also, was equipped as a studio, with the paraphernalia of an artist-designer. A pile of tissue flimsies on the floor beside a drafting table showed where Brett had raced through a series of sketches, tearing off each flimsy, using a new one from the pad beneath as the design took shape. The last sketch in the series – a rear fender style – was pinned to a cork board.

Wingate pointed to it. 'Will that one be for real?'

Brett shook his head. 'You play with ideas, get them out of your system, like belching. Sometimes, that way, you get a notion which will lead to something permanent in the end. This isn't one.' He pulled the flimsy down and crumpled it. 'If you took all the sketches which precede any new car, you could fill Cobo Hall with paper.'

Barbara switched on a light. It was in a corner of the room where an easel stood, covered by a cloth. She removed the cloth carefully.

'And then there's this,' Barbara said. 'This isn't for discarding.'

Beneath the cloth was a painting in oils, almost – but not quite – finished.

'Don't count on it,' Brett said. He added, 'Barbara's very loyal. At time it warps her judgement.'

The tall, grey-haired Negro shook his head. 'Not this time, it hasn't.' He studied the painting with admiration.

It was a collection of automative discards, heaped together. Brett had assembled the materials for his model – laid out on a board ahead of the easel, and lighted by a spotlight – from an auto wrecker's junk pile. There were several burned-brown spark plugs, a broken camshaft, a discarded oil can, the entrails of a carburettor, a battered headlight, a mouldy twelve-volt battery, a window handle, a section of radiator, a broken wrench, some assorted rusty nuts and washers. A steering wheel, its horn ring missing, hung lopsidedly above.

No collection could have been more ordinary, less likely to inspire great art. Yet, remarkably, Brett had made the junk assortment come alive, had conveyed to his canvas both rugged beauty and a mood of sadness and nostalgia. These were broken relics, the painting seemed to say: burned-out, unwanted, all usefulness departed; nothing was ahead save total disintegration. Yet once, however briefly, they had had a life, had functioned, representing dreams, ambitions, achievements of mankind. One knew that all other achievements – past, present, future, no matter how acclaimed – were doomed to end similarly, would write their epilogues in garbage dumps. Yet was not the dream, the brief achievement – of itself – enough?

Leonard Wingate had remained, unmoving, before the canvas. He said slowly, 'I know a little about art. You're good. You could be great.'

'That's what I tell him.' After a moment, Barbara replaced the cloth on the easel and turned out the light. They went back into the living-room.

'What Barbara means,' Brett said, pouring out more Dom Perignon, 'is that I've sold my soul for a mess of pottage.' He glanced around the apartment. 'Or maybe a pot of messuage.'

'Brett might have managed to do designing *and* fine art,' Barbara told Wingate, 'if he hadn't been so darned successful at designing. Now, all he has time to do where painting's concerned is to dabble occasionally. With his talent, it's a tragedy.'

Brett grinned. 'Barbara has never seen the high beam – that designing a car is every bit as creative as painting. Or that cars are my thing.' He remembered what he had told the two students only a few weeks ago: *You breathe, eat, sleep cars . . . wake up in the night, it's cars you think about . . . like a religion.* Well, he still felt the same way himself, didn't he? Maybe not with the same intensity as when he first came to Detroit. But did *anyone* really keep that up? There were days when he looked at others working with him, wondering. Also, if he were honest, there were other reasons why cars should stay his 'thing'. Like what you could do with fifty thousand dollars a year, to say nothing of the fact that he was only twenty-six and much bigger loot would come in a few years more. He asked Barbara lightly, 'Would you still breeze in to cook dinner if I lived in a garret and smelled of turpentine?'

She looked at him directly. 'You know I would.'

While they talked of other things, Brett decided: he *would* finish the canvas, which he hadn't touched in weeks. The reason he had stayed away from it was simple. Once he started painting, it absorbed him totally and there was just so much total absorption which any life could stand.

Over dinner, which tasted as good as it had smelled, Brett steered the conversation to what Leonard Wingate had told him in the bar downtown. Barbara, after hearing of the cheating and victimization of hard core workers, was shocked and even angrier than Brett.

She asked the question which Brett DeLosanto hadn't. 'What colour are they – the instructor and the secretary who took the cheques?'

Wingate raised his eyebrows. 'Does it make a difference?'

'Listen,' Brett said. 'You know damn well it does.'

Wingate answered tersely, 'They're white. What else?'

'They could have been black.' It was Barbara, thoughtfully.

'Yes, but the odds are against it.' Wingate hesitated. 'Look, I'm a guest here . . . '

Brett waved a hand. 'Forget it!'

There was a silence between them, then the grey-haired Negro said, 'I like to make certain things clear, even among friends. So don't let this uniform fool you: the Oxford suit, a college diploma, the job I have. Oh, sure, I'm the real front office nigger, the one they point to when they say: *You see, a black man can go high.* Well, its true for me, because I was one of the few with a daddy who could pay for a real education, which is the only way a black man climbs. So I've climbed, and maybe I'll make it to the top and be a company director yet. I'm still young enough, and I'll admit I'd like it; so would the company. I know one thing. If there's a choice between me and a white man, and providing I can cut the mustard, I'll get the job. That's the way the dice are rolling, baby; they're weighted *my way* because the PR department and some others would just love to shout: *Look at us! We've got a board room black!'*

Leonard Wingate sipped his coffee, which Barbara had brought.

'Well, as I said, don't let the façade fool you. I'm still a member of my race.' Abruptly he put the cup down. Across the dining-table his eyes glared at Brett and Barbara. 'When something happens like it did today, I don't just get angry. I burn and loathe and *hate* – everything that's *white.*'

The glare faded. Wingate raised his coffee cup again, through his hand was shaking.

After a moment he said, 'James Baldwin wrote this: "Negroes in this country are treated as none of you would dream of treating a dog or a cat." And it's true – in Detroit, just as in other places. And for all that's happened in the past few years, nothing's really changed in most white people's attitudes, below the surface. Even the little that's being done to ease white consciences – like hard core hiring, which that white pair tried to screw, and did – is only surface scratching. Schools, housing, medicine, hospitals, are so bad here it's unbelievable – unless you're black; then you believe it because you know, the hard way. But one day, if the auto industry intends to survive in this town – because the auto industry *is* Detroit – it will have to come to grips with improving the black life of the community, because no-one else is going to do it, or has the resources or the brains to.' he added, 'Just the same, I don't believe they will.'

'Then there's nothing,' Barbara said. 'Nothing to hope for.' There was emotion in her voice.

'No harm in hoping,' Leonard Wingate answered. He added mockingly, 'Hope doesn't cost none. But no good fooling yourself either.'

Barbara said slowly, 'Thank you for being honest, for telling it like it is. Not everyone does that, as I've reason to know.'

'Tell him,' Brett urged. 'Tell him about your new assignment.'

'I've been given a job to do,' Barbara told Wingate. 'By the advertising agency I work for, acting for the company. It's to make a film. An honest film about Detroit – the inner city.'

She was aware of the other's instant interest.

'I first heard about it,' Barbara explained, 'six weeks ago.'

She described her briefing in New York by Keith Yates-Brown.

It had been the day after the abortive 'rustle pile' session at which the OJL agency's initial ideas for Orion advertising had been routinely presented and, just as routinely, brushed aside.

As the creative director, Teddy Osch, predicted during their martini-weighted luncheon, Keith Yates-Brown, the account supervisor had sent for Barbara next day.

In his handsome office in the agency's top floor, Yates-Brown had seemed morose in contrast with his genial, showman's manner of the day before. He looked greyer and older, too, and several times in the later stages of their conversation turned towards the office window, looking across the Manhattan skyline towards Long Island Sound, as if a portion of his mind was far away. Perhaps, Barbara thought, the strain of permanent affability with clients required a surly counter-balance now and then.

There had certainly been nothing friendly about Yates-Brown's opening remark after they exchanged 'good mornings'.

'You were snooty with the client yesterday,' he told Barbara. 'I didn't like it, and you should know better.'

She said nothing. She supposed Yates-Brown was referring to her pointed questioning of the company advertising manager: *Was there nothing you liked? Absolutely nothing at all?* Well, she still believed it justified and wasn't going to grovel now. But neither would she antagonize Yates-Brown needlessly until she heard about her new assignment.

'One of the early things you're supposed to learn here,' the account supervisor persisted, 'is to show restraint sometimes and swallow hard.'

'OK, Keith,' Barbara said, 'I'm swallowing now.'

He had had the grace to smile, then returned to coolness.

'What you're being given to do requires restraint; also sound judgement and, naturally, imagination. I suggested you for the assignment, believing you to possess those qualities.

I still do, despite yesterday, which I prefer to think of as a momentary lapse.'

Oh, God! Barbara wanted to exclaim. *Stop making like you're in a pulpit, and get on!* But she had the sense not to say it.

'The project is one which has the personal interest of the client's chairman of the board.' Keith Yates-Brown mouthed 'chairman of the board' with awe and reverence. Barbara was surprised he hadn't stood, saluting, while he said it.

'As a result,' the account chief continued, 'you will have the responsibility – a large responsibility affecting all of us at OJL – of reporting, on occasions, to the chairman personally.'

Well, Barbara could appreciate his feelings there. Reporting directly to the chairman about anything *was* a large responsibility, though it didn't frighten her. But since the chairman – if he chose to exercise it – had a life and death power over which advertising agency the company used, Barbara could picture Keith Yates-Brown and others hovering nervously in the wings.

'The project,' Yates-Brown added, 'is to make a film.'

He had gone on, filling in details as far as they were known. The film would be about Detroit: the inner city and its people, their problems – racial and otherwise – their ways of life, points of view, their needs. It was to be a factual, honest documentary. In no way would it be company or industry propaganda; the company's name would appear only once – on the credits as sponsor. Objective would be to point up urban problems, the need to reactivate the city's role in national life, with Detroit the prime example. The film's first use would be for educational and civic groups and schools across the nation. It would probably be shown on television. If good enough, it might go into movie houses.

The budget would be generous. It would allow a regular film-making organization to be used, but the OJL agency would select the film maker and retain control. A top-flight director could be hired, and a script writer, if needed, though Barbara – in view of her copywriter's experience – might choose to write the script herself.

Barbara would represent the agency and be in over-all charge.

With a sense of rising excitement as Yates-Brown spoke, Barbara remembered Teddy Osch's words of yesterday at lunch. The creative director had said: *All I can tell you is, I wish it were me instead of you.* Now she knew why. Not only was the assignment a substantial compliment to her professionally, it also represented a strong creative challenge which she welcomed. Barbara found herself looking appreciatively – and certainly more tolerantly – on Keith Yates-Brown.

Even the account supervisor's next words diminished her appreciation only slightly.

'You'll work out of the Detroit office as usual,' he had said, 'but we shall want to be informed here of everything that's going on, and I mean everything. Another thing to bear in mind is what we spoke of earlier – restraint. It's to be an honest film, but don't get carried away. I do not believe we want, or the chairman of the board will want, too much of – shall we say? – a Socialist point of view.'

Well, she had let that one go, realizing there would be plenty of ideas, as well as points of view, she would have to fight for eventually, without wasting time on abstract arguments now.

A week later, after other activities she was involved in had been reassigned, Barbara began work on the project, tentatively titled: *Auto City.*

Across Brett DeLosanto's dining-table, Barbara told Leonard Wingate, 'Some of the early things have been done, including choosing a production company and a director. Of course, there'll be more planning before filming can begin, but we hope to start in February or March.'

The tall, greying Negro considered before answering. At length he said, 'I could be cynical and smart, and say that making a film about problems, instead of solving them or trying to, is like Nero fiddling. But being an executive has taught me life isn't always that simple; also, communication is important.' He paused, then added, 'What you intend might do a lot of good. If there's a way I can help, I will.'

'Perhaps there is,' Barbara acknowledged. 'I've already talked with the director, Wes Gropetti, and something we're agreed on is that whatever is said about the inner city must be through people who live there – individuals. One of them, we believe, should be someone coming through the "hard-core" hiring programme.'

Wingate cautioned, 'Hard-core hiring doesn't always work. You might shoot a lot of film about a person who ends up a failure.'

'If that's the way it happens,' Barbara insisted, 'that's the way we'll tell it. We're not doing a remake of *Pollyanna*.'

'Then there might be someone,' Wingate said thoughtfully. 'You remember I told you – one afternoon I trailed the instructor who stole the cheques, then lied to get them endorsed.'

She nodded. 'I remember.'

'Next day I went back to see some of the people he'd visited. I'd noted the addresses; my office matched them up with names.' Leonard Wingate produced a notebook and turned pages. 'One of them was a man I had a feeling about. I'm not sure what kind of feeling, except I've persuaded him to come back to work. Here it is.' He stopped at a page. 'His name is Rollie Knight.'

Earlier, when Barbara arrived at Brett's apartment, she had come by taxi. Late that evening, when Leonard Wingate had gone – after promising that the three of them would meet again soon – Brett drove Barbara home.

The Zaleskis lived in Royal Oak, a middle-class residential suburb south-east of Birmingham. Driving crosstown on Maple, with Barbara on the front seat close beside him, Brett said, 'Nuts to this!' He braked, stopped the car, and put his arms around her. Their kiss was passionate and long.

'Listen!' Brett said; he buried his face in the soft silkiness of her hair, and held her tightly. 'What the hell are we doing headed this way? Come back and stay with me tonight. We both want it, and there's not a reason in the world why you shouldn't.'

He had made the same suggestion earlier, immediately after Wingate left. Also, they had covered this ground many times before.

Barbara sighed. She said softly, 'I'm a great disappointment to you, aren't I?'

'How do I *know* if you're a disappointment, when you've never left me find out?'

She laughed lightly. He had the capacity to make her do that, even at unexpected moments. Barbara reached up, tracing her fingers across Brett's forehead, erasing the frown she sensed was there.

He protested, 'It isn't *fair*! Everybody who knows us just *assumes* we're sleeping together, and you and I are the only ones who know we're not. Even your old man thinks we are. Well, doesn't he?'

'Yes,' she admitted. 'I think Dad does.'

'I know damn well he does. What's more, every time we meet, the old buzzard lets me know he doesn't like it. So I lose out two ways, coming and going.'

'Darling,' Barbara said, 'I know, I *know*.'

'Then why aren't we doing something – right now, tonight? Barb, hon, you're twenty-nine, you can't possibly be a virgin, so what's our hangup? Is it me? Do I smell of modelling clay, or offend you in some other way?'

She shook her head emphatically. 'You attract me in every way, and I mean that just as much as all the other times I've said it.'

'We've said everything so many times.' He added morosely, 'None of the other times made any more sense than this one.'

'Please,' Barbara said, 'let's go home.'

'*My* home?'

She laughed. 'No, mine.'

When the car was moving, she touched Brett's arm. 'I'm not sure either; about making sense, I mean. I guess I'm just not thinking the way everyone else seems to do nowadays; at least, I haven't yet. Maybe it's old-fashioned . . .'

'You mean if I want to get to the honey pot, I have to marry you.'

Barbara said sharply, 'No, I *don't*. I'm not even sure I want to marry anybody; I'm a career gal, remember? And I *know* you're not marriage-minded.'

Brett grinned. 'You're right about that. So why don't we live together?'

She said thoughtfully, 'We might.'

'You're serious?'

'I'm not sure. I think I could be, but I need time.' She hesitated. 'Brett, darling, if you'd like us not to see each other for a while, if you're going to be frustrated every time we meet . . .'

'We tried that, didn't we? It didn't work because I missed you.' He said decisively, 'No, we'll go on this way even if I make like a corralled stallion now and then. Besides,' he added cheerfully, 'you can't hold out for ever.'

There was a silence as they drove. Brett turned on to Woodward Avenue, heading south, then Barbara said, 'Do something for me.'

'What?'

'Finish the painting. The one we looked at tonight.'

He seemed surprised. 'You mean *that* might make a difference to *us*?'

'I'm not sure. I do know it's part of you, a specially important part; something inside that ought to come out.'

'Like a tapeworm?'

She shook her head. 'A great talent, just as Leonard said. One that the auto industry won't ever give its proper chance to, not if you stay with car designing, and grow old that way.'

'Listen! – I'll finish the painting. I intended to, anyway. But you're in the car racket, too. Where's your loyalty?'

'At the office,' Barbara said. 'I only wear it until five o' clock. Right now I'm me, which is why I want you to be you – the best, real Brett DeLosanto.'

'How'd I know him if I met the guy?' Brett mused. 'OK, so painting sends me, sure.

But d'you know what the odds are against an artist, any artist, becoming great, getting recognized and, incidentally, well paid?'

They swung into the driveway of the modest bungalow where Barbara and her father lived. A grey hardtop was in the garage ahead of them. 'Your old man's home,' Brett said. 'It suddenly feels chilly.'

Matt Zaleski was in his orchid atrium, which adjoined the kitchen, and looked up as Brett and Barbara came in through the bungalow's side door.

Matt had built the atrium soon after buying the house eighteen years ago, on migrating here from Wyandotte. At that time the move northward to Royal Oak had represented Matt's economic advancement from his boyhood milieu and that of his Polish parents. The orchid atrium had been intended to provide a soothing hobby, offsetting the mental stress of helping run an auto plant. It seldom had. Instead, while Matt still loved the exotic sight, texture, and sometimes scent of orchids, a growing weariness during his hours at home had changed the care of them from pleasure to a chore, though one which, mentally, he could never quite discard.

Tonight, he had come in an hour ago, having stayed late at the assembly plant because of some critical materials shortages, and after a sketchy supper, realized there was some potting and rearrangement which could be put off no longer. By the time he heard Brett's car arrive, Matt had relocated several plants, the latest a yellow-purple *Masdevallia triangularis*, now placed where air movement and humidity would be better. He was misting the flower tenderly when the two came in.

Brett appeared at the open atrium doorway, 'Hi, Mr Z.'

Matt Zaleski, who disliked being called Mr Z., though several others at the plant addressed him that way, grunted what could have been a greeting. Barbara joined them, kissed her father briefly, then returned to the kitchen and began making a malted drink for them all.

'Gee!' Brett said. Determined to be genial, he inspected the tiers and hanging baskets of orchids. 'It's great to have lots of spare time you can spend on a setup like this.' He failed to notice a tightening of Matt's mouth. Pointing to a *Catasetum saccatum* growing in fir bark on a ledge, Brett commented admiringly, 'That's a beauty! It's like a bird in flight.'

For a moment Matt relaxed, sharing the pleasure of the superb purple-brown bloom, its sepals and petals curving upward. He conceded, 'I guess it is like a bird. I never noticed that.'

Unwittingly, Brett broke the mood. 'Was it a fun day in Assembly, Mr Z.? Did that rolling erector set of yours hold together?'

'If it did,' Matt Zaleski said, 'it's no thanks to the crazy car designs we have to work with.'

'Well, you know how it is. We like to throw you iron pants guys something that's a challenge; otherwise you'd doze off from the monotony.' Good-natured banter was a way of life with Brett, as natural as breathing. Unfortunately, he had never realized that with Barbara's father it was not, and was the reason Matt considered his daughter's friend a smart aleck.

As Matt Zaleski scowled, Brett added, 'You'll get the Orion soon. Now that's a playpen that'll build itself.'

Matt exploded. He said, heavy-handedly, 'Nothing builds itself! That's what you cocksure kids don't realize. Because you and your kind come here with college degrees, you think you know it all, believe everything you put on paper will work out. It doesn't! It's those like me – iron pants, you call us; working slobs – who have to fix it so it does . . . ' The words rolled on.

Behind Matt's outburst was his tiredness of tonight; also the knowledge that, yes, the Orion would be coming his way soon; that the plant where he was second in command would have to build the new car, would be torn apart to do it, then put together so that nothing worked the way it had; that the ordinary problems of production, which were tough enough, would quickly become monumental and, for months, occur around the clock; that Matt himself would draw the toughest trouble-shooting during model changeover, would have little rest, and some nights would be lucky if he got to bed at all; furthermore, he would be blamed when things went wrong. He had been through it all before, more times than he remembered, and the next time – coming soon – seemed one too many.

Matt stopped, realizing that he had not really been talking to this brash kid DeLosanto – much as he disliked him – but that his own emotions, pent up inside, had suddenly burst through. He was about to say so, awkwardly, and add that he was sorry, when Barbara appeared at the atrium door. Her face was white.

'Dad, you'll apologize for everything you just said.'

Obstinacy was his first reaction. 'I'll do what?'

Brett interceded; nothing bothered him for long. He told Barbara, 'It's OK; he doesn't have to. We had a mild misunderstanding. Right, Mr Z.?'

'No!' Barbara, usually patient with her father, stood her ground. She insisted. 'Apologize! If you don't, I'll leave here now. With Brett. I mean it.'

Matt realized she did.

Unhappily, not really understanding anything, including children who grew up and talked disrespectfully to parents, young people generally who behaved the way they did; missing his wife, Freda, now dead a year, who would have never let this happen to begin with, Matt mumbled an apology, then locked the atrium door and went to bed.

Soon after, Brett said good night to Barbara, and left.

12

Now, winter gripped the Motor City. November had gone, then Christmas, and in early January the snow was deep, with skiing in northern Michigan, and ice heaped high and solidly along the shores of Lakes St Clair and Erie.

As the new year came in, so preparations intensified for the Orion's debut, scheduled for mid-September. Manufacturing division, already huddled over plans for months, moved closer to plant conversions which would start in June, to produce the first production run Orion – Job One, as it was called – in August. Then, six weeks of production – shrouded in secrecy – would be needed before the car's public unveiling. Meanwhile, Purchasing nervously coordinated an armada of materials, ordered, and due on vital days, while Sales and Marketing began hardening their endlessly debated, oft-changed plans for dealer introductions and promotion. Public Relations pressed forward with groundwork for its Lucullan free-load which would accompany the Orion's introduction to the Press. Other divisions, in greater or less degree according to their functions, joined in the preparation.

And while the Orion programme progressed, many in the company gave thought to Farstar, which would follow Orion, though its timing, shape, and substance were not yet known. Among these were Adam Trenton and Brett DeLosanto.

Something else which Adam was concerned with in January was the review of his sister Teresa's investment, bequeathed by her dead husband, in the auto dealership of Smokey Stephensen.

Approval from the company for Adam to involve himself with one of its dealers, however tenuously, had taken longer than expected, and had been given grudgingly after discussion by the Conflict of Interest Committee. In the end, Hub Hewitson, executive vice-president, made a favourable ruling after Adam approached him personally. However, now that the time had come to fulfil his promise to Teresa, Adam realized how little he really needed, or wanted, an extra responsibility. His work load had grown, and an awareness of physical tension still bothered him. At home, relations with Erica seemed neither better nor worse, though he accepted the justice of his wife's complaint – repeated recently – that nowadays they had scarcely any time together. Soon, he resolved, he would find a way to put that right, but first, having accepted this new commitment, he would see it through.

Thus, on a Saturday morning, after arrangements made by telephone, Adam paid his first call on Smokey Stephensen.

The Stephensen dealership was in the northern suburbs, close to the boundary lines of Troy and Birmingham. Its location was good – on an important crosstown route, with Woodward Avenue, a main north-west artery, only a few blocks away.

Smokey, who had clearly been watching the street outside, strode through the showroom doorway on to the sidewalk as Adam stepped from his car.

The ex-race driver, heavily bearded and now corpulent in middle-age, boomed, 'Welcome! Welcome!' He wore a dark-blue silk jacket with carefully creased black slacks and a wide, brightly patterned tie.

'Good morning,' Adam said. 'I'm . . .'

'No need to tell me! Seen your picture in *Automotive News*. Step in!'

The dealer held the showroom doorway wide. 'We always say there's only two reasons for a man to pass through here – to get out of the rain or buy himself wheels. I guess you're the exception.' Inside he declared, 'Within half an hour we'll be using first names. I always say, why wait that long?' He held out a bear paw of a hand. 'I'm Smokey.'

'I'm Adam,' Adam said. He managed not to wince as his hand was squeezed.

'Let me have your car keys.' Smokey beckoned a young salesman who hurried across the showroom floor. 'Park Mr Trenton's car carefully, and don't sell it. Also, be sure you treat him with respect. His sister owns forty-nine percent of this joint, and if business don't pick up by noon, I may mail her the other fifty-one.' He winked broadly at Adam.

'It's an anxious time for all of us,' Adam said. He knew, from sales reports, that a post-holiday lull was being felt this year by all auto makers and dealers. Yet, if only car buyers knew, this was the best time in any year to make a favourable financial deal. With dealers heavily stocked with cars forced on them by factories, and sometimes desperate to reduce inventory, a shrewd car buyer might save several hundred dollars on a medium-priced car, compared with buying a month or so later.

'I should be selling colour televisions,' Smokey growled. 'That's what dopes put money in around Christmas and New Year's.'

'But you did well at model changeover.'

'Sure did.' The dealer brightened. 'You seen the figures, Adam?'

'My sister sent them to me.'

'Never fails. You'd think people'd learn. Fortunately for us, they don't.' Smokey glanced at Adam as they walked across the showroom. 'You understand, I'm speaking freely.'

Adam nodded. 'I think we should both do that.'

He knew, of course, what Smokey Stephensen meant. At model introduction time – from September through November – dealers could sell every new car which factories would let them have. Then, instead of protesting the number of cars consigned – as they did at other times of year – dealers pleaded for more. And despite all adverse publicity about automobiles, the public still flocked to buy when models were new, or after major changes. What such buyers didn't know, or didn't care about, was that this was open season on customers, when dealers could be toughest in bargaining; also, the early cars after any production change were invariably less well made than others which would follow a few months later. With any new model, manufacturing snags inevitably arose while engineers, foremen, and hourly workers learned to make the car. Equally predictable were shortages of components or parts, resulting in manufacturing improvisations which ignored quality standards. As a result, an early car was often a poor buy from a quality point of view.

Knowledgeable buyers wanting a new model waited until four to six months after production began. By that time, chances were, they would get a better car because bugs would have been eliminated and production – except for Monday and Friday labour problems which persisted through all seasons – would be smoothly settled down.

Smokey Stephensen declared, 'Everything's wide open to you here, Adam – like a whorehouse with the roof off. You can see our books, files, inventories, you name it; just the way your sister would, as she's entitled to. And ask questions, you'll get straight answers.'

'You can count on questions,' Adam said, 'and later I'll need to see those things you mentioned. What I also want – which may take longer – is to get a feeling about the way you operate.'

'Sure, sure; any way you want is fine with me.' The auto dealer led the way up a flight of stairs to a mezzanine which ran the length of the showroom below. Most of the mezzanine was occupied by offices. At the top of the stairs the two men paused to look down, viewing the cars of various model lines, polished, immaculate, colourful, which dominated the showroom floor. Along one side of the showroom were several cubicle-type offices, glass-panelled, for use by salesmen. An open doorway gave access to a corridor, leading to Parts and Service, out of sight.

Already, at mid-morning, despite the quiet season, several people were viewing the cars, with salesmen hovering nearby.

'Your sister's got a good thing going here – poor old Clyde's dough working for her and all them kids.' Smokey glanced at Adam shrewdly. 'What's Teresa stewing over? She's been getting cheques. We'll have a year-end audited statement soon.'

Adam pointed out, 'Mostly it's the long term Teresa's thinking of. You know I'm here to advise her: should she sell her stock or not?'

'Yeah, I know.' Smokey ruminated. 'I don't mind telling you Adam, if you advise "sell", it'll make things rugged for me.'

'Why?'

'Because I couldn't raise the dough to buy Teresa's stock. Not now, with money tight.'

'As I understand it,' Adam said, 'if Teresa decided to sell her share of the business, you have a sixty-day option to buy her out. If you don't, then she's free to sell elsewhere.'

Smokey acknowledged, 'That's the way of it.' But his tone was glum.

What Smokey didn't relish, obviously, was the possibility of a new partner, perhaps fearing that someone else would want to be active in the business or could prove more troublesome than a widow two thousand miles away. Adam wondered what, precisely, lay behind Smokey's unease. Was it a natural wish to run his own show without interference, or were things happening in the dealership which he preferred others not to know? Whatever the reason, Adam intended to find out if he could.

'Let's go in my office, Adam.' They moved from the open mezzanine into a small but comfortable room, furnished wih green leather armchairs and a sofa. A desk top and a swivel chair had the same material. Smokey saw Adam look around.

'They guy I got to furnish this wanted it all red. I told him, "Nuts to that! The only red'll ever get in this business'll be by accident".'

One side of the office, almost entirely window, fronted the mezzanine. The dealer and Adam stood looking down at the showroom as if from a ship's bridge.

Adam motioned towards the row of sales offices below. 'You have a monitoring system?'

For the first time, Smokey hesitated. 'Yeah.'

'I'd like to listen. The sales booth right there.' In one of the glassed enclosures a young salesman, with a boyish face and a shock of blond hair, faced two prospective customers, a man and a woman. Papers were spread over a desk between them.

'I guess you can.' Smokey was less than enthusiastic. But he opened a sliding panel near his desk to reveal several switches, one of which he clicked. Immediately, voices became audible through a speaker recessed into the wall.

' . . . course, we can order the model you want in Meadow Green.' The voice was obviously the young salesman's. 'Too bad we don't have one in stock.'

Another male voice responded; it had an aggressive nasal quality. 'We can wait. That's if we make a deal here. Or we might go someplace else.'

'I understand that, sir. Tell me something, merely out of interest. The Galahad model, in Meadow Green; the one you were both looking at. How much more do you think that would cost?'

'I already told you,' the nasal voice said. 'A Galahad's out of our price range.'

'But just out of interest – name any figure. How much more?'

Smokey chuckled. 'Attaboy, Pierre! He's selling 'em up.'

The nasal voice said grudgingly, 'Well, maybe two hundred dollars.'

Adam could see the salesman smile. 'Actually,' he said softly, 'it's only seventy-five.'

A woman's voice interceded. 'Dear, if it's only that much . . .'

Smokey guffawed. 'You can hook a woman that way, every time. The dame's already figured she's saved a hundred and twenty five bucks. Pierre hasn't mentioned a cuppla options extra on that Galahad. But he'll get to it.'

The salesman's voice said, 'Why don't we take another look at the car? I'd like to show you . . .'

As the trio rose, Smokey snapped off the switch.

'That salesman,' Adam said. 'I've seen his face . . .'

'Sure. He's Pierre Flodenhale.'

Now Adam remembered. Pierre Flodenhale was a race driver whose name, in the past year or two, had become increasingly well known nationally. Last season he had had several spectacular wins.

'When things are quiet around the tracks,' Smokey said, 'I let Pierre work here. Suits us both. Some people recognize him; they like to have him sell them a car so they can tell their friends. Either way, he's a good sales joe. He'll cinch that deal.'

'Perhaps he'd buy in as a partner. If Teresa drops out.'

Smokey shook his head. 'Not a chance. The kid's always broke; it's why he moonlights here. All race drivers are the same – blow their dough faster'n they make it, even the big winners. Their brains get flooded like carburettors; they figure the purse money'll keep coming in for ever.'

'You didn't.'

'I was a smart cookie. Still am.'

They discussed dealer philosophy. Smokey told Adam, 'This never was a sissie business; now it's getting tougher. Customers are smarter. A dealer has to stay smarter still, but it's big, and you can win big.'

At talk of consumerism, Smokey bridled. 'The "poor consumer" is taking goddam good care of himself. The public was greedy before; consumerism made it worse. Now, everybody wants the best deal ever, with free service for evermore. How about a little "Dealerism" sometime? A dealer has to fight to survive.'

While they talked, Adam continued to watch activity below. Now he pointed to the sales booths again. 'That first one. I'd like to hear.'

The sliding panel had remained open. Smokey reached out and clicked a switch.

' . . . deal. I'm telling you, you won't do better anywhere else.' A salesman's voice again; this time an older man than Pierre Flodenhale, greying, and with a sharper manner. The prospective customer, a woman whom Adam judged to be in her thirties, appeared to be alone. Momentarily he had a guilty sense of snooping, then reminded himself that use of concealed microphones by dealers, to monitor exchanges between salesmen and car buyers, was widespread. Also, only by listening as he was doing now, could Adam judge the quality of communication between Smokey Stephensen's dealership and its clients.

'I'm not as sure as you,' the woman said. 'With the car I'm trading in as good as it is, I think your price is a hundred dollars high.' She started to get up. 'I'd better try somewhere else.'

They heard the salesman sigh. 'I'll go over the figures one more time.' The woman subsided. A pause, then the salesman again. 'You'll be financing the new car, right?'

'Yes.'

'And you'd like us to arrange financing?'

'I expect so.' The woman hesitated. 'Well, yes.'

From his own knowledge, Adam could guess how the salesman's mind was working. With almost every financed sale a dealer received a kickback from the back or finance company, usually a hundred dollars, sometimes more. Banks and others made the payments as a means of getting business, for which competition was keen. In a tight deal, knowledge that the money would be coming could be used to make a last-minute price cut, rather than lose the sale entirely.

As if he had read Adam's mind, Smokey murmured, 'Chuck knows the score. We don't like to lose our kickback, but sometimes we have to.'

'Perhaps we can do a little better.' It was the salesman in the booth again. 'What I've done is, on your trade . . . '

Smokey snapped the switch, cutting the details off.

Several newcomers had appeared in the showroom; now a fresh group moved into another sales booth. But Smokey seemed dissatisfied. 'To make the joint pay I have to sell two thousand five hundred a cars a year, and business is slow, slow.'

Knuckles rapped on the office door outside. As Smokey called, 'Yeah,' it opened to admit the salesman who had been dealing with the woman on her own. He held a sheaf of papers which Smokey took, skimmed over, then said accusingly, 'She out-bluffed you. You didn't have to use all the hundred. She'd have settled for fifty.'

'Not that one.' The salesman glanced at Adam, then away. 'She's a sharpie. Some things you can't see from up here, boss. Like what's in people's eyes. I tell you, hers are hard.'

'How would you know? When you gave my money away, you were probably looking up her skirts, so you let her take you.'

The salesman looked pained.

Smokey scribbled a signature and handed the papers back. 'Get the car delivered.'

They watched the salesman leave the mezzanine and return to the booth where the woman waited.

'Some things to remember about salesmen,' Smokey Stephensen said. 'Pay 'em well, but keep 'em off balance, and never trust one. A good many'll take fifty dollars under the desk for a sweet deal, or for steering finance business, as soon as blow their nose.'

Adam motioned to the switch panel. Once more Smokey touched it and they were listening to the salesman who had left the office moments earlier.

' . . . your copy. We keep this one.'

'Is it properly signed?'

'Sure is.' Now that the deal was made, the salesman was more relaxed; he leaned across the desk, pointing. 'Right there. The boss's fist.'

'Good.' The woman picked up the sales contract, folded it, then announced, 'I've been thinking while you were away, and I've decided not to finance after all. I'll pay cash, with a deposit cheque now and the balance when I pick up the car on Monday.'

There was a silence from the sales booth.

Smokey Stephensen slammed a meaty fist into his palm. 'The smart-ass bitch!'

Adam looked at him inquiringly.

'That lousy broad planned that! She knew all along she wouldn't finance.'

From the booth they heard the salesman hesitate. 'Well . . . that could make a difference.'

'A difference to what? The price of the car?' The woman inquired coolly, 'How could it unless there's some concealed charge you haven't told me about? The Truth in Lending Act . . . '

Smokey stormed from the window to his desk, snatched up an inside phone and dialled. Adam saw the salesman reach for a receiver.

Smokey snarled, 'Let the cow have the car. We'll stand by the deal.' He slammed down the phone, then muttered, 'But let her come back for service after warranty's out, she'll be sorry!'

Adam said mildly, 'Perhaps she'll think of that, too.'

As if she had heard him, the woman looked up towards the mezzanine and smiled.

'There's too many know-it-alls nowadays.' Smokey returned to stand beside Adam. 'Too much written in the newspapers; too many two-bit writers sticking their noses where they've no goddam business. People read that crap.' The dealer leaned forward, surveying the showroom. 'So what happens? Some, like that woman, go to a bank, arrange financing before they get here, but don't tell us till the deal is made. They let us think we're to set up financing. So we figure our take – or some of it – into the sale, then we're hooked, and if a dealer backs out of a signed sales contract, he's in trouble. Same thing with insurance; we like arranging car insurance because our commission's good; life insurance on finance payments is even better.' He added moodily, 'At least the broad didn't take us on insurance, too.'

Each incident so far, Adam thought, had given him a new, inside glimpse of Smokey Stephensen.

'I suppose you could look at it from a customer's point of view,' Adam prompted. 'They want the cheapest financing, most economical insurance, and people are learning they don't get either from a dealer, and that they're better off arranging their own. When there's a payoff to the dealer – finance or insurance – they know it's the customer who pays because the extra money's incorporated in his rates or charges.'

Smokey said dourly 'A dealer's gotta live, too. Besides, what people didn't used to know, they didn't worry after.'

In another sales booth below, an elderly couple were seating themselves, a salesman facing them. A moment earlier, the trio had walked from a demonstrator car they had been examining. As Adam nodded, under Smokey's hand a switch clicked once more.

' . . . really like to have you folks for clients because Mr Stephensen runs a quality dealership and we're happiest when we sell to quality people.'

'That's a nice thing to hear,' the woman said.

'Well, Mr Stephensen's always telling us salesmen, "Just don't think of the car you're selling today. Think of how you can give folks good service; also that they'll be coming back two years from now, and perhaps another two or three after that." '

Adam turned to Smokey. 'Did you say that?'

The dealer grinned. 'If I didn't, I should have.'

Over the next several minutes, while they listened, a trade-in was discussed. The elderly couple was hesitant about committing themselves to a final figure – the difference between an allowance for their used car and the price of a new one. They lived on a fixed income, the husband explained – his retirement pension.

At length the salesman announced, 'Look, folks, like I said, the deal I've written up is the very best we can give anybody. But because you're nice people, I've decided to try something I shouldn't. I'll write an extra sweet deal for you, then see if I can con the boss into okaying it.'

'Well . . . 'The woman sounded doubtful. 'We wouldn't want . . . '

The salesman assured her, 'Let me worry about that. Some days the boss is not as sharp as others; we'll hope this is one. What I'll do is change the figures this way: On the trade . . . '

It amounted to a hundred dollars reduction of the end price. As he switched off, Smokey appeared amused.

Moments later, the salesman knocked on the office door and came in, a filled-in sales contract in his hand.

'Hi, Alex.' Smokey took the proffered contract and introduced Adam, adding, 'It's OK, Alex; he's one of us.'

The salesman shook hands. 'Nice to know you, Mr Trenton.' He nodded to the booth below. 'Were you tuned in, boss?'

'Sure was. Too bad, ain't it, this is one of my sharp days?' The dealer grinned.

'Yeah.' The salesman smiled back. 'Too bad.'

While they chatted, Smokey made alterations to the figures on the sales papers. Afterwards he signed, then glanced at his watch. 'Been gone long enough?'

'I guess so,' the salesman said. 'Nice to have met you, Mr Trenton.'

Together, Smokey and the salesman left the office and stood on the open mezzanine outside.

Adam heard Smokey Stephensen raise his voice to a shout, 'What are you tryin' on? You wanna make a bankrupt outa me?'

'Now, boss, just let me explain.'

'Explain! Who needs it? I read figures; they say this deal means a great fat loss.'

In the showroom below, heads turned, faces glanced upward to the mezzanine. Among them were those of the elderly couple in the first booth.

'Boss, these are nice people.' The salesman was matching Smokey's voice in volume. 'We want their business, don't we?'

'Sure I want business, but this is charity.'

'I was just trying . . . '

'How about trying for a job someplace else?'

'Look, boss, maybe I can fix this up. These are reasonable people . . . '

'Reasonable, so they want my skin!'

'I did it, boss; not them. I just thought maybe . . . '

'We give great deals here. We draw the line at losses. Understand?'

'I understand.'

The exchange was loud as ever. Two of the other salesmen, Adam observed, were smiling surreptitiously. The elderly couple, waiting, looked perturbed.

Again the dealer shouted. 'Hey, gimme back those papers!'

Through the open doorway Adam saw Smokey seize the sales contract and go through motions of writing, though the alterations were already made. Smokey thrust the contract back. 'Here's the very best I'll do. I'm being generous because you put me in a box.' He winked broadly, though the last was visible only on the mezzanine.

The salesman returned the wink. As he went downstairs, Smokey re-entered his office and slammed the door, the sound reverberating below.

Adam said dryly, 'Quite a performance.'

Smokey chuckled. 'Oldest ploy in the book, and still works sometimes.' The listening switch for the first sales booth was still on; he turned the volume up as the salesman rejoined the elderly couple who had risen to their feet.

'Oh, we're so sorry,' The woman said. 'We were embarrassed for you. We wouldn't have that happen . . . '

The salesman's face was suitably downcast. 'I guess you folks heard.'

'Heard!' the older man objected. 'I should think everybody within five blocks heard. He didn't have to talk to you like that.'

The woman asked, 'What about your job?'

'Don't worry; as long as I make a sale today I'll be OK. The boss is a good guy, really. Like I told you, people who deal here find that out. Let's look at the figures.' The salesman spread the contract on the desk, then shook his head. 'We're back to the original deal, I'm afraid, though it's still a good one. Well, I tried.'

'We'll take it,' the man said; he seemed to have forgotten his earlier doubts. 'You've gone to enough trouble . . . '

Smokey said cheerfully, 'In the bag.' He switched off and slumped into one of the green leather chairs, motioning Adam to another. The dealer took a cigar from his pocket and offered one to Adam, who declined and lit a cigarette.

'I said a dealer has to fight,' Smokey said, 'and so he does. But it's a game, too.' He looked at Adam shrewdly. 'I guess a different kind of game than yours.'

Adam acknowledged, 'Yes.'

'Not so fancy pants as over at that think factory, huh?'

Adam made no answer. Smokey contemplated the glowing tip of his cigar, then went on. 'Remember this: a guy who gets to be a car dealer didn't make the game, he doesn't name the rules. He joins the game and plays the way it's played – for real, like strip poker. You know what happens if you lose at strip poker?'

'I guess so.'

'No guessing to it. You end up with a bare ass. It's how I'd end here if I didn't play hard, for real, the way you've seen. And though she'd look nicer 'n me bare-assed' – Smokey chuckled – 'so would that sister of yours. I'll ask you to remember that, Adam.' He stood up. 'Let's play the game some more.'

He was, after all, Adam realized, getting an untrammelled inside view of the dealership in operation. Adam accepted Smokey's viewpoint that trading in cars – new and used – was a tough, competitive business in which a dealer who relaxed or was soft-hearted could disappear from sight quickly, as many had. A car dealership was the firing line of automobile marketing. Like any firing line it was no place for the overly sensitive or anyone obsessed with ethics. On the other hand, an alert, shrewd wheeler-dealer – as Smokey Stephensen appeared to be – could make an exceedingly good living, which was part of the reason for Adam's inquiry now.

Another part was to learn how Smokey might adapt to changes in the future.

Within the next decade, Adam knew, major changes were coming in the present car dealership system, a system which many – inside the industry and out – believed archaic in its present form. So far, existing dealers – a powerful, organized bloc – had resisted change. But if manufacturers and dealers, acting together, failed to initiate reforms in the system soon, it was certain that government would step in, as it had already in other industry areas.

Car dealers had long been the auto industry's least reputable arm, and while direct defrauding had been curbed in recent years, many observers believed the public would be better served if contact between manufacturers and car buyers were more direct, with fewer intermediaries. Likely in the future were central dealership systems, factory-operated, which could deliver cars to customers more efficiently and with less overhead cost than now. For years, a similar system had been used successfully with trucks; more recently, car fleet users and car leasing and rental companies, who bought directly, were demonstrating large economies. Along with such direct sales outlets, factory-operated warranty and service centres were likely to be established, the latter offering more consistent, better-supervised service than many dealers provided now.

What was needed to get such systems started – and what auto companies would secretly welcome – was more external, public pressure.

But while dealerships would change, and some fall by the way, the more efficient, better-operated ones were likely to remain and prosper. One reason was the dealers' most commanding argument for existence – their disposal of used cars.

A question for Adam to decide was: would Smokey Stephensen's – and Teresa's – dealership progress or decline amid the changes of the next few years? He was already debating the question mentally as he followed Smokey from the mezzanine office down the stairway to the showroom floor.

For the next hour Adam stayed close to Smokey Stephensen, watching him in motion. Clearly, while letting his sales staff do their work, Smokey kept a sensitive finger on the pulse of business. Little escaped him. He had an instinct, too, about when his own intervention might nudge a teetering sale to its conclusion.

A lantern-jawed, cadaverous man who had come in from the street without glancing at the cars displayed, was arguing with a salesman about price. The man knew the car he wanted; equally obviously, he had shopped elsewhere.

He had a small card in his hand which he showed to the salesman, who shook his head. Smokey strolled across the showroom. Adam positioned himself so he could observe and hear.

'Let me see.' Smokey reached out, plucking the card deftly from Lantern Jaw's fingers. It was a business card with a dealer insignia on the front; on the back were pencilled figures. Nodding amiably, his manner robbing the action of offence, Smokey studied the figures. No-one bothered with introductions; Smokey's proprietorial air, plus the beard and blue silk jacket were his identification. As he turned the card his eyebrows went up. 'From an Ypsilanti dealer. You live there, friend?'

'No,' Lantern Jaw said. 'But I like to shop around.'

'And where you shop, you ask for a card with the best price difference between your trade-in and the new car. Right?'

The other nodded.

'Be a good sport,' Smokey said. 'Show me the cards from all the other dealers.'

Lantern Jaw hesitated, then shrugged. 'Why not?' From a pocket he produced a handful of cards and gave them to Smokey who counted them, chuckling. Including the one he already held, there were eight. Smokey spread the cards on a desk top nearby, then, with the salesman, craned over them.

'The lowest offer is two thousand dollars,' the salesman read, 'and the highest twenty-three hundred.'

Smokey motioned. 'The report on his trade.'

The salesman passed over a sheet, which Smokey glanced at, then handed back. He told the lantern-jawed man, 'I guess you'd like a card from me, too.'

'Sure would.'

Smokey took out a business card, turned it over, and scribbled on the back.

Lantern Jaw accepted the card, then looked up sharply. 'This says fifteen hundred dollars.'

Smokey said blandly, 'A nice round figure.'

'But you won't sell me a car for that!'

'You're damn right I won't, friend. And I'll tell you something else. Neither will any of those others, not at the prices they put on *their* cards.' Smokey swept the business cards into his hand, then returned them one by one. 'Go back to this place, they'll tell you their price didn't include sales tax. This one – they've left out the cost of options, maybe sales tax, too. Here, they didn't add dealer prep, licence, and some more . . . ' He continued through the cards, pointing to his own last. 'Me, I didn't include wheels and an engine; I'd have got around to it when you came back to talk for real.'

Lantern Jaw looked crestfallen.

'An old dealer trick, friend,' Smokey said, 'designed for shoppers like you, and the name of the game is "Bring 'em back later!" ' He added sharply, 'Do you believe me?'

'Yeah. I believe you.'

Smokey rammed his point home. 'So nine dealers after you started – right here and now – is where you got your first honest news, where somebody levelled with you. Right?'

The other said ruefully, 'Sure looks that way.'

'Great! That's how we run this shop.' Smokey draped a hand genially around Lantern Jaw's shoulders. 'So, friend, now you got the starting flag. What you do next is drive back to all those other dealers for more prices, the real ones, close as you can get.' The man grimaced; Smokey appeared not to notice. 'After that, when you're ready for more honest news, like a driveaway price which includes everything, come back to me.' The dealer held out a beefy hand. 'Good luck!'

'Hold it,' Lantern Jaw said. 'Why not tell me now?'

'Because you aren't serious yet. Because you'd still be wasting my time and yours.'

The man hesitated only briefly. 'I'm serious. What's the honest price?'

Smokey warned him, 'Higher'n any of those fake ones. But my price has the options you want, sales tax, licence, a tank of gas, nothing hidden, the works . . .'

Minutes later they shook hands on twenty-four hundred and fifty dollars. As the salesman began his paper work, Smokey strolled away, continuing to prowl the showroom.

Almost at once Adam saw him stopped by a self-assured, pipe-smoking newcomer, handsomely dressed in a Harris tweed jacket, immaculate slacks and alligator shoes. They talked at length and, after the man left, Smokey returned to Adam, shaking his head. 'No sale there! A doctor! They're the worst to do business with. Want give-away prices; afterwards, priority service, and always with a free loan car, as if I had 'em on the shelf like Band-Aids. Ask any dealer about doctors. You'll touch a nerve.'

He was less critical, soon after, of a stockily built, balding man with a gravelly voice, shopping for a car for his wife. Smokey introduced him to Adam as a local police chief, Wilbur Arenson. Adam, who had encountered the chief's name frequently in newspapers, was aware of cold, blue eyes sizing him up, his identity stored away routinely in the policeman's memory. The two retired to Smokey's office where a deal was consummated – Adam suspected a good one for the customer. When the police chief had gone, Smokey said, 'Stay friendly with the cops. Could cost me plenty if I got parking tickets for all the cars my service department has to leave on the street some days.'

A swarthy, voluble man came in and collected an envelope which was waiting for him in the main floor reception office. On his way out, Smokey intercepted him and shook hands warmly. Afterwards he explained, 'He's a barber, and one of our bird dogs. Gets people in his chair; while he cuts their hair, he talks about how good a deal he got here, how great the service is. Sometimes his customers say they're coming over, and if we make a sale the guy gets his little cut.' He had twenty or so regular bird dogs, Smokey revealed, including service station operators, a druggist, a beauty parlour operator, and an undertaker. As to the last, 'A guy dies, his wife wants to sell his car, maybe get something smaller. More often'n not, the undertaker's got her hypnotized, so she'll go where he says, and if it's here, we take care of him.'

They returned to the mezzanine office for coffee, laced with brandy out of a bottle produced by Smokey from a desk drawer.

Over their drinks the dealer introduced a new subject – the Orion.

'It'll be big when it hits, Adam, and that's the time we'll sell as many Orions here as we can get our hands on. You know how it is.' Smokey swirled the mixture in his cup. 'I was thinking – if you could use your pull to get us an extra allocation, it'd be good for Teresa and them kids.'

Adam said sharply, 'It would also put money in Smokey Stephensen's pocket.'

The dealer shrugged. 'So we help each other.'

'In this case we don't. And I'll ask you not to bring it up, or anything else like it, ever again.'

A moment earlier Adam had tensed, his anger rising at the proposal which was so outrageous that it represented everything the company Conflict of Interest Committee was set up to prevent. Then, amusement creeping in, he settled for the moderate reply. Clearly, where sales and business were concerned, Smokey Stephensen was totally amoral and saw nothing wrong in what had been suggested. Perhaps a car dealer had to be that way. Adam wasn't sure; nor was he sure, yet, what he would recommend to Teresa.

But he had gained the first impressions which he came for. They were mixed; he wanted to digest and think about them.

13

Hank Kreisel, lunching in Dearborn with Brett DeLosanto, represented the out-of-sight portion of an iceberg.

Kreisel, fifty-five-ish, lean, muscular, and towering over most other people like a collie in a pack of terriers, was the owner of his company which manufactured auto parts.

The world, when it thinks of Detroit, does so in terms of name-famed auto manufacturers, dominated by the Big Three. The impression is correct, except that major car makers represent the portion of the iceberg in view. Out of sight are thousands of supplemental firms, some substantial, but most small, and with a surprising segment operating out of holes-in-the-wall on petty cash financing. In the Detroit area they are anywhere and everywhere – downtown, out in suburbs, on side roads, or as satellites to bigger plants. Their work quarters range from snazzy compages to ramshackle warehouses, converted churches or one-room lofts. Some are unionized, many are not, although their total payrolls run to billions yearly. But the thing they have in common is that a Niagara of bits and pieces – some large, but mostly small, many unrecognizable as to purpose except by experts – flow outward to create other parts and, in the end, the finished automobiles. Without parts manufacturers, the Big Three would be like honey processors bereft of bees.

In this sense, Hank Kreisel was a bee. In another sense he was a master sergeant of Marines. He had been a Marine top kick in the Korean War, and still looked the part, with short hair only slightly greying, neatly trimmed moustache, and a ramrod stance when he stood still, though this was seldom. Mostly he moved in urgent, precise, clipped movements – *go, go, go* – and talked the same way, from the time of rising early in his Grosse Pointe home until ending each active day, invariably well into the next. This and other habits had brought him two heart attacks, with a warning from his physician that one more might be fatal. But Hank Kreisel regarded the warning as he would once have reacted to news of a potential enemy ambush in the jungle ahead. He pressed on, hard as ever, trusting in a personal conviction of indestructibility, and luck which had seldom failed him.

It was luck which had given him a lifetime, so far, filled with the two things Hank Kreisel relished most – work and women. Occasionally the luck had failed. Once had been during a fervid affair in rest camp with a colonel's wife, after which her husband personally busted Master Sergeant Kreisel down to private. And later, in his Detroit manufacturing career, disasters had occurred, though successes well outnumbered them.

Brett DeLosanto had met Kreisel when the latter was in the Design-Styling Center one day, demonstrating a new accessory. They had liked each other and, partly through the young designer's genuine curiosity about how the rest of the auto industry worked and lived, had become friends. It was Hank Kreisel whom Brett had planned to meet on the frustrating day downtown when he had had the parking lot encounter with Leonard Wingate. But Kreisel had failed to make it that day and now, two months later, the pair were keeping their postponed luncheon date.

'I've wondered, Hank,' Brett DeLosanto said. 'How'd you get started with the auto parts bit?'

'Long story,' Kreisel reached for the neat sourmash Bourbon which was his habitual drink and took an ample sip. He was relaxing and, while dressed in a well-cut business suit, had the buttons of his vest undone, revealing that he wore both suspenders and a belt. He added, 'Tell you, if you like.'

'Go ahead.' Brett had worked through the past several nights at the Design-Styling Center, had caught up with sleep this morning, and now was relishing the daytime freedom before returning to his design board later this afternoon.

They were in a small private apartment a mile or so from the Henry Ford Museum and Greenfield Village. Because of its proximity, also, to Ford Motor Company headquarters, the apartment appeared on the books of Kreisel's company as his 'Ford liaison office'. In fact, the liaison was not with Ford but with a lissom, leggy brunette named Elsie, who lived in the apartment rent-free, was on the payroll of Kreisel's company though she never went there, and in return made herself available to Hank Kreisel once or twice a week, or more often if he felt like it. The arrangement was easygoing on both sides. Kreisel, a considerate, reasonable man, always telephoned before putting in an appearance, and Elsie saw to it that he had priority.

Unknown to Elsie, Hank Kreisel also had a General Motors and Chrysler liaison office, operating under the same arrangement.

Elsie, who had prepared lunch, was in the kitchen now.

'Hold it!' Kreisel told Brett. 'Just remembered something. You know Adam Trenton?'

'Very well.'

'Like to meet him. Word's out he's a big comer. Never hurts to make high-grade friends in this business.' The statement was characteristic of Kreisel, a mixture of directness and amiable cynicism which men, as well as women, found appealing.

Elsie rejoined them, her every movement an overt sexuality which a simple, tight black dress accentuated. The ex-Marine patted her rump affectionately.

'Sure, I'll fix a meeting.' Brett grinned. 'Here?'

Hank Kreisel shook his head. 'The Higgins Lake cottage. A weekend party. Let's aim at May. You choose a date. I'll do the rest.'

'OK, I'll talk with Adam. Let you know.' When he was with Kreisel, Brett found himself using the same kind of staccato sentences as his host. As to a party, Brett had already attended several at Hank Kreisel's cottage hideaway. They were swinging affairs which he enjoyed.

Elsie seated herself at the table with them and resumed her lunch, her eyes moving between the two men as they talked. Brett knew, because he had been here before, that she liked to listen but seldom joined in.

Brett inquired, 'What made you think of Adam?'

'The Orion. He okayed add-ons, I'm told. Last minute hot stuff. I'm making one of 'em.'

'*You* are! Which one? The brace or floor reinforcement?'

'Brace.'

'Hey, I was in on that! That's a big order.'

Kreisel gave a twisted grin. 'It'll make me or break me. They need five thousand braces fast, like yesterday. After that, ten thousand a month. Wasn't sure I wanted the job. Schedule's tough. Still plenty of headaches. But they figure I'll deliver.'

Brett already knew of Hank Kreisel's reputation for reliability about deliveries, a quality which auto company purchasing departments cherished. One reason for it was a talent for tooling improvisations which slashed time and cost, and while not a qualified engineer himself, Kreisel could leapfrog mentally over many who were.

'I'll be damned!' Brett said. 'You and the Orion.'

'Shouldn't surprise you. Industry's full of people crossing each other's bridges. Sometimes pass each other, don't even know it. Everybody sells to everybody else. GM sells steering gears to Chrysler. Chrysler sells adhesives to GM and Ford. Ford helps out with Plymouth windshields. I know a guy, a sales engineer. Lives in Flint, works for General Motors. Flint's a GM company town. His main customer's Ford in Dearborn – for engineering design of engine accessories. He takes confidential Ford stuff to Flint. GM guards it from their own people who'd give their ears to see it. The guy drives a Ford car – to Ford, his customer. His GM bosses buy it for him.'

Elsie replenished Hank Kreisel's Bourbon; Brett had declined a drink earlier.

Brett told the girl, 'He's always telling me things I didn't know.'

'He knows a lot.' Her eyes, smiling, switched from the young designer's to Kreisel's. Brett sensed a private message pass.

'Hey! You two like me to leave?'

'No hurry.' The ex-Marine produced a pipe and lit it. 'You want to hear about parts?' He glanced at Elsie. 'Not yours, baby.' Plainly he meant: *Those are for me.*

'Auto parts,' Brett said.

'Right.' Kreisel gave his twisted grin. 'Worked in an auto plant before I enlisted. After Korea, went back. Was a punch press operator. Then a foreman.'

'You've made the big leagues fast.'

'Too fast, maybe. Anyway, I'd watched how production worked – metal stampings. The Big Three are all the same. Must have the fanciest machines, high-priced buildings, big overhead, cafeterias, the rest. All that stuff makes a two-cent stamping cost a nickel.'

Hank Kreisel drew on his pipe and wreathed himself in smoke. 'So I went to Purchasing. Saw a guy I know. Told him I figured I could make the same stuff cheaper. On my own.'

'Did they finance you?'

'Not then, not later. Gave me a contract, though. There and then for a million little washers. When I'd quit my job I had two hundred dollars cash. No building, no machinery.' Hank Kreisel chuckled. 'Didn't sleep that night. Dead scared. Next day I tore around. Rented an old billiard hall. Showed a bank the contract and the lease; they loaned me dough to buy scrap machinery. Then I hired two other guys. The three of us fixed the machinery up. They ran it. I rushed out, got more orders.' He added reminiscently, 'Been rushing ever since.'

'You're a saga,' Brett said. He had seen Hank Kreisel's impressive Grosse Pointe home, his half dozen bustling plants, the converted billiard hall still one of them. He supposed, conservatively, Hank Kreisel must be worth two or three million dollars.

'Your friend in Purchasing,' Brett said. 'The one who gave you the first order. Do you ever see him?'

'Sure. He's still there – on salary. Same job. Retires soon. I buy him a meal sometimes.'

Elsie asked, 'What's a saga?'

Kreisel told her, 'It's a guy who makes it to the end of the trail.'

'A legend,' Brett said.

Kreisel shook his head. 'Not me. Not yet.' He stopped, more thoughtful suddenly than Brett had seen him at anytime before. When he spoke again his voice was slower, the words less clipped. 'There's a thing I'd like to do, and may be it could add up to something like that if I could pull it off.' Aware of Brett's curiosity, the ex-Marine shook his head again. Not now. Maybe one day I'll tell you.'

His mood switched back. 'So I made parts and made mistakes. Learned a lot fast. One thing: search out weak spots in the market. Spots where competition's least. So I ignored new parts; two much in-fighting. Started making for repair, replacement, the "after market". But only items no more than twenty inches from the ground. Mostly at front and rear. And costing less than ten dollars.'

'Why the restrictions?'

Kreisel gave his usual knowing grin. 'Most minor accidents happen to fronts and backs of cars. And down below twenty inches, all get damaged more. So more parts are needed, meaning bigger orders. That's where parts makers hit paydirt – on long runs.'

'And the ten-dollar limit?'

'Say you're doing a repair job. Something's damaged. Costs more than ten dollars, you'll try to fix it. Costs less, you'll throw the old part out, use a replacement. There's where I come in. High volume again.'

It was so ingeniously simple, Brett laughed aloud.

'I got into accessories later. And something else I learned. Take on some defence work.'

'Why?'

'Most parts people don't want it. Can be difficult. Usually short runs, not much profit. But can lead to bigger things. And Internal Revenue are easier on you about tax deductions. They won't admit it.' He surveyed his 'Ford liaison office' amusedly. 'But I know.'

'Elsie's right. There's a whole lot you know.' Brett rose, glancing at his watch. 'Back to the chariot factory! Thanks for lunch, Elsie.'

The girl got up too, moved beside him, and took his arm. He was aware of her closeness, a warmth transmitted through the thinness of her dress. Her slim, firm body eased away, then once more pressed against his. Accidentally? He doubted it. His nostrils detected the soft scent of her hair, and Brett envied Hank Kreisel what he suspected would happen as soon as he had gone.

Elsie said softly, 'Come in any time.'

'Hey, Hank!' Brett said. 'You hear that invitation?'

Momentarily the older man looked away, then answered gruffly, 'If you accept, make sure I don't know about it.'

Kreisel joined him at the apartment doorway. Elsie had gone back inside.

'I'll fix that date with Adam,' Brett affirmed. 'Call you tomorrow.'

'OK.' The two shook hands.

'About that other,' Hank Kreisel said. 'Meant exactly what I told you. Don't let me know. Understand?'

'I understand.' Brett had already memorized the number on the apartment telephone, which was unlisted. He had every intention of calling Elsie tomorrow.

As an elevator carried Brett downward, Hank Kreisel closed and locked the apartment door from inside.

Elsie was waiting for him in the bedroom. She had undressed and put on a sheer minikimono, held around her by a silk ribbon. Her dark hair, released, tumbled about her shoulders; her wide mouth smiled, eyes showing pleasurable knowledge of what was to come. They kissed lightly. He took his time about unfastening the ribbon, then, opening the kimono, held her.

After a while she began undressing him, slowly, carefully putting each garment aside and folding it. He had taught her, as he had taught other women in the past, that this was not a gesture of servility but a rite – practised in the East, where he had learned it first – and a mutual whetting of anticipation.

When she had finished they lay down together. Elsie had passed Hank a *happi* coat which he slipped on; it was one of several he had brought home from Japan, was growing threadbare from long use, but still served to prove what Far Easterners knew best: that a garment worn during sexual mating, however light or loose, heightened a man's and a woman's awareness of each other, and their pleasure.

He whispered, 'Love me, baby!'

She moaned softly. 'Love me, Hank!'

He did.

14

'You know what this scumbag world is made of, baby?' Rollie Knight had demanded of May Lou yesterday. When she hadn't answered, he told her. 'Bullshit! There ain't nuthin' in this whole wide world but bullshit.'

The remark was prompted by happenings at the car assembly plant where Rollie was now working. Though he hadn't kept score himself, today was the beginning of his seventh week of employment.

May Lou was new in his life, too. She was (as Rollie put it) a chick he had laid during a weekend, while blowing an early paycheck, and more recently they had shacked up in two rooms of an apartment house on Blaine near 12th. May Lou was currently spending her days there, messing with cook pots, furniture and bits of curtaining, making – as a barfly acquaintance of Rollie's described it – like a bush tit in the nest.

Rollie hadn't taken seriously, and still didn't, what he called May Lou's crapping around at playing house. Just the same he had given her bread, which she spent on the two of them, and to get more of the same, Rollie continued to report most days of the week to the assembly plant.

What started this second go around, after he had copped out of the first training course, was – in Rollie's words – a big Tom nigger in a fancy Dan suit, who had turned up one day, saying his name was Leonard Wingate. That was at Rollie's room in the inner city, and they had a great big gabfest in which Rollie first told the guy to get lost, go screw himself, he'd had enough. But the Tom had been persuasive. He went on to explain, while Rollie listened, fascinated, about the fatso white bastard of an inspector who put one over with the cheques, then got caught. When Rollie inquired, though, Wingate admitted that the white fatso wasn't going to jail the way a black man would have done, which proved that all the bullshit about justice was exactly that – bullshit! Even the black Tom, Wingate, admitted it. And it was just after he had – a bleak, bitter admission which surprised Rollie – that Rollie had somehow, almost before he knew it, agreed to go to work.

It was Leonard Wingate who had told Rollie he could forget about completing the rest of the training course. Wingate, it seemed, had looked up the records which said Rollie was bright and quick-witted, and so (Wingate said) they would put him straight on the assembly line next week, starting Monday, doing a regular job.

That (again, as Rollie told it) turned out to be bullshit, too.

Instead of being given a job in one place, which he might have managed, he was informed he had to be relief man at various stations on the line, which meant moving back and forth like a blue-assed fly, so that as soon as he got used to doing one thing, he was hustled over to another, then to something else, and something else, until his head was spinning. The same thing went on for the first two weeks so that he hardly knew – since the instructions he was given were minimal – what he was supposed to be doing from one minute to the next. Not that he'd have cared that much. Except for what the black guy, Wingate, had said, Rollie Knight – as usual – was not expecting anything. But it just showed that nothing they ever promised worked out the way they said it would. So . . . Bullshit!

Of course, nobody, *but nobody*, had told him about the speed of the assembly line. He'd figured that one for himself – the hard way.

On the first day at work, when Rollie had his initial view of a final car assembly line, the line seemed to be inching forward like a snail's funeral. He'd come to the plant early, reporting in with the day shift. The size of the joint, the mob flooding in from cars, buses, every other kind of wheels, you name it, scared him to begin with; also, everybody except himself seemed to know where they were going – all in one helluva hurry – and why. But he'd found where he had to report, and from there had been sent to a big, metal-roofed building, cleaner than he expected, but noisy. *Oh, man; that noise!* It was all around you, sounding like a hundred rock bands on bad trips.

Anyhow, the car line snaked through the building, with the end and beginning out of sight. And it looked as if there was time aplenty for any of the guys and broads (a few women were working alongside men) to finish whatever their job happened to be on one car, rest a drumbeat, then start work on the next. No sweat! For a cool cat with more than air between his ears, a cincheroo!

In less than an hour, like thousands who had preceded him, Rollie was grimly wiser.

The foreman he had been handed over to on arrival had said simply, 'Number?' The foreman, young and white, but balding, with the harried look of a middle-aged man, had a pencil poised and said peevishly, when Rollie hesitated. 'Social Security!'

Eventually Rollie located a card which a clerk in Personnel had given him. It had the number on it. Impatiently, with the knowledge of twenty other things he had to do immediately, the foreman wrote it down.

He pointed to the last four figures, which were 6469. 'That's what you'll be known as,' the foreman shouted; the line had already started up, and the din made it hard to hear. 'So memorize that number.'

Rollie grinned, and had been tempted to say it was the same way in prison. But he hadn't, and the foreman had motioned for him to follow, then took him to a work station. A partly finished car was moving slowly past, its brightly painted body gleaming. *Some snazzy wheels!* Despite his habit of indifference, Rollie felt his interest quicken.

The foreman bellowed in his ear: 'You got three chassis and trunk bolts to put in. Here, here, and here. Bolts are in the box over there. Use this power wrench.' He thrust it into Rollie's hands. 'Got it?'

Rollie wasn't sure he had. The foreman touched another worker's shoulder. 'Show this new man. He'll take over here. I need you on front suspension. Hurry it up.' The foreman moved away, still looking older than his years.

'Watch me, bub!' The other worker grabbed a handful of bolts and dived into a car doorway with a power wrench, its cord trailing. While Rollie was still craning, trying to see what the man was doing, the other came out backwards, forcefully. He cannoned into Rollie. 'Watch it, bub!' Going around to the back of the car, he dived into the trunk, two more bolts in hand, the wrench still with him.

He shouted back, 'Get the idea?' The other man worked on one more car, then, responding to renewed signals from the foreman, and with an 'All yours, bub,' he disappeared.

Despite the noise, the dozens of people he could see close by, Rollie had never felt more lonely in his life.

'*You! Hey! Get on with it!*' It was the foreman, shouting, waving his arms from the other side of the line.

The car which the first man had worked on was already gone. Incredibly, despite the line's apparent slowness, another had appeared. There was no-one but Rollie to insert the bolts. He grabbed a couple of bolts and jumped into the car. He groped for holes they were supposed to go in, found one, then realized he had forgotten the wrench. He went back for it. As he jumped back in the car the heavy wrench dropped on his hand, his knuckles skinned against the metal floor. He managed to start turning the single bolt; before he could finish, or insert the other, the wrench cord tightened as the car moved forward. The wrench would no longer reach. Rollie left the second bolt on the floor and got out.

With the car after that, he managed to get two bolts in and made a pass at tightening them, though he wasn't sure how well. With the one after that, he did better; also the car following. He was getting the knack of using the wrench, though he found it heavy. He was sweating and had skinned his hands again.

It was not until the fifth car had gone by that he remembered the third bolt he was supposed to insert in the trunk.

Alarmed, Rollie looked around him. No-one had noticed.

At adjoining work positions, one either side of the line, two men were installing wheels. Intent on their own tasks, neither paid the slightest heed to Rollie. He called to one, 'Hey! I left some bolts out.'

Without looking up, the worker shouted back, 'Forget it! Get the next one. Repair guys'll catch the others down the line.' Momentarily he lifted his head and laughed. 'Maybe.'

Rollie began inserting the third bolt through each car trunk to the chassis. He had to increase his pace to do it. It was also necessary to go bodily into the trunk and, emerging the second time, he hit his head on the deck lid. The blow half-stunned him, and he would have liked to rest, but the next car kept coming and he worked on it in a daze.

He was learning: first, the pace of the line was faster than it seemed; second, even more compelling than the speed was its relentlessness. The line came on, and on, and on, unceasing, unyielding, impervious to human weakness or appeal. It was like a tide which nothing stopped except a half-hour lunch break, the end of a shift, or sabotage.

Rollie became a saboteur on his second day.

He had been shifted through several positions by that time, from inserting chassis bolts to making electrical connexions, then to installing steering columns, and afterwards to fitting fenders. He had heard someone say the previous day there was a shortage of workers; hence the panic – a usual thing on Mondays. On Tuesdays he sensed more people were at their regular jobs, but Rollie was still being used by foremen to fill temporary gaps while others were on relief or break. Consequently, there was seldom time to learn anything well, and at each fresh position several cars went by before he learned to do a new job properly. Usually, if a foreman was on hand and noticed, the defective work would be tagged; at other times it simply went on down the line. On a few occasions foremen saw something wrong, but didn't bother.

While it all happened, Rollie Knight grew wearier.

The day before, at the end of work, his frail body had ached all over. His hands were sore; in various other places his skin was bruised or raw. That night he slept more soundly than in years and awakened next morning only because the cheap alarm clock, which Leonard Wingate had left, was loudly insistent. Wondering why he was doing it, Rollie scrambled up, and a few minutes later addressed himself in the cracked mirror over a chipped enamel washbasin. *'You lovin' crazy cat, you dopehead, crawl back in bed and cop some Zs. Or maybe you fixin' to be a white man's nigger.'* He eyed himself contemptuously but had not gone back to bed. Instead he reported to the plant once more.

By early afternoon his tiredness showed. Through the previous hour he had yawned repeatedly.

A young black worker with an Afro hairdo told him, 'Man, you sleeping on your feet.' The two were assigned to engine decking, their job to lower engines on to chassis, then secure them.

Rollie grimaced. 'Them wheels keep comin'. Never did see so many.'

'You need a rest, man. Like a rest when this mean line stops.'

'Ain't never gonna stop, I reckon.'

They manoeuvred a hulking engine from overhead into the forward compartment of one more car, inserting the driveshaft in the transmission extension, like a train being coupled, then released the engine from suspension. Others down the line would bolt it into place.

The worker with the Afro hairdo had his head close to Rollie's. 'You want this here line stopped? I mean it, man.'

'Oh sure, sure.' Rollie felt more like closing his eyes than getting involved in some stupid gabfest.

'Ain't kiddin'. See this.' Out of sight of others nearby, he worked open a fist he had been holding clenched. In his palm was a black, four-inch steel bolt. 'Hey, take it!'

'Why so?'

'Do like I say. Drop it there!' He pointed to a groove in the concrete floor near their feet, housing the assembly line chain drive, an endless belt like a monstrous bicycle chain. The chain drive ran the length of the assembly line and back, impelling the partially completed cars along the line at even speed. At various points it sank underground, rose through extra floors above, passed through paint booths, inspection chambers, or simply changed direction. Whenever it did, the moving chain clanked over cog points.

What the hell, Rollie thought. Anything to pass the time, to help this day end sooner – even a bunch of nothing. He dropped the bolt into the chain drive.

Nothing happened except that the bolt moved forward down the line; in less than a minute it was out of sight. Only then was he aware of heads lifting around him, of faces – mostly black – grinning at his own. Puzzled, he sensed others waiting expectantly. For what?

The assembly line stopped. It stopped without warning, without sudden sound or jolting. The change was so unremarkable that it took several seconds before some, intent on work, were aware that the line was now stationary in front of them instead of passing by.

For perhaps ten seconds there was a lull. During it, the workers around Rollie were grinning even more broadly than before.

Then, bedlam. Alarm bells clanged. Urgent shouts resounded from forward on the line. Soon after, somewhere in the depths of a plant a siren wailed faintly, then increased in volume, growing nearer.

The older hands who had watched, surreptitiously, the exchange between Rollie and the worker with the Afro hairdo knew what had happened.

From Rollie Knight's work station the nearest chain drive cog point was a hundred yards forward on the line. Until that point, the bolt he had inserted in a link of the chain had moved uneventfully. But when it reached the cog, the bolt jammed hard between cog and chain, so that something had to give. The link broke. The chain drive parted. The assembly line stopped. Instantly, seven hundred workers were left idle, their wages at union scale continuing while they waited for the line to start again.

More seconds ticked away. The siren was nearer, louder, travelling fast. In a wide aisle alongside the line, those on foot – supervisors, stockmen, messengers and others – hastily moved clear. Other plant traffic, fork-lifts, power carryalls, executive buggies – pulled aside and stopped. Hurtling around a bend in the building, a yellow truck with flashing red beacon swung into sight. It was a crash repair unit carrying a three-man crew with tools and welding gear. One drove, his foot against the floor; two others hung on, bracing themselves against welding cylinders in the rear. Forward on the line a foreman had arms upraised, signalling where the break had happened. The truck tore past Rollie Knight's work station – a blur of yellow, red, its siren at crescendo. It slowed, then stopped. The crew tumbled out.

In any car assembly plant an unscheduled line stoppage is an emergency, taking second place only to a fire. Every minute of line production lost equates a fortune in wages, administration, factory cost, none of which can ever be recovered. Expressed another way: when an assembly line is running it produces a new car roughly every fifty seconds. With an unplanned stoppage, the same amount of time means the full cost of a new car lost.

Thus the objective is to restart the line first, ask questions later.

The emergency crew, skilled in such contingencies, knew what to do. They located the chain drive break, brought the severed portions together. Cutting free the broken link, they welded in another. Their truck had scarcely stopped before acetylene torches flared. The job was hasty. When necessary, repairmen improvised to get the line moving again. Later, when production halted for a shift change or meal break, the repair would be inspected, a more lasting job done.

One of the repair crew signalled to a foreman – Frank Parkland – connected by telephone with the nearest control point. 'Start up!' The word was passed. Power, which had been cut by circuit breaker, was reapplied. The chain drive clanked over cogs, this time smoothly. The line restarted. Seven hundred employees, most of them grateful for the respite, resumed work.

From the stoppage of the line to its restarting had occupied four minutes fifty-four seconds. Thus five and a half cars had been lost, or more than six thousand dollars.

Rollie Knight, though scared by now, was not sure what had happened.

He found out quickly.

The foreman, Frank Parkland – big-boned, broad-shouldered came striding back along the line, his face set grimly. In his hand was a twisted four-inch bolt which one of the repair crew had given him.

He stopped, asking questions, holding up the mangled bolt. 'It came from this section; it had to. Some place here, between two sets of cogs. Who did it? Who saw it?'

Men shook their heads. Frank Parkland moved on, asking the questions over again.

When he came to the group decking engines, the young worker with the Afro hairdo was doubled up with laughter. Barely able to speak, he pointed to Rollie Knight. 'There he is, boss! Saw him do it.' Others at adjoining work stations were laughing with him.

Though Rollie was the target, he recognized, instinctively, no malice was involved. It was merely a joke, a diversion, a rambunctious prank. Who cared about consequences? Besides, the line had only stopped for minutes. Rollie found himself grinning too, then caught Parkland's eye and froze.

The foreman glared. 'You did it? You put this bolt in?'

Rollie's face betrayed him. His eyes showed white from sudden fear combined with weariness. For once, his outward cockiness was absent.

Parkland ordered, 'Out!'

Rollie Knight moved from his position on the line. The foreman motioned a relief man to replace him.

'Number?'

Rollie repeated the Social Security number he had learned the day before. Parkland asked his name and wrote it down also, his face remaining hard.

'You're new, aren't you?'

'Yeah.' *For Cri-sake!* – it was always the same. Questions, gabbing, never an end. Even when Whitey kicked your ass, he dressed it up with bullshit.

'What you did was sabotage. You know the consequences?'

Rollie shrugged. He had no idea what 'sabotage' meant, though he didn't like the sound of it. With the same resignation he had shown a few weeks earlier, he accepted that his job was gone. All that concerned him now was to wonder: what more could they throw at him? From the way this honky burned, he'd stir trouble if he could.

From behind Parkland, someone said, 'Frank – Mr Zaleski.'

The foreman turned. He watched the approaching stocky figure of the assistant plant manager.

'What was it, Frank?'

'This, Matt.' Parkland held up the twisted bolt.

'Deliberate?'

'I'm finding out.' His tone said, *Let me do it my way!*

'OK.' Zaleski's eyes moved coolly over Rollie Knight. 'But if it's sabotage, we throw the book. The union'll back us up; you know that. Let me have a report, Frank.' He nodded and moved on.

Frank Parkland wasn't sure why he had held back in exposing the man in front of him as a saboteur. He could have done so, and fired him instantly; there would have been no repercussions. But momentarily he had all seemed too easy. The little, half-starved guy looked more a victim than a villain. Besides, someone who knew the score wouldn't leave himself that vulnerable.

He held out the offending bolt. 'Did you know what this would do?'

Rollie looked up at Parkland, towering over him. Normally he would have glared back hate, but was too tired even for that. He shook his head.

'You know now.'

Remembering the shouts, activity, siren, flashing lights, Rollie could not resist a grin. 'Yeah, man!'

'Did somebody tell you to do it?'

He was aware of faces watching from the line, no longer smiling.

The foreman demanded, 'Well, who was it?'

Rollie stayed mute.

'Was it the one who accused you?'

The worker with the Afro hairdo was bent over, decking another engine.

Rollie shook his head. Given the chance, there were debts he would pay back. But this was not the way.

'All right,' Parkland said. 'I don't know why I'm doing this, but I think you got suckered, though maybe I'm the sucker now.' The foreman glared, begrudging his own concession. 'What happened'll go on the record as an accident. But you're being watched; remember that.' He added brusquely, 'Get back to work!'

Rollie, to his great surprise, ended the shift fitting pads under instrument panels.

He knew, though, that the situation couldn't stay the way it was. Next day he was the subject of appraising glances from fellow workers, and the butt of humour. At first the humour was casual and tentative, but he was aware it could get rougher, much rougher, if the idea grew that Rollie Knight was a pushover for pranks or bullying. For someone unlucky or inept enough to get that reputation, life could be miserable, even dangerous, because the monotony of assembly line work made people welcome anything, even brutality, as a diversion.

In the cafeteria on his fourth day of employment there occurred the usual mêlée at lunch break in which several hundred men rushed from work stations, their objective to get in line to be served, and, after waiting, hastily swallow their food, go to the toilet, wash off their dirt and grease if so inclined (it was never practical to wash before eating), then make it back to work all in thirty minutes. Amid the cafeteria crowd he saw the worker with the Afro hairdo surrounded by a group which was laughing, looking at Rollie speculatively. A few minutes later, after getting his own food, he was jostled roughly so that everything he had paid for cascaded to the floor where it was promptly trampled on – apparently an accident, too, though Rollie knew better. He did not eat that day; there was no more time.

During the jostling he heard a click and saw a switchblade flash. Next time, Rollie suspected, the jostling would be rougher, the switchblade used to nick him, or even worse. He wasted no time reasoning that the process was wildly illogical and unjust. A manufacturing plant employing thousands of workers was a jungle, with a jungle's lawlessness, and all that he could do was pick his moment to take a stand.

Though knowing time was against him, Rollie waited. He sensed an opportunity would come. It did.

On Friday, the last day of his working week, he was assigned again to lowering engines on to chassis. Rollie was teamed with an older man who was the engine decker, and among others at adjoining work stations was the worker with the Afro hairdo.

'Man, oh man, I feel somethin' creepy-crawly,' the latter declared when Rollie joined them near the end of a meal break, shortly before the line restarted. 'You gonna give us all a special rest today?' He cuffed Rollie around the shoulders as others nearby howled with laughter. Someone else slapped Rollie from the other side. Both blows could have been good-natured, but instead slammed into Rollie's frailness and left him staggering.

The chance he had planned and waited for occurred an hour later. As well as doing his own work since rejoining the group, Rollie Knight had watched, minute by minute, the movements and positions of the others, which fell into a pattern, but now and then with variations.

Each engine installed was lowered from overhead on chains and pulleys, its manoeuvring and release controlled by three pushbuttons – UP, STOP, DOWN – on a heavy electric cord hanging conveniently above the work station. Normally the engine decker operated the pushbuttons, though Rollie had learned to use them too.

A third man – in this instance the Afro hairdo worker – moved between stations, aiding the other two as needed.

Though the installation team worked fast, each engine was eased into place cautiously and, when almost seated, before the final drop, each man made sure his hands were clear.

As one engine was almost lowered and in place, its fuel and vacuum lines became entangled in the chassis front suspension. The hangup was momentary and occurred occasionally; when it did, the Afro hairdo worker moved in, reaching under the engine to clear the tangled lines. He did so now. The hands of the other two – Rollie and the engine decker – were safely removed.

Watching, choosing his moment, Rollie moved slightly sideways, reached up casually, then depressed and held the DOWN button. Instantly, a heavy, reverberating 'thunk' announced that half a ton of engine and transmission had dropped solidly on to mounts beneath. Rollie released the button and, in the same movement, eased away.

For an infinitesimal fraction of a second the Afro hairdo worker remained silent, staring unbelieving at his hand, its fingers out of sight beneath the engine block. Then he screamed – again and again – a shrieking, demented wail of agony and horror, piercing all other sounds around, so that men working fifty yards away raised their heads and craned uneasily to see the cause. The screams continued, fiendishly, unceasing, while someone hit an alarm button to stop the line, another the UP control to raise the engine assembly. As it lifted, the screams took on a new excruciating edge, while those who were nearest looked with horror at the squashed, mangled jigsaw of blood and bones which seconds earlier had been fingers. As the injured worker's knees buckled, two men held him while his body heaved, his face contorted as tears streamed over lips mouthing incoherent, animal moans. A third worker, his own face ashen, reached for the mashed and pulpy hand, easing loose what he could, though a good deal stayed behind. When what was left of the hand was clear, the assembly line restarted.

The injured worker was carried away on a stretcher, his screams diminishing as morphine took hold. The drug had been administered by a nurse summoned hurriedly from the plant dispensary. She had put a temporary dressing on the hand, and her white uniform was blood-spattered as she walked beside the stretcher, accompanying it to an ambulance waiting out of doors.

Among the workers, no-one looked at Rollie.

The foreman, Frank Parkland, and a plant safety manager questioned those closest to the scene during a work break a few minutes later. A union steward was present.

The plant men demanded: what exactly happened?

It seemed that no-one knew. Those who might have had knowledge claimed to have been looking some other way when the incident occurred.

'It doesn't figure,' Parkland said. He stared hard at Rollie Knight. 'Somebody must have seen.'

The safety man asked, 'Who hit the switch?'

No-one answered. All that happened was an uneasy shuffling of feet, with eyes averted.

'Somebody did,' Frank Parkland said. 'Who was it?'

Still silence.

Then the engine decker spoke. He looked older, greyer, than before, and had been sweating so that short hairs clung damply to his black scalp. 'I reckon it was me. Guess I hit that button, let her drop.' He added, mumbling. 'Thought she was clear, the guy's hands out.'

'You sure? Or are you covering?' Parkland's eyes returned, appraisingly, to Rollie Knight.

'I'm sure.' The engine decker's voice was firmer. He lifted his head; his eyes met the foreman's. 'Was an accident. I'm sorry.'

'You should be,' the safety man said. 'You cost a guy his hand. And look at that!' He pointed to a board which read:

THIS PLANT HAS WORKED
1,897,560 MAN HOURS
WITHOUT AN ACCIDENT

'Now our score goes back to zero,' the safety man said bitterly. He left the strong impression that this was what mattered most.

With the engine decker's firm statement, some of the tenseness had eased.

Some asked. 'What'll happen?'

'It's an accident, so no penalties,' the union man said. He addressed Parkland and the safety man, 'But there's an unsafe condition at this work station. It has to be corrected or we pull everybody out.'

'Take it easy,' Parkland cautioned. 'Nobody's proved that yet.'

'It's unsafe to get out of bed in the morning,' the safety man protested. 'If you do it with your eyes closed.' He glowered again at the engine decker as, still deliberating, the trio moved away.

Soon after, those who had been questioned returned to work, the absent worker replaced by a new man who watched his hands nervously.

From then on, though nothing was ever said, Rollie Knight had no more trouble with his fellow workers. He knew why. Despite denials, those who had been close by were aware of what had happened, and now he had the reputation of being a man not to cross.

At first, when he had seen the smashed, bloody hand of his former tormentor, Rollie, too, was shocked and sickened. But as the stretcher moved away, so did the incident's immediacy, and since it was not in Rollie's nature to dwell on things, by the next working day – with a weekend in between – he had accepted what occurred as belonging in the past, and that was it. He did not fear reprisals. He sensed that, jungle law or not, a certain raw justice was on his side, and others knew it, including the engine decker who protected him.

The incident had other overtones.

In the way that information spreads about someone who has achieved attention, word of Rollie's prison record leaked. But rather than being an embarrassment, it made him, he discovered, something of a folk hero – at least to younger workers.'

'Hear you done big time,' A nineteen-year-old from the inner city told him. 'Guess you give them whitey pigs a run before they gotcha, huh?'

Another youngster asked, 'You carry a piece?'

Although Rollie knew that plenty of workers in the plant carried guns at all times –

allegedly for protection against the frequent muggings which occurred in toilets or in parking lots – Rollie did not, being aware of the stiff sentence he would get if, with his record, a firearm were ever discovered on him. But he answered, noncommittally, 'Quit buggin' me, kid,' and soon another rumour was added to the rest: The little guy, Knight, was always armed. It was an additional cause for respect among the youthful militants.

One of them asked him, 'Hey, you want a joint?'

He accepted. Soon, though not as frequently as some, Rollie was using marijuana on the assembly line, learning that it made a day go faster, the monotony more bearable. About the same time he began playing the numbers.

Later, when there was reason to think about it more, he realized that both drugs and numbers were his introduction to the complex, dangerous understratum of crime in the plant.

The numbers, to begin with, seemed innocent enough.

As Rollie knew, playing the numbers game – especially in auto plants – is, to Detroiters, as natural as breathing. Though the game is Mafia-controlled, demonstrably crooked, and the odds against winning are a thousand to one, it attracts countless bettors daily who wager anything from a nickel to a hundred dollars, occasionally more. The most common daily stake in plants, and the amount which Rollie bet himself, is a dollar.

But whatever the stake, a bettor selects three figures – any three – in the hope they will be the winning combination for that day. In event of a win, the payoff is 500 to 1, except that some bettors gamble on individual digits instead of all three, for which the odds are lower.

What seems to bother no-one who plays numbers in Detroit is that the winning number is selected by betting houses from those combinations which have the least money wagered on them. Only in nearby Pontiac, where the winning number is geared to race results and published pari-mutuel payoffs, is the game – at least in this regard – honest.

Periodically, raids on the so-called 'Detroit numbers ring' are made much of by the FBI, Detroit police, and others. RECORD NUMBERS RAID or BIGGEST RAID IN US HISTORY are apt to be headlines in the *Detroit News* and *Free Press*, but next day, and without much searching, placing a numbers bet is as easy as ever.

As Rollie worked longer, the ways in which numbers operated in the plant became clearer. Janitors were among the many taking bets; in their pails, under dry cloths, were the traditional yellow slips which number writers used, as well as cash collected. Both slips and cash were smuggled from the plant, to be downtown by a deadline – usually race track post time.

A union steward, Rollie learned, was the numbers supervisor for Assembly; his regular duties made it possible for him to move anywhere in the plant without attracting attention. Equally obvious was that betting was a daily addiction which a majority of workers shared, including supervisors, office personnel, and – so an informant assured Rollie – some of the senior managers. Because of the immunity with which the numbers game flourished, the last seemed likely.

A couple of times after the crushed fingers incident, Rollie received oblique suggestions that he himself might participate actively in running numbers, or perhaps one of the other rackets in the plant. The latter, he knew, included loan sharking, drug pushing, and illegal cheque cashing; also, overlapping the milder activities, were organized theft rings, as well as frequent robberies and assaults.

Rollie's criminal record, by now common knowledge, had clearly given him *ex officio* standing among the underworld element directly involved with crime in the plant, as well as those who flirted with it in addition to their jobs. Once, standing beside Rollie at a urinal, a burly, normally taciturn worker known as Big Rufe, announced softly, 'Guys say you dig OK, I should tell you there's ways a smart dude can do better 'n the stinkin' sucker money they pay square Joes here.' He emptied his bladder with a grunt of satisfaction. 'Times, we need help guys who know the score, don't scare easy.' Big Rufe stopped, zipping his fly as someone else came to stand beside them, then turned away, nodding, the nod conveying that sometimes soon the two of them would talk again.

But they hadn't because Rollie had contrived to avoid another meeting, and did the same thing after a second approach by another source. His reasons were mixed. The possibility of a return to prison with a long sentence still haunted him; also he had a feeling that his life, the way it was right now, was as good or better than it had been before, ever. A big thing was the bread. Square Joe sucker money or not, it sure corralled more than Rollie had known in a long time, including booze, food, some grass when he felt like it, and little sexpot May Lou, whom he might tire of sometime, but hadn't yet. She was no grand door prize, no beauty queen, and he knew she had knocked around plenty with other guys who had been there ahead of him. But she could turn Rollie on. It made him horny just to look at her, and he laid pipe, sometimes three times a night, especially when May Lou really went to work, taking his breath away with tricks she knew, which Rollie had heard of but had never had done to him before.

It was the reason, really, he had let May Lou find the two rooms they shared, and hadn't protested when she furnished them. She had done the furnishing without much money, asking Rollie only to sign papers which she brought. He did so indifferently, without reading, and later the furniture appeared, including a colour TV as good as any in a bar.

In another way, though, the price of it all came high – long, weary work days at the assembly plant, nominally five days a week, though sometimes four, and one week only three. Rollie, like others, absented himself on Monday, if hung over after a weekend, or on Friday, if wanting to start one early; but even when that happened, the money next payday was enough to swing with.

As well as the hardness of the work, its monotony persisted, reminding him of advice he had been given early by a fellow worker: 'When you come here, leave your brains at home.'

And yet . . . there was another side.

Despite himself, despite ingrained thought patterns which cautioned against being suckered and becoming a honky lackey, Rollie Knight began taking interest, developing a conscientiousness about the work that he was doing. A basic reason was his quick intelligence plus an instinct for learning, neither of which had had an opportunity to function before, as they were doing now. Another reason – which Rollie would have denied if accused of – was a rapport, based on developing mutual respect, with the foreman, Frank Parkland.

At first, after the two incidents which brought Rollie Knight to his attention, Parkland had been hostile. But as a result of keeping close tab on Rollie, the hostility disappeared, approval replacing it. As Parkland expressed it to Matt Zaleski during one of the assistant plant manager's periodic tours of the assembly line, 'See that little guy? His first week here I figured him for a troublemaker. Now he's as good as anybody I got.'

Zaleski had grunted, barely listening. Recently, at plant management level, several new fronts of troubles had erupted, including a requirement to increase production yet hold down plant costs and somehow raise quality standards. Though the three objectives were basically incompatible, top management was insisting on them, an insistence not helping Matt's duodenal ulcer, an old enemy within. The ulcer, quiescent for a while, now pained him constantly. Thus, Matt Zaleski could not find time for interest in individuals – only in statistics which regiments of individuals, like unconsidered Army privates, added up to.

This – though Zaleski had neither the philosophy to see it, nor power to change the system if he had – was the reason why North American automobiles were generally of poorer quality than those from Germany, where less rigid factory systems gave workers a sense of individuality and craftsmen's pride.

As it was, Frank Parkland did the best he could.

It was Parkland who ended Rollie's status as a relief man and assigned him to a regular line station. Afterwards, Parkland moved Rollie around to other jobs on the assembly line, but at least without the bewildering hour-by-hour changes he endured before. Also, a reason for the moves was that Rollie, increasingly, could handle the more difficult, tricky assignments, and Parkland told him so.

A fact of life which Rollie discovered at this stage was that while most assembly line jobs were hard and demanding, a few were soft touches. Installing windshields was one of the soft ones. Workers doing this, however, were cagey when being watched, and indulged in extra, unneeded motions to make their task look tougher. Rollie worked on windshields, but only for a few days because Parkland moved him back down the line to one of the difficult jobs – scrabbling and twisting around inside car bodies to insert complicated wiring harnesses. Later still, Rollie handled a 'blind operation' – the toughest kind of all, where bolts had to be inserted out of sight, then tightened, also by feel alone.

That was the day Parkland confided to him, 'It isn't a fair system. Guys who work best, who a foreman can rely on, get the stinkingest jobs and a lousy deal. The trouble is, I need somebody on those bolts who I know for sure'll fix 'em and not goof off.'

For Frank Parkland, it was an offhand remark. But to Rollie Knight it represented the first time that someone in authority had levelled with him, had criticized the system, told him something honest, something which he knew to be true, and had done it without bullshit.

Two things resulted. First, Rollie fitted every out-of-sight bolt correctly, utilizing a developing manual skill and an improved physique which regular eating now made possible. Second, he began observing Parkland carefully.

After a while, while not going so far as admiration, he saw the foreman as a non-bullshitter who treated others squarely – black or white, kept his word and stayed honestly clear of the crap and corruption around him. There had been few people in Rollie's life of whom he could say, or think, as much.

Then, as happens when people elevate others beyond the level of human frailty, the image was destroyed.

Rollie had been asked, once more, if he would help run numbers in the plant. The approach was by a lean, intense young black with a scar-marred face, Daddy-o Lester, who worked for stockroom delivery and was known to combine his work with errands for plant numbers bankers and the loan men. Rumour tied the scar, which ran the length of Daddy-o's face, to a knifing after he defaulted a loan. Now he worked at the rackets' opposite end. Daddy-o assured Rollie, leaning into the work station where he had just delivered stock, 'These guys like you. But they get the idea you don't like them, they liable to get rough.'

Unimpressed, Rollie told him, 'Your fat mouth don't scare me none. Beat it!'

Rollie had decided, weeks before, that he would play the numbers, but no more.

Daddy-o persisted, 'A man gotta do somethin' to show he's a man, an' you ain't.' As an afterthought, he added, 'Leastways, not lately.'

More for something to say than with a specific thought, Rollie protested, 'For Cri-sakes, how you fixin' I'd take numbers here, with a foreman around.'

Frank Parkland, at that moment, hove into view.

Daddy-o said contemptuously, 'Screw that motha! He don't make trouble. He gets paid off.'

'You lyin'.'

'If I show you I ain't, that mean you're in?'

Rollie moved from the car he had been working on, spat beside the line, then climbed into the next. For a reason he could not define, uneasy doubts were stirring. He insisted, 'Your word ain't worth nothin'. You show me first.'

Next day, Daddy-o did.

Under pretext of a delivery to Rollie Knight's work station he revealed a grubby, unsealed envelope which he opened sufficiently for Rollie to see the contents – a slip of yellow paper and two twenty-dollar bills.

'OK, fella,' Daddy-o said. 'Now watch!'

He walked to the small, stand-up desk which Parkland used – at the moment unoccupied – and lodged the envelope under a paperweight. Then he approached the foreman, who was down the line, and said something briefly. Parkland nodded. Without obvious haste, though not wasting time, the foreman returned to the desk where he took up the envelope, glanced briefly under the flap, then thrust it in an inside pocket.

Rollie, watching between intervals of working, needed no explanation. Nothing could be plainer than that the money was a bribe, a payoff.

Through the rest of the day, Rollie worked less carefully, missing several bolts entirely and failing to tighten others. *Who the hell cared?* He wondered why he was surprised. Didn't everything stink? It always had. Wasn't everybody on the take in every way? These people; all people. He remembered the course instructor who persuaded him to endorse cheques, then stole Rollie's and other trainees' money. The instructor was one, now Parkland was another, so why should Rollie Knight be different?

That night Rollie told Mary Lou, 'You know what this scumbag world is made of, baby? Bullshit! There ain't nuthin' in this whole wide world but bullshit.'

Later the same week he began working for the plant numbers gang.

15

The portion of northern Michigan which encloses Higgins Lake is described by the local Chamber of Commerce as 'Playtime Country'.

Adam Trenton, Brett DeLosanto, and others attending Frank Kreisel's cottage weekend in late May, found the description apt.

The Kreisel 'cottage' – in fact, a spacious, luxuriously appointed, multi-bedroomed lodge – was on the west shoreline of Higgins Lake's upper section. The entire lake forms a shape resembling a peanut or a foetus, the choice of description depending, perhaps, on the kind of stay a visitor happens to be having.

Adam located the lake and cottage without difficulty after driving alone on Saturday morning by way of Pontiac, Saginaw, Bay City, Midland, and Harrison – most of the two-hundred-mile journey on Interstate 75. Beyond the cities he found the Michigan countryside lushly green, aspen beginning to shimmer and the shadblow in full bloom. The air was sweetly fresh. Sunshine beamed from a near-cloudless sky. Adam had been depressed on leaving home but felt his spirits rise as his wheels devoured the journey northwards.

The depression stemmed from an argument with Erica.

Several weeks ago, when he informed her of the invitation to a stag weekend party, which Brett DeLosanto had conveyed, she merely remarked, 'Well, if they don't want wives, I'll have to find something to do myself, won't I?' At the time, her reasonableness gave Adam second thoughts about going at all; he hadn't been keen to begin with, but yielded to Brett's insistence about wanting Adam to meet Brett's supplier friend, Hank Kreisel. Finally, Adam decided to leave things the way they were.

But Erica had obviously not made plans of her own, and this morning when he got up and began packing a few things, she asked, 'Do you really have to go? When he assured her at this stage he did because he had promised, she inquired pointedly, 'Does "stag" mean no women or merely no wives?'

'No women,' he answered, not knowing if it were true or not, though suspecting not, because he had attended suppliers' weekend parties before.

'I'll bet!' they were in the kitchen by then, Erica brewing coffee and managing to bang the pot about. 'And I suppose there'll be nothing stronger to drink than milk or lemonade.'

He snapped back, 'Whether there is or isn't, it'll be a damn sight more congenial than around here.'

'And who makes it uncongenial?'

Adam had lost his temper then. 'I'll be goddamned if I know. But if it's me, I don't seem to have that effect on others apart from you.'

'Then go to your blasted others!' At that, Erica had thrown a coffee cup at him – fortunately empty – and, also fortunately, he caught it neatly and set it down unbroken. Or perhaps it wasn't fortunate because he had started to laugh, which made Erica madder than ever, and she stormed out, slamming the kitchen door behind her. Thoroughly angry himself by this time, Adam had flung his few things in the car and driven away.

Twenty miles up the road the whole thing seemed ludicrous, as married squabbles so often are in retrospect, and Adam knew if he had stayed home the whole thing would have blown over by mid-morning. Later, near Saginaw, and feeling cheerful because of the kind of day it was, he tried to telephone home, but there was no answer, Erica had obviously gone out. He decided he would call again later.

Hank Kreisel greeted Adam on arrival at the Higgins Lake cottage, Kreisel managing to look simultaneously trim and casual in immaculately pressed Bermuda shorts and an Hawaiian shirt, his lean, lanky figure as militarily erect as always. When they had introduced themselves, Adam parked his car among seven or eight others – all late models in the luxury ranges.

Kreisel nodded towards the car. 'Few people came last night. Some still sleeping. More arriving later.' He took Adam's overnight bag, then escorted him on to a timbered, covered walkway which extended around the cottage from the roadway side. The cottage itself was solidly built, with exterior walls of log siding and a central gable, supported by massive hand-hewn beams. Down at lake level was a floating dock at which several boats were moored.

Adam said, 'I like your place, Hank.'

'Thanks. Not bad, I guess. Didn't build it, though. Bought it from the guy who did. He poured in too much dough, then needed cash.' Kreisel gave a twisted grin. 'Don't we all?'

They stopped at a door, one of several opening on to the walkway. The parts manufacturer strode in, preceding Adam. Directly inside was a bedroom in which polished woodwork gleamed. In a fireplace, facing a double bed, a log fire was laid.

'Be glad of that. Can get cold at night,' Kreisel said. He crossed to a window. 'Gave you a room with a view.'

'You sure did.' Standing beside his host Adam could see the bright clear waters of the lake, superbly blue, shading to green near the sandy shoreline. The Higgins Lake location was in rolling hills – the last few miles of journey had been a steady climb – and around cottage and lake were magnificent stands of jack pines, spruce, balsam, tamarack, yellow pine, and birch. Judging by the panoramic view, Adam guessed he was being given the best bedroom. He wondered why. He was also curious about the other guests.

'When you're ready,' Hank Kreisel announced, 'bar's open. So's the kitchen, Don't have meals here. Just drinks and food twenty-four hours. Anything else can be arranged.' He gave the twisted grin once more as he opened a door on the opposite side of the room from where they had entered. 'There's two doors in 'n out – this and the other. Both lock. Makes for private coming and going.'

'Thanks. If I need to, I'll remember.'

When the other had gone, Adam unpacked the few things he had brought and, soon after, followed his host through the second door. It opened, he discovered, on to a narrow gallery above a central living area designed and furnished in hunting lodge style. The gallery extended around the living-room and connected with a series of stone slab steps which, in turn, formed part of an immense rock fireplace. Adam descended the steps. The living area was unoccupied and he headed for a buzz of voices outside.

He emerged on to a spacious sun deck high above the lake. People, in a group, had been talking; now, one voice raised above others argued heatedly, 'So help me, you people in this industry are acting more and more like nervous Nellies. You've gotten too damn sensitive to criticism and too defensive. You're encouraging the exhibitionists, making like they're big time sages instead of publicity hounds who want their names in papers and on television. Look at your annual meetings! Nowadays they're circuses. Some nut buys one share of the company stock, then tells off the chairman of the board who stands there and takes it. It's like letting a single voter, any voter, go to Washington and sound off on the Senate floor.

'No, it isn't,' Adam said. Without raising his voice he let it penetrate the conversation. 'A voter doesn't have any right on the Senate floor, but a shareholder has rights at an annual meeting, even with one share. That's what our system's all about. And the critics aren't all cranks. If we start thinking so, and stop listening, we'll be back where we were five years ago.'

'Hey!' Brett DeLosanto shouted. 'Listen to those entrance lines, and look who got here!' Brett was wearing an exotic outfit in magenta and yellow, clearly self-designed, and resembling a Roman toga. Curiously, it managed to be dashing and practical. Adam, in slacks and turtle neck, felt conservative by contrast.

Several others who knew Adam greeted him, including Pete O'Hagan, the man who had been speaking when he came in. O'Hagan represented one of the major national magazines in Detroit, his job to court auto industry brass socially – a subtle but effective way of soliciting advertising. Most big magazines had similar representation, their people sometimes becoming cronies of company presidents or others at high level. Such friendships became known to advertising agencies who rarely challenged them; thus, when advertising had to be cut, the publications with top bracket influence were last to be hurt. Typically, despite Adam's blunt contradiction of what had been said, O'Hagan showed no resentment, only smiles.

'Come, meet everybody,' Hank Kreisel said. He steered Adam around the group. Among the guests were a congressman, a judge, a network TV personality, two other parts manufacturers and several senior people from Adam's own company, including a trio of purchasing agents. There was also a young man who offered his hand and smiled engagingly as Adam approached. 'Smokey told me about you, sir. I'm Pierre Flodenhale.'

'Of course.' Adam remembered the youthful race driver whom he had seen, doubling as a car salesman, at Smokey Stephensen's dealership. 'How are your sales?'

'When there's time to work at it, pretty good, sir.'

Adam told him. 'Cut the "sir" stuff. Only first names here. You had bad luck in the Daytona 500.'

'Sure did.' Pierre Flodenhale pushed back his shock of blond hair and grimaced. Two months earlier he had completed 180 gruelling laps at Daytona, was leading with only twenty laps to go, when a blown engine head put him out of the race. 'Felt like stomping on that old car after,' he confided.

'If it had been me, I'd have pushed it off a cliff.'

'Guess maybe I'll do better soon.' The race driver gave a boyish smile; he had the same pleasant manner as when Adam had observed him previously. 'Got a feeling this year I might pull of the Talladega 500.'

'I'll be at Talladega,' Adam said. 'We're exhibiting a concept Orion there. So I'll cheer for you.'

From somewhere behind, Hank Kreisel's voice cut in. 'Adam, this is Stella. She'll do anything for you.'

'Like getting a drink,' A girl's pleasing voice said. Adam found a pretty, petite redhead beside him. She was wearing the scantiest of bikinis. 'Hullo, Mr Trenton.'

'Hullo.' Adam saw two other girls nearby and remembered Erica's question: *Does 'stag' mean no women or merely no wives?*

'I'm glad you like my swimsuit,' Stella told Pierre, whose eyes had been exploring.

The race drive said, 'Hadn't noticed you were wearing one.'

The girl returned to Adam. 'About that drink.'

He ordered a Bloody Mary. 'Don't go 'way,' she told him. 'Be back soon.'

Pierre asked, 'What's a "concept" Orion, Adam?'

'It's a special kind of car made up for showing in advance of the real thing. In the trade we call it a "one off".'

'But the one at Talledega – it won't be a genuine Orion?'

'No,' Adam said. 'The real Orion isn't due until a month later. The "concept" will resemble the Orion, though we're not saying how closely. We'll show it around a lot. The idea is to get people talking, speculating on – how will the final Orion look?' He added, 'You could say it's a sort of teaser.'

'I can play that,' Stella said. She had returned with Adam's drink and one for Pierre.

The congressman moved over to join them. He had flowing white hair, a genial manner and a strong, though pontifical, voice. 'I was interested in what you said about your industry listening, Mr Trenton. I trust some of the listening is to what legislators are saying.'

Adam hesitated. His inclination was to answer bluntly, as usual, but this was a party; he was a guest. He caught the eye of Hank Kreisel who seemed to have a knack of being everywhere and overhearing anything that mattered. 'Feel free,' Kreisel said. 'A few fights won't hurt. We got a doctor coming.'

Adam told the congressman, 'What's coming out of legislatures right now is mostly foolishness from people who want their names in the news and know that blasting the auto industry, whether it makes sense or not, will do the trick.'

The congressman flushed as Adam persisted, 'A US senator wants to ban automobiles in five years' time if they have internal combustion engines, though he hasn't any notion what will replace them. Well, if it happened, the only good thing is, he couldn't get around to make silly speeches. Some states have brought lawsuits in efforts to make us recall all cars built since 1953 and rebuild them to emission standards that didn't exist until 1966 in California, 1968 elsewhere.'

'Those are extremes,' the congressman protested. His speech slurred slightly, and the drink in his hand was clearly not his first of the day.

'I agree they're extremes. But they're representative of what we're hearing from legislators, and that – if I remember – was your question.'

Hank Kreisel, reappearing, said cheerfully, 'Was the question, all right.' He slapped the congressman across the shoulders. 'Watch out, Woody! These young fellas in Detroit got sharp minds. Brighter 'n you're used to in Washington.'

'You'd never think,' the congressman informed the group, 'that when this character Kreisel and I were Marines together, he used to salute me.'

'If that's what you're missing, General . . .' Hank Kreisel, still in his smart Bermuda shorts, snapped to rigid attention and executed a parade ground-style salute. Afterwards he commanded, 'Stella, get the senator another drink.'

'I wasn't a general,' The congressman complained. 'I was a chicken colonel, and I'm not a senator.'

'You were never a chicken, Woody,' Kreisel assured him. 'And you'll make it to senator. Probably over this industry's corpse.'

'Judging by you, and this place, it's a damn healthy corpse.' The congressman returned his gaze to Adam. 'Want to beat any more hell out of politicians?'

'Maybe a little.' Adam smiled. 'Some of us think it's time our law-makers did a few positive things instead of just parroting the critics.'

'Positive like what?'

'Like enacting some public enforcement laws. Take one example: air pollution. OK, anti-pollution standards for new-built cars are here. Most of us in the industry agree they're good, are necessary, and were overdue.' Adam was aware of the size of the group around them increasing, other conversations breaking off. He went on, 'But what people like *you* ask of people like *us* is to produce an anti-pollutant device which won't go wrong, or need checking or adjustment, for the entire life of every car. Well, it can't be done. It's no more logical to expect it than to ask any piece of machinery to work perfectly for ever. So what's needed? A law with teeth, a law requiring regular inspection of car pollutant devices, then repair or replacement when necessary. But it would be an unpopular law because the public doesn't really give two hoots about pollution and only cares about convenience. That's why politicians are afraid of it.'

'The public does care,' the congressman said heatedly. 'I've mail to prove it.'

'Some individuals care. The public doesn't. For more than two years,' Adam insisted, 'we've had pollution control kits available for older cars. The kits cost twenty dollars installed, and we *know* they work. They reduce pollution and make air purer – anywhere. The kits have been promoted, advertised on TV, radio, billboards, but almost nobody buys them. Extras on cars – even old cars – like whitewall tyres or stereo tape decks are selling fine. But nobody wants anti-pollution kits; they're the least selling item we ever made. And the legislators you asked me about, who lecture us about clean air at the drop of a vote, haven't shown the slightest interest either.'

Stella's voice and several others chorused, 'Spare ribs! Spare ribs!'

The group around Adam and the congressman thinned. 'About time,' somebody said. 'We haven't eaten for an hour.'

The sight of piled food, now on a buffet at the rear of the sundeck presided over by a white-capped chef, reminded Adam that he had not had breakfast, due to his fight with Erica, and was hungry. He also remembered he must call home soon.

One of the purchasing agent guests, holding a plate heaped high with food, called out, 'Great eating, Hank!'

'Glad you like it,' his host acknowledged. 'And with you guys here it's all deductible.'

Adam smiled with the others, knowing that what Kreisel had said was true – that the purchasing agents' presence made this a business occasion, to be deducted eventually on Hank Kreisel's income tax return. The reasoning: auto company purchasing agents, who allocated milions of dollars' worth of orders annually, held a life or death authority over parts manufacturers like Kreisel. In older days, because of this, purchasing agents were accustomed to receive munificent gifts – even a lake cruiser or a houseful of furniture – from suppliers whom they favoured. Now, auto companies forbade that kind of graft and an offender, if caught, was fired summarily. Just the same, perks for purchasing agents still existed, and being entertained socially, on occasions like this or privately, was one. Another was having personal hotel bills picked up by suppliers or their salesmen; this was considered safe since neither goods nor money changed hands directly, and later, if necessary, a purchasing agent could deny knowledge, saying he had expected the hotel to bill him. And gifts at Christmastime remained one more.

The Christmas handouts were forbidden annually by auto company managements in memos circulated during November and December. But just as inevitably, purchasing department secretaries prepared lists of purchasing staff home addresses which were handed out to suppliers' salesmen on request, a request considered as routine as saying,

'Merry Christmas!' The secretaries' home addresses were always on the lists and, though purchasing agents allegedly knew nothing of what was going on, somehow their addresses got there, too. The gifts which resulted – none delivered to the office – were not as lavish as in older days, but few suppliers risked failing to bestow them.

Adam was still watching the purchasing agent with the piled plate when a soft, feminine voice murmured, 'Adam Trenton, do you always say just what you're thinking?'

He turned. In front of him, regarding him amusedly, was a girl of twenty-eight or thirty, Adam guessed. Her high-cheekboned face was uptilted, her moist full lips lightly parted in a smile. Intelligent bright eyes met his own directly. He sensed a musky perfume, was aware of a lithe, slender figure with small firm breasts beneath a tailored powder-blue linen dress. She was, Adam thought, one of the most breathtakingly beautiful women he had ever seen. And she was black. Not brown, but black; a deep, rich black, her smooth unblemished skin like ebony. He curbed an impulse to reach out, touching her.

'My name is Rowena,' the girl said. 'I was told yours. And I've been asked to see that you get something to eat.'

'Rowena what?'

He sensed her hesitate. 'Does it matter?' She smiled, so that he was aware of the full redness and moisture of her lips again.

'Besides,' Rowena said, 'I asked you a question first. You haven't answered it.'

Adam remembered she had asked something about – did he always say what he was thinking?

'Not always. I don't believe any of us do really.' He thought: *I'm sure as hell not doing it now*, then added aloud, 'When I do say anything, though, I try to make it honest and what I mean.'

'I know. I was listening to you talking. Not enough of us do that.'

The girl's eyes met his own and held them steadily. He wondered if she sensed her impact on him, and suspected that she did.

The chef at the buffet, with Rowena's aid, filled two plates which they carried to one of the sun-deck tables nearby. Already seated were the judge – a youngish Negro who was on the federal bench in Michigan – and another guest from Adam's company, a middle-aged development engineer named Frazon. Moments later they were joined by Brett DeLosanto, accompanied by an attractive, quiet brunette whom he introduced as Elsie.

'We figured this is where the action is,' Brett said. 'Don't disappoint us.'

Rowena asked, 'What kind do you have in mind?'

'You know us auto people. We've only two interests – business and sex.'

The judge smiled. 'It's early. Perhaps we should take business first.' He addressed Adam. 'A while ago you were talking about company annual meetings. I liked what you said – that people, even with a single share, should be listened to.'

Frazon, the engineer, as if rising to a bait, put down his knife and fork. 'Well, I don't agree with Adam, and there are plenty more who feel the way I do.'

'I know,' the judge said. 'I saw you react. Won't you tell us why?'

Frazon considered, frowning. 'All right. What the loudmouth one-share people want, including consumer groups and the so-called corporate responsibility committee, is to create disruption, and they do it by distortion, lies, and insult. Remember the General Motors annual meeting, when the Nader gang called everybody in the industry "corporate criminals", then talked about our "disregard for law and justice", and said we were part of "a corporate crime wave dwarfing street crime by comparison"? How are we supposed to feel when we hear that? Grateful? How are we supposed to take clowns who mouth that kind of claptrap? Seriously?'

'Say!' Brett DeLosanto interjected. 'You engineering guys were listening. We thought the only thing you ever heard was motor noises.'

'They heard, all right,' Adam said. 'We all heard – those in General Motors, the other companies too. But what a lot of industry people missed was that the very words just quoted' – he motioned towards Frazon – 'were intended to anger and inflame and prevent a reasonable response. The protesting crowd didn't want the auto industry to be reasonable; if it had, we'd have cut the ground from under them. And what they planned, worked. Our people fell for it.'

The judge prompted, 'Then you see invective as a tactic.'

'Of course. It's the language of our times, and the kids who use it – bright young lawyers mostly – know exactly what it does to old men in board rooms. It curls their hair, raises their blood pressure, makes them rigid and unyielding. The chairmen and directors in our industry were reared on politeness; in their heyday, even when you knifed a competitor, you said "excuse me". But not any more. Now the dialogue is harsh and snarly, and points are scored by overstatement, so if you're listening – and smart – you under-react and keep cool. Most of our top people haven't learned that yet.'

'I haven't learned it, and don't intend to,' Frazon said. 'I'll stick with decent manners.'

Brett quipped, 'There speaks an engineer, the ultimate conservative!'

'Adam's an engineer,' Frazon pointed out. 'Trouble is, he's spent too much time around designers.'

The group at the table laughed.

Looking at Adam, Frazon said, 'Surely you're not suggesting we should go along with what the militants at annual meetings want – consumer reps on boards of directors, all the rest?'

Adam answered quickly. 'Why not? It could show we're willing to be flexible, and might be worth a try. Put somebody on a board – or on a jury – they're apt to take it seriously, not be just a maverick. We might end up learning something. Besides, it will happen eventually and we'd be better off if we *made* it happen now instead of being forced into it later.'

Brett asked, 'Judge, what's your verdict now you've heard both sides?'

'Excuse me.' The judge put a hand to his mouth, stifling a yawn. 'For a moment I thought I was in court.' He shook his head in mock solemnity. 'Sorry. I never hand down opinions on weekends.'

'Nor should anyone,' Rowena declared. She touched Adam's hand, letting her fingers travel lightly over his. When he turned towards her, she said softly, 'Will you take me swimming?'

The two of them took a boat from the floating dock – one of Hank Kreisel's with an outboard which Adam used to propel them, unhurriedly, four miles or so towards the lake's eastern shore. Then, within sight of a beach with towering leafy trees behind, he cut the motor and they drifted on the blue translucent water. A few other boats, not many, came into sight and went away. It was mid-afternoon. The sun was high, the air drowsy. Before they left, Rowena had changed into a swimsuit; it was leopard patterned and what it revealed of her figure, as well as the soft-silken blackness of her skin, more than fulfilled the promise of the linen dress she had had on earlier. Adam was in trunks. When they stopped, he lighted cigarettes for them both. They sat beside each other on the cushions of the boat.

'Um,' Rowena said. 'This is nice.' Her head was back, eyes closed agianst the brightness of the sun and lake. Her lips were parted.

He blew a smoke ring lazily. 'It's called getting away from it all. ' His voice, for some reason, was unsteady.

She said softly, with sudden seriousness, 'I know. It doesn't happen often. And it never lasts.'

Adam turned. Instinct told him that if he reached for her she would respond. But for seconds of uncertainty he hesitated.

As if reading his mind, Rowena laughed lightly. She dropped her cigarette into the water. 'We came to swim, remember?'

With a swift, single movement she rose and dived over the side. He had an impression of her lithe dark body, straight-limbed and like an arrow. Then, with a whip-crack sound and splash, she was out of sight. The boat rocked gently.

Adam hesitated again, then dived in too. After the sun's heat, the fresh lake water struck icily cold. He came up with a gasp, shivering, and looked around.

'Hey! Over here!' Rowena was still laughing. She bobbed under the surface, then re-emerged, water streaming down her face and hair. 'Isn't it wonderful?'

'When I get my circulation back, I'll tell you.'

'Your blood needs heating, Adam. I'm going ashore. Coming?'

'I guess so. But we can't leave Hank's boat to drift.'

'Then bring it.' Already swimming strongly towards the beach, Rowena called back, 'That's if you're afraid of being marooned with me.'

More slowly, towing the boat, Adam followed. Ashore, and welcoming the sun's warmth again, he beached the boat, then joined Rowena who was lying on the sand, her hands behind her head. Beyond the beach, sheltered in trees, was a cottage, but shuttered and deserted.

'Since you brought it up,' Adam said, 'at this moment I can't think of anyone I'd sooner be marooned with.' He, too, stretched out on the sand, aware of being more relaxed than he had felt in months.

'You don't know me.'

'You've aroused certain instincts.' He propped himself on an elbow, confirming that the girl beside him was as breathtakingly lovely as she had seemed when he met her several hours ago, then added, 'One of them is curiosity.'

'I'm just someone you met at a party; one of Hank Kreisel's weekend parties where he employs hostesses. And in case you're wondering, that's *all* he employs us for. *Were* you wondering?'

'Yes.'

She gave the soft laugh he had grown used to. 'I knew you were. The difference between you and most men is that the others would have lied and said "no".'

'And the rest of the week, when there aren't parties?'

'I'm a high school teacher.' Rowena stopped. 'Damn! I didn't mean to tell you that.'

'Then we'll even the score,' Adam said. 'There was something I didn't intend to tell *you*.'

'Which is?'

He assured her softly, 'For the first time in my life I know, really know, what it means when they say "Black is Beautiful".'

In the silence which followed, he wondered if he had offended her. He could hear the lapping of the lake, a hum of insects, an outboard motor in the distance. Rowena said nothing. Then, without warning, she leaned over and kissed him fully on the lips.

Before he could respond she sprang up, and ran down the beach towards the lake. From the water's edge she called back, 'Hank said you had the reputation of being a sweet man when he told me to take special care of you. Now let's go back.'

In the boat, heading for the west shore, he asked, 'What else did Hank say?'

Rowena considered. 'Well, he told me you'd be the most important person here and that one day you'll be right at the top of your company.'

This time, Adam laughed.

He was still curious, though, about Kreisel and his motives.

Sunset came, the party at the cottage continuing – and livening – as the hours passed. Before the sun disappeared at last, behind a squad of white birches like silhouetted sentinels, the lake was alive with colour. A breeze stirred its surface, bearing fresh, pine-scented air. Dusk eased in, then darkness. As stars came out, the night air cooled and the party drifted from the deck to indoors where, in the great rock fireplace, heaped brush and logs were blazing.

Hank Kreisel, an affable, attentive host, seemed everywhere, as he had throughout the day. Two bars and the kitchens were staffed and bustling; what Kreisel had said earlier about drinks and food available twenty-four hours each day seemed true. In the spacious, hunting lodge-style living-room the party split into groups, some overlapping. A cluster around Pierre Flodenhale fired auto racing questions. ' . . . *say a race is won or lost in the pits. Is that your experience?*' . . . '*Yes, but a driver's planning does it too. Before the race you plan how you'll run it, lap by lap. In the race you plan the next lap, changing the first plan . . .*' The network TV personality, who had been diffident earlier, had blossomed and was doing a skilful imitation of the US President, supposedly on television with a car maker and an environmentalist, trying to appease both. '*Pollution, with all its faults, is part of our great American know-how . . . My scientific advisers assure me cars are polluting less than they used – at least, they would if there weren't more cars.*' (Cough, cough, cough!) . . . '*I pledge we'll have clean air again in this country. Administration policy is to pipe it to every home . . .*' Among those listening, one of two looked sour, but most laughed.

Some of the girls, including Stella and Elsie, moved from group to group. Rowena stayed close to Adam.

Gradually, as midnight came and went, the numbers thinned. Guests yawned, stretched tiredly, and soon after climbed the stone stairway at the fireplace, some calling down good nights from the gallery to the holdouts who remained below. One or two exited by the sun deck, presumably reaching their rooms by the alternate route which Hank Kreisel had showed to Adam earlier. Eventually, Kreisel himself – carrying a sourmash Bourbon – went upstairs. Soon after, Adam noticed, Elsie disappeared. So did Brett DeLosanto and the redhead, Stella, who had spent the last hour close together.

In the great hearth the fire was burning down to embers. Apart from Adam and Rowena, both on a sofa near the fireplace, only one group remained at the room's opposite end, still drinking, noisy, and obviously with the intention of staying for a long time.

'A nightcap?' Adam asked.

Rowena shook her head. Her last drink – a mild Scotch and water – had lasted her an hour. Through the evening they had talked, mostly about Adam, though not by his choice but because Rowena adroitly parried questions about herself. But he had learned that her teaching speciality was English, which she admitted after laughingly quoting Cervantes: *'My memory is so bad, that many times I forget my own name.'*

Now he stood up. 'Let's go outside.'

'All right.'

As they left, no-one in the other group glanced their way.

The moon had risen. The night was cold and clear. Moonbeams shimmered on the surface of the lake. He felt Rowena shiver, and put an arm around her.

'Almost everyone,' Adam said, 'seems to have gone to bed.'

Again Rowena's gentle laugh. 'I saw you noticing.'

He turned her to him, tilted her head, and kissed her. 'Let's us.'

Their lips met again. He felt her arms around him tighten.

She whispered, 'What I said was true. This isn't in the contract.'

'I know.'

'A girl can make her own arrangements here, but Hank sees to it she doesn't have to.' She snuggled closer. 'Hank would want you to know that. He cares what you think about him.'

'At this moment,' he whispered back, 'I'm not thinking of Hank at all.'

They entered Adam's bedroom from the outside walkway – the route he had used this morning on arrival. Inside, the room was warm. Someone, thoughtfully, had been in to light the fire; now, tongues of flame cast light and shadows on the ceiling. The coverlet was off the double bed, with sheets turned back.

In front of the fire, Adam and Rowena slipped out of what they were wearing. Soon after, he led her to the bed.

He had expected tenderness. He found, instead, a savagery in Rowena which at first amazed, soon after excited and, before long, inflamed him, too. Nothing in his experience had prepared him for the wild, tempestuous passion she unleashed. For both of them, it lasted – with gaps which human limits demanded – through the night.

Near dawn she inquired mischievously, 'Do you still think black is beautiful?'

He told her, and meant it, 'More than ever.'

They had been lying, quietly, side by side. Now Rowena propped herself up and looked at him. She was smiling. 'And for a honky, you're not bad.'

As he had yesterday afternoon, he lit two cigarettes and gave her one. After a while she said, 'I guess black is beautiful, the way they say. But then I guess everything's beautiful if you look at it on the right kind of day.'

'Is this that kind of day?'

'You know what I'd say today? Today, I'd say "ugly is beautiful"!'

It was getting light. Adam said, 'I want to see you again. How do we manage it?'

For the first time, Rowena's voice was sharp. 'We don't, and both of us know it.' When he protested, she put a finger across his lips. 'We haven't lied to each other. Don't let's begin.'

He knew she was right, that what had begun here would end here. Detroit was neither

Paris nor London, nor even New York. At heart, Detroit was a small town still, beginning to tolerate more than it used to, but he could not have Detroit and Rowena – on any terms. The thought saddened him. It continued to, through the day, and as he left Higgins Lake for the return journey southwards late that afternoon.

When he thanked his host before leaving, Hank Kreisel said, 'Haven't talked much, Adam. Wish we'd had more chance. Mind if I call you next week?'

He assured Kreisel that he could.

Rowena, to whom Adam had said goodbye privately, behind two locked doors an hour earlier, was not in sight.

16

'Oh, Christ!' Adam said. 'I forgot to phone my wife.' He remembered, guiltily, intending since Saturday morning to call Erica and patch up the quarrel they had had before he left. Now it was Sunday evening and he still hadn't. In the meantime, of course, there had been Rowena, who eclipsed less immediate matters, and Adam had an unease, too, about facing Erica after *that*.

'Shall we turn off and find a pay phone?' Pierre Foldenhale asked. They were on Interstate 75, south-bound, near the outskirts of Flint, and Pierre was driving Adam's car, as he had been since leaving the Higgins Lake cottage. The young race driver had come to the cottage with someone else who left early, and Adam had been glad to offer him a ride, as well as to have company on the way back to Detroit. Moreover, when Pierre offered to drive, Adam accepted gratefully and had dozed through the early part of the journey.

Now it was growing dark. Their headlights were among many slicing homewards from the country to the city.

'No,' Adam said. 'If we stop, it will waste time. Let's keep going.'

He put out a hand tentatively to the Citizens Band radio beneath the instrument panel. They would be coming within range of Greater Detroit soon, and it was possible that Erica might have switched on the kitchen receiver, as she did on weekdays. Then he let his hand drop, deciding not to call. He was increasingly nervous, he realized, about talking with Erica, a nervousness which increased a half-hour later as they passed Bloomfield Hills, then, soon after, left the freeway and turned west towards Quarton Lake.

He had intended to let Pierre, who lived in Dearborn, take the car on directly after dropping him off. Instead, Adam invited Pierre in and was relieved when he accepted. At least, Adam thought, he would have the foil of a stranger for a while before having to face Erica alone.

He need not have worried.

As the car crunched to a halt on the driveway gravel of the Trentons' house, lights went on, the front door opened, and Erica came out to greet Adam warmly.

'Welcome, darling! I missed you.' She kissed him, and he knew it was her way of showing that Saturday's incident was over and need not be mentioned again.

What Adam did not know was that part of Erica's good spirits stemmed from a dress watch which she was wearing, the watch acquired during a further shoplifting adventure while he had been away.

Pierre Flodenhale climbed out from behind the wheel. Adam introduced him.

Erica gave her most dazzling smile. 'I've seen you race.' She added, 'If I'd known you were driving Adam home, though, I might have been nervous.'

'He's a lot slower than I am,' Adam said. 'Didn't break the speed limit once.'

'How dull! I hope the party was livelier.'

'Not all that much, Mrs Trenton. Compared with some I've been at, it was quiet. Gets that way, I guess, when you only have men.'

Don't push it, pal! Adam wanted to caution. He saw Erica glance at Pierre shrewdly, and suspected the young race driver was not used to the company of highly intelligent, perceptive women. Pierre was clearly impressed with Erica, though, who looked young and beautiful in silk Pucci pyjamas, her long ash-blonde hair falling around her shoulders.

They went into the house, mixed drinks, and took them to the kitchen, where Erica made fried egg sandwiches for them all, and coffee. Adam left the other two briefly – to make a telephone call, and, tired as he was, to collect files he must work on tonight in preparation for the morning. When he returned, Erica was listening attentively to a discourse on auto racing – an extension, apparently, to Pierre's remarks to the group around him at the cottage.

Pierre had a sheet of paper spread out on which he had drawn the layout of a speedway track. ' . . . so heading in to the main stretch in front of the stands, you want the straightest line possible. At two hundred miles an hour, if you let the car wander you lose time bad. Wind's usually across the track, so you stay close to the wall, hug that old wall tight as you can . . . '

'I've seen drivers do it,' Erica said. 'It always frightens me. If you ever hit the wall at a speed like that . . . '

'If you do, you're safer hitting flat, Mrs Trenton. I've been in a few walls . . . '

'Call me Erica,' Erica said. 'Have you really?'

Adam, listening, was amused. He had taken Erica to auto races, but had never known her to show this much concern. He thought: perhaps it was because she and Pierre liked each other instinctively. The fact that they did was obvious, and the young race driver was glowing, responding boyishly to Erica's interest. Adam felt grateful for the chance to regain his own composure without being the focus of his wife's attention. Despite his return home, thoughts of Rowena were still strong in Adam's mind.

'Every track you race on, Erica,' Pierre was saying, 'a driver has to learn to handle it like it was a . . . ' He hesitated for a simile, then added, 'like a violin.'

'Or a woman,' Erica said. They both laughed.

'You have to know where every bump is in that old track, the low spots, what the surface gets like with a real hot sun, or after a sprinkle of rain. So you practise and practise, driving and driving, 'til you find the best way, the fastest line around.'

Seated across the room, his files now beside him, Adam threw in. 'Sounds a lot like life.'

The other two seemed not to have heard. Obviously, Adam decided, they would not mind if he got on with some work.

'When you're in a long race, say five hundred miles,' Erica said, 'does your mind wander? Do you ever think of something else?'

Pierre gave his boyish grin. 'God, no! Not if you figure to win, or even walk away instead of being carried out.' He explained, 'You've a lot to keep checking and remember. How others in the race are doing, your plans for passing guys ahead, or how not to let guys past you. Or maybe there's trouble, like if you scuff a tyre it'll take a tenth of a second off your speed. So you feel it happen, you remember, you do sums in your head, figure everything, then decide when to pit for a tyre change, which can win a race or lose it. You watch oil pressure fifty yards before entering every corner, then, on the back-stretch, check all gauges, and you keep both ears tuned to the way the engine sings. Then there's signals from the pit crew to look out for. Some days you could use a secretary . . . '

Adam, concentrating on memo reading, screened the voices of Pierre and Erica out.

'I never knew all that,' Erica said. 'It will seem different watching now. I'll feel like an insider.'

'I'd like to have you see me race, Erica.' Pierre glanced across the room, then back. He lowered his voice slightly. 'Adam said you'd be at the Talladega 500, but there's other races before that.'

'Where?'

'North Carolina, for one. Maybe you could come.' He looked at her directly and she was aware, for the first time, of a touch of arrogance, the star syndrome, the knowledge that he was a hero to the crowd. She supposed a lot of women had come Pierre's way.

'North Carolina's not so far.' Erica smiled. 'It's something to think about, isn't it?'

Some time later, the fact that Pierre Flodenhale was standing penetrated Adam's consciousness.

'I guess I'll be moving on, Adam,' Pierre said. 'Thanks a lot for the ride and having me in.'

Adam returned a folder to his briefcase – a ten-year population shift estimate, prepared for study in conjunction with consumer car preference trends. He apologized. 'I haven't been much of a host, I hope my wife made up for me.'

'Sure did.'

'You can take my car.' He reached in his pocket for keys. 'If you'll phone my secretary tomorrow, tell her where it is, she'll have it picked up.'

Pierre hesitated. 'Thanks, but Erica said . . . '

Erica bustled into the living-room, pulling a light car coat over her pyjamas. 'I'll drive Pierre home.'

Adam started to say, 'There's no need . . . '

'It's a nice night,' she insisted. 'And I feel like some air.'

Moments later, outside, car doors slammed, an engine revved and receded. The house was silent.

Adam worked a half-hour more, then went upstairs.

He was climbing into bed when he heard the car return and Erica come in, but was asleep by the time she reached the bedroom.

He dreamed of Rowena.

Erica dreamed of Pierre.

17

A belief among automobile product planners is that the most successful ideas for new cars are conceived suddenly, like unannounced star shell bursts, during informal, feet-on-desk bull sessions in the dead of night.

There are precedents proving this true. Ford's Mustang – most startling Detroit trendsetter after the Second World War, and forerunner to an entire generation of Ford, GM, Chrysler, and American Motors products afterwards – had its origins that way, and so, less spectacularly, have others. This is the reason why product teams sometimes linger in offices when others are abed, letting their smoke and conversation drift, and hoping – like prospicient Cinderellas – that magic in some form will touch their minds.

On a night in early June – two weeks after Hank Kreisel's cottage party – Adam Trenton and Brett DeLosanto nurtured the same kind of wish.

Because the Orion, also, was begun at night, they and others hoped that a muse for Farstar – next major project ahead – might be wooed the same way. Over several months past, innumerable think sessions had been held – some involving large groups, others small, and still more composed of duos like Adam and Brett – but from none of them yet had anything emerged to confirm a direction which must be decided on soon. The basement block work (as Brett DeLosanto called it) had been done. Projection papers were assembled which asked and answered, more or less: *Where are we today? Who's selling to whom? What are we doing right? Wrong? What do people think they want in a car? What do they really want? Where will they, and we, be five years from now? Politically? Socially? Intellectually? Sexually? What'll populations be? Tastes? Fashions? What new issues, controversies, will evolve? How will age groups shape up? and who'll be rich? Poor? In between? Where? Why?* All these, and a myriad other questions, facts, statistics, had sped in and out of computers. Now what was needed was something no computer could stimulate: a gut feeling, a hunch, a shaft of insight, a touch of genius.

One problem was: to determine the shape of Farstar, they ought to know how Orion would fare. But the Orion's introduction was still four months away; even then, its impact could not be judged fully until half a year after that. So what the planners must do was what the auto industry had always done because of long lead times required for new models – guess.

Tonight's session, for Adam and Brett, began in the company teardown room.

The teardown room was more than a room; it was a department occupying a closely guarded building – a storehouse of secrets which few outsiders penetrated. Those who did, however, found it a source of unwaveringly honest information, for the teardown room's function was to dissect company products and competitors', then compare them objectively with each other. All big three auto companies had teardown rooms of their own, or comparable systems.

In the teardown environment, if a competitor's car or component was sturdier, lighter, more economical, assembled better, or superior in any other way, the analysts said so. No local loyalties ever swayed a judgement.

Company engineers and designers who had boobed were sometimes embarrassed by teardown room revelations, though they would be even more embarrassed if word leaked out to press or public. It rarely did. Nor did other companies release adverse reports about defects in competitors' cars; they knew it was a tactic which could boomerang tomorrow. In any case, objectives of the teardown room were positive – to police the company's products and designs, and to learn from others.

Adam and Brett had come to study three small cars in their torndown state – the comany's own minicompact, a Volkswagen, and another import, Japanese.

A technician, working late at Adam's request, admitted them through locked outer doors to a lighted lobby, then through more doors to a large high-ceilinged room, lined with recessed racks extending from floor to ceiling.

'Sorry to spoil your evening, Neil,' Adam said. 'We couldn't make it sooner.'

'No sweat, Mr Trenton. I'm on overtime.' The elderly technician, a skilled mechanic who had once worked on assembly lines and now helped take cars apart, led the way to a section of racks, some of which had been pulled out. 'Everything's ready that you asked for.'

Brett DeLosanto looked around him. Though he had been here many times before, the teardown operation never failed to fascinate him.

The department bought cars the way the public did – through dealers. Purchases were in names of individuals, so no dealer ever knew a car that he was selling was for detailed study instead of normal use. The precaution ensured that all cars received were routine production models.

As soon as a car arrived, it was driven to the basement and taken apart. This did not mean merely separating the car's components, but involved total disassembly. As it was done, each item was numbered, listed, described, its weight recorded. Oily, greasy parts were cleaned.

It took four men between ten days and two weeks to reduce a normal car to ordered fragments, mounted on display boards.

A story – no-one really knew how true – was sometimes told about a teardown crew which, as a practical joke, worked in spare time to disassemble a car belonging to one of their number who was holidaying in Europe. When the vacationer returned, the car was in his garage, undamaged, but in several thousand parts. He was a competent mechanic who had learned a good deal as a teardown man, and he determinedly put it together again. It took a year.

Techniques of total disassembly were so specialized that unique tools had been devised – some like a plumber's nightmare.

The display boards containing the torndown vehicles were housed in sliding racks. Thus, like dissected corpses, the industry's current cars were available for private viewing and comparison.

A company engineer might be brought here and told: 'Look at the competition's headlamp cans! They're an integrated part of the radiator support instead of separate, complex pieces. Their method is cheaper and better. Let's get with it!'

It was called value engineering, and it saved money because each single cent of cost lopped from a car design represented thousands of dollars in eventual profit. Once, during the 1960s, Ford saved a mammoth twenty-five cents per car by changing its brake system master cylinder, after studying the master cylinder of General Motors.

Others, like Adam and Brett at this moment, did their viewing to keep abreast of design changes and to seek inspiration.

The Volkswagen on the display boards which the technician had pulled out had been a new one. He reported, with a touch of glumness, 'Been taking VW's apart for years. Every damn time it's the same – quality good as ever.'

Brett nodded in agreement. 'Wish we could say the same of ours.'

'So do I, Mr DeLosanto. But we can't. Leastways, not here.'

At the display boards showing the company's own mini-compact, the custodian said,

'Mind you, ours has come out pretty well this time. If it wasn't for that German bug, we'd look good.'

'That's because American small car assembly's getting more automated,' Adam commented. 'The Vega started a big change with the new Lordstown plant. And the more automation we have, with fewer people, the higher everybody's quality will go.'

'Wherever it's going,' the technician said, 'it ain't gone to Japan – at least not to the plant that produced this clunker. For God's sake, Mr Trenton! Look at that!'

They examined some of the parts of the Japanese import, the third car they had come to review.

'String and baling wire,' Brett announced.

'I'll tell you one thing, sir. I wouldn't want anybody I cared about to be riding round in one of those. It's a motorbike on four wheels, and a poor one at that.'

They remained at the teardown racks, studying the three cars in detail. Later, the elderly technician let them out.

At the doorway he asked, 'What's coming up next, gentlemen? For us, I mean.'

'Glad you reminded me,' Brett said. 'We came over here to ask *you*.'

It would be some kind of small car; that much they all knew. The key question was: *What* kind?

Later, back at staff headquarters, Adam observed, 'For a long time, right up to 1970, a lot of people in this business thought the small car was a fad.'

'I was one,' Elroy Braithwaite, the Product Development vice-president admitted. The Silver Fox had joined them shortly after Adam's and Brett's return from the teardown room. Now, a group of five – Adam, Brett, Braithwaite, two others from product planning staff – was sprawled around Adam's office suit, ostensibly doing little more than shoot the breeze, but in reality hoping, through channelled conversation, to awaken ideas in each other. Discarded coffee cups and overflowing ashtrays littered tables and window ledges. It was after midnight.

'I thought the small car fever wouldn't last,' Braithwaite went on. He put a hand through his silver-grey mane, disordered tonight, which was unusual. 'I was in some pretty high-powered company, too, but we've all been wrong. As far as I can see, this industry will be small-car oriented, with muscle cars on the outs, for a long time to come.'

'Perhaps for ever,' one of the other product planners said. He was a bright young Negro, with large spectacles, named Castaldy, who had been recruited from Yale a year earlier.

'Nothing's for ever,' Brett DeLosanto objected. 'Hemlines or hairstyles or hip language or cars. Right now, though, I agree with Elroy – a small car's the status symbol, and it looks like staying.'

'There are some,' Adam said, 'who believe a small car is a non-symbol. They say people simply don't care about status any more.'

Brett retorted, 'You don't believe that, any more than I do.'

'I don't either,' the Silver Fox said. 'A good many things have changed these past few years, but not basic human nature. Sure, there's a "reverse status" syndrome, which is popular, but it adds up to what it always did – an individual trying to be different or superior. Even a drop-out who doesn't wash is a status seeker of a kind.'

'So maybe,' Adam prompted, 'we need a car which will appeal strongly to the reverse-status seeker.'

The Silver Fox shook his head. 'Not entirely. We still have to consider the squares – that big, solid backlog of buyers.'

Castaldy pointed out, 'But most squares don't like to think of themselves that way. That's why bank presidents wear sideburns.'

'Don't we all?' Braithwaite fingered his own.

Above the mild laughter, Adam injected, 'Maybe that's not so funny. Maybe it points the way to the kind of car we *don't* want. That is – anything looking like a conventional car produced until now.'

'A mighty big order,' the Silver Fox said.

Brett ruminated. 'But not impossible.'

Castaldy, the young Yale man, reminded them, 'Today's environment is part of reverse-status – if we're calling it that. I mean public opinion, dissent, minorities, economic pressures, all the rest.'

'True,' Adam said, then added, 'I know we've been over this a lot of times, but let's list environmental factors again.'

Castaldy looked at some notes. 'Air pollution: people want to do something.'

'Correction,' Brett said. 'They want *other* people to do something. No-one wants to give up personal transportation, riding in his own car. All our surveys say so.'

'Whether that's true or not,' Adam said, 'the car makers are doing something about pollution and there isn't a lot individuals can do.'

'Just the same,' young Castaldy persisted, 'A good many are convinced that a small car pollutes less than a big one, so they think they can contribute that way. Our surveys show that, too.' He glanced back at his notes. 'May I go on?'

'I'll try not to heckle,' Brett said. 'But I won't guarantee it.'

'In economics,' Castaldy continued, 'gas mileage isn't as dominant as it used to be, but parking cost *is*.'

Adam nodded. 'No arguing that. Street parking space gets harder to find, public and private parking costs more and more.'

'But parking lots in a good many cities *are* charging less for small cars, and the idea's spreading.'

The Silver Fox said irritably, 'We know all about that. And we've already agreed we're going the small car route.'

Behind his glasses, Castaldy appeared hurt.

'Elroy,' Brett DeLosanto said, 'The kid's helping us think. So if that's what you want, quit pulling rank.'

'My God!' the Silver Fox complained. 'You birds are sensitive. I was just being myself.'

'Pretend to be a nice guy,' Brett urged. 'Instead of a vice-president.'

'You bastard!' But Braithwaite was grinning. He told Castaldy, 'Sorry! Let's go on.'

'What I really meant, Mr Braithwaite . . . '

'Elroy . . . '

'Yes, sir. What I meant was – it's part of the whole picture.'

They talked about environment and mankind's problems: over-population, a shortage of square footage everywhere, pollution in all forms, antagonisms, rebellion, new concepts and values among young people – the young who would soon rule the world. Yet, despite changes, cars would still be around or the foreseeable future; experience showed it. But what kind of cars? Some would be the same as now, or similar, but there must be other kinds, too, more closely reflecting society's needs.

'Speaking of needs,' Adam queried, 'can we sum them up?'

'If you wanted a word,' Castaldy answered, 'I'd say "utility".'

Brett DeLosanto tried it on his tongue. 'The Age of Utility.'

'I'll buy that in part,' the Silver Fox said. 'But not entirely.' He motioned for silence while gathering thoughts. The others waited. At length he intoned slowly, 'OK, so utility's "in". It's the newest status symbol, or reverse-status – and we're agreed that whatever name you call it means the same thing. I'll concede it's probably for the future, too. But that still doesn't allow for the rest of human nature: the impulse to mobility which is with us from the day we're born, and later a craving for power, speed, excitement which we never grow out of wholly. We're all Walter Mittys somewhere inside, and utility or not, pizzazz is "in", too. It's never been out. It never will be.'

'I go with that,' Brett said. 'To prove your point, look at the guys who build dune buggies. They're small car people who've found a Walter Mitty outlet.'

Castaldy added thoughtfully, 'And there are thousands and thousands of dune buggies. More all the time. Nowadays you even see them in cities.'

The Silver Fox shrugged. 'They take a utility Volkswagen without pizzazz, strip it to the chassis, then build pizzazz on.'

A thought stirred in Adam's mind. It related to what had been said . . . to the torn down Volkswagen he had seen earlier tonight . . . and to something else, hazy: a phrase which eluded him . . . He searched his mind while the others talked.

When the phrase failed to come he remembered a magazine illustration he had seen a day or two ago. The magazine was still in his office. He retrieved it from a pile across the room and opened it. The others watched curiously.

The illustration was in colour. It showed a dune buggy on a rugged beach, in action, banked steeply on its side. All wheels were fighting for traction, sand spewing behind. Cleverly, the photographer had slowed his shutter speed so that the dune buggy was blurred with movement. The text with the picture said the ranks of dune buggy owners were 'growing like mad'; nearly a hundred manufacturers were engaged in building bodies; California alone had eight thousand dune buggies.

Brett, glancing over Adam's shoulder, asked amusedly, 'You're not thinking of building dune buggies?'

Adam shook his head. No matter how large the dune buggy population became, they were still a fad, a specialist's creation, not the Big Three's business. Adam knew that. But the phrase which eluded him was somehow linked . . . Still not remembering, he tossed the magazine on a table, open.

Chance, as happens so often in life, stepped in.

Above the table where Adam tossed the magazine was a framed photo of the Apollo II Lunar Module during the first moon landing. It had been given to Adam, who liked it, and had it framed and hung. In the photo, the module dominated; an astronaut stood beneath.

Brett picked up the magazine with the dune buggy picture and showed it to the others. He remarked, 'Those things go like hell! – I've driven one.' He studied the illustration again. 'But it's an ugly son-of-a-bitch.'

Adam thought: *So was the lunar module.*

Ugly indeed: all edges, corners, projections, oddities, imbalance; little symmetry, few clean curves. But because the lunar module did its job superbly, it defeated ugliness and, in the end, took on a beauty of its own.

The missing phrase came to him.

It was Rowena's. The morning after their night together she had said, 'You know what I'd say today? I'd say "ugly is beautiful".'

Ugly is beautiful!

The lunar module was ugly. So was a dune buggy. But both were functional, utilitarian; they were built for a purpose and performed it. *So why not a car?* Why not a deliberate, daring attempt to produce a car, ugly by existing standards, yet so suited to needs, environment, and present time – the age of Utility – that it would *become* beautiful.

'I may have an idea about Farstar,' Adam said. 'Don't rush me. Let me put it out slowly.'

The others were silent. Marshalling his thoughts, choosing words carefully, Adam began.

They were too experienced – all of them in the group – to go overboard, instantly, for a single idea. Yet he was aware of a sudden tension, missing before, and a quickening interest as he continued to speak. The Silver Fox was thoughtful, his eyes half-closed. Young Castaldy scratched an ear lobe – a habit when he concentrated – while the other product planner, who had said little so far, kept his eyes on Adam steadily. Brett DeLosanto's fingers seemed restless. As if instinctually, Brett drew a sketch pad towards him.

It was Brett, too, who jumped up when Adam finished, and began pacing the room. He tossed off thoughts, incomplete sentences, like fragments of a jigsaw . . . *Artists for centuries have seen beauty in ugliness . . . Consider distorted, tortured sculpture from Michelangelo to Henry Moore . . . And in modern times, scrap metal welded in jumbles – shapeless to some, who scoff, but many don't . . . Take paintings: the* avant-garde *forms; egg crates, soup cans in collages . . . Or life itself! – a pretty young girl or a pregnant hag: which is more beautiful? . . .* It depended always on the way you saw it. Form, symmetry, style, beauty were never arbitrary.

Brett thumped a fist into a palm. 'With Picasso in our nostrils, we've been designing cars like they rolled off a Gainsborough canvas.'

'There's a line in Genesis somewhere,' the Silver Fox said. 'I think it goes, "*Your eyes shall be opened*".' He added cautiously, 'But let's not get carried away. We may have something. Even if we do, though, there's a long road ahead.'

Brett was already sketching, his pencil racing through shapes, then discarding them. As he ripped off sheets from his pad, they dropped to the floor. It was a designer's way of thinking, just as others exchanged ideas through words. Adam reminded himself to retrieve the sheets later and save them; if something came of this night, they would be historic.

But he knew that what Elroy Braithwaite had said was true. The Silver Fox, through more years than any of the others here, had seen new cars develop from first ideas to finished products, but had suffered, too, through projects which looked promising at birth, only to be snuffed out later for unforeseen reasons, or sometimes for no reason at all.

Within the company a new car concept had countless barriers to pass, innumerable critiques to survive, interminable meetings, with opposition to overcome. And even if an idea survived all these, the executive vice-president, president, and chairman of the board had veto powers . . .

But *some* ideas got through and became reality.

The Orion had. So . . . just barely possible . . . might this early, inchoate concept, the seed sown here and now, for Farstar.

Someone brought more coffee, and they talked on, far into the night.

18

The OJL advertising agency, in the person of Keith Yates-Borwn, was nervous and edgy because the documentary film *Auto City* was proceeding without a shooting script.

'There *has* to be a script,' Yates-Brown had protested to Barbara Zaleski on the telephone from New Yrok a day or two ago. 'If there isn't, how can we protect the client's interests from here and make suggestions?'

Barbara, in Detroit, had felt like telling the management supervisor that the last thing the project needed was Madison Avenue meddling. It could transform the honest, perceptive film now taking shape into a glossy, innocuous mélange. But, instead, she repeated the views of the director, Wes Gropetti, a talented man with enough solid credits behind him to make his viewpoint count.

'You won't grab the mood of inner city Detroit by putting a lot of crud on paper because we don't *know* what the mood is yet,' Gropetti had declared. 'We're here with all this fancy camera and sound gear to find out.'

The director, heavily bearded but diminutive in stature, seemed like a shaggy sparrow. He wore a black beret which he was never without, and was less sensitive about words than he was with visual images. He went on, 'I want the inner city jokers, broads, and kids to tell us what they really think about themselves, and how they look on the rest of us lousy bums. That means their hates, hopes, frustrations, joys, as well as how they breathe, eat, sleep, fornicate, sweat, and what they see and smell. I'll get all that on film – their mugs, voices, everything unrehearsed. As to language, we'll let the crud fall where it may. Maybe I'll prick a few people in the ass to get them made, but either way they'll talk, then while they do, I'll let the camera wander like a whore's attention, and we'll see Detroit the way they see it, through inner city eyes.'

And it was working, Barbara assured Yates-Brown.

Using cinéma vérité technique, with hand-held camera and a minimum of paraphernalia to distract, Gropetti was roaming the inner city with a crew, persuading people to talk frankly, freely, and sometimes movingly, on film. Barbara, who usually accompanied the expeditions, knew that part of Gropetti's genius lay in his instinct for selection, then making those he chose forget that a lens and lights were focused on them. No-one knew what the little director whispered into ears before their owners began talking; sometimes he would bend his head down, confidentially, for minutes at a time. But it produced reactions: amusement, defiance, rapport, disagreement, sullenness, impudence, alertness, anger and once – from a young black militant who became impressively eloquent – a blazing hatred.

When he was sure of a reaction, Gropetti would spring instantly back so that the camera – already operating at the director's covert signal – would catch full facial expressions and spontaneous words. Afterwards, with limitless patience, Gropetti would repeat the process until he had what he sought – a glimpse of personality, good or bad, amiable or savage, but vital and real, and without the clumsy intrusion of an interviewer.

Barbara had already seen rushes and rough cuts of the results, and was excited. Photographically, they had the quality and depth of Karsh portraits, plus Gropetti's magic mix of vibrant animation.

'Since we're calling the film *Auto City*,' Keith Yates-Brown had commented when she told him all that, 'maybe you should wise up Gropetti that there are motorcars around as well as people, and we'll expect to see some – preferably our client's – on the screen.'

Barbara sensed that the agency supervisor was having second thoughts about the overall authority she had been given. But he would also know that any film project needed to have someone firmly in charge and, until the OJL agency removed or fired her, Barbara was.

She assured Yates-Brown, 'There *will* be cars in the picture – the client's. We're not emphasizing them, but we're not concealing them either, so most people will recognize the kind they are.' She had gone on to describe the filming already done in the auto company's assembly plant, with emphasis on inner city hard-core hiring – and Rollie Knight.

During the assembly plant filming, other workers nearby had been unaware that Rollie was the centre of the camera's attention. Partly, this was out of consideration for Rollie, who wanted it that way, and partly to keep the atmosphere realistic.

Leonard Wingate of Personnel, who became interested in Barbara's project the night they met at Brett DeLosanto's apartment, had arranged the whole thing without fuss. All that anyone in the plant knew was that a portion of Assembly was being filmed, for purposes unexplained, while regular work went on. Only Wes Gropetti, Barbara, and the camera- and sound-men realized that a good deal of the time they appeared to be shooting, they were not, and that most of the footage taken featured Rollie Knight.

The only sound recording at this point was of assembly plant noises while they happened, and afterwards Barbara had listened to the sound tape played back. It was a nightmare cacophony, incredibly effective as a background to the visual sequence.

Rollie Knight's voice, which would be dubbed in later, was to be recorded during a visit by Gropetti and the film crew to the inner city apartment house where Rollie and May Lou, his girl friend, lived. Leonard Wingate would be there. So – though Barbara did not report the fact to Keith Yates-Brown – would Brett DeLosanto.

On the telephone, Keith Yates-Brown had cautioned, 'Just remember we're spending a lot of the client's money which we'll have to account for.'

'We've stayed within budget,' Barbara reported. 'And the client seems to like what we've done so far. At least, the chairman of the board does.'

She heard a sound on the telephone which could have been Keith Yates-Brown leaping from his chair.

'*You've* been in touch with the client's chairman of the board!' The reaction could not have been greater if she had said the Pope or the President of the United States.

'He came to visit our shooting on location. The day after, Wes Gropetti took some of the film and screened it in the chairman's office.'

'You let that foul-mouthed Gropetti loose on the fifteenth floor!'

'Wes seemed to think that he and the chairman got along well.'

'*He* thought so! You didn't even go yourself?'

'I couldn't that day.'

'Oh, my God!' Barbara could visualize the agency supervisor, his face paling, a hand clapped to his head.

She reminded him, 'You told me yourself that the chairman was interested, and I might report to him occasionally.'

'But not *casually*! Not without letting us know here, in advance, so we could plan what you should say. And as for sending Gropetti on his own . . . '

'I was going to tell you,' Barbara said, 'the client's chairman phoned me next day. He said he thought our agency had shown commendable imagination – those were his words – in getting Wes Gropetti to begin with, and urged us to go on giving Wes his head because this was the kind of thing which ought to be a director's film. The chairman said he was putting all that in a letter to the agency.'

She heard heavy breathing on the line. 'We haven't got the letter yet. When it comes . . . ' A pause. 'Barbara, I guess you're doing fine.' Yates-Brown's voice became pleading. 'But *don't*, please don't, take chances, and let me know *anything instantly* about the client's chairman of the board.'

She had promised that she would, after which Keith Yates-Brown – still nervously – repeated that he wished they had a script.

Now, several days later and scriptless as ever, Wes Gropetti was ready to film the final sequence involving hard-core hiring and Rollie Knight.

Early evening.

Eight of them, altogether, were packed into the stiflingly hot, sketchily furnished room.

For Detroit generally, and especially the inner city, it had been a baking, windless summer day. Even now, with the sun gone, most of the heat – inside and out – remained.

Rolie Knight and May Lou were two of the eight because this was where – for the time being – they lived. Though the room was tiny by any standard, it served the dual purpose of living and sleeping, while a closet-sized 'kitchen' adjoining housed a sink with cold water only, a decrepit gas cooker, and a few plain board shelves. There was no toilet or bath. These facilities, such as they were, were one floor down and shared with a half-dozen other apartments.

Rollie looked morose, as if wishing he had not agreed to be involved with this. May Lou, childlike and seeming to have sprouted like a weed with skinny legs and bony arms, appeared scared, though she was becoming less so as Wes Gropetti, his black beret in place despite the heat, talked quietly to her.

Behind the director were the camera operator and soundman, their equipment deployed awkwardly in the confined space. Barbara Zaleski stood with them, her notebook opened.

Brett DeLosanto, watching, was amused to see that Barbara, as usual, had dark glasses pushed up into her hair.

The camera lights were off. Everyone knew that when they went on, the room would become hotter still.

Leonard Wingate, from the auto maker's Personnel department and also the company's ranking Negro executive, mopped his perspiring face with a fresh linen handkerchief. Both he and Brett were backed against a wall, trying to take as little space as possible.

Suddenly, though only the two technicians had seen Gropetti's signal, the lights blinked on, the sound tape running.

May Lou blinked. But as the director continued to talk softly, she nodded and her face adjusted. Then swiftly, smoothly, Gropetti eased rearward, out of camera range.

May Lou said naturally, as if unaware of anything but her own thoughts, 'Ain't no good worryin', not about no future like they say we should, 'cos it ain't ever looked as if there'd be one for some like us.' She shrugged. 'Don't look no different now.'

Gropetti's voice. 'Cut!'

Camera lights went out. The director moved in, whispering in May Lou's ear once more. After several minutes, while the others waited silently, the camera lights went on. Gropetti slid back.

May Lou's face was animated. 'Sure they took our colour TV.' She glanced across the room towards an empty corner. 'Two guys come for it, said we hadn't made no payments after the first. One of the guys wanted to know, why'd we buy it? I told him, "Mister, if I got a down payment today, I can watch TV tonight. Some days that's all that matters." ' Her voice slipped lower. 'I shoulda told him, "Who knows about tomorrow?" '

'Cut!'

Brett whispered to Leonard Wingate beside him, 'What's this all about?'

The Negro executive was still mopping his face. He said low voiced, 'They're in trouble. The two of them had some real money for the first time in their lives, so they went wild, bought furniture, a colour TV, took on payments they couldn't meet. Now, some of the stuff's been repossessed. That isn't all.'

Ahead of them, Gropetti was having May Lou and Rollie Knight change positions. Now Rollie faced the camera.

Brett asked, still speaking softly, 'What else has happened?'

'The word is "garnishee",' Wingate said. 'It means a lousy, out-of-date law which politicians agree ought to be changed, but nobody does it.'

Wes Gropetti had his head down and was talking to Rollie in his usual way.

Wingate told Brett, 'Knight's had his wages garnisheed once already. This week there was a second court order, and under the union agreement two garnishees mean automatic dismissal.'

'Hell! Can't you do something?'

'Maybe. It depends on Knight. When this is over, I'll talk to him.'

'Should he be spilling his guts on film?'

Leonard Wingate shrugged. 'I told him he didn't have to, that it's his private business. But he didn't seem to mind, neither did the girl. Maybe they don't care; maybe they figure they can help somebody else. I don't know.'

Barbara, who had overheard, turned her head. 'Wes says it's part of the whole scene. Besides, he'll edit sympathetically.'

'If I didn't think so,' Wingate said, 'we wouldn't be here.'

The director was still briefing Rollie.

Wingate, speaking softly but his voice intense, told Barbara and Brett, 'Half the problem with what's happening to Knight is our attitudes – the establishment's; that means people like you two and me. OK, we help somebody like these two kids, but as soon as we do, we expect them to have all our middle-class values which it took us years of living *our* way to acquire. The same goes for money. Even though Knight hasn't been used to it because none ever came his way, we expect him to handle money as if he'd had it all his life, and if he doesn't, what happens? He's shoved into court, his wages garnisheed, he's fired. We forget that plenty of us who've lived with money still run up debts we can't manage. But let this boy do the same thing' – the Negro executive nodded towards Rolllie Knight – 'and our system's all set to throw him back on the garbage heap.'

'You're not going to let it happen,' Barbara murmured.

Wingate shook his head impatiently. 'There's only so much I can do. And Knight's just one of many.'

Camera lights went on. The director glanced their way, a signal for silence. Rollie Knight's voice rose clearly in the quiet, hot room.

'Sure you find out things from livin' here. Like, most of it ain't gonna get better, no matter what they say. Besides that, nuthun' lasts.' Unexpectedly, a smile flashed over Rollie's face; then, as if regretting the smile, a scowl replaced it. 'So best not expect nuthun'. Then it don't hurt none when you lose it.'

Gropetti called, 'Cut!'

Filming continued for another hour, Gropetti coaxing and patient, Rollie speaking of experiences in the inner city and the auto assembly plant where he was still employed. Though the young black worker's words were simple and sometimes stumbling, they conveyed reality and a true picture of himself – not always favourable, but not belittling either. Barbara, who had seen earlier sequences filmed, had a conviction that the answer print would be an eloquently moving document.

When camera lights went out after the concluding shot, Wes Gropetti removed his black beret and mopped his forehead with a large, grubby kerchief. He nodded to the two technicians. 'Strike it! That's a wrap.'

While the others filed out, with brief 'good nights' to Rollie and May Lou, Leonard Wingate stayed behind. Brett DeLosanto, Barbara Zaleski, and Wes Gropetti were going on to the Detroit Press Club for a late supper, where Wingate would join them shortly.

The Negro executive waited until the others had passed through the mean hallway outside, with its single, low-wattage light bulb and peeling paint, and were clattering down the worn wooden stairway to the street below. Through the hallway door, the odour of garbage drifted in. May Lou closed it.

She asked, 'You want a drink, mister?'

Wingate started to shake his head, then changed his mind. 'Yes, please.'

From a shelf in the minuscule kitchen, the girl took a rum bottle with about an inch of liquor in it, which she divided equally between two glasses. Adding ice and Coke, she gave one to Wingate, the other to Rollie. The three of them sat down in the all-purpose room.

'There'll be some money coming to you from the film people for using your place tonight,' Wingate said. 'It won't be much; it never is. But I'll see you get it.'

May Lou gave an unsure smile. Rollie Knight said nothing.

The executive sipped his drink. 'You knew about the garnishee? The second one?'

Rollie still didn't answer.

'Somebody tol' him today at work,' May Lou said. 'They said he don't get his paycheck no more? That right?'

'He doesn't get part of it. But if he loses his job there'll be no more cheques anyway – for anybody.' Wingate went on to explain about garnishees – the attachment of a worker's pay at source by court order, which creditors obtained. He added that, while auto companies and other employers detested the garnishee system, they had no choice but to comply with the law.

As Wingate suspected, neither Rollie nor May Lou had understood the earlier garnishee, nor was Rollie aware that a second one – under company-union rules – could get him fired.

'There's a reason for that,' Wingate said. 'Garnishees make a lot of work for the payroll department, which costs the company money.'

Rollie blurted, 'Bullshit!' He got up and walked around.

Leonard Wingate sighed. 'If you want my honest opinion, I think you're right. It's why I'll try to help you if I can. If you want me to.'

May Lou glanced at Rollie. She moistened her lips. 'He wants you to, mister. He ain't been himself lately. He's been . . . well, real upset.'

Wingate wondered why. If Rollie had learned about the garnishee only today, as May Lou said, obviously he had not been worrying because of that. He decided not to press the point.

'What I can do,' the executive told them, 'and you must understand this is only if you want it, is have someone look over your finances for you, straighten them out if we can, and try to get you started fresh.'

He went on, explaining how the system – devised by Jim Robson, a plant personnel manager for Chrysler, and copied nowadays by other companies – worked.

What they must do, he informed Rollie and May Lou, was give him, here and now, a list of all their debts. He would hand these to a senior Personnel man in Rollie's plant. The Personnel man, who did this extra-curricular job on his own time, would go over everything to see how much was owing. Then he would phone the creditors, one by one, urging them to accept modest payments over a long period and, in return, withdraw their garnishees. Usually they agreed because the alternative was pointed out: that the man concerned would lose his job, in which event they would receive nothing, garnishee or not.

The employee – in this case Rollie Knight – would then be asked: what is the minimum amount of money you can live on weekly?

Once this was decided, Rollie's paycheck would be intercepted each week, and routed to the Personnel Department. There, every Friday, he would report and endorse the cheque over to the Personnel man making the arrangements. The Personnel man's office – Wingate told them – was usually crowded with fifty or so workers who had been in financial trouble and were being helped to straighten out. Most were grateful.

Afterwards, the Personnel man would deposit Rollie's paycheck in a special account – in the Personnel man's name since the company took no official part in the arrangement. From this account he would issue cheques to creditors for the sums arranged, giving Rollie another cheque – for the balance of his wages, on which he must live. Eventually, when all debts were cleared, the Personnel man would blow out and Rollie would receive his paycheck normally.

Records were open to inspection and the service operated solely to help workers in financial trouble, without charge of any kind.

'It won't be easy for you,' Wingate warned. 'To make it work, you'll have to live on very little money.'

Rollie seemed about to protest, but May Lou interjected quickly. 'We kin do it, mister.'

She looked at Rollie, and Wingate was aware of a mixture of authority and childlike affection in her eyes. 'You'll do it,' she insisted. 'Yes, yo' will.'

Half-smiling, Rollie shrugged.

But it was clear that Rollie Knight was still worried – really worried, Leonard Wingate suspected – about something else. Once more he wondered what it was.

'We've been sitting here,' Barbara Zaleski said as Leonard Wingate joined them, 'speculating on whether those two are going to make it.'

Barbara, the only one in the group who was a Press Club member, was host to the other three. She, Brett DeLosanto, and Wes Gropetti had waited at the bar. Now, the four of them moved to a table in the dining-room.

As Press clubs went, Detroit's was among the best in the country. It was small, well-run, with an excellent cuisine, and membership was sought after. Surprisingly, despite an exciting day-to-day affinity with the auto industry, the club's walls were almost bare – self-consciously, some thought – of mementos of the tie. The only one, which greeted visitors on entering, was a downbeat front page from 1947, its headline reading:

FORD DEAD
Dies in Oil-Lit, Unheated House

War and space travel, in contrast, were represented prominently, perhaps proof that newsmen sometimes suffer from hyperopia.

When they had ordered drinks, Wingate answered Barbara's question.

'I wish I could say yes. But I'm not sure, and the reason is the system. We talked about it earlier. People like us can cope with the system, more or less. Mostly, people like them can't.'

'Leonard,' Brett said, 'tonight you've been sounding like a revolutionary.'

'Sounding isn't being one.' Wingate smiled dourly. 'I don't think I have the guts; besides, I'm disqualified. I've a good job, money in the bank. As soon as anyone has those, they want to protect them, not blow it all up. But I'll tell you this: I know what makes people of my race revolutionaries.'

He touched a bulge in the jacket of his suit. It was a collection of papers May Lou had given him before he left. They were invoices, time payment contracts, demands from finance companies. Out of curiosity, Wingate had gone over them briefly in his car, and what he had seen amazed and angered him.

He repeated to the other three the substance of his talk with Rollie and May Lou, omitting figures, which were private, but apart from that the others knew the story anyway, and he was aware they cared.

He said, 'You saw the furniture they had in that room.'

The others nodded. Barbara said, 'It wasn't good, but . . . '

'Be honest,' Wingate told her. 'You know as well as I do, it was a bunch of shoddy junk.'

Brett protested, 'So what! If they can't afford much . . . '

'But you'd never *know* they couldn't, not from the price they paid.' Once more, Wingate touched the papers in his pocket. 'I just saw the invoice, and I'd say the invoice price is at least six times what the furniture was worth. For what they paid, or rather signed a finance contract for, those two could have had quality stuff from a reputable outfit like J. L. Hudson's or Sears.'

Barbara asked, 'Then why didn't they?'

Leonard Wingate put both hands on the table, leaning forward. 'Because, my dear innocent, well-to-do friends, they didn't know any better. Because nobody ever taught them how to shop around or buy carefully. Because there isn't much point learning any of that if you've never had any real money. Because they went to a white-run store in a black neighbourhood, which cheated them – but good! Because there are plenty of those stores, not just in Detroit, but other places too. I know. We've seen other people travel this route.'

There was silence at the table. Their drinks had come, and Wingate sipped a neat Scotch on the rocks. After a moment he went on, 'There's also a little matter of the finance charges on the furniture and some other things they bought. I did some figuring. It looks to me as if the interest rate was between nineteen and twenty per cent.'

Wes Gropetti whistled softly.

Barbara queried, 'When your Personnel man talks to the creditors, the way you said he would, can he do anything to get the furniture bill or finance charges lowered?'

'The finance charges, maybe.' Leonard Wingate nodded. 'I'll probably work on that myself. When we call a finance outfit and use our company's name, they're apt to listen and be reasonable. They know there are ways a big auto manufacturer can put the squeeze on, if we take a mind to. But as to furniture . . . ' He shook his head. 'Not a chance. Those crooks'd laugh. They sell their stuff for as much as they can get, then turn their papers over to a finance company at a discount. It's little buys like Knight – who can't afford it – who pay the difference.'

Barbara asked, 'Will he keep his job? Rollie, I mean.'

'Providing nothing else happens,' Wingate said, 'I think I can promise that.'

Wes Gropetti urged, 'For Christ's sake, that's enough talk! Let's eat!'

Brett DeLosanto, who had been unusually quiet through most of the evening, remained so during the meal which followed. What Brett had seen tonight – the conditions under which Rollie Knight and May Lou lived; their cramped, mean room in the run-down, garbage-reeking apartment house; countless other buildings in the area, either the same or worse; the general malaise and poverty of the major portion of the inner city – had affected him deeply. He had been in the inner city before, and through its streets, but never with the same insight or sense of poignancy he had known within the past few hours.

He had asked Barbara to let him watch tonight's filming, partly from curiosity and partly because she had become so absorbed with the project that he had seen little of her lately. What he had not expected was to be drawn in, mentally, as much as he had.

Not that he had been unaware of ghetto problems of Detroit. When he observed the desperate grimness of housing, he knew better than to ask: *Why don't people move somewhere else?* Brett already knew that economically and socially, people here – specifically, black people – were trapped. High as living costs were in the inner city, in suburbs they were higher still, even if the suburbs would let blacks move there – and some wouldn't, still practising discrimination in a thousand subtle and not-so-subtle ways. Dearborn, for example, in which Ford Motor Company had its headquarers, at last count didn't have a single black resident, due to hostility of white, middle-class families who supported wily manoeuvrings by its solidly established mayor.

Brett knew, too, that efforts to aid the inner city had been made by the well-meaning

New Detroit Committee – more recently, New Detroit, Inc – established after the area's 1967 riots. Funds had been raised, some housing started. But as a committee member put it: 'We're long on proclamations, short on bricks.'

Another had recalled the dying words of Cecil Rhodes: '*So little done – so much to do.*'

Both comments had been from individuals, impatient with the smallness of accomplishments by groups – groups which included the city, state, and federal governments. Though the 1967 riots were now years away, nothing beyond sporadic tinkering had been done to remedy conditions which were the riots' cause. Brett wondered: if so many, collectively, had failed, what could one person, an individual, hope to do?'

Then he remembered: someone had once asked that about Ralph Nader.

Brett sensed Barbara's eyes upon him and turned towards her. She smiled, but made no comment on his quietness; each knew the other well enough by now not to need explanations of moods, or reasons for them. Barbara looked her best tonight, Brett thought. During the discussion earlier her face had been animated, reflecting interest, intelligence, warmth. No other girl of Brett's acquaintance rated quite as high with him, which was why he went on seeing her, despite her continued, obstinate refusal to join him in bed.

Brett knew that Barbara had gained a lot of satisfaction from her involvement with the film, and working with Wes Gropetti.

Now Gropetti pushed back his plate, dabbing a napkin around his mouth and beard. The little film director, still wearing his black beret, had been eating Beef Stroganoff with noodles, washed down generously with Chianti. He gave a grunt of satisfaction.

'Wes,' Brett said, 'do you ever want to get involved – really involved – with subjects you do films about?'

The director looked surprised. 'You mean do crusading crap? Chivvy people up?'

'Yes,' Brett acknowledged, 'that's the kind of crap I mean.'

'A pox on that! Sure, I get interested; I have to be. But after that I take pictures, kiddo. That's all. 'Gropetti rubbed his beard, removing a fragment of noodle which the napkin had missed. He added, 'A buttercup scene or a sewer – once I know it's there, all I want are the right lens, camera angle, lighting, sound synch. Nuts to involvement! Involvement's a full-time job.'

Brett nodded. He said thoughtfully, 'That's what I think, too.'

In his car, driving Barbara home, Brett said, 'It's going well, isn't it? The film.'

'*So* well!' She was near the middle of the front seat, curled close beside him. If he moved his face sideways he could touch her hair, as he had already, several times.

'I'm glad for you. You know that.'

'Yes,' she said. 'I know.'

'I wouldn't want any woman I lived with *not* to do something special, something exclusively her own.'

'If I ever live with you, I'll remember that.'

It was the first time either of them had mentioned the possibility of living together since the night they had talked about it several months ago.

'Have you thought any more?'

'I've thought,' she said. 'That's all.'

Brett waited while he threaded the traffic at the Jefferson entrance to the Chrysler Freeway, then asked, 'Want to talk about it?'

She shook her head negatively.

'How much longer will the film take?'

'Probably another month.'

'You'll be busy?'

'I expect so. Why?'

'I'm taking a trip,' Brett said. 'To California.'

But when she pressed him, he declined to tell her why.

19

The long, black limousine slowed, swung left, then glided smoothly, between weathered stone pillars, into the paved, winding driveway of Hank Kreisel's Grosse Pointe home.

Kreisel's uniformed chauffeur was at the wheel. Behind him, in the plush interior, were Kreisel and his guests, Erica and Adam Trenton. The car's interior contained – among other things – a bar, from which the parts manufacturer had served drinks as they drove.

It was late evening in the last week of July.

They had already dined – at the Detroit Athletic Club downtown. The Trentons had met Kreisel there, and a fourth at dinner had been a gorgeous girl, with flashing eyes and a French accent, whom Kreisel introduced merely as Zoë. He added that she was in charge of his recently opened export liaison office.

Zoë, who proved an engaging companion, excused herself after dinner and left. Then, at Hank Kreisel's suggestion, Adam and Erica accompanied him home, leaving their own car downtown.

This evening's arrangements had been an outcropping of Adam's weekend at Hank Kreisel's lakeside cottage. Following the cottage affair, the parts manufacturer telephoned Adam, as arranged, and they set a date. Inclusion of Erica in the invitation made Adam nervous at first, and he hoped Kreisel would make no references to the cottage weekend in detail, or Rowena in particular. Adam still remembered Rowena vividly, but she was in the past, and prudence and common sense dictated she remain there. He need not have worried. Hank Kreisel was discreet; they talked of other things – next season's prospects for the Detroit Lions, a recent scandal in city government, and later the Orion, some of whose parts Kreisel's company was now manufacturing in enormous quantities. After a while Adam relaxed, though he still wondered what, precisely, Hank Kreisel wanted of him.

That Kreisel wanted something he was sure, because Brett DeLosanto had told him so. Brett and Barbara had been invited tonight but couldn't make it – Barbara was busy at her job; Brett, who was leaving soon for the West Coast, had commitments to finish first. But Brett confided yesterday, 'Hank told me what he's going to ask, and I hope you can do something because there's a lot more to it than just us.' The air of mystery had irritated Adam, but Brett refused to say more.

Now, as the limousine stopped at Kreisel's sprawling, ivy-draped mansion, Adam supposed he would know soon.

The chauffeur came around to open the door and handed Erica out. With their host following, Erica and Adam moved on to the lawn nearby and stood together, the big house behind them, in the growing dusk.

The elegant garden, whose manicured lawn, well-trimmed trees and shrubs wore the patina of professional care, sloped downwards to the uncluttered, boulevarded lanes of Lake Shore Road, the roadway offering no interruption – except for occasional traffic – to a panoramic view of Lake St Clair.

The lake was still visible, though barely; a line of white wavelets marked its edge, and far out from shore, lights of lake freighters flickered. Closer at hand a tardy sailboat, using its outboard as a hurry-home, headed for a Grosse Pointe Yacht Club mooring.

'It's beautiful,' Erica said, 'though I always think, when I come to Grosse Pointe, it isn't really part of Detroit.'

'If you lived here,' Hank Kreisel answered, 'you'd know it was. Plenty of us still smell of gasoline. Or had grease under our fingernails once.'

Adam said dryly, 'Most Grosse Pointe fingernails have been clean for a long time.' But he knew what Kreisel meant. The Grosse Pointes, of which there were five – all separate fiefdoms and traditional enclaves of great wealth – were as much a part of the auto world as any other segment of Greater Detroit. Henry Ford II lived down the street in Grosse Pointe Farms, with other Fords sprinkled nearby like rich spices. Other auto company wealth was here too – Chrysler and General Motors fortunes, as well as those of industry suppliers: big, older names like Fisher, Anderson, Olson, Mullen, and newer ones like Kreisel. The money's current custodians hobnobbed in socially exclusive clubs – at the apex the creaking, overheated Country club, with a waiting list so long that a new, young applicant without family ties could expect to be admitted at senility. Yet for all its exclusiveness, Grosse Pointe was a friendly place – a reason why a *soupçon* of salaried auto executives made it their home, preferring its 'family' scene to the more management-oriented Bloomfield Hills.

Once, older Grosse Pointers looked down patrician noses at automotive money. Now it dominated them, as it dominated all Detroit.

A sudden, night breeze from the lake stirred the air and set leaves rustling overhead. Erica shivered.

Hank Kreisel suggested, 'Let's go in.'

The chauffeur, who appeared to double in butlerage, swung heavy front doors open as they approached the house.

A few yards inside, Adam stopped. He said incredulously, 'I'll be damned!'

Beside him, Erica, equally surprised, stood staring. Then she giggled.

The main floor living-room into which they had stepped had all the accoutrements of elegance – deep broadloom, comfortable chairs, sofas, sideboards, bookshelves, paintings, a hi-fi playing softly, and harmonious lighting. It also had a full-size swimming pool.

The pool, some thirty feet long, was attractively blue tiled, with a deep end, shallow end, and a three-tiered diving board.

Erica said, 'Hank, I shouldn't have laughed. I'm sorry. But it's . . . surprising.'

'No reason not to laugh,' their host said amiably. 'Most people do. Good many think I'm nuts. Fact is, I like to swim. Like to be comfortable, too.'

Adam was looking around him with an amazed expression. 'It's an old house. You must have ripped the inside out.'

'Sure did.'

Erica told Adam, 'Quit making like an engineer and let's go swimming.'

Obviously pleased, Kreisel said, 'You want to?'

'You're looking at an Island girl, I could swim before I could talk.'

He showed her to a corridor. 'Second door down there. Lots of swimsuits, towels.'

Adam followed Kreisel to another changing room.

Minutes later, Erica executed a dazzling swallow dive from the highest board. She surfaced, laughing. 'This is the best living-room I was ever in.'

Hank Kreisel, grinning, dived from a lower board. Adam plunged in from the side.

When they had all swum, Kreisel led the way – the three of them dripping – across the broadloom to deep armchairs over which the butler-chauffeur had spread thick towels.

In a fourth chair was a grey-haired, frail-appearing woman, beside her a tray of coffee cups and liqueurs. Hank Kreisel leaned over, kissing her cheek. He asked, 'How was the day?'

'Peaceful.'

'This is my wife, Dorothy,' Kreisel said. He introduced Erica and Adam.

Adam could understand why Zoë had been left downtown.

Yet, as Mrs Kreisel poured coffee and they chatted, she seemed to find nothing strange in the fact that the others had had a dinner engagement in which – for whatever reason – she was not included. She even inquired how the food had been at the Detroit Athletic Club.

Perhaps, Adam thought, Dorothy Kreisel had come to terms with her husband's other life away from home – his various mistresses in 'liaison offices', which Adam had heard of. In fact Hank Kreisel seemed to make no secret of his arrangements, as witness Zoë tonight.

Erica chattered brightly. Obviously she liked Hank Kreisel, and the evening out, and now the swim, had been good for her. She appeared glowing, her youthfulness evident. She had found a bikini among the available swimwear; it was exactly right for her tall, slim figure, and several times Adam noticed Kreisel's eyes stray interestedly Erica's way.

After a while their host seemed restless. He stood up. 'Adam, like to get changed? There's something I want to show you, maybe talk about.'

So finally, Adam thought, they were coming to the point – whatever the point was.

'You sound mysterious, Hank,' Erica said; she smiled at Dorothy Kreisel. 'Do I get to see this exposition too?'

Hank Kreisel gave his characteristic twisted grin. 'If you did, I'd like it.'

A few minutes later they excused themselves from Mrs Kreisel who remained, placidly sipping coffee, in the living-room.

When they had dressed, Hank Kreisel guided Adam and Erica through the main floor of the house, explaining it had been built by a long-dead auto mogul, a contemporary of Walter Chrysler and Henry Ford. 'Solid. Outside walls as good as Hadrian's. Still are. So I tore the inside apart, put new guts in.' The parts manufacturer opened a panelled doorway, revealing a spiral staircase, going down, then clattered ahead. Erica followed, more cautiously, Adam behind her.

They walked along a basement passageway, then, selecting a key from several on a ring, Hank Kreisel opened a grey metal door. As they entered the room beyond, bright fluorescent lighting flooded on.

They were, Adam saw, in an engineering experimental workshop. It was spacious, organized, among the best-equipped of its kind that he had seen.

'Spend a lot of time in this place. Do pilot stuff,' Kreisel explained. 'When new work comes up for my plants, bring it down here. Then figure out the best way of production at cheapest unit cost. Pays off.'

Adam remembered something which Brett DeLosanto had told him: that Hank Kreisel had no engineering degree, and his only training before beginning business for himself was as a machinist and plant foreman.

'Over here.' Kreisel led the way to a low, wide work table. An object on it was covered by the cloth which he removed. Adam looked curiously at the metal structure underneath – an assemblage of steel rods, sheet metal, and connected internal parts, the size about equal to two bicycles. On the outside was a handle. As Adam turned it, experimentally, parts within the structure moved.

Adam shrugged. 'Hank, I give up. What the hell is it?'

'Obviously,' Erica said, 'it's something he's submitting to the Museum of Modern Art.'

'Maybe that's it. What I ought to do.' Kreisel grinned, then asked, 'Know much about farm machinery, Adam?'

'Not really.' He turned the handle once again.

Hank Kreisel said quietly, 'It's a threshing machine, Adam. Never been one like it, or this small. And it works.' His voice took on an enthusiasm which neither Adam nor Erica had heard before. 'This machine'll thresh any kind of grain – wheat, rice, barley. Three to five bushels an hour. Got pictures proving it . . .'

'I know enough about you,' Adam said. 'If you say it works, it works.'

'Something else works, too. Cost. Mass-produced, it'd sell for a hundred dollars.'

Adam looked doubtful. As a product planner, he knew costs the way a football coach knows standard plays. 'Surely not including your power source.' He stopped. 'What *is* your power source? Batteries? A small gas motor?'

'Thought you'd get around to that,' Hank Kreisel said. 'So I'll tell you. Power source isn't any of those things. It's some guy turning a handle. Same way *you* did just now. Same handle. Except the guy I'm thinking of is an old Eastern geezer in a jungle village. Wearing a slope hat. When his arms get tired, a woman or a kid'll do it. They'll sit there, hours on end, just turn the handle. That's how we'll build this for a hundred bucks.'

'No power source. Too bad we can't build cars that way.' Adam laughed.

Kreisel told him, 'Whatever else you do. Do me a favour now. Don't laugh.'

'OK, I won't. But I still can't see mass-producing, in Detroit of all places, a piece of farm machinery' – Adam nodded towards the thresher – 'where you *turn a handle, for hours on end*, to make it work.'

Hank Kreisel said earnestly, 'If you'd been to places where I have, Adam, maybe you would. Parts of this world are a long way from Detroit. That's half our trouble in this town: we forget those other places. Forget that people don't think like we do. We figure everywhere else is like Detroit, or ought to be, so whatever happens should be our way: the way we see it. If others see different, they have to be wrong *because we're Detroit!* We've been like that about other things. Pollution. Safety. Those got so hot we had to change. But there's a lot more thinking left that's like religion.'

'With high priests,' Erica put in, 'who don't like old beliefs challenged.'

Adam shot her an annoyed glance which said: *Leave this to me.*

709

He pointed out, 'A good many who are moving up in the industry believe in rethinking old ideas and the effect is showing. But when you talk about a hand-operated machine – any kind of machine – *that* isn't a forward change; it's going backwards to the way things were before the first Henry Ford.' He added, 'Anyway, I'm a car and truckman. This is farm machinery.'

'Your company has a farm products division.'

'I'm not involved with it, and don't expect to be.'

'Your people at the top are. And you're involved with them. They listen to you.'

'Tell me something,' Adam said. 'Did you put this up to our farm products people? Did they turn you down?'

The parts manufacturer nodded affirmatively. 'Them and others. Need someone now to get me in a board room. So I can raise interest there. Hoped you'd see it.'

At last it was clear precisely what Hank Kreisel wanted: Adam's help in gaining access to the corporate summit of his company, and presumably the ear of the president or chairman of the board.

Erica said, 'Can't you do it for him?'

Adam shook his head, but it was Hank Kreisel who told her, 'He'd have to believe in the idea first.'

They stood looking at the contraption with its handle, so alien to everything in Adam's own experience.

And yet, Adam knew, auto companies often did become involved in projects having little or nothing to do with their principal activity of producing cars. General Motors had pioneered a mechanical heart for use in surgery, and other medical devices. Ford was working on space satellite communication, Chrysler, dabbling in planned communities. There were other examples, and the reason for such programmes – as Hank Kreisel shrewdly knew – was that someone high in each company had taken a personal interest to begin with.

'Been down to Washington about this thresher,' Kreisel said. 'Sounded out a lot of guys in State. They go for this. Talk of ordering two hundred thousand machines a year for foreign aid. It'd mean a start. But State Department can't do manufacturing.'

'Hank,' Adam said, 'why work through another company at all? If you're convinced, why not build and market this yourself?'

'Two reasons. One's prestige. I don't have the name. Big company like yours does. Has the marketing setup, too. I don't.'

Adam nodded. That much made sense.

'Other reason is finance. I couldn't raise the dough. Not for big production.'

'Surely, with your track record, the banks . . . '

Hank Kreisel chuckled. 'I'm into the banks already. So deep, some days they think I held 'em up. Never had much cash of my own. Surprising what you can do without it.'

Adam understood that, too. Plenty of individuals and companies operated that way, and almost certainly Hank Kreisel's plants, their equipment, inventories, this house, his place at Higgins Lake, were mortgaged heavily. If Kreisel ever sold his business, or a part of it, he could reap millions in cash. Until he did, like others he would continue month by month with cash flow problems.

Again the parts manufacturer turned the thresher handle. Inside, the mechanism moved, though accomplishing nothing now; what it needed was grain to bite on, fed into a quart-size hopper at the top.

'Sure this is offbeat. Could say it's been a dream with me. Had it a long time.' Hank Kreisel hesitated, seeming embarrassed by the admission, but went on, 'Got the idea in Korea. Watched guys 'n dames in villages, pounding grain with rocks. Primitive: lots of muscle, small results. Saw a need, so started figuring this gizmo. Worked on it, on and off, ever since.'

Erica was watching Hank Kreisel's face intently. She, too, knew something of his background, having learned it partly from Adam, partly elsewhere. Suddenly a picture took shape in her mind: of a tough, hard-fighting United States Marine in an alien, hostile land, yet observing native villagers with such understanding and compassion that, years afterwards, an idea born at that time could stay with him like a flame.

'Tell you something, Adam,' Kreisel said. 'You too, Erica. This country's not selling farm machinery overseas. Leastways, not much. Ours is too fancy, too sophisticated. It's like a religion with us – the way I said: everything has to be powered. Must be electric, or use an engine, or whatever. What's forgotten is, Eastern countries have unending labour. You call for a guy to turn a handle, fifty come hurrying like flies – or ants. But we don't like that idea. Don't like to see dams built by coolies carrying stones. Idea offends us. We figure it's inefficient, not American; we say it's the way the pyramids were built. *So what?* Fact is: situation's there. Won't change for a long time, if ever. Another thing: out there, not many places to repair fancy machinery. So machines need to be simple.' He took his hand away from the thresher whose handle he had continued turning. 'This is.'

Adam thought: strangely, while Hank Kreisel had been speaking – eloquently for him – and demonstrating what he had built and believed in, he had a Lincolnesque quality which his tall, lean figure emphasized.

Would the idea work, Adam wondered? *Was* there a need, the way Hank Kreisel claimed? *Was* it a worthwhile project to which one of the Big Three auto companies might lend its world prestige?

Adam began firing questions based on his product planner's training in critical analysis. The questions embraced marketing, expected sales, distribution, local, assembly, costs, parts, techniques for shipping, servicing, repair. Each point Adam raised, Kreisel seemed to have thought of and been prepared for, with the needed figures in his brain, and the responses showed why the parts manufacturer's own business had become the success it was.

Later, Hank Kreisel personally drove Adam and Erica to their car downtown.

Heading home, northwards, on the John Lodge Freeway, Erica asked Adam, 'Will you do what Hank wants? Will you get him to see the chairman and the others?'

'I don't know.' His voice betrayed doubts. 'I'm just not sure.'

'I think you should.'

He glanced sideways, half-amused. 'Just like that?'

Erica said firmly, 'Yes, just like that.'

'Aren't you the one who's always telling me I'm involved with too much already?' Adam was remembering the Orion, its introduction nearing week by week, with demands on his own time increasing, as they would for months ahead. Yet Farstar, now in early phases; was also requiring his concentration and working hours, at the office and at home.

Another thing on his mind was Smokey Stephensen. Adam knew he must resolve soon the question of his sister Teresa's investment in the auto dealership where he was overdue for another visit and a showdown with Smokey over several issues. Somehow, next week, he must try to fit *that* in.

He asked himself: did he really want to take on something more?

Erica said, 'It wouldn't take time. All Hank's asking is for an introduction so he can demonstrate his machine.'

Adam laughed. 'Sorry! It doesn't work that way.' He explained: Any idea passed on for consideration at the summit of the company must have exhaustive analysis and views appended because nothing was ever dumped casually on the president's or chairman's desk. Even working through Elroy Braithwaite and Hub Hewitson, the executive vice-president – as Adam would have to – the ground rules still applied. Neither would authorize approach to the next higher echelon until an entire proposal had been sifted, costs worked out, market potential mapped, specific recommendations made.

And rightly so. Otherwise hundreds of crackpot schemes would clog the policy-making process.

In this instance – though other people might be involved later – Adam, initially, would have to do the work.

Something else: If farm products division had turned down Hank Kreisel's thresher scheme, as he admitted, Adam could make enemies by reviving it, whether success or failure followed. The farm products arm, though small by comparison with automotive operations, was still a part of the company, and making enemies anywhere was never a good idea.

In the end, tonight, Adam had been impressed by his host's demonstration and ideas. But would Adam gain by involvement? Would it be wise or foolish to become Hank Kreisel's sponsor?

Erica's voice cut through his thoughts. 'Even if there were some work, I should think it might be a lot more useful than those other things you do.'

He answered sarcastically, 'I suppose you'd like me to drop the Orion, Farstar . . . '

'Why not? Those won't feed anybody. Hank's machine will.'

'The Orion will feed you and me.'

Even as he said it, Adam knew his last remark was smug and foolish, that they were drifting into a needless argument, but Erica flashed back, 'I suppose that's all you care about.'

'No. It isn't. But there's a whole lot more to think of.'

'For instance, what?'

'For instance, Hank Kreisel's an opportunist.'

'*I* liked him.'

'So I noticed.'

Erica's voice was ice. 'Just what do you mean by that?'

'Oh, hell! – nothing.'

'I said: *What do you mean?*'

'All right,' Adam answered, 'While we were by the pool, he was mentally undressing you. You knew it, too. You didn't seem to mind.'

Erica's cheeks were flushed. 'Yes, I *did* know! And no, I didn't mind! If you want the truth, I liked it.'

He said sourly, 'Well, I didn't.'

'I can't think why.'

'What's that supposed to mean?'

'It means Hank Kreisel's a man, and acts like one. That way, he makes a woman feel a woman.'

'I suppose I don't.'

'No, you bloody well don't!' Her anger filled the car. It shook him. He had the sense to know this had gone far enough.

Adam made his tone conciliatory. 'Look, maybe lately if I haven't been . . .'

'You objected because Hank made me feel good. A woman. Wanted.'

'Then I'm sorry. I suppose I said the wrong thing, didn't think enough about it.' He added, 'Besides, *I* want you.'

'*Do you? Do you?*'

'Of course I do.'

'*Then why don't you take me any more? Don't you know it's two months since you did? Before that, weeks and weeks. And you make me feel so cheap telling you.*'

They had left the freeway. Cosncience-stricken, Adam stopped the car. Erica was sobbing gently, her face against the window on the other side. He reached gently for her hand.

She snatched it back. 'Don't touch me!'

'Look,' Adam said, 'I guess I'm a first-class dope . . .'

'No! Don't say it! Don't say anything!' Erica choked back tears. 'Do you think I want you to take me *now*? After asking? How do you think a woman feels who has to *ask*?'

He waited a while, feeling helpless, not knowing what to do or say. Then he started the car and they drove the rest of the way to Quarton Lake in silence.

As usual, Adam let Erica out before heading into the garage. Leaving, she told him quietly, 'I've thought a lot, and it isn't just tonight. I want a divorce.'

He said, 'We'll talk about it.'

Erica shook her head.

When he came in, she was already in the guest room with the door locked. That night, for the first time since their marriage, they were in the same house and slept apart.

20

'Gimme the bad news,' Smokey Stephensen told Lottie Potts, his book-keeper. 'How much am I out of trust?'

Lottie, who looked and frequently behaved like a female Uriah Heep, but had a mind as a sharp as razor blades, did quick arithmetic with a slim gold pencil.

'Counting those cars we just delivered, Mr Stephensen, sir, forty-three thousand dollars.'

'How much cash is in the bank, Lottie?'

'We can meet the payroll this week and next, Mr Stephensen, sir. Not much more.'

'Um.' Smokey Stephensen rubbed a hand over his heavy beard, then leaned back, lacing his fingers over his belly which had grown larger lately; he reminded himself, absently, that he must do something about his weight soon, like going on a diet, though the thought depressed him.

Characteristically, Smokey was not alarmed about the financial crisis in which, this morning, he suddenly found himself. He had weathered other and would manage this one somehow. He pondered over Lottie's figures, doing further mental calculations of his own.

The day was Tuesday, in the first week of August, and the two of them were in Smokey's mezzanine office at the big suburban car dealership, Smokey behind his desk, wearing the blue silk jacket and brightly patterned tie which were like a uniform. Lottie, across from him, waited deferentially, several accounting ledgers spread open around her.

Smokey thought: there weren't many women around nowadays with Lottie's attitude. But then, if nature snarled at you at birth, making you as ugly as Lottie, you had to compensate in other ways. *By God! – she was a dog.* At thirty-five, or thereabouts, she looked fifty, with her lumpish, lopsided features, buck teeth, the suggestion of a squint, nondescript all-direction hair, appearing as if first grown on a coconut, a voice that grated like metal rims on cobblestones . . . Smokey switched his thoughts away, reminding himself that Lottie was utterly devoted, unquestionably loyal, unfailingly reliable, and that together they had clambered out of scrapes he might never have survived without her staff work.

Smokey had followed a dictum all his life: if you want a woman to stick beside you, pick an ugly one. Pretty girls were a luxury, but fickle. Ugly ones stayed to slice the meat and stir the gravy.

It was another ugly girl who had precipitated this morning's crisis. Smokey was grateful that she had.

Her name was Yolanda and she had telephoned him at home late last night.

Yolanda worked for the downtown bank which Smokey dealt with, and which financed his dealer's inventory of cars. She was a vice-president's secretary, with access to confidential information.

Another thing about Yolanda was that stripped to bra and panties she weighed two hundred pounds.

The moment Smokey had seen her, during a visit to the bank a year ago, he sensed a potential ally. Subsequently he telephoned, invited Yolanda to lunch and from that point let their friendship grow. Now, they met every two months or so; in between he sent her flowers, or candy which she devoured by the pound, and twice Smokey had taken her overnight to a motel. The latter occasion he preferred not to think about too much, but Yolanda – who had few such experiences come her way – remained pathetically grateful, a gratitude she repaid with periodic and useful intelligence from the bank.

'Our adjusters are planning some surprise dealer stock audits,' she advised him on the phone last night. 'I thought you'd want to know – your name is on the list.'

He had asked, instantly alert, 'When do the audits start?'

'First thing tomorrow, though no-one's supposed to know.' Yolanda added, 'I couldn't call sooner because I've been working late and didn't think I should use an office phone.'

'You're a bright kid. How long's the list?'

'Eight dealers are on it. I copied the names. Shall I read them?'

He blessed her thoroughness. 'Please, baby.'

Smokey was relieved to find his own name last but one. If the adjusters took the names in order, which was normal, it meant they wouldn't get to him until three days from now. So he had two days to work with, which wasn't much, but better than having a snap audit pulled tomorrow. He noted the other dealers' names. three were acquaintances whom he would tip off, some other time they might repay the favour.

He told Yolanda, 'You're a sweet kid to call me. We haven't seen enough of each other lately.'

They ended with exchanges of affection, and Smokey sensed this was going to cost him another night at the motel, but it was worth it. Next morning, early, he summoned Lottie, whom he also obliged in basic ways occasionally, but who never, at any time, failed to call him 'Mr Stephensen, sir.' Her report – that the Stephensen dealership was seriously out of trust – resulted.

'Out of trust' meant that Smokey had sold cars, but had not turned the proceeds over to the bank which loaned him the money to buy them to begin with. The cars were the bank's security against its loan; therefore, since it had not been informed otherwise, the bank believed the cars were still safely in Smokey's inventory. In fact, forty-three thousand dollars worth of cars was gone.

Some sales had been reported to the bank over the past few weeks, but by no means all, and an audit of the dealership's stock – which banks and finance companies insisted on periodically – would reveal the deficiency.

The ex-race driver ruminated as he rubbed his beard again.

Smokey knew, as did all auto dealers, that it was normal for a dealership to be out of trust occasionally, and sometimes necessary. The trick was not to go too far, and not get caught.

A reason for the problem was that car dealers had to find cash for each new car they took into stock, usually borrowing from banks or finance companies. But sometimes borrowing was not enough. A dealer's cash might be short, yet cash was needed – to pay for still more cars if the immediate sales outlook was good, or to meet expenses.

What dealers did, of course, was go slow in processing their paper work after any sale was consummated. Thus, a dealer might receive payment from a customer who bought a car, then subsequently the dealer would take a leisurely week or so to report the sale to his own creditors, the bank or finance company. During that time the dealer had the use of the money involved. Furthermore, at the end of it there would be more sales overlapping, which in turn could be processed slowly, so the dealer could use – again temporarily – the money from those. In a way, it was like a juggling act.

Banks and finance companies knew the juggling went on and – within reason – condoned it by allowing dealers to be briefly, if unofficially 'out of trust'. They were unlikely, however, to tolerate an out-of-trust as large as Smokey's was at this moment.

Smokey Stephensen said softly, 'Lottie, we gotta get some cars back in stock before those audit guys get there.'

'I thought you'd say that, Mr Stephensen, sir, so I made a list.' The book-keeper passed two clipped sheets across the desk. 'These are all our customer deliveries for the past two weeks.'

'Good girl!' Smokey scanned the list, noting approvingly that Lottie had included an address and telephone number against each name, as well as noting the model of car purchased and its price. He began ticking addresses which were reasonably near.

'We'll both get on the phone,' Smokey said. 'I've marked fourteen names to start. I'll take the top seven; you call the others. We need cars tomorrow morning, early. You know what to say.'

'Yes, Mr Stephensen, sir.' Lottie, who had been through this before, was copying Smokey's notations on a duplicate list of her own. She would do her telephoning from the downstairs cubicle where she worked.

When Lottie had gone, Smokey Stephensen dialled the first number on his list. A pleasant female voice answered, and he identified himself.

'Just called,' Smokey announced in his most mellifluous man's style, 'to see how you good folks are enjoying that new car we had the privilege of selling you.'

'We like it.' The woman sounded surprised. 'Why? Is anything wrong?'

'Nothing in the least wrong, ma'am. I'm simply making a personal check, the way I do with all my customers, to make sure everybody's happy. That's the way I run my business.'

'Well,' the woman said, 'I guess it's a good way. Not many people seem to care that much nowadays.'

'We care.' Smokey had a cigar going by now; his feet were on the desk, chair tilted back. 'All of us here care very much indeed. And about that, I have a suggestion for you.'

'Yes?'

'Now that you've given your car some initial use, why not run it in to us tomorrow, let our service department give it a thorough check. That way we can see if anything wrong has shown up, as well as adjust anything else that's needed.'

'But we've had the car less than a week . . .'

'All the more reason,' Smokey said expansively, 'for making sure everything's in tiptop shape. We'd like to do it for you; we really would. And there'll be no charge.'

'You're certainly a *different* kind of car dealer, the woman on the phone said.

'I'd like to think that, ma'am. In any case, it's kind of you to say so.'

They arranged that the car would be brought to the service department by eight o'clock the following morning. Smokey explained he wanted to allot one of his best mechanics to the job, and this would be easier if the car came early. The woman's husband, who usually drove to his office downtown, would either ride with someone else or take a bus.

Smokey made another call with similar results. With the two after that, he met resistance – tomorrow would not be convenient to release the cars; sensing firmness, he didn't press the point. Making the fifth call he revised his tactics, though for no particular reason except as a change.

'We're not absolutely certain,' Smokey informed the car's owner – a man who answered the telephone himself – 'but we think your new car may have a defect. Frankly, I'm embarrassed to have to call you, but the way we feel about our customers, we don't like to take the slightest chance.'

'No need to be embarrassed,' the man said. 'I'm glad you did call. What's the trouble?'

'We believe there may be a small exhaust leak, with carbon monoxide seeping into the passenger compartment. You or your passengers wouldn't smell it, but it might be dangerous. To be honest, it's something we've discovered on a couple of cars we received from the factory this week, and we're checking all others we've had recently to be on the safe side. I hate to admit it but it looks as if there may have been a minor factory error.'

'You don't have to tell me; I know how it is,' the man said. 'I'm in business myself, get labour problems all the time. The kind of help you get nowadays, they just don't care. But I sure appreciate your attitude.'

'It's the way I run my shop,' Smokey declared, 'as I'm sure you do yours. So can we count on having your car here tomorrow morning?'

'Sure can. I'll run it in early.'

'That's a big load off my mind. Naturally, there'll be no charge and, by the way, when you use the car between now and tomorrow, do me a favour and drive with a window open.' The artist in Smokey could seldom resist the extra embellishment.

'Thanks for the tip! And I'll tell you something mister – I'm impressed. Shouldn't be surprised if we do business again.'

Smokey hung up, beaming.

At mid-morning, Lottie Potts and her employer compared results. The book-keeper had managed to get four cars promised for next day, Smokey five. The total of nine would have been enough if all the cars arrived, but between now and tomorrow morning some owners might change their minds or have problems arise to prevent them coming. Smokey decided to be safe. He selected another eight names from Lottie's list, and the two of them went back to telephoning. By noon, the owners of thirteen cars, in all, had agreed to return them to the Stephensen dealership early the following day for a variety of reasons.

Next was a conference between Smokey and his service manager, Vince Mixon.

Mixon was a cheerful whippet of a man, bald and in his late sixties, who ran the service department like a skilful maitre d'. He could diagnose instantly the ailments of any car, his organizational work was good, and customers liked him. But Vince Mixon had a weakness: he was an alcoholic. For ten months of each year he stayed on the wagon, twice a year, regularly, he fell off, sometimes with doleful consequences on the job.

No other employer would have tolerated the situation, and Mixon knew it; he also knew that if he lost his job, at his age he would never find another. Smokey, on the other hand, had shrewdly assessed the situation and figured advantages to himself. Vince Mixon was great when he functioned, and when he didn't Smokey managed. Smokey could also rely on his service manager not to be bothersome if ethics were bent occasionally; also Mixon would do anything asked of him in tricky situations, such as now.

Together, they laid plans for tomorrow.

As each of the recalled cars arrived, it would be whisked to the service department and washed, its interior vacuumed, the engine wiped over carefully to ensure a new appearance if the hood was raised. Glove compartments would be emptied of owner's possessions; these were to be stored in plastic bags, the bags tagged so that contents could be replaced later. Licence plates would be removed, their numbers carefully noted to ensure that eventually the right plates went back on the right cars. Tyres must have a coat of black paint to simulate newness, especially where any tread wear showed.

The cars – a dozen, or thereabouts – would then be driven on to the fenced lot behind the dealership where new cars, not yet sold, were stored.

And that was all. No other work, of any kind, would be performed, and two days from now – apart from the cleaning job – the cars would be returned to their owners exactly as brought in.

In the meantime, however, they would be on the premises for counting and inspection by the bank's adjusters who would be satisfied, Smokey hoped, that his inventory of unsold cars was the size it should be.

Smokey said thoughtfully, 'Those bank guys may not get here till the day after tomorrow. But the people'll be expecting their cars back tomorrow night. You'll have to phone everybody in the afternoon, invent a lot of excuses for holding 'em an extra day.'

'Don't worry,' Vince Mixon assured him. 'I'll dream up good reasons.'

717

His employer eyed him sternly, 'I won't worry, long as you lay off the juice.'

The whippet-like service manager held up a hand. 'Not a teaspoonful till this is over. I promise.'

Smokey knew from experience that the promise would be kept, but in exacting it he had ensured that a bender would follow. It was a strategy which the dealer seldom used, but he had to be sure of Vince Mixon for the next forty-eight hours.

'How about odometers?' The service man asked. 'Some of those cars'll have a few hundred miles on by now.'

Smokey pondered. There *was* a danger there; some bank adjusters were wise to dealer tricks and checked everything during a new car audit, odometers included. Yet messing with odometers nowadays was becoming tricky because of state laws; also, those in this year's models were the tamperproof kind.

'Nothing's tamperproof,' Mixon asserted when Smokey remined him of this. From a pocket the service manager produced a set of small, shaped metal keys. 'See these? Made by a tool-and-die outfit called Expert Speciality in Greenville, South Carolina. Anybody can buy 'em and they'll reset odometers any which way; you name it.'

'What about the odometers – with white lines which drop if you change the numbers?'

'The lines are from plastic cases, set to break when you mess with them. But the same people who made those keys sell new plastic cases, which won't break, for a dollar each. I got two dozen outside, more on order.' Mixon grinned. 'Leave it to me, chief. Any odometer in that bunch showing over fifty miles, I'll turn back. Then before the owner gets the car back, I'll fix it the way it was.'

Happily, Smokey clapped his employee on the shoulder. 'Vince we're in great shape!'

By the middle of next morning, it seemed they were.

As Smokey had anticipated, three of the promised cars failed to show, but the other ten were brought in as arranged, and were ample for his purpose. In the service department, washing, cleaning, and tyre painting were going ahead briskly, taking priority over other work. Several of the cars had already been driven on to the storage lot, personally, by Vince Mixon.

Another item of good news was that the bank adjusters were conducting their audits in the order that the eight dealers' names appeared on Yolanda's list. Two of the three dealers whom Smokey tipped off yesterday had telephoned, with news from themselves and other dealerships which made this clear. It meant that Stephensen Motors could be sure of being checked tomorrow, though they would be ready by this afternoon.

Nor did Smokey have any real worries, provided he could get through today and tomorrow with his true stock position undetected. Business generally was excellent, the dealership sound, and he knew he could have his books back in order, and not be seriously out of trust, in a month or so. He admitted to himself he *had* overextended a little, but then, he had gambled before and won, which was a reason he had lasted so long as a successful car dealer.

At 11.30 Smokey was relaxing in his mezzanine office, sipping coffee laced with brandy, when Adam Trenton walked in unannounced.

Smokey Stephensen had become slightly uneasy about Adam's visits, of which there had been several since their first meeting early in the year. He was even less pleased than usual to see Adam now.

'Hi!' he acknowledged. 'Didn't know you were coming in.'

'I've been here an hour,' Adam told him. 'Most of the time in the service department.'

The tone of voice and a certain set to Adam's face made Smokey uneasy. He grumbled, 'Should think you might let me know when you get here. This is my shop.'

'I would have, except you told me at the beginning . . .' Adam opened a black loose-leaf folder which he had carried during his last few visits and turned a page. 'You told me the first time I came: "Everything's wide open to you here, like a whorehouse with the roof off. You can see our books, files, inventories, just the way your sister would, as she's entitled to." And later you said . . .'

Smokey growled. 'Never mind! Didn't know I was talking to a recording machine.' He stared suspiciously. 'Maybe you been using one.'

'If I had, you'd have known about it. I happen to have a clear memory, and when I'm involved in something I keep notes.'

Smokey wondered what else was in the pages of the black folder. He invited Adam, 'Sit down. Coffee?'

'No, thank you, and I'll stand. I came to tell you this is the last time I'll be in. I'm also informing you, because I think you're entitled to know, that I'm recommending my sister to sell her stock in your business. Also' – Adam touched the black loose-leaf folder again – 'I intend to turn this over to our company marketing department.'

'*You what?*'

Adam said quietly, 'I think you heard.'

'*Then what the hell is in there?*'

'Among other things, the fact that your service department is, at this moment, systematically stripping several used cars of owner identification, faking them to look like new, and putting them with genuinely new cars on your storage lot. Your service manager, incidentally, has written bogus work orders on those cars for warranty, which is not being performed but will be charged, no doubt, to our company. Right now I don't know the reason for what's happening, but I think I can guess. However, since Teresa is involved, I'm going to call your bank, report what I've seen, and ask if they can enlighten me.'

Smokey Stephensen said softly, '*Jesus Christ!*'

He knew the roof had fallen in, in a way he had least expected. He realized, too, his own mistake from the beginning: it was in being open with Adam Trenton, in giving him the run of the place the way he had. Smokey had sized up Adam as a bright, pleasant head office guy, undoubtedly good at his job or he wouldn't have it, but naïve in other areas, including the running of an auto dealership. It was why Smokey had reasoned that openness would be a kind of deception because Adam might sense if information was being held back, and it would make him curious, whereas frankness wouldn't. Also, Smokey believed that when Adam realized his sister's interest in the dealership was being dealt with honestly, he would not concern himself with other things. Too late, the dealer was learning he had been wrong on every count.

'Do me one favour,' Smokey urged, 'Gimme a minute to think. Then at least, let's talk.'

Adam answered curtly, 'All you'll be thinking of is a way to stop me, and it won't work. And we've done all the talking needed.'

The dealer's voice rose. 'How the hell you know what I'll be thinking?'

'All right; I don't know. But I know this: that you're a crook.'

'That's a goddam lie! I could take you to court for it.'

719

'I'm perfectly willing,' Adam said, 'to repeat the statement in front of witnesses, and you can summon me into any court you want. But you won't.'

'How a crook?' Smokey supposed he might as well find out what he could.

Adam dropped into a chair facing the desk and opened the black loose-leaf book.

'You want the whole list?'

'Damn right!'

'You cheat on warranty. You charge the manufacturer for work that isn't done. You replace parts that don't need replacing, then put the removed ones back in your own stock to use again.'

Smokey insisted, 'Give me *one* example.'

Adam turned pages. 'I've a lot more than one, but this is typical.' An almost-new car had come into Stephensen Motors' service department, Adam recited, its carburettor needing minor adjustment. But instead of being adjusted, the carburettor was removed, a new one installed, the manufacturer billed for warranty. Afterwards, the removed carburettor had been given the minor repair it needed to begin with, then was placed in the service department's stock from where it was later sold as a new unit. Adam had dates, work order and invoice numbers, the carburettor identification.

Smokey flushed. 'Who said you could go snooping around my service records?'

'You did.'

There were procedures to prevent that kind of fraud, as Adam knew. All Big Three manufacturers had them. But the vastness of organization, as well as the volume of work going through a big service depot, made it possible for dealers like Smokey to foil the system regularly.

He protested, 'I can't keep tabs of everything that goes on in Service.'

'You're responsible. Besides, Vince Mixon runs that shop the way you téll him, the way he's running it today. Incidentally, another thing he does is pad customers' bills for labour. You want examples?'

Smokey shook his head. He had never suspected this son-of-a-bitch would be as thorough, or would even see and understand as much as he had. But even while Smokey listened, he was thinking hard, thinking the way he used to in a close race when he needed to pass or out-manoeuvre someone ahead of him on the track.

'Talking of customers,' Adam said, 'your salesmen still quote finance interest rates at so much a hundred dollars, even though the Truth of Lending Act makes that illegal.'

'People prefer it that way.'

'You mean *you* prefer it. Especially when an interest rate you quote as "nine per cent per hundred" means a *true* interest rate of over sixteen per cent per year.'

Smokey persisted, 'That ain't so bad.'

'I'll concede that. So would other dealers who do the same thing. What they might not like, though, is the way you cheat regularly on dealer sales contests. You postdate sales orders, change dates on others . . . '

Audibly, Smokey groaned. He waved a hand, surrendering. 'Leave it, leave it! . . . '

Adam stopped.

Smokey Stephensen knew: *This guy Trenton had the goods.* Smokey might slide sideways out of some, or even all, the other finagling, but not this. Periodically, auto manufacturers awarded dealer bonuses – usually fifty to a hundred dollars a car – for every new car sale during specified periods. Since thousands of dollars were involved, such contests were carefully policed, but there were ways around the policing and Smokey, at times, had used them all. It was the kind of duplicity which a manufacturer's marketing department, if they learned of it, seldom forgave.

Smokey wondered if Adam knew, too, about the demonstrator cars – last year's models – which the dealership had sold as new after switching odometers. He probably did.

How in hell could one guy find out so much in just that little time?

Adam could have explained. Explained that to a top-flight automotive product planner, such matters as investigative research, detailed follow-through, analysis, the piecing together of fragmentary information, were all like breathing. Also, Adam was used to working fast.

Smokey had his eyes cast down on the desk in front of him; he appeared to be taking the time to think for which he had asked a few minutes ago. Now he lifted his head and inquired softly, 'Whose side you on, anyway? Just whose interests you looking out for?'

Adam had anticipated the question. Last night and earlier today he had asked it of himself.

'I came here representing my sister, Teresa, and her forty-nine per cent financial interest in this business. I still do. But that isn't to say I'll condone dishonesty, and neither would Teresa, or her husband, Clyde, if he were alive. It's why I'll go through with what I told you.'

'About that. First thing you gonna do is call the bank. Right?'

'Right.'

'OK, Mr Smart-ass-noble-high-'n-mighty, let me tell you what'll happen. The bank'll panic. Inspectors'll be around this afternoon, tomorrow they get a court order, padlock this place, seize the stock. OK, next you say you'll hand them notes over to your company sales guys. Know what they'll do?'

'At a guess, I'd say take away your franchise.'

'No guessin'. It'll happen.'

The two men eyed each other. The dealer leaned forward across the desk. 'So where's that leave Teresa and them kids? How much do you think forty-nine per cent of a dead business'd be worth?'

'It wouldn't be a dead business,' Adam said. 'The company would put someone in temporarily until a new dealer could be named.'

'A temporary guy! How well d'you think he'd run a business he doesn't know? – into bankruptcy maybe.'

'Since you've brought up bankrupktcy,' Adam said, 'that seems to be the way you're headed now.'

Smokey slammed down a fist so hard and savagely that everything on his desk top shook. 'There'll be no bankruptcy! Not if I play it my way. Only if we do it yours.'

'So you say.'

'*Never mind what I say!* I'll get my book-keeper here right now! I'll prove it!'

'I've already been over the books with Miss Potts.'

'Then, goddam, you'll go over them again with me!' Smokey was on his feet, raging, towering over Adam. The dealer's hands clenched and unclenched. His eyes were blazing.

Adam shrugged.

Smokey used an inside line to phone Lottie. When she promised to come at once, he slammed the phone down, breathing hard.

It took an hour.

An hour of argument, of assertions by Smokey Stephensen, of the dealer's pencilled calculations with which the desk top was now strewn, of amplification of her book-keeping by Lottie Potts, of examination of financial precedents reaching back to earlier years.

At the end Adam admitted to himself that it *could* be done. Smokey just might, just could, have the business back in shape financially a month from now, allowing for certain unorthodoxies and assuming a continuing upward trend in new car sales. The alternative was a temporary management which – as Smokey pointed out – might prove disastrous.

Yet to accomplish the survival of Stephensen Motors, Adam would be obliged to condone deception and defrauding of the bank's adjusters. He had the knowledge now; it was no longer a matter of guessing. During their rehash of the facts, Smokey admitted his out-of-trust position and his scheming to survive tomorrow's new car audit.

Adam wished he didn't know. He wished fervently that his sister, Teresa, had never involved him in this at all. And for the first time he understood the wisdom of his company's Conflict of Interest rules which forbade auto company employees to become involved, – financially or otherwise – with auto dealerships.

As Lottie Potts gathered together her ledgers and left, Smokey Stephensen stood challengingly, hands on hips, eyes on Adam. 'Well?'

Adam shook his head. 'Nothing's changed.'

'It'll change for Teresa,' Smokey said softly. 'One month a nice fat cheque, next month, maybe, nothing. Another thing – all that stuff you acccused me of. You never said I cheated Teresa.'

'Because you haven't. That's the one area where everything's in order.'

'If I'd wanted to, I could have cheated her. Couldn't I?'

'I suppose so.'

'But I didn't, and ain't that what you came here to find out?'

Adam said wearily. 'Not entirely. My sister wanted to take a long-term view.' He paused, then added, 'I've also an obligation to the company I work for.'

'*They* didn't send you here.'

'I know that. But I didn't expect to discover all I have and now – as a company man – I can't ignore it.'

'You sure you can't? Not for the sake of Teresa and them kids?'

'I'm sure.'

Smokey Stephensen rubbed his beard and ruminated. His outward anger had gone, and when he spoke his voice was low, with a note of pleading. 'I'll ask you to do one thing, Adam – and, sure, it'd help me – but you'd be doing it for Teresa.'

'Doing what?'

Smokey urged, 'Walk out of here right now! Forget what you know about today! Then gimme two months to get finances back in shape because there's nothng wrong with this business that that amount of time won't fix. You know it.'

'I don't know it.'

'But you know the Orion's coming, and you know what it'll do to sales.'

Adam hesitated. The reference to the Orion was like a flag planted in his own back yard. If he believed in the Orion, obviously he believed that, with it, Stephensen Motors would do well.

Adam asked curtly, 'Suppose I agreed. What happens at the end of two months?'

The dealer pointed to the black loose-leaf notebook. 'You hand over them notes to your company marketing guys, the way you said you would. So, OK, I'd have to sell out or lose the franchise, but it'd be a growing business that was sold. Teresa'd get twice as much for her half, maybe more, than she would from a forced sale now.'

Adam hesitated. Though it still involved dishonesty, the compromise held a compelling logic.

'Two months,' the ex-race driver pleaded. 'That ain't so much to ask.'

'One month,' Adam said decisively. 'One month from today; that's all.'

As Smokey visibly relaxed and grinned, Adam knew he had been conned. And now the decision was made, it left Adam depressed because he had acted against his own conscience and good judgement. But he was determined he *would* turn over to his company's marketing department, a month from now, the notes on Stephensen Motors.

Smokey, unlike Adam, was not depressed but buoyant. Though – with a dealers' instinct – he had asked for two months, he had wanted one.

In that time a lot might happen; something new could always turn up.

21

A svelte United Airlines ground hostess brought coffee to Brett DeLosanto who was telephoning from United's 100,000-Mile Club at Detroit Metropolitan Airport. It was close to 9 a.m., and the pleasantly appointed club lounge was quiet in contrast to the noisy, bustling terminal outside. No strident flight announcements were ever made here. The service – as became the VIP crowd – was more personal and muted.

'There's no enormous hurry, Mr DeLosanto,' the girl said as she put the coffee on a table beside the tilt-back chair in which Brett was reclining while he phoned, 'but Flight 81 to Los Angeles will begin boarding in a few minutes.'

'Thanks!' Brett told Adam Trenton with whom he had been conversing for the past few minutes. 'I have to go soon. The bird to Paradise awaits.'

'Never thought of L.A. as being that,' Adam said.

Brett sipped his coffee. 'It's part of California, which viewed from Detroit is Paradise whichever way you slice the oranges.'

Adam was speaking from his office at the company staff building, where Brett had called him. They had been discussing the Orion. A few days ago, with Job One – the first production Orion – only two weeks away, several colour matching problems had arisen affecting soft trim inside the car. A design 'surveillance group', which stayed with any new car through all its stages of production, had reported that some interior plastic delivered for manufacture looked 'icy' – a serious fault – and upholstery, carpeting, and head lining were not the exact match they ought to be.

Colours were always a problem. Any car had as many as a hundred separate pieces which must match a colour key, yet the materials had differing chemical compositions and pigment bases, making it difficult to achieve identical colour shades. Working against a deadline, a design team and representatives from Purchasing and Manufacturing had finally rectified all differences, news just received by Adam with relief.

Brett had been tempted to mention the new project, Farstar, on which work was proceeding excitingly on several fronts. But he caught himself in time, remembering he was on an outside telephone, also that this airline club room, where several other passengers relaxed while awaiting flights, was used by executives from competing companies.

'Something you'll be pleased to know,' Adam told Brett. 'I decided to try to help Hank Kreisel with his thresher. I sent young Castaldy over to Grosse Pointe to look at it; he came back full of enthusiasm, so then I talked with Elroy Braithwaite who seemed favourable. Now, we're preparing a report for Hub.'

'Great!' The young designer's pleasure was genuine. He realized he had let emotion sway judgement in putting pressure on Adam to support Hank Kreisel's scheme, but so what? More and more, nowadays, Brett believed the auto industry had public obligations it was not fulfilling, and something like the thresher gave the industry a chance to utilize its resources in filling an admitted need.

'Of course,' Adam pointed out, 'the whole thing may never get past Hub.'

'Let's hope you pick a "cloud-of-dust" day to tell him.'

Adam understood the reference. Hub Hewitson, the company's executive vice-president, when liking an idea, whirled himself and others into instant, feverish action, raising – as associates put it – clouds of dust. The Orion had been a Hub Hewitson dust cloud, and still was; so had other successes, failures too, though the latter were usually forgotten as fresh Hewitson dust erupted elsewhere.

'I'll look out for one of those days,' Adam promised. 'Have a good trip.'

'So long, friend.' Brett swallowed the remainder of his coffee, patted the airline hostess amiably on the rump as he passed her, then headed for the flight departure gate.

United's Flight 81 – Detroit nonstop to Los Angeles – took off on schedule.

Like many who lived frenetic lives on the ground, Brett enjoyed transcontinental air travel in the luxury of first class. Any such journey assured four or five hours of relaxation, interspersed pleasantly with drinks, good food and service, plus the complacent knowledge of not being reachable by telephone or otherwise, no matter how many urgencies boiled over down below.

Today, Brett used much of the journey merely to think, reviewing aspects of his life – past, present, future – as he saw them. Thus occupied, the time passed quickly and he was surprised to realize, during an announcement from the flight deck, that nearly four hours had elapsed since take-off.

'We're crossing the Colorado River, folks,' the captain's voice rattled on the p.a. 'This is a point where three states meet – California, Nevada, Arizona – and it's a beautiful day in all of them, with visibility about a hundred miles. Those of you sitting on the right can see Las Vegas and the Lake Mead area. If you're on the left, that water down there is Lake Havasu where London Bridge is being rebuilt.'

Brett, on the port side with a seat section to himself, peered downward. The sky was cloudless and though they were high – at thirty-nine thousand feet – he could see, easily and sharply, the shape of the bridge below.

'Funny thing about that bridge,' the captain went on chattily. 'Story is – the people who bought it from the British got their bridges mixed. They thought they were buying the bridge on all those London travel posters, and no-one told them until too late that *that* one is Tower Bridge, and London Bridge was a bitty old bridge upstream. Ha! ha!'

Brett continued to look down, knowing from the terrain below that they were now over

California. He said aloud, 'For ever bless my native state, its sunshine, oranges, screwball politics, religions, and its nuts.'

A passing stewardess inquired, 'Did you say something, sir?' She was young, willowy and tanned, as if her off-duty hours were spent exclusively at the beach.

'Sure did. I asked, "What's a California girl like you doing for dinner tonight?" '

She flashed an impish smle. 'Mostly depends on my husband. Sometimes he likes to eat at home; other times we go . . . '

'OK,' Brett said. 'And the hell with women's lib! At least in the old days, when airlines fired girls who got married, you knew which were the unclipped wing ones.'

'If it makes you feel any better,' she told him, 'if I weren't going home to my husband, I'd be interested.'

He was wondering if that piece of blandishment was in the airline stewardess manual when the p.a. system came alive once more.

'This is your captain again, folks. Guess I should have told you to make the most of that hundred-mile visibility we've been enjoying. We've just received the latest Los Angeles weather. They're reporting heavy smog, with visibility in the L.A. area reduced to one mile or less.'

They would be landing, the captain added, in another fifty minutes.

The first smog traces were evident over the San Bernardino Mountains. With Flight 81 still sixty miles from the Pacific Coast, Brett, looking out, reflected: *Sixty miles!* On his last trip, barely a year ago, no smog had appeared until Ontario, another twenty-five miles westwards. Each time he came here, it seemed, the photochemical smog spread farther inland over the loveliness of the Golden State like an evil fungus. Their Boeing 720 was losing height now for the approach to Los Angeles International, but instead of landmarks below becoming clearer, they were blurring beneath an increasing grey-brown haze which nullified colour, sunshine, seascape. The panoramic view of Santa Monica Bay which approaching air travellers used to behold was mostly, nowadays, a memory. As they continued descending and the smog grew worse, Brett DeLosanto's mood became increasingly melancholy.

Ten miles east of the airport, as the captain had predicted, visibility diminished to a mile, so that at 11.40 a.m. Pacific Daylight Time, the ground was barely visible.

After landing, in the United Terminal a brisk young man named Barclay from the company's regional office was awaiting Brett.

'I have a car for you, Mr DeLosanto. We can drive directly to your hotel, or the college if you wish.'

'Hotel first.' Brett's official purpose in being here was to visit the Art Center College of Design, Los Angeles, but he would go there later.

Though the aerial view of his beloved California under its despoiling, filthy blanket had depressed him, Brett's spirits revived at the sight and sound of the airport's surging ground traffic at closer quarters. Cars, either singly or *en masse*, always excited him, especially in California where mobility was a way of life, with more than eleven per cent of the nation's automobiles crammed within the state. Yet the same source had helped create an air pollution which was inescapable; already, Brett felt an irritation of the eyes, his nostrils prickled; without doubt the unclean brume was deeply in his lungs. He asked Barclay, 'Has it been as bad as this for long?'

'About a week. Seems now, a partly clear day is an exception, a real clear one about as rare as Christmas.' The young man wrinkled his nose. 'We tell people it isn't all made by cars, that a lot is industrial haze.'

'But do we believe it?'

'Hard to know what to believe, Mr DeLosanto. Our own people tell us we have engine emission problems licked. Do you believe *that?*'

'In Detroit I believe it. When I get here I'm not so sure.'

What it came down to, Brett knew, was the balance between economics and numbers. It was possible, now, to build a totally emission-free auto engine, but only at high cost which would make the cars employing it as remote from every day use as a nobleman's carriage once was from the footslogging peasantry. To keep costs reasonable, engineering compromises had to be made, though even with compromises, present emission control was excellent, and better by far than envisioned only a lustrum ago. Yet sheer numbers – the daily, weekly, monthly, yearly proliferation of cars – undid the end effect, as was smoggily evident in California.

They were at the car Brett would use during his stay.

'I'll drive,' Brett said. He took the keys from Barclay.

Later, having checked in at the Beverly Hilton, and shed Barclay, Brett drove alone to the Art Center College of Design on West Third Street. CBS Television City towered nearby, with Farmers' Market huddled behind. Brett was expected, and was received with dual enthusiasm – as a representative of a company which hired many of each year's graduates, and as a distinguished alumnus himself.

The relatively small college buildings were, as usual, busily crowded, with all usable space occupied and nothing wasted on frills. The entrance lobby, though small, was an extension of classrooms and perpetually in use for informal conferences, interviews, and individual study.

The head of Industrial Design, who welcomed Brett amid a buzz of other conversations, told him, 'Maybe some day we'll take time out to plan a quieter cloister.'

'If I thought there was a chance,' Brett rejoined, 'I'd warn you not to. But you won't. This place should stay the pressure cooker it is.'

It was an atmosphere he knew well – perpetually work-oriented, with emphasis on professional discipline. *'This is not for amateurs,'* the college catalogue declared, *'this is for real.'* Unlike many schools, assignments were arduously demanding, requiring students to produce, produce . . . over days, nights, weekends, holidays . . . leaving little time for extra interests, sometimes none. Occasionally, students protested at the unrelenting stress, and a few dropped out, but most adjusted and, as the catalogue put it too: *'Why pretend that the life they are preparing for is easy? It is not and never will be.'*

The emphasis on work and unyielding standards were reasons why auto makers respected the college and kept in touch with faculty and students. Frequently, companies competed for the services of top-line students in advance of graduation. Other design colleges existed elsewhere, but Los Angeles Art Center was the only one with a specific course in auto design, and nowadays at least half of Detroit's annual crop of new designers travelled the L.A. route.

Soon after arrival, surrounded by a group of students, Brett broke off to survey the tree-shaded inner courtyard where they had gathered, and were sipping coffee or soft drinks, and chewing doughnuts.

'Nothing's changed,' he observed. 'It's like coming home.'

'Pretty packed living-room,' one of the students said.

Brett laughed. Like everything else here, the courtyard was too small, the students elbowing for space too many. Yet for all the congestion, only the truly talented were admitted to the school, and only the best survived the gruelling three-year course.

The exchange of talk – a reason why Brett had come – went on.

Inevitably, air pollution was on the minds of students; even in this courtyard there was no escaping it. The sun, which should have been shining brightly from an azure sky, instead filtered dully through the thick grey haze extending from the ground to high above. Here, too, eye and nose irritation were constant and Brett remembered a recent US Public Health warning that breathing New York's polluted air was equal to smoking a pack of cigarettes a day; thus nonsmokers innocently shared a smoker's probability of death from cancer. He presumed the same was true of Los Angeles, perhaps even more so.

On the subject of pollution, Brett urged, 'Tell me what you characters think.' A decade from now students like these would be helping shape industry policy.

'One thing you figure when you live here,' a voice from the rear injected, 'is something has to give. If we go on the way things are, one day everybody in this town will choke to death.'

Brett pointed out, 'Los Angeles is special. Smog is worse because of geography, temperature inversion, and a lot of sunlight.'

'Not so special,' someone else put in. 'Have you been in San Francisco lately?'

'Or New York?'

'Or Chicago?'

'Or Toronto?'

'Or even little country towns on market days?'

Brett called across the chorus, 'Hey! If you feel that way, maybe some of you are headed for the wrong business. Why design cars at all?'

'Because we're nutty about cars. Love 'em! Doesn't stop us thinking, though. Or knowing what's going on, and caring.' The speaker was a gangling young man with untidy blond hair, at the forefront of the group. He put a hand through his hair, revealing the long slender fingers of an artist.

'To hear a lot of people out West, and other places' – Brett was playing the devil's advocate – 'you'd think the only future is in mass transportation.'

'That old chestnut!'

'No-one really wants to use mass transport,' one of the few girls in the group declared. 'Not if a car's practical and they can afford it. Besides, mass transit's a delusion. With subsidies, taxes, and fares, public transport delivers a lot less than automobiles for more money. So everybody gets taken. Ask New Yorkers! Soon – ask San Franciscans.'

Brett smiled. 'They'll love you in Detroit.'

The girl shook her head impatiently. 'I'm not saying it because of that.'

'OK,' Brett told the others, 'let's agree that cars will be the main form of transportation for another half century, probably a lot longer. What kind of cars?'

'Better,' a quiet voice said. 'A lot better than now. And fewer.'

'Not much argument about being better, though the question's always: which way? I'm interested, though, in how you figure fewer.'

'Because we ought to think that way, Mr DeLosanto. That's if we take the long view, which is for our own good in the end.'

Brett looked curiously at the latest speaker who now stepped forward, others near the front easing aside to make room. He, too, was young, but short, swarthy, with the beginning of a pot belly and, on the surface, appearing anything but an intellectual. But his soft voice was compelling and others fell silent as if a spokesman had moved in.

'We have a good many rap sessions here,' the swarthy student said. 'Those of us taking Transportation Design want to be part of the auto industry. We're excited by the idea. Cars turn us on. But it doesn't mean that any one of us is headed for Detroit wearing blinkers.'

'Let's hear the rest of it,' Brett urged. 'Keep talking!' Coming back, listening to forthright student views again – views unencumbered by defeats, disillusion, too much knowledge of practicalities or financial limitations – was an emotional experience like having personal batteries charged.

'A thing about the auto industry nowadays,' the swarthy student said, 'is it's tuned in to responsibility. Someimes the critics won't admit it, but it has. There's a new feeling. Air pollution, safety, quality, all those things aren't just talking subjects any more. Something's being done, this time for real.'

The others were still quiet. Several more students had joined the group; Brett guessed they were from other courses. Though a dozen art specialities beside automotive design were taught here, the subject of cars always evoked general interest within the school.

'Well,' the same student continued, 'the auto industry has some other responsibilities too. One of them is numbers.'

It was curious, Brett thought, that at the airport earlier he had been thinking about numbers himself.

'It's the numbers that eat us up,' the soft-voiced swarthy student said. 'They undo every effort the car people make. Take safety. Safer cars are engineered and built, so what happens? More get on the road; accidents go up, not down. With air pollution it's the same. Cars being made right now have the best engines ever, and they pollute less than any engine ever did before. There are even cleaner ones ahead. Right?'

Brett nodded. 'Right.'

'But the *numbers* keep going up. We're bragging now about producing ten million new cars a year, so no matter how good anybody gets at emission control, the total pollution gets worse. It's wild!'

'Supposing all that's true, what's the alternative? To ration cars?'

Some one said, 'Why not?'

'Let me ask you something, Mr DeLosanto,' the swarthy student said. 'You ever been in Bermuda?'

Brett shook his head.

'It's an island of twenty-one square miles. To make sure they keep room to move around, the Bermuda government does ration cars. First they limit engine capacity, body length and width. Then they allow only one car for every household.'

A voice among the newcomers objected, 'Nuts to that!'

'I'm not saying we should be that strict,' the original speaker persisted. 'I'm simply saying we ought to draw the line somewhere. And it isn't as if the auto industry couldn't stay healthy producing the same number of cars it does now, or that people can't manage. They manage in Bermuda fine.'

'If you tried it here,' Brett said, 'you might have a new American Revolution. Besides, not being able to sell as many cars as people want to buy is an attack on free enterprise.' He grinned, offsetting his own words. 'It's heresy.'

In Detroit, he knew, many *would* view the idea as heretical. But he wondered: was it really? How much longer could the auto industry, at home and overseas, produce vehicles – with whatever kind of power plant – in continually increasing quantity? Wouldn't someone, somewhere, somehow, have to rule, as Bermuda had done: *Enough!* Wasn't the day approaching when a measure of control of numbers would become essential for the common good? Taxis were limited in number everywhere; so, to an extent, were trucks. Why not private cars? And if it didn't happen, North America could consist eventually of one big traffic jam; at times it was close to that already. Therefore, wouldn't auto industry leaders be wiser, more far-sighted and responsible if they took an initiative in self-restraint themselves?

But he doubted if they would.

A fresh voice cut in, 'Not all of us feel the way Harvey does. Some think there's room for lots more cars yet.'

'And we figure to design a few.'

'Damn right!'

'Sorry, Harv! The world's not ready for you.'

But there were several murmurs of dissent, and it was obvious that the swarthy student, Harvey, had a following.

The lanky blond youth who had declared earlier, '*We're nutty about cars,*' called, 'Tell us about the Orion.'

'Get me a pad,' Brett said. 'I'll show you.'

Someone passed one, and heads craned over while he sketched. He drew the Orion swiftly in profile and head-on view, knowing the lines of the car the way a sculptor knows a carving he has toiled on. There were appreciative 'wows', and 'really great!'

Questions followed. Brett answered frankly. When possible, design students were fed these privileged tidbits, like heady bait, to keep their interest high. However, Brett was careful to fold and pocket his drawings afterwards.

As students drifted back to classes, the courtyard session broke up. For the remainder of his time at the Art Center College of Design – through the same day and the next – Brett delivered a formal lecture, interviewed automotive design students individually, and critically appraised experimental car models which student teams had designed and built.

An instinct among this crop of students, Brett discovered, was towards severity of design, allied with function and utility. Curiously, it had been a similar combination of ideas agreed to by Brett, Adam Trenton, Elroy Braithwaite and the others, on the memorable night, two and a half months earlier, when the initial concept for Farstar had emerged. Through the time he had already spent on early Farstar designs, still being laboured over in a closely guarded studio in Detroit, and now here, Brett was struck by the aptness of Adam's phrase: *Ugly is Beautiful!*

History showed that artistic trends – the latticework of all commercial designing – always began subtly and often when least expected. No-one knew why artistic tastes changed, or how, or when the next development would come; it seemed simply that human virtuosity and perception were restless, ready to move on. Observing the students' work now – ignoring a degree of naïveté and imperfection – and remembering his own designs of recent months, Brett felt an exhilaration at being part of an obviously fresh, emerging trend.

Some of his enthusiasm, it seemed, transmitted itself to students whom he interviewed during his second day at the school. Following the interviews, Brett decided to recommend two potential graduates to the company Personnel and Organization staff for eventual hiring. One was the short, swarthy student, Harvey, who had argued forcefully in the courtyard; his design portfolio showed an ability and imagination well above average. Whichever auto company he worked for, Harvey was probably headed for trouble and collisions in Detroit. He was an original thinker, a maverick who would not be silenced, or dissuaded easily from strong opinions. Fortunately, while not always heeding mavericks, the auto industry encouraged them, knowing their value as a hedge against complacent thinking.

Whatever happened, Brett suspected, Detroit and Harvey would find each other interesting.

The other candidate he chose was the gangling youth with untidy blond hair whose talent, too, was obviously large. Brett's suggestion of future employment, so the student said, was the second approach made to him. Another auto firm among the Big Three had already promised him a design job, if he wanted it, on graduation.

'But if there's any chance of working near you, Mr DeLosanto,' the young man said, 'I'll go with your company for sure.'

Brett was touched, and flattered, but uncertain how to answer.

His uncertainty was based on a decision reached alone in his Los Angeles hotel room, the previous night. It was now mid-August, and Brett had decided: at the year end, unless something happened drastically to change his mind, he would quit the auto industry for good.

On the way back East, by air, he made another decision: Barbara Zaleski would be the first to know.

22

Also in August – while Brett DeLosanto was in California – the Detroit assembly plant, where Matt Zaleski was assistant plant manager, was in a state of chaos.

Two weeks earlier, production of cars had ceased. Specialist contractors had promptly moved in, their assignment to dismantle the old assembly line and create a new one on which the Orion would be built.

Four weeks had been allotted for the task. At the end of it, the first production Orion – Job One – would roll off the line, then, in the three or four weeks following, a backlog of cars would be created, ready to meet expected demands after official Orion introduction day in September. After that, if sales prognostications held, the tempo would increase, with Orions flowing from the plant in tens of thousands.

Of the time allowed for plant conversion, two weeks remained and, as always at model changeover time, Matt Zaleski wondered if he would survive them.

Most of the assembly plant's normal labour force was either laid off or enjoying paid vacations, so that only a skeleton staff of hourly paid employees reported in each day. But far from the shutdown making the life of Matt Zaleski and others of the plant management group easier, work loads increased, anxieties multiplied, until an ordinary production day seemed, by comparison, an unruffled sea.

The contractor's staff, like an occupying army, was demanding. So were company headquarters engineers who were advising, assisting, and sometimes hindering the contractors.

The plant manager, Val Reiskind, and Matt were caught in a crossfire of requests for information, hurried conferences, and orders, the latter usually requiring instant execution. Matt handled most matters which involved practical running of the plant, Reiskind being young and new. He had replaced the previous plant manager, McKernon, only a few months earlier and while the new man's engineering and business diplomas were impressive, he lacked Matt's seasoned knowhow acquired during twenty years on the job. Despite Matt's disappointment at failing to get McKernon's job, and having a younger man brought in over him, he liked Reiskind who was smart enough to be aware of his own deficiency and treated Matt decently.

Most headaches centred around new, sophisticated machine tools for assembly, which in theory worked well, but in practice often didn't. Technically, it was the contractor who was responsible for making the whole system function, but Matt Zaleski knew that when contractor's men were gone, he would inherit any inadequate situation they might leave. Therefore he stayed close to the action now.

The greatest enemy of all was time. There was never enough to make a changeover work so smoothly that by pre-assigned completion date it could be said: 'All systems go!' It was like building a house which was never ready on the day set for moving in, except that a house move could be postponed, whereas a car or truck production schedule seldom was.

An unexpected development also added to Matt's burdens. An inventory audit, before production of the previous year's models ceased, had revealed stock shortages so huge as to touch off a major investigation. Losses from theft at any auto plant were always heavy. With thousands of workers changing shifts at the same time, it was a simple matter for thieves – either employees or walk-in intruders – to carry stolen items out.

But this time a major theft ring was obviously at work. Among items missing were more than three hundred four-speed transmissions, hundreds of tyres, as well as substantial quantities of radios, tape players, air conditioners, and other components.

As an aftermath, the plant swarmed with security staff and outside detectives. Matt, though not remotely implicated, had been obliged to spend hours answering detectives' questions about plant procedure. So far there appeared to be no break in the case, though the Chief of Security told Matt, 'We have some ideas, and there are a few of your line workers we want to interrogate when they come back.' Meanwhile the detectives remained underfoot, their presence one more irritant at an arduous time.

Despite everything, Matt had come through so far, except for a small incident concerning himself which fortunately went unnoticed by anyone important at the plant.

He had been in his office the previous Saturday afternoon, seven-day work weeks being normal during model changeover, and one of the older secretaries, Iris Einfeld, who was also working, had brought him coffee. Matt began drinking it gratefully. Suddenly, for no reason he could determine, he was unable to control the cup and it fell from his hand, the coffee spilling over his clothing and the floor.

Angry at himself for what he thought of as carelessness, Matt got up – then fell full length, heavily. Afterwards, when he thought about it, it seemed as if his left leg failed him and he remembered, too, he had been holding the coffee in his left hand.

Mrs Einfeld, who was still in Matt's office, had helped him back into his chair, then wanted to summon aid, but he dissuaded her. Instead, Matt sat for a while, and felt some of the feeling coming back into his left leg and hand, though he knew he would not be able to drive home. Eventually, with some help from Iris Einfeld, he left the office by a back stairway and she drove him home in her car. On the way he persuaded her to keep quiet about the whole thing, being afraid that if word got around he would be treated as an invalid, the last thing he wanted.

Once home, Matt managed to get to bed and stayed there until late Sunday when he felt much better, only occasionally being aware of a slight fluttering sensation in his chest. On Monday morning he was tired, but otherwise normal, and went to work.

The weekend, though, had been lonely. His daughter, Barbara, was away somewhere and Matt Zaleski had had to fend for himself. In the old days, when his wife was alive, she had always helped him over humps like model changeover time with understanding, extra affection, and meals which – no matter how long she waited for him to come home – she prepared with special care. But it seemed so long since he had known any of those things that it was hard to remember Freda had been dead less than two years. Matt realized, sadly, that when she was alive he had not appreciated her half as much as he did now.

He found himself, too, resenting Barbara's preoccupation with her own life and work. Matt would have liked nothing more than to have Barbara remain at home, available whenever he came there, and thus filling – at least in part – her mother's role. For a while after Freda's death Barbara had seemed to do that. She prepared their meal each evening, which she and Matt ate together, but gradually Barbara's outside interests revived, her work at the advertising agency increased, and nowadays they were rarely in the Royal Oak house together except to sleep, and occasionally for a hurried weekday breakfast. Months ago Barbara had urged that they seek a housekeeper, which they could well afford, but Matt resisted the idea. Now, with so much to do for himself, on top of pressures at the plant, he wished he had agreed.

He had already told Barbara, early in August, that he had changed his mind and she could go ahead and hire a housekeeper after all, to which Barbara replied that she would do so when she could, but at the moment was too busy at the agency to take time out to advertise, interview, and get a housekeeper installed. Matt had bristled at that, believing it to be a woman's business – even a daughter's – to run a home, and that a man should not have to become involved, particularly when he was under stress, as Matt was now. Barbara made it clear, however, that she regarded her own work as equally important with her father's, an attitude he could neither accept nor understand.

There was a great deal else, nowadays, that Matt Zaleski failed to understand. He had only to open a newspaper to become alternately angry and bewildered at news of traditional standards set aside, old moralities discarded, established order undermined. No-one, it seemed, respected anything any more – including constituted authority, the courts, law, parents, college presidents, the military, the free enterprise system, or the American flag, under which Matt and others of his generation fought and died in the Second World War.

As Matt Zaleski saw it, it was the young who caused the trouble, and increasingly he hated most of them: those with long hair you couldn't tell from girls (Matt still had a crewcut and wore it like a badge); student know-it-alls, choked up with book learning, spouting McLuhan, Marx, or Ché Guevara; militant blacks, demanding the millennium on the spot and not content to progress slowly; and all other protesters, rioters, contemptuous of everything in sight and beating up those who dared to disagree. The whole bunch of them, in Matt's view, were callow, immature, knowing nothing of real life, contributing nothing . . . When he thought of the young his bile and blood pressure rose together.

And Barbara, while certainly no rebellious student or protester, sympathized openly with most of what went on, which was almost as bad. For this, Matt blamed the people his daughter associated with, including Brett DeLosanto whom he continued to dislike.

In reality, Matt Zaleski – like many of his age group – was the prisoner of his long-held views. In conversations which sometimes became heated arguments, Barbara had tried to persuade him to her own conviction: that a new breadth of outlook had developed, that beliefs and ideas once held immutable had been examined and found false; that what younger people despised was not the morality of their parents' generation, but a façade of morality with duplicity behind; not old standards in themselves, but hypocrisy and self-deception which, all too often, the so-called standards shielded. In fact, it was a time of questing, of exciting intellectual experiment from which mankind could only gain.

Barbara had failed in her attempts. Matt Zaleski, lacking insight, saw the changes around him merely as negative and destroying.

In such a mood, as well as being tired and having a nagging stomach ache, Matt came home late to find Barbara and a guest already in the house. The guest was Rollie Knight.

Earlier that evening, through arrangements made for her by Leonard Wingate, Barbara had met Rollie downtown. Her purpose was to acquire more knowledge about the life and experiences of black people – Rollie in particular – both in the inner city and with the hard-core hiring programme. A spoken commentary to accompany the documentary film *Auto City*, now approaching its final edited form, would be based, in part, on what she learned.

To begin, she had taken Rollie to the Press Club, but the club had been unusually crowded and noisy; also, Rollie had not seemed at ease. So on impulse, Barbara suggested driving to her home. They did.

She had mixed a whisky and water for each of them, and then whipped up a simple meal of eggs and bacon which she served on trays in the living-room; after that, with Rollie increasingly relaxed and helpful, they talked.

Later, Barbara brought the whisky bottle in and poured them each a second drink. Outside, the dusk – climaxing clear, benevolent day – had turned to dark.

Rollie looked around him at the comfortable, tastefully furnished, though unpretentious room. He asked, 'How far we here from Blaine and 12th?'

About eight miles, she told him.

He shook his head and grinned. 'Eight hundred, more like.'

Blaine and 12th was where Rollie lived, and where film scenes had been shot the night Brett DeLosanto and Leonard Wingate watched.

Barbara had scribbled Rollie's thought in a few key words, thinking it might work well as an opening line, when her father walked in.

Matt Zaleski froze.

He looked incredulously at Barbara and Rollie Knight, seated on the same settee, drinks in their hands, a whisky bottle on the floor between them, the discarded dinner trays nearby. In her surprise, Barbara had let the pad on which she had been writing slip from her hand and out of sight.

Rollie Knight and Matt Zaleski, though never having spoken together at the assembly plant, recognized each other instantly. Matt's eyes went, unbelievingly, from Rollie's face to Barbara's. Rollie grinned and downed his drink, making a show of self-assurance, then seemed uncertain. His tongue moistened his lips.

'Hi, Dad!' Barbara said. 'This is . . . '

Matt's voice cut across her words. Glaring at Rollie, he demanded, 'What the hell are you doing in my house, sitting there . . . ?'

Of necessity, through years of managing an auto plant in which a major segment of the work force was black, Matt Zaleski had acquired a patina of racial tolerance. But it was never more than a patina. Beneath the surface he still shared the views of his Polish parents and their Wyandotte neighbours who regarded any Negro as inferior. Now, seeing his own daughter entertaining a black man in Matt's own home, an unreasoning rage possessed him, to which tension and tiredness were an added spur. He spoke and acted without thought of consequences.

'Dad,' Barbara said sharply, 'this is my friend, Mr Knight. I invited him, and don't . . . '

'Shut up!' Matt shouted as he swung towards his daughter. 'I'll deal with you later.'

The colour drained from Barbara's face. 'What do you mean – you'll *deal* with me?'

Matt ignored her. His eyes still boring into Rollie Knight, he pointed to the kitchen door through which he had just come in. 'Out!'

'Dad, don't you dare!'

Barbara was on her feet, moving swiftly towards her father. When she was within reach he slapped her hard across the face.

It was as if they were acting out a classic tragedy, and now it was Barbara who was unbelieving. She thought: *This cannot be happening.* The blow had stung and she guessed there were weal marks on her cheek, though that part was unimportant. What mattered was of the mind. It was as if a rock had been rolled aside, the rock of a century of human progression and understanding, only to reveal a festering rottenness beneath – the unreason, hatred, bigotry living in Matt Zaleski's mind. And Barbara, because she was her father's daughter, at this moment shared his guilt.

Outside, a car stopped.

Rollie, as well, was standing. An instant earlier his confidence had deserted him because he was on unfamiliar ground. Now, as it came back, he told Matt, 'Piss on you, honky!'

Matt's voice trembled. 'I said get out. Now go!'

Barbara closed her eyes. *Piss on you, honky!* Well, why not? Wasn't that how life went, returning hate for hate?

For the second time within a few minutes the house side door opened. Brett DeLosanto came in, announcing cheerfully, 'Couldn't make anybody hear.' He beamed at Barbara and Matt, then observed Rollie Knight. 'Hi, Rollie! Nice surprise to see you. How's the world, good friend?'

At Brett's easy greeting to the young black man, a flicker of doubt crossed Matt Zaleski's face.

'Piss on you too,' Rollie said to Brett. He glanced contemptuously at Barbara. And left.

Brett asked the other two, 'Now what in hell was that about?'

734

He had driven directly across town from Metropolitan Airport when his flight from California landed less than an hour ago. Brett had wanted to see Barbara, to tell her of his personal decision and plans he had begun formulating during the journey home. His spirits had been high and were the reason for his breezy entry. Now, he realized, something serious was wrong.

Barbara shook her head, unable to speak because of tears she was choking back. Brett moved across the room. Putting his arms around her, he urged gently, 'Whatever it is, let go, relax! We can talk about it, later.'

Matt said uncertainly. 'Look, maybe I was . . . '

Barbara's voice overrode him. 'I don't want to hear.'

She had control of herself, and eased away from Brett who volunteered, 'If this is a family mishmash, and you'd prefer me to leave . . . '

'I want you here,' Barbara said. 'And when you go, I'm leaving with you.' She stopped, then regarding him directly, 'You've asked me twice, Brett, to come and live with you. If you still want me to, I will.'

He answered fervently, 'You know I do.'

Matt Zaleski had dropped into a chair. His head came up. '*Live!*'

'That's right,' Barbara affirmed icily. 'We won't be married; neither of us wants to be. We'll merely share the same apartment, the same bed . . . '

'No!' Matt roared. 'By God, no!'

She warned, 'Just try to stop me!'

They faced each other briefly, then her father dropped his eyes and put his head in his hands. His shoulders shook.

'I'll pack a few things for tonight,' Barbara told Brett, 'then come back for the rest tomorrow.'

'Listen' – Brett's eyes were on the dejected figure in the chair – 'I wanted us to get together. You know it. But does it have to be this way?'

She answered crisply, 'When you know what happened, you'll understand. So take me or leave me – now, the way I am. If you won't, I'll go to a hotel.'

He flashed a quick smile. 'I'll take you.'

Barbara went upstairs.

When the two men were alone, Brett said uncomfortably, 'Mr Z., whatever it was went wrong, I'm sorry.'

There was no answer, and he went outside to wait for Barbara in his car.

For almost half an hour Brett and Barbara cruised the streets, nearby, searching for Rollie Knight. In the first few minutes after putting her suitcase in the car and driving away, Barbara explained what had occurred before Brett's arrival. As she talked, his face went grim.

After a while he said, 'Poor little bastard! No wonder he took off at me too.'

'And me.'

'I guess he figures we're all alike inside. Why wouldn't he?'

They drove down another empty street, then, near the end of it, their headlights picked up a shadowy figure, walking. It turned out to be a neighbour of the Zaleskis, going home.

'Rollie's gone.' Brett glanced across the front seat of the car inquiringly. 'We know where he lives.'

Both knew the reason behind Brett's hesitation. It could be dangerous in downtown Detroit at night. Armed holdups and assaults were commonplace.

She shook her head. 'We can't do anything more tonight. Let's go home.'

'First things first.' He pulled to the kerb and they kissed.

'Home for you,' Brett said carefully, 'is a new address – Country Club Manor, West Maple at Telegraph.'

Despite their shared depression from tonight's events, he had an excited, breathless feeling as he swung the car north-west.

Much later, lying beside each other in the darkened bedroom of Brett's apartment, Barbara said softly, 'Are your eyes open?'

'Yes.' A few minutes previously Brett had rolled over on to his back. Now, hands behind his head, he was regarding the dimness of the ceiling.

'What were you thinking?'

'About something clumsy I once said to you. Do you remember?'

'Yes, I remember.'

It had been the night Barbara had prepared dinner here and Brett had brought Leonard Wingate home – the first meeting for the three of them. Afterwards, Brett tried to persuade Barbara to stay the night with him, and when she wouldn't, had declared, '*You're twenty-nine; you can't possibly be a virgin, so what's your hangup?*'

'You didn't say anything when I said that,' Brett pointed out, 'but you were, weren't you?'

He heard her gentle, rippling laughter. 'If anyone's in a position to know . . . '

'OK, OK.' She sensed him smiling, then he turned sideways so that their faces were together once again. 'Why didn't you tell me?'

'Oh, I don't know. It isn't the sort of thing you talk about. Anyway, was it important, really?'

'It's important to me.'

There was a silence, then Barbara said, 'If you must know, it was important to me, too. You see, I always wanted the first time to be with someone I truly loved.' She reached out, her fingers moving lightly down his face. 'In the end, it was.'

Brett's arms went around her, once more their bodies pressed together as he whispered, 'I love you too.'

He had an awareness of savouring one of life's rare and precious moments. He had still not told Barbara of his own decision, made in Los Angeles, or spoken of his future plans. Brett knew that if he did, they would talk until morning, and talk was not what he wanted most tonight.

Then urgent desire, reciprocated, wiped out all other thoughts.

Afterwards, again lying quietly, contentedly, beside each other, Barbara said, 'If you like, I'll tell you something.'

'Go ahead.'

She sighed. 'If I'd known it was as wonderful as this, I wouldn't have waited so long.'

23

Erica Trenton's affair with Pierre Flodenhale had begun early in June. It started shortly after their first encounter, when the young race driver accompanied Adam Trenton home, following the weekend cottage party at Higgins Lake.

A few days after that Sunday night, Pierre telephoned Erica and suggested lunch. She accepted. They met next day at an out-of-the-way restaurant in Sterling Heights.

A week later they met again and this time, after lunch, drove to a motel where Pierre had already checked in. With a minimum of fuss, they got into bed where Pierre proved an entirely satisfactory sex partner, so that when she went home, late that afternoon, Erica felt better, physically and mentally, than she had in months.

Through the remainder of June, and well into July, they continued to meet at every opportunity, both in daytime and during evenings, the latter when Adam had told Erica in advance that he would be working late.

For Erica the occasions were blissful sexual fulfilments of which she had been deprived far too long. She also relished Pierre's youth and freshness, as well as being excited herself by his lusty pleasure in her body.

Their meetings were sharply in contrast with the single assignation she had had, months earlier, with the salesman, Ollie. When Erica thought about that experience – though she preferred not to – it was with disgust, at herself for letting it happen, even though she had been physically frustrated, to the point of desperation, at the time.

There was no desperation now. Erica had no idea how long the affair between herself and Pierre would last, though she knew it would never be more than an affair for either of them, and someday would inevitably end. But for the moment she was enjoying herself uninhibitedly and so, it seemed, was Pierre.

The enjoyment gave each of them a sense of confidence which led, in turn, to a carelessness about being seen together in public.

One of their favourite evening meeting places was in the pleasant colonial surroundings of the Dearborn Inn, where the service was friendly and good. Another attraction at the Dearborn Inn was a cottage – one of several on the grounds – a faithful replica of the one-time home of Edgar Allan Poe. Downstairs, the Poe cottage had two cosy rooms and a kitchen; upstairs, a tiny bedroom under the roof. The upstairs and downstairs portions were self-contained, and rented separately to Inn guests.

On two occasions when Adam was away from Detroit, Pierre Flodenhale occupied the lower portion of the Poe cottage, while Erica checked in upstairs. When the main outside door was locked, it was nobody's business who went up or down the inside staircase.

Erica so loved the historic little cottage, with its antique furnishings, that once she lay back in bed and exclaimed. 'What a perfect place for lovers! It ought not to be used for anything else.'

'Uh, huh,' had been all that Pierre had said, which pointed up his lack of conversation and, in fact, a general absence of interest in anything not connected with motor racing or directly involving sex. About racing, Pierre could, and did converse animatedly and at length. But other subjects bored him. Confronted with current affairs, politics, the arts –

which Erica tried to talk about sometimes – he either yawned or fidgeted like a restless boy whose attention could not be held for more than seconds at a time. Occasionally, and despite all the satisfying sex, Erica wished their relationship could be more rounded.

Around the time that the wish was developing into a mild irritation with Pierre, an item linking their names appeared in the *Detroit News*.

It was in the daily column of Society Editor Eleanor Breitmeyer, whom many considered the best society writer in North American newspaperdom. Almost nothing which went on in the Motor City's social echelons escaped Miss Breitmeyer's intelligence, and her comment read:

> Handsome, debonair race driver Pierre Flodenhale and young and beautiful Erica Trenton – wife of auto product planner Adam – continue to relish each other's company. Last Friday, lunching tête-à-tête at the Steering Wheel, neither, as usual, had as much as a glance for anyone else.

The words on the printed page were a startling jolt to Erica. Her first flustered thought as she read them was of the thousands of people in Greater Detroit – including friends of herself and Adam – who would also see and talk about the column item before the day was out. Suddenly, Erica wanted to run into a closet and hide. She realized how incredibly careless she and Pierre had been, as if they were courting exposure, but now it had happened she wished desperately they hadn't.

The *News* item appeared in late July – a week or so before the Trenton's dinner with Hank Kreisel and their visit to his Grosse Pointe home.

The evening the item was published, Adam had brought the *Detroit News* home, as he usually did, and the two of them shared it, in sections, while having martinis before dinner.

While Erica had the women's section, which included Society, Adam was leafing through the front news portion. But Adam invariably looked over the entire paper systematically, and Erica dreaded his attention turning to the section she was holding.

She decided it would be a mistake to remove any part of the newspaper from the living-room because, however casually she did it, Adam would probably notice.

Instead, Erica went to the kitchen and served dinner immediately, taking a chance that the vegetables were done. They weren't, but when Adam came to the table he still hadn't opened any of the newspaper's back sections.

After dinner, returning to the living-room, Adam opened his briefcase as usual and began work. When Erica had cleared the dining-room, she came in, collected Adam's coffee cup, straightened some magazines and picked up the pieces of newspaper, putting them together to take out.

Adam had looked up. 'Leave the paper. I haven't finished.'

She spent the remainder of the evening on a knife edge of suspense. Pretending to read a book, Erica watched covertly each move which Adam made. When at last he snapped his briefcase closed, her tension mounted until, to Erica's unbelievable relief, he went upstairs to bed, apparently forgetting the newspaper entirely. She hid the paper then, and burned it next day.

But burning a single copy would not, she knew, prevent someone else showing the item to Adam or referring to it in conversation, which amounted to the same thing. Obviously, many on Adam's staff, and others he associated with, had read or been told about the juicy piece of gossip, so for the next few days Erica lived in nervous expectation that when Adam came home he would bring the subject up.

One thing she was sure of: if Adam learned of the item in the *News*, Erica would know. Adam never dodged an issue, nor was he the kind of husband who would form a judgement without giving his wife the chance to state her case. But nothing was said, and when a week had gone by Erica started to relax. Afterwards, she suspected what happened was that everyone assumed Adam knew, and hence avoided the subject out of consideration or embarrassment. For whatever reason, she was grateful.

She was also grateful for an opportunity to assess her relationship with both men: Adam and Pierre. The result – in everything except sex and the small amount of time they spent together, Adam came out far ahead. Unfortunately – or perhaps fortunately – for Erica, sex continued to be important in her life, which was the reason she agreed to meet Pierre again a few days later, though this time cautiously and across the river in Windsor, Canada. But of all their rendezvous, this latest proved the least successful.

The fact was: Adam had the kind of mind which Erica admired. Pierre didn't. Despite Adam's obsessive work habits, he was never out of touch with the sum of life around him; he had strong opinions and a social conscience. Erica enjoyed hearing Adam talk – on subjects other than the auto industry. In contrast, when she asked Pierre for his views on a Detroit civic housing controversy, which had been headline news for weeks, Pierre had never heard of it. 'Figure all that stuff's none of my business,' was a stock reply. Nor had he ever voted. 'Wouldn't know how, and I'm not much interested.'

Erica was learning: an affair, to be successful and satisfying, needed other ingredients than merely fornication.

When she asked herself the question: who, of all the men she knew, would she soonest have an affair with, Erica came up with the revealing answer – Adam.

If *only* Adam would function as an *entire husband*.

But he rarely did.

The thought about Adam stayed foremost in her mind through several more days, carrying over to their evening at Gross Pointe with Hank Kreisel. Somehow, it seemed to Erica, the ex-Marine parts manufacturer managed to bring out all that was best in Adam, and she followed the talk about Hank Kreisel's thresher, including Adam's cogent questioning, with fascination. It was only afterwards, going home, when she remembered the other part of Adam she had once possessed – the eager lover, explorer of her body, now seemingly departed – that despair and anger overwhelmed her.

Her statement, later the same night, that she intended to divorce Adam had been real. It seemed hopeless to go on. Nor, next day, or during others following, had Erica's resolve weakened.

It was true she did nothing specific to set the machinery of divorce in motion, and did not move out of the Quarton Lake house, though she continued sleeping in the guest bedroom. Erica simply felt that she needed a chance, in limbo, to adjust.

Adam did not object – to anything. Obviously he believed that time could heal their differences, though Erica did not. Meanwhile she continued to keep house, and also agreed to meet Pierre, who had telephoned to say he would be briefly in Detroit during an absence from the racing circuit.

'Something's wrong,' Erica said. 'I know it is, so why don't you tell me?'

Pierre appeared uncertain and embarrassed. Along with his boyishness, he had a transparent manner which revealed his moods.

He said, in bed beside her, 'It's nothing, I guess.'

Erica propped herself on an elbow. The motel room was darkened because they had drawn the drapes on coming in. Even so, enough light filtered through for her to see the surroundings clearly, which were much like those of other motels they had been in – characterless, with mass-produced furniture and cheap hardware. She glanced at her watch. It was two in the afternoon, and they were in the suburb of Birmingham because Pierre had said he would not have time to drive across the river into Canada. Outside, the day was dull and the midday forecast had predicted rain.

She turned back to study Pierre whose face she could see clearly too. He flashed a smile, though with a touch of wariness, Erica thought, she noticed that his shock of blond hair was mussed, undoubtedly because she had run her hands through it during their recent love-making.

She had grown genuinely fond of Pierre. For all his lack of intellectual depth, he had proved agreeable, and sexually was every inch a man, which was what Erica had wanted after all. Even the occasional arrogance – the star syndrome she had been aware of at their first meeting – seemed to fit the masculinity.

'Don't mess about,' Erica insisted. 'Tell me whatever's on your mind.'

Pierre turned away, reaching for his trousers beside the bed and searched in their pockets for cigarettes. 'Well,' he said, not looking at her directly, 'I guess it's us.'

'What about us?'

He had a cigarette alight and blew smoke towards the ceiling. 'From now on I'll be more often at the tracks. Won't get to Detroit as much. Thought I ought to tell you.'

There was a silence between them as a coldness gripped Erica which she struggled not to show. At length she said, 'Is that all, or are you trying to tell me something else?'

Pierre looked uneasy. 'Like what?'

'I should think you'd be the one to know that.'

'It's just . . . well, we've been seeing a lot of each other. For a long time.'

'It certainly is a long time,' Erica tried to keep her voice light, knowing hostility would be a mistake. 'It's every bit of two and a half months.'

'Gee! Is that all?' His surprise seemed genuine.

'Obviously, to you it seems longer.'

Pierre managed a smile. 'It isn't like that.'

'Then just how is it?'

'Hell, Erica, all it is – we won't be seeing each other for a while.'

'For how long? A month? Six months? Even a year?'

He answered vaguely, 'Depends how things go, I guess.'

'What things?'

Pierre shrugged.

'And afterwards,' Erica persisted, 'after this indefinite time, will you call me or shall I call you?' She knew she was pushing too hard but had become impatient with his indirectness. When he didn't answer, she added, 'Is the band playing "It's Time to Say Goodbye"? Is this the brush-off? If it is, why not say so and have done with it?'

Clearly, Pierre decided to grasp the opportunity presented. 'Yes,' he said, 'I guess you could say that's the way it is.'

Erica took a deep breath. 'Thank you for finally giving me an honest answer. Now, at least, I know where I stand.'

She supposed she could scarcely complain. She had insisted on knowing and now had been told, even though, from the beginning of the conversation, Erica had sensed the intention in Pierre's mind. At this moment she had a mixture of emotions – the foremost, hurt pride because she had assumed that if either of them chose to end the affair it would be herself. But she wasn't ready to end it, and now, along with the hurt she had a sense of loss, sadness, an awareness of loneliness to come. She was realist enough to know that nothing would be gained by pleading or argument. One thing Erica had learned about Pierre was that he had all the women he needed or wanted; she knew, too, there were others whom Pierre had tired of ahead of herself. Suddenly she felt like crying at the thought of being one more, but willed herself not to. *She'd be damned* if she would feed his ego by letting him see how much she really minded.

Erica said coolly, 'Under the circumstances there doesn't seem much point in staying here.'

'Hey!' Pierre said. 'Don't be mad.' He reached under the bedclothes for her, but she evaded him and slipped from the bed, taking her clothes to the bathroom to dress. Earlier in their relationship, Pierre would have scrambled after her, seized her, and forced her playfully back to the bed, as had happened once before when they quarrelled. Now he didn't, though she had been half-hoping that he would.

Instead, when Erica came out of the bathroom, Pierre was dressed too, and only minutes later they kissed briefly, almost perfunctorily, and parted. He seemed relieved, she thought, that their leave-taking had been accomplished with so little trouble.

Pierre drove away in his car, reaching speed with a squeal of tyres as he left the motel parking lot. Erica followed more slowly in her convertible. Her last glimpse of him was as he waved and smiled.

By the time she reached the first intersection, Pierre's car was out of sight.

She drove another block and a half before realizing she had not the slightest notion where she was going. It was close to three in the afternoon and was now raining drearily, as the forecast said it would. Where to go, what to do? . . . with the rest of the day, with the rest of her life. Suddenly, like a pent-up flood released, the anguish, disappointment, bitterness, all of which she had postponed in the motel, swept over her. She had a sense of rejection and despair as her eyes filled with tears, which she let course down her cheeks unchecked. Still driving the car, mechanically, Erica continued through Birmingham, uncaring where she went.

One place she did not want to go was home to the house at Quarton Lake. It held too many memories, an excess of unfinished business, problems she had no capacity to cope with now. She drove a few more blocks, turned several corners, then realized she had come to Somerset Mall, on Troy, the shopping plaza where, almost a year ago, she had taken the perfume – her first act of shoplifting. It had been the occasion on which she had learned that a combination of intelligence, quickness, and nerve could be rewarding in diverse ways. She parked the car and walked through the rain to the indoor mall.

Inside, she wiped the rain and the tears together from her face.

Most stores within the shopping plaza were moderately busy. Erica wandered into several, glancing at Bally shoes, a display of F.A.O. Schwartz toys, the colourful miscellany of a boutique. But she was going through motions only, wanting nothing that she saw, her mood increasingly listless and depressed. In a luggage store she browsed, and was about to leave when a briefcase caught her attention. It was of English cowhide, gleaming brown. It lay on a glass-topped table at the rear of the store. Erica's eyes moved on, then inexplicably returned. She thought: there was no reason in the world why she should possess a briefcase; she had never needed one, nor was ever likely to. Besides, a briefcase was a symbol of so much that she detested – the tyranny of work brought home, the evenings Adam spent with his own briefcase opened, the countless hours which he and Erica had never shared. Yet she wanted the briefcase she had just seen, wanted it – irrationally – here and now. And intended to have it.

Perhaps, Erica thought, she would give the briefcase to Adam as a parting, splendidly sardonic gift.

But was it necessary to pay for it? She *could* pay, of course, except that it would be more challenging to take what she wanted and walk away, as she had done so skilfully the other times. Doing so would add some zest to the day. There had been little enough so far.

Pretending to examine something else, Erica surveyed the store. As on other occasions when she had shoplifted, she felt a rising excitement, a heady, delicious combination of fear and daring.

There were three salespeople, she observed – a girl and two men, one of the men older and presumably the manager. All were occupied with customers. Two or three other people in the store were, like Erica, browsing. One, a mousy grandmother-type, was examining luggage tags on a card.

By a roundabout route, pausing on the way, Erica sauntered to the display table where the briefcase lay. As if noticing it for the first time, she picked it up and turned it over for inspection. While doing so, a swift glance confirmed that the trio of salesclerks was still busy.

Continuing her inspection of the case, she opened it slightly and nudged two labels on the outside into the interior, out of view. Still casually, Erica lowered the case as if replacing it, but instead let it swing downwards below the display table level, still in her hand. She looked boldly round the store. Two of the people who had been walking around were gone; one of the salesclerks had begun attending to another customer otherwise, everything was the same.

Unhurriedly, swinging the briefcase slightly, she strolled towards the store doorway. Beyond it was the terraced indoor mall, connecting with other stores and protecting shoppers from the weather. She could see a fountain playing and hear its splash of water. Beyond the fountain, she noted, was a uniformed security guard, but he had his back towards the luggage store and was chatting with a child. Even if the guard saw Erica, once she had left the store there was no reason for him to be suspicious. She reached the doorway. No-one had stopped her, or even spoken. Really! – it was all too easy.

'Just a moment!'

The voice – sharp, uncompromising – came from immediately behind. Startled, Erica turned.

It was the mousy grandmother-type who had seemed to be engrossed with luggage tags. Except that now she was neither mousy nor grandmotherly, but with hard eyes and thin lips set in a firm line. She moved swiftly towards Erica, at the same time calling to the store manager, 'Mr Yancy! Over here!' Then Erica found her wrist gripped firmly and when she tried to free it, the grip tightened like a clamp.

Panic flooded through Erica. She protested, flustered, 'Let me go!'

'Be quiet!' the other woman ordered. She was in her forties – not nearly as old as she had dressed herself to look. 'I'm a detective and you've been caught stealing.' As the manager hurried over, she informed him. 'This woman stole that case she's holding. I stopped her as she was leaving.'

'All right,' the manager said, 'we'll go in the back.' His manner, like the woman detective's, was unemotional, as if he knew what to do and would carry a distasteful duty through. He had barely glanced at Erica so that already she felt faceless, like a criminal.

'You heard,' the woman detective said. She tugged at Erica's wrist, turning towards the rear of the store which presumably housed offices out of sight.

'No! No!' Erica set her feet firmly, refusing to move. 'You're making a mistake.'

'Your kind of people make the mistakes, sister,' the woman detective said. She asked the store manager cynically, 'Did you ever meet one who didn't say that?'

The manager looked uncomfortable. Erica had raised her voice; now heads had turned and several people in the store were watching. The manager, clearly wanting the scene removed from view, signalled urgently with his head.

It was at that moment Erica made her crucial mistake. Had she accompanied the other two as they demanded, the procedure following would almost certainly have fitted a pattern. First, she would have been interrogated – probably harshly, by the woman detective – after which, more than likely, Erica would have broken down, admitted her guilt and pleaded for leniency. During the interrogation she would have revealed that her husband was a senior auto executive.

After admitting guilt, she would have been urged to make a signed confession. She would have written this out, however reluctantly, in her own handwriting.

After that she would have been allowed to go home with – so far as Erica was concerned – the incident closed.

Erica's confession would have been sent by the store manager to an investigative bureau of the Retail Merchants Association. If a record of previous offences was on file, prosecution might have been considered. With a first offence – which, officially Erica's was – no action would be taken.

Suburban Detroit stores, especially those near well-to-do areas like Birmingham and Bloomfield Hills, were unhappily familiar with women shoplifters who stole without need. It was not the store operators' business to be psychologists as well as retailers; nonetheless, most knew the reasons behind such stealing included sexual frustrations, loneliness, a need for attention – all of them conditions to which auto executives' wives were exceptionally vulnerable. Something else the stores knew was that prosecution, and publicity which the court appearance of an auto industry big name would bring, could harm their business more than aid them. Auto people were clannish, and a store which persecuted one of their number could easily suffer a general boycott.

Consequently, retail businesses used other methods. Where an offender was observed and known, she was billed for the items taken, and usually such bills were paid without question. At other times, when identity was established, a bill followed in the same way; also, the scare of being detained, plus hostile questioning, were often enough to deter further shoplifting for a life-time. But whichever method was used, the Detroit stores' objective, overall, was quietness and discretion.

Erica, panicky and desperate, left none of the quieter compromises open. Instead, she jerked her wrist free from the woman detective and – still clutching the stolen briefcase – turned and ran.

She ran from the luggage store into the mall, heading for the main outer door by which she had come in. The woman detective and the manager, taken by surprise, did nothing for a second or so. The woman recovered first. She sped after Erica, shouting, 'Stop her! Stop that woman! She's a thief!'

The uniformed security guard in the mall, who had been chatting with a child, swung around at the shouts. The woman detective saw him. She commanded, 'Catch that woman! The one running! Arrest her! She stole that case she's carrying.'

Moving quickly, the guard ran after Erica as shoppers in the mall stood gaping, craning for a view. Others, hearing the shouting, hurried out of stores. But none attempted to stop Erica as she continued running, her heels tap-tap-tapping on the terrazzo floor. She went on, heading towards the outer door, the security guard still pounding behind.

To Erica, the ghastly shouts, people staring as she passed, the pursuing feet, now drawing closer, all were a nightmare. Was this really happening? It couldn't be! In a moment she must wake. But instead of waking, she reached the heavy outer door. Though she pushed hard, it opened with maddening slowness. Then she was outside, in the rain, her car on the parking lot only yards away.

Her heart was pounding, breath coming hard from the exertion of running and from fear. She remembered that fortunately she hadn't locked the car. Tucking the purloined briefcase under her arm, Erica fumbled open her handbag, scrabbling inside for car keys. A stream of objects fell from the handbag; she ignored them but located the keys. She had the ignition key ready as she reached the car, but could see that the security guard, a youngish, sturdily built man, was only yards away. The woman detective was following behind, but the guard was closest. Erica realized – she wouldn't make it! Not get inside the car, start the engine and pull away before he reached her. Terrified, realizing the consequences would be even greater now, despair engulfed her.

At that moment the security guard slipped on the rain-wet parking lot surface and fell. He went down fully, and lay a moment dazed and hurt before he scrambled up.

The guard's misfortune gave Erica the time she needed. Slipping into the car, she started the engine, which fired instantly, and drove away. But even as she left the shoppers' parking lot a new anxiety possessed her: had her pursuers read the car licence number?

They had. As well, they had the car's description – a current model convertible, candy apple red, distinctive as a blossom in winter.

And as if that were not enough, among the items spilled from Erica's handbag and left behind, was a billfold with credit cards and other identification. The woman detective was collecting the fallen items while the security guard, his uniform wet and soiled, and with a painfully sprained ankle, limped to a telephone to call the local police.

It was all so ridiculously easy that the two policemen were grinning as they escorted Erica from her car to theirs. Minutes earlier the police cruiser had pulled alongside the convertible and without fuss, not using flashing lights or siren, one of the policemen had waved her to stop, which she did immediately, knowing that anything else would be insane, just as attempting to run away to begin with had been madly foolish.

The policemen, both young, had been firm but also quiet and polite so that Erica felt less intimidated than by the antagonistic woman detective in the store. In any case, she was now totally resigned to whatever was going to happen. She knew she had brought disaster on herself, and whatever other disasters followed would happen anyway because it was too late to change anything, whatever she said or did.

'Our orders are to take you in, ma'am,' one of the policemen said. 'My partner will drive your car.'

Erica gasped, 'All right.' She went to the rear of the cruiser where the policeman had the door open for her to enter, then shrank back when she realized the interior was barred and she would be locked inside as if in a cell.

The policeman saw her hesitate. 'Regulations,' he explained. 'I'd let you ride up front if I could, but if I did they'd likely put *me* in the back.'

Erica managed a smile. Obviously the two officers had decided she was not a major criminal.

The same policeman asked, 'Ever been arrested before?'

She shook her head.

'Didn't think you had. Nothing to it after the first few times. That is, for people who don't make trouble.'

She entered the cruiser, the door slammed, and she was locked in.

At the suburban police station she had an impression of polished wood, and tile floors, but otherwise was only dully aware of her surroundings. She was cautioned, then questioned about what happened at the store. Erica answered truthfully, knowing the time for evasion was past. She was confronted by the woman detective and the security guard, both hostile, even when Erica confirmed their version of events. She identified the briefcase she had stolen, at the same time wondering why she had ever wanted it. Later, she signed a statement, then was asked if she wished to make a telephone call. To a lawyer? To her husband? She answered no.

After that she was taken to a small room with a barred window at the rear of the police station, locked in, and left alone.

The chief of the suburban police force, Wilbur Arenson, was not a man who hurried needlessly. Many times during his career, Chief Arenson had found that slowness, when it could be managed, paid off later, and thus he had taken his time while reading several reports concerning an alleged shoplifting which occurred earlier in the afternoon, followed by a suspect's attempted flight, a police radio alert and, later, an interception and detention. The detailed suspect, one Erica Marguerite Trenton, age twenty-five, a married woman living at Quarton Lake, had been cooperative, and further had signed a statement admitting the offence.

Under normal procedure the case would have gone ahead routinely, with the suspect charged, a subsequent court appearance and most likely, a conviction. But not everything in a Detroit suburban police station proceeded according to routine.

It was not routine for the chief to review details of a minor criminal case, yet certain cases – at subordinates' discretion – four their way to his desk.

Trenton. The name stirred a chord of memory. The chief was not sure how or when he had heard the name before, but knew his mind would churn out the answer if he didn't rush it. Meanwhile, he continued reading.

Another departure from routine was that the station desk sergeant, familiar with the ways and preferences of his chief, had not so far booked the suspect. Thus no blotter listing yet existed, with a name and charge listed, for Press reporters to peruse.

Several things about the case interested the chief. First, a need of money obviously was not a motive. A billfold, dropped on the shopping plaza parking lot by the fleeing suspect, contained more than a hundred dollars cash as well as American Express and Diners cards, plus credit cards from local stores. A chequebook in the suspect's handbag showed a substantial balance in the account.

Chief Arenson knew all about well-heeled women shoplifters and their supposed motivations, so the money aspect did not surprise him. More interesting was the suspect's unwillingness to give information about her husband or to telephone him when allowed the opportunity.

Not that it made any difference. The interrogating officer had routinely checked out ownership of the car she was driving, which proved to be registered to one of the Big Three auto manufacturers, and a further check with that company's security office revealed it was an official company car, one of two allocated to Mr Adam Trenton.

The company security man had let that item of information about two cars slip out, though he hadn't been asked, and the police officer phoning the inquiry had noted it in his report. Now, Chief Arenson, a stockily built, balding man in his late fifties, sat at his desk and considered the notation.

As the police chief well knew, plenty of auto executives drove company cars. But only a senior executive would have *two* company cars – one for himself, another for his wife.

Thus it required no great deductive powers to conclude that the suspect, Erica Marguerite Trenton, now locked in a small interrogation room instead of a cell – another intuitive move by the desk sergeant – was married to a reasonably important man.

What the chief needed to know was: how important? And how much influence did Mrs Trenton's husband have?

The fact that the chief would take time to consider such questions at all was a reason why suburban Detroit communities insisted on maintaining their own local police forces. Periodically, proposals appeared for a merger of the score or more of separate police forces of Greater Detroit into a single metropolitan force. Such an arrangement, it was argued, would ensure better policing by eliminating duplication, and would also be less costly. The metropolitan system, its advocates pointed out, worked successfully elsewhere.

But the suburbs – Birmingham, Bloomfield Hills, Troy, Dearborn, the Grosse Pointes and others – were always soldidly opposed. As a result, and because residents of those communities had influence where it counted, the proposal always failed.

The existing system of small, independent forces might not be the best means of providing equal justice for all, but it did give local citizens whose names were known a better break when they, their families or friends transgressed the law.

Presto! – the chief remembered where he had heard the name Trenton before. Six or seven months ago, Chief Arenson had bought a car for his wife from the auto dealer, Smokey Stephensen. During the chief's visit to the dealer's showroom – a Saturday, he recalled – Smokey had introduced him to an Adam Trenton from the auto company's head office. Afterwards, and privately, while Smokey and the chief made their deal about the car, Smokey mentioned Trenton again, predicting that he was going higher in the company, and one day would be its president.

Reflecting on the incident, and its implications at this moment, Chief Arenson was glad he had dawdled. Now, not only was he aware that the woman being detained was someone of consequence, but he had the further knowledge of where to get extra information which might be helpful in the case.

Using an outside line on his desk, the chief telephoned Smokey Stephensen.

24

Sir Perceval McDowall Stuyvesant, Bart, and Adam Trenton had known each other and been friends for more than twenty years. It was a loose friendship. Sometimes two years or more slipped by without their meeting, or even communicating, but whenever they were in the same town, which happened occasionally, they got together and picked up the old relationship easily, as if it had never been set down.

A reason, perhaps, for the lasting friendship was their dissimilarity. Adam, while imaginative, was primarily a master of organization, a pragmatist who got things done. Sir Perceval, imaginative too and with a growing reputation as a brilliant scientist, was extensively a dreamer who had trouble mastering each day's practicalities – the kind of man who might invent a zipper but subsequently forget to zip up his own fly.

Their backgrounds were equally at variance. Sir Perceval was the last of a line of English squires, his father dead and the inherited title genuine. Adam's father had been a Buffalo, New York, steelworker.

The two met in college – at Purdue University. They were the same age and graduated together, Adam in Engineering; Perceval, whom his friends called Perce, in Physics. Afterwards, Perce spent several more years gathering scientific degrees as casually as a child gathers daisies, then worked for a while for the same auto company as Adam. This had been in Scientific Research – the 'think tank' – where Perce left his mark by discovering new applications for electron microscopes.

During that period they spent more time together than at any other – it had been before Adam's marriage to Erica, and Perce was a bachelor – and they found each other's company increasingly agreeable.

For a while, Adam became mildly interested in Perce's hobby of manufacturing pseudo-antique violins – into each of which, with peculiar humour, he pasted a Stradivari label – but rejected Perce's suggestion that they learn Russian together. Perce set out on that project alone, solely because someone had given him a subscription to a Soviet magazine, and in less than a year could read Russian with ease.

Sir Perceval Stuyvesant had a lean, spindle-shanked appearance and, to Adam, always looked the same: mournful, which he wasn't, and perpetually abstracted, which he was. He also had an easygoing nature which nothing disturbed, and when concentrating on something scientific was oblivious to everything around him, including seven young and noisy children. This brood had appeared at the rate of one a year since Perce's marriage which took place soon after he left the auto industry. He had wed a pleasant, sexy scatterbrain, now Lady Stuyvesant, and for the past few years the expanding family had lived near San Francisco in a happy madhouse of a home.

It was from San Francisco that Perce had flown to Detroit specifically to see Adam. They met in Adam's office in late afternoon of a day in August.

When Perce had telephoned the previous day to say that he was coming, Adam urged him not to go to a hotel, but to come home to stay at Quarton Lake. Erica liked Perce. Adam hoped that an old friend's arrival would ease some of the tension and uncertainly still persisting between himself and Erica.

But Perce had declined. 'Best if I don't, old boy. If I meet Erica this trip, she'll be curious to know why I'm there, and you'll likely want to tell her yourself in your own way.'

Adam had asked. 'Why *are* you coming?'

'Maybe I want a job.'

But Sir Perceval hadn't wanted a job. As it turned out, he had come to offer one to Adam.'

A West Coast company, involved with advanced electrical and radar technology, required an executive head. Perce, one of the company's founders, was currently its scientific vice-president, and his approach to Adam was on behalf of himself and associates.

He announced, 'President is what we'd make you, old boy. You'd start at the top.'

Adam said dryly, 'That's what Henry Ford told Bunkie Knudsen.'

'This could work out better. One reason – you'd be in a strong stock position.' Perce gave the slightest of frowns as he regarded Adam. 'I'll ask you a favour while I'm here. That's take me seriously.'

'I always have.' That was one of the things about their relationship, Adam thought – based on respect for each other's abilities, and with good reason. Adam had is own solid achievements in the auto industry and Perce, despite vagueness at times and his absent-mindedness about everyday matters, turned everything he touched in scientific fields into notable success. Even before today's encounter, Adam had heard reports about Perce's West Coat company which had gained a solid reputation for advanced research and development, electronically oriented, in a short time.

'We're a small company,' Perce said, 'but growing fast, and that's our problem.'

He went on, explaining that a group of scientific people like himself had banded together in formation of the company, their objective to convert new, advanced knowledge with which the sciences abounded, into practical inventions and technology. A special concern was freshly emerging energy sources and power transmissions. Not only would developments envisaged bring aid to beleaguered cities and industry, they would also augment the world's food supply by massive, powered irrigation. Already the group had scored successes in several fields so that the company was, as Perce expressed it, 'earning bread and butter and some jam.' Much more was expected.

'A good deal of our work is focusing on superconductors,' Perce reported. He asked Adam, 'Know much about that?'

'A little, not much.'

'If there's a major break-through – and some of us believe it can happen – it'll be the most revolutionary power and metallurgical development in a generation. I'll tell you more of that later. It could be our biggest thing.'

At the moment, Perce declared, what the company needed was a top-flight businessman to run it. 'We're scientists, old boy. If I may say so, we've as many science geniuses as you'll find under one umbrella in this country. But we're having to do things we don't want to and are not equipped for – organization, management, budgets, financing, the rest. What *we* want is to stay in our labs, experiment, and *think*.'

But the group didn't want just any businessman, Perce declared. 'We can get accountants by the gross and management consultants in a dump truck. What we need is one oustanding individual – someone with imagination who understands and respects research, can utilize technology, channel invention, establish priorities, run the front office while we take care of the back, and still be a decent human being. In short, old boy, we need *you*.'

It was impossible not to be pleased. Being offered a job by an outside company was no new experience for Adam, any more than it was to most auto executives. But the offer from Perce, because of who and what he was, was something different.

Adam asked, 'How do your other people feel?'

'They've learned to trust my judgement. I may tell you that in considering candidates we made a short list. Very short. Yours was the only name on it.'

Adam said, and meant it, 'I'm touched.'

Sir Perceval Stuyvesant permitted himself one of his rare, slow smiles. 'You might even be touched in other ways. When you wish, we can talk salary, bonus, stock position, options.'

Adam shook his head. 'Not yet, if at all. The thing is, I've never seriously considered leaving the auto business. Cars have been my life. They still are.'

Even now, to Adam, this entire exchange was mere dialectics. Greatly as he respected Perce and strong as their friendship was, for Adam to quit the auto industry voluntarily was inconceivable.

The two were in facing chairs. Perce shifted in his. He had a way of winding and unwinding while seated which made his long, lean figure seem sinuous. Each movement, too, signalled a switch in conversation.

'Ever wonder,' Perce said, 'what they'll put on your tombstone?'

'I'm not at all sure I'll have one.'

Perce waved a hand. 'I speak metaphorically, old boy. We'll all get a tombstone, whether in stone or air. It'll have on it what we did with the time we had, what we've left behind us. Ever thought of yours?'

'I suppose so,' Adam said. 'I guess we all do a little.'

Perce put his fingertips together and regarded them. 'Several things they could say about you, I suppose. For example, "He was an auto company vice-president" or even maybe "president" – that's if your luck holds and you beat out all the other stong contenders. You'd be in good company, of course, even though a *lot* of company. So *many* auto presidents and vice-presidents, old boy. Bit like the population of India.'

'If you're making a point,' Adam said, 'why not get to it?'

'A splendid suggestion, old boy.'

Sometimes, Adam thought, Perce overdid the studied Anglicisms. They had to be studied because, British baronet or not, Perce had lived in the US for a quarter-century and, with the exception of speech, all his tastes and habits were American. But perhaps it showed that everyone had human weaknesses.

Now Perce leaned forward, eyeing Adam earnestly. 'You know what that tombstone of yours might say: "He did something new, different, worthwhile. He was a leader when they carved new pathways, broke fresh gorund. That which he left behind him was important and enduring." '

Perce fell back in his chair as if the amount of talk – unusual in his case – and emotional effort had exhausted him.

Amid the silence which followed, Adam felt more moved than at any other point since the conversation began. In his mind he acknowledged the truth of what Perce had said, and wondered, too, how long the Orion would be remembered after its time and usefulness were ended. Farstar also. Both seemed important now, dominating the lives of many, including his own. But how important would they seem in times to come?

The office suite was quiet. It was late afternoon, and here as elsewhere within the staff building, pressures of the day were easing, secretaries and others beginning to go home. From where Adam sat, glancing outside he could see the freeway traffic, its volume growing as the exodus from plants and offices began.

He had chosen this time of day because Perce had asked particularly that they have at least an hour in which they would be undisturbed.

'Tell me some more,' Adam said, 'about superconductors – the break-through you were speaking of.'

Perce said quietly, 'They represent the means to enormous new energy, a chance to clean up our environment, and to create more abundance than this earth has ever known.'

Across the office, on Adam's desk, a telephone buzzed peremptorily.

Adam glanced towards it with annoyance. Before Perce's arrival he had given Ursula, his secretary, instructions not to disturb them. Perce seemed unhappy about the interruption, too.

But Ursula, Adam knew, would not disregard instructions without good reason. Excusing himself, he crossed the room, sat at his desk and lifted the phone.

'I wouldn't have called you,' his secretary's low pitched voice announced, 'except Mr Stephensen said he has to speak to you, it's extremely urgent.'

'Smokey Stephensen?'

'Yes, sir.'

Adam said irritably, 'Get a number where he'll be later this evening. If I can, I'll call him. But I can't talk now.'

He sensed Ursula's uncertainty. 'Mr Trenton, that's exactly what I said. But he's most insistent. He says when you know what it's about, you won't mind him interrupting.'

'Damn!' Adam glanced apologetically at Perce, then asked Ursula, 'He's on the line now?'

'Yes.'

'Very well, put him on.'

Cupping a hand over the telephone, Adam promised, 'This will take one minute, no more.' The trouble with people like Smokey Stephensen, he thought, was that they always considered their own affairs to have overriding importance.

A click. The auto dealer's voice. 'Adam, that you?'

'Yes, it is.' Adam made no attempt to conceal his displeasure. 'I understand my secretary has already told you I'm busy. Whatever it is will have to wait.'

'Shall I tell that to your wife?'

He answered peevishly. 'What's that supposed to mean?'

'It means, Mr Big Executive too busy to take a phone call from a friend, your wife has been arrested. And not on a traffic charge, in case your wondering. For stealing.'

Adam stopped, in shocked silence, as Smokey went on. 'If you want to help her, and help yourself, right now get free from whatever you're involved in and come to where I'm waiting. Listen carefully. I'll tell you where to go.'

Dazedly, Adam wrote down the directions Smokey gave him.

'We need a lawyer,' Adam said. 'I know several. I'm going to phone one, get him over here.'

He was with Smokey Stephensen, in Smokey's car, on the parking lot of the suburban police station. Adam had not yet been inside. Smokey had persuaded him to remain in the car while he recited the facts concerning Erica, which he had learned on the telephone from Chief Arenson, and during a visit to the chief's office before Adam's arrival. As Adam listened he had grown increasingly tense, his frown of worry deepening.

'Sure, sure,' Smokey said. 'Go phone a lawyer. While you're about it, why not call the *News, Free Press* and *Birmingham Eccentric*? They might even send photographers.'

'What does it matter? Obviously, the police have made a stupid mistake.'

'They ain't made a mistake.'

'My wife would never . . . '

Smokey cut in exasperatedly, 'Your wife *did*. Will you get that through your head? And not only did, she's signed a confession.'

'I can't believe it.'

'You'd better. Chief Arenson told me, he wouldn't lie. Besides, the police aren't fools.'

'No,' Adam said, 'I know they're not.' He took in a deep breath and expelled it slowly, forcing himself to think carefully – for the first time since hastily breaking off the meeting with Perceval Stuyvesant half an hour ago. Perce had been understanding, realizing that something serious had occurred, even though Adam hadn't gone into detail about the sudden phone call. They had arranged that Adam would call Perce at his hotel, either later tonight or tomorrow morning.

Now, beside Adam, Smokey Stephensen waited, puffing on a cigar, so the car reeked of smoke despite its air conditioning. Outside, the rain continued drearily, as it had since afternoon. Dusk was settling in. On vehicles and in buildings lights were coming on.

'All right,' Adam said, 'if Erica did what they say, there has to be something else behind it.'

Out of habit, the auto dealer rubbed a hand over his beard. His greeting to Adam on arrival had been neither friendly nor hostile, and his voice was noncommittal now. 'Whatever that is, I guess it's between you and your wife. The same goes for what's right or wrong; neither one's any business of mine. What we're talking about is the way things are.'

A police cruiser pulled in close to where they were parked. Two uniformed officers got out, escorting a third man between them. The policemen took a hard look at Smokey Stephensen's car and its two occupants; the third man, whom Adam now saw was handcuffed, kept his eyes averted. While Smokey and Adam watched, the trio went inside.

It was an uncomfortable reminder of the kind of business transacted here.

'The way things are,' Adam said, 'Erica's inside there – or so you tell me – and needs help. I can either barge in myself, start throwing weight around and maybe make mistakes, or I can do the sensible thing and get a lawyer.'

'Sensible or not,' Smokey growled, 'you'll likely start something you can't stop, and afterwards wish you'd done it some other way.'

'What other way.'

'Like letting me go in there to begin. To represent you. Like my talking to the chief again. Like seeing what I can work out.'

Wondering why he had not asked before, Adam queried, 'Why did the police call *you*?'

'The chief knows me,' Smokey said. 'We're friends. He knows I know you.' He forbore to tell Adam what he had already learned – that chances were good the store where the shoplifting had occurred would settle for payment of what had been taken and would not press charges; also, that Chief Arenson was aware the case might be sensitive locally, and therefore a favourable disposition might be arranged, depending on the cooperation and discretion of all concerned.

'I'm out of my depth,' Adam said. 'If you think you can do something, go ahead. Do you want me to come with you?'

Smokey sat still. His hands were on the car's steering wheel, his face expressionless.

'Well,' Adam said, 'can you do something or not?'

'Yes,' Smokey acknowledged, 'I guess I could.'

'Then what are we waiting for?'

'The price,' Smokey said softly. 'There's a price for everything, Adam. You, of all people, should know that.'

'If we're discussing bribery . . . '

'Don't even *mention* bribery! Here or in there.' Smokey gestured towards the police headquarters. 'And remember this: Wilbur Arenson's a reasonable guy. But if you offered him *anything*, he'd throw the book at your wife. You, too.'

'I don't intend to.' Adam looked puzzled. 'If it isn't that, then what.'

'*You son-of-a-bitch!*' Smokey shouted the words; his hands, gripping the steering wheel, were white. 'You're putting me out of business, remember? Or is it so unimportant you've forgotten? One month, you said. One month before your sister puts her stock in my business on the block. A month before you turn that sneak's notebook of yours over to your company brass.'

Adam said stiffly, 'We have an agreement. It has nothing to do with this.'

'You're damn right it has to do with this! If you want your wife out of this mess without her name, and yours, smeared all over Michigan you'd best do some fast rethinking.'

'It might be better if you explained what kind.'

'I'm offering a deal, 'Smokey said. 'If it needs explaining, you're not half as smart as I think.'

Adam allowed the contempt he felt to express itself in his voice. 'I suppose I get the picture. Let me see if I have it right. You are prepared to be an intermediary, using your friendship with the chief of police to try to free my wife and have any charges dropped. In return, I'm supposed to tell my sister not to dispose of her investment in your business and then ignore what I know about dishonesty in the way you run it.'

Smokey growled, 'You're pretty free with that word dishonesty. Maybe you should remember you got some in the family.'

Adam ignored the remark. 'Do I, or do I not, have the proposition right?'

'You're smart after all. You got it right.'

'Then the answer's no. Under no circumstances would I change the advice I intend to give my sister. I'd be using her interests to help myself.'

Smokey said quickly, 'That means, then, you might consider the part about the company.'

'I didn't say that.'

'You didn't *not* say it either.'

Adam was silent. Within the car the only sounds were a purr from the idling motor and the air-conditioning hum.

Smokey said, 'I'll take the half of the deal. Never mind Teresa. I'll settle for you not snitching in the company.' He paused, then expanded, 'I'll not even ask for that black notebook of yours. Just that you don't use it.'

Still Adam failed to answer.

'You might say,' Smokey said, 'you're choosing between the company and your wife. Be interesting to see who you put first.'

Bitterly, Adam answered, 'You know I've no choice.'

He was aware that Smokey had tricked him, as had happened the day of their clash in the dealership when Smokey demanded twice as much as expected, then settled for what he had wanted to begin with. It was a hoary dealer's gambit, then as now.

But this time, Adam reminded himself, Erica had had to be thought of. There was no other way.

Or was there? Even at this moment he was tempted to dispense with Smokey's help, to go to the police alone, learn what he could of what still seemed an unreal situation, then discover what, if anything, could be arranged. But it was a risk. The fact was: Smokey *did* know Chief Arenson, and equally obvious was that Smokey knew his way around this kind of situation, which Adam did not. When Adam had said a few minutes ago, '*I'm out of my depth,*' it was true.

But he knew he had acted against his own moral scruples and had compromised with conscience, whether for Erica's sake or not. He suspected, gloomily it would not be the last time, and that personally, as well as in his work, he would make larger compromises as time went on.

Smokey, for his part, was concealing a bubbling cheerfulness within. On the day, only a short time ago, when Adam had threatened to expose him and Smokey won a month's reprieve, he had been convinced something would turn up. He had remained convinced. Now, it seemed, he had been right.

'Adam,' Smokey said. He stubbed out his cigar, trying hard not to laugh. 'Let's go get your missus out of the pokey.'

Formalities were honoured, the rituals observed.

In Adam's presence, Chief Arenson lectured Erica sternly. 'Mrs Trenton, if *ever* this happens again, the full force of the law will be applied. Do you clearly understand that?'

Erica's lips formed a barely audible, 'Yes.'

She and Adam were in separate chairs, facing the chief who was behind his office desk. Despite the sternness, Chief Arenson appeared more like a banker than a policeman. Being seated emphasized his shortness; an overhead light beamed on his balding head.

No-one else was in the room. Smokey Stephensen, who had arranged this meeting and its outcome, was waiting in the corridor outside.

Adam had been here with the chief when Erica was brought in, escorted by a policewoman.

Adam went towards Erica, his arms outstretched. She seemed surprised to see him. 'I didn't tell them to call you, Adam. I didn't want you involved.' Her voice was strained and nervous.

He said, as he held her. 'That's what a husband's for, isn't it?'

At a nod from the chief, the policewoman left. After a moment, at the chief's suggestion, they all sat down.

'Mr Trenton, in case you should have the idea there has been any misunderstanding in this matter, I believe you should read this.' Chief Arenson passed a paper across his desk to Adam. It was a photocopy of Erica's signed statement in which she admitted guilt.

The chief waited while Adam read it, then asked Erica, 'In your husband's presence, Mrs Trenton, I now ask you: were you offered any inducement to make that statement, or was any force or coercion of any kind employed?'

Erica shook her head.

'You are saying, then, that the statement was entirely voluntary?'

'Yes,' Erica avoided Adam's eyes.

'Do you have any complaint, either about your treatment here or concerning the officers who arrested you?'

Again, Erica shook her head.

'Aloud, please. I want your husband to hear.'

'No,' Erica said. 'No, I don't have any complaint.'

'Mrs Trenton,' the chief said. 'I'd like to ask you one other question. You don't have to answer, but it would be helpful to me if you did, and perhaps to your husband, too. I also promise that whatever the answer, nothing will happen as a result of it.'

Erica waited.

'Have you ever stolen before, Mrs Trenton? I mean recently, in the same kind of circumstances as today.'

Erica hesitated. Then she said softly, 'Yes.'

'How many times?'

Adam pointed out, 'You said one question and she answered it.'

Chief Arenson sighed. 'All right. Let it go.'

Adam was aware of Erica glancing his way gratefully, then wondered if he had been wrong to intercede. Perhaps it might have been better if everything came out, since the chief had already promised immunity. Then Adam thought: the place for any more revelations was in private, between himself and Erica.

If Erica chose to tell him. There seemed no certainty she would.

Even now, Adam had no idea how they were going to handle this when he and Erica got home. How *did* you handle the fact that your wife was a thief?

He had a sudden flash of anger: *How could Erica do this to him?*

It was then that Chief Arenson delivered his stern lecture to Erica, which she acknowledged.

The chief continued: 'In this single special instance, because of your husband's standing in the community and the unfortunate effect which a prosecution would have on both of you, the store concerned has been persuaded not to press charges and I have decided to take no further action.'

Adam said, 'We know it was your initiative, Chief, and we're grateful.'

Chief Arenson inclined his head in acknowledgement. 'There are advantages sometimes, Mr Trenton, in having a local suburban police force instead of a big metropolitan one. I can tell you that if this had occurred downtown, with the city police involved, the outcome would have been very different.'

'If ever the question comes up, my wife and I will be among the strongest advocates of keeping a local force.'

The chief made no acknowledgement. Politicking, he thought, should not become too obvious, even though it was good to have gained two more supporters of local autonomy. One day, if this man Trenton was going as high as predicted, he might prove a strong ally. The chief liked being a chief. He intended to do all he could to remain one until retirement, not become a precinct captain – as would happen under a metro force – taking orders from downtown.

He nodded, but did not stand – no sense in overdoing things – as the Trentons went out.

Smokey Stephensen was no longer in the corridor, but waiting in his car outside. He got out as Adam and Erica emerged from police headquarters. It was now dark. The rain had stopped.

While Adam waited as Smokey approached, Erica went on alone to where Adam's car was parked. They had arranged to leave Erica's convertible in the police garage overnight and pick it up tomorrow.

'We owe you some thanks,' Adam told Smokey. 'My wife doesn't feel up to it now, but she'll tell you herself later.' It required an effort to be polite because Adam still resented bitterly the auto dealer's blackmailing tactics. Reason told him, however, that without Smokey on hand he might have fared worse.

Then Adam remembered his anger at Erica inside. Something else she had done, he realized, had been to put him at the mercy of Smokey Stephensen.

Smokey grinned and removed his cigar. 'No need for thanks. So long as you keep your side of the bargain.'

'It will be kept.'

'Just one thing, and maybe you'll tell me it's none of my business, but don't be too hard on your wife.'

'You're right,' Adam said, 'It is none of your business.'

The auto dealer went on unperturbed, 'People do funny things for funny reasons. Worth a second look sometimes to find out what the reasons really were.'

'If I ever need some amateur psychology, I'll call you.' Adam turned away. 'Goodnight.'

Thoughtfully, Smokey watched him go.

They had driven half the way to Quarton Lake.

'You haven't said anything,' Erica said. 'Aren't you going to?' She was looking straight ahead, and though her voice sounded tired, it had an edge of defiance.

'I can say what I have to in just one word: Why?' While driving, Adam had been struggling to control his indignation and temper. Now, both erupted. *In God's name! Why?*

'I've been asking myself that.'

'Well, ask again and see if you can get some kind of sane answer. I'll be damned if I can.'

'You don't have to shout.'

'*You* don't have to steal.'

'If we're only going to fight,' Erica said, 'we won't accomplish much.'

'All I'm trying to accomplish is the answer to a simple question.'

755

'The question being: why?'

'Exactly.'

'If you must know,' Erica said, 'I rather enjoyed doing it. I suppose that shocks you.'

'Yes, it shocks me like hell.'

She went on, musing aloud, as if explaining to herself. 'Of coure, I didn't want to get caught, but there was a thrill in knowing I might be. It made everything exciting and somehow sharper. In a way it was like the feeling you get when you've had one drink too many. Of course, when I *was* caught, it was awful. Much worse than anything I imagined.'

'Well,' Adam said, 'at least we're making a start.'

'If you don't mind, that's all I want to make tonight. I realize you have a lot of questions, and I guess you're entitled to ask them. But could we leave the rest until tomorrow?'

Adam glanced sideways. He saw that Erica had put her head back and her eyes were closed. She looked young and vulnerable and weary. He answered, 'OK.'

She said, so softly that he had to strain to hear, 'And thank you for coming. It's true what I said – I wasn't going to send for you, but I was glad when you were there.'

He reached out and let his hand cover hers. 'You said something' – Erica till spoke dreamily, as if from a distance – 'about making a start. If only we could make a whole new start!'

'In what way?'

'In every way.' She sighed. 'I know we can't.'

On impulse, Adam said, 'Perhaps we can.'

It was strange, he thought, that today of all days Perceval Stuyvesant could have suggested one.

Sir Perceval and Adam were breakfasting together at the Hilton Hotel downtown, where Perce was staying.

Adam had not talked with Erica since their return home last night. She had gone exhausted to bed, fallen asleep immediately and was still sleeping soundly when he left the house early to drive into the city. He had considered waking her, decided against it, then halfway to the breakfast appointment wished he had. He would have gone back, except that Perce had a mid-morning flight to New York – the reason they made the arrangement by telephone last night; also, suddenly, Perce's proposition seemed more relevant and important than it had the day before.

One thing Adam had noticed last night was that while Erica went to sleep alone in the guest bedroom, as she had for the past months, she left the door open, and it was still open when he tiptoed in this morning.

He decided now: he would telephone home in another hour. Then, if Erica wanted to talk, he would arrange his office schedule and go home for part of the morning.

Over their meal, Perce made no reference to the interruption in their talk the previous day; nor did Adam. Briefly Perce inquired about Adam's sons, Greg and Kirk, then they talked about superconductors – the area in which the small scientific company, now offering its presidency to Adam, was hopeful of a break-through.

'One extraordinary thing about superconductors, old boy, is that the public and the Press know so little of them.' Perce sipped his brew of mixed Ceylon and India teas which he carried with him in canisters and had prepared specially wherever he happened to be.

'As you probably know, Adam, a superconductor is a metal or wire which will carry a full load of electriciy without any loss whatever.'

Adam nodded. Like any eighth-grade physics student, he was aware that all present wires and cables caused at least a fifteen per cent loss of power, called resistance.

'So a working superconductor with nil resistance,' Perceval said, 'would revolutionize the entire world's electric power systems. Among other things it would eliminate complex, expensive transmission equipment and provide fantastic amounts of power at unbelievably low cost. What has held back development until now has been the fact that superconductors would only function at very low temperatures – about 450 degrees below zero Fahrenheit.'

Adam said, 'That's pretty darned cold.'

'Quite so. Which is why, in recent years, a scientific dream has been of a superconductor which will function at room temperature.'

'Is it likely to be more than a dream?'

Perce thought before answering. 'We're known each other a good many years, old boy. Have you ever known me to exaggerate?'

'No,' Adam said. 'Very much the reverse. You've always been conservative.'

'I still am.' Perce smiled and drank more tea, then went on. 'Our group has not found a room temperature superconductor, but certain phenomena – the result of experiments we've made – have us excited. We wonder, some days, if we may not be very close.'

'And if you are?'

'If we are, if there *is* a break-through, there's not an area of modern technology which won't be affected and improved. Let me give you two examples.'

Adam listened with increasing fascination.

'I won't go into all the magnetic field hypothesis, but there's something called a superconducting ring. What it is is a wire which will store electric current in large amounts *and hold it intact*, and if we make the other break-through we'll be on top of this one, too. It'll make feasible the transfer of portable electric power in huge amounts, from place to place, by truck or boat or aeroplane. Think of its uses in the desert or the jungle – flown there in a package without a generator in sight, and more to follow when needed. And can you imagine another superconducting ring, this time in an electric operated car, making the battery as out of date as rushlight?'

'Since you ask,' Adam said, 'I have trouble imagining some of that.'

Perce reminded him, 'Not long ago people had trouble imagining atomic energy and space travel.'

True, Adam thought, then pointed out, 'You said two examples.'

'Yes, I did. One of the interesting things about a superconductor is that it's diamagnetic – that's to say, when used in conjunction with more common magnets, immensely large repulsive forces can occur. Do you see the possibilities, old boy? – metals in any kind of machinery nestled close together yet never actually touching. Obviously we'd have frictionless bearings. And you could build a car without metal parts in contact with one another – hence, no wear. Those are just beginning possibilities. Others are endless.'

It was impossible not to share some of Perce's conviction. From anyone else, Adam would have taken most of what was being described either as science fiction of a long-range possibility. But not from Perce Stuyvesant who had a record of good judgement and accomplishment in deeply scientific fields.

'Somewhat fortunately,' Perce said, 'in the areas I've mentioned, and others, our group has been able to move along without attracting much attention. But there'll be attention soon – lots of it. That's another reason why we need you.'

Adam was thinking hard. Perce's report and ideas excited him, though he wondered if the excitement would be as great or as sustained as he had experienced with cars – the Orion and Farstar, for example. Even now, the thought of not being a part of the auto industry was hard to accept. But there had been something in what Perce said yesterday about carving new pathways, breaking fresh ground.

Adam said, 'If we do get down to this seriously, I'll want to come to San Francisco and talk with the rest of your people.'

'We'd be more than delighted, old man, and I urge you to make it soon.' Perce spread his hands in a deprecating gesture. 'Of course, not everything I've described may work out the way we hope, nor is a break-through ever a break-through until it's happened. But there will be *some* important, exciting things; that much we know for sure and that I promise you. Remember that line? – *"There is a tide in the affairs of men, Which, taken at the flood . . . "* and so on.'

'Yes,' Adam said, 'I remember.'

He was wondering about timing, and a tide, for Erica and himself.

25

The initial involvement of Rollie Knight in organized plant crime had begun in February. It started the same week that he saw the foreman Frank Parkland – whom Rollie had come close to admiring – take a bribe, prompting Rollie's later observation to May Lou, 'There ain't nuthun' in this whole wide world but bullshit.'

At first, to Rollie, his participation seemed slight enough. He began by taking and recording numbers bets each day in the area of Assembly where he worked. The money and yellow betting slips were passed by Rollie to the stockroom delivery man, Daddy-o Lester, who got them farther along their route towards a betting house downtown. From overheard remarks Rollie guessed the delivery system tied in with truck deliveries in and out of the plant.

Frank Parkland, still Rollie's foreman, gave him no trouble about occasional absences from his work station which the number running entailed. As long as the absences were brief and not too many, Parkland moved a relief man in without comment; otherwise, he cautioned Rollie mildly. Obviously the foreman was continuing to be paid off.

That was in February. By May, Rollie was working for the loan sharks and cheque cashers – two illegal plant enterprises which interlocked.

A reason for the new activity was that he had borrowed money himself and was having difficulty paying off. Also, the money Rollie was earning from his job, which at first had seemed a fortune, suddenly was no longer enough to keep pace with his own and May Lou's spending. So now Rollie persuaded others to accept loans and helped with their collection.

Such loans were made, and taken, casually – at extortionate rates of interest. A plant worker might borrow twenty dollars early in one week and owe twenty-five dollars by payday of the same week. Incredibly, the demand – including requests for far larger sums – was brisk.

On payday, the loan sharks – company employees like everyone else – would become in-plant unofficial cheque cashers, cashing the paychecks of all who wished, but seeking out those who owed them money.

A cheque casher's fee was the odd cents on any cheque. If a cheque was made out for $100.99, the cheque casher took the 99 cents, though his minimum fee was 25 cents. Because of volume, and the fact that the cheque casher picked up his loans, plus interest, the operation involved big money and it was not unusual for a cheque casher-loan man to carry twenty thousand dollars in cash. When he did, he hired other workers as bodyguards.

Once a loan was made, it was wise for the borrower not to default. Anyone who did would find himself with a broken arm or leg, or worse – and would still owe the money, with more punishment to follow if it remained unpaid. A lucky few, like Rollie, were allowed to work off, in service, part of the interest owed. The principal sum – even for these – had to be repaid.

Thus, Rollie Knight, on all work days and especially paydays, became an intermediary for the flow of loan and cheque money back and forth. Despite this, he continued to be short of money himself.

In June, he began peddling drugs.

Rollie hadn't wanted to. Increasingly, as he became involved with plant rackets, he had a sense of being sucked in against his will, incurring the danger of exposure, arrest and – a dread which haunted him – a return to prison with a long sentence. Others who had no criminal records, though their activities were illegal, ran a lesser risk than himself. If caught and charged, they would be treated as first offenders. Rollie wouldn't.

It had been a growing anxiety on that score which made him morose and worried the night of the *Auto City* filming – also in June – in Rollie's and May Lou's apartment. Leonard Wingate, the company Personnel man, had sensed Rollie's deep-seated worry, but they had not discussed it.

Rollie also discovered, around that time, that it was easier to begin involvement with the rackets than to opt out. Big Rufe made that plain when Rollie demurred after being told he would be a part of the chain which brought marijuana and LSD into plants and distributed the drugs.

Months earlier, when the two had been side by side at a plant urinal, it was Big Rufe who approached Rollie with a hint about recruitment into plant crime. And now that the hint had become fact, it was clear that Big Rufe had a part in most of the illegal action going on.

'Don't cut no slice o' that pie for me,' Rollie had insisted when the subject of drug traffic came up. 'You get some other dude, hear?'

They were on work break, talking behind a row of storage bins near the assembly line, and shielded from the view of others. Big Rufe had scowled. 'You stink scared.'

'Maybe.'

'Boss don't like scared cats. Makes him nervous.'

Rollie knew better than to ask who the boss was. He was certain that one existed – probably somewhere outside the plant – just as it was obvious that an organization existed, Rollie having seen evidence of it not long before.

One night, after his shift ended, instead of leaving, he and a half-dozen others had remained inside the plant gates. Ahead of time they had been warned to make their way singly and inconspicuously to the Scrap and Salvage area. When they arrived, a truck was waiting and the group loaded it with crates and cartons already stacked nearby. It was obvious to Rollie that what was being loaded was new, unused material, and not scrap at all. It included tyres, radios, and air conditioners in cases, and some heavy crates – which required loading with a hoist – and marked as containing transmissions.

The first truck left, a second came, and for three hours altogether the loading went on, openly, and although it was after dark and this portion of the plant saw little night-time traffic, lights were blazing. Only towards the end did Big Rufe, who had appeared and disappeared several times, look around him nervously and urge everyone to hurry. They had, and eventually the second truck had gone too, and everyone went home.

Rollie had been paid two hundred dollars for the three hours he had helped load what was clearly a big haul of stolen goods. Equally evident was that the behind-scenes organization was efficient and large-scale, and there must have been payoffs to get the trucks safely in and out of the plant. Later, Rollie learned that the transmissions and other items could be bought cheaply at some of the many hot-rod shops around Detroit and Cleveland; also that the outflow through the Scrap and Salvage yard had been one of many.

'Guess you bought yourself a pack o' trouble by knowin' too much,' Big Rufe had said when he and Rollie had their talk behind the storage bins. 'That'd make the big boss nervous too, so if he figured you wasn't with us no more, he'd likely arrange a little party on the parking lot.'

Rollie understood the message. So many beatings and muggings had occurred recently on the huge employee parking lots that even security guards went around in pairs. Just the day before, a young black worker had been beaten and robbed – the beating so savage that he was hovering, in hospital, between life and death.

Rollie shuddered.

Big Rufe grunted and spat on the floor. 'Yeah, man, I'd sure think about that if I was you.'

In the end, Rollie went along with the drug peddling, partly because of Big Rufe's threat, but also because he desperately needed money. The second garnishee of his wages in June had been followed by Leonard Wingate's financial austerity programme, which left barely enough each week for Rollie and May Lou to live on, and nothing over to pay back loans.

Actually, the drug arrangement worked out easily, making him wonder if perhaps he had worried too much after all. He was glad that just marijuana and LSD were involved, and not heroin which was a riskier traffic. There *was* horse moving through the plant, and he knew workers who had habits. But a heroin addict was unreliable and likely to get caught, then under interrogation name his supplier.

Marijuana, on the other hand, was a pushover. The FBI and local police had told auto company managements confidentially that they would not investigate marijuana activity where less than one pound of the drug was involved. The reason was simple – a shortage of investigating officers. This information leaked, so that Rollie and others were careful to bring small amounts into the plant each time.

The extent of marijuana use amazed even Rollie. He discovered that more than half of the people working around him smoked two or three joints a day and many admitted it was the drug which kept them going. 'For Cri-sakes,' a regular purchaser from Rollie asserted, 'if a guy wasn't spaced out, how else could he stand this rat run?' Just a half joint, he said, gave him a lift which lasted several hours.

Rollie heard another worker tell a foreman who had cautioned him for being obvious about marijuana use, 'If you fired everybody smoking pot, you wouldn't build any cars around here.'

Another effect of Rollie's drug peddling was that he was able to get squared away with the loan sharks, leaving some spare money which he used to indulge in pot himself. It was true, he found that a day on the assembly line could be endured more easily if you were spaced, and you could get the work done too.

Rollie did manage to work to the continuing satisfaction of Frank Parkland, despite his extra activities which, in fact, took little time.

Because of his lack of seniority, he was laid off during two of the four weeks when the plant shut down for changeover to Orion production, then resumed work when the first Orions began to come down the line.

He took a keen interest in the Orion, describing it to May Lou when he returned from his first day of working on it, as 'Hot pants wheels!' It even seemed to affect Rollie sexually because he added, 'We gonna lay a lotta pipe tonight,' at which May Lou giggled, and later they did, Rollie thinking about wheels most of the time and the chances of getting an Orion himself.

All was going well, it seemed, and for a while Rollie Knight almost forgot his own credo: *Nuthun' lasts.*

Until the last week in August, when he had cause to remember.

The message from Big Rufe came to Rollie's work station via the stock man, Daddy-o Lester. The next night there would be some action. At the end of Rollie's shift tomorrow he was to stay in the plant. Between now and then he would be given more instructions.

Rollie yawned in Daddy-o's face. 'I'll check my engagement book, man.'

'You so smart,' Daddy-o threw back, 'but you don't hipe me. You'll be there.'

Rollie knew he would be, too, and since the last after-shift episode at the Scrap and Salvage area produced an easy two hundred dollars, he assumed tomorrow's would be the same. Next day, however, the instructions he received half an hour before his work day ended were not what he expected. Rollie – so Daddy-o informed him – was to take his time about leaving the assembly line, hang around until the night shift began work, then go to the locker and washup area where others would meet him, including Daddy-o and Big Rufe.

Thus, when the quitting whistle shrilled, instead of joining the normal frenzied scramble for exits to the parking lots and bus stations, Rollie ambled away, stopping at a vending machine area to buy a Coke. This took longer than usual because the machines were temporarily out of use and being emptied of cash by two collectors from the vending company. Rollie watched while a stream of silver coins cascaded into canvas sacks. When a machine was available he bought his drink, waited a few mintues more, then took it to the employees' locker-washup room.

This was drab and cavernous, with a wet cement floor and a permanent stink of urine. A row of big stone washup basins – 'bird baths' – was set centrally, at each of which a dozen men normally performed ablutions at once. Lockers, urinals, toilets without doors, crowded the remaining space.

Rollie rinsed his hands and face at a bird bath and mopped with paper towels. He had the washup area to himself since by now the day shift had gone and, outside, the new shift was settling down to work. Workers from it would begin drifting in here soon, but not yet.

An outside door opened. Big Rufe entered, moving quietly for a man of his bulk. He was scowling and looking at his wrist watch. Big Rufe's sleeves were rolled back, the muscles rippling in his raised forearm. He motioned for silence as Rollie joined him.

Seconds later, Daddy-o Lester came through the same door that Big Rufe had used. The young black was breathing hard, as if he had been running; sweat glistened on his forehead and on the scar running the length of his face.

Big Rufe said accusingly, 'I told you, hurry it . . . '

'I did! They runnin' late. Had trouble at one stand. Somethin' jammed, took longer.' Daddy-o's voice was high-pitched and nervous, his usual swagger gone.

'Where they now?'

'South cafeteria. Leroy's watchin' out. He'll meet us where we said.'

'South cafeteria's those guys' last stop.' Big Rufe told the others, 'Let's move it.'

Rollie stood where he was. 'Move where? An' what?'

'Now get on this fast.' Big Rufe kept his voice low, his eyes on the outer door. 'We gonna bust the vending machine guys. The whole deal's planned – a cincheroo. They carry a big load, 'n we got four guys to their two. You get a cut.'

'I don't want it! Don't know enough.'

'Want it or not, you got it. You got this, too.' Big Rufe pressed a snub-nosed automatic into Rollie's hand.

He protested, 'No!'

'What's the difference? You done time for armed. Now, if you carryin' a piece or you ain't, you get the same.' Big Rufe shoved Rollie ahead of him roughly. As they left the locker-washup room, instinctively Rolie pushed the pistol out of sight into his trousers waistband.

They hastened through the plant, using out-of-the-way routes and keeping clear of observation – not difficult for anyone knowing the layout well. Though Rollie had not been inside the south cafeteria, which was a small one used by supervisors and foremen, he knew where it was. Presumably it had a battery of vending machines, as had the employees' area where he bought his Coke.

Over his shoulder, hurrying with the others, Rollie asked, 'Why me?'

'Could be we like you,' Big Rufe said. 'Or maybe the boss figures the deeper a brother's in, the less chance he'll chicken out.'

'The boss man in this too?'

'I tol' you this piece of action was planned. We bin studyin' them vending guys a month. Hard to figure why nobody knocked 'em off before.'

The last statement was a lie.

It was not hard to figure – at least, for those with inside knowledge – why the vending machine collectors had gone unmolested until now. Big Rufe was among those who possessed such inside knowledge; also, he knew the special risks which he and the other three were running at this moment, and was prepared to accept and challenge them.

Rollie Knight had no such information. If he had, if he had known what Big Rufe failed to tell him, no matter what the consequences he would have turned and run.

The knowledge was: the vending concessions at the plant were Mafia-financed and -operated.

The Mafia in Wayne County, Michigan, of which Detroit is part, has a compass of activities ranging from the outright criminal, such as murder, to semi-legal businesses. In the area, the name Mafia is more appropriate than Cosa Nostra since Sicilian families form its core. The 'semi' of semi-legal is also appropriate since no Mafia-controlled business ever operates without at least some ancilliary knaveries – overpricing, intimidation, bribery, physical violence, or arson.

The Mafia is strong in Detroit's industrial plants, including auto plants. It controls the numbers rackets, finances and controls most loan sharks and takes a cut from others. The organization is behind the bulk of large-scale thefts from factories and helps with resale of stolen items. It has tentacles in plants through surface-legal operations such as service and supply companies, which are usually a cover-up for other activities or a means of hiding cash. Its dollar revenues each year are undoubtedly in the tens of millions.

But in recent years, with an ageing Mafia chieftain declining physically and mentally in Grosse Pointe remoteness, a power struggle has erupted within Detroit Mafia ranks. And since a bloc within the power struggle consists solely of blacks, this substratum – in Detroit as elsewhere – has acquired the title Black Mafia.

Hence, black struggles within the Mafia for recognition and equality parallel the more deserving civil rights struggles of balck people generally.

A cell of the Black Mafia, headed by a militant outside leader who remained under cover, and with Big Rufe as an in-plant deputy, had been testing and challenging the old established family rule. Months earlier, forays had begun into unauthorized areas – a separate numbers operation and increased Black Mafia loan sharking, extending through the inner city and industrial plants. Other operations included organized prostitution and 'protection' shakedowns. All cut across areas where the old regime had once been absolute.

The Black Mafia cell had expected retaliation and it happened. Two black loan men were ambushed in their homes and beaten – one while his terrified wife and children watched – then robbed. Soon after, a Black Mafia numbers organizer was intercepted and pistol-whipped, his car overturned and burned, his records destroyed and money taken. All raids, by their ruthlessness and other hallmarks, were clearly Mafia work, a fact which victims and their associates were intended to recognize.

Now the Black Mafia was striking back. Robbery of the vending machine collectors would be one of a half dozen counter-raids, all carefully timed for today and representing test of strength in the power struggle. Later still, there would be more reprisals on both sides before the white-black Mafia war ended, if it ever did.

And, as in all wars everywhere, the soldiers and other victims would be expendable pawns.

Rollie Knight, Big Rufe, and Daddy-o had come through a basement corridor and were at the foot of a metal stairway. Immediately ahead was a halfway landing between floors, the top of the stairway out of sight.

Big Rufe commanded softly, 'Hold it here!'

A face appeared, looking downwards over the stairway rail. Rollie recognized Leroy Colfax, an intense, fast-talking militant who hung around with Big Rufe's crowd.

Big Rufe kept his voice low. 'Them peckerwoods still there?'

'Yeah. Be two, three minutes more by the looks.'

'OK, we in place. You get clear now, but follow 'em down, 'n stay close. Understand?'

'I got it.' With a nod, Leroy Colfax disappeared from sight.

Big Rufe beckoned Rollie and Daddy-o. 'In here.'

'Here' was a janitor's closet, unlocked and with space for the three of them. As they went inside, Big Rufe left the door slightly ajar. He queried Daddy-o. 'You got the masks?'

'Yeah.' Rollie could see that Daddy-o, the youngest, was nervous and trembling. But he produced three stocking masks from a pocket. Big Rufe took one and slipped it over his head, motioning for the others to do the same.

The basement corridor outside was quiet, the only noise a rumble, distantly above, where the assembly line was operating with the fresh eight-hour shift. This had been a shrewd time to pick. Traffic through the plant was never as great during the night shift as in daytime, and was even lighter than usual this early in the shift.

'You two watch me, move when I do.' Through the mask, Big Rufe's eyes appraised Daddy-o and Rollie. 'Ain't gonna be no trouble if we do this right. When we get them guys in here you both tie 'em up good. Leroy dumped the rope.' He motioned to two coils of thin yellow cord on the closet floor.

They waited silently. As the seconds passed, Rollie found himself with a sense of resigned acceptance. He knew he was in this now, that his participation would not be changed or excused whatever happened, and if there were consequences he would share them equally with the other three. His choices had been limited; in fact, there were really no choices at all, merely decisions made by others and forced on him, which was the way it had always been, for as long as he remembered.

From the coveralls he was wearing, Big Rufe produced a heavy-handled Colt revolver. Daddy-o had a snub-nosed pistol – the same kind Rollie had been given. Reluctantly, reaching into his waistband, Rollie held his too.

Daddy-o tensed as Big Rufe motioned with his hand. They could hear clearly – a clatter of feet coming down the metal stairway, and voices.

The door to the janitor's closet remained almost closed until the footsteps, now on the tile floor, were a few feet away. Then Big Rufe opened the door and the masked trio stepped out, guns raised.

The vending machine collectors looked as startled as any two men could.

Both wore grey uniforms with the vending company's insignia. One had a thatch of red hair and a pale-pink face which, at the moment, had turned even paler; the other, with heavy-lidded eyes, had the features of an Indian. Each carried two burlap bags slung over a shoulder and joined together with a chain and padlock. The pair were big-boned and burly, probably in their thirties, and looked as if they could handle themselves in a fight. Big Rufe gave them no chance.

He levelled his revolver at the red-haired man's chest and motioned with his head to the janitor's closet. 'In there, baby!' He ordered the other, 'You, too!' The words came out muffled through the stocking mask.

The Indian shot a glance behind him, as if to run. Two things happened. He saw a fourth masked figure – Leroy Colfax – armed with a long-bladed hunting knife, leaping down the stairs and cutting off escape. Simultaneously, the muzzle of Big Rufe's revolver slammed into his face, opening his cheek in a gash which spurted blood.

Rollie Knight jammed his own automatic against the ribs of the red-haired man who had swung round, clearly with the intention of aiding his companion. Rollie cautioned, 'Hold it! It ain't gonna work!' All he wanted was to have done with this, without more violence. The red-haired man subsided.

Now the four ambushers shoved the others ahead of them into the little room.

The red-haired man protested, 'Listen, if you guys knew . . . '

'Shaddup!' It was Daddy-o, who seemed to be over his fright. 'Gimme that!' He grabbed the canvas sacks from red-head's shoulder, pushing the man so he tripped backwards over mops and pails.

Leroy Colfax reached for the cash sacks of the other collector. But the Indian, despite his cheek wound, which was bleeding, had spirit. He lunged against Leroy, thrusting a knee into his groin and his left fist hard into the stomach. Then, with his right hand, he reached up and snatched the mask from Leroy's face.

For an instant the two glared at each other.

The vending machine collector hissed, 'Now, I'll know who . . . aaaaaah!'

He screamed – a loud, high-pitched sound which descended to a moan then subsided into nothingness. He fell forward heavily – on the long-bladed hunting knife which Leroy had thrust hard into his belly.

'*Jesus Christ!*' the red-haired man said. He stared down at the slumped, motionless form of his companion of a moment earlier. 'You bastards killed him!'

They were his last words before unconsciousneess as the butt of Big Rufe's gun crashed into his scalp.

Daddy-o, who was trembling more than he had originally, pleaded, 'Did we hafta do that?'

'What's done's done,' Big Rufe said. 'And them two started it.' But he sounded less sure of himself than at the beginning. Picking up two of the chained bags, he ordered, 'Bring them others.'

Leroy Colfax reached for them.

Rollie urged, 'Wait!'

Outside, hurried footsteps were coming down the metal stairs.

Frank Parkland had stayed later than usual at the plant for a foreman's meeting in the office of Matt Zaleski. They discussed Orion production and some problems. Afterwards he went to the south cafeteria where, at lunchtime, he had left a sweater and some personal papers. It was when he had recovered the items, and was leaving, that he heard the scream from below and went down to investigate.

The three bodies were discovered an hour or so later – long after the quartet of Big Rufe, Daddy-o Lester, Leroy Colfax, and Rollie Knight had left the plant by climbing over a wall.

The Indian was dead, the other two barely alive.

26

Matt Zaleski sometimes wondered if anyone outside the auto industry realized how little changed, in principle, a final car assembly line was, compared with the days of the first Henry Ford.

He was walking beside the line where the night shift, which had begun work an hour ago, was building Orions – the company's new cars, still not released to public view. Like others in senior plant management, Matt's own working day did not end when the day shift went home. He stayed on while the next shift settled down, dealing with production snafus as they occurred which inevitably happened while the plant's people – management as well as workers – learned their new assignments.

Some assignments had been discussed during a foremen's meeting, held in Matt's office soon after the change of shifts. The meeting had ended fifteen minutes ago. Now Matt was patrolling – an alert surveillance, his experienced eyes searching for potential trouble spots.

While he walked, his thoughts returned to Henry Ford, the pioneer of mass production auto assembly.

Nowadays, the final assembly line in any auto plant was unfailingly the portion of car manufacturing which fascinated visitors most. Usually a mile long, it was visually impressive because an act of creation could be witnessed. Initially, a few steel bars were brought together, then as if fertilized, they multiplied and grew, taking on familiar shapes like an exposed foetus in a moving womb. The process was slow enough for watchers to assimilate, fast enough to be exciting. The forward movement, like a river, was mostly in straight lines, though occasionally with bends or loops. Among the burgeoning cars, colour, shape, size, features, frills, conveyed individuality and sex. Eventually, with the foetus ready for the world, the car dropped on its tyres. A moment later an ignition key was turned, an engine sprang to life – as impressive, when first witnessed, as a child's first cry – and a newborn vehicle moved from the assembly line's end under its own power.

Matt Zaleski had seen spectators thronging through the plant – in Detroit they came like pilgrims, daily – marvelling at the process and talking, uninformed and glibly, of the wonders of automated mass production. Plant guides, trained to regard each visitor as a potential customer, gave spiels to titillate the sense of wonder. But the irony was: a final assembly plant was scarcely automated at all, in principle it was still an old-fashioned conveyor belt on which pieces of an automobile were hung in sequence like decorations on a Christmas tree. In engineering terms it was the least impressive part of modern automobile production. In terms of quality it could swing this way or that like a wild barometer. And it was wholly susceptible to human error.

By contrast, plants making auto engines, though less impressive visually, were truly automated, with long series of intricate operations performed solely by machines. In most engine plants, row after row of sophisticated machine tools operated on their own, masterminded by computers, with the only humans in sight a few skilled tool men making occasional adjustments. If a machine did something wrong, it switched itself off instantly and summoned help through warning systems. Otherwise it did its job unvaryingly, to hair's breadth standards, and stopped neither for meal breaks, toilet visits, nor to speak to another machine alongside. The system was a reason why engines, in comparison with more generally constructed parts of automobiles, seldom failed until neglected or abused.

If old Henry could come back from his grave, Matt thought, and view a car assembly line of the '70s, he might be amused at how few basic changes had been made.

At the moment, there were no production snags – at least, in view – and Matt Zaleski returned to his glass-panelled office on the mezzanine.

Though he could leave the plant now, if he chose, Matt was reluctant to return to the empty Royal Oak house. Several weeks had gone by since the bitter night of Barbara's departure, but there had been no *rapprochement* between them. Recently Matt had tried not to think about his daughter, concentrating on other thoughts, as he had on Henry Ford a few minutes earlier; despite this, she was seldom far from mind. He wished they could patch up their quarrel somehow, and had hoped Barbara would telephone, but she had not. Matt's own pride, plus a conviction that a parent should not have to make the first move, kept him from calling her. He supposed that Barbara was still living with that designer, DeLosanto, which was something else Matt tried not to think about, but often did.

At his desk, he leafed through the next day's production schedule. Tomorrow was a mid-week day, so several 'specials' would go on the line – cars for company executives, their friends, or others with influence enough to ensure that an automobile they ordered got better-than-ordinary treatment. Foremen had been alerted to the job numbers, so had Quality Control; as a result, all work on those particular cars would be watched with extra care. Body men would be cautioned to install header panels, seats, and interior trim more fussily than usual. Engine and power train sequences would receive close scrutiny. Later, Quality Control would give the cars a thorough going over and order additional work or adjustments before dispatch. 'Specials' were also among the fifteen to thirty cars which plant executives drove home each night, turning in road test reports next morning.

Of course – as Matt Zaleski knew – there were dangers in scheduling 'specials' particularly if a car happened to be for a plant executive. A few workers always had grievances, real or imagined, against management and were delighted at a chance to 'get even with the boss'. Then the legendary soft drink bottle, left loose inside a rocker panel so it would rattle through a car's lifetime, was apt to become reality. A loose tool or chunk of metal served the same purpose. Another trick was to weld the trunk lid closed from inside; a skilled welder, reaching through the back seat could do it in seconds. Or a strategic bolt or two might be left untightened. These were reasons why Matt and others like him used fictitious names when putting their own cars through production.

Matt put the next day's schedule down. There had been no need to review it, anyway, since he had gone over it earlier in the day.

It was time to go home. As he rose from the desk, he thought again of Barbara and wondered where she was. He was suddenly very tired.

On his way down from the mezzanine, Matt Zaleski was aware of some kind of a disturbance – shouting, the sound of running feet. Automatically because most things which happened in the plant were his business, he stopped, searching for the source. It appeared to be near the south cafeteria. He heard an urgent cry: 'For God's sake get somebody from Security!'

Seconds later, as he hurried towards the disturbance, he heard sirens approaching from outside.

A janitor who discovered the huddled bodies of the two vending machine collectors and Frank Parkland, had the good sense to go promptly to a telephone. By the time Matt Zaleski heard the shouts, which were from others who had come on the scene subsequently, an ambulance, plant security men, and outside police were already on the way.

But Matt still reached the janitor's closet of the lower floor before any of the outside aid. Bulling his way through an excited group around it, he was in time to see that one of the three recumbent forms was that of Frank Parkland whom Matt had last seen at the foremen's meeting about an hour and a half before. Parkland's eyes were closed, his skin ashen, except where blood had trickled through his hair and clotted on his face.

One of the night shift office clerks who had run in with a first-aid kit, now lying unused beside him, had Parkland's head cradled in his lap and was feeling for a pulse. The clerk looked up at Matt. 'I guess he's alive, Mr Zaleski; so's one of the others. Though I wouldn't want to say for how long.'

Security and the ambulance people had come in then, and taken charge. The local police – uniformed men first, then plain-clothes detectives – quickly joined them.

There was little for Matt to do, but he could no longer leave the plant, which had been sealed by a cordon of police cars. Obviously the police believed that whoever perpetrated the murder-robbery – it had been confirmed that one of the three victims was dead – might still be inside.

After a while, Matt returned to his office on the mezzanine where he sat, mentally numbed and listless.

The sight of Frank Parkland, who was clearly gravely hurt, had shocked Matt deeply. So had the knife protruding from the body of the man with the Indian face. But the dead man had been unknown to Matt, whereas Parkland was his friend. Though the assistant plant chief and foreman had had run-ins, and once – a year ago – exchanged strong words, such differences had been the result of work pressures. Normally, they liked and respected each other.

Matt thought: why did it have to happen to a good man? There were others he knew over whom he would have grieved less.

At that moment, precisely, Matt Zaleski became aware of a sudden breathlessness and a fluttering in his chest, as if a bird were inside, beating its wings and trying to get out. The sensation frightened him. He sweated with the same kind of fear he had known years before in B-17F bombers over Europe when the German flak was barrelling up, and now, as then, he knew it was the fear of death.

Matt knew, too, he was having some kind of attack and needed help. He began thinking in a detached way: he would telephone, and whoever came and whatever was done, he would ask them to send for Barbara because there was something he wanted to tell her. He was not sure exactly what, but if she came the words would find themselves.

The trouble was, when he made up his mind to reach for the telephone, he discovered he no longer had the power to move. Something strange was happening to his body. On the right side there was no feeling any more; he seemed to have no arm or leg, or any idea where either was. He tried to cry out but found, to his amazement and frustration, he could not. Nor, when he tried again, could he make any sound at all.

Now he knew what it was that he wanted to tell Barbara: that despite the differences they had had, she was still his daughter and he loved her, just as he had loved her mother, whom Barbara resembled in so many ways. He wanted to say, too, that if they could somehow resolve their present quarrel he would try to understand her, and her friends, better from now on . . .

Matt discovered he *did* have some feeling and power of movement in his left side. He tried to get up, using his left arm as a lever, but the rest of his body failed him and he slid to the floor between the desk and chair. It was in that position he was found soon after, conscious, his eyes mirroring an agony of frustration because the words he wanted to say could find no exit route.

Then, for the second time that night, an ambulance was summoned to the plant.

'You're aware,' the doctor at Ford hospital said to Barbara next day, 'that your father had a stroke before.'

She told him, 'I know now. I didn't until today.'

This morning, a plant secretary, Mrs Einfeld, had reported, conscience-stricken, Matt Zaleski's mild attack a few weeks earlier when she had driven him home and he persuaded her to say nothing. The company's Personnel department had passed the information on.

'Taken together,' the doctor said, 'the two incidents fit a classic pattern.' He was a specialist – a cardiologist – balding and sallow-faced, with a slight tic beneath one eye. Like so many in Detroit, Barbara thought, he looked as if he worked too hard.

'If my father hadn't concealed the first stroke, would it have changed anything?'

The specialist shrugged. 'Perhaps, perhaps not. He'd have received medication, but the end result could have been the same. Either way, the question's academic now.'

They were in an annexe to an intensive care unit of the hospital. Through a glass window she could see her father in one of the four beds inside, a red rubber tube running from his mouth to a grey-green respirator on a stand close by. The respirator, wheezing evenly, was breathing for him. Matt Zaleski's eyes were open and the doctor had told Barbara that although her father was presently under sedation, at other times he could undoubtedly see and hear. She wondered if he was aware of the young black woman, also *in extremis*, in the bed nearest to him.

'It's probable,' the doctor said, 'that at some earlier period your father sustained vulvular heart damage. Then, when he had the first mild stroke, a small clot broke off from the heart and went to the right side of his brain which, in a right-handed person, controls the body's left side.'

It was all so impersonal, Barbara thought, as if a routine piece of machinery were being described, and not the sudden breakdown of a human being.

The cardiologist went on: 'With the kind of stroke which your father had first, almost certainly the recovery was only apparent. It wasn't a real recovery. The body's fail-safe mechanism remained damaged and that was why the second stroke, to the left side of the brain, produced the devastating effect it did last night.'

Barbara had been with Brett last night when a message was telephoned that her father had had a sudden stroke and been rushed to hospital. Brett had driven her there, though he waited outside. 'I'll come if you need me,' he had said, taking her hand reassuringly before she went in, 'but your old man doesn't like me, anyway, and being ill isn't going to change his mind. It might upset him more if he saw me with you.'

On the way to the hospital, Barbara had had a guilty feeling, wondering how much her own act of leaving home precipitated whatever had happened to her father. Brett's gentleness, of which she saw more each day and loved him increasingly for, underlined the tragedy that the two men she cared most about had failed to know each other better. On balance, she believed her father mainly to blame; just the same, Barbara wished now that she had telephoned him, as she had considered doing several times since their estrangement.

At the hospital last night they had let her speak to her father briefly, and a young resident told her, 'He can't communicate with you, but he knows you're there.' She had murmured the things she expected Matt would want to hear: that she was sorry about his illness, would not be far away, and would come to the hospital frequently. While speaking, Barbara had looked directly into his eyes and while there was no flicker of recognition she had an impression the eyes were straining to tell her something. Was it imagination? She wondered again now.

Barbara asked the cardiologist, 'What are my father's chances?'

'Of recovery?' He looked at her interrogatively.

'Yes. And please be completely candid. I want to know.'

'Sometimes people don't . . . '

'I do.'

The cardiologist said quietly. 'Your father's chances of any substantial recovery are nil. My prognosis is that he will be a hemiplegic invalid as long as he lives, with complete loss of power on the right side, including speech.'

There was a silence, then Barbara said, 'If you don't mind, I'd like to sit down.'

'Of course.' He guided her to a chair. 'It's a big shock. If you like, I'll give you something.'

She shook her head. 'No.'

'You had to know some time,' the doctor said, 'and you asked.'

They looked, together, through the window of the intensive care unit, at Matt Zaleski, still recumbent, motionless, the machine breathing for him.

The cardiologist said, 'Your father was with the auto industry, wasn't he? In a manufacturing plant, I believe.' For the first time, the doctor seemed warmer, more human than before.

'Yes.'

'I get a good many patients from that source. Too many.' He motioned vaguely beyond the hospital walls towards Detroit. 'It's always seemed to me like a battleground out there, with casualties. Your father, I'm afraid, was one.'

27

No aid was to be given Hank Kreisel in the manufacture or promotion of his thresher.

The decision, by the board of directors' executive policy committee, reached Adam Trenton in a memo routed through the Product Development chief, Elroy Braithwaite.

Braithwaite brought in the memo personally and tossed it on Adam's desk. 'Sorry,' the Silver Fox said, 'I know you were interested. You turned me on, too, and you might like to know we were in good company because the chairman felt the same way.'

The last news was not surprising. The chairman of the board was noted for his wide-ranging interests and liberal views, but only on rare occasions did he make autocratic rulings and obviously this had not been one.

The real pressure for the negative decision, Adam learned later, came from the executive vice-president, Hub Hewitson, who swayed the triumvirate – the chairman, president, and Hewitson himself – which comprised the executive policy committee.

Reportedly, Hub Hewitson argued on the lines: the company's principal business was building cars and trucks. If the thresher didn't look like a money-making item to farm products division, it should not be foisted on any segment of the corporation merely on public-spirited grounds. As to extramural activities generally, there were already enormous problems in coping with public and legislative pressures for increased safety, less air pollution, employment of the disadvantaged, and kindred matters.

The argument concluded: we are not a philanthropic body but a private enterprise whose objective is to make profits for shareholders.

After brief discussion, the president supported Hub Hewitson's view, so that the chairman was outnumbered, and conceded.

'It's been left to us to inform your friend, Kreisel,' the Silver Fox told Adam, 'so you'd better do it.'

On the telephone Hank Kreisel was philosophic when Adam gave him the news. 'Figured the odds weren't the greatest. Thanks, anyway.'

Adam asked, 'Where do you go from here?'

'Can raise dough in more than one oven,' the parts manufacturer said cheerfully. But Adam doubted if he would – at least, for the thresher, in Detroit.

He told Erica about the decision over dinner that evening. She said, 'I'm disappointed because it was a dream with Hank – a good one – and I like him. But at least you tried.'

Erica seemed in good spirits; she was making a conscious effort, Adam realized, even though, almost two weeks after her arrest for shoplifting, and release, their relationship was still unclear, their future undecided.

The day following the painful experience at the suburban police station, Erica had declared, 'If you insist on asking a lot more questions, though I hope you won't, I'll try to answer them. Before you do, though, I'll tell you I'm sorry, most of all, for getting you involved. And if you're worrying about my doing the same thing again – don't. I swear there'll never be anything like it as long as I live.'

He had known she meant it, and that the subject could be closed. But it had seemed a right time to tell Erica about the job offer from Perce Stuyvesant and the fact that Adam was considering it seriously. He added, 'If I do accept it will mean a move, of course – to San Francisco.'

Erica had been incredulous. 'You're considering leaving the auto industry?'

Adam had laughed, feeling curiously lightheaded. 'If I didn't, there'd be problems about dividing my time.'

'You'd do *that* for me?'

He answered quietly, 'Perhaps it would be for both of us.'

Erica had seemed dazed, shaking her head in disbelief, and that subject had been dropped too. However, Adam had telephoned Perce Stuyvesant next day to say he was still interested, but would not be able to fly West until after the Orion's debut in September, now barely a month away. Sir Perceval had agreed to wait.

Another thing that had happened was that Erica moved back into their bedroom from the guest room, at Adam's suggestion. They had even essayed some sex, but there was no escaping that it was not as successful as in the old days, and both knew it. An ingredient was missing. Neither was sure exactly what it was; the only thing they knew with certainty was that in terms of their marriage they were marking time.

Adam hoped there would be a chance for them both to talk things over – away from Detroit – during two days of stock car racing they would be attending soon in Talladega, Alabama.

28

A page one banner headline of the *Anniston Star* ('Alabama's Largest Home-Owned Newspaper') proclaimed:

300 GOES AT 12.30

The news story immediately following began:

> Today's Canebreak 300, as well as tomorrow's Talladega 500, promise some of the hottest competition in stock car racing history.
>
> For the gruelling 300-mile race today, and even tougher 500-mile Sunday, super fast cars and drivers have pushed qualifying speeds close to 190 mph.
>
> What drivers, car owners, mechanics, and auto company observers now wonder is how the power-packed racers will act over the 2.66 miles trioval of Alabama International Speedway, at those speeds, when 50 cars are fighting for position on the track . . .

Lower on the same page was a sidebar story:

Severe Blood Shortage
Will Not Diminish
Big Race Precautions

Local alarm had been manifest (so the secondary news story said) because of an area Blood Bank shortage. The shortage was critical 'because of the possibility of serious injuries to race drivers and a need for transfusions over Saturday's and Sunday's racing'.

Now, to conserve supplies, all elective surgery at Citizens Hospital for which use of blood was predicted had been postponed until after the weekend. Additionally, appeals were being made to race visitors and residents to donate blood at a special clinic, opening Saturday at 8 a.m. Thus, a supply of blood for racing casualties would be assured.

Erica Trenton, who read both news reports while breakfasting in bed at the Downtowner Motor Inn, Anniston, shuddered at the implications of the second, and turned to the paper's inside pages. Among the other race news on page three was an item:

New 'Orion' on Display
This One's a 'Concept'

The Orion's manufacturers, it was reported, were being close-mouthed about how nearly the 'Styling concept' model, currently on view at Talladega, resembled the soon-to-appear, real Orion. However, public interest had been high, with pre-race crowds thronging the infield area where the model could be seen.

Adam would have had the news by now, Erica was sure.

They had come here together yesterday, having flown in on a company plane from Detroit, and this morning Adam left their suite at the motor inn early – almost two hours ago – to visit the Speedway pit area with Hub Hewitson. The executive vice-president, who was the senior company officer attending the two-day race meet, had a rented helicopter at his disposal, which had picked up Hewitson and Adam, and later several more. The same helicopter would make a second series of trips shortly before race time to collect Erica and a few other company wives.

Anniston, a pleasant green-and-white country town, was six miles or so from the Talladega track.

Officially, Adam's company, like other car manufacturers, was not directly involved in auto racing, and the once strongly financed factory teams had been disbanded. Yet no official edict could wipe out an ingrained enthusiasm for racing which most auto executives shared, including Hub Hewitson, Adam, and others in their own and competitive companies. This was one reason why most major auto races attracted strong contingents from Detroit. Another was that auto corporation money continued to flow into racing, through back doors, at division level or lower. In this way – in which General Motors had set a pattern across the years – if a car bearing a manufacturer's name won, its makers could cheer publicly, reaping plaudits and prestige. But if a car carrying their name lost, they merely shrugged and disclaimed association.

Erica got out of bed, took a leisurely bath, and began dressing.

While doing so, she thought about Pierre Flodenhale whose picture had been featured prominently in the morning papers. Pierre, in racing garb and crash helmet, was shown being kissed by two girls at once and was beaming – undoubtedly because of the girls but also, probably, because most prognosticators had picked him as among the two or three drivers likely to win both today's and tomorrow's races.

Adam and others in the company contingent here were also happy about Pierre's prospects, since in both races he would be driving cars with their company's name.

Erica's feelings about Pierre were mixed, as she was reminded when they met briefly last night.

It had been at a crowded cocktail-supper party – one of many such affairs taking place around town, as always happened on the eve of any major auto race. Adam and Erica had been invited to six parties and dropped in on three. At the one where they met Pierre, the young race driver was a centre of attention and surrounded by several glamorous but brassy girls – 'pit pussies', as they were sometimes known – of the type which auto racing and its drivers seemed always to attract.

Pierre had detached himself on seeing Erica, and made his way across the room to where she was standing alone, Adam having moved away to talk with someone else.

'Hi, Erica,' Pierre said easily. He gave his boyish grin. 'Wondered if you'd be around.'

'Well, I am.' She tried to be nonchalant, but unaccountably felt nervous. To cover up, she smiled and said, 'I hope you win. I'll be cheering for you both days.' Even to herself, however, her words sounded strained, and in part, Erica realized, it was because the physical presence of Pierre aroused her sensually, still.

They had gone on chatting, not saying very much, though while they were together Erica was aware of others in the room, including two from Adam's company glancing their way covertly. No doubt some were remembering gossip they had heard, including the *Detroit News* item about Pierre and Erica, which distressed her at the time.

Adam had strolled over to join them briefly, and wished Pierre well. Soon after, Adam moved away again, then Pierre excused himself, saying that because of the race tomorrow he must get to bed. 'You know how it is, Erica,' he said, grinning again, then winked to make sure she did not miss the unsubtle humour.

Even that reference to bed, clumsy as it was, had left an effect, and Erica knew she was far from being completely over her affair with Pierre.

Now, it was noon next day and the first of the two big races – the Canebreak 300 – would begin in half an hour.

Erica left the suite and went downstairs.

In the helicopter, Kathryn Hewitson observed, 'This *is* rather ostentatious. But it beats sitting in traffic, I suppose.'

The helicopter was a small one which could carry only two passengers at a time, and the first to be whirled from Anniston to the Talledega Speedway were the executive vice-president's wife and Erica. Kathryn Hewitson was a handsome, normally self-effacing woman in her early fifties, with a reputation as a devoted wife and mother, but also one who, on occasions, could handle her dynamic husband firmly, as no-one else knowing him could or dared to. Today, as she often did, she had brought along her needlepoint which she worked on, even during their few minutes in the air.

Erica smiled an acknowledgement because the helicopter's noise as they were airborne precluded conversation.

Beneath the machine, the ochre-red earth of Alabama, framing lush meadowland, slid by. The sun was high, the sky unclouded, the air warm with a dry, fresh breeze. Though it would be September in a few days more, no sign of fall was yet apparent. Erica had chosen a light summer dress; so had most other women whom she saw.

They landed in the Speedway infield, already massed with parked vehicles and race fans, some of whom had camped here overnight. Even more cars were streaming in through two double-lane traffic tunnels beneath the track. At the helicopter landing pad, a car and driver were waiting for Kathryn Hewitson and Erica; briefly, traffic in one of the incoming tunnel lanes was halted, the lane control reversed, while they sped through to the grandstand side of the track.

The grandstands too – North, South and Over Hill – were packed with humanity, waiting expectantly in the now hot sun along their mile-long length. As the two women reached one of the several private boxes, a band near the starting line struck up *The Star-Spangled Banner*. A singer's soprano voice floated over the p.a. Wherever they were, most spectators, contestants, and officials stood. The cacophony of speedway noises hushed.

A clergyman with a Deep South drawl intoned. 'Oh God, watch over those in peril who will compete . . . We praise Thee for today's fine weather, and give our thanks for business Thou has brought this area . . . '

'Damn right,' Hub Hewitson asserted in the front row of his company's private box. 'Lots of cash registers jingling, including ours, I hope. Must be a hundred thousand people.' The phalanx of company men and wives surrounding the executive vice-president smiled dutifully.

Hewitson, a small man with close-cropped, jet black hair, whose energy seemed to radiate through his skin, leaned forward so he could better view the throngs which jammed the Speedway. He declared again, 'Motor racing's come up to be the second most popular sport; soon it'll be the first. All of 'em out there are interested in power under the hood, thank God! – and never mind the sanctimonious sons-of-bitches who tell us people aren't.'

Erica was two rows from the front, with Adam beside her. Kathryn Hewitson had gone to the rear of the box, which had tiered seats rising from front to rear, and was sheltered from the sun. Kathryn told Erica as they came in, 'Hub likes me along, but I don't really care for racing. It makes me frightened at times, and sad at others, wondering what's the point of it all.' Erica could see the older woman in the back row now, busy with her needlepoint.

The private box, like several others, was in the South grandstand and commanded a view of the entire Speedway. The start-finish line was immediately in front, banked turns to left and right, the back-stretch visible beyond the infield. On the nearer side of the infield were the pits, now thronged with overalled mechanics. Pit row, as it was known, had ready access to and from the track.

In the company box, among others guests, was Smokey Stephensen, and Adam and Erica had spoken with him briefly. Ordinarily, a dealer would not make it in here with the high command, but Smokey enjoyed privileges at race meets, having once been a big star driver, with many older fans still revering his name.

Next to the company box was the Press enclosure, with long tables and scores of typewriters; also ranged in tiers. The Press reporters, alone among most others present today, self-importantly hadn't stood for the national anthem. Now, most were clattering on typewriters, and Erica, who could view them through a glass window at the side, wondered what they could be writing so much about when the race hadn't even started.

But starting time was close. The praying was done; clergy, parade marshals, drum majorettes, bands, and other non-essentials had removed themselves. Now the track was clear, and fifty competing cars were in starting positions – a long double line. Throughout the Speedway, as always in final moments before a race, tension grew.

Erica saw from her programme that Pierre was in row four of the starting line-up. His car was number 29.

The control tower, high above the track, was the Speedway's nerve centre. From it, by radio closed circuit TV, and telephone were controlled the starters, track signal lights, pace cars, service and emergency vehicles. A race director presided at a console; he was a relaxed and quietly spoken young man in a business suit. In a booth beside him sat a shirt-sleeved commentator whose voice would fill the p.a. system through the race. At a desk behind, two uniformed Alabama State Police officers directed traffic in the non-track areas.

The race director was communicating with his forces: 'Lights work all the way 'round? . . . OK . . . Track clear? . . . all set . . . Tower to pace car: Are you ready to go? . . . All right, fire 'em up!'

Over the Speedway p.a., voiced by a visiting fleet admiral on an infield dais, went the traditional command to drivers: 'Gentlemen, start your engines!'

What followed was racing's most exciting sound: the roar of unmuffled engines, like fifty Wagnerian crescendos, which swamped the Speedway with sound and extended for miles beyond.

A pace car, pennants billowing, swung on to the track, its speed increasing swiftly.

Behind the pace car, competing cars moved out, still two abreast, maintaining their starting line-up as they would for several preliminary, non-scoring laps.

Fifty cars were scheduled to begin the race. Forty-nine did.

The engine of a gleaming, vivid red sedan, its identifying number 06 painted in high visibility gold, wouldn't start. The car's pit crew rushed forward and worked frantically, to no avail. Eventually the car was pushed by hand behind the wall of pit row and, as it went, the disgusted driver flung his helmet after it.

'Poor guy,' somebody in the tower said. 'Was the best-looking car on the field.

The race director cracked, 'He spent too much time polishing it.'

During the second preliminary lap, with the field still bunched together, the director radioed the pace car, 'Pick up the tempo.'

The pace car driver responded. Speeds rose. The engines' thunder grew in intensity.

After a third lap the pace car, its job done, was signalled off the track. It swung into pit row.

At the start-finish line in front of the grandstand, the starter's green flag slashed the air. The 300 miles race – 113 gruelling laps – began.

From the outset the pace was sizzling, competition strong. Within the first five laps a driver named Doolittle, in number 12, charged through massed cars ahead to take the lead. Shooting up behind came car number 38, driven by a jut-jawed Mississippian known to fans as Cutthroat. Both were favourites, with racing pundits and the crowd.

A dark horse rookie driver, Johnny Gerenz in number 44, ran an unexpected third.

Pierre Flodenhale, clearing the pack soon after Gerenz, moved up to fourth in number 29.

For twenty-six laps the lead switched back and forth between the two front cars. Then Doolittle, in 12, pitted twice in quick succession with ignition trouble. It cost him a lap, and later, with smoke pouring from his car, he quit the race.

Doolittle's departure put the rookie, Johnny Gerenz, in 44, in second place. Pierre, in 29, was now third.

In the thirtieth lap a minor mishap, with debris and spilled oil, brought caution flags, slowing the race while the track was cleared and sanded. Johnny Gerenz and Pierre were among those who pitted, taking advantage of the non-competing laps. Both had tyre changes, a fill of gas, and were away again in seconds.

Soon after, the caution flag was lifted. Speed resumed.

Pierre was drafting – staying close behind other cars, using the partial suction they created, saving his own fuel and engine wear. It was a dangerous game but, used skilfully, could help win long races. Experienced onlookers sensed Pierre was holding back, saving a reserve of speed and power for later in the race.

'At least,' Adam told Erica, 'we hope that's what he's doing.'

Pierre was the only one among present leaders in the race who was driving one of the company's cars. Thus, Adam, Hub Hewitson, and others were rooting for Pierre, hopeful that later he would move into the lead.

As always, when she went to auto races, Erica was fascinated by the speed of pit stops – the fact that a crew of five mechanics could change four tyres, replenish gasoline, confer with the driver, and have a car moving out again in one minute, sometimes less.

'They practise,' Adam told her. 'For hours and hours, all year-round. And they never waste a moment, never get in one another's way.'

Their seat neighbour, a manufacturing vice-president, glanced across. 'We could use a few of their kind in Assembly.'

Pit stops, too, as Erica knew, could win or lose a race.

With the race leaders in their forty-seventh lap, a blue-grey car spun out of control on the steeply banked north turn. It came to rest in the infield, right side up, the driver unhurt. In course of its gyrations, however, the blue-grey car clipped another which slid sideways into the track wall amid a shower of sparks, then deep red flames from burning oil. The driver of the second car scrambled out and was supported by ambulance men as he left the track. The oil fire was quickly extinguished. Minutes later the p.a. announced that the second driver had sustained nose lacerations only; except for the two wrecked cars, no other damage had been done.

The race proceeded under a yellow caution flag, competitors holding their positions until the caution signal should be lifted. Meanwhile, wrecking and service crews laboured swiftly to clear the track.

Erica, a little bored by now, took advantage of the lull to move rearwards in the box. Kathryn Hewitson, her head down, was still working on needlepoint, but when she looked up, Erica saw to her surprise that the older woman's eyes were moist with tears.

'I really can't take this,' Kathryn said. 'that man who was just hurt used to race for us when we had the factory team. I know him well, and his wife.'

Erica assured her, 'He's all right. He was only hurt slightly.'

'Yes, I know.' The executive vice-president's wife put her needlepoint away. 'I think I could use a drink. Why don't we have one together?'

They moved to the rear of the private box where a barman was at work.

Soon after, when Erica returned to rejoin Adam, the caution flag had been lifted, the race was running full-out again, under green.

Moments later, Pierre Flodenhale, in 29, crammed on a burst of speed and passed the rookie driver, Johnny Gerenz, in 44, moving into second place.

Pierre was now directly behind Cutthroat, clinging to the lead in number 38, his speed close to 190 mph.

For three laps, with the race in its final quarter, the two fought a blistering duel. Pierre trying to move up, almost succeeding, but Cutthroat holding his position with skill and daring. But in the home-stretch of the eighty-ninth lap, with twenty-four more laps to go, Pierre thundered by. Cheers resounded across the Speedway and in the company box.

The p.a. boomed: '*It's 29, Pierre Flodenhale, out front!*'

It was at that moment, with the lead cars approaching the south turn, directly in front of the South grandstand and private boxes, that it happened.

Afterwards there was disagreement concerning precisely what had occurred. Some said a wind gust caught Pierre, others that he experienced steering trouble entering the turn and overcorrected; a third theory maintained that a piece of metal on another car broke loose and struck 29, diverting it.

Whatever the cause, car 29 snaked suddenly as Pierre fought the wheel, then at the turn slammed head on into the concrete retaining wall. Like a bomb exploding, the car disintegrated, breaking at the fire wall, the two main portions separating. Before either portion had come to rest, car 44, with Johnny Gerenz, ploughed between both. The rookie driver's car spun, rolled, and seconds later was upside down in the infield, its wheels spinning crazily. A second car smashed into the now spread-out wreckage of 29, a third into that. Six cars altogether were in the pile up at the turn; five were eliminated from the race, one limped on for a few laps more before shedding a wheel and being towed to the pits. Apart from Pierre, all other drivers involved were unhurt.

The group in the company box, like others elsewhere, watched in shocked horror as ambulance attendants rushed to the two separate, shattered portions of car 29. A group of ambulance men had surrounded each. They appeared to be bringing objects to a stretcher placed midway between the two. As a company director, with binoculars to his eyes, saw what was happening he paled, dropped the binoculars, and said in a strangled voice, 'Oh, *Jesus Christ!*' He implored his wife, beside him, 'Don't look! Turn away!'

Unlike the director's wife, Erica did not turn away. She watched, not wholly understanding what was happening, but knowing Pierre was dead. Later, doctors declared, he died instantly when car 29 hit the wall.

To Erica, the scene from the moment of the crash onwards was unreal, like a reel of film unspooling, so her personal involvement was removed. With a dulled detachment – the result of shock – she witnessed the race continuing for twenty-or-so laps more, then Cutthroat the winner being acclaimed in Victory Lane. She sensed relief in the crowd. After the fatality the gloom around the course had been almost palpable; now it was cast off as a triumph – any triumph – erased the scar of defeat and death.

In the company box the despondency did not lift, unquestionably because of the emotional impact of the violent death a short time earlier, but also because a car of another manufacturer had gained the Canebreak 300 victory. A degree of talk – quieter than usual – centred around the possibility of success next day in the Talladega 500. Most in the company group, however, dispersed quickly to the hotels.

Only when Erica was back in the privacy of the Motor Inn suite, alone with Adam, did grief weep over her. They had driven together from the Speedway in a company car, Adam saying little, and had come directly here. Now, in the bedroom, Erica flung herself down, hands to her face, and moaned. What she felt was too deep for tears, or even for coherence in her mind. She only knew it had to do with the youthfulness of Pierre, his zest for life, and good-natured charm which on balance outweighed other faults, his love of women, and the tragedy that no woman, anywhere, would ever know or cherish him again.

Erica felt Adam sit beside her on the bed.

He said gently, 'We'll do whatever you want – go back to Detroit right now, or stay tonight and leave tomorrow morning.'

In the end they decided to stay, and had dinner quietly in the suite. Soon after, Erica went to bed and dropped into exhausted sleep.

Next morning, Sunday, Adam assured Erica they could still leave at once if she preferred it. But she had shaken her head, and told him no. An early northwards journey would mean having to pack hurriedly, and would entail an effort which seemed pointless since there was nothing to be gained by rushing to Detroit.

Pierre's funeral, so the *Anniston Star* reported, would be on Wednesday in Dearborn. His remains were to be flown to Detroit today.

Soon after her early morning decision, Erica told Adam, 'You go to the 500. You want to, don't you? I can stay here.'

'If we don't leave, I'd like to see the race,' he admitted. 'Will you be all right alone?'

She told him that she would, and was grateful for the absence of questioning by Adam, both yesterday and today. Obviously he sensed that the experience of watching someone whom she knew die a violent death had been traumatic and, if he was wondering about any extra implications of her grief, he had the wisdom not to voice his thoughts.

But when the time came for Adam to leave for the Speedway, Erica decided she did not want to be alone, and would go with him after all.

They went by car, which took a good deal longer than the helicopter trip the previous day and allowed something of the insulation which had helped her through yesterday to creep over Erica. In any case, she was glad to be out of doors. The weather was glorious, as it had been the entire weekend, the Alabama countryside as lovely as any she had seen.

In the company's private box at the Speedway everything seemed back to normal, as compared with yesterday afternoon, with cheerful talking centring on the fact that two strong favourites in today's Talladega 500 would be driving cars of the company's make. Erica had met one of the drivers briefly; his name was Wayne Onpatti.

If either Onpatti or the other favoured driver, Buddy Undler, won today, it would eclipse yesterday's defeat since the Talladega 500 was the longer and more important race.

Most major races were on Sunday, and manufacturers of cars, tyres, and other equipment acknowleged the dictum: *Win on Sunday, sell on Monday.*

The company box was just as full as yesterday, with Hub Hewitson again in the front row and clearly in good spirits. Kathryn Hewitson, Erica saw, sat alone near the rear, still working on her needlepoint and seldom look up. Erica settled into a corner of the third row, hoping that despite the crowd she could be, to a degree, alone.

Adam stayed in his seat beside Erica, except for a short period when he left the box to talk outside with Smokey Stephensen.

The auto dealer had motioned with his head to Adam just before starting time, when the race preliminaries were in progress. The two of them left the company box by the rear exit, Smokey preceding, then stood outside in the bright, warm sunshine. Though the track was out of sight, they could hear the roar of engines as the pace car and fifty competing cars began to move.

Adam remembered it was on his first visit to Smokey's dealership, near the beginning of the year, that he had met Pierre Flodenhale, then working as a part-time car salesman. He said, 'I'm sorry about Pierre.'

Smokey rubbed a hand across his beard in the gesture Adam had grown used to. 'Kid was like a son to me, some ways. You tell yourself it can always happen, it's part of the game; I knew it in my time, so did he. When it comes, though, don't make it no easier to bear.' Smokey blinked, and Adam was aware of a side to the auto dealer's nature, seldom revealed.

As if to offset it, Smokey said roughly. 'That was yesterday. This is today. What I want to know is – you talked to Teresa yet?'

'No, I haven't.' Adam had been aware that the month's grace he had given Smokey before his sister disposed of her interest in Stephensen Motors would be over soon. But Adam had not acted to inform Teresa. Now he said, 'I'm not sure I intend to – advise my sister to sell out, I mean.'

Smokey Stephensen's eyes searched Adam's face. They were shrewd eyes, and there was little that the dealer missed, as Adam knew. The shrewdness was a reason why Adam had re-examined his convictions about Stephensen Motors over the past two weeks. Many reforms were coming in the auto dealership system, most of them overdue. But Adam believed Smokey would survive such changes because survival was as natural to him as being in his skin. That being so, in terms of an investment, Teresa and her children might find it hard to do better.

'I guess this is a time for the soft sell,' Smokey said. 'So I won't push; I'll just wait, and hope. One thing I know, though. If you change your mind from what you figured to begin with, it'll be for Teresa and not as any favour to me.'

Adam smiled. 'You're right about that.'

Smokey nodded. 'Is your wife all right?'

'I think so,' Adam said.

They could hear the tempo of the race increasing, and went back into the company box.

Auto races, like wines, have vintage years. For the Talladega 500 this proved to be the best year ever – a fast and thrilling contest from its swift-paced outset to a spectacular down-to-the-wire finish. Through a total of 188 laps – a fraction over 500 miles – the lead switched many times. Wayne Onpatti and Buddy Undler, the favourites of Adam's company, stayed near the front, but were challenged strongly by a half-dozen others, among them the previous day's victor, Cutthroat, who was out ahead for a large part of the race. The sizzling pace took its toll of a dozen cars, which quit through the mechanical failure, and several others were wrecked, though no major pile-up occurred as on the previous day, nor was any driver injured. Yellow caution flags and slowdowns were at a minimum; most of the race was full-out, under green.

Near the end, Cutthroat and Wayne Onpatti vied for the lead, with Onpatti slightly ahead, though moans resounded through the company box when Onpatti swung into the pits, stopping for a late tyre change, which cost him half a lap and put Cutthroat solidly out front.

But the tyre change proved wise and gave Onpatti what he needed – an extra bite on turns, so that by the back stretch of the final lap he had caught up with Cutthroat, and the two were side by side. Even thundering down the homestretch together with the finish line in sight, the result was still in doubt. Then, foot by foot, Onpatti eased past Cutthroat, finishing a half a car length ahead – the victor.

During the final laps, most people in the company box had been on their feet, cheering hysterically for Wayne Onpatti, while Hub Hewitson and others jumped up and down like children, in unrestrained excitement.

When the result was known, for a second there was silence, then pandemonium broke.

Cheers, even louder than before, mingled with victorious shouts and laughter. Beaming executives and guests pummelled one another on backs and shoulders; hands were clasped and wrung; in the aisle, between benches, two staid vice-presidents danced a jig. 'Our car won! We won!' echoed around the private box, with other cries. Someone chanted the inevitable, 'Win on Sunday, sell on Monday.' With still more shouts and laughter the chant was taken up. Instead of diminishing, the volume grew.

Erica surveyed it all, at first in detachment, then in disbelief. She could understand the pleasure of a share in winning; despite her own aloofness earlier, in the tense, final moments of the race she had felt involved, had craned forward with the rest to watch the photo finish. But *this* . . . this crazed abandonment of every other thought . . . was something else.

She thought of yesterday: its grief and awful cost; the body of Pierre, at this moment en route for burial. And now, so soon, the quick dismissal . . . '*Win on Sunday; sell on Monday*'

Coldly, clearly, and distinctly, Erica said, '*That's all you care about!*'

The hush was not immediate. But her voice carried over other voices close at hand, so that some paused, and in the partial silence Erica spoke clearly again. 'I said, "That's all you care about!" '

Now, everyone had heard. Inside the box, the noise and other voices stilled. Across the sudden silence someone asked, 'What's wrong with that?'

Erica had not expected this. She had spoken suddenly, from impulse, not wanting to be a focus of attention, and now that it was done, her instinct was to back away, to save Adam more embarrassment, and leave. Then anger surged. Anger at Detroit, its ways – so many of them mirrored in this box; what they had done to Adam and herself. She would *not* let the system shape her to a mould: a complaisant company wife.

Somene had asked: '*What's wrong with that?*'

'It's wrong,' Erica said, 'Because you don't live – *we* don't live – for anything but cars and sales and winning. And if not all the time, then most of it. You forget other things. Such as, yesterday a man died here. Someone we knew. You're so full of winning: "*Win on Sunday!*" . . . *He was Saturday* . . . You've forgotten him already . . .' Her voice trailed off.

She was conscious of Adam regarding her. To Erica's surprise, the expression on his face was not critical. His mouth was even crinkled at the corners.

Adam, from the beginning, caught every word. Now, as if his hearing were heightened, he was aware of external sounds: the race running down, tail end cars completing final laps, fresh cheers for the new champion, Onpatti, heading for the pits and Victory Lane. Adam was conscious, too, that Hub Hewitson was frowning; others were embarrassed, not knowing where to look.

Adam supposed he ought to care. He thought objectively: whatever truth there was in what Erica had said, he doubted if she had picked the best time to say it, and Hub Hewitson's displeasure was not to be taken lightly. But he had discovered moments earlier: *He didn't give a damn! To hell with them all!* He only knew he loved Erica more dearly than at any time since he had known her.

'Adam,' a vice-president said, not unkindly, 'you'd better get your wife out of here.'

Adam nodded. He supposed for Erica's sake – to spare her more – he should.

'Why should he?'

Heads turned – to the rear of the company box from where the interruption came. Kathryn Hewitson, still holding her needlepoint, had moved into the centre aisle and stood facing them all, tight-lipped. She repeated, 'Why should he? Because Erica said what *I* wanted to say, but lacked the moral courage? Because she put into words what every woman here was thinking until the youngest of us all spoke up?' She surveyed the silent faces before her. '*You men!*'

Suddenly Erica was aware of other women looking her way, neither embarrassed nor hostile, but – now the barrier was lifted – with eyes which registered approval.

Kathryn Hewitson said firmly, 'Hubbard!'

Within the company Hub Hewitson was treated, and at times behaved, like a crown prince. But where his wife was concerned he was a husband – no more, no less – who, at certain moments, knew his obligations and his cues. Nodding, no longer frowning, he stepped to Erica and took both her hands. He said, in a voice which carried through the bodx, 'My dear, sometimes in haste, excitement, or for other reasons we forget some simple things which are important. When we do, we need a person of conviction to remind us of our error. Thank you for being here and doing that.'

Then suddenly, all tension gone, they were pouring from the box into the sunshine.

Someone said, 'Hey, let's go over, shake hands with Onpatti.'

Adam and Erica walked away arm in arm, knowing something important had happened to them both. Later, they might talk about it. For the moment there was no need for talk; their closeness wsa all that mattered.

'Mr and Mrs Trenton! Wait, please!'

A company public relations man, out of breath from running, caught them at a ramp to the Speedway parking lot. He announced, between puffs, 'We just called the helicopter in. It'll be landing on the track. Mr Hewitson would like you both to use it for the first trip. If you give me your keys, I'll take care of the car.'

On their way to the track, with his breath more normal, the PR man said, 'There's something else. There are two company planes at Talladega Airport.'

'I know,' Adam said. 'We're going back to Detroit on one.'

'Yes, but Mr Hewitson has the jet, though he won't be using it until tonight. What he wondered is if you would like to have it first. He suggests you fly to Nassau, which he knews is Mrs Trenton's home, then spend a couple of days there. The plane could go down and back, and still pick up Mr Hewitson tonight. We'd send it to Nassau again, for you, on Wednesday.'

'It's a great idea,' Adam said. 'Unfortunately I've a whole string of appointments in Detroit, starting early tomorrow.'

'Mr Hewitson told me you'd probably say that. His message was: For once, forget the company and put your wife first.'

Erica was glowing. Adam laughed. One thing could be said for the executive vice-president: when he did something, he did it handsomely.

Adam said, 'Please tell him we accept with thanks and pleasure.'

What Adam did not say was that he intended to be sure, on Wednesday, he and Erica were in Detroit in time for Pierre's funeral.

They were in the Bahamas, and had swum from Emerald Beach, near Nassau, before the sun went down.

On the patio of their hotel, at sunset, Adam and Erica lingered over drinks. The night was warm, with a soft breeze riffling palm fronds. Few other people were in sight since the mainstream of winter visitors would not arrive here for another month or more.

During her second drink, Erica took an extra breath and said, 'There's something I should tell you.'

'If it's about Pierre,' Adam answered gently, 'I think I already know.'

He told her; someone had mailed him, anonymously in an unmarked envelope, a clipping from the *Detroit News* – the item which caused Erica concern. Adam added, 'Don't ask me why people do these things. I guess some just do.'

'But you didn't say anything.' Erica remembered – she had been convinced that if he found out, he would.

'We seemed to have enough problems, without adding to them.'

'It was all over,' she said. 'Before Pierre died.' Erica recalled, with a stab of conscience, the salesman, Ollie. That was something she would *never* tell Adam. She hoped, one day, she could forget that episode herself.

From across the table dividing them, Adam said, 'Whether it was over or not, I'd still want you back.'

She looked at him, emotion brimming. 'You're a beautiful man. Maybe I haven't been appreciating you as much as I should.'

He said, 'I guess that goes for both of us.'

Later, they made love, to find the old magic had returned.

It was Adam, drowsily, who spoke their epilogue: 'We came close to losing each other, and our way. Let's never take that chance again.'

While Adam slept, Erica lay awake beside him, hearing night sounds through windows opened to the sea. Later still, she too fell asleep; but at daybreak they awoke together and made love again.

29

In early September the Orion made its debut before the Press, company dealers, and the public.

The national Press preview was in Chicago – a lavish, liquor-laced freeload which, it was rumoured, would be the last of its kind. The reason behind the rumour: auto firms were belatedly recognizing that most newsmen wrote the same kind of honest copy whether fed champagne and beluga caviar, or beans and hamburgers. So why bother with big expense?

Nothing in the near future, however, was likely to change the nature of a dealer preview which, for the Orion, was in New Orleans and lasted six days.

It was a spectacular, show biz extravaganza to which seven thousand company dealers, car salesmen, their wives and mistresses were invited, arriving in waves of chartered aircraft, including several Boeing 747s.

All major hotels in the Crescent City were taken over. So was the Rivergate Auditorium – for a nightly musical extravaganza which, as one bemused spectator put it, 'could have run on Broadway for a year'. A stupendous climax to the show was the descent, amid a shimmering Milky Way and to music from a hundred violins, of a huge shining star which, as it touched centre stage, dissolved to an Orion – the signal for a wild ovation.

Other fun, games, and feasting continued through each day, and at nights, fireworks over the harbour, with a magnificent set piece spelling ORION, closed the scene.

Adam and Erica Trenton attended, as did Brett DeLosanto; and Barbara Zaleski flew in to join Brett briefly.

During one of the two nights Barbara was in New Orleans, the four of them had dinner together at Brennan's in the French Quarter. Adam, who had known Matt Zaleski slightly, asked Barbara how her father was.

'He's able to breathe on his own now, and he can move his left arm a little,' she answered. 'Apart from that, he's totally paralyzed.'

Adam and Erica murmured sympathy.

Barbara left unexpressed her daily prayer that her father would die soon, releasing him from the burden and agony she sensed each time she looked into his eyes. But she knew that he might not. She was aware, too, that the elder Joseph Kennedy, one of history's more famous victims of a stroke, had lived for eight years after being totally disabled.

Meanwhile, Barbara told the Trentons, she was making plans to move her father home to the Royal Oak house with full-time nursing care. Then, for a while, she and Brett would divide their time between Royal Oak and Brett's Country Club Manor apartment.

Speaking of the Royal Oak house, Barbara reported, 'Brett's become an orchid grower.'

Smiling, she told Adam and Erica that Brett had taken over the care of her father's orchid atrium, and had even bought books on the subject.

'I dig those orchids' lines, the way they flow,' Brett said. He speared an Oyster Roffignac which had just been served him. 'Maybe there's a whole new generation of cars hung in there. Names, too. How about a two door hardtop called *Aerides masculosum*?'

'We're here for the Orion,' Barbara reminded them. 'Besides, it's easier to spell.'

She did not tell Adam and Erica about one incident which had happened recently, knowing that if she did it would embarrass Brett.

On several occasions after her father's stroke, Barbara and Brett stayed overnight at the Royal Oak house. One evening Brett arrived ther first. She found him at an easel set up, a fresh canvas, and his paints. He had sketched on the canvas, and now was painting, an orchid. Afterwards Brett told her that his model was a *Catesetum, saccatum* – the bloom which he and Matt Zaleski had both admired the night, almost a year ago, when the older man flared up at Brett and, later, Barbara forced her father to apologize. 'Your old man and I agreed it was like a bird in flight,' Brett said. 'I guess it was the only thing we did agree on.'

A little awkwardly Brett had gone on to suggest that when the painting was finished, Barbara might like to take it to her father's room at the hospital and position it where he could see it. 'The old buzzard hasn't got a lot to look at. He enjoyed his orchids, and he might like this.'

Then, for the first time since Matt's affliction, Barbara broke down and wept.

It had been a relief, and afterwards she felt better, aware that her emotions had remained pent up until Brett's simple act of kindness released them. Barbara valued even more what Brett was doing because of the deep involvement with a new car planning project, Farstar, soon to be presented at a top-level strategy meeting for company officers. Farstar was occupying Brett's days and nights, leaving time for little else.

Obliquely, at the New Orleans dinner table, Adam referred to Farstar, though cautiously not naming it. 'I'll be glad when this week is over,' he told Barbara. 'The Orion is Sales and Marketing's baby now. Back at the farm we've new things borning.'

'Only two weeks to the big-you-know-wot parley,' Brett put in, and Adam nodded.

Barbara sensed that Adam and Brett were tremendously caught up in Farstar, and wondered if, after all, Brett would go through with his private plan to leave the auto industry at year end. She knew that Brett had not discussed the possibility yet with Adam who, Barbara was convinced, would try to persuade him to stay.

Barbara revealed some professional news of her own. The documentary film *Auto City*, now complete, had been enthusiastically received at several critical advance showings. The CJL advertising agency, Barbara personally, and the director, Wes Gropetti, had received warm letters of praise from the client's chairman of the board and – even more significant – a major TV network had committed itself to showing *Auto City* as a public service during prime viewing time. As a result, Barbara's own standing at OJL had never been higher, and she and Gropetti had been asked to work together on a new film for another agency client.

The others congratulated her, Brett with obvious pride.

Soon after, the talk returned to the Orion and the dealer preview extravaganza. 'I can't help wondering,' Erica said, 'if all this week is really necessary.'

'It is,' Adam said, 'and I'll tell you why. Dealers and salesmen at a preview see any car at its best – like a jewel in a Tiffany setting. So from that, plus all the carnival, they go back charged up about the product that in a few days will be dropped off in front of their dealerships.'

'Dropped off dusty,' Brett said. 'Or maybe grimy from the journey, with hub caps off, bumpers greasy, stickers and sealing tape all over. A mess.'

Adam nodded. 'Right. But the dealer and salesmen have already seen the car as it should be. They know how great it is when prepared for a showroom. Their enthusiasm doesn't leave them, and they do a better selling job.'

'Not forgetting, advertising helps,' Barbara said. She sighed, 'I know that critics think a lot of the hoopla's corny. But we know it works.'

Erica said softly, 'Then mostly because all three of you care so much, I hope it works for the Orion.'

Under the table, Adam squeezed her hand. He told the others, 'Now we can't miss.'

A week later, when the Orion was on view in dealer showrooms throughout North America, it seemed that he was right.

'Rarely,' reported *Automotive News*, the industry's weekly holy writ, 'has a new car evoked such a remarkable response so soon. Already, a huge backlog of orders has its manufacturers elated, their production men harried, competitors alarmed.'

A press consensus reflected the same view. The *San Francisco Chronicle* declared, 'The Orion has most of the safety and clean air hardware we've been promised for years, and looks beautiful too.' The *Chicago Sun-Times* conceded, 'Yessir! This one's zazzy!' *The New York Times* pontificated, 'Conceivably, the Orion may mark the end of an era which, while admittedly encouraging engineering advances, often subordinated them to styling needs. Now, both out-of-view engineering and external form appear to be proceeding hand-in-hand.'

Newsweek and *Time* both featured Hub Hewitson and the Orion on their covers. 'The last time that happened,' a gleeful PR man told anybody who would listen, 'was with Lee Iacocca and the Mustang.'

Not surprisingly, the company's top echelon was in a happy mood when, soon after the Orion's public introduction, it met to consider Farstar.

It was a final product policy meeting – last of a series of three. The Farstar project had survived the preceding two. Here, it would either go forward as a firm commitment – a new car to be introduced in two years' time – or would be discarded for ever, as many projects were.

The previous meetings had involved intense study, presentations, argument, and tough interrogation, but were relatively informal. The final meeting would still feature the same kind of study and dissection but, as to formality, would be like a black-tie dinner party compared with casual lunch.

The product policy board, which today would total fifteen people, began assembling shortly after 9 a.m. The meeting would commence at 10 a.m. promptly, but it was traditional for informal discussions, between groups of two and three, to occupy most of the hour beforehand.

The meeting place was on the fifteenth floor of the company staff building – a smallish, luxuriously appointed auditorium, with a horseshoe-shaped table of polished walnut. Around the closed end of the horseshoe were five black leather, high-backed chairs for the chairman of the board, president, and three executive vice-presidents of whom Hub Hewitson was senior. In the remaining lower-backed chairs the remaining participants would sit, in no particular order.

At the horseshoe's open end was a raised lectern for use by whoever was making a presentation. Today it would be occupied mainly by Adam Trenton. Behind the lectern was a screen for slide and film projection.

A smaller table beside the horseshoe was for the meeting's two secretaries. In the wings and a projection booth were staff backup men, with thick black notebooks containing – as a wag once put it – every answer known to man.

And as always, despite the prevailing Orion happiness and a surface ease which might deceive an outsider, the underlying tone of the product policy meeting would be deadly serious. For here was where an auto corporation put millions of dollars on the line, along with its reputation and its life. Some of the world's greatest gambles were launched here, and they *were* gambles because, despite research and backup, an 'aye' or 'nay' decision in the end must be based on instinct or a hunch.

Coffee service in the auditorium began with first arrivals. That was traditional, as was a waiting pitcher of chilled orange juice for the chairman of the board who disliked hot drinks in daytime.

The room was filling when Hub Hewitson breezed in near 9.30. He first got coffee for himself, then beckoned Adam and Elroy Braithwaite, who were chatting.

Looking pleased with himself, Hewitson opened a folder he had carried in and spread out several drawings on the horseshoe table. 'Just got these. Timely, eh?'

The Design-Styling vice-president strolled to join them and the four pored over the drawings. No-one needed to ask what they were. Each sheet bore the insignia of another of the Big Three manufacturers and included illustrations and specifications of a new car. Equally obvious was that this was the competitive car which Farstar would face two years from now, if today's proposals were approved.

The Silver Fox whistled softly.

'It's extraordinary,' the Design-Styling vice-president mused, 'how, in some ways, their thinking has paralleled ours.'

Hub Hewitson shrugged. 'They keep an ear to the ground just as we do, read the same newspapers, study trends; they know the way the world's moving. Got some bright boys on their payroll, too.' The executive vice-president shot a glance at Adam. 'What do you say?'

'I say we have a far better car. We'll come out ahead.'

'You're pretty cocky.'

'If that's the way it seems,' Adam said, 'I guess I am.'

Hub Hewitson's face relaxed into a grin. 'I'm cocky, too. We've another good one, let's sell it to the others.'

He began folding the drawings. Later, Adam knew, they would analyse the competitive car in detail, and perhaps make changes in their own as a result.

'I've often wondered,' Adam said, 'what we have to pay to get this stuff.'

Hub Hewitson grinned again. 'Not as much as you'd think. Ever heard of a well-paid spy?'

'I suppose not.' Adam reflected: spying was something which all big auto companies practised, though denying that they did. His own company's espionage centre – under an innocuous name – occupied cramped, cluttered quarters in the Design-Styling Center and was a clearing-house for intelligence from many sources.

For example, research engineers of competitive companies were a mother lode of information. Like all scientific researchers engineers loved to publish, and papers at technical society meetings often contained a phrase or sentence, by itself insignificant, but, taken in conjunction with other fragments from elsewhere, gave clues to a competitor's thinking and direction. Among those engaged in auto espionage it was accepted that 'engineers are innocents'.

Less innocent was a flow of intelligence from the Detroit Athletic Club, where senior and middle-rank executives from all companies drank together. A result of their drinking was that some, relaxed and off-guard, tried to impress others with their knowledge. Across the years, finely tuned ears in the DAC had garnered many tidbits and occasionally news of great importance.

Then there were leakages through tool-and-die companies. Sometimes the same tooling company served two, or even three, major auto makers; thus, a seemingly casual dropper-in to a die-making shop might see work in progress for an auto firm other than his own. An experienced designer looking at the female portion of a die could sometimes tell what the entire rear or front end of a competitor's car looked like – then go away and sketch it.

Other tactics were sometimes used by outside agencies whose *modi operandi* were not scrutinized too closely. They included enlistment of competitors' disaffected employees to purloin papers, and sifting of garbage was not unknown. Once in a while an employee, unconcerned about conflicting loyalties, might be 'planted' in another company. But these were grubby methods which top executives preferred not to hear about in detail.

Adam's thoughts switched back to Farstar and the product policy board.

The auditorium clock showed 9.50 and the company chairman had just arrived, accompanied by the president. The latter, a dynamic leader in the past but now considered 'old school' by Adam and others, would be retiring soon, with Hub Hewitson predicted to succeed him.

A voice beside Adam asked, 'What variances will Farstar have for Canada?' The questioner was head of the company's Canadian subsidiary, invited here today by a courtesy.

'We'll be going into that,' Adam said, but he described the variances anyway. One of the Farstar lines would be given a differing name – Independent – exclusive to Canada, and the exterior hood emblem would be changed to include a maple leaf. Otherwise the car would be identical with Farstar models in the US.

The other nodded. 'As long as we have some differences we can point to, that's the main thing.'

Adam understood. Although Canadians drove US cars, produced by US controlled subsidiaries employing US union labour, national vanity in Canada fostered the delusion of an independent auto industry. The Big Three had humoured these pretensions for years by naming the heads of their Canadian branches presidents, although in fact such presidents were answerable to vice-presidents in Detroit. The companies, too, had introduced a few 'distinctively Canadian' models. Nowadays, however, Canada was being regarded more and more by all auto makers as just another sales district, and the special models – never more than a façade – were being quietly dropped. The 'Canadianized' Farstar Independent would probably be the last.

At a minute to ten, with the fifteen decision-makers seated, the chairman of the board sipped orange juice, then said whimsically, 'Unless anyone has a better suggestion, we might as well begin.' He glanced at Hub Hewitson. 'Who's starting?'

'Elroy.'

Eyes turned to the Product Development vice-president.

'Mr Chairman and gentlemen,' the Silver Fox said crisply, 'today we are presenting Farstar with a recommendation to proceed. You've all read your agendas, you know the plan, and you've seen the models in clay. In a moment we'll get down to details, but first this thought: whatever we call this car, it will not be Farstar. That code name was merely chosen because, compared with Orion, this project seemed a long way distant. But suddenly it isn't distant any more. It's no longer a Farstar; the need is here, or will be in two years' time which in production terms, as we know, is the same thing.'

Elroy Braithwaite paused, passing a hand across his silver mane, then went on, 'We think this kind of car, which some will call revolutionary, is inevitable anyway. And incidentally' – the Silver Fox motioned to the folder of competitors' drawings on the table in front of Hub Hewitson – 'so do our friends on the other side of town. But we also believe that instead of letting Farstar, or something like it, be forced on us the way some of our activities have been in recent years, we can make it happen, now. I, for one, believe that as a company and an industry it's time we took the offensive more strongly once again, and did some way-out pioneering. That, in essence, is what Farstar is about. Now we'll consider details.' Braithwaite nodded to Adam, waiting at the lectern. 'OK, let's go.'

'The slides you are now seeing,' Adam announced as the screen behind him filled, 'show what market research has demonstrated to be a gap in availability, which Farstar will fill, and market potential of that gap two years from now.'

Adam had rehearsed this presentation many times and knew the words by rote. Generally, through the next two hours, he would 'follow the book', now open in front of him, though as usual at these meetings there would be interruptions and pointed, penetrating questions.

As the half-dozen slides went through, with Adam making brief commentaries, he still had time to think of what Elroy Braithwaite had said moments earlier. The remarks about the company taking a strong offensive had surprised Adam, first because it had not been necessary to make a comment of that kind at all, and also because the Silver Fox had a reputation for caginess and gauging wind directions carefully before committing himself to anything. But perhaps Braithwaite, too, was infected with some of the new thinking and impatience pervading the auto industry as old war horses retired or died and younger men moved up.

Braithwaite's phrase 'way-out pioneering' had reminded Adam, too, of similar words used by Sir Perceval Stuyvesant during their own conversation five weeks ago. Since then,

Adam and Perce had spoken by telephone several times. Adam's interest had grown in the possibility of accepting the presidency of Sir Perceval's West Coast company, but Perce continued to agree that any kind of decision be delayed until the Orion's launching and today's presentation of Farstar. After today, however, Adam must decide – whether to go to San Francisco for more discussions or to decline Perce's offer entirely.

Adam had talked with Erica, for the second time, about the proffered West Coast job during their two days in the Bahamas. Erica had been definite. 'It has to be your decision absolutely, darling. Oh, of course I'd love to live in San Francisco. Who wouldn't? But I'd rather have you happy in Detroit than unhappy somewhere else, and either way we'll be together.'

Her declaration cheered him, and even after that he remained in doubt, and was still uncertain now.

Hub Hewitson's voice cut brusquely across the Farstar presentation. 'Let's stop a minute and talk about something we might as well face up to. This Farstar is the ugliest son-of-a-bitch car I ever saw.'

It was typical of Hewitson that, while he might support a programme, he liked to bring out possible objections himself for frank discussion.

Around the horseshoe table there were several murmurs of assent.

Adam said smoothly – the point had been anticipated – 'We have, of course, been aware of that all along.'

He began explaining the philosophy behind the car: a philsophy expressed by Brett DeLosanto during the after-midnight session months earlier when Brett had said, 'With Picasso in our nostrils, we've been designing cars like they rolled off a Gainsborough canvas.' That had been the night when Adam and Brett had gone together to the teardown room, moving on later to the bull session with Elroy Braithwaite and two young product planners, of whom Castaldy was one. They had emerged with the question and concept: why not a deliberate, daring attempt to produce a car, ugly by existing standards, yet so suited to needs, environment, and present time – the Age of Utility – that it would become beautiful?

Though there had been adaptations and changes in outlook since, Farstar had retained its basic concept.

Here and now Adam was circumspect about the words he used because a product policy board meeting was no place to wax overly poetic, and notions about Picasso took second place to pragmatism. Nor could he speak of Rowena, though it had been the thought of her which inspired his own thinking that night. Rowena was still a beautiful memory, and while Adam would never tell Erica about her, he had a conviction that even if he did Erica would understand.

The discussion about the visual look of Farstar ended, though they would return to the subject, Adam knew.

'Where were we?' Hub Hewitson was turning pages of his own agenda.

'Page forty-seven,' Braithwaite prompted.

The chairman nodded. 'Let's get on.'

An hour and a half later, after prolonged and inconclusive discussion, the group vice-president of manufacturing pushed away his papers and leaned forward in his chair. 'If someone had come to me with the idea of this car, I'd not only have thrown it out, but I'd have suggested he looked for employment elsewhere.'

Momentarily, the auditorium was silent. Adam, at the lectern, waited.

The manufacturing head, Nolan Friedheim, was a grizzled auto industry veteran and the dean of vice-presidents at the table. He had a forbidding, craggy face which seldom smiled, and was noted for his bluntness. Like the company president, he was due for retirement soon, except that Freidheim had less than a month of service remaining and his successor, already named, was here today.

While the others waited, the elderly executive filled his pipe and lit it. Everyone present knew that this was the last product policy meeting he would attend. At length he said, 'That's what I'd have done, and if I had, we'd have lost a good man and probably a good car too.'

He puffed his pipe and put it down. 'Maybe that's why my time's come, maybe that's why I'm glad it has. There's a whole lot that's happening nowadays I don't understand; plenty of it I dislike and always will. Lately, though, I've found I don't care as much as I used to. Another thing: whatever we decided today, while you guys are sweating out Farstar – or whatever name it gets eventually – I'll be fishing off the Florida Keys. If you've time, think of me. You probably won't have.'

A ripple of laughter ran around the table.

'I'll leave you with a thought, though,' Nolan Freidheim said. 'I was against this car to begin with. In a way I still am; parts of it, including the way it looks, offend my notion of what a car should be. But down in my gut, where plenty of us have made good decisions before now, I've a feeling that it's right, it's good, it's timely, it'll hit the market when it should.' The manufacturing chief stood up, his coffee cup in hand to replenish it. 'My gut votes "yes". I say we should go with Farstar.'

The chairman of the board observed, 'Thank you, Nolan. I've been feeling that way myself, but you expressed it better than the rest of us.'

The president joined in the assent. So did others who had wavered until now. Minutes later a formal decision was recorded: For Farstar, all lights green!

Adam felt a curious emptiness. An objective had been gained. The next decision was his own.

30

Since the last week of August, Rollie Knight had lived in terror.

The terror began in the janitor's closet at the assembly plant where Leroy Colfax knifed and killed one of the two vending machine collectors, and where the other collector and the foreman, Parkland, were left wounded and unconscious. It continued during a hasty retreat from the plant by the four conspirators – Big Rufe, Colfax, Daddy-o Lester and Rollie. They had scaled a high, chain-link fence, helping each other in the darkness, knowing that to leave through any of the plant gates would invite questioning and identification later.

Rollie gashed his hand badly on the fence wire, and Big Rufe fell heavily, limping afterwards, but they had made it outside. Then, moving separately and avoiding lighted areas, they met in one of the employee parking lots where Big Rufe had a car. Daddy-o had driven because Big Rufe's ankle was swelling fast, and paining him. They left the parking lot without using lights, only turning them on when reaching the roadway outside.

Looking back at the plant, everything seemed normal and there were no outward signs of an alarm being raised.

'Man, oh man,' Daddy-o fretted nervously as he drove. 'If I ain't glad to be clear o' that!'

From the back seat, Big Rufe grunted. 'We ain't clear o' nuthun' yet.'

Rollie, in front with Daddy-o and trying to stem the bleeding of his hand with an oily rag, knew that it was true.

Despite his fall, Big Rufe had managed to get one set of chained cash bags over the fence with him. Leroy Colfax had the other. In the back seat they hacked at the bags with knives, then poured the contents – all silver coins – into several paper sacks. On the freeway, before reaching the city, Colfax and Big Rufe threw the original cash bags out.

In the inner city they parked the car on a dead-end street, then separated. Before they did, Big Rufe warned, 'Remember, all we gotta do is act like there ain't nuthin' different. We play this cool, ain't nobody gonna prove we was there tonight. So tomorrow, everybody shows their faces just like always, same as any other day.' He glared at the other three. 'Somebody don't, that when the pigs start lookin' our way.'

Leroy Colfax said softly, 'Might be smarter to run.'

'You run,' Big Rufe snarled, 'I swear I'll find 'n kill you, the way you did that honky, the way you got us all in this . . . '

Colfax said hastily, 'Ain't gonna run. Just thinkin' is all.'

'Don't think! You showed already you ain't got brains.'

Colfax was silent.

Though he had not spoken, Rollie wished he could run. But to where? There was nowhere, no escape, whichever way you turned. He had a sense of his own life seeping out, the way blood was still seeping from his injured hand. Then he remembered: the chain of happenings leading to tonight had begun a year ago, when the white cop baited him, and the black cop gave a card with a hiring hall address. Rollie's mistake, he recognized, had been to go there. Or had it? If what had overtaken him had not happened this way, there would have been some other.

'Now listen good,' Big Rufe said, 'we all in this together, we stick together. If nobody of us four blabs, we gonna be OK.'

Perhaps the others believed. Rollie hadn't.

They parted then, each taking one of the paper sacks of coins which Big Rufe and Colfax had divided in the back seat of the car. Big Rufe's was bulkier than the others.

Choosing his route cagily, conscious of the implications of the paper sack of coins if he should be stopped by a police patrol, Rollie reached the apartment house on Blaine near 12th.

May Lou wasn't in; she had probably gone to a movie. Rollie bathed the gash in his hand, then bound it roughly with a towel.

After that he counted the money in the paper sack, dividing the coins into piles. It totalled $30.75 – less than a day's pay at the assembly plant.

If Rollie Knight had had the erudition or philosophy, he might have debated, within himself, the nature of risks which human beings take for trifling amounts such as $30.75, and their degrees of losing. There had been earlier risks which frightened him – the risk of refusing to be swept along into deeper involvement with plant crime, and the risk of backing out tonight, which he could have taken, but didn't, when Big Rufe thrust the gun into his hand.

These risks had been real, not just imagined. A savage beating, accompanied by broken limbs, could have been ordered for Rollie by Big Rufe as easily as groceries are ordered from a store. Both men knew it; and that way Rollie would have been a loser too.

But in the end the losing could have been less than the total disaster – life imprisonment for murder – which threatened now.

In essence the risks which Rollie chose to take, and not to take, were those which – in degree – face all men in a free society. But some, within the same society, are born with cruelly limited choices, belying the hoary bromide that 'all men are created equal'. Rollie, and tens of thousands like him, hedged in from birth by poverty, inequality, scant opportunity, and with the sketchiest of education providing poor preparation for such choices as occur, are losers from the beginning. Their degree of losing remains the only thing to be determined.

Thus, the tragedy of Rollie Knight was twofold: the darker side of the earth that he was born to, and society's failure to equip him mentally to break away.

But thinking none of this, knowing only bleak despair and fear of what would come tomorrow, Rollie thrust the $30.75 in silver beneath his bed, and slept. He did not awaken later when May Lou came in.

In the morning, May Lou dressed Rollie's hand with a makeshift bandage, her eyes asking questions which he did not answer. Then Rollie went to work.

At the plant, plenty of talk was circulating about the murder-robbery of the night before, and there had been reports on radio, TV; and in the morning newspaper. Local interest in Rollie's area of Assembly centred on the bludgeoning of Frank Parkland, who was in the hospital, though reportedly with mild concussion only. 'Just proves all foremen are thickheaded,' A humorist pronounced at break time. There was immediate laughter. No-one seemed distressed by the robbery, or greatly concerned about the murdered man, who was otherwise unknown.

Another report said one of the plant managers had had a stroke, brought on by the whole affair plus overwork. However, the last was clearly an exaggeration since everyone knew a manager's job was a soft touch.

Apart from the talk, no other activity concerning the robbery-murder was visible from the assembly line. Nor, as far as Rollie could see, or hear through scuttlebutt, was anyone on the day shift questioned.

No rumours, either, tied any names to the crime.

Despite Big Rufe's warning to the other three, he alone failed to show up at the plant that day. Daddy-o conveyed the news to Rollie at mid-morning that Big Rufe's leg was so swollen he could not walk, and had reported sick, putting out a story of having been drunk the night before and falling downstairs at home.

Daddy-o was shaky and nervous, but had recovered some of his confidence by early afternoon, when he paid a second call to Rollie's work station, obviously wanting to gab.

Rollie had snarled at him, low voice, 'For Cri-sakes quit hangin' round me. And keep that stinkin' mouth shut!' If anyone blabbed, causing word to spread, Rollie feared most of all it would be Daddy-o.

Nothing more that was notable occurred that day. Or on the one after. Or through an entire week following that.

As each day passed, while Rollie's anxiety remained, his relief increased a little. He knew, however, there was still plenty of time for the worst to happen. Also he realized: while the sheer numbers of lesser unsolved crimes caused police investigations to ease or end, murder was in a different league. The police, Rollie reasoned, would not give up quickly.

As it happened, he was partly right and partly wrong.

The timing of the original robbery had been shrewd. It was the timing also which caused police investigation to centre on the plant night shift, even though detectives were unsure that the men they sought were company employees at all. Plenty of auto plant crimes were committed by outsiders, using fake or stolen employee identification badges to get in.

All the police had to work with was a statement by the surviving vending machine collector that four men were involved. All had been masked and armed; he believed that all four were black, he had only the vaguest impressions of their physical size. The surviving collector had not seen the face of the briefly unmasked robber, as had his companion who was knifed.

Frank Parkland, who was struck down instantly on entering the janitor's closet, had observed nothing.

No weapons had been discovered, no fingerprints found. The slashed cash bags were eventually recovered near a freeway, but provided no clue, apart from suggesting that whoever discarded them was headed for the inner city.

A team of four detectives assigned to the case began methodically sifting through names and employment dockets of some three thousand night shift employees. Among these were a sizeable segment with criminal records. All such individuals were questioned, without result. This took time. Also, part way through the investigation the number of detectives was reduced from four to two, and even the remaining pair had other duties to contend with.

The possibility that the wanted men might be part of the day shift, and had remained in the plant to stage the robbery, was not overlooked. It was simply one of several possibilities which the police had neither time nor manpower to cope with all at once.

What investigators really hoped for was a break in the case through an informer, which was the way many serious crimes, in greater Detroit as elsewhere, were solved. But no information came. Either the perpetrators were the only ones who knew the names involved, or others were remaining strangely silent.

The police were aware that the vending concessions at the plant were Mafia-financed and run; they knew, too, that the dead man had Mafia connexions. They suspected, but had no means of proving, that both factors were related to the silence.

After three and a half weeks, because of a need to assign detectives to newer cases, while the plant murder-robbery case was not closed, police activity slackened off.

The same was not true elsewhere.

The Mafia, generally, does not look kindly on any interference with its people. And when interference is from other criminals, repercussions are stern, and of a nature to be a warning against repetition.

From the instant that the man with the Indian features died from the knife wound inflicted by Leroy Colfax, Colfax and his three accomplices were marked for execution.

Doubly assuring this was that they were pawns in the Mafia-Black Mafia war.

When details of the murder-robbery were known, the Detroit Mafia family worked quietly and effectively. It had channels of communications which the police had not.

First, feelers were put out for information. When one resulted, a reward was quietly offered: a thousand dollars.

For that much, in the inner city, a man might sell his mother.

Rollie Knight heard of the Mafia involvement and reward one week and two days after the debacle at the plant. It was at night and he was in a dingy Third Avenue bar, drinking beer. The beer, and the fact that whatever official investigation was going on had not come close to him so far, had relaxed a little of the terror he had lived with for the past nine days. But the news, conveyed by his companion at the bar – a downtown number runner known simply as Mule – increased Rollie's terror tenfold and turned the beer he had drunk into bile, so that he was hard pressed not to vomit there and then. He managed not to.

'Hey!' Mule said, after he conveyed the news of the Mafia-proffered reward. 'Ain't you in that plant, man?'

With an effort, Rollie nodded.

Mule urged, 'You find out who them guys was, I pass the word, we split the dough, OK?'

'I'll listen around,' Rollie promised.

Soon after, he left the bar, his latest beer untouched.

Rollie knew where to find Big Rufe. Entering the rooms where the big man lived, he found himself looking into the muzzle of a gun – the same one, presumably, used nine days before. When he saw who it was, Big Rufe lowered the gun and thrust it in his trousers waistband.

He told Rollie, 'Them crummy wops come, they ain't gonna find no pushover.'

Beyond his readiness, Big Rufe seemed strangely indifferent – probably, Rollie realized later, because he had known of the Mafia danger in the first place, and accepted it.

There was nothing to be gained by staying, or discussion. Rollie left.

From that moment, Rollie's days and nights were filled with a new, more omnipresent dread. He knew that nothing he could do would counter it; he could only wait. For the time being he continued working, since regular work – too late, it seemed – had become a habit.

Though Rollie never knew the details it was Big Rufe who betrayed them all.

He foolishly paid several small gambling debts entirely with silver coins. The fact was noticed, and later reported to a Mafia underling who passed the information on. Other pieces of intelligence, already known about Big Rufe, were found to fit a pattern.

He was seized at night, taken by surprise while sleeping, and given no chance to use his gun. His captors brought him, bound and gagged, to a house in Highland Park where, before being put to death, he was tortured and he talked.

Next morning Big Rufe's body was found on a Hamtramck roadway, a road much travelled at night by heavy trucks. It appeared to have been run over several times, and the death was listed as a traffic casualty.

Others, including Rollie Knight – who heard the news from a terrified, shaking Daddy-o – knew better.

Leroy Colfax went into hiding, protected by politically militant friends. He remained hidden for almost two weeks, at the end of which time it was demonstrated that a militant, like many another politician, has his price. One of Colfax's trusted companions, whom each addressed as brother, quietly sold him out.

Leroy Colfax, too, was seized, then driven to a lonely suburb and shot. When his body was found, an autopsy disclosed six bullets but no other clues. No arrest was ever made.

Daddy-o ran. He bought a bus ticket to New York and tried to lose himself in Harlem. For a while he succeeded, but several months later was tracked down and, soon after, killed by knifing.

Long before that – on hearing of Leroy Colfax's slaying – Rollie Knight began his own time of waiting, and meanwhile went to pieces.

Leonard Wingate had trouble identifying the thin female voice on the telephone. He was also irritated at being called in the evening, at home.

'May Lou *who?*'

'Rollie's woman. Rollie Knight.'

Knight. Wingate remembered now, then asked, 'How did you get my phone number? It isn't listed.'

'You write it on a card, mister. Said if we were in trouble, to call.'

He supposed he had – probably the night of the filming in that inner city apartment house.

'Well, what is it?' Wingate had been about to leave for a Bloomfield Hills dinner party. Now he wished he had gone before the phone rang, or hadn't answered.

May Lou's voice said, 'I guess you know Rollie ain't bin workin'.'

'Now, how in the world would I know that?'

She said uncertainly, 'If he don't show up . . . '

'Ten thousand people work in that plant. As a Personnel executive I'm responsible for most of them, but I don't get reports about individuals . . . '

Leonard Wingate caught sight of himself in a wall mirror and stopped. He addressed himself silently: *OK, you pompous, successful, important bastard with an unlisted phone, so you've let her know what a heel you are, that she's not to assume you've anything in common just because you happen to be the same colour. Now what?*

In his own defence, he thought: it didn't happen often, and he had caught it now; but it showed how an attitude could grow, just as he had heard black people in authority treat other black people like dirt beneath their feet.

'May Lou,' Leonard Wingate said, 'you caught me in a bad moment and I'm sorry. Do you mind if we start again?'

The trouble, she told him, was with Rollie. 'He ain't eatin', sleepin', don't do nuthun'. He won't go out. Just sits and waits.'

'Waits for what?'

'He won't tell me, won't even talk. He looks awful, mister. It's like . . . ' May Lou stopped, groping for words, then said, 'Like he's waitin' to die.'

'How long since he went to work?'

'Two weeks.'

'Did he ask you to call me?'

'He don't ask nuthun'. But he needs help bad. I know he does.'

Wingate hesitated. It really wasn't his concern. It was true he had taken a close interest in hard core hiring, and still did; had involved himself too, in a handful of individual cases. Knight's was one. But there was just so much help that people could be given, and Knight had quit working – voluntarily it seemed – two weeks ago. Yet Leonard Wingate still felt self-critical about his attitude of a few minutes earlier.

'All right,' he said, 'I'm not sure I can do anything, but I'll try to drop by in the next few days.'

Her voice said pleadingly, 'Could you, tonight?'

'I'm afraid that's impossible. I've a dinner engagement which I'm late for already.'

He sensed hesitation, then she asked, 'Mister, you remember me?'

'I already said I do.'

'I ever ask you for anythin' befo'?'

'No, you haven't.' He had the feeling May Lou had never asked much of anyone, or of life, nor received much either.

'I'm askin' now. Please! Tonight. For my Rollie.'

Conflicting motivations pulled him: ties to the past, his ancestry; the present, what he had become and might be still. Ancestry won. Leonard Wingate thought ruefully: It was a good dinner party he would miss. He suspected that his hostess liked to demonstrate her *liberalitas* by having a black face or two at table, but she served good food and wine, and flirted pleasantly.

'All right,' he said into the telephone, 'I'll come, and I think I remember where it is, but you'd better give me the address.'

If May Lou had not warned him before hand, Leonard Wingate thought, he would scarcely have recognized Rollie Knight, who was emaciated, his eyes sunken in a haggard face. Rollie had been sitting at a wooden table facing the outer door and started nervously as Wingate came in, then subsided.

The company Personnel man had had the forethought to bring a bottle of Scotch. Without asking, he went to the closet-like kitchen, found glasses and carried them back. May Lou had slipped out as he arrived, glancing at him gratefully and whispering, 'I'll just be outside.'

Wingate poured two stiff, neat Scotches and pushed one in front of Rollie. 'You'll drink this,' he said, 'and you can take your time about it. But after that, you'll talk.'

Rollie's hand went out to take the drink. He did not look up.

Wingate took a swallow of his own Scotch and felt the liquor burn, then warm him. He put the glass down. 'We might save time if I tell you I know exactly what you think of me. Also, I know all the words, most of them stupid – white nigger, Uncle Tom – as well as you. But whether you like or hate me, my guess is, I'm the only friend you'll see tonight,' Wingate finished his drink, poured another and pushed the bottle towards Rollie. 'So start talking before I finish this, or I'll figure I'm wasting time and go.'

Rollie looked up. 'You act pretty mad. When I ain't said a word.'

'Try some words then. Let's see how it goes.' Wingate leaned forward. 'To start: why'd you quit work?'

Draining the first Scotch poured for him. Rollie replenished his glass, then began talking – and went on. It was as if, through some combination of Leonard Wingate's timing, acts, and speech, a sluice gate had been opened, so that words tumbled out, channelled by questions which Wingate interposed, until the whole story was laid bare. It began with Rollie's first hiring by the company a year ago, continued through his experiences at the plant, involvement with crime – small at first, then larger – to the robbery-murder and its aftermath, then the knowledge of the Mafia and word of his ordained execution which, with fear and resignation, Rollie now awaited.

Leonard Wingate sat listening with a mixture of impatience, pity, frustration, helplessness, and anger – until he could sit no more. Then, while Rollie went on talking. Wingate paced the tiny room.

When the recital was done, the Personnel man's anger exploded first. He stormed, 'You goddam fool! You were given a chance! You had it made! And then you blew it!' Wingate's hands clenched and unclenched with a complex of emotions. '*I could kill you!*'

Rollie's head came up. Briefly, the old impudence and humour flashed. 'Man, you gonna do that, you take card 'n stand in line.'

The remark brought Wingate back to reality. He knew he was faced with an impossible choice. If he helped Rollie Knight to escape his situation, he could compound a crime. Even failing to act on his own knowledge at this moment probably made him an accessory to murder, under the law. But if he failed to help, and merely walked away, Wingate knew enough of the inner city and its jungle law to be aware that he would be leaving Rollie to his death.

Leonard Wingate wished he had ignored the telephone bell tonight, or had not yielded to May Lou's plea to come here. If he had done one or the other, he would now be seated comfortably at a table with congenial people, white napery, and gleaming silver. But he *was* here. He forced himself to think.

He believed what Rollie Knight had told him. Everything. He remembered, too, reading in the press of the discovery of Leroy Colfax's bullet-punctured body, and it had been drawn to his notice in another way because, until recently, Colfax had been an assembly plant employee. That was barely a week ago. Now, with two of the four conspirators dead and a third having dropped from sight, Mafia attention was likely to move to Rollie soon. But how soon? Next week? Tomorrow? Tonight? Wingate found his own eyes going nervously towards the outer door.

He reasoned: What he must have, without delay, was another opinion, a second judgement to reinforce his own. Any decision was too crucial to make unaided. But whose opinion? Wingate was sure that if he went to his own senior in the company, the vice-president of Personnel, the advice given would be coldly legalistic: Murder had been committed, the name of one of the murderers was known; therefore inform the police, who would handle it from there.

Wingate knew – whatever the consequences to himself – he wouldn't do it. Or at least, not without seeking other counsel first. An idea occurred to him: Brett DeLosanto.

Since their first encounter last November, Leonard Wingate, Brett, and Barbara Zaleski had become good friends. In course of an increasing amount of time in one another's company, Wingate had come to admire the young designer's mind, realizing that beneath a surface flippancy he possessed instinctive wisdom, common sense, and a broad compassion. His opinion now might be important. Also, Brett knew Rollie Knight, having met him through Barbara and the *Auto City* filming.

Wingate decided: he would telephone and, if possible, meet Brett tonight.

May Lou had slipped into the apartment unnoticed. Wingate didn't know how much she had heard or knew. He supposed it didn't matter.

He motioned to the door. 'Can you lock that?'

May Lou nodded, 'Yes.'

'I'm going now,' Leonard Wingate told Rollie and May Lou, 'but I'll be back. Lock the door after me and keep it locked. Don't let anyone else in. When I come, I'll identify myself by name and voice. You understand?'

'Yes, mister.' May Lou's eyes met his. Small as she was, scrawny and unimpressive, he was aware of strength.

Not far from the Blaine apartment house, Leonard Wingate found a pay phone in an all-night Laundromat.

He had the phone number of Brett's apartment in a notebook and dialled it. The Laundromat's washers and dryers were noisy and he covered one ear so that he could hear the ringing tone at the other end. The ringing continued unanswered, and he hung up.

Wingate remembered a conversation with Brett a day or two ago in which Brett mentioned that he and Barbara would be meeting Adam and Erica Trenton – whom Leonard Wingate knew slightly – later in the week. Wingate decided to try there.

He called Directory Assistance for the Trenton's suburban number. But when he dialled it, there was no answer either.

More than ever now, he wanted to reach Brett DeLosanto.

Leonard Wingate recalled something else Brett had told him: Barbara's father was still on the critical list at Ford Hospital. Wingate reasoned; the chances were, Barbara and Brett were together, and Barbara would leave word at the hospital about where she could be reached.

He dialled the hospital's number. After waiting several minutes, he spoke with a floor nurse who admitted, yes they did have means of getting in touch with Miss Zaleski.

Wingate knew he would have to lie to get the information. 'I'm her cousin from Denver and I'm calling from the airport.' He hoped the Laundromat's noises sounded sufficiently like aeroplanes. 'I've flown here to see my uncle, but my cousin wanted me to meet her first. She said if I called the hospital you'd always know where I could find her.'

The nurse observed tartly, 'We're not running a message agency here.' But she gave him the information: Miss Zaleski was at the Detroit Symphony tonight with Mr and Mrs Trenton and Mr DeLosanto. Barbara had even left the seat numbers. Wingate blessed her thoroughness.

He had left his car outside the Laundromat. Now he headed for Jefferson Avenue and the Civic Centre, driving fast. A fine rain had begun while he was telephoning; road surfaces were slick.

At Woodward and Jefferson, crowding his chances, he beat an amber light and swung into the forecourt of the Fort Auditorium – blue-pearl-granite-and-marble-faced showplace of the Detroit Symphony Orchestra. Around the Auditorium, other Civic Centre buildings towered – Cobo Hall, Veteran's Memorial, the City-County Building – modern, spacious, brightly floodlit. The Civic Centre area was often spoken of as a fountainhead – the beginning of a vast urban renewal programme for downtown Detroit. Unfortunately, while the head was finished, almost nothing of the body was in sight.

A uniformed attendant by the Auditorium's main doors stepped forward. Before the man could speak, Leonard Wingate told him, 'I have to locate some people who are here. It's an emergency.' In his hand he held the seat numbers he had copied down while speaking with the hospital nurse.

The doorman conceded: since the performance was in progress and there was no other traffic, the car could remain 'just for a few minutes', with the key in the ignition.

Wingate passed inside through two sets of doors. As the second doors closed, music surrounded him.

An usherette turned from watching the stage and the orchestra. She said, low-voiced, 'I won't be able to seat you until intermission, sir. May I see your ticket?'

'I don't have one.' He explained his purpose and showed the girl the seat numbers. A male usher joined them.

The seats, it seemed, were near the front and centre.

'If you'd take me to the row,' Wingate urged, 'I could signal Mr DeLosanto to come out.'

The usher said firmly, 'We couldn't allow that, sir. It would disturb everybody.'

'How long to intermission?'

The ushers were unsure.

For the first time, Wingate was aware of what was being played. He had been a music lover since childhood and recognized Prokofiev's *Romeo and Juliet* Orchestral Suite. Knowing that conductors used varying arrangements of the suite, he asked, 'May I see a programme?' The usherette gave him one.

The passage he had identified was the opening to the 'Death of Tybalt'. With relief, he saw it was the final portion of the work before an intermission.

Even waiting impatiently, the music's magnificence swept over him. The swift-surging opening theme moved on to a quickening timpani solo with strokes of death-like hammer blows . . . *Tybalt had killed Romeo's friend Mercutio. Now, on the dying Tybalt, Romeo wreaked vengeance he had sworn* . . . Horn passages wailed the tragic paradox of human destructiveness and folly; the full orchestra swelled to a crescendo of doom . . .

Wingate's skin prickled, his mind drawing parallels between the music and the reason for his presence here.

The music ended. As a thunder of applause swept through the Auditorium, Leonard Wingate hurried down an aisle, escorted by the usher. Word was passed quickly to Brett DeLosanto whom Wingate saw at once. Brett appeared surprised, but began moving out, followed by Barbara and the Trentons.

In the foyer, they held a hurried conference.

Without wasting time on details, Wingate revealed that his search for Brett had been because of Rollie Knight. And since they were still downtown, Wingate's intention was that the two of them go directly to Rollie and May Lou's apartment.

Brett agreed at once, but Barbara raised difficulties, wanting to go with them. They argued briefly Leonard Wingate opposing the idea, and Brett supported him. In the end it was agreed that Adam would take Erica and Barbara to Brett's Country Club Manor apartment and await the others there. Neither Adam, Erica, nor Barbara felt like returning to the concert.

Outside, Wingate led Brett to his waiting car. The rain had stopped. Brett, who was carrying a topcoat, threw it on the back seat, on top of one of Wingate's already there. As they pulled away, Leonard Wingate began a swift-paced explanation, knowing the journey would be short. Brett listened, asking an occasional question. At the description of the murder-robbery, he whistled softly. Like countless others he had read published reports of the killing at the plant; also, there was a personal link since it seemed likely that events that night had hastened Matt Zaleski's stroke.

Yet Brett felt no emnity towards Rollie Knight. It was true that the young black worker was no innocent, but there were degrees of guilt, whether recognized in law or not.

Wingate obviously believed – and Brett accepted – that Rollie had become enmeshed a little at a time, in part unwillingly, his freedom of choice diminishing like a weakening swimmer drawn towards a vortex. Nonetheless, for what Rollie Knight had done, there were debts he would have to pay. No-one could or should, help him escape them.

'The one thing we can't do,' Brett said, 'is help him get away from Detroit.'

'I figured that, too.' If the crime had been lesser, Wingate thought, they might have chanced it. But not with murder.

'What he needs is something he didn't have those other times – the best lawyer you can get with money.'

'He doesn't have money.'

'Then I'll raise it. I'll put some up myself, and there'll be others.' Brett was already thinking of people to approach – some, outside the usual ranks of charity bestowers, who felt strongly about social justice and racial prejudice.

Wingate said, 'He'll have to surrender to the police; I can't see any other way. But if we've a strong lawyer he can insist on protection in jail.' He wondered – though not aloud – how effective the protection would be, lawyer or not.

'And with a good trial lawyer,' Brett said, 'he might, just might, get a break.'

'Maybe.'

'Will Knight do as we say?'

Wingate nodded. 'He'll do it.'

'Then we'll find a lawyer in the morning. He'll handle the surrender. Tonight, the two of them – the girl as well – had better stay with Barbara and me.'

The Personnel man shot a glance across the car's front seat. 'You sure?'

'I'm sure. Unless you've a better idea.'

Leonard Wingate shook his head. He was glad he had found Brett DeLosanto. Though nothing the young designer had said or done so far was beyond Wingate's own powers of reasoning and decision, Brett's presence and clearheadedness were reassuring. He possessed an instinctive leadership, too, which Wingate, with his training, recognized. He wondered if Brett would be content to remain designing all his years.

They were at the 12th and Blaine intersection. Outside the run-down, paint-peeling apartment house, they got out of the car and Wingate locked it.

As usual, the odour of garbage was strong.

Ascending the worn wooden stairway to the apartment house third floor, Wingate remembered he had told Rollie and May Lou he would identify himself from outside by name and voice. He need not have bothered.

The door he warned them to keep locked was open. Part of the lock was hanging loose where some force – undoubtedly a violent blow – had splintered it.

Leonard Wingate and Brett went in. Only May Lou was inside. She was putting clothes into a cardboard suitcase.

Wingate asked, 'Where's Rollie?'

Without looking up, she answered, 'Gone.'

'Gone where?'

'Some guys come. They took him.'

'How long ago?'

'Right after you went, mister.' She turned her head. They saw she had been crying.

'Listen,' Brett said, 'if we get descriptions we can warn the police.'

Leonard Wingate shook his head. He knew it was too late. He had a feeling it had been too late from the beginning. He knew, too, what he and Brett DeLosanto were going to do now. They would walk away. As so many in Detroit walked away or, like the priest and Levite, crossed over on the other side.

Brett was silent.

Wingate asked May Lou, 'What will you do?'

She closed the cardboard suitcase. 'I'll make out.'

Brett reached into a pocket. With a gesture, Wingate stopped him. 'Let me.'

Without counting them, he took what bills he had and pressed them into May Lou's hand. 'I'm sorry,' he said. 'I guess it doesn't mean much, but I'm sorry.'

They went downstairs.

Outside, when they came to the car, its nearside door hung open. The window glass was broken. The two topcoats which had been on the car's backseat were gone.

Leonard Wingate cradled his head in his arms on the car roof. When he looked up, Brett saw his eyes were wet.

'Oh, God!' Wingate said. He raised his arms beseechingly to the black night sky. '*Oh, God! This heartless city!*'

Rollie Knight's body was never found. He simply disappeared.

31

'It's your life, not mine,' Adam told Brett DeLosanto. 'But I wouldn't be a friend if I didn't say that I think you're being hasty, and making an enormous mistake.'

It was close to midnight, and the five of them – Adam and Erica, Barbara and Brett, and Leonard Wingate – were in the Country Club Manor apartment. Brett and Wingate had joined the others half an hour ago, having driven from the inner city. The conversation had been gloomy. When they had exhausted all that could be said about Rollie Knight, Brett announced his intention to leave the automobile industry and to submit a letter of resignation tomorrow.

Adam persisted, 'In another five years you could be heading up Design-Styling.'

'There was a time,' Brett said, 'when that was the only dream I had – to be a Harley Earl, or a Bill Mitchell, or Gene Bordinat, or an Elwood Engel. Don't misunderstand me – I think they've all been great; some are still. But it isn't for me, that's all.'

Leonard Wingate said. 'There are other reasons, though, aren't there?'

'Yes, there are. I don't think car manufacturers, who do so much long-range planning for themselves, have done more than a thimbleful of planning and service for the community they live in.'

Adam objected. 'That may have been true once; it isn't any more. Everything's changed or changing fast. We see it every day – in management attitudes, community responsibility, the kind of cars we're building, relations with government, acknowledgement of consumers. This isn't the same business it was even two or three years ago.'

'I'd like to believe it,' Brett said, 'if only because obviously you do. But I can't, and I'm not alone. Anyway, from now on I'll be working on the outside.'

Erica asked, 'What will you do?'

'If you want the truth,' Brett told her, 'I'll be damned if I know.'

'It wouldn't surprise me,' Adam said, 'if you got into politics. I'd like you to know that if you do, I'll not only vote for you, I'll contribute to your campaign.'

Wingate said, 'Me, too.' It was strange, he thought, that only this evening he had sensed Brett's leadership and wondered how long he would stay in design.

Brett grinned. 'One of these days that may cost you both. I'll remember.'

'One thing he's going to do,' Barbara told the others, 'is paint. If I have to chain him to an easel and bring his meals. If I have to support the two of us.'

'Speaking of support,' Brett said, 'I've thought of starting a small design business of my own.'

'If you do,' Adam predicted, 'it won't stay small because you can't help being a success. Also, you'll work harder than you ever did.'

Brett sighed. 'That's what I'm afraid of.'

But even if it happened, he thought, he would be his own man, would speak with an independent voice. That was what he wanted most, and so did Barbara. Brett glanced at her with a love which seemed to increase day by day. Whatever unknown quantities were coming, he knew that they would share them.

'There were rumours,' Barbara said to Adam, 'that you might leave the company too.'

'Where did you hear that?'

'Oh, around.'

Adam thought: it was hard to keep any secret in Detroit. He supposed Perce Stuyvesant, or someone close to him, had talked.

Barbara pressed him. 'Well, *are* you leaving?'

'An offer was made to me,' Adam said. 'I thought about it seriously for a while. I decided against it.'

He had telephoned Perce Stuyvesant a day or two ago and explained: there would be no point in going to San Francisco to speak of terms and details; Adam was an automobile man and would remain one.

As Adam saw it, a good deal was wrong with the auto industry, but there was a great deal more that, overwhelmingly, was right. The miracle of the modern automobile was not that it sometimes failed, but that it mostly didn't; not that it was costly, but that – for the marvels of design and engineering it embodied – it cost so little; not that it cluttered highways and polluted air, but that it gave free men and women what, through history, they had mostly craved – a personal mobility.

Nor, for an executive to spend his working life, was there any more exciting milieu.

'All of us see things in differing ways,' Adam told Barbara. 'I guess you could say I voted for Detroit.'

Soon afterwards they said goodnight.

On the short drive from Maple and Telegraph to Quarton Lake, Adam said, 'You didn't say much tonight.'

'I was listening,' Erica answered. 'And thinking. Besides, I wanted you to myself, to tell you something.'

'Tell me now.'

'Well, it rather looks as if I'm pregnant. Look out! – don't swerve like that!'

'Just be glad,' he said, as he pulled into a driveway, 'you didn't tell me on the Lodge at rush hour.'

'Whose driveway is this?'

'Who the hell cares?' He put out his arms, held her, and kissed her tenderly.

Erica was half laughing, half crying. 'You were such a tiger in Nassau. It must have happened there.'

He whispered, 'I'm glad I was,' then thought: It could be the very best thing for them both.

Later, when they were driving again, Erica said, 'I've been wondering how Greg and Kirk will feel. You've two grown sons, then suddenly a baby in the family.'

'They'll love it. Because they love you. Just as I do.' He reached for her hand. 'I'll phone and tell them tomorrow.'

'Well,' she said, 'between us we seem to be creating things.'

It was true, he thought happily. And his life was full.

Tonight he had Erica, and this.

Tomorrow, and in days beyond, there would be Farstar.